TALES

THE COMPLETE SERIES

F T Barbini

Luna Press

PUBLISHING

www.lunapresspublishing.com
ISBN-13: 978-1-913387-29-7

White Child
Text Copyright © 2015 F.T. Barbini
Third Edition 2015
First published 2011.
First published by Luna Press Publishing 2015

The Oracle of Life
Text Copyright © 2015 F.T. Barbini
Third Edition 2015
First published 2012.
First published by Luna Press Publishing 2015

The Nuarn Rift
Text Copyright © 2015 F.T. Barbini
Third Edition 2015
First published 2013.
First published by Luna Press Publishing 2015

Tijara's Heart
Text Copyright © 2015 F.T. Barbini
Second Edition 2015
First published 2015.
First published by Luna Press Publishing 2015

The Guardian's Trail
Text Copyright © 2016 F.T. Barbini
First published by Luna Press Publishing, 2016

The Girl from the Sky
Text Copyright © 2017 F.T. Barbini
First published by Luna Press Publishing, 2017

TIJARAN TALES
BOOK I

WHITE CHILD

CONTENTS

THE TRUTH BEHIND FLYING SOCKS

'Julius McCoy, get your brother off the ceiling!'

Mrs McCoy, despite her kindly nature, was not a woman to be trifled with and, seeing as she was pointing a ladle at him, Julius thought it might be wise to do as she said.

'Down. Now,' she ordered.

Julius had been focussing intently on his younger brother, who was floating happily just beneath the ceiling, but now he relaxed his mental grip. Mrs McCoy stepped underneath Michael, who plummeted into her outstretched arms, giggling delightedly.

'There is little to laugh about, young man,' she said, eyeing him severely. 'And you, Julius, now that you're 12 you should act your age. You don't want to be late for your induction, do you?' She placed Michael on the floor and, after throwing Julius an exasperated look, made her way downstairs.

Julius grinned and winked at his brother, who smiled back before running off to his bedroom.

It had taken only a fraction of his mind-skills to levitate Michael up to the ceiling and guide him perfectly around the set of spotlights. Sure, the descent had been a bit too fast, but he was working on it. Besides, if he was accepted into the Zed Academy, they would teach him how to control his abilities. *If I get in*, he thought anxiously.

A whiff of fresh toast drifted up to his nostrils and Julius's stomach grumbled, teased by the aroma. He quickly made his way to the kitchen. The household was bustling with the usual morning activities. He could hear his mum downstairs preparing breakfast, while his father was doing his best to dress Michael. And *that* was never an easy task, given the boy's tendency for random mind-skill jokes. Julius managed to free himself from the lure of the toast long enough to pop his head into Michael's room, where their dad was trying desperately to reach a pair of socks that were floating high above the floor.

Rory McCoy was a short man in his forties, with light brown hair and dark eyes. Twelve years with his children had given him an almost permanent wrinkling of the brow. Julius used to jokingly tell him that running around after flying socks had helped to keep him in shape, but sometimes he felt genuinely sorry for him and his mum.

Normally, Julius wouldn't have interfered with Michael's routine but this morning was different, since his dad was going to fly him to the Zed Test Centre, so he decided to speed things up a little. He locked his eyes on the socks and, with a small mind-push, thrust them down into his father's hands, before silently retreating back into the corridor. However, by the time Julius reached the kitchen, Mr McCoy was once more being challenged, this time by a pair of airborne shoes.

'I would like five slices of toast,' said Julius, plonking himself down at the table, 'and three eggs please!'

'You're lucky it's such a big day, young man, or I might not have given you even *one* slice,' said his mother setting a glass of milk in front of him and ruffling his hair before turning back to the stove.

Jenny McCoy was a tall, slim woman. Her dark, wavy hair framed a beautiful and elegant face where a pair of bright blue eyes always smiled kindly. Julius strongly resembled her, in that he was tall, had similarly blue eyes and the same aquiline features. Thick dark hair flowed down to his shoulders, except for several jagged strands which hung loosely around his ears and forehead.

'You all set?' she asked.

He nodded, then quietly asked her, 'Do you think they'll take me?'

'I'll sort them out if they *don't*,' she said, while buttering a slice of toast. 'I'm counting on a bit of peace and quiet around here.'

Julius smiled, but he sensed just a hint of sadness and tension in her voice. Over the course of the last 12 years, Jenny and Rory McCoy had been treated to regular displays of their son's mind-skills. He was well aware that they had been eagerly anticipating the day he would be old enough to take the test. In truth, they had known they were in for a rough ride from the start; ever since their first visit to the family Doctor, Dr Flip, all those years ago. He had stared at them from above the rim of his glasses, a mixture of excitement and disbelief on his face.

'I have been a Mind Doctor since 2830,' he had said, waving Julius's Brain Augmentation chart at them, 'and I have never seen such potential in one so young. Incredible – still in diapers, but he's pure Zed Academy material, if ever I've seen one. How many of your ancestors fought in the Chemical War?'

The McCoys had looked at each other, speechless. The War, though it had ended some 300 years earlier, had given rise to certain enhanced mental abilities for generations afterwards. It was in no way consistent – very few actually developed any mind-skills of note – so Julius's results were all the more surprising, since neither they nor their own parents had ever displayed any similar talent. However, after several weeks of intense surprises, such as Julius rocking himself in his cot while hovering a few feet off the ground, they had grown used to it, as any other parents in their position would have. Nonetheless, it had come as a bit of a relief when Dr Flips had announced that the newly born Michael possessed only a hint of his brother's mind-skills. Sure, he would be able to levitate the odd sock or two, but it was unlikely he would ever qualify for the Academy.

Still, Julius suspected the tension in his mother's voice was more due to the strange news that had been popping up lately on the Space Channels than any nerves on her son's behalf. There had been reports of frequent meetings between the Curia – the political heart of Zed – and the Earth Leader, which had caused a series of rumours about an imminent war involving the Zed Academy and the Arneshians. Although the news was probably unfounded, it was a given that they would still be worried about the possibility of their son heading towards trouble.

Just then his father entered the room, closely followed by Michael, who looked awfully pleased with himself.

'I've just got up and I'm already tired,' said Mr McCoy, sounding slightly out of breath. 'I wonder why …' he finished, flashing a disapproving look at Michael.

The boy assumed a sheepish expression and then turned quickly to his mother: 'Can I go with Julius?'

'No, Michael,' she answered. 'You have to go to school. Besides, they wouldn't let you in – you're only ten.'

Michael frowned and bent his head over his cereal bowl. He could smell defeat a mile away.

'I promise I'll tell you everything when I get back tonight,' said Julius, in an effort to cheer him up.

Michael nodded and gave him a little smile.

At that moment, the house computer came online and its metallic voice intoned: 'One female visitor approaching front door, Doorbell will ring in ten, nine, eight ...'

'It's bound to be Morgana. I'll get it Julius. You go and get ready. If we leave early enough, we might beat the traffic,' said Mr McCoy, walking out into the hall.

Julius ran upstairs to his bedroom. He had prepared his bag a week in advance and then checked it every night since. Together with the invitation chip, he was required to bring his Brain Augmentation chart, a document provided by Dr Flip, which certified his brain development since birth. Julius sincerely hoped its contents were good enough for the staff at the test centre. He grabbed his black leather jacket from the wardrobe and swung the backpack over his shoulder. When he returned to the kitchen, a young Asian girl was sitting at the table, drinking a glass of milk.

'*Konnichiwa*, Julius,' she said, smiling from beneath a milky moustache.

'Hey, Morgana. Got everything? Nice 'tache by the way,' said Julius, handing her a napkin from the table.

'Oops. Thanks,' she said, cleaning her lips. 'I've checked three times this morning. The last thing I need is to arrive there without my invitation chip.'

Julius had been friends with Morgana Ruthier ever since her family had moved to Edinburgh eight years ago. She was slightly taller than him, with lovely green eyes, from her Scottish Dad's side, and long, straight, black hair – compliments of her Japanese mother. By all accounts though, she had two mothers, seeing as Mrs McCoy treated her very much like the sister Julius had never had.

'All right children, it's time to go now,' said Mr McCoy, plucking his jacket from the coat stand.

Michael waved goodbye from over his cereal bowl, but kept very quiet. Mrs McCoy walked them outside in her dressing gown, imparting some last minute advice about keeping calm and being polite to their instructors. 'Just do what they ask you to do. Don't show off. And don't ...'

'Yes, yes. As if!' Julius blurted out, rolling his eyes.

Morgana laughed, and while pushing Julius into the back of the fly-car, she turned to Mrs McCoy. 'I'll make sure he behaves. Don't worry.'

'Rory, call me as soon as you know,' said Jenny, retreating back into the doorway.

Mr McCoy waved to his wife and climbed into the driver's seat. Their fly-car, the Bumble Bee 5000, was his latest purchase. He had always been an original when it came to choosing his cars, and this one was no exception. It did look like a giant metal bumblebee for a start, from the stripy black and yellow lines to a pair of tiny wings on the roof – for show rather than functionality, although he always insisted that they helped with the aerodynamics. When it lifted off the road, anyone within a thirty yard radius was treated to the deep buzzing sound of its engine, as if all the neighbourhood had switched on electric razors at the exact same moment.

It was this sound that now filled the air as Mr McCoy guided the car out of their front drive, and Julius's mind wandered off, conjuring up a hundred different pictures of exactly what awaited him at the Academy.

*

The Zed Test Centre for the United Kingdom and Ireland was located in the outskirts of Cumbria, on a plain surrounded by hills. From Edinburgh, it was a flight of roughly forty minutes, following the Air One to Carlisle, then the Wind Four to Maryport. The Air One crossed the Southern Uplands and entered Galloway over the river Esk. It was a lovely journey in the springtime, soaring above the lush green fields dotted with the white shapes of newborn lambs below.

Although the traffic on the skyway wasn't too heavy, several other vehicles were whizzing past at different speeds and altitudes, some quite recklessly too. They, however, were floating peacefully along. The sun was shining down, unhindered by any clouds, making the car's outer shell glimmer. As an added little flourish, all Bumble Bee fly-cars had their own unique brand of paint, which smelled incredibly like honey. The heat of the mid-morning sun was intensifying that delicious smell so much that a number of seagulls had actually tried to peck at the paint before flying off in disgust.

Inside the car, the passengers had been quiet ever since leaving town. Morgana, who normally loved the countryside, was far too nervous to admire the view and was twisting and stretching a corner of her shirt with sweaty hands. When she could no longer bear the silence, she turned to Julius. 'I'm so nervous. I spoke with Kaori yesterday. She told me that I shouldn't worry because the test isn't really that difficult. But I can't help it.'

Kaori was Morgana's sister, and a third year student at Tuala, one of Zed's three schools. Of course, Morgana devoured any and all news she could pry from Kaori, and was always more than happy to excitedly pass that information on to Julius. No one was allowed within Zed's grounds except its members, but in Satras, its only civilian town, school students could receive visits from their families. As such, Morgana had been able to visit her sister twice during the mid-winter holidays, and both times she had faithfully reported back all that she had seen and done there to a decidedly envious Julius.

Today, though, he wasn't overly keen on talking about Zed. With the test looming so near, he felt it better not to jinx anything by assuming he would pass – just in case. So he nodded absently to her as she talked and kept his thoughts to himself. He was getting terribly anxious now. His stomach felt like it was on fire, while his skin was covered in goose bumps. He turned his attention to the skyway and realised they had just hopped onto the Wind Four. After a further ten minutes of whizzing along, they came across a blue signpost on the left of the skyway which read: "ZED TEST CENTRE. Reduce altitude now."

'Over there,' cried Mr McCoy, pointing to the ground excitedly.

Julius and Morgana simultaneously leapt over to the left window, causing the Bumble Bee to tilt to one side. There, below them, the Zed Test Centre came into view. As they drew closer, Julius noted how it was divided into three sectors – a landing area enclosed within long rows of shrubs, a car park next to it, and the main building. What caught his attention most, however, was the round, metallic silver building in the far sector. The lower curve of the sphere disappeared into the ground where four black iron arms emerged from the surrounding flowerbeds and hooked into it, holding the entire structure in place. What appeared to be the main entrance – a large circular doorway – yawned open above a flight of metal stairs that led up to it from a paved square, which Julius saw was bustling with movement.

The Bumble Bee slowly descended towards the runway and headed for the landing area, which was flanked by two rows of tiny yellow lights embedded in the concrete. The fly-car landed smoothly and hovered along the track towards a line of toll booths, where it stopped.

'Good morning, sir. Two for the test?' called the guard, nodding at Julius and Morgana.

'Oh, no – it's just me. They're here for moral support,' replied Mr McCoy with a grin. The guard stared back at him and raised one eyebrow quizzically.

'Dad!' Julius implored through clenched teeth. 'Not really the time.'

Mr McCoy cleared his throat and quickly handed over the invitation chips. The guard looked suspiciously at him and inserted them into his computer. A few seconds later, a holographic screen flickered to life in the space between the booth and the fly-car with pictures and personal details of the two children.

He quickly switched his gaze from the screen to the youngsters. 'Well, I don't know about your driver here, but you two certainly appear to be in order. Enter the car park via C sector. Your space is number fourteen. Have a good day,' he said, flashing a cheeky smile at them.

Mr McCoy laughed nervously as he took the chips back and handed them over to Julius. Steering the Bumble Bee forward, he followed the road to the left and brought them to a halt at their allocated space. There, they quickly exited the car and headed along the walkway. The fly-car park was already filled with the most bizarre and colourful vehicles on the market. While Mr McCoy passed comment on the latest models – 'The Dung Beetle 1000, now that's an interesting piece of machinery, but you can bet it doesn't smell as nice as my Bee!' – Julius and Morgana were gazing at the main building, where dozens of children were making their way through its entrance.

Julius noticed that the adults weren't going in with them but were instead being directed to a small waiting room to the right. He pointed this out to his father, who was satisfied once he saw that it had windows all around so that he could continue admiring the fly-cars.

Once in the square, Mr McCoy stopped. 'I'll be waiting for you next door. You will both do well. Just stay focused.' He started towards the waiting room but after a few steps turned around and called back to his son. 'Oh, and Julius, try to leave the building standing once you're done, will you?'

Julius grinned and waved him away. Together with Morgana, he walked towards the main door and looked up. The oval emblem of Zed towered over the entrance. It showed the Moon, glowing white and full in a starry black sky. The Zed lunar perimeter was a shimmering dot in its centre.

Morgana drew a deep breath and said, 'Come on Julius – let's go book our tickets to the Moon.'

THE ZED TEST

When Julius entered the building, he found himself in a large, well-lit reception area. A guard in a grey uniform was directing everybody to join a long, snake-like line to the enrolment desk. Except for a female voice shouting 'NEXT!' at regular intervals, the room was surprisingly quiet.

Julius looked around. The walls on either side of the hall were covered with portraits of people that he didn't recognise. All of them were wearing black suits with numerous medals pinned to their chests. Under each frame, was a small golden plaque bearing the name of the person portrayed. He noticed that one picture was much larger than the rest and was placed on its own high above the reception desk. Although it was quite far for him to read the inscription, he instantly knew who the man in the portrait was. In fact, there was not one person on Earth who didn't know of him: Marcus Tijara. He was the man who had almost singlehandedly brought Earth into the Space Era, researched the White and Grey Arts and most important of all in Julius's opinion, created the Zed Lunar Perimeter.

'Julius, look,' said Morgana tapping excitedly on his shoulder.

She was pointing at three full-size portraits to their left. 'This is Roland Kloister, the Grand Master of Kaori's school, Tuala. And this is Edwina Milson, the Head of Sield School. Which means that this man here is Carlos Freja, the current Grand Master of Tijara School. Kaori said that people speak of him as being the true heir of Marcus Tijara.'

Julius stared, fascinated by Freja's portrait. It was difficult to tell what his age was. His body looked tall and sturdy, his hair dark and short, but his face seemed worn and his intense grey eyes were surrounded by lines. Julius thought that, if he was accepted into Zed, he would want to go to Tijara and study under Carlos Freja. In that moment, he felt such admiration for this man who he did not even know that a sense of guilt crept over him because he realised that he had never felt like that about anyone, not even his own father. Ashamed, he pulled his eyes away from the picture.

Beside him, Morgana was looking above the heads of the other children in an effort to see how far they were from the desk.

'At least the queue is moving quickly,' she said.

'Good, 'cause I *really* need the toilet,' said a voice behind them.

Julius and Morgana turned around and then looked upward. Seated in a hovering wheelchair, a grinning boy looked down at them. Beneath a bed of tangled brown hair, two hazelnut eyes moved nervously from Julius to Morgana. After a brief awkward silence, the boy offered his hand.

'Hi. I'm Faith. From Ireland.'

Morgana, who had always been more relaxed with strangers than Julius, grabbed his hand and shook it vigorously. 'Hi. I'm Morgana, and this is Julius. From here. Well kinda – I'm actually from Japan, but my Dad is Scottish. That's why I'm doing the test here.'

The boys nodded to each other. Morgana seemed quite happy to talk away while they were waiting but Julius was still too nervous for that. So he kept quiet and occasionally dragged Morgana forward in the queue by her arm.

'That's a really flashy transport you've got there,' said Morgana, examining Faith's wheelchair from every angle. 'A Lady Bird 300, but with the electric core of an early Grass Hopper model. How unusual.'

'Wow, I'm impressed,' replied Faith. 'I haven't met many people who would know the model of me chair, let alone noticing that the core was different. Are you into engineering?'

'She's going to be a spaceship pilot,' cut in Julius from over his shoulder.

Morgana blushed a little and smiled. 'I'd like to.'

'That's wonderful,' said Faith. 'It's no easy job either. I wanna be a spaceship architect and engineer, and build the most amazing ships you'll ever see. Meantime, I'm practising on me chair. By using different parts, not only can I get it to spin, but also to hover and jump. I'm working on making it fly right now. I've kept the wheels functioning though, 'cause you just never know. Me friend Roy Bray back home – that would be Dublin by the way – broke down one day and his wheels were only there for show so I had to tow him all the way to his house. By the time we got there, his tires had gone and he was sending sparks everywhere like a firework,' finished Faith in a fit of laughter.

'A right sight, I bet,' said Morgana, giggling.

Even Julius was smiling despite his nervousness. Under the puzzled stares of several people, and because they were getting closer to the desk, they managed to pull themselves together.

Eventually, it was Julius's turn to enrol. A long faced lady stared gravely at him from behind the desk.

'Name-chip-documents,' she cried, in one breath.

'Julius McCoy,' blurted out Julius, startled.

He quickly handed her his folder. She didn't seem willing to wait for even one second.

She's probably been doing this since dawn, thought Julius.

The lady kept hold of his invitation chip and folder and slammed a visitor pass onto the desk. Before Julius could even say thanks, she raised her face and shouted, 'NEXT!'

Beyond the desk, a guard asked Julius to enter a room on the left. He waved back at Morgana and did so. The new space was long and bare, and had all sorts of monitors and what looked like a metallic tunnel structure on the far end. Eight boys were already sitting along the wall near the entrance. Julius moved next to a square-faced boy, with rather large shoulders and an expression of boredom on his face. The visitor pass around his thick neck said that his name was Billy Somers. Julius was about to sit down when a whistling Faith entered the room and positioned himself next to him.

Somers glanced over at Faith. 'If *he's* not worried about the physical test, we really shouldn't be,' he said with a snigger, to no one in particular and clearly without any concern that he might be heard.

Faith stared blankly at him for a few seconds and suddenly broke out into a broad grin. He then turned his attention to the various devices in the room as if nothing had happened.

Somers, like Julius and the rest of the boys, was caught off guard for a moment by Faith's reaction, but any further retaliation was cut short by two men in white coats who entered the room and shut the door behind them. One of them was carrying a small pile of folders and walked directly towards a desk at the back of the room where he sat down; the other one stopped in front of the boys.

'Gentlemen, this is your physical test. We don't have time to waste so when I call your name step forward to the Tunnel Scan and walk – I repeat *walk* – through it.' He then looked at a small blonde boy. 'Taun, Roger. Follow me.'

He turned and walked towards the large device, with the little boy hurrying behind him. Julius watched Roger Taun approach the Tunnel Scan and disappear under its thick metal arch. He noticed that everybody else was watching intently, except Faith, who was examining his fingernails. The doctors worked fast. Julius watched each boy walk through the tunnel and leave the room, until his turn came. When he stepped under the Tunnel Scan one of the doctors told him to look straight ahead. The tunnel was about six metres long and rather dark. Inside, numerous coloured lights blinked on and off around him, accompanied by tiny beeping sounds. When he stepped outside, he saw a wide and long screen to his left that showed all the information they had gathered from his body. He didn't have time to read any of it though because his full skeleton suddenly appeared on the screen, staring back at him. The word "PASS" flashed in green across it.

'Move along now. Leave through that door,' said one of the doctors, pointing at the exit.

Julius returned to the corridor and joined the others, who were waiting for everyone to finish their medical tests. They were all quiet and he was pleased to see he wasn't the only fidgety one. He looked towards the reception, noting that it was still crowded, while dozens more people were swarming through the front door. Julius briefly thought that at that very moment, across the planet and on each of the Earth colonies, all children aged 12 were being examined in their own country's Zed Test Centre. Only one hundred of them would make it to Zed though, and he strongly hoped that Morgana and he were good enough to be among the chosen ones.

The medical test had been fine and that was no small relief, but the hardest part was about to begin. They were going to test his mind-skills, on which his chances of entering Zed would rest entirely. How they would do that, however, Julius had no idea.

I hope they ask me to start a fire or move something with my mind, he thought, but that immediately made him recall that he still wasn't very good at putting the fires out afterwards, and that Michael's landing that very morning had not gone too smoothly. For the next few minutes, Julius mentally went through all the skills he'd ever used and concentrated on the correct dose of energy to use for each of them. Like his father had said, he really didn't want to destroy anything, which *had* been known to happen.

When Faith finally joined them, a different man in a grey uniform walked towards them.

'Follow me gentlemen. Single file and do not lag behind.' He then turned and started down a staircase.

They hurried after him, Julius accompanied by the gentle hum of Faith's chair behind him. A few minutes later they reached a small room. It was unfurnished, except for several bulky cardboard boxes spread to one side of the room. Some of them were flattened and piled against one of the walls. A gangly man with dark hair starkly flattened against his head grabbed a handful of small black objects from an open box and stamped them indelicately to each of the boys' foreheads.

'Thethe are thelf-adhethive micro-chipth,' he said in a bored voice.

Everyone looked at each other puzzled, while someone grunted in the back. Even the guard was straining to suppress a laugh. The man, clearly oblivious of the reaction to his lisp, took no notice and continued with his chant: 'Do not remove them until you are told to do tho. Your brain activity will be tranthmitted through them and recorded on thenthor boxeth during your tetht. There are five luminouth pointh on the chip. When all of them turn red, you will hear a beeping thound in your head. That ith your cue to move to the exit.'

'I can't really see me own forehead, sir,' ventured Faith.

'I'm thure your friend will tell you,' he replied, uninterested.

Julius nodded, trying to keep a straight face.

Once out of the room the guard led them along a narrow, descending corridor.

'We must be underground,' said. It was an obvious statement to make but now that the laughter had passed he felt anxiety creeping back. Between the medical test, the chip on his forehead and walking along artificially illuminated, empty corridors, he felt as if he was on a conveyer belt.

I can see why Kaori said that the test's not really difficult, thought Julius, frustrated. He was being scanned and tagged, but nobody was interacting with him or asking him to prove himself. He was about to share his feelings with Faith when the guard huddled them all in front of a double door. He then pushed a button and a wall came down behind them, enclosing them in a small space. A few seconds later, the door in front of them opened and Julius felt a wave of energy passing through him that made his hair stand on end, while his ears were trying to adjust to the loud noises assaulting him from every direction. He was staring at the biggest room he had ever seen.

'Holy Fagioli! This room's gotta be at least fifteen meters high,' shouted Faith.

'No kidding,' replied Julius. If Faith's estimation was anything to go by, then the room must have been easily 100 meters long. He saw dozens of sensor-boxes all along the walls; beneath them numerous adults in white coats and helmets were busy typing notes on their pads. In the corners, large computerised panels flashed constantly. If Julius thought that the sidelines were busy, the middle of the room was positively chaotic. Hordes of boys were running around while boxes, chairs and the occasional desk zoomed along the ceiling. Several small fires burned brightly here and there. From what he could tell, they were seemingly using their mind-skills for an obstacle course of some sort, only there was no *visible* course. Each person was acting independently, performing whatever task they chose, from shifting objects with their minds, to starting fires. Some just stared blankly at the teachers. The lights on their foreheads were showing different colours. The majority of them were yellow, some were green, and only one boy, Julius noticed, had two red lights on his forehead.

'They look like little running Christmas trees,' said Faith.

'What are they doing?' asked Julius, incredulous.

Without warning, the guard behind them blew a whistle.

'Your turn. Move it!' he shouted.

They stepped into the crowd anxiously, as if they were walking through a panic-stricken herd of buffaloes, but it took Julius only a few moments to adjust to the chaos around him.

'I suppose they just want me to show my skills,' thought Julius. At that moment, he heard a loud and clear voice inside his head: '*Make them fly!*'

He didn't recognise the voice but he instinctively knew it was a command. In front of him, he saw two little boys attempting to create a fire. Julius concentrated and fixed his gaze on them. Instantly they both levitated off the ground, puzzled expressions on their faces. When they were a meter above the floor and bouncing like yo-yos in midair, they started to scream, but among all the chaos no one heard them. Julius kept his mind locked on them and shot them across the room. When he thought that they looked green enough, he gently landed them back on the floor. He then touched his forehead, trying to figure out if his sensors had gone off, but to his frustration he couldn't tell. He sidestepped as a box flew past his head and glanced around, looking for the next challenge. Suddenly the same voice popped into his head: '*Quick, danger above you!*'

Julius looked up – a fire extinguisher was plummeting through the air towards Faith, who was busy turning someone else's small fire into a blazing furnace. Behind him, the owner of the fire extinguisher was running with his nose pointed to the ceiling trying to regain control of it, oblivious of Faith's bonfire. Julius locked his eyes onto the fire extinguisher and stopped it a couple of meters above Faith's head. At the same time, he ordered Faith to halt the boy behind him. He did this wordlessly, with his mind. Faith promptly extended his hand towards the boy, who stopped dead in his tracks as if he had hit an invisible wall. Julius then landed the extinguisher gently on Faith's lap, who took it and put out his fire. Julius let out a sigh of relief and, walking towards Faith, looked down at the ashes of the bonfire – a bright crimson flame instantly sprung from the ground, lighting up the room.

'Show off,' said Faith laughing.

At that moment, Julius felt a strong buzzing sensation in his head.

'Your sensors are all red! Am I lit up too?' shouted Faith over the noise.

'Yeah! That was quick. We've gotta get out of here,' replied Julius. 'Lead on.'

They jostled their way through the crowd, Julius moving people out of their path with small mind-pushes. Once out of the room, the buzzing in their ears stopped. There were ten cubicles lined in front of them. A man told them to queue at different ones.

'Good luck,' said Julius.

'Same to you,' answered Faith before they got separated.

When Julius finally sat down, a young lady in a white coat smiled at him and, with a pair of tweezers, peeled the chip off his forehead. He was knotting his hands together, unable to sit still.

'Are you nervous?' she asked him, kindly.

Julius nodded and tried to smile, but his mouth had dried up. He watched her place the chip into a machine that looked like a microwave. She then closed the door and a red light flashed on. He sat there for what seemed like an age. Seconds felt like years. He was glad to be in a cubicle where no one could see him, for in that moment he was sure he had failed and that the lady was going to tell him that they were sorry but he just wasn't good enough. Finally, a green light blinked on and the machine printed out several pages of charts and symbols that Julius couldn't understand. He looked at the woman. She looked at the charts, wide-eyed. With an encouraging, surprised smile she looked back at Julius. 'I believe congratulations are in order.'

Julius's face broke into the biggest grin, totally at a loss for words.

'Follow the corridor,' said the lady, 'There is a waiting room two floors up and on the left. Someone will need to see you before you can go.'

Julius thanked her and walked past her desk into the corridor beyond. The noise slowly subsided behind him. He went up the stairs in a blissful trance and eventually found himself in front of the waiting room. As he entered the room, he was relieved to see that Morgana was already there, talking enthusiastically to a red-haired girl. When she saw him, she ran towards him, grabbed his shirt and looked into his eyes.

'Do you know what this means?' whispered Morgana excitedly. 'It means that WE-ARE-IN!'

Julius was beaming. He still couldn't believe it. His stomach was full of butterflies. He was so charged up that he felt as if he could have lifted the roof off the building with just a blink of his eye. He looked around and saw two people chatting at one of the tables and, in another corner on his own, sat a very smug-looking Billy Somers intently reading a magazine.

Julius realised that, of all the dozens of children he had seen that morning, only six were sitting in that room. He was proud to be among them and more so because Morgana was there too. He also hoped that Faith would join them soon since, without him, Julius could not have displayed his abilities so clearly or finished the test so quickly. Besides, Faith had performed well and had shown that he was surprisingly receptive to Julius's mind-messages. Before then, only Morgana had ever responded so quickly to Julius, and they had known each other for many years.

As if in answer to his wish, the waiting room door opened. With the happiest expression, Faith entered the room followed by an officer, who took a seat in the corner. Julius and Morgana went over to congratulate him. As they walked past where Somers was sitting, Julius noticed his smugness had been replaced by a mixed expression of shock and disgust. He looked as if he was about to burst, but obviously thought better of saying anything with an officer present. As Faith took his place next to Julius, he flashed a cheeky grin in the direction of the now positively furious Billy Somers.

For the next two hours everyone in the room, with the exception of Somers, chatted about the events of that morning, sharing detailed descriptions of their tasks. They all agreed on how lucky they had been to make it through.

'Anyway, what's the story with that room of chaos? People could have hurt themselves,' said the red-haired girl in a thick Welsh accent. Morgana had introduced her as Leslie Rogan.

'It's so they can test your skills under pressure of course,' answered Faith. 'They figure that when you're in trouble you don't have time to think, so they want people who are quick. Speaking of which, Julius, next time you send me a mind e-mail like you did before, do it gently. You almost blew me brain off!'

'Oh, I'm sorry. Next time I'll come and ask your permission first.'

'Did you really speak with Faith?' asked Alan Cross, one of the other selected people. 'I mean, I could hear the messages from the teachers, but I couldn't really speak back.'

'Sure he did,' cut in Morgana. 'Julius is very good at that. When we were six, we used to team up at card games and cheat all our parents' friends out of their small change. I would challenge them, he would stand behind them, look at their cards, and then tell me what they were with his mind.'

'Remind me never to play cards with you, Julius,' said Faith, raising an eyebrow.

Finally, the door opened. A man in a navy blue uniform entered and stopped in the middle of the room, facing the group. He was tall and athletic and, although his expression was rather stern, he had a young, attractive face. He looked at each of them in turn and for a few moments not a sound could be heard. Julius grew a little uncomfortable under his gaze. As his eyes moved to the next person, Julius could have sworn that he had smiled almost imperceptibly at him.

'I am Master Cress, Second in Command of the Tijara School,' he said. His clear voice echoed in the room. 'You have been selected to join the Zed Academy. It is a great honour but also the end of life as you know it.'

With that, he reached into his pocket and drew out several small envelopes. 'Marion Lloyd and Billy Somers, step forward. You are to join the Sield School.'

He handed them an envelope each, which they took before stepping back again.

'Alan Cross and Lesley Rogan – Tuala School,' he continued.

Julius could see that Morgana was quite disappointed, because she had really wanted to join her sister, Kaori, at Tuala.

'Julius McCoy, Morgana Ruthier and Faith Shanigan – Tijara School.' They moved forward to receive their envelopes. Julius was pleased to see that he wasn't the only one who was trembling nervously – Faith's chair was practically vibrating beneath the excitement of its owner.

Julius looked at the envelope that had his name printed on it. Next to it, they had written "1MJ". Morgana had told him that all first and second year students were called Mizki Junior, and that Mizki was the name of the scientist who had first studied mind-skills alongside Marcus Tijara.

'The envelope contains all the necessary information that you and your parents need to read,' continued Cress. 'On Sunday, the 31st of August, you are to report here at 08:00 hours. A shuttle will fly you to the Zed departure centre in Prague. Latecomers will, of course, remain here. You are now free to go,' he finished. With that he nodded to the group and left the room without so much as a second glance.

'That guy needs to chill,' exclaimed Faith, once the door had closed.

That made them all burst into laughter. All except Somers, that is, who simply walked out of the room with his nose upturned.

'And he could do with the same therapy,' added Julius, pointing to Somers, adding fuel to their laughter.

He could feel the tension of the morning ebbing slowly away and being replaced by a sense of relief. Julius was struck by a certainty that he would always remember this moment as one of genuine, shared happiness between a group of people who had just realised their greatest dream.

*

Nathan Cress stood peering through the window of his office, which overlooked the main entrance. His eyes followed Julius as he left the building. As soon as the boy had disappeared into the fly-car park, a beeping noise caught his attention. He turned towards the centre of the room and crossed his arms in front of him.

'Good day, Carlos.'

The holographic shape of the Grand Master Tijara, Carlos Freja, appeared in the middle of the room.

'And to you, Nathan,' said Freja. 'I trust you have good news.'

'You were right. The boy's mind-skills are off the charts and balanced right across the board. And he hasn't even started his training yet,' said Cress with a tinge of excitement in his voice. 'He is a natural White Child.'

Freja nodded. 'Perfect. Salgoria must not know, or she will go after him too. Her threat is growing as we speak, but we shall be ready for her when the time comes. Train him hard; keep him safe. You know what to do.'

'Of course. Leave that to me,' said Cress, as the hologram slowly faded.

THE ROAD TO THE MOON

On the morning of the 31st of August, heavy black clouds covered the sky above the Zed Test Centre. Nothing could be seen around the building but pouring water. Julius stood at the window of a waiting room, watching the rain draining away into the flowerbeds. At that moment, Morgana came running across the paved square. Before entering through the circular door, she turned and waved to her family, who were standing near their fly-car, huddled under an umbrella. Because parents were not allowed into the centre, Julius had had to say goodbye in the Bumble Bee. The McCoys had enjoyed a long and cheerful meal together the night before, during which Jenny and Rory had given Julius plenty of good advice. Mrs McCoy had shed a few tears that morning and decided to give Julius his yearly dosage of kisses and hugs, all the way from Edinburgh to Maryport. Mr McCoy had been very excited ever since the beginning of that week. He hadn't even seemed to mind that Julius, impatient for his departure, had gone a little out of control with his skills. The only time that he'd had to reprimand his son was when half of the bathtub had disappeared, while he was in it. Michael, on the other hand, seemed to have taken Julius's leaving very badly. When his brother had told him about his test back in April, Michael had been very excited, but as the months had passed, he had grown quieter and quieter. The realisation that it would be another two long years before he would have the chance to join Zed, and therefore be reunited with his brother again, had put him in a miserable mood.

'You can come and visit me in mid-winter,' Julius had told him in the fly-car. 'I'll show you Satras and the Hologram Palace, and we can play games all day.'

The idea of playing with his brother in a Hologram Palace had had a soothing effect on Michael, who had squeezed his brother tightly. 'You're the best Julius … and not just because of the Hologram Palace.'

'I love you, Mickey,' Julius had said, hugging him tighter.

Thinking of Michael made Julius smile. He had promised him that he would write as often as he could and he intended to keep to his word.

Just then, Morgana walked into the room, leaving behind a trail of water.

'I have now crossed the line between being wet and being water,' she said, dumping her soaking rucksack on the floor.

Julius helped her remove her coat. 'Seen anybody else in the parking lot?' he asked.

'Yes. There were five fly-cars all steamed up,' answered Morgana. 'I think there was a lot of talking and crying going on. It took me a good hour to leave home. My granny didn't want to let me go. She was so upset that in the end my Mum decided to stay behind with her.'

'I will miss your granny,' said Julius, 'especially her amazing choc-toffee-coffee pie. Who knows what they're going to feed us up there.'

'Only the best cuisine!' exclaimed Faith, entering the room and turning Morgana's trail of water into a puddle. 'It was in the chip that Cress gave us. You haven't read it, have you? Tut, tut.'

'Hi Faith, does that chair of yours float too?' asked Julius, watching water drip off it and onto the floor.

'Yes, and it's also waterproof,' he answered. 'However, I am not. Can you help me to get this coat off please? It weights a ton.'

Julius helped him while Morgana took his rucksack and put it next to hers.

'What did you guys bring in the end?' she asked. 'It took me forever to decide.'

'That's because you're a girl,' teased Julius.

'And you mister, are very predictable. I bet you brought music, history books and your Tolkien collection, which by the way, you must have read at least thirty times already,' answered Morgana wryly.

Each student was only allowed to bring one bag, weighing no more than five kilograms. The school would provide every essential, from toothbrush to underwear, to classroom materials. They were also told not to bring any spare clothing. It was true that Julius had packed quickly and that Morgana had been mostly right: he had packed everything that she had said and also an extra chip containing the addresses of his friends and family. His rucksack was pretty light, but he knew that whatever he might need could be found in Satras.

'What's in your bag then? I bet you brought pictures of airports,' said Julius, dismissing her last remark.

'Actually, I put some music and books on my chips. I also brought a copy of my favourite world landscapes and the encyclopaedia of the history of aviation,' said Morgana.

'Books and music for me too,' added Faith. 'Plus me trusty repair kit for the chair. I never leave the house without it.'

Gradually the other four students arrived. Billy Somers continued to avoid any interaction with the group, as if it would contaminate him somehow. Julius was grateful for Somers's quiet attitude – this was an exciting day for everyone, and nobody needed a spoiler.

At eight o' clock sharp, the door opened and a middle-aged woman in a grey suit entered the room. 'Attention please,' she said in a firm voice. 'Behind you are two doors leading to changing rooms – left for the ladies and right for the gentlemen. Inside you will find a bag with your name on it. I want you to change into your uniform and place your civilian clothes in the bag. Leave them there. They will be sent back to your families. You have 15 minutes.'

Julius grabbed his rucksack and followed Alan Cross into the changing room. There were four grey packs lined up in the centre of the room. Julius found his own one and dragged it to the nearest bench. Excited, he pulled out a pair of combat trousers, a long sleeved cotton t-shirt, a jumper, a pair of socks, boxer shorts, and a pair of sturdy boots. Each item was navy blue. There was a label on the left sleeve of both the jumper and the t-shirt. Julius grinned with pride as he read the silver letters: 'Julius McCoy – 1MJ – Tijara School'. He was about to remove his own jumper when a sudden thought made him stop – would Faith need help getting changed? And how was he supposed to ask without embarrassing him in front of the others?

Unfortunately, Somers seemed to have had the same thought and was now turning towards Faith. 'Shanigan, do you want me to call that nice lady to help you out?' he asked with a sneer.

Julius froze, unable to believe what he had just heard. He knew that kids often mocked each other for a laugh, but in certain cases you just didn't. It was a line no one with even a hint of decency would ever cross. For that reason, the changing room had suddenly gone quiet and all eyes were fixed on Billy and Faith.

'Thank you Somers,' said Faith, smiling suddenly. 'But I'm already waiting for your sister.'

Somers's face turned danger-red and he advanced towards Faith, fists clenched. Julius and Alan Cross immediately jumped between them.

'Let me at him!' cried Somers, trying to remove Cross from his path.

'Yeah, let him come!' shouted Faith, waving his fists in the air.

'He insulted my sister!'

'That's 'cause you insulted him first!' shouted back Julius, trying to keep Faith's chair from advancing.

At that moment, an angry female voice bellowed out from a speaker in the room: 'If I hear another sound coming from that room, none of you gentlemen will leave this Zed Centre. Ever!'

Julius felt Faith's chair stop, and released his hold. Somers threw Faith a nasty look and went back to his bench.

'I don't need help,' said Faith, his cheeks now slightly flushed. With that, he turned around and started to undress.

Julius did likewise, but kept glancing towards Faith to check that he really could do it by himself. To his surprise, he did so very smoothly. His chair had special in-built arms that could lift Faith's body and legs while he changed his trousers.

Once ready, Julius folded his old clothes and placed them inside the grey pack. There was a mirror in the room and, when Julius caught sight of his reflection, he instantly knew that this uniform was the symbol of a new life. Julius and Faith both had navy blue uniforms. Alan Cross's was dark red and Billy Somers's was olive green. They went back to the waiting room where the girls were already waiting. Morgana's uniform was also navy blue, but under the jumper she was wearing a pleated, knee-length skirt and a pair of tall leather boots with flat heels.

The grey-uniformed woman threw a hard look at the boys. 'Everyone follow me now,' she said sternly and led them out of the room past the reception desk.

Crossing over the paved square, they walked past the visitor's building where their parents had waited for them during their test, and arrived at a runway. There, a small white shuttle was waiting for them. It was perched on three wheels, with a set of steps leading to an opening in its side.

The rain was still lashing down so everybody ran to the steps, covering their heads with their rucksacks. Faith waited behind for the others to embark, and then hovered directly inside.

Once aboard, they were told to sit near the front. Faith moved over to the designated area, where he locked his chair in place. The woman checked that all their seatbelts were fastened while the shuttle prepared for takeoff. Julius looked out of the window to see if the Bumble Bee was still there but the rain was too heavy to make anything out. The shuttle engines hummed into life and several minutes later they were airborne.

The flight to Prague was only thirty minutes long. Julius watched the landscape rolling by quickly, with Morgana's head resting on his shoulder. Below him, he saw other vehicles criss-crossing in the air and knew that none of them were allowed to fly anywhere near their Zed shuttle. When Julius was eight, Mr McCoy had explained to him that there were three different flying systems in the world. The lower one was used by fly-cars; the second system, at a higher altitude, was for private aircraft and fly-buses; the third one, an exclusive, high-speed system, was only to be used by Zed personnel. Any trespassers risked being sucked into the jet-stream of the fastest aircrafts on Earth, and if they were still alive after that and had no good reason for trespassing in the first place, being deported to the infamous Halls of Ahriman. Mr McCoy had not been too sure about where Ahriman was or where it had gained its reputation from, but the general opinion was that it was a damned place and for the young Julius it was enough to decide that he would never trespass in the Zed high-speed system.

They were flying over the German border when the pilot announced that they would be landing in the next few minutes. Morgana leaned over Julius to look down. It was a beautiful sunny day and they could see Prague below with the river Vltava dividing the city into two halves.

'Look, that's Charles Bridge, and that one is Prague Castle,' said Julius.

They watched the west side of the city passing by, while the shuttle slowly descended towards the Zed departure centre. Upon landing, the aircraft kept moving along the runway and disappeared inside a tunnel. When it finally came to a halt, the woman led them all out.

The departure centre was a large hall with metal walls and a stained glass roof. Sunrays were streaming through its glass panels, creating beautiful rainbows on the floor below. Julius saw several doors leading out from the main area, some marked "ZED PERSONNEL ONLY" and others "CIVILIAN PERSONNEL ONLY". There was also a café, lit up in purple neon, and a number of world restaurants. The main hall was crawling with boys and girls of all nationalities. Julius saw that in the middle of the hall, hovering in mid-air, there were three silver signs. Each of them represented one of the three Zed schools. Below each sign, three squared sectors had been created with metal rails to gather the respective students. Julius's group followed the woman with the grey uniform through the noisy crowd. She stopped before a small gate, behind which was Tijara's sector. A tall officer, wearing a Tijaran uniform, took three microchips from the woman and ushered Julius, Morgana and Faith inside.

'See you in Satras,' said Morgana, waving to the girls.

'Bye Julius. Bye Faith,' Alan Cross called after them.

'Yes, Shanigan, see you later,' added Somers sarcastically.

The woman pushed Somers forward unceremoniously before Faith could reply.

'What was that about?' asked Morgana, holding the gate open for Faith. She suddenly heard Julius's voice in her head: '*Somers has been on his back ever since last spring, and Faith has his own wonderful way of dealing with provocation.*' He then gave her a quick summary of that morning's skirmish in the changing room. Morgana shook her head and muttered something about boys and brains.

When they entered the sector, a few smiling faces turned towards them.

Julius, Faith and Morgana smiled back and moved towards the side of the perimeter.

'There must be about sixty of us in all the sectors and more are coming out from the aircrafts,' said Faith, hovering high above their heads, until the Tijaran officer told him to land immediately.

Twenty minutes later, they heard the officer talking into an earpiece, confirming that his students were all present. Julius looked around him and counted 30 people in his group. He was curious to know where they were all from but knew better than to browse around in other people's minds. His parents had taught him very early in life about the importance of freedom and privacy. 'How would you like it if Morgana knew all your secrets and told them to your friends?' Mr McCoy had asked him. Julius had blushed furiously at the thought and since then had tried very hard to not take his skills lightly. However, there were occasional moments in which he could unintentionally perceive other people's thoughts, especially when he was relaxed, and that made him very uncomfortable.

Slowly, the area between the sectors and the runway cleared. All the students were inside the perimeters and Julius watched as the Tijaran officer joined them and locked the gate behind him. Suddenly, the platform on which they were standing began to descend through the floor. Julius grabbed hold of the rail to steady himself and Morgana held on to Faith's chair. He felt the platform changing direction several times as it followed its underground track before coming to a halt in front of a wall where a single door stood. The officer spoke again into his earpiece and the door opened. He then turned towards the students.

'My name is Captain Foster. I am in charge of Tijara's security. Every year I volunteer to collect the new students from Earth so that I have the chance to memorise each and every face. Make sure you do not have reason to meet me again, except for official receptions … or war.' He paused and fixed them all with an icy look.

Julius thought that his voice alone had been enough to carry his point home, even without the killer stare, but obviously he wasn't going to bring that up.

'Once through this door,' continued Foster, 'you will be inside the Zed shuttle. I want you to occupy seats one to thirty. Lift off is at 10:00 hours. In two hours, you will be in Zed. Shanigan, you go first. Move it!'

The group parted quickly to let Faith pass, and Julius and Morgana followed him. They entered from a side door near the front of the shuttle. There were two long rows of seats, three-by-three, divided by a corridor. To his left, Julius saw the other students embarking, the Tuala group in the centre and the Sields at the back. Faith moved to the top of the left row and locked his chair in place. Julius and Morgana took the seats behind him, leaving an empty one near the corridor.

'I'm glad there has been some progress in gravity research,' said Julius, fastening his seatbelt. 'Can you imagine travelling to the Moon in one of those ancient rockets?'

'Aye, it must have been murder,' said Morgana, examining the shuttle. 'These models look just like normal aircrafts, but the magic is in the engines.'

'As always,' said Faith. 'However, I would improve it with a touch or two, starting with the thrusters setup that is …'

At that moment, a boy walked up to them. He had a bush of brown curly hair and a dark tan.

'*Aloha*, mind if I sit here?' he asked, smiling.

'Not at all,' said Morgana, who as always was the first to socialise with strangers. '*Konnichiwa!*'

'Wow! Was that Japanese?' asked the boy.

'Yes it was. But it's easier if we keep using the common speech. I'm Morgana. These two are Julius and Faith.'

'I'm Lopaka Liway, from Hawaii. Good to meet you!'

'Hawaii?' cried Faith. 'Do you surf by any chance?'

'Even when I sleep,' replied Lopaka.

'Then you are me man. Come, sit. We have much to discuss,' said Faith, excitedly.

Julius and Morgana looked at each other, puzzled. Even Lopaka appeared to be surprised but, since he clearly loved the sport so much, he was more than happy to pass the time discussing waves, waxes and boards.

When the shuttle lifted off, Julius barely noticed it, but he knew that he was rising above the clouds and making a straight line for the stars. The idea that he was leaving the Earth's orbit was slowly sinking in and he felt a new wave of excitement rushing through his body. He was happy to be there, happy to be alive and even ashamedly happy that there had been a Chemical War, since it was the only reason he was now on his way to the Moon.

As Morgana had gone to meet some of the girls behind them, Julius joined Faith and Lopaka in their surfing chat. They had been flying for over an hour when Morgana came back and dropped herself into her seat with a big smile on her face.

'I've met some of the girls in our class,' she explained happily to Julius. 'Many of them come from the colonies and they were telling me all about it. Maybe one day we'll be able to visit them. Wouldn't that be great?'

'And maybe you'll be piloting the ship that takes us there.'

'One day I will. Right now though, I want to watch this Zed video with you. When I went to visit Kaori before, it wasn't on our shuttle. Put on your headphones.' Morgana pushed a button on the armrest of her chair and a holoscreen appeared in front of them. She put on her own headphones and plugged Julius's in next to hers. A few seconds later, the head of a young pretty woman with a blonde bob appeared on the screen.

'Good morning, and welcome to space! Please select the topic of interest from the choices below.'

Three touch-pads appeared over her smiling face: 'Moon', 'Marcus Tijara' and 'Zed Lunar Perimeter'. Morgana touched the first one and the screen faded slowly to black. As different pictures of the Moon started to scroll past, the lady's voice told them all sorts of information. Julius knew most of the things she was telling them about but he did manage to learn some new facts.

'As seen from the Earth, the Moon appears to have bright and dark patches – the bright ones are craters and mountains which can catch the Sun's light, and the dark ones are low-lying plains. Centuries ago, those plains were thought to be seas, or *mária*, and today we still call them by their first given names, such as Sea of Rains or Ocean of Storms, although in truth the Moon is entirely without water.

'The Moon does not have atmosphere, which means several things: the edges of the shadows are sharp as razors, since there is no mist to make them softer; there is no sound, since this needs air to travel; there is no protection from the Sun during the day and no way to imprison heat during the night, creating great extremes of temperature. Along the Equator, the daily temperature is 100 degrees Celsius, whereas the night temperature can fall to -160 degrees.'

'Whoa,' cried Julius. 'That's almost as low as liquid air!'

'Well, I'm not planning any trekking outside the Lunar Perimeter,' added Morgana quickly.

'Let's hear about Marcus Tijara,' said Julius, touching the screen. The woman's smiling face reappeared and so did the three options. He pressed the next button and the screen faded once more to be replaced by the face of Marcus Tijara.

'Marcus Tijara was the first scientist to research the effects caused by the Chemical War of the 25th century. Tijara himself was granted the gift, or curse as some would call it, of highly developed mind-skills. By 2620, Tijara, who had become highly esteemed in the eyes of the Earth Leader, was granted permission to build the Zed Lunar Perimeter on the Moon. The Perimeter was to become home to the Curia and to the Zed Academy, a base for exploration of the galaxy and a defence system to maintain the hard won peace on planet Earth.' The blurb finished and the main menu reappeared.

'Is that all?' asked Julius, disappointed. 'I thought she was going to tell us about Marcus's battle with Clodagh Arnesh, and of how they both died.'

'We'll probably study that in class.'

Julius pressed the last button.

'This is the Zed Lunar Perimeter,' said the woman. 'Only Zed Members and Curia personnel are allowed to live in the Perimeter. Students of the schools are given special permission to reside in Zed until completion of their six years of training, which will qualify them as Zed Members. They will study for two years as Mizki Juniors, two years as Apprentices and two years as Seniors. The only habitable lunar area, Zed has been developed across four low-plains. As you can see from the picture, the plain at the top is the Sea of Serenity, where you will find the Zed Docks. Below it is the Sea of Tranquillity, where you can relax in the bustling and friendly Satras. Who said that the Moon doesn't have atmosphere?' added the voice with a giggle.

'I can't believe she said that,' said Julius, in a deadpan voice.

'She did, she did,' added Morgana, equally serious.

'… Just to the right of the Sea of Tranquillity,' continued the woman, 'we have the Sea of Fertility, where the Zed schools are situated: Tuala, Sield and of course Tijara, where Marcus himself was Grand Master. In the schools, selected students can develop their mind-skills in the form of White and Grey Arts. Finally, the plain at the bottom is the Sea of Nectar, home to the Curia, where the headquarters of Colonial Affairs are located.'

The woman's head flashed up for the last time, 'If you require any further information, visit us in Satras, at the information kiosk. Thank you for your attention and, once again, welcome to Zed,' she said, as the holoscreen disappeared.

'It's all so exciting,' said Morgana, putting their headsets away.

'Learned anything new?' asked Faith, now that they had finished.

'Yeah. The lady here recommended going for a walk outside Zed around midday,' said Julius.

Faith looked a bit puzzled, but Morgana shook her head and rolled her eyes. 'Don't listen to him. She didn't say that. However, she *did* say some interesting stuff.' Morgana then promptly filled Faith in on her latest discoveries.

Ten minutes later, a voice came through the speakers which were fitted above each row. 'All students return to their seats immediately and fasten their seatbelts for landing.'

Excited murmurs spread through the shuttle as everyone ran back to their seats. Unfortunately, he couldn't see much through the small windows, so Julius had to be content with sitting back comfortably, closing his eyes and imagining his very first landing on the Moon.

A NEW HOME

The shuttle came to a halt at the Zed Docks at 12:00 hours. The students were so excited that half of them threw off their seatbelts the instant they landed. Captain Foster, who was in charge of the Tijaran students, stood in the middle of their section with his hands behind his back. A single glance from him was all it took to get everybody's attention.

'We are about to board the Zed Intra-Rail system,' he said. 'It will take us to Tijara. Where I go, you go. Keep your eyes on me at all times and don't make me come and find you. I also strongly recommend that you practice your school's salute.'

Julius threw a worried look at Morgana, because he couldn't remember what the salute was. By the look in her eyes, it was clear that she wasn't going to be much help.

'Have either of you two actually read that chip?' asked Faith with a theatrical sigh. 'What are you like. Come on, I'll show you what to do once we get on the train.'

The students poured into the corridor and Julius let Morgana and Faith go ahead of him. The shuttle door opened onto a platform inside a brightly lit gallery, where the train was already waiting.

'Shame, I thought we would land in the centre of our own docks,' said Morgana, disappointed. 'This is where any old visitor from Earth lands.'

Julius looked to his right, where a metallic gate blocked the tunnel. Behind it, he thought with excitement, were all the spaceships that he would soon be flying. He had just enough time to see the other schools' students boarding the two train compartments behind his own, before he was dragged inside by Morgana.

'I feel like I'm inside a suppository,' said Faith looking around, and indeed the train carriages did have that exact shape. With the exception of the metallic floor, the three sections were completely made of glass, no doubt to give a better view on the journey.

The train left the tunnel and made its way out of the Sea of Serenity. Not one of the students uttered a word; they were too busy staring all around them, mouths gaping in wonder. Julius wasn't sure that his brain was actually registering where he was. The surface of the Moon was bright grey and interrupted by small ridges, gaps and channels – the old scars left behind by the meteorites that had collided with it eons ago.

'Look above you, guys. That shield is the coolest of all! I wish I had invented it,' exclaimed Faith.

Julius and Morgana looked up as Faith enthusiastically imparted his technical wisdom on them. 'See, the shield recreates Earth's atmosphere and covers the whole of Zed. Not only does it block out the sunlight, which would turn us into toast otherwise, but it's also the reason why we can breathe and why we have gravity … and see those little dots there, and there and … anyway, that's the illumination system. It gives us night and day as we'd have on Earth and keeps the temperature constantly mild.'

Julius noticed that Morgana was listening to this description in a sort of trance, as if

Faith had been describing a succulent fudge cake. He smiled knowingly – for Morgana, technological wonders were as tasty as honey was to bears.

'That's really great, Faith, but now show us that salute thingy,' said Julius, lowering his voice and checking that nobody was listening.

'Oh, it's quite simple really. You place your right fist on your heart, or was it the left … no wait …'

'Faith,' cut in Julius, 'can you visualise what you saw in that chip?'

'Sure. Why?'

'I'll try to break in.'

'You what?' said Faith, sounding very worried.

'You won't feel a thing, promise. Just close your eyes. Morgana, give me your hand. You too, Faith. On three. One … two … three!' Julius closed his eyes.

From the darkness, a familiar single point of light emerged, growing slowly into a tunnel. Julius projected the tunnel mentally forward until he came across Morgana's mind-link. He joined it to his own and together they shot forward into Faith's mind. There, an image began to form: hundreds of people stood in orderly rows. Julius concentrated on a boy at the front. His right arm was pressed against his body, fist clenched, while the other hand rested on the shoulder of the person to his left. A voice cried, "In your heart!" and everyone shouted back, "Tijara!". Julius saw that on pronouncing the last syllable, the boy slammed his right fist against his heart and stamped his right foot on the ground. Then the image faded and he drew back from Faith.

'I got goose bumps,' said Morgana. 'That looked positively … charging.'

'I got goose bumps too,' said Faith, 'but only because I feel violated! It's incredible that you can do that, Julius. Just remember to ask first, all right?'

When the train approached Satras station, it didn't stop, but turned left towards the Sea of Fertility, where the schools awaited. Slightly puzzled, Julius watched as Morgana started to climb the back of Faith's chair.

'Can you fly up a bit, Faith?' she asked, tapping him on the shoulder. 'I want to see if I can spot Tijara.'

'You'll bang your head on the ceiling, woman!' said Faith, hovering upwards.

'There it is! I see it. It's soooo beautiful,' cried Morgana with her hands and nose pressed against the glass roof. At those words, the other students turned to the left and let out a gasp as Tijara appeared from behind a bend.

An outer wall of sandstone surrounded a tall glass dome, whose upper portion touched the Zed shield and merged with it. From the top of the dome, water slid down the glass and fell in gentle waterfalls over the sandstone walls, ending in a placid moat that surrounded the school, making it appear as if it was on an island. Embedded in the wall were large stained glass windows, framed by luscious tropical plants and multi coloured flowers which stretched towards the sky. The reflections created by the artificial light as they bounced off the water made the school glow like an oasis in the middle of a desert.

Julius turned around just in time to see Captain Foster watching the students, a rare little smile on his face. Then he straightened up and resumed his usual seriousness.

'Tijaran students, time to get your bags, double quick! Miss Ruthier,' he said looking at Morgana. 'I think you've trespassed enough on Mr Shanigan's hospitality.'

Morgana leapt off Faith's chair onto the floor, almost landing on a boy who was standing nearby. The boy steadied her and smiled. She looked into his green eyes and Julius noticed her turning very red indeed. He also saw something else – a faint wisp of pink rising above her head. Julius had seen wisps like that before; he had long since figured that they must be emotions and generally that was his cue to look away because, when people displayed their feelings so strongly, it was easier for him to look into their minds.

When the train came to a halt, he shouldered his rucksack and followed as the Tijaran students stepped out onto the platform.

'Are you sure we're not in the Caribbean?' asked Faith, stretching his arms contentedly.

After hours spent cooped up inside buildings and shuttles, Julius was loving the warmth of the air on his skin. The rain of Scotland, which only that morning had soaked through his clothes, was already a distant memory.

The platform led them towards the main gate of Tijara, creating a bridge over the moat, which was protected from the waterfalls by large sheets of glass. Captain Foster ordered them into a single line and ushered them inside one by one through a small barrier on the right side of the entrance. When Julius's turn arrived, the Captain told him to look left into a dark, square gap. He saw a red dot and knew that his retinas were being scanned. There was a beeping noise and the barrier opened. He moved forward into the reception area, where a man in a grey uniform was gathering the students in front of a glass door. His badge read "James Leven, Front Gate Guard". To the left of the barrier Julius saw a waiting room furnished with sofas and armchairs. It was a pleasant area where the light streamed through stained glass windows, creating a warm atmosphere. Behind the sofas, a staircase disappeared into the floor. Above it, a sign read "TIJARA – HANGAR ACCESS".

'That'll be my bedroom then!' said Morgana, pointing at it.

'You should get them to change the sign then. For privacy, you know,' added Faith.

At that moment, Captain Foster brushed past them and touched a button to the left of the door, which slid open noiselessly. They stepped into a large circular promenade, tiled in white marble. Potted plants stood between sliding glass doors, which opened at regular intervals along the perimeter. In the centre of the promenade, a black cylindrical structure rose all the way up to the ceiling. At the point where it merged with the dome, water trickled down over its slick surface, creating an encircling pool at its base, which was lined with benches. The double doors of this inner structure opened as they approached, and Foster ushered them inside.

The brightness that had accompanied them throughout Zed disappeared unexpectedly and it took a few seconds for Julius to adjust to the dim light of the hall. Ahead of him, he could see a raised podium with a handful of seats behind it while the rest of the hall was occupied by rows of chairs, facing towards it.

Foster motioned for them to sit at the front. Julius and Morgana did so, deliberately choosing seats at the end of the first row, so that Faith could stop next to them. When everyone was settled, they heard a noise above their heads and watched in astonishment as the ceiling parted, revealing the black and starry sky beyond the Zed shield.

'Welcome to space,' said a voice suddenly.

All heads turned towards the stage, where the Grand Master of Tijara stood. Julius recognised Carlos Freja immediately from the portrait he had seen in the Test Centre. If the man in the picture had produced a sense of admiration in Julius, the real one made him want to hide behind his seat, for the sheer intensity of his grey eyes alone. Every bit of Freja screamed order and discipline: his short hair, his pristine blue uniform, his posture. Even his voice had sounded powerful without being overly loud. Julius watched, enraptured as Freja scanned the students with his piercing eyes and, when they came to rest upon him, he could have sworn that they had widened imperceptibly. Gradually, the Grand Master let his face relax a little, and the faintest hint of a smile appeared on his lips. Julius heard Morgana, and several others behind him, let out a sigh of relief at this change.

'I trust your journey has been pleasant. Judging by Captain Foster's report, I believe you were all pleased at the sight of Tijara.' As he said this, he looked towards Morgana and Faith with an eyebrow raised and Julius saw his friends blushing wildly.

'Tijara is the soul of Zed,' continued Freja, 'the first creation of Marcus Tijara on this incredible satellite that is the Moon. And Zed is a gift, born from the mistakes of mankind, for the salvation of mankind. It is a reminder of how low we humans can sink, and of how high we can rise when we set our hearts to following their true path: that of defending the greatest gift of all – life.

'Only thirty of you stand before me today, the thirty most gifted 12 year-olds that Earth and its colonies have to offer. Wear your pride upon your face, for you will carry the traditions of Zed forward. And at the same time, coat your heart with humility, for the journey of life is long and your learning will never end.'

As Freja's words were still lingering in the air, Nathan Cress walked up the central aisle and stopped under the podium, where he turned to face the students. 'Mizki, stand for the salute,' he ordered, standing to attention.

Julius scrambled to his feet along with the others. He put his right arm at his side and his left hand on Faith's shoulder.

'In your heart!' cried Freja.

'TI-JA-RA!' they cried back in unison. As the echo of their voices and stamping feet faded, Julius felt a rush of energy shooting through his body. For the first time since his test, the reality of his new life struck him fully, and he felt tears of pride swelling in his eyes.

Freja nodded, impressed, and left the hall.

'All female students,' said Cress, 'make your way to the promenade and follow Miss Child to your dorms.'

'See you later, guys,' said Morgana, grabbing her bag.

Once the girls had left, Cress got the boys moving too. Waiting outside was an older boy wearing a well pressed uniform and sporting a sharply cropped hairstyle. Julius looked at the label on his left sleeve and saw that he was a final year student, a 6 Mizki Senior, named Tony Tower. He asked them to follow him and then set off. They headed off to the right and walked past a door, which a sign identified as the staff quarters. The boys' dorm was the one after, followed by the girls'. Tower led them on and stopped in a small atrium.

'Each dorm has six underground floors – lift or stairs, it's up to you. Each year has its floor: the first years sleep on level -6. Every room is shared by two students. You'll find your names on the door tags. To open the door, look into the keyhole – it has a sensor that scans your retina. Every security door in Zed works like this and, if you are authorised to enter, it will open. You can make your way down now to leave your bags. You will need to report to the mess hall at 14:00 for lunch. Do not be late.'

As Tower left them, Julius stepped into one of the four lifts with Faith and a few of the other students. When they reached their floor, they found themselves at the beginning of a long bright corridor, with doors to either side. At the end of it, a blue sky could be seen through a large window.

'Aren't we underground?' asked Julius, perplexed.

'It's probably one of those funky scenery screens. Anyway, this is me room right he-'

At that moment, a muffled voice called out for help from inside the room. Faith looked into the scanner quickly and the door opened. Julius stepped back, startled by the sight that greeted him. Partition walls inside the room were sliding back and forth, out of control. Beds and chairs were appearing and disappearing from holes in the floor, while various computer screens were flipping frantically through the side walls. A small boy was stuck in the bathroom at the far end of the room, a look of total panic on his face.

'Press the red button near the door. Make it stop, please!' cried the boy.

Julius, being careful not to get squashed in between the partition walls, reached out his arm to the control panel and slammed his hand against the red button. Everything stopped and all the partitions slid back into place.

'That was close,' said the boy, walking towards them.

'Are you ok?' asked Julius, trying not to laugh.

'Yeah, sorry about that … must have pressed the wrong combination … I'm Bartholomeus Smit – Barth if you please, from Holland.'

'I'm Faith, your Irish roommate. This is Julius McCoy from Scotland.'

'Nice meeting you, and thanks for … you know …'

'No worries, but we should try to get this room sussed before we go to bed,' said Faith with a grin.

'You do that. I'll go find my room,' said Julius, leaving Barth and Faith on the threshold cautiously pressing various buttons.

Julius's room was the third on the right. The name "Skye Miller" was written underneath his. He looked into the keyhole and the door slid open. His new roommate was already there, emptying the contents of his rucksack into the drawers of his desk. Julius recognised him from the train as the one who Morgana had landed on earlier. He had messy blonde hair and green eyes. Julius felt a good vibe coming from him and smiled involuntarily. It didn't happen often, but when it did it was always a good sign. As he walked in, the boy stood up and stretched his hand out.

'How's it going? I'm Skye.'

'Julius. Nice to meet you.'

'Hope you don't mind if I sleep on this side.'

'Not at all. Did you figure out the controls?'

'Sure. Come here in the corner and I'll show you.'

They moved over to the control panel next to the door and Skye pressed the red reset button. His desk disappeared into the wall, leaving the room completely empty.

'This is the starting stage,' said Skye. 'See here, there are two rows of buttons, one for you and one for me. When you press the first button, the partitions come up creating two distinct areas, which are our rooms. Then the second button gets the beds up from the floor. The ceiling is actually a scenery screen, so you can sleep under a starry sky if you like.'

As Skye pushed the second button, Julius entered inside his own area.

'There's a drawer at the bottom of the bed for your clothes,' explained Skye.

Julius opened it and saw that there were two sections.

'It says here to put your dirty clothes on the right,' he said.

'They probably get picked up by someone when the bed is back in the floor,' said Skye. 'Anyway, step away from the bed. The third button opens a section in the wall where your desk and computer terminal are stored. And finally, this last button is definitely my favourite.'

Julius leapt backwards as a large reclining chair came up from the floor while a multi-purpose screen flipped out from the wall.

'This is just!' cried Julius.

Skye joined him inside his space. 'Neat, huh? And once the partitions are up, you can change your room from the inside,' he said, pointing to a small panel on the wall.

At that moment, there was a knock at the door. Julius opened it and Faith hovered inside.

'Is this room something or what?' asked Faith.

'For sure! Hey Faith, this is Skye.'

'Hi. Nice chair, mate,' said Skye, shaking Faith's hand.

'Thanks. I'm quite proud of it you know. Built it all by meself.'

'Faith is very technical,' added Julius.

'Indeed I am, but I'm also famished. Shall we go up?'

They all readily agreed and made their way up to the promenade. With the exception of the other first year students, the place was empty. They walked past the girls' dorm and quickly checked the lounge, a vast room with sofas and tables, and a large fireplace. At the mess hall entrance, Tower was handing out booklets to the students as they walked past him. Julius rolled his up, put it in one of his trouser leg pockets and joined the queue for the food.

The mess hall was a huge area filled with artificial sunlight from the shield. Ten long tables occupied the right hand side, and on the left a food counter separated the hall from the kitchen. Julius could see at least five cooks dishing out mouth-watering platters at incredible speed. To the back of the hall, a glass door opened into what looked like a small garden. Julius could make out trees, benches and even a stream, winding its way around various pathways.

'That looks positively girly …' said Faith, who was looking in the same direction.

Julius nodded. He was sure that Morgana would be quite delighted to spend her free time in there.

Above the tables, mounted against the far wall, was a large screen with messages and name charts scrolling across it. At the top of the screen, the word "Hologram Palace" flashed in bright red letters.

'Look at that, guys!' cried Julius. 'It shows all the top scores from the Satras games.'

'Me name will be there soon,' said Faith.

'And you can check results by school, by team and by individual as well,' added Skye. 'Shame that we aren't allowed on Satras until next month.'

They each grabbed a tray of food, sat down at one of the tables and started reading their booklets. Inside was a black and white map of Zed and another of Tijara. Julius saw that the infirmary was next to the mess hall, followed by the library, the holographic sector, the classrooms for the White and Grey Arts, and the offices. Every sector went deep underground, like the dorms. The booklet also contained information on the

Fyver, the official currency of Zed. It said that, at the end of each week, students would receive up to ten Fyvers that could be spent in Satras, and that the amount gained was tied to how well the student performed during that week.

'Outstanding students,' said Faith in a solemn voice, 'will receive commendations in their files, but act like Billy Somers and you'll get expelled.'

'Who's Somers?' asked Skye.

'A stuck-up nasty number, all the way from the sewers of Earth.'

'He's at Sield,' added Julius, relieved.

Faith continued his scan of the booklet aloud until he found a paragraph on personal conduct: 'Always preserve the school's reputation and remember rule number one, be very careful and thoughtful if ...'

'If what, Faith?' asked Julius, chewing his grilled halloumi salad with gusto.

'... if you decide to start a relationship,' finished Faith, almost in a whisper.

After a few seconds of general silence, Julius swallowed.

'As if ...' he said, looking quickly away.

'Yeah,' butted in Faith even more quickly, 'that's girl's stuff!'

At the end of the meal, Julius placed his empty tray on a trolley and saw Morgana waving to him from the garden.

'Did you eat outside?' asked Julius, sitting down on the grass beside her.

'It's so beautiful here. The sun, the sound of the water, the smell of the trees. I love it!' said Morgana lying down.

'I thought you would.'

Faith and Skye joined them and Faith introduced their new friend to her. Julius saw that Morgana had recognised him from the train, but was relieved to notice that there was no pink wisp above her head this time. He had to admit that the garden was really relaxing and, as all the other students were there too, they spent the entire afternoon lying on the grass, talking and laughing. Thanks to Morgana's friendliness, they also managed to meet most of the students from their year and, when they went back into the mess hall to eat their supper, Julius's table was awash with new faces.

Faith had discovered that Skye liked surfing too, and together they had cornered Lopaka Liway into sharing techniques with them over a crème brûlée. Julius was deep in conversation with a Hungarian boy called Ferenc Orbán who, like him, had a real passion for history. Only when they had discussed the most important monarchs, rulers and dictators of Hungarian history – 'My favourite is Matthias "The Raven"' – 'Agreed. He's the coolest.' – 'What about Zsigmond?' – 'Yeah, but he didn't stop the Ottomans.' – did they feel satisfied and ready to go to sleep.

As he lay on his new bed that night, Julius watched the Milky Way drift past on his scenery screen. His mind was so full of the things he had seen that day, and of the people he had met, that it took him a while to wind down. Eventually his eyes closed and he fell asleep with a big smile on his face.

LIFE IN TIJARA

At seven o'clock, a violent alarm sound woke the entire floor up. A loud voice called for the students to get dressed and lined up in the corridor in three minutes. Julius awoke with a jolt, leapt out of his bed and ran from his area, colliding with Skye in front of their bathroom.

'Where am I? Who are you?' blurted out Skye, his eyes still half closed.

It took them a few seconds to realise what was going on and to retreat hastily back into their areas. Julius grabbed his clothes and ran into the corridor, hoping sincerely that it wasn't going to be like this every morning for the next six years. Outside, Tony Tower was standing by the lift waiting for them.

'Good morning gentlemen. Glad to see you are all present,' he said, looking up and down the two rows of students. Julius did likewise and noticed that yes, they were all present, but most of them were also half naked, except for Faith, who looked as neat and pristine as Tower did.

'From tomorrow,' continued Tower, 'you will be able to set your own alarm, but if one of you is ever late for class, the whole floor will lose that privilege for a week. Breakfast is between 07:00 and 08:30 and you must be INSIDE the class by 09:00. When we greet a teacher or a superior in general, we bow our heads as a sign of respect; they will bow to you in return. Get dressed now, *properly*, and make your way to the mess hall. There I shall hand out your timetables.'

Tower bowed his head slightly and they all bowed back. When Julius got to the mess hall he saw that it was teeming with older students – they had all returned for the start of the new school year. He found Faith and Morgana, sitting at one of the tables, already eating.

'Morning lot,' he said sitting down. 'Did you girls get the alarm from hell too?'

'Aye. You should have seen us: hair everywhere, boots in hands and blurry eyes … not charming.'

'Same here … except for Shanigan.'

'I was already awake,' said Faith defensively. 'I didn't know what time we were supposed to be up, and since it takes me a while … but do not fear! In case of emergency, I shall fight in nothing but me underwear.'

'That's the spirit!' said Skye, joining them. 'Here, these are the timetables.'

Julius grabbed his with excitement but that didn't last long.

'Three hours of Meditation on a Monday morning? You've got to be kidding me!' he said, distressed. '*And* we have to write diary entries for all of the subjects …'

'Telekinesis and … what the heck is Draw?' asked Faith.

'Three hours of Spaceology on a Wednesday morning …' echoed Skye feebly.

'At least it's followed by Martial Arts. And on Friday it's all Pilot Training!' said Morgana excitedly.

That last bit of news was good enough for them, and when they left the mess hall they were in a much cheerier mood.

At 08:40, they made their way to the holographic sector where a man in a Tijaran uniform, by the name of Gabriel List, told them to go one floor down to room one. This area was large and completely white, with no chairs or desks. The students walked in uncertainly, as if they were expecting the whole place to suddenly disappear. The floor seemed to be made of glass, and Julius found himself probing it with his foot to make sure it was thick enough to support their weight.

'It will hold, Mr McCoy, do not worry,' said a kindly voice from behind him.

Julius turned and saw an old Chinese man standing by the door. His head was completely bald, but a thin white goatee reached to his chest. He wore a loose tunic over baggy trousers and a pair of training slippers. Every item of his clothing was as white as his goatee. The man knelt down on the floor and with his arms he gestured for the students to do likewise, in a semi circle around him. He then bowed his head to them and the students bowed back.

'I am Professor Len Lao-tzu,' he said. His voice was calm and well paced, his face relaxed. 'Can one of you tell me your definition of Meditation?'

After a brief nervous silence, a boy put his hand up. Julius had met him the day before – Dumisai Chiddy, from Zimbabwe.

'Sir, is a state of contemplation … Sir.'

'Very good. Any additions to that?'

'Sir,' said Morgana, 'a state of extended reflection or contemplation.'

'Thank you Miss Ruthier. Indeed, reflecting or contemplating for extended periods of time is what we practice in Meditation. There are good reasons for it, obviously. In a meditative state, the body consumes less oxygen and expends less energy. Your brain pattern will show mainly alpha waves: they are the electrical activity of one who is awake, but relaxed.

'In this school, you will learn to develop and control the White Arts. Meditation, being the most basic of them, is also the means to do just that. Being able to relax your mind at will allows you to perform under pressure. This brings us to your aim for this year – to master this art in order to achieve a perfect state of relaxation in less than one minute.'

Lao-tzu stood and asked the students to rise and line up along the walls. Julius heard a buzzing noise coming from under his feet and suddenly the floor split into several different panels, each one large enough for a person to lie on.

'As you can see there are a number of scenery screens on the floor. I would like you to choose the one that best brings forth a feeling of relaxation in you. Then sit on it and wait for the others,' said Lao-tzu.

Julius scanned the floor quickly. There were many country settings, with and without sheep; there was one completely black panel and another with only water. In the far right corner of the room he finally saw one that he liked and moved towards it. It showed a solitary, stony tower rising from the top of a hill towards the night sky. Julius sat down and looked around. Next to him, Skye had chosen the water picture and was watching the fishes swimming below him. Morgana – 'Very predictable,' thought Julius – was sitting on a picture of a forest clearing, with a stream cutting through it and a cloud of butterflies flitting in and out of view. He noticed that Faith's picture was a single fluffy cloud against a blue sky.

'Now that you are all settled,' said Lao-tzu, 'place your finger on the spot where you would like to land. As it is your first time in a holographic environment of this kind, I recommend you close your eyes during the activation – it could be somewhat disorientating.'

He clapped his hands once and each screen, and its occupant, became instantly enveloped in what looked like a soap bubble. Excited, Julius placed his finger on the top of the tower and closed his eyes. Suddenly, he felt a gush of fresh air in his face and, as all other noises faded into the distance, he found himself enveloped by the stillness of the night. Lao-tzu's soothing voice came to him and he opened his eyes.

'Breathe deeply, slowly. Clear your mind of everything and let the night embrace you.'

Julius measured his breathing and focused on a distant point in front of him. After a few minutes though, he realised that it wasn't working at all. He couldn't get his mind to relax, full as it was with all that had happened in the last two days. He tried closing his eyes, he tried lying down, he even tried standing up, but with no success – the night wasn't coming anywhere near him.

'That's great,' he muttered, sitting down again. The thought of spending the next three hours perched on that tower like a vulture made him quite depressed. Eventually he lay down and, without realising it, drifted into sleep. When he opened his eyes again, he saw that he was back in the room. He sat up, embarrassed, but quickly noticed that all of his classmates were also asleep. Faith's head was lolling to one side, while Skye was snoring profoundly next to him. Professor Lao-tzu was sitting facing them, and when Julius met his eyes he felt himself blushing.

'Sorry Professor,' he managed to mumble in the direction of his teacher.

Lao-tzu just smiled and kept still. Eventually the others woke up too and from the general silence, Julius knew that they were feeling as awkward as he was.

'You may go now,' said Lao-tzu.

They bowed to him and left the room in silence. Once in the corridor Faith, Skye and Morgana joined Julius.

'I can't believe I fell asleep,' said Morgana dejectedly.

'We all did,' said Faith.

'Yeah, but I'm the one who's supposed to love hanging around in woods!' she cried.

'What was the point of that? Why didn't he wake us up?' asked Skye.

'Who knows? Mind you, I feel refreshed after that extended nap,' added Julius. 'But I really hope it's going to get better.'

They all nodded in agreement and headed off to the mess hall. The warmth of the garden was too enticing to ignore, so they took their lunch with them and sat on the grass.

Faith was eyeing his diary suspiciously. 'What am I supposed to write?' he said to no one in particular.

'Dear diary,' said Skye, 'I had my first Meditation class today. I slept for three hours. It was great!'

They all laughed at that and Julius felt that he could cope much better with his shameful performance, knowing that he wasn't alone.

After lunch they made their way back to the holographic sector for their Telekinesis class. A man was already there waiting for them. He was tall and imposing, with broad shoulders and thick legs. His face, devoid of any facial hair, was plump and red, as if a heart attack was never too far away. The corners of his blue eyes stretched into tiny smile-wrinkles, a sign of many hours spent in laughter, it seemed to Julius. With an inviting gesture, the man gathered the group around him and they bowed to each other.

'I am Professor Paul King,' he began with a booming voice. 'Telekinesis can be defined as movement from afar. It is the ability to manipulate objects mentally and, since you are standing in front of me, it is safe to assume that you all have that ability.'

Julius thought about his brother, Michael, and of the many times he had made him fly around the bedroom. At least this was something he was good at, so he wouldn't embarrass himself as he had done that morning.

'The possibilities of this particular White Art are endless, starting with your personal defence. Moreover, a highly trained mind can even pilot a spaceship remotely.'

'Now that's interesting,' thought Julius. He'd never known that something like that was actually possible.

'Obviously what makes this skill hard to manage is not so much *moving* the object, as *controlling* that movement. That will be your aim for this year, to perfect the ability to control.' As he said that, he uncovered a crate behind him. 'Take one of these objects and line up at the back wall, then place it at your feet.'

Julius grabbed the first thing he found, a cube made of soft material. When they were ready, King told them to make their objects slide across the floor to the other end of the room. Julius locked his eyes on his cube and felt a familiar click inside his head. Then he pushed. The cube crossed the floor in a straight line, without lifting from the ground. He looked around and was pleased to discover that he had been the first. Faith's cube was rolling over the floor and Morgana's was floating to its destination. Only Skye had it sliding along the surface, but not in a straight line.

King let them try it a few more times before splitting them into pairs. Julius was paired with Faith, and they were told to go to opposite sides of the room and face each other. They were then instructed to send the object back and forth between them. After several minutes however, Faith was still struggling to keep the cube from rolling and Julius was getting bored, so he started to pull Faith toward him along with the cube. At first Faith couldn't understand what was happening, but when he saw Julius laughing, he slammed his brakes on.

'I'd like to see you try that now, smarty. This baby's got hydraulic brakes!'

Obviously it was a tempting invitation and Julius obliged him. Not knowing what kind of resistance Faith's chair would pose, he pulled a little harder than normal and before he knew it he found himself pinned to the wall by Faith and his chair. They burst out laughing, quickly followed by the rest of the class, who had stopped to see what had happened.

'As you can see,' said King with a raised eyebrow, 'the possibilities are *indeed* endless.'

The rest of the lesson flew by and when they left, Julius and Faith started laughing again, thinking of how they would record the incident in their diaries.

*

On Tuesday morning, Julius awoke at eight, leaving plenty of time to wash and get dressed – he really wasn't a morning person. Feeling slightly more human, he joined his friends in the mess hall for a quick breakfast. Once finished, they headed off to their very first Draw lesson, still trying to figure out exactly what the "draw" in question was. Faith was convinced that they were supposed to paint using only their minds; Skye and Julius thought it was where they would learn how to draw up legal documents, in case they ended up working for the Curia; Morgana reckoned that it must be something to do with extracting information from people, using some undefined power. Their teacher, a wiry middle-aged woman with a remarkably long nose, by the name of Professor Cathy Turner, put them out of their misery a few minutes later, leaving them all dumbstruck.

'The power of drawing,' explained Turner, looking over her spectacles, 'is one of the most difficult White Arts to master. It allows the recipient to draw energy – life, if you like – from another living organism.' She paused for a moment, to let the words sink in more effectively. 'Using White Arts depletes energy. Should you find yourself in a combat situation, the presence of something as small as a flower could save your life. Marcus Tijara himself was the first to discover and study this art. Every person who has been affected by the Chemical War carries the genes that allow the draw, but as with every other art, and perhaps more so, drawing requires an incredible amount of control: should you use it untamed, on another human being, you could kill them.'

Professor Turner seemed satisfied with the look of horror on the students' faces and proceeded to distribute little cactus plants among them.

'Since you have just woken up and had breakfast, your energy levels are at their fullest. Therefore, you shall not be able to draw too much. Your cacti have flowers – if the draw is successful, one of the flowers should wither.' As she spoke, she placed a plant on her desk and stood over it while the students gathered around her. She cupped her hands around the plant, as if to shelter it from a wind. Julius watched her fingertips, which were moving slightly, as if feeling for something imperceptible. Suddenly she took a deep breath and held it for a few seconds. At that moment, several students pointed at the cactus, whispering. Julius watched, mouth open, as one of the pink flowers began to wither before falling onto the desk – she had sucked the life from it. After the demonstration, Professor Turner sent the students back to their desks. She then made her way around the class, trying to explain to each of them in turn how they were meant to accomplish the draw.

Julius saw that both Skye and Faith successfully withered their flowers a little. When Turner stopped at Julius's desk, he had recovered from his initial surprise, and since the others were busy writing down first impressions or trying the draw again, he felt ready enough to try.

'Now Mr McCoy, are you relaxed?' she asked him. Julius nodded and she continued. 'Every living organism is surrounded by an energy field. Your fingertips need to feel it. When you have found it, you have to concentrate and *pull* that energy into you. A sudden, deep inhalation is all that it takes to draw. I'm going to connect this energy receiver to your arm, to record how much you draw.'

She placed an electrode on his forearm and Julius tried to relax. He placed his hands around the plant, closed his eyes and started to feel for the energy. It took him a minute before he could feel anything, and when he did, he took a sudden, deep breath and held it. In his mind he could see a blue smoky fluid entering his fingertips, and spreading all the way up his arms to his shoulders, accompanied by a tingling sensation.

He slowly opened his eyes and looked at the plant. To his disappointment however, the flowers were all still attached and looking distinctly perky. The colours had possibly faded a little, but that was all. He looked at Professor Turner, starting to apologise, but stopped in mid-sentence. She was staring, slack-jawed, at his energy receiver over the rim of her glasses. Julius looked at the little needle on the monitor and saw that it was stuck all the way up to the maximum. Somehow, he had charged it completely without killing the plant.

His teacher's hands were still firmly planted on the desk. Julius was trying to decide whether to say something, when he noticed that her digital watch had stopped. Right at that moment, Professor Turner shook herself from her reverie, hurriedly gave Julius a new energy receiver, shovelled three new pots of cacti onto his desk and gathered the old one up in her arms.

'Keep trying, class. I'll return shortly,' she said, rushing out of the room.

The other students turned curiously towards Julius, who shrugged his shoulders, not knowing himself what had happened.

Professor Turner returned twenty minutes later, and the lesson continued without further incident. When the bell rang, she dismissed them with a quick bow.

'Could someone close the door please,' she called to her students.

Julius was the last to leave and as he grabbed the handle to pull the door shut behind him, an electric discharge shot through his fingers. The door swung from his grasp, pushed by this jolt, slammed against the wall and banged shut an inch from his face. He stood there, dumbstruck until he heard Professor Turner's footsteps advancing menacingly towards the door.

'Who is the student who wants a detention so much, that he feels the need to slam my door?'

Julius didn't wait for her to find out, but turned on his heels and headed for the exit at a gallop. When he joined the others in the mess hall, Morgana asked about his draw.

'Even when Professor Turner came back, she was still rather distracted,' said Morgana over her soup. 'I mean, she actually put her hands on the spikes of the cactus during my demonstration. What did you do, Julius?'

'I'm not sure. I did draw some energy, but the flower stayed on.' It was true enough and, although the fact that Professor Turner's watch had stopped was still puzzling him, he really didn't understand what had happened and decided not to share that information with them.

'How much energy did you draw?' asked Faith.

'I maxed out the receiver,' muttered Julius.

'And the plant?'

'Nothing happened to it. No withering.'

They kept eating in silence for a while. Then Skye turned to Julius: 'You could check it out, you know? In the library I saw a chip about drawing. If Marcus Tijara was involved in it, he might have left some notes.'

Julius thought that sounded like a good idea, and decided to check it out sometime before the next Draw class.

That afternoon's much anticipated first Martial Arts lesson, turned out to be a major disappointment as Professor Lee Chan was out of school for the day on business. Instead they ended up in a Grey Art classroom studying anatomy of the human body, supervised by a very serious Nathan Cress.

Wednesday arrived and nobody, except Morgana, was looking forward to that morning's lesson. The Spaceology teacher, Lucy Brown, was an ageing woman with long white hair, who spoke excitedly about every facet of the stars and planets. The first lesson was about the Solar System, and as Professor Brown started to explain that the Sun contained about 99.9 per cent of the System's total mass, Julius's attention sunk by about that percentage. To pass the time, he started to move pens and rulers with his mind over to Faith and Skye, occasionally hitting a classmate along the way. Morgana was furiously taking notes, since this subject bore great relevance to her dream career as a spaceship pilot, and was throwing furious glances over to the boys every time an eraser hit her on the head.

Afterwards, during lunch, they were relieved to find out that Professor Lee Chan had returned, and so they changed into their tracksuits before entering the holographic sector.

The room had taken on the appearance of a dojo, with wooden floors and padded walls. Professor Chan could have been the lost twin brother of Len Lao-tzu – the only difference was that his clothes were all black and his goatee was still brown. When they were all kneeling on the floor, he began.

'I apologise for my absence yesterday, however, I understand you all had a chance to revise anatomy and knowing how our bodies work is fundamental to this discipline. We study this Grey Art for various reasons: fitness, mental discipline, self-defence and combat skills. Although there are many martial arts, the one that will concern us is the Mindkata. A kata is a set routine of techniques performed alone, or sometimes with a partner. The development of your mind-skills, or White Arts, as we call them, is a major part of your training. Therefore our katas are devised for their benefit. Miss Louisa Call,' he said to a small, red haired girl. 'Volunteer, if you please.'

Louisa walked forward, looking more than a little worried. Chan placed a wooden chair in front of her and then asked her to step back.

'If you were to remove an object from your path using telekinesis, what position would you assume?'

Louisa extended one arm forward, open palm facing the chair. Chan asked her to push the chair backwards and she did. It slid to the end of the room and bounced off the wall.

'Thank you, Miss Call. You may rejoin your classmates. How many of you assume that same position?' asked Chan.

Almost every student put their hand up.

'As a martial artist, you will learn a more effective technique for performing that action.' Chan pulled the chair back to its original position, with his mind. He stood with his legs slightly apart, left foot forward. Both his arms were bent by his sides, parallel with his feet. His left hand was bunched into a fist and, of his right hand, only the index and middle finger were outstretched, the other two bent under the thumb. Quick as a cat, he shot both his right hand and foot forward simultaneously. As he did so, he let out a sharp breath, like a gust of wind, and in an instant the chair smashed against the back wall.

'Rapid!' said Faith, ecstatically.

'Quite so, Mr Shanigan,' said Chan, turning to face them. 'What did I just do, Mr McCoy?'

'You used your fingers as … a channel?' answered Julius tentatively.

'Correct, although your entire body is a channel. The powers that you unleash outwards come from within, therefore you can freely choose what means you use to release them. Arms, fingers and legs, because of their shape, create a perfect channel for shooting energy. Next year, you will be introduced to the Gauntlet – it is a device worn on the back of your hand, an outlet for your energy. It gives a colour to it, allowing you to see and control its direction.'

'I wonder,' whispered Faith to Julius, 'can you use your nose as an outlet?'

'I thought your bum would do better!' answered Julius, trying hard not to laugh.

'I could turn me chair into a rocket!' The picture of Faith lifting off was enough to bring tears to both their eyes.

'Perhaps we should give that a try, Mr Shanigan,' Chan's voice suddenly thundered over their heads.

Julius and Faith tried hard to pull themselves together, but their teacher wasn't moved, and as punishment they ended up doing weights for one hour. That night, Julius was quite unable to walk. His entire body was aching and following a quick bite and a shower, he decided to call it a day. When he entered his room, Skye was sitting at his desk, writing. Julius nodded to him and slowly lowered himself onto his reclining chair.

'You don't look too shiny, mate,' said Skye putting down his pen.

'Never mind … what are you up to?'

'Oh, just writing home. If Mum doesn't hear from me regularly, she'll think I'm dead … or worse.'

Julius nodded and thought about the promise he had made to Michael. He couldn't have written to him that night anyway, given that he was unable to even lift his arms and that he had to drink his soup through a straw. So he made a mental note for the end of the week and collapsed exhausted on his bed.

That Friday morning, he and the rest of his classmates were lined up outside the holographic classroom by 08:30 sharp, for their first Pilot Training lesson. When their teacher arrived, Julius could see that he was clearly pleased.

'I have had eager students before, but thirty minutes early? It's a record!' he said with a smile, and ushered them inside the room.

The Professor introduced himself as Farid Clavel, a young man from Lebanon. His uniform was as tidy as was expected of all Zed officers, but Julius thought that his face had a pleasant, relaxed look to it.

The classroom had already been prepared, with thirty simulation cockpits all facing Professor Clavel in two semi-circles.

'Before we start,' said Clavel, 'there is someone I would like you to meet.' As he said that, an old black man with candid white hair stepped inside the room.

'This is Mr Pete Kingston from Mississippi, the owner of Pit-Stop Pete,' said Clavel. Pete smiled at the class.

'Mr Kingston runs an outer docking base in our orbit. Ships come from all over to use his services – from refuelling, to repairs, to construction. No doubt someone in this class will choose to spend their summer camp doing work experience at Pete's'.

Julius could see that Faith was smiling at Pete unashamedly and knew already that his friend would put his tent up in that dock for the whole summer. Pete told them they were all welcome to visit him at any time and, before leaving, Julius watched as he whispered to Professor Clavel, throwing occasional glances at Faith. He found that odd, but perhaps it was just a coincidence.

The lesson finally started, and when Julius sat down in his cockpit, he was really excited. They spent the morning familiarising themselves with all the buttons, levers, panels and screens, over and over again. In the afternoon, Professor Clavel made them work in pairs, so they could question each other about what button did what, route-finding and how to set coordinates for a hyperjump, a facility that all Zed aircraft possessed.

Julius had thoroughly enjoyed the day, even when Faith tried to swap all the controls around because apparently he knew a way of making them more functional. By four o'clock, he knew how to start a spaceship without destroying the engines. As he sat in his room that night, Julius read over his diary entries again. Then he took his laptop and began to write to his brother, Michael, about all the excitement of his very first week at the Zed Academy.

A BIRTHDAY'S BEST GIFT

'I can't believe we've been here a month already,' said Julius one Friday at lunchtime.

He was lying under an oak tree in the garden with his mates, digesting a particularly heavy lunch. The school had become as familiar to him as his own home, and he had settled into the routine quite easily. Nothing ever seemed to change in Tijara, from the spring-like temperature to the sunny sky. Yet, he felt like he had done and learned more in the past month than in all of his 12 years on Earth.

The lessons *had* picked up pace, however, and the teachers had been giving them plenty of homework. Most evenings he could be found in the library doing research or in the holographic sector improving his Mindkata techniques and telepathic control. Professor Turner had made no further comments on his first draw, so he had put the whole cactus incident out of his mind. Besides, he was now able to draw some energy from the little flowers like most of his classmates.

In Meditation, Professor Lao-tzu had let him fall asleep for three weeks, before Julius could exhort himself to stay awake, even if no relaxation had been achieved as yet. Out of their class, only Morgana had managed to stay awake from the second week, but Julius wasn't surprised by that. For many years Morgana had forced him to walk with her in the Highlands, or to sit along the shore of Loch Lomond for hours on end, just soaking up the surroundings – she positively thrived on those sensations.

Morgana was sitting against the oak tree, staring at the stream and looking quite content. Julius knew why: her sister Kaori had just left, having shared lunch with them. She was two years older than Morgana but they were very much alike in both personality and looks. Julius had spent some time with Kaori back home, but as they grew up, the difference in age had become more prominent and she had found an older group of friends. On the subject of friends, Julius had found himself reflecting quite often about how lucky he had been to meet Faith and Skye. They were quite different from each other, Faith with his quirkiness and Skye with his natural enthusiasm, but they were both honest, straightforward people, which Julius appreciated a lot.

Lost in these thoughts, he suddenly remembered that the day after tomorrow would be Faith's birthday. He would have to speak with Morgana and Skye to organise him a present, and quickly. Turning towards Morgana, he called her with his mind. She flinched a little, startled.

'*I need to talk to you,*' he thought.

'*What's up?*' she thought back, still looking at the stream.

'*It's Faith's birthday on Sunday and, maybe if you take him away for a little while, I can organise something with Skye.*'

'*Sure. I'll get him over to the holographic sector or something. Can you let me hear what you say to Skye?*'

'*Hey, I'm not a conference network facility you know!*'

'All right, but let me know what you decide.'

'Sure. Thanks a lot.'

Morgana stood up and, with the excuse of revising flight techniques before that afternoon's pilot lesson, she managed to lure Faith away. As they were leaving, Julius noticed that Skye was about to stand up as well, so he quickly sent him a mind message: *'Don't move. And don't say anything!'*

Skye couldn't have moved even if had wanted to. He had never received a mind message from Julius before and so sat where he was, petrified.

Once the other two had disappeared, Julius turned to him: 'Sorry. I didn't mean to scare you.'

'That was freaky. For a moment I thought my father was behind me.'

Julius explained the situation to him quickly, aware that they only had a few minutes left of their lunchtime.

'How many Fyvers do we have?' asked Skye.

'I managed to get 30 for September. But we can only go to Satras in two weeks' time.'

'Hey, why don't we give some Fyvers to Kaori? I'm sure she can get us something before Sunday.'

'That's a good idea. I'll give Morgana a tenner tonight then, with a list of possible presents. She can get them to Kaori.'

With the present organised, they headed off to class. The first thing they noticed when they entered was that their cockpits had been replaced with individual desks. When Julius sat down, he saw that the surface of the desk was in fact a touch screen.

Farid Clavel waited for them all to be seated before beginning the lesson. 'As you know, all weapons have been banned since the Chemical War. Because over half of the population was decimated during that period, the Earth Leader, together with the five Voices of Earth, representing each continent, successfully implemented the ban. Only the White and Grey Arts were allowed to be used as protection for the human race. In Space, we have not been involved in a large scale conflict since the Arneshians' attack on Zed, back in Marcus Tijara's time. However, one of the purposes of Zed is that we be ready, should that threat, or any other, arise again.'

Julius watched Clavel closely. Since the rumours of a possible conflict between Zed and the Arneshians had begun that April, he had not heard any further news. Clavel's face, however, was unusually serious while he discussed the topic, and it occurred to Julius that perhaps the Space Channel had not been too far off in its predictions.

'If you look at your screen, you will see that I have uploaded some schematics for you,' continued Clavel. 'Spaceship combat is possible because of this device, the ship catalyst. Professor Chan has mentioned the Gauntlet to you – this device is its equivalent. A ship can have as many catalysts as is needed but it is important to remember that a person is required to operate each one. The device channels your energies and amplifies them as much as required.'

Just then Professor Chan entered the classroom and, after a short exchange with Clavel, with several glances thrown in the direction of Faith, he turned to the class: 'Mr Shanigan, please follow me.'

Julius saw that Morgana was looking at him, puzzled, but he could only shrug his shoulders in reply, feeling as clueless as she was. Faith hovered over to Chan and followed him out of the room. Julius could have sworn that there was a look of anxiety on his face. He remembered that there had been a similar exchange between Pit-Stop Pete and Clavel, during their first week in Tijara, and he hoped Faith wasn't in any kind of trouble. In fact, he was so preoccupied that by the time the lesson ended he had very little recollection of what they had been shown.

By nine o'clock that night, however, they were all worried because Faith had still not returned. Resolved to find out what was going on, Julius, Morgana and Skye started along the corridor towards the teachers' offices, in search of someone who could help them. As they were approaching the main gate, Professor Chan crossed their path.

'Professor,' said Julius with a quick bow, 'could you tell us where Faith Shanigan is?'

'Mr Shanigan will spend tonight in the infirmary room.'

'Is he all right?' asked Morgana, clearly flustered.

'He is quite well, Miss Ruthier. He only needs to … get used to his new situation,' said Chan with a smile. 'You can visit him in the morning though.'

With that, he bowed and walked away, leaving them even more puzzled than before. They waited for him to disappear into the staff dorms, and then ran to the infirmary sector, only to find it shut.

'Julius, can't you send him one of your freaky mind messages?' asked Skye, trying to force the door open.

'I was trying but I can't get through,' answered Julius, shouldering the door.

'Boys, leave that door standing, please,' said Morgana looking behind her. 'If Foster catches us, he'll probably throw us out of an airlock or something.' The Head of Security's name was scary enough to make them stop, and so they decided to leave.

'At least we know he's fine,' said Julius, but that night he couldn't stop wondering about Faith's "new situation".

At eight o'clock the following morning, Julius and Skye picked up Morgana and made their way to the infirmary. As they entered, an incredible sight greeted them – Faith was gliding towards them in an upright position.

'Guys,' he cried ecstatically, 'check out me birthday present. It's rapid!'

Julius stopped in his tracks, eyes wide open. Faith was wearing what looked like a long, conical shaped skirt. It was blue like their uniforms and seemed to be made out of horizontal panels, slightly overlapping each other. They couldn't see his feet, just a small gap between the bottom of the skirt and the floor.

'Well that's a new situation and no mistakes,' said Julius, grinning.

Faith explained to them how the school had ordered this new prototype for him, from Pit-Stop Pete. Professor Chan had spent the afternoon teaching him how to use it and Dr Dritan Walliser, the resident physician, had inserted a number of sensors into his legs. Since that last piece of news had made his friends drop their jaws, Faith decided to show them exactly what he meant.

'See, the skirt-frame is fixed to me waist like a belt, and harnessed underneath. The bottom of the frame has the same devices as me old chair: I can hover or glide, or use the emergency wheels – just in case – and if I have to sit down,' he said, gliding towards a bench, 'me brain interacts with the magnetic field of the frame which will make me legs bend accordingly, by activating the corresponding sensors.' He bent forward slightly and, as he did so, the bottom panels began to slide upwards, the lower ones under the ones above them. When they reached Faith's knees, they stopped. He was still hovering, but then his knees started to bend and the frame landed him gently on the seat.

Julius had been speechless throughout this demonstration while Morgana, holding her hands to her chest, had a little tear rolling down her cheek.

'Oh Faith,' was all she managed to say.

Faith noticed her reaction and turned vaguely to Julius and Skye, slightly red in the face.

'This is just!' said Julius. 'Come on, we're going to show you off.'

They left the infirmary and went straight to the mess hall. Needless to say, Faith and his "skirt" became the centre of attention for the whole weekend. They couldn't walk anywhere without being stopped by groups of students asking for a demonstration. Faith happily obliged them each time, and by Sunday night his control of the frame was as smooth as could be. In light of this development, Julius had agreed with the others to postpone buying the birthday present until they went to Satras themselves, so that Faith could choose some new gadget for his skirt. On Sunday night, they gave Faith a card instead and promised to take him shopping soon.

As their first visit to Satras was approaching, the Hologram Palace was all the 1 Mizki Juniors could talk about. Every meal time would see the first year students huddled in groups, discussing the latest scores and arguing about who was the best of the best. One Friday evening, Julius was having a snack in the garden with Skye and two other students from their year, Gustavo Perez and Yuri Slovich, both from the colonies. Perez had gathered information about the games from an older student and was sharing his knowledge enthusiastically.

'You can compete in different formats, but the ultimate glory comes from playing Solo, and being good at it. Or else you can play regular games as a team – it can be as large or as small as you like. It can represent a year, a nation, or even a continent. Or it can be just you and your roommate if you like.'

'Obviously only teams from the same category can compete against each other,' added Yuri. 'So, for example, you and Skye couldn't compete against a national team.'

'Yes we could,' cried Skye, 'and we would kick ...'

'Yeah, yeah,' cut in Yuri. 'Wait until you start before you boast. There's nasty competition out there.'

'Like who?' asked Julius.

'See that guy over by the stream?' said Yuri, pointing over his shoulder.

'What, the one surrounded by girls?' said Skye in awe.

'The very one: Bernard Docherty, a 5 Mizki Senior. He's the Solo Champion for the whole of Zed. Only the top ten high scores are displayed for the Solo game – the first is his, the other nine have been there for the last fifty years.'

Julius watched as Docherty sat on a bench, his long legs stretched out before him. A small crowd was gathered around him. He must have been talking about something exceptionally interesting, judging by the look of admiration from the boys, and by the adoring glances of the girls.

'What are the team games like?' asked Julius, still looking at Docherty.

'The main difference,' Gustavo answered, 'is that in team games you use your Grey Arts, like piloting or martial arts, whereas in Solo it's all about your White Skills and how strong your mind powers are. There are different kinds of group games. Broadly speaking, you can divide them into two categories: combat simulation and flight, which are racing games. But, even if you should race fifty times in a row, the tracks always change – the computer randomises it that way.'

'That's another way that Solo games are different,' added Yuri. 'They can be race, fight, or a bit of both, only you don't get to decide. But, whatever comes up when you enter the simulator, the difficulty level remains the same.' He glanced at his watch and said, 'Anyway guys, we need to go. And Skye, my mum says that your mum wants you to write to her, or she'll chuck all of your surfboards into a black hole.'

'Right, thanks Yuri,' said Skye, looking distressed.

'What's it like on the colonies?' asked Julius, after Yuri and Gustavo had left.

Skye propped himself up on his elbows and plucked the grass blades around his hands. 'Weird,' he said, smiling at Julius. 'People think that, just because we're far away from the Curia and Earth, we sing and dance all day.'

'Don't you?' asked Julius, teasingly.

'Maybe on the *actual* colonies they do, but not where I come from. My home is on Terra 3, one of the Zed space stations in the Indus constellation.'

'I thought that all space settlements belonged to Earth,' said Julius, a little confused.

'The colonies do, but they were formed after the three Zed space stations were built. Only an active member of Zed, graduated from the schools, can live on them. My dad for example, studied at Tuala and now works on Terra 3. When he married, my mum moved there too, and when he retires they have to move back to Earth, or to one of the colonies.'

'What if you have a brother who doesn't get selected for the Academy?'

'Then, when he's sixteen, he has to move out and start a life for himself.'

'Can you find work in these places?'

'Sure. There's always something needing done when humans are around – you can open a hairdresser's if you really want! Obviously you can't live in a villa surrounded by trees, but if you fancy a day in the country you just use the holodeck.'

'Being out there,' said Julius, creasing his eyebrows, 'weren't you ever afraid of being attacked by the Arneshians?'

'I thought about it sometimes. But Dad said they wouldn't dare. The space stations are well protected and, besides, the Arneshians would have to pass by Zed before reaching us. *And* they don't have any mind-skills.'

'None?' asked Julius.

'Don't they teach you space history on Earth?' asked Skye.

'I would have studied that in high school, if I hadn't been selected for Zed. As it is, I haven't had a chance yet. Wanna bring me up to scratch, oh smart one?'

'For you? Sure,' said Skye, flashing him a wink and sitting up. 'Lesson one: Clodagh Arnesh – she was Marcus Tijara's friend and colleague. They researched the mind-skills together – only Arnesh didn't have any. Instead, she was incredibly gifted at everything technological, which was also a knock-on effect of the Chemical War. When they opened the Zed Academy, Arnesh established the Grey Arts and taught them in this very school. She invented Mindkata and was one hell of an engineer. Faith would have loved her. Then fame went to her head and she desired to become the Earth Leader, since she had done so much for it with her studies. But, with no mind-skills, she needed Marcus's support. She tried to convince him to join her in her power quest, but Marcus refused. Arnesh was envious of his talents, and so were her supporters: all folks with no mind-skills, just like her. They fought, until Marcus banished Clodagh and her followers to the Taurus constellation. She settled on a planet in the Pleiades star cluster and named it Arnesh. A few years later, Marcus created some sort of powerful weapon to use as a defence in case Arnesh decided to return, which she did. Marcus's weapon did work, however both he and Clodagh were killed. Nobody really knows how or why, although my dad believes that someone does know, but they just won't tell us. Some of her followers survived obviously, and they retreated to Arnesh to bide their time.'

'So, even if they were banished, they could still come back?' asked Julius.

'Of course. Since Clodagh's death, there's always been a ruler on Arnesh who has tried to complete her quest – now they have Queen Salgoria, a direct descendant of Clodagh Arnesh, who's been walking in her great-great-great-grandmother's footsteps. Heck, we've even had our fair share of kidnappings in Satras.'

'What?' said Julius, taken aback.

'Well, at least it's thought that it was the Arneshians, although it can't be proved. The last person disappeared four years ago. He was Tuala's Master at the time, Bastiaan Grant. That one really shook things up in the Curia and they tried hard to cover it up with the Space Channel.'

'Did they ever find him?'

'Kinda. He was dead.'

'But why would the Arneshians kidnap folks?'

'Who knows. Although, I remember one of my dad's conversations back home, after they found Grant. He was talking about some kind of experiments that had been done on his body. Anyway, don't worry about it – our borders are well guarded by the fleet. If they did try to re-enter, we would know.'

A sudden shiver ran down Julius's back. He didn't feel like sitting outside anymore. The black sky seemed quite ominous to him after their conversation and he wanted to be back within the safety of the school's walls. Later that night, as he was tossing and turning in his bed, he struggled to shake the feeling that the Arneshians could in fact re-enter their galaxy somehow. If the Space Channel reports were anything to go by, it could already have happened.

SATRAS

On Saturday morning, Julius and one hundred other students gathered at the train stop outside Tijara's gates. The crowd was so excited that, when the train arrived, Julius was almost lifted off the floor and had to elbow his way into the compartment. By the next stop, when another 100 students boarded from the Tuala School stop, they were all jammed in like sardines in a tin. The train finally stopped at the Satras platform, which lay at the opening of a large cave situated at the centre of a gentle ridge. Julius wedged his way out of the carriage with some difficulty, only to find himself piled against a mass of bodies in the queue for the security checkpoint. Together with Skye he tried to protect Faith from getting squashed, skirt and all, while Morgana and Siena, a pretty Italian brunette in their year, pushed forward through the crowd ahead of them to create some space. When they finally reached the entrance, they had to separate and walk single file through a set of turnstiles, as if they were entering a football stadium, only instead of handing over their tickets they had to look into a retinal scanner.

When they finally emerged on the other side, they found themselves standing on a large terrace overlooking Satras. Julius gasped in wonder, as it was more amazing than he had ever imagined. The town itself was carved into the rocky mantle of the Moon, rather than above the surface, and its look reminded him of the inside of the Colosseo of Rome. Someone had excavated tunnels and caves all around, now occupied by shops, cafes, restaurants and hotels, all covered in neon lights. Thin bridges criss-crossed in mid-air, linking all the facilities. They were packed with students running from one level to the other. Streams of emerald green water flowed out from hollows, cascading over the rocks and crashing with a roar into a large central lake. All around its shores were small tables with benches, where visitors could sit and enjoy the view of the waterfalls and the little wooden boats floating peacefully on the surface of the pool below. It was always night in Satras but, with the neon lights and the emerald water, the whole town glowed like an eerie light bulb.

The town had been built at the same time as the Curia and the schools. It was a place that served numerous functions: the ministers would meet there to conduct business, to welcome delegations from the colonies and to hold official receptions. As only Zed members were allowed inside the schools or the Curia, all visitors would converge here, where they could be accommodated in one of the many hotels. The students would come to spend their hard earned Fyvers in the various shops and cafes of Satras, but mainly in the famous Hologram Palace. There were also rumours of unofficial, secretive business transactions being conducted once all the students had returned to their respective schools, although no employee would ever have admitted to that.

'Look there – on the other side!' cried Julius.

Opposite the terrace and across the lake was a tall tower protruding out of the

Moon's jagged rocks and stretching all the way to the ceiling. Above the entry archway, the words "Hologram Palace" were carved into the rocky face.

'Let's get down there. Come on!' said Skye, running towards the platform-lifts at the side of the terrace.

There were six lifts in total, continuously moving in a loop from the entrance to the ground floor. A man stood by the lifts, helping people step carefully over the gap. Julius was suddenly reminded of the ferris wheel back home, which was mounted every year in Princes Street gardens for the Hogmanay celebrations. Together with Michael, he would pester his dad to take them there with the repeated and often broken promise that they would not use their skills to make the wheel go faster.

Julius and Skye stepped lightly onto the lift, Skye giving his hand to Morgana in a proper, gentlemanly manner, while Faith smoothly hovered his way over.

'You know,' said Julius, eyeing Faith's skirt, 'if this thing crashes you'd be the only one left alive, with that gliding gadget of yours.'

'I hope not – you still owe me a birthday present!'

'Oh, really?' said Skye. 'How would you like a pink ribbon to go with your bloomers?'

That made them laugh so much that the lift shook beneath their feet. Several of their fellow passengers shot frightened stares at them as a result, so they quickly calmed down.

'We'll look for your present later,' said Julius to Faith. 'Let's go shake that tower up first.'

Once on the ground, they stepped off the lift and pushed their way through the crowd, oblivious to all the bustling around them. Reaching the gate of the Palace, Julius stopped and looked up. The tower was so tall that he couldn't see its top, his view further hindered by the green reflections thrown up by the water. They walked through the Palace gate and into a well lit hall. Small monitors were fitted all along its walls so that visitors could check the availability of the rooms and sign up for games. There was also a smaller section of screens where rooms could be booked for other functions, such as entertaining guests, worshipping or simply relaxing. In the centre of the hall was a kiosk, manned by an extremely wrinkled old lady. Her name badge identified her as Mrs Mayflower. Above her head, a sign read "Information and bookings". Three arches yawned out behind the kiosk – signposts indicated that the side ones led to the hologram rooms and the central one to the arena.

They walked through the middle arch into the inner ring, which was cluttered with small groups of students. Some of them were debating what to play and who should play what; others were just sitting on the large steps, watching the games unfold on the giant screens surrounding the arena.

'I think we should go for a racing game,' said Skye after a few minutes.

'Excellent idea!' said Morgana excitedly. 'I feel like showing off a little.'

'I'm in,' said Julius. 'What about the teams? Two against two, or …'

Julius broke off as Billy Somers barged his way through the crowd, followed by three other Sield students.

'I think you should race against us,' he said to Julius, with a smirk. 'And we'll play with a girl too, to make up for the guy in the skirt.'

Julius didn't reply but instead looked at Faith with an "Are you going to let him get away with that?" expression on his face. Faith smiled in his usual unconcerned fashion and gestured for Somers to lead the way.

As the Sield students walked past them, the girl turned to Faith and stopped. 'I can't really stand his big mouth,' she said in a light French accent, pointing at Somers. 'I only want to play. I'm Amelie by ze way, and zey are Ben Clatt and Eric Offson.'

Faith was clearly pleased by that remark of support and immediately introduced her to Julius and the others. Together they walked to the kiosk, where Somers had already booked a game.

'The game's a race,' said Somers. 'Two teams, eight planes. Last pilot standing wins. Let's go!' Somers started towards the left door, calling his team to him with an arrogant snap of his fingers.

Julius's eyes widened in disbelief. 'Did you see that?'

'How anyone can stand that pompous bore is beyond my comprehension,' added Morgana with a shake of her head.

Somers's team mates weren't impressed either.

'Does he think we're his dogs or something?' said Eric.

'This is the first and last time I play with him,' answered Ben, snapping his fingers back in the direction of Somers.

Julius was standing just behind them and listened to their outraged comments with delight.

Beyond the left door, a set of stairs led them downward until the corridor split into two paths. Julius saw that the one on the left was signed "Combat" and the other "Flight". They followed the right corridor, which led into a spacious room where several other 1 Mizki Juniors were already gathered.

'If I can have your attention please,' a male voice cried over the group. 'My name is Mr Smith, the Flight sector technician. As this is your first time in the Hologram Palace, you need to listen up. Every time you play in teams you will come to this floor. Behind me are two changing rooms – girls to the right – where you will be given your holosuit. Get changed and wait inside until your team is called. Leave through the green portal and a technician will lead you to your individual holosphere. During flight games, you will pilot a one-man vessel through a series of obstacles. This plane is built exactly like a Cougar, which is Zed's fastest aircraft.'

Morgana tugged excitedly at Julius's sleeve when she heard that, while he actively ignored her and continued listening to Mr Smith's instruction.

'To remove the obstacles and the enemies out of your path, you will use only the plane's laser gun. Now, to remove an enemy Cougar from the game, first you have to shoot them – if you hit them in the right spot, a circle will appear above the plane; second, you have to fly your plane through your enemy's circle. When you've accomplished both of those tasks, they will disappear from the game. Your own mind-skills will be blocked off and cannot be used during team games. If you want to show off, you'll have to play Solo. Now, get changed!'

The buzz of excitement accompanying that last order was tangible. The technician watched the students entering their changing rooms and, as Julius's group approached the door, he called Faith to one side. 'When you've collected your holosuit, keep walking to the end of the room. There's a space there where you can get changed more comfortably.'

Faith nodded and glided inside. Julius was pleased to hear that, since he really didn't want to see a repeat of what had happened in the changing rooms at the Zed

Test Centre back in August.

The holosuit desk was near the door and Julius awaited his turn eagerly. When he reached the desk, the technician measured him with a critical eye and selected a holosuit from under the counter. Grabbing it, he walked inside. The changing room was long, with lockers along both walls and metal benches running down its centre. The front of each locker had a small screen fixed to it. Opposite the entrance, were two doors to either side of the green portal. The one to the left must have led to shower rooms, thought Julius, judging by the cloud of steam puffing out of the door; the other one was the area where Faith had been directed to get changed.

'This looks just like my wetsuit,' said Skye, 'Only funkier!'

Julius examined his own holosuit – it was black, with bright blue sensors covering almost every inch of it, feet included, all the way up to the neck. He had never surfed in his life, so he copied Skye as he changed, trying not to look too clumsy as he did so.

'It's easier if you sit down,' said Skye. 'Start from your feet and work your way up, like when girls put tights on.

'How do *you* know how girls put their tights on?' asked Julius with a raised eyebrow.

Skye turned slightly red and with a wave of his hand said, 'Never mind that. It's a long story. Anyway, once around the waist put your arms in the sleeves. Zip is at the back.'

Julius followed the instructions quickly and then pulled the zip as far as he could. He felt a piece of cord hanging from its end, so with his other hand he grabbed hold of it from over his shoulder and pulled it up the rest of the way.

'You're a natural,' said Skye. 'You should come surfing with us sometime.'

'Maybe I will. By the way, we didn't really give a team name at the desk, did we?'

'I think Somers might have done it for us,' said Skye, looking slightly worried.

And sure enough, a few minutes later the loudspeaker called out the teams. 'Somers's Gang and the Skirts, make your way through the green portal.'

Keeping their heads very low, embarrassed as they were by their wonderful team name, Julius and Skye followed Somers toward the exit, muttering various unkind remarks behind his back. At the sight of the vast area that stretched out beyond the portal, however, all other thoughts left Julius's mind in a flash.

Contained within the vast area beyond were dozens of long rows of machines reaching to the other side of the room. These were obviously the holospheres that Morgana had told him about. The light was quite dim, but he thought that this floor could easily contain at least 300 players.

Morgana and Amelie emerged from their dressing rooms just in time, as a technician was calling their teams over to the left hand side of the floor. Julius followed them.

The metallic base of each holosphere was fixed to the floor with large bolts. Hovering above its base, a metal ring was glowing pale blue – it was inside this structure that the player had to go. Julius saw the technician lifting Faith off the floor and swiftly hoisting him up inside the ring. Faith grabbed two handles to either side of his head and raised himself up while the technician secured him quickly in place with a waist harness that was in turn attached to the ring. Next, he pressed a button on the back of the skirt and its panels retracted upwards, creating a thick belt around Faith's waist. The man then pushed a button on a remote control, activating the holosphere. Instantly, a magnetic field enveloped Faith, creating a shimmering bubble.

'You lot take the next seven,' said the man to the rest of the group.

Julius went for the holosphere next to Faith's, winking at him as he walked past. He lifted himself up using the handles and placed his feet onto two platforms. When everyone was ready, the technician activated all the spheres at once and all sound disappeared. Julius felt something tightening around his hands, waist and feet, but couldn't actually see any straps. Then a headrest slid down behind him. The pale blue field began to shake madly, sending ripples downward, and as the light became increasingly brighter Julius had to close his eyes tightly. Suddenly he felt as if his body had become weightless and he was no longer secured to the inner ring of the sphere. He opened one eye cautiously, just in time to see himself being lowered delicately inside his Cougar, which was just large enough to contain a comfortable leather seat and a small control panel. He sat there, mesmerised by the vast number of stars glittering in the infinite, dark expanse in front of him. During pilot training with Professor Clavel, they had never done a proper flight simulation in a hologram room. Usually, all that Julius could see from his training station was his classmates. Today for the first time, however, he would be experiencing what it was like to be a pilot on a real plane, and so far it felt great.

A red, intermittent light appeared in the darkness of the aircraft. Julius pushed it and all the controls came to life, illuminating the navigation helm.

'Julius, can you hear me?' Morgana's voice resounded in the aircraft.

'Loud and clear. Skye?'

'Yep. Faith?'

'Does Somers smell like a wet baboon?'

There was a brief snigger across the line.

'That would be a yes then. Morgana,' continued Julius, 'since you're the only one who's been here before, can you tell us what bit of the enemy's ship you have to hit to get the target circle to appear?'

'Actually, no. The sensor changes in every game, so you have to keep firing till you find it. It's half the fun. And mind the obstacles … they tend to be quite vicious. Use them as shields if you can, but shoot whatever you need to.'

'If I get hit,' said Faith 'take out Somers for me, will ya, guys?'

There was no doubt that Julius would give it his all. He knew that it was just a game, nonetheless he still felt quite nervous. Suddenly a robotic voice echoed in his ear, counting down from five. Julius grabbed the handles of the u-shaped steering mechanism and took a deep breath. As the voice reached zero, he felt a mighty acceleration rush through the aircraft and he was shoved against his seat. He began to steady the Cougar into a straight line. There was no clear path that he could see, but his aircraft seemed to know exactly where to go, following some sort of spiralling, hyperactive rollercoaster track. As Julius couldn't see any obstacles coming his way, he started to practice some basic navigation movements. The controls were incredibly sensitive and the response was immediate.

'Julius, is that you driving like a drunken loony?' asked Faith.

'Sorry, I was just getting used to the system,' apologised Julius, steering away from Faith's aircraft.

'Hey!' cried Skye. 'I can see you both. I'm right below you. This is flashy!'

'When you're done fooling around,' said Morgana seriously, 'how about we go wipe them out?'

'Is she always this aggressive?' asked Skye, a hint of concern in his voice.

'Only when she's driving,' whispered back Julius.

'I heard that,' said Morgana speeding past them and disappearing from view in a downward spiral.

'Let's get them!' cried Skye, accelerating after her.

Julius let Faith fly ahead and then followed closely behind. Now that he was getting used to the navigation system, he had completely forgotten about being nervous. He looked over his shoulder through the glass hatch, which extended all the way to the tail of the Cougar, but there was no trace of Somers's group.

'Watch out!' said Morgana.

Julius looked up. Approaching fast, a group of meteorites was blocking the path. He saw Morgana's aircraft smoothly slipping through them and disappearing on the other side. He decided to follow her and accelerated towards a lower section, where the rocks were thinner. He tilted to one side and dived. Suddenly, a bright light flashed to his left and a delighted laugh echoed all around him.

'Did you see that?' cried Skye. 'I blasted my way through!'

Julius pulled level with Skye and gave him the thumbs up. He then accelerated forward to tail Morgana again.

It wasn't long before the next obstacle appeared in front of them. It looked like a giant windmill and it was blocking the entire track. Julius tried to judge the speed at which the blades were rotating, but that wasn't easy given that he was accelerating towards them at such a swift pace.

'Here goes nothing,' he said and dived straight between two blades as a gap appeared in front of him. He was sure his aircraft had scraped something, but he had made it through and his controls still seemed to be working fine. He could feel sweat on his face now and had to wipe it from his eyes with the back of his hand.

'Tornado right ahead!' cried Morgana. 'It'll swing you forward. Don't fight it.'

At the sight of the huge tower of swirling grey clouds, Julius automatically reduced his speed. Unperturbed, Faith whizzed past him and straight into the vortex.

'I'm through!' cried Faith excitedly a few seconds later.

Julius accelerated again and entered the grey column. He felt himself being pushed against the left hand side of his seat as the Cougar was treated to a full spin in the tornado. Then he was propelled forward and shot out like a stone from a sling. He steadied his aircraft as best he could, readying himself for the next surprise.

'Oh boy,' said Skye in a quivering voice. 'I think my breakfast is coming back up …'

'Breathe deeply,' said Julius, 'and do it quickly. I can see the next set.'

A large metal plate was blocking the entire track and the only way past it appeared to be through one of the many openings on its surface. Julius picked the uppermost one, but once inside he realised that it wasn't just a hole, but the beginning of a transparent pipe, twisting itself over and above the others. He couldn't steer more than a fraction to either side, which was probably a good thing since the track was really showing him the meaning of "evil rollercoaster". Suddenly, inside a pipe running level with his, he noticed another aircraft which Amelie was piloting. Julius felt a rush of adrenaline as he realised she had not yet spotted him. He slowed down just enough to let her fly ahead and ensure that her aircraft would come out first. After a few more seconds of inverted loops and sharp bends taken at furious speeds, Julius saw the end of his pipe. As he shot out of it, Amelie's Cougar was still ahead, to his right. He pulled up behind her and opened fire. Her aircraft swerved abruptly in panicked surprise. She started to fly unsteadily, but Julius kept on her tail and didn't stop firing. There were no visible objects ahead that she could use to shield herself and a few seconds later a bright yellow circle appeared above her aircraft.

'Don't lose her now,' Julius said to himself. He wasn't sure how long the target would remain active, so he quickly flew above her and lunged forward through the circle.

'Enemy destroyed,' said the robotic voice flatly.

'Hey, what happened?' said Morgana. 'Who did what to whom?'

'I got Amelie!' cried Julius ecstatically.

'Well done mate,' said Faith. 'One down and three to go!'

'Yes Julius, well d … oh damn!' cried Skye.

'What's the matter?' asked Julius, alarmed.

'It's Somers. He's right behind me!'

'Where are you? I can't see you.'

'I've just come out of the pipes of doom. He's firing like a maniac!'

'Hold on Skye!' said Faith. 'I can see you. Speed up!'

Julius slowed, wanting to give them some back up, but just then the next obstacle loomed into view. It was a giant humanoid robot, standing in the middle of the track and firing quick laser bursts from its eyes. Julius swerved all the way to the right, but the robot kept firing at him. He saw that the gap between its legs was the easiest way to pass him, so he banked sharply towards the centre of the track. Putting his aircraft into a horizontal spin to avoid getting hit, he shot through its leg without so much as a scratch. He was aware that the boys were still trying to shake Somers off, but they were well behind him now.

'Morgana, where are you?' said Julius.

'I've done a fast lap. There's one more obstacle after the robot. I've opened a path through it: bottom right corner. Hey, I can see Eric!'

'Go get him, girl.'

'Roger that!'

Julius kept looking back over his shoulder for Faith and Skye with no joy. The tension was mounting quickly. Then he heard Faith's voice coming through over the line: 'Skye, your target is up. Bend right!'

'I'm trying!' answered Skye. 'Oh bug …'

'Allied destroyed,' said the now familiar robot-voice.

'Faith?' called Julius.

'Skye's gone, but I'm all over Somers like a rash!'

Julius was incredibly frustrated at not being able to see what was happening.

'I got his target up!' cried Faith. 'You are so mine, Somers.'

'Get him, Faith!' shouted Julius.

'I'm almost in … almost … almost … Gotcha!'

'Enemy destroyed.'

Julius joined Faith in a bout of celebratory whooping.

'Enemy destroyed,' droned the voice once more.

'Sorry, that was me,' said Morgana cheerily. 'Eric is no more.'

'All hail the skirts of the team,' laughed Faith.

Julius was approaching the last obstacle now – a solid wall of overlapping plates. He saw the gap that Morgana had made and, with a big grin on his face, he flew straight in. Little did he know that Ben Clatt's aircraft was waiting in the darkness on the other side. At first Julius saw only a shadow to his left. It was only once he had returned to the middle of the track that Ben opened fire on him. His heart skipped a beat in surprise. Looking over his shoulder, he saw Ben's Cougar right on his tail.

'Get off me!' cried Julius, trying to shake him off.

He dived as fast as he could, then steered his Cougar into several twists and spirals, but Clatt was never too far behind. The first obstacle was approaching again and Julius noticed that many of the meteorites had disappeared from the bank, so he flew straight through a large central gap and kept accelerating. True to his memory, the windmill appeared soon afterwards. He opened fire against its blades and managed to blast open a safe passage without slowing down. As soon as he made it to the other side a red alert sound echoed inside his aircraft.

'Target activated,' said the voice flatly.

Julius maintained his breakneck speed, but Clatt's laser fire was all around him. Sweat poured down his face as he made a desperate sprint towards the tornado.

'Come on!' he told himself as the swirling column loomed closer.

For one brief moment, Julius really believed he would make it to the other side, but it was just then that Ben's aircraft flew straight through his target. Everything went dark and he felt as if a massive weight had entered his body, dragging him down into the seat. He opened his eyes and found himself back inside his holosphere. The technician walked over to him and deactivated his restraints.

'Game over, I'm afraid,' he said, helping Julius down. 'Make your way to the changing room so you can watch the end of the game.'

Julius nodded and headed for the exit, trying to keep his legs steady. He walked past Faith's holosphere and thought that he looked like someone in a deep sleep, but with a very agitated dream going on inside his head.

'Julius, come here quick!' called Skye from a corner of the changing room.

He was standing there with the upper part of his holosuit hanging around his waist, intently watching the screen on his locker with Eric.

'That was some chase man,' he said to Julius.

'Don't tell me. I must have sweated a couple of buckets.'

'Not as much as Clatt is sweating right now. Faith and Morgana are all over him. He doesn't stand a chance.'

Julius watched as the three aircrafts sped beneath the giant robot, trying to avoid being hit by its lasers. Once past it, Ben ended up between Faith, who was firing mercilessly from the left hand side, and Morgana, firing from the right. A few seconds later Clatt's yellow target appeared and Faith flew out in front of him, forcing him to pull back. As he did, Morgana, who was poised behind him, flew through the target and Ben's aircraft disappeared from view.

A line of writing scrolled across the screen: "The Skirts have won the game". Julius and Skye celebrated with a low five and shook hands with Eric. Somers, predictably, had already skulked off towards the showers.

Half an hour later Julius, Faith and Skye were sitting on the steps of the arena waiting for Morgana and, when she arrived, she ran to them with the biggest of smiles.

'That was some flying, lady,' said Faith, nodding in admiration.

'Yeah. I bet you'll become the best pilot in our year,' added Skye.

Morgana blushed slightly and gave a little bow.

'Well, I don't know about that, but we can definitely be the best team in our year!'

'As soon as we learn how not to get shot!' said Julius, looking towards Skye and laughing.

'Come on, you guys were great too,' answered Morgana. 'Besides, Julius, you're in the charts for first kill.'

'That will save my honour, this time at least.'

They left the Hologram Palace, still talking about their race, and Julius was surprised to find that he didn't really mind too much about having been eliminated – he'd just had the greatest time with his mates and nothing could have spoiled that.

As it was almost lunchtime, they decided to look for somewhere to eat. Satras had filled up even more since that morning and Julius was taken aback by all the different nationalities of the people around him. He found that comforting and was sure that Marcus Tijara would have loved to have seen his dream of a united Earth come true.

They were about to step onto one of the bridges when Faith suddenly stopped: 'Look guys, it's Pit-Stop Pete! I'm gonna go thank him for the skirt.'

They were quite happy to join him and take a closer look at this famous character of Zed. However, as they drew nearer, they realised that Pete was locked in deep conversation with two other men, and he seemed quite upset. They stopped a little distance away, waiting for him to finish. Julius caught a glimpse of a black wisp rising from Pete's head. He shook his head slightly and the wisp disappeared – he didn't need his powers to see that Pete was having an argument. One of the men, who was wearing a red cap down to his brow, stood in front of Pete with a calm, almost mocking expression on his face. Julius felt that something was not quite right about him.

'He feels ... different,' he thought, although how so, he couldn't say.

Eventually the men left and Pete remained there, shaking his head. Faith advanced slowly towards the old man and the group followed him.

'Excuse me, sir,' said Faith timidly.

The full head of snow white hair turned suddenly around. As soon as he saw the skirt his face lit up.

'Mr Shanigan,' he said in his pleasant drawl. 'How good t' see ya out an' about.'

'I don't know how to thank you for me gift,' said Faith blushing, 'but it means the world to me.'

Pete's smile widened.

'Then I'm even gladder I made it, son. Nothing can come between us an' our dreams. You remember that.'

'He sure will,' said Morgana, moving forward. 'He just won his first race in the Palace!'

'Is that right? Wanna be a pilot?'

'Morgana is the pilot really. I want to build Zed's spaceships,' answered Faith, with more confidence in his voice.

'I'm sure you will. But be prepared, in this here line o' work ya'll have to swallow a lotta dirt, kid.'

'You mean like the two guys that you were talking to?' asked Julius earnestly.

Morgana nudged him in the ribs and he realised that he had been too forward.

'I'm sorry, I didn't mean to ...'

'It's all right, son,' cut in Pete kindly. 'My dockin' base is always full an' very busy. The last thing I need's a ship parked there for no reason, takin' up precious space, unloadin' stock that's not even for me. But that's how the Curia wants it, an' there ain't nothin' I can do about it. That's what I mean by dirt. Well, don't you go worryin' about it, now. You enjoy your new gadget, Mr Shanigan, an' I'm sure I'll see ya soon for a little work experience, right?'

Faith nodded enthusiastically and shook his hand with evident admiration. Pete waved to them all and hobbled off into the crowd. Julius followed him with his eyes. Pete had tried to dismiss the incident, but the black wisp had reappeared above his head.

THE HOLOPAL

The opening of the game season had sent Julius and his classmates into a frenzy as they looked to spend as much time as possible in the Hologram Palace. Students were allowed in Satras every day, although they had a curfew of eight pm from Sunday to Thursday and nine pm on Fridays and Saturdays. The Skirts – they had unanimously decided to keep the name that had brought them such good luck in their first game – had managed to squeeze in several sessions after classes, as training for the weekend. At Julius' suggestion, they had agreed to concentrate on racing games for that year and to play only against each other during their weekly training. The extra practice had paid off, as over the following weekends their stats had improved greatly among the 1 Mizki players. To Faith's immense pleasure, Billy Somers' name was nowhere to be seen in the charts.

The Skirts' quick rise to fame had even been noticed by Professor Clavel, who had made several positive remarks during their pilot training lessons. One such afternoon, Julius and his classmates were logging off from their computer terminals, concluding a hard day of work on basic engine maintenance theory.

'Your attention, Mizki,' said Clavel to the class. 'How many of you have used the race simulation games?'

A forest of arms quickly shot up. Julius looked around and noticed that only four girls and Barth, Faith's roommate, had not put their hands up.

'As a *suggestion*,' continued Clavel, 'I would recommend that everyone get at least a few games under their belts before the end of term. Our first flight sim-lesson in school won't be until February and a little experience will be greatly advantageous.' With that he looked directly at Julius and his team mates. 'I have noticed that some among you have taken a particular liking to racing games. Isn't that right, Miss Ruthier?'

'Yes sir!' answered Morgana, evidently delighted at the direct acknowledgement from a teacher.

'I am very pleased,' answered Clavel. 'Incidentally, how did you come up with your team name?'

Morgana blushed and looked over at Faith.

'It was a good, good friend of ours who suggested it, sir. We didn't want to disappoint him,' answered Faith, with one of his trademark grins.

Clavel nodded and dismissed the class, ignoring the fact that both Julius and Skye could barely contain their laughter.

Unfortunately, as they went deeper into November, Julius noticed a sudden increase in the level of homework they were receiving from their teachers. The game practices had to be cut to twice a week, since most evenings they were either mapping the Milky Way in the library or practising their draws until they had finally run out of cactus plants.

The Martial Arts lessons had become more and more exhausting. Professor Chan had set a fixed routine schedule for the students until the end of term. On Tuesday afternoons, they would run countless laps around the dojo, lift weights and do umpteen push-ups and pull-ups until their arms and legs gave in. On Wednesdays, Chan made them practice Mindkatas for the entire three hours. Following a brief warm up, Julius would face a holographic target and practice his katas against it until the target was eliminated and immediately replaced by a new one. He had to channel his powers through his legs and arms, in sets of one hundred per limb. Then, he would restart the cycle all over again. One time he was so exhausted after training that he fell asleep in the changing room shower, and it was only because Skye had found him twenty minutes later that his skin hadn't completely prunified. After that, the Skirts decided unanimously to cancel game practice on Tuesdays and Wednesdays.

'Heck,' said Skye that afternoon, as they lay sprawled out under the oak tree in the garden, 'I can't even lift my pen to write in my diary, never mind convincing my legs to carry me as far as Satras.'

'I hear you,' added Faith. 'Julius, you might have fallen asleep in the shower today, but last night I fell asleep in me skirt, standing like a horse. Unfortunately Barth decided to wake me up, but given his still appalling knowledge of the room control panel, instead of switching the light on he got the bed out of the wall, which rammed into me waist and sent me wheeling against the wall!'

'Oh boy,' said Morgana, with a snort, 'did you hurt yourself?'

'Nah, but Barth was mortified. He couldn't stop apologising. He's a bit of a menace that one. I don't know if I would trust him with a shopping trolley, never mind a space ship.'

'Maybe you could invite him to practise with us sometime,' said Julius.

'Yeah, maybe – when I'm feeling suicidal!'

*

On Monday morning, after a breakfast of honey-poached figs and spicy potato cakes, Julius made his way to the White Arts sector. Since the beginning of term, he had arrived later and later in the mess hall and often the others would already have left by the time he had finished his breakfast. He really couldn't get himself out of bed early, but since he had never been late for class, no one had ever complained. Monday mornings had also become the worst days for Julius. Although he liked Professor Lao-tzu very much, Meditation was his least favourite subject. He felt that achieving a perfect meditative state in less than a minute was way beyond his abilities. He had tried to change the landscape to see if it would help, but in the end the stone tower on top of the hill had proven to be the only place where he really felt comfortable. Neither Faith nor Skye had managed to go below the time limit, but they had achieved a brief meditative state nonetheless. He didn't even want to consider Morgana, who could get into a trance in 57 seconds, setting the record for the whole class.

As he descended to the classroom that morning, he found his classmates already kneeling on the floor in a circle waiting for Lao-tzu. He squeezed between Morgana and Skye and prepared himself for another dreadful performance. A few minutes later the professor entered the room, kneeled and bowed to the students. He was carrying a small leather box, which he placed on the floor in front of him.

'Good morning to you all,' he said in his usual tranquil voice. 'Before we begin our practice, I would like to introduce you to a very interesting device.' As he said that, he opened the box and lifted out an object similar to a hair band, but made entirely of glass. At its extremities were two pea sized spheres.

'This is a Scrambler, a device built by Clodagh Arnesh herself when she was still a teacher in Tijara.'

The class fell silent and Julius found himself leaning in slightly towards Lao-tzu.

'As you know, Clodagh Arnesh did not possess a single White Art skill. However, she was a genius when it came to technology. It was she who created the Grey Arts. Her friend Marcus Tijara had it all: he was a natural talent with all the White Arts and a very apt pupil when it came to learning the Grey ones. Arnesh felt incomplete compared to him. So she decided that, if she could not master both Arts, she would be the only one who could access the full potential of the Grey Arts. She became paranoid that Marcus, or anyone else with similar abilities, would read her mind and steal her technological secrets. It was at that time that she invented the Scrambler, a machine that creates a field of high frequency interference within the mind of the wearer, making telesthesia practically impossible.'

'Sir,' said Lopaka Liway, 'what is telesthesia?'

'It is a rare White Art ability that lets you perceive the thoughts of people around you, among other things, without the use of your normal sensory system. As well as blocking an outsider from reading your thoughts, the Scrambler was also devised to confuse the minds of those who came near it, which brings us back to meditation. As you work towards your goal of achieving relaxation, trance and balance, you effectively minimise the risks of being affected by one of these gadgets. You will have a chance to practice with Scramblers, once you have achieved your time limit goal.' Lao-tzu then stood and invited the students to choose their landscape for the day.

Julius walked automatically towards the top right corner of the room, sat down on his screen and closed his eyes. His mind was fully distracted by the Scramblers and by what Lao-tzu had said about telesthesia. It was a rare skill, but had he not experienced it many times before? It had always happened unintentionally and for brief spells, but he had been able to do it. He also knew that, when he did perceive other people's thoughts, he always felt very relaxed.

'If only I could figure out how to recreate that relaxation,' he thought.

However, the more he tried the tenser he became, and by the end of the lesson he was utterly depressed. Unfortunately, a new set of worries was about to settle on the class. Before leaving, Professor Lao-tzu asked them to stay behind a few more minutes. Tony Tower entered the room, bowed to the students and kneeled before them.

'Mizki, I have been sent to inform you that you are all up for review this week.'

The entire class let out a collective gasp at those words.

'Every November and June,' continued Tower, 'all Tijaran students meet with the heads of their year. They will discuss your progress with you and the subjects that you need to improve on. Where necessary, extra work will be assigned. As you know, there are no exams at the end of each year, but you are still required to demonstrate your proficiency in all first and second year courses if you want to continue your life on Zed. After today's lessons, there will be a schedule for the meetings in the school lounge at level -3. Find your name and the date of your appointment. Whatever you do, don't be late. Class dismissed.'

Julius felt a cold shiver run down his spine. For all the progress he had made since August, Meditation was still his Achilles' heel and he knew that his review would suffer for it. As the afternoon crawled on, that sense of chill had not left him and, when the last class ended, he rushed to the lounge unable to contain himself any longer. As he entered, Julius realised that he had rarely been in that area since arriving on Tijara. It was softly lit, filled with comfortable sofas and armchairs. A fireplace occupied the far wall – it was large enough that it could easily have fitted five students standing abreast. The large windows around the room were in fact scenery screens and, as Julius looked at them, he noticed that it had begun to snow. On the right hand side of the entrance, a set of stairs led to the underground levels. As he made his way down, a buzz of students' voices rose up to meet him. He realised that the students were all Mizki Seniors, judging by their height, and that Tony Tower and Bernard Docherty were among them. He kept going, throwing just a glance at the people gathered on level -2.

'Those must be the 3 and 4 Mizki Apprentices,' thought Julius, without stopping. Finally he arrived at the Juniors' level. A large group of 2MJ were already huddled against the wall, looking for their names on the list. He tried to peek over their shoulders, but he was still too far away to read anything.

'There you are Julius,' said Faith, appearing suddenly behind him. 'You must have been very keen to get down here.'

'Faith,' said Julius, pulling him closer, 'can you lift us above them?'

'Sure. Hop on.'

Julius climbed the rim of the Skirt and held on to Faith as they hovered slowly upwards. The other students were pushing and pulling below them, hitting the Skirt as they tried to protect their heads from Faith's feet.

'I found the first year's schedule,' said Julius stretching his neck towards the list.

'Good, so you can read mine too. I'm kinda struggling to keep us still, here.'

'Smock … Slovich … Shanigan! Your appointment is tomorrow at noon in the office, level -1 with Mrs Cruci. Same for me, except I'll see her at 12:30. OK, get us down Faith.'

Faith landed them in the centre of the lounge and they made their way to the mess hall. When Morgana and Skye joined them for tea, Julius was almost relieved to discover that they too were feeling as tense as he was. No one felt like going to Satras – instead they spent their evening in the garden, looking through their school diaries and discussing their individual performances in the various subjects. By the time he went to bed that night, Julius was a little more relaxed, comforted by the fact that at least he wasn't alone in his worries.

The following morning, Julius' class was unusually quiet. All the students were feeling very nervous as their individual meetings approached. A little before midday, Faith left the Draw class to attend his appointment. Morgana's review had been earlier that morning, but Julius had not been able to discuss it with her since Professor Turner had kept them busy drawing from saplings.

Julius didn't feel like eating before his meeting with Mrs Cruci so, when the lesson ended, he walked over to the office and sat on the long circular bench that surrounded the fountain around the assembly hall. Morgana joined him shortly afterwards.

'I thought you might be here,' she said, sitting down next to him.

'How did your meeting go?'

'It was fine, I guess. Mrs Cruci is a really nice woman and made me feel completely at ease. In general I'm doing all right. I have to improve in Draw and make more effort in Martial Arts, but I'm top of the class in Meditation.'

'No surprise there. You always had a knack for it,' said Julius, looking down at his feet.

'Is Meditation what's troubling you?'

'Yeah … and I don't know how to make it better. Morgana, how do you slip into a trance so quickly?'

'Practice, I guess.'

'Yes, but what *exactly* do you do?'

'Well, you concentrate on something so completely that you stop being aware of anything else, even yourself,' she answered evenly.

'But if you're not aware of yourself, how do you know? I mean, once you realise you're in a trance then surely you are also aware of yourself?'

'For one, I don't ask myself if I'm in a trance or not. I just *feel* it and I stay there, until I'm calm and relaxed.'

Julius nodded, but he was still worried.

'Mrs Cruci will help you, I'm sure. Besides, Julius, you're one of the best in every other subject. It's unlikely they'll kick you out of Zed. Listen,' she said, standing up, 'I'm going to have some food now. Before you enter, take a deep breath and calm down. You'll be fine.'

Julius watched her leave, then stood up and approached the office area. Quietly, he opened the main door and entered. Inside was a corridor that ended in a window overlooking Tijara's main entrance. The waterfall outside fashioned a curtain of rain against the glass, creating wavy reflections on the marble floor. To the left of the window, a set of stairs led downwards, presumably to the lower levels. There were two doors to either side of the corridor, and Julius gasped when he saw the name plaque on the right hand door – behind that, the Grand Master Tijara was sitting at his desk. Julius had just begun to wonder if Freja knew about his dreadful performance in Meditation, when the other door opened. He turned on his heels in a flash and found himself staring at Master Cress.

'Good afternoon, Mr McCoy. Step inside my office please.'

Julius was so taken aback by the sudden appearance of Cress that he didn't know what to do.

'Sir, I have a meeting with Mrs Cruci in a short while.'

'I know. However, Mrs Cruci must attend to other business as soon as she is finished with Mr Shanigan; therefore I shall do your review in her place.'

Julius's heartbeat instantly went from a canter to a gallop at that news. There was nothing he could do, though, but follow Cress into his office. As he sat, he noticed several framed pictures on the wall, each containing younger versions of Cress as he made his career in Zed. He smiled at one of the pictures because, if he wasn't mistaken, there was a Mizki Junior Cress standing in the centre of it, flanked by two others boys. Julius followed the sequence on the wall: Cress holding a trophy outside the Hologram Palace; graduating from Tijara; shaking hands with Freja; being made Master; sitting inside a jet plane, a huge smile on his face.

'I feel as if those pictures were taken only yesterday,' said Cress quietly.

Julius was almost positive that Cress wasn't particularly old, so seeing all that he had accomplished in such a short period of time, left him slightly in awe of the Master.

'You must have been very determined, sir,' said Julius before he'd even had time to consider whether or not it was appropriate to make such a remark.

'And you are not, Mr McCoy?' replied Cress, staring intently at him. 'I heard from your teachers that you are, and that is always a good start, especially when certain problems need to be addressed.'

Julius didn't know what to say, so he simply nodded, hoping that Cress would put him out of his misery as soon as possible. The Master activated his desk. Its flat, glass face was soon filled with information, menus and buttons, all moving slowly across its surface. Cress pressed one of the menus and instantly Julius' file opened. He read the report quietly for a few minutes, before looking up at Julius. 'I see you have taken quite a fancy to racing games, Mr McCoy. You and your team have made impressive progress in the game world. All that after-school training has definitely paid off.'

'Thank you, sir,' said Julius, pleasantly surprised. He had not expected Cress to take any interest in the students' out of school activities.

'Game achievements are monitored by teachers,' said Cress, as if he had read Julius' mind. 'We can tell a lot about our students by the way they behave during them – combat and flight skills, leadership, they all count towards forming a complete individual. Moreover, the fact that you have enough Fyvers to play and practise means that your performance in class must also be good. You eat healthily and regularly enough and your body is in good shape, according to Professor Chan. This is also important. *Mens sana in corpore sano*. It's Latin, and it means "a healthy mind in a healthy body". Never forget that. You have a regular sleep pattern, normal for a developing boy such as yourself. That said, I can see that you do rather like to wake up at the last possible minute.'

Julius shifted uncomfortably in his chair. He'd thought that Cress would only be discussing his subjects with him but instead he felt completely exposed, as if there was nothing he could do without the whole of Tijara knowing about it.

'All of your teachers have been satisfied with your performance so far, all except one. Do you know who might that be?'

'Professor Lao-tzu, sir?' answered Julius sheepishly.

'Correct. Your teacher has told me that you have not been able to achieve any sort of meditative state as yet. You seem restless and out of focus when you enter his class. Does this reflect your feelings for Professor Lao-tzu, Mr McCoy?'

'Not at all, sir. I like him very much. I just …' Julius tried to express how he felt, but no words came to his mouth.

Cress looked at him for a moment, then spoke into his headset: 'Mr List, this is Master Cress. Please ready a holopal for Mr McCoy, 1MJ, by the end of today. I shall send you the configuration within the hour.'

Julius looked at Cress with a puzzled expression.

'You must defeat this obstacle, Mr McCoy. The holopal is a program designed specifically for helping students overcome any subject related difficulties. You shall have morning meetings with your holopal, Monday to Friday, starting from tomorrow. You will meet in one of the hologram rooms between 05:00 and 07:00. If you are ever late, you will be given detention. On Monday mornings, you will study Meditation with your classmates, as usual. I am giving you until the end of February. If there are still no improvements, we will perhaps have to reconsider your training on Zed. Am I clear, Mr McCoy?'

'Sir, yes, sir,' said Julius, devastated. He couldn't believe his ears. For a start, he really wasn't a morning person. Plus, Morgana had just told him that no one could kick him out of Tijara for having trouble in one subject, yet here he was, having just been given an ultimatum by Master Cress himself.

'The holopal can be configured to look like anyone you wish,' continued Cress seriously. 'Normally a shape that is conducive to your aim, in this case, achieving relaxation and a meditative state. Now, Mr McCoy, I read in your file that you are quite passionate about Earth history and have a keen interest in Japanese culture, am I right?'

'Yes sir,' answered Julius promptly.

'In that case, I suggest a Zen master to be your holopal. As a matter of fact, we have already used this specific shape in the past, with successful results. Will you give it a try?'

Julius nodded.

'Very well, Mr McCoy. Report to Mr List tonight at 20:00 hours. You are free to go now.'

'Thank you, sir,' said Julius, standing up. He bowed to Cress and left his office.

*

'I still can't believe you had your review with Cress.' said Skye, clearly dumbstruck.

Julius had met up with the others in the garden, after their Martial Arts lesson. He had told them all about his meeting and the holopal.

'Were any of you given remedial classes?' asked Julius rather miserably.

Morgana looked at Faith and Skye, and by their looks Julius knew that the answer was no.

'Great. I bet I'm the only one in our year that was.'

'So what?' said Morgana. 'It's only until February anyway. By then, I'm sure you'll be fine. Besides it shows that they care about us. It's their job to make us the best that we can be.'

'I think Morgana is right,' said Faith. 'I mean about the caring stuff. I might not have remedial classes, but ... they put me on a diet ... from chocolate ...'

'What?' said Skye. 'But you're skinny, man!'

'Well, it's for the Skirt. I need to check me weight, so that I can still fit in this thing. Also, pilots' chairs are not that big and, with all the different pressures and null gravity and the like, being fit is kinda compulsory.'

The image of a fat blob walking around in the Skirt made Julius smile. 'I guess you're right and, anyway, there's nothing I can do about it.'

They spent the rest of the afternoon lazing around on the grass, filling in their diaries and discussing new racing strategies. As the sun set, they went inside for their meal, after which Julius took his leave.

'You gotta tell me everything about the holopal when you get back,' said Faith excitedly.

'For sure, I'll catch you guys later.'

Julius left the mess hall and made his way to the holographic sector. When he got there, Gabriel List was sitting at the front desk.

'Mr McCoy,' he said in an official tone of voice, 'follow me please.'

They went down to level -1, where List stopped outside a door marked "Technician's

Den". He looked at the retinal scanner and the door opened. The "den" was effectively a staff room for List and his colleagues, and was by far the most chaotic room Julius had seen anywhere inside the school. Tiny little robots whisked around the floor, picking up pieces of paper, gum wrappers and fluffs of dust. The many shelves surrounding the room were crammed with beeping silver gadgets, whose function totally escaped Julius. He noticed that the walls were actually writing screens, filled with mathematical equations and scarily long formulae.

'Don't mind the mess,' said List, kicking one of the robots out of his way. 'We seem to concentrate better in this environment.'

Julius smiled as he watched a robot the size of his foot attempting to pick up a peanut butter sandwich that was practically glued to the floor.

'My friend Faith would love this room.'

'Is he the guy with Pete's Skirt?' asked List, ushering Julius into a smaller, empty room.

'Yes. He's very good with gadgets and the like.'

'Maybe I should invite him over sometime.'

'He'd like that, sir.'

'In here you can call me Gabriel. Zed is far too formal for my taste.' He gave Julius a big smile and guided him into one of the classrooms.

'I've received Cress's configuration for a Zen master and I took the liberty of doing a little research on the topic in order to find you a suitable one. I want you to try it out. Remember, the holopal is state of the art VI ‒ virtual intelligence ‒ it thinks, it has a nanosecond reaction time to process info, it makes decisions and can physically interact with its surroundings.' List pulled a watch out of his pocket and gave it to Julius. 'Put it on, and when you are ready I want you to place your finger on the centre of the screen.'

Julius followed the instructions and an old Japanese man appeared, kneeling opposite him.

'Let me introduce you to Master Isshin,' said List, retreating quietly out of the room.

Julius stared at the man, unable to say a word. He couldn't read the expression on his face. Isshin seemed to possess both the tranquillity of Lao-tzu and the sharpness of Chan. His eyes were small and dark, but penetrating. He wore a blue kimono over his bent, aged body. Julius shifted uncomfortably, wondering if he was supposed to say or do something. Suddenly the man lifted a hand and waved it in the air between them. The familiar sensation of displacement that Julius felt whenever he sat atop his tower in Lao-tzu's class swept over him, as he found himself in a forest in the early evening dusk. Isshin stood effortlessly and gestured for Julius to follow him. As he walked behind the master, Julius breathed in, enjoying the smell of the evening around him and the moss of the trees. A small wooden temple appeared just ahead of them, with four pillars holding up a pagoda-style roof. Isshin led him towards it. Julius removed his boots outside the entrance, as the master removed his shoes. A white tatami covered the floor, with two rows of cushions on it. Sticks of sandalwood incense were burning swiftly, permeating the air around them.

'Please sit in the lotus position, Mr McCoy.'

Isshin's voice was friendly and surprisingly young, thought Julius. He followed the instruction as best as he could, but lost his balance trying to cross his legs in the appropriate fashion.

'Perhaps the half lotus will do for now,' said Isshin, easing into that position himself. 'I want you to keep your spine relaxed but straight, and your head level. Your eyes must remain half closed, to avoid falling asleep.'

Julius thought that between the warm, lulling air, the sweet incense and that afternoon's Martial Arts lesson, there was no way he would stay awake, so he was more than happy when Master Isshin continued to talk.

'What do you know about Zen, Mr McCoy?'

'It's a Japanese form of Buddhism, where meditation is very important.'

'You are quite correct. Professor Lao-tzu's methods are successful with most students. However, for some the practice of more ancient methods is best, which is why you are here. Using meditation, Zen Buddhists would try to achieve enlightenment, a flash of insight, an awakening of the mind beyond logical comprehension. Interestingly, these *satori*, these flashes, seem to come during everyday activities, when the mind is relaxed, rather than when one is trying too hard to concentrate.'

Julius's eyes widened imperceptibly, but still enough for Master Isshin to notice.

'I believe, Mr McCoy, that you have experienced telesthesia before, am I right?'

'Yes sir. I have never done it on purpose though. It just happens.'

'That is a strength,' said Isshin, 'and we are going to use it to our advantage. Tell me, what happens within you as you sit on top of the tower?'

'I breathe deeply, close my eyes and try to clear away all thoughts,' answered Julius. 'It doesn't work though. Either my thoughts get more chaotic or I fall asleep.'

Master Isshin nodded. 'If you are looking at a pool of clear water and someone throws a handful of dirt in it, what would be the quickest way to restore its clearness?'

'Not to touch it?' said Julius tentatively.

'Correct. You let it settle by itself. If you stir it, or try to move it away, it may never do that. During our sessions, I want you to do just that. Don't fight away your thoughts, but follow them, observe them, relax with them. They are part of you.'

Julius nodded.

'Very well, Mr McCoy. I shall meet you here tomorrow morning at 05:00. You can deactivate me by touching your watch whenever you are ready to leave.'

Julius felt quite awkward. He knew that Isshin wasn't real and he could just switch him off at will, but somehow that just didn't feel right. In the end he stood and bowed respectfully to the master, before touching his watch. Walking out of the hologram sector, he felt a little confidence returning, as this new method seemed to be more fitting for him. Frankly, given the choice between waking at the crack of dawn and being thrown of out of Zed, he knew which one to choose, even if it meant sleeping in the Technician's Den.

GOING SOLO

As Julius entered the last week of November, he had never felt more tired in his whole life. The homework had doubled in all subjects and Professor Chan continued to train them as hard as if they were an Olympic team. He had to abandon his cosy bed at an outrageous hour, while Skye would be snoring peacefully from under his blanket. The thought that he could only have breakfast after two hours of staring at trees and bees during meditation made his stomach rumble and his temper rise. On top of all this, Professor Turner started to observe Julius's draws a little too closely for his liking. She would try to be casual about it – tiptoeing around behind his back, looking over his shoulder – but Julius wasn't fooled. He knew that, ever since his first draw attempt, her interest in his ability had increased significantly, even though he wasn't quite sure why.

At last, after an excruciating session of Martial Arts, he approached his mates in the mess hall and made a painful announcement: 'I'm sorry, guys. I'll have to give up the weekly training for a little while.'

'Frankly I'm surprised you've lasted so long, man,' said Faith over his carrot salad.

Julius dropped down onto a chair with his head in his hands. '… nasty alarm is killing me …'

'Don't worry about it,' said Skye. 'We all have tonnes of homework anyway.'

'Besides, I'm sure you'll master meditation long before the winter break,' added Morgana, trying to sound cheerful.

'Will I? Really?' asked Julius, frustrated. 'The way I see it, that holopal of mine is not really doing what it's supposed to. I think it's so bored by the whole thing that it's started to flicker on me on purpose – which is very upsetting by the way. This morning it disappeared after dragging me to the top of Mount Fuji. I had to wait an hour before Gabriel List realised something was wrong and rescued me. Perched on that peak like a bird and all I could think of was blinking bacon and eggs!'

They stared at him for a moment before bursting into laughter. Julius couldn't help but join in. They spent the rest of the evening in the Juniors' lounge helping each other with an essay on the Galilean Moons, trying to figure out which one was which.

'I'm telling you,' said Faith waving his pencil at Skye, 'the big one is Callisto!'

'But Callisto is all dark and this is kinda lightish,' answered Skye, shoving a picture under Faith's nose.

'Then it must be Europa.'

'Can't be,' added Julius. 'It's far too big.'

They all looked at Morgana, as if waiting for the right answer.

'What?' she said, peering over her book. 'What are you looking at me for?'

'Well, you're the pilot,' said Skye. 'You're supposed to know.'

Morgana shook her head and grabbed the picture from Skye's hand. 'It's Ganymede.

It's got dark patches and lighter grooves and it's the largest moon in the Solar System.'

'That settles it,' said Faith matter of factly. 'That leaves Io, the yellow one.'

'That's sulphur,' added Morgana vaguely.

'It could be me grandmother's custard for all I care. I'm too tired, guys. I'm gonna call it a night.'

'Hear, hear!' said Skye, packing up.

Julius agreed wholeheartedly and followed them back to the dormitories. Unfortunately, he was so looking forward to his bed that he forgot to set the alarm. At 05:00 hours, the lights in the room came on. Julius sprung up from the bed, blurry eyed. Skye was fast asleep and, in the corridor, all was silent. Suddenly his eyes widened in a mixture of surprise and fear.

'Oh no, I'm dead!' he kept repeating aloud as he jumped out of bed and scooped his clothes from the floor. He flew out of the room and up the stairs, trying to shove his head through one of the sleeves of his jumper as he went. The main corridor was empty and he ran as fast as he could, doing his best to ignore the smell of breakfast coming from the mess hall. When he finally arrived at the hologram sector, the door was closed. He only just managed to slow down before he could crash into the wall. It was then that he saw the note on the door:

> "Mr McCoy,
> Arriving late for the morning sessions was NOT in the agreement. You shall spend your afternoon in the detention room in the library.
>
> Master Cress."

'I was only a few minutes late!' shouted Julius at the door. 'It's not fair!'

Nobody answered him, however. The only noise in the corridor was that of the waterfall trickling over the black marble wall of the assembly room. Dejectedly, he headed over to the mess hall.

'At least I'm getting an early breakfast this morning,' he thought, trying unconvincingly to cheer himself up.

A couple of hours later, Julius was awoken by Morgana and realised that he had fallen asleep on one of the benches in the canteen.

She sat down next to him and shook him gently by the shoulder. 'You don't look too happy. What's up?'

Julius rubbed his eyes and told her what had happened.

'How can he do this? I've never been late before!'

'Come on Julius, don't be mad. There's no point really. Look what I brought you,' she said, rummaging in her bag and handing him a chip. 'It's my relaxing music collection. I thought it might help you get into the right frame of mind.'

'Thanks Morgana,' he said, feeling slightly less grumpy.

'I made a copy, so you can keep that one.'

'I might use it for my afternoon detention. You never know.'

'Let's get some breakfast now. I'm starving,' she said, dragging him by the arm.

As with every Thursday, his only class was three hours of Telekinesis in the morning. Julius thoroughly enjoyed these lessons with Professor King, seeing as he was quite good at this subject. That, however, meant that time passed even quicker and before he knew it he found himself outside the library for his detention.

Miss Evelyne Dubois was the young librarian who welcomed Julius at the door. Students were allowed in this particular section of the microchip library only with special permission or, as in this case, for detention. The room was cosy and welcoming, simply furnished, with slick black terminals attached to ten separate mahogany desks. There were four other senior students in the room with him and they all looked up briefly as he entered the room and walked over to one of the empty desks. With a big sigh, he pulled out his diary, deciding that he would use the time to update his daily progress. He also took out Morgana's music chip to listen to.

After two hours of solid work, Julius put his pen down and looked up towards Miss Dubois. He wasn't sure how long his detention was supposed to last for and, as he was about to go and ask, his eyes fell on a stack of chips at the bottom of a shelf. The label above them simply read "Draw". Julius suddenly remembered the conversation he had with Skye about Tijara's notes on the subject. He had never gotten around to checking them out as he had been meaning to do. He scanned the chips quickly until he came across one labelled "Marcus Tijara and the White Art of Drawing". He saw that Miss Dubois was busy talking with a student and was facing the door. Carefully, Julius picked up the chip and inserted it into a slot in the side of the monitor.

Julius scanned through the various chapters. He knew most of the information from his lessons, but kept reading. Eventually he found a short chapter called "Drawing from inorganic matter". In it, Marcus Tijara explained how it was still a largely unexplored field with only a handful of recorded case studies. Despite the lack of documented evidence, however, it was indeed possible. Only once had Tijara come across a subject who had been able to perform a draw from a microwave oven. The subject had later discharged a small electric shock upon touching a metal object. Julius' eyes widened at that. Suddenly the memory of his first draw flooded back to him and, with it, the image of Professor Turner's digital watch, stopped, on her wrist. What if he had actually caused the watch to stop? Had he really drawn from it? The energy receiver had been charged to the full, but his cactus had not withered. Where had that energy come from? Julius looked back at the screen. Tijara said that the subject had released an electric shock onto a metal object. He remembered clearly how he had touched the door handle of Miss Turner's classroom and how it had flown out of his hand, slamming against the wall as if pushed by an unseen force. His heartbeat quickened and he continued reading:

"Shortly after this episode, the subject's health deteriorated at a dramatic rate. His body went into shock and eventually shut down completely before we could intervene. We could only watch as his skin started to burn from the inside. It was as if a bolt of lightning had entered his body and stayed there. He died almost immediately. Although an isolated event, this dreadful experience has at least confirmed that inorganic drawing is possible. If another human should be able to recreate this act, he or she would be strongly advised to discharge the energy as soon as possible, in order to avoid a similar fate to that of our test subject. We are in no position to know if, in case of survival, the subject would have suffered or developed side-effects. What we do know is that, like the other subjects capable of inorganic drawing, all his White skills were incredibly powerful. Finally, as a word of caution, if another individual with this power is discovered, they should be brought to the attention of the Grand Masters as a security measure."

Julius slumped back in his chair. It was all so difficult to believe, but deep down he had no doubts. He was now certain that he had drawn from a lifeless object.

'Mr McCoy,' called Miss Dubois from her desk.

Julius almost jumped out of his chair at that, engrossed as he was in his thoughts.

'Your detention is over. You can leave now.'

Julius switched off the monitor and placed the chip back on the shelf. He left the library without looking up, not knowing where to go. He felt strangely alone, as if the discovery of his ability had placed him in an empty slot, isolating him somehow from his friends. Yet he felt that he needed them now more than ever. He wasn't sure if he would tell them about Tijara's chip, but he did know he needed their company right then. He searched the dorms, the lounge and the garden, but couldn't find any of them. Frustrated, he walked towards the exit, thinking that they might have gone to Satras. He boarded the Intra-Rail System, oblivious of the students laughing around him. All he could think of were the last words written by Tijara, about how anyone like him should be reported for security. What was he to do? Tell Cress? What if they asked him to leave Zed? He couldn't bear that. As he stepped off the main lift inside Satras, and started to walk beside the lake, a thought came to him which made him feel a little more hopeful. The day he had drawn from Professor Turner's watch, she had been standing over him. She knew exactly what Julius had done and, no doubt, had reported her findings. Yet, no one had ever talked to him about it, as if it wasn't important at all.

'Well,' Julius said to himself, 'if they aren't bothered, then neither am I.'

Dismissing his fears, Julius stopped and looked around, but there was still no trace of Morgana or the others. He realised that he was standing outside the Hologram Palace and decided to check inside before going back to Tijara. In the arena, there were only a few students sitting on the large steps and most of the game screens were inactive. He checked the boards but the Skirts' names weren't on any of them either. As he was walking past the booking kiosk, a wrinkled old hand shot out and grabbed him by the arm. Julius almost let out a scream and staggered backwards.

'Heeee! Sorry lad. Didn't mean to scare you.'

Julius looked up at old Mrs Mayflower, startled. He had seen her quite regularly since he had started playing and couldn't believe that someone with so many wrinkles could actually have enough energy for such a fast movement.

'It's all right. I was distracted. I ... can I help you?'

'I thought you just needed a little encouragement,' she said with a smile.

'For what?'

'But for playing Solo of course, my dear. Why else would you be walking this empty courtyard without your team?'

'Actually, I wasn't really ...'

'Come, come lad. I have been running this kiosk for 60 years. I have seen plenty of young hopeful students coming this way, in the middle of the week, alone, looking for a shot at glory,' she said with a knowing wink. 'Take young Mr Docherty for instance – he came here when he was a 3 Mizki Apprentice. A scrawny little thing he was, a little taller than you perhaps. He arrived alone, on a midweek evening, just like you. And from that moment, his life changed. He made it into the top ten Solo records, at number one. The first new blood in fifty years!' she clapped her old hands together delightedly, as if speaking of the past made her feel young again. 'So, Julius lad, what will you do?'

'About what?'

'Eeeeh! I thought you were smart. Taking a shot at Solo. What else?'

'No, really. I … I don't think it's a good idea at all.'

'Come on. No one will know. If you don't make it into the top ten, your name won't even appear on the board. You have nothing to lose.'

Julius thought about it for a moment. To tell the truth, he was really curious about Solo. He had wanted to try it ever since his arrival on Zed and, given that he was on his own, and still trying to digest what he had learned in the library, perhaps it wasn't a bad idea after all.

'All right, sign me in.'

'One Solo ticket coming up! Go through the right door and good luck.'

Julius thanked her and made his way to the entrance, throwing one last glance over his shoulder to check that nobody had seen him. He followed the stairs down to a small room, where a man was sitting behind a desk reading a comic book. He looked up as Julius entered.

'Hey, the first customer of the day. Come in!'

Julius walked forward, trying not to look too scared.

'Hi, I'm Mr Preston. First time, huh?'

'Is it that obvious?'

'Don't worry, I've seen worse.'

'So, what do I do?'

'Well, you get your holosuit in the changing room and then wait to be called, like in the group games. I'll set you up. The main difference in Solo is that you don't get to choose your challenge against the simulator. You could be racing, or you could be fighting, or both, and you *will* be using your actual mind-skills. The difficulty level has been the same since Marcus Tijara's time. Just so you know, it was him and that traitor Arnesh, may she rot in space, who built this Palace.'

'How difficult is it?'

'Pretty nasty, but don't worry – you can't actually die. There's a safety protocol written into the program. Right this way then,' he said, ushering Julius into the dressing room.

Julius was given a holosuit, exactly like the one he used for the group games, and an object that looked like a glass mask, with a thick rubber rim around its edge.

'This is a face shield,' said Preston. 'Put it on when I tell you to. It will allow you to breathe. Good luck.'

Julius nodded and started to undress. He looked apprehensively at the face shield and wondered why he would need any kind of breathing device at all. A few minutes later he was called to make his way through the green door.

The Solo area itself seemed really small compared to the group game floor, and very different. There were no holospheres to begin with, but instead Julius counted twenty cubic tanks, which looked much like aquariums, each one as big as his bedroom. Preston motioned him towards the first of the containers where they stepped onto a platform which raised them both to the top of the tank. Julius peered into it and saw that it was filled with a transparent jelly-like substance.

'Put your shield on now,' said Preston.

Julius felt a slight suction as its rim closed around his face. He tried to breathe but it was oddly difficult and was just about to take off the mask when Preston pushed him unceremoniously into the tank. He slid into the clear jelly, feeling very much like a tadpole slinking its way through mud.

'Can you hear me?' said Preston, his voice now slightly muffled.

Julius looked up and nodded.

'Great. Take a deep breath.'

Julius did and the oxygen entered his lungs immediately, slowing his heartbeat to a steady rhythm. He slowly moved about, to test his new surroundings. The more he did so, the more he realised that the substance in the tank was actually far less viscous than jelly, lending him a sensation of weightlessness.

'Once the game starts, you'll have five seconds to get your bearings,' Preston continued, 'after that, all hell breaks loose ... and you better be ready. Clear?'

Julius gave him the thumbs up.

'On my mark then – three ... two ... one ... activate!'

The tank began to shake furiously and the now familiar white light, which marked the beginning of a simulation, flooded the space around him.

When Julius was finally able to open his eyes, he found himself staring at a most unexpected sight: he was standing in the middle of a vast green field, under a blue, sunny sky, a warm gentle breeze ruffling his hair.

'What the ...?' he gasped.

He took a few cautious steps forward, all the while trying to assess the situation and check for any signs of danger.

'This must be a combat game,' he said.

Immediately he assumed the combat stance that Professor Chan had taught them in their first Martial Art lesson: his right index and middle finger extended; the other fingers under the thumb. He felt his muscles tensing and his skin tingling. Julius was so absorbed by the sense of that moment that he didn't even notice the tiny electrical discharges sparking off his fingertips.

Up ahead of him was a small forest and he walked towards it, lightly treading on the thick grass. As he entered the shadows of the trees, the air grew still and all went quiet, as if all sound had been sucked into a vacuum. He could see a clearing on the other side and headed in that direction, glancing from side to side as he went. Suddenly, a flock of birds took flight from a nearby tree. Julius froze in his tracks: there was a rumble in the distance, growing ever louder as each second passed, and the ground shook as if a herd of buffaloes was roaring towards him. He staggered backwards and turned to face the source of the noise – instead of buffaloes, a group of at least ten samurai in full armour were hurtling at him. They unsheathed their swords as they ran and let out a battle cry, more like the screams of banshees than of humans.

Julius whirled and sprinted towards the clearing, hurdling dead branches and boulders as he went. He was vaguely aware of a small, calmer part of himself that was unconsciously lifting obstacles from his path and flinging them at the chasing pack. In retaliation, a flurry of arrows whistled past his ears. One of them skimmed by inches from his cheek, close enough to fill him with the certainty that he had to get out of the open and find shelter as quickly as possible.

Up ahead he saw a hill crowned by a rocky wall, which looked as good a place as any for him to mount a counterattack. He scampered up to the top where he spun and looked down. The samurai emerged from the line of trees and charged up the hill. At the same time, Julius bent his mind and will into a vision of a roaring fire and, extending his right arm, he unleashed all the energy he could muster. Flames erupted from the ground, lighting the fallen branches and creating a crimson ring at the base of the hill. The samurai skidded to a halt before leaping away from the heat. Julius didn't wait for them to regroup, but instead ran down the other side of the hill. Their screams were still in the air when he was abruptly scooped upward as if by an invisible hand and engulfed by white light. A few seconds later, he found himself on top of the very same hill. Panting, he surveyed the area but there was no trace of the forest or the samurai.

'What next?' he said to no one in particular, wiping sweat from his forehead.

Night was closing in fast and, as darkness crept over the hill, a group of isolated lights appeared in the valley below. Julius, certain that nobody was following him, ran towards them. As he drew nearer, he could hear a faint melody in the air. The source of the music and the lights was a small village. Two rows of wooden houses flanked a dusty main street, which opened out into a square. There was a bonfire at the centre of it, fuelled by thick logs. As Julius walked towards it, he could just about make out the shapes of people dancing on a stage. The delicious smell of popcorn and candy filled his nostrils. He made his way past a burger stall and realised that all the people around him were old and wrinkly, like Mrs Mayflower. When he reached the bonfire, Julius stopped abruptly. What he had mistaken for logs were in fact the scorched bodies of the samurai that had chased him through the forest, their armour piled up to one side.

'No . . .' he said, stumbling forward.

The music stopped and petrified, Julius watched as the villagers turned to face him. The sweet, plump faces of the old ladies had become grave and sullen, staring at him in eerie silence.

'Stay back!' shouted Julius, even though nobody had moved.

He extended his combat arm in front of him as he backed towards the edge of the square. In unison, the villagers let out a blood-curdling laugh, their mouths agape as they mocked and pointed at him. Julius looked on in horror as their mouths continued to open way beyond human range, so much that their faces were disappearing behind them.

All of a sudden, a voice spoke clearly in his head: '*Don't let them morph. Hit them now!*'

Julius was startled by the voice, but quickly gathered his wits. He bent his mind to the first villager in sight, a haggard old man with alternating teeth, and pushed, sending him flying backward with such force that he took two others with him. Julius switched his attention to three more villagers as they advanced towards him. He lifted one up, just as he had done with Michael back home, and dropped him on top of two ladies. They crashed to the floor and didn't rise again. He had to keep reminding himself that they weren't really old people, but simulated enemies. Several villagers at the back of the group had almost completed their morph. As Julius continued to frantically push people back with his mind, he caught a glimpse of one of them changing, his mouth bent backwards and over his own head. It encircled his body and peeled away, skin and all, revealing a black mass of teeth and hair underneath. The dark shape fell down on all fours, howling with rage.

'You've got to be kidding!' cried Julius. He was exhausted but was still somehow managing to keep the few remaining villagers at bay.

One of the beasts was stalking towards him, its tongue out and its teeth bared in a snarl. Julius knew instantly there was no way he could outrun it. There was only one way out. He backed away from the still morphing villagers and used his remaining strength to bend his mind against the lone beast. He locked his eyes on the creature's and pushed against its mental barriers with all his might, trying to control it. He had never attempted something like this before and, as the pain in his head intensified, he prayed that he would never have to again. The beast kept walking towards him, but its eyes were glazing over and its stride growing heavy. Its head lolled from side to side and, by the time it slumped at Julius's feet, it was utterly defeated.

'*Get up!*' he ordered with his mind. '*You must carry us to safety!*'

Julius climbed on its back as the beast struggled back up again.

'Come on! Run!' he shouted, seeing that the rest of the villagers had completed their transformation and were closing in on them.

Julius grabbed a clump of its grimy fur and spurred the creature on. They tore through the main street, aiming for the valley that stretched out beyond it. Turning, he saw the pack snapping and snarling at his heels. He aimed his fingers at the closest one, meaning to knock it off course with a shock wave, but managed only to slow it down, as his energy was now almost depleted. One of the beasts caught up with him, so Julius locked his legs around his own creature's chest, threw his hands over the other one and grabbed its ears. He was going to draw from it.

'Share the love, puppy,' he said through gritted teeth.

He felt its energy field pulsing beneath his fingertips and without hesitation took a deep breath and held it. As with his previous draws, he closed his eyes and in his mind's eye saw the blue smoky fluid entering his fingers and his body, replenishing his energy. The beast lost pace dramatically. He was about to release its head when his own ride was knocked down and he was sent crashing to the ground. The last thing he saw were sharp teeth snapping at his flesh as he began to scream. Then the white light enveloped him.

'Hey. Wake up!' Julius heard the voice travelling to him as if from a great distance. Groggily, he opened his eyes, struggling to remember where he was. Through the liquid haze, he saw Preston's face – he was banging his fist against the tank. As memory flooded back Julius kicked upwards to the surface and grabbed the edge of the tank. Preston jumped onto the platform and joined him there.

'Judging by your state, you must've had one hell of a ride,' said Preston, removing the face shield and helping him out of the tank.

'What happened? How did I do?' asked Julius, checking that his body had not been mutilated by the pack of beasts.

'Dunno kid. The computer is analysing your trip. It will be ready by this evening. Go get changed now.'

Julius was exhausted and felt bruised, even though there were no physical signs that he had been hurt in any way.

'That didn't go too well,' he said to himself as he walked into the shower. He was truly relieved that no one would ever know about his defeat.

RED CAP

Julius decided to go into the courtyard for a moment of rest, but what he found was a quite unexpected sight – Morgana, Faith and Skye were all standing there. Morgana had been crying, judging by her eyes, and the boys were staring at him, speechless.

'What happened?' asked Julius, alarmed. 'Morgana, why are you crying? Is it Kaori?'

'I thought … those beasts had hurt you for real,' she said, sobbing. With that she threw her arms around him and cried some more.

Julius realised then that they must have been watching his Solo game on one of the screens. He stood there in awkward silence, patting Morgana's back until she was ready to let go.

'It was only a game, silly,' said Julius with a smile. 'Sorry I didn't tell you guys, but I couldn't find you and I came here looking for you and then …'

'Man, don't worry. I'm not speechless because of that,' said Skye. 'You were really great!'

'Got killed though,' said Julius, blushing slightly.

'Who cares? That was some hardcore stuff, to be sure!' added Faith excitedly. 'I thought I was watching a horror movie.'

'Yeah, it was brutal,' said Skye.

'I think it's wrong what they turned those lovely old people into,' said Morgana, shaking her head.

'By the way, Skye,' said Julius sheepishly, 'I might have nightmares for a month after tonight. You know, just in case you hear me scream in the middle of the night.'

'I got your back. Come on, let's go for an ice cream. I wanna hear everything.'

Satras was quiet that night. There were only a handful of students doing some last minute shopping and a few other visitors strolling around the lake. Skye had taken them to Mario's Ice-Land, an ice cream parlour on the third level. After furnishing themselves with a matching set of chocolate moustaches, courtesy of Mario's infamous Gut Wrencher Sundae, they all sat back happily as Julius told them about his game. He tried his best to explain how it had felt being chased by the samurai, and the sensation of mentally pushing away the creatures in the village – that had been the really difficult part. He didn't care to admit how scared he had been though or how easy it had been to forget that he was in a simulated combat. Thankfully they didn't ask too many questions on that score, so Julius was able to skirt around it and concentrate instead on the skills he had used.

'Well, mate,' said Faith laying down his spoon, 'you did it. Now we all have to take a shot.'

'Speak for yourself,' said Morgana. 'I'll stick with my flying games for now.'

'I'm with Faith,' said Skye, 'but I'm not telling you when I go either.'

'Speaking of going, we better move. It's almost eight o'clock. I'll get this,' said Morgana, pulling out her wallet.

Julius finished the last of his ice cream and led the way back down. At the Satras station they became quite nervous, as they only had ten minutes left before Foster would lock Tijara's gate.

'Finally, here's the stupid train!' said Faith, hovering above the tracks.

As the train pulled in and drew to a halt, Julius became aware of two men who had queued up ahead of them. Immediately he recognised them as the unpleasant fellows who had been arguing with Pit-Stop Pete on the day of their first game, back in October. Once inside, he leaned against the glass surface of the train and looked over at them. The taller of the two was still wearing the red cap down to his brow and was talking animatedly to the other. The sense of unease that Julius had felt the first time he had seen them was back, stronger than before. There was definitely something not right about them. He decided to do a little mind probing, just for a few seconds, to see if he could pick up any clues as to why he felt so guarded. Locking his eyes on Red Cap, he tried a light mind push. Normally, Julius would have been able to perceive something, but not this time, so he pushed a little harder, but again to no effect. He tried with the other man – same blank.

'That's impossible,' he mumbled.

'What's wrong, Julius?' asked Morgana. She followed his gaze towards the two men.

'Weren't they the ones who upset Pete, back in Satras?' asked Skye.

'The very same. There's something wrong about them. I don't like it,' said Julius, 'and I can't link to either of them.'

The train was now approaching the Zed docks. As it slowed, the men moved towards the door.

'Flaps!' Look there,' whispered Faith, pointing to something outside the train.

They turned to see what had caught Faith's attention and saw a man, crouched by the sensor lock on one of the dock's side doors, unmistakably trying to force it open. Red Cap and his partner had disembarked and were walking straight towards him.

'We've gotta tell someone,' said Morgana, a hint of panic in her voice.

'There's no time,' answered Julius, 'I'm going to stop them.'

'WE are going to stop them,' said Skye emphatically, 'You had your fun with Solo. This is team work. Morgana, go back to Tijara and tell Foster.'

'Hey, I'm in the team too, you know!' she answered resentfully.

'Stop bickering! Let's go before the train leaves. They're already in,' said Julius.

And with that, he darted forward. Faith's skirt hummed behind him, accompanied by the hurried footsteps of Skye and Morgana. Julius stopped outside the door and saw burn marks around the sensor lock. Cautiously, he peered inside and saw the three men walking towards the centre of a large hangar. Motioning for the others to follow, he quietly made his way forward.

The men stopped next to a Cougar where Red Cap uncovered a small green crate by the wall and handed it to one of his accomplices.

'You know what to do,' he said.

His comrade headed towards the end of the hangar at a run. Seeing this, Julius leapt into the light, combat hand at the ready.

'Hey, this area is for Zed members only!' shouted Julius.

Skye, Faith and Morgana came forward and stood by his side.

Red Cap turned to face them, a dangerous smirk on his face. 'Hmph, it's the granny-killer,' he scoffed.

Julius barely had time to register what he had just been called before Red Cap whipped something from his pocket and threw it at the Cougar next to him. There was a small explosion that blew one of its wings off and dark smoke billowed out into the hangar. Julius covered his face just in time to protect himself from metal fragments that were flying through the air. Through the smoke, he was relieved to see that Faith had shielded Morgana with his skirt. He ran towards Red Cap with Faith in tow while Skye and Morgana went for the other man, who was trying to hide behind the crippled plane.

Julius tried to push Red Cap off balance, by hitting him with a volley of short energy bursts, but to his dismay they weren't inflicting any damage. His shockwaves rippled through the air, passed harmlessly through Red Cap and dispersed against the far wall. Faith's efforts were also in vain. Either they had both suddenly lost their mind-skills or this guy was protected by some invisible shield.

Red Cap let out a spiteful laugh and threw another bomb at them. Luckily Faith had seen it coming and with remarkably quick reflexes flew straight at Julius, lifted him off his feet and dived for the safety of a nearby column. The device exploded just behind them, sending them flying. They landed hard and Julius sprang to his feet just in time to see Red Cap disappearing through the back door of the hangar.

Julius turned to his right and saw that Morgana and Skye were still fighting against the last of their enemy, who just stood there, motionless. Their attacks were proving as ineffective as his had been. He sprinted forward and, for no logical reason, scrambled onto a crate and dived at the man. But, as Julius closed his arms around his neck, he grasped nothing but fresh air and ended up sprawled across the floor. As he landed with a thud, a bright red light lit up the room for a second and blinked out just as quickly. Then all was still.

'Julius, are you OK man?' asked Skye, helping him up.

'Yeah, I'm fine … I think. Where's that guy gone?'

'He just … vanished,' said Morgana, struggling to catch her breath.

'Not before dropping this,' said Faith, holding up a small red box. 'It fell off as you passed through him.'

'What's that?' asked Skye, shaking some dust from his hair.

'No idea. Maybe …' Faith was cut short by the sound of feet running toward them.

Captain Foster had just entered the hangar, closely followed by ten security guards. He stood there flabbergasted, looking from the four dusty students to the crippled Cougar leaning on its one remaining wing. After a few seconds, he seemed to regain some composure and turned to his men.

'Alert the Grand Master that there's been a security breach in the Zed docks. I shall be along shortly with the students. And send a repair team to the hangar, pronto!'

Julius looked at the others anxiously. How they were going to explain this to Freja was anybody's guess, and judging by Foster's stern expression, he was sure they were in big trouble.

*

Twenty minutes later, they were all standing to attention in Cress' office, their uniforms singed from the explosions and greyed by the dust. Julius's eyes kept flicking towards Freja, who was sitting silently behind Cress' desk. He was staring at the red box in his hands, his eyes focused and grave. Julius felt positively petrified – being in the presence of the Grand Master was intimidating enough as it was without the added burden of this unpleasant incident. Master Cress, who was standing by Freja's side, listened into his earpiece for a few moments before addressing the students: 'I believe an explanation is in order. Mr Miller?'

Skye began to talk. He told how they had seen the men arguing with Pete back in October and then noticed them again on the train. To Julius's surprise, Skye made no mention of his failed mind-linking attempts and skipped straight to how Faith had seen them breaking into the hangar and everything that had followed.

'But, instead of alerting security from aboard the Intra-Rail System,' said Cress seriously, 'you decided to take it upon yourselves to eliminate the threat. Who may we thank for the partial destruction of the hangar, the Cougar and the possible death of four Tijara students?'

'It was me, sir,' said Julius quickly, 'I am the one responsible.'

'This isn't the Hologram Palace, Mr McCoy. Leave heroic stunts for your Solo games. In real life, you belong to Zed and we act as a collective.'

Julius felt his cheeks burning with shame but somehow managed to keep his eyes fixed on the Master.

Cress stared at them in silence for several excruciating seconds.

'You are all banned from Satras until the mid-winter break. From tomorrow, for the next three weeks, between 17:00 and 20:00 hours, you shall report daily to Professor Chan for extra Martial Arts lessons. You are under direct order not to mention any of today's events to anybody ... and that includes the red box. Understood?'

'Yes sir,' they answered promptly.

'Report to Dr Walliser in the infirmary. Dismissed.'

They bowed low and left the room. Once in the corridor, Julius stopped and quietly pressed his ear against the closed door.

'Are you crazy?' whispered Skye.

Julius hushed him and gestured for the others to join him. He could see they were all anxious, but their sense of curiosity was obviously stronger than their fear because they moved closer without hesitation.

'Nathan,' Freja's slightly muffled voice said, 'retrieve the footage from the dock's surveillance cameras. I want exterior and interior views. And have List examine this box immediately.'

'Do you think it's ...'

'Salgoria. Who else?'

Julius stiffened at the mention of the Queen of Arnesh. There was a sharp intake of breath behind him – probably Morgana. He heard steps approaching the door, so brusquely he pushed the others along the corridor until they were clear of the office block. Nobody said anything but, judging by their expressions, Julius knew they were as worried as he was. The idea that Salgoria's men had infiltrated Zed right under their noses was scarier than any detention.

In the infirmary, the nurses took them all into separate rooms. Dr Walliser disinfected a few cuts and bruises on Julius's arms and face and then released him. He made his way to the mess hall where he was going to meet the others for some food, a chat about what they had just heard and perhaps a little rant about what seemed like an undeserved detention. But, as he approached, he heard raucous laughter and chanting, as if someone was having a huge party. Curious, he stepped into the room and, before he had time to understand what was going on, the cheering doubled in volume and he was instantly surrounded by his entire year. Hands pulled at him from all directions – a sea of laughing faces danced in front of him as his classmates patted him on the back and heartily congratulated him. Julius was totally mystified by the situation and it wasn't until he saw Skye bouncing merrily on one of the benches, pointing at the Solo screen, that he realised what was going on. He looked up and saw his own name on the ninth rank of the board. A beautiful smile lit up his face and, as he pushed his way towards Skye, he was positively beaming.

'Paint me green and call me a leprechaun. You did it!' shouted Faith, gliding over the tables.

Skye leapt from the table and landed in Julius's arms hooting, while Morgana clapped and cheered with Siena. Julius shook hands with most of the students in the mess hall, answered questions and vaguely dodged a few of the older girls who were trying to hug him. Thankfully Morgana came to the rescue, announcing, businesslike, to the crowd that his food was getting cold. When Julius went to bed that night, he was still grinning, the fear of Salgoria forgotten for a while.

*

The three weeks before the mid-winter break went by quicker than Julius could have anticipated. The news of his Solo score had spread like wildfire. Someone had apparently made an illegal copy of the footage from his game and circulated it among the three schools. Kaori had reported that his game was the most viewed inside the Palace arena, which made Julius mighty pleased with himself. During his breaks, he was often surrounded by small crowds eager to hear all about the morphing grannies and the skills he had used.

Not once had his friends complained about their detention, which Julius thought was only fair and decent of them given that, although he had been the one to start the chase in the hangars, he had not obliged them to follow. They had made their choice and were paying the consequences just as he was.

With all the extra Martial Arts training, they were getting fitter and stronger, which made a big difference in their regular classes. Banned as they were from Satras, their only chance of getting anywhere near a plane's cockpit was during their Pilot Training on Fridays, and they enjoyed the lessons all the more for it. Spaceology was still rather boring for most of the students in comparison to the other subjects, except for Morgana of course. On the last Wednesday morning before the holidays, after being hit on her head for the umpteenth time by an eraser, courtesy of Skye, she stood up and stopped Professor Brown.

'Excuse me, Professor,' she said throwing an evil glance at Skye, 'I can't quite hear you from here. Shall I move to a closer desk?'

Professor Brown looked a little puzzled, especially after seeing three of her students stifling a laugh.

'Of course, Miss Ruthier. Take a seat. Now, as I was saying,' she continued, 'Kratos is an artificial disc, built by Zed around fifty years ago. Its purpose was that of a storage facility for the Academy. However, it has never been utilised due to its gravitational instability whenever a solar flare occurs. It is very close to our sector and its atmosphere is breathable thanks to a shield, much like Zed's. However ...'

The bell cut her short and she dismissed the class with a frustrated expression, given that most of the students were already at the door. But, while Professor Brown had seemed oblivious of the holiday spirit among the students, Professor King, the Telekinesis teacher, had embraced it a little too enthusiastically. The following morning, Julius's class was divided into two groups for a massive mental tug-of-war session. Professor King, sporting a Santa Claus hat, was instructing them from the back of an embalmed reindeer called Jeff, which was gliding along the classroom under his telekinetic guidance.

'Show off,' said Faith under his breath.

'I want the teams in two rows facing each other, two yards away from the white line. Once in position, you must hold hands. On my signal, you shall try to bring the other team towards you and over the line. Since it's your first time I would advise you to concentrate on the student directly opposite you.' King stopped his steed between the teams. 'Ho, ho, ho! Ready...steady...go!'

Julius felt a sudden tugging sensation in his chest, which pulled him forward slightly. He regained his footing and concentrated on Skye, who was standing opposite him. Pulling with his mind was harder than he had thought and it felt very weird indeed. Holding hands with fourteen other people meant that his efforts were being spread right across the line. He felt like an electric conductor, with the energy of his team mates passing through his body. Professor King was laughing his head off, which didn't help Julius's concentration at all.

'If you could see yourselves! Here, let me take a picture,' he said, laughing even harder, while pulling a camera out of his pocket.

Julius could only imagine why. The class was totally silent, without the shouting and the cheering that would normally accompany an activity such as this. All any spectator would see was thirty people grunting in concentration, their faces red and their brows dangerously close to their mouths. Julius forced these thoughts out of his mind and focused instead on Skye. He could see the other team advancing unevenly towards the line, which allowed him to see who was pulling the hardest. Morgana, who was holding his left hand, started to slide forward too, thanks to the efforts of Yuri Slovich. Julius redoubled his pull, and after several painful minutes, the other team began to slip forward faster and faster. Skye, who was holding his ground stoically, was forced across the line by the people to either side of him. The first cry in the room came from Barth, who literally flew over the line compliments of Faith.

'I think I've ruptured a blood vessel,' said Skye, rubbing his forehead.

Professor King was spurring his dead steed across the room, dismissing the class with one final "Ho, ho, ho!".

'He needs a holiday more than we do ...' whispered Morgana as they left.

OF PARTIES AND JUNKYARDS

The last day of term came and went and, by dinner time, Julius was as happy as he could be. He had finally managed his first brief trance, during that morning's session with Master Isshin.

'I'm so glad for you, Julius,' said Morgana, nimbly picking at her vegetable tempura with a pair of chopsticks. 'I knew you could do it.'

'What did the holopal do – hit you over the head with a hammer?' asked Skye with a grin.

'He was tempted, but no. I was actually considering giving up, thinking that I would try again after the holiday, when all of a sudden I just zoned out. I think I was so relaxed about it that it just happened by itself.'

'Was Master Isshin pleased?' asked Morgana.

'Yes … for about two seconds. Then he flickered and disappeared on me again. I bet there's something wrong with this watch. Maybe I've damaged it or something.'

'Who cares,' said Skye. 'Now that you've done it, Cress will be satisfied and you'll be able to sleep again in the morning.'

'I hope so, oh so much.'

And, sure enough, when he returned to his quarters Julius found his computer monitor beeping – there was a message from Gabriel List asking him to return the watch in the morning, as he wouldn't need it anymore. With deep satisfaction, he deactivated his alarm clock and buried himself under the blanket.

It was close to midday by the time Julius dragged himself out of bed and headed for the holographic sector. He knocked on the technicians' door, while undoing the strap of his watch.

'Mr McCoy,' said List after opening the door, 'I see you got my message. Come inside.'

Upon entering, Gabriel dropped all formalities, as he had done before. He invited Julius to sit, shoved a cup of hot chocolate into his hands and asked about his experiences with the holopal. As Julius recounted the details of his sessions, List became ever more animated. It reminded him incredibly of how excited Faith got whenever he talked about anything to do with the latest gadgets and gizmos, and he made a mental note to introduce the pair of them at the earliest opportunity.

'I am glad Master Isshin was able to help,' said List, sipping from his cup.

'You're telling me. By the way, you might need to check the program.'

'You mean it disappeared on you again?'

'Yes, just after my trance. Maybe the excitement was too much and he blew a circuit, or something.'

'It is possible,' said List, half smiling, 'except it's not the first watch that's packed up on us this month. I better go check the VI core. Anyway, if you should need Master

Isshin again, you know where to find him.'

Julius thanked him and headed to the mess hall, where he grabbed some food and took it with him to the garden. Morgana, Faith and Skye were lying on the grass. Skye waved as he approached.

'About time,' he said, making space beside him.

'Thanks for letting me sleep this morning,' said Julius.

'I figured you'd kill me if I didn't.'

'Too true. So what's up?'

'At breakfast, they gave us the schedule for our mid-winter family meals,' said Skye. 'And here's the really cool bit – we get to have them in the Hologram Palace.'

'Yeah,' said Morgana, sitting up, 'we can program in any setting we want! The slot for our year is on the 28th.'

'Sounds good,' said Julius.

'Not really,' said Faith gloomily, ''cause it means that the Palace will be off limits from now until New Year.'

'Shoot,' said Julius, disappointed. 'My little brother will be gutted.'

'I know,' said Morgana. 'But at least Michael will have a meal in there. Why don't you let him choose the program, Julius?'

'Good idea. He'll like that. What are you guys going for?'

'Well,' said Skye, 'all of the Terra 3 people have a meal together every year. Apparently, it's a tradition as old as the Zed space stations.'

'Who else is from Terra 3 in our year?' asked Julius.

'Louisa Call, Yuri Slovich, Annette Valeris and Morgana's friend, Isolde Frey. I grew up with them. I mean, there are only so many places you can go to when you're on a space station. But hey, it's home,' said Skye with a shrug of his shoulders. 'What about you, Faith?'

'I thought of going somewhere in the Hawaiian Archipelagos. You know, sun, sand and surf. Besides, me Ma' loves to sunbathe.'

'That sounds better than my party,' said Skye. 'You don't mind if I barge in, do you?'

'To be sure.'

'We're going to have our usual traditional Japanese meal,' said Morgana. 'My mum bought us all new kimonos when she visited Kyoto last month. I think she got one for you too, Julius,' she said, turning towards him.

'Excellent! I'm looking forward to seeing her.'

'You guys been friends long?' asked Skye.

'Morgana is practically my sister,' said Julius, trying to steal one of the dried apricots she was snacking on.

'I prefer to think of myself as his good conscience,' she said, quickly moving the food out of reach. 'We grew up on the same street, went to the same school and all the rest. So you *could* say we're like family.' As she said that, she lightly ran her fingers through his hair and ruffled them.

Julius took his chance and lunged at the apricots, grabbing a handful as he rolled across the grass before leaping up triumphantly. 'Thank you. Thank you very much. I'm here all week,' he said, bowing to an invisible crowd. 'I'm off to speak to Michael. See you later guys.'

Morgana waved him away with a mock expression of frustration and, lying back, resumed reading her book. As Julius was about to turn away, he caught Skye looking at her and noticed a light pink wisp above his head. He turned the other way, suddenly very embarrassed.

'I really don't need to know,' he muttered to himself as he hastily left the garden.

It took about two hours of messaging back and forth before Michael finally decided what program he wanted for the holiday meal. With this information, Julius went to Satras to book a slot. Mrs Mayflower was all smiles and praise for his Solo score when she saw him and Julius, who was surrounded by several queuing students, blushed nervously and wished she would just get on with it. It was bad enough that Bernard Docherty was staring at him from the sidelines – Julius thought he resented him for making it onto the score board – but it got worse when he placed his order for the holosuite. For reasons unknown to Julius, Michael had decided to have the meal in the middle of a junkyard.

'Do you want a tetanus shot with that?' Mrs Mayflower asked with a concerned look.

Their parents had tried to dissuade Michael in every way and with numerous bribes, but he had not budged.

'A junkyard?' asked Faith over his tea that night.

'Has he gone mad?' said Morgana.

'Suddenly my shindig with the colonists sounds like fun,' added Skye, with a perplexed look on his face.

'Faith, I forbid you to mention Hawaii to me until the end of the year,' said Julius, brandishing a turkey leg at him.

'I'll try mate,' said Faith, seriously. 'So, you gonna eat *junk* food?'

The four of them looked at each other and burst out laughing, while Julius pelted Faith with turkey bones.

The following week Satras was packed with visitors, day and night. Each student's family was allowed to stay only for 24 hours, to avoid overcrowding. With the Hologram Palace closed, Julius and his mates spent most of their days walking around Satras, catching up with other classmates, visiting Mario's Ice-Land and exploring the many shops scattered across the various levels.

On the morning of the 28th, Julius went to pick his family up from the docks. As he waited for their shuttle, his mind turned to the fight with Red Cap and his men. Cress had not mentioned the incident even once, as if he wanted them to forget all about it. As far as he knew, it had remained a secret from the rest of Zed too. It wasn't as if Julius thought about it constantly, but it was hard to forget that he had been involved in a serious incident like that – the memories were there, stored in the back of his head.

'Julius!' cried Michael, jumping off the shuttle and running wildly towards his brother.

Julius caught him in his arms and squeezed him. Jenny and Rory McCoy followed their youngest son a little more elegantly, although Julius could see his dad's eyes keenly scanning the area. After several minutes of hugs, kisses and more hugs – Hasn't our son grown so much, Rory? – Julius led them aboard the Intra-Rail System that would take them to their hotel in Satras.

Julius couldn't help but smile as he watched them soaking in the new surroundings with sheer delight on their faces. It strongly reminded him of his own excitement when he had first seen Zed. Satras surely was a mighty sight for them and one day was not nearly enough to enjoy all of its amusements. After checking in they set off for their meal, deciding that they would do some exploring later.

As they reached the Palace, they were directed by security guards to use the left door and to go two floors down. Julius explained to Michael that this was the same entrance he used for the games. His brother was looking everywhere and touching everything, overjoyed to be there at last. When they reached their floor, they stopped behind Dhara Sundaram, an Indian girl in his year. Julius watched as Dhara and her family stepped onto a lift. Its metal doors closed as soon as they were in and slid away before disappearing behind the wall to their left, before being promptly replaced by a new lift. Julius, who had read the instructions several times that morning, walked confidently towards it. He cleared his throat and gave the command: 'Computer, activate 1MJ McCoy.'

Julius invited his family to enter the lift and as they stepped inside, the door shut behind them and the floor began to move. When the lift stopped, another door opened revealing the biggest junkyard the McCoys had ever seen.

Even with all of his holographic experience, Julius was blown away. The junkyard seemed to spread out forever in pile upon pile of trash of every kind. Tiny fairy lights gave a festive glow to the drabness of the place, creating fantastic shadows all around. At the centre of an empty area, they saw a table laden with an impossible amount of food and drinks. The table itself was sculpted from the oddest pieces of junk compressed together. Julius could distinguish a fridge door, a fly-car seat and even a teddy bear. The backs of the chairs curled upwards, creating tall, elegant metal frames.

'Shall we?' said Rory, inviting his family to sit down.

'Is it safe to eat this food, Julius?' asked Jenny anxiously.

'Of course it is, dear,' cut in Rory, 'perfectly safe. Michael and I were so excited about coming here that we looked it up, didn't we son?'

Michael nodded his agreement, but his mouth was already too crammed with food to add any comment. As they began their meal, Rory explained to his wife how the holosuite was programmed to convert energy to matter and back again, which allowed them to physically interact with their surroundings.

'The food you're eating darling, is the same as you would get on a spaceship. It's replicated through a protein re-sequencer ...'

At that point Julius had to stifle a laugh, as he realised that his mum couldn't understand half of what Mr McCoy was saying.

'Dad, I think you've confused her enough,' said Julius, helping himself to a large portion of mash.

'Maybe you're right, son. Why don't you tell us about you now?' said Rory jovially.

Julius was glad to finally be able to speak to them in person about his new life. Writing or talking through a sat-cam wasn't really the same. He had always spoken to his parents about everything, knowing that they would listen and try to understand, no matter what he was going through. But, as he told them about his friends, his success in the game world and his failure in Meditation, it dawned on him that he wasn't going to be able to tell them about his fight in the docks. He had been ordered not to mention it to anyone and, being a Zed student, he had to follow the rules. Knowing that, however, didn't make it any easier to keep it from his parents.

When he had finished, Jenny shared the news from home, which Julius was eager to hear. After lunch, Michael spent a good hour rummaging in the piles of junk, assembling the weirdest gadgets and toys. It broke his heart, but Julius had to tell his brother that, once out of the holosuite, all his possessions would disappear.

'I know,' said Michael sadly. 'It's the matter-energy conversion. I've looked it up.'

'I'm impressed. What say we go shopping for some real gadgets in Satras?'

'Excellent. Let's go!' said Michael, rushing everyone off their seats.

'That's a good idea,' said Jenny. 'I think I've had enough of the junkyard. Besides, I want to try and find some lunar memorabilia for your granny.'

They spent the rest of the afternoon walking around Satras and, in the evening, went to Mario's to meet up with Morgana, Kaori and their parents. Julius was beaming when Mrs Ruthier gave him his kimono, and Michael begged her to bring one back for him the next time she was in Japan.

'I'll save the money. I promise,' he said sincerely.

They stayed up quite late but, even with their parents there, Julius and Morgana had to return to Tijara by midnight. The morning after, the two families caught the shuttle back to Earth together, leaving Julius, Morgana and Kaori waving goodbye to them from the platform.

'That was fun,' said Morgana, watching the shuttle take off. 'Too bad it was only one day.'

'We'll see them soon enough Hana-chan,' said Kaori, putting an arm around Morgana's shoulders as they boarded the train back to the schools. 'Besides, we still have two exciting events coming up – the New Year party and your birthday.'

'Too right. I'm so looking forward to it!'

'How does the party work?' asked Julius.

'Each school has their own one, normally in the assembly hall.'

'Oh,' said Morgana, clearly disappointed. 'I thought that we'd be together.'

'I know,' said Kaori, 'I would have liked that too. There are so few events that get all three schools together, like the ceremony for a new Grand Master for example. But I'll see you during the day and I'm sure you'll have a great time at the party, even without your big sister. You'll take care of that, won't you Julius?'

'Sure thing. And we've even prepared a little surprise for you.'

Morgana smiled and clapped her hands together excitedly.

'See? All sorted, sis.'

The train slowed down and stopped at Tijara, so they said goodbye to Kaori and went in search of their friends.

On the afternoon of New Year's Eve, Julius' dorm was in a state of total panic. Apparently not one of the first years was able to make an acceptable bowtie and in the end they unanimously decided that Lopaka Liway would fetch Tony Tower and bring him there, by force if necessary. To their relief, Tower arrived along with three of his mates, and they happily went from room to room making sure that all the young students looked impeccable.

Julius and Skye were standing in front of the mirror, meticulously smoothing the creases from their jackets. For the New Year party, all students had to wear a black, tailored dinner suit, with white shirt and black tie. Julius had collected his own after lunch, from Twitch and Stitch, the schools' uniform supplier in Satras.

'Don't we look just!' said Skye, combing his hair.

'Just,' said Julius feeling rather anxious. He was always self-conscious at these kinds of formal events and was hoping to find a table in the darkest corner of the room.

'Are you guys ready?' asked Faith, knocking on the door.

'Come in,' said Skye with one last futile attempt to flatten his wavy hair.

Faith glided into the room, his metallic skirt as black as his jacket.

'How did you do that?' asked Julius, surprised.

'It was Pete. He left a tub of dark polish at Twitch and Stitch, in case I felt like … coordinating!'

'Just watch you don't get too close to any of the girls' dresses,' said Skye.

'Oh, no worries. It's already dry. Anyway, I doubt anybody would ask me to dance.'

'We'll dance with you, Faith,' said Skye with a wink.

'Speak for yourself,' said Julius, pushing them both out of the room.

They made their way up to the hall, checking that their bowties were still facing the right direction. As he stepped out of the lift, Julius was startled by the large crowd in the main corridor. There were 180 Mizki students in Tijara, and tonight they would all be gathered in the same place. They were huddled in small groups, some sitting by the fountain that ran around the black walls of the assembly room, and others just milling about. Everyone looked exceptionally smart and very official, but Julius could tell there was a sense of anxious anticipation in the air. He didn't even need to concentrate to see the little wisps of pink rising above the heads of the senior boys as they discreetly ogled the girls mingling in the crowd.

'Hey guys,' said Morgana from behind them.

Julius turned and saw her and Siena approaching them.

'Ladies, you look wonderful,' said Faith, bowing ceremoniously.

'Thank you,' they both answered, blushing.

Julius also thought that they looked really pretty, but he most definitely wasn't going to share that thought with them. Morgana was wearing a long, strapless, emerald green satin dress. The folds of the gown draped smoothly towards the ground, making Julius think of soft tropical waves. Around her shoulder, she wore a velvet stole of the same colour.

'Happy birthday, Morgana,' Julius said cheerfully. Then he sent a quick mind message to Skye, who was staring at the girls with the glazed expression of a sloth.

'*Close your mouth, you ape!*'

Skye was startled out of his reverie, but managed to recompose himself without the girls noticing.

At that moment, the doors of the assembly hall opened and the students started to file in. When Julius entered the hall, his eyes wandered up to the ceiling. The roof panels had been slid open, allowing them to see the bright stars beyond the Zed shield. The room looked different from their first visit. All the chairs had been replaced by circular tables, covered with white linen and silver candleholders. The flickering lights created intimate glows and cast shadows all around. The tables formed a semi-circle facing the stage, where a long table had been prepared for the teachers.

'There's a free table over there,' said Morgana, pointing to her left.

They hurried in that direction and Julius headed straight for the most hidden of the chairs. That left three empty seats, which were soon taken by Lopaka, Isolde and her roommate Femi Mubarak, a girl from Egypt. Waiters in white uniforms moved swiftly from table to table, bringing filled champagne flutes to all the Mizki. Watching them dodge the students with remarkable agility, Julius thought about the first and only time he had tasted champagne, at his parents' wedding anniversary, but he couldn't remember whether he had liked it or not.

As the last of the students found their seats, Master Cress entered the hall. He walked over to the stage and faced the Mizki.

'All rise,' he said aloud, lifting his hands upwards.

The students rose quickly to their feet and the noise died down. Julius followed Cress's gaze toward the main door, where the Grand Master of Tijara was standing, impeccably dressed. Freja stepped into the room followed by the teachers, all wearing black – even Chan and Lao-tzu had swapped their usual tunics for dark suits. They walked to their table and stood behind their chairs.

'Please, be seated,' Freja said to all.

Julius sat down, trying to shake off the shameful memory of his last meeting with him.

'It is with great honour that I welcome you all to this special event,' said Freja, bowing his head to the assembly. 'Two hundred and thirty-five years ago, Marcus Tijara stood on this very stage, addressing the first ever Mizki students. Much time has passed since then, but his dream of building a peaceful society has never died and it continues to shape Zed's ethos, even today. I would like you to raise your glasses with me, to the teachers and staff of Tijara, for their constant contribution to that dream.'

Freja and the Mizki raised their glasses together to the teachers, who were bowing to them in return.

'Tonight,' continued Freja, 'we celebrate the end of another year spent in peace and prosperity. May the year 2856 be as peaceful and prosperous.'

'So let it be,' answered the assembly in unison.

Freja took his seat and the waiters began to serve dinner. As the evening progressed, Julius felt his anxiety ebbing away and sensed that this night would be a fine one. He was having a mighty good time with his mates; the food was excellent and his ego had been suitably boosted, as several Mizki Seniors had made their way over to the table to congratulate him personally on his Solo score. After dessert, fifteen couples, made up entirely of 6 Mizki Seniors, moved to the empty floor and opened the dances to the notes of Strauss's waltz.

'My sister told me it's a tradition for the final year students to open the dances,' Morgana told her girlfriends with an excited giggle.

'They look so beautiful,' said Siena dreamily.

Given that the girls were all busy watching the dancers, Julius decided it was the perfect moment to bring out Morgana's surprise. He had arranged everything with the chef that very afternoon and, with a nod of his head, he signalled to the waiter that they were ready. As the last notes of the music faded away, a beautiful birthday cake made its way to their table. Morgana's eyes grew wide and bright when she saw it, and so great was her joy that she remained speechless. The table started to sing "Happy Birthday" not so loud as to attract the attention of the entire room, but enough so that the adjacent tables joined in.

'Thank you, guys,' said Morgana tearfully. 'Thank you so much.'

'Come on, make a wish,' said Skye with a big smile.

Morgana closed her eyes for few seconds, then blew out the candles in one go, all thirteen of them. Julius started to clap and everybody else joined in with loud cheers. He knew that Morgana had been well and truly pleased with the surprise because, as she looked at him, he could see a bright aura spreading all around her head and shoulders like a glittering cape.

'I wish they could see that,' thought Julius with a smile. In his mind that was the best thank you, better than any words she could have said.

As midnight drew near, Julius watched the students dancing wildly all around the room. It seemed that the dance floor was too small for all of them. Morgana and Isolde were also in the crowd, with Faith doing a mad hover-dance between them.

'I hope that skirt holds him up,' said Julius with a grin.

'Come on. Let's go and make sure it does,' said Skye, dragging him to the dance floor.

With ten seconds left before the bells, the DJ began the countdown and everyone joined in. As the clock struck midnight the hall erupted in joyful cheers, while a formation of Zed's Cougars flew across the sky. Their sharp turns and twists generated a huge roar from the crowd and they all clapped wildly.

'Happy Hogmanay, Julius,' said Morgana hugging him tightly.

'To our first space party,' said Faith, spinning out of control above their heads.

The music started again for a celebration that would continue into the small hours of the night.

Around one o'clock, Julius and Faith left Morgana and Skye on the dance floor, to make a quick visit to the restroom behind the main stage. Suddenly, as they were coming out again, Faith grabbed Julius by the arm and pushed him behind a thick curtain.

'What the ...' started Julius.

Faith clamped his hand over Julius's mouth and pointed to his left where Freja and Cress were standing, engrossed in what appeared to be an intense discussion. Julius moved quietly towards them and peeked out of a gap in the curtains. Although they were keeping their voices low, Julius and Faith could hear them well enough.

'Are you sure, Nathan?' asked Freja. His voice sounded worried and tense.

'Positive. Salgoria's troops have occupied Kratos. We just don't know why.'

'What about the red box?'

'That's the worst news of all. It's a hologram remote control, with the added power of a scrambler. It's very advanced technology. Salgoria is a proper Arneshian. But ... you don't seem surprised, Carlos.'

'I've examined the CCTV footage from the hangar. The scan analysis has revealed two distinct electromagnetic interferences.'

'McCoy and his friends were telling the truth then.'

'Yes, but we never doubted that. In the meantime, order a scan of all holographic devices on Zed. List said he's been having some problems recently.'

Julius froze as he remembered the numerous times when Master Isshin had flickered and vanished during their meditation training.

'Are they here for him, Marcus?'

'Yes. Somehow they've found out.'

'I'll have him followed then.'

'Do it. We cannot risk another Bastiaan Grant. Not this time. And especially not with him.'

'Anything else?'

'That will be all for now, Nathan.'

As they walked away, Julius and Faith moved back towards the restroom.

'We've gotta tell the others,' said Julius seriously. 'Let's go.'

Ten minutes later, they were all sitting in the garden, the cheerfulness gone from their faces.

'I can't believe we fought against holograms,' said Skye, shaking his head.

'It makes sense,' answered Julius. 'All our mind-skills went right through them.'

'And when you knocked the device from that thing's head, it just disappeared,' added Faith.

'They were using the holonet,' said Julius, 'that's why Master Isshin wasn't working properly and why Red Cap called me a "granny-killer" – he was in the net. He knew exactly what I was doing in that Solo game.'

'Given that it worked as a scrambler, it's no wonder you couldn't read their minds, Julius, not in Satras and not in the train,' said Morgana.

'What were they doing here, anyway?' asked Skye. 'Testing that remote device?'

'I think they were doing more than that,' said Julius. 'Freja mentioned Bastiaan Grant. You know what that means.'

'Wasn't he the Tuala Master that disappeared a few years back?' asked Morgana. 'Kaori told me about it.'

'They think the Arneshians are here to kidnap someone else?' asked Skye.

'Yes. And they seem to know who he is, because Freja has asked to have him followed.'

'Right,' said Faith, 'but what about the hologram that ran away with that box? Where did it go? Is their ship still at Pete's dock? And why are the Arneshians occupying Kratos?'

'Remember what Professor Brown said before the winter break?' said Morgana. 'She told us that Kratos is an empty man-made disc and that it's very close to our sector.'

'Then it's no coincidence, whatever their reasons are,' said Faith.

They discussed the matter further but still couldn't find answers to the many questions. To avoid suspicion they returned to the party, the thought of dancing completely gone from their minds.

They continued to discuss the news until two o'clock, when the last song faded away and the students were asked to retire for the night.

As he lay in bed, in the darkness, Julius felt the threat of Salgoria creeping over him.

'What a way to end the year,' he said to Skye.

'Amen to that.'

FLIGHT TIME

With the mild-winter break over, life in the school returned to normal. On their first Monday back, Julius attended his Meditation lesson without the usual dread and sure enough he managed to slip into a trance within the set target of a minute. Although Morgana was still the quickest in their year – thirty seconds – Julius was at least even with Skye and Faith, which gave Professor Lao-tzu reason to congratulate him on his achievement.

After lunch, they walked to the holographic sector for their Telekinesis lesson. As they entered, Professor King asked them to sit.

'It is customary at this time of year to introduce the 1 Mizki Juniors to the Spring Missions,' he said.

At that announcement the silence was interrupted by a buzz of excited whispers.

'As you may know,' continued King, 'the curriculum for the two junior years is the same for all students. In third year, on the other hand, you will be able to choose specialised subjects. The Spring Missions and the Summer Camps are opportunities for you to sample the different paths available to Zed graduates.'

'Guess where I'm going,' whispered Morgana eagerly to Julius.

'However, there has been a change of plans,' continued Professor King seriously.

The class fell silent again. Julius threw a glance at Faith, and received an equally worried look in return.

'From this year, the school will be deciding the nature of your first mission. It has been agreed that all Mizki Juniors will spend two weeks on the Earth colonies. More details will be given in due course.'

Some of the students seemed excited by that prospect, but others weren't quite sure what to think about the change, judging by their perplexed faces. Julius, however, had more than a clear idea of why this was happening, and he wasn't the only one.

'We should have seen it coming,' said Morgana once the lesson was over.

They were walking back to the lounge to finish an essay on ship catalysts for Professor Clavel, which was due by the end of the week.

'They're sending all MJ's as far away as possible from any action,' said Julius, annoyed.

'If anything happens,' said Morgana, 'the Arneshians will have to pass through Zed and its colonies before they get to us. I guess it's understandable that they want us out of the way. Shame though, I was really looking forward to some real flight training.'

'It's not fair. We're probably the only four students in the whole of Zed with any idea of what's going on and they don't even bother asking us if we want to do our part,' continued Julius animatedly. 'I mean, we actually fought against Salgoria's men … things!'

'Speaking of four,' said Skye looking around, 'where's Shanigan got to?'

'I don't know. He was behind us when we left class,' said Morgana, checking the lounge. 'Anyway, let's not talk in here. Remember we're under orders not to discuss the situation with anybody. I don't want to get into any more trouble if I can help it.'

Julius nodded in agreement, but he was still frustrated. It wasn't so much that he couldn't choose his mission – after all, visiting the regular colonies was a great experience – the truth was that the fight in the hangar had left him craving more action. That, and the fact that Red Cap had mocked and defeated him. If he had shared any of these feelings with the others, they would surely have told him to let it go; that he couldn't have known they were holograms; he had only just started training and he was lucky to be alive. Julius knew all of this already. Perhaps it simply boiled down to the fact that he hated losing and Red Cap reminded him all too much of people like Billy Somers – the sneering, taunting characters who loved to make others feel useless. It seemed unfair that, as soon as Somers had been put in his place by his own bravado and disappeared from the scene, Red Cap had come along to cause a whole new set of problems.

Four hours later, Julius, Skye and Morgana were sitting in the mess hall, having their dinner. Skye was swallowing freshly made ravioli like there was no tomorrow.

'Good grief, boy!' said Morgana looking at him, her face caught somewhere between disgust and amazement. 'Why don't you eat space and time while you're at it?'

'That's not a mouth,' added Julius, 'it's a black hole.'

'But I'm hungry!' said Skye shrugging his shoulders. 'Anyway, still no sign of Faith. I bet you a Fyver he's gone to try out Solo.'

'And you would lose that bet,' answered Faith, patting him on the shoulder.

'Where did you go?' asked Morgana, moving her bag from the chair so Faith could sit next to her.

'I paid a visit to Mr Pete,' said Faith with an enigmatic smile.

'Well?' asked Julius. 'What did you find out?'

'After class I went to Satras. Pete has a shop on the second tier. They sell tools and spare parts and the like. He's rarely there, but the attendant can contact him. So I told him who I was and made an excuse that I needed to see him.'

'What excuse?' asked Julius suspiciously.

'I tore off a panel from the back of me skirt actually.'

'You're a maniac!' said Skye giving him the thumbs up.

'And it worked. Pete came to see me and fixed it, no problem. As he was working, I took the liberty of asking a few questions … the right questions might I add. When I mentioned those guys, he went mental. He said they'd disappeared and nobody had come to collect those boxes they left behind, but they too mysteriously disappeared one day. And on New Year's Eve, their ship also left his dock but nobody actually saw the pilot entering the docking area!'

'Boy, wasn't Pete chatty,' said Morgana.

'Maybe it's 'cause he was so mad,' answered Faith.

'We already knew those holograms had left,' said Skye. 'One escaped with the green box; one was eliminated by Julius's acrobatics and the one with the red cap made a run for it.'

'What about their ship?' asked Julius.

'Maybe it was a hologram too,' said Skye.

'It can't have been. They saw it taking off from the dock,' answered Faith.

'Besides, if they do manage to kidnap this person, they're gonna need a real ship to transport him. Now we have two holos, a box and a ship missing,' recapped Morgana flatly. 'What are they gonna do – kamikaze themselves into the mess hall?'

'We can only keep our ears open,' said Julius with a sigh. 'But, between this latest news and the new Spring Mission rules, I bet Freja isn't sleeping all that well.'

'No one is,' added Faith seriously. 'Satras was packed with Zed officers. I've never seen so many since we got here.'

When they resumed their visits to the Hologram Palace, Julius saw that Faith had not exaggerated about the amount of Zed personnel patrolling the Lunar Perimeter. The Intra-Rail System was always crammed with men and women in uniform, sombre expressions on their faces. They would get off at Tijara, Tuala and Sield, at Satras and at the Docks, but the majority stopped at the Sea of Nectar, where the Curia was situated. The Hologram Palace was possibly the only place in Satras without officers present. The Mizki, it seemed, were still its main residents. The Skirts had picked up where they had left off with their winning streak and were still the leading team on the group charts. Often they simply played among themselves, other times they would sit in the courtyard, waiting for other students to challenge them or vice versa. It was a good way of meeting the Mizki from Tuala and Sield and, although they had decided to play only against groups from their year, they had been approached by older students as well, which really boosted their confidence. With the first proper flight simulation approaching, Julius had proposed that they lend a hand to any of their classmates who still weren't confident enough. Barth had been the first to gratefully accept their offer and, although the first few flights had gone horribly wrong, he had eventually managed to hold his plane on course and to stop himself shooting team-mates by mistake.

On the first Friday of February, the 1MJ's made their way to level -5 of the holographic sector, where Professor Clavel was standing beside a closed door.

'Good morning Mizki. In the room behind me, you will find thirty Sim-Cougars waiting for you. Choose one, take your seat and strap yourself in. Don't touch anything else until I say so. On you go.'

Morgana was so excited that she pushed Faith and Skye unceremoniously out of the way.

'She's supposed to do that,' explained Julius, shaking his head.

They had never been in this particular room before, and Julius was really surprised by how large it was. Thirty aircrafts were lined up in rows of ten, all facing a raised podium at the foot of a huge white screen. Julius found an empty plane and stood there looking at it. The Cougar was metallic black with a transparent cover over the cockpit. He reckoned it was a good eight feet long, with a wing span of at least twenty feet. The wings bent backwards, like outstretched arms protecting the main body. It was shaped like a slim, elongated dewdrop, the tip of which was sharp and thin. The rounded back section hosted the engine.

Julius passed his hand over the slick surface of the Cougar, a smile breaking out on his face. There was a step ladder next to each plane and Julius used his to climb inside, being careful not to kick the plane. It was a tight fit but familiar nonetheless – the aircrafts in the Hologram Palace were modelled on the Cougars, and he had plenty experience with those. He pulled the seatbelt across his lap and waited. To his right, he saw Faith hovering over his plane and gently landing in her seat. When all the

Mizki were ready, Professor Clavel climbed the steps to the podium. Julius saw that the teacher had a control panel in front of him and, as he pressed a button, all of the stepladders disappeared under the floor.

'You are sitting in the most advanced flight simulation program there is,' said Clavel. 'These Sim-Cougars are exact replicas of the real ones and, once we start, you will be able to manoeuvre them as you would if you were in space. For today you will not interact with each other, but instead concentrate on getting familiar and confident with your Cougars. This morning I want you to work on orientating around our lunar orbit, changing direction and controlling your speed, like we practiced in class. As you have learned in class, all Zed aircraft are capable of FTL, faster than light speed, no matter their size. Although you know how to engage FTL, it will be disabled for these simulations. The program will give you instructions as you progress through the various levels. Until you have satisfactorily mastered a task, you will not be allowed to progress further. Are you ready Mizki?'

'Yes, sir!' they all answered.

The hatch on Julius's plane closed down around him and locked into place.

'Good job I'm not claustrophobic,' he thought, taking a deep breath.

Slowly, four white walls emerged from the floor around his aircraft and rose all the way up to the ceiling. He guessed that he was now in a tank similar to those used for the Solo games in the Hologram Palace. The black body of his Cougar stood out sharply in all that white. Suddenly the light blinked out and Julius felt the plane lifting off the floor, the engine purring gently to life. A well lit runway appeared out of the darkness in front of him and the computer came on line.

'Prepare for launch,' said a voice from the console.

Julius followed the order and entered the launch sequence, as he had done in class so many times before.

'Engine engaged,' he said. 'Ready for departure.'

'Permission granted,' replied the computer flatly.

Julius pressed the thruster button and he was pushed against his seat by the G-force as the Cougar sprang forward towards the darkness at the end of the runway. As he entered the lunar orbit, his body relaxed again. He was aware that his surroundings were simulated, but the illusion was perfect. Decreasing his speed, he began to orient his plane toward the Moon. Zed, with all its buildings gathered under the shield, stood out clearly against its surface. He cheered loudly as a sense of joy overwhelmed him. Surely this was his coolest experience yet.

'Input Zed base coordinates from this position,' ordered the voice.

Julius complied. Now he could start his orientation training. The computer gave him the coordinates of different points in space to reach. Julius then had to find the correct spots, confirm their location and move onto the next one. He was curious to see how the others were doing, but all communications had been cut off. After about 20 correctly executed trips, he was allowed to return to base coordinates. With his Cougar still pointed at Tijara, he began to try some manoeuvres. Initially he had to practice using the thrusters to move his plane sideways, up and down. Julius was immediately aware that the controllers were set to a much higher sensitivity than those of the Cougars in the Hologram Palace. He continued to move his aircraft around until he felt confident. Then he was allowed to progress and practise turning at different angles.

'McCoy,' said Professor Clavel over the intercom.

'Yes, sir?' said Julius, a little startled.

'I want you to try a reverse 360 degree rotation from stationary, if you please.'

'Sir?'

'A back flip, McCoy! You do remember the sequence, I hope.'

'Yes, sir,' he answered, a small bead of sweat forming on his forehead.

In the Palace, he had never tried that manoeuvre before. He entered the command on the panel and gripped the control stick. The Cougar replied swiftly and Julius didn't even have time to realise he was upside down for a second or two before he was level again.

'Good,' said Clavel. 'Do a few more and then try a few forward flips.'

'Yes, sir.'

Full of confidence, Julius followed the instruction promptly. Next came the twists and those were a no-brainer for him. Finally, he was allowed to practise controlling the Cougar's speed. The aircraft was fast beyond imagination and even a simple acceleration made for an exhilarating experience. He spent the last hour combining all the different sections of that morning's training and after one final fast lap, ending in a back flip, a twist and a tight left turn, Julius made his way to the simulated hangar. As the program ended, he wasn't the only one to come out of the Cougar visibly excited. Morgana was jumping up and down while leaning on Faith, who was also bobbing out of control as a result.

'Miss Ruthier,' said Professor Clavel, suppressing a smile, 'I think Mr Shanigan's suspensions may require a little more grace on your part.'

'I'm sorry, Professor, but this was the best lesson ever!' she said, beaming.

'And it won't be the last. This training is all you Mizki will be doing until your Spring Mission,' he said to the class. 'We are done for now. We shall resume at 14:00 hours. Dismissed.'

The excitement continued throughout their lunch. Julius and his mates didn't actually manage to eat much as they were too busy telling each other about their own performances. When the afternoon session resumed, they were all eager for more and Professor Clavel happily complied, programming the computer so that one scenario would follow the other without rest.

As the lessons continued throughout that February, they were eventually allowed to fly in teams. The Skirts were flying again, alternating the leadership of their squad every hour. The computer would set them scenarios – sometimes as simple as flying around moving obstacles, sometimes more complex like evading enemy ships, which were similar to the Cougars, only white. They couldn't use the catalysts yet, but they had plenty of other things to worry about as it was. When in charge, Julius had to check fuel levels and give instructions to his fighters to ensure that they would all survive the virtual attack. Evasive manoeuvres were becoming ever more important, and the simulator increased the difficulties of the scenarios with every tactical decision they made.

March brought an entirely new challenge for Julius and his classmates as Professor Clavel properly introduced them to the ship catalysts.

'About time,' whispered Skye, visibly thrilled.

For that lesson, Julius was flying by himself once again. As he waited in lunar orbit, Professor Clavel opened the intercom to all students.

'As you have probably noticed, there are two additions today. To your left and right, you will see the ship catalysts. They are the transparent levers protruding from the control panel. You will be using them to project your White skills. You cannot use the Mindkatas in this type of combat; therefore it is your Meditation training that you must rely on for focus and precision.'

'Glad I've got that sorted then,' said Julius, relieved.

'To fire, just do what you normally would. Aim the catalyst and focus your mind on the target. If you do this correctly, you will see your raw energy shooting out in a yellow beam. Now, for the real surprise of the day. As far as piloting is concerned, on a one-man vessel such as the Cougar, the controls change. When you are using the catalysts, you will be flying the ship using only your mind-skills.'

Shocked, Julius froze for a moment, as they had not been taught any such thing before.

'Before you panic, Mizki,' resumed Clavel, sounding slightly amused, 'the catalysts are very sensitive. They channel your energies through touch, but they also *feel* your will to move in whatever direction you want and take you there. Give it a try. Activate the combat program when you're ready.'

As soon as the intercom went silent, Julius started the firing simulation immediately. He was very eager to try out his skills on the catalysts.

'Proceed to the following coordinates to begin your training,' the computer intoned to him.

Julius quickly input them and flew towards a group of rocks. He chose a particularly large one and positioned his Cougar in a direct line opposite it. Closing his hands around the catalysts, he tightened his grip. As he touched the levers, a white circular target appeared on the glass in front of him. Instinctively, he thought that the Cougar needed to be a little over to the right. Immediately, he felt the ship shift to the right, exactly as he had wanted it to.

'This is just! It feels my thoughts,' he said, incredulous.

He adjusted the catalysts, until the crosshair glowed red and locked onto the rock. Julius focused his mind on it and pushed. He felt the familiar sensation of energy leaving his body and watched, open mouthed, as a bright yellow beam shot out from the tip of the Cougar and blasted the rock to smithereens.

'Who's the daddy!' he shouted excitedly.

He immediately moved on to the next rock, and the next, until they were all gone. The computer then challenged Julius to find and fire at enemy ships. As he engaged the different enemies, Julius was surprised to realise that he had been piloting the ship using only his mind, as his hands had never once let go of the catalysts. He spent the whole afternoon improving his single-fighter tactics and by the end of the lesson he had quite the sore head from concentrating and was a little on the weak side from using up so much energy.

These individual training sessions were entertaining enough but, after only a couple of them, Julius was itching to fly again with his mates. Professor Clavel, pleased with their progress, allowed them to try four-fighter squads. It was like being back in the Palace, only the Skirts were far more fluid now that they were using mind-skills to pilot and fight. Their confidence bordered on recklessness at times, which forced Clavel to hail them during training to remind them of where they were.

Whenever he reprimanded them, it was along the lines of, 'Skirts, get back into position and follow protocol. This is no game!' or 'Do I have to remind you of the difference between games and reality? If you die out there, it really is game over. Use your heads or I'll split your team up!'

That threat usually worked and they would all calm down again, until the next time. Except for the occasional *recommendations* from Clavel, Julius knew that he was making great progress in this subject. He was placing incredible demands on both his mind and body, but he knew it was worth it. Despite the tiredness, he never forgot to write home and tell Michael all about the Cougars, which made his brother really happy. He was careful not to mention anything about Salgoria's plans though, as he had the feeling that all correspondence would be monitored at a time like this. Although the Lunar Perimeter was not officially in a state of alert, Julius was aware of the increase in space traffic. At night, when he relaxed in the garden with the others, he could see dozens of Cougars flying over Zed every hour. By the end of March, their presence had become so much a part of the landscape that Julius hardly even noticed them as much anymore.

On top of this, two odd additions were introduced to their study programme. Professors Brown and Clavel gave a simulation lesson together, which involved learning to pilot and man a Stork, an eight-people carrier, on the routes from Zed to the regular colonies.

'This is very fishy,' said Morgana at the end of the lesson.

'What's fishy?' asked Julius.

'Well, Stork training and route lessons are not supposed to happen 'til third year. Kaori told me that she started them this past autumn. Why would they change the programme?'

'Maybe they want to make sure that even the MJ know enough to do their part if something happens,' suggested Skye.

Julius listened in silence. Skye's answer was as good as they were going to get and probably correct. What was bothering him, however, was something else. Ever since Faith had told them Pete's news, especially concerning the missing ship, Julius was unable to think about much else. When he lay in his bed at night, he would go over all the information in his head to try and make some sense out of it. In his mind he could clearly see the various pieces of the puzzle – the hologram remote control, the Scrambler, Red Cap, the missing ship, Kratos, even the flickering of Master Isshin – they were all linked somehow. He just couldn't see how. Sometimes he had the feeling that the answer was on the tip of his tongue but, before he could grasp it, it was gone.

In the second week of April, Professor King announced to the class that their Spring Mission would be carried out on Colonial 1, which instantly transformed Zolin Acalan, a 1MJ who happened to be from there, into an information kiosk. The poor boy was surrounded at all times of the day by classmates hoping to find out everything there was to know about the colony. A few days later, letters containing details of their mission were delivered to the students. Julius opened his at the dinner table and felt his stomach sink to his feet.

'Great,' he said gloomily.

'What's the matter? You look like a rain cloud,' said Faith worriedly.

'It says here that we leave on the 18th.'

'Hey, that's your birthday,' said Morgana, smiling.

'At 07:00 hours,' he continued grimly. 'An early rise – it's the present I've always wanted.'

'Cheer up, Julius,' grinned Skye, patting him on the back. 'We'll make it a birthday to remember!'

THE DRAW

Julius opened one blurry eye and poked his head out from under the cover. He could hear voices around him, but couldn't make the words out. Prising open his other eye, he was just in time to see Skye and Faith looming over his head. Faith was holding a blueberry muffin topped with a tiny lit candle.

'Happy birthday, sleeping beauty!' cried Faith happily.

'Make a wish,' said Skye.

Julius's brain took a few seconds to realise what was going on. He could feel in his bones that it was very-early-o'clock, but when they struck up an impressively off key "Happy Birthday" in his honour, he couldn't restrain his smile.

'That was the nastiest birthday song I've ever heard. Thank you guys,' he said, sitting up in the bed.

'I thought we were doing quite well,' said Faith to Skye.

'Me too. Clearly he hasn't washed his ears yet.'

'That must surely be it,' said Julius.

'Here,' said Faith, passing the muffin to Julius. 'Make a wish and get dressed – it's already 06:30. We'll wait in the foyer.'

Julius looked at his candle. As the boys closed the door behind them, the flame flickered and went out.

'Hey, I haven't made a wish yet!' he said, disappointed. Given that he was going to wish for an extra hour in bed and knowing that was impossible, he shook his head and ate the muffin instead.

At 07:00 hours, Julius joined his classmates in Tijara's foyer. He had packed his rucksack the night before, just to gain some extra sleeping time, and he knew how to be quick when needed. Morgana gave him a big hug and wished him a happy birthday so loudly that all of the Mizki heard her. Faith didn't miss out on the opportunity for more singing.

'All together now,' he cried, hovering over the crowd, 'happy birthday to youuu …'

Julius felt his cheeks burning and his ears melting. This chorus was even worse than Faith and Skye's earlier duet. Still, he managed a diplomatic smile and thanked everyone.

'If the celebrations are over, maybe we can begin the boarding procedure.' It was Captain Foster, wearing his usual "I'm not easily amused" expression.

The Mizki fell silent at once and bowed to Foster.

'In a moment, we shall make our way to the hangar,' said Foster. 'There are five Storks waiting there for you, piloted by our 5 Mizki Seniors. There will be a Zed officer to welcome you at Colonial 1. Remember, once you leave the Lunar Perimeter, you become a Zed representative. The reputation of us all depends on you. Be a gracious guest and a keen learner. Understood?'

'Yes, sir!' they answered in unison.

'Very well. Follow me,' said Foster, before opening the hangar gate and descending the stairs.

Julius shouldered his rucksack and followed his classmates. The access to Tijara's hangar was a brightly lit, white tunnel. Several corridors branched off to either side of them at regular intervals, but Julius couldn't see where they went to.

'A few signposts would have been good here,' said Faith, looking around curiously.

Morgana was visibly delighted to finally be able to see the school's hangar.

'I thought I heard an engine going, over there,' she said, as Julius dragged her back in line.

'It's a hangar, Morgana! What did you expect – your granny in a wheelbarrow?' he answered, pushing her forward.

'But it sounded *big*.'

Eventually the corridor opened onto a platform overlooking a shaft that was larger even than Satras. Julius walked to the rail, gaping in wonder, and looked down. He could see five different decks below him, each one lower than the previous one, opening outward like a giant fan. The first three of these decks had Cougars stationed on them; the last two were for the Storks. Dozens of Tijaran maintenance staff bustled to and fro, busy with upkeep and repairs for the planes. At the end of each deck, was a launch ramp built within a long tunnel and, from where he stood, Julius was able to witness a couple of breakneck Cougar re-entries, each one accompanied by Morgana's cheers and Faith's hollers.

'Let's move, Mizki,' called Foster, starting down a ladder that led off from the platform.

This time Julius literally had to pry Morgana's fingers away from the rail and drag her down the stairs, while Skye required the full weight of his body to push Faith along, much to the amusement of their classmates.

'Honestly, woman,' said Julius, shaking his head. 'You'll have your chance soon enough.'

'But they are sooo beautiful,' she sighed longingly.

When they reached the fourth deck, Foster motioned for them to board the Storks, and then walked all the way to the ship nearest the runway, where the 5MS pilots were waiting.

Julius and Skye, followed by Barth, boarded the last Stork left available, closest to the stairs. Faith and Morgana couldn't resist one last spot of sightseeing before boarding themselves. As they waited, Julius had a look around. The Stork was exactly the same as the one they had used during simulation. The two pilot chairs were at the front, with access to the various control panels. Behind them were the passenger seats, in two lines of four, facing each other. The access hatch was on the rear left hand side. There were two locked panels between the pilot and passenger seats on either side of the cabin, which Julius recognised as the access points for the ship's catalysts.

'You know,' said Morgana, stepping inside the Stork, 'we could have boarded one of the ships at the top.'

'Yes, we could've,' said Skye with a raised eyebrow, 'but we were too busy dragging you two gawping goons down here. Weren't we, Julius?'

'As a matter of –' Julius froze in mid sentence, his eyes fixed on the deck entrance.

'What's the matter?' asked Faith, hovering towards the hatch.

Julius had been watching two officers offloading crates at the mouth of a corridor leading off from the rear of the deck. Under the shadow of the stairs, he had not been able to see their faces, but as soon as they stepped into the light Julius's heart skipped a beat. As much as he wanted to be wrong, there could be no mistaking either of them – Master Isshin and Red Cap.

'Wait a minute ... isn't that Red Cap?' asked Faith, suddenly sounding very worried.

'Yes, together with my holopal,' said Julius.

'Why are they wearing Tijaran uniforms?'

'Whatever the reason, it can't be good.'

'What's going on?' whimpered Barth from his seat.

'Over there, at their feet,' said Morgana, looking out of one of the windows, 'it's the missing crate!'

Julius quickly spotted it, just as Red Cap looked up and took a step forward.

'Right on time,' he snarled, his eyes fixed on Julius. 'Try and catch me, White Child.'

Without hesitation, Julius leapt from the Stork, meaning to rush at him, when suddenly one of the crates exploded. He was hurled back inside the Stork, where he landed heavily on Skye. As he tried to regain his feet a second, much larger explosion shook the entire hangar. Julius managed to grab Morgana before she could crash into the hull plating.

'What's happening?' cried Barth, his whimpering replaced by sheer panic.

Julius gripped the edge of the door and leaned outside. There was debris everywhere and a number of small fires had broken out on the deck below. Several feet to the right, Captain Foster lay unconscious on the ground – Julius was relieved to see that two pilots were attending to him. A wailing siren filled the air and black smoke rose from those ships that had been damaged in the explosion. He could hear shouting all around him, as Tijaran security officers came pouring down the stairs.

'Attention!' a voice ordered from the hangar's loudspeaker. 'All Mizki return to Tijara assembly hall, immediately. All personnel to action stations.'

As the announcement was repeated again, Julius stepped onto the deck and continued searching for Red Cap and Isshin, but there was no trace of them.

'Barth, stop!' cried Morgana suddenly.

Julius turned and jumped out of the way just in time to avoid a full on collision with Barth, who was running towards the corridor entrance, where the missing crate had been left.

'Watch out!' shouted Skye, pointing to the walkway above Barth.

Julius looked up and saw a metal platform plunging towards the ground, directly where Barth was heading. He locked his eyes on Barth and gave him a mighty shove with his mind, sending him tumbling into the corridor as the platform crashed over the crate, blocking the entrance.

'Are you all right?' Julius shouted towards him.

Barth sat up and looked at him. He wore a dazed expression on his face and was breathing heavily.

'Yes, I... I think I tripped over this box,' he said, sounding confused.

Julius looked down and instinctively took a step back. The floor was littered with dozens of small red boxes, which he recognised as the holograms' remote controls.

The moment Skye and Faith arrived by Julius's side, the red boxes started to vibrate madly, and in a matter of seconds they had all produced holographic humanoids in Tijaran uniforms.

'Barth, run!' cried Faith, gliding away from the crate and dragging Julius and Skye with him.

Barth didn't need to be asked twice and scampered down the corridor in a flash.

'Get back to the Stork!' yelled Julius.

As soon as the Arneshian holograms materialised, they started to scatter in all directions, mixing with the real Tijaran officers. Julius saw them boarding the Cougars and the few Storks left on the decks below them. As the ships took off some headed out into orbit, but a few of them deliberately crashed against the main hangar structure, hitting the stairs and blocking the corridors.

'We gotta get to the exit!' cried Skye, sheltering under a Stork wing.

'There's no time,' said Julius. 'The Stork is our only chance.'

He turned to Morgana and grabbed her shaking hands.

'Now's the time to show us what you've got. We need you to fly us out into orbit.'

Morgana looked at him, her eyes widened in panic. Gathering herself together, she took a deep breath and nodded.

'Get in boys. Faith,' she called to him, 'I'm gonna need your help.'

Faith followed her to the pilot seats.

'Skye, you and I will man the catalysts,' said Julius.

Skye closed the hatch and took his station. Julius unlocked his panel and pulled the catalyst towards him. As the radar screen lit up, he fastened the safety harness to keep himself steady.

'Hold on back there,' said Morgana, initiating the lift-off sequence. 'Faith, polarise the hull.'

The Stork vibrated slightly and hovered upward. Morgana was moving the ship forward when a Cougar cut them off, sending them veering downwards.

'Head for that runway below us!' cried Faith.

Morgana veered right and accelerated towards it. The Stork shot through the tunnel at such speed that the onboard computer self-activated.

'Reduce speed in hangar,' it said. 'You are breaking safety protocol 7.3.'

'Shut up!' cried Morgana, accelerating even more.

'Watch out for that rock! And for that one! And that one!' cried Faith, pointing in different directions all at once.

'Enough! Faith, you're supposed to calm me down here!' said Morgana, her voice almost hysterical.

'Sorry. You're doing just fine. You're the best pilot there is. You're great,' said Faith, sweating profusely.

'Get ready, guys,' she shouted over her shoulder as they sped towards the exit.

As the Stork entered orbit, Julius felt his lungs deflating slightly. Zed's space was riddled with ships – Tijara's, Tuala's and Sield's – all fighting against each other.

'This is a slaughter,' said Julius, as he watched a Cougar diving into the side of a Tuala Stork.

'I hope the others made it out in time,' whispered Morgana.

'The Zed shield has been hit!' cried Skye.

Julius looked on in dismay. The shield was flickering on and off as it absorbed stray hits from the fighting above it. He saw the individual shields of all Zed structures being activated for extra protection. Morgana flew the Stork higher, steering them out of harm's way.

'How can they drive?' said Faith, frustrated. 'They're not real.'

Julius looked at the battle raging below and suddenly it hit him. As the pieces of the puzzle fell into place, his face lit up. 'That's it!' he cried. 'They can't, but their remote controls can.'

'What are you talking about?' asked Morgana.

'Don't you see? Professor King said that, with powerful telekinetic skills, you can even pilot a spaceship from a distant location. The Arneshians don't have White Arts, so they're using VI technology instead!'

'That's impossible,' said Faith. 'You'd need some seriously powerful machines to remotely control those red boxes, and Arnesh is too far away for that.'

'But Kratos isn't. That's why they've occupied it!'

Julius looked at his friends as the reality of his words dawned on them.

'I'm going there,' he said steadily. 'Anyone wants to pull out, now's the time.'

'I'm in,' said Skye flatly, holding Julius's gaze.

'My sister is down there,' said Morgana. 'There's no way I'm not coming. Faith?'

'All the way, Skirts.'

Julius felt a weight lifting from his heart. 'Morgana, set a course for Kratos. Faith, send a transmission to Cress. Tell him to scan the fleet. The ships without any bio signatures are piloted by holograms. Skye and I will be on defence.'

Skye nodded and moved back to his station. Morgana entered the coordinates for Kratos into the computer and they slipped out of Zed orbit undetected.

'Done,' said Faith, pressing a button. 'I've sent the message. Let's hope he gets it.'

A minute later, Cress's voice echoed in the ship. 'Stork 9, this is Tijara. We've received your message. Re-enter Zed orbit immediately. I'm sending the coordinates for a safe rendezvous.'

Faith shook his head as he began to jam the transmission. 'Tijara, this is Stork 9. We're having trouble reading you. Repeat.'

Cress's voice started to crackle. 'Stork 9 ... ordered ... immediately ...'

'Sorry sir, I can't hear you,' Faith said.

Finally the line went dead.

'I can't believe I just did that,' he said, looking nervously at the others. 'They'll take away me skirt and give me leaded bloomers for this.'

That thought made them laugh so much that Morgana had to activate the autopilot.

'Yeah, yeah. Laugh it up,' said Faith, but he couldn't hold back a smile either.

'How long till we get there, Morgana?' asked Julius once the laughter had subsided.

'Well, according to the computer, Kratos is 0.01953125 light years away.'

'In English please?' asked Skye.

'Och, a hyperjump will get us there in a tick. Why?'

'Because, if I'm reading this radar right, we've got company,' said Julius.

'I see it,' said Faith, checking the scan readings, 'but I don't recognise the ship.'

'Friendly?' asked Morgana nervously.

'No bio signatures onboard. It's a nasty.'

Julius looked through the rear hatch window. The ship was as large as the Zed shuttle that had taken them to the Moon. It was speeding towards them but, instead of opening fire, a ramp opened outward and downward, like a giant mouth.

'Why isn't it engaging us?' asked Morgana, keeping the Stork clear of it.

'Because it can't,' answered Julius. 'You can't use the catalyst without mind–skills. Besides, that doesn't even look like a Zed vessel.'

'It's trying to scoop us up,' said Morgana.

'Ahead!' cried Faith. 'It's an asteroid field. Let's lose it in there before we make the jump. I don't fancy playing cat-and-mouse in hyperspace.'

'Put some air between us, Morgana,' yelled Skye. 'Give us a chance at a clear shot.'

The Stork accelerated and entered the field from below. The rocks were hurtling past them, some of them spinning erratically. Julius could see droplets of sweat forming on Morgana's brow.

'Just like in the games, Morgana,' encouraged Skye. 'We know you can do it.'

Julius saw the vessel approaching on their right, with only a large asteroid between them.

'Morgana, get ready to slow down at my command!' he cried. 'Skye, it's gonna come out in front of us.'

Julius followed the ship on his radar and saw it converging toward their trajectory. He held tight to the catalyst and adjusted his grip.

'Three … two … one … now!'

The Stork suddenly decelerated, just in time to avoid crashing into the enemy, which had popped out just in front of them. Julius concentrated on his target. Even though he was sure the pilot wasn't Red Cap, it was his face that he imagined. He pushed hard with his mind and felt the familiar sensation of energy coursing from his body and into the catalyst. At the same time, two yellow beams – his and Skye's – shot out of the Stork and struck the ship directly on its engine. The explosion rocked the Stork, shaking it off course, but it was nothing that Morgana couldn't handle.

'Come to mama!' shouted Skye, giving Julius a high-five.

'The Skirts are back,' laughed Faith, patting Morgana on the shoulder. 'Nice bit of flying, girly-o.'

She relaxed, looking exhilarated. 'It's time to jump, guys. Just hold on to something.'

'Wait a minute,' Faith stammered nervously, 'are you sure you know how to do this? I mean, we've never actually done it bef …'

Morgana didn't allow him to finish his argument and fired up the hyperdrive.

Julius was overwhelmed by a strange sensation of displacement, like he had temporarily stepped outside of his body. Fortunately, it lasted no more than a couple of seconds before the feeling subsided and a giant metallic disc appeared in front of them.

'Looks like Kratos's shield is still operational,' said Faith, pointing at the shimmering layer that cupped the disc. 'I'm going to scan the surface.'

'Check for bio signs too,' said Julius. 'The Arneshians may be there.'

'No humanoid presence. In fact, no life forms whatsoever,' said Faith, after a short pause. 'The only thing I'm picking up is a small cubic structure. It must be the holocontrol station we're looking for.'

'I'll take us right above it,' said Morgana.

The Stork approached the Arneshian outpost and brought them through the shield unscathed. Morgana steadied the ship and landed it next to their target.

'It doesn't look like much,' said Morgana. 'Is the computer inside?'

'Kids,' said Faith seriously, 'we have a problem. According to our scanner, that cube is the main computer. And we can't blow it up. It's made of some sort of extra-strong inorganic alloy.'

'What if all four of us link to the catalysts?' asked Skye.

'That could work … if you were able to go nuclear.'

'Then we disable the mainframe manually.'

'Not possible. It's right in the core,' answered Faith, pointing at the schematics on his screen.

'So what, we just go back?' cried Skye, frustrated.

'No we don't,' said Julius calmly. 'There is another way.'

From the moment Faith had mentioned the word "inorganic", Julius's mind had instinctively zoomed in on his draw ability, and the day he had stopped Professor Turner's watch. It was a long shot, and a dangerous one at that, but he couldn't think of any other way. Marcus Tijara himself had proven that it was possible.

'I think I can draw from it,' continued Julius.

'From a non-living source? You're kidding, right?' said Faith.

'No I'm not. But you better be ready to fly us out on the double 'cause I don't know how long I can hold on to that energy for.'

'Forget it, mate. It's too risky. It could kill you,' said Faith seriously.

'I've done it before, Faith. I can release the cube's energy through the catalyst. It's the only chance we've got and we're wasting time. You have to trust me on this one.'

They stared at him in silence and he saw dark wisps rising from their heads. Julius looked away and opened the hatch. They were scared and he couldn't risk getting his mind muddled up with fear as well. He needed all the focus he could muster.

'Just be ready,' he said.

Julius climbed out of the Stork and walked over to the computer. As he moved towards it, the black exterior of the cube shimmered in the artificial sunlight from its shield. Julius stopped in front of it and watched as algorithms and dim flickering lights passed over its shiny surface. He walked around the cube a few times, hoping to find a focal point, and eventually stopped at its east side. Here was a darker area, which the scrolling information was streaming into, almost as if it was an entrance to the inner core itself. There was no way to be absolutely sure, but he had to make a decision.

Vigorously, he rubbed his hands together, trying to get the blood flowing through his fingertips, and placed them near the surface. His fingertips did not touch it, but he could still feel his skin tingling all over from being so close to the cube's energy field. He closed his mind to everything else around him, to the noises, the light and the faces of his mates. He let the air out of his lungs gently and, when there was no more to push out, he took a deep, steady breath and held it in. His mind was immediately filled with images of a blue, smoky fluid, moving up through his fingers and arms like a snake. The sensation was far more overpowering than that first draw in class had ever been. The fluid moved into his chest where it gathered in his lungs. When his whole body felt like it was on fire, Julius knew he had to stop.

Forcing his eyes open, he released the air from his lungs. His legs were shaking so much that Julius fell to his knees, breathing heavily. He felt sick, as if he had just drunk some sort of poison but, when he looked at the cube again, a pained grin touched his lips. The computer had gone almost totally dark, with only a handful of lights still visible. Julius forced himself back to his feet and staggered in the direction of the Stork.

Skye had jumped out of the ship, and had his arms outstretched, reaching for him.

'Let me help you.'

'Don't touch me!' said Julius, recoiling from him.

Skye looked down at Julius's hands – the palms were raw-red and wet.

'OK. I won't touch you, but I'll help you along.'

Julius felt his body being lifted from the ground and pushed smoothly towards the Stork and knew that it was Skye's doing. Then Faith appeared at the hatch and locked his eyes on Julius too. He floated right inside the Stork and landed gently in front of one of the catalysts. He glanced at Morgana, who looked like she had just stopped crying, and managed a tired smile in her direction.

'Let's go, pilots,' said Skye, closing the door.

The Stork took off immediately and shot away from the cube, sending ripples through the shield's membrane. Julius knew that, if he held onto the computer's energy for even one more minute, he would explode. Grabbing the catalyst, he focused on the target and discharged all the energy in one mighty push. A thick yellow beam shot out of the Stork, disintegrating the cube in a massive explosion. The Stork was propelled forward by the blast and it was only thanks to Skye's quick reflexes that Julius wasn't thrown around like a ragdoll. Kratos's disc had snapped in two and the pieces were slowly drifting off into space.

'You did it!' shouted Morgana. She jumped from her seat and swung her arms around Julius. 'Your mum will never forgive me,' she said, half crying and half laughing. 'I promised her I'd keep you out of trouble!'

'That was amazing,' said Skye. 'If you make it back alive, they'll put you in a museum.'

Julius couldn't help but smile, even though he was still dazed and his hands were in agony. Thankfully, Morgana had found a first aid kit and was carefully bandaging them.

'Hey guys,' called Faith from the front of the Stork, 'the cavalry has just arrived, and they're all human.'

A fleet of Cougars had just entered Kratos's airspace and was closing in on the Stork.

'Open a channel, Faith,' said Skye, moving toward the cockpit.

'Tijara, this is Stork 9,' announced Faith confidently. 'The enemy is down. Mission accomplished, and thank you very much. Oh, we also got rid of that useless disc for you, by the way.'

Julius and the others looked at him, shaking their heads in a mixture of disbelief and amusement.

Faith turned to face them, sporting his characteristic grin. 'I'll be deported to the Halls of Ahriman for that but, heck, it was worth it!'

'I told you we'd give you a birthday to remember, McCoy,' said Skye, sitting down next to Julius.

'Yeah,' said Julius wearily. 'But please, let's make it a bit less memorable next year.'

BELONGING

Julius dozed in and out of sleep during the brief journey back. His head was throbbing and his muscles were sore and stiff. Everyone was quiet, but he knew their silence was deceptive. They were all aware of the importance of what they had just done on Kratos and the number of people they had potentially saved, but they weren't going to brag about it. Somehow, it didn't feel like the right thing to do.

As their ship entered the lunar orbit, Julius could see debris floating everywhere – the remains of the defeated Cougars. Dozens of Sky-Jets zoomed in and out of Pete's docking base, salvaging what they could. Morgana landed the Stork in Tijara's hangar, which was being repaired at an impressive speed. Captain Foster was waiting for them on the runway. His head was bandaged, but he looked his usual stern self.

'Come with me, Mizki,' he said, bowing slightly to them.

They followed him in silence back to Tijara, all the way to the hall outside Cress's office, where he left them without a word.

'Humph. He could've at least said something nice,' said Faith once Foster had left.

'Did you expect a brass band?' answered Skye, dropping heavily onto a seat.

'No, but a "Thank you for saving our lives" type of thing would have been good.'

'It'll be a miracle if they don't court martial us.'

Morgana had just helped Julius to sit down, when suddenly the office door opened, making them all jump up in surprise.

'Inside,' said Cress curtly.

They filed into the office and waited quietly before the Grand Master. Cress walked behind his desk and stood by Freja's side. They both looked extremely serious.

'Miss Ruthier,' said Cress, 'I want a full account of your actions, from the moment you entered Tijara's hangar. Don't leave anything out, not even Mr Shanigan's amazing ability for jamming fleet channels.'

Julius saw a red wisp shooting out of Faith's head, but managed to keep a straight face. As Morgana recounted the day's events, Julius became increasingly aware of Freja's gaze on him. When she reached the part in which he had drawn from the computer, he saw Freja's eyes widen, just for a second. When Morgana finished her account, nobody spoke for a short while. Freja and Cress studied the desk panel. Julius watched Freja touching various areas of the screen, sorting through data and grouping information into folders. Finally, he looked at Cress and nodded.

'I thought we'd already discussed the Zed protocol of acting as a collective,' said Cress.

'Permission to speak freely, sir,' said Julius, trying his best to not sound rude.

'Granted,' answered Cress.

'I am aware that we are only 1MJ, sir, but we understand teamwork.' As he said that, he looked quickly at his friends, who all nodded encouragingly. 'The thing with being a Zed officer is that life is not so much about choice, but more about duty. We had the choice of turning back the Stork and watching the slaughter of our fellow Mizki, but we had the duty, the knowledge and the opportunity to put a stop to it. So we did. And for that we take full responsibility.'

The room fell silent for a few seconds.

Finally, the Grand Master spoke: 'The list of infractions committed today is more than enough to have you expelled.'

Julius felt Skye shifting uncomfortably next to him.

'However,' continued Freja, visibly relaxing, 'we also need to recognise the importance of individual initiative, especially when that initiative is undertaken for the greater good of our family. You have all displayed incredible skills today. Miss Ruthier's evasive manoeuvres would have matched those of an experienced pilot.'

Morgana blushed instantly and stared at her feet.

'Mr Shanigan's co-piloting and Mr Miller's use of the catalyst in combat were also of the highest standard.'

Faith and Skye allowed themselves a shy grin.

'And, of course, Mr McCoy's leadership skills, and the clever use of the rare gift that is inorganic drawing, were just exceptional.'

Julius bowed his head, a flush of pride awoken in him by those words.

'Foiling Salgoria's plot was a remarkable achievement, Mizki. No charges will be pressed against any of you. All I will say is that you must learn to trust in your family from now on. It is unity that makes us stronger. And now, follow Master Cress to the infirmary. Mr McCoy, please stay a little longer. Dismissed.'

Apprehensively, Julius watched his friends leave. He had never been alone with the Grand Master and he hoped Freja wasn't going to give him some kind of special punishment, given that he had already singled him out as the "leader".

'As your Stork was re-entering Tijara, Mr List came looking for me quite urgently,' said Freja, opening a drawer.

Julius watched as he placed a box on the desk and, when he opened it, Julius's heart sank. There was a red cap inside it.

'I believe this was left for you,' said Freja, handing it to him.

Julius took it and noticed a piece of paper pinned to the inside lining. It read "I'll get you McCoy. You can't run forever, White Child."

'Where did they find it, sir?' asked Julius, stunned, the happiness of a moment ago completely gone.

'Apparently Master Isshin's VI program activated itself in the presence of Mr List. It lasted only a few seconds but, as it vanished, it left behind one of the red control boxes and this. I remembered your previous encounter with the hologram you called "Red Cap" in the hangar and, of course, he played a rather big part in today's events according to Miss Ruthier's account. Am I correct to assume that it taunted you?'

Julius nodded, his mouth too dry to say anything.

'Don't let it get to you. Never let emotions cloud your harmony. If you are meant to meet it again, you will. But remember, this hologram, as intelligent as it seems, is still just a program, not real. Salgoria, on the other hand, is our main concern. Have a seat, Mr McCoy.'

Julius was grateful for the offer, as he was feeling rather light headed.

'Do you know what a White Child is?' asked Freja, easing the chair in behind the desk.

'No, sir. But ... Red Cap called me that this morning, inside the hangar.'

Freja nodded. 'I shall tell you what we know on this topic, since it concerns you personally. It is no secret that the Arneshians have tried to gain power over humanity since Zed was created. Over the centuries, their rulers devised different plans to achieve their objective but, fortunately for us and thanks to Zed, they were never successful. When Salgoria became queen, she changed her tactics. No longer would control be gained by useless open war, but by using the very abilities that made the Arneshians so gifted in the first place – the Grey Arts, or advanced technological and logical skills. The holographic remote control is just one example of the devices they can invent. When it comes to new technology, they are still unbeatable.

'In recent years, however, Salgoria has also begun meddling with genetic engineering – manipulating the DNA of an organism. Tell me, McCoy, have you heard of Bastiaan Grant?'

'Yes, sir. I was told he was one of the people who got kidnapped and that he died, possibly because of some sort of medical experiment.'

'Precisely. The people abducted were all Zed members, with very advanced mind-skills. I was one of the crew members who found Angra Mainyu, the Arneshian lab where Mr Grant was experimented upon. We also discovered the bodies of those who disappeared before him. Most shocking was the discovery of many lifeless infants. The notes left behind by their medical team confirmed what we had already started to realise: Salgoria was trying to craft the perfect being. This perfect DNA would be genetically created through the unwilling donations of people like Grant and the Arneshians themselves. Remember, she needs an Arneshian because only one of them can fully reach the maximum potential of the Grey Arts.

'However, things did not go according to plan. The experiments failed and Salgoria decided that, in order to succeed, she would need someone as gifted as Tijara himself had been, someone who would possess the most powerful White and Grey Arts and would be called by Tijara's own nickname – a White Child.'

Julius was staring at Freja, dumbstruck. 'Sir,' he said, 'you cannot possibly mean that I am one of those. There must be a mistake. I mean, I even had to take remedial meditation!'

'Your Brain Augmentation chart, Red Cap's actions, and the way you foiled Salgoria's plans beg to differ, Mr McCoy. It is also apparent to me that the ship that pursued you was clearly there to kidnap you. Don't forget, you're only thirteen and have a lot of training ahead of you to fully unlock your potential. Salgoria will not be in a hurry to try such direct tactics again, now that she knows what you're capable of. But be on your toes, for people like you are always on her radar.'

Freja stood up and Julius respectfully did likewise.

'I didn't mean for us to have this conversation so soon, or to make you aware of your potential in such a fashion, but circumstances forced my hand. Perhaps it is for the best. Off you go now. I believe Dr Walliser will want to run some tests on you. The draw you performed today will fill up several library chips.'

'Thank you, sir,' said Julius, bowing his head.

As he opened the door, he glanced at the Grand Master one last time. Freja's grey eyes looked back and Julius was filled with that same sense of admiration that he had felt upon first seeing his portrait back on Earth. He was indeed very proud to belong to the Tijaran family.

By the end of April, news of the attack on Kratos had made its way around all of Zed, and the Skirts had become well known, even outside the gaming circle. Julius had told only Morgana about his conversation with Freja. Somehow, he was embarrassed to admit to the guys that he had been at the centre of the Queen of Arnesh's plans and that she had singled him out as a White Child. He most definitely wasn't going to tell his parents about it either – he was sure they would rush to fetch him, out of fear for his life. He would be careful, as Freja had said, and that was all he could do. There was no way he would let anybody, even an evil queen, ruin his dream of becoming a Zed officer.

Although Julius and his friends had decided to keep it quiet, or "play it cool" as Skye had put it, Barth had not been able to refrain from telling his classmates about how Julius had saved him in the hangar. Naturally, none of the Mizki could rest until they knew more, and so they had badgered and pestered the Skirts, until the whole story had come out and was then spread to the entire school. Kaori, who was understandably very proud of her little sister, had seen to it that Tuala also knew all about it, and it was only a matter of time before the Sield students were in the loop too.

By mid-May, it had become impossible for Julius to go anywhere without being cornered and questioned about their fight, and especially about his draw. He wasn't really the public speaker type and, although he was proud of their achievement, he really wished they would just give it a rest and let him get on with things. When Dr Walliser released the first part of his research on Julius' draw to Tijara's library, an incredible amount of students and workers from the Curia flocked there to read it. Fortunately, this release gave Julius a welcome break from being interrogated at every possible opportunity. In fact, the students seemed to be so in awe of him that they appeared hesitant to approach him anymore, which suited Julius perfectly.

On the 31st of May, the spring term ended and the Mizki were all packed and ready for departure to their summer camps. Faith would spend his three months at Pit-Stop Pete, learning about the everyday running of a docking station and the various maintenance routines of the fleet. Morgana was going with him for two months before joining, under special permission, the apprentice flying camp in the Canis Major constellation. Julius, with the personal approval of Master Cress, had decided to go to the Fornax constellation, where Zed held intensive training courses on the different uses for ship catalysts. He was really looking forward to it for two reasons: on the one hand he would be travelling 46 light years away from Earth, his very first interstellar journey and the fulfilment of a childhood dream; on the other he would have a chance to fully test his mind-skills. As an added bonus, he wasn't going alone, as Skye had decided to join him.

Julius and his classmates walked to the Zed dock, where they would soon board the transports to their various destinations. Julius watched the students saying their goodbyes to each other. There were plenty of pats on the back for the boys and emotional hugs between the girls.

To Julius it looked just about right: out here they were all family after all.

'It seems like yesterday that I first landed on the Moon,' said Morgana, reminiscing.

'Actually, that was Neil Armstrong,' said Faith with a grin.

Morgana looked at him in mock exasperation.

'She's right,' said Skye, 'and what a great year it's been.'

'Hear, hear,' cried Faith.

'And you know what made it so good?' said Julius, beaming. 'The Skirts did. And it's only the beginning.'

TIJARAN TALES

BOOK II

THE ORACLE

OF LIFE

CONTENTS

RE-ENTRY

Julius McCoy woke up with a jolt. It took him a few seconds to remember where he was. As the burbling of voices outside his cabin and the familiar drone of the engines carried to his ears, he relaxed and lay back again, rubbing his eyes wearily.

'Attention students,' bellowed a voice over the intercom system. 'We will be entering Zed orbit in ten minutes. Collect your belongings and report to deck B.'

Julius couldn't believe they had arrived already. He had left Alpha Fornacis just three hours earlier and yet here he was, 46 light years later, back in his own solar system. 'That's hyperjump for you,' he mumbled, groggily.

He dragged himself out of his bunk and moved to the small metal sink by the window. There he washed his face with cold water and ran his wet hands through his dark hair. *I could do with a haircut,* he thought to himself – the jagged strands were looking more unruly than usual. It wasn't his fault though. At Summer Camp, he had been constantly occupied with spaceship catalysts and how to use them during Combat. It had been pretty difficult at times but, then again, it was an advanced course designed for Mizki Seniors. And it was only because Julius had shown how capable he was in Flight fighting that he had been given special permission to join the older students. His friend, Skye, had also been allowed to go with him, for similar reasons. There was no question that they had both proven their skills in the past year.

He dried his face and looked out of the window. The stars, yellow dots in the pitch black sky, streamed by him, glowing eerily. He had been kept busy that summer, but no matter how tired he had felt when he went to bed, his last thoughts had always strayed back to Queen Salgoria and the events of the previous April.

He remembered clearly their fight with the Arneshian hologram army, led by Salgoria's henchman, Red Cap; how he, Skye, Faith and Morgana had escaped from the hangar; the desperate flight to the Arneshian outpost, where the remote control for their army had been positioned, and the draw he had performed to destroy it. It amazed him still that he had even survived that. As much as he had done though, he knew what he owed to his three friends for their part in that battle.

'McCoy, are you decent?' called Skye from outside the cabin.

'Coming,' shouted Julius over his shoulder.

He grabbed his backpack and moved towards the door, which slid open silently. Skye was leaning against the opposite wall, his blonde curls partly hiding his light grey eyes.

'Are we there yet?' asked Julius, who had set off in the direction of deck B.

'Almost,' said Skye, hurrying to catch up with him. 'The Seniors are all assembled. I thought you might be asleep, as usual.'

'I was, actually. Mind you, I don't think I managed more than an hour or two, but it's better than nothing.'

'Why do you sleep so much? There'll be plenty time for that when you're dead.'

'That's a cheery thought. Thanks.'

'Besides, there are other things to do here,' said Skye with a sly grin.

'What are you on about?'

'Ife Alika,' he said quietly.

'What's that?'

'Not what – *who*.'

Julius stopped and looked at him. 'Is that what you've been doing all those hours in the hangar – chatting the pilots up?'

'Not quite. You can't chat up a Senior just like that. It could be quite embarrassing … and possibly dangerous. You have to play to your strengths. I'm young, you see; inexperienced but willing to learn and, of course, interested in *everything* she has to say. That way she thinks I'm cute and likes talking to me. She feels … understood, and in control. Believe me McCoy, that's how you do it,' he finished, like a professor who had just explained some highly advanced scientific fact to an ignorant pupil.

Julius opened his mouth to say something, but he knew there was no point, so instead just shook his head and continued walking. Skye didn't seem at all bothered by that, and proceeded to list Ife's many fine qualities, then abruptly stopped again as soon as they reached the deck where the Seniors were. Skye, who had just spotted Ife, nudged Julius in the ribs and pointed her out to him. Julius had to admit that she really was very pretty indeed. The only useful information he had gathered from Skye's admiring words was that she came from Nigeria and was among the best of the 5 Mizki Senior pilots. She was surrounded by a group of giggling girls just then, and when she saw Skye, she gestured for him to join them. 'Come with me,' said Skye to Julius under his breath, and wandered over to them.

Julius stayed where he was, feeling partly amused but also quite nervous. He had never been much good at socialising with strangers, especially older girls, so instead of joining his friend, he retreated to one of the hatches by the opposite wall. Ever since the draw incident, he had the feeling most people were unsure what to say to him; so generally they avoided talking to him altogether. That suited Julius just fine, and he had spent his time concentrating on ship catalysts instead.

The only Senior who had been chatting to him at all was Bernard Docherty, a 6MS student. Up until the previous November, Docherty had been the only student from Tijara School to make it into the top ten of the all-time Solo rankings: a simulated single player competition that tested an individual's mind-skills to the very limit, by way of Combat scenarios, Flight games, or a mixture of the two. In fact, he was currently the reigning champion for the whole of Zed. Just making it into the rankings was an achievement, given how difficult the Solo games were. To his surprise, Julius had managed to shoot straight into the charts in ninth, the youngest ever from Tijara. He shuddered, thinking about that game and his battle with the weird, morphing villagers. Certainly, it had caused quite a stir among the other students when they had viewed replays of it afterwards.

The group games were much more enjoyable for him though – something to do with the fact that no one was allowed to use their mind-skills in them and they had to work together in teams. His thoughts turned to his own team, the Skirts, so formed and named almost by accident on their first visit to Satras's famous Hologram Palace. A smile crept onto his lips as he remembered how he and Skye, along with Faith and

Morgana, had gained quite a reputation for their gaming skills.

The ship juddered slightly as it entered orbit and Julius peered out of the porthole next to him. The Zed Lunar Perimeter was just coming into view, sitting proudly on the surface of the Moon. He stared beyond it for a minute, to where Earth shone blue, green and white in the distance and he wondered for a moment how his parents and his little brother Michael were getting on.

As the ship continued its descent towards Zed's dock, Skye joined him by the hatch. 'Today is our first Mooniversary, you know?' he said, pointing out the window.

'Yup,' said Julius. 'Exactly one year ago we were just arriving, and we didn't even know each other then. Do you think we'll get our new uniforms tonight?'

'Hope so, buddy boy,' said Skye, throwing an arm over Julius' shoulders. 'We're 2 Mizki Juniors as of today.'

'Bet your life we are,' said Julius with a grin. 'Listen, remind me to write to my folks later, OK? They'll be worried sick wondering if I've survived the summer. Have you written home at all?'

'Yeah,' answered Skye, stepping to the side and turning to prop his back against the wall. 'You can send messages between all of Zed's space stations. It's only the relay to Earth that doesn't work from so far away. Besides, you can be sure my Mum would've had a search party out if I didn't get in touch.'

'Imagine what *that* would have done for your star-rep with the ladies,' said Julius, with a wink.

Skye shivered at the thought, 'Don't even joke about it.'

*

By the time they docked, it was almost seven o'clock. The Zed shield's artificial illumination had grown dark, mimicking the twilight sky of the last day of August on Earth. Julius and Skye hurried off the ship and boarded the Intra-Rail train which, after a brief stop at Satras, delivered them to the outskirts of their school. Julius stretched and drew in a breath of Zed's warm air. After two months on a cold space station, the heat felt like absolute bliss to him. Tijara looked as inviting as always, a spherical sandstone structure with the appearance of a tropical island, covered as it was in palm trees and gentle waterfalls. They walked over to the security entrance, where their retinas were scanned by Tijara's front-gate guards, the Leven twins, who were never seen anywhere without each other, much to the puzzlement of all the students.

Once through, Julius and Skye headed straight for the boys' dorm and boarded the lift.

'Remember to press -5. We're one level up this year,' said Julius to Skye. He was getting quite excited at the idea of seeing his new bedroom and uniform.

The dorms had six underground levels in all. 1MJs slept on -6, as Julius had the previous year. As a person progressed through each new school year, so they were moved higher up the levels, getting ever closer to the ground floor.

The lift came to a stop at their floor and opened onto one end of a long corridor, which had four closed doors on each wall. All school-level groups were limited to thirty students each, with an equal number of boys and girls, so there was never any need for more than eight rooms per year. The same rule applied for the girls' dorm.

They exited the lift and stopped in front of the third door on the right. 'Here we are, darling,' said Skye. 'Just like last year.'

'Allow me, dear,' said Julius, looking into the retinal scanner that acted as security lock for the room.

The bedroom had the same layout as their previous one, with a control panel for electronically raising or lowering partitions and furniture. Neatly folded on each of their tables were their new Tijaran uniforms. Julius grabbed one of the blue jumpers and looked for the label on the left sleeve. Written in silver, the letters spelled out "Julius McCoy-2MJ-Tijara".

'This is just!' he said excitedly.

'Hey, there's a message from Faith,' said Skye, who was checking his personal holoscreen. 'He's with Morgana in the garden. They'll meet us for tea around eight.'

'Great. I've got time to wash up then. I want to wear my new clothes.'

After a refreshing shower, as he waited for Skye to get ready, Julius sent a quick message home. A few minutes later, feeling crisp and refreshed, the boys made their way up in the lift and emerged onto the school's circular promenade. When they arrived in the mess hall, they saw that most of the tables had been taken up by the latest batch of 1MJ recruits, who had just spent their very first day on the Moon. Judging by their expressions, they had been having a great time of it so far.

'Wait till they get their timetables tomorrow morning,' said Julius to Skye, with a wry smile.

Just then, Morgana and Faith waved to them from the back of a long queue for the food. Morgana was so happy to see Julius again that she was positively beaming, her lovely almond-shaped, green eyes shining brightly. They had met many years ago when her family had moved from Japan to Scotland, her father's homeland, and had always looked out for of each other as they grew up together. When Julius was close enough, she threw her arms around his neck; Morgana was the only girl in the whole world who would actually be allowed to do that, given how naturally reserved Julius was.

As she turned to greet Skye, who was visibly pleased at being considered hug-worthy as well, Faith hovered towards them, sporting his now famous conical, metallic skirt. It was amazing to Julius thinking about how, when he had met Faith the year before, he had been restricted to a wheelchair. Not that a wheelchair could *actually* limit someone as technologically gifted as Faith who, even at that young age, had already managed to alter the chair so it could hover and fly about. The 'skirt', as everyone called it, was an invention of Pit-Stop Pete's, the owner of a docking base in lunar orbit, where Faith had just spent his Summer Camp. Julius knew that it had made a great difference in his life and, even if Faith didn't ever talk or make a fuss about his disability, it was clear how happy he was just to be able to stand up like the rest of them.

'How's it going, boys?' asked Morgana.

'Had a great time in Fornax,' answered Julius, truthfully. 'But it was hard work. We spent every waking hour with a catalyst in our hands, shooting anything that moved.'

'That sounds fun,' said Morgana. 'I did a fair amount of flying myself this past month. The apprentice camp is *really* advanced. I don't know why they gave me permission to join them so early. At least I didn't crash any of the Cougars though. And Kaori was there too, which was brilliant of course.'

'How *is* your sister?' asked Julius, edging slowly forward in the queue.

'She's good, thanks. She says hi.'

'What about you, Faith?' asked Skye.

'I spent the best part of the summer zooming in and out of Pete's dock on a sky-jet, salvaging debris from the battle with the Arneshians.'

'A what?' asked Julius.

'A sky-jet. It's a jet-propelled personal aircraft, or to put it simply, a space-scooter. Pete has hundreds of them. They're actually really fun to drive.'

'I got a shot at it too, when I was there in June,' added Morgana. 'There were so many Cougar parts floating about, it was getting dangerous for everyone. So, as part of our Summer Camp, Pete made all of us go retrieve them.'

'Sounds like you actually did something useful and had fun,' said Julius.

'To be sure. The luck of us Irish is never-ending,' said Faith, with a theatrical wink.

Finally they reached the counter, where the resident chef, Felice Buongustaio, was dishing out *tagliatelle al ragù*, a dish of fresh pasta dressed in tomato and mince sauce.

'Can I have a double portion please, Felice?' pleaded Skye, almost on his knees, much to the amusement of the first year students.

'*Va bene, va bene!* Of course,' cried the chef in a thick Italian accent. 'But only because you remind-a me of my son and you've spent three months on-a that piece of floating junk in-a outer space. What have they been feeding you, eh? You look-a too skinny. You're a boy in full growth. You need-a to eat. Eat, I say!' he finished with a flourish of his hands.

'You're very right and I'm so glad to be back, Felice. It's like going home to my dad when I see you,' said Skye, pursing his lips as if he was about to cry for all the emotion he was feeling.

It was all too much for Felice, who couldn't resist being called a father, and proceeded to dish out a portion of pasta sufficient enough to feed a small platoon. Skye walked away with a large smile and a humongous plate of food, leaving the others standing there quite stunned.

'I'm gonna call him the *Black Hole*, from now on,' said Julius.

'Where does he put it?' asked Morgana.

'Who knows,' said Faith. 'If I ate that much I wouldn't fit in me skirt. Mind you, I think I must have grown a bit over the summer, 'cause it feels tighter around the waist.'

'Tell me about it,' said Morgana. 'I feel like all my clothes are getting smaller in the oddest places.'

Julius and Faith froze, looked at her, and then quickly glanced away.

'What?' asked Morgana. 'What's the matter?'

It was only when the boys had turned a dark shade of red around the ears that she understood. 'Honestly, guys,' she said, pragmatically. 'It's called puberty, and it's going to happen a lot from now on, to *all* of us. You better get used to it.'

Julius and Faith mumbled an apology, but it was clear from their faces that the embarrassment wouldn't fade away so quickly. Come to think of it, Julius *had* started to notice a few changes to his own body over the past few months and, looking at some of his classmates he had become aware of more than one boy developing a slight moustache shadow.

Once dinner was finished, they all moved to Tijara's private garden, where they lay down on the grass under their favourite oak tree. The other 2MJs were also milling about and Julius took the chance to chat with most of his classmates, discussing the new gaming season in Satras and exchanging stories about the various Summer Camps. Everyone seemed to have had a great break. None of them talked much about the fight with the Arneshians anymore. Julius supposed that was understandable, given that ultimately they were completely unaware of the real reason for that attack on Zed. How could they, when they knew nothing of Salgoria's secret experiments, or how he was the *White Child* she had been trying so desperately to kidnap?

Tijara's Grand Master, Carlos Freja, had revealed as much to him following the attack. Salgoria had discovered about the existence of a White Child, someone with the exact blend of DNA that she needed. Julius had just joined the Zed Academy at that point, to train in the White and Grey Arts: the White to develop his mind-control abilities; the Grey to enhance the logical side of his brain. Arneshians, by their nature, were highly skilled only in the Grey Arts. The White Arts, however, were a gift that only a small portion of the Organic population possessed, and Julius was that rarest of things: an exact blend of both Arts.

If they had succeeded in grabbing hold of him, and mixing his DNA with an Arneshian's, Salgoria would have been able to create a being powerful enough to finally help her overthrow Earth's leadership. Morgana was the only other person Julius had shared this information with and he was sure she had kept this to herself, as he had asked her to. She didn't even discuss it with him, unless he brought it up. Still, Julius knew it was playing on her mind. He could tell she was worried by the grey wisps of smoke rising from her head when she looked at him silently. He had come to rely on the colourful wisps he saw above people; they helped show him their true and deepest feelings.

*

At seven o'clock the next morning, Julius' alarm marked the beginning of a new year in Tijara. To his surprise, he awoke rather more easily than usual, and for the first time he was dressed and out the door before Skye. As he walked along to the mess hall, he met Morgana in the corridor.

'You're up early,' she said.

'I thought I might start the year properly this time,' he replied. 'Besides I want some extra time to digest the timetable, you know, in case it's nasty.'

As they reached the mess hall entrance, Julius saw a table with two trays lying on it, one for each junior year. He picked up two copies from the second tray, placed them in his back pocket and headed to the food counter. Once they had finished eating, Julius pulled them out onto the table.

'Here,' he said handing one to Morgana. 'Break it to me gently.'

Morgana glanced over hers. 'Sorry. We have two extra hours of lessons and we *still* need to keep a diary for each subject.'

Julius sighed and scanned his own copy. 'Spaceology, Draw, Telekinesis, Meditation, Martial Arts and Pilot Training,' he read aloud. 'Plus two new subjects: Shield and Telepathy. What's Shield?'

'Did I just walk in during an episode of "*There's No Such Thing As A Silly Question*"?' asked a familiar voice from behind him.

'Morning smarty-metallic-pants,' said Julius, shifting along the bench to let Faith in.

'Morning, lovelies,' he said. 'To tell the truth, I was actually wondering the same thing.'

'It's probably a defence course, or something. As for Telepathy … it sounds straightforward enough,' added Morgana with a shrug of her shoulders.

'We've not got either of them till Monday though,' said Julius.

'What's the story for today then?' asked Faith over his cereal bowl.

'Let's see. Wednesday … double Spaceology, double Draw and, after lunch, double Telekinesis,' said Julius. 'Not too bad.'

'Ooh, I almost forgot,' said Morgana suddenly. 'You'll never guess what happened to Billy Somers.'

As the name was mentioned, the boys stopped eating abruptly and plonked their forks down on their plates. Somers was a token of everything a Mizki student shouldn't be. Considering how much grief he had given them when they had met him at the Zed Test Center back on Earth, it was a surprise to them that he had even got in. And sure enough, once enrolled, he had continued his obnoxious behaviour towards everyone he met, not least of all Faith. Fortunately they had not heard much from him in a good while.

'What's he done now?' asked Faith, pretending not to care.

'Remember Marion Lloyd, the girl who passed the test with us?' continued Morgana in a conspiratorial tone. 'I met her yesterday in the dock, and she told me Somers left Zed last year!'

'He what?' said Julius. 'Why would he do that?'

'That's the thing. No one knows,' she answered. 'It happened a few weeks after that first game we had against him last year. Marion just said one day he was called out of class and that was the last anyone saw of him.'

'He probably got kicked out for being a prat,' said Faith, 'and was too ashamed to show his ugly face around Zed again.'

'It's still weird though,' said Julius. 'Not that I miss him. Thankfully, bullies like him are few and far between, and they stick out like sore thumbs. But Faith's right, I'm sure: he probably got booted.'

Certainly, it seemed obvious that Somers had not been missed by anyone at the school, and Julius was sure he wouldn't lose any sleep over it either. He returned his attention to his new timetable, while the mess hall slowly filled up.

When Skye finally joined them, it was time to head to their first lesson. Professor Lucy Brown was waiting for them outside her class, in the Grey Arts sector. She was an excitable, aging English lady in a blue Tijaran uniform, with long white hair gathered in a plait. Julius, followed by Faith and Skye, took a seat as far towards the back as he possibly could, knowing that his eyes might close involuntarily at some point during the lesson, while Morgana moved quickly towards the front, since this was a favourite subject among aspiring pilots like her.

'Welcome back, 2MJs,' she said, bowing to the students.

They all bowed back respectfully and then sat down.

'This year we will be concentrating on the constellations, all 88 of them, as defined by the International Astronomical Union back in 1930, long before the Chemical War of 2550. Now, can anyone tell me who the astronomer was who listed the *first* 48 constellations?'

A hand shot up timidly, that of Barth Smit, Faith's professionally clumsy Dutch roommate. They all looked at him in surprise, since Barth had yet to excel in any particular subject.

'It was Ptolemy the Greek,' he said in a squeaky voice. 'He listed them in *The Almagest*, in 150 CE.'

Everyone in the classroom stared incredulously at him, clearly impressed.

'Well, Mr Smit, that was quite the answer. I take it you like the topic, then?'

But Barth was too embarrassed to speak and simply nodded his head rapidly.

'In that case you might want to keep your eyes on a career as a navigator,' she said, smiling kindly at him and resuming the lesson. 'During the course of the year, you shall learn the system of names, letters and numbers used to recognise the celestial objects present within each constellation, and the fastest routes between us and them.'

Julius let his head fall heavily to the desk. With all due respect to Professor Brown, he would rather have been eaten by mutant grannies in a Solo game than learn to do a job that a computer was going to do for him anyway. Faith and Skye seemed to be of that opinion too, since they promptly began a match of Mindless. This was a game that Julius had invented the year before, during a lesson about the moons of Jupiter. It required two players, who had to mind-push a small ball of paper towards the other's nostrils, and score as many of these goals as possible. Obviously, retrieving the ball was the harshest part of the game, which included a lot of sneezing from both players, and the occasional nosebleed.

The two hours eventually passed and the 2MJs walked over to the White Arts sector for their Draw lesson. There, they bowed to Professor Cathy Turner, who was standing fidgeting by the door, wearing her white lab coat. Julius, Faith, Skye and Morgana moved automatically towards their usual counter, where a set of leafy pot plants awaited them.

'She seems more wired than usual. Are we sure she's not on drugs?' whispered Skye to the others.

'I think her nose is getting longer,' added Faith.

'Hey! You two,' said Morgana, 'Cut it out. She's a nice lady.'

'And she's coming this way,' added Julius under his breath.

Professor Turner was indeed moving closer to their station, where she stopped in front of Julius.

'Mr McCoy,' she said quietly. 'I need to inform you that over the summer you have been officially registered with the Curia and the Grand Masters of the three schools, for the inorganic draw you performed last April.'

'Oh ... thanks,' said Julius. He knew this was going to happen, but he still felt a little embarrassed.

'I would have liked seeing that very much indeed. Ever since the day you made my digital watch stop, I figured there was something different about your draw ability. I've read all the papers published by Doctor Walliser on your draw. It was fascinating. Most of all though, I'm glad that you are alive, McCoy. It was a tremendous risk you took back there.'

Julius nodded. 'Thanks, Professor. I'm glad to be here too.'

The teacher smiled at him and then turned towards the rest of the class. '2MJs, it's a pleasure to have you all back. You have completed your first year of Draw training with excellent results. Now that we all know *how* to perform a draw, we are going to practise the fine art of controlling *the amount* of energy we need to obtain from a target.' She paced between the counters and pointed at the various pot plants in front of each student as she walked. 'These specimens are more delicate than your average cactus plant, so we shall work on them for a while. Let's start by drawing just enough energy to wither only the tip of each leaf.'

For the rest of the lesson, they worked in silence, while Professor Turner moved around the class replacing any dead plants with new ones. It seemed that everyone was finding it hard to control their draw. Even Julius wasn't able to limit his to smaller quantities – it was always the entire leaf. By lunch, no one had managed to fulfil the criteria.

'Not to worry, Mizkis,' said Professor Turner as they left the classroom. 'You'll manage. Just keep trying.'

'You've gotta love her optimism,' said Faith, once in the corridor. 'She managed to smile even after bringing me the fourteenth plant.'

They all agreed and used up their lunch time trying to guess where she kept her seemingly infinite stash of shrubbery. The last two hours of the day were spent with Professor Paul King, the Telekinesis teacher. He had decided to celebrate the beginning of the year in his typical *unusual* style.

'Today, we shall move a meteorite!' he cried ecstatically, his face growing deeply red – in stark contrast to the blue of his uniform. 'I want to see the powers seeping from your skin, permeating the air. Focus! Concentrate!'

Julius and his classmates could only stand there, transfixed by Professor King's drive and ambition, but most of all by the mammoth-sized rock before them.

'How the heck are we supposed to do that?' whispered Morgana.

'I think I know why he's always so red: he gets internal bleeding every time he tries to move something bigger than him,' said Skye.

'If I try to move that thing, it'll be me brains seeping through me nostrils and permeating the floor,' added Faith.

'I'll probably pee myself,' finished Julius miserably, trying not to think about the numerous glasses of orange juice he had drunk at lunch.

The recommended approach, according to the Professor, was for the whole class to try it all together, which they did for the next two hours. The meteorite moved roughly five inches, while the students strained themselves so much that in the end the majority had to go to the infirmary to get headache shots.

Five minutes from the end of the lesson, an anonymous student even succeeded in getting an enthusiastic holler from Professor King, for farting loudly under the strain. 'Air biscuit!' he cried jovially. 'We have ourselves an official air biscuit!'

That did it – Julius and his classmates collapsed on the floor in hysterics, which prompted the Professor to call it a day. He strolled off nonchalantly and left them there, like a bunch of gasping fish, struggling to regain their composure. By the time that evening arrived, news of the "air biscuit" had made its way throughout the entire school. Some of the 6MS pupils had even promised a cash reward to the proud owner of said biscuit but, no matter how many Fyvers had been promised, nobody came forward to claim the prize.

*

That Thursday morning, the 2MJ students started the day with Professor Len Lao-Tzu, who helped them ease back into their meditation routine, seeing as they were quite rusty from the long summer break. His classroom had the peaceful atmosphere of a temple, and indeed looked like one too. He was kneeling in front of them, clad in a loose white tunic and trousers. In his usual serene manner, he calmly announced that they were all expected to lower their trance threshold from one minute to thirty seconds. That really worried Julius, seeing as the previous year he had been required to attend remedial lessons just to get his time down to *one* minute, never mind *half a minute*. He sincerely hoped he didn't have to endure private tutoring again. It wasn't even so much that his VI tutor had ended up helping the Arneshians invade Zed, but more because he had been forced to wake up at 05:00 every morning for a month to do those extra lessons. That was just *not on*, in his book.

As serene and quiet as that morning was, that afternoon in the martial arts dojo was far more energetic. Professor Lee Chan, the only other one of the teachers who didn't wear the official Tijaran uniform, welcomed them back to their Mindkata lessons in high spirits, running them through a training session designed specifically for a seasoned athlete, with the promise of many more wonderful surprises to come, starting the following Monday. By the end of training, Julius was too exhausted to think about surprises and went to bed straight after dinner, aching all over.

*

As was the case the previous year, Fridays were wholly devoted to Pilot training, everyone's favourite subject. Professor Farid Clavel met them in Tijara's underground holographic sector, where the Sim-Cougars were kept. Naturally, Morgana was waiting outside the classroom by eight thirty, eager as always to fly. When Julius didn't see her at breakfast, he grabbed two brioches and a latte and went to meet her.

'Thanks! How did you know I was here?' she asked, biting into her pastry.

'Not difficult, really,' he said, sitting down on the floor next to her. 'It's Friday, and a full Clavel day. Where else *would* you be?'

'It's just in case he gets here early, so I can go in and do some warm-up. You know me,' she said.

'Yes, I sure do,' said Julius with an exaggerated sigh.

As if in answer to her prayers, Professor Clavel did indeed arrive a few minutes early, dressed as ever in his pristine uniform.

'Miss Ruthier,' he said holding out his hand and helping her up. 'Why am I not surprised? And Mr McCoy, it's a pleasure to see you again.'

Julius liked Clavel. He had a warm smile and always managed to make him feel comfortable. 'Likewise, Professor,' he said with a quick bow.

Clavel invited them inside, listening with genuine curiosity to Morgana's tales of her Summer Camp.

'Sounds like you had a good summer, Miss Ruthier. I hope you won't find my lessons too easy now,' he said.

'Not at all!' she answered vehemently. 'I really enjoy you ... I mean ... your lessons!'

'Excellent,' said Clavel, clearly pleased by her enthusiasm.

Julius noticed a thick pink stream of smoke shooting upwards from her head; he recognised it as Morgana's "embarrassing moments" wisp, his cue to remove her from the scene before she could dig herself an even bigger hole.

'I can't believe I said that,' she whispered to Julius as he led her away by the elbow.

'Well, you did. Now, let's go look at the pretty Cougars, yes?'

Mercifully for Morgana, the rest of the class joined them soon after and, by the time the lesson had started, there was not a pink wisp to be seen. Clavel had decided to use their first training session of the new year to revise all the flying techniques they had previously learned. Not all of the students had had the opportunity to fly during their Summer Camps, and he needed them all to be comfortable with their Sim-Cougars. By the end of the day, the 2MJs had left the holographic sector with renewed confidence. Julius was in particularly high spirits. Tijara was beginning to feel increasingly like home to him. Plus, next year, his brother Michael would be able to join the Zed Academy, hopefully even the same school as him too. Thinking about it made Julius eager to speak to his family again, so he hurried back to his room and spent the next two hours talking to them on his computer.

That night, he slept peacefully. Yes, it was really good to be back.

AUGMENTATIONS

That Monday morning, the 2MJs gathered in a classroom on level -5 of the Grey Arts sector. Everyone was visibly excited, as they would soon be meeting a new teacher. Julius, Morgana, Faith and Skye were chatting in a corner when the door suddenly opened. The students fell silent at once and bowed towards the entrance.

'Good morning, Mizkis. I am Professor Calandra Morales and this is your first Shield lesson. Welcome.'

Julius didn't need help in identifying her accent as Spanish and could quickly tell that Professor Morales had a vibrant demeanour. She had long, dark wavy hair that covered her shoulders and a pair of large, smiling brown eyes.

'This course will teach you how to protect yourself, and others, against different types of external attacks. We will have lessons in this room in the morning, when you will be studying the theory of the various Shield techniques. Then, after lunch, we will continue our training in the dojo. There you will learn to use your own shields while using your Mindkatas in a more flexible way. After January we will also use most of the mornings for practice. Sounds fun, no?'

Julius certainly thought so. On Mondays he did prefer more active subjects, as there was less risk of him falling asleep.

'Now, here's the best part,' said Professor Morales stepping into the centre of the room. To all of their surprise, she removed her blue jumper, boots and socks, remaining bare footed in her Combat trousers and t-shirt. She bent her left arm and brought it up in front of her chest, parallel to the floor. 'Watch,' she said.

Suddenly a shimmering magnetic field sprung out of her forearm, creating a shield that protected her from head to toe. The class let out a gasp.

'How did you do *that*?' said Lopaka Liway, completely forgetting protocol.

Professor Morales smiled and continued her demonstration. With the same ease, she produced another shield from her right forearm and proceeded to walk among the students, moving her arms in a smooth flow around her torso. It was obvious from this demonstration that it would require a high level of agility to use the shields properly. To stun the Mizkis even more, she produced two further shields from the tops of her feet. Then, just as quickly as they had appeared, they all vanished. The students erupted into applause, while several of them were shouting for more.

'*Muchas gracias*. Thank you,' she replied, bowing. 'The shield is powered by my own mind-skills, but it *isn't* created from out of nothing. Today, we are going to Dr Walliser and each one of you will be fitted with a special microchip in both forearms. Those chips are for your shields.'

Julius, like the rest of the class, was too surprised to say anything. They were still in a dazed silence as Professor Morales put her shoes back on and led them out of the class, to the infirmary.

'How come Kaori never told me about the shields?' asked Morgana. She didn't seem very pleased.

'Maybe she didn't want to spoil the surprise for you,' answered Faith.

'And how come I've never seen Calandra before?' said Skye, following her every move with his eyes. 'She's *muy caliente.*'

'Don't you start with her too, you hear?' whispered Julius. 'And don't call her Calandra. She's our teacher, man!'

'I need to learn some more Spanish,' continued Skye, oblivious of what Julius had just said. 'Hey, Valdez! Come here a second.'

Manuel Valdez, a short, dark-haired boy, walked back towards Skye.

'Valdez, you speak Spanish, right?'

'I'm Mexican, chico,' replied Manuel, raising an eyebrow at him. 'What do you need?'

'Give me something clever to tell *her*,' he said, pointing at Professor Morales.

'*Ay caramba, amigo!* You wanna play with fire, huh?' said Manuel with a grin. 'Come with me.' He dragged Skye away from the others and began chatting quietly to him.

'What's got into him?' said Morgana, amused.

'His hormones, that's what,' said Julius, half exasperated. 'He's spent the summer chasing this girl called Ife, which is risky enough 'cause she's a Senior. But the teacher … he could get expelled!'

'He's a nutter,' said Morgana.

'At least *he* has a chance,' replied Faith. He looked at Julius and Morgana and pointed at his skirt. 'A lot more chance than I'll ever have.'

Julius was taken aback, as this was the first time he could remember Faith making any sort of negative comment about his situation.

'Faith, that's not true,' said Morgana, putting her arm around his shoulders. 'Who cares if you can't walk, right? That's not what makes someone special. Besides, how many people do you know who can hover?'

Julius saw Faith's smile grow a little wider. Only Morgana could have made someone feel better so easily, and he had seen her doing that ever since the first day they had met.

When they reached the infirmary, Dr Walliser was standing in the foyer with the nursing team. 'Good morning,' he said to the students. 'Today is a special day for the 2MJs, because you will not only receive your shield-chips, but also for the first time ever, all Zed students will be fitted with a PIP-chip.'

The Mizkis seemed understandably confused, so Dr Walliser extended his left hand in front of him, touched the centre of the left palm with his right index finger and activated a small, circular holoscreen which popped into life above his hand.

'This Personal Information Planner, or PIP, contains all the information that you would normally access from any of the Tijaran terminals. Among other things, it has your timetable, an alarm clock and a map of Zed, and it will link you to any other student in the Lunar Perimeter. Plus, you can type notes on it, by simply touching the screen, which will take a bit of getting used to because it feels like you're touching fresh air.'

'Paint me pink and call me an android,' said Faith, shaking his head. 'Last year I ended up metal-plated and fitted with sensors all through me legs. This year they're implanting more chips in me arms and hands. By the time I graduate, there'll be nothing left of me!'

That made everyone within earshot giggle.

'Well I'm glad you're all so comfortable with the thought,' said Faith, half seriously.

'There are a couple of things still to tell, Mizkis,' said Professor Morales. 'The good news is that there's a nice shop in Satras called Going Spare, which sells upgrades for all your chips. You might want a different colour for your shield's magnetic field, yes? Or some extra functions for your planner, like spare memory in case you want to store books, movies or music.'

'There you go, guys,' said Skye. 'That shop will be the go-to place for all our birthday presents this year.'

'Agreed; absolutely; bet your butt,' answered Julius, Morgana and Faith, almost in unison.

'The bad news,' said Morales, 'is that, in order to allow your shield implants to properly bond with your muscles, you will not be able to use them or play any games in Satras until November.'

A chorus of disappointed grunts echoed through the infirmary at that news.

'However,' continued the Professor, 'for this very same reason, all your Monday afternoon classes will be cancelled until November, to give your body a chance to rest.'

'Now that's what I call good news,' said Faith.

Dr Walliser began to call the students one by one, in alphabetical order. When it was his turn, Julius went into a room with a nurse by the name of Federica Primula.

'Lift your sleeves, please,' she said, typing his name into the terminal. 'Place both arms inside this tube, palms down.'

Julius did as instructed. The tubes were transparent, so he watched curiously as two green lasers marked a spot in the middle of each of his forearms. Next, a pair of small metal boxes was lowered automatically over both marks. As they touched his skin, he felt a sudden sharp pain, similar to an injection. 'Ouch!' he said, jerking his arms back.

'Don't worry. It'll pass,' she said, disinfecting the two red marks on his skin. 'See? You can barely notice them. Now, where do you want your PIP-chip?'

'I'm right handed,' he answered.

'In your left hand then. Palm up.'

Julius gritted his teeth and inserted his hand into the tube once again. The pain was sharper this time, but it was also thankfully brief. Once the nurse had disinfected the skin on his palm, he left the room.

By the time the remaining 2MJs had been fitted with chips, it was already midday. Professor Morales told them to make good use of the free time and practise using their PIP-chips. The Mizkis were more than happy to oblige, and for the rest of that afternoon there was not one boy or girl from their class who didn't have his or her nose buried in their PIP. That evening in the garden, when Julius finally lifted his eyes to look around, he felt like he was in the middle of a firefly convention, as all that was visible was a myriad of yellow circular holoscreens, glowing dimly among the trees.

*

When Julius woke up on Tuesday morning, his forearms still felt quite bruised and sore, thanks to the shield implants. As he walked over to the shower, he couldn't help but muse over how the invention of body augmentations had helped humans to enhance themselves with everyday tasks, but *also* how it was surely moving them a step closer to the creation of a different species altogether. Julius, who loved Earth history, had studied extensively on this topic from a young age. He remembered that, ever since the twentieth century, humans had been talking about cyborgs, fictional beings that were part robot, part human. The subject had been widely discussed in popular literature and entertainment, while tentatively experimenting with the technology in existence at the time. Slowly but surely, advances in bio-mechanics had started a revolution that had eventually led to the use of chip-implants to fulfil many different tasks, like sending and receiving data and curing various previously incurable diseases. And now he too was being sent down the path of augmentation – he didn't mind too much though, as long as the "real" Julius still owned the majority of his body.

When he had finished getting ready and arrived in the mess hall for breakfast, Faith waved at him from a table in the corner, where the rest of the gang was also sitting. Julius grabbed some porridge from the counter, covered it in honey and ginger puree, and headed over to join them.

'Morning, folks,' he said, sitting down.

He got general nods in reply from Morgana, Faith and Skye, who were all busy swallowing or chewing.

'So, does anyone have any idea who the Telepathy teacher is?' asked Julius.

'Kaori didn't tell me much,' said Morgana. 'All I know is that he's called Oleron Beloi and he's from Russia. And he doesn't actually *speak*.'

'What do you mean?' said Faith.

'I'm not sure if he can't or just won't, but he never utters a word. Apparently he's also the best Telepathist the world has ever known.'

'This White Art should be right up your alley, Julius,' said Faith, through a mouth full of toast.

'Yes,' added Morgana. 'You do mind-talking all the time.'

Julius nodded. 'Guess so. But so do you guys.'

'Sure,' said Faith. 'Maybe not as well as you, but we do. What *you* do that I can't, though, is that scary e*ntering-my-mind-to-see-what-I-see thing.*'

Julius grinned. 'I've only done it once, with your permission. Last year on the train to Tijara, when you couldn't describe the school salute to us, remember?'

'Oh, I remember all right. I felt so violated!'

'*2MJs. Please report to holographic sector, Level -5 ,*' said a male voice, inside Julius' head.

'What the …' cried Julius, jumping up in surprise.

'What's happening?' said Morgana, looking worried.

Julius looked around. 'Did you hear that voice?' he asked them.

Morgana and Skye nodded.

'I think it was the teacher,' said Faith.

Julius noticed that all the 2MJs looked just as traumatised as him.

'I take it we need to go to class then … ten minutes early too,' said Skye gathering up his things. 'Come on, guys. Best we obey the voice.'

'I hope he didn't hear my reaction,' said Lopaka Liway, walking past them. 'I wasn't kind, or polite.'

With that, they hurried from the mess hall and headed left along the promenade. Gabriel List, the senior technician, was at his desk at the entrance of the sector, welcoming the students. When he saw Julius, he smiled.

'Mr McCoy,' he called. 'How are you? Did you have a good summer?'

'Yes, thanks Mr List. And you?'

'I was kept very busy repairing our Holopals because of … well, you know. Any more problems with Meditation?'

'No. The first lesson went fine. I think I'll be all right.'

'Good. On you go now. Professor Beloi doesn't like to be kept waiting.'

Julius went back to the others and together they caught the elevator down. When they reached Level -5 there was only one door open, so they headed inside.

'Whoa,' Julius gasped, looking around him with wide eyes.

Morgana, Faith and Skye stared, awestruck at the sights in front of them.

They were standing on a stone ledge no more than a few feet wide, overlooking a massive labyrinth of mirrors. The ledge ran off to either side of them, and followed the edges of the square room. As the rest of the Mizkis arrived for class, Julius and several others were running excitedly here and there along it, exploring the labyrinth with their eyes. The light was reflecting off the mirrors in all directions, creating shiny shapes against the walls.

'*Good morning, Mizkis,*' said the same voice in Julius' mind.

He looked around, searching for the source of it. Without the sound, it was impossible to tell where it was coming from.

'Over there!' cried Lopaka, pointing at a small circular platform, which was hovering above the labyrinth.

The students faced towards it and bowed. The platform moved closer to where they were gathered, along the ledge, and Professor Beloi bowed in return to the students. He was a tall man, with broad shoulders and a short, thick neck. His eyes and hair were dark brown, and he had a quite remarkable handlebar moustache.

'*Since, no doubt, you will be wondering why I do not speak, let me explain it to you now. I have always believed that actions are better than words when it comes to learning. Therefore, forty years ago, I decided to stop talking altogether. Telepathy was to become my sole means of communication, and, if I was to master it to perfection, I was going to have to practise it constantly.*'

Julius was stupefied. He couldn't imagine spending even one hour without talking, never mind forty years. No wonder this guy was the best in the world.

'*You are all capable of receiving messages from experienced teachers like myself, but less so at transmitting to, or communicating with, other less accomplished people. This year, we shall practise transmission, and the many valuable uses of this White Art. I understand that it might be frustrating at times, but necessity is the very best reason for learning.*'

Julius watched, enthralled, as Beloi moved closer to the ledge.

'*I want you to pair up now. One person from each couple will join me on my platform and I will place them in random parts of the labyrinth, while the rest of you up here will guide them toward the centre of it, using only your minds to communicate the directions to them. As you can see, the ledge follows the room around, so make good use of it.*'

Julius was sure all the others would probably try to pair up with him, given his skills, but in fact the four of them just stood there facing each other.

'This is ridiculous,' said Morgana, shaking her head. 'We can't all pair off with Julius. Skye, you want to join me?'

'Madam,' he replied, with a little bow.

Julius looked at Faith. 'What's it going to be?'

'I've got a bit of a sore head, actually,' said Faith with a sly grin. 'I'll go in and you guide me out, methinks.'

'*OK*,' said the Professor, in their heads again. '*The fifteen who are going into the labyrinth, come with me.*'

So Faith, Morgana and another thirteen students hopped onto Professor Beloi's platform, and were dropped off at different points along the labyrinth's perimeter.

'*Remember, guides, you cannot talk and you cannot use your hands either. To the person in the labyrinth, I would suggest a little meditation for a few minutes, to clear your mind. It'll make things easier.*'

While Faith meditated, Julius took the opportunity to study the labyrinth's layout. It seemed simple enough and, by the time Faith was ready, Julius had almost memorised the path to the centre.

'*OK, fly-boy,*' said Julius to Faith. '*Can you hear me?*'

'*Loud ... clear ... you?*' Faith's voice in his head sounded a little disjointed and faraway.

'*Sort of. Try to concentrate harder on each individual word. Visualise them in your mind.*'

'*I'll try. That better?*'

'*Yes, much. You ready?*'

'*Is me skirt metal? Sure am.*'

Julius smiled. '*Keep facing that direction. Start walking and take the first left.*'

Faith began to move, and spent the next twenty minutes following Julius' directions. Occasionally, Julius would ask him to focus more, especially when he took the opposite path to the one advised, or got so disorientated that he would walk straight into a mirror. But he was still the only student in the labyrinth making any progress at all.

'*Almost there. Take the next left, then the second on the right and Spock's your uncle.*'

'*Ain't you handy to have around?*' said Faith, emerging in the centre of the labyrinth. '*I'll just sit here then, and wait.*'

Julius smiled contentedly. He had wanted to make a good impression on the teacher and was sure he had done just that. As he looked at the other students, he had to hold back his grin. Barth Smit, notorious menace, was bouncing from mirror to mirror and was sporting a swollen forehead as a result. Siena Migliori and Astra Evangelou were both trapped in the same corner – in the absence of any clear directions, they were trying to feel their way out. Morgana, meanwhile, was advancing slowly but steadily along the maze, while some others were still sitting at their starting positions, like Jiao Yu, her new roommate. The temptation to give them a hand was strong, but Julius thought better of it.

When all the stragglers – some with the teacher's help – had finally been rounded up in the centre of the labyrinth, Professor Beloi gave them a fifteen minute break, and then made them swap roles. It was Faith's turn to guide Julius through the maze, and he did so rather well. It wasn't quite as quick as when he had been doing the guiding but, despite that, he was the first to the end point.

'*I still think it's 'cause you're good at receiving,*' said Faith, while they were waiting for the others to finish.

'*Maybe, but you know how to use telepathy, Faith, or you wouldn't be here on Zed. You can do just as well as me.*' Faith made no reply so Julius let the topic drop.

By the end of their first lesson, everyone had tried both roles, with different degrees of success. Professor Beloi had not made any individual evaluations, probably a good thing given that some of the students hadn't actually made it to the centre, but he promised them more of the same for the next few lessons.

*

For the next three weeks, Julius and the Mizkis got busy adapting to their second year subjects, both the old and new ones. So far, there were no troubling topics for him – in fact, he was doing rather well. It made him think that perhaps Freja had done a good thing by telling him that he was a White Child; he felt as if that knowledge had given him a little more confidence when it came to learning new things. Morgana had noticed this too, and had mentioned it to Julius on a few occasions. But then again, Morgana had *always* believed in him and his abilities, so maybe she didn't really count. What was beyond question, though, was that Julius was very happy with his start of term and hoped to keep it that way for the rest of the year.

September quickly came and went, and October brought glimpses of Satras and of a new gaming season. They were only to be allowed back on the third weekend of the month, which for Faith meant no birthday presents for another two weeks. Despite that, Julius, Morgana and Skye made sure he got a nice chocolate and carrot gateau for his birthday dinner – courtesy of Felice Buongustaio – with fourteen candles to blow out.

'Thanks, guys,' he said that night, passing slices of cake around the table.

Julius, Morgana and Skye had transferred fifteen Fyvers into Faith's account, as a present.

'Any idea what you're going to buy?' asked Morgana, licking her fingers.

'Actually, between upgrades for the PIP-chip and the shields, I have no idea. I guess I'll just have to wait and see what they're selling in Going Spare.'

'What about your skirt?' asked Julius, 'Can you still get gadgets for it?'

'I think so, but I forgot to mention it. Pit-Stop Pete wants to see me for a skirt-service.'

'That sounds fun,' said Skye, ramming an entire slice of cake into his mouth.

'Very,' said Faith, 'if I was a Ferrari. By the way Skye, you can't eat the candles.'

Skye stopped chewing, produced a blue wax ball from his mouth and put it down on his plate, while the others observed him with silent, comical looks on their faces.

'You really are a human trash compactor – you know that, right?' said Julius, amused.

*

On Saturday, the 16th of October, Julius met the others at Tijara's main gate at eight o'clock sharp. It meant getting up as early as a normal school day but, given the number of people that would soon be clogging up the Intra-Rail System, it was well worth it. A handful of 1MJ students were also waiting for the train, chaperoned by a couple of Mizki Seniors.

'I wish someone had warned *us* last year to make sure we got here before the masses,' said Morgana.

'I almost got me new skirt torn off of me, the crowds were so bad!' added Faith, reminiscing.

'That might happen again, and worse, if you don't move away from the tracks by the way,' said Julius, dragging him back away from the edge of the platform.

When the train arrived, they boarded it without any difficulties and, following two brief stops for the early birds from the Tuala and Sield schools, they reached their destination. After a whole summer away, walking through the gates of Satras and standing on the terrace overlooking the emerald lake felt like a sweet homecoming to them.

'I so missed this place,' sighed Morgana.

Julius looked past the lake and the hundreds of shops flooded in neon lights, to a tall tower protruding from the Moon's jagged rocks and stretching all the way to the ceiling – the Hologram Palace, home of the Skirts.

'I know we can't play yet,' he said to the others, 'but let's go sit in the arena later on. I wanna check the score boards and see what's been going on.'

'Ah aid someone's beaten your Solo score?' said a voice behind him.

Julius whirled around in surprise, and saw Bernard Docherty standing there.

'Hi Julius, how's things?'

'Bernard. Have you met my friends?'

'*Everyone* knows the Skirts,' he said jovially.

Julius noticed the pinkish wisps emanating from the tops of his friends' heads. It seemed a compliment from Docherty was enough to get them blushing.

'So, what's up, McCoy?'

'Just shopping. They've implanted our shields, so we can't play until November.'

'I remember that day, all right. It'll be worse when you get the chips in your feet, trust me. Well, maybe we'll meet in there this year,' he said pointing at the Palace. 'Enjoy your day.'

They watched as he boarded one of the platform lifts into Satras with two other Mizki Seniors, and waited for the next one so they could go too.

'He's a nice guy,' said Morgana, observing him from afar. 'I mean, he's made Zed history with his Solo record so he could easily have been a real stuck-up number because of that. But, in fact, he's quite the opposite.'

Julius nodded in agreement. He remembered the first time he had seen him, in the garden of Tijara. He had been surrounded by girls and boys, all positively spellbound by him. Now it made sense. He was a gracious winner, in true Tijaran style, and he hoped that one day he could follow suit.

As they stepped off the elevator, a unanimous vote called for an opulent breakfast at Global Brioche, the only place in Satras where you could find all of the different foods used for breakfasts around the world. A few minutes later, armed with custard-filled doughnuts in one hand and lattes in the other, the Skirts discussed the plan of attack for the day. Once they had managed to prise Skye from the pastry display, they headed straight for Going Spare, which they were very keen to explore. As he stepped inside the shop, Julius was immediately struck by the number of gadgets and gizmos spread over the seemingly hundreds of shelves.

'I could waste the whole day in here,' he said to no one in particular.

There was no answer from the others. Like a flock of oversized magpies, they were completely mesmerised by the shiny objects. Knowing that he needed to do other things that morning, he decided it would be best to ask for help, and walked towards one of the shop assistants. He asked to see the colour choices for the shields and was led towards a display.

'Choose the one you like,' said the man, 'and then put your arms inside these tubes, with the chips under the light. I'll do the rest.'

His favourite colour was sapphire blue, so he told the assistant and placed his arms in the tubes. The man selected the required tones for the colour and when the light shone over the scars on Julius' forearms, he pressed a button and a needle shot down into the chips. Julius flinched, expecting to feel the usual sharp pain, but it didn't arrive.

'Is that it?' he asked, quickly massaging each of the tiny scars.

'Yes. When you use the shields for the first time, you'll see. It's beautiful. Anything else I can help you with?'

'I would like more memory for the PIP, a different colour for my holoscreen – red this time – and an Earth Link so I can video-call home, please.'

'Coming right up,' said the man.

In ten minutes, he had fulfilled all of Julius' requests, for the price of thirty Fyvers. Each week the students could earn up to ten Fyvers to spend in Satras, depending on how well they had performed in class and, since Julius had done really well and couldn't spend any of his money on games, he had enough for the upgrades and a long overdue haircut.

'Guys, I'm going to head over to the *Barber of Seville*,' he said to the others.

'Wait for me,' said Faith from where he was standing, by the till. 'I need a trim too.'

'I'm meeting Kaori for more shopping and lunch,' said Morgana, who was still browsing over the merchandise. 'How about we meet at one in the Palace arena?'

'Fine by me,' said Skye, 'This morning I'm sort of busy … with … just busy.'

'Who are you meeting?' asked Julius with a knowing grin.

'No one,' said Skye, vaguely.

Julius and Faith quickly moved over and cornered him.

'Go on! Tell us,' said Faith.

'Wait!' said Julius. 'Don't tell me – it's Ife, right?'

'Maybe. Well, OK. Ife is far too old for me, so I decided to bring it down a level or two.'

'Yes but *who* then?' persisted Faith.

'You don't know her. She's from Sield School: Pippa Coleman, 3 Mizki Apprentice.'

'And when did you meet her?' asked Julius in surprise. 'You haven't really left Tijara that much.'

'I'm good at social networking,' said Skye, proudly. 'That's one good use of the PIP-chip.'

'You're quite something, you know that?' said Faith, amused. 'Will we see you at one?'

'Of course. Friends before girls, right?'

'Don't let Morgana hear you saying that, ever, if you know what's good for you,' said Julius, 'OK then, we'll see you later.'

They waved to Morgana and left the shop and then burst into laughter. It took a while before they were able to stop again.

'What is he like?' said Faith. 'And how many crushes is this now?'

'The third since August, including the teacher. But never fear, we have another seven months until the end of the school year.'

'Anything could happen between now and then,' added Faith, grinning.

When they entered the barber shop, a short, dark haired man came quickly to welcome them in and ushered them into two of his high leather chairs.

'Good morning, gentlemen,' he said with an obsequious bow and the vocal flourish of a tenor. 'My name is Figaro Rossini, factotum and owner of this fine establishment.

Now, from the obvious absence of facial hair, I assume that you are here for a haircut, no?'

'To be sure,' said Faith. 'See if you can untangle this brown carpet parked over me head please. Not too short though.'

'Right away, sir,' said Figaro, tipping Faith's head back and beginning to wash his hair in a basin of water that was attached to the back of the chair.

Julius relaxed in his own seat, which Figaro had reclined to make him more comfortable.

'Sir,' asked Faith, 'I don't mean to be out of place, but am I right in saying that your name is related to the name of this shop?'

'Why, yes! Figaro *was* the barber of Seville, in the opera by the Italian composer Rossini, my ancestor. Hence my name. My family built this shop in the days when Marcus Tijara and Clodagh Arnesh were first founding the Zed Lunar Perimeter. But I am very surprised that you know of this opera.'

'I'm Irish, see, but me mum's family is Italian. They used to play loads of opera in the house.'

'Well, good for you! It's truly a balm for the spirit.' As he said this, he turned on the stereo and selected the opera in question.

Julius waited patiently for his turn, enjoying the music and the smell of aftershave permeating the leather of his chair. Figaro meanwhile had removed the basin of water and was vigorously drying Faith's hair. The sound of the barber working as he rapidly snipped away at his friend's locks was almost hypnotic.

When Figaro finished with Faith, he moved over to Julius, attached a clean basin of water and washed his hair, then tilted the chair upright once again. 'What shall it be for you, young master?'

'I like my hair longish, but the jagged strands are getting out of control. They need to be less Amazon Forest and more botanical garden type of vegetation.'

'I'm sorry, but I have no idea what you're talking about.'

'Just tidy it up, please,' said Julius.

When they left Figaro, Julius and Faith looked a lot neater than when they had entered.

'Let's just grab some food and go to the Hologram Palace. There'll be plenty of entertainment there, till the others arrive,' said Faith.

'Sure, and it's free. I don't want to finish all of my money today.'

So they stopped by one of the many stalls along the Emerald Lake and bought sandwiches and a litre of freshly squeezed carrot juice to share. When they reached the Palace, dozens of 1MJ boys and girls were populating the courtyard, some looking rather lost and scared.

'Surely *we* weren't like that, last year?' said Julius, sitting down on one of the large steps of the arena.

'Of course not,' answered Faith, unconvincingly. 'Besides, I was too busy dealing with Somers – he did have a way of gettin' me goat up.'

'You always managed to put him in his place though, Faith.'

'But it's a shame I lost me temper with him – he wasn't really worth it. I should have known better.'

'No one could blame you for that. He insulted you at every opportunity. Heck, I would have done the same thing.'

'I'm fine with me disability, Julius. Well, at least I'm comfortably resigned to it. I've gotten used to the stares, the pity and sometimes even being treated like I'm second class, or a freak,' said Faith. 'Certain things you can't change, and the more I get upset or frustrated about it, the more time I waste, when I could be using that time to find ways of getting around me problems. You would have thought that, with all the technological discoveries we have, somebody would have invented a cure for folks like me, but no.'

Julius stared at his feet for a moment, reflecting on Faith's words. For a start, he was surprised at how much Faith had just told him. This year Julius had already been taken by surprise with the remark about his lack of chances with girls, and now this. Julius thought he sensed a hint of frustration in his friend's voice but, try as he might, he couldn't actually see any form of coloured wisp above Faith's head, a sign that he was probably suppressing his emotions pretty well. Still, he was glad that he had opened up to him. It meant he was trusted at least.

'Ah, don't be too harsh on yourself, mate,' he said, eventually. 'You're a really funny guy so even the worst of your wisecracks makes people like Somers look like the idiots they are. See, that's one way of getting around the problem. Besides, everyone needs to let off steam sometimes. We're only human, after all! Well OK, maybe not you – you're pretty much a cyborg already.'

Faith laughed heartily and punched Julius on the shoulder. 'Don't worry. You'll get there too one day.'

'At the rate they're going with these augmentations, it'll be earlier than we think.'

They finished their food in silence while staring at the scoreboards in the arena. Julius was curious to know exactly why Faith was unable to walk, but he knew better than to ask, or to probe around in his head with the aid of mind-skills. Faith would tell him when he was good and ready, so Julius would simply wait until then.

At one o'clock, Morgana and Skye joined them on the steps. According to the charts, the Skirts still held the record for flying games among the first year students.

'Guys, what do you say we start this year with a fight?' said Morgana, looking at the scoreboards for the team fighting contests. 'There aren't any particularly impressive records up there, and I bet you no one will be able to beat our Flight score for a long time.'

'I like that idea,' said Faith.

'Why don't we play the first one against the computer?' said Julius, 'To see what it's like.'

'Sound,' said Skye. 'Are we still only competing against teams from our own year?'

'I'd prefer that, if it's all right with you guys,' said Morgana. 'At least for now.'

Julius and the others nodded in agreement. They spent the afternoon wandering around the arena, checking out newcomers and meeting up with students from the other schools. Julius and Faith even managed to drag Skye away from the crowd to enquire about his date, but he was rather mysterious about it and would not share any particulars, with the excuse that it wasn't the gentlemanly thing to do. Julius told Skye it was very thoughtful of him to not kiss-and-tell and so they stopped pestering him. It was just before eight o'clock when they returned to Tijara for dinner. Given that his wrist wasn't hurting too much anymore and that he was dying to use some of his gadgets for the PIP, Julius spent the evening chatting with his family on his new Earth Link from the comfort of the Juniors' common room.

THE FIRST ORACLE

The first week of November felt a century long to Julius, so eager was he for the weekend to arrive. This was in no short part down to the knowledge that on Saturday the 2MJ students would finally be allowed back into the Hologram Palace, now that their shield implants had been given a chance to fully merge with their muscular tissue.

'Merged or not, I'm going to the Palace tomorrow,' said Julius during the Friday evening meal.

'I'll follow you even if me arms fall off,' added Faith, eagerly.

This enthusiasm was shared by all of their classmates, and there was plenty of game-talk that night, as the students decided who to team up with and who to challenge. So it was no great surprise that the Tijaran train stop was packed to the hilt by 08:00 the following morning. Still half asleep, the Skirts had managed to beat all the queues, thanks to sneaking out of school one hour before the others. So while their classmates struggled like so many sardines to cram themselves onto the Intra-Rail System, Julius and his friends were enjoying a small breakfast in the quiet of the arena.

Julius drained the last drops of his latte and stood up. 'Are we ready, Skirts?'

The others nodded. Skye collected everyone's cups and threw them in a nearby nullify-bin, where the rubbish was instantly dematerialised.

When they reached the information kiosk, old Mrs Mayflower greeted Julius with her usual cheeky smile.

'Good morning, madam,' said Julius. 'We would like to sign up for a Combat game please.'

'Now, that's a first for the Skirts. It's good to see you back,' she said smiling at the others. 'We've missed you here at the Palace.'

'We've missed it too, Mrs Mayflower. Like you wouldn't believe,' said Morgana.

'But of course. Well, you're back now. Here's your ticket. Miss Logan will tell you what to do. Good luck!'

They said goodbye to her and passed through the entrance for the group games. The previous year, they had always followed the underground corridor to the right, where the Flight sector technician, Mr Smith, would be waiting to set them up with their holosuits; today however, they took the left path which was marked "Combat". At the end of the corridor, they found a room with two doors and a desk between them. A young blonde woman was sitting on top of it, reading something on her PIP. When she saw them, she closed her hand and got off the desk. Julius handed her their ticket.

'Morning all. I'm Miss Logan. First time in Combat, huh?' she asked, with an encouraging smile. 'Well, no need to fear – it's the same routine as for Flight. Get in, get changed, wait to get called, get holosphered and of course, do your best. You can't use your mind-skills in here, as you know, 'cause this isn't Solo. The big difference is that you don't have a Sim-Cougar to attack your enemies, so you'll be given a Sim-

Gauntlet instead. You heard of them before?'

'Well, we've heard of *the* Gauntlet,' answered Morgana. 'Last year, Professor Chan explained that it's a device you wear on the back of your hand, which works like the catalyst on a Cougar, so your mind-skills get channelled through it and you can aim it at a target. But we haven't done any training with it yet.'

'You'll start today then. The energies you use in Combat games aren't your own anyway. They are already pre-programmed into the Sim-Gauntlet. You'll see them coming out in a blue beam. All you need to do is aim and tighten your fist to shoot. Remember, these types of sessions have a set time limit. You have thirty minutes to create as much havoc as possible. You ready then?'

They nodded excitedly and hurried to the respective dressing rooms. Inside, Faith headed straight for the back room, where he could change with a bit more privacy. Julius and Skye quickly changed out of their uniforms and into the holosuits, then waited by the door to be called. As they sat there, Julius examined the Sim-Gauntlet on his right hand. It was made from a hard plastic material, which covered the back of his hand and gathered up into a thin central ridge starting at his wrist and coming to a stop just above the third knuckle. There was a tiny hole set into this end, which was clearly where the beams shot out.

A few minutes after Faith had finished up and joined them, the loudspeaker called for the Skirts to enter the arena through the green portal. As soon as they had done so, they instantly recognised the familiar vast room, with its dozens of long rows of holospheres stretching across the arena. Julius was pretty sure this was every bit as large as the Flight game sector.

'I didn't think it would be possible to have *two* such massive areas,' he gasped.

'Between these holospheres and the Flight ones we could have every single Zed student gaming at once,' said Faith, in awe. 'How rapid would that be?'

Once Morgana had joined them, a floor technician showed them to their holospheres. Julius climbed nimbly onto the hovering, metal ring-frame of his sphere, as he had done many times before. Grabbing the handles to either side of him, he placed his feet onto the two small platforms below him and rested his head back against the support. When they were all ready, the technician activated the controls and the lights went dim. Julius felt a familiar tightening sensation around his hands, waist and feet, as the pale blue magnetic field enveloping him began to tremble. Seconds later, the dusk of the room gave way to a growing ball of light and he shut his eyes against its brightness. His body became weightless and he felt himself being lowered gently down onto hard ground. He opened his eyes and quickly jumped back, as he found himself staring over the edge of a precipice.

Behind him, he heard Faith shouting excitedly. 'Me legs! Me legs! I can see me legs! Guys, I can walk!'

Julius turned around and watched, mouth open, as Faith improvised a merry Irish jig. There was a thick green wisp emanating from his head, which Julius immediately recognised as a telltale sign that Faith was genuinely overjoyed.

'This simulator is well cool,' said Skye, who was standing just to the left of Faith and grinning brightly as he watched the dance. 'Just don't go knocking us off this platform OK, you crazy kid.'

As he said that, Julius and Morgana had a proper look around them, and realised that they were indeed standing on a grassy platform, roughly the size of a king-sized bed, which was flying across a clear blue sky.

'I wonder where we're heading,' said Julius. He didn't fully trust the peaceful atmosphere around them. This was a Combat game after all, so it struck him as a good idea for them to stay sharp.

As if they had read his thoughts, Morgana and Skye began to scout the horizon, and Julius did likewise. It took Faith a little longer to recompose himself, but none of them were about to complain about that, seeing as he was so understandably excited about his very own functioning legs. It was Morgana who first spotted something.

'Over there,' she said, pointing with her finger at a spot just below and ahead of them.

The others edged over beside her and looked down.

'Is that a tower?' asked Julius.

'It looks like it,' answered Skye. 'There are people all around its base. What are they doing?'

'It's a siege!' said Faith. 'See there – they're putting ladders against the tower, so they can climb it.'

'But why?' said Morgana, 'There's nowhere to go from its top.'

'I think,' said Julius, worriedly, 'the more important question is, why are *we* heading towards them?'

Suddenly, as if prompted by the words, the platform veered left and started its descent towards the peak of the tower.

'Oh boy,' said Faith, 'Um, guys … I think they've seen us.'

Julius glanced anxiously at the mob below, who were waving pitchforks and slingshots over their heads and glaring angrily back at him. Without warning, the platform stopped abruptly above the tower and began, slowly but steadily, tilting to the left.

'Shoot!' cried Julius, stepping to the right side of the platform in an effort to counteract the tilt.

'Woah,' exclaimed Morgana, who was losing the battle to stay on her feet. Just in time, Julius grabbed her hand and pulled her back.

'Sit down everyone!' shouted Skye.

'Quick. The roof of the tower – we're going to have to slide down onto it,' said Julius. 'There's no other way.'

'I can't believe I'm saying this, but …' said Faith scrambling backwards, 'I miss me skiiiirt …' And with that, he slid off onto the top of the tower.

The others tumbled down right behind him and landed face first on the hard stone floor.

'I hope we get bonus points for this,' groaned Julius, checking his nose to see if it was still intact.

'What was that ab … ouch!' exclaimed Morgana, massaging the right side of her face with her hand. 'I don't believe it. They just threw a beehive at me!'

'I hope it's empt … ouch!' cried Skye, shielding his face with his left hand and picking up the projectile with the other. 'It's a blinking pine cone!'

'Death to the ogres!' the crowd shouted as one from the base of the tower.

'Kill the monsters!' added another lone voice, just for good measure.

'Steady on now, you pesky peasants,' called Faith, who was obviously feeling rather put out by all of this and marched over to the edge of the tower. 'I'll have you know that me friends here have a mean aim, especially under pressure. Isn't that right, guys?'

'Too right,' said Julius. 'Come on Skirts, this is *our* game. Pick a side and give 'em grief!'

The rallying call worked wonders and, less than ten seconds later, the air was filled with blue beams of energy firing off in every direction. Every time they hit someone, the target would instantly disappear. Despite their heavy losses however, the attacking horde continued their assault, throwing every manner of weird projectile. At one point, Julius could have sworn that he saw a chicken whizz past his head, closely followed by what appeared to be a loaf of bread.

'Hey!' cried Morgana in between shots. 'They've put a ladder up.'

Julius ran over to her side and took aim at a man who was scrambling up towards them. He squeezed his fist tightly and a blue jet shot out, hitting the man square on his nose. The puzzled expression on his face was the last thing Julius saw before the peasant disappeared into thin air. It took several more minutes of intense firing but at last they managed to eliminate all of the attackers.

'That was hard work and no mistake,' said Skye, panting.

'And you haven't seen anything yet,' said Julius ominously, pointing north. 'It looks like their friends are coming to the party.'

'We've gotta get out of here,' said Morgana. 'Look, there's a forest over there. We *could* try to lose them in it.'

'Works for me,' said Julius. 'Come on. This side. It was nice of them to leave a ladder for us.'

Julius waited for his friends to climb down and then rushed after them. Together, they sprinted for the forest, accompanied by Faith's hollers as he savoured the joy of running with his own legs.

'Keep going!' called Julius, hurrying them on. 'They're catching up.'

As they hurtled through the forest they kept turning and firing at random, hoping to get lucky and hit some of the chasing pack. Some of the shots actually did find their target but, as many as they hit, there were still more who stayed hot on their tails.

'There's an opening to the right,' cried Skye, swerving in that direction.

Julius veered off to follow him, then half stopped and glanced back towards Morgana and Faith, who had stopped briefly to fire off a volley of shots at their pursuers.

'This way. Come on!' he shouted to them. Then, seeing that they were following, he took off after Skye again.

Up ahead, the trees were parting off to either side while the ground sloped steadily downwards. A flurry of pine cones and other random missiles whisked past his head. He wasn't really paying proper attention to where he was going so, when Skye suddenly stopped, Julius simply rammed into the back of him.

'What's the matter with you?' cried Julius in surprise.

That's when he noticed that they had stopped just in time to avoid going over the edge of a cliff. Far below them was a lake that was fed by a large waterfall to their left.

'That was too clo ...' began Skye.

He never managed to finish his sentence though, as just then, Faith and Morgana belted out of the trees and crashed into Julius and Skye, sending the two of them flying through the air and over the cliff.

'AAAAHHHH!' cried Julius, arms flailing.

As he fell, he braced as best as he could for impact and just hoped he wouldn't land on top of Skye. Seconds later he splashed into the lake. The water, which was freezing cold, swirled all around his head and ears. Struggling to orientate himself, he searched desperately for the surface. Finally, he spotted a ray of sunshine filtering down through the water and he kicked upwards, towards it. He emerged in time to see Morgana and Faith jumping off the cliff together just as a line of the pine cone wielding peasants screeched to a halt at its edge. To his left, Skye was swimming for the shore and calling to them as he went. Julius treaded water for a moment, waiting to check that the other two resurfaced safely. He was also slightly worried about Faith and how he would cope with the novelty of swimming. Fortunately they were both fine though and, as soon as they caught sight of Julius, they began to swim in his direction.

'I'm so glad I wore trousers today,' said Morgana, as they reached the shore and heaved themselves out of the water.

'I'm so not,' said Faith, seriously.

Julius chuckled, and then pointed towards the cliff, where a small group of the peasants had just leapt into the lake. 'They're coming. We need to keep going.'

Before them, the forest continued all along the left shore so they hurried inside it, with Julius leading the way. He could tell that the crowd wasn't far behind, because their stomping feet were shaking the ground beneath him. He knew that they needed to somehow either lose them or else find a place to stand their ground and fight.

Just then, he sensed something to his right, and a mental picture appeared in his mind of a cave and a long tunnel. He veered off in that direction and shouted back to his friends: 'Come on, there's a cave here! Let's go – we can hide inside it.'

Behind him, the others skidded to a halt and dived after him. There was a large weeping willow in front of them, its leaves hanging over like a curtain of green. They swatted them aside and scrambled up an embankment that had a rock wall at its head, with the mouth of a cave yawning open there. They hurried inside and pressed their backs against the wall, trying hard to control their heavy breathing. A moment later, the angry hubbub of the mob echoed through the cave, then slowly died off and disappeared. Julius drew a sigh of relief.

The air about them was cool and damp, which wasn't ideal given how wet they all were. As his eyes adjusted to the darkness around him, Julius realised that this wasn't just a small cave they had ducked into – it was a vast cavern, which stretched off into what appeared to be a long tunnel.

'How did you spot this place?' said Morgana to Julius. 'None of us saw it, especially with that tree in the way.'

He shrugged. 'I didn't – it appeared in my mind.'

She looked quizzically at him. 'Hmm, OK. Well, what do we do now?'

Faith peered outside, and quickly pulled his head back inside. 'Some of 'em are still out there,' he whispered. 'Looks like they're searching for us.'

'Well, we can't go that way then,' said Skye, wringing some water out of his shirt.

Julius stood up and took a few tentative steps in the direction of the tunnel. There was a faint glow coming from the far end, possibly from another opening.

'I think there may be a way out up that way,' he said.

Morgana looked distrustfully at the tunnel. 'That's all very good, but we need a torch or something. It's pitch black in there.'

'Problem solved,' said Faith. He was tapping a small button on his Sim-Gauntlet, which was causing a small blue light to blink on and off. 'Try yours.'

They each quickly found the lights on their own Gauntlets and flicked them on.
'You guys check it out,' said Skye. 'I'll wait here and keep watch.'

Julius hesitated, not wanting to leave his friend behind, but also realising it would be better to have at least some kind of warning if their hiding place was discovered. 'OK,' he said after a minute, 'but the first sight of trouble, you come after us you hear?'

'With bells on,' Skye answered, with a reassuring grin, then added, 'Go on, I'll be fine,' after seeing Morgana's and Faith's doubtful expressions.

They nodded and turned to Julius, who was staring purposefully into the darkness. He felt Morgana grab hold of the back of his t-shirt, while Faith in turn drew closer to them. Cautiously, they set off through the cavern, making sure to be careful where they placed their feet on the uneven ground. As they moved further along the tunnel, the faint light from the outside world behind them gradually faded away, leaving them with only their pale lights to illuminate their surroundings and the outcrops of red rock all around. As they went, they became aware of faint squeaking noises above them.

'Bats,' gasped Morgana, looking up at the ceiling, 'My hair hates bats.'

'Do you get them often?' asked Faith, with a chuckle.

'If we keep our voices down, they won't bother us,' whispered Julius.

Eventually the path split into two tunnels, one heading downwards – its entrance half blocked by a couple of collapsed wooden beams – and the other bending right and upwards.

'I don't want to go any deeper into this thing,' said Faith.

'I hear you. Let's try the right tunnel,' said Julius, heading in that direction. He took only a few steps around the bend and then froze where he was.

'What's wrong?' asked Faith.

'Get back,' hissed Julius. 'Now!'

In the darkness ahead, two large yellow dots were advancing towards them, swaying slightly from one side to the other as they approached.

'What is it?' whispered Morgana, anxiety creeping into her voice.

'And what's that stench?' added Faith, slowly backtracking.

There was no way for Julius to tell, but he could hear clicking noises on the ground, like nails or claws, tapping against the rocky surface. Gradually, he raised his right arm in front of him, and prepared to shoot.

'Aim between the eyes,' he said.

Faith and Morgana, who were also slowly retreating, nodded and raised their Sim-Gauntlets in front of them. As they reached the point where the path had split, there was the sound of footsteps hurrying towards them from the direction of the cave entrance.

'They've found us!' cried Skye.

At that moment, several things happened at once: a huge black bear emerged from the tunnel, raised itself up on its hind legs and roared threateningly at the intruders. Meanwhile the bats, who had been peacefully lining the cave ceiling, burst into a chaotic flutter of wings and shrieks, further obscuring the already dim light. Julius squeezed his fist and fired at the bear, aided by Morgana who, to her eternal credit, was somehow managing to ignore the bats. Faith and Skye turned towards the angry mob, their backs touching Julius and Morgana's. A small part in the back of Julius' mind took note of how they had taken that instinctively protective formation, without any prior decision, and the thought of how efficient they were together filled him with a sense of exhilaration. He continued firing at the bear with renewed zeal and, when he saw that the animal was almost finished, turned and said to Morgana, 'Help the others.'

Morgana's arm swung promptly to the left, in the direction of the mob.

'Julius,' cried Skye. 'When you're done playing with that oversized cub, aim for the rocks above the door. We need to stop them from coming in.'

Julius hardly thought "cub" was a suitable description for the hairy beast in front of him, but this definitely wasn't the time to argue about it. He squeezed hard one last time and watched the bear crash to the ground, then whirled around to face the advancing mob. They were still pressing forward but, between the cloud of bats and the sterling efforts of the Skirts, they weren't managing to make any serious inroads yet. Julius looked up at an outcrop of rocks just above the entrance, aimed at them and squeezed his fist. The blue beam shot through the air and exploded against the wall of the cave. Chunks of rocks tumbled onto the crowd, while a growing rumble filled the air. A sudden tearing sound ripped through the cavern, and they all stared up, not daring to breathe, as the entire section of stones above the entrance teetered, then came crashing down, plunging them into darkness.

'Are you guys all right?' cried Julius.

'Shoot first. Ask questions later,' shouted Skye, knowing that some of the mob may have been trapped inside too.

Julius pointed his light at the pile of rubble. There were a few survivors, some still brandishing their bizarre missiles, but Morgana, Faith and Skye quickly eliminated the last of them.

'That was intense,' said Julius, pulling a strand of hair behind his ear.

'I think we're going to get loads of points for this one,' said Skye.

'By the way, how long have we got left?' asked Faith. 'The thirty minutes should be up by now, surely.'

'If my PIP is correct, the simulation should end in the next two minutes,' answered Morgana.

Julius walked back and popped his head into the tunnel that the bear had emerged from. It was a dead end. He returned to the collapsed wall and tried to shift some of the rocks, but none of them would budge. The others had plonked themselves down in exhaustion opposite the split in the path, so he joined them.

'Hmm …' said Faith, sounding worried. 'Time's up, but we're still here.'

'Maybe they're having some sort of delay. A glitch perhaps,' added Skye.

'Well, I hope it's not something we've done, shooting the place up like that,' said Faith.

They sat waiting for a few more minutes, discussing their performance and how they could improve it for the next game. Suddenly Julius, who had been leaning back on his hands, sat bolt upright; he felt something, a presence of some sort, but he couldn't quite put his finger on exactly what it was. He stood up and glanced around the cave, half expecting to see some crazy new game character come charging out of the shadows. The others looked at him.

'What's up, McCoy?' asked Skye.

'Not sure,' answered Julius. 'Could have sworn I felt something.'

The others immediately jumped to their feet and began to look in all directions.

'There!' said Julius, pointing at the left tunnel. 'There's something through there,

I'm sure of it.'

'Guys,' said Morgana, 'haven't we had enough for one day?'

Julius shook his head. 'I say we check it out. There's nowhere else to go and besides, when they extract us from the game, it won't matter where we are.'

'Better than sitting here, I suppose,' agreed Faith.

'The Skirts never run from a challenge, right?' said Skye, not waiting for a reply and moving towards the tunnel entrance. 'Stand back!' he called. With two quick bursts of energy from his Sim-Gauntlet, he pulverised the wooden beams blocking the way.

Julius moved next to him, stretching his right hand forward to illuminate the downward path. Morgana stepped behind Skye, followed by Faith and they set off. The path stretched on and they walked in silence along it for what seemed like an eternity.

'I can hear water dripping,' said Morgana eventually.

'There's also a weird glow ahead,' added Faith.

'Hey, come on!' shouted Julius excitedly. 'There's some kind of chamber along there.'

They had reached the end of the path. At the bottom of a slope in front of them lay a small pool of water, surrounded by a number of tunnel entrances. Water was falling from the jutting rocks into the pool in gentle trickles, creating echoes all around the cave. Right in the centre of this tiny lake was a flat rock, half covered in algae.

'It's kinda pretty, in a strange way,' said Morgana.

'Yeah, but what is it?' Julius asked, and headed down the slope while the others stood and examined the chamber. He stooped over and looked closely at the rock, then stepped back quickly – there was a click, followed by a whirring sound, and a mechanical device, which looked like a scanner of some sort, popped out of the rock. Sure enough, it emitted a flat beam of turquoise light, which spread out in a straight line at his feet, then slowly rose up his body and continued upwards until it reached the top of his head. He stood, transfixed. Then, just as quickly as it had appeared, it was gone.

'What in the name of ...' began Skye. He was cut short as a blinding flash of light filled the cave, forcing them all to flinch and shield their eyes with their hands. When they opened them again they saw, to their amazement, that there was a luminous woman standing on the rock in front of them.

'Um, are we *sure* time is up?' said Morgana.

'Yeah, but maybe this is a bonus level or something,' offered Skye.

'It's a hologram – I'm pretty certain of that – but who is she?' asked Julius, stepping closer.

'Careful there,' called Faith.

As Julius got closer, the woman looked at him and smiled. She appeared to be in her mid-thirties, with long blonde hair outlining her beautiful, delicate face. She wore a flowing, silver tunic with large sleeves.

'I've been waiting for you,' she said.

Julius jumped back in surprise, while the others readied their Sim-Gauntlets.

'Do not be afraid,' she said with a gentle smile. 'I kept telling myself you would come back to me, and here you are.'

'Who are you?' asked Julius. The woman didn't answer, but kept staring in front of her, the same warm smile fixed on her face.

'I don't think we can actually interact with it,' said Faith. 'This could just be a standard holo-message relay station, which, in this case, looks like a lady.'

'Meaning?' asked Skye.

'Well, like I said before, it's just a bonus event that we've found inside the game. We've activated it, but it isn't specifically for us.'

'OK, but what's the point? What do we do with it?'

'Hush,' said Morgana, as the holo-lady began to speak again.

'I am the first Oracle and I will set you on the right path. My time is short, so hear my words. We shall meet again in fifty-five days from now, in the last five minutes of the day.'

Morgana began to type away speedily on her PIP as the lady spoke.

'Go to Lake Smaragdus, where it all began,' continued the Oracle. 'At the feet of the lovers you shall see me, if you can. You will heed my words three more times. Remember, only the bravest can reach the end. Farewell, my bringer of life.'

With those words, the Oracle flickered and vanished.

'Flashy! We got ourselves a little treasure hunt,' said Skye.

Julius was just about to reply when he suddenly felt himself being sucked backwards, and the next moment he was gone.

*

'Apologies, guys,' the technician said, as he helped Faith out of his holosphere. 'The system went mental for a while and we couldn't get you back. I hope you didn't mind waiting too much.'

'No problem,' answered Julius. 'The game has some nice surprises if you have time to find them.'

'I suppose so,' he said, furrowing his brow quizzically. 'Anyway, you'll need to move along. Sorry, but I've got several other kids to retrieve now that the system is back online.'

They thanked him and headed for the dressing rooms. Half an hour later, they sat on the steps of the arena, eagerly waiting for their score to come up as an ever growing number of students queued up for the games.

'I'm so glad we got here early this morning,' said Morgana, watching Mrs Mayflower looking increasingly stressed as the crowd around her kiosk multiplied.

'See Yuri, what did I tell you? I knew they would be here already.'

'Hi Gustavo; Yuri. Always a pleasure,' said Julius, looking over at the two boys as they appeared from the crowd.

Like Skye, Yuri Slovich and Gustavo Perez came from the Zed space stations, and had become a sort of double act, in that they were inseparable. They acted as if they were brothers, but physically they couldn't have been more different from each other: Yuri had a definite eastern European paleness to him, with light eyes and hair, while Gustavo was simply the opposite, with darker skin and hair.

'Why aren't you queuing? Have you played already?' asked Yuri in surprise.

'Got here at the crack of dawn, actually,' answered Faith.

'I didn't think it would be this busy,' said Gustavo.

'Well, it is Saturday, plus you know every 2MJ in Zed has been chomping at the bit for a game,' said Julius.

Yuri chuckled and nodded. 'So, what are the Skirts up to this year then?'

'We've decided to start off with Combat actually, but only with teams from our own year,' explained Morgana.

'And how did it go?'

'Well, it was just us early birds this time. We're still waiting for the score,' said Skye. 'There was a problem with the simulator this morning and we got stuck in it, well past our game time.'

'No kidding?' asked Yuri.

'Yep. I was a little worried at first,' said Morgana. 'But then, as we were waiting, we found a bonus level inside the game.'

'Really? I've never heard of anything like that before. Maybe it's a new thing.'

'Perhaps,' answered Skye. 'Hey, look. The score is coming up.'

Julius turned towards the central screen, where that morning's scores were being compiled. The chart started with the first-year results. For Flight, the Skirts were still leading the table, unbeaten since the previous school term. They cheered as soon as they saw it. When the second-year chart appeared, their cheering grew even louder – they had made it to number one in the Combat game category, edging out a team called The Zedinators.

'How good are we?' said Faith, giving low-fives to each of his team mates.

'This is just!' cried Julius, who was beaming happily.

'You are no fun,' said Yuri, shaking his head. 'But I gotta hand it to you, you did well. Congrats.'

'Thanks, you guys,' said Morgana.

'Well, Yuri,' said Gustavo, putting a hand against his friend's back and leading him off towards Mrs Mayflower's kiosk. 'I think it's about time we assembled a team so we can kick their little skirted butts.'

'You wish,' shouted Skye, with a cheeky grin.

'See you guys later,' called Julius.

'So,' said Faith, once they had left. 'What do we do about that bonus thingy?'

'The lady said she'll be back in 55 days,' said Julius. 'That's Morgana's birthday.'

Morgana, who was scanning the scoreboard, turned her head and looked at Julius. '31st of December?'

'Yes. At five to midnight.'

'It'll be right in the middle of the New Year's ball,' said Morgana. 'It might be tricky to get away.'

'Never mind that – we need to figure out where we're going, first of all,' answered Skye. 'But not now, please. I'm starving and it's getting far too busy in here. Let's go to Global Brioche.'

'You'll turn into a global brioche if you're not careful,' quipped Faith.

'Funny guy, hey,' said Skye, throwing an arm around his neck and pulling him along in the direction of the shops. 'I'll pull your skirt over your head if you don't watch it.'

Julius and Morgana grinned at each other and followed them. It was tricky going, trying to find a path through the packs of students, but Julius hardly noticed it, so lost was he in happy thoughts of their Combat result and the news that would surely soon be spreading throughout Satras – the Skirts were back.

VANISHING ACTS

November had started in the best of ways, as far as Julius was concerned. He was still performing well in all of his subjects, the Palace was currently holding not one, but two records for the Skirts, and his Solo score remained unbeaten from the previous year. On top of this, the Space Channel had not reported any sightings of Arneshian fleets. It was as if their defeat in the summer had been enough to send them home with their tails between their legs. Julius didn't really believe that he had seen the last of them, however, but he was pretty sure that they wouldn't try another open attack again anytime soon. With these thoughts in his head, he headed to Chan's dojo for his Mindkata session, looking forward to trying to use his shield for the first time. There, Professor Morales was waiting for the students. Professor Chan stood to one side, leaving his colleague to lead the lesson.

'Good afternoon, Mizkis,' she said, bowing. 'Please kneel.'

Julius noticed how quickly everyone obeyed, eager as they all were to finally try out their shields.

'We have spent the last two months learning the theory behind basic Shield techniques,' continued Morales. 'From today, until the holiday, you will learn to use and control your shields as you walk, run and perform basic kata movements. In January, if Professor Chan believes that you are ready, then we can begin experimenting with defence and attack.'

An excited murmur spread through the dojo.

'I'm going to ask you to fan out in a long row. Make sure you have enough space on either side to safely activate your shields.'

Julius positioned himself between Faith and Barth. Although, being all too aware of Barth's propensity for disasters, he put a bit of extra distance between him and the young Dutchman as a precaution. He noted how Lopaka had done the same thing on Barth's other side.

'Now, do as I do, please,' Morales said, bending her arms parallel in front of her, fist against fist and then waiting for the students to do the same. 'Each shield chip is activated by your mind-skills. The actual resistance of the shields is already calibrated into your chips, so you can all withstand the same level of attacks. As you move through the Mizki ranks, your shields will be improved and made more resistant. Take a deep breath now, and *will* your shields into life.'

Julius concentrated on the chips beneath his skin, and soon felt a light jolt of current running up his forearms. Suddenly, a pair of sapphire-blue magnetic fields sprung into being, creating two long, oval walls, from above his head right down to his feet.

'Amazing,' gasped Julius.

The dojo had turned into a multicoloured forest. It appeared that all of his classmates had paid a visit to Going Spare, because every single shield had been personalised with a different tint. Morgana had chosen a delicate shade of lilac. Faith had gone for a lively green, while Skye had turned his shield silver.

'Very good, Mizkis,' called Morales. 'Now, try walking around the dojo for a bit, without bumping into each other.'

Julius began to move slowly, being very careful to avoid the other students.

'You can stop focusing on the shield, by the way,' added Morales. 'It'll stay active for as long as you want.'

'Or until you faint, or die, or get hurt,' added Professor Chan from the corner.

'Yes, thank you, Professor,' said Morales, eyeing him sideways.

'I thought they should know,' he replied, shrugging his shoulders innocently.

Julius relaxed his mind, concentrating more on his own movement than on the shields, and indeed they did stay up. Occasionally there was a zapping sound – the kind of crackling noise a fly made when it hit an electrified zapper – whenever two students allowed their shields to touch. Following these contacts, the shields would normally disappear, given that the students tended to get a fright and instinctively turn them off whenever this happened. Variations on "Sorry", or "Get out of my way – I can't control this thing" could be heard throughout the dojo during that first lesson.

'Very good, Mizkis – you're doing well,' encouraged Morales.

'Carry on as you are,' called Professor Chan to the class. 'Professor Morales and I are going to start moving around the room. Your job is to try to avoid us.'

And, with that, they began to dart here and there among the students, forcing them into swift changes in direction. Julius noticed that Faith was managing to turn more fluidly than anyone else, aided by his ability to hover. With his smooth movements and the green shields surrounding him, it was like watching him waltz with an emerald ghost.

'Stop-stop-stop!' cried Morgana, suddenly.

Julius and the other students turned to see what was happening, and were treated to a curious picture. Several strands of Morgana's hair were being yanked upwards by Barth's shield, who had somehow managed to entangle them inside the magnetic field.

'Oops, I'm sorry. Wait, let me help!' pleaded Barth, trying to pull his arms away and free her.

Obviously that was only making things worse, as Julius could tell by the single tear running down Morgana's cheek.

'Mr Smit, stop moving!' ordered Professor Morales, hurrying over to them.

Barth froze like a statue but continued apologising as he stood there. Julius almost had more sympathy for him than Morgana; the look of anxious worry on his face was that great.

'Now Mr Smit, listen to me carefully,' continued Morales. 'Whenever such a situation occurs, one has to stop, focus on their shield and simply switch it off. This is what I want you to do, on the count of three – one, two, three!'

Barth closed his eyes and took a deep breath ... but nothing happened. Julius stood watching, mesmerised by the scene. He knew how much Morgana loved her hair. She tended to it daily, so that its "Japanese shine", as she called it, would remain untarnished.

'OK,' said Morales, trying to remain calm. 'That didn't work, and unfortunately I can't retract your shields for you, so we'll just have to take you to see Dr Walliser. Try to walk side by side. Yes, that's good.'

Morgana let out a yelp of pain as the Professor led them slowly out of the dojo. Barth immediately hurried out another stream of apologies.

'If anything happens to my hair, you'll be sorry for sure,' warned Morgana, through gritted teeth.

The students waited for the three of them to leave the room, and then collapsed into fits of laughter.

'I can see remedial classes coming his way,' sighed Professor Chan, shaking his head.

It took all of his authority to get the class under control again. It was needed, as it was soon clear that giggling and trying to control a magnetic field at the same time wasn't a particularly good idea. The lesson was punctuated by several more clumsy collisions, but fortunately there were no further tangled hair incidents. At 16:00 hours, they were dismissed from class. Julius, Faith and Skye headed off to find Morgana. Ten minutes later she emerged from the infirmary, looking quite menacing, grasping a bunch of black hair in her fist.

'Don't speak to me!' she growled, storming along the concourse toward the garden.

Julius and Skye exchanged a quick glance, each stifling an amused grin, but they knew better than to pass any kind of comment. Apparently, Faith didn't.

'Don't worry,' he said reassuringly, gliding after her. 'It's just a tiny patch of hair. Who's going to notice such a silly little thing?'

Without turning or breaking stride, Morgana elbowed him hard in the ribs, sending him sprawling into a large pot plant.

'What did I say?' he asked.

'The wrong thing,' answered Skye, helping him out of the shrubbery.

*

It took Morgana the best part of November before she was able to work anywhere near Barth again. Whenever she saw him, her hand would nervously shoot up to her head, where the clutch of hair had been cut off. Julius agreed with Faith that it was barely noticeable, but he kept very quiet about it. As Faith had discovered, girls were quite funny, and unpredictable, when it came to their flowing locks.

But, if Morgana was a bit distracted during Professor Morales's classes, Skye was the complete opposite. Every time he was in a Shield lesson, he turned into an overexcited bundle of happiness, an apparent expert in Shield techniques and lover of all things Spanish. Never mind that every Monday morning Julius woke up to an insane smell of perfume, vile enough to kill a llama, that Manuel Valdez had told him was just the right essence for anyone wanting to attract a Mediterranean women.

'If I ever turn into a moron over some girl, I give you full authorisation to throw me out of an airlock,' uttered Julius to Faith, at the end of yet another Shield class.

'I'll make a note of that,' answered Faith.

'Hey guys,' said Morgana, emerging from the dojo and joining them.

'Hey,' answered Julius, who was not entirely sure whether her mood had improved at all, and was subtly trying to gauge if it was safe to speak to her again. 'Wanna come with us to the garden?'

He obviously wasn't subtle enough, though, as Morgana quickly noticed the hesitant tone in his voice. 'Don't worry, I'm OK now. I had lunch with Barth earlier and told him to forget about it – I wouldn't do anything nasty to him.'

'That was mighty nice of you,' said Faith.

'Maybe,' she said, with a shrug of her shoulders. 'You know, he may be a complete klutz but he just can't help it I guess. Sorry about elbowing you, by the way.'

'No probs. I always wanted to know what was behind that plant anyway,' Faith said, and winked at her.

'So, did you hear the news?' asked Julius, happily moving the conversation along now that all seemed fine.

'I sure did,' answered Morgana. 'We're getting our November reviews done this coming Friday.'

'Yep,' said Faith. 'We've got Mrs Cruci again.'

'I haven't met her yet,' said Julius. 'Last year, I got Master Cress. But not this time, hopefully. I'm pretty sure they won't give me any extra classes. I've been a good boy.'

'Same here,' said Faith.

'I'm fine too. So's Skye – apart from that perfume he's been wearing,' added Morgana, creasing her nose up. 'I'm worried for Barth though. That's another reason why I spoke to him today.'

'Why, is he nervous about some of the subjects?' asked Julius.

'When we were in the infirmary he was really upset – I mean, so was I – but he was really unhappy. He just kept saying that he'd really done it this time and he would be sent packing for sure.'

'Can they do that?' asked Faith, aghast.

'I don't know. It seems they just give you extra lessons if you're not up to scratch, as Julius knows, but …'

'Yeah, you can never tell,' said Julius. 'He's got the mind-skills though, or he wouldn't be here in the first place. Maybe they'll advise him to go for a desk job. He's a complete menace when it comes to the physical stuff, but he *is* also a smart kid.'

'Well, we'll just have to see. Anyway, if you get a chance, he could do with some cheering up,' said Morgana.

'I'll talk to him,' said Faith. 'He's my roommate, after all. I'll do it before the meeting with Mrs Cruci.'

'Thanks, Faith,' said Morgana, and smiled.

Julius soon realised that Barth wasn't the only one who could benefit from a chat before the reviews. All 2MJ students were required to state their preferences for which subjects they wanted to follow during their next two Apprentice years. Although the actual choice wouldn't be made until the following September, they needed to have a vague idea ready, in order for Mrs Cruci to give them the relevant details. So it was no surprise that, every night of that third week in November, they would meet in the common room to eagerly exchange ideas and information on career choices. Morgana, unsurprisingly, had already decided that she wanted to be a fleet pilot. Faith wanted to become an engineer and Skye was torn between the idea of joining the fleet as a catalyst specialist and a career in politics – Morgana and Faith believed this had everything to do with the fact that these were both considered to be quite sexy career paths by many of the girls in Tijara. Julius, for very different reasons, liked the idea of becoming a catalyst specialist too. It was not only that he was particularly good at it, but also because the idea of joining the fleet to become a strategist, diplomat, or even better, a captain, was a very alluring one. He hoped he wasn't aiming too high though. Freja had intimated to him that a White Child had more chance than others of reaching the highest ranks, but that was no guarantee that he actually *would* make it.

So, when Friday finally arrived, Julius nervously went off to meet with Mrs Cruci. She was a kind, pleasant woman, and quickly put him at ease.

Julius explained his plans to her and watched as his file appeared on the slick screen built into her desktop. Mrs Cruci opened the folder with a tap of her finger and proceeded to type his information into a document simply entitled "Julius McCoy – ?MJ". After she was finished she moved it to one side with a gentle flick and looked up at Julius.

'It may be worthwhile to consider spending the summer serving on a Zed vessel, so you can get a better idea of what it's like doing the kind of work you're looking at,' she said,

'Thanks, I'll definitely think about that,' he answered.

'Well, that's us for now then,' she said with a smile. 'Grand Master Freja is very pleased with your progress, so keep it up and good luck with whatever you decide to do.'

Julius thanked her and stood up to go. He was a little surprised about the personal message from Freja. Then again, he thought as he walked to the door, maybe it wasn't such a shock. He *was* the Grand Master of Tijara, so it was surely only natural that he maintained an interest in how the students were getting on. After all, his deputy, Master Cress, even kept track of how much Julius weighed at any one time and how many hours he slept each night.

He left the office and wandered off back to his dorm, feeling very pleased with how well his review had gone. With that out of the way, his mind drifted to another matter that he had pushed to the back of his thoughts for the past week. Lest he forget, there was a treasure hunt to be solved.

*

The following Wednesday afternoon, the Skirts found themselves sitting at Mario's, drinking milkshakes and searching on their PIPs for information about Smaragdus.

'I have looked at every single name of every blinking sea on the blinking Moon, and found precisely zilch,' cried Morgana in exasperation, throwing herself against the back of her chair.

'What were you hoping to find – the Double Chocolate Ice Cream Sea?' asked Faith, stirring the last remnants of his strawberry shake with a straw.

'Mmm, chocolate,' sighed Skye, greedily slurping down his Nutty Blitz and then scrunching his face as the resulting brain-freeze hit him.

Morgana sighed and said, 'Well, Smaragdus *is* Latin and on the Moon all of the craters have Latin names, so it was worth a shot.'

'Yes, but they're also called "*seas*", and the lady in the cave said "*lake*",' replied Julius.

'Anyway, what does Smaragdus mean?' asked Faith.

'My PIP says "*emerald*",' answered Morgana.

'So, it's like an emerald lake,' chipped in Skye, who was still rubbing his forehead.

'That's it!' exclaimed Julius, sitting up and slapping his friend on the back. Skye coughed and glared at him. Julius, oblivious to this, carried on: 'An *emerald lake* – don't we have one of those here, in Satras?'

The others looked at him, their eyes growing wide with comprehension.

'It would make sense,' said Morgana. 'It's the only *genuine* body of water on the Moon and it does have a rather emerald-ish colour to it.'

'So, who are these "*lovers*" she was going on about?' asked Faith.

They fell silent for a minute and stared out of the cafe window, which stretched from floor to ceiling and overlooked Satras's main courtyard below them.

'Right there,' said Skye suddenly, jumping up from his chair and pointing at the far shore of the lake that lay at the foot of the Hologram Palace. 'How did I not think of it before?'

'What are you on about?' asked Julius, peering out of the window. Then he spotted it – a statue of a man and a woman gently embracing, their lips lightly touching. He had surely seen it at least a hundred times, but never before paid much attention to it.

'The first time we went shopping at Going Spare, I went for a date with Pippa Coleman, didn't I?' answered Skye. 'Well, she met me there, under the kissing lovers.' He was beginning to blush a little now.

'*A date?*' parroted Morgana, and grinned at him. 'Well, you guys do have your little secrets, don't you?'

They all looked innocently in different directions; Skye had suddenly found something very interesting on the ceiling to stare at. They were spared any further interrogation, though, as Mario approached their table and began to clear up the glasses.

'Mr Mario,' asked Julius, turning to face him. 'What's the *actual* name of Satras's lake?'

Mario seemed a bit taken aback by the question and stroked his bushy moustache distractedly. 'Why, it's Emerald Lake. Only, those big pompous heads back in the day called it by its Latin name, which incidentally I can't pronounce.' He stopped for a moment, lost in thought, and then mumbled, 'Such a funny thing.'

'What's a funny thing?' asked Julius.

Mario shook his head. 'Oh, nothing. I was just thinking that it's funny how sometimes such beautiful things can come from the ugliest of people.'

'What do you mean?' asked Faith.

'Well, this entire place was Clodagh Arnesh's idea. Satras was her baby – the Palace included.' The cafe owner looked at them each in turn and, seeing how they were now hanging on his every word, continued. 'My ancestor Carmine, *may-he-rest-in-peace*, was given a special invite from Clodagh herself to leave his ice cream parlour in Naples and move his business to Zed. He had tonnes of pictures of her eating in here. Good for business, you understand. Well, back then it was. Quite often, she would pop in just to get an ice cream cone to take down to the lake, so she could eat it on one of those little boats. They've got some of the pictures stored away in the Curia's archives, as far as I know.'

He stopped and looked at them but they were still just staring back, dumbfounded, at him.

'Anyway, it's been nice speaking to you, but I've got ice creams to cream and milkshakes to shake,' Mario said, skilfully scooping up the rest of the glasses. He stopped for one further second, then mumbled something about strange kids and left.

Once he was gone, Julius leaned forward and said, 'It's incredible how easy it is to forget that Marcus Tijara didn't actually build Zed by himself,' said Julius.

'At least now we know where to go for the next clue,' said Morgana.

'Yes, but we need to figure out how to get back here on New Year's Eve without being seen,' added Faith.

However they were to do it, thought Julius, it wasn't going to be easy. Just before seven-thirty, they boarded the Intra-Rail back to Tijara, in time for curfew. As they approached the station, they noticed a group of men in official uniforms clustered outside the school entrance.

'Hey, what's going on over there?' said Skye, moving closer to the window.

'Looks like Security's out,' replied Faith.

And sure enough Julius could see Tijara's front-gate guards, the Leven twins, talking to the Chief of Security, Lieutenant Foster, who was a living nightmare for any student who dared to step over the line.

'Look, Freja and Cress are there too,' said Julius. 'And Professor Chan.'

As soon as the train came to a halt, Julius leapt out. There was a large crowd of students gathering at the entrance to the school. He pushed through them to the front of the throng, followed closely by the others. Two girls, who Julius recognised as 5 Mizki Seniors, were sitting to one side, crying on each other's shoulders while Nurse Primula attended to them.

'Skye,' called Julius, pointing at another girl, who was standing separately, a few feet away from them, by herself. 'Isn't she one of Ife's friends? We met her this summer during the camp.'

'You're right. It's Betty,' Skye answered. 'Let's go ask her if she knows what's going on.'

When they approached her, she seemed to recognise Skye immediately, and walked towards him with her arms open.

'Oh Skye, it's horrible!' she said, hugging him tightly as tears streamed down her face.

'What's the matter, Betty?' he asked.

'It's Ife,' she sobbed.

'What happened to her?' said Skye, now also visibly worried.

'We were on our way back to school, when these men jumped out from behind the hedge and pushed us to the ground. We didn't have time to do anything, it happened so quickly.'

'What do you mean? What did they do?' asked Skye.

'We ... we picked ourselves up and ... and we looked around, but Ife ... she wasn't there. She was gone!' And with that, Betty's tears became an uncontrollable torrent.

Skye, for once, didn't know what to say, so he just stood there, holding her. Julius felt his heart turn cold. He looked over at Grand Master Freja, who was standing, arms crossed, surveying the children. Julius had not seen him in six months, but it was noticeable how tired he looked. Just then, their eyes met and Freja motioned for him to come closer. Despite his surprise, Julius didn't hesitate and went immediately.

'Sir,' he said, bowing.

'Mr McCoy,' replied Freja, bowing back.

'Is this Salgoria's doing, sir?'

'We don't know yet, but we have to consider the possibility. In the meantime, I need you to remain sharp, and look out for each other. Remember last year, McCoy. Salgoria can be very determined when she wants something.'

'Yes, sir,' Julius said. There was a multitude of questions he wanted to ask, but as Freja seemed quite preoccupied just then, he pushed them to one side.

The Grand Master dismissed Julius, then walked back to his deputy and began speaking privately to him. Lieutenant Foster meanwhile, briskly ushered the students inside the school gates.

Julius knew that it wouldn't take long for the news to spread, so he was not surprised when all of the Tijaran Mizki pupils were called to assembly that same evening. It was Master Cress who entered the hall to address them and, as he did, all eyes were fixed firmly on him. He bowed to the students and motioned for them to sit.

'At this very moment, the Masters for all three schools are making this same announcement. As you have no doubt heard, one of our students was removed from these premises against her will earlier this evening. Ife Alika, a 5 Mizki Senior, was returning to school for dinner when five men attacked her party and, it seems clear, kidnapped her.'

A buzz of whispering erupted throughout the hall.

Cress waited for the students to quiet down before resuming. 'We do not know the identity of those behind this terrible act but, as a safety measure, we would like for all of you to be extra cautious and look after each other. Respect all curfews and keep your PIPs on standby, so your location can be pinpointed at all times. The Grand Master is at this moment talking to the Alika family, and requests that you all keep them in your thoughts during this worrying time.'

*

'This is bad,' said Faith, sitting down on Julius' bed.

After Cress had dismissed the students, they had wandered back to their rooms in eerie, near silence.

'They don't want to say it, but Salgoria is behind this,' said Skye. 'Remember what I told you last year, about those kidnappings? The Arneshians were to blame for them. Now they've started again.'

Julius was stretched back in his Lazy Boy, playing with a corner of his t-shirt. Of the four members of the Skirts, only Morgana and he knew that Salgoria had in fact resumed her kidnapping ways much earlier – the previous year to be precise, when she had tried to nab Julius. For some reason, though, he still didn't feel ready to tell the other two about this.

'All those folks who got kidnapped, they were found dead,' continued Skye. 'She will die too.'

'We don't know that!' blurted out Julius. 'If it is Salgoria, she might have another need this time. She might need her alive.'

'Julius is right,' said Faith. 'It isn't much to wish for, but his guess is as good as yours. Better, actually.'

Skye nodded. There really was nothing they could do about it, except wait for more information. That night Julius didn't sleep much and, from the faint glow of Skye's PIP, he knew he wasn't the only one. He thought about Ife's family – what they must be going through – and hoped against hope that they would find her soon.

*

December was a joyous time for the students, as they were allowed to reunite with their families in Satras – the only time of year this happened. However, the normal heightened atmosphere of anticipation, which the holidays usually brought, seemed to have been considerably dampened. There had been no new developments in Ife's case, a situation that was not easing anyone's mind. Unfortunately, things were about to get worse, as the people of Zed were soon to find out.

On the evening of Sunday the 12th of December, Julius was having dinner with Faith when the mess hall screens switched from the Hologram Palace score charts to Zed News. This was an internal channel that reported on life on the Moon, exclusively for Zed's citizens. As the breaking news logo appeared, the students instantly fell silent. Morgana and Skye stood rooted to the spot in the middle of the hall, with their food trays still perched in their hands.

'This is Iryana Mielowa, reporting live from Satras Intra-Rail station. Tonight, at 19:00 hours, there was another kidnapping: 4 Mizki Apprentice Sharon Dally, from Sield School, was snatched from this very platform. Mrs Mayflower, a worker in the Hologram Palace and long time resident of Satras, was also attacked during the incident.'

Julius and Faith looked at each other, astonished.

'We understand, from Mrs Mayflower's account, that three men sneaked up on her and Miss Dally as they waited for the train to arrive. Mrs Mayflower managed to fight off her assailant, but was thrown across the ground where she lay, unable to aid the young girl as she was dragged away along the rail tracks. Although there are no confirmed leads as to who is behind this attack, the common consensus is that this episode is indeed related to the disappearance of Ife Alika two weeks ago. The possible involvement of the Arneshians is also being seriously considered, although in the minds of many this is already a certainty. Here now is a recording of Mrs Mayflower's statement as she was carried away to Satras Hospital.'

The image switched to a crowd of people gathered around a stretcher. Upon it, Mrs Mayflower was resting, clutching a handbag to her chest. There were photographers all around her, illuminating the platform with the flashes from their cameras. Several security officers were huddled around her, trying to hold back the eager reporters. Ms Mielowa, being the most intrepid of them, had managed to force her way through and push a microphone under the old lady's nose.

'They didn't want *me*!' Mrs Mayflower was explaining. 'One of them grabbed hold of me and started to drag me away, but one of the others told him to stop because they only wanted the girl. So the one who was attacking me said, "But she's a woman too", and the other answered, "She's far too old to be of any use to *her*". Too old? *Moi*? No manners these days, I tell you.'

At that point, a group of official Curia representatives stepped in, flashing their badges, bringing the interview to an abrupt end and hurrying the stretcher away.

The image switched back to Ms Mielowa. 'The Curia has, of course, recommended extreme vigilance from all residents of Zed. We'll be back with further news at midnight.'

'You are joking me,' gasped Faith, leaning back in his chair.

Morgana and Skye walked over to the table and sat down.

'How much you wanna bet the Arneshians are behind this?' said Skye.

'I bet Freja is going to ground us all, just in case anyone else disappears, and that means goodbye Satras,' said Faith.

'I get the feeling that I'm the one who'll be needing some protection,' said Morgana.

The boys looked quizzically at her, not understanding what she meant by that.

'Weren't you listening?' she asked. 'Mrs Mayflower said those thugs were after *women*. And one of the attackers also mentioned that old women were no use to "*her*".'

'*Her*? Salgoria, you mean? But you're right,' agreed Julius. 'Ife, Sharon – both female; both young.'

'And both students,' added Morgana.

'I'm not so sure that matters,' answered Julius. 'The only reason they didn't take Mrs Mayflower was because of her age.'

'True,' said Morgana.

'In any case, all we can do is not let you out of our sight when we're outside Tijara's walls,' said Julius. Right, guys?'

'Of course,' replied Faith instantly. 'And Morgana, you may want to talk to the girls in your dorm and tell them to stick together too.'

'I could volunteer myself for bodyguard duty for one or two of your female friends,' said Skye, winking cheekily. 'Like Siena and Isolde, for example.'

'What are you like?' she said, rolling her eyes in mock exasperation. 'What about looking out for me?'

'Only kidding,' he said. 'I have my assignment, Miss Ruthier. You will be well guarded. The Skirts stick together.'

'Absolutely. Best you remember that, young man,' she said.

Julius finished his dinner in silence, only half listening to their banter. He couldn't even begin to imagine what he would do if anything ever happened to Morgana.

THE MID-WINTER ORACLE

'It's an ugly statue and no mistake,' said Faith, looking up at the kissing lovers.

Julius and Morgana were also looking at the sculpture, their heads tilted to one side.

'That's because you haven't done any kissing yet,' said Skye. 'You'll have a different opinion one of these days.'

'Yeah well, find me a girl that can see past this skirt first, then I'll let you know if I've changed me mind,' answered Faith, sounding quite unconcerned about it.

Julius looked at the foot of the statue. There was a small slab of marble with a short phrase cut into it, reading: "To M. Forever yours, C."

'That's *so* romantic,' said Morgana, with a long sigh. 'I hope, someday, someone will do the same for me.'

'Zed to Morgana, please reply,' said Julius, clicking his fingers under her nose. 'How are we going to get here on New Year's Eve?'

'We'll need to sneak past the Leven twins and maybe Foster too. Plus, enter Satras without security asking why we aren't at the school ball,' said Faith.

'And don't forget about the kidnappings,' added Julius. 'They'll never let us out. Especially not you, Morgana. Also, everyone knows it's your birthday on the 31st, so it'll look weird if you're not there.'

'I knew you would say that,' she huffed.

'I know it's a pain, but I'm right, and you know it,' he said.

'Oh, all right,' she agreed. 'I'll stay behind, but only this once. And anyway, why would the game give us clues that require being out after curfew?'

Skye shrugged his shoulders and said, 'I guess it's the only way to test how *brave* someone really is.'

'For sure,' said Julius. 'And don't worry, Morgana, we're claiming this prize for *all* of the Skirts. You'll be playing your part anyway.'

'Speaking of skirts,' said Faith. 'I think I have an idea.'

'Which is?' asked Julius.

'I can foresee me skirt having a little malfunction, at around seven-thirty pm, on the last day of the year.'

'And?' said Skye.

'See, officer,' said Faith, pretending to plead with one of the Satras security guards, 'I was collecting me uniform for the ball when I fell into the lake and this skirt got waterlogged. So naturally, me friend here went off to find some help. But then a couple on a boat came along and gave me a lift so, when he got back, he couldn't find me. Then we both decided to look for each other, him at the bottom of the lake, me up on the shopping level.'

'That's very convoluted,' said Morgana, 'And a bit silly.'

'What if we come here as normal to get our uniforms and only one of us stays behind, hides and retrieves the message?' offered Skye.

'He's got a point,' said Morgana. 'The fewer of us missing, the better. It'll raise fewer suspicions back in Tijara.'

The boys looked at each other and nodded.

'I'll do it,' said Julius.

'No, I will,' said Skye.

'We'll draw straws then,' said Faith. He hovered over to a nearby juice stand and asked the owner for three long straws. They watched as he cut the end off one of them. Then he turned around quickly and, when he turned back to face them, the straws were all neatly lined up, sticking out of his clenched fist. He offered first pick to Skye.

He pried one out, instantly realised it was a long straw and cried, 'Shoot! That's so unfair!'

'Heh, heh, heh,' cackled Faith dramatically. 'It's just the two of us now, pretty boy.'

Julius looked at the closed fist and picked the straw on the left.

'Yes!' he cried triumphantly.

'Double shoot!' said Faith. 'Can you believe the luck of this guy?'

'Oh yeah, baby,' said Julius, doing a little victory dance just to rub it in a bit more.

'Just make sure you keep your PIP on at all times,' said Morgana. 'We want to see everything.'

'Besides, we'll need to be able to tell you if they find out you're not in school and you're in serious trouble,' said Skye.

'Seriously, though,' said Faith. 'You may want to think of an excuse in case they catch you.'

'I'll just say that the Oracle made me do it,' he said, grinning.

'That's a one-way ticket to the loony house,' answered Faith.

*

'What do you mean you're not coming?' Julius was sitting by the terminal in his room. Skye was dozing in his bed, and he could hear him breathing through the partition that separated their room in two. It was the last Sunday before the midwinter break. That morning, Julius had received a message on his PIP from his mother, asking him to call her back after lunch. Julius had done so, and was now staring at the screen with an extremely disappointed expression on his face.

'I'm so sorry, honey,' said Jenny. 'Your father broke his leg and the doctor said he can't leave the house, let alone leave orbit.'

'How did he do that?'

'Do the words *chasing Michael* and *flight of steps* mean anything to you?'

Julius pursed his lips, trying to suppress a grin. 'He didn't see the steps?'

'Nope,' she said, exasperated. 'There were too many pairs of socks floating around the hallway, obscuring the stairs from view.'

'Jeepers. What is it with that kid and making his socks fly?'

'Who knows,' she replied. 'But, ever since you went away, Michael has been trying hard to fill your shoes, bless him. At least he hasn't set fire to the bed, like you used to do when you were little.'

'I don't remember that.'

'Whenever you had a nightmare, the bed would start smoking. We had to install a smoke detector in your room.'

'That bad, huh?'

'You were hard work all right,' she said. 'But I wouldn't want you any different.'

Julius smiled shyly. 'Well, why can't you just bring Michael and the two of you can visit at least?'

Mrs McCoy sighed deeply. 'Trust me, I would love to, but your Dad's finding it very difficult to move about easily. And you know how terrible he is with cooking as it is. I wouldn't want him burning the house down.'

'OK then, why not send Michael to me, by himself? You could get a couple of days of peace and quiet with Dad. It sounds like you both need it.'

'I don't know Julius, he's still very young.'

'He won't get lost, honestly! Put him on the shuttle and I'll pick him up at this end. Where could he go anyway? Moon walking?'

'Funny man you are. What about the kidnappings? Tijara told all parents about it, even though, of course, we can't tell another living soul.'

'It's girls they're after. Michael will be fine.'

'Where will he sleep, though? He can't stay in Tijara at night.'

'Stop worrying, Mum! Look, why don't you ask Morgana's folks? I'm sure they'll be happy to take care of him.'

'That could work, actually,' said Jenny, relaxing a little. 'I'll ask them and let you know.'

'Thanks, Mum.'

'We'll miss you, darling. Take care now, and say hi to Morgana.'

'I will. Say hi to Dad.'

The video screen went blank. Julius was pretty sure the Ruthiers would be more than happy to bring Michael with them. Feeling a bit more content, and a little sleepy, he decided to follow Skye's example and have a short nap. '*At least I'll get to see one of my family,*' he thought to himself as he drifted off.

*

For their last Telepathy lesson, on Tuesday morning, Professor Beloi told them to pair up as usual, and then spread them throughout the maze. This time Julius worked with Morgana, while Skye and Faith joined forces for a change.

'*Pay attention now,*' said Beloi's voice in their heads. '*Does anyone remember what a Scrambler is?*'

All hands shot up simultaneously, to the delight of their teacher.

'*Mr Kashny?*'

'*A Scrambler is a device like a hair band. It was created by Clodagh Arnesh when she was a teacher in Tijara. When you wear it, it creates interference in your brain waves, so that no one can read your thoughts.*'

'*That is correct. What else does it do? Miss Sundaram?*'

'*It can confuse the mind of anyone who comes too near the wearer, sir.*'

'*Very good. Today, you shall try to be reunited with your other half using Telepathy. However, I have fitted several Scrambler devices throughout the maze, with the sole purpose of hindering your efforts.*'

'Great,' muttered a depressed boy's voice to the left side of Julius, causing a few stifled giggles among the students.

'*Indeed, Mr Yuran,*' boomed Beloi's voice, making the Mizkis grab their heads in surprise.

'Sorry, sir ...' said Grigor Yuran, sheepishly.

Julius thought the task would be easy enough, despite the interference. However, it took more than twenty minutes before he was able to pick up even the faintest thought from Morgana. The Scramblers were viciously powerful, sending countless different signals through the air at the same time. No matter how hard Julius tried to focus on Morgana, he just couldn't reach her. Very occasionally, he caught a hint of her voice in the chaos and tried to follow it. He also tried sending powerful signals out to her, the equivalent of mind-shouts – but even that didn't always work. By the time the lesson ended, three hours later, not one pair had been rejoined, creating much frustrated chatter among the pupils the rest of that day.

The next few days passed uneventfully. Julius wasn't sure if it was just because of the missing girls, but a solemn atmosphere hung over the school, in stark contrast to the previous year. The teachers smiled very little, their faces often imbued with worry. As far as Professor Beloi was concerned, Julius wasn't sure what to think, given that he was very good at keeping his innermost thoughts to himself. Even Professor King, who was easily the most cheerful man Julius had ever met, was quite subdued. His embalmed reindeer, known to the students as Jeff, was parked in a corner of the classroom, looking sadly at the Mizkis through its glass eyes. Julius remembered with a smile how last year King had taken it for a crazy joyride above their heads, simply using his telekinetic abilities. The fact that he wasn't up to any similar tomfoolery this year was proof enough of his dampened spirit. The only teacher who seemed unaffected by the gloomy atmosphere was Professor Chan, who kept training them in the dojo at Olympic levels.

'I think this whole thing has made him worse,' said Skye, at the end of a particularly painful abs workout.

'If that's even possible,' replied Julius from the floor. He was just lying there, panting in exhaustion.

'Someone needs to push me back to me room,' said Faith, resting his head against the wall, his arms hanging limply at his sides. 'Even the skirt is refusing to move.'

'Fat chance, mate,' said Skye. 'We'll have to sleep here tonight.'

'Class, on your feet!' cried Chan.

'Professor, please,' pleaded Lopaka feebly. 'I think I'm going to pass out, sir.'

Professor Chan examined the students sternly. Every single Mizki was sprawled out somewhere. Julius thought that they looked like bodies left behind after an explosion. Chan seemed to have reached the same conclusion, because his expression softened a little.

'In my days, children were made of stronger stuff,' he said. 'Where you are, just kneel and face me, please.'

The students complied as quickly as their sore limbs would allow.

'We train hard because what's happening out there is hard,' said Chan.

Julius noticed a subtle shift in the mood at those words. The groans eased up a bit and everyone seemed to listen intently.

'Over the mid-winter break, you will spend a lot of time outside Tijara. I don't need to remind you how serious the situation is, so I am asking you to be particularly careful. The ladies should not be left by themselves at any time. Respect the curfew and, if you spot anything or anyone suspicious, report it immediately. You'll find that the security in Satras is greatly increased these days, although they may be wearing regular clothes so as not to attract attention. Understood, Mizkis?'

'Yes, sir,' the class replied in unison.

'Very well,' said Chan, standing up. 'You have worked well this year. Enjoy your break. Dismissed!'

The students stood and bowed to him before leaving the dojo.

'Did you hear that?' asked Morgana, once they were outside in the promenade. 'Increased security. Are you sure it's a good idea going after that Oracle thing?'

'We knew there would be security, right?' answered Julius.

'Yes, but a normal level of it. Not undercover officers,' she replied.

'I'm curious, Julius,' said Faith. 'I want to know what this Oracle is all about. But you're the one risking getting caught. It's your call, mate.'

'I'm curious too, truth be told,' said Skye. 'If you decide to go, I'll share the blame if something happens.'

'Likewise,' said Faith.

'Of course, guys,' nodded Morgana.

'Thanks,' said Julius. 'Then it's settled. I'll go as planned.' Julius was touched by the show of support, but he sincerely hoped there would be no need at all to test their friendship.

*

It was a Zed tradition that during the week before New Year, all Mizkis were allowed 24 hours to spend with their visiting family. All games at the Hologram Palace were suspended, so that its holodecks could be used by the students and their guests for their main meals. It had been decided that, this year, the 2MJs would be hosting on the 26th of December. Morgana had told Julius that Michael would be coming up with her family and that they would have a traditional Japanese New Year meal. This news greatly excited Julius. For one thing, he loved Japanese history and culture, but he was also dying to wear his new kimono, a present he had received the previous year from Morgana's parents. Skye would be having the usual annual meal, hosted by the head of the Terra 3 space station. He wasn't particularly happy about their visit, though, and was showing all the visible excitement of a dead body. Faith, meanwhile, had decided that he would indulge his mid-winter craving for all things sun, sand and surf by taking his family for a virtual trip to Brazil.

On the morning of the last Sunday Julius, Morgana and her sister Kaori, headed to the Zed docks to collect their families. Julius' classmates were all there too, eagerly waiting for their relations. Minutes later, the Earth shuttle arrived and, when its doors opened, a river of smiling faces poured out onto the platform. Julius spotted the Ruthiers immediately. Alistair Ruthier was a tall man in his forties, broad of shoulders and rosy cheeked. Fujiko, his wife, was quite the opposite – a small woman also in her forties, with a face as smoothly perfect as a doll, and eyes as black as coal. It was easy to see which features Morgana had inherited from each of them: she had her dad's green eyes and physique and her mum's straight raven-black hair and delicate facial appearance.

'Hana-chan! Sakura-chan!' cried Mrs Ruthier as soon as she spotted her daughters.

Julius smiled as he heard the pet names. Morgana was Hana-chan, meaning "flower", while Kaori was Sakura-chan – "cherry blossom". Then Michael came pelting out of the shuttle, dodging a nearby family by a few inches, and ran to his brother. The hug he gave was as heartfelt as ever, but Julius noticed how he pulled away a bit quicker than normal, perhaps a sign that he was growing up and so becoming more self-conscious when it came to showing affection. However, there was no hiding his enthusiasm at being back in Satras. He was all big eyes and barely contained excitement as he stood there in front of his brother. Julius turned to Fujiko and Alistair, gave them a warm hug each and thanked them again for bringing Michael along.

'It is our pleasure,' she said. 'Besides, he was so excited about getting a chance to wear his new kimono!'

'Can you believe it, Julius?' said Michael, beaming. 'She got me one too!'

'I'll help you both to fit them properly tonight, before the meal,' said Alistair.

'We'll need the help, for sure,' answered Julius.

After collecting their luggage, they walked off together to the Moon-Hole Inn. It was the oldest of the hotels on the Moon capital and inside it was done up in the style of a large, wooden Swiss house. Its simple but charming interiors lent it a quaint, homely atmosphere. After checking in and receiving their room numbers at reception, they quickly dumped their belongings and headed out again towards the shopping area. Julius had told Mr and Mrs Ruthier that he wanted to spend some time alone with his brother, before they all met up again at the hotel to get changed for the meal. Of course, they were quite content with that, as they seemed just as eager to have some quality time with their girls.

Michael wanted to see all the gadget shops in Satras, lover of all things technological as he was. Julius was happy to oblige and took him to browse at Going Spare before proudly showing off his new PIP and shields, which left Michael positively green with envy. The meal was set to start at 15:00 hours, so Julius knew to avoid eating too much at lunch. With that in mind, they picked up a glass of freshly squeezed pomegranate juice each, along with a handful of falafels, and went down to the lake to eat them aboard one of the rowing boats.

'This lake is cool,' said Michael, touching the water with his fingers. 'It's so green and shiny.'

'Well, soon you'll be able to see it every day,' said Julius, finishing the last dregs of his juice.

'Yeah, I'll have to wait until the August session to do the test though, 'cause I'm not twelve until July.'

Julius thought he heard a little apprehension in his brother's voice. He looked at him closely, and sure enough he could see a tiny dark wisp floating above his head. 'You're not worried, are you Mickey?'

'A bit.'

'I was worried too, remember?'

'I know, but I'm not you, Julius. My skills are different, I don't even know if they're there sometimes. I mean, sure I'm great at making socks fly, but that's about it. You used to liquefy the bathtub!'

'I wouldn't be too concerned about it. Doctor Flip has always said that mind-skills come out at random times, and that adolescence can trigger certain abilities that may have been dormant before. I mean, there's this guy in my year, Barth – nice guy, and he has his moments, but he's a menace. His skills are nowhere near the class average, yet he's still here. I think you've definitely got more potential than someone like him.'

'Really?' said Michael, hopefully.

'Faith can tell you – he's his roommate. But just don't ask Morgana about him. Barth almost cut half her hair off with his shields.'

'And he's still alive?'

'Just.'

'Well, maybe you're right. I guess my skills will get stronger at some point.'

'Sure they will. You'll see.'

Julius thought for a moment about Michael's abilities. It was true that he had never noticed a wide variety of skills in his brother's repertoire but, then again, it was also true that different people developed in different ways. If nothing else, he was sure Michael would make an excellent technician and have a career in engineering, just like Faith. He looked at his brother again, and saw that the wisp above his head had turned from black to yellow.

'Ah, Michael-san,' said Julius, slipping into a mock Japanese accent, 'let us go get changed. Tonight, we wear kimono with honour, *neh*?'

'*Hai*, Julius-sama!'

They fixed each other with matching stern expressions and then broke into a fit of laughter. Calming themselves a little, they rowed to the side of the lake and disembarked. By the time they arrived at the hotel, they were in a great mood. At 14:00 hours, when they knocked on the Ruthier's door, Alistair answered – he was already magnificently decked out from head to toe in the traditional Japanese garb.

'Wow!' said Michael. 'You look just like a samurai!'

'Thank you,' he replied, and gave a polite bow. 'I've put the kimonos in your room, Michael. Let's get changed in there and leave the girls to do their thing.'

They went to the room next door, where Michael begged to be the first to get kitted out. Julius was happy enough to watch, as Alistair was so skilled at it that it was a pleasure to observe him. Michael was soon ready – his vibrant blue kimono making him look very smart indeed.

'Can I go show the others, please, please, please?'

Mr Ruthier chuckled. 'OK, go on then.' Once Michael had shuffled out of the room, he turned his attention to Julius. 'Your turn now.'

As Julius stood, arms in the air, being wrapped in the various layers, he tried to memorise the movements so he could attempt it himself next time.

'Very important,' said Mr Ruthier. 'Always drape the left over the right side. The other way is how you would dress a dead man for his funeral.'

'Good to know,' replied Julius.

'There now, you're ready,' said Alistair, tightening the sash and moving him over to the mirror.

'That's just! Thanks.'

They stood there in silence for a moment in front of their reflections, admiring the fine craftsmanship of the kimonos.

'I can't believe how grown up you are,' said Mr Ruthier. 'You know, it seems like yesterday that you and Morgana first met. You were just five years old then, when we moved in next door to you. Do you remember that day, Julius?'

Julius turned to face him and was surprised to see how worried he suddenly looked. Smoky wisps were pouring out from the top of his head.

'Kind of,' said Julius uncertainly, trying to recall. He hadn't thought about it in years.

'She was sitting in our front garden, playing with her doll, while we were unloading the car,' continued Alistair. 'Mr Johnson from across the street; his dog – I forget its name – got loose and ran across the road, barking like crazy. Fujiko had taken Kaori inside and I was carrying a chair. But you had seen everything and, as I turned my head, realising with dread that I would never get Morgana out of the way in time, there you came, striding across our lawn with your hand stretched out in front of you. I'll never forget how you shouted at that silly mutt, "Get away from her!", and next thing the dog flew backwards, as if someone had fired it out of a slingshot. Then Morgana ran up behind you and gave you the biggest hug, and you both just stood there, without saying anything, watching as the dog yelped all the way back to Mr Johnson. The look on his face – it was priceless – but I was in too much shock to laugh at the time.'

As Julius listened to the story, the memory of it came flooding back to him. It was strange to think how, in that one moment, as he stood with this girl he had never met before hugging his back, he instantly knew that she was someone he wanted to have around him forever.

'There's something awful happening in Zed,' said Mr Ruthier, his tone becoming very serious, 'and I bet the Arneshians are behind it. You *will* take care of my girls won't you, son?'

'Of course I will,' said Julius, sincerely. 'They are my family.'

Alistair nodded, satisfied. 'Glad to hear it.'

Just then, the door opened and Michael entered the room.

'Ah, right on time,' said Alistair. 'Are the ladies ready?'

Michael shook his head. 'Not yet. They say they need five minutes, and that yes that does really mean five minutes, and that I look great, and we should wait for them downstairs.'

'Well, that's a lot of information for one sentence,' said Mr Ruthier, grinning at the young boy. 'But I think I got it all. Come on then, let's go.'

With that, they left the room and caught the elevator down to the hotel foyer. Julius felt quite proud that Morgana's dad was showing such trust in him, to look after her and Kaori. But there was no doubt in his own mind that he would do everything in his power to keep them both safe, no matter the cost.

There were various people, guests and staff, milling about in the foyer. When the girls arrived, ten minutes later, everyone stopped what they were doing and turned to admire them. Morgana was wearing a lilac kimono with a striking, red-and-white pattern design on it, which Julius liked very much.

'*Good thing Skye's not here,*' he said to her, using a mind-message, as they walked through Satras towards the Hologram Palace. '*If he saw you dressed like that, he'd be developing a crush on you right now.*'

'*Shut up!*' she answered in the same way, blushing slightly.

Julius grinned and observed with curiosity the admiring looks thrown in the direction of Morgana and Kaori by the older Mizkis. He had to admit, they did look beautiful in their kimonos, with their dark hair gathered up in picturesque swirls at the tops of their heads. Julius noticed a few of the students also looking at him, but he wasn't sure exactly why. Perhaps it was to do with the stories of the inorganic draw he had performed last year, or his Solo record, which had given him a level of unwanted fame in Tijara. Maybe it was for no other reason than the novelty of him being dressed in a kimono, escorting the two pretty girls to either side of him. Whatever the reason, he began to feel quite uncomfortable and hurried his steps toward the Palace.

When they arrived, the security guards invited them to use the door on the left. Morgana led the way downstairs, until they reached the lift that would take them to their holodeck.

Kaori stepped in front of the metal door and gave the command: 'Computer – activate 4MA Ruthier.'

The door opened and they all stepped inside the lift. A few seconds later, the opposite door opened, leaving Julius and Michael gaping in wonder at the site beyond it.

'Welcome to Ritsurin-Kōen garden,' said Morgana and Kaori together, stepping out and turning to bow to the others.

'What a wonderful choice, girls,' said Fujiko, clapping delightedly.

'And it's all ours for the night,' added Kaori.

As Julius took a few steps into the garden, the crisp, fresh air hit his nostrils and awoke his senses. He breathed deeply, enjoying the smell of wet pine trees, his eyes basking in the brilliant, virtual landscape. A walking path wound its way around and over several koi-filled ponds and islands, which all interconnected by wooden bridges. He ambled along behind the others, fully distracted by the beauty of the trees, until Morgana joined him.

'I knew you'd like it here,' she said.

'It was the perfect choice to inaugurate my new kimono. By the way, where is this exactly?'

'Takamatsu. It's in the Shikoku province.'

Julius nodded. They were now approaching a *ryokan* – a traditional Japanese house. It was a low wooden structure, raised up a few steps from the ground. Outside the doors were two pots, each containing three sawn-off bamboo shoots surrounded by pine tree sprigs.

'This is called *kadomatsu*, Julius,' said Kaori, pointing at one of them. 'It's a traditional decoration of the New Year Holiday. We place two of them in front of homes to welcome the *kami* – the spirit – of the harvest, so that the next crop will be bountiful.'

Julius absorbed every detail and piece of information he was given, eager as he was to learn more about this fascinating culture. By now he knew that, as he entered the house, he had to remove his shoes before stepping onto the *tatami*, a woven rush-grass mat used for covering the floor. Everyone wore *tabi*, the split-toed socks used for walking around inside the house.

Fujiko bowed to the holomaids that would attend to them, waited as they slid the *shoji* screen-door open and then entered the dining room. Julius followed her, stopping to bow slightly as he passed the maids. Inside was a low, short-legged table in the centre of the room, surrounded by several floor-cushions. Julius was directed to kneel between Alistair and Michael. As everyone settled, he let his eyes wander around the room. The paper screen walls enclosed them on all sides, except one that instead gave way to a large window overlooking a well tended Zen garden. It was surrounded by three red brick walls, the furthest of which had an alcove set into it, housing a hanging picture-scroll and a delicate flower arrangement.

'*Akemashte omedetō gozaimas!*' said Fujiko.

'*Tanjōbi omedetō gozaimas, Morgana,*' added Kaori.

Julius and Michael stared blankly at them, not understanding what had just been said.

'Happy New Year,' explained Morgana. 'We never seem to be together for that *and* my birthday, which is what Kaori was saying, so we use this occasion to celebrate both.'

'Well, happy New Year and happy birthday, then!' said Michael.

Soon, the holomaids brought them a hot towel each to wipe their hands and faces, along with some warm *sake* and *oolong* tea. Next came the food, which was laid out on heated plates at the centre of the table.

'During New Year,' explained Fujiko, 'we eat a special selection of dishes called *osechi*. Right now on the table you can see rice, boiled seaweed, fish cakes, mashed sweet potatoes with chestnut and sweetened black soya beans. But nowadays people will also have whatever other food they want. I've asked the girls to order some *sushi* and *sashimi* for you, Julius, since I know that you like them so much.'

'*Dōmo arigatō gozaimas, Fujiko,*' said Julius bowing his head. 'This is just!'

The meal continued through the afternoon in a festive atmosphere. It felt very much like it was really New Year's Eve, which Julius thought was probably a good thing, since he knew he was going to miss the actual party on the night, thanks to the Oracle-quest. For the present, though, he lost himself in the day. He knew that the food itself was generated by a magnetic field and that they were only able to eat it because of the energy-to-matter conversion, but he was still astounded by the quality and flavour of it.

After the meal, they took a stroll through the garden to digest and savour the tranquillity of the place. The Ruthiers wanted to hear about everything that was going on in Zed, and how each of them was doing in, and out of, school. Jenny and Rory McCoy had specifically asked them to check how everything was going with Julius, or as Jenny had put it: "Please make sure you tell him I say he must eat properly – no good him nurturing his mind-skills if he's going hungry." And so, after a good hour discussing the kidnapping situation, Julius was put through a series of questions about any possible ailments, injuries or mental fatigue he may have been suffering, which made Michael laugh a lot as he watched his brother being interrogated like that.

'Laugh all you like, bro,' said Julius, with a raised eyebrow. 'Next year it will be you under the microscope. Never mind Mum and Dad – the school is worse. They even keep tabs on how many times you go to the loo.'

'They do?' asked Michael, looking genuinely worried.

'He's kidding you,' said Kaori, leaning towards him.

Michael glared at Julius, who was grinning cheekily, and then pounced on his older brother. Next thing he knew, Julius found himself in a headlock and his scalp getting the full knuckle-rubbing treatment from Michael.

'Geroffme!' laughed Julius, trying unsuccessfully to shake his brother off without using his powers, and thinking to himself, '*Man, the little tyke's getting strong.*'

Although Morgana had witnessed their little wrestling matches many times before, they always made her giggle, especially this time with the comical sight of Julius getting bested by his little brother like that. In fact, it made her laugh so much that she had to sit down.

The rest of the evening was spent playing games and eating sweets inside the house. By the time they finally left the holodeck it was well past eleven. Julius, Morgana and Kaori insisted on accompanying their guests to the hotel. Julius saw Michael back to his room, to be sure he had everything he needed. Michael barely managed to get himself changed into his pyjamas, sleepily half-brushed his teeth and then slumped onto the bed and instantly slipped off into dreamland. Julius stood there for a few seconds, listening to his gentle snoring, and a tiny smile touched his lips. He switched off the light and closed the door gently behind him as he left the room.

'*What a perfect evening,*' he thought to himself, as he padded along to the Ruthier's room, where he stopped and knocked lightly on the door.

'Morgana answered – she was looking a little bleary eyed, obviously tired out from the long day.

'You ready?' he whispered.

She nodded and, a few seconds later, Kaori joined them out in the passageway.

Mr Ruthier stuck his head out and said, 'Good night, son. And remember, keep your eyes open, OK?'

'I certainly will, sir,' answered Julius.

With that, the three of them headed back to Tijara for the night.

*

'It was great to see you, Julius,' said Alistair the following morning.

They were all standing on the dock platform, saying their farewells.

'You too,' said Julius. 'It was so nice to share your reunion with all of you. And thanks again for bringing Michael along.'

'That was our pleasure,' said Fujiko, taking a quick break from embracing her daughters. 'You know you two are like family anyway. Now come on, Ali – let's leave these fine young men to say goodbye to each other.'

She gave him a hug and then turned back to the girls, who were quickly swallowed up in a blanket of cuddles from their parents.

'Hey, bro,' said Julius, kneeling in front of Michael. 'Make sure Dad's leg heals fine. No more sock jokes for a while, OK?'

'OK,' he replied with a grin. 'I'll be careful.'

'Excellent. I'll see you in September, right here, on this platform. I'll come pick you up myself.'

'I hope so, Julius,' he said in a tiny voice, which was quite unusual for him.

'Come here,' said Julius, pulling him close. 'You'll be fine. You are a real McCoy, you hear me?'

Michael nodded, his face still buried in Julius' shoulder.

'We need to go now,' said Alistair.

Julius let his brother go, and watched as he boarded the shuttle. Morgana and Kaori stood by his side and waved to their family, until they had disappeared inside the ship.

'You're so sweet with your brother, Julius,' said Kaori, smiling.

Julius, who was entirely embarrassed about being mentioned in the same sentence as "sweet", turned a shade of crimson and headed for the nearest exit, trying hard to hide his face from her.

'I think it's lovely,' she said, ignoring his reaction. 'Well, I'm off, sis. See you for your birthday.'

Morgana waved to her as she left and then turned to Julius. 'Come on you, let's get back. And stop all that blushing or I might start thinking you have a crush on my big sister!'

Julius, now turning so red that he looked sunburnt, kept his head turned away and followed her back to the train.

*

On Friday the 31st, Julius woke up with a knot of anxiety in the pit of his stomach, which he was unable to rid himself of for the rest of the day. After lunch, he made his way into Satras with the rest of the gang, where they stopped by Twitch & Stitch to collect their evening suits for the New Year ball. He picked his up as normal knowing that, if he didn't, there would soon be word sent to Tijara. So, once out of the shop, he rolled up the new clothes and stuffed them unceremoniously into his rucksack. At six o'clock, they all headed over to Mario's for an ice cream.

'I've got a bad feeling about this,' said Morgana, sipping the last of her milkshake.

'You're not helping,' said Julius. 'Look, we said we'd do it, and this is the best way of going about it. I'll be careful and keep a low profile.'

'Let's synchronize our PIPs, guys,' said Faith. 'Time's a-tickin' and I need to get back and change. You know it takes me a bit longer. Julius, activate your video-cam option.'

Julius switched on his PIP and the familiar circular panel materialised above the palm of his left hand. With his right finger he scrolled through the menu options, until he found the video-cam, and selected it.

'I found a way to secure a channel just for us,' continued Faith. 'Select channel fourteen, Morgana's age.'

'Thanks, Faith. I feel ... remembered,' she said drily.

'My pleasure. Activate it now.'

Julius followed the instructions and was pleasantly surprised to see Faith's face pop into view on his monitor. He moved his hand in front of him, watching as the image moved over to Skye and then Morgana.

'It seems to be working,' said Skye, who had just activated his PIP. 'I can see what he's seeing now.'

'So can I,' added Morgana, peering at her own screen. 'Hmm ... my hair looks far too messy. Can't have that on my birthday, now can I?'

'We're all set then,' said Julius. 'Come on, let's get moving.' He walked the others to the exit, which was now packed with students, then made his way back to the lake and hopped into one of the boats that was moored by the shore. Rowing out to the centre of the lake, he concealed himself beneath one of the many small bridges and waited for the Mizkis to return to their schools. The ball normally started at 20:00 hours, which meant that very soon he would be alone. He could see plenty of adults, with and without Zed uniforms, walking about, but none of them seemed to take any notice of him. Julius lay back in the boat, underneath the seats, selected an e-magazine on his PIP screen, and began his vigil.

*

'Julius, come in,' said Morgana's hushed voice.

Julius sat up, startled. He had fallen asleep without even noticing. He lifted his palm and blinked at the PIP, which was displaying an image of Morgana's face.

'Did you fall asleep?' she asked, concerned.

'Obviously,' answered Julius groggily. He felt sore all over from lying on the hard wooden floor of the boat for so long.

'It's almost midnight.'

'Really?' said Julius, suddenly wide awake. He checked his watch and realised he had fifteen minutes to go. 'Shoot! Any news from your end?'

'No. No one's noticed your absence. Mind you, we've kept a very low profile. Apart from Skye, who's been dancing with every girl he could find, of course.'

'No surprises there, then,' said Julius. 'Here's been quiet enough. There aren't many people about. Most folks are either in the Palace or in the bars upstairs.'

'How are you going to get near the stat … ouch! Skye, watch those dancing feet of yours, will you?'

'Sorry. Where is he?' he heard Skye ask, then: 'Faith, come here quick!'

For a few seconds there was a bit of confusion as first Skye and then Faith squeezed their faces into view next to Morgana's.

'You could use your own PIP, you know?' said Morgana, getting slightly crushed between their heads.

'But this is much more cosy!' said Skye, merrily.

Julius shook his head, and said, 'Happy birthday, Morgana. What are you guys doing?'

'Making sure you don't fall asleep again, by the sound of things! And moral support, of course,' answered Faith. 'We snuck out into the garden. Are you still out on the lake? It's almost time. Hurry!'

'I'm afraid to sit up, in case someone sees me,' whispered Julius.

'Switch to video-cam mode and hold your PIP up,' said Skye. 'We'll check for you. A holoscreen will be less visible than your big head.'

Julius lifted his hand slowly above him, until the screen was sticking up over the rim of the boat.

'All clear, mate,' said Faith. 'I think it's time for you to pull a Jeff.'

Julius understood what was meant by that. He needed to use his telekinetic skills to move the boat near the statue, just like Professor King had done the previous year with his now infamous dead reindeer. First though, he would have to pinpoint exactly where the statue was. 'Where do I go, guys?'

'From your position, you need to go east,' said Skye.

'No, it's west,' added Morgana.

'Good job I'm the navigator,' said Faith. 'Go north.'

Julius, who was now totally confused, thought it would be best if he had a look for himself and so quickly popped his head up, checked where the statue was and then lay back down again. 'Guys, I'm going south,' he said.

'I knew that,' mumbled Faith.

'Shhh!' said Morgana. 'Let him concentrate.'

Julius focused his mind on the prow of the boat, as he needed to turn it to face in the right direction first. Once he had successfully done that, he willed the boat towards the statue. He had to move really slowly, so as to mimic the speed of a drifting object and not arouse any suspicion from anyone who might happen to be passing by. There was no sound from his PIP, as the others had gone deathly quiet. Julius could tell they were feeling as tense as he was. Occasionally, he would bring his hand up, so they could check he was moving in the right direction, and that no one was staring curiously at the boat.

'Slow down,' whispered Morgana. 'You're almost there.'

Gently, Julius brought the boat to a halt. He felt a slight thud against the keel as it bumped against the side of the lake and came to a stop.

'The statue's just there,' said Skye. 'Keep your head down and your PIP up. We'll watch what happens for you.'

'And I'll keep an eye out,' added Morgana.

Julius nodded. He pressed the record button on his monitor, propped his hand on his bent knee and adjusted its position so that they could see the foot of the statue. There were only a few minutes left, but it felt like ages to him as he lay there, trying hard not to move a muscle. Looking up, towards the ceiling, he traced the outlines of the various bridges that criss-crossed high above him, linking the upper tiers of Satras. He could hear various soft melodies drifting down from the different restaurants and bars, and his thoughts turned to food, which instantly made his stomach grumble.

Suddenly, Julius caught a hint of movement out of the corner of his eye, and he tensed up. He could have sworn that he had seen a shadowy figure peeking over the handrail of one of the bridges which passed just above the statue. But, as soon as he had looked up at it, the shadow had instantly retracted. His heartbeat quickened as he lay there, wondering what he had seen, but he didn't dare move. It could have been no more than a reflection from the water, or just someone passing by, he tried to reassure himself. After all it was New Year's Eve, so of course there would be people about. Since the figure hadn't reappeared, Julius forced himself to relax, although in the back of his mind he couldn't quite shake the feeling of being watched.

'Here she comes,' said Skye, excitedly.

Julius closed his eyes and focused only on her words. 'Well met,' he heard the soft voice of the Oracle say. 'I am glad you could join me again, here at our favourite spot. I am the second Oracle, and I will set you on the right path. My time is short, so hear my words. We shall meet again in fifty-five days from now, in the last five minutes of the day. Go to Pèsaro and touch the sea. The door that is revealed to you there will lead you once more to me. You will heed my words two more times. Remember, only the bravest can reach the end. Farewell, my bringer of life.'

Julius lay there for a moment, in case there was any more, but there was nothing to be heard except the intermingled music from the restaurants.

'The coast's clear, Julius,' said Morgana. 'Come on. Get yourself back to Tijara now.'

Julius quickly swung himself over the edge of the boat. He landed in the water, but here by the shore, the depth was low enough that his combat boots easily kept him dry. Moving stealthily, he zipped across to the far wall. Keeping himself close to it, he hurried towards the exit, hoping not to bump into any guards.

'Take the stairs,' said Skye. 'They're tucked away nicely. Besides, the lifts don't have any walls, so anyone would easily be able to spot you.'

Julius flipped his palm up and looked at the screen. He had almost forgotten about it still being on. 'Good thinking, mate. Surprised you managed to spot that with my PIP turned upside down and all.'

'Well, I've always been a bit different in the way I see things,' answered Skye with a grin.

Julius smirked. 'OK, I'm going to have to move fast now, so the view may get a little blurry. I want to keep my PIP on though. You make handy lookouts.'

'Quite right,' said Morgana. 'Now stop talking and get moving.'

Julius nodded and took the stairs in long strides, two at a time, almost running now. Once he reached the top of them, he crouched down behind a nearby pillar and scanned the broad terrace that overlooked Satras. It was empty. He was just beginning to edge forward when suddenly a mighty roar broke the air around him, and he leapt in fright. Then he heard the sound of raucous music, mixed in with cheering voices and realised that the bell must have struck twelve.

'Happy 2857, Julius!' he heard Morgana, Faith and Skye say in unison.

'Thanks,' he said, turning his screen upright again. 'Do you mind if I get out of here first?'

'Um, of course not. Sorry, mate,' said Faith sheepishly. 'Carry on.'

Fortunately for Julius, the security guard at Satras's main gate was so busy trying to hug a blonde female officer that it gifted him the perfect opportunity to slip past without being noticed. Not that Morgana and Faith were helping matters any.

'They're going to see him!' said Faith anxiously.

'He's turning! No, wait!' added Morgana.

'Look the other way! The *other* other way!'

'Wait a minute – she's not kissing him back!'

'Will you two shut up, or I really will have to turn this thing off!' hissed Julius, pressing his mouth against the monitor. 'They'll hear me for sure if you keep that up!'

'Sorry,' they both said, and fell quiet.

Once on the Intra-Rail platform, Julius waited for the train in the shadows of the nearby trees, only daring to emerge when it had come to a full stop and was about to leave again. In a flash, he leapt from his hiding place and darted inside, just before the doors shut.

'Good work,' said Skye. 'And now for the hard part.'

'Damn it!' cried Julius, slapping his forehead in frustration. 'Of course. How am I going to get past the Leven twins? We really should have planned this better. I'm dead now, for sure.'

'Well, before you go writing out your last will and testament, would you listen to us?' said Faith. 'It's not like we spent the night eating and dancing, you know.'

'That we did, actually,' said Skye. 'Especially dancing.'

'The point is,' interrupted Morgana, 'that we *also* figured out a way to distract the twins. So when you get off the train, hide somewhere until we tell you to move. And, by the way, put your suit on. We'll be quick. Over and out.'

Julius relaxed slightly, and once he reached the stop for Tijara, he did as Morgana had told him to. As he climbed off the train, he spotted a convenient and suitably large clump of bushes, which he hid behind and began to undress. His suit was badly wrinkled, but somehow he didn't think people would take much notice of that. He was just about to get changed into it when he heard Morgana's voice yelling from the direction of the school entrance. He looked up in alarm, and without thinking twice, sprinted for the gate, clutching his suit, dressed in nothing but his underwear.

'*Something's wrong. Oh, please don't let her be kidnapped!*' He thought desperately to himself as he ran.

He could hear an almighty commotion of some sort coming from the foyer and, when he passed through the gate, he saw the Levens running towards the promenade. Julius sprinted after them, still oblivious of the fact that he was wearing next to nothing. When he reached the corridor he almost tripped over the twins who, for some reason, were lying on the floor. He managed to hurdle them, but landed in a puddle of water, skidded madly and careened face-first into the large fountain which surrounded the assembly hall, creating a tidal wave that soaked the floor. He sat up, feeling completely bedraggled – spluttering and spurting water out of his mouth. He wiped his eyes and saw Morgana, Faith and Skye standing under the waterfall, soaked from head-to-toe. As if that wasn't enough, just then Captain Foster entered the scene and stood there, arms folded, surveying the carnage in ominous silence.

Ten minutes later they all found themselves standing in Foster's office, waiting to discover just how bad their punishment would be. They each had towels wrapped around their shoulders and were trying to dry out as best they could. They looked like a line of well drowned rats.

'I have been working in this school for many, many years,' said Foster, standing up behind his desk. 'But I have *never* witnessed a scene like tonight's. Would anyone care to tell me what you were doing in that fountain, *with or without* your clothes on?'

Julius, who had no idea what had happened in the seconds preceding his amazing entrance, decided to let this one pass. Besides, he had already done quite enough work for one night, so he thought it only fair that someone else do the explanations for this one.

'Sir, it was just an accident,' said Faith, putting on his best "responsible adult" voice. 'We were a little overexcited about the whole New Year thing, and so we thought we'd start the year off with a dare. So Mr McCoy, Mr Miller and meself challenged each other to a little *mind-swim* race in the fountain, to see who could do the fastest lap around the assembly hall. Very silly, I know. We apologise profusely for that.'

'And?' said Foster, clearly not satisfied with the story.

'I slipped and fell into the water before I was able to deactivate me skirt, sir. So Mr Miller jumped in to rescue me, so I wouldn't rust and sink to the bottom like a lost pirate's treasure. Then Miss Ruthier came looking for us, and seeing that we were clearly in distress, she jumped in to try help us as well.'

'*And?*' said Foster. Some of the edge had left his voice – he was obviously gathering some amusement from the situation.

'When our brave security officers heard the commotion, they rushed to see what was happening and slipped on the wet floor.'

Foster turned his head towards Julius, and then looked back at Faith. It was clear that he wanted an explanation for the half-naked student standing in his office. Faith swallowed, and nodded. 'Me Mum used to say that one should never go swimming with clothes on – me old crazy Uncle Jim used to do it all the time – anyway, Mr McCoy must also have been taught that. Unlike me, he decided to put those words into practice. He's very wise for his age,' he finished with a nervous grin.

It was taking Julius all of his strength to keep from bursting into laughter. He could feel a tear squeezing its way out of his eye, while he struggled to control the muscles in his face. To top it all off, his empty stomach let out an almighty rumble that ripped through the silence for a good few seconds.

'So sorry, sir,' he said, looking down. 'Swimming makes me very hungry.'

And that was it. Foster gave them a week-long ban from Satras, for inappropriate behaviour, and an extra week for cheek.

Faith started to say something, but the Captain fixed him with such a stare that he quickly clamped his mouth shut again. 'Count yourselves lucky I'm in a good mood tonight. Now, leave! Get yourselves dried up before you catch pneumonia.'

Once outside, as they walked back to their dorms, Morgana elbowed Julius in the ribs. 'You silly sod, I told you we were going to distract the twins. You should have just slipped in through the gate while you had the chance. What on earth were you doing running around in your undies?'

'I *was* getting changed when I heard you yelling and I thought, well … I didn't know what to think. I can't help it if you're such a great actor that you even fooled me.'

She smiled and put her arm around him. 'Well, I suppose I can't blame you for looking out for me, hey? Anyway, I'm tired now,' she said, yawning. 'I'll see you guys tomorrow. We can talk about what that Oracle said another time. We sure went to enough trouble for it.'

The boys waved goodbye as they went their separate ways.

'Come on,' said Skye. 'I've brought some food back to the room for you.'

Julius barely had time to get himself dried up, fed and into bed – he was fast asleep as soon as his head hit the pillow. All in all, it had been quite a night.

AN OLD FRIEND

'Fifteen days without games,' groaned Skye.

It was the first day of the year and, after a long lie-in, the Skirts had met under the oak tree, in the garden. Julius was munching on a slice of lemon and walnut cake, the last remnant of what had been a huge breakfast, even by Skye's standards. Now, with the entirely convincing midday sun shining down through the branches from Zed's shield, creating magical sparkling reflections on the surface of the stream, Julius felt finally and positively jam packed.

'I think we got lucky, actually,' said Faith. 'The Leven twins didn't even realise that Julius came from the front gate in the first place.'

'Narrow escape, if you ask me,' agreed Julius. 'I'll tell you what though, if the next clue turns out to be another curfew breaker, outside of the school's walls, I'm going to become very suspicious.'

'Speaking of the next clue,' said Morgana. 'I can't understand it at all. What's Pez ... Pesr ... and what sea are we supposed to touch?'

Julius activated his PIP and watched the recording he had made of the second Oracle. Faith, who was sitting by his side, leaned in to look.

'What's that word she's saying?' asked Julius? 'It starts with "P".'

'It sounds Italian to me,' added Faith.

'How do you know?' asked Skye in surprise.

'Me mum's family is Italian, remember, and this word sounds Mediterranean for sure. Let me check.'

Julius watched as Faith activated his PIP. Using a holographic screen meant a lot of finger-walking in midair, one of the peculiar things that Julius had observed about their new toys.

'Here it is,' said Faith, turning the screen towards the others. 'Lady and gentlemen, this is *Pèsaro*.'

'Are you sure that's what the Oracle said?' asked Morgana. 'I mean, that looks like a city ... on Earth.'

'In Italy, yeah. I'm fairly sure it is.'

'So, I take it this town is near the sea?' asked Julius.

'To be sure,' answered Faith. 'It's on the Adriatic coast.'

Julius looked at the others with a raised eyebrow and, judging from the silence, he knew they were all just as surprised as he was.

'That's that then,' said Skye. 'There's no way we can board a shuttle and head to Italy. End of story.'

'Yeah,' added Julius. 'That *is* a bit too much to ask.'

'Shame though,' sighed Morgana. 'I was enjoying this little treasure hunt. I guess we can check with the Hologram Palace and ask them what the prize was.'

'Hold on, guys,' said Faith, his nose remaining buried in his holoscreen. 'I don't think we need to go anywhere, except perhaps to Satras.'

'How come?' asked Julius.

'I know it's a long stretch, but hear me out. There's a connection between the town of *Pèsaro* and our local barber shop.'

'The *Barber of Seville?*' asked Skye, confused.

'Yes. The owner of the shop is this chap called Figaro Rossini, who told us that he's a descendant of *the* Rossini.'

'Who is ...' said Skye.

'Giacomo Rossini was a famous Italian composer. Centuries ago, mind you.'

'The guy that wrote the Barber of Seville!' said Morgana. 'That's a clever choice for his shop name.'

'OK, but I still don't see the connection,' said Julius.

'Rossini was born in *Pèsaro*,' concluded Faith.

Julius' mouth formed an O as he realised the meaning of this information. 'So the third Oracle could be *inside* his shop?'

'I think so,' said Faith. 'I can't really see how we're going to touch the sea, though.'

'Well, given that it's the only lead we have,' said Morgana, 'I think it's worth a try. We'll have to check the shop out as soon as this silly detention is over.'

Everyone agreed. Julius felt a tingling excitement creeping over him. Even if the lead turned out to be a dead end, he was glad they at least had *some* hope of finding the next clue. He was growing increasingly intrigued by the mysterious silver-clad lady.

*

As the lessons resumed that year, the students quickly slipped back into their routine. There was a strange sense of eagerness to learn in the air. Julius put it down to the two kidnappings. After all, none of them would want to be caught off-guard if it should happen again. There was a lot of talk in the boys' changing rooms about what they would do if they had to defend any of the girls from an assailant, and what mind-skills were best to use. There was no hint of false bravado in any of these discussions either. Julius genuinely believed that Mizkis were all about watching each other's backs.

He could only imagine what the conversations were like in the girls' dorm, given that they had the most to be worried about. He had been careful to keep a close eye on Morgana recently, and he knew that Faith and Skye had been doing the same. Whenever they were out in Satras, she was never left alone and even on the rare occasions when she went somewhere that they couldn't follow, like the ladies' room, there was always at least one of them close at hand, just in case. Julius wondered if she had noticed but, since she had not made any complaints about feeling "stalked", he had decided to not even broach the subject. Since Ife's disappearance, it also seemed like Skye had calmed down with his schoolboy crushes. Although he had only briefly become fascinated with her, during the previous Summer Camp, Julius knew her disappearance had affected him. A few times he had noticed Skye staring off into the distance, at nothing in particular, especially when he thought no one was watching. Once again, Julius had decided it was best not to bring it up, but to make sure his friend knew he was there if he needed to talk about anything. Julius wasn't particularly good with the whole bonding thing when it came to people who weren't his direct family, or Morgana. Regardless of that, he knew deep down that Faith and Skye were becoming close enough to him that they may as well have been his brothers.

On a Tuesday afternoon, after changing into his tracksuit, Julius headed for the dojo. Professor Chan motioned the students to enter and kneel in three rows before him. All eyes were turned to the wooden box at his feet, as today they would finally be given the famous Gauntlet.

'As promised, Mizkis,' began the Professor, 'today you shall receive your own personal Gauntlet. How many of you have used a Sim-Gauntlet in Satras before?'

Julius and the rest of the Skirts immediately raised their hands, followed by about half of the class.

Professor Chan nodded, then opened the top lid of the box and started handing the Gauntlets out to the students. Once he received his, Julius was pleased to see that it looked largely the same as the one he had used before in the Hologram Palace.

'During your Combat games,' continued Professor Chan, 'you aim and tighten your fist in order to shoot. It is the same with a real Gauntlet. Moreover, as the energy leaves your body, it will be coloured, normally in yellow, same as the ship catalyst's beam. Now, before you put them on, I want you to listen to me very, very – and one more time – very carefully, without touching anything until I tell you to.'

The class looked up at Chan, puzzled by the unusual request.

'There is a red dot at the beginning of the hard ridge, right above your wrist. That is the safety button. To make it active you need to press it with your finger. Each safety has been built with your own unique fingerprint programmed into its memory, so it will only work when it is being used by its rightful owner. The reason for all these precautions is that this device is not a toy. When you wear it, you must always check that the safety is on. A few years back, an actor was performing for our Zed officers in Satras. He was killed by a round of applause from an excitable individual who had forgotten to do this.'

Julius stared at Chan, horrified.

'I trust, 'continued Chan, obviously enjoying the facial expressions of his students, 'no one here wants to kill their friend with a handshake, correct?'

The Mizkis shook their heads earnestly.

'I thought so. Put them on now and go line up against the back wall.'

Julius stood between Skye and Faith, while Morgana made sure that she was as far away from Barth as possible, without actually leaving the dojo altogether. Chan clapped his hands twice and, out of thin air, thirty dummies materialised – one to each student.

'Activate your Gauntlets now and, when you're ready, you can begin. To start with, just try to aim and hit your target.'

Julius watched as Chan moved swiftly out of the way, then he pressed the red safety button. The Gauntlet instantly began to vibrate and tightened slightly around his right hand. Making a fist, he took aim at the dummy's head and squeezed. Immediately, a yellow beam shot outwards and crashed into the chest of his target, propelling it backwards.

'Wow!' he cried, and turned to watch his friends.

'Try harder,' ordered Chan over the noise. 'I want to see those dummies crash against the opposite wall.'

Julius didn't need to be told twice. This time he focused harder and squeezed his fist closed even tighter. The dummy flew backwards as if hit by a meteor, striking the wall like a freight train.

'This is incredible!' yelled Barth, waving his armed hand about excitedly. 'Oops, sorry,' he then added, quickly lowering his hand after noticing how everyone had ducked down, covering their heads.

'Mr Smit!' shouted Professor Chan. 'If I so much as see you even vaguely pointing that at anything other than the dummy in front of you, you'll be taking its place while I use you for target practice! Is that clear?'

Barth gulped hard and nodded anxiously. His arm shot upwards like a bolt, pointed directly ahead of him. Sure enough, the next few beams he fired were deadly accurate, perhaps propelled by his fear of the Professor's wrath as much as anything else.

Fortunately, the lesson continued without any further incident. Julius was doing a good job of pushing his dummy back against the wall every time he tried, so Chan told him to try control his energy now, by moving the target back only a few feet at a time. Julius found this more challenging but, since controlling energy was also part of his training during Draw lessons, he figured this could only help.

'Good, Mizkis,' said Chan a while later. 'A suggestion though: it is all very good shooting with one hand when you, and your target, are standing still but, when you are moving around, as you would in a real combat situation, it is more stable if you do like so.' The Professor lifted his right arm in front of him and rested it on top of his left, wrist to wrist. 'This is better. Now try it.'

They all mimicked him and sure enough, by the end of the second hour, everyone was easily able to hit their mark. So, when they returned the following Thursday, Chan had them practising their Mindkatas, only this time using their Gauntlets. The 2MJs were positively abuzz with talk of it, so thrilled were they by this new gadget. Surprisingly, Morgana couldn't even stop talking about it during Pilot training that Friday – her favourite class. She was closely examining the Cougar's catalyst, asking if Professor Clavel would show her its inside. She wanted to know exactly how it worked and if there was any way it could be assembled onto a Gauntlet. Faith thought this a jolly good idea indeed, and insisted that they should find a way of doing so without delay. They were so obsessed with this idea that they didn't even notice Clavel trying to explain how there was a high probability that their brains would explode as a result of a reverse stream of energy, should their new invention overheat. Julius and the rest of the class listened with great amusement to this heated debate, while calibrating their own catalysts.

On Monday the 17th of January, the last bell rang, signalling Julius and his friends to rush from their Shield lesson as if the classroom had been set on fire. Two weeks away from Satras was a hard price to pay for any detention. Their eagerness was even more heightened because they were desperate to test their theory about the third Oracle. They headed straight for the Intra-Rail platform, where they boarded the train and were in Satras a few short minutes later. Julius led them towards the barber shop, navigating along the shortest and least crowded route among the maze of paths and bridges that was the main shopping area.

'Here we are,' he said, stopping outside the entrance to the *Barber of Seville*. The shop was empty, except for one man who was having his face slapped with aftershave. 'What are we going to say to him?'

'I'll ask him some questions about music,' answered Faith. 'But I think someone should get a haircut too.'

'Don't look at me,' said Morgana defensively. 'Especially not after the Barth catastrophe.'

'Fair enough,' said Julius. 'Skye will do it then.'

'Why me?'

'Because Julius and I have already had one,' said Faith. 'While you were busy kissy-facing that Pippa Coleman girl from Sield School.'

'All right then,' said Skye, resigned to his fate.

Faith opened the door and waited for the others to enter, before following them in. As had happened the last time he had been in the barber shop, Julius was immediately enveloped in a cloud of soothing aromas, from the smell of the leather on the swivel chairs, to the aftershave.

'Hello! *Benvenuti*,' cried Mr Rossini, with his usual joviality. 'Have a seat and I will be with you shortly.'

They entered quietly and sat down on the chairs lining the back wall. As they waited, Julius casually inspected the room with his eyes. One thing he had not noticed on his previous visit was that the shop also seemed to be a kind of small museum of barber history. As well as the typical shelves containing various hair products – razors, scissors and towels – there were also glass cabinets containing heavily rusted iron blades and old, dishevelled brushes. He noticed a single, closed door at the other end of the shop, and felt sure that they would have to check it out somehow, to see where it led.

'So, what can I do for you today?' asked Mr Rossini, bowing with a flourish to them.

'I would like a trim, please,' said Skye, trying to sound like he sincerely wanted one.

'Excellent. Come this way then.'

'Mr Rossini,' said Faith, following them to the chair. 'If you don't mind, could I ask you about your ancestor, the composer?'

'But of course!' Rossini answered, seeming very pleased. 'Ask away, my boy. I knew it when I saw you last time – you have a very keen ear for music. So, what would you like to know?'

Faith proceeded to ask the most bizarre questions he could think of, so as to keep the barber's mind focused on Skye's hair and the topic at hand. Meantime, Julius and Morgana strolled around the shop, acting as if they were merely looking at the curious displays spread around the room.

'*Morgana*,' said Julius, with his mind.

'*I can hear you,*' she said, walking over to him, still pretending to observe the items in the glass cases.

'*I don't see much in this room that could help us,*' said Julius. '*But there is a door in the back that we should check out.*'

'*I see it,*' said Morgana, glancing in that direction. '*I'll go. You keep him busy.*' Then Morgana turned to the barber. 'Sir, can I use your bathroom please?'

'Sure. It's in the back,' he said pointing towards the door with his head.

Julius grinned and walked towards the opposite end of the room, where he stopped in front of one of the cases, containing a particularly old foam brush which had very few bristles left on it.

'Mr Rossini,' he said. 'Why did you keep this old brush?'

The barber turned towards him, scissors in midair, and looked at the display. 'That "old brush", as you call it, belonged to Marcus Tijara, young man,' said Rossini proudly.

'No way!' cried Julius, pressing both palms against the glass.

'This business has been here since the beginning of Zed, and many important backsides have sat on these very chairs – well, the cushions have to be changed every fifty years or so, but the chair frames are the original ones.'

'*It's a bit dark in here!*' Julius heard Morgana's voice say in his head.

He moved away from the display with the brush and resumed his stroll around the shop. '*Use the light from your PIP!*'

'*Good idea.*'

Suddenly, Julius stopped. Through one of the glass cabinets he had spotted a framed picture hanging from the wall. He moved as close as the glass would allow, his nose pressed against it, and squinted his eyes. It was a panoramic image of a seaside town, with the sun shining down on a calm, blue sea. A shiver ran down his back.

'Mr Rossini?' he said, continuing to stare at the picture. 'What town is this?'

The barber turned his head, still holding a strand of Skye's hair between two of his fingers. 'Why, that's Pèsaro,' he answered. 'It's the birth city of my family, the Rossinis. It's in Italy, you know?'

Julius nodded politely, but his mind was miles away. This had to be it – the Oracle's clue. But what exactly was he supposed to do with it? He concentrated, recalling the lady's words in his memory: something about going to Pèsaro and touching the sea, followed by something else, about a door being revealed. Trying to act casual, he stretched his arm behind the glass case and placed his fingers against the portion of sea in the picture. Nothing happened.

'Great,' he muttered under his breath.

'*What was that?*' said Morgana, in his mind.

'*What was what? Are you OK?*'

'*Yeah yeah, I'm fine. But I heard a click just then, somewhere in this room, like when a catch is released.*'

Julius looked at the picture again: '"*The door that is revealed there to you will lead you once more to me". That's what she said. Hang on, I'm going to do it again. I want you to try and figure out where the sound is coming from.*'

'*OK,*' answered Morgana.

He pressed his finger against the blue sea again and again, each time asking Morgana if she had managed to find the secret door. It took several attempts, but eventually she did.

'*Wait,*' she said. '*I can feel a draught coming from the floor – it's a trapdoor. I'm going to check it out quickly.*'

Julius couldn't do much more than wait and hope that no noise would filter through and alert Rossini. Five minutes later, Morgana reappeared in the shop, long strands of cobweb hanging from her hair and clothes.

As soon as Julius saw her, he grabbed her arm and dragged her out of the shop in a hurry, throwing a "We'll be back" in the direction of his friends. It took him a while to clean all the clinging threads off her, not least because she was jumping hysterically from one foot to the other, shaking herself as if she was covered in repulsive bugs.

'I hate insects! Especially in my hair,' she whimpered, trying to calm herself down.

Julius chuckled.

'I'm all right now,' she said, ignoring him.

Five minutes later, Faith and Skye walked out of the barber shop.

'What happened in there?' asked Faith, looking at the small pile of cobwebs and dust curls at Morgana's feet.

'Forget that,' she said. 'Let's move away from here.'

They walked over to the nearest bench, in the middle of one of the bridges, overlooking the lake.

'So I touched the sea in the *Pèsaro* picture,' said Julius, 'and it opened a trapdoor in the back room, which Morgana found.'

'It was in the corner of the room,' explained Morgana. 'It was half hidden by boxes, and judging by the layer of dust on the floor, it had been undisturbed for a while. So I had a look inside it. There was a ladder, which led down into a large empty room. It had no exits that I could see.'

'And you don't think Mr Rossini has been down there at all?' asked Skye.

'No way. I mean, the place was full of cobwebs and the air was stale. I could see a wall of dust in the light of my PIP and when I walked around the room I left the kind of footprints you would leave behind on the sand. I don't think anybody has been down there for at least a few years. We'll need to go back there one night, when the shop's closed.'

Julius stood up and shook his head. 'This is game over then.'

'What do you mean?' asked Skye.

'It's one thing breaking curfew ...' began Julius.

'... and another breaking and entering,' finished Faith.

Absolutely,' said Julius. 'Let's go speak to someone at the Palace. This is getting far too fishy.'

No one argued with him – they all knew he was right. You just didn't do these kinds of things on Zed. So, they made their way down to the Palace, hoping to find some answers.

As they entered through the gate, it became apparent that Mrs Mayflower had still not resumed her duties at the kiosk since the attack. Another woman was there working in her place but, seeing as they didn't really know her, they decided instead to speak to Mr Smith, the technician in charge of Flight games. They walked down to the right sector and approached his desk. He was busy signing in a group of 3MA students, so they waited in line for him to finish.

'Look who we have here,' said Mr Smith, happily. 'I haven't seen you guys since last year. What took you so long?'

'Hello,' said Morgana. 'We haven't abandoned you. This year we've just been trying our luck with the Combat games.'

'I know you are. The Skirts are already at the top of that scoreboard too, as you well know. I'm very impressed. So, are you here to fly?'

'Actually not,' replied Julius. 'We would like to ask you something, but I'm afraid it may sound a bit strange.'

'Ask away,' he answered.

'Is there some kind of bonus level built into the games?'

'What do you mean?' he asked, looking puzzled.

'For example, if you do really well during a Combat game, then a hologram appears with a puzzle and if you can figure it out, you get a prize.'

'Not that I know of,' he said.

'What about a treasure hunt?' asked Morgana, directly.

'No, sorry,' he said. 'But you know, an in-game bonus is actually a good idea. You don't mind if I run it by my colleagues, do you?'

'Be our guest,' said Faith.

'Mr Smith,' said Julius, 'are you sure there's nothing like that going on already?'

'McCoy, I don't know what you're trying to find out, but I'm telling you again, there are no bonus levels or treasure hunts present in our games. There never has been and I'm sure I would have been notified of any changes if they had been made, since I am one of the game programmers. Satisfied?'

Julius nodded and wandered off back to the arena, with the others in tow. Once there, they sat down in a quiet corner. None of them had said a word since they had left Mr Smith. Julius' mind was conjuring up all sorts of explanations. He really wasn't sure what to make of it. 'It's a prank, or an Arneshian stunt,' he said finally.

'Either way,' said Skye, 'shouldn't we tell someone? I mean, it doesn't seem likely that we can go meet the third Oracle now, does it?'

'I don't feel like telling anyone yet,' said Faith.

'I agree, actually,' said Julius. 'On New Year's Eve, the Oracle said she would meet us twice more. After Rossini's clue, there would be only one to go. Are we sure we want to give up now?'

'Of course not,' said Morgana. 'Besides, if we go to Cress now, he's going to find out about our last out-of-hours escapade and, if this turns out to be a hoax we'll have got ourselves into trouble for nothing.'

'OK, fine,' said Skye. 'How are we planning to keep this date with the third Oracle then? Because I'm telling you, I'd rather not get another detention. My mum has already "donated" one of my surfboards to a black hole, she was so angry about the last one.'

'That's easy enough,' said Julius. 'We're not going to be there at all.'

'I'm a tad confused,' said Faith.

'We're going to rig Rossini's basement with cameras, and watch the show from the comfort of our dorms,' said Julius.

'You know, McCoy,' said Faith, patting him on the knee, 'I thought you were dumb like a dumbbell, but I was wrong.'

'That's a brilliant idea, Julius,' said Morgana. 'It's agreed then.'

Julius couldn't help feeling rather pleased with his fine suggestion. All they needed to decide now was who was going to get the next haircut.

*

Early on Saturday the 5th of February, the Skirts left Tijara carrying a rucksack each. They got off the train at Satras station and headed straight for Pit-Stop Pete's shop, where they purchased ten night-vision mini-cameras, along with some cables and a few rolls of duct tape. Then they went to Going Spare, where Faith bought a special connector for his PIP, plus a handful of various other gadgets. Julius had no idea how all the pieces were meant to fit together, but that was Faith's area of expertise. From the moment they had decided to rig the basement, Faith's brain had gone into overdrive and he had spent the last three weeks devising the best way of building their surveillance system. Once he had finished his blueprint, his face had lit up with pride and he had handed the shopping list to them. Thankfully, between the four of them, they had enough Fyvers to allow them to buy all the stuff, and it was decided that they would proceed with their plan on the first available date.

'Here we go again,' said Julius, standing outside The Barber of Seville. 'Who's getting the haircut, then?'

'You are,' answered Morgana. 'Faith has to rig the basement, Skye has had one recently and, well, I'm a girl, so I don't need one right now, and certainly *not* from a barber.'

'OK, I get it,' sighed Julius. 'Come on, let's go.'

As they stepped into the shop, Mr Rossini stood up and opened his arms to them.

'My friends! What a pleasant surprise!' he cried.

'Good morning, sir,' said Morgana, smiling her most charming smile. 'The boys just can't get enough of you.'

'You honour me with your presence,' he said with a bow. 'Who will it be today?'

'Me,' said Julius walking towards the chair. 'Not too short please, but less wild.'

'Mr Rossini,' said Faith in a small voice, 'is it OK if I use your bathroom for a moment? It's me skirt, see, there's something wrong with one of the panels and it's hurting me leg quite badly.'

'But of course,' said the barber, looking at Faith with concern. 'Right at the back and take your time, brave young man.'

'Thanks, sir,' he answered. Then he collected everyone's rucksacks and disappeared with a "*They're for me spare parts.*"

'Does he always have to carry those bags around?' asked Mr Rossini, after Faith had gone.

'Today he's travelling light, actually,' answered Julius, looking extremely serious, and leaving Rossini speechless. 'But let's worry about my haircut now.'

'And since we are here,' added Skye, 'why don't you tell us more about your famous ancestor, Giacomo Rossini?'

Mr Rossini looked like his birthday had come early; he was more than happy to indulge them, and started a long and colourful story that covered most of the 19th century and all of the 20th. However, by the time Julius was ready, Faith had still not re-emerged from the basement and so they allowed Mr Rossini to carry on with his musical history to cover the 21st century too. Although the barber had a knack for storytelling, Julius was ready to pass out there and then from sheer boredom. Just as he was beginning to despair, Faith joined them again, with a triumphant smile and four empty rucksacks.

'Thank you, sir,' said Faith, 'I really needed that.'

'Don't you worry. This shop will always be open to you and your friends. Well, come back and see me when your hair gangs up on you again.'

'Thanks. Will do.' said Julius as they left the shop.

Once they had put a safe distance between them and the barber shop, they stopped.

'All done,' said Faith. 'I was able to create a circular rig on the ceiling, so we've got all angles covered.'

'Good job you had the skirt so you could hover upwards,' said Skye. 'Because trying to pass a stepladder off as a repair kit for your skirt would have been a real stretch.'

They laughed and walked back down to Satras's main floor area. To celebrate their success, they decided to challenge each other to a Flight game, for old times' sake, an idea that yielded another top time record among the 2MJs of Zed.

*

The live feed from the cameras was only accessible through Faith's PIP, so it became quite common to see Julius, Skye and Morgana – individually, or together – staring into Faith's holoscreen at every opportunity. After a while, they even stopped asking him for permission and would sometimes just grab his hand as they passed him in the corridor, for quick peeks. At mealtimes, Morgana could be found sitting next to Faith, a fork in her left hand, which she used to distractedly eat her food, and her right holding up his hand so she could stare at his holoscreen. Sometimes she would pass his hand over, like a box of sweets, to Julius or Skye. Faith didn't seem to mind, strangely enough. In fact, he had got into the habit of leaving his PIP tuned into the surveillance channel and become adept at doing pretty much everything with his right hand only.

Thankfully, their classmates didn't seem to have picked up on this odd behaviour which, according to Skye, was probably because the Skirts were becoming known as a naturally odd bunch anyway. There was only one occasion, when Ferenc Orban and Lopaka Liway had asked them what on earth they were up to. They had merely been told that it was important, top secret experimental research on Faith's skirt, as authorised by Pit-Stop Pete, supreme maker of said skirt. Faith's serious look discouraged them from asking any further questions.

Julius soon grew certain, as did the other three, that there was no fear of Mr Rossini finding the cameras. In fact, they were pretty sure he didn't even *know* that there was a basement in his shop to begin with. Watching the feed so regularly was just a way of biding time, like the way a person would sometimes unconsciously keep checking their watch, as if that would hurry time itself.

Once though, Julius and Faith could have sworn they had seen a shadow moving in a corner of the room. They rewound the footage and checked it several times. Then they showed it to Morgana and Skye, not telling them what to look for, to see if they too would catch a glimpse of the mysterious shadow. In the end they had all agreed that something had indeed moved in front of the camera, but since it wasn't spotted again on any of the other footage, they let it go.

After what seemed an eternity, Thursday the 24th finally arrived. Julius was very excited and quite unable to concentrate for more than a few minutes at a time, which, funnily enough, turned out not to be a problem during that morning's Meditation lesson. Professor Lao-tzu had asked half of his students, including Julius, to wear Scramblers while trying to communicate with a partner. So when Barth, who had been paired with Julius, was unable to perceive even half a thought and was getting redder and redder from the effort of concentrating, it was attributed to the Scrambler's powers, rather than to the fact that Julius wasn't really trying at all.

Lunchtime was spent peering over Faith's shoulder for the usual checks of the "just in case" variety. Thankfully they had Martial Arts in the afternoon, so were kept seriously busy by Professor Chan and the fresh excitement of fighting with the Gauntlet. As they sat down for dinner that night, Faith decided that he needed to rest his left hand and kept his fist closed for the whole meal.

'So, where are we going to meet tonight?' asked Julius, wiping his mouth and leaning back in his chair.

'If it wasn't for the small issue of Morgana's gender, I'd say the boys' dorm,' said Faith.

'That's OK,' said Morgana, with a cheeky grin, 'I feel up for some mischief tonight. Besides, I've been left on the bench too much already. Coming over to your dorm is not going to be a problem.'

'What's the penalty if they catch you in a boy's room?' asked Skye, 'I'd just like to know for, um, future reference.'

Julius, Faith and Morgana stared at him in silence.

'Never mind,' said Skye, 'Just kidding.'

'Well I don't know what would happen, but I'm pretty sure it's not allowed. I'll be careful,' she said.

'I'll tell you what,' said Faith, 'I can feel a plan hatching. Meet me in the foyer of the girls' dorm at 23:30. Oh, and wear trousers.'

'OK,' said Morgana, looking suspiciously at him.

Julius decided that it was better not to ask. The others disappeared off, but he spent another hour relaxing in the garden discussing extravagant Ottoman rulers with Ferenc Orbán who, like Julius, had a passion for ancient history. Gustavo Perez and Yuri Slovich sat nearby, staring mystified at them, as Julius and Ferenc eagerly discussed whether Selim the Sot had *really* drowned after drinking too much champagne, and about how Ibrahim the Mad had lost his marbles after being imprisoned by his brothers for twenty-two years. They ended off with an animated debate on who had been the best sultan – Süleyman the Magnificent or Mehmet the Conqueror – before retiring for the night.

Later that evening, there was a knock on his door. 'I told Barth we were filling in our diaries,' said Faith, entering the room and closing the door behind him.

Julius was sitting at his desk, finishing off a letter home. 'Good,' he said, swivelling in his chair to look at Faith. 'I've checked, and all the 2MJs have turned in for the night. You shouldn't meet anyone from our year at least.'

'I'm really curious to know how you're going to sneak Morgana in here undetected,' said Skye, sitting up in his bed, where he had been lounging and watching a movie on his PIP. 'If it works, I might use it sometime in the future … for another purpose.'

'Just make sure I'm not here when you do that, you hear?' said Julius.

'Of course. My brain is already plotting the perfect plan,' said Skye.

'Yeah, we know where your brain is all right,' replied Julius.

'That would be in your pants, in case you're wondering,' added Faith.

Julius and Skye couldn't help but snigger at that, and were still laughing as Faith made to leave. 'I'm gonna go wait in me room, he said, pausing in the doorway. 'I'll keep a channel open, so you may wanna switch over when you're finished laughing.'

As soon as Faith was gone, Julius moved over to Skye's bed and plonked himself down next to him. Skye had turned to the open channel and Julius shoved him to the side so he could see the holoscreen properly.

'He's right, you know?' said Julius.

'What, you mean about my brain?' said Skye. 'I can't help it. Girls just have this effect on me. It's like I need them to know that they can count on me, that I can protect them. They're so different to boys; so adorable and … uh, I don't know. It's difficult to explain, I guess.'

'Ah, we're just messing with you. We know you mean well. Besides, I reckon every girl needs a gent like you around. Although, I doubt most of them would be happy to share you with the competition.'

'Yeah, I've already learnt that lesson with Pippa,' said Skye. 'She got all jealous and upset, 'cause I asked her about her roommate.'

'When?'

'On our first date – the one by the lovers' statue?'

'You're kidding, right?'

'Nope. She just got into a huff and cut our date short.'

'No wonder! I mean, come on. I'm no expert at this dating stuff, but even I know that one at a time is the decent thing to do. You're some guy, you know that?'

'I agree,' said Faith's voice from the PIP.

'Me too,' said Morgana. 'I hope you knew I was online by the way.'

'Uh huh … sure,' said Skye, clearing his throat and fidgeting nervously. 'No problem.'

'One bit of advice though,' said Morgana. 'Keeping your options open is of course an option, but I would highly recommend that you make that clear to whoever you're dating at the time, 'cause hurt feelings aren't funny.'

Julius stared at Skye with an expression that clearly said, "I told you so."

'Of course,' answered Skye, feeling glad that she couldn't see him blushing.

'Right, now, everyone shut it,' said Faith. 'Press the mute button. I don't want anybody hearing your voices. Morgana, I'll be there in a minute.'

Skye muted the sound on his holoscreen and the two boys watched as Faith left his room. To all of their amazement, they saw that he was carrying a wakeboard, which he placed on the floor in the middle of the corridor. He hovered over it, slipped his feet inside the straps and tightened them as much as he could above his boots. When he floated upwards, the board went with him.

'What the … Hey! That's the board I use in the Palace for waterskiing!' said Skye.

'It'll be all right. He normally knows what he's doing,' said Julius, trying to sound reassuring.

'Yeah, normally.'

Faith continued his ascent, looking as if he was actually riding waves and enjoying the sun. When he reached the promenade, he continued in the same fashion towards the girls' dorm.

Julius saw Morgana's mouth drop open as Faith appeared in the foyer. She had been hiding behind a plant and emerged into the open as he stopped in front of her. Faith freed his feet and gestured for Morgana to sit down in the middle of the board. Despite the lack of sound on Skye's screen, it was clear from Morgana's hand gestures that she was saying something along the lines of "Are you out of your mind?". Faith, in reply, pointed at his watch and made as if he was about to turn away. Morgana quickly stopped him, then stepped onto the board, gathered her legs up and buried her head between her knees.

'Tell me he's not really going to …' started Julius.

Sure enough, Faith hovered above Morgana and gently descended over her, his conical skirt covering her like a tea cosy.

'He's unbelievable,' said Skye, sounding impressed.

'Yeah, and *she's* awfully brave,' added Julius. 'Let's hope he doesn't let one out, or we might have a blue, comatose girl coming our way.'

It took Skye a few seconds to realise what that remark meant, but as it sunk in, he howled with laughter, while Julius tried to keep his friend's hand steady so he could continue watching the PIP.

Faith, meanwhile, slipped his feet back into the straps and shakily took off again. He was swaying a little from the effort of keeping his balance but he soon managed to inch forward in the direction of the boys' dorm.

Skye had managed to pull himself together and was now glued to the screen again. In fact, he and Julius had grown so tense that neither of them had realised they were clutching each other's forearms. It was a bit like watching a silent horror movie, with Faith's various expressions their only indication of what was going on. Suddenly, he stopped in the middle of the promenade and stared intently ahead of him.

'What's happening?' said Julius.

'Is someone there?' asked Skye, tightening his grip on Julius' arm.

'Ouch! How should I know? I'm sitting here with you, remember!'

Faith looked around anxiously, then flew back into the girls' dorm foyer, and hid behind the wall.

That was when Julius and Skye managed to catch a glimpse of exactly what the problem was: three of the Professors – Morales, Chan and King – were taking an evening stroll through Tijara.

'They're really stuck now,' said Skye.

'We've got time. He just needs to be careful,' replied Julius, only half convinced by his own words.

Julius turned his thoughts to the layout of the school. All areas opened onto the promenade which encircled the assembly hall. Its black marble walls were in turn overlaid by the cascading water that ran into a fountain all around the base of the walls – the same fountain where they'd had their little incident on New Year's Eve. On the screen, he could see that the teachers had stopped between the entrances to the dorms, and were giving no sign of moving anytime soon. He knew they would have to distract them somehow, so that Faith and Morgana could sneak past safely.

'Skye, I think maybe you should go ask Professor Morales if she can help you with your Spanish.'

Skye didn't need to be asked twice. He leapt from the bed, stopped briefly in front of the mirror to smooth down his curls and dashed out of the door.

'I was kidding ...' said Julius. 'Oh, never mind.'

Two minutes later, Faith's camera zoomed in on Skye approaching the Professors. A few seconds after that, Julius was treated to a brief cameo of Faith staring into the camera and mouthing words that he took to be, "He's completely bonkers".

Whatever Skye had said or done, however, it seemed to have worked, as shortly afterwards Faith and his cargo were able to leave their hiding place and hover to a now empty corridor. When he turned into the foyer of the boys' dorm undetected, Julius let out a long sigh of relief. He hurriedly opened the door and ushered the crazy surfer into the room, then closed it again as soon as he had scanned the corridor to make sure that no one had woken up and noticed.

'Let me out!' said Morgana, knocking on the inside of Faith's metal skirt.

'Just a moment, woman. I need to land first!' he said, setting the board down. He hastily loosened the straps and hovered upwards. As he did so, Morgana rolled out onto the floor.

'I thought I was going to be stuck in there forever,' she said, stretching and breathing in deeply.

'Where's Skye?' asked Julius.

'That man, honestly,' said Faith. 'He greeted everyone, apologised for the late hour and asked to speak to Morales about an urgent matter.'

'Which was?' asked Julius.

'Apparently his brother is about to marry some two-timing Spanish woman, and he has decided to save the family honour by writing a letter, in Spanish, warning her to change her "wily" ways or risk being exposed to the whole family.'

'What did she say to that?' asked Julius, his eyes widening.

'She just put a hand on his shoulder, told him how brave he was and how many girls would appreciate that kind of attitude when he's older.'

'What? Is she completely dumb?'

'You gotta give it to him. He's got the whole puppy-eyes routine mastered,' said Faith.

'Apparently so,' agreed Julius.

'Then she took him off to the canteen so they could sit down and talk about it,' continued Morgana.

'Well, if he misses the Oracle, I guess he can just watch the recording,' said Julius. 'Speaking of, shall we get ready?'

They all sat down on Julius' bed, with Faith in the middle so they could watch his screen.

'I got a little upgrade just for the occasion,' said Faith, smiling proudly and switching on his PIP. The screen appeared to be twice as large as it had been before.

'That's just,' said Julius, impressed.

'That's what you're getting for your birthday,' said Morgana to Julius.

'OK guys, here we go,' said Faith, holding his hand out slightly in front of him so the screen was clearly visible to everyone.

The image they saw was the main angle from the trapdoor into the centre of the room, which they thought was the likeliest place for the Oracle to appear. Just to be sure though, Faith had placed the remaining cameras in positions that also covered the four corners of the room. Those other views were now minimised to icon size at the bottom of the screen. The night vision light created an eerie atmosphere: everything had a curious green tinge about it. Specks of dust floated around like snowflakes, before falling into the vague outlines of the shoeprints left behind by Morgana and Faith. Their eyes were soon drawn to the centre of the room, where the dust had begun to swirl and converge.

'There she is,' whispered Morgana.

Slowly, the shape of the lady began to form in front of their eyes, her silver mantle tinged by the green light. She looked up, straight into the main camera, almost as if she knew that it was there. Julius held his breath in anticipation of the new message.

'Well met,' said the Oracle. 'I am glad you could join me again. I am the third Oracle and I will set you on the right path. My time is short, so hear my words. He left Artemis speechless when he told her, "Be my bride"; or so Sir Pierre believed when he found her gift, and sighed. We shall meet again in fifty-five days from now, in the last five minutes of the day. You will heed my words one more time. Remember, only the bravest can reach the end. Farewell, my bringer of life.' She finished with a smile in their direction, and then slowly faded into nothingness.

'This one sounds tricky. We're going to need to analyse it word by-,' she began, and then stopped abruptly.

Julius turned his head to look at her. She was staring wide eyed at the screen, so he followed her gaze and froze.

The shadow of a man had appeared in the middle of the room, staring at the spot where the lady had been standing just seconds earlier. He took a few steps away from the main camera and then turned, slowly. Julius felt all the air rush out of his lungs and his jaw dropped open in disbelief as the face came into focus. 'Red Cap,' he whispered.

Red Cap looked around him, then up towards the main camera. They watched silently, still in shock, as he stretched out his hand and tore it loose. The feed disappeared. The remaining four quickly followed suit.

Just then, the door flew open and a flush-faced Skye stumbled into the room. 'What did I miss?' he asked, and was greeted only by their white faces.

'You'd better sit down,' said Morgana.

GASSENDI'S ROCK

'What happened?' asked Skye, who was obviously quite alarmed by the odd reception he had received. 'Did the feed fail?'

Julius, who was sitting on the bed in silence staring into nothing, promptly stood up and, without a word, left the room. He headed straight for the stairs, not caring if he bumped into the Grand Master himself. When he reached the promenade, he turned left and headed for the mess hall. The kitchen was empty, its surfaces freshly clean and shiny for the morning breakfast. He marched over to the hot drinks dispenser and ordered the first thing that came to mind: 'Hot chocolate. No sugar.'

He spilled a little and almost dropped the cup, his hands were shaking so badly. Fortunately, a hand reached out from the left and steadied it just in time. It was Morgana – she had left the room right after him and followed in silence.

'Go sit down,' she said. 'I'll bring it over.'

Julius wiped his hands with a paper towel and sat down at one of the smaller tables. Morgana joined him a couple of minutes later, carrying two cups.

'What's going on, Morgana?' said Julius, clearly upset.

'I don't know,' she said, gloomily. 'I don't know why Red Cap is back or what he's up to.'

'Do you think the Oracle is just one of his tricks? Have we been played for fools all along?'

'Maybe he's just involved with the kidnappings. That was, after all, why he was here last year.'

Julius took a sip of chocolate. 'What if he's come back for … well, for me?'

'What, because you're a White Child?' she asked, looking at him with some concern.

Julius nodded.

'Could be. But, it doesn't *feel* like last time. It seems like they're only targeting girls. Also, we haven't had any sign of Red Cap since last April, or seen anything that suggests he's directly involved in this business. And the Oracle seems far too nice to be involved with the Arneshians.'

Julius thought about it. 'So you're saying that Red Cap just happened to stumble into that basement by mistake?'

'Not by mistake. But … he could have followed us, maybe.'

Julius knotted his eyebrows. 'When I was lying on the boat, by the lovers' statue, I had this feeling like I was being watched. Then I saw a shadow moving, on the bridge above me.'

'There you go,' said Morgana. 'It was our friendly holo-psycho. He heard the Oracle's clue and decided to check it out, especially because *you* were involved.'

'You could be right, you know. Still, I'm pretty sure Red Cap has something to do with these kidnappings, but it doesn't seem like they have anything to do with the Oracle.'

Morgana looked at him, sipping her drink in silence. Julius could tell she wanted to say something, but left her to talk when she was ready. Sure enough, a moment later she put the cup down and looked up.

'Listen Julius, what about the guys? Don't you think you should tell them about this White Child business? It would make things easier if they knew.'

'Maybe, but it doesn't seem necessary for others to know about this.'

'"Others"?' said Morgana, flushing slightly. 'I'm not talking about just anyone here, Julius. It's Faith and Skye, our friends. A few months ago they risked their lives on Kratos with you, remember? You owe them an explanation.'

Julius was taken aback by her reaction, but he knew she was right. He had postponed this chat for far too long. He would much rather have kept it a secret, but they *had* risked life and limb because of him. What's more, with Red Cap back in the picture, it was entirely possible that Julius might be in danger again, and his friends too by association, so at the very least he needed to warn them. 'All right, all right, I'll tell them tomorrow.'

'No! Tell them now.'

'Tell us what?' said Faith, hovering over to the table, followed by Skye.

Julius motioned for them to sit and took a deep breath. For the next while, there was no other sound in the mess hall other than Julius' own voice. The more he said, the lighter he felt, as if an invisible weight had been lifted from his shoulders. He told them all about the conversation with Freja, the day the Grand Master had revealed his true nature as a White child. Then he recounted how Queen Salgoria had been kidnapping highly skilled Zed officers in order to splice their DNA together with the Arneshian's own genes, and how those experiments had failed, causing the deaths of so many in the process. Then he moved onto the bits they didn't know about the attack on Zed the previous year; the plot to kidnap him, led by Red Cap, in order to use his special DNA and that of an Arneshian to create the perfect being. He finished off by telling them of Freja's warning to be careful, in case Red Cap came back for him, no matter how unlikely that had seemed at the time.

'A *White Child*,' said Faith in astonishment. 'Well, paint me red and call me a beetroot.'

They chuckled at the quip, and immediately felt the sombre mood lift a little.

'McCoy's a White Child. Who would have thought?' said Skye, obviously pleased. 'He is a little pale, it's true.' He grinned at Julius, who punched him on the arm.

'Actually, we should have at least suspected as much after that Draw stunt he pulled on Kratos,' said Morgana, who seemed relieved now that Julius had shared the whole story with the other two.

'Guys,' said Julius, 'you have to swear you won't tell a soul.'

'Of course, mate,' said Skye. 'But I reserve the right to call you WC.'

'You do that, and I'll tell every girl on Zed that you still wet the bed.'

'OK,' said Morgana, standing up. 'And on that note, I think I can call it a night.'

'I'm shattered too,' said Faith. 'Let's discuss the situation another time, guys. I think a major piece of news like that is enough for one day.'

Julius followed them back to the dorm, feeling tired but much happier. The anger he had felt when he had seen Red Cap on the screen had almost completely dissipated.

Morgana had been right, after all. It was much better now that the others knew everything he did. However, he had his doubts about how that would make things any easier. Being a White Child wasn't necessarily a burden, but he wondered if it would make the others look more to him for leadership. It wasn't a thought he was entirely comfortable with. As much as he valued having them around, when it came to making decisions, he still felt like a Solo player.

*

During the last few days of February, Julius found himself fighting an internal battle: should he tell Freja about Red Cap, or not? The others had not said very much on the topic, but he was certain that they were considering the consequences as he was. There was no mistaking what a big decision it was, and he didn't feel like making it alone. So, on Tuesday the 1st of March, he called a meeting under the oak tree, in Tijara's garden.

'I think you all know what we need to decide, guys,' he said. 'Do we tell Freja?'

'I say no,' said Faith.

'No for me,' said Skye.

'No,' said Julius.

'Ditto for me,' added Morgana.

Julius looked at them each in turn, feeling strangely relieved at the unanimous vote. 'If we told Freja, we would have to explain why we had surveillance cameras in Mr Rossini's basement, which could get us all into a lot of trouble. And, with Red Cap thrown into the picture, I could see me being completely grounded and out of action, for my own protection. Not to mention being totally cut off from the rest of the treasure hunt. Red Cap escaped me once already and I really don't want to give him another chance to do it a second time.'

'OK, so what reasons are there for why we *should* tell him?' continued Morgana.

'Because of Ife and Sharon,' said Skye. 'If Red Cap is tied to the kidnapping, and chances are that he is, then we really ought to.'

'This information could save their lives,' agreed Morgana.

'They'll never allow us to continue with the treasure hunt,' said Faith. 'Especially since the Hologram Palace staff doesn't even know anything about any in-game bonus.'

'Shoot,' said Julius, slumping back on the grass. 'We're trapped.'

Lacing his fingers together, he placed the back of his hands over his eyes and breathed deeply. The cold grass was doing a good job of soothing the tense muscles in his neck, while a few of the longer blades tickled his ears pleasantly. He remembered Freja's words from the previous year. He had asked Julius then to trust in his new family – the Tijaran family.

'We have no choice,' said Julius, sitting up.

'No, we don't,' said Morgana. 'Not when there are lives at stake.'

'We tell the whole story,' said Skye, 'and we share the consequences.'

*

As they arrived at the senior staff area, they bumped into Master Cress, who was just exiting his office.

'Sir,' said Julius, bowing. 'We wish to speak to Grand Master Freja.'

'He's busy right now, McCoy. Is there something I can help you with?'

Julius knew that Freja trusted Cress completely, but he wanted to talk to the Grand Master directly. There was sure to be some form of punishment because of their treasure hunt, so he at least wanted the chance to tell the story face to face. 'We wish to speak to him directly, sir, if you don't mind.'

Cress looked at them, puzzled. 'He's in a meeting and I ...'

'It's about Red Cap, sir,' Morgana blurted out, interrupting him.

Cress' face instantly took on a look of concern. 'Very well. Wait here. I'll call you when he's ready.'

Julius sat down in one of the armchairs that lined the corridor, while Master Cress disappeared into Freja's office. Waiting for Freja was never a pleasant experience. No matter the reason for seeing him, Julius always felt like a naughty boy who had done some terrible mischief and was duly about to be punished for it. Thankfully, the wait didn't last too long. Five minutes later, Cress opened the door and invited them in.

Freja's office was made up of two rooms, separated by a large archway. The main door opened onto a living room, which was furnished with three grey leather sofas facing a long, glass-top coffee table. There was a trolley with bottles and glasses on the other side of the room, no doubt for use when he was entertaining guests. To Julius' delight, the walls of the room were obscured by several large bookshelves housing a seemingly endless amount of books. This was a precious sight indeed, since books made of real paper had become extremely rare over the course of the last 500 years. The books themselves were shielded by transparent protective panels, making Julius feel as if he had just stepped into a museum like the ones his parents loved so much, back on Earth.

As they reached the main part of the office, the bookshelves gave way to mounted pictures, shelves laden with trophies and various other objects, which Julius did not have time to examine properly. Behind a large mahogany desk at the end of the room, stood Carlos Freja, in typically pristine uniform and sporting his usual impenetrable gaze.

Julius and the others stopped as they drew near, and bowed their heads.

'At ease,' said the Grand Master, extending his hand out in front of him. 'Sit, please.'

Four chairs had already been set out for them, so they quickly obeyed. Julius was aware that Master Cress had sat down on a chair behind them and that, as he had foreseen, he would be listening to their news.

'I have a recording you should see, sir,' said Faith, activating his PIP.

'Send it through, Mr Shanigan,' said Freja. He motioned for Cress to join him and, activating his own PIP, he placed his left hand in front of him for them both to watch.

Julius sat in silence as the video was transferred to Freja's device and then carefully studied. The voice of the Oracle resounded clearly in the stillness of the office, her latest clue unresolved. Then, after a brief silence, they heard the sound of footsteps on a squeaky floor board, and the noise of the camera being ripped from the ceiling, which signalled the end of the recording. Freja and Cress looked quite stunned, a little too much for Julius' liking. Freja stared intently at Cress for a moment and Julius was sure that a mind-message had just been passed between them. It had been so quick and unexpected that he had only caught a brief hint of what sounded like a murmur.

'I think you ought to explain some of the background to this video, Mizkis,' said Freja. 'Tell me everything – I want every last detail, even if you don't think it's important.'

Faith began to tell the story, starting with how Julius had sensed something in the cave, to the scanner in the chamber and the first Oracle that had appeared there. Freja looked at Julius intently as he listened to that part, but said nothing. Faith continued on, as the Grand Master switched his gaze back to him, recounting everything that had happened up to and including New Year's Eve. At that point, Freja looked at Julius and said, 'We were wondering where you had *really* been that night, Mr McCoy. Weren't we, Master Cress?'

'And it does explain the performance that you put on for Captain Foster,' added Cress, raising an eyebrow.

Julius sunk into his chair, reddening and hoping that Faith would hurry up and finish. The story then turned to all of the events surrounding Mr Rossini and his barber shop, ending with the appearance of Red Cap in the basement.

'Sir,' said Skye, 'We don't think that the Oracle has anything to do with the Arneshians, but we do feel that Red Cap is tied to the kidnappings.'

'We came to you because it was the right thing to do,' said Julius, 'but, now that Red Cap has seen the Oracle, we wish to see the treasure hunt through before he does. Please don't take it away from us.'

'In the light of what we have just seen, I cannot grant such a concession lightly, Mr McCoy.'

'Sir, please,' said Julius, trying hard to sound determined, rather than confrontational. 'She said that we will only see her one more time before the end. We've come so far. Let us finish this.'

Freja searched him with his grey eyes for a few seconds. 'I will consider your request.'

Julius sighed in relief. It wasn't a "yes", but it was certainly better than an outright "no".

'There is also another matter to consider,' said Cress. 'That of your trespassing on private property and, of course, breaking curfew.'

'*Here we go,*' thought Julius. '*That's another detention for sure.*'

'We shall take into account the various factors that have prompted your actions,' continued Cress. 'You will be informed of our decision in due course. Dismissed.'

They bowed and left the room in single file, feeling quite surprised that they had escaped without having the books, and a few shelves thrown at them, at least for the moment.

*

Once they had gone and the door shut behind them, Cress turned to Freja, looking incredulous. 'They *really* didn't recognise her.'

'Surprising, isn't it,' said Freja, leaning back in his chair.

'I know we don't teach History and Politics until third year, but I had to admit, I was quite astonished by their ignorance.'

'It's been a long time, Nathan. Besides, she did look rather young in that video. Their misplaced trust in the Oracle may just give us the advantage we need though. It's probably better if they *don't* know who she is.'

'Are you going to let them continue the hunt then?'

'Yes, I am. This discovery is an unexpected victory for Zed. Besides, I suspect that we need to follow this lead to the end if we want to find the missing girls. The two paths lead to one shared destination; there's no doubt in my mind about that. There's also that scanner they mentioned. It could be nothing – an activation device of some sort – but I just wonder ...'

Cress waited for him to finish, but he seemed lost in thought. 'Maybe we should take over from here then. It could be dangerous for them.'

Freja looked at him and shook his head. 'I fear that, if we do that, we'll lose the scent. For whatever reason, they were the ones who found the hologram – I have a feeling that we need to let them see this one through. Besides, McCoy is like a hound that has just smelled blood. He will not stop until Red Cap is finished.'

Cress nodded. 'They certainly have done well with the clues so far.'

'Indeed,' said Freja, a little smile curling one corner of his mouth. 'They showed remarkable wit to overcome those obstacles. Tell them to continue and to report all progress on the next clue to you directly. We'll take some extra precautions too.'

'I understand. And what about the other matter?'

'Captain Foster has already dealt with the infringement on New Year's Eve. I'm sure you'll find the correct recourse for their inappropriate behaviour towards Mr Rossini.'

Cress nodded. Freja eased back in his chair and passed his hands over his face, his gaze fixed on nothing in particular.

'You look tired, Carlos,' said Cress.

'I am, Nathan,' sighed Freja. 'I spent most of the day in a videoconference with the Curia, the other Grand Masters and the family of the missing girls.'

'How are they coping?'

'Well enough, given the circumstances,' said Freja. 'I mean, the Curia asked them not to disclose news of the kidnappings to any journalists, while the Curio Maximus is practically blackmailing them with a guilt trip: if they talk, there's a chance their daughters could be harmed in retaliation. Then there's us, promising that we'll do everything in our power to get them back but, given our previous record, the chances are *not* in our favour.'

Cress watched as Freja walked over to the water fountain and poured himself a glass of water.

'I want McCoy under constant surveillance, Nathan,' said Freja, turning to him. 'I know it sounds awful but, as a White Child, *he's* the one we can't afford to lose. Do what you must.'

*

'Detention or not,' said Skye, once back in the promenade, 'we did the right thing.'

'Of course we did,' said Morgana. 'If there's even a small chance that our video can help Freja find the girls, then it's worth it.'

Julius nodded. He agreed with them, of course he did, but apparently Red Cap still had the power to get under his skin. Last year, Freja had told him to let it go, that he was only a hologram, a slave of Salgoria's. But, for Julius, that wasn't so easy. Since his reappearance, Red Cap's face had haunted his dreams almost every night. Sometimes, in those dreams, Julius didn't manage to escape and was captured at the end of a futile struggle.

'I really hope they'll let us finish,' said Faith.

'I don't care what he says,' said Julius, 'because this time, if Red Cap crosses my path, I won't let him get away.' There was enough anger in his voice to stop the others dead in their tracks. 'I'm not kidding.'

They believed him, and none of them found anything to reply.

*

The following Monday afternoon, the 2MJs were finally treated to their first class of Martial Arts, in which they would be able to fight using both a shield and the Gauntlet. Professor Morales was waiting at the dojo entrance, welcoming the students with her usual smile, while Professor Chan stood by her side with furled eyebrows, a double act that the Mizkis had become quite accustomed to. Faith had been calling them "the odd couple" since November, due to the plainly evident difference in the two teachers' personalities. Morales' natural bubbliness could hardly be more in contrast to Chan's serious nature. It seemed that the more she smiled at him the closer his eyebrows got to each other, creating a mono-brow effect.

'Oh boy,' whispered Faith, looking at Chan. 'He's wearing his constipated face again. I foresee severe pain of the muscles and cracking of the joints for tonight.'

'You know what?' said Morgana, observing the teachers closely. 'I think he fancies her.'

'Who? Morales?' asked Julius, horrified.

'Why? What's wrong with that?' said Morgana. 'She's an attractive woman.'

'But, but … they can't,' stuttered Julius.

'Why not?'

'They're teachers,' he answered, as if that should clearly prove his point.

'No-uh,' said Morgana, shaking her finger under his nose. 'They are as human as you are.'

'Julius is right,' added Skye. 'Besides, she's in love with me. I'm far more charming than Chan.'

'Is that right?' said Morgana, chuckling.

'How do you know he likes her?' asked Faith, genuinely curious. 'I mean, it looks more like the opposite, actually. He never smiles at her, or even looks her in the eye.'

'That's *exactly* it,' said Morgana, knowingly. 'Pretending that you don't care for someone normally means the opposite. You want to arouse their curiosity as to why you don't like them, which in turn makes them think about you, often with astonishing results. I'm not saying it's a good method, but it has been known to work.'

'Wow,' said Faith, 'Remind me to ask you a couple of questions later on.'

'How do you know all this stuff?' asked Julius.

'WC,' said Skye, nudging Julius in the ribs, 'she's a woman. Of course she knows this stuff. It's a genetic thing. It's how they wile their way into our hearts.'

'Don't call me WC, or I'll tell Chan he's got competition, and then he'll use his constipated secret move on your a …'

As Skye grabbed Julius into a head lock, the door of the dojo closed. The students immediately faced the teachers and bowed.

'First things first, Mizkis,' said Chan, 'I want you to use a Sim-Gauntlet for today's lesson. Since you'll be practising against each other, I really would like to avoid burying anyone tonight.'

As the students walked over to the shelf, Chan moved to the centre of the room, clapped twice and quickly moved his hands up and to the side. To their general astonishment, the dojo stretched itself instantly, turning into a much larger and wider room.

'I want fifteen students on the left and fifteen on the right of the room,' called Chan. 'Professor Morales will give each of you a coloured armband that contains a sensor. Anytime you are shot by one of the Sim-Gauntlets, the sensor will go off and you must step to the side of the main floor area immediately. Keep in mind, this exercise is about teamwork. Now, go to your stations and get ready.'

Julius and Morgana were each given a yellow armband, while Faith and Skye got red ones. The two teams moved to opposite sides of the dojo, where they were given a few minutes to prepare.

'Morgana,' said Julius, talking quickly. 'We need to stick together. My left shield will cover my side and front; my right one will do the same when I'm not shooting, but I can't protect my back. You'll have the same problem, so we walk back to back. That way, we'll be able to cover all directions. Why are you smiling?'

'Your eyes shine when you organise people,' she said, straightening her armband. 'You'll make a great captain one day.'

Julius blushed slightly and, not knowing what to say, he stood up and gave her his hand. Morgana grabbed it and jumped to her feet. She didn't add anything else, but he could see a little smile curling the corners of her mouth.

'Mizkis, activate your shields,' cried Chan.

A dull, electric noise ran simultaneously through the dojo, as all the shields came online.

'I want a clean fight,' added Morales. 'May the best team win.'

Her words had barely left her lips when the Mizkis began to advance toward the middle of the room, letting out battle cries as they went. Morgana moved quickly into position at Julius' back, ready to fire on anyone who dared approach them. Soon the dojo had transformed into a confusing battlefield, with students shooting at each other without any clear plan or tactic. The armbands of those who got hit flashed brightly before emitting a shrill beeping sound. As Julius dodged a few attacks and shot three of his classmates, he was strongly reminded of his test at the Zed Center almost two years before, where he had managed to prove his worth to the Lunar Perimeter selection panel amid the chaos of children trying to survive long enough to get through.

'Barth!' cried Morgana suddenly, grabbing Julius' t-shirt. 'Let's go get him.'

For a moment, Julius thought that she wanted to shoot Barth just to get him out of the training, as a safety measure. Then he spotted him, and understood that Morgana meant to rescue him. Barth was kneeling in the centre of the dojo, his shields on, desperately trying to protect himself. No one had made a move against him, which was surprising given that he was such an easy target. But Julius knew why: it was part of the Zed honour code – you didn't kick someone who was already down.

'All right,' he said to her, over his shoulder. 'Let's blast our way over there.'

She gave him the thumbs-up and they began to move rapidly sideways. Julius' right shield and Morgana's left one had created a wall to protect them, while the opening gap was covered by the quick bursts of light from their weapons. They shot at anyone who crossed their path, sometimes jumping over students who had been hit and were now trying to get to the sidelines by crawling on all fours. They saw others who had also been eliminated trying to get clear by ramming their way through the crowd.

'Barth, get up!' cried Julius, towering over his classmate.

'It's not safe,' said a little voice from under his shields.

'Barth Smit!' shouted Julius over the noise. 'You stand up right now and join us, or I'll shoot you myself.'

Morgana threw a look at Julius that clearly said, "Like that's going to help."

'I can't!' said Barth.

'Yes you can,' said Julius, a little more gently this time. 'We're covering you. Just use your shields to protect your open side. You'll be fine, honestly.'

Barth glanced up, looking pretty shaken, but gradually he started to shift towards Julius' legs and stood up cautiously.

'Attaboy,' said Julius, nodding his approval. Barth smiled and, just then, inexplicably decided to scratch his head. As he did, his shield lifted upwards, leaving Julius' entire right side unprotected. He looked up and, too late, saw that Faith had him in his sights. It all happened so fast that he could do nothing to prevent it. Faith grinned and squeezed his fist, the shot hitting Julius square on his hip.

'Sorry mate!' cried Faith, before retreating towards the few survivors left in his team.

Julius stood, looking with resignation at his flashing sensor then, without a second glance at Barth, made his way towards the sidelines.

'Come sit here,' said Lopaka, with a big grin. 'Man, that sucks. I can't believe he got you shot.'

'It's Barth,' said Julius, plonking himself on the ground by Lopaka's side. 'I should have known better.'

'Don't worry, no one's gonna think any less of you. You did the decent thing, trying to help him.'

'It was Morgana's idea, actually. I would have probably just left him there, but Morgana's different. Her heart's in the right place.'

'She's got a few other things in the right places too,' said Lopaka, watching her shoot her way through a group of Mizkis.

'Excuse me,' said Julius, with a comical look of shock on his face. 'I don't think I wanna hear any of that.'

'Oh, come on,' said Lopaka, nudging him in the rib. 'I don't know if you've noticed or not, but a few of our Mizki ladies are growing up fast. It's kinda hard to miss. Besides, why does it bother you? Are you guys going out?'

'What?!' said Julius, now looking even more shocked. 'No way! She's like my sister, honestly. And I really don't need to picture any of her round bits in my mind, thank you very much.'

'So you did notice she's got round bits,' teased Lopaka, undeterred.

As Julius' face continued to grow redder and redder, he realised with horror that Morgana was presently walking towards them, laughing happily, with one arm around Siena's shoulders. Julius' eyes took on a mind of their own and gave the two girls a proper once-over. Embarrassed, as he had never been before, he suddenly stood up and scurried over to Faith and Skye, hoping that by the time he reached them his colour would be back to normal.

*

Later that night, as the Skirts headed along the promenade towards the mess hall, they were approached by Master Cress.

'Mizkis,' he said. 'The Grand Master has granted your request.'

Julius felt a wave of relief wash over him at that news.

'You shall report directly to me on this matter,' continued Cress. 'And, in case you haven't noticed yet, your next meeting with the Oracle will fall during your Spring Mission. You have until the 20th of March to figure out the next location.' Cress bowed quickly, and then headed back towards his office.

'Jeepers,' said Julius, turning to the others. 'We only have thirteen days left.'

'We'll work it out,' said Faith. 'I'm sure of it. But not right now, please. I'm feeling Chan's workout effects right down to me pinkie toes. That is, if I could feel me pinkie toes.' With that, he left, whistling to himself as he hovered away, leaving the three of them standing there in awkward silence.

Julius looked at the others with a shrug of his shoulders. 'It's Faith. That was normal for him.'

*

In the days that followed, Julius found himself busier than ever. Between homework, making a record of each lesson in his diary and the occasional visit to the Hologram Palace for a quick fight with the Skirts, there was not much time for anything else. It was only when Professor King reminded the students that he needed their choices for the Spring Missions by the end of the week, that Julius realised how urgent it was to put their heads together and identify the next location, as that would obviously decide where they went for the break. So, on Tuesday the 15th of March, he rallied the others together to spend the evening working on the clue.

'Come on, guys,' said Skye. 'Let's go talk over some dinner. I'm starving and I think Felice has made *gnocchi con burro e salvia tonight.*'

'What, you speak Italian now?' asked Julius in amusement.

'Felice likes to speak it, and I like Felice,' explained Skye.

'Well, whatever this *con burro salivation* thing is you're talking about, it sounds yummy,' said Faith. 'Besides, I think better on a full stomach.'

Julius nodded in agreement. He was tired, but the afternoon's training had also left him rather famished. Plus, he needed to remind himself of the details of the last message because, with all the recent events, it had grown quite hazy in his memory. And so, after they had wolfed down the quite delicious gnocchi, Julius felt ready to absorb himself into a discussion about the riddle. First, though, they had to stop Skye refilling his plate for the fourth time.

'Honestly, you're going to explode if you don't stop,' said Julius. 'These things tend to expand once they hit your stomach.'

'I just have two left, and then I'm done,' said Skye, swallowing the last mouthful. 'Mom always told me that I have the metabolism of a hummingbird, and that's 100 times faster than an elephant's.'

'Yeah,' added Faith. 'And, by the look of things, I bet you ate the damn bird and the elephant too, just for good measure.'

Julius threw his head back and let out a burst of laughter, quickly followed by Faith and Morgana. Skye threw him a look of mock indignation, but couldn't keep a straight face for long.

'You're funny, Irishman,' said Skye, wiping a tear from the corner of his eye. 'I'll let you live another year.'

'Thank you, Oh Royal Bottomless Pitness. And now, if you've done eating, we should probably crack on with solving that clue.'

'Right, let's go to the garden,' said Morgana, standing up. 'It'll be quieter there.'

Julius brought his food tray back to the rack, grabbed a glass of fresh apple juice and headed for the oak tree, followed by the others.

Once they were all seated, they activated their PIPs and settled down to watch the recording.

'*He left Artemis speechless when he told her, "Be my bride"; or so Sir Pierre believed when he found her gift, and sighed.*' As the words faded into the night, Morgana pressed a spot on her holoscreen, activating a holographic keyboard.

'I need to take some notes,' she said sitting up properly. 'This is definitely the hardest one so far.'

'We need to figure out who these Artemis and Pierre characters are,' said Skye.

Julius activated the Zed personnel database. So far, all the clues had led to lunar locations and he strongly believed this one would turn out to be no exception to that. He typed the name "Pierre" into his keyboard and pressed enter. For a few seconds he watched as page upon page of information scrolled rapidly in front of his eyes. When a series of pictures sprung into view, he touched the screen to slow it down. Carefully, he scanned the names under each photo, all of men named Pierre who had either worked or studied on Zed at one point or another over the years, going back as far as the year 2620.

'I've got at least 300 Pierre's here,' said Julius. 'But without any point of reference they're quite useless to us. We need to narrow it down a bit.'

'And I've found no trace of a woman called Artemis,' added Faith.

'Guys, let's read the riddle properly,' said Skye. 'It looks to me like a guy called Pierre asked this Artemis to marry him, right? So, shouldn't we be searching for *a couple* with those names, rather than two separate people?'

'No,' answered Faith, squinting at his screen. 'Not Pierre.'

'What do you mean?' asked Morgana.

'Faith's right,' said Julius. '*Someone else* asked Artemis to marry him. Pierre is just the person who found her gift.'

'OK, well what's the gift then?' asked Skye.

'How about this: when you ask for someone's hand in marriage, normally you give them an engagement ring, right?' said Morgana. 'A ring with a stone in it.'

'So you're thinking that, for some reason, Pierre found Artemis's engagement ring here on Zed,' said Julius. 'This is mental. Surely the Oracle can't be expecting us to pry into the private life and history of every single Pierre that's ever passed through here.'

'OK then,' said Morgana, 'let's do a search with these names, within Zed, but *not* in the personnel files. Maybe we need to think outside the box a little.'

Julius shrugged his shoulders and activated the search engine on his PIP. He typed in "Artemis" and waited, not feeling overly optimistic about what the results would be. Sure enough, three pages of random information appeared, all containing the name.

He ran his eyes over the main titles of the various articles, trying to spot anything that stuck out from the rest, which wasn't easy given that he wasn't exactly sure what he was looking for. However, on the last results page, one particular heading caught his attention: something to do with ancient Greek mythology. Julius suddenly became very alert. He was already well aware that Artemis was a Greek name, thanks to his passion for Earth history, which had started when he was just a young child. His father, being a bit of a fanatic himself, had taken Julius to visit a different museum each weekend, and explained to his son how the story of Earth's people was passed on through what they left behind. Rory's enthusiasm had affected him so much that, as soon as Michael was old enough to walk, Julius had insisted that he come along on their little field trips too. For his seventh birthday, his dad had given him a book of stories about ancient Greece and its gods, which he had read over and over again.

'I know who Artemis is,' he announced to the others, with a hint of satisfaction in his voice. 'We're sitting on it.'

'What?' said Skye, looking puzzled.

'It's the moon,' explained Julius. 'In Greek mythology, Artemis is the goddess of the moon, among other things.'

'Get outta here,' said Faith.

'I'm serious. The Romans called her Diana, and she also was the goddess of the moon. Besides, it doesn't look like there's ever been any actual person with that name in the whole history of Zed,' finished Julius.

'How can someone propose to a goddess?' asked Skye.

'And how can someone propose to the moon?' added Faith.

Julius shook his head. 'I'm not sure, but that's my best guess.'

'OK,' said Morgana. 'Let's run with it. If the Oracle used Artemis as a nickname for the moon, then this Pierre guy is somehow linked to it. Not to Zed, but the moon itself. Let's see if we can find a link in the database within the history of the moon.'

Julius lay down next to Faith and let him do the searching. Faith's right hand moved quickly over the holoscreen, selecting pages and moving icons in and out of view with quick swipes of his fingers.

'Hold it!' cried Faith, suddenly.

Julius sat up, his gaze drawn to the article that his friend had enlarged on the screen.

'Pierre Gassendi,' said Faith, with a broad smile. 'He's a French chap who named a crater here on the moon, called … well, called *Gassendi*!'

'Guys, have a look at this picture of the crater,' said Julius excitedly.

Morgana and Skye crawled quickly over beside them and peered at the screen.

'It's the engagement ring!' gasped Morgana. 'Read what it says, Faith.'

'"Gassendi – named after Pierre Gassendi, French astronomer, 1592-1655. Large lunar crater at the northern edge of the Sea of Moisture. From above, the crater resembles a *diamond ring*. Gassendi is currently linked to the Zed Lunar Perimeter via a subway system. Gassendi has been an active mineral research facility since the construction of Zed."'

'So it was a meteorite that married Artemis,' said Skye. 'Go figure.'

'Exactly,' said Morgana. 'It gave her a precious *gift* and, centuries later, Pierre discovered the crater, which was eventually named after him. I think we've got it.'

'Makes sense to me,' said Faith. 'Let's run it by Cress though, and see what he reckons.'

We'll need to check if we're actually allowed to spend the Spring Mission in Gassendi.'

It was getting late, so they decided it was best to leave it until the next day. It was agreed that Julius would go see Cress during their lunch break. As he walked back to his room, Julius felt a deep sense of satisfaction spreading through him. Solving the riddles was pleasing enough, and knowing that they had the blessing of the Tijaran Grand Master was a great relief on top of that. Despite this, there was a part of him that couldn't quite understand why Freja was actually allowing them to continue with the hunt, especially now that Red Cap had made a comeback. Still, more than anything, he was determined to repay the trust that Freja had shown in him and reach the final Oracle. And if Red Cap decided to get in the way, he would just deal with him too.

*

The following day, Julius wanted to catch Cress before he went for lunch so, straight after his Draw class, he hurried to the Master's office. Now, standing outside, he knocked on the door and waited.

'Come in,' he heard a muffled voice say, and the door slid open.

Julius stepped in and bowed.

'McCoy, have a seat,' said Cress, beckoning to a chair in front of his desk.

'Thank you, sir.'

'I take it you solved the riddle.'

'We think so, sir. The location of the next Oracle is in Gassendi.'

Cress raised an eyebrow, looking surprised. He then tapped a space on the holoscreen set into his desk, which opened up a document. With the tip of his finger, he slid it across to Julius.

Julius dragged the virtual document towards him and rotated it so it was facing the right way up. He realised immediately that it was a list of locations on the moon: Gassendi was the first name on it.

'You mean you figured the same thing, sir?' asked Julius, his eyes growing wide.

'Well … naturally, we did a little research of our own,' explained Cress. 'The Grand Master loves a puzzle, you see. Gassendi was at the top of both of our lists. So, with yours, that makes three exact same guesses. I think we can safely assume it must be where the next Oracle will appear.'

Julius nodded, feeling quite pleased that they had all arrived at the same conclusion.

'Speak to Professor King about the Spring Mission. You will sign up to join the Gassendi crew. And, if any of your fellow students should ask, you're going there to study up close exactly how a mineral research facility works. We don't need a crowd following you. Understood?'

'Yes, sir.'

'You may go now,' concluded Cress, bowing his head briefly.

Julius bowed back, stood and left the room with a smile on his face. All in all, things were falling into place very nicely.

*

On Sunday the 20th of March, Julius and the rest of his classmates queued outside Professor King's office at midday. The Mizkis had been given a list of potential destinations that Friday and told to carefully examine all missions before deciding. Julius knew that, from the following year, their subjects would become much more specialised, in line with the specific career they would choose for themselves. This mission then, together with the Summer Camp, was vitally important because it would provide them with a taste of what was to come. Obviously this was not the case for Julius, though, seeing as the choice had been made for him once they had figured out the Oracle's clue. Not that he was complaining – after all, he was already pretty sure what he wanted to be once he left the Academy.

He glanced at his friends, who were lined up in front of him. The four of them must have looked rather out of place in that queue. It seemed that they were the only ones who were quietly waiting to be called, while all around them the rest of the Mizkis were noisily exchanging last minute information in the loudest possible manner.

'Morgana, finally!' cried Siena Migliori, pushing her way over to them.

'Hey, Siena – everything all right?' said Morgana.

'Yeah, all good. Except, I can't decide where to go this spring. What are you doing?'

'Errr … mineral research facility of some sort … boring really.'

'What? I thought you'd want to go to Flight School or something. Anyway, what about you guys?' she asked, turning to the boys.

'Same,' answered Julius, looking distractedly at his feet.

'Yeah, we're going there too,' said Skye, waving his thumb at himself and Faith.

'Well, where is this hot spot then?'

'It's called Gassendi,' answered Morgana. 'I'm not sure you'd like it.'

'Morgana Ruthier, is there something you're not telling me?' said Siena, eyeing her suspiciously.

'No, no! Honest. It's just that we …'

'We've been given detention,' whispered Faith, hoping she would buy the lie. 'Please don't tell anyone.'

'*Again?*' said Siena, with a smile. 'OK. I'm not even gonna ask.'

'Sorry,' continued Morgana. 'But this place is *really* dull and just outside the perimeter.'

'Yeah,' added Julius. 'We don't even get to leave orbit. I don't think you'd like it.'

'I suppose,' said Siena, looking down at the list she was holding in her hands.

Julius watched as she inspected the document, holding his breath. In the meantime, the queue was slowly moving forward, and Morgana was trying her best to recommend other "nice places" to her. Eventually, they arrived at the desk, where Professor King was making the bookings.

Siena marched over ahead of them. 'Five for Gassendi, please,' she said with a triumphant smile. 'I'd rather be bored with you lot than be by myself.'

'Five for Gassendi?' asked Professor King, furrowing his brow and looking at her in surprise. 'I didn't even know Gassendi was on the list. Why on earth would you want to spend two weeks there? I thought you lot were more the pilot or fighter types; not the artsy ones!'

Julius looked at the others, quite at a loss for words. He had hoped that Cress would inform the Professor in advance, but that was clearly not the case. And what exactly did King mean by "artsy"?

'Sir,' said Faith, 'we decided that, before we completely rule out a career in a lab, we should really experience it first.'

Professor King stared at him, looking entirely unconvinced. 'I see. So, what's the real reason?'

'They got detention, and I'm accompanying them out of the goodness of my heart,' whispered Siena, leaning in close to the desk.

'Ah!' said King, raising his left hand. 'Say no more. Five tickets for Gassendi coming right up!'

*

Over the course of the next four weeks, Julius poured over the schematics of Gassendi every day, hoping to identify a likely place where the Oracle would make her appearance. However, without physically being there, this was easier said than done, so in the end he was forced to leave it be until he actually got there. The time couldn't pass quickly enough though, he and the rest of the Skirts were so distracted by the anticipation of what the final Oracle would reveal to them. They were so excited that they didn't even remember to think about what they would actually be doing during their mission.

Unfortunately for them, Master Cress had not forgotten about their *real* detention – the one they were due for trespassing on Mr. Rossini's property. It turned out to be working shifts in the barber shop, by way of punishment. They were to spend three full weekends as apprentices for the barber, who was extremely happy to receive the extra help. Master Cress had not mentioned the genuine reason for their detention to Mr. Rossini – an omission that Julius and the others were relieved about. After all, they had grown quite fond of the barber, and so it would have been a shame to lose his friendship.

Eventually, the day of their departure finally arrived. Julius eagerly packed his rucksack and remembered for a moment what he had been doing the previous year. '*At least this year I won't have to get up at a silly hour on my birthday,*' he thought happily to himself.

JULIUS' WORST FEAR

'This train is really something,' said Faith, sounding completely awestruck.

'It sure is,' replied Morgana in a similar tone.

Julius threw a glance at Skye and said, 'Here we go again.'

Watching Morgana and Faith slaver over the latest technology was something that Julius and Skye had grown used to and, judging by the knowing smile on Siena's lips, it must have been normal for her too.

Currently, they were sitting on the shuttle to Gassendi, waiting patiently to depart. The seats themselves were very comfortable, furnished, as they were, in supple leather. There were six chairs in total, set side by side in two rows of three each. These were fixed onto a clear, glass platform beneath their feet. Skye and Siena were to Julius' right; Morgana and Faith behind him. They had been told that the trip wouldn't take long at all but, according to Cress, it was a ride worthy of the Hologram Palace. Now, as Julius sat taking note of how there seemed to be no cabin enclosing the train, no tracks on the floor and only the entrance to a well lit tunnel stretching out into the distance in front of them, he wondered if maybe it was time to get a little worried.

'You should have seen Morgana's face last year, the first time she saw her dorm room,' said Siena to Julius. 'I thought she was going to short-circuit the entire floor, the way she kept pushing every button in the room.'

Julius grinned and nodded his head – he could imagine her expression well enough. To be fair, though, this was a remarkable train, entirely different to the Intra-Rail System they normally used. In fact, so far, *everything* was different about this Spring Mission. Last year, there had been the threat of the Arneshians, which had forced the Zed Grand Masters into sending all junior Mizkis to the colonies for their missions. Not that any of them had ever actually left in the first place, given how all hell had broken loose as soon as they had reached the Tijaran dock.

'*Well,*' thought Julius, '*I'll be seeing somewhere new this time.*'

'Seatbelt check, Mizkis!' an operator called out from the platform to his left, making Julius jump a little.

'Yessir!' shouted Morgana enthusiastically.

'Can you make it go fast, please?' pleaded Faith.

'Not sure you'd like that, kid,' answered the operator, a burly man who had the appearance of someone who would rather be on holiday somewhere with actual sunshine.

'Just this once,' implored Morgana.

'Don't do it on my account,' added Skye, turning to the man and shaking his head vigorously.

The operator sniffed and half-smiled. 'Don't you worry kids, this thing will go fast enough, so you'd better buckle up.' With that, he wandered off back to the control station.

Julius gulped, quickly tightened his seatbelt and gripped the armrests of his seat. As he breathed in, the surface beneath his feet began to vibrate and they lifted slowly into the air, until the train was centred in line with the middle of the tunnel entrance. They hovered there for a minute, while an electromagnetic field began to form around their seats, starting from the bottom of the vehicle, spreading to either side and in front of them, and finally up over their heads, creating a cocoon of sorts. As the blue energy threads uncoiled around them, Julius felt every hair on his body stand to attention. At the same time, their seats started to tilt slowly back.

'This is amazing!' cried Morgana.

'I know! Me heart might explode!' added Faith.

Julius had just started to turn around to say something to the two weirdoes behind him, when the train suddenly shot off. The acceleration was so strong that he was slammed straight back into his seat.

'WAAAHHH!' he shouted, unable to manage anything else. This was accompanied by a surround-sound chorus of screams from his own row and some joyful hollering from the back.

Julius couldn't see very much, save for flashing lines of white light streaming past his head. He felt as if he was trapped inside a bolt of lightning, which had somehow been harnessed and funnelled into an energy conduit. Sharp bends and twists flashed past him at a pace more appropriate to a ship at warp speed than to a public transport vehicle. He was starting to regret the eight pancakes he had wolfed down that morning.

Mercifully, the train began to slow and gradually came to a halt, easing to a complete stop beside a long platform to their right. The energy bubble around them made a static, crackling noise and faded away. Julius unbuckled his seatbelt and turned to the others feeling that, if his eyes got any wider, they would pop like two tiny balloons. Every hair on their heads was standing on end, and tiny sparks of static were fizzing all about them.

'Um Skye, you look a bit green,' said Julius, eyeing his friend suspiciously.

On cue, Skye bent over and threw up between his knees.

'Aah, man!' cried Julius, lifting his legs as quickly as he could.

Siena fiddled desperately with her seatbelt buckle and only just managed to get free and escape the tiny, spreading pool of ooze. Morgana followed suit but, as she leapt out onto the platform, her legs wobbled and she stumbled on her feet, landing unceremoniously in a heap on the floor. Faith had quite simply passed out where he sat. It took three security officers to drag the five of them out of the train station and into their rooms, where they lay in embarrassed silence for a while.

When Julius felt steady enough to stand without holding on to the bed, he tottered over to a large glass desk in one corner of the room and sat down on the small chair in front of it. A bottle of water and a tray of glasses had been placed there. Julius gratefully filled one of the tumblers to the brim and gulped back several mouthfuls.

The living quarters were designed in much the same way as their dorm rooms back on Zed, except that they were quite a bit larger, so more people could fit inside. There were four beds in total. Faith and Skye lay sprawled out on two of them nearest to Julius' bed, which was set next to the far right wall.

'Wha … where am I?' groaned Faith from his bed.

'You passed out on the train, which you deserve; and that there is your new bed for the next two weeks, which you *don't* deserve, quite frankly,' answered Julius.

'I can't help it that I got excited about the ride. I thought it was gonna be fun,' groaned Faith feebly.

'I'm *walking* back to Tijara. Never again,' groaned Skye, carefully sitting up in his bed.

'Bleah!' said Julius, pulling a face. 'I can smell your breath from here. Brush your teeth, man. It's the least you can do, seeing how you almost puke-washed my boots before, *and* Siena's.'

'Oh man. I forgot about that. That's *so* embarrassing.'

'Yeah, but it could have been worse,' replied Julius, who was beginning to feel a little sorry for Skye now.

'How? My star-rep is officially ruined.'

'Julius is right,' said Faith, hovering over to the table, swaying a little as he went. 'You could have thrown up on yourself; or on *her*; or peed your pants *and* thrown up; or all of the above.'

'Now that you put it that way, I guess ...'

At that moment, there was a knock at the door.

'Come in,' said Julius.

Morgana walked into the room, still looking a little pale. 'Not a word, please.'

'Yeah, it's better that way,' answered Julius, pouring her a glass of water.

'Siena is resting, so I figured now's a good time to have a talk about the Oracle.'

Julius nodded and activated the desk computer. As soon as the menu lit up on the glass surface, he searched for a map of Gassendi and opened the file. As seen from above, the research facility created a figure of eight, with the upper circle proportionally much smaller than the lower one.

'Just like an engagement ring,' commented Morgana.

The entire building was enclosed within a metal dome and each section was conjoined by long tunnels. The sleeping quarters were in the eastern portion of Gassendi's main body.

'We'll need to go there and try to find the exact location,' said Morgana. 'We can't do it now though. We're supposed to meet the head of the facility, Ms Davies, to get our duties for the mission, and we're already late as it is.'

'They won't mind us exploring Gassendi, surely,' said Faith.

'Yeah, but Siena will be with us,' said Skye.

'A little telepathy goes a long way,' said Julius.

'All right then,' said Morgana, 'but we need to do it sooner rather than later. We only have two days left till the Oracle's message.'

They all nodded in agreement. Morgana hurried off to fetch Siena and, together with the boys, they headed to Ms Davies's office. Julius was getting quite curious as to exactly what kind of research went on in Gassendi. All he knew was that they mined moon rocks for one purpose or another.

*

'Welcome to Gassendi, darlings!'

The tall, elegant lady who met them as they entered the office caught them all off guard with her casually exuberant greeting. She opened her arms wide and said, 'Please, sit down and be my guests.'

Julius couldn't help but smile. Almost everyone had manners here, but she seemed to be a step beyond that. With her posh English accent, long blonde hair and sophisticated gestures, she reminded him more of a movie diva than a Zed teacher.

She perched herself on the desk and leaned on one arm, legs crossed, her right foot dangling freely. 'I have to confess, I am surprised by your presence here. For years, not even one student has chosen Gassendi. Now I have *five*. I was starting to worry about my lab. Why, without any new blood to replace us old cronies, there would be no future for mind-art.'

'Mind-art?' blurted out Faith. Then quickly he added, 'Beggin' your pardon, madam.'

'Of course,' she answered, passing a jewelled hand through her wavy hair. 'Gassendi is the artistic hub of Zed. And you, my darlings, are our new sculptors in the making.'

Julius' jaw dropped, and his wasn't the only one.

'Are you surprised that I should know of your hidden talents?' continued Ms Davies. 'Master Cress did say you were rather shy when it came to discussing your passion for mind-art.'

'Did he?' asked Julius.

'Indeed, and you know what else he told me?'

'Surprise us,' said Faith, looking worried.

'That it's someone's fourteenth birthday tomorrow!'

'You don't say,' answered Julius unenthusiastically.

'You'll have a fabulous surprise, darling,' she said, pointing at him.

'I can't wait.'

'Marvellous. Now, if you follow me, I shall give you the tour of our little cradle of inspiration.' She sprung lightly off the table and headed for the door, followed by five dubious faces.

Ms Davies led them along several illuminated corridors, calling their attention to the left and right every now and then – to the workshops, as she called them – where men and women in lab coats were staring at blocks of various sizes and moving around them as if they were performing some kind of tribal dance. Julius noticed a couple of men in blue overalls milling about as they moved along the corridor. They were young, well kept and definitely didn't appear to be artists.

'Ms Davies,' he said, catching up to her as she walked. 'Who are those official looking guys I saw? They didn't seem like they were teachers or anything.'

She stared down at him, looking a little confused, and then her face lit up as she realised who he was talking about. 'Oh, don't worry about them, dear. They're security guards sent over from Tijara a couple of days ago. There's another two about somewhere. I personally didn't see the need for them, but they insisted. I guess this whole dreadful business with the kidnappings has made them extra cautious, seeing as you all are going to be staying for a while.'

'Makes sense,' he said, trying to sound blasé. 'Can't hurt to be careful.'

'Quite right,' she said, nodding approvingly. 'A wise boy you are.'

After a few minutes, she stopped next to a small platform, where a middle-aged man was preparing to create something.

'Every working space,' she explained, accentuating each sentence with extravagant waves of her hands, 'is surrounded by protective force-fields, so that pieces of the lunar rock don't go zipping off about the room and harming others; this field can actually trap those pieces too. Mind-art requires years of practice, darlings, and *serious* fine-tuning of your White Arts. Essentially, what a regular sculptor would do with a hammer and chisel, you are doing with your minds. Even creating something as small as the petal on a rose requires carefully dosed energy bursts, or you risk blasting the whole thing off. What a tragedy that would be, hmm. Now, watch him.'

The artist on the platform was carefully studying the slab of rock. Julius took note of how the man's gaze intensified, and knew this was the same kind of focus someone would have when they were about to use their mind-skills. Suddenly, a small piece of rock flew off the slab and became trapped inside the force-field in front of where they were standing, making them all jump back in surprise. When Julius looked again, a perfectly sculpted nose had appeared, so elegant and fine that it looked almost real.

'Follow me, darlings,' said Ms Davies.

They resumed their tour, and Julius realised that they were now heading towards the smaller, upper portion of the building. As they approached a split in the corridor, Ms Davies took the path to the right.

'This is a *very* special section of Gassendi,' she explained. 'There is only one room here – the most important of them all.'

She stopped in front of a large doorway. Two sets of stairs fed off to either side of it, curving steadily upwards on an inward arc. They peered inside the room, which was a softly lit, empty area encased within a huge glass dome. Through it, they could see the stairs continuing their ascent, until they met to form what appeared to be a landing overlooking the glass bubble.

'Notice how wide the landing area is up there – that's where observers can stand – and how the stairs almost *embrace* the centre workspace,' said Ms Davies. 'In every generation, only two people are authorised to work using real lunar rock inside here. I, as the chief of Gassendi, am one of them.'

'I don't understand,' said Julius. 'What are the other workers using then?'

'It's a synthetic replica of the lunar rock. It's so similar that the untrained eye cannot tell the difference.'

'But why?' asked Skye.

'We can't very well keep drilling the Moon forever, my dear boy. Zed was built some 233 years ago. Imagine the size of *that* hole! Besides it keeps the artists on their toes; they know that only the greatest of them will claim the ultimate prize. This room is as precious as the diamond it represents.'

'Come again … madam?' said Julius eagerly.

'Surely you know about Gassendi's shape, don't you, darlings? The engagement ring?'

They nodded.

'Well, this room is at the exact centre of the diamond … if this really *was* a ring, that is.'

Julius' face lit up, and he threw a satisfied glance at the others.

'However, right on the opposite side of the main body, there is also a smaller circular room, inside a lesser crater; almost as if it were another diamond crowning Gassendi: a tiny, twin diamond.'

Julius' heart sank at those words. Surely, this is where the Oracle's clue was leading them, but which of the rooms was the right one? It was definitely going to complicate matters. It seemed odd to Julius that it hadn't been in the plans they had studied earlier. Perhaps they were out of date.

'Can we see the other one, please?' asked Faith.

'Sure,' answered Ms Davies, looking a little surprised. 'There isn't much to see really but, if you wish, you can even do your training in there.'

Julius' ears perked up. Knowing that the second room was not off limits to them certainly helped things. On the other hand, the presence of the two possible locations meant that they would undoubtedly need to split up.

'Come along then. Let's have a quick look at the other room. Time's marching on and we've so much to do, darling ones.' With that, she strode onwards and they hurried after her.

They moved along a corridor, which veered off right. It ended and met the beginning of another passageway, which led off to the left and then straight again. It was quite apparent that these walkways cut through the middle of the crater that Gassendi was situated within. Julius made a quick mental note of the route, which seemed simple enough, but he knew how easy it was to get lost in unfamiliar surroundings.

A few minutes later, they came to a doorway on their right. Ms Davies stopped and said, 'Well, there you go. As I said, not much to see.'

They looked inside. Indeed, the room was quite unremarkable, not much more than a circular space and nothing else.

'Happy?' she asked.

They nodded and followed as she led them back along the corridor. The next couple of hours were spent being introduced to the various artists who worked on Gassendi. They were largely eccentric types, but they all seemed friendly enough, and quite happy to see a new batch of students taking an interest in their craft. Ms Davies paired each of them with a sculptor, before taking them to the mess hall for lunch.

'Your training will start this afternoon, darlings,' she said. 'Your tutors will pick you up from here and take you to your work stations. As artists, we don't follow a strict working routine, but you are encouraged to train beyond your school hours. So, if you feel the need to sculpt at midnight, be my guests.'

'Great!' cried Morgana, her face lighting up. 'I mean, you never know when inspiration will strike you.'

'That's the spirit,' said Ms Davies with equal enthusiasm. 'I can feel it. You will do very well on Gassendi. Let me know if you need anything.' And, with that, she left them to their meal.

Julius wished they could talk freely about all the news they had just gathered but, with Siena sitting at their table, it wasn't possible and, given that their tutors were due to pick them up shortly, he knew that all planning would have to wait until the evening.

*

Julius' tutor was a man in his fifties, by the name of Walter Treat. Walter had spent the last thirty years of his life training in Gassendi, hoping that one day his luck would turn and he would create the ultimate masterwork that would gain him a place among the lunar rock sculptors.

'But don't feel sad for me if it doesn't, boy,' he said with a wink. 'I get to live in a fantastic place, doing the work I love, surrounded by likeminded people who always understand how I feel. And, believe me, that is a rare thing in life.'

Julius smiled, warming to Walter's optimism and passion for art. As someone who loved history, Julius had seen a few masterpieces in his life, and appreciated the intrinsic value of each of them. So, when he was placed in front of his first block of fake rock, there was no doubting that he would give it his best shot. To his surprise, the afternoon flew by, and it was only when Walter pointed out that it was past dinner time, that he stepped back to admire his sculpture. He crossed his arms and tilted his head to the right. Walter joined him and did likewise.

'I take it you meant to give it four legs, right?' asked Walter, delicately.

'Of course,' said Julius, trying to sound convincing.

'In that case, well done. You've just created your first four-legged, armless human being.'

Julius grinned, thanked Walter for his help and headed to the mess hall. Faith, Morgana and Skye were sitting at a table in the corner so he joined them.

'Hey, where's Siena?' he asked.

'She went to bed early,' answered Morgana. 'To tell you the truth, I'm tired too, but I waited for you so we can talk about the Oracle.'

Julius sat down. 'Sorry, I got caught up creating a masterpiece. I'll get something to eat later. Thanks for waiting though.'

'No prob,' said Morgana.

'Looks like Cress sent some reinforcements this time,' he said.

Morgana raised an eyebrow at him. 'What? Oh, the security guards. Yes. Do you think they'll complicate things?'

Julius shook his head. 'Don't think so. I'm sure they've been briefed to help us – don't see why they would stop us from doing what we came here to do.'

'Yeah,' agreed Faith. 'Sounds about right. Anyway, looks like this time it's pretty straightforward. We're free to roam around at any time, which means no need for sneaking about.'

'We've been *so* good at that up till now,' said Skye, sarcastically. 'Always seems to end in a detention. Seriously though, we'll have to split into two groups so we cover all possible areas.'

'Julius, how about you and Skye take the smaller diamond crater, on the other side, while Faith and I take the main one?'

'I don't know,' said Julius. 'Maybe I should take the main room, just in case.'

Morgana glared at him. 'In case of what? In case that's where she appears? You always get to do the fun part, Julius. Besides, there's a 50-50 chance. Knowing my luck, you'll get the room where the Oracle is.'

Julius looked at her and began to say something, then thought better of it. Morgana was a relaxed person but, when she made her mind up about something, she wasn't to be trifled with.

'OK, OK. Easy, tiger,' he said with a grin. 'Anyway, so I take it you and Siena are sharing a room?'

'Yes, but she normally falls asleep early. It won't be a problem coming out at night.'

'Then it's settled,' said Faith. 'We meet at eleven, here in the mess hall. Have your PIPs ready to record.'

'Tomorrow I'll let Master Cress know about our plan,' added Morgana. 'But right now, I'm off to bed.'

Satisfied now that they were organised, the boys were finally able to relax. Julius grabbed some food – grilled sole with a double helping of new potatoes – while Faith and Skye checked the latest Hologram Palace scores on their PIPs. They were suitably pleased that their records for team Flight and Combat were still unbeaten among the 2MJs, and chatted about possible tactics for future games until they could no longer keep their eyes open. Then they shuffled back to their bedroom and turned in for the night.

*

On the morning of his birthday, Julius woke up much earlier than he would have liked, with the unsettled feeling of someone who has just had a particularly bad dream. He checked his PIP and saw that it was only seven in the morning.

'That's the worst present ever,' he mumbled.

He lay there, looking at the ceiling, a sense of anxiety gnawing at the pit of his stomach. He knew why, even as he recalled the details of his nightmare. In it, Red Cap had been on Gassendi, in one of the workshops. Julius had tried hard to recognise the room, but it kept eluding him. Red Cap was sculpting something, assisted by Walter Treat. Julius wanted to shout at his tutor to stay away, Red Cap wasn't a friend, but no sound escaped his lips and he was unable to move, because he was trapped inside one of the protective force-fields. Walter had given the Arneshian a hammer and a chisel to use on an authentic block of lunar rock. But, as Julius watched, he realised that the surface of it wasn't grey, as it should have been. Instead it was transparent, like glass.

Red Cap chipped away, bit by bit, until he had finished and proudly held out his creation in the palm of his hand, for Julius to see. It was a sphere, and inside it something was moving and wriggling about, like a tadpole. Red Cap looked up at Julius and said, 'It shall be mine.'

Julius tried to shout again, harder than before, but still nothing could be heard inside the containment field. He was powerless to do anything as Red Cap walked away, escorted by Walter. That was when he had woken up.

As far as he could recall, he had never had premonitions before, and he wasn't the type to get scared easily just because of a bad dream. Yet, the reality was that Red Cap really had been back in Zed and obviously knew what Julius and the others were up to. There was every possibility that he would pop up in Gassendi too. They would have to be extra careful this time.

Since sleep was no longer an option, he decided to get up and treat himself to a nice breakfast. It was past eight o'clock when the others joined him, singing their usual tone deaf version of *Happy Birthday*, much to the amusement of the various staff members who were dotted about the mess hall. Ms Davies, true to her word, delivered his "fabulous present" as promised: permission to work inside Gassendi's special room for the day. He was overcome by a sudden, irrational fear that he would somehow end up stepping on the Oracle by mistake and making an almighty mess of the entire treasure hunt. He smiled nervously, aware of what a huge honour this was, and thanked her. She seemed convinced enough and left him to finish his breakfast.

Morgana, though, noticed his distress. When he told her what the problem was, she quickly reminded him that people had been working in the room for years already, so it was unlikely he could cause any damage that hadn't already been done. Besides, it would be a perfect opportunity to see if he could spot anything out of the ordinary about the place. It was enough to convince Julius to go in and he spent the day chipping away at a brand new slab of synthetic rock, or "listening to the block", as Walter liked to say. He sincerely believed that all blocks already contained an idea, which was a bit like their soul. By listening carefully to it, the sculptor was the *medium* who freed that idea, rather than its *creator*. This, he said, was the true path of an artist. By the looks of his sculpture at the end of the day, Julius wasn't entirely convinced that the idea he had just unleashed on the world made very much sense.

Later that evening, at dinner, Julius was treated to a lovely custard and nut birthday cake with fourteen candles, ordered especially by Morgana from Felice Buongustaio. But the *real* surprise of the day was that each of his friends had sculpted something just for him.

'Here,' said Siena, placing her present on the table in front of him. 'It's not great, but I know how you like history, so I made you a little replica of the *Duomo* in Siena, the cathedral of my city, in Italy.'

'Wow, this is really good,' said Julius turning the rock in his hands. 'It must have been difficult to make all those spires at the top. You did great. Thanks.'

Siena was visibly pleased when she sat down. Next, Skye and Faith stood up together.

'Ours is a linked present,' said Skye. 'I give you my home, Terra 3. May you be my guest one day.' He handed Julius an object resembling an elongated spinning top.

'Thanks man. I'd really like that,' answered Julius, gratefully accepting the gift. 'By the way, what's this flat tongue sticking out on the right?'

'That's my surfboard – the one my mum always threatens to chuck out of the airlock.'

'And here's me present,' said Faith. 'You'll be needing one of these if you're gonna go visit ol' mad goose Miller's home, that's for sure.'

Faith handed him a beautifully carved spaceship, in a model he did not recognise. It reminded him of a shuriken, the throwing stars that ninjas used, only the wings appeared to be much thinner than was normal. Julius could see that his friend had also done his best to create the entry hatches, the engines and the portholes.

'I invented it especially for you,' said Faith, with a hint of pride in his voice. 'When I've come up with a cool name for it, I'll let you know.'

Julius looked at him in amazement. 'Mate, you may be bonkers, but you're also a genius ... deep, deep down ... very deep down.'

'I'll take that as a compliment then!'

'And to complete the series,' said Morgana, stepping forward, 'here's your very own *Maneki Neko*!' She handed him a small, grey cat with an upright paw – a symbol of good luck in Japan.

'Good thinking, Morgana,' said Julius. 'Given the Red Cap situation, we could do with some luck, I think. Thanks.'

'What red cap?' asked Siena.

Julius stared blankly at her for a moment, silently cursing himself for the slip.

'Skye lost his cap,' said Faith, quickly.

'My favourite red one,' added Skye, trying to sound upset. 'It was Julius' fault, as usual.'

'I gave Julius the lucky charm, so he could find Skye's hat again,' finished Morgana

Siena looked quizzically at each of them in turn and Julius was convinced she hadn't bought any of it. Then her face relaxed and she turned to Morgana. 'Good thinking, girl.'

'By the way, McCoy,' said Skye, handing him a microchip, 'this is a voucher for Going Spare as well, since we'd agreed we would all use that shop for our birthday presents.'

'Thanks guys. This is just. Come on, let's have some cake.'

As he sat eating a slice, it dawned on him that his birthday had passed without any major crisis or disaster, as had happened the previous year. Tonight, he would chat to his parents from his room, as opposed to from the infirmary lounge, pleased to report that he was still in one piece. He smiled, happily enjoying the company of his friends, his earlier nightmare forgotten.

*

When the morning of the 20th of April finally arrived, everyone at the breakfast table, except Siena, felt slightly on edge. Julius knew they were all thinking about that evening, when the last Oracle would be revealed to them. He could see greyish wisps emanating from their heads, and knew it was a sign of the anxiety they were feeling. He looked down at his hands and saw a thin layer of the same colour covering his skin. He was glad that the others couldn't see this. Somehow, he felt that he needed to at least appear calm, despite how nervous he was. He had not shared his dream about Red Cap with them, as he didn't think it necessary to add any extra worries into the mix.

The best that he could do to make the day go by quickly was keep his mind occupied on his sculpting, and chatting to Walter a little in between. There was nothing more to plan – everyone knew their tasks. So, when at last eleven pm came, they met in the mess hall for a final chat over a cup of hot chocolate.

'Did you stroke the cat, Julius?' asked Skye, half seriously.

'Nope. Is that bad?'

'Basically it means that, if something happens to one of us, it's your fault,' said Faith.

'Thank you. Thank you kindly, sir,' said Julius bowing his head. 'I feel so much better now.'

'Don't mention it. I aim to please.'

Morgana looked at Faith with a raised eyebrow. 'I think it's time for us to leave.' And with that, she dragged him towards the exit.

Julius was smiling but, as they were about to disappear behind the corner, a sudden anxious thought hit him and he called after them. 'Faith, take care of Morgana, all right.'

'Roger,' he answered. 'Although it's more likely it'll be the other way around.'

Morgana hesitated for a minute, turned and looked curiously back at Julius. Then she smiled at him and disappeared around the corner.

'We should go too,' said Skye.

Julius nodded and together they headed towards the smaller crater. The corridors were eerily quiet at night, making Julius acutely aware of their footsteps echoing in the empty workshops. He was too used to the bustle of Satras, which never stopped, day or night, so he found this contrast a little unnerving. There was something a little odd about Gassendi too, beginning with the fact that it was not the kind of place one would expect to find in a military base.

'Why would Marcus Tijara want an artistic studio on Zed?'

'Kinda odd, isn't it?' said Skye. 'My dad says that, if you aren't that good a fighter, this is where you'll end up.'

'Seriously?'

'Nah. At least I don't think so. Besides, my tutor told me it was Clodagh Arnesh who got this place up and running, just a month before she was banned from the lunar perimeter.'

'That woman built an awful lot of Zed, it seems.'

'The girly stuff, you mean,' said Skye, sounding a little annoyed. 'Let's see, there's the ice cream parlour, the barber shop, the statue of the lovers and ... oh yes, an art club.'

'You're wrong, mate. You told me yourself she didn't become famous for her fluffy bunny collection.'

'Did I say that?'

'Well, not the bunny thing but, yes you did. You know just like I do that her brain was a match for Marcus Tijara himself.'

'I know, I know. But don't you go defending her because of the *good* stuff she did. She isn't a hero!'

'I wasn't ...'

'When you grow up on a space station like I did,' cut in Skye, 'the Arneshians aren't a topic for polite conversation, you know?'

'I know, but I didn't ...'

'Maybe on Earth it's easy to forget, but out there they're always on your mind. They could blast us all to smithereens without Earth, or Zed, even knowing it!'

Julius stopped in his tracks, waiting for Skye to finish. 'You done?' he asked.

'Yes,' he replied, lowering his voice. 'Sorry, I guess.'

'Never mind that. You're right, Skye. I have no idea what it feels like living out in the middle of the galaxy, far from Earth and Zed. But I'm here for the same reason you are: the Arneshians are traitors and as long as they want to control us, they are our enemies, no matter how clever they are or how many things they invent. I'm not defending Clodagh Arnesh, but you've got to know your enemies if you want to beat them.'

'Did Freja tell you that?'

'No. It was Master Isshin actually – before he went berserk and tried to kill us all last year.'

Skye smiled and held his right hand out to Julius. 'Ah man, I didn't mean to take it out on you. Sorry, but I can't stomach those traitors.'

Julius nodded and gripped his hand. He couldn't argue with that. 'Listen, last year you did a good job convincing me that the Arneshians couldn't even pee without us knowing about it, remember?' he said, lightly. 'What's with the sudden change of opinion?'

'That was before Zed nearly got wiped out last summer,' said Skye, starting to move again.

Julius took a few steps, and then stopped again suddenly. He cocked his head to the side, listening carefully.

'What's wrong,' whispered Skye. 'You hear something?'

Julius stood for a few seconds more and then began to walk again. 'I don't think so. Probably just the nerves.'

They walked the last few feet in silence and, when they reached their destination, they quickly checked that the area was clear. Once they were sure no one else was around, they sat down inside the small circular room, at opposite ends. Julius activated his PIP and made sure it was pointing towards the centre of the room, where he thought it most likely that the Oracle would appear, and Skye did likewise. Then, they waited in silence.

The minutes seemed to pass by way too slowly. Julius could feel himself getting tired, as his body began to relax, slumped against the wall. He looked over at Skye, who was also clearly growing sleepy, judging by the way his head was resting on his knees. Julius made an effort to focus and found his mind wandering back to his nightmare from the other night. His memory of the dream had been a little fuzzy when he had first woken up, he had been so disturbed by it, but now little details were coming into focus. He thought about the room he had been in, and the more he remembered, the more familiar the place seemed.

Suddenly, he sat bolt upright, his eyes widening in dismay as he was struck by the revelation that the room in the dream was indeed Gassendi's special workshop – the heart of the main diamond. A feeling of deep dread crept over him, banishing any hint of sleep from his head. Was he waiting in the wrong place? And why had he let Morgana persuade him that she should go to the main room, which was much more likely to contain the Oracle and quite possibly the danger of Red Cap appearing there too? His unease was growing stronger by the minute and he stood up.

'Whatsa matter?' mumbled Skye, startled out of his nap.

'Something's not right,' said Julius.

'What? According to my watch we still have a minute to go.'

'I don't think it's *here*,' said Julius, pacing around the room. 'It's gotta be in the main room.'

'Relax. Morgana and Faith will get it.'

'It's not the Oracle I'm worried ab- '

Julius' words died in his throat as the sound of a scream pierced through the night.

'Morgana!' he shouted, and ran out of the room, closely followed by Skye. The sound of several sets of running footsteps echoed behind him. He turned his head, not breaking pace, and saw Skye just behind him, with two of the security guards further back.

'Come on!' shouted Julius.

Just then, another scream filled the air.

'That's Siena!' cried Skye.

A brief thought flashed through Julius' mind: '*What's Siena doing with them?*' But he let it go – there was no time for that now.

Gassendi had appeared to be such a small compound the other day, but now it seemed to stretch endlessly ahead as they rushed frantically along the pathway. Julius bounced off the wall as he swerved around a bend, he was running so fast, all the while reaching out desperately with his mind to Morgana, but there was no answer – not even a hint of her thoughts.

As they turned the last corner and the door to the main workshop came into view, a cold shiver ran through Julius as he saw what was happening. An ominous figure, unmistakably that of Red Cap, was standing in the middle of the room with his back to the door. The two guards they had seen the other day were standing to either side of the door, looking in but not moving. Morgana, Siena and Faith were all immobilized, floating in midair at the far end of the room, their arms pressed against their sides as if they were bound by some invisible rope. Their fearful eyes followed Red Cap's every movement. Julius had only a few seconds to take all of this in. Had he had longer to stop and properly assess the situation, he might have hesitated. But right then, seeing them like that, he felt a bright rage surge through him.

'What are you doing?' he shouted at the guards as he drew closer. 'Get him!'

They turned and the one to his left shouted, 'McCoy, wait!'

But there was no waiting – he charged and leapt at Red Cap, aiming to grip hold of his back and pummel him with as many physical and mental blows as he could manage. But, instead of flying through the atmosphere as he should have, he stopped in midair, as if he had hit an invisible bed of jelly, and hung there, in the middle of the doorway.

Everything after that seemed to happen in slow motion. He tried frantically to move but every effort was in vain, as he remained trapped and powerless. He heard Skye's voice from the corridor behind him, but it sounded muffled and far away. Then it dawned on him: Red Cap had activated the protective force-field that the Gassendi artists used during their work, so preventing anyone from reaching him. That's why the guards hadn't rushed in, and Julius had leapt straight into the trap. He cursed inwardly as he hung suspended, forced to watch helplessly, exactly like in his nightmare.

Red Cap ignored him; his right hand was held out at his side, palm facing towards Faith and the girls. It was clear that, whatever he was doing, he was controlling their bonds and keeping them from intervening. The Oracle floated in front of Red Cap, delivering her message. Julius saw her lips moving but couldn't quite make out anything that was said. She finished, and his heart sank as he saw a small hole open up in the ground at her feet, and a little container rising up from within it. Red Cap leaned over and picked it up. His hand disappeared momentarily – Julius' view was blocked by Red Cap's back – and, when it appeared again, the container was gone.

Julius cried out in frustration. Red Cap, possibly attracted by the muffled noise, straightened up and half-turned, keeping his right hand pointed at the others. He edged towards Julius and drew his face close. Julius knew those despicable features far too well, the memory of them etched deeply into his mind. The cruel mouth; the harsh, square jaw line; most of all, the mocking eyes. The panic Julius had been feeling a moment ago subsided and violent anger flared up in him again. But there was nothing he could do to stop the Arneshian, and they both knew it.

'White Child, you're late,' said Red Cap, shaking his head like a disappointed parent. His voice was still slightly muffled but Julius could just about hear every word he said. Then his eyes shifted, focusing on something behind Julius. 'Too bad they can't help you. Time to go now, but make sure you come and find me – we'll have a little party.'

Red Cap moved towards the rear of the room, where Morgana, Siena and Faith were still hanging like flies in a spider's web. Julius became aware that someone must have raised the alarm, as several of the teachers and the two security guards were trying to push through the force-field, then pulling away quickly as they realised it was impossible to do so. Out of the corners of his eyes, he could make out people standing on the two stairwells and the observation deck at the top, staring helplessly down at them.

'Stop him!' he tried to shout. 'Somebody! Help them!'

Red Cap lowered his right hand and the three hostages fell to the floor. Without waiting for them to stand, he scooped up Morgana and Siena, one under each arm. Tightening his grip on them, he lowered his head, as if lost in concentration. Faith leapt up and tried to rush at him but Red Cap kicked him – he flew back and landed in a heap. The girls looked pleadingly at Julius. Panic and fear were etched all over their faces, as they struggled frantically to get away from the Arneshian hologram, but there was nowhere to go. The last Julius saw of them was Morgana's terrified eyes staring at him. Then they vanished into thin air.

CLODAGH ARNESH

Julius' throat was burning. Dr Walliser had wrapped a Heal-O collar around his neck, to soothe his voice box, and told him not to speak for an hour. Faith and Skye were also sitting in Gassendi's infirmary, more for moral support than anything else, since neither of them had actually suffered any injuries during the incident. Both Grand Master Freja and Master Cress had arrived on the first transport to Gassendi, as soon as word had been sent to them of what had happened, along with the doctor.

'I'm done,' said the physician to Freja and Cress. 'The boys are fine, but a few hours' sleep will go a long way right now. I gave them something to help them relax.'

'Thank you, Doctor,' said the Grand Master. 'We will join you shortly.'

Dr Walliser bowed his head and left them alone in the room.

'Gentlemen,' said Freja. 'Losing two more students was not in our plans. We are deeply saddened by this and we have informed the girls' families. Be assured, none of you is to be held responsible for tonight's events.'

Julius looked up at Freja and, unable to speak, sent him a mind-message. '*Sir, we need to find them.We can't just stay here!*'

'Mr McCoy,' said Freja, nodding in Julius' direction, 'says we should begin our rescue mission now. We are in full agreement there.'

'We've already been briefed by the guards we sent to watch over you,' said Cress. 'Two of them were up on the viewing area, keeping watch but, when they tried to rush down to stop Red Cap, he activated the force-field. He must have overridden the control box somehow – he's a smart holo, certainly the smartest I've come across. No matter,' he continued, shaking his head. 'We must be smarter. We will begin by retrieving and examining the recordings from each of your PIPs, plus the footage from the surveillance cameras in the room. That will hopefully help us determine the best course of action.'

The boys nodded. The mood had lifted a fraction – it was a relief for them having the heads of Tijara there, taking charge of matters.

'However,' added Freja, 'while we do that, I must ask you to remain here until I call for you. You need some rest and there is nothing you can do in Tijara.'

'But, sir-' began Skye, standing up.

'Mr Miller, this is not a request. It is an order!' said Cress.

'Yes, sir,' answered Skye, backing down.

Julius stepped towards Freja. '*Please, sir,*' he told him. '*Don't keep us waiting too long. Morgana ... she ...*' He had to stop, as a wave of emotion threatened to overwhelm him.

Freja put his hand on Julius' shoulder. 'I know. We will do everything we can for the girls – we will not rest until we have them all back.' He turned on his heels and, followed by Cress, exited the room.

Julius looked at Faith and Skye. Even if he could speak, he didn't know what to say and was suddenly feeling very tired. The shock of the night's events was hitting home hard now, leaving him quite unable to think of any clear plan.

'We all need some rest,' said Faith, gliding past in the direction of the door. He looked truly wretched.

Skye put his hand on Julius' arm and squeezed. 'We'll find them.'

Julius moved his head up and down a couple of times. Just then, he didn't want to think about anything – only forget his pain for a few hours in the arms of sleep. They trundled off to the dorm in silence.

*

In all, Julius managed a good eight hours of sleep, thanks to Dr Walliser's medicine. His voice was also back; his throat was a lot better and his mind felt much clearer. Of course, his first thought when he woke up was of Morgana. How would he be able to face Kaori or her parents, especially after the promise he had made to Mr Ruthier not too long ago? It was a sickening thought but, despite this, he felt strangely calm. '*We're going to find her!*' he said to himself, and he believed it. He had to.

An hour later, he met Skye in the mess hall. He was sitting at one of the tables, drinking a cup of coffee.

'Hey,' said Julius, sitting down.

'Your voice is back,' said Skye, pouring some coffee for him from the flask next to him.

'Yeah. Have you seen Faith?'

'He's right behind you,' answered Skye, looking over Julius' left shoulder.

Faith had just entered the hall. He hovered over and sat down at the table. He was still looking downcast.

'Are you all right?' asked Julius.

'I'm sorry, guys,' said Faith. 'It's all me fault. I should have stopped him. I should have seen him coming!'

'Faith, don't,' said Julius. 'I don't think any of us could have done better.'

'Yes, but I was there with them. I was supposed to protect them,' continued Faith, miserably.

Julius shook his head. 'Freja is right. It's not our fault. Let's just concentrate on finding her ... them.'

'You heard his order,' said Skye. 'We can't leave Gassendi.'

'Yes, but we *can* start our homework, right?' said Julius, tapping the PIP chip under his skin.

Faith nodded. 'I can pull up the CCTV footage from the room too. It shouldn't be too difficult to access it from here.'

'Great,' said Julius. 'Let's go to our room. I don't want to attract any more attention.'

'Sure,' said Faith. 'You know, it's strange we haven't heard anything from Ms Davies yet. I wonder what Freja told her about all of this.'

'That reminds me,' said Skye, standing up, 'she wants to see us, before we do anything else. She came by when you guys weren't here. I don't think she knows about the Oracle. As far as she knows, we were working late and the girls were just victims of the Zed kidnappers.'

They headed over to see her and indeed, when they entered her office, there was nothing in her behaviour to suggest that she knew any differently. Julius even concentrated on her aura, looking for any tell-tale wisps of colours that would indicate her being suspicious, but all seemed normal, save for a slightly grey wisp above her head that showed that she must have been quite upset about what had happened.

'I am so sorry, my darlings,' she said.

Julius noticed that her eyes were bloodshot.

'I feel responsible for what has happened, as you were all guests in my facility. Yet, as the Grand Master says, we cannot control fate itself. It seems he was right.'

'Madam,' said Faith. 'I know it may sound a strange request, but could we take a look at the footage from last night?'

Ms Davies looked at them for a few seconds before answering. 'I don't see why not. I already made a copy for the Grand Master yesterday. You can have one too.'

Faith thanked her, activated his PIP and moved closer to her desk. She pulled the file up from her desk computer, pinching it delicately between her fingers, and pushed it towards Faith – it floated in mid-air for a second before it got close enough to the PIP's receiver and was sucked into it like water down a drain.

'Thank you, madam,' said Faith, stepping back.

'You're welcome,' she replied. 'At the very least, this kidnapping has absolutely confirmed the involvement of the Arneshians.'

Julius looked quickly at Skye and Faith, then back at the teacher, putting on a puzzled expression. 'What do you mean ... madam?'

'Well, that holo with the funny red cap obviously worked for the Arneshians. He was talking to Clodagh Arnesh, after all.'

Julius gaped at her, suddenly feeling as if someone had just dropped a boulder into the pit of his stomach.

'What?' asked Skye.

Ms Davies looked at them in surprise. 'Clodagh Arnesh. You *have* heard about the founder of the Arneshian Empire, right?'

'We know who she is. I meant, was she there? Where?' asked Skye impatiently – he appeared to be so flabbergasted that he had completely forgotten about all protocol and formalities.

'Right in the centre of the room, my dear. Where else? It was only her holographic representation obviously. She *is* dead after all.'

Julius felt his whole body grow heavy and he slumped down onto one of the chairs in front of Ms Davies's desk. 'The lady in grey: the hologram – that was Clodagh Arnesh?'

'Of course! I know her face well. It was a young Clodagh though. I would say from right around the time she left Zed.'

'Thank you, Ms Davies,' said Faith, sounding rather shaken.

'That's quite all right. I'm not sure how much it will help though. You'll have to excuse me now, darlings. I have urgent matters I have to attend to. Incidentally, if you need the day off, I quite understand.'

*

'How thick can we possibly be?' said Skye, his face buried in his hands.

They had returned to their room in complete, astonished silence. The realisation of how big their oversight had been was just beginning to sink in.

'It was them from the start,' said Faith, who was hovering back and forth distractedly. 'The Oracle, the kidnappings, Red Cap, it was all the Arneshians. We've been played for fools.'

'Freja must have known,' said Skye, lifting his head up and shifting uncomfortably on his bed.

'Damn right he knew,' said Julius, drumming his fingers on the table. 'And so did Cress, but they didn't say anything. For some reason, they let us carry on believing that the Oracle had nothing to do with the Arneshians. Why?'

'You'll have to ask next time you see them,' said Skye, shrugging his shoulders. 'But, if Freja believes this hunt is worth finishing no matter the cost, he must reckon it can help us find the girls. You can be sure of that.'

'So what do we do with this tape?' asked Faith. 'We gonna take a look?'

'Sure,' said Julius. 'I want to know what she said.'

Faith switched on his PIP. He swiftly transferred both his recording and the CCTV footage into the desk computer. Once that was done, he plucked the virtual file from Ms Davies between his fingers and shifted it into the middle of the room. 'Computer, activate file. On screen,' he said. The tiny folder suddenly expanded and transformed into a holographic projection screen.

Julius sat back in his chair and took a deep breath. Seeing Morgana like that again wasn't going to be easy.

When the video started, it was quickly apparent that the camera had been positioned just above the door, inside the glass dome, looking towards the centre of the room. Faith and Morgana were standing by the back wall, looking rather excited, with their PIPs activated. Suddenly, though, their expressions changed – fear and panic were written on their faces as two more figures came into view, and Morgana screamed - it chilled Julius' bones hearing it again. Red Cap was holding Siena in a headlock and, when he reached the middle of the room, he shoved her at Morgana, who just about managed to steady her. At the top of the image, the two guards emerged from the shadows on the viewing platform and ran down the stairs to the left, rushing to get to the entrance of the room. Red Cap produced a controller of some sort and pointed it at the door. Immediately, the force-field sprung into life at the edges of the dome.

He turned around again, just in time to see Faith thrusting his right hand outwards, clearly preparing to hit Red Cap with a mind-blast. It was already too late though – as the holo lifted his right hand up, the three of them were lifted off the ground and bound by whatever energy-force the Arneshian was using.

'See, Faith,' whispered Julius, 'you did all you could.'

Faith looked down and didn't answer. Julius switched his attention back to the video, where Red Cap was standing in the centre of the room, with his back to the exit. 'Where's McCoy?' he said. 'You were all supposed to be here. Wasn't the clue clear enough for him? And who's this little eavesdropper?' He pointed his left hand at Siena.

'Kiss me metal skirt,' said Faith defiantly.

Red Cap sniffed derisively at him. 'No matter – I'll find a use for all of you, don't you worry.' Then he stepped back and waited.

When Clodagh Arnesh appeared a minute later, he bowed deeply. Julius looked closely at her, almost as if he was seeing her for the first time. There was no denying that she was an incredibly attractive woman but, where before that had seemed quite normal for a harmless Oracle, as they had believed her to be, now it didn't feel right at all. In fact, it seemed completely wrong to Julius that the person responsible for so much hurt, and two centuries of hostilities, should be so strikingly beautiful.

'Well met,' said Clodagh's smiling hologram, 'I am the last Oracle and I will grant you what you seek. To you who have found me and accompanied me on this journey, hear my words, for my time is short. On the exact date of my birthday, deliver my most precious possession to the wandering heart of Ahriman. Remember, only the bravest can reach the end. Farewell, my bringer of life.'

There was a muffled noise from somewhere out of shot, and Faith, Morgana and Siena turned their heads to face a point slightly to the left of Red Cap. Julius knew that it must have been when he had become trapped in the force-field. Unperturbed, Red Cap picked up the Oracle's treasure. From the elevated angle of the camera, Julius was now able to see what the Arneshian holo had done with it: his hand disappeared inside his belly and then reappeared without it. That was when he had turned towards the door, where Julius was hovering out-of-shot, like an insect trapped in a drop of water.

'Stop the video, please,' said Julius. 'I don't want to see the rest.'

Faith did so immediately, and let out a deep sigh. 'Well, at least it picked up what the Oracle said, right?'

Julius leaned back in his chair and closed his eyes. He forced the image of Morgana's terrified face out of his mind for a moment and focused instead on Clodagh's words. 'When is this birthday of hers, then?'

'We can look it up, but I'm sure Freja will know that already,' said Faith, searching the database on the desk computer. 'Here it is. According to this record, she was born on the 15th of May at 20:37.'

'We have 24 days left then,' said Julius. 'I'm willing to bet that Freja will want us to finish the Spring Mission in Gassendi. Mind you, I feel horrible saying this, but I don't think I'm ready to face Kaori as it is.'

'Well,' said Skye, 'there would be nothing else for us to do until then anyway.'

'I wonder if the clue means that we have to go to Ahriman, as in the *Halls* of Ahriman,' said Faith, who was looking a bit worried.

'It's the only Ahriman I know of,' said Julius, who was also quite nervous at the thought of it. 'Although she did talk of the *wandering* heart of Ahriman. Maybe it's not there?'

'Guys, before you start researching,' said Skye, 'know this: everything to do with Ahriman is top secret. You'll find no information on anything related to it.'

'Do we know *anything* about the place?' asked Julius.

'Other than it's used to scare kids, not really,' said Skye. 'It belongs to the Arneshians, and they build … things there, I know that much.'

'Me dad always said that, if you break the law, that's where they'll send you,' added Faith.

Julius had heard that one before, from his own dad but, given that he now knew it belonged to the enemy, he doubted very much that earthlings would ever really be sent there.

'Well,' said Faith, 'that pretty much ends our hunt and leaves us totally at the mercy of Freja. If he decides to leave us out of it, there's nothing we can do about it.'

As much as he hated to admit it, Julius knew that Faith was right. He couldn't see them being allowed to return to Tijara until the end of the mission, or Freja even necessarily calling to update them on the situation. All they could do was wait and talk to the Grand Master on their return. And, if Freja decided to leave them behind, they would just have to find another way.

*

The journey back was mercifully not as bad as their trip *to* Gassendi. Either the technicians had noticed the absence of the girls or they merely didn't want to deal with another pool of regurgitated breakfast. Whichever it was, Julius was grateful for the smoother ride. Over the last few days, his mind had been running amok with visions of Morgana's family waiting for him on the Zed dock platform, dressed in full samurai garb, their katana swords at the ready. As he got off the transporter and entered the main dock area, he mentally prepared himself for a barrage of insults and accusatory stares. However, all he found was Kaori, sitting alone on a bench, looking completely crestfallen. He stopped in his tracks, not sure what to say or do. Faith and Skye patted him on the back and waited quietly behind him.

'We're here, mate,' said Skye.

Looking up and spotting them, Kaori jumped up and ran towards Julius, who braced himself for a blow. But, instead, she opened her arms and threw them around him, gripping him tight as a flood of tears gushed out of her. Julius stood there with his arms by his sides, and allowed himself to be hugged, surprised and relieved that she wasn't angry at him.

'It's not your fault, Julius,' she said, as her sobbing eased a little. She turned her face first to Faith, and then Skye, 'None of you.'

Julius sighed, as all his earlier anxiety melted away. Now, feeling slightly awkward, he managed to raise his hands to her shoulders, not quite sure whether he should stroke or pat them. In the end, he just rested his hands gently on them, waiting for her tears to stop.

'Come with me,' she said to them a minute later.

Julius exchanged a quick glance with the others, and they nodded. They followed her and hopped onto the Intra-Rail. As they reached Satras, Kaori told them to get off. The buzz of noise as the door opened was in stark contrast to the quiet environments of Gassendi that they had grown used to over the last few weeks. In his present state of mind, Julius didn't really appreciate it. Kaori led them along the path beside the lake, past the Hologram Palace, until they reached an opening in the lunar rock. Julius had noticed it before, but had never thought to check inside it. It was a small grotto, with four wooden benches facing what looked like an altar of sorts. On its surface someone had placed a small projector pointing upwards, so that the pictures of the girls who had been kidnapped were displayed above it. Morgana was portrayed wearing her kimono, in a picture that Julius recognised as being from last December's annual meal. Her smiling face was lit up by the trembling flames of several holographic candles. The amount of mementos and small items laid out there was a little overwhelming – there were cards and good luck charms of all varieties, from students and staff alike, spread all across the surface of the shrine.

'Mrs Mayflower started it,' explained Kaori, sitting down on the front bench. 'She called it "The Wall of Remembrance".'

Julius took a seat next to her, while Faith and Skye sat down on the bench behind them.

'I didn't even know this grotto existed,' said Julius, quietly.

'It's always been here, as far as I know,' said Kaori, 'but the memorial started after Sharon Dally was taken.'

Julius sat silently, lost in his thoughts for a moment. The grotto kept the outside noise of Satras muffled, almost as if its walls were soundproofed. He appreciated the peacefulness of the place, and was deeply touched looking at the signs of friendship left there by so many different people. 'I'm sorry, Kaori' he said quietly. 'If only I- '

'Don't, Julius,' she replied instantly. 'I know you well enough to believe that everything you could have done, you did. My parents believe that too. What we need to concentrate on now is getting her back; getting them all back! Morgana's a strong girl – she'll hold on until we get there.'

Julius held her gaze. Kaori was right: there was no time for regret or guilt now. He would get her back, no matter what it took. Failure was not an option.

*

That night in the mess hall, each of the 2MJs came over in turn to where Julius, Skye and Faith were sitting, to show their support. Although they still had to keep the real reason for their presence in Gassendi a secret – the excuse that it had been a detention still seemed the best one at that stage – they did still answer a few questions about what had happened during the kidnapping.

'Man, that must have been scary,' said Lopaka afterwards, shaking his head. 'You guys could have been hurt.'

Julius nodded absently, but said nothing.

The mood around the Academy was understandably muted. The usual banter and mealtime commotion was at a minimum. Recent events, especially coming after last year's attack, had made the students quite edgy. It seemed that there was no completely safe place on Zed anymore. The disappearance of Morgana and Siena had also left Evita Suarez and Jiao Yu without roommates, so Evita had moved in with Jiao for moral support. It was just until the girls were rescued and returned safely to Zed, they assured each other. Everyone held firm to that hope, despite their fears that they would never see the missing girls again.

'Julius,' said Barth quietly, once the majority of the Mizkis had left. 'You'll find a way to get them back, right?'

'I will,' he said. 'You can count on it.'

Barth smiled, looking reassured. 'We'll see them soon, then. I know you'll succeed.'

'Thanks Barth, but ...' He paused in midsentence as an image of Red Cap's leering smile flashed into his head.

'But?' asked Barth.

'Nothing,' said Julius, pushing the image out of his mind. 'We'll get them back – that's all there is to it.'

*

On Monday morning, all classes resumed as normal. Julius, Faith and Skye headed to their Shield lesson. As soon as all of the students had filtered into the classroom,

Professor Morales called them to attention.

'Mizkis,' she said, 'I can't tell you how saddened I am by the disappearance of your classmates. This is a tough time for all of us. But I *can* tell you I have no doubt that our Grand Master will do everything in his power to get them back.

'In the meantime, though,' she continued, 'we will train twice as hard. Girls, it's no use pretending you aren't targets for the Arneshians now. Our advantage is that they seem to think you are *easy* targets. You are not! If they come for you, make sure you give them plenty of reasons to regret it.'

Julius was heartened by the way the girls all nodded their heads firmly in agreement. It was obvious that they had been in need of words like this from a strong woman like Morales. In fact, they seemed to take her message a little too much to heart because, as soon as training began, they set about the boys as if they were Arneshians. The lesson proceeded at a ferocious pace, girls against boys, except for Julius and Skye, who were set to work together, to compensate for the fact that the girls were now two short.

'Calm down!' cried Ferenc Orban, as the session neared its end. He had been paired up with Leanne Nord, a stout, blonde Canadian girl, and was presently trapped in a corner, kneeling under his shield, trying to fend off her increasingly fierce attacks.

'No! I have to train hard and you … will … not … get … me!' she said through gritted teeth, punctuating her words with frightening bursts of energy.

Immediately, Professor Morales had to step in and release the poor boy from his predicament. 'Excellent job, Ms Nord,' she said, leading Leanne away. 'You've got that move properly sussed out.'

'No nasty Arneshian's going to kidnap *me*,' she declared, scrunching her forehead and swatting her fringe away with one hand.

'Yeah, and no one's going to ask you out either,' added Skye, under his breath.

Julius kicked him on the shin, and Faith slapped her hand on Skye's mouth, but neither of them could restrain their grins either.

'Ouch,' complained Skye, stroking his leg.

'Shush – you deserved that,' said Julius, wryly.

'I think that's enough for today, Mizkis,' said Morales, who was standing at the head of the classroom. 'Well done, all of you. And remember, look out for each other, OK.'

As the students were packing up for lunch, Professor Morales received a call on her PIP. Julius was just gathering his things when he heard the teacher's voice in his head: '*McCoy, Miller and Shanigan – stay behind please.*' Startled, he looked up and noticed Faith and Skye doing the same.

Once the rest of the class had gone, Professor Morales called the three of them over. 'The Grand Master wishes to speak to you all now, in his office. Dismissed.'

They bowed and left the room. None of them said anything, but Julius sensed that they were all thinking the same thing: surely Freja was calling them in to reveal the plan for rescuing the girls. They were so full of anxious excitement that, by the time they reached the staff offices, they were practically running.

Julius knocked on Freja's office door and, once again, it was Master Cress who opened it to greet them. 'Come in, Mizkis. Go through – the Grand Master is waiting for you'

They headed into the main office, where Freja was sitting behind his desk. Three chairs were laid out in front of it. '*There should be four,*' thought Julius, and lowered his head as a knot formed in his throat.

'Did you watch the footage?' Freja asked, once the boys had bowed and seated themselves.

'Yes sir,' answered Faith. 'Ms Davies let us look at it.'

Julius looked at Freja directly. 'Permission to speak freely, sir.'

'Granted,' replied Freja.

'I take it there's a reason why we weren't informed of the true identity of the Oracle, sir.'

Skye shifted uncomfortably in his seat, and Faith elbowed Julius lightly. Evidently they didn't think it was appropriate to question the Grand Master in this manner.

'Does it bother you, Mr McCoy?' replied Freja, nothing in his voice indicating that he had taken the question as being impertinent. He held Julius' gaze, observing him in his usual calm manner. 'Or rather, would it have made any difference to the way you approached your hunt, had you known that Clodagh Arnesh herself had created it all and there was a good chance this was all linked to the kidnappings?'

Julius thought about it for a few seconds. 'I still wouldn't have backed down, but I also wouldn't have …' He stopped, unable to finish.

'Wouldn't have what?' said Freja. 'Let Miss Ruthier come along? I believe that, Mr McCoy. I also believe, however, that Red Cap still has a lot of influence on your behaviour, to the point where you lose sight of logic and, of course, control of your mind-skills. Had you known that he had been sent by Queen Salgoria to oversee the kidnappings and to personally take care of the Oracle's hunt, wouldn't that have affected you?'

'Maybe, sir,' answered Julius, still looking at Freja directly. 'But, like you said, I wouldn't have put Morgana in harm's way either.'

'Mr McCoy, I thought you knew Miss Ruthier better than that,' answered Freja, raising an eyebrow. 'You would not have succeeded. Miss Ruthier is just as headstrong as you are when it comes to finishing a job. You cannot make those decisions for her.'

Julius didn't answer, but inside he knew that Freja was right. Morgana would never have let him go to Gassendi without her. She was a Skirt through and through, as she had demonstrated last year, when they had first challenged Red Cap and his cronies in the Zed hangar. He had tried to send her away then to get help and she had almost ripped his head off for even thinking of protecting her like that. So yes, Freja was definitely right: Morgana would have insisted on going with them, no matter what he had said. 'But *you* could have stopped her, sir!' said Julius, staring intently at the Grand Master. Beside him, he heard a sharp intake of air from Skye.

Freja sighed and sat back. 'Don't think that doesn't bother me, McCoy. But there was a lot I had to take into consideration. We already had two girls missing and it seemed that you four had stumbled onto possibly the only clue that might lead to their whereabouts. Certainly those Oracle messages weren't meant for you. If I had started interfering and sending members of staff instead, Red Cap might have figured out that we were onto him and seriously jeopardised the mission. Our advantage, I thought, was that he *didn't* know that you had told us about your *treasure* hunt.'

Freja stopped momentarily and looked at Cress, who was standing behind the boys. 'Of course, we had hoped that the guards we sent would be able to protect you. They were some of our finest men – but it seems none of us accounted for the force-field, or for Red Cap being one step ahead of us. We *won't* make that mistake again.'

'That's right,' said Cress. 'And now, Mizkis, let's move on to what we called you here to discuss. What did you make of the Oracle's last message?'

'Not much, sir,' answered Skye. 'We know that Clodagh's birthday is on the 15th of May at 20:37 and that whatever she gave to Red Cap has to be returned to her on that exact date. As far as the location is concerned, we're not too sure. Ahriman is an Arneshian facility and all information on it is classified, so surely you know more than we do about it, sir.'

'Thank you, Mr Miller,' said Master Cress. 'This is all correct, except for one particular. Clodagh mentioned "the *wandering* heart of Ahriman" and that is *not* within the Halls of Ahriman.'

'You know where that is, sir?' asked Julius, hopefully.

'We know far too well where that is,' answered Freja, gravely. 'I myself was there once. The wandering heart is *Angra Mainyu*.'

Realisation dawned in Julius' mind, and quickly gave way to cloying fear. He remembered the name from a conversation he had had with Freja the previous summer. He noticed that Skye's knuckles had turned white, his fists were so tightly clenched, and a dark, wispy cloud was seeping from the crown of his head.

'I don't understand,' said Faith. 'What's an Angry Mineyew?'

'Angra Mainyu,' said Julius, flatly. 'It's the Arneshian lab where they experimented on those kidnapped people years ago.'

'It's where they found Bastiaan Grant's body,' said Skye.

Faith slumped back in his chair.

'When we boarded Angra Mainyu,' continued Freja, 'we became aware that Salgoria's ultimate goal was to create a perfect being by mixing the DNA of a powerful Arneshian, like her, with that of a White Child.' As he said these last two words, Freja quickly switched his gaze from Julius to the other boys.

'They know,' said Julius, aware that the Grand Master was trying not to draw attention to the fact that Julius was just such a person. 'It was best that I told them everything.'

Freja nodded. 'So, of course, this is why she tried to kidnap Mr McCoy last year. As you are aware, that attempt failed, and Salgoria's plan it seems, took on an unexpected new shape.'

Freja got up and walked over to the window of his office, which overlooked the school entrance. There, he crossed his arms and stood silently. The three boys were barely aware that they had leaned forward in their chairs, eagerly waiting to hear what this new plan was.

'It was our initial decision,' said Freja, 'that you should have no part in the last mission aboard Angra Mainyu,' said Freja, still staring out the window. 'Although we are well aware of your abilities and willingness to help, you are young and not even fully trained.' Julius was about to say something, but Freja raised his right hand, indicating for him to remain quiet. 'I said it *was* our initial decision, Mr McCoy. You see, the last Oracle is preventing us from leaving you behind.'

Julius looked at Skye and Faith, who appeared to be as confused as he was.

'"*To you who have found me and accompanied me on this journey, hear my words*",' said Freja, quoting Clodagh's message. '"*To you who have found me.*"'

'I'm not sure I follow, sir,' said Julius.

'Well, it's that part of her message, plus a couple of other things. When you first told me about the way the first Oracle scanned you before she appeared, it made me think.'

'About what, sir?' said Skye.

'That kind of technology has been around for some time; the retina scanners outside your rooms work on a similar basis. Except, the one that you found doesn't seem to have been programmed to identify any one particular person: it seems that it was more like a tagging device – the molecular signature of whoever was there would then have been stored in its memory banks. I'm guessing it's a way of ensuring that the person who started the mission was the one there at the end.'

'Wait a minute,' said Faith. 'Beggin' your pardon, sir, but none of the other Oracles used scanners.'

'True,' said Freja. 'That's very observant of you Mr Shanigan; except, they wouldn't need to. The three Oracles that followed must have been programmed to activate at the assigned times once the first Oracle delivered her message.'

'Why go to all that trouble though?' asked Julius. 'And how do we know the last Oracle will use a scanner too?'

The Grand Master moved back to his desk and sat down again. 'Think about it: if the last Oracle could be easily activated, the Arneshians surely would have found it before now. As we already know, they've been using Angra Mainyu, on and off, for some time. It follows that Clodagh must have put some safety measures in place to ensure that whoever was going to claim her prize would have to show their worth by jumping through a few hoops before that. Those were very specific clues too. They certainly weren't meant for you Mizkis.'

'If they weren't meant for us, sir,' said Faith, 'then why wasn't the scanner programmed to only respond to an Arneshian?'

Freja smiled enigmatically. 'We don't think it was meant exclusively for Arneshians either.'

'Then who?' said Julius.

'Ah,' said Freja, 'we're not a hundred percent sure yet. We've got an idea about that, but we have to check a few more things before we can say for sure. There's one other telling factor, which I'm sure you can guess, Mr McCoy. Something Red Cap said to you on Gassendi.'

Julius stared at him and then his eyes grew wide as he began to understand. 'He said I must come and find him. At first I thought he was just taunting me, but he was giving me a message, wasn't he? He knows that I ... we need to be there.'

Freja nodded. 'You were right the first time, Mr McCoy. *You* have to be there. In the Gassendi footage, Red Cap seemed upset by your absence. One of the first things he asked was where you were. When things went wrong, he grabbed Miss Ruthier because he couldn't get to you, knowing you would do everything in your power to get her back. It goes against my better judgement, but there is no alternative: you must go.'

'Wait a minute!' said Skye, standing up. 'What about us – Faith and I? We're not letting him go on his own.'

'Sit down, Mr Miller!' cut in Master Cress.

'Sorry, sir,' said Skye, obeying the command. 'But ...'

'But nothing,' Freja interrupted. 'There's no need for you to be there. The first Oracle only scanned Mr McCoy.'

'But there could have been other scanners, sir ...' argued Skye.

'Yeah, yeah – I'm sure I saw one of those things scanning us too,' chipped in Faith, unconvincingly.

'Please, sir,' said Julius. 'There *could* have been some other tagging device we didn't know about. Before the first Oracle appeared we saw more than one light in the cave. We can't afford to go all the way to Angra Mainyu without them and find out that they needed to be there too. Plus, remember when the Arneshians tried to invade us: I wouldn't have got anywhere without them – I need them.'

'That tells me more about you as a person than their *actual* need to be there, McCoy,' said Freja, sitting back in his chair and looking at Cress. For a minute, the boys sat in anxious silence. Then Freja sighed and sat forward. 'Very well.'

'Yes!' exclaimed Skye and Faith in unison, then quickly controlled themselves again.

'There's something else,' continued Freja. 'Since Red Cap now has Clodagh's gift, it means that we cannot finish this without him either.'

'Red Cap ...' said Julius, under his breath. 'Do you think he was there right from the start, sir?'

'Indeed,' said Freja. 'He was sent for the Oracle by Salgoria and it was only by a fortuitous chance that you four stumbled upon it during your game. I'm pretty sure he must have been there when you received the first message, even though you didn't see him. So he must have been following the clues and plotting to grab hold of you on Gassendi, Mr McCoy.'

'That means that Morgana is definitely still OK then, right?' said Julius. 'He won't harm her because he needs her as bait.'

Freja nodded. 'I think so but, more than that, I think all of the girls are still all right. Their kidnappings are definitely linked to this Oracle business.'

'Sir, what do you think Salgoria is up to?' asked Julius.

'All in good time, Mr McCoy,' replied Freja. 'We shall depart on the evening of the 14th of May. The Grand Masters of Sield and Tuala will also be onboard, as this matter concerns them greatly. There will be a briefing on the way, once we leave Zed. It's safer if you don't know too much at this stage.'

'Mizkis,' said Cress. 'I trust you understand the need for complete silence on this matter.'

They all nodded.

'Very well. You are dismissed,' said Cress, bowing his head.

Once outside the office, they walked along the promenade towards the mess hall.

'What do you think?' asked Julius. He was still quite wound up from everything that had been discussed – he felt a pressing need to clear his head and see what the others made of it all.

'Well, Freja obviously knows the score and has a plan,' said Faith. 'That *is* good news.'

'The *other* good news,' said Skye, 'is that we're going too.'

'Yeah,' said Julius. 'That is *great* news. And we're going in with all three Grand Masters, no less.'

'I wish Freja had told us something about the plan though,' said Faith. 'This way, we're left guessing for the next twelve days.'

Julius agreed with Faith, but unfortunately there was nothing any of them could do about it. He would just have to endure the anticipation as best he could. One thought in particular kept popping into his mind, though, no matter how hard he tried to restrain it. Last year, Freja had told him that the previous time they had boarded Angra Mainyu all they had found were notes and the bodies of the kidnapped victims, a fact that the Grand Master had been careful not to mention this time. *'Remember, they need Morgana. She'll be OK,'* he kept reassuring himself. But, even if that was the case, what about Siena and the other girls? There was no guarantee of their safety. All Julius could do, however, was hope that they weren't too late already.

*

To their relief, the days passed by mercifully quickly. Julius, Faith and Skye guessed that the other teachers must have been told what was happening by Freja because, in all of their lessons, the three of them had every possible defence and attack application drilled into their brains. None of the Professors had openly admitted as much to them, although Professor Chan had offered them extra classes to teach them several new katas, and Professor Beloi had offered them unlimited use of the labyrinth in the evenings, to help strengthen their mind-channels. They had willingly accepted and were not at all surprised when, during these extra classes, they were also joined by random members of staff. Thankfully, they had been discreet enough not to attract any unwanted attention from the other Mizkis. When Saturday the 14th arrived, Julius was pumped up and raring to go, like before a big game. He found it impossible to sit still and spent most of that morning pacing up and down in his room. Eventually, he was growing so impatient that he decided he needed to do *something*.

'I need to get out of here. I'm going to go to Satras,' he said to Skye, who had been working away on his computer and doing a good job of ignoring his restless friend.

'Yeah, good idea,' replied Skye. 'Let's take our stuff with us – no sense in coming back here before we leave.'

They quickly packed a few essentials into a couple of light backpacks, including their own Gauntlets, which Professor Morales had insisted they take with them. Fifteen minutes later, they were out the door, and stopped by Faith's room to fetch him. He had been tinkering away on his skirt, which Julius guessed was probably more to do with keeping himself occupied than making any real adjustments. En route, he typed out a message on his PIP and sent it to Kaori, asking her to meet him in the grotto. Although they had sworn to keep the mission secret, Julius had filled her in on what he knew a few days before. He figured she deserved that much and, besides, he knew she could be trusted not to talk about it with anyone else.

When they arrived at the grotto, Kaori was sitting waiting on the front bench. She turned around as they entered and smiled weakly at them.

'You look tired, Kaori,' said Julius.

'It'll all be over soon,' she replied. There was no uncertainty in her voice. 'When do you leave?'

'Shortly,' said Faith. 'We need to be at the docks in twenty minutes. Cress told us to board the ship before everyone else, just in case someone sees us and wonders what's going on.'

Julius opened his pack and pulled out the *Maneki Neko* that Morgana had made for him back in Gassendi. He walked over to the altar and placed it there, next to the other gifts.

'Don't forget to stroke it,' said Kaori.

Julius did so. Regardless of whether he believed in luck or not, it was still something that Morgana had given to him, and touching it somehow made her feel a little nearer. Julius sat down next to Kaori, and Skye moved over to the altar. He placed something on it that Julius couldn't see, but he guessed that it must have been for Ife.

Faith had nothing to leave, but he did stop in front of the altar for a second and stroked the cat, lightly. 'I'll take the luck of the Irish, and the Japanese, just to be sure,' he said, turning to face them. 'Come on now – we need to go, or we're going to miss the flight.'

As they made to leave, Kaori hugged each of them in turn. 'Good luck, all of you,' she said, a single tear spilling down her right cheek. 'Thanks for being such good friends. Morgana couldn't have wished for more.'

Julius squeezed her hand quickly and then ducked out the opening of the grotto. Together, the three boys headed up to the Intra-Rail stop outside Satras. They were soon at the Zed docks, where a strangely subdued Captain Foster was waiting for them. He led the way towards the shuttle pod that would be taking them into orbit, where they would be rendezvousing with the ship that would be taking them to Angra Mainyu.

'Mizkis,' he said, as they were boarding. 'Good luck.'

They all bowed, grateful for the gesture. A few minutes later, the shuttle took off, leaving the Lunar Perimeter far behind.

'Nice,' said Faith some time later, staring wide eyed out of the porthole beside him. 'Check out our ride.'

Julius, who had been lost in his own thoughts, unstrapped his seatbelt and crossed over to where Faith was seated. He leaned and looked through the window. They were just coming into dock alongside a large spaceship. Its outer hull was pitch black, like the open space around it. Several small lights were fitted against its shell, marking the outline of the ship. It looked much like a Cougar, except many times bigger, but it still retained the flat, raindrop shape of the smaller, one-man version. Their shuttle floated smoothly in through a large rectangular opening at the back of the ship and came to rest beside a long platform within the dock. They hurried over to the shuttle exit, eager to get a proper look at the inside of the spaceship, the first proper naval vessel that any of them had ever been on.

The hatch opened and, as they stepped outside, they were greeted by a Zed officer: a tall, stocky man whose name badge read "John Hardy". He bowed as they stepped onto the platform. 'Gentlemen, welcome aboard the Ahura Mazda.'

THE LOVERS' SHADOW

The officer escorted them to their quarters, which he had informed them were located on the upper deck. While they were walking, they passed several officers in the long corridors of the ship. Like John Hardy, most were quite tall and looked like they were at least a good twenty years older than the boys. All of them carried the air of seasoned professionals, completely at ease with each other and their surroundings – Julius knew that they had most likely been out here in space for who knows how long. The Ahura Mazda was probably more like a home to them than wherever they had originally come from. Certainly, as they drew closer to the upper section of the ship, where the main crew lodgings were situated, Julius immediately noticed how each of the berths had been decorated with personal items and pictures.

They reached the end of the corridor and Hardy stopped in front of a door on the right wall. 'These are your quarters for the next two days. The mess hall is back the way we came. You can get your food there from 19:00 hours. The Grand Master wants to meet you at 20:00 hours. Don't be late.'

They bowed as he left, and stepped into the room. It was nothing glamorous – not much more than a cubicle with bunk beds on both sides and a small lavatory area at the back. Julius dumped his backpack on the floor next to the door and threw himself onto the lower left bed. He was suddenly feeling quite tired – it had been a long day and the adrenaline that had made him feel like a caged tiger earlier on had faded away. The worries he had been carrying with him ever since Morgana's kidnapping were also starting to take their toll. It seemed that Faith and Skye were in need of some downtime too, because they both followed suit – Faith took the lower bunk opposite Julius and Skye the one above it – and were soon navigating their PIPs in silence.

Without realising it, Julius dozed off and was woken an hour later by Skye. 'Come on – I'm so hungry I could eat darkness. Let's get something from the mess hall before our meeting.'

Julius sprang up. He felt better – well rested. 'I really must have needed that,' he said, washing his face in the small sink at the back of the room.

'I bet the food here isn't as good as in Tijara,' said Skye, gloomily.

'Here we go again,' said Faith, pushing him out of the room. 'If it isn't girls, it's food. If it isn't food, it's girls, and so on and on and on, forever and ever and ever and ever …'

Julius chuckled and, closing the door behind him, followed them down the corridor. They found their way to the canteen easily enough. As they entered, every one of the officers turned towards them, making the boys stop dead in their tracks. Julius looked around self-consciously.

'Who the heck are these guys?' growled a man, sitting at one of the long tables to their right. He had a long, jagged scar running along his left cheek.

'Don't you know – that's for that babysitting job you applied for,' answered a curly-haired man to his right, which was greeted by a smattering of laughter.

'What's *he* wearing?' continued the first one, pointing his fork at Faith.

'Your sister's Sunday best, that's what I'm wearing,' answered Faith indignantly.

The scar-faced man's eyes grew wide, and a threatening hush fell over the room. Then he let out a booming laugh, quickly followed by everyone else in the room. Julius breathed a sigh of relief – for one instant he had been sure they weren't going to make it out of there alive.

'Knock it off, Kelly,' said a female officer, who was sitting next to him.

'All right, all right,' he said, wiping a tear from his eye. 'Just having a laugh, Elian.'

The woman named Elian motioned for the boys to come over to the table. 'Sorry about that,' she said. 'They're a good bunch, most of the time.'

'Hi,' said Julius, shaking her hand. 'For a moment, I thought we were on the wrong ship.'

'Don't worry about me,' said Faith. 'I can hold me own.'

'I noticed,' she said, grinning. 'Good for you.'

'Hi, I'm Skye,' he said, stepping forward. Maybe it was because of the surprisingly deep voice that came out of him, but Julius and Faith whirled around as if they were expecting to see someone else entirely. When all they saw standing there was the one and only Mr Skye Miller, they realised that their friend had no doubt just developed another one of his crushes. This was further backed up by the way he was suavely cocking his left eyebrow.

'Hello, handsome,' said Elian, with a smile, evidently playing along. 'Call me back in a few years' time, will you?'

'I'm already counting the days,' he replied in the same low drawl.

Elian laughed. 'Grab some food and join us,' she said.

The boys headed for the food counter, where a selection of reasonably appetising platters had been laid out.

'Skye,' said Julius, 'what happened to you when you were young?'

'She is *so* hot,' cooed Skye, ignoring him.

'Forget it, man,' said Faith to Julius. 'He's possessed by his own hormones. When they take over like this, you just gotta wait till it's over.'

Julius shook his head, and patted Skye on his shoulder as he scooped a helping of mashed potatoes onto his plate. 'I won't tell Morales, I promise.'

After grabbing a tray of food each, they returned to the table and sat down opposite Elian and Kelly, who properly introduced himself. 'Welcome aboard, Mizkis. No hard feelings, I hope.'

'I'm sorry to hear about Morgana,' said Elian, brushing a lock of her long, chestnut hair behind her ear.

Julius looked up in surprise. 'Do you know her?'

'I met her last summer, in the Canis Major. I was one of the instructors at the apprentice flying camp. I've never seen talent like that in someone so young before.'

'Yeah, she's the best,' Julius said.

'We'll get them all back,' said Kelly, quietly. 'You'll see.'

Julius stared for a few seconds at the man as he slowly ate his food. The scar extended from his left jaw up to his cheekbone. Whatever had caused the injury, it had missed his eye by no more than half an inch. Surprisingly, it made Julius feel more at ease, knowing that he was clearly in the presence of someone who had seen some proper action before, and so was more likely to know what to do if things turned bad. And, judging by the number of officers onboard, it seemed that a bad scenario was definitely on the menu.

For the next while, their conversation steered away from the mission ahead. It was as if they had made a silent agreement to keep the chat light and give themselves a chance to relax before the meeting. At 19:50, Cress arrived in the mess hall.

'First Officer on deck!' cried Kelly, standing swiftly to attention.

Julius, Faith and Skye quickly did likewise and bowed to the Tijaran Master.

'At ease,' said Cress, bowing back to them. 'Mizkis, if you are done we should make our way to the ready room.'

The boys immediately moved over to the door and waited for Cress.

'Second Officer Kelly, your presence is also requested.'

'Yes, sir,' he answered, promptly.

Julius waited as Cress and Kelly exited, and then followed them with the others. He was vaguely aware that his heart had begun to beat rapidly, as the thought dawned on him that soon he would be in the same room as all three of Zed's Grand Masters.

The ready room was near the front deck of the ship. As they entered, Julius was relieved to find they were the first ones in – he hadn't been looking forward to having all eyes trained on him when he arrived. A glass-top table occupied the middle of the room, surrounded by several black leather armchairs running down either side of the table, which stretched from a few feet in front of the door to the far wall to their right. Cress walked around the head of the table, where a single chair had been placed, and indicated for the rest of them to join him. Kelly sat down next to Cress, with Faith to his left, followed by Julius and Skye at the end.

Julius looked around him as they waited silently for the others to arrive. The walls were covered in monitors of various sizes and all manner of control panels. There was also a metal plaque on the wall opposite him, which read "Ahura Mazda – Captain John D Kelly".

'*Faith!*' said Julius, calling to his friend with his mind. '*It says on that plaque that Kelly is the Captain of the ship! Didn't Cress call him Second Officer?*'

'*Yes, but the Grand Masters are also onboard, remember,*' answered Faith, pretending to look at his fingernails. '*Kelly may very well be the Captain normally, but the crew on this ship would still answer to the Heads of the schools. So, if they're here too, then they're the highest ranked.*'

'*Do you think maybe Elian is his girlfriend, then?*'

'*Probably, given how much of a liberty she took before, shutting Kelly up like that.*'

'Hey! She didn't shut me up!' said Kelly, out loud. Julius and Faith froze and looked at him, blushing wildly.

'How did you …' began Julius.

'First off,' said Kelly, looking quite amused, 'give me *some* credit at least. I did study on Zed too, you know. Secondly, you guys aren't exactly subtle.'

'He's right,' said Master Cress, trying to look serious. 'I heard you from here. You may want to use a Scrambler next time. It'll give you some privacy.'

Julius and Faith turned a shade of magenta and sunk deeper into their chairs.

'I take it I missed something there, right?' asked Skye, leaning in towards Julius.

'Later,' whispered Julius, making a shooing gesture with his hand.

When the clock struck eight, the door of the ready room swished open and Freja entered. Kelly promptly stood up and called, 'Captain on deck!'

Everyone, including Cress this time, stood and bowed. Freja dipped his head and then waited by the entrance for his guests to step inside.

'Grand Master Sield – Edwina Milson,' announced Kelly, and then bowed.

Everyone else in the room followed suit as a stout, distinguished woman walked in. She responded in the same fashion, and then stood by her seat, just across from Julius.

'Grand Master Tuala – Roland Kloister,' continued Kelly, as a broad-shouldered man of average height entered the room.

Once again, there was an exchange of bows and Kloister stepped over to the seat beside Milson. Freja moved away from the entrance, to the chair at Kloister's left hand. There was now only one seat left empty – the one at the head of the table. After a brief pause, Kelly made a final introduction: 'Curio Maximus – Aldobrando Roversi.'

As he said this, a holographic image appeared in the empty seat, that of a tall, grey-haired man. Julius, who was feeling distinctly awestruck, seeing as he was now in the presence of the head of the Curia, bowed low.

'At ease,' said Freja and invited them all to sit.

Julius was filled with wonder as it hit home just how remarkable a line-up was assembled there at the table. Kloister, a sturdy, middle aged Austrian, was wearing the dark red uniform of his school. His fair, cropped hair and bright blue eyes gave a pleasant youthfulness to his face, which compensated for his stern gaze.

Julius had been told that Edwina Milson was from South Africa, and that she was the only Grand Master ever to continue playing in the Hologram Palace after being elected as Head of a school, which of course made her rather popular among her students. She was also dressed in full uniform, sporting Sield's official colour, a lively olive-green shade.

Although being in the same room as the heads of Tuala and Sield for the first time was a genuine treat, the real highlight for Julius was the presence of Roversi. The Curio Maximus rarely visited Satras, and only then for certain formal occasions. From his studies, Julius was well aware of how important the Curia was, being the political heart of Zed and a major link between Earth and the rest of the galaxy. He remembered reading about how the Curia had been formed with the express purpose of developing Earth's defences and overseeing the running of Zed and the colonies. This was in direct response to the defection of the Arneshians and the deaths of Marcus Tijara and Clodagh Arnesh back in 2628. Over time, its remit had changed, as responsibility for Earth's military protection had been handed over to the three Grand Masters, leaving the Curia in charge of diplomatic affairs and the exploration of the galaxy through its Colonial Affairs division.

'Thank you all for coming,' said Freja. 'I am reminded at times like this how grateful I am for Zed and the work we do. As you know, we are gathered here tonight to discuss a most pressing matter: the Oracle of Life. Each one of us sitting here in this council knows some part, but not the entirety, of this complex story. Therefore, for the benefit of us all, we shall begin by laying it out in full. Mr McCoy, would you tell us about your discovery, please?'

Julius took a deep breath and tried to fight back the embarrassment of having to speak in front of such an important audience. He began to recount their first chance encounter with Clodagh Arnesh, and spoke of how they had successfully managed to work their way through each clue, until that last fateful night in Gassendi. Admitting to breaking curfew, barging into private property and lying to superiors in front of these people, was probably the hardest thing that Julius had ever been asked to do; knowing Freja though, it could have been his idea of a *moral* punishment. He was mindful not to leave anything out, even admitting about how they hadn't recognised that the Oracle was actually Clodagh Arnesh. However, when it came to Red Cap and his part in all of it, Julius hesitated and looked over at Freja. The Grand Master nodded his head understandingly in reply.

'The hologram responsible for the Gassendi kidnappings,' said Julius, 'is the same one that organised the attack on Tijara last April. I call him Red Cap, but I have no idea who he really is.'

'Yes,' said Milson. 'Freja told us about him. He must be quite an important piece of Salgoria's puzzle to have spared him after the attack failed.'

'Carlos,' said Roversi, 'I take it you invited this young man here tonight on account of him being a White Child, am I right? But what of the other two?'

'You're partly right, Aldobrando,' answered Freja. 'Clodagh Arnesh herself made the other half of the decision for us. You see, the last message indicated that those who had been there at the beginning must be there to deliver her gift at the end. These three Mizkis, along with Miss Ruthier and Red Cap, were there at the start.'

The Curio Maximus seemed content enough with Freja's explanation, and Julius wasn't about to add anything else on that front. Besides, he was feeling quite distracted by how casually he had been referred to as a White Child. It was noticeable too how no one had flinched when they heard that. Obviously his secret was more widespread than he had thought. Even this Kelly guy knew, and they had only just met. Why would Freja tell *him* something like that? He was only a spaceship captain, after all.

'Very well,' said Roversi. 'Please continue.'

'We come now to the crucial question,' said Freja. 'What is the true nature of this "precious possession" of hers, and why exactly did Clodagh Arnesh go to the painstaking trouble of hiding it in such an involved way. Kloister, if you will.'

Grand Master Kloister straightened up in his chair. 'Thank you, Freja; I'll be brief. The three Grand Masters have long been entrusted with Marcus Tijara's legacy: his original scripts, notes, files, the lot. The majority of these items are in the public domain, accessible to Mizkis, officers and even the general public. Of these, there are a few which remain highly classified, known of only by the Grand Masters. One such secret, I will reveal now to the rest of this council.

'Everyone around this table knows that Marcus Tijara and Clodagh Arnesh built Zed together in 2620. We know all about their mind-skills and their unsurpassed talent for using them to their very fullest. We also know that, at some point between the foundation of Zed and the banishment of the Arneshians five years later, Tijara and Arnesh became lovers.'

Julius' mouth fell open. Of all the endless possibilities for what was about to be revealed to them, he had certainly not seen *that one* coming. Even Kelly looked a little flustered.

'However, gentlemen,' continued Kloister, 'this is *not* the secret. The fact that you didn't know about their relationship is merely a symptom of the passing years. It seems that, 200 years later, their love affair doesn't make headlines anymore. Next time you're in Satras, though, look around at the various tell-tale signs of their affection.

You see, Clodagh built Satras as a place in which to express her love for Tijara, from the emerald lake to the ice cream parlour – ice cream was Marcus's favourite treat after all. There's even a statue by the lake, which was commissioned for their first anniversary and made in Gassendi, another of Clodagh's favourite places.'

'"To M. Forever yours, C.",' said Skye, almost in a trance.

'Correct, Mr Miller,' said Milson, 'I'm glad *somebody* noticed that.'

'I must have seen that inscription a hundred times … but I never knew,' he replied

'Well, now you do,' she said. 'And it may be worth your while to refresh the memories of the younger Mizkis when you return to school. You too, Captain Kelly. History should not be forgotten, no matter how shocking the truth of it.'

Skye shifted in his chair, and Julius saw a greyish wisp floating above his head. It was obvious to him that his friend wasn't particularly enthused by this idea. He thought back to Skye's angry reaction, in Gassendi, when Julius had dared to mention *anything* good about Clodagh. So he very much doubted that Skye would be in any great hurry to spread this story back in Satras.

'What I am about to tell you,' continued Kloister, 'is something that is known only to the Grand Masters, and which the rest of you are obliged to not share with *anyone* outside this council. Not your fellow Mizkis, boys; nor your crew members, Captain Kelly; not even your staff at Colonial Affairs, Curio Maximus.'

'But of course,' replied Roversi.

'Understood, sir,' answered Kelly.

Julius, Faith and Skye simply bowed their heads in acceptance of this obligation.

'This information was discovered among Tijara's private papers, written by his own hand and confirmed by a series of medical records that accompanied those papers. It appears that, in the year 2624, Clodagh Arnesh fell pregnant.'

Julius stared in disbelief at the Grand Master, his brain working double shifts as it registered this latest news on top of the previous revelation, which had been shocking enough.

'Marcus was absolutely delighted,' said Kloister, 'and he expressed these feelings in his diary. He even decided to propose to her. However, it was around this time that Clodagh decided to steer her course away from peace, and to strive instead for dominion over Earth.'

'We don't believe this idea came to her suddenly either,' added Milson. 'Rather that it had been growing in her for some time. Already, she had gathered a big following, something that Marcus had been largely oblivious of, it seems, or at least the true nature of that following. Love *is* blind, as they say. And it worked both ways – perhaps the joy of Clodagh's union with Marcus made her mistakenly believe that he wouldn't refuse to join her.'

'But refuse he did,' said Kloister. 'And it seems he tried hard to persuade her to let go of her evil thoughts and instead think about their life together as a family. Clodagh was having none of it though. It would cost Marcus everything he held dear, but still he threatened to banish her from Zed if she didn't change her mind.'

Julius thought suddenly of Morgana, and pictured how she surely would have been crying by this point of the story, had she been there with them.

'It was then that Clodagh decided to leave. Marcus' rejection of her was too much to bear. The hatred she nurtured for his mind-skills drove her mad and she did the unthinkable: the medical records show that the two-month-old foetus inside her was removed from her womb and frozen in a secure, secret location on Zed.'

'Say what?' blurted out Faith.

'He meant to say "*sir*", sir,' added Skye quickly.

'Of course, sir,' said Faith, blushing wildly.

'It's quite understandable, Mr Shanigan,' said Milson. 'The gentlemen around this table seem to share those sentiments too.'

Indeed, as Julius looked around him, shock was written large on the faces of those in the room who were finding all this out for the first time.

'As you know,' resumed Kloister, 'in January 2625, Clodagh was banned from Zed, the Earth and all of their colonies. She took her favourite ship, the Angra Mainyu, while her followers were given enough vessels to take them all far away, and enough resources to terraform a new planet. Eventually, she did find a new home in the Taurus constellation, and called it Arnesh. Three years later, Clodagh and Marcus were both dead … but that is another tale.'

'After she first left,' said Freja, picking the story up, 'Marcus discovered a note, left behind by Clodagh. In it, she begged him to reconsider and join her. If he wanted to do so, he could find her and their child through the Oracle of Life. We had never understood that part, up until recent events.'

'The messages we heard were for *him*!' said Julius, as realisation dawned in his mind. 'The first time we met her, she said, "*I knew you would come back to me*" and the second time, at the lovers' statue, she said we were at their favourite spot. She was talking to Marcus Tijara!'

'Yes, Mr McCoy,' said Freja. 'She believed that, in the end, he would come back to her.'

'Sir,' asked Skye, 'how did Salgoria know about the Oracle?'

'We're not sure,' said Freja, 'but the most likely answer would be from Clodagh herself. Maybe, when Marcus continued to ignore her pleas, she decided to leave some kind of record of it for her own Arneshian successors. This is all guesswork of course, but it seems the most logical explanation.'

'But what can Salgoria possibly do with Clodagh's foetus, anyway?' asked Skye.

'She can build the army she's always wanted,' answered Julius. 'She won't need me or any other White Child.'

'If she's capable of reviving the foetus,' explained Milson, 'Salgoria would have the perfect being in her hands – the child of the two most powerful practitioners of the White and Grey Arts. The DNA would be astounding, you can imagine. She could clone it as many times as she needs.'

'Wait a minute; what do they want the girls for, then?' asked Faith.

Freja looked at the other Grand Masters, then back at the Mizkis. 'She needs a mother, a female carrier: my guess is they've taken a few so they can select the most suitable one.'

A deep silence descended upon the room. It took Julius a few moments to fully realise the dreadful meaning of Freja's words. Then, an idea started to form in his mind, like a growing ray of light. 'That really *does* mean the girls are still OK, right?' he said excitedly. 'They can't harm *any* of the girls until the Oracle's … I mean, Clodagh's gift is delivered, and by then we'll be there to stop them!'

'I believe you are correct,' said Freja. 'It's what we're counting on, anyway.'

'And now for our plan,' said Kloister, clearing his throat and turning to the Curio

Maximus. 'We have managed to track down the precise co-ordinates of Angra Mainyu. Between our present warp-speed and a further hyperjump, which we'll use for the last leg to catch them by surprise, we believe we *will* reach it in time. Clodagh's precise birthday is at 20:37 tomorrow night so, all going according to plan, we will board the ship ten minutes before then. We have no way of knowing what we'll find waiting for us onboard, but the three Mizkis should be with us. I wish we could avoid taking them altogether, but Freja is right: they may be needed to trigger the final Oracle message.'

'What do you intend to do with the foetus and the ship?' asked Roversi.

'Destroy them both,' replied Freja.

'The Grand Masters of Zed don't need the Curia's approval in these matters of course,' said Roversi. 'But, for what it's worth, you have our support. You are free to act in the best interests of Earth and Zed.'

Freja, Kloister and Milson bowed their heads courteously to the Curio Maximus.

'Cress will return to Tijara,' said Freja, 'and inform Master Lim and Master Carrero of our plans.' Then he turned to the boys. 'Mizkis, you are dismissed and at liberty until tomorrow evening. At 19:00 hours, you will meet Lieutenant Elian Flywheel in the mess hall. She will equip you for the mission. This council is now adjourned.'

Julius, Faith and Skye stood up, bowed to the others and quietly filed out of the room. None of them were quite able to believe what they had just heard. They wandered over to the mess hall, grabbed three cups of hot barley and returned to their cabin. There they sat for the next couple of hours discussing everything they had just heard, trying to somehow digest these revelations and, most of all, to fathom the consequences of what the Arneshians were planning to do with the kidnapped girls.

Julius could feel rage growing in him. How could he have led Morgana into this awful situation? He should have protected her better, but instead he had failed and she was now facing the incredible prospect of becoming the surrogate mother of Tijara's own son. The thought of it was so hard to comprehend that he was unable to dwell on it that night for too long. It was easy to tell that Faith and Skye felt the same – every time the conversation turned to Salgoria's plan, little grey wisps sprung up around their heads and hung there for a few seconds before dissipating again into thin air. Eventually, they grew tired of talking and lay back in their beds, each one lost in their own thoughts. Julius could feel a headache coming on, so he closed his eyes and slowly drifted off into a restless sleep.

*

The following evening, Julius sat anxiously waiting in the ready room. It was ten minutes until mission time. Faith and Skye were sitting at the opposite end of the table, in the seats that Cress and Kelly had been using the day before, looking every bit as nervous as he felt. They had all been equipped with special protective gear: a type of uniform that none of them had ever seen before on Zed. Elian had given them each a small button-like gadget, called an Exoskin, to fix onto their jumpers, over their hearts. When they pressed it, their bodies were instantly wrapped in what felt and looked like energy fields, but which quickly transformed into solid armour. The device also had a setting to extend this armour over the head, like a helmet. Its neutral colour was a dark shade of silver but, if it was pressed a second time, it created a chameleon effect and blended perfectly with the surrounding environment: this cloaking device could render a subject practically invisible. It was incredibly light in weight, to the point where Julius couldn't tell whether it was activated or not, unless he looked at it. They were all wearing their Gauntlets, which under different circumstances might have been quite enthralling, being entrusted with them like that outside the classroom for the first time. Not that that seemed to register much with Faith, he was so ecstatic about the new gadget Elian had given them. He kept pressing away on it, marvelling at its various functions, especially the chameleon setting. It was quite amusing to Julius, every time Faith activated it, seeing his friend blink in and out of visibility.

After watching Faith for a few minutes, Julius got up and stood in front of the plaque on the wall. He passed his fingers lightly over the ship's name and smiled. He liked it here. The crew seemed like a well-knit, close unit, and he thought that if one day he was ever given command of a ship, he would want it to be like this one. Maybe he would have Faith adjust a few bits and pieces on it, but the essentials were already there.

'What do you think of the name – Ahura Mazda?' said Kelly, entering the ready room.

Faith and Skye instantly stood and bowed to the Captain. Julius turned, bowed, and watched as Kelly approached him.

'It's a strange one, sir. What does it mean?' he replied.

'It's taken from ancient Iran – it represents the principles of goodness and truth. Do you want to know the name of its opposite, the principle of darkness?'

Julius nodded, his curiosity fully piqued.

'Angra Mainyu.'

Julius gasped in surprise. 'Salgoria's ship!'

'Yes,' continued Kelly. 'They were designed as mirror images of each other. Both ships were built at the same time, in a place that today we call The Halls of Ahriman.'

'Are the Halls really as bad as they say, Captain Kelly?' asked Faith.

'I'm afraid I can't discuss that. Still, the two ships are identical. One was built for Clodagh and the other for Marcus. She took hers with her when she was banished, and Zed kept the Ahura Mazda.'

'It must be an honour to pilot this ship then, if it belonged to Tijara,' said Julius.

'Oh, it is. I fought hard to become its commander.' As he said this, Kelly unconsciously rubbed the scar on his face. Julius took note of it but, although he was really curious to ask about it, he decided it was best left for some other time.

'I want to command a ship like this one day,' said Julius.

Kelly didn't answer, but observed him silently, as if he was sizing him up. Julius was just beginning to feel a little awkward, when finally the Captain turned to the door and beckoned for the three of them to follow him.

He guided them along a passageway which led onto a landing by the boarding hatch. A large window was set into the hatch, so they could see out into the space outside. The landing was brimming with officers. The Grand Masters were all there, standing off to the right, flanked by several stern faced officers. Julius noticed that everyone there had the Exoskins fixed to their uniforms.

'We're ready for FTL whenever you are,' said Elian, over the intercom.

'Very good, Helmsman. Wait for my order,' said Freja loudly, and then turned to face the boys. 'When we board Angra Mainyu, you three will go with Captain Kelly and his team. Under no circumstances do I want you out of his sight, unless he gives you a direct order. Understood?'

'Yes, sir,' they answered in unison.

'The Grand Masters and I will be with Lieutenant Parker and his team,' continued Freja. 'There will be four more teams on standby, led by Lieutenants Sanders, Molloy, Trond and Berger.' Five men, who had been standing off to the side of them, stepped forward and bowed to the Grand Master. 'May our mission succeed, for the sake of our people!' said Freja solemnly.

'So let it be!' the officers answered, as one.

Kelly led the boys to the left hand side of the room and said, 'Hold on to the banister, Mizkis!'

'FTL engaged,' called Elian over the intercom, 'in five, four, three, two, one. Skip!'

Julius felt as if he just stepped out of his body, exactly like before, when Morgana had fired up the Stork's hyperjump during their fateful flight to Kratos. The sensation didn't last long thankfully and, as he drew a deep breath to steady his stomach, the shape of Angra Mainyu loomed into view through the hatch window. The Ahura Mazda drifted towards it, carefully manoeuvring the airlock so it lined up with that of the Arneshian ship. A couple of minutes later, Julius heard a click and a green light flashed on above the hatch.

'Kelly's team, go!' ordered Freja.

'Mizkis, gear up!' shouted Kelly, pressing the device on his jumper, and then releasing the airlock door.

The boys activated their armour and flicked the safety off on their Gauntlets. At once, Julius, Faith and Skye were surrounded by twelve muscular officers, who formed a ring around them, shielding them completely.

'Skirts!' called Julius, turning to his friends and holding his left hand out to them.

First Faith, and then Skye, clamped their left hands over his. Julius saw scarlet wisps of excitement enveloping their bodies. The hunt had begun.

ANGRA MAINYU

When the airlock opened, Julius was completely taken aback. He knew that the two ships were identical, but to actually step into a darker version of the Ahura Mazda was particularly eerie. Even without the bright lights, Julius could see that the observation deck on the Angra Mainyu was a carbon copy of the Ahura's, and he was willing to bet that the internal layouts similarly mirrored each other. He suddenly wished that someone had told him about this design quirk earlier than Kelly had, because he would have spent some time checking out the blueprints for the Ahura if he had known. Now, however, they would have to rely on the officers around them to navigate.

'This way,' said Kelly, leading them through the hatch and down a corridor to the left.

Julius, Faith and Skye lifted their Gauntlets in front of them, and adopted combat stances, with their right wrists perched on their left arms for support, like Professor Chan had taught them. Faith's skirt hummed gently as he hovered by their side.

Julius heard light footsteps from the airlock behind them. He turned his head and saw Freja and his team heading right. Tiny beads of sweat were starting to form on his forehead and he wiped them off with the back of his arm. The silence in the ship only added to the tension he could feel creeping up on him like a ghostly presence, making the hairs on his arms stand up straight. It was discomforting, the absence of sound in a ship of this size – surely it wasn't natural. He tried to still his mind and tune his senses into everything around him, hoping for some small noise or sign that could lead them towards Morgana and the other girls.

Kelly stopped at the end of the wall on his right side, crouched down and peeked around the corner. When he was sure it was safe, he led them on, around the angle of the wall and up a flight of stairs that jagged back in the direction they had come from. As they reached the floor above, they saw Freja's team emerging from the top of a set of stairs to their left.

The boys watched on as Kelly and Parker nodded to each other and then indicated for each of their teams to split into two smaller units, with quick, precise gestures of their hands. They were now gathered outside an archway which was shrouded in dim shadow. They filed in and moved to the left and right of the chamber beyond – Julius, Faith and Skye with the group on the left – while the sub-teams moved swiftly ahead to secure the farthest sides of the area.

Julius kept looking around him for clues to Morgana's whereabouts but, in the poor light, he couldn't really see much. He could just about make out some kind of pedestal in the centre of the room. It was positioned in the middle of a raised, square platform that had four curved control-desks at each of its corners. Behind this area, Julius could see Freja, Kloister and Milson also staring intently at it.

'*Listen carefully, all of you.*' Freja's voice popped suddenly into Julius' head, startling him a little. He had never heard the Grand Master communicating in this way before, and he was amazed by how clear and strong it sounded. *'This is it: the core of the ship. The package will be here in about four minutes,'* he continued. Julius instinctively picked up on how Freja had used the word "package", obviously to avoid revealing the nature of its contents to the other officers.

'The Mizkis are present in the room, so Red Cap should be able to activate the last Oracle and deliver the item. We will let him do just that.'

'Sir?' There was a murmur of surprise from several of the officers. Clearly Julius wasn't the only one thinking that might not be such a good idea. Even Kelly was looking a little puzzled.

'In order to fully eliminate the threat of the package, it must be activated and its contents exposed. As soon as Red Cap does that, Kelly's team will take care of him.'

'Yes, sir,' said Julius, along with the other officers. He still wasn't entirely convinced that the best course of action was to actually allow the delivery to go ahead, but he was fully aware that he had also just been authorised to go after Red Cap once that was done.

'No one moves until I give the order – no matter what happens – understood?'

There was a chorus of *"yes, sir!"*, which gave a strange echo effect in Julius' head. He was quickly discovering how disconcerting mind-talking could be among large groups like this.

Everyone fell silent again, an air of anticipation hanging over the room. They didn't have to wait too long as, a few minutes later, a door at the top of the chamber opened and Red Cap entered. He walked casually to the centre of the room and onto the platform, and then stopped.

'I wouldn't move if I were you,' he said in an unconcerned voice, to no one in particular, although it was clear that he was aware of his audience, despite their camouflage.

'There goes the element of surprise,' whispered Skye.

Red Cap began his preparations on the central pedestal. At either side of the chamber, no one moved – Julius knew that, unless Freja gave the order, it would stay that way.

'So,' called Red Cap, 'did you bring the White Child, or should we just call this thing off now?'

He was met only by silence. Red Cap sniggered. It was obvious that he already knew the answer to his question and was just taunting them. Not only that, but he had just revealed that there was a "White Child" in the room – word of that would quickly spread among the officers afterwards. Julius was aware that this was a deliberate ploy. Red Cap's arrogance infuriated him and he struggled to contain the anger that was bubbling up inside him like a raging volcano. He thought of everything they had been subjected to by the Arneshians: the girls who had been kidnapped to use like meaningless vessels and discarded as Salgoria saw fit; he thought of the Ruthiers and the other parents – the desperation and worry they must be feeling – and it burned through him. The time had come to settle this score once and for all.

He was so consumed by the thought of vengeance that he was oblivious to how the adrenaline had begun to pump through his veins: waves of energy were rising up in him, causing tiny sparks at the tips of his fingers, creating the illusion that energy was actually dripping from his hands. He didn't even notice how the officers around him were edging away from him. Even Faith and Skye, who had witnessed Julius' abilities at first hand, were unable to stay close to him. It was as if they were being pushed aside by a growing orb of energy around their friend. But Julius remained unaware of this; his mind bent solely on Red Cap. As he watched, every sinew tensed, like a wolf waiting to pounce on its prey, the Arneshian holo spoke again.

'Come now, White Child – enough of the games. Step forward. We both know nothing happens if you don't.'

Julius tried to calm himself and waited for Freja to give him some kind of order, but there was nothing. Maybe the Grand Master was waiting for him to make a move. He decided the only way forward was to see this one out, and he *was* itching to get at Red Cap. He stood up and began to walk forward.

'*Only* you!' said Red Cap menacingly. 'Or your friends don't see another school year.' With that, he held up a small silver controller in his left hand and pointed up to the ceiling. It had been shrouded in darkness before but now bright light illuminated it.

Julius looked up and gasped. High in the air, four pods could be seen gently bobbing below the domed ceiling. He strained his eyes and saw that inside them were the four kidnapped Mizkis: Ife, Sharon, Siena and Morgana, whose dark hair was floating ethereally around her face, as if her pod was filled with some kind of liquid. Red Cap pointed his right hand upwards and shot a small blast of energy towards them – it struck just below them and rippled in the air, revealing for a minute an underlying field of energy.

'If you hurt them-' shouted Julius. To his left, Faith and Skye sprang forward and then stopped dead as Julius shot a mind-message at them: '*Don't! That won't help.*' He wondered why none of the officers had moved yet.

'As long as you're a good boy, and your soldier friends stay where they are, I won't do anything to them. Think fast – time is short, little one,' Red Cap finished mockingly.

A sense of utter desperation filled Julius. This wasn't how it was supposed to go. And what was Freja doing? There was still not even a hint of an order from him. He looked up at the girls again and walked towards him – there really was no other choice. Red Cap smiled and waved Julius closer. He inched forward hesitantly onto the platform; being so near to the Arneshian was a torture in itself. His muscles trembled from the effort of controlling himself.

A few seconds later, a small hole appeared in the pedestal. A ray of turquoise light, like the one that had appeared in the cave before the first Oracle appeared, emanated out of it, scanned Julius from head to toe and blinked out again. There was a loud beep and the last Oracle sprang into dazzling life.

'You fill my heart with joy, my love,' she said, spreading her arms out.

Julius studied Clodagh's face: so beautiful and yet forever tainted now that he knew what she had done, and the suffering that her obsession had caused for so many. In that brief instance, however, her expression was a picture of tenderness and anticipation, a woman longing for a lost love to return to her.

'*She really believed he would come back,*' thought Julius to himself. There was no empathy in that knowledge though – in the grand scheme of things, he couldn't bring himself to feel sorry for her.

'Give it to me,' she said, extending her hands, 'and I shall create it for us.'

Red Cap reached into his chest and pulled out the container, then gently placed it on her outstretched palms. Clodagh's hands closed around it and drew it in towards her belly, where it vanished inside her holographic body.

'*Now!*' he heard Freja's voice in his mind. He swung his head from left to right and saw the officers who had been waiting on either side burst forward towards them.

'No, no,' said Red Cap calmly, extending his left hand outwards and flicking a red button on the silver controller. A blue, electric force-field sprung up around the edges of the raised area, blocking them all out and trapping Julius inside with Red Cap. As this happened, a loud buzzing sound filled the room, and an army of Arneshian holograms materialised at the back of the chamber. Julius pointed his Gauntlet at Red Cap but the holo knocked him back with a thrust of energy from his right hand 'This time we win,' he said, raising the controller up above his head.

'I don't think so!' Freja's voice rang out, clear and commanding, from Julius' right. The outline of a man's shape could just be made out against the inside of the control-desk in that corner.

'*He was hiding there all along,*' thought Julius incredulously,

The Grand Master's camouflage melted away and, quick as lightning, he made a grabbing gesture with his left hand. The controller flew out of Red Cap's hand and into Freja's. Without missing a beat, he fired an energy burst, which the Arneshian just managed to deflect, but the force of it knocked him back against the desk behind him. An instant later, Freja clicked the button on the controller and the force-field disappeared. 'The Oracle!' he shouted and immediately two white rays of energy, coming from the other Grand Masters, enveloped Clodagh, forming a cocoon around her and dragging her slowly toward the right sideline.

The Zed officers were now engaged in a full-on battle with the Arneshian holograms. The room was ablaze with the light of the energy-bursts from their Gauntlets. Julius had been so stunned by how quickly everything had happened, never mind the shock of seeing Freja appear seemingly from out of thin air, that he had been completely caught off guard. Now, clarity returned to his mind and he searched with his eyes for his old enemy. Red Cap had recovered and was on his feet again. He briefly made as if he was going to attack Freja, but hesitated. Instead he swung around, leapt up on the controller desk and hurdled over the heads of a group of soldiers behind it. He landed effortlessly beyond them and sprinted for a door in the far corner of the right wall. A red mist descended over Julius and he dashed after him.

'McCoy! Wait for us!' he heard Kelly shout from his left, but there was no stopping him now.

'Let's go! Let's go!' cried Skye, motioning for Kelly to follow as he took off after Julius.

'Get your blinking shield up, Julius!' shouted Faith, switching his own one on and zooming over to his friend's side to protect him from any stray fire. Julius managed to activate his just in time to block a shot from Red Cap as he sprinted through the door after him.

Kelly and his team advanced after them. A handful of the men crouched down in a row, their shields held out in front of them like a protective wall, and fired at a clump of holos that were trying to stop them. The rest targeted a group that was attempting to follow. Their shots, despite them being on the move, hit their marks and several of the holograms disappeared in an instant.

Julius, Faith and Skye, meanwhile, had just turned a corner in the passageway beyond the doorway. They suddenly found themselves in a large room that was brimming with more of the Arneshian soldiers.

'Aim for the boxes above their heads!' yelled Julius, keeping his eyes fixed on Red Cap. He moved over to Skye, their shields side by side to shelter them from the volley of energy-bursts that the hologram army was firing at them. Kelly's men had fought their way out of the chamber and were now streaming into the room, their defences up to form a barricade, and were advancing steadily forward.

'Wait, where's Faith?' said Skye, and then stopped, his eyes growing wide as he spotted him.

While the Arneshians had been distracted by Julius, Skye and Kelly's team, Faith had taken full advantage of the situation and stealthily snuck over to the centre of the room. There he stopped, hovering just above the ground, and shouted, 'Duck!'

Everyone hit the ground, and the holograms whirled around, suddenly aware of this new threat. It was too late though, as Faith launched himself into a spin, his Gauntlet held out in front of him, firing off a volley of energy while he twirled on the spot, spreading devastation among the holos. 'Behold, the rotating fury!' he cried.

'He's absolutely bonkers!' said Kelly, booming with laughter. 'I like it!'

The holograms were swept away by the carousel of energy crashing into them, their small red controller-boxes clattering to the floor as they blinked out of existence. It was only when there was a small handful of them left that they decided to retreat through the side exit. Kelly and his men leapt to their feet and ran after them.

'Mizkis, follow us!' he shouted, as he led his team out, not stopping to check that they were behind him. So he didn't notice that Julius, Faith and Skye had no intention of following.

Julius stepped into the middle of the room, hot rage coursing through him. 'Show yourself!' he yelled.

'I'm right here, White Child,' said Red Cap, stepping out of the shadows. 'You children have been a nuisance for far too long. How about you all just die now?'

Before any of them had a chance to react, he flung his hands outwards in a pushing motion, and the boys flew across the room. Like an arrow, Faith careened out the door and crashed into a group of Zed officers in the passageway beyond it. Skye smashed into the back wall and was knocked out cold.

Julius landed in a heap on the floor several feet from where he had been standing, his upper teeth biting down as he hit the floor, splitting his lower lip open. He dragged himself up, wiping the blood from his mouth with the back of his hand.

'Is that it?' he shouted. 'You Arneshians are nothing but cowards. Look at you, sending a bunch of bully holos to do your dirty work. You're nothing, you hear me? You don't even exist!'

'Such anger,' said Red Cap, shaking his head in disappointment. He lifted his right hand and Julius was scooped up high into the air, where he hung suspended, wriggling and twisting desperately to try to free himself.

While this was happening, Faith had recovered and rushed back into the room. He hurried over to where Skye was lying and knelt in front of him so they were both protected by his shield. From there, he fired several shots at Red Cap. The holo easily blocked them with his empty hand, however, and deflected them back at Faith, who had to duck behind his shield to avoid being killed by his own energy-bursts.

'Wha ... what hit me?' groaned Skye, regaining consciousness.

'If you're done napping, we could use your help,' said Faith, not turning to look at him.

Skye shook his head, suddenly remembering where he was. He flicked his shield on as he scrambled to his feet, and started to shoot at Red Cap. Unfazed, Red Cap continued to block them with his left hand. As he did this, he began to rotate his right hand in increasingly rapid arcs. Invisible cords of energy wrapped around Julius' upper body and bright dots filled his vision as the breath was squeezed out of him. '*I have to stop him,*' he thought desperately, but there was nothing he could do – he couldn't lift his Gauntlet because his arms were trapped behind his back.

Just as he was beginning to black out he saw, as if through a haze, Kelly and two men rush into the room and charge. It was enough to briefly distract Red Cap and Julius felt the grip around his chest loosen. He strained with all his might and managed to pull his right arm free. With his Gauntlet drawn up in front of him, he took aim and shouted with his mind, for all in the room to hear, '*Shoot his box! The controller box!*'

Red Cap couldn't hear this, but he must have felt something because his head turned toward Julius, a confused expression on his face. Julius stared coldly at him. 'Party's over. Time you were leaving!'

'No-' Red Cap began, but he was cut short as six beams of energy flashed through him, knocking the remote device off his head. His eyes widened in disbelief, and then he was gone.

Julius fell to the floor and quickly got to his feet again. 'Come on – let's finish this,' he said, walking over to the red box lying on the floor.

Captain Kelly, Faith and Skye moved over to his side, surrounding the device. They readied their Gauntlets and pointed them at it.

'On three,' said Julius, breathing heavily. 'One ... two ... t-'

Suddenly the red box whisked past them, off to the right, as if pulled by a magnetic force.

'What the-' said Kelly, as they turned on their heels to follow it.

Standing by the door, covered in dust and scratches, Grand Master Kloister was holding the box in his left hand. 'Come with me,' he ordered. 'I'll show you how we're going to do this. And we need a few extra hands over there.'

They looked quickly at each other and then set off after Kloister, who led them along the passageway, back to the central chamber.

'Wow,' said Faith, as they entered the room. 'You guys really didn't like the furniture, did you?'

They stood there, admiring the devastation that had been rained down on the place. The floor was littered with red boxes, some torn in half, some still smoking. Large chunks had been blown out of the control-desks on the platform and the pedestal had been completely destroyed. The Clodagh hologram was nowhere to be seen. Julius looked around and saw Freja and Milson huddled together in quiet discussion. The Grand Masters had their backs to them, making it impossible to hear what they were saying. Julius, like everyone else, waited in anticipation for them to finish, his eyes darting from them to Morgana and back. A minute later, Milson stood up and silently left the chamber.

'Gentlemen,' said Kloister, turning to the teams. 'What say we get our girls down and see how they're doing?'

They all gathered around him. Freja joined them and pushed a blue button on the silver controller he had yanked away from Red Cap. The field of energy below the girls fizzled out, but the pods remained where they were.

'All together now,' said Freja. 'Hold them steady.'

They fixed onto the pods with their minds and dragged them gently downwards. As they touched the ground, the pods exploded with small popping sounds, leaving the girls lying on the floor, covered in a goo-like substance. Morgana opened her eyes and let out a couple of wet coughs. She tried to get to her feet, but then thought better of it and instead knelt there, blinking at the mess around her. A second later she was enfolded by two arms.

'Wai … wha …' she mumbled weakly.

'Welcome back,' said Julius, squeezing her tight and grinning with delight.

Morgana hugged him, then pushed him gently away and looked at her dripping clothes, before gazing around blankly at the room. When she saw Siena, kneeling off to her left, shivering like a bedraggled cat, she finally remembered. Looking Julius in the eyes, she said, 'You guys came for us.'

'Actually,' said Faith, hovering over to them, with Skye just behind, 'we were tempted to leave you with the Arneshians. But then I figured, if I let the best pilot on Zed go, then who's going to fly me ships?'

'Come here you,' said Morgana, shaking her head and holding her arms out to them. 'Both of you.' They hurried over and she hugged them tight, while tears streamed down her face.

Julius sat with his legs stretched out, his trousers drenched from the liquid that had oozed out of the pods, but he didn't care. He was far too tired, and happy, to worry about a soggy bottom.

'We're not quite finished yet,' said Freja, gently. 'Let's get back to our ship.'

Kelly lifted Morgana off the floor in an easy gesture and carried her off. Three other officers gathered the remaining girls in their arms and followed him. Skye walked beside the man who was carrying Ife, holding her hand in his.

'Grand Master Freja,' said Julius, as they were leaving the chamber.

Freja stopped and turned to him, with a look of contentment which Julius had never seen before, on his face.

'Which one is Red Cap's box, sir?'

'That one there, by the broken pedestal,' he answered. 'Kloister thought it was an appropriate resting place.'

Julius looked back at it. He longed to shoot it himself, there and then, just to be sure. But Kloister had already decided its fate, and it was not for Julius to ignore a Grand Master's wish.

'It's over, McCoy. You did it, and you can finally put *him* out of your mind. Let's go now. I can't wait to blow this vessel to smithereens.'

'I couldn't agree more,' said Julius. 'You know, sir, you were pretty impressive back there, if you don't mind me saying.'

Freja smiled at him. 'I've still got a few tricks up my sleeve, McCoy.'

They walked down to the lower level and, by the time they reached the exit, Julius had just one nagging question that was begging to be answered. 'Sir?'

'Yes, McCoy?'

'Do you think Captain Kelly would let me join him for part of the Summer Camp?' Freja turned to look at him and, as always, seemed to pierce right through him with his gaze.

'Sorry, sir,' said Julius, turning red. 'It was a silly idea. Captain Kelly probably doesn't-'

'I'll see what I can do,' answered Freja, cutting him off.

*

Once they were back on the Ahura Mazda, the Mizkis were told to go to the observation deck. The resident doctor, upon hearing of their success, had hurried up to meet them, and said that he needed to check the girls immediately to make sure they were definitely all right. However, Freja insisted that they be allowed to watch the destruction of the Angra Mainyu – it was, in his opinion, the best possible medicine. Given that they were all now back on their feet, walking unassisted, and seemed to be suffering no obvious after-effects, the doctor relented and agreed to wait a few minutes.

Morgana stood between Julius and Faith, a blanket wrapped around her shoulders. Skye was standing with Ife, while Sharon and Siena sat by the window.

Julius watched the ship slowly moving away from them. When the explosion came, the Ahura Mazda didn't even twitch. A bright, silent wave washed over the hull of their vessel, so intense that Julius had to shield his eyes for a moment. Knowing that Red Cap would forever be buried with it did seem quite fitting now that he thought about it.

Clodagh's spaceship, and everything in it, was destroyed in that blast; its debris destined to travel through space for all eternity.

LEGACY

For the second time in a year, Julius was about to disembark in the Zed docks with dread in his heart. The first time he had been afraid to face Kaori, right after Morgana had been kidnapped. Today, he would be facing her entire family and, although the rescue mission had been successful, there would be a lot of apologising to do.

The Grand Masters had sent word of the successful rescue mission to the girls' immediate families, along with special permission for them to fly in and stay with their daughters in Satras for a few days. Julius thought that was a particularly good idea, especially since the girls were bound to be subjected to a barrage of questions from the Mizkis once they returned to school. Julius had been in that position the year before, so he had a great deal of sympathy for them. It had been a tiring experience. Moreover, before leaving the Ahura Mazda, each of the four girls had to swear, under oath, that the presence of McCoy, Shanigan and Miller would be kept secret. Ife, Sharon and Siena had seemed a little surprised by that, but none of them had objected.

When the doors opened, the three Grand Masters filed out in their pristine uniforms and headed straight for the waiting parents. Through a porthole on the deck, Julius could see numerous handshakes being exchanged, along with heartfelt thanks for bringing back their daughters. Then, it was the girls' turn to emerge from the ship. As soon as they appeared, all composure left their parents and they were swept up in a whirlpool of joyful tears and crushing embraces. Julius, Faith and Skye waited for a while in the shadows and, when they were sure that no one was paying attention, they hurriedly disembarked. They had just managed to make it to the nearest exit, when a man called out, 'Julius!'

He stopped and turned – it was Morgana's dad. Mr Ruthier jogged towards him and Julius held his breath. Then he noticed a telltale white wisp floating above Mr Ruthier's head and a wave of relief washed over him. A feeling of guilt still lingered but, as he opened his mouth to apologise, he was left speechless by the intensity of the hug that met him. Julius squeezed back gratefully and, for a few seconds, they stood there like that.

Mr Ruthier stepped back and Julius saw that Morgana and the rest of her family were standing there; the same bright, wispy light was surrounding Fujiko and her daughters. As one, they bowed to him, a sign of respect passed on from centuries long gone.

'Thank you, son,' said Mr Ruthier. 'I knew you would bring her back.'

'I ... I'm sorry. I shouldn't have let this happen in the first place,' said Julius. 'I promised I would take care of them, but instead I let you all down.'

'Don't say that, lad,' replied Mr Ruthier kindly. 'We've been shown the footage of Morgana's kidnapping. Grand Master Freja also sent me a message to tell me what went on inside Angra Mainyu. You've done everything in your power to protect her, and then rescue her. I couldn't have asked for more, and most certainly I could not have done what you did. If I *really* wanted to blame someone, I could point to Zed's lack of security. But, since the day my daughters were selected to join the schools, I knew their safety was no longer in my hands, as hard as that may be to accept. They belong to Zed now, and so do you.'

Julius bowed his head gratefully. Deep down, he knew that Mr Ruthier was right, but to actually hear him saying it made a big difference. They shook hands and Julius watched as he led his family away. He waved to Morgana and sent her a quick mind-message: *'I'll see you in a few days.'* She waved back and nodded.

Julius grabbed his bag and turned back towards the exit, where Faith and Skye were waiting for him.

'So,' said Julius, patting Faith on the shoulder. 'Care to explain where you learned to do that "rotating fury" stunt?'

'Yeah,' said Skye, 'and I'd like to know exactly what was behind that "rabbit in the headlights" glance you threw at Siena back on the shuttle.'

'I'd almost forgotten about that – I wanna know too,' said Julius, laughing and elbowing Faith in the ribs.

'She was going to hug me!' exclaimed Faith defensively, and darted into the Intra-Rail station.

'Come back, *Fury*!' called Julius, who was grinning wildly. 'We wanna know more!'

It was a long train journey back to Tijara for poor old Faith, who was ribbed mercilessly all the way by his two friends.

*

It was nearing midday on that day – Monday, the 16th of May – as the train arrived at their destination. While Julius, Faith and Skye were heading over to their dorms to unpack and freshen up, the rest of the 2MJs were just finishing their Shield lesson with Professor Morales. The boys knew their classmates would want to know why they had skipped class that morning, so they had agreed to simply say that Freja had given them permission to go to the docks with the girls' families and welcome them back. After all, they had been there when Morgana and Siena had been kidnapped.

The story worked, and not one of the Mizkis raised any objections over lunch when they heard this explanation. Julius guessed they were all just too happy that the girls were safe, even though the students would have to wait until they returned to school that Wednesday to hear all about their ordeal. In fact, the excitement was so much that Barth decided to organise a little welcome back party in Tijara's garden for them. The idea turned out to be a great success, with all the teachers in attendance, as were the older students. Even Cress and Freja stopped by for a few minutes. Felice Buongustaio prepared a mouth-watering buffet, which was spread out on a long picnic table in the middle of the garden, and was serving slices of cake to the hungry crowd. The trees had been decorated with colourful fairy lights, compliments of the many students who had volunteered to chip in.

Julius was sitting on a chair under a tree, one foot propped against another seat. Hands in pockets, he watched with delight as the night unfolded. He still found himself feeling a little shy in among such large crowds, so he was quite content to sit there on the outskirts – he wouldn't have missed it for the world.

Not too far from him, Professor Chan was congratulating Faith on his "rotating fury" move, saying that he had showed remarkable skill adapting a kata to complement the advantages his skirt offered. He even added that he would be teaching that very move to any other student who was accepted into Zed and had to be fitted with a similar skirt. Faith was so pleased with this that he couldn't find anything to say, except to fumble a small thank you.

A few feet to Julius' right, Skye was quietly, but dramatically, explaining to Professor Morales how dangerous the fight on Angra Mainyu had been, and how he had managed to save several soldiers with his Shield manoeuvres. Julius grinned and shook his head.

Further away, Morgana and Siena were at the centre of an ever changing group of people, who flocked around them to hear all about their ordeal. Julius felt sorry for them, but he figured, after that, they'd surely be left in peace again. Eventually, the throng of people thinned out, and Siena walked over to Julius.

'Hey,' she said.

'Hey, Siena,' replied Julius, lifting his feet off the chair and offering her the seat.

'No thanks,' she replied. 'We kept missing each other on the way back home – that ship's huge. Anyway, I've already thanked Faith and Skye, but I wanted to thank you too.'

'That's fine,' said Julius. 'We just did whatever we could.'

She nodded her head and turned to leave but, as she did, Julius said, 'You know, there was one thing I was wondering though.'

She stopped. 'What's that?'

'That night, back in Gassendi, what were you doing in the room? I thought you had gone to bed.'

'I did,' she replied. 'I had a bad dream and then, when I woke up and didn't see Morgana, I went to find her. I guess that's what I get for being curious.'

Julius nodded and Siena wandered off to rejoin Morgana. The rest of the evening went smoothly and, when midnight came, the Mizkis returned to their dorms, tired but happy.

*

There were only twelve days left until the end of the year, and the students had to choose their Summer Camp destinations once again. On the last Saturday of May, the Skirts were sitting under the oak tree, munching on toasted sunflower seeds.

'You lucky sod!' said Faith, throwing a seed at Julius.

As it turned out, Freja had managed to convince Captain Kelly to take Julius with him, and not just for a week or two, but for the entire summer.

'Yeah,' answered Julius, beaming. 'I have no idea how he managed that, but I'm not going to complain about it.'

'I think the real revelation is Skye,' said Morgana. 'Mr Smooth-talk here is going to spend his summer in the Curia!'

'What?' said Faith and Julius in unison.

'Let's just say that I've decided to try something different this year. Hone my talking skills, if you like. And I've heard that girls like a powerful man.'

'I knew there had to be a reason for it,' said Julius, rolling his eyes. 'Seriously, though, you want to be a politician?'

'I'm thinking about it. Maybe a diplomat. Who knows?'

'Well, mate,' said Faith, 'if there's one person who could sell stars to the universe, that person is you. And it *would* be handy to have a friend in Colonial Affairs.'

'So you approve?'

'Of course,' said Morgana. 'And you don't need our approval. We'll support you no matter what.'

'Well said, Morgana,' added Julius. 'Besides, the Skirts already have one fighter.' As he said that, he pretended to shine his fingernails on his jumper, in mock smugness.

'All right then,' said Skye. 'And you guys?'

'Faith and I will stick with last year's plan,' explained Morgana. 'I'll go with him to Pete's, and then head off to meet Elian at the apprentice flying camp.'

'I like Elian,' said Skye, with a long sigh. 'I would so go out with her.'

'Who *wouldn't* you go out with?' asked Julius.

'Err ... your ugly face?'

The words were barely out of his mouth before Julius had pounced and wrestled with him, crying, "Revenge!". Faith promptly hovered over them and plonked himself down on their legs, trapping them both and leaving Morgana laughing her head off under the tree.

*

When the last day of term finally arrived, Julius stood on the Zed dock, pushing his rucksack towards the shuttle door with his foot, while sending a message to Faith on his PIP. Suddenly, his bag lifted off the floor and levitated over his head. Julius, who was distracted, didn't realise what had happened and continued to push away at an invisible object for a few steps. When he realised that his foot was finding only fresh air, he stopped and looked down.

'Hey!' he said, searching for his bag.

'You could always wear it on your shoulders, you know?'

Julius turned in the direction of the voice and saw Bernard Docherty standing there, looking rather pleased with himself. The older boy looked up and Julius followed the direction of his gaze: the bag was hovering a few feet above his head. He stretched out his arms and the rucksack fell into them.

'Is that you leaving then?' Julius asked him.

'Yep. It's over.'

'What next?'

'I'm going home to California for the summer. Then back here to start my new job in the Curia.'

'Politics, huh? I can see that.'

'Can you?' asked Bernard, half-smiling at him.

'Sure. You have charisma. Haven't you noticed how people listen to you?'

'You're doing all right for yourself too, you know. Though, you do need to work on your leadership skills a bit more. You're still too shy for a captain.'

'A captain?'

'And a brilliant one you'd make, if I've read you right.'

Julius wasn't sure what to say, but he was quietly pleased with what Bernard had said.

'Anyway, I need to give you something,' said Docherty, pulling out a little box. 'Take it – it's yours.'

Julius took the box, opened it and emptied its contents into the palm of his left hand. It was a black metal ring, with the word "*Solo*" engraved on its inner side.

'Only one person at a time can wear that ring,' explained Bernard. 'If someone overtakes you while you're still in school, you must hand it over to them.'

'What if no one makes it before I leave?'

'Then you hand it back to Master Cress. Marcus himself made it for the Solo champions. It's Zed legacy.'

Julius nodded and slipped the ring onto the middle finger of his right hand. The band, which was loose at first, tightened gently until it fitted him. 'This is just!' he said, admiring it.

'Cool, huh? And everyone knows what it means. It'll earn you respect,' said Bernard.

'Thanks, and good luck.'

'You too, McCoy,' said Bernard. 'I'll see you around.'

Julius stood on the platform, watching him board the shuttle to Earth. It was a shame that he had never managed to challenge him in the Hologram Palace; it could have been fun.

'*The shuttle for Pit-Stop Pete's is departing from dock bay 5. Passengers must make their way to the gate for immediate boarding,*' called a voice over the loudspeaker.

Julius tightened his fist, making the black ring on his finger shine under the artificial light of the Zed shield. It was going to be a great summer. He shouldered his rucksack and headed for the shuttle.

EPILOGUE

Edwina Milson removed the feeding bottle from the heater and let a few drops of milk fall onto the back of her hand. The temperature seemed fine, as far as she could tell. The last time she had fed a baby – her niece – she had still been living in South Africa with her sister. She walked over to the crib and looked at the child wrapped in the sand coloured blanket. The tiny infant was staring up at her with its big blue eyes, its tiny fists pressed against its mouth. The sight of this caused a deep sense of broodiness in Edwina, and she briefly felt a sting of regret in her heart, for letting her career take over her life at the expense of raising a family of her own.

'It is as it was meant to be,' she said. There was a light knock at the door. 'Come in,' she called, but not too loudly – she didn't want to scare the baby, after all.

Freja and Kloister entered the room and walked quietly to her side.

'So,' said Kloister, 'what is it?'

'A girl,' answered Milson. 'Disappointed, Roland?'

'You know me better than that,' he said gently, leaning over the crib and touching one of the tiny fists with his finger. A little smile appeared at the edges of his mouth. 'She's growing faster than I thought.'

'I don't think we've seen just *how* fast she can grow yet,' she said; then to Freja, 'Have we done the right thing, Carlos?'

'We have given her a chance to live,' answered Freja. 'No more, no less. And we'll do our best to ensure she takes after her father's side of the family.'

'Speaking of Tijara,' said Roland, 'I think our holo friend should be kept in *your* school. Here you go.'

Freja opened his hand and Kloister handed him a small, singed red box.

'This is one Pandora's Box I never want to see opened again,' said Kloister.

'Let's hope not, Roland. But you just never know – it may prove useful one day.'

The baby stirred a little and Edwina held a finger up to her lips to shush them. They leaned over the crib again, marvelling in silence at this innocent child who had caused so much fuss.

For the moment, at least, everything was as it was meant to be.

TIJARAN TALES
BOOK III

THE NUARN RIFT

CONTENTS

A BOLT FROM THE BLUE

Captain JD Kelly was leaning against a large porthole, on the observation deck. His head rested on the cold, pressurised glass panel, arms crossed in front of him. He was enjoying a moment of peace, a rare occurrence in what was the otherwise busy environment of his spaceship. With the exception of the six years developing his mind-skills in Tijara School, Kelly had grown up on the Zed space station Terra I, before he had been appointed to the ship Ahura Mazda, working his way through the ranks until he became its captain. He was used to airlocks, holodecks, nullifying bins and resequencers and he knew the gentle noise of his ship's engine – the way it purred under his feet while he walked the corridors. His whole life had been spent in space, without even a single day on Earth.

Every so often he would fancifully plan a visit to one of the old continents, telling himself that the next leave would be different and he would actually go. Perhaps he would even take Lieutenant Elian Flywheel with him, if she would consider going anywhere with her superior officer. He didn't believe he was the worst man of the lot, but he feared a beautiful, intelligent woman like Elian would never settle for a rough case like him. They were close in age, but for some reason 38 looked more like 48 on him. Maybe it was the scar that ran from his left jaw up to his cheekbone which made him doubt his chances with her; maybe it was the sheer dread of being refused, but after 12 years he had still not found the guts to ask her out.

The life of a captain sure was tough, and a lonely one at that. There was always something to do, a new location to explore or, as had been the case for the last three months, someone to train. On the first of July 2857, a 2 Mizki Junior from the Tijara School had been sent to his ship, the Ahura Mazda, for his Summer Camp. Kelly had been sceptical at first, since no Mizki had ever been allowed on board his ship for training before, but the request had come from the Grand Master of Tijara himself, Carlos Freja, and no one could refuse Freja, especially not Kelly. Fortunately for him though, the boy in question was more than just your average 14 year old; in fact, Julius McCoy was anything but.

Since joining the Zed Academy two years before, the boy had not only proven himself as a natural White Child – someone with incredibly strong mind-skills – but he had also played a vital part in defeating the Arneshians, sworn enemies of all Earthlings. After foiling their queen's plans twice, Julius McCoy, who dreamt one day of becoming a Starfleet commander, had just spent three intense months on board, learning with the same passion and eagerness that Kelly himself had demonstrated at that age. Kelly was convinced that the boy would go far; the talent was plain to see – it had only to be harnessed. Now, Summer Camp was drawing to a close and tomorrow Julius would return to Tijara to begin his third year at the school, as a 3 Mizki Apprentice, with a whole world of opportunities at his feet.

When he heard the door slide open, Kelly looked up. 'Over here, McCoy.'

Julius bowed his head respectfully and moved over to the porthole. 'Captain,' he said.

'Did you pack your bag?' asked Kelly.

'I'll do it later. I don't have much,' he answered.

Kelly watched as Julius leaned against the glass panel, staring intently at the Moon, with its orbiting docking station and the surrounding protective bubble that was the Zed Lunar Perimeter. He thought that the boy had grown a bit over the summer – a good two inches perhaps. His messy black hair hung down in jagged, loose strands, framing his bright blue eyes. He switched his gaze back to the Moon outside the window. 'They've started,' he said, pointing at Zed.

Julius looked toward the lunar perimeter, where several wide, flat ships were moving into place in a tight formation around the upper portion of the shield. 'What's going on?' he asked.

'Zed is getting a revamp, and about time too.'

'Why?'

'The defence systems needed some updating, as well as some serious repairs, especially after the last attack.'

'That's good, right?'

'Sure, but it should have been done a few years ago.'

'Why wasn't it? What happened?'

'It's more like, what didn't happen,' Kelly answered. 'Queen Salgoria and the Arneshians lulled us into a false sense of security. They'd been quiet for so long that we stupidly believed we were at peace. Until the last couple of years, of course, when they caught us with our trousers down. We've been at red alert ever since.'

Julius nodded his head, knowingly.

'They began relocating Sield School back in June and they're almost done. Tuala is next,' said Kelly.

'Are they moving us?' asked Julius, pressing his hands against the glass.

'Yes, they are. But Tijara won't go till January.'

'Where will they take us?'

'See that round space station in the lunar orbit? That's where. It'll just be for a few weeks though.'

'A bit like a school trip, then.'

'Yeah, something like that,' said Kelly. Then he shook his head. 'Heck kid, you picked the wrong time to join the Academy. I don't like it where we are with the Arneshians, this calm before the storm. I can feel it brewing. Salgoria is planning something big and I don't like it one bit.'

'I'd rather be here than stuck on Earth worrying about them. I don't know how my parents can stand it.'

'Simple. They don't really know.'

'What do you mean, sir?'

'They only get the news that the Curia deems suitable to release. Telling the Earth leader the whole story about kidnappings and genetic experiments isn't really something that ranks as a priority for Colonial Affairs.'

'But folks have the right to know.'

'For what purpose, McCoy? Why worry, when there's nothing you can do about it?

If Zed is defeated, Earth would be lost in an instant. We are the defence system. Let us worry for everyone else.'

'It still seems unfair.'

'It's one of those diplomatic decisions. I'm not too good at that stuff. I'm a man of action; I leave politics to the politicians.'

'My friend, Skye Miller, has gone to the Curia, for his Summer Camp.'

'Has he then? I remember him, of course. Miller didn't strike me as the desk type.'

'I guess he was curious. But he probably also did it for his star-rep. He says girls are attracted to power.'

Kelly burst out laughing. 'He's got that right!'

'Not all girls, surely?' said Julius, sounding slightly defensive. 'Morgana isn't like that at all.'

'Who, your friend the pilot?'

Julius nodded.

Kelly thought briefly of Elian, and how easygoing she was with everyone, no matter what rank they held. 'Maybe you're right. But if that's the case, she's a rare one. I would keep her close if I were you, and judging by the way she hugged you last year, after we rescued her from Angra Mainyu, she wants you to keep her close too, if you know what I'm saying!'

'Naaaah! She doesn't ... I don't ... I mean, she's like a sister, or ...'

The captain laughed again and patted Julius on the back, hard enough to make him bump against the glass. 'Blessed youth!' he said. 'All right, all right. So where's the fourth musketeer, anyway? The big-mouthed Irish kid.'

'Faith spent the Summer Camp at Pit-Stop Pete's, as always, assembling engines. He'd stay there the whole year if they let him.'

'A techie, huh?'

'He's great. He says he'll build me the best spaceship ever one day.'

'No one can beat the Ahura Mazda, kid.'

'I'm prepared to bet on it, Captain.'

'You're on. But I'll believe it when I see it, and by then I'll probably be long dead.'

Julius grinned at him and they both looked out at Zed again as the ship drew closer to it. Kelly returned to his thoughts. It had been a good summer. He would be sorry to see McCoy go, although he knew it wouldn't be long before the next time. Just then, the boy activated his Personal Information Planner and looked down at its small holographic screen, which was hovering over the palm of his left hand. He seemed anxious. 'Everything all right?'

'I'm waiting for my folks to call me. Michael – my little brother – is having his Zed admission test today. But there are no messages on my PIP yet.'

'Wait – aren't the tests done in April anymore?'

'They are. It's just that he only turned 12 in July, so he had to wait for the end of August session.'

'I see. He'll be fine, I'm sure. With a brother like you ...'

'I hope so, Captain. I really do.'

Kelly thought he detected just a hint of doubt in Julius' voice, though.

*

'Why aren't they calling?' growled Julius to himself. He was now feeling utterly frustrated. He had been pacing up and down in his cabin since leaving Captain Kelly on the bridge two hours ago. He had tried the home line several times, but no one had been there to answer. He couldn't understand why his parents hadn't called yet; after all, the test should have finished by now. He sagged heavily onto his bed, where he lay, staring at the ceiling and trying to calm himself down. After a couple of minutes, his PIP screen lit up, signalling an incoming vidcall. In a flash, Julius was on his feet again. 'On screen!'

'Ahoy, there!' said Faith's smiling face.

'Oh, it's only you.'

'Thanks! It's good to see you too, mate,' answered Faith sarcastically. He was busy polishing his conical hover-skirt, which allowed him to stand despite his disability.

'Sorry. I haven't heard anything about Michael yet,' said Julius, anxiously.

'Bummer,' said Faith.

'I don't understand why it's taking so long. It's almost ten at night, and they're still not home.'

'You sure they didn't go out to celebrate, or something?'

'Without telling me? Unlikely. I'm starting to think that-' Just then, a second incoming vidcall made his PIP vibrate. 'It's them, Faith. Gotta go, gotta go!'

'Right you are. Call me later,' said Faith, before disappearing from view.

Julius took a deep breath. 'On screen.' His dad's face came into view, and he felt his stomach sink around his ankles as soon as he saw the downcast expression on his features.

'Hi son,' said Rory McCoy, who was sporting two dark bags beneath his eyes. 'You'd better sit down.'

Julius didn't need to be asked twice. He plucked the holographic image of his dad's head between the fingertips of his right hand, and threw it into the centre of the room, where it expanded to full length, showing Rory in all his tired glory, bumble bee-shaped slippers and all. While Julius sat back on his bed, his father's hologram sank down onto a chair.

'He didn't make it, did he?' asked Julius, quietly.

Rory shook his head. 'No, he didn't. Between getting in for the medical examination and being escorted out of the main premises, it took about ten minutes.'

'Escorted out?' said Julius, visibly alarmed. 'What do you mean? Did he play some silly tricks on the officers?'

'No Julius, he didn't.' Rory passed a hand through his hair. He looked completely worn out. Julius could see thin white strands among the familiar brown ones. 'Your mother and I were waiting with the other parents – like I did when you and Morgana were doing your test – when suddenly an officer came into the waiting room, asking for the McCoys. Everyone was looking at us, wondering what had happened. We thought that Michael had had an accident. He couldn't give us any information, so we followed him to another office, behind the main test centre. When we entered, Michael was waiting there, looking confused and scared. Other than that, he seemed fine, even though he kept saying that he hadn't done anything wrong. Eventually, after waiting for almost half an hour without a clue as to what was happening, one of your Tijaran teachers came in to meet us.'

'Who was it?' asked Julius.

'Master Cress.'

At any other time, Julius wouldn't have seen anything odd in that, given that it had been Master Cress himself who had told Julius about being accepted into Zed, at the end of his own test. But these were not normal circumstances, it seemed. 'Go on,' he prompted his father.

'He introduced himself, apologised for the situation and, on a screen, showed us a series of tests that had been run on Michael during the medical exam. I don't know how to say this Julius ...'

'Say what, Dad?'

'Michael is ...' he paused, and drooped his head.

'Michael is what?' asked Julius, unable to suppress the impatience in his voice.

'He's an Arneshian!' Rory blurted out.

Julius looked at his father, stunned, waiting for him to say that he was only joking, but there was only an uncomfortable silence. His mouth had gone dry. 'An Arneshian! What are you talking about?' sputtered Julius. 'He can't be an Arneshian! He's one of us.'

'Yes ... Of course he is, son. Sorry, I'm not explaining this very well - he's a *Nuarn*.'

Julius flinched at that word: Nuarn was the term used to describe any Earthling born with the advanced technological Grey Arts skills of an Arneshian after Clodagh Arnesh's banishment.

'How ... how is this possible?'

'They don't know. They even tested your mum and me, to see if we carried some weird gene, but from their first analysis it looks like we're just plain humans.'

'Wait a sec ... what about the socks? He always made the socks fly. Surely that counts as telekinesis, and that's a mind-skill, right?'

'Yes, they did find that odd, but apparently it can happen with Nuarns. The side of his brain that controls logic,' continued Rory, 'computation and all sorts of Grey Arts, is off the charts. His technological skills are very advanced, with very little presence of mind-skill development. You had plenty of both, that's why you made it into Zed.'

'What's going to happen now?' asked Julius, incredulous.

'Nothing is going to happen, Julius. It's not like Nuarns are shipped off to Queen Salgoria. Master Cress said that your brother is not allowed on Zed, except to visit you during the mid-winter break. He'll just live here like any other human. There are many Arneshians on Earth, you know. They just blend in.'

'But he did get tagged.'

'Yes. They gave him the choker,' said Rory, more than a trace of sadness in his voice.

Julius nodded. He knew all about the later generations of Arneshians on Earth, but it wasn't really big news back home. People didn't tend to discuss their presence; in fact, it was safer to say that they were practically ignored – except for the choker, a device which blocked all Grey skills. He had never liked those grey, metallic neck bands, a constant reminder that the person wearing it was someone potentially dangerous, and essentially an outcast. 'Where is Michael? Can I talk to him?'

'Not just now. He was so upset that the doctor gave him a sedative. Your mum is with him. She says she'll speak to you soon.'

'All right. Tell him I'm thinking of him, and when he feels ready, tell him to call me.'

'Of course. Are you all set for tomorrow?' asked Mr McCoy, quickly changing the subject.

'Yes. I'll be back in school by tea time,' replied Julius, absently.

'Good. Take care, son. Your mother and I wish you all the best for the new year ahead. We're very proud of you, son.'

'Thanks Dad,' said Julius, attempting to smile.

'We'll get through this together. Don't worry.'

Julius nodded half-heartedly. 'Good night, Dad.' When his dad's hologram vanished, he rubbed his eyes with the heels of his hands. How could this be happening to his family? There was obviously nothing wrong with his parents, as today's tests had shown. Yet, both of their children had turned out to be at opposite ends of the spectrum of mind-alterations – the long-lasting legacy of the Chemical War of 2550.

The Arneshians represented all that Zed and its officers stood against. For 232 years the Earthlings had fought with this breakaway sect of humanity, who were devoid of mind-skills, but rich in technological know-how, for control of the planet. In the last two years of his life, Julius and his friends had been at the forefront of that battle twice already, sending Queen Salgoria and her holographic army packing.

For months, Julius had formed an image in his mind; one in which he and his brother would be fighting the enemy together, side by side. He had even created a folder on his PIP, containing a personal guide to life on Zed, which he had been planning on giving to Michael upon arrival, as a late birthday present. In between lessons and games, Julius had listed the coolest shops to visit on Satras, tips on how to win in the games at the Hologram Palace and the best ways to earn Fyvers at school.

All of this was worthless now, shattered by a medical exam. Michael would never get to use the information in that folder and he would never be able to receive Zed officer training. Not only that, but he was also tainted in such a way that would forever be greeted with distrust by his fellow humans. Mind-alterations of any kind made a person "abnormal"; the difference was that if someone had mind-skills, they were set for life, with a future career in space guaranteed, but if someone was a Nuarn, then the only place for them was Earth, under constant surveillance.

Julius suddenly felt very tired and confused. He decided not to call Faith back, but to rather leave it until the next day. He knew he'd have to tell his friends sooner or later, but he couldn't bring himself to do it when it all still seemed so impossible to him. He took a quick shower, slipped under the covers of his bed and let himself drift off into an uneasy sleep.

MIZKI APPRENTICE

'Computer, terminate session 2MJ McCoy,' said Julius aloud. The holoscreen on the desk in his room flickered for a moment, and then vanished. His last day aboard the Ahura Mazda was at its end. Julius stretched lazily in the chair, and ran his fingers through his hair. The three months of his Summer Camp had flown by and although he would have loved to remain with Captain Kelly and his crew, he was eager to see his friends. Trying to digest the news about Michael was proving very difficult. His sleep had been restless and he had woken up several times with a deep sense of dread in his heart. Dreams of Michael being taken away by Zed officers, and shipped off to the planet Arnesh like a traitor, had filled his night.

At breakfast that morning, Kelly had taken one look at him and immediately realised that something was wrong. Julius hadn't been able to bring himself to lie about the fact that Michael had failed the test, but he certainly hadn't wanted to share the rest of the news with him either. Still, he had had to spend the entire day avoiding Kelly's curious glances.

Julius stood up and moved to the locker where his bag was waiting, already packed, then swung it over his shoulder and headed for the door. Before leaving the room he had a good, last look around, partly to check that he hadn't left anything behind, and partly to say goodbye. He was pretty sure he would be back, but not before next summer.

When he reached the docking bay, Captain Kelly and Lieutenant Flywheel were waiting by the small shuttle pod that would be taking him back to Zed. 'Captain. Lieutenant,' he said, bowing to them.

'I'm sad to see you go, Julius,' said Elian, sincerely. 'It's been great having you here.'

'I really enjoyed the summer. Thanks for all your help. And thanks for having me, Captain Kelly.'

'You did good, kid. You've earned your placement for next year, if you're still interested in stealing my job,' said Kelly.

Julius grinned. 'Sure.'

'Run along now.'

With a last quick bow, Julius boarded the shuttle pod and strapped himself into the free seat next to the pilot. The hatch closed silently, and a few minutes later the engine hummed into life. The bay outside quickly emptied, and the large airlock below the pod yawned open. Julius' stomach turned a little as the shuttle dropped into space; their descent only lasted a few seconds thankfully, before the pilot steered them towards the Moon, setting their course for the Zed docks.

As they entered orbit, Julius threw a quick glance at the platforms stationed above a section of the shield encasing Zed's lunar perimeter. To their left, he could see Pit-Stop Pete, which served as the orbital repair station. It was a flat disc, with a central spherical structure set in its middle. Several ships were docked all around its edge which, to Julius, made it look a bit like a giant daisy. Behind Pete's core floated the repair bays, rectangular metal frames which encased a spacecraft during its maintenance. There was plenty of activity going on, with numerous sky-jets zooming in and out of hatches, carrying people and various bits of equipment. Faith and Morgana had already driven one of those space-scooters during their first Summer Camp at Pete's, the previous year. The students had been asked to help out retrieving all the debris left behind after the battle between Zed's Cougars and the Arneshian fleet. Julius was sure Skye would also have had a shot at it, seeing as he had grown up on a space station, which meant that he was the only one of their group who still had not tried it. Perhaps he could ask Faith to take him with, next time he visited Pete.

Slowly, the shuttle pod began to pass through the shield. Julius had the impression that its membrane was stretching over their windscreen like a thin layer of jelly, which was pliable enough to allow them to push through it but at the same time not allow any room for the air inside to seep out. The Zed shield had many useful functions: as well as protecting them from attacks and the harshness of the space environment outside, it generated the air they breathed, using specially designed filters. It was also equipped with an illumination system that mimicked the sunrise and sunset of Earth, as timed at the Greenwich meridian. Seasonal changes in temperature were the only thing that Zed lacked, but Julius didn't mind the perennial spring too much; besides, if he really wanted to have cold feet and see his breath puff up in little clouds, all he had to do was enter a simulation room.

A few minutes later, the pilot landed smoothly inside Zed's dock, and the hatch swung open. Julius grabbed his bag, thanked the pilot, and disembarked. He headed straight for the Intra-Rail System, hoping not to meet any of his classmates. He had been so sure that he would soon be welcoming Michael to Zed, that he had told everyone in his year group about the test, so he knew there would be questions about what had happened. Julius had already decided that when anyone asked, he would give the same explanation he had given Captain Kelly: his brother just didn't have enough mind-skills. Yet, as soon as this thought formulated in his mind, Julius felt a pang of guilt as he realised the truth was he was ashamed to tell people that Michael was an Arneshian. He really needed to work on it, because spending the rest of his life lying about it was definitely not an option.

As soon as the train arrived, he jumped on board and in the short time it took him to reach Tijara, he used his PIP to send a note to Morgana, Faith and Skye, who were listed under "Skirts" in his contact list, the name their gang had adopted from their gaming sessions. In the message, he asked them to meet him in the school garden, at the foot of their favourite oak tree, in twenty minutes. Given that he had been incommunicado since the night before, he knew they had probably already guessed that something was up. They were his closest friends after all and, with them at least, he was ready to come clean.

*

'Surely they've made a mistake,' said Skye, staring at Julius and sounding completely bewildered.

'Nope. Michael has been certified and tagged,' answered Julius, grimly.

'What are the odds?' added Faith. 'A White Child and a Nuarn, both from the same parents.'

'I'm so sorry, Julius,' said Morgana, squeezing his arm gently. 'How is Michael?'

'I haven't spoken with him yet. He's still very upset. Mum will let me know when he's ready to talk.'

'Have you ever noticed anything odd about him?' asked Faith.

'Michael has always been odd,' answered Julius. 'But if you mean, Arneshian-odd, then no. Sure, he's very talented when it comes to building things, but other than that ...'

'Man, I would be gutted,' said Skye, shaking his head. 'Do pass our ... our ...'

'See,' said Julius, the frustration he was feeling seeping out into his voice, 'that's the thing – I don't even know how to feel! What should I pass on to him? Our pity? Our best wishes for a swift recovery? He's not dead, he's not ill and he's certainly not going to get better. Yet, he's everything we hate.'

'Come on now,' said Faith. 'That's too harsh. Plenty of Nuarns have lived among us in the past 200 years, and not one of them has ever done anything wrong or shameful.'

'Faith is right,' added Morgana. 'They may be singled out, but they get by just fine.'

'Get by, huh?' said Julius. 'Is this what I have to wish for my little brother's future? That he gets by?'

'What did you have in mind?' asked Skye. 'Did you think he would become the next Grand Master of Tijara, or something?'

'And what if I did?' said Julius, a little louder than he meant to. A couple of Seniors and a group of first years sitting nearby, turned their heads towards him. Julius saw them and, lowering his voice, he turned to Skye once more. 'What are *you* hoping to do with your life? Get by?'

'Hey, I'm just happy to exist, man. Everything on top of that is a bonus for me. We all get by. Some of us better than others, but we all do. And since when did this conversation become about me, anyway?'

Julius leaned back against the oak. 'Sorry. I didn't mean to take it out on you.'

'I know, mate.'

'That's why we're here, Julius,' said Morgana. 'Vent away.'

Julius breathed deeply. 'This one is gonna be hard to digest.'

'Have you told anyone else?' asked Faith.

'Cress and Freja know, of course. As for the others, I'll just say he didn't make it. For now anyway.'

'Of course,' said Morgana, quickly. 'We'll back that up.'

The boys nodded in agreement.

'Look,' said Morgana, pointing at the garden entrance. 'The rest of our year is arriving. Let's go say hi.' She stood up and held her hand out to Julius. 'He'll be ok.'

Julius looked her in the eyes for a few seconds, wanting with all his heart to believe her. Then he grabbed her hand and pulled himself up. 'I hope you're right.'

Seeing his classmates after the long summer gap was always good for Julius; it felt like a reunion party for old friends, with everyone eager to share their stories from the past few months. There were a few recurring after-dinner activities among the students that night. One of these was the moustache check, where all the boys' faces were scanned for the faintest trace of hair, something that they seemed to find hilarious. Of course, Skye being Skye, he quickly grew bored with talk of facial hair and instead took to examining something he found far more interesting: the girls' body development. This was the cue for Julius and Faith to let him talk by himself while trying not to look at whatever he was so blatantly pointing at.

All night, Morgana was surrounded by her closest girlfriends, Isolde Frey and Siena Migliori, and they chatted excitedly right up until bedtime. Julius often wondered what could have possibly happened to them over the summer that justified such an intense conversation, especially since he knew that it would be like this for the entire year. But it quickly occurred to him that he didn't much care to know anyway, given that it was most likely about clothing or hair or whatever else girls discussed. The fact that they may be discussing the boys was something that rarely crossed his mind since, in his opinion, Morgana would always be too young to be interested in relationships.

In a corner of the mess hall, Barth "The Menace" Smit was comparing scars, bumps and scabs with Lopaka Liway. All of Lopaka's were surf-related – something that he was definitely proud of. In Barth's case though, they were all the result of sheer clumsiness and, judging by the grin on his face, it seemed that Barth was beginning to embrace his awkwardness a little too much, in Julius' opinion.

Before the evening was over however, Julius knew that most of the students would be discussing the games in the Hologram Palace. Everyone on Zed knew who the best players were: the Skirts. As a group, they were formidable and had already set unbeaten records among the first and second year students, in both the Flight and Combat simulations. It was only natural that all eyes would be on them this coming year, as they entered the third year competitions. Technically, they were allowed to compete against any age group, but the Skirts had decided they would stick to their level, and no one had been able to make them change their minds, much to the frustration of the older students who were itching to challenge them. As if this wasn't enough, Julius had also set a personal record for Solo, the single player version of the regular games, where players used their actual mind-skills to fight against the computer. As the reigning champion, he was allowed to wear the black metal ring on his finger, which had the word "Solo" engraved on its inner surface.

Strangely enough, no one had asked Julius about Michael yet. Whether they had simply forgotten, or just noticed how he was keeping to himself and so drawn their own conclusions from that, he couldn't tell. Either way, he was grateful for it.

Eventually, it was time to retire for the night. As 3 Mizki Apprentices, their year group would now have their dorms on level -4.

'Another three years, and we'll make it to the surface,' said Faith, waving goodbye for the night and following Barth into their shared room.

'Not quite to the surface,' added Skye. 'I feel like a mole sometimes.'

'You are a mole,' said Julius, pushing him along the corridor. 'And I'll take the bed nearest the door.'

There was a brief struggle, as the two of them tried to squeeze through their bedroom door at the same time, much to the amusement of the rest of the boys in their dorm.

'Come on – I want to see our new uniforms,' said Skye excitedly, even though Julius' hand was parked on his face. 'Look, they're on my bed!'

'It's *my* bed,' said Julius, who had Skye's thumb lodged firmly in his right ear. He managed to pull Skye back by his jumper and rushed to claim the bed he wanted. Julius' new wardrobe was neatly laid out. There were new socks and underwear, two pairs of tracksuits, a pair of combat trousers, short and long-sleeved t-shirts, two round-neck jumpers, a pair of trainers and some new boots. Everything was navy blue: Tijara's official colour. All of the outer garments had labels on them with the words "Julius McCoy – 3MA –Tijara", written in silver. The sight of those tags brought home his new reality to him: his two Apprentice years had officially begun.

*

On the morning of Thursday the 1st of September, Julius woke up feeling rested and decidedly more cheery than he had been the previous two days. He had been thinking about it a lot and had decided that there was no reason why he should feel embarrassed about Michael's situation. He knew that it would take time to fully accept it, but to be sad, or ashamed, was not fair on his brother, who had done nothing to deserve that. He would talk to Michael and let him know there was absolutely nothing to worry about and that he could still realise his dreams, even if it meant doing it through an institute other than Zed.

By the time Julius was showered and dressed, Skye and Faith were patiently waiting outside in the hallway, sporting their new uniforms. Faith's metallic, panelled skirt had even been freshly polished for the occasion.

'You finished putting your makeup on, Julia McCoy?' teased Skye.

'You look … sparkly,' said Julius, ignoring him and admiring the hovering device wrapped around Faith's waist. 'Very shiny.'

'Fresh start and all that,' said Faith, pirouetting for his friends. 'However, I do seem to have a problem.'

'What's that?' asked Skye.

'Me legs are outgrowing the skirt,' explained Faith, hovering upwards slightly and pointing at his feet.

Julius looked down and, sure enough, he could see feet and ankles dangling from the bottom of the skirt. Then he turned to Skye, and chuckled.

'I look funny, do I?' said Faith, in a deadpan voice. 'I'll show you funny; I'll turn you into the Flying Scotsman, McCoy.' He charged towards Julius, who spun on his heels and made a dash for the stairs. Faith quickly caught up, deftly slipped his arms under Julius' armpits and, gripping him tightly, lifted him off the floor and whisked him up the stairs.

'Let me down, you crazy Irishman!' cried Julius, thrashing about in the air.

Soon enough, the commotion attracted students from all the other dorms. As they zoomed up the stairs, Julius had to face a barrage of flashes as the Mizkis snapped away on their PIP cameras at each floor landing. Skye and some of the 3MAs led a parade behind them, hollering and clapping away. Gustavo Perez, one of their classmates from Terra 2, was walking beside Skye, grunting and crying with laughter.

'That's it,' said Julius, once they reached the level -1 landing. Stretching out his hand, he aimed for the wall directly ahead and gave a strong mind-push. He immediately felt the energy rush out of his body, and although no one could see the actual stream, they all heard the whooshing sound and a thump as it rebounded off the wall. To the general amusement of everyone, Julius and Faith were blasted backwards by the strength of Julius' push and sent tumble-weeding down the stairs.

'I've recorded it, Skye! I've recorded it!' Manuel Valdez, a dark haired Mexican boy who had proved a valuable source of Spanish pick up lines in the past for Skye, was loudly crying out while leaping about excitedly. '*Tus amigos son locos!*'

Julius and Faith couldn't even disentangle themselves from each other, for how hard they were laughing and how sore they were. Eventually, Skye and Lopaka had to pull them apart.

'You girls can carry on messing about if you like but I'm starving,' said Skye. 'We've only got twenty minutes until first class. I could eat a space freighter.' And with that he started up the stairs.

The thought of being left without food until break, combined with the sudden urge to discover what subjects they would be studying that year, spurred Julius and Faith into action and they hurried after him. As they approached the mess hall entrance, the smell of bacon and pastries grew maddeningly strong and inviting.

Julius noticed that no timetables had been left for them by the door, as had happened the previous year, but instead there was only a single message on the monitor beside the doorway, instructing all 3MAs to assemble in the garden at 09:00 hours.

Faith and Skye shrugged their shoulders and motioned for Julius to hurry up.

The canteen was packed with all the returning students and a fresh batch of 1 Mizki Juniors, who were all intently studying their new timetables. Julius grabbed a large latte, plus a carrot-and-hazelnut muffin, and headed for a table which was occupied by Morgana and Siena, followed by Skye and Faith.

'Hi guys!' said Morgana, cheerily.

'Ladies,' said Julius, sitting down next to her.

'Hi Siena,' said Faith. 'Good to see you again. How was your summer?'

Suddenly, Julius noticed a little wisp of bright pink shooting out of Siena's head, like a tiny firework. He flinched, caught off guard by it. The wisps and threads that came out of people's heads were something that apparently only Julius could see, as far as he knew anyway. It didn't always happen, but when it did, Julius was able to tell what a person was feeling at that moment.

'What's the matter?' asked Skye, noticing his friend's discomfort.

'Oh, nothing,' answered Julius quickly. 'Just banged my knee against the table.' He really didn't want to share what he had seen; besides, if he had read that wisp correctly, then Siena had a crush on Faith and Julius certainly didn't want to get involved in that. He had never been the best when it came to girls and their strange ways.

As the start of period one approached, all the Mizkis began to slowly file away and head to their respective classes. Julius looked around and realised that only his year group had remained behind.

'Let's go, guys,' said Morgana to her table and stood up.

They quickly returned their empty trays to the counter and headed outside. Julius stretched happily in the morning sunshine. He knew that the heat he was feeling wasn't really from the sun, but the illusion of it was good enough to make it seem real. As he walked into the clearing at the centre of the garden, he spotted a man there, sitting cross-legged and beckoning to them with his right hand.

'Over here, Mizkis,' called the man, pleasantly.

They walked towards him and were invited to take a seat on the grass. Faith's skirt, interacting with the sensors implanted in his legs, was able to make him kneel quite easily and he gently lowered himself to the ground. Julius sat next to him, and turned his attention to the stranger. He wondered who this man was and where was he from.

His skin was slightly darker than Julius', and his hair was jet black.

Once all eyes were fixed on him, the man bowed to them, and they bowed in return, as was customary on Zed. 'Good morning Mizkis, and welcome to the first of your Apprentice years. My name is Hamza Patel, and I will be your guidance teacher for the next two years.'

'Sir,' Dhara Sundaram, a petite girl with long straight hair, said shyly. 'Are you Indian, sir?'

'Indeed, Miss Sundaram,' answered Mr Patel, amiably. 'From a village not too far from yours, actually.'

Dhara looked pleased, and nodded her head.

'Mrs Cruci has passed all of your files on to me, and with them your ideas for possible careers,' said Mr Patel, his eyes examining them. 'As you know, from this year you will be able to select two of your subjects, according to your own wishes, while the rest of the timetable will be the same for all of you. As always, you are required to keep a record of all of your classes in your student log, as it allows you to analyse the choices you make, as well as the weaknesses and strengths you may have in any given area.'

'Sir,' said Morgana, eagerly. 'When can we choose our new classes?'

'That is what you'll be doing today and tomorrow, Miss Ruthier,' answered Patel. 'We have prepared a special career fair in the assembly hall, where the relevant teachers will be answering all of your questions. We have also invited representatives from different professions, so you can pick their brains about the ins and outs of each job. How does that sound?'

An excited whisper ran through the group.

'What a nice way to start the year,' said Faith, merrily. 'Two extra days off!'

'Double agreement,' added Julius.

'Now,' continued Patel, visibly satisfied by their reaction, 'as you enter into the hall, scan your PIP chip on the sensor by the entrance, and a map of the fair will be downloaded into its memory. It's a bio-interactive app, which responds differently to every individual. Your own special set of mind-skills will make certain career paths flash brightly if they are suited to you.'

'What if you like a subject that doesn't suit you, sir?' asked Barth, sounding very worried.

Patel smiled affably. 'Then choose it. In October, and again at the end of the year, we will have our usual reviews and if you've changed your mind, so be it.'

Barth looked relieved at that, as did a few of the other students.

'Visit every station. By 16:00 you must make an initial selection, which you will submit to me, via your PIP. Tomorrow morning I will send it back to you, confirming the subjects that you are allowed to take, and if there are any that you need to change. It is very rare that you aren't allowed to do a certain subject, but it can happen. The final decision rests with Grand Master Freja.' Patel stood up, nimbly. 'Let's go Mizkis. I'll be at the fair with you if you need to ask me anything.'

Julius waited for Faith, Skye and Morgana to join him, and together they headed indoors. A small queue formed as they approached the black doors of the main hall. Julius watched eagerly as the Mizkis ahead slowed down by the entrance, before disappearing inside. When it was his turn, Julius scanned his PIP chip on the sensor and felt a little shiver run up his arm. He moved inside and stood off to the side, waiting for the others.

The rows of chairs that normally occupied the hall had been replaced with a multitude of colourful stands, peppered across the floor. Each station was shared by the particular subject teacher and the representatives for each job. The lighting inside the hall had been turned to its full brightness, in contrast to the usual softer ambience.

'I say we divide and conquer,' said Skye, examining his new map, which was hovering above the palm of his hand.

'Good idea,' added Morgana. 'Later,' she said, walking away towards the centre of the room.

'All right then,' said Julius, activating his own map. As it flashed into life, he was surprised to see that every single stand was glowing brightly. 'Great,' he said, disheartened. Being a White Child sure had its downsides: according to the screen, no matter what he chose, he would do well, so there was no guidance for him there. He decided to approach the floor the old fashioned way, stand by stand, left to right. The first one in his path, he was pleased to see, was occupied by none other than Captain Kelly himself.

'McCoy, are you following me?' said Kelly, pretending to be serious. 'I've told you a thousand times, I will never let you anywhere near a spaceship.'

'Good morning, Captain,' answered Julius, grinning. 'I didn't expect to see you here.'

'The Grand Master asked me to,' he answered, dropping the joke. 'It's hard to say no to him.'

'I bet,' said Julius, under his breath.

'Anyway, McCoy. What are you doing here? You know you'll pick this subject, so go visit the other stands. You're not having second thoughts, are you?'

'Oh no, Captain,' answered Julius quickly. 'I'm just exploring, that's all.'

'Good. Why don't you go and meet your new teacher, then?' said Kelly, pointing at the next section.

'I wouldn't want to presume that I get to do this subject, Captain.'

'Presume away, and get lost,' said Kelly, half seriously. 'I have other candidates to meet.'

Julius bowed and moved to the right. There was a woman in the next section, under a sign that read "Starship Management". Julius approached her hesitantly. 'Good morning,' he said, politely. The woman turned towards him, and bowed. She was tall, with auburn hair gathered in a tight bun behind her head; her nose was thin, its tip pointed slightly downward, and her eyes were wide and black. Julius knew he had seen her before, coming and going in Tijara, but he had never properly met her.

'Good morning,' she replied cordially. 'I'm Professor Farshid, Starship Management.'

'Julius McCoy.'

'Pleased to meet you. Are you interested in becoming a captain?'

'Yes, very much,' answered Julius.

'This is the course for you then. It's very comprehensive and will teach you all the different aspects you need in order to successfully command a ship and its crew. From leadership skills, diplomacy, intergalactic protocols – in case we should ever encounter another race – to the everyday run of the mill stuff: what you need, who you need, basic maintenance and, of course, piloting. You will have a helmsman for that, but it is important you are an excellent pilot yourself. You will also have all sorts of technicians and civilian personnel to direct.'

'It sounds pretty full on,' said Julius.

'It is, but in my opinion, it's *the* job to have. Nothing beats it!' said Farshid, brimming with infectious confidence. 'Here,' she said, holding a hand-held device out for Julius. 'Bring your PIP-chip closer. I'm transferring the prospectus to you. It contains everything you need to know about this course and the career options at the end of it. Read it before you sign on.'

Once the transfer was done, he withdrew his hand. 'Thanks, Professor.'

'You're very welcome.'

Julius bowed, touched by her comment, and moved along to his right. The next three stations were marked as Starship Engineering for Pilots, Technicians and Architects respectively. Sure enough, Julius spotted Morgana anxiously jumping up and down in the queue for the first of them and Faith desperately trying to keep his place in both the second and third queues, by zooming between them. 'Mental, those two,' he chuckled to himself. He decided to skip those stations for the time being, given how busy they were, and headed for the far side of the hall, opposite the entrance. There were two stations there: Pilot, and Catalyst Training. Julius did like flying and was very good at it too, but given a choice between the two courses, he knew his strengths leaned more towards the use of catalysts and therefore, combat. He still stopped by the first one though, where Professor Clavel, who also taught Pilot Training as a core subject, was handing out his own prospectus. 'Can I have one, Professor?' called Julius, over the heads of the classmates gathered there in front of him.

'Here you are, McCoy,' said Clavel, holding out his device over Yuri Slovich's head.

Julius stretched his hand towards it to receive the file. He was pleasantly surprised to see that one of the real life pilots at this stand was none other than Lieutenant Elian Flywheel but, seeing as she was completely surrounded by students, Julius didn't stop to say hi, and moved on to the next stand. The Catalyst station was shared by four men that Julius had never seen before. The first one on the left was holding the same kind of device that Clavel and Farshid had, so Julius assumed that he must be the teacher. He was a man of broad build, with dirty-blonde hair and small chestnut eyes. Julius walked up to him and bowed. 'Julius McCoy, sir,' he said. 'Could I have one of those, please?'

The man looked at Julius with curiosity. 'I am Professor Gould. Your PIP, please.' As Julius did so, Gould added, 'I was wondering when you'd turn up.'

'Were you?' asked Julius.

'When a Mizki Junior is allowed to spend his first Summer Camp in the Fornax constellation doing an intensive Catalyst Training course, believe me, I am the first to know about it.'

'That was a brilliant summer, sir,' said Julius excitedly.

'If you pick this course you'll get more of the same.'

Julius nodded. 'Oh, I will, sir.'

'I would still like you to read the prospectus though.'

'Of course. Thank you,' said Julius. He quickly bowed and left.

There was no real need for him to stop by the catalyst operators, since he had already met a fair few of them during that first summer. Along the right side of the assembly hall, there were just two large stations: Colonial Affairs, and History and

Politics. Julius saw Skye talking with one of the female Curia workers, at the Colonial Affairs desk, and couldn't suppress a chuckle. He was leaning over the counter, his head resting on the heel of his hand, looking dreamily at the young woman. In the three years Julius had known Skye he had come to accept the fact that his friend was a magnet for girls and, most importantly, that he knew exactly what to say to attract them. No matter who they were – students, Zed officers or teachers – if he liked them, he would work his way into their consciousness somehow. At the tender age of fourteen, Skye "Black Hole" Miller – as he had been affectionately dubbed, due to the amazing amount of food he could consume – was the guy you talked to, if you needed advice on relationships. Julius grinned and moved along. Working at the Curia wasn't really that appealing to him since, in his opinion, there was nothing exciting about being stuck behind a desk. However, perhaps History and Politics would be a nice change, he thought, since he liked history anyway, so he stopped to pick up a prospectus, just in case.

The last station sat in the middle of the assembly hall and seemed rather empty in comparison to the others. It was Spaceology and, at the sight of Professor Lucy Brown, Julius let out a groan. He had fallen asleep more times than he could remember during her core classes, so there was no way he was going to choose it as one of his extra subjects. He stopped at the stand though, more out of diligence than any other reason.

As he finished and headed out of the hall entrance, Mr Patel took him aside. 'McCoy, I was asked to tell you that you'll be busy in the infirmary every Thursday at 11:00.'

'What for, sir?' asked Julius, shocked.

'The Grand Master has his reasons, of course, but Dr Walliser will be able to explain them to you at your first session.'

'When will that be?'

'Probably not until October, but they'll notify you.'

Julius nodded, feeling quite annoyed that Freja had made plans without discussing them with him first. Unfortunately, he knew complaining about it wouldn't make any difference, so he pushed the news to the back of his mind and began to count the prospectuses he had collected. He was required to gather some more before he could leave the room, so he began his sweep from the left again and stopped at the stations he hadn't visited during his first round. By the time he finished up and reached the mess hall, it was eleven o'clock. He grabbed some fresh orange juice and headed for the garden, where he lay under the oak tree, with his PIP switched on. Morgana and Faith joined him an hour later, eventually followed by Skye. The four of them sat there for the rest of the afternoon, comparing ideas and advising each other on what they thought were the best courses. Lunch came and went, and by four o'clock they had still not made a choice.

'There's too much to take in,' said Morgana, sounding thoroughly frustrated.

'Everything seems interesting,' said Skye, flipping from prospectus to prospectus on his holoscreen. 'I really don't know what to pick.'

'I like a couple of courses,' said Faith, looking dejected, 'but they clash on the timetable, so I have to settle for one, which is easier said than done.'

Julius opened his blank timetable and noticed that some of the spaces were greyed out. 'Those must be our core lessons then,' he said.

Faith leaned in to look at it. 'The personal choices are every Tuesday and Wednesday morning.'

Julius looked at his options and, although he really wanted to share as many classes as possible with the others, he knew he had to decide what was best for him.

'Come on, let's do this!' said Morgana practically. 'Tuesday mornings – I'll go for Starship Engineering for Pilots.'

'SS Management for me,' added Julius.

'Technician's path, here,' said Faith.

'Colonial Affairs,' finished Skye.

'Next, Wednesday Mornings,' called Morgana again. 'Pilot Training all the way, boys.'

'I thought so,' said Julius. 'Catalyst Training for me.'

'SS Architecture, if you had any doubts,' said Faith.

'I must do History and Politics. No choice there,' said Skye.

'Shame we can't be together,' said Morgana. She pressed a few buttons and sent her programme off to Mr Patel.

'I know, but can you imagine me sitting in Colonial Affairs?' said Faith, mimicking slipping a rope around his neck and giving it a tug upwards.

Julius laughed, and sent his schedule off. 'Well, that's that then,' he thought to himself.

*

That evening, the 3MAs were abuzz with discussions about their timetables, trying to find out who chose what, and why. The excitement was such that, on the Friday morning they just couldn't wait until nine, and pleaded with Mr Patel to start earlier. Fortunately, the guidance teacher had no problem with that, since all he had to do was send them their approved schedules back.

When Julius opened his, he was delighted to see that his subjects had been confirmed.

With the course choices out of the way, Mr Patel, to the great surprise of the Mizkis, left them free to do as they pleased. As Apprentices, they weren't allowed on Satras until the second weekend of October however, so they had to find other things to do, to pass the time.

Morgana went off to meet up with her girlfriends, so they could resume their seemingly endless, cosy conversations. Julius, Faith and Skye, together with seven other classmates, started a match of five-a-side mind-ball in the garden, the Zed version of football, whereby instead of using their feet, the players would pass the ball overhead using only their Telekinetic abilities. Needless to say, Barth managed to run straight into a tree, giving himself a bloody nose and a severe headache as reward for his clumsiness. Every time ten points were scored, some of the other Mizkis would substitute in, to give everyone a chance to play, and the ones who had been playing a welcome breather. After lunch, even Morgana decided to join in, challenging the class to a boys-against-girls competition. The game got so intense that, when the Friday lessons ended, most of the Tijaran students ended up gathered around to watch and cheer. Eventually, tea time came, and they decided to call it a night, with the boys' team leading, 568 to 540.

Julius and Faith were dripping with sweat, so they headed back to their rooms for a quick shower, and then headed back up towards the mess hall for dinner. As they were walking, they passed a group of 5MS girls, and caught a snippet of their conversation.

'Yeah,' said a red haired girl, 'and she told me that Skye Miller saved them all single-handedly from the evil Arneshians.'

'It would be so exciting to have someone like him come to your rescue!' giggled a brunette.

'She told me that after Skye rescued her, he took her out on a date! And then they …' whispered a third one, her voice tapering off as the two boys moved away.

Faith and Julius stared at each other, stupefied. Apart from the fact that no one was supposed to know the details of their mission, to believe that Skye had rescued the girls all on his own was quite preposterous. There were tears in their eyes, and they were making particularly odd noises as they tried hard to suppress their amusement. Once they were sure they were out of earshot of the girls, they fell against each other and howled with laughter. It was too funny not to share, so when they got inside and spotted Skye, Morgana and Siena, they quickly sat down at their table and shared the tale.

While Skye and Morgana were suitably amused, Julius thought that Siena didn't really look like she was enjoying the joke, but maybe she just hadn't found it that funny. After all, she had been one of the kidnapped girls, along with Morgana, and she knew all too well the real scale of the rescue mission, which had required the intervention of a whole team of officers, as well as the three boy members of the Skirts.

'And you know what's even funnier, Miller?' said Faith, waving a fork in the air. 'It's the fact that you sit here, stinking to high heaven after twelve hours of physical exercise, and not one of these girls here has said anything. Me Irish sense of comprehension is officially baffled.'

'It's nothing to do with "Stinky" here,' answered Morgana, promptly. 'It's more to do with the fact that we haven't washed either.'

'*Fanks Mofgana,*' said Skye, chewing noisily.

'No, seriously, look at him,' she said, her voice caught halfway between mirth and mock disgust.

'Yeah, yeah,' said Faith, still looking unconvinced.

*

The morning after brought more mind-ball in the garden; this time the other year groups joined in too, creating an improvised mini tournament that ran throughout the entire weekend. By the time that Sunday night arrived, there were plenty of sore necks among the students, as running around with their heads tilted back, fixed on the hovering ball, was seriously hard work.

One curious episode that left the Skirts puzzled, was that by bed time the story of Skye Miller rescuing the hostages had somehow changed. According to the female consensus, the unsung hero of that day was now none other than Faith "The Skirt" Shanigan.

'What can I say,' said Faith, still chuckling about it. 'It's me Irish charm.'

Given the sudden satisfied grin on Siena's face, Julius wasn't too sure that his charm had had anything to do with this strange turn of events.

THE AMBASSADOR

On Monday the 5th of September, the 3MAs gathered in the mess hall for breakfast. There was an air of anticipation among the Apprentice and Senior Mizkis, as they awaited their new timetables.

Julius had just started his honey and cinnamon porridge, when his PIP vibrated, announcing an incoming message. Judging by the sudden drop in noise in the room, it was clear that the rest of the students had also received one. There was a rush to activate their devices, followed by a general chorus of comments that ranged from enthusiastic to horror-stricken. Julius avidly scanned his new schedule.

'We're starting Pyrokinesis!' cried Skye excitedly.

'Finally!' added Faith, exchanging a high five with Julius. 'Bring on the heat!'

'Ahem,' coughed Morgana. 'I don't mean to be a spoilsport, but it says here that we don't start Pyrokinesis until January.'

'What?' said Julius, double-checking his planner. 'Why?'

'It doesn't say,' answered Morgana.

'On a Friday morning there's a class of Biomathematics, run by Cress,' said Skye.

'It says here that it's an opt-in subject,' said Julius.

'That's right,' added Morgana. 'Kaori told me that MAs can study towards a medical career if they want to.'

'Hmm,' said Julius, not convinced. 'It doesn't sound like much fun to me.'

'Probably because it isn't,' replied Skye.

Julius nodded. 'So, what exactly do we study in this Bio-thingy anyway?'

'It's math applied to biology,' explained Faith, simply. 'They use it for genetic research and computer simulations ... among other things, but that's as much as I know.'

'Wow,' said Julius. 'That's a lot more than I care to know.' Then he remembered his conversation with Patel the previous day. 'Speaking of doctors, apparently Freja wants me to see Walliser every Thursday morning.'

'Really?' asked Morgana. 'When did he tell you that?'

'Yesterday.'

'I get it,' said Faith, patting him hard on the shoulder. 'It's the W.C. business again!'

'Don't call me W.C.,' said Julius, flicking a lump of porridge at his friend with the tip of his spoon.

Just then, the loudspeaker bellowed, 'Attention Mizkis – all 3MAs must report to the infirmary at 09:00.'

Julius looked around the room, feeling quite puzzled. A table of senior students were chuckling away disconcertingly, and pointing at them.

'Infirmary?' gulped Faith. 'Why the infirmary?'

Skye shook his head. 'No idea, mate.'

'Please don't tell me they're going to add a few more gadgets to me body,' continued Faith, the distress obvious in his voice.

Body augmentations were a necessary part of their Zed training, and they were always done to enhance the students' abilities. In his second year Julius was implanted with the Personal Information Planner chip into his left hand and two shield chips — one in each of his forearms. He could understand Faith's anxiety, though. Because of his disability, the school had already given him his famous Skirt, which responded to the many sensors embedded all along his legs. Julius had joked with him before about how he was slowly being turned into a cyborg.

They tried to guess, and even resorted to begging some of the Seniors to tell them what was happening, but no one was able to extract even a hint from them, so the 3MAs made their way to the infirmary feeling a mixture of curiosity, and suspicion.

Dr Walliser, the Tijaran physician, was waiting for the students. Resident nurses Ms Federica Primula and Mr Dorian Finch were by his side, together with ten other members of staff. The students were invited to take a seat on the many sofas occupying the waiting area. When they had all done so, Dr Walliser bowed to them. 'Good morning,' he said, 'and welcome to your Apprentice years.'

The students bowed back to him, still looking quite anxious.

'As you can see from your timetables, the first two hours of lessons on Mondays are for Pyrokinesis, but you will not be able to do this training until January.'

A few murmurs of complaint ran through the room.

'I know it seems unfair but, trust me, you must be physically prepared for the intense pressure you will be putting your body through once you start.' Dr Walliser began to stroll in front of them, hands nestled in his lab coat pockets. 'I'm sure all of you have experimented with your Pyrokinetic skills at one point or another but, of course, always during simulated game play. You will be trained to a completely different level, pushing boundaries you didn't even know you had. To do this, you must prepare, and that is why every Monday morning you shall come to the infirmary for your Pre-Pyro dose.'

More whispers spread around the room.

'I don't want anyone to worry unnecessarily though,' the doctor continued. 'All you will be required to do is to lie on a bed while we administer the treatment. There is a very important reason why all students undergo this procedure. Using Pyrokinetic abilities on a regular basis exerts sustained and irrevocable harm on all internal body organs, and to the circulatory system, due to the heat that is generated by your mind-skills. In the past, Mizkis were not able to fully develop this White Art, as they could end up severely damaged by it. Today's technology however, has allowed us to bypass these problems, and that is why we must properly prepare your bodies.'

'It doesn't sound too bad,' ventured Julius unconvincingly.

'I know what you're really thinking about, McCoy,' said Faith. 'An extra chance to sleep.'

Julius grinned and winked at him.

'The treatment lasts approximately 90 minutes, so we are going to start right away. Wait here until your name is called. Zolin Acalan, come with me.'

Zolin, a short boy with brown hair, stood up quickly and moved over in front of the doctor. Julius watched as he was led off into one of the rooms. As soon as he had gone, the nurses started to call names alphabetically, and the next twelve students were summoned. Julius was among them, and followed his designated nurse to a nearby room.

The doctor hadn't lied – all Julius was asked to do was lie on a bed and relax. He watched intently as Ms Primula inserted a needle into his left arm, flinching just a little when it went in. The little tube was attached to a machine, which Julius assumed was the Pre-Pyro dispenser.

The nurse pressed a few buttons on the machine, until a long steady beep was heard. 'There, you're all set. If you want to watch something, the screen in front of you is voice activated. Just say the channel and it'll select it for you. Any problems, here's the call button, by the bedside. I'll be back in a little while.'

Julius nodded. Once the nurse had closed the door, he decided a little nap was just the thing for him, so he closed his eyes and dozed off.

*

'Wake up, McCoy.'

The voice brought Julius back to full consciousness. He looked at his arm and saw that the needle was gone.

'There's some juice in the waiting room,' said Ms Primula. 'Have a drink; it'll make you feel better.'

Julius stretched slowly, before jumping off the bed. He stood still for a few seconds, to see if he could feel anything weird about his body. Everything seemed fine however, so he left the room. A few of the other students were already in the waiting area. Julius grabbed a glass, filled it with juice from a jug and sat down on one of the sofas. It was true: the tangy liquid gave him a nice kick, which awoke all his senses. It wasn't long before all the 3MAs were out of their rooms, sipping some juice and comparing first impressions of the Pre-Pyro treatment. All in all, it hadn't been a bad experience; strange perhaps, but perfectly acceptable.

When Dr Walliser released them at 11:00 hours, the Mizkis headed straight to the Grey Arts sector for their Draw lesson. Professor Cathy Turner was waiting by her door, spectacles precariously propped on her long, bony nose.

'Welcome back, Mizkis,' she said, twitching in her usual manner. 'Let me show you to your new classroom.'

Julius followed her eagerly, wondering what new plant she would let them use to practice their draws. So far they had worked on cacti and more delicate pot plants, trying to control the amount of energy drawn each time.

'I hope we get to practice on a big ol' tree,' said Julius, rubbing his hands together.

'I agree,' said Faith. 'I'm tired of stinky, puny sticks. I want me hands on a right trunk.'

There was a snort, followed by a chortle from behind. Skye and Manuel Valdez were turning redder by the second.

'What?' asked Faith, puzzled, 'What did I say?'

Morgana, shaking her head, leaned closer to Faith and whispered something in his ear which made him turn crimson.

'You guys are bad!' said Faith pointing at them both but, by then even Julius and Morgana had joined in. Faith shrugged, and began to chuckle himself.

Amidst the laughter, Julius noticed that they had descended a couple of floors, and that Professor Turner was now standing in front of a new entrance, ushering the Mizkis inside. When Julius stepped through the double door, the sight before him took his breath away.

'Is this a zoo?' asked Morgana, clearly impressed.

'As close as we can get to one on the Moon, Miss Ruthier,' replied Professor Turner. 'Come, let's go and sit at those picnic tables for a moment.'

The students followed her and took a seat, exploring the environment around them with their eyes.

Even after two years on Zed, the holographic facilities of the Lunar Perimeter never failed to astonish Julius. The virtual zoo was set inside a vast park, with green hills rolling off in the distance under a blue sky. Rows of trees stretched off in every direction, and a cacophony of mixed animal voices echoed through the air.

'This simulation room is specifically calibrated to perform draws on animals,' explained Turner. 'As Apprentices, you must now learn to take advantage of different types of life forms, in a responsible manner. As I explained to you in your first year, the smallest amount of energy can save your life in combat.' She then turned to her right and whistled sharply. From a nearby path, something scampered her way.

Julius glanced in that direction and found himself staring at a bouncing Border collie.

A chorus of 'Awww!' came from the girls, but to their disappointment, the dog didn't even notice them, and instead sat obediently at Professor Turner's feet.

Julius knew very well what was coming, since he had also performed a draw on a sim-wolf during his first Solo game, some two years ago. He watched as Professor Turner placed her hands on either side of the dog's head, her face fixed in concentration, looking the animal directly in its eyes. She then took a long, deep breath and held it. Julius saw several yellowish threads of energy passing from the animal's fur to Turner's fingertips, which then spread over her hands until they were completely absorbed into her skin. The collie yelped weakly and swayed to the left, before hunching down in exhaustion.

'Just enough for a pick-me-up,' said Turner, satisfied.

And indeed, she did look perkier than before, in direct contrast with the dog, who was now practically asleep.

'So, for this year's training, you will be free to choose an animal for your weekly practice. Start small, and work your way up. And to stress the importance of responsible drawing, every time you harm a sim-animal by drawing too much, Fyvers will be docked off your account, so be careful, or you'll be left with nothing but a string of detentions.'

Lopaka Liway raised his hand.

'Yes?'

'Professor, I don't mean to be cheeky, but … what are the odds of finding an elephant on a spacecraft?'

'Fair question,' answered Turner. 'However, you seem to forget the importance of the exploration and repopulation programmes that Zed has been conducting throughout the galaxy. There are many habitable planets out there, and although no one has seen an elephant on a space station, more than three million animals live on Kapaldi 22. So, you see, Mr Liway, it is better to be prepared than sorry. And now Mizkis, go explore the zoo and find your first animal. And don't forget to update your logs as you go along. Off you go.'

Julius exchanged a glance with the rest of the gang. 'Not too bad for a Monday morning.'

'Agreed,' said Skye, 'but let's try not to kill anything, or we can say goodbye to the game season this year.'

Julius nodded eagerly. In fact, he was so worried about the idea of having Fyvers removed from his weekly wage that he decided to try his draw only on the sturdiest of any small animals he could find. So it was that he ended up spending the rest of the morning staring intently at a particularly uncooperative tapir.

Professor Turner had given each of them an energy receiver, so that by the end of the lesson they had a precise log of the type of animals used and the amount of energy drawn each time. At lunchtime, as the students returned their receivers to the teacher, they saw Barth walking up the path, soaked from head to toe.

'What happened to you?' asked Faith.

'That nasty platypus just wouldn't stand still,' he said, trailing water all over the place. All the Mizkis collapsed into fits of laughter so contagious that even Professor Turner found it hard to stifle a giggle.

After their meal, Julius and his classmates made their way to Professor Clavel's classroom in eager anticipation of their Pilot Training lesson.

'I wonder what we'll be doing this year,' said Morgana to no one in particular, as she was bouncing along the promenade.

'Look at her,' said Skye, nodding in her direction. 'We aren't even in class, and she's already hyper.'

'Wait until she starts her chosen subjects,' said Julius. 'Then you'll see her really take off. Her head will be so high up in the clouds she won't even notice us lot.'

'Huh?' asked Morgana, suddenly turning around. 'Did someone say something?'

They looked at her in amusement.

'See? What did I tell you?' said Julius to the boys; then to Morgana, 'Nothing dear, just talking about the weather.'

When they arrived at their classroom, Clavel was already inside.

'Welcome back Mizkis,' he said. 'I'm glad to see that even after two years you're still punctual.'

Julius looked around at the enthusiastic faces of his classmates. There was no doubt that Clavel was one of the most liked teachers in Tijara, so their constant punctuality didn't surprise him at all.

'We have a very special destination set for you this year, and this is what you'll need to pilot in order to get there,' he said, touching a section of his desk. Immediately, a holographic image appeared in the space behind him.

Julius looked up and saw a shuttle pod revolving slowly on its own axis. He had been in one of them before: a four-seater used to carry people to and from spaceships.

'I wondered when we would get to piloting them,' said Faith, sounding quite pleased at the prospect.

'What's the destination we're going to, Professor?' asked Morgana, who looked about ready to leap up and down in her seat with excitement.

'Your destination,' continued Clavel, 'is Gea One – our very own space station.' A new holographic image appeared above his head, leaving the students in stunned silence. The Gea was a metal sphere, surrounded by two rings crossing over each other in a perpetual motion. 'The Gea can hold 300 people, and for three months it will be Tijara's new school.'

'Holy Fagioli!' cried Faith, shaking Julius by the shoulders. He looked at Clavel. 'Professor, please, no more! Me heart can't take it!'

'Too bad, Mr Shanigan,' said Clavel, 'since I was about to show you the last surprise. But if you don't want to …'

'No, no! Don't listen to him,' cut in Morgana, flushed cheeks and all. 'Tell us, Professor!'

'Here it is, then,' he said, smiling and pointing upwards. 'The Heron.' The two holograms suddenly shrunk and moved to the side, leaving centre stage to a starship.

Julius had seen this model before, and he was aware of it being a larger version of the Cougars. The Heron was a water drop-shaped, flat ship with two fins sticking out from the middle of its upper and lower sides, capable of carrying 100 passengers.

'Awesome,' whispered Barth, full of wonder.

Although Julius had already been given the heads up by Captain Kelly about their impending stay in orbit, his concerns about Michael had driven it clear out of his mind, which was why he had not mentioned it to the others. Remembering his chat with Kelly however, made him think of his brother again, and the sadness that fell over him dampened his excitement about Gea One. In the confusion around him though, no one had noticed his sudden change of mood, so Julius had a chance to breathe deeply, compose himself and force a smile onto his face.

For the rest of the lesson, the Mizkis explored the contents of their class programmes in some depth, so that they had a schedule of what lay ahead in the coming weeks. Learning to pilot and maintain the shuttle pod was going to be their focus until the mid-winter break.

*

On Tuesday morning Julius woke up well before his eight o'clock alarm. After a quick shower, he headed for the mess-hall, and bumped into Faith in the food queue.

'Really looking forward to me new classes, mate,' said Faith, filling his plate with scrambled eggs and smoked salmon.

'Same here,' said Julius. 'Starship Management: I wonder who else has chosen it.'

'I know that Lopaka's in me class. I didn't think he'd like engineering. Apparently it's a family thing. Go figure.'

'Shame we have to split, though.'

'It sucks, actually. At least it's only for a couple of mornings.'

Julius nodded. He didn't like the idea, but there was nothing to be done about it. He would never have chosen engineering just to be with Faith for a few hours on a Tuesday morning; he would have hated it and probably failed the course. Besides, they would have plenty of time to catch up afterwards.

At 08:50, Julius went to the holographic sector, on level -6, and waited for Professor Farshid to arrive. A few minutes later, three of his classmates – Zolin Acalan, Kaleb Kashny and Yuri Slovich – came around the corner, and greeted him cheerfully. Julius waved back.

'Great!' said Yuri. 'I knew you'd be here, McCoy.'

'Julius,' said Kaleb, 'it looks like it's us two against these spacemen. All-boys teams.'

Julius smiled at the joke: he and Kaleb both came from Earth, while Zolin was from Colonial 1 and Yuri, like Skye, was from Terra 3.

'Ahem.' The group turned to look in the direction of the sound. 'Did you really think there would be no ladies present?' said Leanne Nord, walking towards them in her usual confident stride.

'You know, Leanne,' said Jiao Yu, who was walking next to her, 'I think they did.'

'Tut, tut,' added Astra Evangelou, who was a few steps behind the other two girls. 'I bet we can teach you a thing or two.'

'I bet you could,' answered Zolin, grinning cheekily. 'Right, guys?'

'You're so immature,' said Leanne, shaking her head, and pretending to be offended.

The banter continued like that for the next few minutes, with more goodhearted retaliation from the boys, matched equally by the girls. Julius, who still wasn't much good at chatting with girls, found himself suddenly wishing for Morgana's reassuring presence. Seeing as that wasn't possible right then, he quietly stepped back, happy to watch them from the sidelines.

It wasn't long before Professor Farshid arrived and opened up the classroom. Inside, it had already been set up with eight single desks, forming a circle. Julius sat between Yuri and Astra, facing Kaleb.

'My, my – seven students,' said Farshid, raising an eyebrow. 'More than I was expecting.'

Julius tried to read her, but couldn't quite get any sense of whether she was genuinely pleased by the turnout, or not. She seemed quite different from his other teachers, that was certain. She didn't have the warmth of Morales, or the natural ease of King and Clavel; at the same time she wasn't as stern as Chan or Beloi either. Truth to be told, the only person Julius could compare her to was none other than Grand Master Freja: someone who inspired authority, but still managed to be quite accessible at the same time. You wouldn't want to joke around with Freja, but you could be sure he would help you when the chips were down. Were those the qualities of a good captain? Julius wasn't entirely sure, but he knew that was what he was here to find out.

'This tends to be a small class,' explained Farshid. 'Five is the average number of students who generally sign up. Being a captain is a dream for many, but a reality for few.' She let her words hang in the air for a moment, to let them sink in. 'It's not my intention to scare you, Mizkis, but you need to know that if your ship is under attack, its shields are down and the engines offline, every single crew member will be looking at you, demanding a solution. And you must give it to them. In the face of death, you must be larger than life. It is unthinkable for a captain to be anything less than that.'

Julius felt a shiver run down his spine – her words had definitely hit home for him.

Professor Farshid looked down and touched a point on her desk. Suddenly, the room disappeared, and was instantly replaced with what looked like the engine room of a large spaceship. There was a collective gasp from the students at the sudden change, since they were now sitting in the middle of a bustling environment, with holographic crew members hurrying to and fro, and a massive plasma core engine to one side.

Julius shifted in his chair, looking wide-eyed at the scene unfolding all around him. His classmates were equally captivated by their surroundings, their heads turning left and right, trying to take everything in.

'A captain has many responsibilities,' she continued. 'Although you will not be expected to actually fix an engine, attend to a sick crew member, cook a meal or even pilot your ship, you must know everything that goes on onboard.' As she spoke, she continued pressing different points on her desktop, and every time she did, the scene around them altered.

From the engine room they found themselves in the sick bay, followed by the canteen, and the bridge. In each of these areas, there were always dozens of the holo crew walking around them, and even sometimes through them, attending to their duties.

'During the course of this year,' said Farshid, 'you will familiarise yourself with all the areas that make up a spaceship, from the living quarters to the bridge; the amount of staff required to man these areas and the tasks of each individual under your command, whether they be your tactical officers, your science officers, or your chefs.'

Julius continued looking around avidly, even though he had already been on spaceships before, and had a pretty good idea of what was expected from a captain, thanks to Kelly's help.

'Check your PIP before coming to class,' continued Farshid. 'Some days we will work in here, others in the Grey Arts sector. So Mizkis, still think you have what it takes?'

'Yes, Ma'am,' they replied as one.

'So let it be,' nodded the teacher, satisfied.

Certainly, Julius knew in his heart that this was his calling; it would be hard, but he was up for it. The simulation faded slowly away, and on each desk appeared a blueprint for the Heron.

'Professor Clavel has already told you that you'll soon be manning this ship,' said Farshid. 'I want you to go over every nook and cranny of it, taking extensive notes of the different sectors. In two weeks time I want you each to hand in a detailed report on the essential areas required to create a fully functional ship, and the minimum number of crew members needed to man them.'

The students liked the idea of this so much that, when Julius asked if they could start straight away, they all eagerly backed him up.

Farshid had no problem with that, and spent the next three hours answering their questions and raising any issues with their planning. 'I know it spoils your design, Mr Kashny,' she said tapping on Kaleb's sketch, 'but a toilet is a necessary part of a spaceship, and the bridge is not the right place for it.'

Julius was pleased to see how easily this new subgroup was forming a bond right from the start, though he suspected that at some point there would come a time for competitiveness. But ultimately, each of them wanted to be Zed captains, and so were all on the same side.

That afternoon, at lunch, The Skirts met up as usual, and had to force themselves to take it in turns telling each other about their morning, since they were trying to all talk at the same time. The excitement was so great that, when Morales took them to the infirmary for their annual shield-chip update, Faith didn't complain, and instead volunteered to go first. His good mood wasn't even dampened when Dr Walliser asked him to remain behind to fit his skirt with an extra panel at the bottom (to make up for his growing height), along with the corresponding sensors inside his legs. To Julius' amazement, he was still chatting away about engineering when he joined them later for tea, seemingly oblivious of the fact that he had just spent the afternoon being poked and cut in various parts of his body.

*

Wednesday morning saw the 3MAs maintaining the same level of excitement as the previous day, as they went along to the first sessions of their second chosen subjects.

Julius headed for the holographic sector, to meet Professor Jeremy Gould, who was head of Catalyst Training in Tijara. As he stepped into the room, he was surprised to see Isolde Frey there. He had never thought of her as a fighter.

'Hi Julius,' she said, her long, dark braid swaying behind her shoulders as she turned. 'Guess who the only two Mizkis attending this class are?'

'Hi,' he replied. 'Just us two, huh?'

'Yes. And you look surprised to see me, I'd say. Or maybe you're just disappointed.'

'Uh, no ... well, ok, yes. A little,' he answered, awkwardly. Then, realising his blunder, he hurried forward, waving his hands in the air. 'I didn't mean that! I'm not disappointed, honest. I meant what you said first, surpr-'

'Whatever,' Isolde interrupted, turning away from him, the cheeriness gone from her voice.

Julius rolled his eyes, mouthing the word "idiot" to himself, then sat at the desk to her right. This was just perfect, he thought. By the look of things, Tuesday mornings would see him stuck in the middle a bunch of hormonal classmates, happily engaged in romantic bantering, while Wednesdays would see him one-to-one with a touchy girl. All in all, two of Julius' worst nightmares. On the bright side, he knew Isolde a little better than the girls in his other class, on account of her being such close friends with Morgana.

Professor Gould arrived at 09:00, on the dot, and nodded curtly to his students before activating his terminal. Julius had discovered that Gould was from Terra 1, same as Grand Master Freja; the only two Tijaran teachers from outer space. There was a long-held rumour about him, supported by many of the Senior Mizkis, that he slept with his Gauntlet under his pillow, just in case. Julius thought that, if it was true, he must either be one hardcore fighter, or a complete pillock.

'Miss Frey,' said Gould, examining a file on his desk, 'Professor Clavel believes you capable of becoming a catalyst specialist.'

'Yes, sir,' she replied.

'And what practical experience have you had so far?'

Julius looked at Isolde, also quite curious to find out.

'As well as maintaining excellent grades in class, sir,' said Isolde, a hint of nerves in her voice, 'I have used the Hologram Palace regularly, each week, for the past two years. I rank third overall in the female Fight chart for the whole of Zed.'

Julius was definitely impressed by that. He regularly checked the Solo scores and the progress of the Skirts against similar teams, but he had never thought to check any of the other types of charts, which was why Isolde's record caught him completely by surprise.

Professor Gould nodded. 'It's a good start.' Then he turned to Julius. 'Mr McCoy, you come highly recommended for this course. Between your Solo record, the Skirts' endeavours, and your past two Summer Camp experiences, I am sure you can easily prove your worth to me. Remember though, arriving at the top isn't difficult; remaining there is. Don't become complacent in your success, or you may lose your status before you even realise it.'

'Yes, sir,' answered Julius, glad that Gould, while acknowledging his past achievements, hadn't made too much of a big deal about it.

Professor Gould picked up two virtual files from his desktop, pinching each one between thumb and forefinger. 'Open your PIPs, please.'

Julius activated his, and watched as Gould flicked the file in his left hand toward him. To the eye, these data files always appeared like luminous, tiny specs of gold, as they travelled between two points. Julius knew though, that they contained a massive storage of information. The file floated briskly towards his activated PIP, accelerating as it got closer, and was rapidly sucked into the holographic screen on his palm.

'This is your 3MA programme,' said Gould. 'I want you to read it before next Wednesday. As well as a breakdown of topics, it has the dates of a series of checkpoints scattered throughout the year. We don't have exams on Zed, as you know, but by each checkpoint you must have mastered the topics up to that date, or you will not be able to progress. If, by the end of the year, you have not cleared all of them, you will not be allowed to continue on this course as a 4MA. Is this clear?'

'Yes, sir,' they quickly answered.

'Good. Let's start from scratch.' A screen flickered to life behind his head, displaying an image of a Zed officer manning a spaceship catalyst. His hands were clenched tight around the lever, seemingly releasing a vast amount of energy. 'As you know, a catalyst channels your energies and shoots them out in the form of a yellow laser beam. Meditation is what gives you focus and precision for shooting; this White Art is especially useful when you are piloting a Cougar. Why is that, Miss Frey?'

'Because, on a one-man vessel, such as a Cougar, you fly it using only your mind-skills, since your hands are busy operating the catalyst,' she answered promptly. 'Therefore Meditation is vital, as it helps you concentrate on doing the right things at the right time.'

'Correct, Miss Frey. A fleet is only as strong as the fighters in it; if you're having a bad day, or you're distracted for whatever reason, and without a way of replenishing your energies, you will not be able to attack an enemy, or defend your ship.' The image behind Gould slowly changed to one of a fighter looking increasingly tired, while the beam from his catalyst was growing weaker. 'You must know how to manage your powers, and how to reload quickly.' Again, the image changed. This time the fighter was firing short bursts of energy, rather than one continuous stream, and intermittently drinking some kind of liquid from a long tube connected to the wall right behind the catalyst. He appeared to be very lively now. Professor Gould dismissed the screen with a wave of his hand, and looked at the two Mizkis. 'A catalyst is just a piece of metal – you are the real weapon.'

Even if he hadn't been able to see the orange wisps in Gould's aura, it was clear enough to Julius that the professor was passionate about his work. As the teacher talked, it wasn't just words that Julius heard; behind every gesture and facial expression, there was a story to tell. To Julius, being described as a weapon was particularly strange, especially now, in a society where conventional weapons no longer existed.

Before the Chemical War of 2550, someone like Julius or Isolde would have been seen as a threat to humanity, or as someone to be used in the then common wars between nations. The death of some twelve billion people in that war had changed all that though, leaving the remaining three billion-odd to face up to their own mortality. After a global promise of never again, weapons had been completely banned and the planet became the D.R.E., the Democratic Republic of Earth, under the guidance of the Earth Leader and the five Voices of the Earth, representing each of the five agreed continents. It was only because of the Arneshians that words like "weapons", and "military" had been reintroduced into everyday vocabulary, although Julius was glad they were now more commonly used in reference to defence, rather than offence.

'We shall start this course by examining a catalyst up close and personal,' said Professor Gould. 'Behind you, there are three basic types of catalyst, one set for each of you. You've seen them before, during Pilot Training. Today, instead of using them, I want you to take them apart.' He walked towards the back of the room, motioning for them to follow.

Julius let Isolde choose first, and then moved to the remaining empty table with the catalysts propped on it. There were all manner of screwdrivers, pliers and tools of different shapes and sizes that Julius had never seen before, all neatly arranged on a large tray to the side of them. Julius looked at them with apprehension. 'Faith would be able to do this in a jiff,' he whispered to Isolde.

'Yeah, and we need to learn how to do it just as well as he would,' she replied.

He was pleased to notice that some of the coldness had left her voice.

'I want you to make a note of the name and function of each individual piece,' said Gould. 'By the end of October you must be able to assemble each one of them in less than a minute; this will be your first checkpoint. And now, to work!'

'To work then,' repeated Julius softly, looking at his catalysts, not sure where to begin.

By one o'clock neither he, nor Isolde, had managed to finish the task. Professor Gould however, wasn't especially displeased and pointed out that to fully catalogue each piece and understand its function for the first time certainly wasn't a job for one lesson. Those words reassured Julius greatly and, judging by the greenish wisps visible in Isolde's aura, they had had the same effect on her.

*

Later that day, Julius bumped into the rest of the Skirts in the promenade, and they headed for lunch together, once again eagerly sharing every detail of their new subjects with the others.

'Wow,' said Skye, swallowing his last French fry whole. 'Isolde's a fighter. Who would have thought?'

'You should have paid more attention to the girls' charts,' said Morgana.

'No, please,' cut in Julius. 'He already pays enough attention to girls as it is.'

'I'm honing my diplomatic skills,' answered Skye, defensively. 'In my position it's very handy to be as close as possible to as many people as possible, I'll have you know.'

'I'm not even gonna ask what position that is,' muttered Julius.

'Your *position*?' said Faith. 'Have you already replaced the Curio Maximus, then?'

'Not yet,' said Skye, with a cheeky grin, 'but I'm working on it. I found out that his daughter works at Colonial Affairs too.'

'You're unbelievable,' said Morgana, rolling her eyes.

'Moving on,' said Julius, punching Skye on the shoulder, 'how was Starship Architecture, Faith?'

'Really grand,' he answered. 'It's going to be the best course yet for me, and there's this competition as well, you know.'

'What competition?' asked Morgana.

'Apparently every few years Pit-Stop Pete runs it and you have to design a spaceship from scratch. It's open to all Mizki Apprentices and Seniors and, if you win, they actually build it as a one-off.'

'That's just, Faith,' enthused Julius.

'You should definitely go for it, mate,' added Skye. 'Who better than you?'

'I'm not too sure,' said Faith, sounding a bit worried. 'It's packed with older Mizkis and I really don't want to shame meself by making something horrible. I mean, I just started the course, I couldn't possibly-'

'Faith,' interrupted Morgana, 'when was the last competition held?'

'Nine years ago.'

'So this could be your only chance to realise the biggest dream you've ever had, and you're still debating about entering?'

'Well ...'

'That's it,' she said, standing up abruptly. 'You've lost your marbles. Come with me, now!'

'What ... hey!' uttered Faith, as Morgana grabbed him by the waist of his skirt and dragged him out of the mess hall, fork still in hand, past the staring eyes of a group of 1MJs.

'That girl's a handful,' said Lopaka Liway, stopping next to their table, holding an empty tray. He was looking at Morgana with a longing expression on his face.

'Too big of a handful for you, my friend,' said Skye, standing up and patting him on the shoulder.

'I'll show you both a handful, if you don't drop that kind of talk right now!' said Julius, brushing past them and returning his tray to the counter.

'What's with him?' asked Lopaka. 'I can never talk about girls with him.'

'Late puberty,' said Skye.

'I heard that,' Julius called from behind them.

'Oops. Better go,' he whispered to Lopaka. Then to Julius, 'Coming dear!'

When Morgana and Faith joined the others in Professor Beloi's Telepathy class, Faith was positively beaming. 'Professor de Boer said that Pete was counting on me signing up,' he told them, clearly chuffed by that.

Morgana just sat there, a little satisfied smile on her face.

'*Well done, you,*' Julius told her with his mind.

'*Someone had to,*' she replied.

Professor Beloi announced himself to the students in his customary way, with a sudden mind-message, taking them all by surprise. They should have known better by now really, especially since their Russian teacher had not uttered a single word in forty-one years, which was probably the reason why he was the best telepathist the world had ever known. '*Good afternoon, Mizkis,*' he said, entering the classroom. '*Take a seat.*'

The students quickly complied.

'*In light of our recent encounters with the Arneshians, we are going to step up the pace this year. I have already sent my programme to each of you, and I expect all of you to-* '

'All personnel and Mizkis, please activate Space Channel one immediately!' a voice boomed over the loudspeaker.

The students looked at Beloi, who appeared to be as surprised as they were. '*Very well,*' he said, and activated a large screen on the front wall, so the entire class could see it.

Julius exchanged a worried look with the others. Interrupting lessons so the whole school could watch the Space Channel wasn't exactly an omen of good news, and judging by the grey wisps above Beloi's head, that was exactly what he was thinking too. There was complete silence as the words "Breaking News" rolled across the screen.

'Good afternoon Zed,' said the anchorwoman, Iryana Mielowa.

Julius recognised her immediately, with her dark wavy hair and bright red lipstick — she was probably the most familiar face on the Lunar Perimeter. She was sometimes also half-jokingly referred to as "the harbinger of moon".

'We are interrupting our regular broadcast to report an unprecedented event: less than thirty minutes ago Earth Channel News received a recorded vidcall from Manuel T'Rogon, the High Ambassador of the Arneshians.'

'The what of who?' said Faith, incredulous.

'The video has already spread like wildfire throughout Earth and the regular colonies,' continued Ms Mielowa, 'creating considerable unrest. Here, now, we will be showing it on the Space Channel in its entirety.'

Julius shifted uncomfortably in his seat with a growing sense of unease. What could the Arneshian ambassador possibly have to say to Earth? He could feel the tension in the air, as no one uttered a sound.

Professor Beloi had also taken a seat next to Barth, and was staring at the screen like the rest of them.

The image switched from Ms Mielowa to that of a hefty man, seated behind a dark, mahogany desk. When Julius saw him, he unconsciously leaned forward, so as to observe him better; after all, this was the first time he was seeing an *actual* Arneshian, as opposed to one of their holographic servants. To his surprise however, Manuel T'Rogon looked just like any other human, and nothing in his features suggested otherwise: he had pale blue eyes and a thin, pointy nose; his short, pearl-white hair shimmered as the light caught it. He was wearing a metal circlet around his head, while his body was garbed in what appeared to be a long silver tunic, with gold details embroidered on the front. Still, there was something odd about him, but Julius couldn't quite pinpoint what. All in all though, T'Rogon was a bit disappointing, perhaps because a tiny part of Julius' brain had half-expected to see tentacles sprouting out of his head or, at the very least, an extra set of ears.

'Earthlings, on behalf of Queen Salgoria of Arnesh, I bring tidings of peace and goodwill,' said the ambassador.

His voice was calm and welcoming and Julius immediately noticed a distinct absence of any accent. T'Rogon was using the common speech in its purest form, untouched by the regional variations that he was used to hearing on Zed.

'For the past 200 years our people have been at war. No more, we say. Let us bury the hatchet of hatred and division, in favour of a new era of prosperity and peace. Let us build bridges, not walls. Let us bring to life the dream once shared by Clodagh Arnesh and Marcus Tijara. Words cannot fully express the sentiment of regret that we Arneshians feel for what we have done against Earth, our mother world. Nonetheless, I am here to formally lay at your door the most heartfelt apologies from my queen and my people, with the hope that you will allow us to demonstrate our sincerity. Thank you,' he concluded, bowing his head.

The image faded to black, then switched back to Mielowa. 'Ambassador T'Rogon and his entourage will enter the lunar orbit within the next two weeks. More news in tonight's edition. Iryana Mielowa, reporting live from the Space Channel.'

'Is this a joke?' said Skye, breaking the astonished silence.

'*I'm afraid not, Mr Miller,*' answered Beloi, returning to his desk.

'He's not seriously expecting us to let him waltz in and park his ship in our backyard, is he?'

'*But that's exactly what he'll do,*' answered Beloi. '*He has diplomatic immunity, and he is going to use it.*'

'I don't believe this!' cried Skye, jumping up, his cheeks flushed.

Morgana delicately placed a hand on his forearm, to calm him. It had the desired effect, because he took a deep breath and slowly sat back down.

Julius knew how sensitive Skye was when it came to the Arneshians – his opinion was very much black-and-white when it came to taking sides in that regard. As was the case with anyone who had grown up on a Zed space station, he had been raised with the fear that attack could befall them at any minute; he had never forgiven the Arneshians for letting him, his family and friends grow up in such way. 'Professor,' said Julius, 'isn't there a danger that they may try to attack us while in our orbit?'

'Yes!' added Barth, looking agitated. 'What if they detonate their ship near Pit-Stop Pete?'

'Oh no, they won't!' answered Faith quickly, fist in the air. He was very protective when it came to Pete Kingston.

'*Mizkis,*' said Beloi, '*do not fret. There will be no explosion, at Pete's or anywhere else. Every visiting ship that comes within our orbit is always completely encased within a magnetic field, for everyone's peace of mind. And if they do "detonate", Mr Smit, they would be blown to smithereens within their own containment field. Now please, excuse me for a few minutes.*' Excited whispering broke out among the students, while Beloi moved towards the back of the room and activated his PIP.

The Mizkis gathered up into small groups, to discuss the situation and try to figure out what T'Rogon's real intentions were. Skye continued to vent his frustration with those students who, like him, had grown up in outer space, feeling that only they could truly understand what it meant to feel the enemy's breath on the back of their necks. Faith and the other engineers, who were apparently not convinced by Beloi's reassurances, were discussing the defence system of Pete's docking station and just how big an explosion it could sustain, while Morgana was simply listening to his words and at the same time keeping a worried eye on Julius, who had fallen completely silent.

Julius' mind had left his classmates' concerns far behind and had drifted off in a different direction: he was focused only on Michael. Had his brother already seen this video? How would he react to it, now that he knew he was one of them too? Would he even understand properly what any of this meant? Julius had no answers to those questions, but deep down he had a feeling this abrupt change of heart from the Arneshians was not going to play out easily at all.

LONG LOST FRIENDS

In the weeks that followed I 'Rogon's video appearance, all conversation boiled down to just one topic: the armistice with the Arneshians. Every inhabitant on the Lunar Perimeter was very sceptical about the idea of any possible truce. There was no great love of the need for any military action, but their distrust of Salgoria's people had grown deep over the last two centuries.

Many of Julius' classmates were quite prepared to voice their views on the Space Channel, should they be asked, but all the students had been instructed to refrain from doing anything of the sort until the official position of the Curia was known. Still, that didn't prevent the Mizkis spending most of their waking hours discussing the Arneshians' real intentions, much to the annoyance of their teachers, who found it difficult to get them to focus on even their most basic exercises.

On Monday the 26th of September, Julius and Faith were in the Apprentices' lounge, tackling their homework. Even though they were enrolled in different subjects, studying together still made things easier. Faith was lying on one of the sofas with an e-book about plasma cores propped on his belly, and his metallic skirt flattened around his legs; Julius had taken over the large rug in the middle of the room, with the various bits and pieces required for assembling a catalyst spread out in front of him. Professor Gould had set the first of their checkpoints for the end of October and occasionally, Faith would offer Julius advice on quicker ways of doing things, which was gratefully received.

Later that evening, Skye and Morgana entered the lounge in a hurry, followed by Barth and Siena.

'They're here,' said Skye, heading straight for the large TV screen on the back wall, and switching it on.

Julius instantly knew who he was referring to, and a little shiver ran down his back. They had been waiting the whole day for this: the Arneshian delegation was about to enter lunar orbit. Faith sat up, making space for Morgana and Siena next to him. Skye and Barth sat down on the floor beside Julius. No one spoke as Iryana Mielowa appeared on the screen.

'I'm standing inside the Zed docks, surrounded by the lunar leaders, awaiting the most anticipated event in modern human history: the visit of the Arneshian delegation. The tension here is tangible, and the last of the preparations have now been completed. The Curio Maximus, Aldobrando Roversi, has just arrived, accompanied by some of the Curiates. Behind me, you can see them talking to the Grand Masters and the Masters of the three schools.'

'Wait a minute,' said Morgana. 'What are the Cur ... the uh, Curi ... the whatchamacallems doing there?'

'The Curiates,' volunteered Skye. 'They help Roversi make important decisions.

They're like his council, that's why they're here. I've just studied that actually, but don't ask me their names.'

Morgana nodded, clearly impressed.

Julius scanned the people in the background and easily spotted the faces which were familiar to him: apart from Freja and Cress, he recognised Roversi and the other Grand Masters, Kloister and Milson, having met them a few months earlier, during their rescue mission aboard Angra Mainyu. That left seven people he had never seen before, and he guessed that five were the Curiates, and two would have to be the Masters of Tuala and Sield.

A minute later, the image switched to a view looking out into space, with Pit-Stop Pete's docking station in the left of the screen. Mielowa continued her commentary of events but, for the moment at least, nothing was happening.

'Where are they?' asked Morgana impatiently.

Suddenly, as if in answer, a large, dark blob blinked into view, filling the screen. Mielowa's tiny yelp of surprise was most likely echoed by numerous others watching the coverage. Slowly, the formless mass began to stretch out in all directions, and gradually took on a spherical shape, until it was a hulking, solid, steel structure, which looked big enough to fit the entire lunar perimeter inside it.

'Oh my,' gasped Siena.

'Will you look at that,' said Faith, his jaw dropping open in sheer admiration.

'It's just a ship,' added Skye, pretending not to care.

'Miller, that is *not* just a ship,' Faith retorted. 'I would guess that Zed has never seen the likes of her. I get how you feel about those fools, but when it comes to starships, man, they seem to know what they're doing.'

Skye shook his head and didn't reply.

Julius was with Faith on this one. He didn't even know that starships could morph like that, never mind that it seemed it had made the journey to Zed in a shapeless state. 'How's that even possible?' he said, pointing at it.

'I'm dying to find out,' replied Faith, leaning forward towards the screen. 'And I bet Pete is pretty keen too.'

'Taurus One,' said Morgana. 'Look, the name is written under that hatch there.'

'Maybe it's because they come from the Taurus constellation,' offered Barth.

'I would so love to pilot one of those,' continued Morgana. 'Mind you, I can't even tell where the front of this thing is.'

'You know,' said Siena, sounding puzzled, 'for a diplomatic mission, they sure brought a large ship with them.'

Skye snorted in reply and crossed his arms, a disapproving expression etched all over his face. 'Diplomatic mission

my a-'

'Look,' cut in Julius. 'There's a port opening up.'

They all watched as a cavity appeared, creating a dark patch in the steel body. A small shuttle pod emerged from it, making a direct course for the Zed docks. The camera followed the vessel until it crossed the Zed shield, then switched to Iryana Mielowa, back on the platform. She had moved closer to the landing area where, being the only TV station allowed access, there was no need for the cameramen to fight for a good spot.

'Look at Freja's face,' said Barth. 'He doesn't seem very happy about this.'

'Who would be?' snorted Skye. 'He's probably wondering where the trap is.'

Julius had no way of knowing what his Grand Master was thinking about, but he could see plenty of dull, grey wisps radiating from him, and the others around him, causing a kind of ghostly puddle on the concrete floor beneath them. They were definitely worried about something and, on that score, Skye was correct – who wouldn't be?

Silently, the shuttle pod landed and everyone held their breath. The hatch slid open noiselessly, and a moccasin-clad foot appeared. The Arneshian ambassador stepped out, the thin metal circlet on his head glistening in the light. Manuel T'Rogon had arrived.

Julius stared, transfixed, at the screen. The ambassador was wearing the same gold-detailed tunic that he had on the day of the first broadcast; he could see now that it reached almost to his feet. He was taller than Julius had previously thought, and broadly built. His head was held up with pride, his stern features softened a little by just a hint of an enigmatic smile. Roversi, Freja and the other Zed leaders bowed their heads in the customary lunar fashion. T'Rogon responded in kind.

'Is it just me, or is his skin slightly … greyish?' asked Morgana.

'That's it!' said Julius, slapping his thigh. 'I knew there was something odd about him during that broadcast, but I couldn't tell what.'

'Apparently it's to do with the atmosphere on Arnesh,' explained Barth, timidly.

'Well well, look who's been doing his homework,' said Faith. 'I'm impressed.'

Barth blushed vividly, smiled, and resumed his viewing in silence.

Once all the protocols for receiving guests had been followed, four more Arneshian delegates stepped out from the shuttle pod. They were clothed in similar robes, and each had matching circlets around their heads. After they had all been greeted, Roversi and T'Rogon led the way, followed by the Grand Masters, while the Masters and Curiates escorted the remaining Arneshian delegates. As they disappeared off the screen, the cameraman zoomed in on Ms Mielowa. She was positively beaming, no doubt fully aware what a honour it was to be giving witness to such an event. 'You saw it here first, ladies and gentlemen. Iryana Mielowa, for the Space Channel.'

*

'Don't you think it's odd,' said Morgana, a week later over breakfast, 'that people back on Earth seem to be a wee bit too positive about this whole ceasefire thing?'

'To be sure,' agreed Faith. 'You would have thought they'd be more concerned about their real intentions. I mean, everyone knows how dirty they've played recently.'

'Actually they don't really,' said Julius, looking up from his food and meeting their surprised gazes. 'I was talking to Captain Kelly about it, and he told me that the Curia doesn't pass all information on to Earth. They only communicate with the students' parents, as you know.'

'But, that's not right,' said Morgana.

'That's exactly what I told Kelly,' answered Julius

'What do you mean?' asked Skye. 'Why?'

'Well, he says it's because there's no point scaring folks with stories of kidnappings and the like when they can't do anything about it.'

'Good grief,' said Faith. 'Can you imagine if they did ever find out about the kidnappings? Not to mention the truth about old Bastiaan Grant's death all those years ago. They would have kittens!'

'It certainly wouldn't look too good for Colonial Affairs,' said Julius.

'Or Zed,' added Faith. 'Let's hope they never find out.'

'I think it may be too late for that,' said Skye, pointing at one of the mess hall screens. 'Look.'

Julius, Faith and Morgana turned quickly in that direction, while from a nearby table, Leanne Nord shouted, 'Everybody! Quiet.'

Iryana Mielowa was speaking above a "Breaking News" sign, with "T'Rogon reveals Grant's fate at last" written underneath that. As someone turned up the volume on the TV, the seriousness of this latest report immediately became apparent. 'As a token of goodwill, Ambassador T'Rogon has delivered several top secret files to Earth Leader, Paulo Trent. These files include the shocking truth behind the death of Bastiaan Grant, the Tuala Master who disappeared six years ago, and the recent series of abductions from Zed, all at the hands of the Arneshians. In a statement, T'Rogon said, "We wish to come clean about all of this". As the contents of these top secret files leak their way around the global media, we are hearing more and more reports of people in favour of peace negotiations with the Arneshians, while the Curia's reputation seems to be at a major low for the first time in the history of Zed.'

'I can't believe he gave those files to Trent,' said Morgana, sounding completely stunned.

'Oh, he has his reasons, I'm sure,' said Skye bitterly. 'No doubt he wants to discredit us in the eyes of our own people.'

'He's very clever,' agreed Julius. 'By apologising for what they've done wrong, they're showing their good side, while we look like the ones scheming to keep secrets from Earth.'

'If you think about it,' said Faith, 'not even me relatives back home – apart from Mum and Dad – knew what happened to those girls last year. Did you tell your aunt or uncle, Julius?'

'No, I didn't. Academy honour code, rule five: a student may only report to their immediate family, and they must not disclose anything therein to anyone else.'

'Exactly. And now that code has landed us in deep trouble. I bet you anything, every Zed student will be getting a call from home asking if it's true,' continued Faith.

'Yes, and straight after their kids, they'll be calling the schools, demanding an explanation,' concluded Julius.

'If you ask me,' said Morgana, 'the Curia brought this on itself. They're supposed to be the bridge between Earth and Space, not the gate.

'I wonder what's going to happen now,' said Skye.

'Whatever it is, it won't be good,' answered Julius with a sigh.

*

Julius realised just how accurate his prediction had been only a few days later. On Wednesday the 5th of October, it was Faith's fifteenth birthday, and thoughts of the recent events were put on hold for a little while. Skye, who had puppy-eyed his way into the heart of Felice Buongustaio, Zed's head chef, over the course of the previous two years, had now convinced him to create his deliciously deadly Supernova, a cake so called because of the untold amount of calories it contained. It was crammed with so much chocolate, nuts and fudge, that it could stall a nuclear reactor. It was, in fact, the only cake that carried warnings about its possible side effects, which included violent cramps, rashes on the scalp, and gout. Felice had made this cake only twice before and, after each occasion, he had promised Dr Walliser he wouldn't do it again. However, when it came to Skye, the chef had no will of his own.

Although Faith's party was being organised by his classmates, there were also other Mizkis in the garden, all of whom had heard of the Supernova at one point or another, but never actually seen one. When the 3MAs caught sight of the brown monster being carried into the garden, their cries of "Happy Birthday" abruptly died in their throats, giving way to a deferential silence.

'It does exist,' whispered Yuri Slovich and Ferenc Orban in chorus.

'Am I supposed to say thanks for that?' asked Faith, breaking out in a cold sweat.

Carefully, Felice placed the cake on a table, while the Mizkis gathered around. He looked at Faith and opened his hands. 'I could-a say Happy Birth-a-day, but-a maybe good luck it's-a better,' he said.

Faith looked at the 15 fat candles sticking out of the glossy, chocolate coated top, which looked more like lit sticks of dynamite, and gulped.

'Make a wish-a!' said Felice.

'I wish to still be alive tomorrow,' said Faith, looking at the cake with dread.

'Too bad-a,' said Felice. 'You told us the wish-a. Now it don't work no more.'

'What?!' gasped Faith.

By then Felice had already turned around and was heading back towards the kitchen, while the others laughed nervously.

'Miller!' cried Faith. 'This is all your fault. You go first.'

'No way. It's your party, dude.'

'Go on Faith,' said Julius. 'We'll all have a bite. Right guys?'

'Yeah, go on!' said Morgana.

'I've alerted Nurse Primula,' added Julius. 'She's on standby for the night.'

'Great,' said Faith, half-heartedly. He took a deep breath and blew out the candles while his friends cheered. Morgana and Siena removed them, being careful not to pour the hot wax over the surface of the cake. When they had removed the last one, Faith picked up the knife and placed it over the centre of the cake, looking very nervous.

'It won't explode, you know,' said Lopaka.

'Are you sure about that?'

Just then, a boy cried out from one corner of the garden, making Faith freeze. 'This can't be true!'

There was enough panic in his voice to instantly claim the attention of all present.

Julius looked to his left and saw a 4MA Mizki standing there, staring wide-eyed at his PIP screen, which was hovering above the boy's left hand.

'What's happened?' asked Morgana.

'They've stopped recruitment,' the boy said, his eyes not leaving the screen.

'What recruitment?' said Julius.

'The Zed Test Centres on Earth have all been shut down.'

Julius activated his PIP immediately, quickly followed by most of his classmates. Faith leaned in to look at Julius' screen. Sure enough, as soon as Julius clicked onto the News page there it was: the familiar "Breaking News" banner emblazoned beneath a picture of a test centre. Julius pushed the play button and watched as the video showed security personnel closing and locking the gates of the building.

'In an unprecedented move,' said Iryana Mielowa, 'Earth Leader Paulo Trent has declared that all Zed recruitment should be suspended until further notice. A full enquiry is to be launched into the various revelations contained in the files from Ambassador T' Rogon, to judge Zed's actions in all these matters.' The images continued to show the closure of various test centres around the world. Julius recognised the British one as it flashed up briefly. 'After the shocking discoveries of the past few days, more and more people are warming to the idea of negotiation with the Arneshians, with many growing extremely uneasy about the level of secrecy which has developed in the Lunar Perimeter. The decision to suspend recruitment was issued this afternoon and, although the consensus is still mixed, there seems to be many who would support a total closure of Zed.'

Julius closed his PIP. 'I can't believe this.' As he glanced around, most of the 3MAs had also finished watching the report, and were looking quite bewildered.

'Can they actually do that?' asked Morgana. 'I mean, Zed isn't controlled by the Earth Leader.'

'Aye, but we come from Earth,' said Julius. 'Obviously they must have some sort of power.'

'What if they keep them closed forever?' asked Barth.

'Unlikely,' replied Skye. 'They can't just abandon the space program. They'll need the technology, and it's all here.'

'What if they get the gear from the Arneshians?' asked Siena. 'We all know they're a lot more advanced than us.'

'And what?' said Faith quickly. 'Bypass us completely, like we don't exist?'

'They couldn't shut down Zed,' said Julius. 'Freja wouldn't let them, and neither would I.'

Faith sighed. 'Happy birthday to me. I think I'm ready for the Supernova now.'

'I think I may need a slice too,' said Skye. 'This news sucks, big time.'

'Well,' said Julius patting Faith on the shoulder, 'normally it's my birthday being spoiled by some Arneshian trick but this year the honour's all yours.'

'There's still time, McCoy,' he said glumly, raising an eyebrow. 'Mark my words.'

After Julius had finished a slice of the cake, which was indeed delicious, but which had also given him quite the sugar rush, he realised there was no way he would be able to eat any dinner. So he decided to instead call home and see how the latest news had been affecting his family. He was also hoping he would finally be able to talk to Michael, and see firsthand how he was coping with his new reality. To his surprise Skye, who was looking oddly indisposed, headed back to the room with him.

'You ok?' Julius asked.

'Not sure, actually. I don't think I should've had those slices.'

'Slices? How many did you have?'

'Four … or five?'

'You know,' said Julius, opening the door to their room and allowing his friend to enter first, 'if you're sick tonight, you deserve it.'

Skye walked straight into the toilet and closed the door behind him.

'Shout if you need me to fetch the doctor,' called Julius, taking a seat at his desk. 'Computer, call home,' he said.

After a few seconds, Jenny McCoy's face appeared in the panel. 'Darling,' she said, a smile lighting up her features. 'I'm so glad you've called. We were just thinking about you!' She turned her back to Julius momentarily. 'Rory! Come here, quick. It's our boy!'

'Did you hear the news?' asked Julius, scanning the living room behind his mother, hoping that he would see Michael there somewhere.

'All of the news,' she replied. 'But I still can't believe Trent would want to stop recruiting like this.'

'Hiya son,' said Rory, taking a seat next to his wife.

'Hi Dad. How are things?'

'I guess we're all a wee bit shaken up. That T'Rogon though, I don't like the looks of him. It's fishy what he did with those secret files. Makes Zed look bad.'

'That's what we think he's trying to do,' agreed Julius.

'Is it true about Bastiaan Grant?' asked Jenny, sounding a little alarmed.

Julius nodded. 'Everything they've said is true. Hey, so where's Michael? Why hasn't he called me yet?'

'Your brother has been so gloomy since the test,' said Jenny. 'He really wants to talk to you, but I think he feels ashamed, because he failed.'

'But it's me. I don't care what they say he is.'

'That's the problem, Julius. It's because it is you and not some other random person,' said Jenny.

'I don't understand.'

'I thought you would have by now. Michael idolises you. He's always wanted to be like you. So to then fail that test, for him, it's like letting you down.'

'But I'm not perfect. I make mistakes: big ones too!'

'Julius darling, you'll always be his hero, no matter what you do.'

Julius wasn't sure what to answer. He felt genuinely touched but, at the same time, undeserving of such admiration. 'So, he won't talk to me?'

'Just give him a little more time. We'll tell him you called, and that you love him very much.'

Julius nodded sadly. 'Have you told anyone else about him being an Arneshian?'

'Some,' answered Rory, 'but no one really needs to be told, thanks to the choker he has to wear.'

'Has he had any problems because of it?'

'Not at all. Of course, people are surprised when they find out, but he's not the first, nor will he be the last. To a certain extent, it's only Michael who has to find a way to get over it. Everyone else isn't really that bothered.'

Julius, however, wasn't entirely convinced.

'Believe me son, here on Earth folks have a very different opinion of the Arneshians.'

'What's that? You don't approve of them, do you?' said Julius, sounding a bit more defensive than he meant to.

'It's not what you think darling,' said Jenny. 'We don't get to see the enemies of Zed, like you all do out there. We only know the Nuarns who live with us; the ones who work alongside us and contribute to our society. That's why people have a different perception here; it's a matter of habit.'

'Sure,' said Julius curtly. 'That's why they put collars around their necks, to remind them who's boss, right?'

'That's not the reason and you know it,' said Rory, calmly. 'The only reason Zed wants them to wear the chokers is because it blocks their Grey Arts. It prevents them from developing too fast, and ensures they don't-'

'Don't what, Dad?' blurted out Julius, realising that the conversation was taking a wrong turn, but unable to stop himself.

'That they don't become a threat,' finished Rory simply.

'A threat,' repeated Julius. 'That's what Michael is: a potential threat. You can embellish the story as much as you like, but no one treats them the same. Not even you, and he's your own son.'

Jenny's eyes began to fill with tears. She quickly stood up and disappeared from view.

'Mum!' Julius called. He leaned back against his chair, shaking his head. 'I … I didn't mean it's her fault.'

'She knows that,' said Rory. He sounded exhausted. 'Look, we've been through some pretty big changes in the last month, all of us. Everyone's on edge. You have your own worries up there without having to deal with all this. Michael will come around, you'll see. As far as T'Rogon is concerned, he's done as much damage as he can. We'll recover and move on. Zed is still part of Earth and it won't be dismissed lightly. You, on the other hand, I know that you can't always tell us what happens in Tijara, but your mum and I would really appreciate some more news from you. I think any parent deserves that.'

'Sure,' he said. 'Listen, I need to go now, Dad. Say hi to Michael for me.'

'I … yes, of course son. You take care now.'

Julius waved and closed the link. With the unhealthy sounds that Skye was producing next door, and the cake still rocking his stomach, he realised that maybe calling home just then hadn't been such a great idea. He had upset his mum for no good reason and he now felt quite miserable himself. Perhaps it was true: the people back home didn't think of the Arneshians as a constant threat, but as the guy or the girl next door. So when T'Rogon had come waltzing in, asking to make peace, no wonder they didn't really think there was anything odd about it. And on top of that, Zed was being made to look like it had something to hide, with no accountability to Earth or its citizens. Morgana was right: the Curia had brought this on itself.

Before retiring for the evening, Julius switched on his PIP, opened a new message addressed to his mum, and sent it. In it, he wrote just four words: *Sorry. I love you.*

THE CHALLENGE

The morning after Faith's birthday, Professor Lao-Tzu had to cancel his Meditation lesson on account of more than two-thirds of his students being under the care of Dr Walliser. News soon spread around Tijara that the after-effects of the Supernova were taking their toll, which only added to the legendary status of Felice's cake. Julius wasn't feeling great but, since he had only eaten one small slice, he succeeded in removing the nasty aftertaste with a long lie-in and a glass of fresh mint water. With three hours of Martial Arts in the afternoon, he decided that he really should eat a little because, cake or no cake, Professor Chan would no doubt relentlessly put him through his paces. That said, given the amount of calories unleashed by the single slice Julius had eaten, he knew he could do with some serious exercise to help work it off.

When he got to class, Morgana was also there, along with Siena – the three of them bringing the class number up to five. The professor had activated the scenery panels in the walls, floor and ceiling so that they were now displaying a park, the leaves on the trees tinged with yellow-brown hues of Autumn. Clumps of the fallen virtual leaves swirled around their ankles as they jogged along the path for their warm up.

'So glad I only had a little taste of that dratted cake,' said Morgana, who was running with Julius on her right and Siena to her left.

'I thought more girls would have done the same thing,' said Julius.

'Why's that?' asked Morgana.

'You know … waistline and all that. Skye says you girls are always talking about fitness and … stuff.'

'Does he now?' replied Siena stiffly. 'That's not all we talk about, I'll have you know.'

Julius began to regret even mentioning anything about it. Was he supposed to ask about their other interests at this point, he wondered. He looked at Morgana, but her gaze stayed fixed ahead of her, a little smile curling one corner of her mouth.

'Hmm, what else do you talk about then?' he asked.

'Loads of stuff,' answered Siena. 'Life, school, love.'

Morgana giggled and Julius could feel his cheeks flushing. Why had he let himself get dragged into this?

'Come on, Julius,' said Siena. 'Don't you guys talk about girls too?'

'Not really. I mean, Skye does, and others, but we … I don't … Girls like Skye, and … um …. no one's quite like him,' he finished awkwardly.

They laughed at his answer, in a friendly manner, and Julius knew there was nothing mocking about it. Still, he felt so embarrassed that he would have given anything for a change of topic just then, or even an Arneshian attack.

'McCoy,' said Siena, 'do you mean to tell me that you're completely unaware of the way some of the girls look at you? Because if that's the case, let's just drop this chat right now and re-open it when you wise up a little.'

He felt so stupid. Of course he did, he wasn't that blind. But right now he just wanted this conversation over, so he played dumb and shook his head. Thankfully, that was enough for Siena and she didn't push the subject any further. For the rest of the lesson, as they went through various training drills, the two girls chatted away about future shopping trips to Satras and various party ideas, while Julius tried his best to blend in with the walls, especially when they started discussing bra sizes.

As dinner time drew near that evening, the rest of the students were dismissed from their respective classes and Julius was gratefully reunited with Faith and Skye. He had never been so happy to chat with them about engines and plasma cores.

*

As the first week of October came and went, Julius felt the familiar anticipation for the gaming season ahead growing in his mind. He had been working extra hard in class to earn as many Fyvers as he could. Plus, he and the rest of the Skirts had managed to avoid killing any sim-animals during their Draw sessions, so none of them had lost anything either. On Monday the 10th, as they made their way to the infirmary for their Pre-Pyro therapy, they eagerly discussed what games they would be playing that Saturday.

'Ok so, first year we did Flight,' said Julius, as they waited in the lounge for the nurses to arrive. 'Last year it was Combat. Maybe we could go back to Flight again.'

'I don't know,' said Skye. 'I did enjoy the Combat scene more, to be honest.'

'I'd always choose Flight over Combat,' said Morgana, 'but I guess you know that, right?'

'And there's another issue to consider too,' added Faith. 'Are we sticking to the usual plan of competing only against students from our year?'

'Aye,' said Morgana.

'Definitely,' agreed Skye. 'Besides, it's a great way for us to hold on to top spot.'

'I bet the Seniors are gonna say we're too scared to play against them,' said Faith.

'Let them,' answered Morgana. 'They said the same thing last year. Who cares?'

'They're just jealous because we're top of the chart overall, and they can't get there,' continued Skye. 'If they're as good as they think they are, their names would be up there, instead of ours.'

'Right then, let's think about an action plan, and at lunch we can decide,' concluded Julius.

The others agreed and moved off to their respective areas for their treatments.

Ms Primula was waiting for Julius as he entered the room that had been assigned to him. 'Good morning Julius, how are you today?'

'All good, thanks. And you?'

'Still recovering from Wednesday's night shift, actually.'

'Supernova night?' asked Julius, and he couldn't help but laugh. 'That bad, huh?'

'Felice should know better,' she replied, her hand inserting the needle with practiced experience as Julius lay back on the bed. 'Dr Walliser went mental when he saw the first patient. He knew it immediately, even before that poor Irish boy could open his mouth. I think it was his birthday, actually.'

'It was. My roommate Skye wasn't feeling too good either.'

'I remember him. He came in around five in the morning, and he had to be put on a drip.'

'Yeah. I did hear him … uh, losing loads of fluids that night. But that's his prize for eating five slices!'

'Did you say five?' asked the nurse, sounding understandably startled. 'I don't think we've ever met anyone who ate more than two and wasn't sick for a week.'

'Well, we don't call him The Black Hole for nothing.'

'I need to tell the doctor right away. We may need to study him more closely. Call if you need anything,' she said, leaving the room in a fluster.

Julius grinned and closed his eyes. Hearing about all the post-Supernova ailments made him even more grateful that he had only just had a taste of it. 'Faith will remember this birthday for a while,' he thought. Maybe they should buy him something in Satras, just to cheer him up a bit. After all, it couldn't have been great spending his birthday suffering from severe cramps, in a semi-conscious state. Julius opened his left hand and activated his PIP. The screen sprang to life, hovering over his palm. He selected the Hologram Palace page from his bookmarks and started browsing the charts, to remind himself of where everyone had been sitting in the rankings before the summer break. He was halfway through the Mizki Juniors when his PIP vibrated, signalling an incoming vidcall.

'On screen,' he said. Morgana came into view. 'Hey, what's up?'

'Go to the Space Channel, now,' she said, hurriedly.

'O … Ok,' he said. Then, to the empty room, 'Computer, Space Channel News.'

T'Rogon's toothy smile instantly appeared on the room screen. Julius pushed a button on the side table, and the top half of the bed rose up, allowing him to sit properly. 'Now what?' he said. It was too early for this kind of surprise. Julius quickly saw that T'Rogon was being interviewed by Iryana Mielowa, who today was wearing the reddest shade of lipstick he had ever seen. Her dark hair had been gathered upwards, and she was batting her eyelashes much too seductively for his liking. 'Is she flirting with him?'

'My thoughts, precisely,' said Morgana disapprovingly from his PIP. 'Apparently the programme started forty minutes ago and is also being broadcast on Earth.'

The camera panned to the left of Mielowa and focused on Paulo Trent, or at least his holographic image. Julius had seen him on TV many times before – he had grizzled hair and dark eyes. Trent had been elected to lead the Democratic Republic of Earth when Julius was just eight but, despite his young age, he still remembered watching coverage of the exciting party that had been thrown for him in his homeland, Brazil – having the Earth Leader come from your country was a huge honour. Sitting next to Trent were Grand Masters Freja, Kloister and Milson, each wearing their particular school's uniform.

'Moving on from the issue of the Zed Test Centres,' said Mielowa, 'we now come to the last item on today's agenda. Mr T'Rogon, tell us about the children you brought with you from Arnesh.'

'What children?' cried Julius and Morgana in unison.

'But of course,' answered T'Rogon, flashing a bright smile at her. 'It was the wish of my Queen that you should meet our offspring. After all, we are proud parents too. They represent the best in us, and are the most advanced of our civilisation.'

Julius watched Freja intently: as the ambassador spoke those words, the Grand

Master had not moved a muscle; his face was a blank mask, in stark contrast to Trent's cheeriness.

'If we are to begin dialogue,' continued T'Rogon, 'then the new generations should be involved. They had no part in all that went on before; their hands are clean.'

Ms Mielowa was nodding her head vigorously in agreement, reminding Julius of one of those toys with the springs in their necks, which people sometimes placed in the rear windows of their fly-cars.

'Ambassador,' Mielowa asked, 'what are your children like?'

'Just the same as yours, Iryana – may I call you Iryana?' he replied, making her blush furiously.

'Oh, p-lease!' groaned Morgana, rolling her eyes.

'Children are children,' continued T'Rogon. 'They like to learn, build, expand their minds and most of all, they like to play. As a matter of fact, just last night, they were expressing their interest in your magnificent Hologram Palace. After all, it was their ancestor, Clodagh Arnesh, who built it.'

'Well Ambassador,' said Trent, 'in that case I think that a visit is in order!' He turned to the Grand Masters. 'Don't you think so?'

Edwina Milson forced out a smile that could have grated steel, and nodded. Kloister looked at Freja, then back at Trent.

Eventually, it was Freja that spoke. 'Mr Trent is right,' he said, calmly. 'What do you have in mind, Ambassador?'

'A challenge, perhaps?' replied T'Rogon. 'Wouldn't it be great if our peace negotiations were to start with a friendly game between our children?'

'I think it's a marvellous idea, Ambassador!' said Trent, looking pleased. 'And I am sure that our facilities will be perfectly able to accommodate such an event.'

'What type of challenge would that be, Ambassador?' asked Mielowa. 'One on one, perhaps?'

'I was more inclined toward a team effort, actually,' answered T'Rogon. 'We have ten of our best youths onboard the Taurus One and they would all love to compete.'

'Then it's settled,' said Trent. 'Freja, why don't you choose ten of our best players and- '

'Oh no,' cut in T'Rogon. 'Not Freja. We want this challenge to be as fair as possible now, don't we?'

'I can't believe he said that!' cried Morgana.

'What does he even mean?' said Julius, feeling completely outraged. 'Is he expecting Freja to select ten crappy students?'

'Let your best player select the team,' he continued. 'And from what I've heard, you do have a Solo champion at your school.'

Julius' mouth fell open involuntarily. 'Wha …' was all he could manage to say.

'Who is he, Freja?' asked Trent, seeming more and more like a kid in a candy store with each passing minute.

Freja seemed unwilling to answer at first, but eventually he did. 'Julius McCoy, one of our third year students.'

'Yes – McCoy,' said T'Rogon. 'He's quite the celebrity on Arnesh.'

'Is he now, Ambassador?' asked Trent, sounding quite chuffed.

'Oh yes, didn't Freja tell you? He's very much responsible for disrupting our plans over the last two years … of which we are very glad, I might add. He's what you call a ...'

'No!' cried Julius at the screen, realising with horror what the ambassador was about to reveal.

'... White Child,' finished T'Rogon.

Julius slumped back, feeling as if someone had punched the air out of him. Everyone who was watching this interview would know now: his parents, Michael, all his classmates; even old Mrs Mayflower. Freja, Kloister and Milson, however, hadn't so much as flinched, and Julius wondered how hard they must be trying to not betray any emotion.

'Is this true, Carlos?' asked Trent.

Freja simply nodded.

'We are very grateful for him, you know,' said the ambassador. 'It was, in fact, McCoy's efforts which made Queen Salgoria rethink her actions. How could she allow the destruction of such talent; such skills? Do you want to know what she said to me?' T'Rogon leaned towards Mielowa, who was hanging on his every word by that point. She nodded, captivated, so he continued. 'She said to me, "T'Rogon, my friend, go to Earth and make peace! I have realised the beauty of the human race once more and I want the dream of Clodagh and Marcus to finally come true. T'Rogon, I don't have much longer left to live – make this my lasting legacy."'

'Salgoria's dying?' sputtered Trent.

Even the Grand Masters flinched at that.

'Not quite,' explained T'Rogon quickly. 'But she's getting on in years; we all are.'

'Well folks,' said Mielowa, wrapping up the interview with a triumphant smile. 'You heard it here first. This is Iryana Mielowa, from the Space Channel.'

Julius shut his PIP off abruptly, forgetting that Morgana was still online, and ordered the room monitor to switch off. He lay back and stared up at the ceiling, too astonished to do anything else. Thankfully, the Pre-Pyro session wouldn't be over for another hour, so he had some time to try regain his composure. He felt torn in two: on one hand T'Rogon had just revealed his secret to the entire world, which would no doubt expose him to the unwanted attention of people who didn't even know him, and for that he hated the ambassador's guts; on the other hand though, the ambassador had selected him, over everyone else, to lead a team in the most important challenge Zed had ever faced. As he brooded over the events, his PIP vibrated, signalling an incoming message. Julius opened it and saw that it was from his dad.

"Is it true?" is all it read.

"Aye. Sorry I was asked not to tell," he typed back.

"I knew it! Be more careful than ever, J."

"Will do."

"Very proud."

He closed the screen once more. 'That was quick,' he said to himself. His parents had always known that his mind-skills were strong, ever since his first visit to the family Mind Doctor and he felt very grateful to his dad for dealing with the news so quickly and simply. He wondered what Michael would make of it; he was afraid that it could make him feel even worse. But there was no helping it now. T'Rogon had seen to that.

At 10:30, Nurse Primula came into the room and removed the needle from Julius' arm. He was expecting some sort of remark, but she didn't say anything, so he went back to the infirmary waiting room for the usual orange juice and biscuits. The rest of his classmates were just finishing up, and Julius grew conscious of the darting glances directed at him and the quiet whispering. He saw numerous wisps of mixed reds and greys floating throughout their auras, as if their excitement at the news was tainted by a sense of apprehension. When Faith, Skye and Morgana emerged from their rooms, they immediately joined him on the sofa.

'That was so OTT,' said Morgana. 'He practically insulted Freja and led Trent and Mielowa about by their noses.'

'I thought those two were the worst,' said Faith. 'At least the GMs were cool as cucumbers, rather than jumping through the hoops T'Rogon was holding out for them.'

'He really knows how to take centre stage,' said Skye. 'I hate to admit it, but he's good at his job.'

'What job?' asked Faith, sarcastically.

'Undermining Zed's credibility,' answered Julius, dryly. 'And steering opinion in favour of this armistice. But I don't buy it.'

'I think you've got more pressing matters than that now, Julius,' said Morgana.

'The challenge,' he said. 'I know.'

'At least that shouldn't be a problem,' said Skye. 'I mean, we are pretty good … aren't we?'

'For starters, I've never been responsible for more than three people in a team – none of us has; second, we don't know zilch about these Arneshians or their abilities; and third, who says I'm gonna pick you?'

Skye was momentarily lost for words, but then he saw Julius, Faith and Morgana chuckling, and he punched Julius on the arm.

'Seriously though,' said Julius, 'this is one big responsibility I could do without. I mean, Earth against Arnesh!'

'McCoy,' said Faith, 'do you want to be a captain or not? If I'm going to entrust one of me babies into your care, I want to make sure you don't chicken out at the first problem.'

Morgana laughed. 'He's right, you know? Show us your stuff!'

Julius sighed and was about to reply, when he saw Dr Walliser approaching them.

'Master Cress would like to see you in his office at 11:00 hours,' the doctor said. 'All four of you.'

'Thanks Dr Walliser,' said Morgana, as he left them.

'I guess we'll be missing Draw then,' said Faith. 'Shame, I was looking forward to seeing me monkey.'

'Come on, let's go,' said Julius standing up. He was all too aware of numerous eyes following them out of the infirmary.

*

Julius knocked on Cress' door, which immediately slid open. He entered, followed directly by the others, and found the Master waiting behind his desk. They bowed to him and four chairs materialised in the centre of the room, courtesy of the inbuilt replicator.

'I take it you watched the interview,' said Cress.

'Yes sir,' answered Morgana.

'I won't deny that he has put us in quite a spot with this challenge. I take it you will be picking all of the Skirts, yes McCoy?'

'Yes sir,' answered Julius.

Cress nodded. 'Given the Arneshians' lack of mind-skills, it has been agreed that you will face each other with Sim-Gauntlets in a mixed flight/fight simulation, to the last man, or woman, standing. McCoy, you are the leader of a toon of ten players, chosen from across each of the three schools and all year groups.'

'Sorry, a what, sir?' asked Julius.

'A toon,' repeated Cress. 'As in a platoon.'

'Of course,' said Julius. 'How will I select the players, sir?'

'Gabriel List and the technical department have arranged a video conference for tonight at 20:00 hours.'

'A conference?' said Julius, suddenly worried.

'Yes McCoy, a conference. Speaking to people and all that?' said Cress, sounding amused. 'You better overcome that particular fear soon. Mr Miller can teach you how, I am sure.'

'Yes, sir,' answered Julius, ignoring the stifled giggles to his left.

Then Morgana's voice popped into his head: '*Told ya!*'

'Talk about how you will be selecting the players, and what roles you will be looking for. The Tijaran students will be physically present; the students from Tuala and Sield will see you as a hologram in their respective Assembly Halls. Should you choose someone from the Sield School, they will be housed in Tijara until the day of the challenge since, as you know, they are currently in a space station orbiting us. Once the Zed toon is created, the Grand Masters will need to approve it.'

'Zed Toon ...' said Faith. 'I like the name. Can we use it?'

'Go right ahead.'

'When is this event taking place, sir?' asked Skye.

'On Saturday the 5th of November; you have twenty-five days to prepare. I've booked a room exclusively for your practices in the Palace. Mrs Mayflower will give you the details. You are not allowed to skip lessons, but your team can stay behind to practice beyond curfew if needed; once you're allowed to game again of course.'

'Thank you, sir,' said Julius.

Cress stood up, walked around his desk, and stopped in front of them. 'Everyone would just love to see you win this challenge, Mizkis, but there's more than the Skirts' reputation at stake this time. The Arneshians are looking for ways of discrediting us in the eyes of Earth and we cannot afford that. Play fair and be careful. Dismissed.'

*

'The hall is absolutely heaving!' said Morgana.

'Don't need to know,' said Julius, dusting off his clothes and flattening his hair. He couldn't remember ever being so nervous. They had jotted down a few selection rules during lunchtime, and then Morgana had spent the last two hours helping Julius to calm down with some meditation. It was only after Faith had accused him of being worse than a pregnant woman an hour before delivery, that he had forced himself to regain some composure.

At 19:55 Gabriel List fetched him and led him to a spot near the stage. 'The link is ready. Just take a deep breath and remember there are worse things in life than this.'

'Like what?'

'I could be testing the mic by telling everyone that our very own White Child had to take remedial Meditation lessons, in first year,' said List with a grin.

'Thanks Gabriel, and I thought you were my friend,' he answered back.

'So did I! Jokes aside, how did the Mizkis take it?'

'Funnily enough, no one has said anything to me about this White Child business. I see them looking at me, but they don't come forward. I think they're scared.'

'Of you? Nah. Go on now – it's time.' List gently pushed him forward. 'Good luck!'

As Julius stepped onto the platform, the voices hushed down, until there was complete silence. Julius moved over to the centre of the stage and stopped before the podium that had been placed there. He pressed a button set into its top ledge and activated a screen which displayed the notes he had written up that day. Having so many Mizkis staring at him was rather intimidating; however, he knew that right then they were looking at the leader of a unique squad, a leader chosen because of his particular abilities, so he couldn't afford to show any weakness or doubt.

'Good evening Mizkis,' he started. His voice cracked a little, but he cleared it with a small cough. 'As of tonight, we will start the selection for the Zed Toon. Anyone who is interested can send their names and game stats to me. I am looking for the best nine players on Zed, to compete in a flight/fight simulation. Therefore, the squad will need to be balanced. You all saw the interview today, so you know what is at stake. If you are chosen, you will represent Zed and Earth in a unique competition. Do not enter lightly!' That was it. He had said all he needed and, knowing that, allowed himself to relax a little. 'Are there any questions?'

A few hands shot up. Julius pointed to a blonde boy in the third row, who he thought he recognised as a 4MA student.

'Are the Skirts taking part?' he asked.

'Their names have been entered.'

'So you're not really looking for nine players, then. Figures,' said the boy wryly. There were a few chuckles at that.

Julius raised an eyebrow: who did this guy think he was? Suddenly he didn't feel so shy that he couldn't answer back. 'I'm sorry, I didn't catch your name. Is it because you're not in the gaming charts, unlike The Skirts?' A much larger burst of laughter greeted Julius' reply, which encouraged him immensely. 'Miller, Ruthier and Shanigan are at the top of the overall and individual charts, and they have been there for the last two years straight. No one can contest that. Next!'

There was a smattering of applause which quickly faded away, but it gave him a few seconds to calm himself again. The mixture of adrenaline and nerves had made him grip the podium tightly, and he could see his knuckles turning white. Once again, he took a deep breath and continued answering questions. Fortunately, no one made any more silly remarks, and the conference ended just before 21:00 hours, which left Julius and the Skirts free to grab a bite to eat.

'That went well,' said Faith, once they were seated with their food.

'Thanks for sticking up for us, Julius,' said Morgana.

'No problem. Who was that guy anyway?'

'Forget about it,' said Skye, 'and rather check the mail. I want to see if anyone has applied yet.'

Julius activated his PIP, and as soon as he did, his inbox filled up with 123 messages. 'This is going to be harder than we thought. Look how many already, and they keep arriving.'

'I don't think picking people will be a problem,' said Morgana, waving her chopstick in the air. 'I'd be more concerned with those you don't pick.'

As she said that, Julius looked around the mess hall. Suddenly, he was very aware of tiny little smiles and looks of approval being thrown at him, which were soon followed by numerous friendly shoulder pats and thumbs up as people passed by his table.

'You have a whole bunch of new friends now, McCoy,' said Skye.

Julius knew then just how right Morgana was. This was not going to be an easy job.

*

With less than a month to go, and no access to Satras for another week, the Skirts decided to spend the next few days selecting the players. Faith was in charge of filtering the entries, according to their individual placing in the charts. Anyone below tenth rank was automatically excluded. Julius and Skye had decided to focus on the fighters, and Morgana and Faith on the pilots.

As well as poring over player files, one Wednesday evening Julius received a call to see Dr Walliser the following morning. With everything that was happening on Zed, he really could have done without this extra treatment, or whatever it was that Freja wanted him to do. At the end of their Meditation class he quickly mentioned where he was going to his friends, promising that he would tell them all as soon as he got back.

Dr Walliser was waiting for him in the foyer. 'Mr McCoy, follow me.'

Julius was taken into one of the familiar rooms, where he sat on the bed.

'You must be sick and tired of this place,' said the doctor. 'Second time this week?'

'Third,' specified Julius.

Walliser nodded. 'Grand Master Freja has decided to use one of our gene therapy enhancement procedures on you.'

'A what procedure, sir?' asked Julius.

'The simplest way to explain it, is that we want to improve your DNA, McCoy.'

'I don't understand,' said Julius, trying to hide the concern in his voice. 'Why me?'

'As a White Child, you will receive certain special treatments during your development on Zed,' answered Walliser, preparing a tray with various instruments. 'Not that we've had that many like you, though. You are special, as far as Zed officers go, and a most precious asset for our defences. Salgoria has already moved twice to get you and, even though she has failed, we need you strong and in peak condition. I have to admit, I've never met a White Child in my career, so I'm really looking forward to our weekly meetings. So McCoy, what do you say?'

'Do I have choice?'

'Do you want out?'

'No, sir,' answered Julius.

'Then you don't,' said the doctor, not unkindly. 'Shoes and socks off, please.'

Julius removed his boots and lay down on the bed. Walliser got to work, nimbly attaching sensors around Julius' head and neck, and on the backs of his feet and hands.

'Thanks to the advances in Biomathematics,' explained the doctor, 'all you need now is a quick injection in the neck, and a small pill.'

Julius looked suspiciously at the red pill that Walliser was handing to him on a dish. He put it in his mouth and swallowed. 'Ugh,' he said, disgusted. 'It tastes horrible.'

'Here, have some juice,' said Walliser.

Julius drank gratefully, trying to remove all trace of the acrid taste.

'You'll need to stay in here for half an hour, McCoy. That's all that's required from you for this treatment. Ms Primula will let you know when the time is up.'

'Thanks doctor,' said Julius, lying back down. With time to kill, he decided to carry on his player search so, once he was alone in the room, he activated his PIP and skimmed through the files. The thirty minutes flew by and soon the nurse came to let him know he could leave. In fact, it took him more time to explain what had happened to him to the Skirts, than to actually do the treatment. Faith had far too many questions about it that Julius couldn't answer and, in the end, he told him he should ask Cress during their next Biomaths lesson since, no doubt, the Tijaran Master would know a lot more than Julius ever could about it. Skye found the whole thing quite cool, while Morgana seemed a little anxious about it, but didn't say anything.

*

On Friday the 14th, Julius and Morgana were sitting under the oak tree in the garden, looking over pilot choices. Skye had to finish an assignment for the following Monday, while Faith was developing his project for Pete's competition.

'I'm not sure who to go for,' said Julius, switching between three files. 'Who would you choose?'

'Charlie Dolan, 5MS Tuala. He's the best of the three,' answered Morgana quickly. 'But if you're looking for a pilot-slash-fighter, then it's between our Isolde, or Celia, from 6MS Sield.'

Julius closed Charlie's file and read over the stats for Isolde and Celia.

'You know Julius, I think we should go for Isolde. She does have a good reputation and, besides that, she'd love to fight by your side.'

'How so?'

'I think she fancies you, which wouldn't surprise me in the least. I mean, most of the girls in our year think you're cute,' she said, matter-of-factly.

'I wish you hadn't told me that,' he said, shaking his head. 'How am I going to look at her in class now? It's just the two of us!'

'You're far too shy for your own good, you know? When it comes to ladies, I mean.'

'It's just a distraction, and I don't need that.'

'Don't forget what they say – behind every great man, there's a great woman!' she said, teasing him. Before he could think of a reply, she promptly stood up and left him there under the tree.

Julius looked at Celia's file again, and then at Isolde's. If he picked her, there would be nothing strange about it; after all, she was good and had high stats. And she *was* pretty, he had to admit. 'See – just a distraction,' he said to the empty garden, then stood up and headed inside for dinner.

It was during dessert that the final list was decided. Julius sent it to Freja, and they waited patiently for a reply. At 21:00 hours, the list was returned to him with a seal of approval from the three Grand Masters, and a personal note from Edwina Milson, the only GM who still played in the Hologram Palace. '"Excellent choice, McCoy. Good luck.",' said Julius, reading out the message. 'That was nice of her.'

'And here's the message for the lucky winners,' said Faith, clearing his throat. 'Congratulations, such-and-such. You have been selected to represent your planet in the most exciting challenge ever! The Zed Toon depends on you. No pressure. Meet tomorrow morning at 09:00 hours by Mrs Mayflower's kiosk. Signed, JMWC.'

'What's that last bit?' asked Julius, suspiciously.

'JM, that's you; WC, for White Child,' answered Faith, with a grin.

'Oh no you don't! No one is going to call me WC. Off my case, Irish,' growled Julius.

'You're no fun,' said Faith, typing on his PIP. 'There, just JM. Better?'

'Much better. Right – let's send them.'

As soon as Faith had pressed the send button, Julius felt as if a weight had lifted from his chest. Tomorrow morning they would start training and he really hoped that the new toon would blend well.

*

The next morning, Isolde joined the Skirts on the Intra-Rail platform, looking suitably excited. Morgana was very happy to have her there, since she was one of her two best friends. When the train arrived, Julius looked around the carriage hoping to see the other players and, sure enough, huddled in a group at the back were five faces that he recognised immediately, having poured over their files for an entire week.

'Hey there,' he called.

The five Mizkis waved back and moved over to the front to join them. Wearing the dark red Tuala uniform were Maks Suraev, a blue eyed 5MS from Russia, who was renowned for his piloting skills, and Nalani Liway, Lopaka's big sister. She had been chosen by Faith once he had found out that, like her brother, Nalani had a real passion for technology, not to mention her seriously deep dark eyes, which grabbed Faith's attention a little too often. The three fighters who had been chosen were all from Sield. They were, a lively American girl called Ellie Gibson from fifth year, plus two 6MS: the tanned Inigo Vega from Spain, and the red haired Maya Berg from Norway.

'I hope you guys don't have any problems with me being in charge,' said Julius, after they had all shaken hands. 'I mean, I'm only a 3MA after all.'

'You're kidding, right?' said Maks. 'You're a Solo champion and a White Child. I'm more than happy to leave you in charge.'

The others readily agreed, making Julius feel more at ease. 'I'll do my best, I can promise you that, but it won't be easy. There will be plenty of eyes on us for this game, so let's make sure we give it our all.' As he looked at the newly assembled Zed Toon, he started to get a good feeling about them. The new guys seemed friendly enough and, if they were as good as their stats suggested, then his job wouldn't be too hard. Of course, he also had the Skirts there to help him out.

*

As the days passed, and the 5th of November drew closer, things started to get pretty hectic. Faith was dividing what little free time he had between extra practices and his competition, often not going to sleep until the small hours of the morning, while Julius worked on assembling and disassembling catalysts with Isolde. With them working together both in school and in gaming, Isolde soon forgot about Julius' earlier blunder in class and became much more relaxed around him. However, after the conversation he had had with Morgana about Isolde's apparent feelings for him, Julius started to feel a bit more awkward around her.

Morgana and Skye were also dealing with their fair share of homework and practice. And, not being totally blind, Julius had also begun to notice Skye's extra-curricular activities with Maya Berg which, as Faith had put it, had been only a matter of time really. To everyone's delight though, their practice sessions were going well, and they all seemed to be working with, and around, each other in a pleasingly fluid way.

When the time came, Julius and Isolde sat, and passed, their checkpoint exam with Professor Gould, managing to assemble three different types of catalyst within a minute. Julius felt so good about it that he didn't even flinch when Isolde gave him a congratulatory hug, on their way out of class.

The night before the big game, Julius called home and was delighted to be greeted by the sight of Michael's face appearing on screen first. Although they didn't exchange too many words, just the fact that his brother was sitting there, between his parents, was the best possible way to end his day. They told Julius that they would be watching the game with Morgana's family, over at their place. As he signed off that night, and got ready for bed, Julius felt on such a high that he was ready to take on the entire world.

ZED TOON

On the morning of the challenge, Julius met his team by old Mrs Mayflower's kiosk in the Hologram Palace. The game would not start until midday, but they had been asked to arrive three hours early to avoid the crowd and leave time for last minute preparations.

'Eeeeh! Look who's here,' said Mrs Mayflower, flashing her usual cheeky, although less toothed, smile at them.

'Good morning!' said Morgana. 'Will you cheer for us, Mrs Mayflower?'

'I will be doing more than that, dear!' Saying this, she turned around, disappeared beneath her counter and re-emerged holding a silver-grey t-shirt, with ZED TOON emblazoned on it. 'Ta-daa! What do you think?'

'Brilliant!' said Ellie and Nalani together.

'Really shiny,' added Skye.

'They will be on sale in every shop in Satras, and not just for today. They'll become serious memorabilia.'

'Make sure you keep some for us,' said Faith. 'I'm sure me mum would love one.'

'Have the Arneshians arrived yet?' asked Julius.

'Yes. They got here an hour ago and went straight to their dressing room.'

'What do they look like?' asked Maks.

'Kids,' she said, simply. 'A bit greyish perhaps, but just like you.'

Julius nodded. 'So, what's the deal today?'

'The cameras will go live when the game begins. There will be a small ceremony at the start, where you will meet your opponents for the first time. It'll be a fast paced game, but you can do it. However, first things first, there's breakfast waiting for you downstairs, courtesy of Global Brioche.'

'All right!' said Skye, clearly pleased with that last bit of information.

'Thanks Mrs Mayflower,' said Morgana. 'Where do we go?'

'Follow the corridor to Combat,' she said, pointing at the stairs that led down towards the simulation levels. 'They're waiting for you.'

Julius led the way, and when they reached the split in the corridor they took a left. Once at their destination they were met by Miss Logan, the blonde technician in charge of that sector, and Mr Smith, who took care of Flight simulation.

'This way please,' said Miss Logan. 'Have your breakfast in here, before you get changed.'

Julius was surprised by all the trouble they seemed to have gone to for them. The normally bare reception room had been fitted with three small tables and ten chairs; each table was laden with juice, coffee, milk and at least eight different types of pastries. Julius loved Global Brioche, purely because of their ability to cater for whatever type of sweet you craved, from Turkish Baklava, to Hungarian Dobosh, and even Polynesian Malasadas, which Julius liked very much. He looked at the spread eagerly, but he knew that he must not overindulge, no matter how tempting it was. 'Miller, don't-' he started.

'I know,' Skye cut in quickly. 'I promise I'll leave space for dessert.'

For the next two hours, they went over the possible scenarios they may encounter, hoping that the computer hadn't inserted too many surprises for the occasion. At 11:00, Julius couldn't wait any longer and walked over to the desk. Mr Smith gave him a holosuit and he went to get changed.

The monitors in the dressing room were switched on, but instead of broadcasting the games, as they would normally do, they showed Satras and the Hologram Palace arena, packed with students and Zed officers glued to whatever screen they could find. Julius saw his classmates in a corner of the main courtyard. They were all wearing the silver grey t-shirts over their uniforms; he was overwhelmed by the sight, and it was then that he truly realised what this game actually meant for the Lunar Perimeter.

Slowly, the rest of the boys joined him and with ten minutes to go, the familiar green light appeared on the side door. As they entered onto the game-floor, an eerie silence met them. On a Saturday morning the whole place would have been teeming with Mizkis, but not today; it had all been shut down because of this game.

'This way,' said Mr Smith, leading them towards the closest row of machines.

Julius stopped by the first one and waited as each member of his team passed by, giving them high fives as they did. Morgana was the last, and she winked at him on her way to her sphere. He grinned back before quickly climbing into his own frame, as he had done countless times before. He then placed his feet on the two small platforms and grabbed the handles. When the holosphere was activated, all sound disappeared; the headrest slipped behind his head, while invisible straps secured his hands, ankles and waist. The sphere's membrane became visible and slowly began to vibrate. Julius shifted in his restraints and closed his eyes, feeling weightlessness entering his body. It was time.

*

He came to in a town square, surrounded by the quaint facades of small, brick houses. He looked around and saw that his team was all there. In-game, they were now clothed in silver, fitted jumpsuits, with their surnames printed in shimmering white on the front and back, which Julius guessed must be for the benefit of the spectators. Faith had regained the use of his legs, exactly as had happened during last year's games, which made him mighty pleased. They all had triangular devices pinned on their chests, above their hearts: Julius knew these were their com-links, which were small communication devices.

'That colour really suits you,' said Skye, winking at Maya. 'It goes nicely with your eyes.'

Faith pretended to puke behind his back, making everyone snigger.

'I would refrain from doing that in front of the cameras, Mr Shanigan,' said a voice suddenly. 'The audience will not be able to hear you, but they will see you quite clearly.'

They all turned and saw Professor Chan atop a small podium. He was wearing his usual loose, black tunic, and standing there with his hands behind his back.

'Professor,' said Julius, surprised. 'What are you doing here?'

'I will be the master of ceremonies for this game. The Arneshians are about to arrive and, as soon as they do, the game will go live. Create a row in front of me now; gaze forward. McCoy, you first.'

Julius stood before Chan, and the other players positioned themselves in a line behind him. Chan examined them thoroughly, and looked pleased. 'Remember who you represent today.'

'Yes sir,' they answered as one.

Suddenly, there was a flash of light and ten figures appeared in the square. As tempted as he was to stare and examine them, Julius continued looking ahead, hoping to look professional. After all, from that moment, the world's eyes would be fixed on them.

'Arnesh Glory, welcome,' said Chan. 'Please stand next to a member of the Zed Toon, your leader at the front.'

Julius was aware of feet approaching and, out of the corner of his eye, saw that someone had stopped just to his left.

'Face each other and bow,' ordered Chan.

Julius turned left and found himself staring at a boy taller than he was. He was wearing a black jumpsuit, with the com-link device pinned to his chest; his eyes were blue and his hair pure white – it shimmered in the same way as T'Rogon's. To top it off, a thin circlet crowned his head. In the sunlight his skin looked slightly dull and greyish. The name printed on his suit identified him as K'Ssander. The boy kept his face straight, betraying no emotion. Julius wondered just how old he was because, quite frankly, he didn't look much like a "youth", as T'Rogon had said; not quite an adult, but certainly not as young as the Zed students. He quickly threw a glance at the other Arneshians, and was taken aback when he saw that, as well as having the same hair colour as their leader, they were all as tall and looked just as old too. The surprise must have been visible on his face, because suddenly he heard Chan's voice in his mind, '*Don't show any weakness, McCoy.*' He immediately relaxed his face and stared back at the other captain.

'Players, I want a fair game from you. You all have Sim-Gauntlets and, as per usual, all mind-skills have been blocked, so you are now equal. The com-link on your chest will allow you to communicate with your own team. Every time you hit a player, their health bar will decrease, until it's depleted and the person will then disappear from the game. The last player standing will represent the winning team. Are you ready?'

'Yes, sir!' they all cried.

'Let the game commence.'

As Chan pronounced those words, a white light engulfed the square once more and, as Julius opened his eyes for the second time, he found himself sitting on a tree branch with Faith, in the middle of an empty field. 'What the …' he started.

'Where's everyone?' asked Faith, sounding worried.

Julius touched his com-link. 'Zed Toon, state your position,' he said, scouting his surroundings and looking down carefully.

'Skye and Inigo, standing in a pond,' replied Skye.

'Morgana and Maks, chicken house,' said Morgana.

'I'm with Maya in a tunnel,' added Isolde.

'Nalani and I are in a stinky bakery,' said Ellie.

Julius looked at Faith, feeling totally at loss.

'So much for teamwork,' said Faith.

'Look for a big landmark, anywhere around you,' said Julius. He began to scout the horizon as well, until his eyes rested on a tall building in the distance. 'Toon, can you see the building with the neon sign at its top?'

'The one that says, "Fly me"?' asked Skye.

'That's the one,' answered Julius.

The others confirmed that they could see it too.

'Right. Let's meet there and shoot anything that moves along the way. Good luck.' He turned to Faith. 'We have to jump. Are you ready?'

Faith nodded and slid off the branch until he was dangling by his hands. After a brief hesitation, he let go. Julius followed suit.

'Now what?' asked Faith.

'Now we run!' said Julius, suddenly grabbing him by the arm.

'Wait, what-' Faith turned his head and saw an armour plated stegosaur pelting towards them, making the ground shake. 'Why is it looking at us like that? Doesn't it eat grass?'

'I refuse to stand here and discuss dietary habits with it!' shouted Julius. 'Run!' Julius leapt forward in the direction of the landmark ahead, keeping an eye out for any possible Arneshian attacks. The two boys had been sprinting for almost a minute, the dinosaur's footsteps booming behind them, when finally Julius spotted a large clump of trees to his left. 'Over there. We'll hide and ambush it!' They instantly steered in that direction and, as Julius made a sharp bend behind one of the thick tree trunks, he saw a jet-bike parked in its shadow.

'Move over,' said Faith, jumping on the vehicle and pressing the start button. It roared to life and slowly rose from the floor. 'Hop on!'

Julius swung his right leg over, hooked his left arm around Faith's waist and turned to look back, Gauntlet at the ready. Faith accelerated and the jet-bike zoomed forward. A few seconds later, the stegosaur broke through the tree line.

'Shoot it!' cried Faith, while he sped in the direction of a nearby rocky terrain, hoping to discourage the animal from following any further.

Julius tried to steady his right arm but, with all the tight turns that Faith was having to make, that was easier said than done. He aimed as best as he could and, when he thought the beast was more or less centred, he fired. The first energy ray whisked past it, well above its head; Julius continued shooting at it, and slowly lowered his arm until he hit the stegosaur's forehead. The animal stumbled, let out a primeval roar, and crashed to earth in a cloud of dust. Seeing that it wasn't about to get up again, Julius turned forward and patted Faith on the shoulder. 'Good driving, speedy. Now, take us to that building.'

As the landmark loomed closer, Julius saw that it was set in the middle of a ruined city. As they arrived at the edge of it, Faith stopped the bike. The place was eerily quiet, except for the occasional chattering of the birds that had made a home in the long abandoned structures. Where the road began, cracked asphalt replaced dying blades of grass. 'Zed Toon,' said Julius over his com-link, 'we've just reached a ghost town. I'd say it's about 3000 feet to the meeting point.'

'How did you get there so quickly?' asked Inigo. 'We just made it out of the pond!'

'About that,' interrupted Skye, 'we would have been a lot quicker if it wasn't for the giant octopus that tried to drown us.'

'Giant octopus?' said Morgana. 'For real?'

'We believe you, Skye,' said Faith. 'Julius just downed a dinosaur.'

'These games get weirder by the day,' commented Nalani. 'Anyway, we're out of the bakery and right under the building. If you-' Nalani's voice cut out abruptly and was replaced by the sound of screams and running footsteps.

'What's happening?' shouted Julius. 'Nalani? Ellie?'

Faith revved the engine. 'Hold on!' He lurched forward, aiming for the building.

'Ellie?' Julius kept calling her name over the com-link. 'Nalani, come in!' No one answered his call, but he could hear hurried steps and voices he didn't recognise.

'Can you see them, Julius?' asked Morgana, breathing heavily – it sounded like she was running.

'Not yet, but we are getting closer,' he replied.

Faith had the jet-bike at full speed, and Julius had to hold on to him with both arms to avoid being blown backward by the wind. They were forced to zip in between the fly-car carcasses and sometimes just above them; for some reason their ride wouldn't take them higher than ten feet above the ground.

'Ellie!' screamed Nalani. 'Stop, no!' Then silence.

Faith spotted the bakery and skidded to a halt outside it.

'Zed Toon: Gibson, Liway, eliminated,' the monotone voice of the computer announced over the com-link. 'Arnesh Glory: F'Saner, eliminated.'

'Shoot!' cried Julius, running a hand through his hair.

'At least they took one of theirs with them,' said Faith. 'Let's get inside our meeting point. We're too exposed out here.'

'Toon,' Julius said, 'we are going in. Meet us there.'

Cautiously, keeping their Sim-Gauntlets at the ready, they backed into the building. Faith checked that the foyer was clear before letting Julius in. Once inside, they secured the ground floor, checking behind any closed doors and corners.

'I'll go check upstairs,' said Faith, heading toward the stairwell.

Julius crouched by the main glass door, sheltered by the branches of a pot plant. Losing two players so early wasn't good, but there was nothing to be done about it now; they would just have to be extra careful from here on.

'Julius,' whispered Isolde, over the com-link. 'Can you hear me?'

'Yes, where are you?'

'Across the road from you. See the wrecked Bumble-Bee? We're right behind it.'

Julius identified the fly-car immediately, as it was the same model as his dad's, and saw two pairs of feet shuffling beneath it. 'I see you. Want me to cover you?'

'That would be just swell,' she replied.

Julius shifted over to the door, opened it slightly and had a quick glance around. He couldn't see any movement. 'Ready … Go!'

Isolde and Maya jumped up and slid over the roof of the car, and ran as fast as they could towards Julius, who was waiting, ready to open the door wide for them. That was when the shooting began.

'Run!' he shouted at the girls. Isolde ducked down and Maya shielded her head with her arms. Julius spotted K'Ssander leaning out of a window on the first floor of the building opposite them. He lifted his Gauntlet and returned fire. A further series of energy bursts streamed at the girls from his left, this time from inside a burnt-out fly-car. He began to panic as he realised he wouldn't be able to hold off both attackers.

To make things worse, the girls had stopped running and were now caught smack bang in the middle of the crossfire.

'Faith!' Julius shouted over his shoulder. 'Could do with some help here!'

A few seconds later, Faith had joined him and started firing at the opponent to their left.

'They won't be able to resist much longer,' said Julius.

'Hey!' cried Morgana suddenly. 'Over here, you big bullies!'

Julius looked right, and saw her standing over a capsized nullifying bin, her Sim-Gauntlet aimed at the Arneshian leader, a look of stern defiance on her face. The energy beams shifted towards her, but Morgana was quicker. She back-flipped and landed effortlessly a few feet back, then sprinted towards the side of the building with the neon sign.

'That's what I call a crowd pleaser,' whooped Faith enthusiastically.

'Where did she learn that?' said Julius, wide-eyed.

At the same time that Morgana was attracting the shooters' attention, Skye, Maks and Inigo had entered the fray; shielding their sides with scrap pieces of metal, they ran towards the girls, grabbed them by their arms and dragged them inside the building, where Julius was waiting, and slammed the door shut behind them.

'That was close,' panted Maks, slumping down, exhausted.

'We must have lost a lot of life back there,' said Isolde, who was also breathing heavily.

'At least we're still here,' said Maya. She walked up to Skye and thanked him with a big kiss on his cheek for saving her.

Inigo and Maks grinned and winked at Julius and Faith.

'It's the Miller charm,' whispered Faith. 'You get used to it.'

Suddenly, there was a loud thumping noise, which made them all jump. They whirled to the source of the sound and saw Morgana standing on the other side of a full-length window, hiding in the shadows.

Julius touched his com-link. 'Are you ok?'

'Yes. I think I lost them for now, but you need to let me in.'

'Stay back,' he replied. He aimed his Gauntlet at the bottom of the glass panel and fired a single blast at it; the window shattered and came crashing down. Morgana hurried inside and re-joined the group. They stood for a bit, not saying much and all was quiet. The respite didn't last long however as, a few minutes later, the ominous sound of a low rumble, growing slowly louder, was heard from outside.

'What is that?' asked Inigo, walking over to the main door.

Julius and the others moved cautiously forward and peered into the distance. A billowing cloud of dust hung above the road, rolling slowly in their direction. As it drew closer, the various small pieces of junk sprawled on the floor around them began to vibrate and rattle.

'Look at the fly-cars!' gasped Inigo, pointing.

Julius involuntarily took a step back as he watched one of the vehicles tilt precariously forward, then backwards, then forward again, as if it was perched on the edge of a precipice. It teetered like that for a few seconds, then nose dived and disappeared from view. 'The road is collapsing!' he said.

'It's happening all around us!' cried Inigo.

'Upstairs, quick!' shouted Julius, ushering them up the stairwell.

'Won't we be trapped?' said Maya, holding on to Skye's hand.

'The sign on the roof,' replied Julius. 'It says, "Fly me". I bet there's a way out up there.'

'It's fly-time!' cheered Morgana. 'Let's go, let's go!'

Faith turned to Inigo and Maks, pointed at Morgana and said with a smile, 'That, is also something you get used to.'

'My kind of girl,' said Maks.

Julius tried to ignore the comment, and the fact that there were little red wisps shooting out of Maks's head as he looked admiringly at Morgana. A couple of minutes later, they had reached the roof.

Julius was relieved to see that there were indeed four aircraft parked there, similar in design to the Sim-Cougars, but slightly longer, so as to accommodate two people in each. 'Morgana, Maks, Isolde and Faith,' called Julius. 'You're piloting – take us out of here.'

'Aye, aye Captain,' answered Morgana enthusiastically, rushing towards the first plane with Skye in tow.

Julius followed Faith towards the second one; Inigo went with Isolde and Maya with Maks. The engines fired up simultaneously and the four Cougars lifted upwards.

Julius grabbed the catalyst and began to scout the sky. His seat was raised slightly, allowing him to see over the pilot's head; as in the real Cougars, the top cover was transparent, so that there were no blind spots. 'Morgana,' called Julius. 'Follow us west. Isolde and Maks, head east. Let's find them.'

'Roger,' answered the pilots.

Isolde and Maks performed a perfect 180 degree reverse rotation – just as they had been taught in first year – and headed eastward, still in the upside down position, twisting themselves to face the right way up as they flew. From up above, Julius now had the chance to see the abandoned city in its entirety, or at least what was left of it. The cloud of dust had almost completely settled and he was able to make out the long, black strips of nothing that had replaced the roads. Not a car was in sight, only the buildings, jutting out of the concrete like rotten teeth.

'Where are they?' said Faith, frustrated.

'I bet they're hiding,' answered Julius. 'Keep circling the city, Faith.'

'Guys,' said Maks over the com-link, 'I see movement ahead.'

'There are people on one of the rooftops,' said Maya. 'It's them! I recognise their shimmery hair.'

'Send us the coordinates, Maks,' said Julius. 'Let's go say hi.'

Faith veered right and zoomed forward, lowering his altitude until he was level with the rooftops.

Julius looked into the distance and spotted five small aircrafts, taking off from one of the tallest buildings. 'Faith,' he said quietly, 'take us to ground level. I want to hit them from below.'

'Sneaky! I like it,' grinned Faith, before diving between two houses.

Julius readjusted his grip on the catalyst and kept his eyes on the sky above, while the Cougar moved silently closer to their targets. 'I see them,' he said, a few seconds later. 'Aim for the rearguard one.'

'Roger,' answered Faith. He steered upwards and, as stealthily as he could, positioned himself right below the last Arneshian aircraft, nose pointing at its core.

'Go!' cried Julius.

Faith accelerated instantly, flattening both of them against their seats. Julius took aim and opened fire. Caught by surprise, the Arneshian craft swayed desperately and set off at pace, leaving its group behind. 'Stay with him, Faith!' shouted Julius, still shooting.

'Come to daddy, you shell-head,' said Faith, sticking hot on its tail.

The Arneshian craft twisted and swerved, in and out of empty buildings, in an effort to lose them in the ruins, but Faith was relentless in his chase. As they emerged from one of the buildings, an energy burst rocked their plane.

'We have company,' said Faith. 'Two nasties right behind us.'

'Don't lose him, Faith,' said Julius. Then to the com-link, 'Guys, we need some help here.'

'I'm on it,' said Morgana.

'We'll take care of them,' said Isolde.

'They're all yours, ladies,' answered Faith. 'I've got me hands full with this one.'

Julius continued shooting, and thanks to Faith's flying, he managed to keep a constant stream aimed at the enemy craft. He wasn't quite sure how that would affect the pilots inside it but, since no target had appeared above the plane, as it would have in a regular flying game, he believed that the craft must also have a separate energy bar. 'Come on,' he said through gritted teeth. 'Will you just die already?' As if in answer to his plea, the Arneshian plane suddenly exploded, the force of it enough to knock them slightly off course.

'Arnesh Glory: C'Tardid, T'Namen, eliminated,' announced the computer.

'Yes!' cheered Julius. 'Well done mate,' he said, patting Faith's shoulder.

'Likewise,' said Faith, grinning.

'Congrats,' said Maks over the com-link, 'but leave the champagne on ice for now. I've got two aggros right behind me.'

'On our way,' answered Faith, speeding up. 'Send coordinates.'

'Incoming,' replied Maya.

Faith veered upward and headed back toward the city.

'Hmm ...' said Julius after awhile. 'They should be here, but I can't see them.'

'We're here!' cried Maya. 'Look up!'

'Where?' asked Faith.

Julius craned his neck around until he caught sight of a fast-moving shadow in the lining of a cloud. 'There!' he said, pointing.

Suddenly, Maks's Cougar burst out of the cloud, followed by two enemy craft. He was twisting and spinning skilfully to avoid being hit. Faith accelerated and positioned his craft behind the Arneshians.

As he did so, Julius began to shoot. 'Stay still, damn you,' he said through gritted teeth. To his frustration, the two planes in front of him were zipping nimbly around each other, making them incredibly difficult to hit.

A minute later, the computer came back online – 'Zed Toon: Frey, Montoya, eliminated.'

'Shoot!' cried Julius. 'Morgana, what's happening?'

'Just ... a ... sec ... almost ... there!' she answered.

'Arnesh Glory: A'Trid, P'Lankot, eliminated.'

'All right!' said Skye. 'Bring 'em on!'

'Well done, guys,' said Julius. 'Come join us.'

'On our way,' answered Morgana.

Julius was still firing determinedly at the planes in front of him, and wondering how low their energy bars were now; unfortunately there was no way to tell, and they seemed to be going just as strong as when the chase had started. He had five players left while K'Ssander had four, and that was a good start, but he knew they really couldn't afford to lose any more.

Without warning, the Cougar banked left sharply. 'Faith, where are you going? I'm in the middle of shooting that guy!'

'It isn't me,' answered Faith. 'I can't control it.'

'What's happening?' said Morgana.

Julius looked around and saw that all the planes, including those of the Arneshians, were now flying in an orderly manner in the same direction, creating a V-formation. He let go of the catalyst and wiped the palms of his hands against his suit. He wouldn't admit it out loud, but this unplanned rest was more than welcome: aiming and shooting was hard enough work, even without the constant spinning and twisting of the last few minutes.

'What's that, right ahead?' asked Maks. 'Can you make it out?'

Julius peered into the distance and saw six tall dark shapes, split into two groups of three. With the sun in his eyes, it was difficult to tell exactly what they were, but soon the shapes began to take on an unmistakable humanoid outline. His mouth fell open, while his brain tried to process what he was actually seeing. 'That can't be.'

'Well, wax me back and call me a surfboard,' said Faith, hypnotised by the view.

As they drew closer, each shape became perfectly clear and visible; standing at roughly 150 feet above the ground were six giant robots, in full armour plating. The three on the right bore the Zed oval emblem on their chests – Julius instantly recognised the full moon in a starry dark sky – while the remaining ones had a symbol that Julius had never seen before: a triangle with a straight line balanced at its peak, contained within a circle. Although he could guess that it must be the Arneshian symbol, he had no idea as to its meaning, and no time to figure it out either, so he pushed it out of his mind for the time being. He focused his attention on the nearest of the Zed robots. The paint on the metal created the illusion that the machine was wearing clothes. Its torso, pelvis, forearms and the sections from the knees down were coated in blue, while the rest of the area was metallic grey; red and gold designs were embossed throughout giving it a vibrant look. Its head was crowned with a spiked, gold circlet. Julius was blown away by the look of it, and judging by the total silence on the com-link, the rest of the toon were just as stunned as he was.

The plane bearing him and Faith steered itself away from the formation and headed for the robot to their far right. They levelled up to it at waist height and slowly ascended toward the head. As they did so, Julius observed the perfect details of its armour. The sun reflected off its surface, creating a kaleidoscope of colours inside their Cougar. When they reached its face, Julius found himself staring at two large black eyes, which had a menacing look about them courtesy of the arched metal eyebrows above them. The nose was straight and almost triangular; the mouth thin, but perfectly shaped. They hovered there for a few seconds, and then the craft began to slide sideways, moving in an orbit around the head, until it was facing the back of it. They rose a couple of feet, paused in front of a large opening, and slowly moved forward, slotting comfortably into the hole, where it locked into place.

'I always knew I was the brains of the operation,' said Faith.

Julius chuckled nervously; they were now literally sitting inside the skull of the robot. There was a gentle humming noise and a new type of control panel materialised over the Cougar's own, and solidified.

'Am I supposed to drive this thing?' asked Faith, looking back over his shoulder.

'I guess,' answered Julius, shrugging his shoulders. He picked up two controllers from his own panel and, as he began to rotate them, the arms of the robot did exactly the same. 'Whoa! It looks like I can control his arms.'

'That means that I've got the legs. I think I need to put me feet in these stirrups here,' said Faith. He added, as an afterthought, 'Good job I've got me legs on today.'

Julius watched as Faith stepped cautiously forward into the empty space below his seat; as he did this, it was mimicked perfectly by the robot. Guided by Julius, the robot lifted both arms and, when he squeezed the catalysts, two violent bursts of energy pelted out of the hands, crashing into a tree in front of them, blowing it to smithereens. 'This is just!'

'There's a funny button here,' said Faith. 'It says UP. I might just press it, you know?'

'Sure, go a-' began Julius, but the words caught in his throat as the robot zoomed upwards into the sky. 'OK, now we're flying again.'

'Incoming!' said Morgana cheerfully, as her robot came to a halt in midair before theirs. 'Come on up, Maks!'

The third Zed robot quickly joined them and, as they regrouped, the Arneshians did the same.

'Let's get 'em!' cried Morgana, leading the attack.

Faith guided the robot after her; Skye and Maya quickly followed suit, and they all released a volley of energy bursts at their targets. The Arneshians weren't about to stand still though, and launched towards them, lasers blazing away in response.

'Guys, I can sense a head-on collision coming our way,' said Faith. 'Shouldn't we move, maybe?'

'Hold your course!' ordered Julius. 'They will move.'

'If you're sure,' replied Faith, sounding unconvinced.

'I'll take the one in the middle,' said Morgana. 'You're so mine.'

'She's a little intimidating sometimes,' whispered Maya, over the com-link.

'Girl, you ain't seen nothing yet,' said Morgana. '*Banzai!*' Her robot hurtled on and collided with the furthest forward of the Arneshians. The sound of clashing metal echoed through the air.

'I'm gonna close me eyes now,' said Faith. 'Here we go!'

Julius felt a rush of adrenaline surge through him, but kept his hand steady as he continued shooting from his catalyst. He braced himself for the impact and, as the Arneshian robot loomed large in front of theirs, he also shut his eyes. As they crashed against each other, Julius was grateful that his shoulder straps kept him safely cushioned in his seat, even though the jolt made the entire robot shake. He opened his eyes and realised that he had grabbed the Arneshian vehicle by its arms, and now had it in a lock.

'Hold on to him. I want to slam-dunk him to the ground,' called Faith excitedly.

Julius kept his hands steady, while Faith manoeuvred into place. Several seconds later, they were in free fall, the ground speeding up to meet them. This time, the landing impact was considerably more brutal, and the two robots were bounced clear of each other.

'I feel like I'm in me mum's washing machine,' whined Faith, rubbing his neck.

From the ground where they were lying, Julius began to shoot again – a steady, powerful stream of energy directed at his opponent's head. Faith wrestled with the controls and managed to get the robot upright again. The Arneshian machine was trying hard to stand up, but was struggling futilely.

'We haven't killed them for real, have we?' asked Faith, walking slowly towards it.

They were within a few feet of it when it flashed brightly and then disappeared, catching them by surprise.

'Arneshian Glory,' announced the computer. 'B'Nold, M'Tard, eliminated.'

'What's with these people and the missing vowels in their names?' said Faith.

'Vowels are so last year, F'Th,' said Julius, grinning.

'Oi, comedians,' cried Skye, 'why don't you come up and play with the big boys?'

'On our way,' replied Faith, taking off.

'Guys,' said Maks, 'we need some serious help here.'

Julius looked around and saw one of the Arneshian robots hovering high in the air, and swinging Maks's robot around by the legs.

'I'm gonna be sick soon,' groaned Maya. 'I'm not kidding!'

Faith lowered his altitude and zoomed up toward the feet of the Arneshian.

'Hold on tight, guys,' shouted Julius. He lifted the arms and fired, blasting the enemy robot up and backwards. Its grip didn't falter though and, as it fell, it took Maks down with it.

'It's gonna land on top of them,' cried Faith, diving down in pursuit.

As they sped closer, Julius grabbed at the Arneshian with the robot's arms, but it was too late; when Maks's robot crashed to the ground, its attacker crunched down on top of it. Faith managed to pull out of their nosedive just in time, narrowly avoiding joining the pile-up.

Julius craned his neck and looked down. The Arneshian robot was slowly getting back to its feet. 'Maks, Maya,' he called. 'Are you OK?'

'Sort of,' answered Maks, 'but this machine has gone dead. It won't move.'

'What about the Sim-Cougar?'

'Gone too.'

'Then get out of there! We're coming down to shield you.'

'Julius,' said Faith, sounding oddly calm, 'I don't want to sound repetitive but, once again, I am not in control of the steering.'

'What do you mean?' asked Julius anxiously.

'We're free falling, and there's nothing I can do about it.'

Julius looked down and saw that indeed, they were plummeting to earth, in the direction of their teammates. 'Guys, get out of there. Now!'

'Julius!' cried Morgana. 'We can't control this thing!'

'Brace yourself and join the club,' replied Julius. 'Looks like we're all going down.'

Maks and Maya scampered out of the back of their robot's head. Thankfully, Maks grabbed hold of Maya's hand just in time to pull her clear of the landing area.

Julius gripped his shoulder straps, bracing himself as they crashed into the ground. As the dust settled, he groaned and opened his eyes slowly. 'Are you all right?'

'I'm fine,' answered Faith, yanking himself free of his seat. 'This is the harshest game, by far.'

'Morgana, Skye, can you hear me?'

'Yes,' answered Skye. 'We're getting out now.'

Julius nodded, relieved that they were all at least still in the game. Hurriedly, he unlocked his seatbelt and opened the hatch in the ceiling. He let Faith go first, then crawled out quickly. When he stood up and looked around, he immediately realised that something was wrong. 'Wait a minute – how come the Arneshian robots are still flying?'

'Hey,' cried Maya indignantly. 'That's not fair!'

The others looked up and, sure enough, the two robots were circling the sky above their heads.

'I don't understand,' said Morgana, shielding her eyes from the sun.

'Well, we can't ask questions now,' said Julius, rallying them. 'We need to go. Head towards that forest. Come on!'

They followed as he ran towards the trees; there weren't really many alternatives. Unexpectedly, a burst of energy struck the ground a few feet in front of them, sending debris flying in all directions and opening up a large hole.

'They're shooting at us,' cried Maya.

No sooner had the words left her mouth when a second shot hit just to their right, creating a huge cloud of dust. Julius skidded to a halt, unable to make out what was around him anymore. Then he heard the computer's voice. 'Zed Toon: Shanigan, Suraev, eliminated.'

'We can't stay together!' he cried. 'Skye, Maya, head east. We'll meet inside the forest.'

Skye grabbed Maya's hand and sped off to the left; Morgana and Julius headed right. Above them, the Arneshians split up and followed, firing relentlessly as they went.

Morgana was to Julius' left, keeping pace as they ran. Out of the corner of his eye he saw a dark shape descending towards her. He threw a glance over his shoulder and saw a large metal hand coming to scoop her up. Desperately, he veered in her direction, leapt forward, caught her in his arms and dragged her to the floor, just as the hand swooped over their heads. They rolled a few feet, then quickly sprang up again and ran.

'I don't think I can go on much longer!' cried Morgana.

'We're almost there. Come on!'

A new explosion opened the ground before them, sending them both tumbling into the newly formed crater. When the second blast hit, Julius was lifted off the ground and sent crashing against the edge of the hole. He kept his eyes shut as he flew through the air, waiting for the inevitable thud as he landed. He knew that, unless the in-game safety protocol failed, he couldn't really get hurt; still, as he landed on his chest, the air was pushed out of his lungs.

'Zed Toon: Ruthier, eliminated.'

'Damn it!' cried Julius.

'Julius, where are you?' said Skye. 'We made it through the forest, but that thing is still above us.'

Julius blinked and searched around him. Spotting a hole in the side of the crater, he quickly scampered inside it. The cloud of dust had not settled yet, giving him a few brief moments of shelter. 'It's not good guys,' he replied. 'Their advantage is far too great. We can't outrun them, so stay put as much as you can, Skye. After a while the computer is bound to give us another way out. It always does.'

'All right, we'll find a hideout, somewhere in-'

An explosion rocked the ground, and Julius felt bits of earth falling on top of his head and shoulders.

'Zed Toon: Miller, Berg, eliminated.'

'Skye, answer me!' called Julius. But he knew that it was too late. He was on his own and couldn't afford to stay where he was, waiting to be picked off. He wiped the dust from his face and caught sight of the forest. Half of it was ablaze. Deciding to try take advantage of the low visibility, he climbed out and made a run for it. As the first line of trees drew closer, he became aware of a shadow descending on him. He only had a brief chance to look up before a large net fell over him. He stumbled to the ground and flailed around inside the meshing. A giant hand came down, plucked him from the floor and lifted him in the air. Julius held on to the net and watched as the ground sank fast below him. When he looked up again, he was staring at the giant eyes of a robot and, above its brow, at the smirking face of the Arneshian leader, K'Ssander. 'What are you waiting for?' shouted Julius. 'End this now!'

The robot stretched out its left arm, dangling Julius in front of it. Its right arm then lifted, laser at the ready, and aimed at the net. Julius took a deep breath and stared back at K'Ssander, waiting for the blast.

FRACTURES

Julius' eyes flew open, as if he had just woken sharply from a bad dream. He moved about as much as he could in his restraints, to get the blood pumping and the feeling back in his limbs. Looking around, he noticed the empty holospheres around him and wondered if they had forgotten about him. Just as he was considering calling out to try get someone's attention, Mr Smith came to let him out.

'That was a heck of a ride, McCoy,' he said, deactivating the magnetic field. 'You gave it your best shot, so be proud of it.'

Julius nodded. 'It would be better if we'd won, though.'

'Next time,' he said, patting Julius' shoulder.

Julius clambered clear of the sphere. He was just on his way to the exit when he heard a commotion erupt up ahead of him. He moved forward quickly to find out what all the noise was about and, as the door came into full view, stopped dead in his tracks, stunned. It was like a freeze-frame from a movie, but all the more surreal because of where he was and who was involved in it: K'Ssander was gripping Morgana by her forearm, holding her behind him, while his free arm was stretched forward, index finger shoved against Skye's chest. Skye had his arms down by his side, fists clenched, leaning forward towards K'Ssander. Four of the Arneshian players were standing around them, watching, and looking very smug.

'Let me go!' cried Morgana.

'You heard the lady, grey skin,' said Skye through gritted teeth.

'Make me,' replied K'Ssander calmly.

The Arneshian leader's answer was enough to jolt Julius out of his momentary trance and he stomped towards them. However, as he started to move, Maks came striding out of nowhere and landed a right hook on K'Ssander's face. There was a sharp thwacking sound as Maks's knuckles connected, and a tiny groan escaped from K'Ssander's lips. Morgana, who was straining to get free, fell to the floor as he let go of her arm. In a flash, the watching Arneshians launched themselves at Maks, sending him sprawling to the floor, and they all collapsed in a heap.

As if moved by the same hand, Julius and Skye threw themselves into the fray, trying to pull the attackers off. Julius locked his arms around the neck of one of the Arneshians, narrowly ducking his head out of the way of a stray punch from the left and a loose kick aimed at him to his right. However, as he did that, his chin collided with someone's heel, making him see stars.

Just then, he heard Professor Chan's voice loud and clear in his mind: '*Get Miller out of there. Now!*' The commanding tone in the professor's voice snapped Julius to attention. He immediately let go of the Arneshian, jumped up, and looked for Skye. Spotting his friend, he grabbed him by the shoulders and pulled him clear, fists still flailing.

Maks, meanwhile, had regained his feet, and was promptly floored again as K'Ssander, who had quickly come back to his senses, launched himself at the Mizki Senior. The two of them were wrestling furiously when Chan and Mr Smith reached them.

'We don't treat ladies like that on this planet,' cried Maks, rolling onto K'Ssander. 'I'll teach you some respect.'

'No you won't!' said Chan imperiously, scooping Maks up by the collar of his shirt. 'Stop! Arneshian Glory, go back to your dressing room. That's an order!' He extended his left hand to Morgana, who was still sitting on the floor, and helped her to her feet. 'You too, Miss Ruthier.'

The Arneshians grabbed hold of their captain and trundled sulkily away.

When they had completely disappeared from view, Chan released Maks. 'What were you thinking?' said Chan angrily, turning to face him. 'Have you any idea of the consequences of your actions, Mr Suraev?'

'He was just protecting Morgana, sir,' argued Skye.

'Be quiet, Mr Miller,' said Chan. 'I did not give you permission to speak.'

'But, sir-' continued Skye.

'Quiet!' ordered Chan. The professor returned his attention to Maks. 'I know very well what that boy was doing, but that does not excuse your childish behaviour. You are a Zed student Mr Suraev, and we don't train you to engage in street brawls! K'Ssander wouldn't have harmed Miss Ruthier – he was just trying to goad you into doing something silly, and he succeeded perfectly.'

Maks shifted uncomfortably on his feet, but not once did he take his eyes away from Chan. Watching him, Julius had to agree that Maks had been reckless, but he had guts too, that much was sure.

'A common brawl!' said Chan, raising his hands in frustration at the ceiling. 'You could have at least used your blinking Mindkatas! Get changed, all of you. And rest assured, this doesn't end here. They will never allow that.'

As Chan stormed out of the room, Julius and Skye turned to Maks and patted him on the back.

'Great job, mate,' said Skye.

'That K'Ssander, man,' said Maks, rubbing his left shoulder and grimacing. 'It was like wrestling with a big rock. I'll get some grief for it, but Morgana's worth it. Sorry Julius, I hope I didn't screw things up too much.'

Julius shook his head, purposely ignoring the remark about Morgana. 'Don't worry about it, Maks. He was well out of order. To tell the truth, I'm more concerned with that game. Something fishy went on in there.'

'Yeah, those bloody robots,' said Skye, rubbing his left cheekbone, which was already starting to swell. 'Why were ours the only ones that stopped working? Do you think they pulled some dirty Arneshian trick on us?'

'I *know* they did,' answered Julius. 'But we need to prove it before we go making any accusations.'

Maks and Skye nodded. That was surely something that could not be resolved with a brawl.

*

'Take it easy next time, you hear me?' said Ms Primula, disinfecting a cut on Julius' chin. She picked up a handheld device and placed it an inch over the wounded area. 'Don't worry – it's just a Derma-Fix tool. It'll make you heal faster, but the scar will remain for a while. Hold still.'

Julius felt a tickling sensation spreading over his chin, accompanied by a buzzing noise. He guessed that the light, or whatever was in the light, was repairing his damaged skin cells and that, in a few minutes, the cut would be completely gone; the throbbing however, would stay with him for a few more hours. Right now though, Julius wasn't thinking about his chin, but rather about the reception they had received, as he and the rest of the Zed Toon had emerged from the Hologram Palace. Although he had been dreading that moment, it had not been too bad. A few of the watching crowd had shaken their heads miserably; others had actually applauded, and some had even stepped forward to shake their hands. Sure enough, the bloody cuts on their faces had raised a few eyebrows but, no questions were asked. Just before they had joined the crowd, Julius had taken the rest of his toon aside and told them what had happened at the end of the game.

'That pig!' Maya had said, indignantly.

'When this story comes out,' Julius had replied, 'and folks start to bad-mouth us about being sore losers or something, I want you to tell the students in your schools what really happened. Tell your family, your friends, and everyone you know. I'll take my punishment a lot better knowing that at least our people know the truth. Agreed?'

They had nodded, without hesitation. It was only when he had seen Chan talking to Freja and the other Grand Masters that his heart had started to race. What would the head of Tijara make of his leadership skills? Fortunately, they hadn't been pulled up there, in front of the crowd. Freja had simply glared at them, clearly not very pleased about it all, and had allowed them to return to their respective schools. Now, lying on the infirmary bed, Julius realised that this brief rest would soon be over, as he had just received a message, summoning him to Freja's office, along with Skye and Morgana.

*

'Miss Ruthier,' said Freja, from behind his large, glass desk, 'would you care to explain how this incident played out?'

Julius saw Morgana shifting in her chair. Reddish wisps were filling her aura, a sign that she was quite embarrassed.

'I was walking towards the changing room, behind Skye, when K'Ssander grabbed my arm. I asked him to let go, but he wouldn't. Skye turned around and told him to stop, while the other Arneshians just stood there, watching. Skye confronted him, but didn't engage him physically, at least not until Maks appeared out of nowhere and ... punched him. It forced K'Ssander to let go of my arm and I lost my balance. That's when Skye and Julius intervened and, uh, tried to stop the fight.'

Cress, who was standing to the right of the Grand Master, raised an eyebrow and said, 'Stop it? Join it, more likely.'

'That's not what we were trying to do, sir,' said Julius, quickly. 'I swear!'

'Be that as it may,' said Freja, shaking his head, 'it is not how it will be presented to the world.' He stood up and paced the floor. 'In case it's not clear enough, McCoy, this is what will most likely happen as a result of your actions: Mr Suraev will be used as a scapegoat, because he started the fight, regardless of how admirable his intentions were; you two will receive a serious case of bad press, and by default, so too will Tijara and Zed; worst of all, our already precarious reputation will take another blow, giving more support to the decision of the Earth Leader to close Zed recruitment. Is this clear enough for you?'

Julius looked back at him, trying to stay calm. He knew Freja was right, but the unfairness of it all, coupled with the fact that he had just lost the most important game of his life, was starting to take its toll. 'And the fact that they cheated to win makes no never mind to anyone, I suppose?'

Freja exchanged a quick look with Cress. 'Where's the proof of this, McCoy?' he asked.

'Everyone saw the robots – our robots – stop working in the middle of the game. Surely that should count for something.'

'Such an accusation, just after losing a challenge,' said Freja, 'can only worsen our position, especially when we have no evidence to back it up. Half the world probably think it was bad decision-making on your team's part.'

'You know that's not true,' said Morgana. 'Please Grand Master, have Mr List analyse the footage, or the game records. We can't let them get away with this.'

'We'll look into it, Miss Ruthier, but be prepared, because the worst is yet to come. Dismissed.'

*

With November truly underway, Julius arrived at the conclusion that Freja's prediction about their immediate future had been right: things were going from bad to outright horrid. Although the Space Channel had tried to remain neutral while describing the events following the game, the terrestrial ones had not been so soft. Blame was placed at Julius' feet for failing to properly direct his team in battle, and for allowing one of his team members to vent his frustration in such a "barbaric" way, as they put it. This made Julius mad, more so because there was nothing he could say or do to defend himself or his friends. Freja had been clear on that score – no public actions were to be taken on this matter until it was resolved at a higher level.

On top of that, T'Rogon had done his best to enhance the image of a manipulative Lunar Perimeter, rife with dangerous learners and a serious lack of space protocol on the part of the Grand Masters, placing so much trust in those students. Rumour had it that Maks had been forced to apologise in person to K'Ssander and his team, before starting a month-long ban from Satras, and an even longer one from the Hologram Palace. Morgana had been particularly crushed by that news. Skye and Faith had told her over and over again that there was nothing to blame herself for, but she couldn't help feeling that she had been the cause of this whole mess.

At least the Zed Toon had kept their promise about spreading the real story as much as possible, which pleased Julius, although he knew they were preaching to the converted: every last Zed student would, of course, side with them. The real problem was back home, on Earth. How were they going to get them to realise that T'Rogon was a wolf in sheep's clothing? Freja was right: they couldn't kick and scream about it without seeming like sore losers. They would have to wait and hope for some evidence before even considering speaking out. Surely Gabriel List would manage to find something in the game log that could be used to unmask those Arneshian cheats publicly. In the meantime though, they would just have to keep a low profile and hope there would be no more surprises.

*

Three weeks later, Julius was in the garden, stretched out against the oak tree, reading up on the personnel that was needed on the bridge in a spaceship, while Morgana was lying with her head resting on his right thigh, as she checked her mail. Julius heard a beeping noise coming from her PIP, and looked over at it.

'It's a message,' she said, rising up and perching on one elbow. 'It says to watch the Space Channel.'

'Not again,' groaned Julius, getting worried.

Morgana tuned her PIP into the news channel and moved her hand a little so that Julius could also see it. Iryana Mielowa was sitting in the Space Channel studio, facing T'Rogon. The first thing that was noticeable was that there was none of the recent cheeriness in her expression; even her lipstick was of a more modest shade. Julius didn't think that was a good sign at all.

'Ambassador,' she said. 'You called for this vidcon in order to make an important announcement. We are listening.'

T'Rogon smiled. He seemed confident and strong. To Julius, in that moment, he looked more like Salgoria's right hand than a simple messenger. Even Julius' old nemesis, Red Cap, had not exuded this much power.

'Thank you, Ms Mielowa. Over the past few weeks we have greatly enjoyed your hospitality. We have learned much of your recent history, both Earth's, and the Lunar Perimeter's. We have met some truly outstanding Earthlings during our visit.' He bowed his head once, towards the camera. 'My people and I have been aware for some time now that among you live quite a vast number of late generation Arneshians, or Nuarns as you call them. I have to admit, we thought that it showed remarkable qualities on your part to be so welcoming of a people who have not done particularly well by you. Up until now, that is. For this, my Queen is forever grateful.

'A powerful feeling came over my colleagues and I when we found out just how many Arneshians are currently living on Earth – 50 million, if I'm not mistaken – and we felt that we couldn't really leave without extending a formal invitation to each and every one of them, to come meet us aboard our ship.'

Julius shuddered. All he could think of was Michael.

'And what exactly would be the purpose of this visit?' asked Mielowa.

'To meet their own people, naturally.'

'Their own people? I'm sorry Ambassador, but aren't they already living with their families?'

'You tell him, girl,' whispered Morgana, totally absorbed in the interview.

'Well, they are biologically related to their parents, of course. But are they really the same as them? No, they are not. Now, for the first time in their lives, they have the opportunity to fully comprehend what it means to be an Arneshian; to encounter likeminded people who appreciate the extent of their gifts.'

'Gifts?' asked Mielowa suspiciously.

'The Grey Arts of course, my dear. Our unique talent for scientific logic is something to be nurtured, not feared.'

'And what gives you the impression that the Arneshians living on Earth are so feared by us?'

'Wrong question,' muttered Julius, shaking his head.

T'Rogon looked at her with a triumphant smile. 'What about the chokers they are forced to wear, Ms Mielowa? Isn't that a sign of fear? Suppressing the natural development of their brain, just in case an individual chooses to do wrong – as if doing wrong was only possible for an Arneshian. What about the others? Shouldn't we put a choker on everyone with mind-skills then, so nobody can do harm?'

Julius caught the briefest hint of dark shadow passing over T'Rogon's face as he said that last sentence, but he quickly regained his composure. Julius wondered if anyone else had noticed it.

'Ambassador,' said Mielowa, after a brief pause, 'exactly what do you have in mind for these visits?'

'All we ask is that any Arneshians wishing to meet with us, send us their files. We would then organise their visits and, of course, pay for all their travel expenses.'

'You tricky b-'

'Shhh,' said Morgana, leaning closer to the screen.

'How long would these visits last for?'

'Why, as long as they want them to. In fact, if they so wish, they could simply decide to return to Arnesh with us. Our ship, Taurus One, is rather large, and it can accommodate everyone quite easily.'

'That's why he brought that mammoth ship!' cried Julius, feeling completely outraged. 'He knew it all along.'

'Back to Arnesh?' asked Mielowa, sounding understandably flabbergasted.

'Why not? If they should wish to live in a world where being an Arneshian is the norm, who are you to stop them? We have made some terrible mistakes, I know, but those days are behind us now.' Seeing as Ms Mielowa had gone silent and seemingly incapable of answering back, T'Rogon continued with his recruitment pitch. He looked straight at the camera, as if he was addressing the Nuarns directly. 'If you stay here you will never be able to enjoy a career in space, nor to develop your true path. Most of all, you may never get to meet anyone who will love you as an equal. Salgoria is giving you the chance for a new life, a new career. Who can stand in your path? No one can.'

Ms Mielowa gulped and turned to the camera, looking totally shell-shocked. 'You saw it here first. Iryana Mielowa, Space Channel.'

'That was unbelievable,' said Morgana, turning her PIP off. 'Julius? Hey, where are you going?'

But he had already disappeared inside the school.

*

A few minutes later, Julius was sitting at his desk, talking to his family. 'What did Michael do when he heard the news?'

'Nothing, actually,' said Rory. 'He just stared at the screen, as if we weren't in the room at all, but I could tell he was upset.'

Julius breathed a little easier. As ridiculous as the thought was, he had half feared that his brother would say he wanted to go visit the Arneshians.

'So he really had nothing to say?'

Rory shook his head. 'He's been even quieter lately, like there's something on his mind. He won't talk to us though. And he's been watching the Space Channel. Regularly.'

'You're kidding,' said Julius, knowing how little interest Michael had for anything remotely factual. Mentioning the news to Michael was like mentioning Spaceology to Julius: a sure way of sending them both to sleep.

'Your mum has tried to ask him about it, but he just shrugs his shoulders and changes topic.'

Julius sighed. 'Can T'Rogon cause any *more* problems?'

'What really worries me,' said Rory, 'is the way that Paulo Trent has just laid down the red carpet for him. He's supposed to represent us and our best interests but, so far, he hasn't done much of that. If he doesn't stand his ground soon, T'Rogon could start a schism.'

'A what?'

'A separation. He's trying to bring division among us, to create a rift between Earthlings.'

'What a mess,' said Julius. 'I wish I could talk to Michael in person. I feel so bad being out of reach like this.'

'We'll all come up for the mid-winter holiday, son. You'll have your chance then. It'll be good for Michael to see you.'

'Definitely,' agreed Julius. 'Just try not to break your leg again, Dad.'

'As long as your brother stays away from stairs and socks, I'll be fine. Just book us somewhere nice this time, no junkyards please.'

Julius chuckled. Two years ago, Michael had insisted that they have their meal in a massive holographic junkyard, which didn't go down well with Jenny. 'I'll take care of it. Don't worry.'

'Good. Stay out of trouble, Julius.'

'Yeah, I'll see what I can do,' he replied. 'But apparently I'm "an irresponsible boy, lacking in leadership skills", in case you haven't read the latest news.'

'I always knew you'd make us proud,' said Rory, with a grin.

'Thanks. Bye, Dad,' said Julius.

Rory waved and the image faded to black.

*

'Never rains – it pours, ay?' said Faith.

'What?' said Julius, finishing off his daily entry in his logbook. 'You talking about having the Arneshians as our new friendly neighbours, or the fact that they'll soon be recruiting an army from among our very own families?'

'Well yes, there is that of course,' said Faith, who was sporting two big bags under his eyes. 'But right now I've got this assignment to finish for Beloi on synaptic junctions for tomorrow, and the deadline for Pete's competition is the day after that. I need a holiday already.'

'I thought your design was finished,' said Julius.

'It's presentable, but I feel like it'll never be done. I keep finding bits that are missing, or need to be changed.'

'I think you're worrying too much. You've been pouring over those schematics for months now.'

'But what if I've forgotten something essential and the ship blows up?'

'Faith, you don't actually have to *build* the thing. Let Pete worry about the details.'

'I can't, Julius. I'm designing it, so it's me responsibility.' And with that he hunched over his screen again and started to scan every inch of the blueprint.

'I'll leave you to it, then …' said Julius, packing up his things. Faith was so absorbed in his work that he didn't even notice him leaving. Julius headed out of the lounge and over to the mess hall, aiming to have a little downtime with a book before dinner. He had been so busy lately that he was still on the same page he had started three weeks ago. He crossed the mess hall, passing by a small group of 4MAs huddled at one of the long tables, fully engaged in game chat. The kitchen wasn't open yet, so he walked outside into the garden. A few students were milling about here and there, but there was no trace of Skye or Morgana. Now that he thought of it, he hadn't seen either of them since the end of their Shield class but, given that all he wanted to do was chill out and read, it wasn't necessarily a bad thing. He sat down, switched on his PIP and looked through his files, until he found the book he was reading – an ancient classic about androids and electric animals. Just as he had settled down and started the new chapter, his PIP vibrated to indicate an incoming vidcall. He sighed and pressed the Onscreen button. 'What's up, Miller?'

'Jules! You wouldn't believe where I've been!'

'Erm … Satras?'

'Yeah, yeah, but where, exactly?'

'I don't-'

'Never mind – you couldn't begin to guess, anyway. Gabriel List asked me to test the very latest sim-dating programme to hit the holo-world!'

'Wow,' said Julius, not quite sure what to make of that. 'I'm not even gonna ask why he picked you.'

'I know, right?' said Skye, obviously pleased with himself. 'Anyway, stay where you are, 'cause I've got loads to tell you!'

'All right. I'll see you soon,' he answered, closing the link. 'Honestly.' He shook his head and went back to his book. He had barely managed to read four lines, when his PIP vibrated again. He rolled his eyes, then accepted the vidcall. 'Hi Morgana.'

'*Kombanwa*,' she said, greeting him in Japanese. 'I'm on my way back. Where are you? Wait, I can see the oak tree behind your head. I'll be there shortly. Got loads to tell you.'

'Where have you been?'

'Tuala, visiting Maks.'

'Why?' The question was out of his mouth, before he could stop himself.

'What do you mean, why?' asked Morgana, sounding genuinely puzzled.

'I meant, I thought he was in detention or something,' Julius responded, trying to sound casual about it.

'Yeah, he's banned from Satras, but not from his friends! Besides, it's partly my fault, so I figured he'd appreciate the gesture.'

'Oh, I bet he does,' mumbled Julius.

'You OK? You seem a bit weird,' she asked, her head cocked to one side.

'I'm good. Just tired, that's all. I'll see you at dinner, all right?'

'Soon,' she said cheerfully, and signed off.

Julius found his bookmark for the second time but, no matter how much he tried, he had lost his focus. 'She didn't need to go see him, really,' he muttered to no one in particular. 'He's only in detention. And why am I even bothered? I'm not her guardian. I just don't want her to get hurt, that's all … and now I'm talking to myself. Great.' Shaking his head, he forced himself to concentrate, leaned back against the tree trunk, and resumed his story.

'McCoy!' shouted Skye, barely thirty seconds later, from the entrance to the mess hall. 'You've got to hear this!'

Julius sighed in resignation and closed his PIP. 'I'll never finish this blinking book.' He stood up, brushed the grass from his trousers and headed back inside.

Skye managed to entertain most of the 3MAs throughout that evening, with every last little detail of the new sim-dating programme. It wasn't going to be available until the following year but, judging by the keen interest among the students, Julius could guess how successful it was going to be.

'So, what can you do with it?' asked Leanne.

'Many things,' replied Skye, sounding as confident as a seasoned salesman. 'Not only can it create the perfect date, according to your specific requirements – it can also help build up your confidence.'

'How?' asked Barth, immediately interested.

'Let's say you've never dated before, or you don't know how to dance, or how to do small talk; the programme can teach you, using one of its own super-duper holos. Once you've downloaded the software onto your PIP, you're free to create any holo-character you like.'

'Can you make it look like someone you know?' asked Siena.

'Absolutely. You just upload the matrix and the software will do the rest. You thinking of anybody I know?' he added, mischievously.

'None of your business,' she said quickly, blushing furiously.

'Did you actually try it?' asked Lopaka, in awe.

'Oh yeah,' said Skye. 'And believe me, you can't tell the difference.'

There were several murmurs of approval at that.

'Where will it be, Skye?' asked Gustavo.

'Mr List says it's primarily been created for the crews that have to go on deep space journeys, to minimise their loneliness. On Zed, you can get it at the Palace; you just book a room and, once you're there, you download the programme onto your PIP. Easy as that.'

'Nice one. I've got to tell Yuri!' said Gustavo, and hurried off.

Excited by the news, most of the Mizkis went back to their own activities, leaving Barth with the Skirts.

'Sounds grand,' said Faith, cracking open a pistachio.

'Hmm … I don't know,' said Morgana. 'Surely it can't replace the real thing. What if you get all flustered and bothered, and then you go – hold on, this thing is fake?'

'Well, I do wanna get flustered and bothered, if you don't mind,' said Faith, making everyone laugh.

'He's right,' added Barth, thoughtfully. 'For some of us it may well be our only chance.'

'That's not true,' answered Morgana. 'You'll find your other half, one day.'

'And when I do, I need to make sure I don't cut her hair off by accident, like I did with you!'

Even Morgana had to join in on that one, despite how upset she had been about it at the time. 'All right, you win. The programme could help you be a little less-'

'Dangerous!' finished Faith.

'And you, Julius?' asked Skye. 'Are you gonna give it a go?'

'I don't seem to have a good relationship with holos,' he said half-heartedly. 'In case you forgot, Master Isshin tried to kill us all two years ago.'

'That was different,' said Skye, dismissing his answer with a wave of his hand.

'Well, if I do I'm not going to tell you,' said Julius, grinning.

'Oh, come on!'

Julius just looked back at him and grinned.

That night, after Skye had turned off the light, Julius found his thoughts turning to the sim-date programme. As the silhouette of his perfect date began advancing towards him, he realised that maybe, just maybe, he *would* try it out.

MID-WINTER BLUES

Julius, Skye and Morgana were standing outside Pete's shop, in Satras, waiting for Faith. It was Thursday the 1st of December, the deadline for the spaceship competition. Faith had been so eager to hand in his project that he had left Tijara right after his Martial Arts class without even stopping to take a shower. The others decided to do likewise, and boarded the Intra-Rail, trying to keep out of the other passengers' nostrils as much as possible.

'It's done,' said Faith, finally hovering out of the shop.

'When will you know?' asked Julius.

'Mid-summer, probably. It depends how many entries they get.'

'I bet you feel relieved,' said Skye, patting him on the shoulder.

'You have no idea,' he said. 'I don't think I've ever worked so hard in me life.'

'Then you deserve a prize,' said Morgana. 'How about an ice-cream?'

'I think I fancy something savoury, actually.'

'I know just the place,' said Morgana. 'It's this new deli, on the fourth tier. It's called "Hallouminati: The People of the Cheese". Kaori says it's yummy!'

'What the heck kind of a name is that?' asked Skye.

'Sounds good to me,' said Julius. 'Let's go.'

When they got there, they found a small queue of people waiting to be served, so they joined in. Intrigued by the various pungent smells, Julius peered inside. The shop had several deli counters; four of which were filled to the brim with cheeses from all over the Earth. Julius read some of the labels, Parmigiano, Camembert, Emmental, Pecorino, and a variety of blue cheeses; a fifth counter contained several different types of bread, everything from rolls, to baguettes, to large, brown crusted loaves; finally, a sixth one contained fresh fruits, cut into slices. This sight, especially after three hours of exercise, made him simply ravenous. He looked at the menus on the walls, trying to decide what to order.

'Half a baguette with Pecorino and pears, please,' asked Julius, once he reached the till. He was just about drooling by then. He handed over two Fyvers and scurried along to the counter, where two men were preparing the food with practiced care.

'There you are,' said one of them, handing him a plate.

Julius thanked him and headed for one of the small circular tables outside the shop. Soon, the others joined him.

'Come to papa,' said Skye, lifting his filled roll in both hands.

'You look like an anaconda trying to eat a sheep,' said Julius, staring at Skye's cavernous mouth.

'It's called cranial kinesis,' said Skye, pausing for a moment. 'That's why snakes can eat animals that are bigger than them. I looked it up 'cause I wanted to know if I could do it too, but no.'

'You're kidding, right?' asked Morgana.

Skye just winked at her and bit into his food.

'Hey look,' said Faith, pointing to his right, along the path. 'The GMs.'

When he turned around, Julius was surprised to see Freja, Kloister and Milson walking along the path, seemingly window shopping. Then he realised that it wasn't just the three of them; they were accompanied by a young couple and a small girl which he guessed must be their daughter.

'How odd to see them outside of school like this,' said Morgana.

Julius agreed with that but, then again, of course they must also have an actual life. 'Maybe one of them is related to the couple,' he said.

'Wow,' said Faith. 'Check her out.'

He was pointing at the girl, who was standing in front of a large flower pot, which was twice her size. Her blond curls were held back by a red hair band, highlighting the delicate features of her young face; she was wearing a white and red dress, with black, shiny shoes and short white socks. All in all, she had a doll-like look about her. She couldn't have been more than seven years old, but Julius could tell that she was Zed material: one of her little hands was stretched towards the pot and, with no apparent difficulty, she was lifting it up and spinning it in a small circle.

'Farrah!' called her mother, hurrying towards her.

As the child was scooped up, Kloister was quick to freeze the pot in midair, before it could crash back down again.

'Nice save,' said Faith, turning back to his food.

Julius watched Edwina Milson caress the little girl's cheek, before the whole group resumed their stroll, and eventually disappeared from view.

*

With December came the realisation that the Earth President was not going to do anything to stop T'Rogon's open invitation to the Nuarns. Whether he wouldn't, or couldn't do so, Julius didn't know but, as the weeks passed, an increasing number of them began to apply for the trip to Taurus One. The 14th was the date set for the first group of travellers to journey into Zed orbit, and Julius had been scanning the news since early that morning. The Space Channel had sent its reporters to all the Zed departure centres involved, to gather as many interviews as they could. By lunchtime, there were at least fifty of these in the archives, and Julius scanned through them eagerly on his PIP.

'Let's watch that one,' said Faith, leaning closer to him. 'It's from the centre where we took off from Earth.'

Julius obliged him, while slowly eating his lentil soup. As he pressed the button, the Prague departure centre appeared in the background, where a man carrying a suitcase was being interviewed. The first thing Julius noticed was the man's choker, which was still visible under his shirt.

'Mr Schneider,' said a man's voice from out of shot, 'you are the ten-millionth Nuarn to have booked this trip. What made you decide to visit the Taurus One?'

'Mainly curiosity, I guess,' answered the man. Although he spoke in the common speech, his accent sounded northern European to Julius. 'As it is, I would never have been allowed to leave Earth otherwise. T'Rogon is giving me that opportunity.'

'Aren't you afraid of boarding what we always believed to be an enemy ship?'

'I don't know about being afraid, but an enemy ship? I don't think so. Ambassador T'Rogon said it right: we are alike. I have nothing to fear from them.'

'How long do you plan to stay on board?'

'As long as they let me. This may well be my only chance, so I intend to take full advantage of it.'

'Why the large suitcase?'

'I might just decide to stay ... indefinitely. In any case, I would like to be prepared.'

The interviewer thanked Mr Schneider, who picked up his luggage and headed for his shuttle.

Julius closed his palm, deactivating his PIP, and shook his head. 'We should have seen this coming.'

'You heard Beloi,' said Faith. 'Diplomatic immunity. We couldn't have prevented their visit.'

'Dad said Salgoria is trying to create a schism, a division among us.'

'That sounds about right,' said Faith, finishing his breaded escalope. 'There's three billion of us and about 50 million Nuarns on Earth, and T'Rogon wants to separate us.'

'Well, he's not getting Michael, that's for sure,' Julius said bitterly.

'Has he said anything?' asked Faith, quietly.

'He won't talk about it,' answered Julius. 'I'm hoping to have a chat at our midwinter meal. It's long overdue.'

Faith nodded. 'If there's anything I can do ...'

'Thanks, mate. I'll keep that in mind.'

*

The last day of term flew by quicker than Julius could have expected. By all accounts, Friday the 24th was supposed to be an exciting day from start to finish: there were only two hours of lessons in the morning – Telekinesis with Professor King and his infamous stuffed reindeer, Jeff – followed by a free afternoon to spend in the Palace before it was shut down for the mid-winter meals. Yet, Julius wasn't as thrilled as the others were, his mind preoccupied with his brother's visit.

Because of the Tijaran school's upcoming relocation to Gea One in a week's time, the Mizkis had to see their families earlier than previous years, that coming weekend, leaving Julius with less than two days to decide what to book for his meal.

'I think I'll go somewhere in Polynesia,' said Faith to the others, at lunch.

They had gone back to the Hallouminati shop which, incidentally, was the only place with a few free tables.

'I want a very Earthy place this time,' said Julius.

'Why?' asked Morgana, slicing her roll into smaller, more manageable pieces.

Julius looked at the Palace, in the distance. He was trying to voice the thoughts that had been bouncing around in his mind over the last few days. 'If Michael ... if he should decide to go to Taurus One, they would probably give him as much technology as he wants.'

'But they can't give him Earth,' Faith finished for him.

Skye and Morgana nodded in agreement.

Julius looked at them, relieved that they had understood him so quickly. 'Earth is his home, and if we go somewhere that feels like it, then maybe Michael …'

'Makes sense,' Skye cut in. 'It'll help him see what he would be missing.'

'Anywhere special come to mind?' asked Faith.

Julius thought back to their childhood and the things they had done together. 'We used to go camping up north – I mean in the Highlands – Glen Affric.'

'Oh Julius, it's so beautiful up there!' cooed Morgana.

'Michael loved it there too,' said Julius. 'He would spend the whole day chasing red squirrels and watching out for Golden Eagles; Dad would fish for our dinner and Mum would get the barbecue going.'

'It sounds like a grand place,' said Faith. 'Go on and book it.'

Julius nodded. There were many other places that brought back good memories, but somehow Glen Affric felt right.

As soon as they had finished their food, they headed for the Palace, where they had to queue for ten minutes before they could all make their reservations. With that concern out of their minds, the Skirts treated themselves to their last Fight game of the year.

*

When Michael stepped out of the shuttle, Julius was caught by surprise: the person standing between Rory and Jenny wasn't the sweet little kid that Julius had seen the year before on this very same platform, but a young teenager almost as tall as he was, with a long, light brown fringe hiding his dark eyes. He had a troubled look on his face, as if some mental struggle was raging inside his head and a little crease had formed between his eyebrows, similar to the one his dad had had for years. There were no two ways about it – Michael looked older.

It was Jenny who hugged Julius first – something his brother had eagerly done in previous years – followed by an affectionate embrace from Rory. In stark contrast, Michael's arms felt almost limp around Julius' shoulders, and his smile had lost some of its natural warmth. As he stood there, holding his brother, Julius felt as if there were so many things he wanted to say, but no words were actually coming out. On second thoughts, that was probably a good thing: the Zed docks were hardly the right place for a deep and meaningful chat.

'How was the trip?' asked Julius, grabbing his mum's case.

'Great!' answered Rory, beaming. 'But I'm looking forward to getting to our hotel right now. I'm knackered.'

'I'm so happy to see you, Julius,' said Jenny, squashing him against her and kissing his cheek.

'Mu-um!' he said, blushing. 'Not here.'

Jenny laughed amiably. 'You'll never be too old for your mum's kisses, my boy!'

'He probably has a girlfriend around here, somewhere,' said Rory cheekily. 'You'll ruin his star-rep.'

'No way!' answered Julius quickly. 'That's Skye's thing. I'm busy as it is, anyway.'

'He's only fourteen, Rory,' said Jenny. 'Let him enjoy his youth without the pangs of the heart. Speaking of, how's Morgana? I saw a picture of her the other day, and she looks so beautiful.'

'Speaking of? What's she on about?' thought Julius to himself; then out loud, 'She's good. Her folks arrived early this morning.'

'You give her a big kiss from me, if I don't manage to see her.'

'A kiss? Unlikely,' he said, horrified.

'It's just an expression!' said Jenny, sounding amused.

Rory laughed. 'Don't worry dear, he'll not be so horrified at that thought soon enough.'

'Can we just change topic, please?' Julius implored.

'All right,' said his dad, grinning. 'So, what did you book for us this time?'

'I thought it would be nice to go up north,' he said.

'Are we going to Glen Affric?' said Michael suddenly.

Julius was overjoyed to see a smile light up his brother's face; he had chosen well after all. 'Aye. I got us our usual cabin and kept all the dragonflies, but completely left out the midges.'

'Nice one,' said Michael, visibly relaxing.

'Excellent choice, son,' said Rory. 'We all love that place.'

Feeling heartened by their reaction, Julius led them to their hotel with a lighter step, anticipating a really good mid-winter meal.

*

The midday sun was shining down on the glen, the heat intensifying the smell of the surrounding pines, birches and oaks; the grass was green and punctuated by many colourful plants, from creeping ladies' tresses to twinflowers. The cottage stood by the shore of Loch Beinn a' Mheadhain, whose still surface reflected the eagles soaring above it. Rory and his sons were standing by the water, armed with fishing rods and patience, while Jenny was getting the barbecues going and preparing the side dishes.

Julius had ensured there would be plenty of fish and meat in the fridge since, simulation or not, it wasn't guaranteed that they would actually catch anything. He felt good standing there, barefoot on the fresh grass, surrounded by his family. He had calibrated the artificial sun to give off a moderate warmth, and when both him and Michael had taken their t-shirts off, he had to work hard to convince his mum that they didn't need any sunscreen.

'It's only a programme!' he said, trying to avoid the dollop of cream that she was chasing him with.

'You're Scottish, dear,' she said, unconvinced. 'You would burn under a desk lamp.'

Eventually, Julius had to let her have her way, so that he could carry on fishing in peace.

They sat down for their meal around two in the afternoon, under the branches of an old pine tree. The air was fresh and filled with the smell of grilled meat. Julius found himself answering the usual barrage of questions in front of a kingly food spread: sausages, lamb cutlets, trout, salmon, pickles, coleslaw and fresh bread. He had even remembered to order dessert, so the family was treated to a delicious wild berry cheesecake, with plenty of coffee and fresh juice to go with it.

As the afternoon passed in a sort of peaceful haze, Julius realised that he would have to pluck up the courage to have a proper chat with Michael. He felt that the day had been relaxed enough to put his brother in the right mood for talking, or at least he hoped so.

'Hey bro,' he said, sitting up in his deck chair. 'Why don't we give those two some privacy and go for a walk?'

Michael seemed unsure.

'Come on. We can go check if the squirrel house is still there,' said Julius. 'Besides, I need to walk off all that food.'

'All right,' he said, standing up.

Julius threw a glance at his folks, and saw his dad nodding knowingly. They started off along the shore, following a small path which skirted the edge of the forest. A group of dragonflies hovered above the water while, in the forest, a Scottish crossbill sung its unique song.

Julius had been thinking all morning about an ice-breaker to use with Michael, but now he was completely at loss for what to say. Eventually, it was Michael that took the lead.

'Did you tell your friends about me?' he said.

'Of course. As soon as I got back to school.'

'And what did they say?'

'They were really sorry that you couldn't join us. They were looking forward to you being on Zed.'

'It didn't bother them knowing I'm a Nuarn?'

'Why should it? You're still Michael to them,' said Julius.

'And to you? Am I still your brother, Julius?'

Julius stopped abruptly and turned to face him, putting both hands on his shoulders. 'Yes, you are. And don't you ever doubt that, you hear me? What I said last year is still true: you are a real McCoy, no more, no less.'

Michael looked at him and nodded. Then he carried on walking. Julius followed him, aware of the fact that his brother had a worried look back on his face.

'I always wanted a career in space-'

'But you still can, Michael.'

'Let me finish,' he said, a bit louder.

Julius was startled by the seriousness and hurt in his voice. No twelve-year-old should feel like that.

'I wanted to build ships and watch them fly across the galaxies. I wanted to live on the Zed space stations and teach others how to fix things. That was my dream, and it's all gone now.'

'You can still do that,' said Julius, aware of the pleading in his own voice.

'No I can't, and you know it. Nuarns aren't allowed in space. The closest I can get to it is by visiting you on Satras. And that will also end when you graduate, in three years time. All I can do on Earth is build spare parts for shuttles; end of story.'

'How do you know all this?' asked Julius, genuinely surprised.

'It was in the leaflets I got from Taurus One.'

Julius' jaw dropped an inch. 'From the Ambassador?'

'Yes. They sent them to all us Nuarns, explaining about the travelling procedures.'

'But ... but you're not really thinking of going, are you?' he said, stopping dead in his tracks. 'T'Rogon is a manipulative oaf, who's trying to take you away from us, your families, for some nasty reason of his own. They've already cheated during our game and now they're trying to trick you all!'

Michael paused, lost in thought for a moment, but it didn't last long. 'T'Rogon said that I can be an engineer if I want, or a pilot. There are no restrictions on Arnesh for what I can or can't do.'

'Arnesh ...' Julius' jaw had dropped another inch, while his eyes were widening in disbelief.

'They would get rid of this ... dog collar, for a start, and give me a circlet.'

'A circlet?'

'Yeah, like the one T'Rogon wears; that all Arneshians wear. It's like a crown that amplifies our Grey skills.'

Julius' surprise gave way to anger and he felt it slowly mounting in his body. Trying hard to keep his voice level, he asked, 'And what else is he going to give you?'

'A job, a school to go to – like Zed, but for kids like me. He can give me a future I'll never get here.'

'Michael, are you seriously telling me that you would leave all of us behind, your real family, to join a bunch of folks who have been trying to kill us for the last 230 years? Folks who can't even win a game fair and square?'

'He told us that you people would say that.'

'*You people?*' Julius was furious. He could feel hot energy surging along his arms, making his fingertips tingle. The last time that had happened, he had been facing Red Cap. But Michael was not an Arneshian, only a scared kid who had just been given a shortcut, right out of the frying pan and into the fire. He needed to calm down, before his powers messed up this situation even more. He took a deep breath and started walking again. Eventually, Michael followed him.

'I realise this must have been tough for you.'

'You do, Julius? How exactly? How can a White Child, the Solo champion of Zed, possibly know what it feels like to be a Nuarn, to be destined to a second class life, while everyone else around him has it all? How can you?'

Julius was stunned to a halt again. Where was this bitterness coming from? It was as if a dam had been broken, and all his brother's feelings from the last few months had finally been unleashed. 'Michael, bad things happen to everyone in life. Look at Faith, without the use of his legs forever, without a chance to get back the freedom he so wants, and yet he copes! Why can't you adapt too?'

'Because I have a choice!' he shouted.

Julius watched as the tears gushed out and ran down Michael's cheeks, glistening in the afternoon sun. Everything was silent around them, except for the buzzing of the dragonflies. Michael dropped to his knees and buried his face in his hands, sobbing. Julius' anger immediately dissipated and he knelt down by his brother's side, hugging him tightly, like he had done so many times over the years.

'Why?' he kept saying as he sobbed. 'All I wanted was to join Zed ... with you.'

'I wanted that too Mickey and I'm so, so sorry. You have to believe me. If there was anything I could do to change this I would.'

Julius held him until he stopped shaking, then he let him go and sat on the ground. 'Mum and Dad, do they know?'

'No!' he said, panicking. 'Please don't say anything about this.'

'I won't. Why don't you find out about other careers in the Development Bureau? There's one on George Street, by Charlotte Square.'

'I only read what the Ambassador sent. I thought it would be the same thing.'

'Somehow I doubt it. Listen Mickey, if I were in your shoes I would also be curious to visit Taurus One. That, I can understand. I'm not sure how much Mum and Dad have been telling you, but in the last two years the Arneshians have tried to kill me and everyone else on Zed, at least twice. They even kidnapped Morgana.'

Michael looked quite stunned by that, but not as much as Julius would have hoped.

'And now they're here, like nothing ever happened. Well, forgive me, but I don't believe them one bit. Most of all, I don't want you in harm's way; that's why I'd rather you didn't go meet T'Rogon.'

'Well … I'll ask Dad to take me to the bureau,' Michael said half-heartedly.

Julius had to be content with that for the moment. 'All right. Let's go back. They'll be waiting for us.' He stood up and helped Michael back to his feet. Somehow, this didn't feel like a victory to Julius.

The rest of the day flew by and Rory decided they should go for an ice-cream at Mario's Ice-Land. Jenny wanted to pick up a few things to take back with her, so after a quick supper, they said goodbye to their cabin and Glen Affric.

*

Julius and his family left the Moon-Hole Inn around 10:00, the morning after, and went for breakfast at Global Brioche. By the time they reached the docks it was close to midday. As they stood by their shuttle, Jenny performed her last-minute dispensing of hugs while Rory made the usual list of recommendations. It always pained Julius watching his parents go away; he missed them very much, but there was little he could do about it.

Before seeing his brother off, Julius took him to one side. 'I know I'm not around as much as I would like,' said Julius, 'but if you ever need to talk about something – anything – you call me, all right?'

Michael nodded. He looked a bit better than yesterday, but he was still unusually quiet.

'Will you remember to check the bureau tomorrow?' asked Julius, hopefully.

'I will.'

It wasn't much, but it would have to do. 'Take care, little bro.'

'You too, Julius,' he said.

As he turned, Julius saw Ambassador T'Rogon walking along the platform, and realised with dread that he was about to walk past them, escorted by two of his men. Alarmed, Julius tried to think of a way to hide Michael from view, but couldn't, at least not without making the situation worse. A few seconds later, Julius found himself face to face with T'Rogon.

The Ambassador seemed as surprised as Julius was to be meeting him like this. Instinctively, Julius had shoved his brother behind his back, worrying that the Arneshians would see Michael's choker and try to use it as ammunition against him later on. There was an awkward moment of silence, where they all stood there, not knowing what to say. Julius knew that T'Rogon could see Michael very well, but he still hoped the choker would remain hidden from his view.

Just then, to Julius' relief, Master Cress emerged out of nowhere and stepped between them. 'Ambassador, a word if I may,' he said firmly.

Julius, who couldn't afford to forget protocol, bowed quickly. But, as he straightened up, he was certain that T'Rogon had clearly seen Michael's choker. A tiny snarl curled the corner of the Ambassador's mouth briefly, making Julius' skin crawl.

'Was that really T'Rogon?' asked Michael, once they had moved away.

'Yes,' said Julius, trying to calm his nerves.

'He looks so normal,' said Michael.

'He's not a nice guy, believe me.'

'Why did you hide me from him? Are you ashamed of being seen with a Nuarn?'

'No. It's not that. I had to because-'

'Never mind. I don't need your explanations,' he said.

'Michael, please,' said Julius, trying to grab his arm.

His brother shook him off curtly, and boarded the shuttle without turning back.

GEA ONE

On Saturday the 31st of December, all students had to collect their uniforms for the ball from Twitch and Stitch, an operation that took up the best part of the morning. It seemed that most of the Mizkis had left this task to the very last minute. After a stop at Going Spare, so Morgana could choose her birthday present, and a quick bite at Hallouminati, the Skirts headed back to school.

The Tijaran Mizkis had been asked to assemble in the hangar by 14:00. When Julius arrived on the main platform overlooking the shaft, he leaned over the rail to look down. The five decks, stacked one beneath the other, opened outwards like a huge fan. The first three decks were for the Cougars, and the last two for the Storks.

'Look! The decks are moving,' said Morgana, pointing down.

Julius watched as the decks shifted to the right, exactly like a fan would fold in on itself. From the bottom of the shaft a new, long deck began to surface, coming to a stop where the first one had been just a moment before. Smoothly, six different new decks fanned out to the left, each one riddled with small shuttle pods.

'Mizkis,' called Captain Foster, from a raised ledge.

The students turned to face him and fell silent at once.

'First years to the first deck; seconds to the second deck, and so on and so forth.'

'Let's go, let's go!' chirped Morgana, visibly thrilled.

'Here we go again,' said Julius, allowing her to drag him by the arm.

The Mizkis headed for the stairs and the lifts, trying to negotiate the crowd as they went. It took a while to reach the third deck, but eventually the 3MAs were all accounted for. Eight students had been previously selected by Clavel to pilot the shuttles and, of course, Morgana was among them. She headed for the closest one and hopped on, followed by Siena, Isolde and Jiao, all looking as giddy as she was.

'Over here, guys,' shouted Lopaka, boarding another shuttle.

Faith hovered inside and sat next to Lopaka, while Julius and Skye took the back seats.

Julius was beginning to feel a bit more relaxed, allowing the excitement of the weeks ahead to sink in. The shuttle itself wasn't all that thrilling, but it was part of the journey, after all. Professor Clavel had been teaching them how to pilot these crafts since September, to the point that, after four months, Julius couldn't stand the sight of them much anymore. They were effectively smaller versions of the Storks, but not as fast; their main purpose was for carrying people to and from space stations or starships.

'3MA Liway, requesting permission to take off,' said Lopaka into his microphone.

'Permission granted,' the control tower answered.

There were plenty of runways to choose from, so Lopaka picked the closest free one and hovered over to it. Julius remembered how Morgana had managed to trigger the safety speed protocol the last time they had flown through here, but then again, the Arneshians had been hot on their heels. This time though, Lopaka navigated the brightly lit tunnel surely and safely, flying steady behind Morgana's shuttle.

'So, Lopaka,' said Faith, trying to sound casual, 'how's your sister?'

Lopaka threw him a sideways glance. 'Nalani's good, thanks.' Then, with a grin, 'Should I tell her you're asking?'

'Mr Shanigan!' said Skye, patting his friend on the shoulder. 'Is there something you'd like to tell us?'

Faith was blushing slightly, but still managed a smile. 'So what? She's a lovely girl. Isn't that right, Lopaka?'

'That she is. And if your intentions are beyond gentlemanly, I'll cut your head off.'

Julius and Skye burst out laughing.

'I'm only kidding, Faith,' said Lopaka. 'I'd like you as a brother-in-law.'

'Thanks man, I appreciate the vote of confidence. But, uh, let's not get ahead of ourselves.'

'Siena may have some competition after all,' thought Julius with a grin.

The banter continued all the way into orbit, where the shuttle pod slowed down in the proximity of Gea One.

'Look at her,' said Faith, craning his head to take in the sight. 'She's so big.'

'She's tiny compared to my Terra 3,' said Skye. 'But she's pretty, I grant you that.'

As all of the shuttle pods reached the orbiting space station, they halted, waiting for permission to dock. Abruptly, the rotating outer rings halted, and several docking bay hatches opened simultaneously.

'3MA Liway, proceed to bay 36,' said the computer.

'Acknowledged,' answered Lopaka. He moved forward, steering gently into the opening; a large docking arm latched onto their shuttle and dragged it safely inside, while the pressure door closed behind them.

With the pod securely parked, Julius disembarked with the others, hoisting his rucksack up on his shoulder, and followed the rest of the students out of the hangar.

'Welcome aboard, Mizkis,' greeted Captain Foster over an intercom. 'There are six coloured lines flashing on the walls, each with the year group written underneath. I want you to follow yours back to the dorms on deck four. Find your rooms, drop your bags and report to the lounge, on deck three. There, you will collect the welcome pack for your PIP. It has an interactive map of Gea, your schedule for the rest of the day, the location of your classes, and the safety protocols. Read them thoroughly, and STAY OUT OF TROUBLE!'

'Will he ever tire of reminding us?' sighed Skye, shaking his head.

'As if,' added Julius.

'We're green,' said Faith. 'Me favourite colour.'

The 3MAs began to shuffle forward, their numbers swelling as more students joined in from different corridors. After a while, the green strip veered off to the right, along deck four. An archway opened onto a straight corridor, with eight doors to the left and eight to the right.

'Hey guys!' said Morgana, joining them. 'We're all on the same floor!'

'I bet that was Miller's idea,' said Julius.

'Anything to be close to the ladies,' said Skye, with a wink.

'That's us,' said Morgana, pointing at a door with her name on it. 'Jiao! Over here!'

'Catch you in a bit,' said Julius, waving goodbye before following Skye.

A minute later he was standing inside a well lit room, split into two distinct areas which mirrored each other. Julius took the bed to the right. It had a bedside table beside it and a metal chest at its feet. A door led off to the side, which he guessed must be for the bathroom, while a long rectangular window covered the length of the back wall, looking out into the vast expanses of space surrounding Gea One.

'Nice view,' said Julius peering out of it. He really did love it out here, with the calming hum of the engines, surrounded by stars, and knew that he was thoroughly addicted to life in space – it was impossible for him to now even begin to imagine his life without Zed. He felt a twinge of sadness as he tried to guess what he would have done if he had found himself denied the opportunity, like Michael had been.

'Ready Jules?' said Skye, snapping him away from his thoughts.

He nodded and together they headed out, collecting Faith and Morgana on the way. The green strips on the wall were proving to be very handy as, between the stairs, the lifts and the numerous decks, getting lost would be all too easy. They followed them to the lounge, where Julius was surprised at how large the area was. it seemed that the entire school was now assembled there, and there was still room to spare.

'Over here,' said Faith, hovering toward the left side.

Julius saw something resembling a hand-dryer attached to the wall; it had a yellow screen on its front, with the words "Welcome Packs" emblazoned on its face. Faith activated his PIP and held his hand under the scanner, until it beeped.

'That was easy,' said Julius, as soon as he had downloaded his pack.

Once they had all gathered theirs, they moved to a group of sofas at the far side of the room.

'Hey, look: they've got a Juice-Maid table!' said Morgana excitedly.

'A what?' asked Julius.

'Yeah, I've heard of them,' said Faith. 'Go on – show us how it works.'

Morgana sat up and placed her hand, palm down, on the glass top. 'Ginger Beer, Organic.' To the boys' surprise, a small hatch opened underneath her hand, and a glass filled with fizzy, opaque liquid pushed upwards into her grip. 'Cheers!' she said, curling her legs up under her.

'This is just!' said Julius, putting his hand on the machine. 'Peach tea, iced.' A glass promptly rose up from the hatch and he sipped it thirstily.

Skye quickly ordered a coconut milkshake, and Faith then ordered a lemonade.

'So, Julius,' said Morgana, 'you didn't really tell us about your mid-winter meal. How did it go with Michael?'

'I'm not too sure, actually,' he said, setting his glass down and checking that no one around them was in earshot. It was true, he still hadn't spoken to them about what had happened during, and after, their visit to the virtual Glen Affric. He had been waiting for the right moment but, for one reason or another, it had never come. 'I'm telling you guys, I've never seen Michael so bothered,' said Julius. 'It's like he's got the weight of the world on his shoulders.'

'But he didn't actually say he *was* going to join them though, did he?' asked Morgana.

'At first it was clear that he was going to,' answered Julius. 'Then, after our chat, he didn't seem quite so sure anymore. But I swear, for a moment there, I thought I was going to lose it.'

'What do you mean?' asked Skye. 'With Michael?'

'Yeah. You should've heard the stuff he was throwing at me. The bitterness in his voice. He said I couldn't possibly understand him, because of who I am, and that only T'Rogon had the solution to all his problems.'

'That's harsh,' said Skye.

'Maybe, but it's also normal,' said Faith. 'He's a twelve-year-old who's had his dreams shattered and, just when he's starting to deal with it, T'Rogon arrives and suddenly there's a way of getting those dreams back online. Wouldn't you have done the same?'

'Maybe … if I had never left Earth, or if I hadn't been here to see the things they did to us …' said Julius.

'Never. Not if you had been born on Terra 3 like me,' said Skye firmly.

'He received a leaflet from T'Rogon as well,' said Julius.

'The Ambassador's sure done his homework, hasn't he?' said Faith. 'With the kind of technology they've got, I bet that leaflet looks mighty appealing to a Nuarn.'

'What could they possibly have that we don't?' said Julius, throwing himself against the sofa in a huff. 'So far we've seen a psychotic V.I., a bunch of holos, and a few grey skinned folks; but what else?'

'I think it's simply that they're super-smart,' said Morgana.

'But what does that even mean?' said Julius. 'Aren't we smart too? We have Grey skills like them, and we know how to use them too. Look at Faith!'

'Thanks, buddy,' said Faith, raising his glass to him. 'But, it's more to do with faster brain processing and what they do with the knowledge. Their technology is much better than ours.'

'How so?' asked Morgana, sounding genuinely curious.

'During our engineering lessons, Professor de Boer told us a few things that … well, if you think what we have here on Zed is cool, think again, 'cause the Arneshian stuff is way ahead.'

'Like what?' asked Julius.

'Their ships can travel twice as fast as ours can; like, they can do 10,000 light years in five years.'

'No way,' said Morgana.

'Yes way,' continued Faith. 'And they use some kind of mystery power source for their drive cores, which we still can't identify. Plus, records from Marcus Tijara's own time said that their biggest ships were protected by some sort of barrier that could easily deflect the firepower of a small fleet.'

'Have we ever taken one of them down?' asked Julius, finding himself very much captivated by the discussion.

'Apparently so, but you need to get real close.'

'I bet their destructive power is mental,' added Morgana.

'Nuclear-like,' said Faith.

'And on that note, I'm off,' said Skye, quickly standing up.

'Where are you going?' asked Morgana.

'Somewhere else, where there's no admiring talk of Arneshian technology.'

'That's not what we were doing, mate,' said Faith, looking a bit hurt.

'I'd be careful then if I were you, or people may question your allegiance.'

'Come off it, Miller,' said Faith, testily.

'I question your sanity sometimes,' added Julius, with a raised eyebrow.

Skye waved his hand in front of him. 'Forget it guys. You know me and my views. I'll go have a chat with Valentina – she's prettier than you two. But not you, darling; no one is prettier than you,' he ended off, blowing a kiss at Morgana.

'Hang on a minute: who's this Valentina, now?' asked Julius, following Skye with his eyes as he walked away.

'5MS,' replied Morgana, shaking her head.

'What's got into him?' said Faith. 'We can never talk about Arneshians when he's around.'

'Maybe he's got space station syndrome or something,' offered Morgana.

'It's his thing,' said Julius. 'Forget about it.'

'I hope Michael doesn't buy into this recruitment nonsense, anyway,' said Morgana.

'I hope so too,' agreed Julius. 'But it's done now. I told him it would be a really bad choice. He's not stupid; he'll see it for himself. Besides, my folks would never let him.'

'That's good then,' said Morgana. 'It means that you can look forward to the New Year's party without any worries; and to my birthday cake!'

'As long as it's not a Supernova,' added Faith quickly.

'No chance! I'm expecting a dance too, by the way, with both of you.'

'With pleasure, milady,' said Faith.

Julius smiled. He was trying to relax his mind as much as he could; but, as long as the Taurus One stayed in orbit, he wouldn't truly be at ease. He wanted to know that T'Rogon was far away enough to pose no threat to his family.

They spent the rest of that afternoon going over their new schedules, checking out the Gea One's facilities and chatting with their classmates. Around 18:00, they decided to return to their dorms to get ready for the ball. Julius was really looking forward to it, especially because he had missed the previous one, following Clodagh Arnesh's hologram around Satras.

*

The main hall on Deck six had been chosen as the venue for the New Year party. The circular room was filled with round tables, covered with silver tablecloths, leaving space for a large dance floor in the middle. Even the teachers' usual long table had been replaced with two small ones, and moved to one side.

Julius, Skye, Lopaka and Faith arrived at 19:00 sharp, looking very smart in their dark dinner jackets. Once again, Faith had blackened the panels on his skirt to match everyone else's attire.

As the Tijaran Mizkis started to pour inside the hall, Julius decided that it was time to find a table. 'Let's get this one,' he said, moving to the right hand side.

The others quickly followed him, and stood beside the table. It wasn't long before a group of 3MAs girls entered the hall. Julius caught a glimpse of lilac satin emerging from between Siena and Isolde, and knew it was Morgana, sporting her favourite colour.

'Isn't she something,' said Lopaka, sounding quite awestruck.

'Yeah,' added Julius, completely transfixed.

'Who are you talking about?' asked Faith, looking at the pair of them.

Julius was startled out of his reverie and quickly looked at Lopaka. 'Um … they all do, right?'

Lopaka nodded happily. 'I wouldn't know who to pick, quite frankly.'

'Where are you: at the fruit market?' thundered Leanne Nord from behind them, before shouldering her way through the boys' ranks.

Julius had to quickly retrieve Faith, who had been sent drifting away as a result.

'I wouldn't pick you if you were the last apple on the Moon,' mouthed Lopaka. 'Unless I wanted a concussion, that is.'

Skye chuckled and waved to Morgana to join them. She smiled when she saw him and brought Siena and Isolde over with her.

'*Konnichiwa*,' she said.

Morgana was positively beaming, and why shouldn't she be, thought Julius: it was her fifteenth birthday, New Year's Eve, and she looked great.

'Ladies,' said Faith, with his usual flare, 'you're more beautiful every year.'

They all giggled and Siena began to blush too. Julius wondered how long it would take Faith to realise he had an admirer.

Soon, a group of waiters began to circle around the tables, serving champagne for the toast, a sign that the teachers would be arriving shortly. Five minutes later, Master Cress stepped into the hall and all Mizkis rose from their seats to face the door. Led by Grand Master Freja, the Tijaran teachers made their entrance, and headed to their tables.

'Please, be seated,' said Freja.

They all sat down and, within a few seconds, the hall was quiet.

'I welcome you all to celebrate New Year here tonight. This is the first time since I've been Tijara's Grand Master, that it will be taking place outside the walls of our school. And, I must say, the staff of Gea One have done a marvellous job, making us feel right at home.

'It has been quite the year, Mizkis. No Earthling had seen an Arneshian up close for 230 years, until now, and you have all been witnesses to this unprecedented event. We do not know how this story will unfold but, no matter the outcome, we will stay true to Tijara's code and, we shall lead our lives under the banners of honour, respect, loyalty and courage. A toast then, that the year 2858 be a peaceful and prosperous one for all mankind.'

'So let it be,' answered the students as one, before raising their glasses.

Once Freja was seated, the waiters filed in and began to serve the dinner. As always, the food was plentiful and excellent and, by the time the 6 Mizki Seniors stood up to open the dances, as per tradition, Julius was positively stuffed and content.

'Me skirt is about to burst,' said Faith grinning at Siena and patting his belly. 'I might just have to spread out, 'cause this food-baby is having a fit!'

She glanced at him, looking slightly disgusted.

'I don't think she needs to know that,' whispered Skye, leaning towards him.

'Huh?' said Faith.

'He's right, you know?' added Julius, holding his glass in front of his mouth.

'Your typical after-dinner chat with a lady should not include anything about digestion or bursting at the seams,' said Skye. 'It's not, uh, conducive.'

'Conducive to what?' asked Faith, sounding genuinely puzzled.

Skye looked at Julius, and rolled his eyes. 'McCoy, why don't you organise Morgana's cake while I explain a thing or two to this muppet about courting.'

'But I don't need-' started Faith.

'Shush,' said Skye. 'It's on the house.'

Julius grinned and left them there. Fortunately the girls were too engrossed in watching the 6MS students dancing to Strauss' waltz to notice what had been happening on the other side of the table. It took Julius a few minutes before he found a free waiter, but finally he managed to flag one down, and asked him to bring Felice Buongustaio's package to their table. Before leaving Zed, Julius had placed an order with Tijara's chef for Morgana's cake, as they did every year; only, this time, he had been too busy worrying about Michael to actually think of a specific request, so he had left it to Felice to choose. Now, as he returned to the table, he sincerely hoped they weren't going to get another Supernova. So, Julius was pleasantly surprised when the waiter arrived with a tray of chocolate cupcakes, topped with white icing in the shape of snowflakes, each one sporting a small sparkler.

'They're gorgeous!' cried Morgana, clapping her hands. 'Thank you so much!'

Once dinner was over, most of the Mizkis began to move to other tables, to visit their friends, while others took over the dance floor and began the partying.

'See you later guys,' said Skye, flattening his curls.

'And where are you off to?' asked Julius.

'Got a date with Valentina tonight,' he said. 'Don't wait up, dear.'

'Behave yourself, darling' said Julius, adjusting Skye's bow tie.

'Who's for a dance?' asked Isolde, looking in Julius' direction.

'Let's go!' said Faith, dragging Morgana and Siena to the dance floor.

'Um, I'll be right there,' said Julius vaguely. 'Gotta go see someone about something first. Bye.' And, with that, he rushed off, leaving a distinctly long-faced Isolde with the grinning Lopaka.

The evening passed by smoothly and pleasantly. As midnight arrived, Julius was engrossed in chat with a group of 4MAs who, just like him, had more interest in discussing the Zed Toon game than dancing about the place. He could hardly believe it when he checked his PIP and saw that it was past one o'clock. The party would finish at two and he was looking forward to a long lie-in the next day.

Refilling his glass at a Juice-Maid on one of the side tables, he moved over to the far wall and leaned against it, looking out at the dance floor. Faith was hover-dancing here, there and everywhere, accommodating as many requests from the girls as he could. All of them loved standing on his skirt's metallic hem and being whisked around, none more so than Siena, who was never far away. At one point in the course of the evening, Faith had even tried to see how many girls he could carry at any one time; that is, until Captain Foster threw one of his famous ice-stares in his direction, making it clear that there shouldn't be any more such experiments. Skye had spent the entire evening dancing and chatting with his new flame, Valentina, seemingly oblivious of the venomous stares that some of the other girls were throwing in her general direction. Julius hoped he wouldn't be treated to too many details over the next few days, especially because he could have sworn that the two of them had disappeared off for around an hour and a half before the bells had sounded at midnight.

All in all, it had been a good night. The Gea One had provided a smart setting for the party; Julius had chatted with loads of people, including some of the older Mizkis, and he had managed to stay away from any unnecessary dancing by starting random conversations whenever a girl came anywhere near his seat. A very good party indeed, by his standards. He was just beginning to think about bed, when Morgana emerged from the crowd and walked over to him, beaming from ear to ear.

'You've been rather popular tonight,' she said, grabbing his glass and taking a big gulp of juice. 'I heard a few girls complaining that they couldn't get you to dance at all! I wonder why that is.'

Julius smiled, 'I was bone-tired.'

'I'm afraid that doesn't work with me. And since you promised, will you give me the honour of this dance?' she said, bowing.

'Only 'cause it's your birthday,' he answered.

'Come on then,' she said, placing the glass down on the table and leading him to the dance floor by the hand.

The rest of the Mizkis were flitting around trying to find a partner for the final dances of the evening. Julius noticed Isolde on the edge of the room, whispering to another girl; judging by the cold stare she threw his way when she saw him on the dance floor with Morgana, it was clear she wasn't best pleased. He did feel a little sorry for her, but he couldn't exactly pretend to be interested in her when he wasn't.

'So,' he said, turning his attention to Morgana, 'good birthday then?'

'Cracking,' she answered.

Her head was resting on Julius' shoulder, so he couldn't see her face, but he could tell from her voice that she had had a great time.

'I love my presents, my cup cakes, and this place. I've danced and laughed a lot, plus I got such a lovely birthday card from Maks.'

Julius managed to not betray his surprise, and didn't reply.

'He wished me a great night, and said that he wanted to be here so badly,' she told him, with a giggle.

Julius became aware of a cascade of pink threads pouring out of Morgana's head as she spoke. He stretched his left hand out, behind her back, and saw that it was wrapped in the smoky wisps. He would rather have not noticed it, but there it was, plain as day: Morgana definitely had a crush on Maks.

'He's so sweet,' she continued.

'Mph ...' grunted Julius.

'Morgana lifted her head off his shoulder. 'What's wrong?'

'Nothing ...' he said, trying to sound convincing.

Morgana stopped dancing and looked Julius in the eyes. 'Are you playing big brother with me?'

'What ... No!' he said, but he could feel himself beginning to blush.

'Are you sure?' she asked again. 'Because every time I mention Maks you go all mumble-grumble on me.'

Julius saw a hint of amusement on her face and it dawned on him that his odd behaviour had been interpreted as him being protective, which was probably a good thing. Right then however, his brain was working solo, taking notice of a whole different set of things which were well and truly outside of Julius' control; and definitely not listed under the "big brother" category. Morgana's arms were still resting on his shoulders, and her face was a little too close for comfort to his own. He was also very aware now of how his hands had become glued to her back, the fingertips resting partly against the satin of her dress and, more distractingly, partly against her skin, which incidentally was the softest thing he had ever touched. And why were her eyes shining like that? Did her lips just look like juicy strawberries, or was it possible they also tasted like them?

'Julius? Hello? Anybody there?'

Her voice came out of nowhere, calling him back to reality. 'Sorry … I …'

'Never mind,' she said with a grin. She put her head back on his shoulder and began to dance again. 'You always were like a big brother anyway.'

'Great,' he thought. At this point he decided that it was best to finish the dance and leave the floor while he still had his dignity intact. He moved his hands so that they were resting completely against the surface of her dress, rather than her skin, and forced himself to think about Professor Gould's next checkpoint. But, try as he might, his thoughts kept creeping back to her raven black hair, tickling his face, and the alluring fragrance that wafted to meet him every time he leaned closer to her neck.

'Damn and blast!' erupted Faith, next to them.

Julius and Morgana turned to see what was going on.

'Me skirt is stuck,' he said, looking very apologetic. 'Sorry Siena, I think me dancing night is over. Julius, could you give me a hand?'

'Uh, yeah, yeah. Sure,' he answered, secretly relieved to be cutting his awkward dance short.

'Happy birthday,' he said to Morgana once more, letting her go.

She smiled at him and planted a light kiss on his cheek. 'Thank you,' she said.

A wave of shivers ran down his back. He turned away quickly, bumped into Faith, and self-consciously smoothed the creases on his shirt. Aware that he was acting a little weird at this point, he quickly wheeled the crestfallen Faith out of the room, stopping only to gather their dinner jackets under one arm. Morgana and Siena were left standing on the dance floor by themselves, not quite sure what to make of the odd couple that had just beaten a hasty retreat from the ball.

Once the two boys had reached their dorm, Faith turned to Julius. 'Sorry for interrupting you there, mate.'

'It's fine. I was done, anyway.'

'What an embarrassment. I really need to see Pete.'

'Are you gonna be all right?'

'Yeah. Thanks for the lift.'

'No worries. I'll see you tomorrow then.'

Faith nodded and entered his room. Julius, deciding that he'd had quite enough of the party and unfamiliar sensations in the pit of his belly for one night, also returned to his quarters. He stayed up to write a quick message to his family wishing them a happy new year, then watched the Zed Channel for a bit, which was showing scenes from the celebrations on Earth. It was only after he had showered and slipped under the covers that Skye walked in, and threw himself down on his own bed, smiling tiredly at the ceiling. His hair looked ruffled and there were faint traces of lipstick on his neck. Julius had his hand on the light switch, when Skye turned to face him.

'You like her, don't you?'

Julius felt his stomach contracting. 'Who?'

'You know who. I saw you on the dance floor.'

'She likes Maks.'

'That's not what I asked you.'

Julius looked at him for a few seconds, then rolled over and switched off the light. 'Good night, Skye.'

PLAYING WITH FIRE

For the first time in his life, but most likely not the last, Julius began the new year inside a space station. The Gea One was not as large as Zed but, for some reason, it never felt like a crowded environment to him. In eight days, normal lessons would resume, so he decided to make the most of his free time by reading, sleeping and generally relaxing with the rest of the Mizkis. The lounge on deck three was large enough to accommodate most of the students easily; there were cosy booths dotted about, equipped with soft sofas, screens, music systems, snack dispensers and Juice-Maids. In fact, there were so many of these that, whenever Julius agreed to meet the Skirts in one of the booths, they had to be very specific about which one, or they risked getting lost.

Julius was finally able to finish the book he had been trying to read since December – it left him thinking that being a bounty hunter would actually be a pretty cool job – and started a new one, another old saga, all about a dark tower. Reading allowed him to stop thinking about Michael, and that was a much-needed relief. The exodus of Nuarns had gathered pace and continued throughout the festive period, with hundreds of thousands of them leaving Earth every week. Iryana Mielowa had mentioned that as many as 40 million Nuarns had already left for good. Whenever the thought of it became overwhelming, Julius remembered that at least Michael was still at home. He clung to that thread of hope with all his might.

Thinking about his new feelings for Morgana was also something he was trying to avoid but, since Maks was constantly sending messages to her PIP, making her blush and giggle every time, this was proving easier said than done. Since New Year's Eve, he had been making a fair stab at figuring out what was going on in his head – and other parts of his body too.

Girls had never really meant much in his life up until then, in that sense anyway; he preferred friends to girlfriends, as that seemed a lot less complicated than a relationship. Even knowing that Isolde was interested in him had not changed that. He could see how she looked at him whenever their paths crossed, but he didn't have any strong feelings for her, except a slight discomfort at the thought that she wasn't happy because of him. Maybe the reason why Morgana had awoken these sensations in him, was due to their long-standing friendship, and the fact that he had always been able to relax around her.

'I'm not jealous,' he thought. 'I've always taken care of her, and I don't want her to get hurt.' Julius kept repeating these words in his head, like a mantra, over and over again, until eventually he convinced himself it was true. And if Maks ever did anything stupid, well, he would just show him what a White Child could do.

*

'Really looking forward to our first Pyro class,' said Skye, who was stretched out on one of the sofas in the lounge. It was the last Sunday of the mid-winter break and he was determined to enjoy every last minute of it by doing precisely nothing.

Julius was sitting on the opposite sofa, his legs resting on the coffee table, with Barth and Faith on either side. Morgana and Siena were reading a magazine on her PIP, scoring all the latest Earth fashion tips.

'I'm excited too!' said Barth.

Morgana looked at him. 'Now, remember Barth, where do you go and stand when we get to Pyro class?'

'On the opposite side of wherever you are?' he said, hesitantly.

"Atta boy!' She nodded and returned to her magazine.

'Who would have thought that Chan does Pyro classes too?' said Faith.

'Yeah, but who else is nuts enough for it,' said Skye.

'Maybe Gould?' ventured Julius. 'He does sleep with his Gauntlet under his pillow, after all.'

'No, no! According to Valentina, this is a side of Chan that we haven't seen yet.'

'You expect us to believe that you two actually *talk?*' said Faith, making the others chuckle.

'Laugh all you like,' answered Skye, with a "speak-to-me-when-you-reach-my-star-rep" look, followed by another that seemed to say, "as if".

'What time is it?' asked Faith, stretching. 'Me tummy's growling.'

'Let's go to the mess hall,' said Julius. 'I'm starting to get a wee bit peckish myself.'

'Ladies?' said Faith, turning to them.

'Later, thanks,' answered Morgana, without lifting her head from her PIP.

Julius thought that Siena looked sorely tempted to join them but, seeing as Morgana wasn't going, she seemed resigned to staying behind, and shook her head.

'I'll be there in a minute,' said Skye, who was busy texting on his PIP.

Faith motioned for Barth to come with them, and he leapt up, clearly pleased at being asked – Julius saw a green wisp rising from his head, a sure sign of his happiness, and smiled, seeing how much being included in their group meant to Barth.

When they entered the mess hall on deck two, many of the Mizkis were already assembled there, looking positively agitated. The students were talking to each others in hurried, low voices. Puzzled, Julius walked towards Lopaka's table, followed by the others.

'Hey guys,' he said, 'has something happened?'

Lopaka, Gustavo and Yuri made space for them on their bench.

'Some of the Arneshians have just come aboard,' whispered Lopaka; he pointed to his left. 'Over there.'

Julius spotted them immediately, and his jaw dropped. Seated at one of the corner tables were K'Ssander, his friend A'Trid, and one of T'Rogon's colleagues. They were eating with Master Cress and Professor Clavel.

'Why on Earth are they here?' asked Julius, not caring much just then if they overheard him.

'Who knows,' answered Yuri. 'I got here earlier on and saw them. Freja and T'Rogon were just leaving.'

'It looks like they're visiting us, or something,' said Gustavo.

Faith shook his head. 'How could Freja allow those cheating traitors onboard?'

'I don't think he has a lot of choice,' said Lopaka. 'With Paulo Trent opening Earth up like that, he's probably pressured the Curia into doing the same thing.'

'Or it could be a bargaining chip, for reopening the schools,' said Julius.

'How?' asked Barth.

'A show of good faith on Zed's part,' explained Julius. 'We show Trent that we're good hosts, with nothing to hide, and maybe he'll open up recruitment again.'

'So, basically we're sucking up to Trent,' summarised Gustavo.

Julius nodded. That was it, and it would probably continue that way until T'Rogon left orbit; judging by the impressive, steady numbers of Nuarns leaving each week, that could be sooner rather than later.

*

By the following morning, news of the Arneshian visitors had spread around the Gea like wildfire. Kept at bay by their teachers, the Mizkis had tried hard not to show any anger at their presence, but that was as much as the students were willing to give. As the Arneshians entered the mess hall, they were greeted by a wall of quiet disdain. Julius and the Skirts decided to make breakfast a quick business, and left as soon as they had finished their food, without even a glance in the direction of the visitors.

Once out of the mess hall, Faith touched one of the wall pads and said, '3MA, Pyro class, 09:00.'

Immediately, a green cursor appeared onto the right wall and shot ahead, indicating the path to their class. All lessons were to be held on deck five, which was spacious enough to hold both White and Grey Arts classes. They hopped into the lift; three floors down, as the doors opened, the green cursor was flashing for them to follow. It led them along a corridor, first right, then left, until eventually it came to a stop outside their classroom.

They stepped inside, and found themselves in a large room with metal walls. There were scorch-marks on all sides; most of all, on the ceiling. Several fire extinguishers were placed all around the floor, obviously ready to be used in case of things going wrong. Julius walked up to one of them and had a good look: it was shaped like an old style handgun; it was red and had several settings to choose from, according to the kind of fire that needed extinguishing. This one was already prepped for 'Pyro', and Julius wondered how the fire they would be creating in this class was any different from a natural one.

'Housekeeping is slacking a bit, I say,' said Faith, sliding a fingertip over the surface of the wall, which revealed a shinier surface beneath a layer of soot. Unable to resist, he hovered upwards, all the way to the ceiling, and began to graffiti the dark surface.

'Faith,' said Morgana, 'what are you doing?'

'Just a little piece of art,' he said, the tip of his tongue sticking out as he concentrated. 'There, that's much better,' he said, admiring his work from floating-distance.

Julius looked up, and started to laugh, quickly followed by Skye and Morgana.

Faith had sketched an Arneshian boy – K'Ssander, judging by the gigantic "K" on the front of his top – being chased by a robot version of Faith, seemingly intent on zapping his backside with his Gauntlet. The boy was shielding his rear as he ran, while a speech bubble floated above the robot's head, reading, "Eat me skirt!"

'Superb!' applauded Skye, wiping a tear from his eye.

'I didn't know you could draw like that, Faith,' said Morgana. 'I'm impressed.'

Faith hovered back down to the ground, savouring the moment. 'There's more where that came from,' he added.

Just then, they heard voices and steps approaching the door and, shortly after, their classmates filed into the room. Julius was still doubled over, laughing and pointing at the ceiling, so it didn't take long for them to join in.

Mariam Richards, a quiet 3MA from Lebanon, who was standing by the door admiring the sketch, glanced over her right shoulder and suddenly became very serious. 'Psst! Chan is coming!'

Everyone assembled, facing the door. The lights had dimmed a little outside in the corridor, and everyone had quietened right down inside the room. Julius heard a faint rustling, growing louder with each passing second. He tuned in and quickly realised that it was the sound a burning fire made. He supposed that he shouldn't have been surprised by that, given that they were about to start a Pyro lesson, but he certainly hadn't expected to hear it out there in the corridor.

When Professor Chan entered the room, there was a collective gasp: he was completely enveloped by tongues of flame, dancing around him, but showing no sign of causing any harm to his skin. The Mizkis stepped back, wide eyed in admiration.

'He certainly knows how to make an entrance,' said Skye, starting to clap. 'Go, Professor!'

Chan stopped in the middle of the room and bowed, the flames still encircling him. Then, he closed his eyes and, very slowly, the fire began to diminish, until the flames fizzled out and completely vanished. The Mizkis bowed, their respect for him now swelled to a huge level.

Unexpectedly, Chan turned toward the door, and said, 'Please, step inside and take those seats along the left wall.'

Everyone looked at the entrance expectantly, and all of their enthusiasm instantly disappeared like a soap bubble popping, as K'Ssander and A'Trid strolled into the room. Julius felt a surge of anger stir beneath his skin and, as K'Ssander's eyes passed in his direction, he instinctively moved to shield Morgana from sight. The Arneshian was obviously loving his visitor privileges, as the arrogant smirk on his face clearly illustrated. Julius knew well enough that they weren't to cause any trouble but still, he decided that K'Ssander should at least get a glimpse of how the Mizkis really felt. Holding the Arneshian's attention, he motioned with his head toward the ceiling. It took K'Ssander a few seconds before he saw the sketch but, as he did, the smirk slipped off his face, and his greyish complexion was momentarily flushed with fury. Julius had a grin of his own as he returned his attention to the teacher.

'Be seated,' said Chan, kneeling in front of the students.

'What you just witnessed will be the reward for some of you, if you work hard and follow my training properly. I say some because Pyrokinesis, or the ability to create fire, is not a given. Just because you've made it into Zed, does not mean you have this ability. And if you do have it, it still may never develop beyond the creation of a mere candlelight of flame.

'Our Arneshian guests are here to observe our lesson today since, as you all know, they are gifted with Grey skills, but not White ones, and will therefore never be able to make use of their inner energies, like you can.'

Julius caught sight of a wisp of gold shooting from Chan's head: it seemed the professor was proud of this difference, which gave them a clear advantage over the Arneshians.

'Before we start, Mizkis, I must impress on your young minds that, under no circumstances, will you use this mind-skill against a fellow human being. It is strictly forbidden, and carries the heaviest of penalties. As Mizkis, you have plenty of ammunition to use against a foe, without resorting to murder.'

'Why worry?' K'Ssander's question caused all heads to turn his way. 'If your life is in danger, you should use all you have, even if it means harming a human.'

Professor Chan regarded him for a moment. 'That, Mr K'Ssander, is a major difference between our people and yours.'

'Kick-ass, Chan,' Faith whispered into Julius' ear, who nodded, deeply satisfied by the Arneshians' lack of reply.

'And now,' continued Chan, as if nothing had happened, 'I am going to split you into three working groups, according to the strength of your Pyro abilities.' He turned to one side of the room, and made a shooing motion with his hands; in response, the wall seamlessly retreated a few hundred feet, leaving the students quite astonished.

'How big *is* Gea?' asked Morgana.

'Deck five and six are massive holographic structures,' explained Faith. 'And they can expand at will.'

'I will call you up one at a time and, when I do, you will create and throw a fireball at the far end, using a basic mind-kata. Understood?'

'Sir, yes sir,' replied the Mizkis.

'Warm up for a moment then.'

Julius was beginning to feel a bit uneasy. Showing the Arneshians their powers was a bit like showing your cards to an opponent before the game was even over. Thanks to the extra treatments he was receiving each week, he was sure that his skills had developed quite a lot recently, and he feared revealing what he was capable of to them. Then again, he couldn't be entirely certain what would happen, since he had not used any Pyro skills since he had left Earth. '*Should we be doing this, in front of them?*' he asked Morgana with a mind-message.

Morgana looked up, startled, but quickly regained her composure and continued her warm-up. '*I don't see why not,*' she answered. '*The Arneshians have known about our Pyro skills for centuries now.*'

'*What about us, though? Should we be showing off what we can do so freely?*'

'*They already know you're a White Child, if that's what's worrying you. Besides, it's also likely that K'Ssander knows what you did last year on Angra Mainyu.*'

'*But what if they're recording us?*'

'*Then give 'em a show they won't easily forget.*'

Julius didn't know what else to say. Morgana was right, of course, but he still wasn't comfortable with this unplanned showcase they were putting on.

'Let's start from the bottom of the alphabet,' said Chan. 'Mr Yuran, if you please.'

Grigor Yuran moved to the centre of the room, looking quite nervous. Julius could understood why: after two years of sharing personal Pyro stories, they were all now going to see what everyone could really do, with the added pressure of an Arneshian audience.

Grigor took a deep breath and lifted his right hand, palm up. Slowly, a speck of light appeared above the skin and became a small flame, which steadily grew until it was the size of an apple.

'Very good, Mr Yuran,' said Chan. 'Take your time now, and focus.'

The class was completely still now; even the Arneshians were watching intently. With a quick flick of his hand, Grigor flung the fireball as far as he could. All eyes followed its luminous stream as it sailed through the air, before disappearing in a puff and being replaced by a flashing red number.

'230 feet!' said Chan, patting him on the shoulder. 'Well done. You are in group two, range of 100 to 300 feet.'

Chan activated a sign with a "2" written on it, which was hovering in midair, and pushed it back towards the left wall. The number crossed the air until it reached its destination and then hung there, suspended above the ground.

'Next: Miss Yu,' called Chan.

One after another, the Mizkis were tested and assigned to the three different groups, covering a wide range of distances. Annette Valeris was the first to be assigned to group one, for a range of 0 to 100 feet. Even the fireball she had generated had been small; no more than the size of a walnut.

The final group, in the 300+ range, was opened by Felicity Steep, who managed to throw a fireball the size of a basketball a distance of 306 feet away. By the time Julius' turn came round, Barth, Morgana, Faith and Siena had joined group one, while Skye had gone to group two.

'Mr McCoy,' called Chan.

Julius walked up beside him and lifted his right hand. Closing his eyes, he concentrated on his inner energy, focusing on the flow of it through his veins, which was slow and steady; he closed his mind to everything around him, trying to silence any thoughts of the Mizkis, and Arneshians, in the room. Maintaining his concentration, he visualised an opening on the palm of his hand, and let the heat seep out through it.

'Uh, is the flame meant to get that big?' he heard Faith ask a few seconds later. There was more than a hint of worry in his voice.

Julius opened his eyes, and instinctively recoiled backwards away from his hand when he saw what had concerned Faith so much: he was staring at a ball of fire which was easily two feet in diameter.

'Steady McCoy,' said Chan, placing a hand on Julius' shoulder.

Julius carefully bent his wrist downward, so that the burning orb was directed away from him. The air around him was beginning to heat up, to the degree where he was finding it hard to breathe.

'Control it, McCoy!' said Chan. 'Focus on the fireball and withdraw some of your energy.'

'Sir,' said Julius, now extremely agitated, 'I'm not sure how.'

'Do it McCoy, focus now!'

Julius imagined the globe as a helium balloon, with a release valve at the bottom. In his mind, he opened the valve, and allowed some of the energy to course back inside him. As soon as he did this, however, he felt as if his veins were catching fire, as if the effort of trying to draw the already unleashed energies back was entirely the wrong thing to do. Without a second thought, he opened his left hand, and rerouted the simmering energy to its empty palm, which created another fireball.

'Everyone, step back!' ordered Chan. 'Shields up, Mizkis, and make sure our guests are sheltered. That's an order.'

Julius heard the shuffling of feet behind him, followed by the sound of many shields humming into life. Chan then activated his right arm-shield, positioned himself next to Julius, and brought the shield up to rest against Julius' forearms, creating a barrier to protect them both from the heat of the fireballs.

'McCoy, you must relax now,' said Chan, calmly. 'Everyone is safe.'

'Professor, I can't reduce the flow. When I draw it back in, it burns me.'

'Then close it off completely. On the count of three, I'll shut my shield down and you will release the fireballs. I'll help you … and don't worry about the distance please. After this stunt, you'll be in a group all of your own anyway. Here we go: one … two … three!'

Chan's shield deactivated on three and, as it disappeared, Julius whipped both of his hands forward with as much strength as he could muster. The fireballs zoomed away from him, their speed amplified by Chan's Telekinetic powers, and hurtled into the far wall. A red number flashed up indicating 400 feet.

'Woah!' cried Skye in astonishment.

The Mizkis erupted, hollering and whooping, so impressed were they with the distance Julius had managed. He and Chan were slumped forward, breathing hard as they recovered from their effort. Julius' t-shirt was sticking to his body, and there were pearls of sweat beaded across his brow.

'I take it the DNA enhancement treatment is working then, McCoy,' said Chan, patting him on the back. 'You singed my eyebrows.'

Julius nodded, still too tired to reply. He turned to look at his classmates, who were still enthusiastically cheering for him, and couldn't restrain a grin. The smile quickly disappeared though, as he spotted K'Ssander and A'Trid deep in quiet conversation.

*

The Skirts quickly grew used to life on the Gea One, and soon it felt like a second home to them. The only things they truly missed were Satras and the Hologram Palace. Deck six did have several holodecks for private use, but they tended to be occupied by the Mizki Seniors most of the time, which Julius thought was highly unfair.

Unfortunately, K'Ssander and A'Trid were still onboard, although the teachers saw to it that they were moved around as much as possible, so as not to unsettle any one class for too long. All in all, the 3MAs had three visits from them and, on reflection, Julius thought that it could have been worse. With help from Faith and Skye, he made sure that Morgana was never left alone when the Arneshians were in the same room, not even for a second. No one liked having them there, but Freja had given his orders and, as such, the guests were to be treated with courtesy, so they just kept their chins up and waited for their visit to be over.

All of their lessons restarted in full during January, sometimes in a classroom, and other times in a holoroom. Julius' extra treatments with Walliser continued as normal, although the changes he was experiencing in his ability levels were getting weirder by the day. It was like his skills had suddenly skipped a stage of their evolution, as he was now able to perform to a level exceeding even the seniors. All of his teachers and classmates were, of course, aware of his treatment, so the fact that in his Draw lessons, he could now successfully gather energy from a rhino, rather than the koala he had been drawing from before, didn't much surprise anyone; they were becoming accustomed to having a White Child in their class. Catering for this, Professor King started to train Julius' telekinetic skills in the cargo bay, where he would practice moving crates from one side of the bay, and stacking them on the other. Sometimes, if King was in the mood, he would get Julius' classmates to sit on top of the crates, and throw small objects for him to deflect, while he was levitating them.

The really bizarre stuff however, first began during one of Beloi's classes, when the Mizkis had been split into small groups, placed in a room and instructed to have conversations with one another, using only their minds. Julius had asked a series of questions, and received replies, not only from his own team, but also from about twenty other Mizkis, who all thought that the questions were being directed at them. It took a few minutes for Beloi to understand what was happening and move Julius, and his group, into an isolated section of deck five.

After that, these surges of power cropped up at random moments. Once, Professor Farshid had sent her students to explore Gea One's command centre. Julius had soon returned to her, complaining of a splitting headache, which had been caused by him being able to hear the constant chatter of various conversations across the six decks; he was picking them up like a radio.

Eventually, Dr Walliser and Freja decided that it would be best to suspend his treatment for a while, to give his DNA more of a chance to adapt to the enhancements, which made Julius happy, not least because he was starting to lose sleep. It was also agreed that Professor Lao-tzu would work on some specialised meditation techniques to help him find a way of shielding himself from this bombardment of "white noise". It took until the beginning of February before Julius started to feel that he was once again back in control of his own head.

*

It was Tuesday the 8th of February, and Julius was having a long, hot shower. Professors Morales and Chan, had put the class through yet another intense Shield lesson, and all his muscles were aching. He was just beginning to drift off, savouring the feel of the refreshing water against his skin, when the sound of the doorbell echoed in the bathroom. He threw a towel around his waist and went to answer the door.

Faith was hovering there. 'I'm starving,' he said.

'Come in,' said Julius. 'I'm almost done.'

Faith zoomed inside and waited by the window, while Julius went to finish up. 'Are you still hearing voices, W.C.?'

'No,' shouted Julius from the bathroom. 'At least, not as much.' He emerged a couple of minutes later, now fully dressed, a towel draped around his neck. He sat down on the chair, slipped his boots on, and began to dry his hair. Suddenly remembering, he stopped and looked at Faith. 'And don't call me-'

'W.C.,' Faith finished for him. 'Just because I'm in a good mood tonight, I'll do what you ask.'

'And what's the occasion?' asked Julius, throwing the wet towel into the laundry chute.

Just then, the terminal beeped, signalling an incoming vidcall. 'Hold that thought,' said Julius. 'On screen.'

His mother's face popped into view, her cheeks strewn with tears. 'Oh Julius,' she sniffed.

'Mum! What's happened?' cried Julius, moving towards the terminal.

'It's ... Michael,' she sobbed.

'Is he all right?' he asked, startled by the fear in his own voice.

'He's applied to visit the ... the Taurus One and ... and a letter of acceptance has arrived this morning.' With that, she burst into a fit of tears.

Faith made as if to leave the room, but Julius indicated for him to stay. The possibility he had been secretly dreading, but which he had forced himself to believe would never happen, was suddenly becoming a reality. He waited for his mum to calm down, while his stomach tightened into a knot. He could see black, wispy threads pouring from her head which left him in no doubt that she was feeling quite terrified.

'Mum, where are Dad and Michael now?'

'They had a fight this morning, as soon as that damn letter arrived. Michael left in a huff and went off to the Nuarn office, while your dad went to file a complaint with the City Chambers,' she said, dabbing her face with a handkerchief.

'What did they say at the Chambers? Can they do something to stop him?'

Jenny shook her head. 'Rory called me at lunchtime. They told him they will try, but the chances are slim.'

'But he's only twelve; how can he decide for himself?'

'It's because he's a Nuarn, Julius. Different laws apply now.'

Julius was stunned and quite unable to believe what he was hearing. 'What can we do, then?'

Jenny shrugged her shoulders, looking very tired. 'I don't know what there is to do, honey. Your dad has gone to pick him up now. Maybe I'll have more to tell you when they get home.'

Julius felt thoroughly miserable now. 'Ask Dad to call me as soon as they're back. We'll sort something out, you'll see. Please don't cry, Mum.'

Jenny took a deep breath, kissed her fingers and touched them against the screen. Julius placed his on hers, and closed the link.

'I'm so sorry, mate,' said Faith, from the corner of the room.

Julius sighed, and shook his head. 'You know, I really thought our mid-winter chat had made a difference.'

'He may still change his mind,' offered Faith. 'And if he does end up going, maybe that'll be enough. He'll see what it's like and then go home again.'

'Maybe,' said Julius, not convinced.

'I do have an idea though.'

Julius looked up at him. 'What is it?'

'I figure if we, the Skirts and Siena I mean, each write a letter to Michael telling him about our own personal encounters with the Arneshians, maybe it'll help him understand what they're really like.'

'You could be right, you know,' said Julius, suddenly hopeful.

'Let's go find the others then,' said Faith, heading for the door.

Sure enough, Skye, Morgana and Siena were more than happy to help and, to Julius' delight, they started writing their letters on the spot, so they could all send them before dinner. It took the best part of an hour, but eventually they were all done.

'I hope you don't mind a few swearwords here and there, McCoy,' said Skye, transferring his file over to Julius' PIP.

'No worries. I know how you feel about the Arneshians, and hopefully he'll feel it too. Thanks, guys,' he said, turning to them. 'I'll put them all together and send them as one. By the way Faith, what did you want to tell me before?'

'The spaceship model I designed has been shortlisted,' he said, shyly.

'That's amazing!' said Morgana.

'Congrats, mate,' added Julius. 'We knew you could do it.'

Siena looked like she was about ready to cry from her excitement, which pleased Faith immensely. 'Thank you, guys,' he said, turning a little red.

'See, Julius,' said Morgana. 'This is a good omen for us. Send the letters now, with our good vibes. We'll wait for you in the mess hall.'

Julius nodded and started to write his own little introduction to the messages. When he was satisfied with it – he wanted it to sound fair and logical – he attached all of the other files to his own, and sent it directly to Michael. With that done, all he could do was wait and see.

*

When Julius stood up and headed to the mess hall, he failed to notice the two visitors in the next booth. K'Ssander and A'Trid had been sitting there for nearly two hours, quietly unobserved and patiently waiting.

As soon as Julius had sent his message, K'Ssander's own portable device had glowed red, instantly redirecting it to him. He placed a trace on Julius' mail system, so that all future messages to Michael's address would be intercepted, and skimmed through the message, the smirk on his face growing larger as he read. 'Little brother doesn't need any help,' he said coldly. 'He's already decided his path.' He quickly made a copy of the message, and sent it to T'Rogon.

*

Every day of that second week of February Julius called home, and every day Michael refused to talk to him. This obstinate silence on his brother's part hurt him far more than his decision to visit the Taurus, because he had shut him out of his life. Rory had explained several times already why they could do nothing to prevent the visit; in fact, the Nuarn office had told him that, if he did, he could be prosecuted for breaching Nuarn rights. To add to the frustration, Jenny and Rory hadn't been able to check if Julius' letter had arrived, as Michael flat out refused to talk about his brother.

'When is his visit scheduled for?' Julius asked his parents one night.

'We don't know yet,' answered Jenny.

'After February probably,' said Rory.

Julius nodded. The possibility of losing Michael to the Arneshians was causing a sense of unease in him like he had never experienced before.

'I'm sorry, darling,' said Jenny, after a long pause. 'We've been so worried about Michael that I haven't even asked how you're doing.'

'You don't have to worry about me, Mum,' said Julius. 'I'm fine, really.'

'My gorgeous White Child,' she said, smiling tenderly. 'You work so hard to keep us safe … How could Michael do this to you, after all you've been through? It makes me so mad.'

Julius wouldn't admit it out loud but, now that his mum had said it for him, he realised just how upset he too was at his brother's lack of appreciation for Zed. It was a cold comfort hearing her say that.

'I hear you have some Arneshians onboard, son,' said Rory.

'You do? Really?' asked Jenny anxiously.

'Aye, they've been here since January,' replied Julius. 'Sorry, I should've mentioned it, but with all the rest going on …' he opened his hands, '… it's not a big deal right now.'

'Be that as it may,' said Rory, 'keep an eye on them, you hear?'

'I will, Dad.'

*

It was the last Tuesday of the month, and the Mizkis were in the mess hall finishing their breakfast.

'3MAs, please report to the lounge, at 09:00,' announced a voice over the intercom.

'Let's hope it's not another augmentation,' said Faith, wiping his mouth and standing up.

Julius, Skye and Morgana followed him out of the room and to the lift, curious about the change of program. When they got to deck three, Professor Farshid and Clavel were sitting in the centre of the room, waiting for the students to arrive.

'Mizkis!' called Farshid. 'Over here. Take a seat,' she said, gesturing to the tables surrounding her.

Morgana chose the table closest to Clavel, where she sat, beaming at her favourite teacher.

'I can see your wisdom teeth, woman,' said Julius, nudging her in the ribs.

'I can't help it if he's so charming and magnificent,' she answered, dreamily.

'Is she going the Miller route?' asked Faith, joining the table. 'Having one teacher-stalker in our team is quite enough, I say.'

'At least she's not wearing that awful, stinky perfume Skye wore for Morales last year,' added Julius.

'I heard that,' said Skye, sitting down next to him. 'I'll have you know that was the latest love fragrance from Earth, that was.'

'Sure, if you were looking to attract a warthog,' said Faith.

'Shush,' said Morgana. 'They're starting.'

'Good morning, Mizkis,' said Clavel, standing up. 'Professor Farshid and I have a surprise for you. We have decided to take advantage of our present location and start the Spring Mission a month early.'

The Mizkis reacted with excited murmurs, making Clavel and Farshid nod with satisfaction.

'Given the course choices you have made, back in September,' continued Clavel, 'we have decided to combine this year's Spring Mission with a test of your progress so far.'

At the word "test", the air of excitement faded a little. Missions were supposed to be fun, but tests certainly weren't.

Professor Clavel seemed to sense the change in atmosphere, and proceeded to reassure the Mizkis. 'As you recall, Mr Patel told you that you would be able to change your career path if you were unhappy with your courses. Consider this test just such an opportunity.' He turned to his colleague. 'Professor Farshid, if you please.'

Amira Farshid stood up, and Clavel took his seat again. 'Next Monday, you will board the Heron for 12 days of simulated training, during which each of you will be assigned a role in line with your course choice and the abilities you have demonstrated so far.'

'Yes!' said Julius, slapping his thigh. Looking around, he could see that his classmates were thinking the same thing: the Heron model wasn't perhaps as cool a spaceship as the likes of the Ahura Mazda, but it was still a real ship, which could take a crew of up to 100 members.

'Over the next few days, Professor Clavel and I, together with your other teachers, will review your achievements in class so far and decide your individual roles for the mission, of which you will be notified at the weekend.' She pointed at Leanne as the girl raised her hand. 'Yes, Miss Nord.'

'Will we be able to break orbit, Professor?'

'You will be allowed to roam freely within our solar system of course, but no further than that.'

Julius grinned at the group. 'This is just!'

'I'm so excited I'm going to faint,' said Morgana, breathing deeply.

'Wait until they finish,' said Faith, hushing her.

'With all of you occupied in central roles, the rest of the crew will be made up by the ship's V.I. system, which will see that all basic necessities are taken care of. I'm talking about chefs, cleaners and the like. Believe me, you will feel just like real crew members.'

'It will be a great experience,' said Clavel, standing up. 'So make the most of it. Dismissed!'

The Mizkis stood and bowed to their teachers, before heading to their lessons in high spirits.

*

The Spring Mission was all the Mizkis could talk about that week. Yuri and Gustavo had set up a PIP app which allowed students to place bets on the Mizkis and the roles they were likely to get, and sent it to all of the 3MAs.

'Julius,' said Skye, one evening, 'you're represented in every category, you know?'

And so he was, although not necessarily as first choice for all of them. Still, it was a nice feeling knowing that the others thought him capable of doing pretty much everything. As good news as that was, he was still worried about the fact that it appeared his letter had still not been delivered to Michael yet, according to his dad, so he sent it again, hoping to reach his brother before it was too late.

Finally, that Sunday morning, the Mizkis received their duty-slips. Julius opened his in his room, and his heart literally skipped a beat when he saw Captain written next to his name. He was, naturally, overjoyed and headed out into the corridor, where he saw Faith hovering towards him, with a massive grin on his face.

'I'm Chief-Engineer!' he cried, giving Julius a high-five.

'That's cracking, mate!'

'Captain?' Faith asked him, nodding, as if he already knew the answer.

'Captain,' confirmed Julius ecstatically.

'Guys!' cried Morgana, from the opposite end of the corridor. Siena was with her, and they were running excitedly down the corridor towards them, arms opened wide.

Julius and Faith stood there, watching as the girls pelted down the corridor. Julius could see emerald green wisps of happiness spreading all around them as they ran, unceremoniously knocking any passing Mizkis out of their way. Faith, who was slightly to the side and behind Julius, spread his arms, ready to catch at least one of them, still grinning madly. Julius, however, was suddenly overcome by a sense of pure panic. In his mind, he saw Morgana's wild run ending in his arms, and her soft body slamming against him. So, as she leapt at him, he did the only reasonable thing he could think of in that moment: he stepped out of the way. Morgana and Siena shot through the air, both now aimed at Faith. Julius turned around just in time to see the Irish boy's grin turn into an O, as the girls crashed into him, projecting them all out of the door at the far end of the dorm, holding on to his skirt. Julius heard a crash and a second later Faith shouted, 'McCooooooy!'

He decided it would be best not to wait around, and hastily retreated back into his room.

THE HERON

On Monday the 5th of March, the 3MAs were instructed to assemble in the docking bay by 09:00 to board the Heron. As captain, Julius was required to be aboard an hour earlier than the rest of his crew, together with his first officer, Yuri Slovich.

'Aren't you excited, McCoy?' asked Yuri, as they entered the hangar.

'Scared, more like,' said Julius. 'Aren't you?'

Yuri looked at him sideways, 'If you promise to keep it to yourself, I'll admit that I'm petrified.'

'It's wild, isn't it? After two and a half years of training, here we are, about to man our first spaceship.' He walked quietly down the gangway for a minute, then spoke again. 'The truth is that I'm not bothered about commanding the Heron. I think that's the easy part. It's T'Rogon that worries me.'

'How so?'

'I feel like I can't make even the tiniest mistake for fear of getting Zed into more trouble. I mean, on Earth they already think I'm a liability as it is, thanks to T'Rogon, imagine if-' Julius stopped abruptly where he stood, and grabbed Yuri by the arm.

'Wha-' started Yuri, swinging around to face him.

Julius motioned for him to look ahead.

'What are *they* doing here?' asked Yuri.

K'Ssander and A'Trid were stepping out of one of the Heron's hatches, their visitor passes in clear view on their chests. Julius felt a pang of anger spreading through his body as he watched them strolling freely, in and out of Zed's facilities. They had no right to be here and he decided that, pass or no pass, he was going challenge their presence. 'Yuri, call security. Hurry,' he said without taking his eyes off the Arneshians.

Yuri didn't need to be told twice, and darted back the way they had come from.

'Well, well,' said K'Ssander, attracted by the noise. 'If it isn't Captain McCoy,' he said, walking slowly forward. He squared up in front of Julius, while A'Trid leaned against the wall, hands in pockets, enjoying the scene.

Julius didn't give any ground, and dropped his bag on the floor. 'You have no business here.'

K'Ssander smirked at him. 'Says who?'

'I do and I don't give a damn about that piece of plastic around your neck. You are not welcome here.'

The serious tone in Julius' voice obviously made K'Ssander think twice and drop his cocky attitude, but still he stayed where he was. Julius was aware of a tingling sensation spreading down his arms. He knew all too well what it meant, and didn't need to look down to know that tiny sparks were now spurting from his fingertips. He was mad, all right.

A'Trid must have noticed it too, because he stopped smiling and began to move away from Julius. 'Don't be stupid, McCoy,' he said.

Julius was breathing deeply, trying to keep the build-up of energy at bay. His intention was to scare, not hurt them, but they didn't need to know that.

'Does it bother you that we can come and go as we please?' asked K'Ssander, unconcerned by A'Trid's apprehension. 'Your boss says we can.'

Julius moved closer. 'My boss isn't here now, is he? And neither is yours.'

'Come McCoy, we are your guests.'

'You may fool Trent and a bunch of civilians, but you can't fool Zed. We know why you're here, like we both know you cheated your way through that game.'

'Still dwelling on it, I see,' he said, squaring up to Julius. 'You need to prove it, don't you?'

'Oh, I will,' said Julius steadily.

Only a few inches separated their faces, but neither of them were prepared to budge. Suddenly K'Ssander's hand jerked up, and grabbed Julius' t-shirt.

It took only a fraction of a second for Julius to do the same thing. The knuckles on his hand were just starting to turn white, he was pushing them so hard into K'Ssander's chest, when they heard Foster's booming voice behind them.

'What's going on here?'

Startled, they let go of each other, and turned in his direction.

'Miss Petri!' thundered Foster. 'Mr Miller, put your hands where I can see them!'

'It's not what you think, sir,' said a muffled voice.

Julius couldn't understand what was going on, and stood there baffled, watching Foster as he glowered at a niche in the wall to his right.

Just then, Yuri came running along the corridor towards them. 'Captain Foster, you got them!'

'Oh yes, I did,' he answered. He stretched his arms forward and, when he pulled them back, he had Skye by his left ear and Valentina by her right. She looked utterly embarrassed.

Julius couldn't believe his eyes.

'And what exactly were you up to?' asked Foster, menacingly.

'Sir, we … uh … we were just checking that panel over there … ow!' said Skye, trying unsuccessfully to weasel his way out of the pickle he was in.

'Impossible, Mr Miller,' thundered Foster. 'You didn't have any free hands for that.' Then he headed toward Julius, dragging the two young lovers behind him. 'Mr McCoy, is this element one of your crew?'

'Yes, sir. He's my tactical officer.'

'Since you are his captain, McCoy, you shouldn't be needing to call me for breaches of good conduct. You must learn to deal with indiscipline yourself. A day in the brig should do it.'

'That's not why we called you, sir,' said Julius. He turned to point at the Arneshians, and saw that they had disappeared. Frustrated, he looked around him, scanning the corridors for any sign of them, but to no avail. 'Damn it,' he thought, wondering where they had gone. He looked back at Foster, aware of the inquisitive gaze, and to Skye, who looked particularly dejected. 'We … uh … called you because she's not one of ours, and I'm too busy to escort her back to her quarters.'

'Very well,' answered Foster. 'I'll see to it.' And with that, he pushed Skye at Julius unceremoniously, and headed back, still grasping Valentina by her ear.

'Call me ... ouch!' she said over her shoulder.

Skye blew her a kiss, looking theatrically sad, while massaging his bright red, sore ear. Once Foster was out of sight, he spun around and glared at Julius in disbelief. 'What did you do that for? Are you so heartless that I can't even spend my last few free moments in the arms of my beloved?'

Julius crossed his arms and looked at his friend, trying to remain calm. 'First off, she's not your *beloved*, but just one of the many girls with a seasonal ticket to your pants. And secondly, we didn't call Foster to break up your lip-wrestling session, but to come fetch that pain in the backside K'Ssander, and his pal, A'Trid.'

Skye look suitably astounded. 'What?'

'We saw them coming out of the Heron,' explained Yuri. 'That's why I called Foster.'

'How could they just board our ship like that?' asked Skye.

Julius shook his head. He was tempted to say that, had it not been for Skye and Valentina, they could have found out from Foster, but decided instead to let it go. 'I'll ask Faith to check our security cameras when he gets here. Come on now, it's getting late.' He grabbed his bag and walked up to the hatch of the Heron. The day hadn't even started yet and he was already stressed out. That just wouldn't cut it though: it was his first day as captain, and he needed all his wits about him. Like Professor Farshid had told them at the beginning of the year, no matter what happened, a captain had to be larger than life. So Julius forced himself to focus on the day ahead. He drew a couple of deep breaths and stepped inside the ship.

*

By mid-morning all 3MAs had boarded, and the V.I. crew of the Heron had been activated. Julius watched his holographic chefs at work in the galley with slight apprehension, wondering if any of them would turn sour and lead a rebellion. It was silly, of course, but the memory of Master Isshin's betrayal two years before, was still vivid in his mind.

The Heron was not meant to break orbit until midday, so Julius walked throughout the ship all morning making sure that everyone was fine, as he supposed a good captain should do. He visited Faith in engineering, drawing some amusement from the Mizkis calling him Chief and allowing him to direct them at will; then popped his head in at the War-deck, where Skye and Isolde were discussing security and checking the catalysts' upkeep. Finally, he arrived at the bridge, where he jumped a little as someone shouted, 'Attention on deck!', followed by a standing salute from all present.

'At ease,' he said, once he realised they were addressing him. It looked like everyone was taking their roles very seriously, so he decided it was only proper to play his part too.

Morgana, beaming like it was her birthday, was doing a great job as first pilot, checking her station, and guiding Barth and Siena through their duties as navigation support officers.

Julius nodded in satisfaction and strolled over to Yuri, who was carefully examining an electronic log. 'Commander Slovich, what's our status?'

'We are on schedule, Captain. All supplies are onboard, the Mizkis are at their stations, and our Chief has confirmed that all V.I. systems have been activated.'

'What about sickbay?'

'All in order. Doctor Flox has given us the all-clear.'

'Flox, is he a human or ...'

'V.I.'

'Thank you, Commander. Order the crew to change into fleet uniform. Then report our progress to Master Cress and confirm our departure time as midday.'

'Aye, Captain. And don't forget your log,' he added quietly.

Julius had indeed forgotten his log, but he wasn't about to mention that to Yuri. Now that everything was ready, he moved off to examine his own quarters, which were just off the bridge. He grabbed his bag, which he had left outside his door that morning, and let the security sensor scan his eyes. The door slid open silently, revealing a large, luminous room. To his left was a desk, fitted with a monitor, and a comfy leather chair; to his right was an L-shaped sofa, with a glass top coffee table in front of it. A huge window ran along the length of the back wall, with tea lights dotted along its windowsill. There were pictures on the walls, one showing the Lunar Perimeter under construction, another Marcus Tijara standing outside the Hologram Palace, and an evocative one of Earth, taken from space.

Julius knelt next to his bag, and opened it. He rummaged in it for a minute, until he had retrieved an electronic picture frame, which he placed on his new desk. Sitting down in his chair, he touched a pressure pad on the side of the frame and a series of images began to scroll slowly across the glass. He smiled as he saw one of Michael hanging from Julius' neck like a small monkey. He remembered the occasion well: they had been in the Meadows, in Edinburgh, having a picnic for his brother's seventh birthday. 'Computer,' he said, leaning back. 'Activate 3MA McCoy.'

'Online. Welcome aboard, Captain,' answered the ship computer.

Julius coughed a little, to clear his voice. 'Captain's log. Stardate 5-3-58. Err ... so ... we are all aboard and ... hmm ... engine looks good, according to Faith – Chief Engineer, I mean – and ... computer pause!' he said, shaking his head. As far as first logs went, that was pretty rubbish, he thought. He would need to work on it, especially since Farshid could very well choose to broadcast it to the whole of Zed, just to teach him a lesson. He stood up and paced to the far right corner, where another door led on to a conjoining bedroom. Being the captain had its perks, judging by the size of his bed, and the fact that he didn't have to share a room with anyone. The latest Zed fleet uniform had been laid out on the bed: a fitted, navy blue jumpsuit, with his name and rank on the left sleeve, and a com-link on the chest. Feeling more and more like a real captain, he grabbed it and got changed.

At 11:50, Julius entered the bridge; this time he was prepared for the formal salute, and took his place at the large chair in the centre of the room. Skye and Isolde occupied the control panels to his left; Yuri was at his right, along with Barth and Siena; Morgana sat at the front of the ship, where her pilot chair was set between a kaleidoscope of holographic panels of varying sizes.

The front end of the bridge was transparent, giving a breathtaking view of space. The large window wasn't strictly necessary, in the way that a windscreen was on a fly-car, but it did add to the experience.

As the clock ticked down to midday, Julius felt the excitement mounting and knew he wasn't the only one, judging by the large grins on various faces on deck; there was perhaps a little apprehension too, as Barth's white knuckles proved. Julius pressed the Heron's intercom button. 'Heron One, this is the captain speaking.' He paused for a moment, trying to steady his voice. 'Prepare for departure.' Finally, he turned to Morgana. 'Lieutenant Ruthier, take her out.'

'Aye, Captain,' she answered.

Julius watched as she pushed and slid various levers and buttons on the holopanels surrounding her. With her left hand, she grabbed the shift handle, and pushed it forward with slow, controlled speed; her right hand continued tapping away speedily on the screen in front of her, adjusting the trajectory as she went, until the Heron broke orbit.

It took no more than a couple of minutes, but to Julius it seemed longer. He knew that Farshid and Clavel were watching, and probably so too were Freja and Cress – by now, he knew that very little escaped the Grand Master. From the point of view of the Spring Mission, he needed to prove to Farshid that he had what he took to be a leader. It didn't matter to him that Zed would need more than one captain for its fleet; Julius wanted to be the best.

'Straight and steady she goes,' called Morgana, proudly. 'Heron's docking has been cleared. Where to, Captain?'

Julius realised that he hadn't actually thought about that, so he looked over at Barth, hoping for his navigational skills. 'Ensign Smit,' he called.

Barth looked up quickly, looking guilty.

'What would you recommend as a first stop?' asked Julius.

Barth's face lit up with relief. 'Venus is supposed to be beautiful at this time of the year, sir. I would suggest we start there, and then visit the rest of our planets … sir.'

'Ensign Migliori,' said Julius.

'Aye, Captain?' answered Siena.

'What speed would you recommend for that?'

'Light speed, sir. It will be two light minutes to Venus, four to Mars, thirty to Jupiter; then it's one light hour to Saturn and four to Neptune. By the end of the week, we will have seen all our planets, with time to spare. And, if we're in a hurry, there's always the hyperjump option.'

'Very well. Set a course for Venus.'

'Aye, Captain,' she said, visibly pleased at having been asked for her input.

'*That was nicely done, Julius,*' Morgana told him with her mind. '*You're doing a grand job.*'

Julius grinned a little, grateful for the show of support and, he had to admit, for the private moment she had just shared with him.

*

The next few days passed by smoothly, and all the Mizkis seemed to be having a great time. Barth's itinerary had worked out well, and they had managed to visit all of the planets, moons, and satellites in their solar system. They gathered samples from the rings of Saturn, practiced shooting at small asteroid fields, and watched Morgana taking hundreds of pictures for her latest project: creating her very own Vbook on the most scenic routes between planets.

Every evening, for an hour, Julius would report to Professor Farshid, and study the data she had gathered during the day from each student. She would advise Julius on the best ways of improving an individual's performance, and how to teach them the right way to complete a task, in a professional manner. Afterwards, she would comment on Julius' own actions, what he had done well, and what he needed to improve on. Lastly, she would go over the list of requests made by Commander Slovich, from daily supplies to crew requests, approving the ones she saw fit and explaining to Julius why she had selected some over others. That time spent with Farshid was really important to Julius, and he came to look forward to it every day. He really wanted to impress her, so he strove to do his best in all his actions and decisions. By the end of the second week, he had the feeling that he had aced the Spring Mission, and was looking forward to seeing his final report.

On Thursday the 15th of March, they re-entered Zed's orbit, and stopped within range of the Gea One. That evening, after his usual meeting with Professor Farshid, Julius was up on the deck, scanning their checklist for the following day, which would also be their last. Morgana had told him she would wait for him to finish, so she kept herself busy at the helm, showing Faith a few minor adjustments that she wanted for the shift handle. Julius was almost done when he received a message on his PIP, so he quickly finished his work, and checked it. The message was short, but as he saw who it was from, his eyes grew bigger. It read: "Check the Space Channel. K'Ssander."

Julius looked up, 'Faith. Is there a screen for the Space Channel in here?'

'Yeah,' he replied, hovering over to the captain's chair. There, he pressed a couple of buttons and the front window of the deck turned into a large screen.

Morgana looked up and took a few steps back so she could see properly as well. 'What's the matter?'

Julius didn't answer, but sat up straight in his chair as the Space Channel's evening edition began. A sense of anxiety was creeping up on him, making the hair on his arms stand up. Why would K'Ssander be messaging him for this?

Faith and Morgana must have noticed his odd expression, because they moved and quietly stood to either side of him, watching the screen intently. The view was that of the Prague Departure Centre for Zed, and it looked like another busy evening.

'We are here in Prague to follow the latest wave of departures for the Taurus One.' Julius recognised the speaker's voice as belonging to the man who had interviewed the Nuarns before. His heartbeat sped up.

'More than 45 million Nuarns have already left Earth,' continued the man, 'and many are wondering if this exodus will continue until the very last one has joined Ambassador T'Rogon. So far, only a few thousand have returned to Earth. I'm going to try and talk with some of the travellers who are here tonight,' he said.

Julius watched as the camera swung to the right, and headed straight for a group of people standing at the back of a long queue.

'Excuse me,' called the reporter. 'May I have a word, for the Space Channel?'

The two people standing at the back turned around at the same time, and faced the camera. Julius felt all the air escaping his lungs, and a cold grip closing around his heart; Faith let out a sharp intake of breath, while Morgana's hand tightened on Julius' shoulder.

Seeing Michael's face on camera was the last thing that Julius had expected, and even less so the boy standing to his brother's side: it was none other than Billy Somers, looking as full of himself as ever. He was taller, but his square face and large shoulders were the same; a puffed up version of the bully they had met two years before. In comparison, Michael looked rather slender, although it seemed to Julius that he was a few inches taller than when he had last seen him. But, what was Somers doing there, with his brother?

'What is your name, young man?' asked the speaker, out of shot.

'Billy Somers, and this here is Michael McCoy,' he said, smugly.

'May I see your t-shirt?'

'Yeah,' he replied, stretching the bottom corners of it so it was clearly visible for the camera. 'And in case you can't read it, it says, "Zed Sucks".'

'The cheek,' whispered Faith.

'Why the animosity toward Zed, Mr Somers?' asked the reporter.

'Because they're a bunch of losers, with second class technology and staff so inept that it took them almost a year before they realised I was a Nuarn!'

'What?' cried Morgana to the screen.

'What do you mean?' asked the speaker.

'They tested me, enrolled me, and shipped me off to Sield school. They wasted nine months of my precious life – which I will never get back – before they realised that I wasn't gifted enough for them. So they booted me back to Earth.'

'You must have been devastated,' commented the reporter.

'Quite the contrary. Who would want to be with that Mizki trash when I can be with the Arneshians, my own people? They will give us back our freedom and our dignity. See this boy here?' he said, grabbing Michael by the shoulder and pulling him close. 'This boy is Julius McCoy's brother, and you know what Zed's precious White Child did when he found out? He got him collared like a dog, like everyone else does on Earth, when they have a Nuarn in the family. If his brother doesn't care for his own blood, and if my parents don't care for me, why should we stay here? Answer me that!'

'How can you do that ...' Morgana's voice was trembling.

'Mr Somers, what are your plans now?' asked the speaker.

'To leave this dump you call home. For good.'

'Are you joining the Arneshians in their journey back home?'

'Damn right I am. We both are. We're boarding that shuttle tonight, all the way to Pit-Stop Pete, and tomorrow morning we'll be on the Taurus One, on our way to Arnesh.'

'And what about you, young man?'

Michael looked up, looking quite unconcerned. 'I believe the Ambassador can give me a better future.'

Julius had remained quiet during the interview. Now, he stood up, walked past his friends and headed to his quarters without saying a word. Soon after, the interview ended.

'Faith, what should we do?' asked Morgana, wiping a tear from her cheek.

'Leave him be, for now. I'll tell Yuri to take charge for tonight.'

In silence, they left the bridge and headed to the canteen.

*

'Julius, it's me,' said Morgana, knocking at his door.

Julius was startled out of sleep, and heaved himself up on his elbows.

'Julius?'

He stretched his hand towards the control on the wall and unlocked his door, before slumping back on the covers. He heard steps out in the front room, then something being placed down on the glass table.

'Have a shower and come out, please. I need to talk to you.'

He checked his PIP and saw that it was 06:40. He had slept the whole night through, without eating or even undressing. Slowly, he rolled out of bed and headed to the bathroom. Fifteen minutes later he emerged into the lounge, wearing a clean uniform. Morgana was sitting on one side of the sofa, legs gathered under her; she had brought him a latte and a couple of pastries. He sat down next to her and grabbed the coffee.

'Rough night, huh?' she said.

Julius took a long sip, then put the cup down. 'I really believed he wouldn't go,' he said, looking at a point on the floor, between his feet. 'Have the others ...'

'Yes, they saw it,' she answered. 'Most of them were pretty astonished about Somers's revelation, to tell the truth.'

Julius nodded absently. Of course, to see Somers there had been a surprise, but in the face of Michael leaving, he couldn't care less if Billy had claimed to be the reincarnation of Marcus Tijara.

'As for Michael,' she said, 'our lot knew he was a Nuarn. Even my roommate Jiao has a Nuarn cousin who left last month. I guess they thought it could happen. They've all been thinking of you, Julius.'

He buried his face in his hands and rubbed his eyes, tiredly. Then he looked up at her. 'How could he do that, Morgana? How could he leave his own family like that?'

She shook her head. 'He's only a child-'

'Don't give me that! We were his age when we destroyed Kratos and saved Zed, or have you forgotten?'

'People are different, Jules. Situations are different. He'll never have our chances, and he really believes that T'Rogon is going to give him what he wants. Can you blame him?'

Julius had gone over that argument a thousand times the night before. What didn't sit right with him wasn't so much that Michael had made the life-changing choice he had, but more the fact that he may never see him again and, knowing this, his brother had made no effort to see him one last time. That, more than anything, had really shaken Julius quite badly. He hadn't felt up to actually speaking to his parents after the interview, so he had messaged them instead. Judging by his dad's short reply, that had probably been for the best: they were both still in shock, and needed time to try process the pain of Michael leaving.

'He's safe at least,' added Morgana.

Julius looked at her, not knowing what she meant.

'He's one of them, Julius. They won't harm him.'

Part of him knew she was right. At least that was one positive thing out of this whole mess. But still, his heart felt like it was being weighed down by a brick.

'Right now though, we need you, Captain McCoy,' she said, standing up. 'You have one last job to finish and a crew to take home. I know this may seem like a joke in the light of last night, but it isn't. If you really care about your future in Zed, you better rise to this challenge.'

Julius knew all too well what his duties were, but he was grateful to Morgana for being there for him, to remind him. She had always been his voice of reason. He grabbed one of the pastries and took a bite, and realised he was absolutely famished.

'That's better,' she said. She ruffled his hair as she stepped past him, and left the room.

*

At 08:00, Julius was standing on the bridge, waiting for his officers. Skye walked in first and momentarily put a hand on his shoulder. He didn't say anything, just gave a light squeeze, and resumed his post. Shortly after, all the deck's crew had reported for duty. When Julius' PIP beeped to indicate an incoming call, he was fearful that it would be more bad news. But it was only Isolde, offering her ear, should he need to talk to someone. It was a kind offer, but he would rather talk to the Skirts if he really needed to. Besides, he thought it best not to give her the wrong impression, just in case she took it as a sign that he was letting her into his private space. He looked at her and nodded his thanks, which caused all sorts of pink and green wisps to shoot out of her head. No, he definitely couldn't talk to her. A few minutes later, Yuri confirmed that all sectors had checked in, including engineering. Julius hailed the Gea One, and requested permission to dock.

'Heron, you may dock in bay 15.'

'Copy that, Gea. We'll be there in ten minutes.' He turned to Morgana. 'Take us home, Lieutenant.'

'Aye, Captain.'

Julius was holding on to the fact that very soon he would have three full days of rest, in which he didn't need to be responsible for anybody and could just be by himself if he wanted to. This Spring Mission had really spelled out what Farshid had meant when she said that a captain must be larger than life: come hell or high water, his crew would always rely on him to keep them safe and take them home in the end. He wondered if Captain Kelly had ever felt that way before, and made a mental note to ask him the next time they met.

He looked past Morgana's station, into space. It was some view from the bridge. He could see a slice of Earth beyond the Moon and Pit-Stop Pete, with its busy docks. Further away, to the right, was the Taurus One, lurking like a silent, evil giant. It was even bigger out here than it had looked on video; by now it was carrying almost 50 million Nuarns. 'And soon, my brother too,' thought Julius glumly. Why would T'Rogon need a ship that size though, wondered Julius. Even with all the Nuarns on board, it was simply massive. There was also its uncanny ability to morph.

Suddenly, he noticed that the image in front of him was shifting slightly to the right, like when a camera pans sideways in a movie. 'Lieutenant?' he said to Morgana.

'Ensigns,' called Morgana to her officers, 'check our course.'

'It's not us,' said Siena, looking worried.

Morgana pressed a few buttons, scanned the sensors, and turned to Julius. 'The Heron has changed course, Captain.'

Julius saw grey wisps surrounding her aura, and knew it wasn't a good sign. He looked at Skye and Isolde, but they only shook their heads in dismay.

'Do we have *any* control over the ship?' asked Julius.

'None,' said Morgana.

'And where are we heading?'

'Pit-Stop Pete,' said Barth, turning rather white. 'If we can't change course, we'll cut right through it in less than five minutes.'

'McCoy to engineering,' said Julius.

'Go ahead, Captain,' said Faith. 'What's happening?'

'Right now,' answered Julius calmly, 'it looks like a repeat of the Zed Toon game. Do you know what I mean?'

There was a brief pause. 'It's not us steering, is it?'

'Correct. You need to shut down the engines from there, before your beloved Pete Kingston gets blown to smithereens.'

'What?' cried Faith, suddenly fully alert. 'I'll take care of it, Captain!'

Julius kept his eyes on their route. The Heron had now completely shifted and Pete's docking station was perfectly centred in the middle of the window. 'Morgana, anything?'

'No. I'm still locked out of the controls.'

'Damn it,' said Julius, slamming his fist on the armrest of his chair.

'Oh no,' said Barth, feebly.

'What is it?' asked Julius.

'We're shifting again,' he answered.

Julius looked out and saw Pete's station moving to the left, while an Arneshian spaceship was detaching from it at the same time. The Heron was unmistakably heading for a new target. 'Faith!' cried Julius. 'Why aren't we stopping?'

'Because I wasn't in charge of designing this piece of junk, that's why! If I had, we wouldn't be having this conversation.'

'Yes but, can you stop it?'

'I'm trying McCoy, trust me.'

'Julius,' called Morgana, 'that shuttle … our new target …'

'What about it?'

'I've just checked; according to the dock logs there's only one shuttle due out today. '

'So?' urged Julius.

'It … it's the one carrying Michael!'

Suddenly, everything made sense: K'Ssander and A'Trid's visit to the Heron had had a very specific reason. Somehow, they had managed to rig his ship, just like they had during the game, to their robots. Zed was no longer in control of the helm; Arnesh was, and if Julius didn't do something quickly he was going to lose his brother, and cause a diplomatic incident. Dismayed, he also realised that, in the excitement of the mission, he had completely forgotten to ask Faith to check their internal security cameras when they first boarded the ship, and mentally cursed himself for it. If only he had performed his duties as captain properly, none of this would be happening. He felt like he had failed them all. Still, he couldn't allow himself to dwell on it; if ever there was a time to get his act together, it was then. He needed to stop the Heron. 'Morgana, how much time to impact?'

'Less than two minutes.'

'Heron,' called Julius over the ship's intercom, 'I want every single Mizki on War-deck, right now. Faith, stay where you are and work on the engine – keep whatever help you need. Morgana, go to tactical alert and contact Master Cress immediately. Everyone else, move!' He headed for the door, motioning for Skye, Isolde, Siena and Barth to follow him.

'War-deck?' asked Skye, catching up with him. 'What are you thinking of doing?'

'We're going to give the shuttle a little push,' he said, tapping his head.

A smile spread over Skye's face. 'Professor King would be proud!'

The Mizkis were filing in from the different decks and corridors. Julius hoped that linking the telekinetic skills of more than 25 students would give them a better chance of clearing their path, before it was too late. The War-deck was positioned above the bridge, and was where all the Heron's catalysts were fitted. The walls and ceilings were made of unique transparent panelling, to give a perfect view of outside.

'Are we using the catalysts?' asked Lopaka.

'Not unless you want to blow that shuttle up,' answered Julius.

'We are going to push it away,' explained Skye, 'using our powers, and *Julius* as a catalyst.'

'What?' gasped Lopaka, wide-eyed.

'Face the shuttle and hold each other's hands,' said Julius. 'You're going to focus on me. When I tell you, start pushing and I'll channel our energies towards the shuttle's port. Clear?'

'Are you sure we're not going to just end up blasting your brains out?' asked Gustavo.

'Trust me, you won't.'

'All right, let's do it,' called Leanne Nord, pushing her way to the front of the room. She took Julius' left hand in her right, and gave her other hand to Skye.

The rest of the Mizkis grabbed each others' hands, and silence fell on the room. Julius closed his eyes and began to breathe deeply. He was aware of the clock ticking and the sound of the impact alarm blaring throughout the Heron; he pushed the noise to the back of his mind, until it became soft, and faraway. As had happened before, they were creating a human conduit, the energies of his classmates filling his mind, making his hair stand on end. He could feel a greater control over his body this time though, probably as a result of his latest augmentations, and he was glad because he would need all his strength to avert the crash. Slowly, he opened his eyes, and saw the Arneshian shuttle drawing closer and closer. He stretched his right hand forward, toward the port of the shuttle, holding Leanne's hand tight in his left. This was the moment. 'Push!' he urged the Mizkis.

The energy streamed out of Julius' hand with all the strength of a cork popping out of a bottle of champagne, making him stagger backwards a little. The Heron stuttered and, although it didn't completely stop, Julius could feel that it had slowed down. He focused on the small vessel in front of him, and pushed as hard as he could. It was almost as if a cushion of air had formed between the Heron and the shuttle, stopping them from coming any closer. For one fleeting moment, Julius believed they had managed it. Then he saw that they were still moving towards the target.

'Faith, report!' said Morgana over the intercom.

'I'm almost done!' he answered.

'Come on guys,' thought Julius.

'30 seconds to impact!' shouted Morgana.

'Keep pushing, Mizkis!' called Faith over the intercom. 'We can do it together, but we're cutting it real fine!'

The Mizkis all pushed with renewed vigour. Julius felt an incredible surge of energy leaving his body, and wondered how long they could maintain this for.

'Done!' cried a victorious Faith. 'Morgana, steer us away!'

No answer came from the helm, but Julius felt the ship veering right. The engine had stopped now, but they were still travelling toward the shuttle.

'It's too late,' whispered Julius.

The Heron had stopped, but it was still drifting and Julius realised that Morgana wouldn't make the turn in time.

'Captain to all hands,' he cried. 'Hold on!'

The impact shook the whole ship, sending the Mizkis sprawling to the floor. They had thankfully slowed down enough to avoid an explosion, but not to prevent a head-on collision. Julius scrambled to his feet and realised just how close he was to the Arneshian shuttle: he could now read the serial number on one of its portholes.

'Skye,' called Faith, 'seal off the lower decks. We're losing oxygen.'

'Breached hulls, sealed.'

'Everyone, back to stations,' ordered Julius. He rushed to the bridge, feeling very light headed, but knowing he couldn't stop now.

'Isolde, report,' he said, once he was back in his chair.

'Decks one to four are breached, but contained. We're fine, Julius. And so is the Arneshian shuttle.'

'Captain, the Grand Master is hailing us,' said Siena.

'Put him through,' said Julius.

Freja appeared on the front screen of the ship, looking worried. 'McCoy, is the crew all right?'

'Yes, sir. I'll have Flox check us out in a minute. Sir, it wasn't our fault. The ship's engine and helm were out of our control.'

'What are you saying?'

'I'm saying that this is a repeat of the game.'

Freja looked flustered. He turned around and began to talk quietly to the Master. Eventually, they saw Cress leave in a hurry. 'McCoy, there will be an enquiry.'

'An enquiry? It is clearly not our fault!' said Julius angrily.

'Be that as it may, it is protocol. The 3MAs are forbidden to leave the Heron, or to attempt to remove the ship from the Arneshian shuttle's port until the end of proceedings. We will make sure that you have all the supplies you need for your extended stay.'

'But, sir-'

'You have your orders, Captain,' cut in Freja.

'Sir,' answered Julius, realising there was nothing else he could do. At least Michael's shuttle was still there too. Maybe, just maybe, he would at least get a chance to try change his brother's mind.

REALITY BITES

In the following hours, all of the news channels were ablaze with vicious verbal attacks from the Arneshians against Julius and his crew. Not one hour passed without a flurry of new, spiteful words from T'Rogon. Even though Earth knew full well that the Curia was examining all the recordings from the collision and that there was a full enquiry on the go, Paulo Trent and the Voices of the Earth seemed to have added weight to the Ambassador's opinion that Zed's incompetence, and Freja's recklessness, were ultimately responsible for this diplomatic incident.

'And we cannot excuse the White Child,' said T'Rogon during an on-air face to face with the Curio Maximus, Roversi, the morning after the incident. 'McCoy may still be in training, but the fact that he is so gifted should make him even more accountable for what has happened. If you can't control him, then you are guilty too.'

Julius and the Skirts were seated on the sofa in the captain's quarters, watching all of this. Iryana Mielowa was hosting the meeting in the Space Channel studio.

'Ambassador,' began Roversi, clearly straining to keep control of his temper, though his nostrils were still twitching, 'surely you can't be serious. Accidents can happen on a training mission. You have students too; you should know.'

'You have said it, Curio. We have students, but you seem to be training bitter children, and McCoy is a classic example of that. Or have you forgotten about the fight after the game? In fact, let us remind the people of Earth about that ignominious moment; let's show them what *really* happened.'

'We don't actually have any footage of that event, Ambassador,' said Mielowa, curtly.

'No matter,' answered T'Rogon. 'I do.'

To everyone's astonishment, T'Rogon placed two fingers against his left temple and pressed: the circular Arneshian symbol lit up on the back of his hand, and a holographic screen appeared in front of him, large enough to be seen clearly by all present.

'What kind of bio-technology is that?' muttered Faith, awestruck.

'I don't care if that screen comes out of his rear-end,' said Skye, growing livid. 'He's going to show that stupid fight again. Why don't they stop him?'

It looked like Mielowa was wondering the same thing, because she was looking imploringly behind her, possibly for her station aids, to see why they weren't intervening.

As was to be expected, the fight was shown very much from an Arneshian perspective: it started, in fact, with Maks storming in and punching K'Ssander, and then being joined by Julius and Skye.

'That's not fair!' cried Morgana, indignantly.

'See there?' continued T'Rogon. 'Your pupils are out of control. That boy just stormed in and hit one of my students for no reason; well, for no other apparent reason than they had just lost a very important game.'

Roversi seemed at loss for what to say. It was as if he had never been briefed about the full story of what had really happened, and was now being confronted with something he didn't know how to handle diplomatically. 'Boys will be boys, Ambassador,' he said, trying to shift the focus onto something else.

'Really?' he said, sitting up in his chair like he was preparing to take off at a sprint. 'Let me tell you something more, Curio, that may finally open your eyes and change the lax attitude with which you run this Lunar Perimeter of yours. You should really get to know your Mizkis better than this. That McCoy, as well as being a sore loser and a lousy leader, will stop at nothing to get his way.'

Julius bristled with anger, and sat up in his seat. What was T'Rogon on about this time?

'When he found out that his brother was a Nuarn, instead of encouraging him to strive for something better in life, he tried to stop him any way he could from fulfilling his dreams. To begin with, he threatened him with false letters written with the help of his friends.' As he said this, he touched his temple again, and a series of emails began to scroll down on his personal holoscreen, which was still sitting open before him.

'How did he get those?' cried Julius, standing up. He knew full well that T'Rogon had seen Michael's choker that day at the docks, during the mid-winter break, but how could he have known about those letters?

'No wonder Michael never got them,' said Faith.

'Then,' continued T'Rogon, looking quite pleased with the effect he was having on Mielowa and Roversi, who both seemed spellbound by his words, 'when the letters didn't work, he attacked the very shuttle his brother Michael was using to travel to the Taurus One.'

Julius slammed his fist on his thigh, 'How dare you?' he yelled in frustration, throwing a kick at the holoscreen, right at T'Rogon's face. Yellow sparks of energy were falling from his fingertips onto the floor, where they fizzed out.

Morgana switched off the feed and stood up. 'We've wasted enough time. I think we need to make a little enquiry of our own.'

'She's right,' added Faith. 'We're probably the only ones who actually believe that this was foul play. Julius, you said K'Ssander and A'Trid came out of the Heron before we left; I'm going to put a team together and start examining all communication channels in, and out, of this ship.'

'Good idea,' said Skye. 'Isolde and I will check the cameras, from two hours before we saw the Arneshians. I think we can safely assume they didn't sleep in here, but if I can't find something, I'll search back further.'

'Do that,' said Faith, 'and get the Mizkis to search the entire ship for anything out of place. Morgana, I need you to map the exact trajectory of the Heron in the ten minutes before the collision; I want to see if I can match it with my findings.'

'All right,' she said, turning to Julius, 'And you, glowing boy, need to calm down and resume your captain's duties. There's a long list of people waiting to talk to you, starting with Professor Farshid. Help them help us out of this mess.'

Julius nodded. He really wanted to lend a hand onboard, but that was not how a captain helped. 'Sure thing. I'm on it.'

They left him in his quarters, eager to start their duties. Julius sat at his desk, pushing his anger about T'Rogon's accusations out of his mind. It wasn't easy, but he couldn't afford to let the Arneshian get the upper hand at a time like this. 'I am the root of this tree,' he said to himself. 'They depend on me, and I will not fail them again.'

*

Faith had spent the best part of two days inside engineering. He had instructed Lopaka to direct their classmates Annette, Femi and Barbel to scour the security channel, while he himself had started by thoroughly examining Julius' PIP chip, thanks to Dr Flox, in sick bay, who had removed the chip from Julius' hand for a while. It hadn't taken him long to isolate the tracing code which K'Ssander had tacked on to Julius' bio-software. Julius had been quite gobsmacked when he saw it flashing up on the screen. Faith had then returned to engineering, to ensure he found a way of recording the code so it could be processed as evidence.

It was towards the end of the second day, around 22:00 hours, when Femi called her team to her. 'I think I've found something,' she said.

'Don't play it yet,' said Faith, on a hunch. 'Patch it through our earpieces, channel one.'

Lopaka looked at him, puzzled, but quickly complied. He sat down on the floor, next to the girls, while Faith hovered back and forth anxiously. Then Femi pressed play.

'*It is done, Ambassador,*' said K'Ssander's voice.

'*Very well,*' answered T'Rogon. '*Salgoria is extremely pleased with your efforts. And you know how forthcoming she can be towards her faithful.*'

'*It was an honour to serve her.*'

'*Don't be modest, Mr K'Ssander. It took skill to plant those devices on their robots in the middle of a game. They didn't even notice. As they will also not notice us steering the Heron.*'

'*They're not as advanced as I thought they'd be, Ambassador,*' K'Ssander scoffed contemptuously. '*It was like stealing candy from a child.*'

Faith stopped his pacing, and clenched his fists.

'*Yes, quite,*' continued T'Rogon. '*Our mission is almost complete. We have enough Nuarns to last us a lifetime of experiments.*'

'*When can we break orbit?*'

'*As soon as the minefield is in place and activated, which will not be long now. We will be ready in time for the last shuttle delivery; the shuttle which I'm standing in now.*'

'*You mean, the one that will be carrying the McCoy boy?*'

'*The very one.*'

'*Will the field be enough to …*'

'*Enough to blow them to the four corners of the galaxy? Why yes, I believe it will.*'

The recording stopped there, leaving the Mizkis staring at each other in silent fear.

'Femi,' said Faith, after a couple of minutes, 'show me the matrix for this dialogue.'

Femi stood up, her legs shaking a little. She pressed a few buttons and a long code streamed onto the screen in front of her. Faith moved closer, activated his PIP, and displayed the tracing code he had found inside Julius' PIP chip, alongside this new one. 'I want you to look for this inside the dialogue code.'

'Isn't that the tr-' started Lopaka.

Quickly, Faith placed his hand on Lopaka's mouth, gesturing for everyone to be quite. Lopaka looked at him, mystified, but nodded. The girls did likewise. Faith pointed at the air above him, then at his ear and chest, and mouthed the words, 'They are listening to us.'

Everyone's eyes grew large with understanding, and they began the search. Eventually, Barbel pointed at the screen, a satisfied grin on her face. The code was there all right, embedded in the Arneshian dialogue. Faith needed to warn the others immediately. 'Come with me,' he said, before heading for the bridge.

*

When Julius saw Faith and his team rushing onto the bridge all flushed and flustered, he leapt up from his chair in alarm, only to be shushed by the waving of Faith's hand. Morgana, Skye, and everyone else on deck looked at them, dying to know what was going on. Faith went straight to the security panel, shoving Skye hastily out of his way, and pressed several buttons in quick succession.

In the meantime, Lopaka casually plonked himself down in the captain's high chair and flicked on the intercom. 'Aloha folks! This is Mr Liway from the deck,' he said, winking once at Julius. 'The Captain has a surprise for you all, and is cordially inviting you up on the bridge right now!'

Morgana stared blankly at Julius, hoping for answers, but he could only shrug and shake his head in reply. Annette Valeris and Barbel Frank stood at either side of the entry door, motioning for the Mizkis to be quiet as they stepped inside. Soon, the deck was packed with 25 very perplexed students.

'Done,' said Faith finally, letting out a sigh of relief. 'You can talk now.'

'What was that all about?' asked Julius.

'The Heron is bugged,' replied Lopaka.

'What?' cried Skye.

'And there's more,' said Faith, preparing his PIP. 'You all need to hear this.' The 3MAs listened to the recording of the dialogue in silence, until Faith stopped it. 'K'Ssander and A'Trid have bugged the entire ship,' he explained. 'Right now, only the deck is safe.'

'Wait,' said Julius. 'Does that mean they know you've heard their dialogue in engineering?'

'No,' answered Faith. 'I had a hunch and got my team to put on headsets the first time we listened to it. They also don't know we've found out about the bugs on the Heron. I've just patched a virus through the deck relay. We have about twenty minutes before they can listen in on us again in this room, so we need to be quick.'

'How did you find out, Faith?' asked Siena.

'Julius' PIP chip was bugged. I just had a feeling that they could have done the same to the Heron.'

Siena looked at him proudly.

'This is the proof we need against the Arneshians,' cried Leanne Nord. 'We must broadcast this dialogue through the Space Channel.'

'Not without a confirmed signature on their voices, we can't,' said Faith.

'He's right,' added Julius. 'We must link this recording to the Taurus One shuttle, or they'll think we made it up.'

'And how do you propose we do that, Chief?' asked Skye.

'We can get K'Ssander easily, since he was standing right here on the Heron. For the shuttle though, that's a different story; we can only get T'Rogon's signature directly from the relay he used.'

Julius fell silent for a minute, lost in his thoughts. This was the chance he had been waiting for – an opportunity to board the shuttle and see his brother again. But it wouldn't be easy. 'We need a way to avoid being seen once onboard. Judging by the shuttle's size, there could be about 50 people standing between us and the relay.'

'We could use the Exoskin suits,' said Skye. 'We have a couple on board.'

Julius nodded, he looked at the rest of his classmates. 'As captain, I have decided to board the shuttle; not just because my brother is on it, but also, if I had done my duty properly, this accident may never have happened.'

The Mizkis looked at him, listening intently as he carried on.

'The day we departed from Gea, I saw two of the Arneshians stepping out of the Heron. I should have requested a full scan, but ... in the confusion beforehand, I didn't. I'm sorry.'

'Actually,' added Yuri, sounding a little sheepish, 'I was standing right by your side and I forgot too. It's also my fault.'

'Ahem,' coughed Skye. 'I believe the biggest blame lies with me actually, since I ... distracted you all.'

'I am the captain,' said Julius. 'It was my responsibility.'

Skye and Yuri seemed set to disagree, when Morgana put an end to it. 'And now that you've done your confessions guys, we need to vote for who goes on this mission; I vote for Julius and Skye – and if I have to explain the reasons why it should be them, then you've chosen the wrong career path,' she ended, crossing her arms and tapping her foot rapidly on the floor.

'I agree,' said Manuel Valdez, quickly followed by a general nodding of heads from the rest of the Mizkis.

'Bossy lady is right,' said Leanne, seriously. 'What do you want us to do in the meantime? And let's decide quickly. If the Arneshians are really listening, they'll be wondering where the heck we all went.'

'Faith?' said Julius, indicating for him to carry on. He had done a great job up until now, and he had a better overview of the technical situation.

Faith seemed very pleased to be given the lead on the mission, and moved to the centre of the deck. 'Right, those of you with bridge duties, stay here. Lopaka, take a team to engineering, and start repairing the engine. Leanne, you're in charge of fixing the breached hulls – we may need to make a hasty retreat. Everyone else is on security detail. Keep scanning every nook and cranny of this ship for anything out of the ordinary – we can't afford to miss anything else.'

'Watch what you say everyone, and watch what you send through your PIPs,' added Julius. 'Use your mind-skills for private stuff. This is our last chance to prove what the Arneshians are really up to.'

As the crew filed quietly away, Jiao Yu stopped by Julius' side. 'Is it true what they said about experimenting on the Nuarns?'

Julius looked at her and saw that she had been crying. Then he remembered that her cousin had boarded the Taurus One already. 'Don't worry, Jiao; we won't let them get away with it.'

Jiao looked at him for a few seconds, until she seemed convinced that he could really do something, then nodded and walked away.

When the other Mizkis had all left, the meeting continued.

'Once you two access the relay,' explained Faith, 'they'll find out pretty soon.'

'What kind of equipment are we dealing with?' asked Isolde.

'I don't know; which leads to another issue: our com-links may not work inside an Arneshian vessel.'

'And the PIP?' asked Morgana.

'Same thing.'

'What about telepathy?' asked Skye.

'Possibly,' said Faith.

'What, from *another ship?*' asked Isolde.

'I think I could,' said Julius. 'At least I can try.'

'Good, because right now it's the only option we have,' said Faith.

'What about those mines T'Rogon was talking about?' asked Morgana. 'We need to tell Freja.'

'Faith, are you sure there's no video surveillance on the deck?' said Julius.

'Positive. I've checked the room and it's clean.'

'All right. Get Cress on the line, and keep him talking.'

'What should I say?'

'Improvise, but be careful, the 20 minutes are up in a few seconds.'

Faith hailed the Gea One, requesting permission to talk to Cress, who came on screen shortly after.

'Chief Shanigan, what can I do for you at this late hour?'

'Master Cress! What a pleasure to see you again!'

'Cut to the chase, please. In case you haven't noticed, we are rather busy trying to get you out of there.'

'But of course. I'll be brief,' he said, starting to hover randomly across the deck. 'Tonight, I couldn't sleep. Me tummy was really upset, and I was wondering what in the name of ...'

Julius saw that Cress was about to interrupt, so he jumped in front of the screen and waved to get the Master's attention. Just for good measure, he shushed him too. The expression on Cress' face in response to this disrespectful behaviour was a frightening cross between shock and bewilderment.

'...me great-great-great uncle Phil who, bless his soul, had an unnatural likeness to a mountain troll ...' said Faith, unperturbed.

Julius began to type quickly on his PIP, his screen facing Master Cress, so it served as a notice board to transmit his message: "Cannot send. Heron bugged. Call Freja."

Cress read the screen carefully, then activated his own PIP, and nodded to Julius.

'... In fact, not just any mountain troll, but a mountain troll with a very ugly mother, and possibly a gorilla for a father ...'

'Mr Miller,' said Cress, trying his best to play along with the farce, 'I believe that your chief engineer is having problems. Could it be something he ate?'

'Possibly, sir. I should go fetch Captain McCoy, perhaps.'

'Yes, maybe you should.'

'Surely it couldn't have been that leftover mutton leg I found floating in the plasma core the other day ...' Faith rambled.

When Grand Master Freja joined Cress, he caught the last bit of Faith's monologue and his left eyebrow shot upwards. Cress pressed a button to close the audio channel between them and the Heron, and briefed Freja. Julius saw comprehension dawning on the Grand Master's face and leaned close as Freja typed something quickly on his own PIP and held it up for Julius to read.

"Explain."

Julius quickly typed his response: "Found chat between T and K. It proves Heron/Game compromised. Nuarns wanted for experiments. Faith can retrieve signature from relay on shuttle."

"Do it. How can we help?"

"No need. You find the minefield around Zed!" Freja's face grew dark at that, and Julius added, "T said mines all linked and set to go off."

"When?"

"When Michael's shuttle reaches Iaurus One."

'… but then I say, how can it be? Me stomach can digest cement and spiders, surely the mutton …'

'That's enough, Mr Shanigan,' said Cress. 'Mr Miller, I order you to lock your engineer in the brig until next year.'

Morgana and Siena had their hands clamped over their mouths, trying to stifle their laughter.

'Yes, sir!' said Skye, staying exactly where he was.

"Be careful," wrote Freja. "We'll take care of the minefield."

Julius nodded, relieved. Finally, they had a chance to set the record straight once and for all. He bowed to Freja and Cress, and motioned for Faith to stop acting.

'I have no more time to waste,' said Cress. 'Tell McCoy I want an official apology for this insult.' He looked at them, with a hint of a smile. The show had definitely amused him.

When the screen went dark Skye stepped closer to Julius and sent him a mind-message, 'I've noticed you didn't mention to Freja that we need to be onboard the shuttle to fetch that signature.'

'It must have escaped my mind,' answered Julius vaguely.

DECEPTION

In the early hours of the 19th of March, Julius and Skye had fixed the Exoskin devices onto their uniforms, and were standing on deck two, where a portion of the Heron was lodged firmly inside the Arneshian shuttle. Annette Valeris had just cut into the metal, creating an opening big enough to let the boys pass through it. With the aid of a handheld sonar device, she had been able to locate a passage that would open into one of the service conduits, allowing the team a safe entry point.

'*I've downloaded the layout for the shuttle onto your PIP, based on my best guess, plus details of all the Arneshian relay schematics known to Zed,*' explained Faith telepathically. '*Just bear in mind, I don't know exactly what you'll find over there. It would be easier if you took me with you.*'

'We need you here,' said Julius. '*You're the only one that can safely retrieve the signature once we access it, and patch it straight through to Zed.*'

'*I know. It's hard being a genius.*'

Julius smiled, then said aloud, 'Annette! Skye and I are going to have a game of chess. Leave us alone for awhile, will you?'

'I think I'll go for a nap,' said Faith.

'Of course. I'll make sure no one bothers you,' said Annette, with a wink.

Julius and Skye pressed their Exoskin buttons once, to activate the suits. Instantly, their bodies were wrapped in energy fields, which transformed into dark, solid armour.

Morgana was standing to the side, looking anxiously at him. Julius wanted to hold her right then, just to soothe her, and put her mind at ease, but he settled instead for a brief smile.

He looked at Faith. '*I want you to seal this port once we're in.*'

'*What if you need to make a hasty retreat?*'

'*You could be needing to do that yourself, and you're now responsible for the lives of 28 Mizkis.*'

Faith considered that for a moment. '*All right, but if you need to, I want you to breach the lower decks. We'll depressurise after you. Clear?*'

'*Clear,*' he replied. Without further word, he tapped Skye on the shoulder, prompting him forward, and through the hole. As they crouched inside the service conduit on the other side, Julius stopped to watch Annette seal the gap shut behind them. She was quickly done, and they were shrouded in darkness. He flipped the safety off on his Gauntlet, waiting as his eyes adjusted. It took a few moments, but eventually a light began to filter through grids into the shaft.

'Which way?' whispered Skye, activating the light on his Gauntlet, and shining it first in one direction, then the other.

'The closest relay station which can give us access to the bridge should be south of here,' answered Julius. 'Let's go.'

Stooping, they cautiously made their way along the conduit, lightly testing the panels ahead of them with their feet, trying to keep to the edges and avoid stepping on the lighter centre areas which might give off telltale noises under their weight. The light from Skye's Gauntlet wasn't particularly strong, but they avoided using anything brighter, for fear of it being spotted through the hairline cracks in the duct; for all they knew, this service conduit could have been passing over the middle of a restroom.

As they went, Julius intermittently paused to check the map on his PIP, whenever they came to a fork in the path. 'We're almost there,' he said. 'about 30 feet.' They carried on, but there was now a sense of unease steadily growing in Julius' mind. It felt as if some important piece of information was trying to get to the forefront of his thoughts but, as much as he tried, he couldn't quite put his finger on it. He was still dwelling on this when they reached the relay panel. Skye moved closer, and pulled out a small, rectangular handheld tool from his pocket.

'What is that?' whispered quietly Julius. He had never seen anything like it before.

'It's an Omni-gizmo,' answered Skye, pushing a lever on its surface, which caused a small blade to pop out. 'Valentina got it from Pete's shop, in Satras.'

He watched as Skye wedged the blade into the side of the relay, and popped the cover off it. There was a circuit board beneath it, with all manner of tiny bright lights blinking away busily. Julius activated his PIP, and selected the file with the schematics that Faith had given him, tilting his screen towards Skye, so they could both examine it. They scanned the various blueprints, comparing them with the board in front of them, but with no joy. Desperately, they checked it again, but still couldn't find one that would match the shuttle's relay.

'Jules, I think you need to contact Faith,' said Skye. 'Morgana told me she would be helping him meditate, so he would hear you better.'

'Let's hope it works,' Julius replied. He took a deep breath. This was going to be another first for him and, as far as he knew, a first for any Mizki. He had certainly never heard of anyone ever successfully communicating telepathically from ship to ship; the vast reaches of space had proven just too big an obstacle to be conquered in that way. However, he knew that his skills had been seriously boosted of late and, if what he had accomplished in the first Pyro lesson was anything to go by, he believed he could truly pull this off.

He focused his mind on Faith, visualising his friend's green eyes staring into his own. He zoomed his mind's eye in on the pupils of Faith's eyes, until the blackness of them was filling his entire vision. Then he began to call to him. It wasn't strong at first, but rather soft, and probing; it was as if Julius was trying to tune a radio, and every time he called his friend, he got a little closer to the right frequency. He didn't try to rush this, knowing that it would take time for Faith to hear him, and do his own tuning-in.

'... ius,' a voice whispered at the back of his mind. It was faint, but definitely Faith's.

Julius twitched, a little surprised that he had actually managed it. He reached out for the voice and found it. 'I'm here,' he said. There was a hint of pain in his head at first, like a pulse, then it was gone.

'... lius ... Julius,' repeated Faith.

'Can you hear me?' asked Julius.

'Now I can,' answered Faith.

'I need your help with the relay station. I don't know how to access it.'

'*Describe it to me, or maybe … Remember three years ago, when we landed on the Moon? You saw through my eyes. Can you make me see through yours?*'

Julius wasn't sure if it was possible, but just then it seemed like the only solution left. '*I'll try, but Faith, you have to focus.*' He took a deep breath and examined the relay station, exploring its angles and lines with his eyes; every one of its lights and patterns, until it was all firmly embedded in his mind.

'*I see it, Julius!*' cried Faith. '*One moment.*'

Julius hoped this would work and, especially, that Faith would be quick about it. The pulsing pain in his head had returned, and this time it was staying put. Still, he didn't dare let his concentration falter.

'*Press the second light from the bottom,*' said Faith.

Julius focused and did what he was told, as Faith continued to issue instructions for the next few minutes while, all the time, the throbbing pain in his head grew relentlessly.

'*The last part now,*' said Faith. '*The amber button: press it. It will send T'Rogon's signature to the Heron.*'

Julius did so, and relaxed; his headache subsided just a touch. '*Done.*'

'*Great. Now get the heck outta there. You've no doubt set off all the alarms in their network.*'

'*On our way,*' said Julius, shaking his head and massaging his temples.

Skye placed the cover over the panel, and turned back the way they had come. Julius put a hand on his shoulder, and stopped him.

'What's wrong?' asked Skye, quietly.

'I'm not coming yet. I need to find Michael.'

Skye stared at him, as if he was set to argue, but stopped himself, obviously realising that he wouldn't have been able to change Julius' mind, no matter how hard he tried. 'Right. Over there,' he said, eventually. 'There's a grid we can use.'

Julius looked along the duct leading off to their left, to where Skye was pointing. According to their map, it led right onto the bridge. They inched forward and, a minute later, Skye stopped. He crouched down, motioning for Julius to do the same. There was a meshed grille under their noses which looked down onto the floor below them.

'I think the coast is clear,' said Skye.

It certainly appeared that way, but that same nagging doubt of earlier had crept back over Julius' mind. Skye was right: there was no one in sight below, but why was that? Faith had seemed certain that, by accessing the relay station, they had blown their cover. So then, where was everybody? However, there wasn't much choice in the matter, as far as he was concerned – he had to get to his brother.

Gingerly, he lifted the grille and propped it against the side of the conduit to his right. Next, he activated his helmet and tapped the Exoskin button on his chest twice, triggering the cloaking mechanism, making him instantly invisible. Cautiously, he stuck his head through the hole and scanned the room; it was empty. He grabbed the edge of the opening in front of him, rolled head-over-heels through the gap and landed agilely below it. A couple of seconds later, he heard Skye drop down next to him.

He quickly lifted his Gauntlet, and inspected around him, double-checking that they really were alone. '*Scan the shuttle,*' he said to Skye's mind.

'*The bridge is clear,*' said Skye, a few moments later, moving the scanner in his PIP from side to side. '*There are no bio-signs.*'

'What about holos?'

'No electromagnetic interferences, either.'

'What's the radius on that scan?'

'About 500 feet, I'd s-'

'It's empty,' interrupted Julius, out loud.

'Shhh!' urged Skye.

'The shuttle is empty,' repeated Julius, not caring. Now he knew why he had felt so odd. Even though they had been careful, and the shuttle was moderately big, there was surely no way the sound of their passage could have gone completely undetected. When Faith had checked with Cress earlier, it had been confirmed that the transport had left Pit-Stop Pete with a full cargo. 'There should be 50 people in here.'

'Well, we should first make sure we definitely are alone,' whispered Skye.

'That won't be necessary!' They jumped as T'Rogon's voice filled the air suddenly.

Julius and Skye spun around quickly, Gauntlets at the ready. Behind the main control panel was a platform, with the holographic image of the Arneshian ambassador staring contemptuously at them.

'Now Mizkis, where are your manners?' said T'Rogon. 'I like to look my enemies in the eyes. Is that too much to ask?'

Julius pressed the Exoskin button on his chest, deactivating his helmet and camouflage. 'Glad you know that we are enemies,' he said, gesturing for Skye to reveal himself. 'Where is everybody? Where's Michael?'

'Why? Were you expecting to find him here?' taunted the ambassador.

'You said he would be. We have a recording of the discussion between you and K'Ssander, and very soon, the whole world will hear it too.'

T'Rogon laughed heartily, as if he had just been told a particularly funny joke. Julius bristled; the throbbing pain in his head had returned and, to make things worse, T'Rogon was now laughing at him.

'What's so funny?' growled Skye.

'I'm sorry,' said T'Rogon, recomposing himself. 'How very rude of me. There is a big difference, you know, between what you heard, and what actually is.'

'Is this some kind of a joke?' said Julius but, by now, he was getting a pretty clear idea of what the ambassador meant. Not only was the shuttle really empty, but Julius was now sure that there had never been any Nuarns, or Arneshians, on it. 'Why lead us to believe there were people onboard? Why the set up?'

'My Queen said this to me: "This White Child has been a thorn in our side twice already, T'Rogon; that is twice too many. Make sure he is out of the way when you do what you are really there to accomplish." And so, you are here. Does that answer your question?'

'You mean, your conversation with K'Ssander ...'

'Was a diversion? Yes. Of course, what we said about the game being fixed is true. The same goes for the Heron's sabotage. But you knew that already, didn't you? Alas, these things won't matter, soon enough. Our mission is almost complete.'

'What mission?' said Julius, fists clenched tightly at his sides.

'I'd rather not say, except that, you should keep an eye on Earth: it will be the show of the century. By the way, did you tell Freja about the mines? Of course you did. Thank you, dear boy. Now even the Grand Master of Tijara is busy elsewhere, on a fool's errand.'

'Fool's errand?' repeated Skye.

'Yes, chasing the imaginary minefield.'

Julius looked at Skye, astonished. Surely this couldn't possibly be true.

'*Tempus fugit,*' said T'Rogon. 'I'll leave you with a piece of good news, and some bad news. The good news is that some friends of yours didn't want to leave without saying goodbye: K'Ssander, A'Trid, B'Nold, step out if you please.'

From a darkened corner of the bridge, the three Arneshians walked forward.

'But the scanner; it didn't-' began Skye.

'Earth technology really isn't that great, you know,' said K'Ssander, with a smirk.

'I'm dying to hear the bad news,' said Julius drily.

'Oh, you will. This shuttle will self-destruct in ten minutes, starting now. Goodbye,' said T'Rogon, before his hologram vanished.

'*I have to warn Faith,*' Julius mind-messaged to Skye.

'*I'll keep them busy. Do it now!*' he replied.

Julius touched his Exoskin twice, selecting the full helmet and camouflage. There were two exits, one to each side of him; he sprinted for the one on the left, and leapt between A'Trid and B'Nold. To make sure that they would follow him, he stretched out his Gauntlet behind him and shot out a single, small fireball.

'Damn it!' Julius heard A'Trid cry out behind him, and hoped that he had slowed him down.

Julius ran through the exit and veered right, trying desperately to clear his mind of all T'Rogon's words. He was feeling far too much anger, and he needed to get rid of it if he hoped to use his skills properly. He focused on Faith and began to mentally reach out to him. '*Faith! Can you hear me?*' he cried. In his mind, he saw his words smashing against rocks. '*Faith!*' he tried again, more urgent this time. Again, nothing.

Suddenly, he saw a shadow advancing on him; he skidded to a stop and hurtled down a corridor leading off to his left, shooting a fireball behind him. Reaching the end of the corridor, he realised that it was a dead end, and started to turn back, but stopped as he saw A'Trid closing in on him. If he shot a fireball now, in such close quarters, he could seriously wound the Arneshian, so instead, he activated his shields and created a barrier between them.

'That's not fair,' shouted A'Trid in frustration, as he struck the shields with a flurry of powerful kicks and punches.

Julius ignored him, breathed deeply, and called out again with his mind to Faith.

'*You almost blew me head off!*' said Faith.

'*Get the Heron clear. Now! ... tell Freja ... minefield is ... ake!*'

'*Is what? I can't understand! I'll come and get you.*'

'*NO! Get them out!*' shouted Julius. His head flared with searing pain. He lost his focus, and the channel with Faith. At that moment, he knew that he had also lost his last chance of getting away: if he couldn't find an escape pod, he and Skye would both surely die on the shuttle.

A'Trid abruptly stopped his physical attack, opened his right hand and pointed it at Julius' shield; the symbol of Arnesh lit up in the middle of his palm, making the skin look almost transparent. He waved his hand and a stream of electricity surged outwards, striking the magnetic field in front of Julius.

Julius felt the shields quivering, as if the combination of the two energies had created something quite unstable. He knew he couldn't remain like that much longer, so he mustered as much strength as he could manage and shoved forward with his mind. It was too much for A'Trid to resist; he flew backwards, and smashed against the far wall, before landing on the floor unconscious.

Julius closed his shields, and rushed back to the bridge, trying to ignore the bright pain filling his head. When he got there, he saw B'Nold holding Skye by his arms, with K'Ssander standing in front of him, his right palm pointed menacingly. Julius caught a glimpse of the disk embedded in K'Ssander's hand. The Arneshian raised the disk to Skye's head, who began to twitch, as if a current of electricity was suddenly passing through him. Skye's cries of agony drove Julius into action. He stretched his right hand forward and mind-pushed K'Ssander away, then rushed at the Arneshian, springing onto him and dragging him to the floor.

That gave Skye the chance he needed. He wriggled free of B'Nold, spun around, and pushed him backwards with several short, powerful bursts of energy. The Arneshian jerked wildly, as Skye advanced forward, pummelling him out of the room and knocking him out cold. Julius, meanwhile, was feeling completely drained, and was struggling in vain to hold onto K'Ssander. The Arneshian broke away from his grip, and rushed at Skye.

'Watch it!' shouted Julius.

Skye heard the shout too late; as he stepped back inside the room, a strong arm wrapped itself around his neck.

'Let him go!' cried Julius. Slowly, he lifted his Gauntlet, and aimed it at the Arneshian's head.

Skye was tearing at K'Ssander's arm, trying desperately to prise it away from his windpipe.

'What do you care if he dies, McCoy?' he replied coldly. 'I thought you were here to save your little brother. Shame you won't get to see him one last time because, once they start the experiments on him, he'll never be the same ever again. Then he'll really be like us.'

'Leave Michael out of this,' warned Julius, through gritted teeth.

K'Ssander tightened his grip and moved his head behind Skye. He lifted his right hand and placed it against Skye's head; the disk in his palm glowing to show that it was active.

Julius could see that Skye was in agony, while his face was turning purple. He wasn't sure how much more his friend could take, but he was certain he wouldn't last much longer. Julius felt anger surging through his veins, and made no effort to restrain it this time; it was washing away the pain in his head and lending him some much-needed strength. As happened so often when he was that furious, the energy was dripping from his hands now, circling his arms like golden wisps.

'The ship is about to explode,' said Julius, steadying himself. 'We can finish this elsewhere.'

'I'm not afraid to die, McCoy. That's the difference between you and me.'

Julius saw Skye's eyes roll upwards and knew there was no time left. He didn't think twice about what to do next. 'So be it then,' he said, opening his left hand and beginning to draw from the Arneshian.

K'Ssander, who was clearly expecting a direct attack of some sort, was taken completely by surprise. Not knowing what was happening to him, his eyes grew large, like he had just realised something very important. His mouth fell open, but still he wouldn't let go of Skye. His skin, which was already greyish in colour, turned a good shade darker as he gasped for air.

Skye was still clawing at the Arneshian's arm, but weakly now; he didn't have much fight left in him.

'Let him go!' cried Julius again.

Whether or not K'Ssander could actually hear him was hard to tell, but he continued gripping Skye tightly. It was as if time itself had frozen in that one horrible moment: Skye's hands fell down by his sides and his head slumped forward. K'Ssander wheezed one last intake of air, before finally letting go, and crumpling onto the floor.

As that happened, a hand grabbed Julius' wrist from the side, immediately stopping the Draw. 'Enough,' a familiar voice said, gently.

Julius turned, wide-eyed, and saw Kelly standing next to him. A spark of hope lit up his heart, and he realised that he wasn't going to die on that shuttle after all.

'Skye!' he said, launching himself forward. But an officer appeared from behind him, grabbed him by the shoulders, and started to walk him away from the bridge. Julius, however, refused to leave without knowing whether Skye was alive or not, so he turned and held his ground, as Kelly knelt beside his friend.

'Is he all right?' asked Julius, his voice wavering.

Kelly scanned the boy quickly with a portable medical scanner. Then he placed a strange mask over his face. 'He's ok.'

Julius exhaled in relief. Then his eyes grew wide. 'T'Rogon rigged the shuttle to blow; we'd better get out of here!'

'Well, come on then; let's go!' said Kelly, scooping Skye up and running toward the exit. Three more officers quickly followed, each carrying one of the Arneshian boys.

'How did you know we were here?' asked Julius, as they ran.

'Freja told me to keep an eye on you,' he replied. 'And I figured, if you want to take my place some day, I better keep you alive.'

Julius looked at K'Ssander, who was dangling limply in the arms of one of Kelly's men, his skin still abnormally dark. A shiver ran through Julius; certainly, he had meant to severely hurt the Arneshian, and he would have finished him off to save Skye, but what would Freja think of him when he found out that he had used his Draw powers against a human being? All those lessons about being responsible with his skills had been flung out the window in a matter of seconds. Most of all, just then, Professor Chan's words echoed in his mind, like ghosts in a haunted house: "That, Mr K'Ssander, is the difference between our people and yours." Julius felt he had surely just proven that they were no different, or better than the Arneshians. The only thing he could be sure of right at that moment though, was that, when he had been given a choice between Skye's life or K'Ssander's, his heart had made the decision for him.

'Move it everybody!' urged Kelly. 'This joint is about to blow!'

They rushed toward the shuttle port, and through it into the Ahura Mazda, which was attached like a limpet. An officer sealed the port shut behind them, and the ship pulled away from the shuttle.

'Hold on, kid!' shouted Kelly to Julius.

Julius grabbed hold of the nearest railing, just in time. The blast of the shuttle explosion shoved the Ahura forward, like a stone from a slingshot. Julius turned to Kelly. 'Captain, we have to warn Freja!'

'He knows about the mines, Julius. Don't worry, the whole of Zed is mobilised, looking for them.'

'It's a trick, a decoy!'

'What do you mean?'

'T'Rogon told us that it was all a diversion, to get us out of the way. There's never been a minefield.'

Kelly stared at Julius, weighing the situation. 'Stay here.'

Julius nodded, and went over to Skye. The doctor was wrapping a Heal-O Collar around his neck, but not before Julius caught sight of the large dark bruises beginning to appear on his skin. 'He could have killed him,' he thought. Julius stood up, looking for the Arneshians, but couldn't see them anywhere. It was probably for the best though, given that he had almost regained his full strength now, thanks to the Draw he had done, and he was still feeling pretty angry.

'McCoy,' called Kelly. 'Come over to the bridge.'

Julius sprinted up the steps and joined the captain.

'The Grand Master is onscreen. Tell him what you know.'

Julius bowed quickly to Freja, trying not to think about the fact that he hadn't really been given permission to board the shuttle like he had. 'Sir, T'Rogon tricked us. The shuttle was empty and he said that there was never a minefield; it was just a way of keeping us busy. He said to keep our eyes on Earth, because the real show would be there.'

Freja stared back at Julius thoughtfully, then switched his gaze to Kelly. 'I want the Taurus One o-'

Before he could finish, the Ahura Mazda began to tremble like a frightened animal. Julius saw Freja grab hold of the arm of his chair, inside his own ship.

'What's happening?' said Julius.

'Lieutenant, report!' ordered Kelly.

Elian Flywheel, from the pilot's seat near the front of the ship, was trying unsuccessfully to steer the Ahura Mazda on a straight course. 'We're stuck, Captain. I can't move her an inch.'

'It's the Arneshians,' said Julius. 'They did the same thing to the Heron.'

'It looks like the entire Zed fleet is immobilised,' said Elian.

Suddenly, all the lights in the ship flickered and went out, leaving them in darkness.

'Sir, whatever's keeping us still seems to have drained all the power out of our ship,' said an officer to Kelly's right.

The trembling slowly subsided, allowing Julius to stand without having to hold onto something. The only light filtering in was from beyond the front window of the ship where, in the distance, the near side of the Earth was bathed in sunlight.

'S-sir,' said Elian, almost in a whisper. 'You've got to see this.'

Julius followed as Kelly moved over beside her. What he saw, out in space beyond the Ahura, froze him to the spot. He gripped the left arm of Elian's seat, a clawing sense of dread spreading over him.

Silent and lethal, the Taurus One had left its moorings, and was moving through space like a jellyfish through water. Every ship in its path was being pushed gently aside, as if carried by the crest of a small wave. For the previous few months, it had maintained its spherical shape, making Starfleet quite forget about its ability to morph. Now, as it glided past the Moon toward Earth, it began to seamlessly transform and stretch, until it had become a vast, flat disk, its surface so great that it obscured the sun. Not one of the Zed ships was intervening, trapped by the invisible energy field that was holding them all at bay.

The Arneshian disk continued on its relentless course, until it was directly above Earth, where it stopped, and hovered like a giant hat, blocking the planet from the rays of the sun. Oceans, mountains, plains and deserts had all turned a sickly grey hue, swathed in the shadow of the disk; they seemed to have lost their vitality and life. The disk sat there, silent and ominous for a moment, then began to morph again. Like a silk scarf covering a ball, it melted over the surface of the Earth, until it had completely enveloped it, creating a perfect, gigantic cocoon.

Julius' knees gave in and he slumped to the ground. Thinking of his parents, witnessing all this from within it, was too much to handle, and his brain shut down.

The Taurus One began to glow, dimly at first, then brighter, until it was so fierce that the bridge of the Ahura Mazda was flooded in light, forcing everyone onboard to shield their eyes behind their arms. Then, just as it seemed it couldn't get any brighter, the light dimmed again. The cocoon gently opened, and began to rise up, until Earth was freed once more from its grasp. The Taurus floated there for a brief moment, and then continued to rise, up and up into space. Its task completed, it entered into warp and, in a flash, it was gone.

The lights on the bridge flickered back to life a second later, and the crew stood blinking at each other in stunned silence.

'The power is back online, Captain,' said Elian, snapping out of it.

'Take us closer to Earth, Lieutenant. Run a scan,' ordered Kelly.

The Ahura Mazda moved within range, and Kelly strode over to his tactical officer. 'Report. Have they hurt our people?'

'Sir,' gulped the officer, turning white. 'There are no people. Sir … all the humans are gone!'

NO MAN'S LAND

Julius' footsteps echoed in the abandoned street. The sky was clear, the kind of blue he hadn't seen in three whole years. There were no clouds to be seen, and no gulls or birds of any sort. Edinburgh Castle was sitting proudly atop its rock, unconcerned by the lack of tourists and the eerie absence of the one o'clock gun, a memory of centuries past.

The air here seemed fresher to Julius than on Zed; the smell of the trees, the grass and the sea mingled together, filling his lungs. He could see his house halfway down the lane, his dad's Bumble Bee fly-car parked out front, its little wings reflecting the July sun. Julius stopped beside it and looked at the garden. The weeds had grown significantly in the last three months, suffocating some of the flowers that Jenny McCoy loved to grow along the edges of the stone path. If he had had more time, he could have cut the weeds back a little, but then, what was the point really? He stepped forward, toward the front door, looked into the retina scanner to its left, and pressed the entry button.

The buzzing noise of the door opening startled Julius. It almost seemed inappropriate in that silence, like talking loudly at someone's wake. He stepped inside and was immediately hit by the smell of rotten food and stale air. He stopped breathing through his nose and said, 'Computer, activate ventilation system.'

A jet of fresh air streamed into the living room, confirming that at least the house computer was still working. A thick layer of dust had settled over all the furniture and pictures, giving the place a horribly abandoned feeling. In the absence of its normal occupants, it appeared that a family of little spiders had moved in, and Julius had to duck to avoid a clutch of cobwebs as he climbed the stairs.

He pushed his bedroom door open and walked in. It had been a long time since he had last seen it, but everything was just the way he had left it. Sunlight streamed in through the window, illuminating his bed. He noticed something sticking out from under his pillow, and he grabbed it; it was a sealed envelope, labeled, "To Julius. M.".

Julius stood there for a moment, staring at the familiar handwriting. Michael could have chosen to send him a message over the net, but hadn't. Instead, he had chosen something a lot more personal, which was why this, more than anything, was hurting him the most. He pocketed the envelope without opening it, knowing that he couldn't really cope with it just then.

Before going back downstairs, he checked the other bedrooms. His brother's bed was made, which didn't surprise him, and so too was his parents' bed. He wondered how much sleep they had managed since Michael's departure, and gently closed their door.

When he arrived in the kitchen and saw the dining table, his heart skipped a beat. At the moment in which the Taurus One had closed over Earth, Jenny and Rory must have been sitting down for breakfast. The table was set for two; a couple of slices of old mouldy toast were on a separate plate in the middle of it, and there were dead flies in the marmalade jar, which had been left open. There was also a spoon on the floor beside one of the chairs, with bits of what looked like dried food stuck to it. It was as if his dad – because Julius knew that that was his seat – was moving the spoon towards his mouth when it had happened.

Julius activated his PIP and selected the bio-particle detector. All of the Mizkis had been given one before they left Zed to come down here, so they could scan their homes for human traces. He passed the chip in his hand over the chairs, table and floor, without noticing anything out of the ordinary. When he finally sent the readings back to Tijara, he let out a sigh of relief; the Arneshians had not vapourised them.

'Julius? Are you in here?' called Morgana from the front door.

He gave a last look around before leaving the kitchen. Morgana was standing by the door, looking tired. Julius saw that her eyes were red from crying, and guessed that the emotion of seeing her empty house must have proved too much.

'How did they do it?' she asked.

Julius shook his head. He had been wondering the same thing. 'I take it you didn't find any traces either.'

'None, thankfully. Let's walk back, please. I don't want to stay here a minute longer.'

Julius stepped outside and locked the door, knowing that the house computer would also shut down. 'Kaori?'

'She's gone to check her roommate's place, near Tollcross. She'll make her own way back.'

They walked in silence, side by side. Julius was so overwhelmed by the emptiness that he didn't even flinch when Morgana hooked her arm in his. Right then, the gesture felt like the most normal thing in the world. He unhooked his arm and placed it over her shoulders – it felt good when she leaned her head against his shoulder, and wrapped an arm around his waist.

'It's too late,' she said. 'Now that the truth is out, it's too late.'

Julius knew she was right. The recording of T'Rogon had been broadcast to all the Earth, and Zed, colonies, and Mr List had been able to prove that the game had been compromised. But the people who really needed to hear this, people like Paulo Trent and his brother, weren't around anymore. So it didn't matter.

'What's Freja going to do?' she asked.

'They'll shield the planet at the end of June. It'll give it a chance to take a break … from us, I guess. They think that by the time we return, it will have renewed the land.'

'Can we really get them back?'

Julius could hear a hint of tears in her voice, and held her tighter. 'We'll get them *all* back.'

'How are we going to do that, Julius?'

'We're going after them.'

Morgana stopped, looked up at him and, after a few seconds, nodded once, her gaze sure and confident.

They began to walk again, heading towards the shuttle. Julius had no idea how they were going to accomplish the rescue, but he felt sure that Freja would find a way.

Still, for now, the Arneshians had won.

TIJARAN TALES
BOOK IV

TIJARA'S HEART

CONTENTS

PROLOGUE

Carlos Freja ended the vidcall with a pained expression on his face. He had been dialling his sister Clelia's number every day for the past five months, and watched the vidmessage on her answer-phone, fully aware that she wouldn't be picking up. Her house had been empty ever since the 19th of March 2858: the day humanity had completely disappeared from Earth. Calling her was neither logical nor rational, but seeing her warm smile had kept him going during that long summer, as he set about organising the largest rescue mission Zed had ever planned. Freja needed his own hope to remain strong; the hope that he would be able to find three billion people still alive and bring them home safely. His students would be counting on him, as too would Clelia. If only he knew where to start looking.

He stood up and strolled over to the only window in his office. He could see Tijara's entrance from there, with its luscious ferns crawling over the walls, and the gurgling blue waters of the surrounding moat. A group of 2 Mizki Juniors were waiting on the Intra-Rail platform, probably heading to Satras. Normally they would have been in class at this hour, but the start of term had been rescheduled to allow for all the preparations. He was going to miss this place, he thought.

A beep made Freja turn. 'Come in.'

The office door slid quietly open and Master Cress entered and bowed to the Tijaran Grand Master.

Freja bowed back and invited him to sit on one of the grey leather sofas. 'Coffee, Nathan?'

'Industrial strength, please.'

Freja poured two cups from the freshly filled pot and handed one to Cress, as the intoxicating aroma spread through the room. 'Let's hear it,' he said, sitting down.

'Some good news at last. List says we'll be ready for departure by the end of September, now that we know how to use those Arneshian portals. It wasn't easy to hack into their operational systems, but we've managed it. It means that when we find our people we can teleport them back here.'

Freja nodded, satisfied. He still couldn't believe that teleportation was actually possible, but it also didn't surprise him in the least that the Arneshians had discovered it; after all, they had been born with advanced technological skills. 'What else?'

'We've managed to replicate the static field they used against our fleet, back in March. It still needs to be properly studied, but we know it can stop anything in its tracks. Plus, we can create a protective cloak with it.'

'Excellent,' said Freja. 'We can activate it around Earth and use it to reinforce our own shield, here on Zed. We don't know how long we'll be gone for and I don't want to find any surprises when we get back.'

'On that note, List has requested to stay behind. He says someone has to work the main portal at this end.'

'Agreed. Tell him to assemble his team and pass on any other requests. I also want someone to check that our animals on Kapaldi 22 don't go killing each other off while we're away — at least not any more than nature intended.'

'How long do you think we'll be away for?'

'It's five months from here to Arnesh, at warp speed. Then we need to find our people, and who knows where we'll be by then. And let's not forget our *other mission*.'

Cress looked suddenly tense. 'Do you still intend to rebuild Tijara's Heart?'

'I do.' Freja's mood darkened a little. 'We don't have any time left. Salgoria will overwhelm us if we don't act now.'

'The Curia has agreed then?'

'Yes: on the condition that I build the crystal too, which was also my requirement.'

'The crystal … how do we know it'll work this time? McCoy could—'

'It *will* work,' Freja cut in. 'We have no choice. We waited three years … and for what? Our people have gone and it's our duty to find them; at all costs.' He stood up and walked back to the window. The warmth of the artificial sun soothed his skin and restored some sense of calm in him. 'These students are the best humanity has to offer, Nathan, and McCoy is the brightest star of them all. We have to take the risk. If he can't do it, no one can.'

'Does he need to know?' asked Cress, standing.

'Not until the time comes. Everything will be ready by then.'

'Very well,' said Cress.

As he left Freja's office, Cress felt the pressure of what was to come settling heavily on his heart. Still, he knew he would cope with it, as he had always done. But this time was different, because his anxiety came from the knowledge that Julius McCoy had just been chosen as Tijara's next sacrifice.

MOONRISING

The crate sailed smoothly through the air, taking a sharp right turn at the centre of Tijara's hangar and headed straight for the west side, where dozens of similar containers were already neatly stacked against the wall. As it reached the top layer of them, it hovered there for a few seconds, then floated slightly to the left.

Julius McCoy was adjusting the crate's angle with his mind — an operation that he had performed at least four dozen times that morning — his right hand stretched out toward it, holding it suspended in midair. Once he was satisfied with its positioning, he gently lowered it into place and let out a sigh of relief.

'Excellent, mate,' said Faith, hovering over to him with the aid of his metal skirt. 'That was the last one.'

'For now,' said Julius, rubbing his temples. Using mind-skills for long periods of time always gave him a slight headache, even after three years of training.

'Then let's go grab some lunch. Me stomach is a-rumbling.'

Julius plucked his jumper up from the floor and dusted it off, paying particular attention to the new label on the left sleeve, which had "Julius McCoy – 4MA –Tijara" emblazoned on it in silver letters.

When the two boys arrived in the mess hall, they saw various small groups of students having their lunches and talking quietly among themselves. It was in stark contrast to the excited mealtime chatter of previous years. Julius had grown used to the dampened atmosphere of that summer and found it quite understandable considering the circumstances: loved ones, family members, friends — every last one of them had suffered during their latest encounter with the Arneshians, whisked away in the blink of an eye, victims of their enemy's technological superiority. Still, Julius was sure each of his fellow students hung from his same thread of hope: that somehow they would see them all again.

The Nuarns — later generations of Arneshians who had been raised on Earth — had been taken too, including Julius' own brother, Michael. What made it worse for Julius was that Michael, unlike his parents, had decided to leave Earth of his own free will, long before the Arneshians' final move; like 50 million other Nuarns, he thought that he was going *home*, to live with his own kind. If only they had listened to Zed's warnings about accepting the Arneshians' invitation, everything would have been different. But the Academy's words had fallen on deaf ears, and by the time the truth had been uncovered for all to see, it had been too late: earthlings and Nuarns alike had realised their mistake from the inside of an enemy ship.

Julius hated it when his thoughts took a trip of their own, revisiting the unpleasant events of the 19th of March, the day he had been unable to stop Ambassador T'Rogon from carrying out his plan, and when he had fought K'Ssander, the Arneshian boy, almost to the end. If Captain Kelly hadn't arrived when he had, Julius could have killed

K'Ssander. 'Would have,' he thought to himself. 'He had Skye in a headlock and wasn't going to let him go. I gave him plenty of chances. What did he think, that I would let my friend get hurt without a figh–'

'Julius!' called Morgana, from a nearby table. 'Over here.'

He snapped back to the present and turned around. Faith had already been served and was sitting by Morgana's side, eating, while Julius was still standing, daydreaming at the counter, with an empty tray in his hands. He grabbed a plate of boiled carrot sticks and went to join them.

'Did you fall asleep or something?' asked Faith, amused.

'Just tired, that's all,' he answered.

Morgana looked at him, a concerned expression on her face. 'Still not sleeping?'

'On and off.' He nibbled half-heartedly on a carrot. 'It's all so different this year. No Summer Camp, no new timetables, no 1MJs to fill up the -6 dorm.'

'Aye, that's the creepiest thing,' said Morgana. 'All three schools are short of 30 students each — it's hard to believe there's no kids left.'

'I never thought I would say this,' added Faith, 'but I miss me classes. Especially Professor De Boer's. The only thing they've done so far is to insert those shield-chip implants into our feet, back in June. And they still hurt!'

'I wish they'd tell us something,' said Julius, feeling peeved. 'All we do is pack, move cargo and prep the fleet, but what's the plan?'

'I hear you,' said Faith. 'Personally I could do with a date.'

'And it would be about time too!' said Skye, arriving as if on cue and dumping himself on the bench next to Faith.

'Mr Miller,' said Faith, shifting to try make some space for himself. 'What an honour to see you.'

'I know, right,' he replied, stealing one of Julius' carrots. 'I'm telling you, I feel like I'm getting to know the Curia more intimately than I ever would have thought possible.'

'What?' said Julius. 'Is that your roundabout way of saying you've scored with Roversi's daughter already?'

'Nah. I've decided that going after the Curio Maximus' most prized possession could be a career breaker.'

'Or maker,' added Morgana. 'You could marry her, you know?'

Skye shivered. 'Don't even go there. Anyway, Faith, what's with the date request, then?'

'It's not that kind of date,' said Julius. 'We just want to know when the action is going to start.'

'And I have an answer for you,' replied Skye, winking.

'For real?' asked Julius, suddenly fully awake.

'Yep. But you guys can't tell anyone, OK? It'll be on the news later, anyway.'

'When?' urged Faith and Morgana in unison.

'28th of September.'

'In two days?' cried Julius.

'Shhh!' said Skye, hushing him and looking around nervously. 'I don't want to lose my future job!'

'This is awesome,' said Julius, lowering his voice. 'So what are they saying at the Curia?'

'I don't know where we're going — or how — but apparently they've found a lead as to where some of our people may be.'

'How did they do it?' asked Morgana, her food forgotten.

'Not sure, but it's what has kept us back this whole time. At least Gabriel List and his men have been able to work that teleportation thingy.'

'Wow,' said Faith. 'That technology is really something else. Sorry Skye, but when it must be said, it must.'

They all knew how Skye's hatred for everything Arneshian made him pretty touchy about anything resembling a compliment to them, so they simply avoided discussing how good their enemy's scientific knowledge was.

'It's fine,' he said. 'This is way too big to ignore. Did you know that List is staying behind, to activate the Zed portal?'

'No way,' said Julius. 'I didn't think Freja would leave anyone behind.'

'Someone has to, though,' said Morgana, assertively, 'for when our people return.'

'Who else is staying, Skye?' asked Faith.

'Part of the Curia, a few medics, Gassendi's crew and most of Satras.'

'And what about us? What will they want us to do?'

'Not sure yet, but all the schools are going. Believe me, we won't be idle. The whole fleet is coming with.'

'I'm glad my sister Kaori is still in school,' said Morgana. 'All her older friends have already been given active duties.'

'That's right,' said Skye. 'Maya, from last year's Zed Toon, graduated in May and she's been assigned to one of the Herons.'

'She'll be fine, I'm sure,' added Morgana, noticing how his brow creased.

'Sure. I bet you're glad that your Maks is still in school. You guys going out, or what?'

She nodded enthusiastically, half blushing.

Julius coughed and almost choked on one of his carrots.

'*I knew it,*' continued Skye, cheekily. 'I saw you the other night in Satras, by the lake.'

'Really?' she said, fully blushing this time. 'Where were you?'

'Just passing by. I would have stopped to say hi too, if it wasn't for the fact that I couldn't actually see his hands?'

'Get out of here,' she said, giggling.

Even Faith began to laugh, as Morgana turned ever redder.

Julius, on the other hand, was only pretending — badly — to enjoy the banter. Inside his head, he was watching an image of himself wrecking the mess hall, dragging Maks Suraev by the hair, to behind the food counter, opening the oven door and throwing him inside, before shutting the door and raising the temperature to the max. Over the last couple of months he had managed to push his half-feelings for Morgana — with no small amount of effort — to the very back of his mind. Still, he really didn't need all this talk of "*your* Maks" and "disappearing hands" in the same sentence as "Morgana".

'Look at her, Jules,' said Skye. 'Isn't it funny how red she gets?'

'Hilarious,' he mumbled, renewing his attack on the carrot sticks.

'Speaking of … this stuff,' said Faith, looking serious, 'and I may be totally off base here, but I think that … maybe … perhaps Siena likes me … a little?'

The other three stared at him in perfect silence for a few seconds, and then started to laugh.

'What?' asked Faith, blushing every bit as red as Morgana had.

'I never thought I would see the day,' cried Skye, slapping his thigh.

'Bah … you're probably right, I am mad,' he added sheepishly. 'I mean, I can't even walk.'

'No, no, no!' said Morgana, putting one hand on his arm. 'Quite the contrary. We're laughing because she's fancied you for ages, hovering skirt and all!'

'Does she?' he asked, eyes growing wide.

It took the best part of lunch to convince Faith that they weren't kidding, but when they returned to work that afternoon, he was sporting the most delighted smile they had seen in a long time.

By that evening, rumours of the impending departure had been officially confirmed, lifting the mood right across Zed. All the Mizkis received a message to gather in the assembly hall by 10:00 hours of the following morning, for a short briefing. So it was that, after a late breakfast, Julius arrived at the hall with his classmates, and waited eagerly for the Grand Master's appearance.

The empty rows at the back were a painful reminder of the absence of the 1MJs and sure enough, when Freja entered, Julius noticed him glancing sadly at those very seats. The Mizkis stood up as Freja climbed the four steps to the podium. As he bowed in acknowledgement to them, they bowed back.

'Be seated,' he said.

It occurred to Julius that Freja looked in much higher spirits today than he had over the course of the summer. The Tijaran Grand Master, who had been busy with preparations, had occasionally appeared on the Space Channel, always looking tired and strained. But not today, thought Julius. Today, he looked as strong as the first time he had seen him, right there in that same hall.

'Mizkis,' Freja began, 'for the past three years, the Lunar Perimeter has been at the centre of events that will live forever in history. After decades of seemingly peaceful existence, Queen Salgoria and her people twice tried, and failed, to shake our world, but succeeded in the end.' Freja let his words echo in the stillness of the hall. 'We have all suffered much these last few months, dealing with the loss of our families and friends, afraid that we would never know what became of them. When I think that I at least know where one of my family, my own son, is, I cannot help but feel a little guilty, knowing that most of you sitting here before me have no such luck.'

'He has a son?' whispered Julius into Skye's ear, but his friend looked just as surprised.

'You have all worked hard this summer, helping Zed prepare for its biggest ever mission, and for that I thank you. Mizkis, you have made us proud.'

Murmurs of assent broke the silence and Julius could have sworn he heard a few sniffles from the back.

'Tomorrow at noon,' continued Freja, 'we will leave the Moon and our own solar system. I cannot tell you when we will return, nor if all of us ever will but, wherever we go, we shall carry the legacy of Marcus Tijara with us.'

'On your feet, Mizkis!' cried Master Cress, who was standing a little behind, and to the right of Freja.

Julius was startled, as he hadn't noticed him entering the room. The ceiling began to retract and the lights dimmed. He looked up, as the vastness of space filled his view, separated only by the Zed shield. Then he saw a vast shadow, slowly obscuring the starlight.

'Behold the might of Moonrising!' declared Freja.

Julius' mouth formed an O, as a sense of awe fell over him.

'It's a battlestar ...' uttered Faith, mesmerised by the sight of it.

Towering over their heads was the most majestic spaceship that Julius had ever seen. Dark as the night, it reminded him of a shark, as viewed from below. It was exceptionally tall — *thick*, was the word that came to mind — and he was able to make out five distinct layers, which appeared as if they had been designed to fit snugly together, as they were now, but still able to separate when needed.

'Mizkis,' said Cress, 'let's hear it for our new home.'

Julius prepared for the school salute, pressing his right arm against his body, with his left hand resting on Skye's right shoulder.

Cress shouted, 'In your heart!'

Julius cried back, 'TI-JA-RA!' as he slammed his right fist against his chest and stomped his right foot on the ground, at the same time. Just like the first day he had done the salute, he felt a rush of energy fire through him.

Freja looked at the students. 'A new chapter of history lies before us. May we return home, victorious!'

'So let it be,' answered the assembly.

The Grand Master bowed and left the hall, while Master Cress took his place on the podium. The excitement was tangible, and it was a few minutes before silence could be restored.

'You will receive the blueprints for Battlestar Moonrising later today. Pack your belongings and say your goodbyes. Boarding procedures will commence tomorrow morning at 08:00 hours from the school's hangar. Dismissed!'

*

That afternoon Julius thought it only appropriate that the Skirts have one last game in the Hologram Palace before leaving. Unfortunately, it seemed every other student on Zed had the same idea, so they ended up having an ice-cream at Mario's Ice-land instead, before returning to the school to lounge in the garden, under their favourite oak tree.

'It says here that it can carry 5,000 people,' marvelled Faith, reading from the holoscreen floating over the palm of his hand.

'What's in each of its layers?' asked Julius, pulling himself closer to Faith.

'Tijara, Tuala and Sield schools are in the top three. Then one is shared by the Curia and the Hospital, and the last one is occupied by New Satras; says here it can carry 3,000 peeps by itself!'

'Not bad,' said Julius. 'That's why it looks massive.'

'When all the ships are together,' read Morgana from her own screen, 'they call it the Citadel, and hyperjump is offline.'

'Not warp, I hope,' remarked Faith.

'That one's fine. But all units must split before a skip.'

'And what about our fleet?' asked Skye, lying on the grass, staring up at the oak's long and luscious branches.

'There will be Cougars onboard each hangar,' answered Morgana, quickly retrieving the information. 'Plus a fleet of Herons, 10,000 strong.'

'Talk about the solitude of space,' said Julius, impressed by the numbers.

'Hey guys,' said Skye, 'I picked up something for us to mark the occasion.'

'Is it legal?' asked Faith.

'Come closer,' he said, and knelt next to the oak's trunk.

Julius watched as Skye pulled a small metal plaque from his pocket, together with his trusty Omni-gizmo which was currently on its screwdriver setting. He held the plaque against the tree and fixed it to the wood. Selecting the laser setting next, he proceeded to write, "The Skirts were here" on it, followed by his own name.

'I didn't think you were the sentimental type,' said Faith, taking the gizmo from Skye's hand and etching his name below his.

Julius and Morgana followed suit, adding their names as best they could.

'That was a lovely idea, Skye,' said Morgana.

Julius thought so too. At least there was some mark of them having been there, left behind. After all, no matter how mighty Moonrising had looked to him, there was no guarantee they would return victorious, as Freja had wished. Even with all the optimism in the universe, there was still a chance they may not return at all.

THE NEW SOLO CHAMPION

Leaving Tijara had not been easy for Julius, who had been surprised by the sense of loss he had felt that morning. For months he had been waiting for the rescue mission to begin, without sparing much thought to what he would be giving up by leaving. He stared at his school through the Stork's small porthole window, as it disappeared slowly from view below him, lost in the shimmering waves of Zed's shield. 'I wonder if we'll make it back for graduation,' he said, quietly.'

Faith followed his gaze out to the Moon. 'You think it'll take us that long?'

'Who knows,' he answered. 'But if it does ... then today was the last time we'll ever get to wake up in Tijara. We can't go back once we're officers.'

'I hadn't thought about it,' said Faith. 'You're making me sad, McCoy. And I don't want to be sad on me birthday week. Already I feel like there's not a lot to celebrate.'

'Sixteen is a good one, Faith,' said Julius. 'At the very least let us take you to New Satras for some food.'

'All right, but no Supernova, please,' he added quickly, remembering the stomach-bursting cake they had got for him on his previous birthday. 'I think me guts are still suffering last year's side effects.'

'Yeah,' grinned Julius, 'Nurse Primula mentioned your *indisposition*.'

'I never wished so badly to be a cow, like I did that night, McCoy. I tell you, I could have really done with an extra stomach.'

Julius laughed. 'Did you wish to be a cow on more than one occasion? Don't worry mate, no cake for you this year.' With his mood uplifted, Julius readied himself for boarding Moonrising.

The anticipation of the impending mission had spread throughout the Mizkis, renewing their hope and strengthening their hearts. Julius could see thick wisps of green and grey floating below the ceiling, a sign of their excitement, mixed in with a twinge of anxiety. By the time the Stork docked inside the battlestar, the wisps were filling the entire shuttle.

*

'This place is bigger than Pete's'!' cried Faith, hovering into the hangar without even bothering to pick his bag up.

When she heard that, Morgana rushed outside, leaving Julius and Skye to carry all of their stuff.

'Here we go again,' said Julius, shrugging and shouldering her rucksack.

Skye shook his head and picked up Faith's. 'Some things never change.'

As it was, the hangar was much larger than Julius had imagined, with high ceilings, mezzanines, gangways and plenty of wide, open spaces. As he walked towards the exit, he passed row upon row of black Cougars, silently waiting, like animals ready to pounce; he knew there were even more of them in the levels above and below him, without counting those carried by the other two schools. Including the thousands of Herons following them, Zed was really travelling with a mighty fleet this time. And that, Julius kept thinking, was bound to help. On leaving the hangar, he saw a large screen on the wall, with the full layout of Tijara. He quickly noticed familiar flashing red dots set into the walls, and figured that they were there to direct them to the central section of the ship where, no doubt, the dorms, galley, mess hall and engine room were located. To the left of this were the bridge and the War-deck, plus the staff and officers' quarters; to the right were the training areas for the White and Grey Arts classes.

'How do we get to New Satras?' called out Lopaka, a question which was promptly echoed by most of his classmates.

'Wouldn't you like to know, Mr Liway,' Hamza Patel answered cheerily. The guidance teacher of the Mizki Apprentices had just joined them and was now motioning for them to follow him.

As they trooped after Patel, Julius tried to keep track of their route, but each new corridor looked the same as the previous one, with dull, grey metal features everywhere. The whole vessel felt weird: it lacked the cosiness of the Ahura Mazda and the comforts of Gea One. Maybe it was just the sheer size of it, or perhaps it was just its nature — after all, Moonrising *was* a battleship. In one word, Julius would have described it as *gritty*.

Eventually, after numerous turns and sets of stairs, they arrived at their dorms.

'3MAs,' called Patel, 'left corridor. 4MAs, to the right. Girls' rooms first, then boys, same pairs as always. Drop your belongings and meet me back here in five minutes. Go!'

The Mizkis shuffled along, filing into their respective corridors. Julius and Skye headed to their room, which, like on Zed, was the third one on the right.

Skye looked into the retina sensor and the door slid open silently. 'This is shabby as anything,' he said, trudging over to the farther of the two beds in the room.

Julius dropped his bag on the floor and looked around. There were no windows, but the wall had one large scenery screen, which also acted as a display. The room was certainly smaller than what they usually had, but he didn't figure he would be spending much time there anyway.

'The bathroom is tiny,' said Skye, peering into a back room. 'I hope Faith can fit in his one, with his skirt.'

'Surely they've thought of that,' said Julius, heading for the door. 'Come on. Let's get going.'

As it turned out, Faith was more than satisfied with his extra-large facilities, an unexpected benefit which made his roommate Barth a very happy Mizki indeed.

Once all the Apprentices were back, Patel led them up the stairs, into the mess hall.

'This is a bit … dismal,' groaned Morgana, miserably observing the shabby grey decor all around.

Julius was sure he was going to have to change his one word description of Moonrising from *gritty* to *depressing*. 'Did they run out of money or something?'

'Please, let the food be all right,' added Skye, sounding concerned.

Julius, who was now feeling particularly grumpy, took a seat on one of the hard, iron benches. 'If this is it, I'm not looking forward to seeing New Satras at all,' he muttered.

Patel was waiting for the students to sit, all the time observing them with an amused little smile. 'Welcome to BM Tijara, Mizkis,' he began. 'I trust you found your dorms welcoming and cheerful.'

'Has he *seen* the dorms?' whispered Morgana.

'The stylish interior design,' continued Patel, 'is especially visible in common areas, such as this mess hall. The vibrancy of the colours simply jumps out at you, doesn't it?'

'Is he even on the same ship as us?' said Leanne Nord, not quietly enough.

Patel seemed to be greatly enjoying their puzzlement, until he could no longer disguise it and began to laugh.

'That's it,' said Faith, 'he's banged his head somewhere. Julius, get Nurse Primula.'

'I'm sorry, Mizkis,' said Patel, regaining some composure. 'What you see is a battlestar in safe mode, where all power is converged in its core. This can happen during hyperjump or in combat. Normally though, part of the power is re-routed to the holonet, which makes this place feel a little more homely.'

Julius was still unsure about how that would actually work, but three years on Zed had, if nothing else, taught him to expect the improbable.

'MAs,' said Patel. 'I give you the *real* Moonrising.'

At those words a wave of crackling static shot through the room, striking across every single surface in the mess hall. As it passed over, it laid a kaleidoscope of colours across the furniture, floor, ceiling and walls, transforming the dreary hall into a first class lounge area.

'Plug me in and call me a floor lamp,' said Faith, hovering upwards and twirling on the spot in delight as he admired the changes.

Julius was every bit as astonished as everyone else at what he saw. Thanks to the soft wall lights, the atmosphere had been transformed into something far more relaxed: pastel tones of blue and green helped with the new uplifting ambience of the place, while leafy virtual plants lent the sitting areas an air of privacy and comfort.

Patel enjoyed the Mizkis' reaction a little longer, before regaining their attention. 'Given the circumstances we find ourselves in, the school year will revolve around the rescue mission. Your timetables will be reduced to only the essentials and, most importantly, it will be flexible. Some of your teachers are on active duties, like Professor Farshid, so, when they're needed, your classes will be cancelled at a moment's notice. That said, there is a weekly programme of studies for all of you, which will be sent to your PIPs.'

'We'd completely understand if you happened to forget to do that,' added Faith, innocently.

'Thank you, Mr Shanigan. I'll make sure *I don't* forget,' replied Patel, drawing a few laughs from the students. 'Teachers or not, you still need to complete your training.'

'Good try, Faith,' said Julius, patting him on the shoulder.

'And now, for your timetables.' Patel activated his PIP and dabbed the screen a few times. 'Open your mail, please.'

A moment later Julius received Patel's message and opened it. He quickly saw that his chosen subjects – Spaceship Management and Catalyst training – were on Monday and Wednesday mornings.

'Here's the new subject,' cried Skye excitedly. 'It's called Twist.'

'Wait,' said Julius. 'Isn't that like, an old dance?'

'I doubt it's the same thing,' said Morgana. 'It's says here that Professor Morales will be taking it.'

'Followed by an hour of Gene Therapy for yours truly,' added Julius.

'They're still playing with your DNA, huh?' asked Faith, leaning in to examine his planner.

'Apparently so,' replied Julius, who wasn't too happy about it.

'Better you than me.'

'Cheers.'

'It looks like Fridays are free,' said Skye.

Julius checked and noticed the empty space. The weekly programme seemed greatly reduced compared to previous years — not that he minded that too much.

Patel allowed them a few minutes to examine the message, then spoke again. 'Until 17:00, Monday to Friday, you must remain within Tijara, as you could be assigned to internal active duties. Outside of these times, you are free to visit New Satras although, for this week, you must wait until Saturday morning. Curfew is at the usual 20:00, Sunday to Thursday, and 21:00 at weekends. As for today, you'll start your timetable at 14:00.'

'Do we still need to keep a log of each lesson?' asked Isolde, clearly hoping for a negative answer.

'You do, Miss Frey,' he said, shattering that little dream. 'And now you're free to go.'

With lunchtime approaching, Julius and the others decided to remain in the hall, and moved over to a group of sofas, where they were soon joined by Siena and Isolde.

At one point Morgana nudged Julius in the ribs, and pointed at Faith, a cheeky grin on her face. When Julius looked up he saw that Faith was peering at Siena through the transparent holoscreen on his hand, pretending to read something.

'*Caught you!*' said Julius, inside Faith's mind.

Faith jolted, and fumbled with his screen, clearly flustered.

Julius and Morgana tried to stifle a laugh as Faith attempted to reactivate his PIP as if nothing had happened, all the time throwing them daggers with his eyes.

Just as Julius was returning to examine his class schedule, Gustavo Perez's voice rang through the mess hall. 'Blimey, McCoy! Have you seen the Solo chart?'

The whole room went quiet and, judging by Gustavo's face, it was easy to tell that it wasn't good news.

Julius removed the timetable from the screen with a flick of his finger and selected the Game Charts app. Without realising it, he was now literally on the edge of his seat and his palms had grown sweaty. After almost two years as the reigning Solo champion of Zed, another Mizki had beaten Julius: appearing at rank 1 was the unknown F.H., from Sield School. He re-read the chart again, just to make sure he had it right, but no matter how many times he checked it, F.H. was still there, for a game played the evening before, during their last night on Zed. Julius was too stunned to say anything and largely ignored the sympathetic pats on the shoulder from his classmates.

By lunchtime, he was still staring blankly at the screen, so Morgana went to fill his tray for him, while Faith and Skye led him by his arms to the table. Julius was processing the news, while having his food, which quite clearly wasn't happening, as he demonstrated by trying to eat his soup with a fork.

'Are you all right?' asked Morgana tentatively.

'Here, mate,' said Skye, handing him a spoon. 'You'll never finish it at this rate.'

Julius stared blankly at the spoon, then at Skye, then stood and banged his fists on the table. 'How could I let that happen?' he cried in frustration. 'Aaargh!' And with that, he strode off in a huff, returned to the table to grab a pork rib before storming off again, leaving the Skirts in resigned perplexity.

'What just happened?' asked Professor Chan, passing by the table, carrying a tray.

'Someone beat him at Solo,' answered Skye. 'A certain F.H., from Sield.'

Chan laughed. 'Ah! Imagine his face when he finds out that he was beaten by a girl! No offence, Miss Ruthier.'

'None taken,' she replied.

As soon as Chan had gone, they looked at each other, mouths gaping.

'Morgana,' said Skye, 'ask Maks who she is. Come on!'

She quickly sent Maks a message, begging him for a reply as soon as possible.

*

During pilot training that afternoon, Julius went through the motions, unable to focus and not even realising that Moonrising had just broken orbit. Luckily Professor Clavel had asked them to do some revision on Cougar maintenance, which meant that he simply had to stare at the manual in order to appear busy.

The news that F.H. was a girl had spread through Tijara like wildfire and, by dinner time that evening, Maks had replied to Morgana, confirming that her name was Farrah Hendricks, a 4MA. More than that, he didn't know, as she had only joined Sield that year.

Just when Julius thought that it couldn't get any worse, his PIP beeped. The message was short and to the point: 'Meet me in New Satras, Rowan Square; Sat at noon. Bring the ring. Farrah XXX.'

Faith grabbed Julius' hand and turned it so he could read the message, then got the others at the table to lean and have a look. 'Oh no, not the *ring*,' he teased.

'Ouch!' said Skye. 'At least she signed off with three kisses.'

'Let me see that!' said Morgana, suddenly very curious. She grabbed his hand and pulled him halfway across the table.

'Steady there!' said Julius, trying to avoid her plate of mash. 'It's attached to me, remember.'

'You never know, McCoy,' said Skye, winking. 'Something good *can* come of this, you know.'

'Nonsense,' said Morgana, a little too loudly. Realising that they were all looking at her, she let go of Julius' hand. 'She's … the enemy. Julius couldn't possibly fraternise with the enemy now, could he? It would look … odd, so soon after he's lost.' Seeing as they were still staring at her, she stood up, flicked her black hair behind her shoulders and huffed, 'It's late. I'm going to bed.' And with that, she stormed off.

'I bet it's the hormones,' added Skye, as an afterthought. 'It'll pass.'

To Julius however, it felt more like a hint of jealousy which, in his mind, was the best news he had had all day.

*

On Tuesday morning, Julius arrived at breakfast sporting two big bags under his eyes, and carrying two mugs of black coffee.

'Rough night, huh?' asked Morgana, looking a lot more relaxed than the previous evening.

Julius nodded. 'And I deserve it too.'

'Why's that?' asked Faith, biting into his toast.

'Och, it's something Professor Gould told me last year in class,' explained Julius. 'He said that getting to the top isn't hard, but staying on top is. I've just proved his point.'

'Fair enough,' said Morgana. 'But you know, it's not like we've had a lot of time to play lately.'

'I know,' he said. 'It still sucks, though.'

'At least you can say you've been on that chart,' said Faith, brandishing the half eaten toast in his direction. 'Cheer up, mate.'

In the end, Julius had to let it go, or at least managed to push it to the back of his mind enough to face his first full day of lessons.

Returning to a routine felt oddly comforting to him. There was so much going on outside Moonrising — what with the mission, the concern over his family and friends and more potential attacks from the Arneshians — that the timetable gave him a sense of familiarity, of something that was safe.

Professor Lao-tzu invited the Mizkis to use his class on a Friday, to meditate, since with the pressure of possible combat situations, he wanted everyone to be as focused as they could. Morgana clapped cheerily at the news, meditation being one of her favourite pastimes.

'Guess where I'll *not* be on a Friday,' whispered Julius to Faith.

Unfortunately for Julius, however, there was no escaping the Tuesday morning hour in the infirmary, for his DNA augmentation, which he decided to pass with a cheeky snooze.

Professor Morales and Professor Chan helped the Mizkis learn how to use the latest shield implants. The students had found walking and fighting with two implants hard enough and it had taken them more than a year to master; now, they had to deal with four, two of which sprung out of their feet.

Morales showed them how these behaved differently from the chips in their arms: for one thing, they dissolved whenever they crossed one of their body parts or the upper shields — the sensors were programmed to recognise their owner's DNA — making their protection less reliable; on the other hand, they created a formidable barrier when the person was standing still, allowing them to protect an entire group efficiently.

Needless to say, Professor Chan planned their Martial Arts classes to include plenty of excruciating leg work. Even Faith wasn't exempt from this, as Chan taught him how to retract the bottom panels of his skirt, allowing him to use the shields in his feet as well.

As for Professor King, who was redder and jollier than ever, he had decided that, in celebration of them being on a battleship, they would hone their telekinetic skills by pushing Cougars along the runways.

'A *Cougar*?' cried Faith in astonishment. 'That spells hemorrhoids to me.'

Professor King found that remark hilarious and patted Faith on the shoulder hard enough to send him flying sideways, before demonstrating what to do on a nearby plane.

'I'll go retrieve Faith,' said Lopaka, quietly.

Julius nodded. 'Thanks mate.' He looked back at King, and shook his head. He had to admit, his teacher was as crazy as it got, but he was also very good. The Cougar began to roll along on its wheels slowly, but steadily, leaving a puzzled mechanic, who was lying flat on his back beneath the plane, holding his tools in midair, watching as the engine he was working on moved away from above his nose.

To complete what had proved to be a very full day, Professor Beloi — who had reached his forty-second birthday without uttering a single word — promised them stress, anxiety and more pressure for the rest of the year, as he discussed his plans for improving their telepathic skills.

All in all, it had been a busy day, thought Julius that night. But, as with every other 4MA, he was really looking forward to his first Twist lesson, and wondering what exactly he would be doing in it.

On Thursday morning, at 09:00, the Skirts, along with Siena, made their way to Morales' classroom. Mercifully, Skye had stopped wearing his awful aftershave, finally acknowledging that not only did it not attract Morales, but instead repelled every female in a 30 feet radius.

'Good morning, Mizkis,' greeted Morales, with a bow to the class. 'Sit, please.'

Julius sat down on the floor and watched as she casually retrieved three balls from the back of the room, using her mind-skills.

'From this year, we start training on the Sub-molecular Distortion Field — Twist, as we call it. So, how many of you have managed to unbind molecules before?'

Julius looked around him, and slowly raised his hand, hoping he wasn't the only one. To his surprise, George Lowet and Femi Mubarak also raised their hands.

'That's quite a number,' said Morales, sounding pleased. 'Normally, we have none. Can you tell us: what is the biggest object you have ever twisted, please?'

Femi answered, 'A plate, ma'am.'

'A pillow,' said George.

'Er ... a bathtub?' offered Julius, reddening slightly.

'Oh!' said Morales. 'Was anyone in it at the time?'

'Um ... yeah. My dad,' he admitted, shyly.

'I remember that!' said Morgana, laughing. 'That story went around the whole neighbourhood!'

'Very good, Mizkis,' continued Morales. 'Can you three come up here, please?'

Julius, Femi and George walked up to the centre of the room.

Morales bounced one of the balls a couple of times, then threw all of them up, froze them in midair with her mind, and said, 'Take one each and Twist it. On three.'

Julius stepped to the one closest to him and nodded at the other two, feeling a little nervous. The class had gone silent in anticipation, making him realise that some of them had never seen this skill in action before. He stretched his hand towards the ball and, on Morales' signal, he locked his mind on the ball and felt it ripping apart, as he envisioned the molecules being pulled in different directions.

The effect of the Twist made the class gasp. There were three soft thudding sounds, then the balls were reduced to thousands of tiny fragments, all suspended in front of the standing students.

'Where are the balls?' asked Barth, sounding suitably stupefied.

'Those *bits*, Mr Smit,' explained Morales, 'are the ball.' She turned to Julius. 'Can you re-bind them?'

'Sort of,' he answered, 'but not that well.'

Morales looked questioningly at Femi and George, who both shook their heads.

'Very well,' she said, stretching her hand towards the pieces; as they all watched in amazement, she bound them back together, into three solid balls once more. 'Thank you, Mizkis.'

There were a few cheers from their impressed classmates as they sat back down.

'There's a catch, however, with this particular mind-skill,' continued Morales. 'As you saw, your three colleagues can unbind molecules and keep them suspended, which means that, as well as practicing Twist, they will also focus on rebinding objects. In the meantime, though, I'll need to test everyone else and, if you don't have the Twist gene active in your DNA, I'm afraid you'll need to spend a few lessons with Doctor Walliser, who will unlock it for you.'

'Will we still be able to do it then?' asked Isolde, hopefully.

'Of course,' replied Morales. 'If you are here, then you are all carriers, Miss Frey. You may just need a little push in the right direction, is all. Besides, you wouldn't want to leave all the fun to these three, would you?'

Soon, Morales began testing the rest of the class. Julius, Femi and George stood to one side while she did this, watching as their classmates tried to unbind the ball, without a single one of them succeeding. By the end of the second hour, Morales had scheduled them all in for treatment with the doctor, starting from the following week.

'I knew they would find a way to send me to the infirmary again,' moaned Faith, as they left the room at the end of the class.

'At least you'll be done in a few weeks,' said Julius. 'I've got the whole year to spend in that place for my treatment. Speaking of, I'd better go. Catch you later.'

*

Saturday the 6th of October finally came around and, as Julius awoke that morning, he immediately remembered what lay ahead. Skye must have also remembered because, even before he was out of bed he said, 'Do you want us to come with you to meet Farrah?'

Julius thought about it for a moment. 'I'm fine, don't worry. I'll see you guys afterwards, for Faith's birthday lunch. What did we get him in the end?'

'The best present ever,' said Skye. 'A voucher for a session in the sim-dating programme.'

'No way!'

'It'll be awesome.'

'Just don't give it to him in front of Siena, please.'

'Good point. Let's make tracks, it's almost eleven o'clock and your date is in an hour.'

'It's *not* a date,' growled Julius, throwing his pillow at Skye, which hit him perfectly in the face.

'All right, I get it!' laughed Skye, hopping out of bed.

'You go first,' said Julius, pointing to the bathroom. As his friend went off to shower, he lay there, staring at the scenery screen, where an autumnal morning sun had replaced the starry darkness of space. The Solo ring on his finger felt cold to the touch; he was just about to pull it off, but hesitated. 'Just a little longer,' he said to himself.

*

At 11:30, Julius, Skye and Faith met Morgana and Siena at the rear exit of Tijara. There were three sets of lifts that linked each of the four layers of Moonrising: one at the front, one at the centre and one at the back, all of which were working at full capacity today. They managed to squeeze inside, despite having to fight for space with the other Mizkis, who were also anxious to see New Satras.

When the door opened, Julius was pushed out of the lift and against the side wall by a human wave. 'This reminds me of our first time in Satras,' he cried to Skye, who was stuck behind a boisterous group of Mizki Juniors.

Faith was happily hovering above the crowd, directing Morgana and Siena towards Julius.

'At least *he's* having fun,' said Skye, pointing at Faith, while trying to grab hold of Morgana's hand.

Julius couldn't go anywhere for the moment, so he flattened himself against a recess in the wall, using a nearby doorframe for shelter. As he did so, he heard a loud clicking noise and felt a strong sensation of heat against his neck. He jerked his head away and turned to face the door. Its surface was unremarkably flat, sporting only a single plaque in the centre of it which read, "TH – Off Limits" followed by a drawing of four stars – one at the top, two below it to either side, and one at the bottom – joined together by straight lines to form a diamond. Julius passed his fingers over the plaque, and was surprised to find that it was cold to the touch. 'Strange,' he thought.

'Over here, Julius!' called Faith.

'Coming,' he replied, leaving the door behind and joining his friends.

As they made it past the main entrance, they stopped in front of a large map of New Satras, which showed four floors of shops, bars and restaurants, with a holofloor that extended right down to level -5.

Julius checked the time and realised that he was going to be late. Quickly, he typed out "Rowan Square" on one of the information pads on the wall, and an area of level -3 lit up in green. 'I've got five minutes to get there, guys.'

'Want me to carry you?' volunteered Faith.

'That wouldn't do much for my dignity, but thanks.'

'Let's meet back here in one hour,' said Skye, pointing at a place on the map.

'*Eat Your Mama Blind?*' read Morgana. 'What kind of a place is that?'

'If they serve food,' said Skye, dragging her away, 'it's my kind of place, lady.'

'See you later, Julius,' she called, waving to him.

He waved back, then headed for the lower levels. He didn't have a lot of time to look around just then, but New Satras appeared to be a lot like a fancy shopping mall, very much like the ones they had back on Earth. It was certainly full of life and colour, but without the wide, open spaces of the real Satras.

When Julius arrived at level -3, he checked a nearby map and saw that Rowan Square was right at the centre of this floor. He hurried along the main path, and it suddenly dawned on him that he didn't even know what this girl looked like; secretly he hoped that he would miss her altogether, so he could keep the ring for a little longer: after all, Bernard Docherty had waited until the end of the year before he had passed it on to Julius.

As he reached Rowan Square, he quickly noted how it was the first green area he had seen so far in New Satras. The path opened up into a medium sized park, complete with wooden benches, grass and, unsurprisingly, numerous rowan trees. Julius wondered if they were real or just another trick of the simulator, but either way they looked good and made the place feel more alive. The scenery ceiling above the park showed a beautiful blue sky, further adding to the illusion of this being an outside area. Julius stepped onto the grass and strolled towards the big tree at the centre of the park, all the time playing nervously with the ring. He checked the time and saw that it was 12:05. There were a few Mizkis sitting on the benches, busily chatting or eating. He expected that she would be alone or, at the very least, on the lookout for him too.

Just when he was about to give up and leave, he noticed a girl walking slowly across the grass, coming towards him. It is fair to say that, at that moment, Julius experienced a quite unexpected lowering of his jaw, which left him gawping for several seconds in a most unbecoming manner. Thankfully for him, she was still too far away to see this, giving him time to recompose himself, flatten his hair and straighten his clothes. He coughed, breathed in deeply, and leaned casually against the tree trunk. When she saw him, her lips formed the most beautiful smile and Julius almost slid off the trunk. With every step she took, her honey blonde hair danced around her shoulders, while her smooth skin seemed to reflect the light around her.

She stopped right in front of him and stretched out her hand. 'Farrah Hendricks.'

Julius simply stared back, wondering if he had ever seen eyes quite so blue before. He looked at her hand and, mustering all of his courage — more so, it seemed, than he had needed to face Red Cap — he grabbed hold of it with his own. 'Julius McCoy.'

She smiled and held his hand for a few moments, before letting go.

Julius decided that if he wanted to make it out of there without completely embarrassing himself, he would need to pull himself together double-quick. 'Coffee?' he asked her.

'Sure. There's a cart over there,' she pointed. 'Just black.'

Julius nodded and headed for the vendor, breathing deeply as he went. 'Don't screw this up, McCoy,' he said to himself.

When he returned, Farrah was sitting on the grass, her long legs gathered under her.

'Here you go,' he said, passing her the paper cup.

'Thanks.'

Getting the drinks had been a good idea, as Julius began to feel a bit more relaxed and in charge of his jaw. For some curious reason, he found himself wanting to make a good impression. He might have lost the Solo title, but he wasn't a *total* loss. 'I guess congrats are in order.'

She bowed her head, and smiled. 'I was really surprised when I saw the score, believe me.'

'How come your Solo video isn't out yet?'

'I don't know. Maybe a problem with the recordings?'

'Shame. I would have liked to see you in action.'

'Yours was pretty cool.'

'You mean you watched it?' said Julius, feeling a surge of pride at that.

'Many times,' she replied. 'You could say I've studied it thoroughly. I wanted to ask you so many things about it …'

'Why didn't you?' he said quickly, forgetting that they had only just met.

Farrah looked down and plucked delicately at a blade of grass. 'I wasn't well.'

'Oh,' he said. 'Is that why you weren't at school last year? I mean, my friend Maks told me you had just joined us.'

'That's right. I had to be in hospital for a while. My folks have a business on Satras so, when I wasn't ill, I stayed with them. Then, this summer, the doctors said I could try out for Sield and see if I managed to get in.'

'Well, you managed it all right,' said Julius. 'I mean, you come back to school and the first thing you do is steal the Solo title! I think I need to have a word with your doctor.'

'I'm so sorry,' she said, teasing him. As she laughed, she put her hand on Julius' arm, sending shivers all over his body.

'So, uh … were you, uh, very ill?' he stammered.

'I can't quite remember my time in hospital, to tell the truth. The doctor said it's a characteristic of my disorder. I'm fine now though, but I still need to be checked every month or so.'

'You look … plenty healthy to me,' he added.

'Thank you. My mum would agree,' she said, cheerfully. 'She told me so just this morning.'

'Your parents are here, then?'

'Yes. One level above us,' she said, pointing up. 'Yours? Were they …?'

'Aye.'

'I'm sorry. How many of your family?'

'My folks, my granny, and my brother. He's a Nuarn actually, so he *chose* to go.' As those words left his lips, Julius realised just how easy it had been to tell her about Michael. He was rather surprised by that.

'Is that the Solo ring?' she said, tactfully changing topic.

'The very one,' answered Julius. He took it off, gave it a quick wipe with a corner of his t-shirt and held it up. 'I forgot the box.'

'It's OK. I'll wear it now, anyway,' she said holding her hand out to him.

Julius felt slightly awkward, but she was still smiling at him. So, for the second time that morning, he took her hand and put the ring on it.

The black band automatically adjusted to fit her finger. She held it to her heart, batted her eyelashes a few times, and sweetly sighed, 'Oh darling! But of course I accept!'

Julius panicked. 'What … No … I …'

'Got you!' she said, laughing. 'It'll take more than a ring to woo me. Hey, how about a picture to mark the occasion?'

He nodded, feeling slightly out of his depth and very much not in control of the situation once more. Farrah opened up her PIP screen, stretched her arm out in front of them, and placed her head on his shoulder, the hand with the Solo ring held up between them. 'Cheese!'

Julius wasn't quite sure about the quality of his own smile, but he gave it his best shot, considering the circumstances.

'There,' she said, closing the PIP. 'I've just sent it to you. Must treasure every moment.'

For the first time, Julius detected a hint of sadness in her voice, but it passed away as quickly as it had arrived.

'I must go now,' she said, standing up.

'Sure, me too. It was my friend's birthday yesterday, and we're having lunch together,' he said. 'Will I see you around?'

Farrah looked at him, almost as if she was studying his face. 'Why not? You have my number.' With that, she waved, and walked off.

Julius didn't move until a few minutes later; he was feeling slightly worried about the fact that his heart was still beating hard in his chest.

When he joined the others — in what turned out to be a Jamaican restaurant — it took all of his willpower to refrain from telling Skye and Faith how the meeting really went, because Morgana was there too. Even though she was going out with Maks, he still felt a little too uncomfortable to talk about Farrah in front of her, and maybe even a little guilty. The guys didn't need to know *everything* anyway, and particularly not about his gaping mouth or his out-of-control heartbeat, so he decided to play it cool and keep his thoughts about her to himself for a little longer.

OUTER SPACE THRILLS

The next morning Julius was up and running rather early, which made Skye very suspicious. 'Are you OK?' he asked as Julius emerged from the bathroom, fully dressed and ready to go.

'For sure,' Julius replied, offhand. 'Why?'

'Because it's 8 o'clock *and* it's Sunday morning?'

'So?'

Skye brushed his fringe out of his eyes, and stared intently at Julius. 'There's something you're not telling me.'

'It's our first chance to try the Moonrising's holospheres! I don't want to queue forever. Do you?'

Skye didn't seem too convinced. 'Fine,' he said, and swung his legs over the side of the bed. 'Give me a moment.'

As soon as he had disappeared into the bathroom, Julius switched his PIP on and, leaning against the room's scenery screen — which was broadcasting sunrise over the ocean — he opened up the picture of Farrah, and let out a long sigh. There was something the matter with him all right, but he had no intention of admitting it. Deep down, he was even a little afraid that Skye would make a move on her, just because he was, well, Skye Miller.

Julius had spent the night thinking up all sorts of excuses for going to Satras, while avoiding sounding too desperate, and in the end he had settled on the games, which were always a good enough reason for the Skirts. As Skye got ready, Julius sent a message to Faith and Morgana, arranging for them to meet them in the mess hall at 08:30. Luckily, neither of them found the request strange and happily agreed to the plan.

*

When they reached the holofloor in New Satras, a familiar face waved at them from the information kiosk.

'Mrs Mayflower!' cried Morgana, running towards her. 'It's so good to see you!'

'Eeeeh! Look who's here,' said the old lady excitedly. 'My favourite team.'

'I didn't know you were coming along as well,' said Julius, noticing that her wrinkles had multiplied greatly, since the summer.

'There was nothing much left to do in Satras,' she explained. 'No customers, no fun. I'd rather be here, in the thick of it. Besides, I owe those Arneshians a lesson on how to treat old ladies!' she said, punching her left palm with her other fist.

'That's the spirit!' said Faith.

Julius grinned. True enough, she had almost been kidnapped two years before but, judging by her resolute attitude, she was definitely on good form. 'Well, we're glad you're here.'

'Thank you, my dearies,' she said, sounding genuinely moved. 'So, did you come to look at our facilities?'

'Yes,' answered Faith. 'What's the story on New Satras?'

'Very similar to home, really,' explained Mrs Mayflower. 'Only, there are far less holospheres and fewer games going on at any one time. They do it to save power, but also in case of emergency. Players need to be able to get out of their spheres quickly and you can't afford to have 300 people stuck in there at the same time if anything goes wrong.'

'Fair enough,' said Faith. 'Do you have a little space for us today?'

'Of course. Fight or Flight?'

'Flight!' cried Morgana. 'Everyone for themselves.'

'One Flight token coming up. Enjoy!'

'Julius?' called Skye. 'Are you coming or not?'

Julius, who was currently facing away from the booth for some reason, turned around, looking oddly surprised. 'Wha … oh! Yeah. I was just-'

'You're weird, you know that?' said Skye, dragging him into the changing rooms.

Julius had, of course, been distracted as he looked for Farrah, in the off chance she had decided to take a walk down there. Unfortunately, his focus didn't improve very much in the games and he ended up getting shot down so many times by everyone else that it was almost embarrassing.

'McCoy!' shouted Morgana, after destroying Julius for the tenth time in a row. 'What the heck was that? Do you even want to play?'

'Sorry guys,' he said, trying to sound like he was under the weather. 'I don't feel too well. I think I'll just wait for you outside. If I take another turn I'll probably throw up in my lap.'

'Good grief,' said Faith. 'That's never a good idea, as me grandma Allappa used to say, whenever someone threatened to throw up on themselves … or their friends for that matter.'

Julius stared ahead blankly, pondering Faith's words for a minute, and then shook his head. 'I'll see you shortly.' He disconnected from the game and climbed out of his holosphere. He was feeling perfectly fine, but it was obvious that his mind was focused elsewhere, so he got changed and exited out into the courtyard, where he sat watching the rest of the Skirts' games on one of the large arena screens.

'I've seen you do a lot better than that.'

Julius turned and saw a Zed officer sitting at the top of the steps, holding a takeaway cup of coffee. He didn't recognise the man, but he had three pale blue stripes on each of the sleeves of his jacket: the symbol for all Curiates. Julius guessed that he must then have been at the docks, the year before, when Ambassador T'Rogon had landed on the Moon. The man had rather an official air about him, with his tightly cropped hair and pristine uniform.

Julius stood and bowed, and watched as the man did the same.

'Ben Hastings,' he said, shaking Julius' hand. 'Do you mind if I sit with you for a while?'

'Not at all,' answered Julius, feeling quite intrigued and chuffed that he was being approached by such an important man.

'The Skirts are on top form today,' he said, pointing at the screen.

'Apart from me, obviously,' Julius added in a low-key manner.

'We all have our off days, you know.'

Hastings had a warm smile, which reminded Julius of Clavel's. Like the professor, he seemed to have an easy-going attitude. It was evident in his eyes, and by the many orange-coloured wisps which were floating around him. Those, in particular, put Julius at ease. 'I guess so. Do you play, sir?'

'Don't bother with the *sir*, please. We're just having a friendly chat,' he replied, amicably. 'I used to play but, since I joined the Curia, time has become a precious commodity for me. Not to mention this whole mess with the Arneshians.'

Julius nodded, understanding him all too well.

'Hey, I hope I didn't offend you before. I know very well what you can do, in case you're wondering.'

'It's OK. I can safely admit that I was pretty rubbish back there.'

'In the office we have bets on student teams, and I picked you guys from the start.'

'Really?'

'We need to have some R&R too, you know? Anyway, I just wanted to say that the Skirts are the best team we've seen on Satras for many, many years. And, if I may, you are the star of the team.'

'I wouldn't be without the others,' answered Julius, reddening slightly.

'Don't be modest, Julius,' said Ben, jovially. 'Your team is everything, I know. But you have been gifted beyond hope. Take pride in it, and use your gift to bring hope back to us. Be a White Child.'

Julius couldn't help but feel mightily pleased. To receive such a compliment from one of the Curiates was quite an honour.

Just then, the screen announced the end of the game, and Hastings stood up. 'I have to get back now. Don't tell Miller that I said you're the star, or he'll come storming into my office.'

'I won't,' said Julius, getting to his feet. 'I promise.'

'It was good meeting you finally.' And with that, he left.

It was a nice way to right the wrongs of a bad game and, as Julius waited for his friends, he imagined what it would have felt like if Farrah had been there next to him, listening with admiration to the Curiate's words. When the Skirts emerged from the changing rooms, they found him daydreaming on the steps, looking chuffed.

Much to his frustration however, Julius didn't manage to bump into Farrah that weekend so, when Monday arrived, as well as being distracted, he had also started to become a little touchy. Luckily, Professor Farshid had decided to take the students for a full tour of Moonrising; from the top of the ship to the bottom. That gave Julius a further chance to look for Farrah, both inside BM Sield, and in New Satras. He didn't spot her anywhere, but he felt better just for trying. It was only during Professor Clavel's class, that afternoon, that Julius' mind was able to focus properly on the task at hand.

'Mizkis,' said Clavel, 'given our re-location, it is time to introduce you to a new space vehicle.'

A few whispers broke out among the students.

'I know that some of you have had a chance already,' he said pointing at Morgana and Faith.'

'It's the sky-jet!' cried Skye, excitedly.

Clavel nodded, and that was enough to send the Mizkis into a frenzy.

'Finally!' said Julius, giving Faith a high-five.

'Here's how we're going to do it,' said Clavel, hushing them. 'Moonrising's current low speed will allow us to use the next couple of hours for some real practice; no simulation.'

Both Julius and Faith had to place their hands on Morgana's shoulders, to stop her from bouncing up and down in her seat.

'Our 5 and 6MSs will provide aerial support, while you're out there. In case of emergency, they will bring you back in. Follow me to the hangar now.'

Julius was really looking forward to this. It was hard to believe that, shortly, he would be out in space, far from his solar system, driving a sky-jet alongside a battleship. As he walked through the hangar with the other students, he tried to take in all the bits of advice that Faith and Morgana were sharing, learnt during their Summer Camp experience at Pete's. To Julius' surprise, he found out that Skye hadn't yet tried it out, despite the fact he had been raised on a space station. Due to age-restrictions, he wasn't allowed, which was why he was now looking every bit as excited as Julius.

In the hangars, Professor Clavel took them up a flight of stairs, to a mezzanine level. The ceiling was much lower here but, from the edges of the platform, there was a great view of the Cougars below.

For the first time, Julius was able to appreciate just how many machines there were onboard, and the sheer amount of engineers and mechanics, who were zooming busily between the aircrafts.

'Here we are,' said Clavel, pointing towards an area below and to the opposite side of the Cougars. 'Welcome to Sky-Jet Central.'

The Mizkis rushed to the banister and looked with amazement at the sea of space-scooters waiting there for them.

'Pick any one you like, from the front row, please,' Clavel instructed them.

Julius hurtled down the steps, three at a time, clearing the last four with one leap, while Faith hovered nonchalantly over his head. He stopped beside the first available one and walked around it, studying all of its parts. It looked very much like the everyday fly-scooters that could be bought back on Earth. The seat was long enough to take two people, and it ended in a high back that rose up above head-height. There was a gap for the legs, between the seat and the handlebars, with a small storage compartment underneath it. The jet was the colour of hard coal: a deep, dark grey that would blend perfectly with the dark expanses of space. The words, "BM Tijara" were etched into the front panel, above the emblem of Zed.

'Hop on, so I can show you the controls,' said Clavel.

Julius took his seat and was glad to find that it was soft and comfortable.

'Essentially, the sky-jet drives like a scooter,' explained Clavel. 'We use it to carry people outside a space station; to collect items and deliver them around the orbital space. They are never used for fighting though. To move forward, you rev the right throttle, and use the handbrakes to stop. You can also reverse by pressing the red button on the left handle.'

Julius identified all of the mentioned parts, and found the reverse button on the left, which could be activated with a flick of the thumb.

'There's a menu on your central touch-screen. Activate it now, please.'

Julius did so, and it lit up in green. The words, "New User – Log in" flashed up briefly, before being replaced by an empty box and keyboard.

'Today, Mizkis,' said Clavel, 'you have the opportunity to create your tag-names, which will be used every time you participate in a mission.'

'I've dreamt of this day since I was a little girl …' enthused Morgana. 'I still do!'

Skye glanced sideways at her. 'You need to get out more, woman. I'm gonna have a word with Maks, that's what I'll do.'

Morgana was far too mesmerised by the green screen to take any notice of him, and kept wringing her hands together.

Julius began to rack his brain for a name to use. It would have to be short and have a cool ring to it, he reckoned. 'I wish Clavel had given us the heads up for this,' he whispered to Faith, who simply nodded thoughtfully.

'Hey, why don't we choose a theme,' proposed Skye, 'as members of the Skirts?'

'Good idea,' said Faith. 'Like animals or metals, you mean?'

'Exactly,' answered Skye. 'What about birds?'

'I knew you'd say that …' said Julius.

'I like it,' said Morgana. 'Can I be "Swan"?'

'Better you than me,' chirped Faith.

'I was thinking more along the lines of birds of prey, you know?' said Skye. 'Something a bit more … ferocious than a swan.'

'You'll be a vulture then, Miller,' said Faith. 'On account of your eating habits.'

'Hey, I don't eat corpses,' he grumbled.

'That's because you haven't run out of food yet.'

Skye pondered the remark. 'Hmm … You know what? I like it. I'll be Vulture.'

'Good man,' said Faith. 'I'll take Baza.'

'I'll be Goshawk,' said Julius.

'Nice one,' said Morgana. 'I'm going for Kite then.'

Julius typed his tag name into the box and pressed his thumb against the starting pad, to tie it to his personal profile. The name immediately flashed up on a small screen at the front of his jet.

Once all the Mizkis had picked their names, Clavel continued the lesson. 'From the menu, you can select your front light, send distress codes, open the intercom, and several other functions that we will explore as we go. Last, but not least, you will need to activate your cupolas. A cupola is the name of the protective field that allows you to be *out there* without a spacesuit. I want you to activate those now, and keep your feet inside the vehicle.'

Julius selected his, and the field sprung up, promptly cutting off all outside noise. He looked at the shimmering dome above his head and touched it cautiously; although it did have some give, it was still pretty solid. His screen blinked, asking him to open the inter-con.

A second after he did so, Clavel came on-air. 'You're now ready to go,' he said. 'Follow me outside, in single file, one after the other.'

Julius watched as Clavel hopped onto one of the sky-jets and fired up the machine. As its cupola appeared, its lights came on and it lifted off the floor.

'Engines on, Mizkis. You can talk to each other, by calling up the respective tag names on screen; you can select as many as you want at any one time. These machines have a fairly long range, but you may lose contact in certain areas of space. All right, let's move it.'

Julius turned the engine on; it made a whooshing noise as it came to life, which faded to a gentle rumble, reminding him of the power contained within the machine's turbines. As soon as Morgana started to move away, Julius edged his sky-jet forward behind her. It was extremely responsive, and he didn't need to give it too much power to make it go fast. He slowed down to the designated safety speed that all pilots were told to use within the hangar; he was already beginning to adjust well to the machine.

Clavel stopped and gathered the Mizkis together inside one of the airlocks; once the last student was safely sealed inside, he opened up the port door.

Julius was completely awestruck as he inched forward. This was different to the other times he had been outside, in the Stork, and the various transport vessels. In those, there had been ceilings and walls which felt quite reassuring, but in the sky-jet, the only thing separating him from the vastness of space was a thin shield. He realised that he was, in reality, just a little creature, and was suddenly conscious of his own fragility. He could hear his heart beating fast in his chest, in the silence within his jet's cupola. Although the temperature had remained constant and warm, he shivered instinctively on seeing the dark emptiness around him.

He steadied himself, and continued following Clavel, aware that a large number of Cougars had just left BM Tijara, and were slowly patrolling the surrounding space area.

His intercom crackled on, and Clavel spoke. 'You have about 90 minutes to get to know your jets. Try manoeuvres, different speeds, turns, and whatever else you want. We aren't going to have too much practice time after this, so you need to be really confident as soon as possible. Those of you with experience should help the others. Off you go!'

Julius began by turning his sky-jet around, so he could admire the full might of Moonrising, as it towered before him. He wasn't able to actually take it all in, at such close quarters, but he figured if he wanted to get a proper view of the ship in its entirety, he would probably need to stray quite far, something he was pretty sure they weren't allowed to do.

He opened up a com-channel with the Skirts and, together, they began to try all sorts of drills involving twists, bends and mad chases. The sky-jets were fast and easy to pilot, which made the session incredibly varied. Every so often — or regularly in the case of Barth — a couple of Cougars had to intervene and round up the stragglers, any time they forgot to keep up with Moonrising, which was naturally moving forward on its set course. At the end of the lesson, the Mizkis were still having so much fun that it took Clavel another 20 minutes before he could get them all safely inside the airlock, and even that only happened after he had threatened to order the Cougars to open fire.

That evening, after dinner, the excitement still hadn't died down, so most of the 4MAs went to the lounge to write up their logs, exchange tips, and compare notes. After a couple of hours of intense conversations, Julius decided to get himself a hot chocolate and went over to the counter. As he waited for his drink, he opened his PIP to look at the picture Farrah had taken of them, which had now become quite a regular thing. He was so engrossed in this, that he didn't notice Skye walk up behind him.

'Gotcha!' he said, over his shoulder.

Julius closed his PIP abruptly, and his cheeks flushed red. 'Don't, Miller.'

'*Now* I understand what's been going on with you lately, you sly dog,' he said, with a cheeky wink.

Julius couldn't suppress a half-smile, but he still didn't want to encourage Skye's taunts, so he forced a straight face.

'Can we at least talk about it?' Skye asked him, simply. 'You're my best mate, Jules, so I'm not going to mess with you about this. Please?'

Julius grabbed his cup and moved to one of the empty tables, motioning for Skye to follow him. Once seated, he opened up the picture again and showed it to him.

Skye looked at it for a long time, then said, 'You're in serious trouble my friend. And any guy would beg to have such trouble.'

'Tell me about it,' said Julius. Gradually, he began to open up to Skye, and described their first meeting, and how he had felt when she had put her head on his shoulder, or touched his arm.

'Your smile looks a bit weird in that pic ... were you feeling ok? Anyway, she's stunning, man. And she kicked your butt at Solo. When's your next date? Or proper first date?'

'Date?' gulped Julius, panicking. 'No ... we didn't arrange a date.'

'What? How did you leave things, when you parted ways? Did you tell her to have a nice life, or something? Please tell me you didn't!'

'No, actually. I asked her if I would see her around and all she said was, "Why not. You have my number".'

'Unbelievable,' said Skye, slapping his forehead. 'You've managed to memorise her last words, but you still don't have a date. Are you man or amoeba? Why haven't you called her? You don't need an excuse, you know?'

'I don't?'

'Do you?'

'Well, I thought that it would look less ... pushy if I did.'

Skye put on his best affairs-of-the-heart face. 'What do you have, to use as a reason for calling her? Let's have it.'

'Well, there's the Solo ring box, which I haven't given her yet.'

'Use it. Perfect excuse. Send her a message, right this instant. Tell her something like, apologies for not getting back sooner, but you had internal active duties that kept you up all night.'

'But that's not true,' protested Julius, feeling a bit like he was being swept up by a whirlwind.

'Silence! You've let more than 48 hours pass without making contact, and although a little waiting is healthy, too much can cheese a girl off, big time. Besides, active duties is one of those magic bunch of words that makes you look good, and competent.'

'It's two words, actually.'

'That's beside the point. So, as I was saying, you then ask her how she is and when it'll be convenient for her to meet up, so you can give her the box.'

'Then what?'

'Then the ball is in her court, and we wait. You can't plan everything, McCoy.'

Julius sighed and nodded, trying to remember all of Skye's recommendations for the message. 'Ok, thanks. But you must keep this to yourself, you understand me?'

'Count on it,' he replied. He stood up and was about to go rejoin the others, when he stopped and turned to Julius again. 'I've got to ask, man: what about Morgana?'

'What about her?' he answered, blankly.

'You know what I mean.'

'She made her choice, didn't she?'

Skye looked at him, 'I guess she did. You *both* did.'

That evening, after saying goodnight, Julius returned to his room, eager to put together his message for Farrah. It took him almost half an hour to write 10 lines, but he wanted to make absolutely sure he had included all of Skye's suggestions. Eventually, after re-reading it five times, he sent it, and drew a long breath. 'What will be, will be.'

*

The first thing Julius did the next morning was to check his PIP but, to his dismay, there was no reply from Farrah yet.

'She's probably still asleep,' said Skye, trying to sound convincing, while yawning.

Unfortunately, the story was the same every morning that week, right into the weekend, and the week after. By the time Sunday the 21st of October had come around, Julius had become truly miserable and Skye's excuses for Farrah's silence were running dry. He had even considered checking with Maks, but the thought of Morgana finding out was enough to put him off and encourage him to try come up with another plan.

It was around lunchtime of that day that people began to hear rumours about the mission. There was an increasingly common one that some of the Earthlings had been located at last, in the Delphinus constellation.

Julius, like everyone else on board, finally had something else to focus on, and even Farrah's reply — or rather lack thereof — was put to one side for the moment.

The Skirts, along with Siena, Isolde and Barth, were having lunch at the Jamaican restaurant, which had become quite popular with their group.

'I hate waiting,' said Skye, eating a double portion of goat curry. 'And I hate rumours.'

Julius was munching a chicken leg, lost in thought, when the "Breaking News" sign flashed up on the large TV screen at the far end of the restaurant.

'Look,' said Morgana. 'It's Mielowa. I didn't know she came with us.'

But there she was, Iryana Mielowa, the Space Channel's very own roving reporter, sporting a new auburn bob with a razor-sharp edged fringe, and a dark brown shade lipstick.

'Good afternoon, Moonrising,' she said, with a charming smile. 'The Space Channel has been officially authorised to report that some of our people have been located at last, in a nearby classified location.'

An excited buzz ran through the restaurant. Mielowa turned to her right, and the camera panned to include Aldobrando Roversi. Julius thought that he looked pretty much the same as he had last year, but perhaps with a touch more grey hair than before.

'I'm here with the Curio Maximus,' Mielowa continued, introducing her guest, 'to find out more about our recent discovery. Mr Roversi, what can you tell us about it?'

'We are extremely pleased with our progress, Ms Mielowa,' he said, confidently. 'It took us the best part of five months to track this location, but we have done it.'

'How was that achieved, Curio?' said Mielowa.

'Our enemies have left behind a particularly strong signature, which has allowed us to track them through space. Incidentally, the very technology they have used against us — from the static field that ground us to a halt, to the teleportation devices — have also been put to good use. Thanks to our brilliant technicians, we now know how to use them and we *will* use this knowledge to send our people back.'

'This is marvellous news, Curio,' said Mielowa, all smiles. 'Tell us, how have you been able to confirm where our people actually are? I understand that we're talking about a sizeable area on a small planet.'

'Given the circumstances,' said Roversi, affably, 'I can afford to disclose just a few more details. We tracked their signature all the way to their location, then used a sensor scan to detect that indeed there were bio-signatures present. After that, we used their very own teleportation technology to relay a message into the midst of the group. We had to wait several days before someone took charge, worked out our instructions, and sent a reply. And there's more.'

'Yes?' said Mielowa, totally engrossed.

'The person who replied was none other than Mr Chris High, Voice of the Earth for Oceania.'

'No!' cried Mielowa, clasping her hands to her chest. 'Does this mean that …?'

'Exactly. Mr High has confirmed he is still in the company of the people who were in Oceania at the time of the abduction.'

'How many people are we talking about here?'

'20 million, give or take,' said Roversi.

Mielowa dabbed a finger to the side of her right eye, as if she was drying a little tear. Then she turned to the camera. 'You heard it here first. Iryana Mielowa, Space Channel.'

Raucous cheers erupted from every table in the restaurant. Even the passersby, who had stopped to watch the broadcast, were now clapping and chattering away in animated fashion.

'This is just!' cried Julius, waving the half-eaten chicken leg around, while Siena and Morgana tearfully embraced each other.

'We *have* to go find George and Felicity,' said Morgana, leaping up suddenly.

'Let's go,' agreed Siena. 'Later, guys!'

Julius knew why, and appreciated what a nice gesture it was from the girls. Their classmates George Lowet and Felicity Steep, were from Australia and New Zealand respectively, so they were bound to be emotionally involved in the rescue mission, more than anyone else in their class. On the down side, however, it seemed clear that they hadn't found Europe's former inhabitants yet. Julius looked up at Faith, and saw the same disappointed expression in his eyes. 'I guess we should be pleased for them,' was all he could muster.

'Sure. But I just want me family back.'

'Have the Arneshians split them up according to their continents, or something?' asked Skye, cleaning his plate with a healthy chunk of fresh bread.

'Maybe,' answered Julius, leaning back in his chair. '20 million though. How are we going to get them all back?'

'It's going to take forever,' added Skye.

'Not necessarily,' said Faith. 'We have their teleportation technology now, and we know how to use it. What bothers me is how we actually found out about their location.'

'You heard the Curio,' said Skye. 'We followed the Taurus One's signature.'

Faith shook his head. 'That day, by the time we were able to move again, the Taurus One had gone to warp and if the Arneshians have two brain cells between them that work properly, they would have also used hyperjump a few times, just for good measure. On top of that, our people have been kept on that planet for six months, if not more, some 100 light years away.'

'So?' asked Julius, not liking where this was heading.

'So, there is no known device that can track and follow a ship's signature under those circumstances. If you ask me, the Curia had another lead, and they're just telling us a story to fill in the gaps.'

'But why?' asked Skye.

'I don't know. Maybe they want to keep some details classified, in case there's a spy on board — either human, or holo.'

'On Moonrising?' said Skye. 'It's practically Zed on holiday. There are no strangers on board. Surely, we would have noticed an intruder.'

'Mind you,' added Julius. 'They've been able to sneak Arneshians into Zed before, remember. I guess I don't mind them being a little cautious, if that's the case.'

There was no disagreeing with that, so they continued to discuss the impending rescue mission for the rest of the afternoon. When dinner time arrived, they remained where they were, ordered some more food and were joined by more of the 4MAs. Morgana also returned, accompanied by Maks. Soon enough, Julius found himself chatting to him, all the while trying hard to ignore his arm around Morgana's shoulder, which irritated him greatly. At the same time, he was still hoping to spot Farrah, among the crowd but, as curfew approached, he realised that yet another day had passed by with no word from her.

ON THE USE OF POWER

After a typically exhausting session practicing with their shield implants, the 4MAs made their way to the mess hall, for a much deserved lunch.

Julius was limping slightly, as he recovered from a cramp in his left leg, thanks to Morales and Chan's intense training. 'I swear,' he said, massaging his sore calf. 'Those two were meant for each other.'

'And I thought Morales was nice,' added Skye. 'She's worse than him! Did you see the lack of pity on her face when I fell over in agony?'

'Yeah,' added Faith. 'But that's probably because it was the fourth time you were trying that stunt on her to get out of class.'

'So? It should have worked the first time,' said Skye, looking disappointed. 'I'm losing my touch with her.'

'Whatever you do,' added Morgana quickly, 'don't you go wearing that awful perfume again, please.'

'Nah,' he replied. 'I think it would be too late anyway. She's under his spell now. I see the way she looks at him. The man in black has won.'

'I bet it was his pointy goatee that did it,' said Morgana, nudging him in the ribs. 'He's more mature, and that's what a woman needs: a mature person by her side. Someone to rely on in dire straits.'

Julius was about to say something about Maks not being there for her when it mattered, but bit his lip.

'I could grow a goatee too,' said Skye, defensively, 'if I wanted too.'

'Yeah right,' she said, grinning. Then she screamed and ran on ahead, as Skye turned suddenly and began to tickle her.

'Baby face! Baby face!' she chanted, goading him and laughing all the while.

Faith seemed to enjoy the chase, while Julius' eyes were mainly focused on Skye's hands and their exact whereabouts as he proceeded to subdue Morgana. He knew they were only joking around, but why did he need to joke so blinking close to her body? And why was she giggling like that? And why- His PIP suddenly vibrated, interrupting his thoughts. He looked down and froze on the spot; there was an incoming vidcall from Farrah. He swallowed, forgot about everything else and said, 'Go ahead guys, I'll catch up in a minute.'

Skye stopped in mid tickle, still holding onto Morgana, who was staring at him, and wondering what had happened. Skye's eyes met Julius' and it was clear that he had realised exactly what was distracting his friend. There wasn't any need for telepathic skills to figure that one out.

'We'll see you in the mess hall,' said Skye, dragging Morgana away, despite her protests.

'What's happening?' she asked, aware that something had passed between Julius and Skye.

'Never you mind, Miss "If-he's-not-old-as-my-grandpa-I-won't-date-him".'

Julius watched them walk away, while a hot flush ran over him. With a trembling finger, he pressed the onscreen button and opened the channel.

'Hi Julius!' she said, her lovely smile filling the screen.

Julius was once again taken aback by her beauty. Even though he hadn't seen her for almost three weeks, she was exactly like he remembered her, except she was perhaps looking a little tired, he thought. 'Hey Farrah,' he said, trying to sound as natural as possible. 'It's good to see you. I thought my message had gotten lost or something.'

'I'm so, so sorry, Julius,' she replied and, by all accounts, it looked like she really meant it. 'I only saw it this morning.'

'Oh. Was your PIP down or something?'

'They shut it down … I was in hospital again.'

Realising now that the reason she hadn't replied had nothing to do with him made him feel incredibly relieved. 'Are you ok now?'

'Back to normal, I guess,' she said, shrugging her shoulders.

'If I'd known I would have come visit you.'

'You're sweet. I wish you had known … I would have liked that very much,' she said, lowering her eyes.

Julius was vaguely aware that his cheeks were becoming pretty warm, and surely turning a dark shade of red, but quite frankly he didn't seem to care that much. The open way she was talking to him, as if they had known each other for more than just three weeks, made him feel completely at ease and more eager to see her than ever before. 'I've been carrying the box with me ever since I wrote you. Do you think we could meet? I mean, if it's OK with you.'

'Are you kidding?' she laughed. 'I'd love to see you again!'

Julius tried hard, and quickly realised that he couldn't really find a suitable reply to that.

His oversized smile must have done the trick, however, because she nodded happily and said, 'Great! Why don't you meet me by my parents' shop, on Saturday afternoon, at 2 o'clock? It's called Auld Oddities.'

'It's a da- a … plan, I mean. Yeah, great. Yeah.' At that point he made the decision to hang up before he could embarrass himself. 'Till Saturday, then.'

'Till then,' she said.

*

The moment he stepped inside the mess hall, he knew he wasn't going to be able to hide the elation he felt swelling in his chest. It was written all over his face, which was why Skye just nodded, as he came to meet him at the door, and gave him a congratulatory double pat on the shoulder. 'Saturday afternoon,' was all Julius could say.

'Nice work, McCoy. Hey, listen,' said Skye, as they walked back to the others, 'Morgana was nagging me about what was going on, and Faith was getting pretty curious too. All I said is that it was this Solo girl you'd met, and you needed to give her the box back.'

Julius thought about it for a moment. 'It's fine, don't worry. In fact, it's probably easier if they know.'

'Besides Julius, who did you think you would fool with *that* grin?' he added, cheekily. 'You could see it from Earth.'

When they got to the table, Morgana simply waved at him and continued her conversation with Siena. If she was pretending not to be interested, she was doing a pretty good job of it, thought Julius. Faith, on the other hand, wanted to be brought up to scratch, while Skye was anxious to find out what they had said to each other. It made for a rather intense lunch chat, or, in Julius' case, just chat, since he was so absorbed by recounting and revisiting their call, that food was the last thing on his mind.

Talking to Farrah had had the effect of a month's worth of gene therapy on Julius, whose powers peaked superbly that afternoon, to the astonishment of both Professors King, and Beloi.

For their telekinesis lesson, King had created an obstacle course in the cargo bay, and asked the students to pair up. Julius ended up with Faith, and his job was to levitate and manoeuvre him past each obstacle, without letting him drop to the floor. His powers were so heightened, that not only did he literally zoom Faith from A to B in record time, but he then proceeded to fire him back to A, then back to B, then A, and so on and so forth, faster and faster, until eventually Faith put a stop to it by throwing up indecently all over the floor.

When he arrived in Beloi's class for their last hour of lesson, Julius finished his day with a superior display of telepathic skills. The famous mirror labyrinth, in which they had been practicing since second year, had been reassembled on Moonrising, and Professor Beloi had gone the extra mile to make it as challenging as their present mission called for. When Beloi asked them to find a partner, Faith refused point blank to work with Julius, which forced a nervous Skye to take his place.

They were told to guide their partners around, and out of, the maze; only, this time, they wouldn't just be hindered by scramblers, but also by Arneshian holos, which the Mizkis had to fight off their path. Julius whisked Skye through the labyrinth, destroying all obstacles for him, and a few of his classmates' opponents too, just for good measure. The scramblers didn't even begin to bother him, his thoughts were so loud and clear that they were heard by all the students in the labyrinth, preventing them from hearing their own guides. Surprisingly, Professor Beloi seemed quite amused by this, and urged the other students to try and block Julius' voice from their minds. Unfortunately, no one was able to do so and, at the end of the hour, all of his classmates, bar Skye, were still stuck in the labyrinth being chased by holos.

'*McCoy,*' said Beloi, before Julius could leave at the end of the lesson. '*Who is this pretty blonde girl, called Farrah?*'

Julius did a double take and was mighty relieved that Beloi spoke only telepathically, so no one else had heard him. '*She's a friend of mine, Sir. How do you know about her?*'

'*She's all over your brain. Quite hard to miss,*' said Beloi. '*I would recommend you see her before every mission: she makes a hell of a fighter out of you.*'

Julius couldn't agree more, and made a mental note to tell her that on Saturday. That is, if he could resist for another three days.

He checked the time and saw that he had more than two hours to go before curfew. After a quick shower, instead of heading back to the lounge, he made a run for the lifts and headed down to New Satras. He was intent on finding out exactly where Farrah's parents' shop was, so he wouldn't be late on Saturday. He looked at the floor chart near the entrance, and scanned the list of businesses on level -2. 'Auld Oddities,' read

Julius, when he spotted it. 'Right above Rowan Square.' That was a start. He took the escalator to the right level, trying to think up a convincing excuse, in case he actually bumped into her. Fortunately, the floor was quite busy that afternoon, and Julius found it easy to move around without drawing too much attention to himself.

As he approached the shop, he slowed down and cautiously peered through the glass window. There was a tall lady behind the counter, probably Mrs Hendricks, wrapping something for a Tuala student. Julius studied her for a while, but failed to see any resemblance to Farrah, except perhaps for the wavy hair. 'Maybe she takes after her dad,' he thought.

He took a good look at the strange and unusual objects on the shelves, and realised that it was an antique shop. Some of the gadgets were completely unfamiliar to Julius, but some he recognised quite easily. There were music playing devices, phones of various sizes, and clocks; there was also a range of mirrors, number plates and jewellery. He would have liked very much to browse the place properly, but he was too afraid that Farrah might walk in. Perhaps on Saturday he would get a chance.

Unsure of what to do next, he headed towards a small cafe across the road from the shop. As he was about to enter, he saw Ben Hastings, sipping coffee at one of the tables. The Curiate was talking to someone on his PIP but, when he saw Julius, he smiled and motioned for him to come closer and have a seat.

Julius figured that talking to Ben was the perfect excuse for waiting around a while longer, on the off chance Farrah showed up, so he sat down gratefully.

'Of course, Aldobrando,' said Ben, into his mouthpiece. 'I'll join you in a short while … Very well … I'll take care of it.'

'Hello, Mr Hastings,' greeted Julius. 'How's the Curio Maximus?'

'Good of you to join me,' he replied, affably. 'The Curio is well. I'll tell him you asked after him. So, what brings you here tonight?'

'Och, just taking a walk,' said Julius, innocently. 'It's been a long day at school.'

Ben nodded. 'Busy at work too. I hate this war,' he said. 'I hate the Arneshians.'

Julius was surprised to hear a Zed officer express his opinion so strongly but, at the same time, he found it quite refreshing as well.

'If only Marcus had never fallen for Clodagh, we wouldn't be in this mess. Women … The moment she stepped out of line, with her dreams of world domination, he should have neutralised her, right there and then. But he didn't, and he died because of it.'

Julius knew all about that particular tragic love story, although how exactly Marcus had died was not quite so well known.

'She was very clever,' continued Ben, 'I'll grant you that, but no mind-skills. And what is a person without powers? I'm sorry if I seem harsh to you, but that's what I believe.'

Julius wasn't quite sure how to reply. He sensed that Ben had just needed to let off some steam, rather than have a proper conversation about the issue, so he decided not to challenge him on anything he had said. One thing, however, he *did* feel the need to say. 'My brother is a Nuarn.'

'I know, Julius. So was mine,' he replied. 'There's very little I don't know, in my line of work, especially when it concerns you.'

Julius wasn't really shocked by that, even though he knew this was how Zed worked, and that there weren't many secrets in this particular family. 'Did your brother also join T'Rogon?'

'No. He died a few years back.'

'I'm sorry,' said Julius. 'Do you ever wonder what he would have done in my brother's place?'

'I think he would have gone too, or at least, that's what I would have done.'

That really caught Julius' attention, and he sat up straight in his chair.

'What choice did he have, anyway? Without mind-skills, he would have been at the mercy of others — a kind mercy perhaps, but still, at their mercy. And what if he had decided to be loyal to his family and stay behind? He would have been kidnapped along with the others, and been at the mercy of someone else. Would you have liked that?'

'No,' said Julius, quickly. 'Not at all.'

'Neither would he, I imagine. He made his choice, according to his powers and talents, in the same way as you've made your choices, according to your powers. Never feel guilty about your mind-skills, because there's a reason for everything in this world. Michael wasn't meant to have them, but you were. At least that's what I believe.' He finished the last sip of his coffee, and stood up. 'I'm off to dinner with the Curiates, tonight. What about you?'

'I'll head back too,' answered Julius. 'Curfew soon.'

'Good talking to you again, Julius. See you around.'

Julius bowed and watched him disappear into the crowd. It was strange hearing it from someone else, but he agreed with what Ben had said about his powers. The thought that he could have been born normal had always bothered Julius, and he had grown up fully aware of just how special his life was, even without the whole White Child business.

*

As they headed to their Martial Arts class, on Wednesday afternoon, the 4MAs were surprised to find Professor Clavel, instead of Chan, waiting for them.

'What's going on?' asked Faith.

None of their classmates seem to know either, so they sat down in front of the teacher, and waited to be clued in. Julius noticed how tense Clavel looked — he could see it in his aura, which was stricken with red wisps.

'Mizkis,' he began, 'from this moment forward, you are on official duties, and all lessons are suspended.'

Julius turned to the others, wide eyed. It seemed the moment had finally arrived.

'I'm here to brief you on Operation Oceania, so please open your PIPs now.'

The class promptly followed his instruction.

'I'm downloading the schematics of the area where our people are being held. It has been decided that all Mizkis from 4th year up, will be flying the Cougars, together with our Zed fighters.'

Morgana looked at Julius, excitement all over her face.

'As students, you will be required to provide aerial support to our Storks, Herons and, most important of all, to our portals, which we will be using to teleport people back to Earth. And you will *not* land on that planet, or engage the enemy without permission. Understood?'

'Sir, yes Sir,' cried the students.

'We have divided the airspace into sectors. Each one of you will be assigned one, and there you will remain for the entire duration of the mission, or until you are personally recalled back to Moonrising. Each sector has a number of portals and aircrafts to protect. You will be told who your charge is in due course.'

'Sir,' said Isolde, 'when do we start?'

'Soon, Miss Frey. Before this weekend is over, we will get our people back.'

The Mizkis cheered at that, and several of them moved over to George and Felicity, and patted them on their backs in a show of support.

Clavel let the class calm down before continuing. 'Let's take a look at this place then.' He pressed a few buttons on the wall, and ten touch-table tops emerged from the floor, dotted all around the room. 'Group up around a table.'

Julius, Faith, Skye and Morgana headed for the nearest one.

'I wonder if they'll keep our class in the same sector,' said Skye.

'I hope so, guys,' said Morgana. She activated their table top, and a large blueprint popped into view.

Julius studied it and quickly realised that it was a massive facility with multiple areas, extending over many miles. 'And that's only the ground floor,' he said, feeling slightly disheartened.

'This can't be right,' said Skye, pressing the "depth" button. 'It says that there are *twenty* underground levels.'

'It means each one is large enough to contain roughly 1 million people,' said Morgana.

'If they've kept our people split into continents, like we think,' said Faith, 'just how big will the other rescue missions be?'

'The remaining continents have between 500, and 900, million people each,' said Julius. 'That is, if they've kept the Americas as one.'

'It'll take us forever,' said Skye.

'Guys, let's just focus on this one first,' said Morgana, being practical. 'I'm sure they'll find a way of doing things quickly, if they can.'

Julius nodded, knowing that she was right. He looked at the respective airspace areas and carefully studied each sector; there were also several pictures of teleportation gates, which he studied thoroughly.

Clavel walked around the room, stopping by each of the tables, and answering any questions. Eventually, he made it to the Skirts. 'How does it look?'

'Busy like an anthill,' answered Faith.

'You'd better not crash into each other, then,' said Clavel.

'Sir,' said Julius, 'are we expecting any hostiles?'

The others looked up at Clavel, with worried expressions.

'I would say so,' he replied, simply.

Julius nodded. 'We'll fight back, then.'

'We may have to, yes,' agreed Clavel. 'We are deploying the Mizkis to border patrol, to ensure that none of the Arneshian ships come close to Moonrising. It's a big task, but you will at least have a safe harbour behind you, in case of emergency.'

'Will we fly together, sir?' asked Morgana, pointing at the Skirts.

'I don't see why not, Miss Ruthier,' said Clavel. 'But it's not a time for bravado, understood?'

'Us?' said Faith, pretending to be mildly offended. 'Would we ever?'

4

Clavel looked at him, with one raised eyebrow, then moved forward to the next table.

Julius turned to the others and grinned, trying to look relaxed. But, deep down, he felt a rush of nervous adrenaline coursing through him. After all, combat often brought with it casualties.

*

As it turned out, Faith got a chance to prove Clavel right the day after. All Mizkis had been asked to check their Cougars, to ensure that they were ready to go at a moment's notice.

Faith, being Faith, had spent the whole day maintaining his aircraft, as well as those of his classmates. The 4MAs trusted him so much that, even if a qualified Zed engineer had deemed their Cougars fit to fly, they still wanted to hear it from Faith too. Siena seemed to be finding the oddest little noises coming from her plane, which left him having to check her engines at least twice every hour — not that he was complaining much about it, of course.

Around dinnertime, most of the students had left the hangar, leaving only Julius and Faith behind.

'Come on, Irish!' said Julius, impatiently. 'It's eight o'clock and I'm *really* hungry.'

'Almost there,' said Faith, hovering high above, his head buried inside one of the engines. 'I just need to tighten that pressure gauge … over there … nasty thing …'

Julius sighed and, crossing his arms, he slumped to the floor and leaned back wearily against a tool trolley. A few minutes passed by, and he felt his head lolling forward, as it grew heavy.

'That guy is so weird.'

Julius' sat up quickly, startled awake by the sound of a boy's voice from behind him.

'I know, right?' said another one. 'How's *he* gonna fight?'

'He can't really. They keep him around as a handyman.'

'I can't stand the Skirts. Just because they win a bunch of games, they think they can do whatever they want.'

Julius realised they hadn't seen him sitting there, and decided that was probably a good thing. As long as Faith kept his head in the engine, he wouldn't even notice them, and he could just let them pass by. Knowing Faith, he figured, if he could avoid a confrontation, it would be for the best.

'That McCoy is the worst of the lot,' said the first boy. 'He wouldn't admit it last year, but that team selection for the challenge was rigged.'

That was when Julius recognised the voice: it was the blonde boy who had accused him of favouritism when he had chosen the team for the game against the Arneshians.

'Nah. The worst one is that cripple over there, if you ask me,' added his friend.

Hearing them use the word "cripple" acted like a wakeup call, because both Faith and Julius, straightened up at the same time and faced the two boys.

'Who are you calling a *cripple*?' asked Faith, flatly.

Julius looked at their uniform tags, and saw that they were both 5MSs. The blond boy's name was Sheldon Luner, and his big-mouthed friend was Ernie Dillon. Julius' first instinct was to give them a piece of his mind-skills, but thought better of it, while Faith, whose judgment was probably affected by the long, tiring day of work, flew directly at them, charging like a bull.

Julius had to duck as his friend passed over his head, at the same time trying to grab him by the skirt. Unfortunately, he barely brushed the edges of it, allowing Faith to park his fists in the middle of each of the seniors' faces. There was a loud *crunch*, which Julius recognised as the unmistakable sound of a nose being broken.

'By dose ...' cried Ernie Dillon, in agony. 'You broge by dose!'

Julius saw blood trickling through Ernie's fingers, as he clutched his hands to his face. Sheldon Luner, meanwhile, was lying flat on the floor, out cold, with Faith hovering in mid-air above him, breathing heavily. Julius could almost see the steam coming out of his nostrils, while his clenched fists had turned red from the impact, and Dillon's blood. In four years of friendship, Julius had never seen Faith lose his temper like that. Not even Adrian Sewell had been able to get him so upset; then again, that had been a long time ago, and Faith was a very different person now. He wasn't sure what he should do, but the arrival of an angry-looking Captain Foster resolved the problem for all of them.

*

Julius, Faith, Sheldon and Ernie were standing in Foster's office, while the Captain laid into them like there was no tomorrow. Faith wasn't uttering a single word, still visibly furious, so Julius volunteered to explain what had set his friend off.

Foster turned dangerously scarlet, and seemed shocked, appalled and flustered all at once. 'In forty years of service I have NEVER witnessed such behaviour between students! *Especially* students from the same school! How can we fight the Arneshians if we don't have a united front inside our own house?'

Julius just kept looking straight ahead, wondering what on earth was he doing there, since he hadn't actually done anything wrong.

'Luner, Dillon,' cried Foster. 'You will be referred to Master Cress for your idiocy. Shanigan, you and McCoy will put your hands to better use by cleaning the storage cupboard until midnight. And no dinner until then!'

'But, sir,' started Julius, 'what have I done?'

'You weren't quick enough to stop your friend from descending to animal level. What kind of a White Child are you, if you can't even use Stasis on a person!'

'What's Stasis?' said Julius, feeling crushed by the unfairness of all this.

'Sir,' whispered Luner, sheepishly, 'we do Stasis in fifth year.'

'So?' growled Foster.

'They're in *fourth* year.'

Foster seemed taken aback. Then he looked at Julius, unabashed, and resumed the shouting. 'What kind of a White Child are you if you can't even use Telekinesis on a person?'

Julius didn't even bother to reply at that point since, quite clearly, Foster was bent on giving him a punishment.

Twenty minutes later, Julius and Faith were cleaning dusty shelves in a cramped little room, just off the training sector of Tijara. It was a storage area for microchips, which had been boxed back on Zed, and were now needing unpacking.

Julius wiped down one of the bottom shelves, opened a box, and took out a stack of the chips. He began to place them upright against the back wall, without any specific order. He raised an eyebrow when he noticed a strange title, "Tijara's Ultimate Sacrifice" above an odd-looking logo, but he was too annoyed to think about it properly, and dismissed it as just another documentary about the death of Marcus Tijara.

It took Faith a long time, but eventually he broke the silence. 'Sorry, mate.'

Julius looked up, with a stack of containers in his hands, and shrugged his shoulders. 'Don't worry about it.'

'You shouldn't be here,' he replied. 'You had nothing to do with it.'

Julius knew that well enough but, frankly, he was more concerned with the seriousness in Faith's voice than the lack of food. 'I just didn't see it coming is all,' said Julius. 'You're the one that usually shrugs people like that off, not take them on.'

Faith hovered upwards, carrying a box. 'I spent five years of me life being laughed at because of me chair. Always last, always left out of every damn game or trip. People don't need to call you a cripple to make you feel like one.' He paused for a moment, unpacking a few of the items onto a higher shelf. 'When I came here I knew it would be different, and I said to meself that no one would ever treat me like that again. Dillon and Luner are just more of the Somers of this world, cowardly bullies, but I didn't expect to find any of them here, on Zed.'

'People are people, no matter where you are,' said Julius. 'I think we *are* lucky here, though. Douchebags like them are few and far between.'

Faith nodded. 'If I feel down, I can go to the Hologram Palace and get a room where I can … walk again, and be just like you. But, outside I have to survive and fend for meself. That's why I shrug them off, like you said. I try to find some sort of inner strength, and it works most of the time.'

'Except tonight,' said Julius.

'Yeah, except tonight. Tonight me legs have been more useless than usual.' He paused for a second, as if mustering his courage. 'I was seven, you know.'

Julius stopped what he was doing, realising that Faith was about to tell him exactly what had happened to him.

'Me parents had gone to the house next door, leaving me little cousin Patty and I at home. She went outside, chasing after a ball. I was right behind her, so when she got in the middle of the road and that fly-car showed up at top speed, I knew what would happen. Me powers weren't strong enough to push her out of the way — heck, I didn't even know what powers I had back then — so I did the only thing I *could* do. I ran to her, shoved her off the road, and got hit in her place. It happened so fast …' Faith shook his head. 'And the thing is, *she's* me inner strength. Whenever I feel down in the dumps because I can't walk, I think of her. If I had to choose all over again, between saving Patty's life, or not being able to walk, I'd never hesitate — I would *always* choose her over me. We all have responsibilities. She was mine.'

Julius was left speechless, and all he could do was place a reassuring hand on the bottom of his skirt. 'You're a good guy, Faith.'

That night, as Julius lay in his bed, he couldn't help but think about Faith's words. He had done what he had because it was his duty, and he never questioned it, no matter what the consequences. Ben Hastings had told him that a person without powers was destined to a shallow existence, but was it true? Faith had lost a most precious gift, the freedom to walk and run, and yet, his life was richer than that of many people he had met. In his place, he may well have at least blamed his parents for leaving him alone at such a young age, with an even younger kid to look after, or the driver of the fly-car for being so reckless. But not Faith. His inner strength kept him going, and he was braver even than Julius. How would he have coped without his powers? And never mind his legs because, in his mind he agreed with Ben, his skills were the most important thing there was.

OCEANIA

Julius spent the next couple of days in a state of anxiety, fuelled by the impending mission and, of course, his meeting with Farrah. He wasn't the only one however, to feel the strain, and a sense of calm before the storm had permeated throughout Moonrising. Since the interview with Roversi, Iryana Mielowa had embarked on a live marathon of minute-by-minute updates on the situation, seemingly sleeping only a mere four hours per night. Yet, she always looked impeccable, which drew amazed comments from the female students, who were not looking quite so refreshed by the long wait.

The 4MAs had eventually been assigned to sector 7, and divided into 6 groups – the Skirts, plus Isolde, had been named as the fourth toon. With them was a mixture of 5 and 6MSs from Tijara, alongside several Zed officers, all responsible for the defence of their zone. Julius had also discovered that Captain Kelly and the Ahura Mazda would be working much closer to the planet; knowing that Kelly was around made him feel much more confident.

On Saturday morning, the 4MAs had officially been told that they would be the armed escort for the Storks, their size being smaller and so more appropriate to their rank as apprentices. After a hurried lunch, Julius couldn't take the wait any longer and decided to head to New Satras, taking Skye along for moral support. He could feel a tight knot in the pit of his stomach as he arrived at level -2. Unconsciously, he kept flattening his hair, in between drying his palms on the sides of his trousers, and straightening his uniform.

'I'm going to head to that cafe over there, all right?' said Skye. 'Keep calm and you'll be fine.'

Julius nodded. He took the box out of his leg pocket and removed a bit of fluff which was stuck in one of the corners. Composing himself, he began to walk determinedly towards Auld Oddities. Just as he had reached the centre of the square, a loud siren exploded to life, followed by an announcement: 'All Mizkis and Zed officers report for duty immediately!'

Julius stopped dead in his tracks. 'Damn,' he cried. Suddenly, all the colours and decor began to fade around him, like fresh paint being washed away by rain, as Moonrising entered into battle mode. He turned around, looking for Skye and saw that he was running towards him.

'She's there!' shouted Skye, over the noise, pointing at the shop. 'Let's go!'

Julius looked, and felt a rush of blood flooding his face, as he spotted Farrah hurriedly closing her parents' shop door behind her. 'Farrah!' he called, heading towards her.

She heard his voice and, when she saw him, she waved in his direction.

As they met, Julius was sorely tempted to throw his arms around her, but thought better of it, so he stopped short of bumping into her and put one hand on her arm instead.

'Right on time,' she said. 'I thought I'd *never* see that box!'

'Come on,' said Julius, grinning, 'we'll talk on the way.' As he turned and began to power-walk, his hand slid down her arm; when he found her hand, he grabbed it, and was relieved to feel her locking her fingers between his. His heart skipped a beat. 'Uh … this is Skye, by the way.'

'Hi there,' said Skye, shoving a few people out of the way, as they headed for the lifts. 'I've heard so much about you, and such a description that I had started to believe you didn't exist!'

Farrah smiled, blushing slightly as she threw a glance at Julius. 'Nice to meet you, Skye.'

'When he told me that he had stumbled upon the most beautif- ouch!' he yelped, as Julius' elbow shot into his ribcage. 'Never mind …' he whispered, feebly.

Farrah looked at the pair of them, and giggled. 'I need to take the lift at the far end. It's quicker for me.'

They took the stairs at a run, and came to a stop when they reached the transporter for Tijara. Even with the confusion all around, Julius still took note of how perfectly Farrah's olive-green uniform suited her hair colour and skin complexion.

'We should go out for a meal, all together,' said Skye, waving to her as he held the lift door open.

'Sounds great,' she replied, and then to Julius, 'Thanks for the box.'

He didn't want to let go of her hand, but he had no choice. 'Hey,' he said, moving closer to her. If his heart had been skipping beats before, it was now pounding furiously, as her face drew nearer. 'Be careful out there, all right? Cause I *really* would like to see you again.'

Before Julius could say anything else, she placed a light kiss on his cheek. 'Likewise,' she answered. With that, she turned and ran to her lift.

Skye had to drag Julius inside, as he was still rooted to the spot, turning a healthy beetroot colour.

'You'd better clean that lip balm off!' he said, grinning cheekily.

'No way. It'll be my lucky charm for today.'

*

When they reached the hangar, Faith, Morgana and Isolde were already there, waiting by the Cougars. The siren was still blaring, but, by now, it had become background noise.

As Julius and Skye joined their group, Clavel approached them. 'Who's in charge of toon 4?'

All faces turned to Julius.

'McCoy, get your guys ready to go in five,' said Clavel, moving quickly to the next group.

Julius nodded, and faced the others. Solemnly, he put his hand forward, palm down. 'We will bring them back,' he said.

'So let it be!' they replied, as one, and placed their hands on top of Julius'.

They held there together for a moment. Julius could see red wisps pouring from their auras. 'Channel your fear and make it work for you,' he said. 'Failure is not an option. Let's go.' He watched as they all boarded their planes, throwing a last glance at Morgana. No matter what was going on elsewhere, he would always care for her, whether she knew it or not.

He climbed inside his Cougar, and placed his thumb on the recognition plate. As he did so, his tag name appeared in bright, yellow letters on both side-displays of the craft. 'Goshawk, ready to roll,' he said. When he looked at Isolde's plane, he saw that she had chosen "Ruby", as her tag name. He quickly created a channel for his toon, and one for the Zed officers, knowing that any communication from Moonrising would come through whether or not there was a free channel. He then opened a tab with all of his toon's vitals, and the state of their Cougars, which appeared as vertical red lines; he hoped he wouldn't have need to check that too often. 'Toon 4, this is Goshawk. Ready check and standby.' Immediately, the red lines turned green, one by one, giving Julius the go-ahead. 'Moonrising, this is Toon 4. We're ready to go.'

'Initiating departure procedure, Toon 4. Hunt hard,' a voice replied from the bridge.

Julius touched the tips of his right fingers to the smear of lip balm that Farrah had left on his cheek. A fresh whiff of cocoa wafted up to his nostrils, which immediately made him think of sand, sea, and sun cream lotion. He was so electrified by the memory of his encounters with Farrah that, right then, he felt like he could have stormed the planet all by himself. He was still buzzing about the fact that she hadn't let go of his hand *and* agreed to go out for dinner. He couldn't let those good signs go to waste; but, first, they had a continent to rescue. He switched on his engine and rolled onto the short runway, followed by his toon.

The outer airlock ports were all open; a thin membrane, similar to the Zed shield, protected the inner hangar from outer space, preventing the deck from depressurizing. The Cougars, however, could just fly straight through it to get out, or get back in.

Julius took hold of the ship's catalysts, and willed his Cougar forward. Immediately, it accelerated and broke through the membrane, out into space.

'It's rush hour, people,' said Faith, as the rest of the toon joined him outside Moonrising.

Julius looked up, through the transparent roof of his plane, and watched several layers of black Cougars positioning themselves in their own respective zones. Julius knew, somewhere among them, was Farrah; he wished now that he had asked her what sector she would be working in, or even what her tag name was. He touched his screen, bringing up the coordinates for sector 7, and led his toon towards it. He could see his classmates' Cougars heading in his general direction, all flying together in tight formations. As they moved further away from Moonrising, groups of the planes detached and veered off to their posts, where Zed officers were already patrolling.

As he approached his zone, Julius spotted a teleportation gate. 'Look, guys!' he said. 'It's our portal.'

'Wow,' said Isolde. 'Will it really work?'

'I know, right?' said Morgana. 'I never even thought it would be possible.'

'It's slightly scary, if you ask me,' said Skye. 'How do you know you won't just end up ... *dispersing* yourself in the course of the journey?'

'It worked well enough for the Arneshians,' answered Faith. 'We only have to hope that List has properly recreated it.'

'What do you mean?' said Skye, in alarm. 'Hasn't this thing been tested yet?'

'It'll be fine, mate,' said Faith. 'I'm sure they've done homework aplenty before risking sending 20 million people through it.'

Skye didn't reply, but Julius understood his nervousness well enough, because he had also had the same concerns. This was, after all, a first for humans — or at least the non-Arneshian portion of mankind — and, although Zed had already been testing it for a few months, there was still no guarantee that all would go smoothly. Plus, there was the fact that it wouldn't just be *one* portal, but a series of them, as each carrier was taken back to Earth, quadrant by quadrant. Yes, thought Julius, there was reason for concern all right.

The portal was a massive 8 shaped structure, with each of the two circles functioning as a one-directional access path to and from Zed. Its silver metal frame shone bright in the darkness of space; tiny green lights marked the way in, while red ones dotted the way out. Julius guessed that, to get back home, the Storks would need to pick the green ones.

'Baza, Ruby,' said Julius, hailing Faith and Isolde. 'Keep your eyes on the planet, and alert us when the Storks begin to arrive.'

'Aye, aye, captain,' replied Isolde, veering her Cougar towards the edge of their zone, as close to the planet's airspace as they were allowed to go.

'Kite and Vulture,' called Julius again, 'you're with me on sector patrol. Make sure no one sneaks in from the shadows.'

'On it, Goshawk,' replied Morgana, promptly.

Julius steered his plane in the opposite direction and began to circle around the portal. Occasionally, he came across one of the seniors, who just nodded in his direction, before moving on. Julius could read all sorts of mixed emotions in their eyes, from fear to anxiety, not to mention the ashen-grey wisps swirling about in many of their cockpits. Only the auras of the Zed officers were mainly green, a clear sign of excitement, which was most likely thanks to their many years of training and experience. It was certainly good to have them around.

'Guys,' called Faith, after a while, 'I think they've started.'

Julius brought his plane about and zoomed in on the planet, using his scanner. There were so many planes above the rescue area that it was difficult to tell exactly what was going on. Then he noticed the Ahura, which was firing over a side section of the camp, where a large grey building stood. It was surrounded by barren land, which stretched for several thousand yards.

'Why are they shooting?' asked Isolde.

'According to Mielowa,' explained Faith, 'they're creating openings to let our ships go through.'

'Mielowa?' said everyone else, at the same time.

'Yes? She's on the radio doing a live report,' said Faith, defensively. 'At least I know what's going on.'

'Channel, please?' said Morgana.

'Well,' answered Faith, evasively, 'technically you don't have that kind of radio on a Cougar ...'

'But ... *you* do?'

'Just a little modification. You know me.'

'Yes, we know you, Baza,' said Julius. 'Keep us in the loop, then.'

'With pleasure,' replied Faith.

Julius shook his head, and wondered what else could be installed on a Cougar, if left in Faith's hands for long enough.

With the updates starting to come in fast from Faith, Julius resumed his patrol towards the furthest part of the sector, making sure to scan ahead for any unwanted visitors.

'They've just ceased firing on the camp,' said Faith. 'The Ahura Mazda has landed, together with the rest of the infantry party. They're going in!'

Julius took a deep breath, and stretched his hands, cracking his knuckles one by one, to ease the mounting tension. A sense of unease had drifted through his area, further heightening the sense of anticipation, and seemingly dragging time to a standstill.

'The transporters are now getting ready to land,' said Faith. 'There are thousands of them all lined up ... but there's some resistance ... wait ...'

'What's happening, Faith?' implored Skye.

'There's some fighting going on.'

'Oh no,' said Morgana, sounding suitably worried.

'Faith?' urged Julius.

'Hold on,' he said. 'They won't allow our ships to land until the coast is clear. The combat troops have met the Arneshian guards, it seems.'

Julius was getting restless now. There was a battle not too far away, and here he was, having to rely on second hand radio updates to know what was happening, circling the portal like a caged animal with nowhere to go. Minutes passed by without news, as Mielowa herself waited to hear from the foot soldiers.

An hour went by before, eventually, Faith's voice filled their planes. 'The transporters are landing!' he cried. 'They've cleared the first level!'

'All right,' said Julius, sighing in relief. He knew that the infantry's job had only just started but, as they worked their way down, through the subterranean levels, the ground floor would be able to begin the evacuation. 'Talk to me, Faith.'

'They're loading the Storks and the Herons ... They're starting to take off. Guys, they're on my scanner. The first ships are breaking orbit.'

'Goshawk, this is Commander Fletcher,' said a new voice. 'Arrange your toon along these coordinates, to flank the Storks as they come in.'

'Understood, Sir,' replied Julius. Then he quickly forwarded the location to the others, and took up position near the portal. 'Be ready, everyone.'

As the first Stork approached sector 7, Julius felt a lump in his throat, as he thought of how close they were to getting some of their people back. He wondered about his parents. Where were they? Was someone taking care of them? He hoped they would be with people they knew from back home. As for Michael's whereabouts ... well, that was everybody's guess.

He watched as the Stork moved closer and closer to the portal; as soon as it entered the green-lit path, it disappeared in a fizz of static discharge before his eyes. 'This is just,' he whispered, in disbelief.

'Unbelievable,' said Morgana, obviously as stunned as he was.

'Look alive, guys,' said Skye. 'There are more incoming.'

Slowly, but steadily, the number of Storks heading for their portal increased, and so did the number of Cougars along the transports routes, which were there to cover them. To actually see them arriving, one after the other, and disappearing like packages at the end of a conveyer belt, made Julius realise that this operation was going to take a long time to complete. He looked at his watch, and noticed that they had been working for almost two hours already. He knew that when his toon needed to re-fuel or rest, they would be recalled to the hangar, while another toon took their place, and so on in rotating shifts as needed, until it was done.

It took the Zed infantry the best part of the next 7 hours to reach the last sub level of the camp. By then, news of a few casualties on both sides had reached Moonrising and the pilots. It understandably dampened the mood and, for a while after, there was virtual silence on the channels, save for vital pieces of information.

At 22:30, Julius and his toon were sitting in their Cougars inside the hangar, ready to begin their third shift after an hour break. He was thinking now about Captain Kelly, wondering where he was, and if he had also infiltrated the site. Julius had seen him in action a couple of times, and he knew that he could fend for himself. Still, he would have hated to hear about anything bad had happening to him. He checked the news screen on his PIP, and scanned the casualty list. As was to be expected, Zed losses were all among the ground troops, and all names that Julius didn't know. But, he knew, they had been students just like him, once upon a time, probably with families to whom they'd never return. Saddened, he selected the mission page, where a counter indicated that 6 million people had been rescued so far. Commander Fletcher had estimated that, all going well, they would finish around midday on Sunday.

Julius' next shift was going to be a shorter one and, at midnight, he would be allowed four hours of sleep. As he sat waiting in his Cougar, before closing his PIP, he went into his messages, opened a new one, on which he wrote one word, "Hey", before sending it to Farrah. 'Toon 4, ready check and stand by,' he said to the others. The lights turned green, and the bridge authorised them for take-off. 'Come on, guys. One more shift till Bedshire.'

Once back out in space, they resumed their positions, replacing one of the toons that was due a break. The Storks were still flowing along to the nearby portal, only with a bit more speed and frequency. Perhaps, after several hours, they had become more efficient at loading passengers, whisking them through to Earth, and making the journey back to here.

'At least Mielowa hasn't reported anyone as missing,' said Morgana.

'Yes,' commented Faith. 'It seems like the portals are working well, thankfully.'

'What about the pilots who are going back and forth?' asked Skye, who was still a little unsure about the new technology.

'Nothing to report on that one either,' answered Faith. 'But we'll probably find out tomor-'

'Faith?' asked Morgana. 'You there?'

'Hmm … that's strange,' he said, after a pause.

'What is?' asked Julius, now fully alert.

'I have a very weird reading coming from the far side of the camp.'

'You do?' asked Isolde. 'And how can you tell from here?'

'Faith,' said Julius, 'did you alter the Cougars' long range scanners, by any chance?'

'Maybe … but that's not the point. I'm telling you, I've picked up something odd, an object of some sort, which has left the camp and is heading east.'

Julius thought about it for a moment, then opened a channel to Commander Fletcher. 'Sir,' he said. 'We're picking up an unusual reading here.'

'What is it, Goshawk?' said Fletcher.

'It looks like an unidentified ship has left the camp, heading east. I'm sending you the trace,' said Julius, transferring Faith's findings.

'You may be right,' said Fletcher. 'Although, how you got this information is beyond me.'

Julius acted innocent, and ignored the last part of his comment.

'I'll go check it out. You guys stay here and keep your eyes open. You're doing a grand job, Toon 4.'

'Aww ... That was nice of him,' said Morgana, cheered by the compliment.

'What do you think it was, Faith?' asked Skye.

'Me best guess would be an Arneshian shuttle, trying to sneak away.'

'Why would they do that?' asked Isolde.

'To save their butts?' volunteered Skye. 'It doesn't look like they're winning, does it?'

'Attention pilots,' called Commander Fletcher to all the Cougars in his sector. 'Arneshian shuttle on its way to sector 7. I'm in pursuit.'

'What?' cried Skye.

Julius frantically began to scan the airspace, but couldn't see anything.

'I've got it!' said Faith. 'Incoming, on these coordinates. Sending them through.'

Julius locked them in to his radar and suddenly a blinking point appeared before him. 'We need to stop the Storks, Faith!'

'I'm on it,' he said. 'Moonrising, this is Baza 4. The Storks must be rerouted: we have an incoming bogey on its way here. Looks like it's heading for the portal.'

'Roger, Baza 4. All Storks are being diverted to adjacent portals. All Mizkis, retreat immediately to Moonrising. All Zed officers, support Commander Fletcher.'

Julius looked at the radar and saw that the Mizkis were following orders on the double, while the officers had gone to Fletcher's aid.

Suddenly, a blinding light flashed past them. Julius had to shield his eyes with his arms, for how strong it was. He blinked and looked at his screen; according to his radar, it had come from the Arneshian shuttle.

'What the heck was that?' shouted Skye.

'A pulse of some kind,' answered Faith. 'And it just knocked down all communication channels. Neither Fletcher, nor Moonrising are responding.'

'Then how come *we're* still talking to each other?' asked Morgana.

'It's 'cause I'm *the* Faith, little lady. Our toon has a special channel,' he added.

Morgana giggled nervously. 'Wait until I tell Siena about this!'

'You do that!' said Faith, enthusiastically.

'Hey,' said Julius, 'who's gonna protect the portal, if we leave too?'

'No one apparently,' replied Isolde. 'Come on, guys. We need to retreat.'

'Julius is right,' said Faith. 'Me radar's reading everyone pursuing the bogey, but no one blocking it, or coming this way. What if they don't catch it before it arrives at the portal?'

'And what do you propose we do?' asked Morgana. 'Park sideways in front of the path?'

'Julius, we need to retreat!' insisted Isolde. 'Clavel was clear, we can't engage the enemy.'

'We're not going to,' he said. 'We'll switch off the portal, instead.'

'What, did you bring a spacesuit or something?' asked Skye.

'He meant with our skills, Dumbo,' said Faith, cheekily.

'I knew that,' answered Skye, vaguely.

'What's the plan, then?' asked Morgana.

'We'll let it get to the portal, and at the last second we cut off the power, so it goes right through it and into the docking bay on the other side. Isolde, will you help us?'

She didn't answer straight away, but eventually replied, 'All right, I'll do it.'

'Good girl,' said Faith, pleased. 'The more, the merrier.'

'Come on then,' said Julius, hurrying them. 'Spread out, around the core of the portal.'

'Which is?' asked Skye.

'It's that large sphere at the centre of the structure, linking the two rings,' answered Faith.

'We need to blow it off,' said Julius, 'but not too early. They must see the green lights, until the very last second.' He positioned his Cougar above the core section, and focused his mind on it, then he took a deep breath and waited. The dot on his radar was drawing closer with every blink. 'Hold it steady,' he said to the others. Out of the corner of his eye, he spotted the Arneshian shuttle approaching fast, pursued by a large number of Cougars. 'Here it comes. Ready … Steady … Now!'

Five yellow beams shot out of the Cougars, striking the portal's core just as the enemy shuttle was about to hit it. There was a small explosion which sent sparks flying, and made the portal shake and wobble. The Arneshian pilot, just as Julius had foreseen, shot straight through and kept on going toward Moonrising. The Zed Cougars had veered off at the last minute, but were now returning to the portal.

Julius watched the enemy shuttle trying to veer upwards, to avoid Moonrising's opened bay, but it was going too fast, and simply didn't have enough time to pull out. A few seconds later, the Arneshian ship was swallowed up by the battlestar. Commander Fletcher, followed by several Cougars, flew straight past toon 4, and followed into the hangar, probably to make sure that the pilot was apprehended.

'We did it!' cried Morgana.

A Cougar pulled up next to Julius; the pilot, who Julius didn't recognise, gestured for him to go back to Moonrising.

'Guys, we've been recalled,' said Julius. 'Head back to the hangar.' It was then that he noticed something floating upwards from the portal, soon to be lost in space. 'What is that?' he said to himself. He took off after it, trying to get close, but not so close as to touch it with his ship.

'Julius, where are you going?' asked Morgana.

'I'll be right there,' he replied. He was getting ever nearer the object, but couldn't tell exactly what it was, as it spun freely on its own axis, reflecting Moonrising's external lights back at Julius. He locked his mind on it and, using the catalyst, gently pulled it close to him, until it bumped against the Cougar's body, and came to a rest on its nose. He kept it there, using a portion of his powers, making sure to keep enough of his mind focused on piloting the plane back into the hangar. When he climbed out of his cockpit, there was a commotion around the Arneshian plane. He ignored it and called for Faith. 'Can you get that thing down?' he said, pointing at the nose of his Cougar.

'What did you find?' asked Faith, hovering upwards, and reaching for the item. As he landed back on the ground again, Morgana, Skye and Isolde came running towards them.

'It was a holo pilot!' said Morgana. 'As always, they're not brave enough for- Hey! What is that?'

Faith held it out, and they all examined it. The mysterious silver object was cross-shaped, with small cubes, spheres and triangles grouped at the ends of each of its four arms; it was glowing, lit by some sort of internal, green luminescence. In the centre, where the arms met, was a black sphere. The arms had a series of holes along their length, placed at random intervals. Julius noticed how the smaller parts were all assembled symmetrically, following the same pattern: each arm ended in a silver sphere; a triangle grew out of it and, at each of its base corners, was a smaller sphere. From each of these, three further little arms shot out, each terminating in a cube.

'It reminds me of one of those molecular model sets that I used in Chemistry class,' said Faith.

'One section seems to be switched off,' observed Morgana. She pointed at the three cubes at the end of the part in question, and their connecting ball. 'See?'

'I have no idea what it is,' said Julius, after a while. 'But I think it was ejected from the shuttle.'

'Why?' asked Isolde.

'Maybe the pilot didn't want us to find it,' replied Julius.

'Whatever it is, I hope it's good enough to get us out of trouble,' said Skye, looking up. 'Clavel is heading this way, and he doesn't look at all pleased.'

'McCoy! Shanigan!' shouted Clavel striding up to them. 'Cress' office. Now! And bring that thing with you,' he finished, pointing at the mysterious object.

Julius swallowed, and threw a worried glance at Faith.

'Good luck,' whispered Morgana, as they walked away. 'We'll be in the lounge.'

Clavel, who was normally a very peaceful and relaxed man, seemed to have lost all of his usual poise, and was now striding ahead of them, sending red and black wisps every which way.

'*He's really mad,*' said Julius, to Faith, with his mind.

Faith simply nodded, and gulped.

Clavel led them out of Tijara's hangar, and all the way to the front of the ship, where the school staff had their quarters.

Moonrising was still in safe mode so, whatever this place looked like when it was full of colour was anybody's guess. Just now, however, it looked pretty shabby.

They had just taken the corridor which led to Cress's office, when a door swung open and the furious Master jumped out in front of them. 'Inside!' he bellowed.

'Yes, sir,' replied Julius and Faith together, before hurrying after him.

They stood to attention in the middle of the room, while Clavel and Cress towered in front of them.

'The artifact, McCoy!' said Cress.

Julius handed it to him, and watched as the Master placed it delicately on his desk. There was a strange look on his face as he handled it, and a thick green wisp had just emerged from the crown of his head.

'I'm extremely disappointed, and so is Professor Clavel,' said Cress. 'Of all the times you could have chosen to disobey orders and pull one of your stunts, you really picked the wrong one. Explain yourself!'

Julius felt slightly miffed by this particular ticking off. Hadn't they just prevented an enemy ship from entering the portal to Earth? What was he on about? 'Sir, after the pulse attack, we were cut off from Moonrising, and Commander Fletcher. When we saw that the portal was going to be left defenceless we … I, gave the order to deactivate it, to prevent the Arneshian's escape. And it worked.'

Cress was breathing deeply through his nostrils now. He made Julius think of a bull who was preparing to charge, which was most unlike the Master of Tijara. Surely there was more to this than he was letting on.

'Let me tell you the story from our perspective, McCoy,' said Cress. 'Toon 4 warns Commander Fletcher of a strange reading, which the officer pursues, as per protocol. And that's OK, because he's trained for it. Then, Toon 4 receives a direct order from the bridge of Moonrising, to pull back, which doesn't happen. And that's not OK, because you lack the training. Orders from superior officers must be followed!'

Julius could see that Cress was getting more worked up with every sentence, and he didn't like where this was going.

'If Mr Shanigan here hadn't tampered with the Cougars' com-links, you would have been able to hear us loud and clear, because, funnily enough, we have the technology to bypass a pulse attack! But you couldn't, because *his* system was fighting *ours*!' he said, pointing at Faith. 'So, Fletcher couldn't tell you to get out of the way, but kept pushing the Arneshian towards the portal, because WE-HAD-A-PLAN! An entire team was waiting for this dratted shuttle on the other side of the portal, ready to catch it, but it never arrived! And, do you know why? Because *you* broke the damn portal! It will take us hours to fix that core engine, delaying the entire mission by half a day! The artifact would have been retrieved on the other side, end of story. Satisfied?'

Julius and Faith just stood there, speechless, trying to digest Cress' words.

'Just who do you think you are?' continued Cress loudly, still in obvious need to let off steam. 'After four years of training, you still treat us like we're the enemy, the people to contradict! There is nothing that we do on Zed that is meant to hurt you. Nothing! We are your family.' And with that, he stomped around the table and sat down in his chair.

'Your flight support to the mission is over,' said Clavel. 'You will assist in the hangar with repairs and maintenance. You will *not* take part in the next rescue mission, whenever that may be and, if needed, the biggest thing you'll fly will be a sky-jet. There will be no leaving Tijara and no access to New Satras until further notice. That goes for the rest of your toon as well.'

'Please, sir!' cried Faith, arms in the air.

'Sir!' started Julius.

'Sir, nothing,' said Clavel. 'They are not puppets. They chose the same way as you did, and so they'll pay the consequences for their actions. You have three hours left before your next shift. I suggest you retire. Dismissed.'

'Yes, sir,' said Julius. He threw a last glance at Cress, and left the room.

'I'm sorry, Julius,' said Faith, as they walked back to the lounge. 'It's all me fault. If I hadn't added that stupid extra channel, we wouldn't be in this mess.'

'If you hadn't added that long range sensor, we would never have caught that shuttle, so don't apologise. Beside, have you seen the way Cress reacted, when he saw that thing?'

'No. What do you mean?'

'Never mind that, now. Cress seemed *thrilled* to have it on his desk. That alone, if you ask me, is the reason why we're not out of the rescue missions altogether, washing Felice's dishes in the galley.'

When they reached the lounge, the rest of the toon was waiting in one of the booths, sipping hot chocolate.

'Go get us a hot drink, and I'll tell them,' said Faith.

Julius nodded, grateful at not having to do that part. When he returned, he realised that Faith hadn't told them either. Not really, anyway. He had recorded the entire scene on his PIP, and was now letting Master Cress do the telling, and the shouting, aided by Clavel.

'Shoot,' said Skye, in frustration. 'Can you believe that? No New Satras? Maintenance duties? No offence, Faith.'

'None taken. And, by the way, Morgana, I wouldn't mention this to Siena.'

'I think the story has already done the rounds twice,' said Morgana. 'Too late, Faith.'

Isolde stood up. 'I should have left when the order came. I feel like it's your fault, Julius, but I have no one to blame but myself.'

'Isolde, I'm sorry,' replied Julius, standing up.

She just looked at him, and left.

'Isolde, wait,' he called.

'Let her go,' said Morgana. 'We're all tired now, and we need some rest. I'll talk to her tomorrow.'

'Here, let me send you a copy of tonight's episode of the Cress' show, in case you can't sleep,' said Faith.

'Gee, thanks,' said Julius. As he opened his PIP to check that it had arrived, he saw a new message from Farrah. He opened it and read, "You. X". He smiled. At least the day was closing on a bit of a high.

NIGHT CRAWLING

Morgana had been right about their story being common knowledge. As soon as they resumed their shift at 4 in the morning, they were welcomed by a few cheers of sympathy from some of their classmates and some not so encouraging looks from the Mizki Seniors. The toon just kept their heads down and took to refueling and repairing the Cougars, avoiding too much banter and generally keeping a low profile.

Julius was particularly annoyed at the New Satras ban, since that was the only place where he could have met up with Farrah. Moreover, Cress' accusations about treating them like they were the enemy still rang in his ears, making him even more upset. Sure enough, in hindsight, he realised he had screwed up royally, but certainly not with the intention of hurting Zed. His intentions had been good; he had just been trying to protect the portal and whoever was on the other side. How could Cress and Clavel not see that? He shook his head, glad at least that Freja hadn't been summoned about this. And — considering it was already the second time that he had been in trouble in the past month — that was a bit of a miracle.

Early Sunday evening, the Oceania Mission officially ended, bringing with it widespread relief and a welcome sense of accomplishment. Moonrising regained its colourful appearance, while a big dinner party was held in Tijara's lounge. Staff and students were finally allowed to relax and exchange their experiences and impressions, while pictures of the Oceanic countries scrolled across the many screens dotted around the ship.

Mielowa was reporting moving stories of people returning to their homes after the many months that had passed. There were tears of joy, and of sadness, as some of them had died in captivity, mainly due to illness or old age. George Lowet and Felicity Steep were both huddled in a booth, talking to their families via their PIPs.

One thing which piqued everyone's curiosity, was that every single one of the rescued Earth folk were wearing Arneshian circlets around their heads, just like the one T'Rogon had been sporting, the previous year. The captive had reported that these circlets shone with some sort of inner light, which went off as soon as they were removed from the compound. None of them were able to offer an explanation for it but, since they were removed with no apparent discomfort to the wearer, the matter was pushed to one side, as nothing more than an Arneshian oddity.

'Last year Michael told me that they wear them to amplify their Grey Skills,' explained Julius.

'But these are humans, with no skills to amplify,' replied Morgana.

'Maybe they wanted everyone to look like them,' offered Skye.

Julius doubted that, but he had no better explanation for it.

That night passed quickly and, at two o'clock, the Mizkis were asked to retire, and were given the Monday off.

'It's so unfair,' Julius said to Skye, once they were back in their room. 'A whole day that I could spend with Farrah, and I'm not even allowed to leave Tijara.'

'Well, at least *one of us* will get to see his lady tomorrow,' said Skye, winking cheekily.

'Still with Valentina, huh?'

'And we'll be celebrating, oh yeah!'

'Great,' huffed Julius. 'Just what I needed to hear.'

'You'd better text Farrah and let her know, by the way.'

'I will,' said Julius. Now that they had made a start of sorts, he certainly didn't want to risk losing her over some silly reason. He opened his PIP and began to type.

*

The last day of October finally arrived, and Julius headed to Professor Chan's Pyrokinesis class, which was held in a massive area at the back of BM Tijara. Since last year, he had learned to control the amount of fire his body generated and, now that his gene therapy had increased his skill so considerably, Julius was much better at creating the size of fireball he wanted, without singeing Chan's eyebrows.

'Gather up, Mizkis,' called Chan. 'There's something we need to discuss before we start our lesson. Can anyone tell me, is fire able to burn in space?'

Everyone raised their hands.

'Mr Liway?'

'There's no oxygen in space, sir, so if you just have fuel it won't burn.'

'Very good. And why does the Sun, or any of the stars, appear to be *burning* then, Miss Migliori?'

'They don't burn because of a chemical reaction, sir,' explained Siena, 'but by nuclear fusion, where an atom's nucleus bonds with another nucleus; that way, they don't need oxygen. Stars are like nuclear bombs which are continuously exploding, for billions and billions of years.'

'Good,' said Chan. 'Although we tend to stay indoors out here, there may be times where you may need to use this particular skill in open space.'

'We're going nuclear, sir?' asked Faith, worried as usual about them needing any type of augmentation.

'You already have, Mr Shanigan. Your Pre-Pyro treatment, last year, has given you the ability to create fusion. Just now, it's lying dormant, and it will remain so, until you need it.'

'He's kidding, right?' Faith whispered sideways to Julius.

'Sir,' said Barth. 'Isn't there a risk that we, you know, end up blowing the whole place up?'

'That would be regrettable, Mr Smit, but the fusion only functions in the vacuum of space, when it detects the absence of oxygen, and it's only as powerful as your own individual Pyro skill.'

'Good,' said Barth, hesitantly. 'It's just that, me being me and all, I'm a little concerned that-'

'I see, Mr Smit, and you may be right,' said Chan, raising an eyebrow. 'I guess it's your choice at this point. Do you want to keep avoiding the challenges that life throws at you, or are you willing to step up to them? Personally, I'd feel safe knowing that you're my navigator, but I'd still like to know that you have at least given this mind-skill a try. Only then will you know if it's for you or not. Remember, we all have talents, and it's our duty to use them. But first, you have to discover those talents.'

Barth stared intently at Chan as he spoke, and Julius noticed a little golden wisp coiling around his classmate's head. 'Good on you, Professor,' he thought to himself. Chan's compliment and words of encouragement had obviously made an impression.

'Now,' resumed Chan, 'after a year of creating fireballs of all different sizes and shapes, I want you to learn how to *direct* these projectiles, using your telekinetic skills. Split up into your usual range groups and pick a lane.'

Julius joined the 300 + feet group, which was made up of Leanne Nord, Felicity Steep, Ferenc Orban, Kaleb Kashny, and Isolde. He let them go first, they all managed to generate their fireballs, and releasing them, but they weren't able to guide them at all.

After several unsuccessful attempts, Ferenc turned to Julius. 'What am I doing wrong?'

Julius was surprised that *he* was the one being asked like that, what with Professor Chan just at a few feet away from them. He stood, and walked up to the line, vaguely aware that Isolde was still giving him the cold shoulder, annoyed as she was about their ongoing detention. 'I think you need to release it slowly, so you can actually guide it. If you're too fast, it's harder to control.'

'Show me,' said Ferenc.

The others made space, leaving Julius alone at the front of the lane. He took up his usual stance: right hand lifted, palm facing up and bent slightly outwards. He could feel the energy starting to flow through his veins, converging towards the palm of his hand. He had learned to be careful about how much of this energy he let out because, having to reduce the size of the fireball after release, which required drawing some of the power back in, caused a painful burning sensation all up his arm.

Once he had created a sphere the size of a football, he pulled his hand back, then forward, and gently released it; the ball floated forward steadily away from him. He locked his mind on it, and guided it first up, then downwards and finally to the left and right. When it reached the end of the lane he summoned it back to him, this time making it follow an undulating line. To finish off, he pushed it up above his head and slapped it forward like a volleyball. The fireball disintegrated an instant later against the far wall.

Happy with the performance, he turned around, and realised that the entire class was watching, with gaping mouths.

'McCoy, you've just invented a new game,' said Faith, excitedly. 'Professor! We should have a school competition, a tournament of fire-volleyball. And the final can be in space, like a nuclear final!'

Chan stared at Faith, with an intense monobrow.

'Or not …' added Faith. 'I'll shut up, now,' he finished, and resumed his training.

Julius' group was extremely eager to learn how he had done that, all except for Isolde, who had moved off to train by herself, without a word to anyone else.

'What's her problem?' wondered Julius, shrugging his shoulders. Whatever it was, he decided it was just going to have to take care of itself. After all, he already had Farrah to think about, and Morgana to look after, so he really didn't need to worry about Isolde too.

*

When the first weekend of December arrived, Julius tried to distract himself by going to the gym and working out until he was completely exhausted. He would have invited the others, but they were nowhere to be found.

It was only on Saturday afternoon that Faith joined him at the dojo, just as Julius was emerging from the changing room. 'There you are!' said Faith. 'I've been looking everywhere for you.'

'Just passing time, really,' said Julius, grabbing his bag. 'The others?'

'Skye's been practicing mouth-to-mouth with Valentina all day, and will probably continue to do so for the rest of the weekend. I was fixing Cougars, *supervised*,' he added, with a grunt.

'Morgana with Isolde?'

'Isolde was with Siena, actually. I haven't seen Morgana since last night.'

That was strange, thought Julius. Maybe she was having some time off, meditating in a holosuite or something.

They headed to the lounge and, while Faith went to fetch them a couple of cold drinks, Julius plunged himself onto one of the sofas, feeling particularly tired and achy. Had Cress *really* said that the ban from Satras applied through December too? Maybe they had misheard him; as desperate as it was, Julius thought he'd check the recording again, just to be sure. He opened his PIP and played the video back. As the camera's point of view was from Faith's palm — who had understandably been trying to be inconspicuous about it — the angle was a little odd, and at times fixed on Master Cress' crotch, which Julius really didn't have any interest in staring at. So he let his eyes wander around the room, checking the shelves, the decor and the pictures on the wall. Finally, it arrived at the bit he was looking for, and Clavel clearly said: "No access to New Satras until further notice. That goes for the rest of your toon as well."

Right then, in the video, Faith threw his arms in the air; as he did this, Julius was given a brief glimpse of Cress' desktop from above, which had several electronic folders moving across the display that was its top. 'Freeze,' he cried, suddenly. He magnified the still a little and had a closer look. There was no mistaking it: one of the files clearly had "McCoy – Classified" written across its cover.

'What's with that face?' said Faith, as he arrived. He placed the glasses down on the table next to the sofa and leaned over to have a look at Julius' PIP.

'I have no idea what it is,' replied Julius, pointing at the folder. 'Can you make it clearer?'

Faith sat down on the edge of the sofa, called up the video, and got Julius to show him the point that had caught his attention. He tried out a few of his software add-ons on the footage, and was able to make the image slightly larger. 'This is the best I can do,' he said finally, showing it to Julius.

There was no doubting what the file title read, but why was it there and, more importantly, why was it classified? 'I want to find that file and read it. Tonight, at dinner time,' said Julius, firmly.

'Excuse me! You want to break into Cress' office? Am I hearing you right?'

'The info in there is about me. I want to know what it's about. And anyway, can't we access his terminal from here?'

'We? I'm getting the feeling that you want this detention to last *forever*.' He stared at his friend for a moment, who was unflinching in his resolve. He sighed in resignation. 'All right, I'll help you access his desk, but we need to be inside his office. On Satras we could have used any public terminal, but from here they'll trace us in a sec.'

Julius nodded. Faith was right — this wasn't going to be easy.

*

'Don't these people ever sleep?' said Faith, hovering along in front of Julius, that night.

It was 20:00 hours, and most of the staff were at dinner. Now that Moonrising was out of safe mode, the colours had returned, allowing them to see just how beautifully decorated the staff and officers' quarters really were. They had reached the front portion of Tijara, walking along casually enough, but making sure to be quiet about it. It had been agreed that they would pretend to actually have business with one of their teachers, if anybody decided to stop them.

'The office is along the next corridor to the right,' said Julius.

'Shoot,' said Faith, through gritted teeth. 'Officer coming this way.'

Julius had a quick look, and continued walking casually forward. 'Cress is going to be very pleased when he sees this report, won't he?' he said, loudly.

Faith cottoned on straight away, and maintained the act. 'Of course he will. Besides, he did ask us to *personally* deliver it to him when it was ready.'

'Yes,' said Julius, smiling in the direction of the officer as they passed him. 'He wanted us, *personally*.'

'Evening, sir,' said Faith, bowing his head.

The officer bowed back, but didn't give them a second look.

'Phew,' said Julius. 'That was lucky. Come on, we're here.' They turned into the corridor and walked up to the door of the office.

'Knock,' said Faith, 'just like we rehearsed.'

Julius rapped on the door, but there was no answer from inside.

'Let's hope he's eating a big meal,' said Faith. He quickly set to hack the entry mechanism, and a few seconds later they had access.

Julius waited for his friend to go inside, then closed the door behind him, and began to wait. He took a seat on one of the chairs along the corridor, which was sheltered by a large, holographic pot plant. If someone should happen to pass by, he wouldn't be noticed. As the minutes ticked away, he kept nervously checking the time; he hoped Faith would be able to find the file without too many difficulties. 'Come on, Faith,' he whispered.

A few moments later, his PIP bleeped to signal an incoming message. He opened it quickly and grinned. It was a copy of the file. He leapt up and moved to the end of the corridor, to check that the coast was clear, but as he put his head around the corner he practically smacked straight into Cress' chest.

'McCoy,' said Cress, in surprise. 'What are you doing here?'

'I'm sorry, sir,' said Julius, bowing. 'I was looking for you.'

'Right, let's go to my office then,' said Cress, striding to the door.

'Oh, it won't take long, sir,' said Julius, loudly, hoping that Faith would hear him and find a place to hide.

'What is it?'

'I would like to ask you to lift the ban from New Satras ...' began Julius, but when he saw Cress' face growing thunderous, he changed tactic, '... for my toon, sir. It wasn't their idea. I was their leader and they obeyed orders. They've paid enough for it, sir.'

Cress looked at him, dubiously. 'Very well. But the ban is still in place for you and Mr Shanigan, until I see fit to lift it.' And with that he turned and entered his office.

Julius ran to the door, waiting to hear shouting or cries coming from inside, but there was total silence. He tried to focus on Faith and searched for his friend's mind, calling out to him mentally. '*Faith ... Can you hear me?*'

A faint answer carried to him, and he honed in on it. '*Faith?*'

'*I can hear you. Did you get the file?*'

'*Yes. Where are you?*'

'*I'm lying on the floor, between the sofa and the wall,*' he replied angrily. '*Can't you get him out of this room?*'

'*What is he doing?*'

'*How should I know? All I can see is the blinking ceiling!*'

'*OK, OK. I'll think of something, but it may take a while.*'

'*Whatever you do, do it fast. And don't even think about leaving me here all night!*'

'*The guy is gonna need to sleep at some point,*' said Julius, defensively. '*Oh no!*'

'*What? What's happening?*'

'*Foster is staring right at me ...*'

'*Julius, no! Don't you dare ...*'

'Good evening, Captain Foster,' said Julius, 'I was just with Master Cress and heading back to my quarters.'

Foster looked at him, with the special suspicious look he reserved only for members of the Skirts. 'Move along,' he growled.

Julius bowed and left, aware that the captain was only a few steps behind him. 'Poor Faith,' he thought. There was nothing else to do, so he went up to the lounge, hoping that Cress would go to bed soon.

With no Morgana or Skye in sight, he grabbed an empty booth and opened up his PIP to read the file, being careful to shield it from any nearby Mizkis. The cover was exactly like he'd seen in Faith's video before, with a tiny little symbol at the bottom, 4 stars connected by lines to form a diamond; he opened the folder with a flick of his finger. There was only one document in it, and it was all about him. Across the page, a red APPROVED seal stood out clearly. Both Freja and Cress had signed it. Julius focused on the main text. In it, the Grand Master was discussing the fact that, after four years of observation and intense gene therapy, Julius was the ideal and only candidate for Tijara's Heart. Confused, Julius continued reading. They obviously wanted him to take part in some sort of mission, but then, why hadn't they told him about it? Cress had talked a lot about how important communication between the head staff and the Mizkis was, yet now it seemed that Cress was the first to hold back. Annoyed, Julius scanned the rest of the paragraph, but found nothing worth remembering. As he reached the end of the document his eyes stopped on an added comment at the bottom of the page, which he definitely wasn't expecting to find there. It read, "Keep him away from FH as much as possible". Only one person, among Julius' friends at least, had those initials, and that was Farrah: Farrah Hendricks. Completely baffled, he re-read the document, making sure there was nothing else attached.

It was almost midnight when Faith showed up at Julius' booth, carrying a tray of whatever food he'd been able to find at that hour.

'Sorry, mate,' said Julius. 'Foster did his best.'

'I know,' answered Faith. 'But you owe me one, big time.'

'For sure. How did you get out?'

'You don't want to know. Anyway, was it worth it?'

Julius thought about it, then sent him the file. 'See for yourself.'

Discreetly, Faith opened his own screen and began to read. 'What's this symbol, on the cover?'

'Don't know. And before you ask, I also don't know what they're talking about.'

Faith scoured the file; when he saw the last line he looked up. 'Can this be your girlfriend they're talking about?'

'She's not my girlfriend, actually. But she is the only one I know with those initials.'

'But why? Surely you can date whoever you want?'

'Who said anything about dating?'

Faith looked at him blankly.

'OK, maybe,' admitted Julius. 'But it beats me why it can't be her. Anyway, I guess you heard Cress' answer about the ban.'

'Yep. Skye and Morgana will be happy.'

'Isolde too. She's been a right grouch lately.'

'It's because she likes you,' said Faith, simply. 'She wants to hate you for the mess you got her into, but she also wants to suck your lips off. And that makes her all sour-faced.'

'You've been spending too much time with Miller, you know?'

'Skye? Not likely. If I ever need advice, I'd feel safer asking Morgana, I think. She's got that female insight thingy and she's getting loads of practice lately, if you get me drift,' he said, chuckling. He quickly stopped though, when he saw how unamused Julius' was. 'Uh, heh. Just kidding …'

*

Skye, Morgana and Isolde had, of course, been grateful to Julius and Faith, for the lift on their bans. Julius knew that Morgana would once again start disappearing off to meet Maks whenever she could, which made him wonder what exactly had possessed him to request some leniency from Cress as he had, and not something else entirely.

Naturally, they were also curious to hear all about Julius' classified file, and tried their best to figure out what it could possibly mean, but without success. When Julius shared the note at the bottom of the page, Morgana didn't say anything, while Skye made similar comments to the ones made by Faith.

Fortunately, Julius was soon distracted from thoughts of bans and detentions, as Moonrising was treated to the news that the next planet had been located for the second of their rescue missions. Although there was no information as to how Zed had found it, the little luscious planet stood at the center of a small solar system, in the Capricornus constellation. Thrilled by their success with Oceania, Mizkis and officers alike were rearing to take it on. As November got underway, more details about the mission began to emerge, until finally it was confirmed that there were about 600 million bio-signatures on the planet.

'Professor Clavel, do we know who they are?' asked Faith, during a piloting lesson.

Clavel was still upset with the Skirts, but he was their teacher after all, and therefore treated them the same as before. 'If the Arneshians are indeed keeping them grouped by continent, we can guess from the number that they may be from the Americas. But we haven't established that yet.'

'I hope so,' said Lopaka. 'My folks would be there at least — that is, if they've put the Hawaiians in with the rest of them.'

'Mine will be there,' said Leanne, without her usual brio. 'My whole family lives in Canada.'

'What about you Mizkis?' Clavel asked, looking at Manuel Valdez and Evita Suarez.

'Yes,' answered Evita, 'mine are all in Argentina.'

'Mexico and Peru,' said Manuel. 'They should be there.'

'This one is going to last for ages,' commented Skye.

'About a month, Mr Miller. Imagine if we had to do it centuries ago, when the population was *twice* that number.'

'At least now we know what to expect,' said Lopaka.

'I wouldn't be too sure, Mr Liway,' said Clavel. 'This mission is far bigger and this time the Arneshians will be expecting us. Security will be tighter, mark my words.'

'What's our plan, sir?' asked Morgana.

'We need to stay out of scanner range for the moment. Scouts will be deployed to assess the situation from within. We need to know what our infantry will be facing when they land. Planning is ever more important this time around, Miss Ruthier.'

The seriousness in Clavel's voice had dampened their spirits somewhat, so the students returned to studying flight tactics scenarios, harder than ever.

'I wonder who they'll send to infiltrate the settlement,' said Julius.

'Whoever they are, it's a dangerous job,' said Morgana.

'But also exciting,' added Skye.

'I hate waiting,' said Julius, frustrated. 'We don't even know if they'll let us take part at all. And if they do, we're either gonna be in here, fixing engines, or out there on a sky-jet!'

'It's done, now,' said Morgana. 'Let it go, Julius.'

*

Julius was really looking forward to seeing the back of this year, which had been one of the toughest he had ever experienced.

News relating to the rescue mission had become increasingly rare, to the point where even Mielowa had started to urge the Curia to release any information they had on the scouting plan, to appease Moonrising's unsettled crew.

Julius spent most of his free time practicing sky-jet manoeuvres with the Skirts, or in the gym working out. Every day he would also text Farrah, although he tried not to overdo it, under Skye's advice. That was easier said than done though, especially every time Morgana announced that she was off to dinner with Maks, or going to take a walk with Maks, or going shopping with Maks. Julius had to admit it, at least to himself: it wasn't easy letting someone else look after her, no matter how hard he tried.

The evening of Sunday, the 30th of December, was one such night. They had tried coming up with new ways of using sky-jets in combat since earlier in the day, and by 20:00 they were getting tired and quite stroppy.

'That's enough for today, guys,' said Morgana, picking up her bag. 'I need to go get changed.'

'But we haven't finished yet,' said Julius. 'We've still got the last scenario to run through.'

'I'm tired,' said Morgana, 'I can't focus anymore and I'm late.'

'Late for what?' asked Julius, sounding more annoyed than was necessary.

'Late for a *date*, if you must know.'

'You're spending enough time with Maks as it is these days, doing Zed knows what, while we need to practice these formations.'

'I resent what you're implying,' cried Morgana.

'I wasn't implying, I was telling!'

'I know what I'm doing, thank you very much!' replied Morgana, outraged. 'And one more thing, mind your own business!' With that, she stormed out of the hangar, without looking back.

'Ouch…' said Skye. You really have a way with women, McCoy.'

'I felt the chill right down me bones, so I did,' added Faith, with a shiver.

'You shouldn't talk,' snapped Julius. 'What have *you* done about Siena, huh? Nothing, that's what.'

'I'm getting there,' said Faith, defensively.

'Cut it out, you two,' said Skye. 'Let's just go to eat before I lock you both inside the sim-dating programme.'

Julius agreed that the sensible thing to do right now, so he switched off the desktop screen and picked up his bag.

'McCoy,' called Mr Simmons, a short, bald engineer, who was in charge of the sky-jet sector. He walked briskly towards them. 'Before you go, the Ahura Mazda needs a few sky-jets onboard. Can you guys deliver them?'

Julius looked at the others, grinning. 'Of course we can, sir.'

'Very well. The ship is just outside our docking bay. Don't keep her waiting.'

'We're on it!' whooped Faith.

The three of them ran toward their sky-jets, their hunger and tiredness forgotten.

'We may even get to see Captain Kelly,' said Julius.

'I hope so,' answered Skye, hopping onto one of the jets. 'Imagine if he invites us to stay for New Year!'

'That would be awesome!' agreed Julius. 'Goshawk, ready to go,' he said, lifting off.

'Baza, ready,' said Faith.

'Vulture, ready,' said Skye.

'Let's go,' called Julius, excited to be finally doing something useful.

They passed through the protective membrane and were soon out in space. The Ahura Mazda was literally in front of them and, although Julius was itching to take his jet for a ride, he knew that he had to make the delivery without any delays, so he headed for the ship's docking bay.

Once all three of them had entered, the port below them closed, and the bay was re-pressurised. When the light turned green, Julius knew it was safe to remove the jet's protective cupola.

'Welcome aboard,' Captain Kelly greeted them, and bowed.

Julius, Faith and Skye bowed back, before breaking into large smiles.

'It's good to see you again, boys,' said Kelly, amiably.

'Good to see you too, Captain,' said Julius. He had always liked Kelly. In a strange sense that he couldn't explain, the captain felt like a big brother to Julius, and even more strangely, he felt the sudden urge to tell him *everything* about Farrah.

'Come eat with us,' he said. 'Elian would love to see you.'

The boys looked at each other, obviously eager to stay.

'Could someone tell Mr Simmons, in engineering, please?' asked Julius. 'We … um … are already in a spot of trouble with Cress and … um …could do without the aggravation?'

Kelly let out one of his booming laughs, and patted Julius hard on the shoulder. 'I'll take care of it, but I want to hear all about it. Come on up.'

Julius and the others followed him up to the mess hall, unable to believe their luck at being on the Ahura Mazda again. 'I bet Morgana will be *furious* when she finds out,' thought Julius, feeling a little pleased about that.

Elian was indeed happy to see them, and the whole crew made them feel right at home. Julius was, of course, no stranger to them, and Skye and Faith had been on board long enough to remember their way around.

Kelly chatted away to them, asking all about how things were going on Moonrising. As soon as he heard that they didn't have any plans for New Year, he called the battlestar's engineer, requesting the boys' presence on board for active duties, as well as training, for the whole weekend.

Mr Simmons saw no reason to refuse the captain's request, and wrote a note next to their names, in the Tijaran manifest, so that if someone came looking for them, they would know where they were.

With that out of the way, the evening got properly started. Skye was entertaining half of the male crew, with stories of his various conquests, and all about the creation of the sim-dating programme, which had been built under his specifications — a piece of news that immensely raised his status among the Ahura's officers. Faith was deep in conversation with the engineers, telling them about his entry into Pit-Stop Pete's competition, of which he hadn't heard much lately, but that he was sure would grant him at least second place nonetheless.

Julius, Kelly and Elian moved to the bridge after dinner, where there was a beautiful view of the planet where the humans were being held. The indoor lights were switched off, so they could properly admire the star-ridden space outside.

Eventually, later on in the evening, Elian stretched in her chair, then sat up. 'How is Morgana?' she asked. 'I was surprised not to see her with you tonight.'

'She, uh, had to go away, so when they told us to make the delivery she wasn't around,' he said, unwilling to add anything else.

'I see,' she said, standing up. 'You tell her I was asking after her.'

'I will.'

'Goodnight Julius, I'll see you tomorrow.'

'Goodnight, Lieutenant.'

'I'll be right back,' said Kelly, following her out of the room, his aura wrapped in pink wisps.

Curious, Julius peeked over the back of his chair, as inconspicuously as he could, and peered down the dim corridor beyond the exit. It was quite dark, but the vibrancy of the colourful wisps laced among the shadows left no room for doubt; as his eyes adjusted to the dark, he could just about make out Kelly holding Elian, tight in his arms, and kissing her with such passion that Julius was startled for a moment. He quickly turned in his chair to face the front again, feeling his cheeks flushing.

Kelly returned, minutes later, and took his seat again. 'So, how have things been, apart from the detention?'

'Good,' said Julius, trying not betray his surprise at what he had just witnessed. 'I'm still Dr Walliser's lab-rat, but at least now they've got their dosage right, so I don't *interfere* with the running of the ship. Lessons are good too. I like Pyrokinesis and I wish we could do more Twist lessons, but we hadn't had a chance lately, with all this going on.'

'Yeah, I liked that subject too. And how's mad Chan?'

'Still mad,' said Julius, grinning. 'I bet that man would survive anything.'

'We should send *him* to scout the planet, I'm telling you.'

'Yes, we should.'

'You look bulkier, McCoy. Have you been working out?'

'You think so?' asked Julius, flexing his bicep. 'I don't know what else to do. Between Chan's hardcore lessons and the ban from New Satras, I've got plenty of spare time.'

'It doesn't hurt taking care of your body but, what do you mean, nothing else to do? You not seeing anyone?'

'Well, sort of,' he replied. 'There's this girl, from Sield, and she's ... she's ...' At that point, totally unable to describe her any further without embarrassing himself, he decided to just show Kelly the only picture he had of her. 'Here,' he said, holding the PIP screen up to Kelly. 'This is Farrah Hendricks.'

Kelly looked at the picture, and let out a long whistle. 'Wow, and what exactly have you done to deserve *her*?'

'I know, right?' said Julius, pleased that Kelly approved. 'And I forgot to mention, she's the new Solo champion.'

'So, are you guys going out?'

'We've only met once ... and a half. Plus texts.'

'What?'

'Long story, but I was trying to ask her out, when the alarm went off and the mission started. Then I got the detention. But she wants to see me again, and she let me hold her hand, and she said she'll come out to eat with us!'

'It looks like someone is in love, to me,' said Kelly, cheekily.

Julius was surprised to realise that he didn't mind the captain saying that, even though he couldn't quite put a word to his feelings just yet. 'I don't know if it's *love*, but I sure like her ... a lot.'

'I bet you do. The room is dark and I can see you glowing red like a little campfire.'

'Although, I don't know why, but I feel that ... some people wouldn't like that.'

'It wouldn't be the first time, trust me.'

'Hmm?'

'Never mind,' said Kelly. 'If you like her, just go for it. Some things are worth fighting for. That's a lesson I learned the hard way.' Kelly stood up and walked to the window. 'We'll use the sky-jets to approach the planet. We need something small and undetectable to reach the security tower. Once there, we can teleport a com-link inside the camp, and find out what's going on. We have a few hard weeks ahead of us.'

He turned to Julius. 'You can have your old room if you like, unless you want to bunk with your mates.'

'I'll stay with them, thanks. It was good to see you again, Captain.'

'Goodnight, kiddo.'

Julius went back to the room he had shared with Skye and Faith, two years ago, thinking about how things had changed since then. His friends were already fast asleep. As he lay down for the night, his mind wandered to Kelly and Elian, embracing in the shadows of the corridor, only it wasn't really *them* he saw, but himself and Farrah instead. 'A man's gotta dream,' he thought. With those pleasant images in his head, he drifted off to sleep.

THINGS WORTH FIGHTING FOR

'I will not let you risk your life like that, Elian!'

Julius sat up in bed, startled out of sleep by the shouting, and in his disorientated state, tried to place the source of the voice. It seemed to have come from the corridor. There was no mistaking that it had been Captain Kelly.

'Wha—' started Faith.

'Shhh!' said Julius.

'You have no right to keep me behind!' shouted Elian.

Skye had now also woken up, and was avidly listening to the exchange.

'I believe I do, actually. We have no idea what's waiting for us in that tower, and I don't intend for *you* to find out. End of story,' said Kelly.

'I am an officer too, JD, and I will not step down just because we … we … you know.'

Skye looked at Julius, puzzled, who indicated that Elian and Kelly were together, by nodding and tapping the sides of his index fingers together a few times.

'It's my job to protect you, Elian. Call me selfish, but I won't put your life at risk. And that's an order!'

'Any of these guys' lives are just as important as mine!'

'That's not the point!'

'You're their captain!'

'And you're my wife!'

'No way,' gasped Faith.

Julius realised that he was munching away at his fingernails, completely caught up in the argument.

Silence followed Kelly's last statement, save for a few thumps and bumps.

'What's happening?' whispered Skye, eager to hear more. 'Where are they? What are they doing?' He moved to the door and pressed his ear to it.

Julius and Faith followed suit, scampering over each other to get a better ear position. It was at that point that one of them accidentally bumped the door release button, which caused it to zip open sideways, sending all three of them tumbling out into the corridor, where they landed in a heap.

When Julius looked up, Kelly and Elian were staring at them, wrapped in each other's arms.

'Top of the morning, Captain,' said Faith, cheerily, from the bottom of the pile. 'Lieutenant! You look radiant as ever. May I add our sincere congrats for such a happy event?'

Julius scampered to his feet, and gave Skye and Faith a hand up. 'Sorry, we kinda heard … from the room.'

Elian smiled. 'It's our fault, really. Besides, I'm glad someone finally knows.' She threw a sideways glance at Kelly and walked away.

'We forgot you guys were here. This wing has been empty for a while,' explained Kelly. 'I would appreciate ... er ... if you would keep this to yourselves, please.'

'You don't need to worry about us, Captain,' said Skye. 'Kudos to you! She's your perfect match.'

'Try telling that to my dad,' replied Kelly.

'Is that why she said we're the only ones who know?' asked Julius.

Kelly nodded, looking a little downcast.

'No wonder she's pi- ahem, upset,' said Skye, matter-of-factly. 'Women love to spread the news about things like this. Como, Captain,' said Skye, leading Kelly along the corridor. 'Let's go get a coffee, shall we? There's a couple of things you need to know.'

'How old are you, kid?' said Kelly, still being pushed gently forward by Skye.

'Old enough,' he replied, reaching up and patting Kelly's shoulder. 'Old enough.'

Julius stood speechless in the middle of the corridor, watching as the two of them disappeared from sight.

Faith moved over to his side. 'I wonder how long it'll take Miller to realise he's only wearing his underpants.'

*

After breakfast, Kelly had plenty to attend to on the war deck, so he asked the Skirts to show his ground troops the latest upgrades for the new sky-jets. The crew was to be divided into small groups, with each group receiving a 30 minute lesson at some point that morning.

When the first team arrived, Julius and Skye stepped back, allowing Faith to lead the session. As he hovered beside one of the scooters, surrounded by ten officers, he demonstrated everything that was new to these models, and fielded all questions professionally and with ease.

'The sky-jets you've been using so far,' explained Faith, 'required you to wear a spacesuit. With these models, you don't have to, because they have the cupola, which keeps you protected against outer space.'

'He really knows his stuff, doesn't he?' whispered Skye to Julius.

'He's a Skirt, after all,' answered Julius.

'Now, if my esteemed colleagues would like to step up to their jets,' said Faith, 'you can split into three groups and practice departure procedures.'

Julius and Skye were more than happy to oblige, as they were finally beginning to feel useful for something actually related to the next mission.

The morning passed quickly, and they were eager to continue straight after lunch.

At 17:00, the last group came in, accompanied by Elian.

'I know I'm not allowed to go,' she said quietly to the Mizkis, 'but I can at least have the training, right?'

Faith started the lesson for the last time that day, and was grateful for it too, as he was starting to feel pretty tired.

'This here is the com-link that one of you will be taking to the tower,' he said to the group. 'It has been adjusted so that it can self-teleport from the tower into the main compound. Captain Kelly needs you to activate the terminal inside the tower, use the map it contains to find a safe internal location, then input those co-ordinates into this com-link, and send it to said location, where hopefully it will be used by our people to contact Moonrising.'

'Thanks for the briefing, Chief,' said Elian, with a smile.

'You're very welcome,' replied Faith, grinning.

'How many people can you seat on one of these jets?' asked a black-haired officer.

'Ideally, just one, although, if necessary, you can have two,' answered Faith. 'But it's not very comfy. Look,' he said, sitting down on the jet, with his skirt retracted. 'McCoy, come here.'

Julius hurried over and sat behind him, keeping his feet inside as much as possible, so that Faith could activate the cupola.

As the glass closed over them, there was a snapping sound, and the two boys found themselves with very little space to move in.

'You look like the inside of a can of tuna,' said Skye, chuckling.

'Yeah,' said Julius, with his head squashed against the glass. 'Not comfy, is about right. Can you let us out now?'

'Agreed,' said Faith, whose nose was pressed against the front screen. 'Just a sec 'cause it's not working.'

'Are you OK, guys?' asked Elian, walking over to them.

Skye and the officers were practically howling with laughter by this point, although one of them did manage to control himself enough to lend a hand.

'I think me skirt is stuck in something,' said Faith.

'All right, don't panic,' said Elian, trying to maintain a straight face. 'I'll go get some tools and be right back.'

Skye, in the meantime, decided this was the perfect opportunity for the officers to take a few pictures of him, sitting atop the cupola, above the tangled bodies of his mates. 'I'll make a few bucks from these, thank you very much.'

'Wait until I get out!' cried Julius, shaking his fist in the air, all of about 0.10 inch away from his head, which was as much space as was left in the cupola-cage.

'Relax, McCoy,' said Skye, stretching out over the cupola, with a teasing smile. 'We'll use the money to go out for dinner, with our ladies, you know?'

Faith was banging his head against the glass, in protest, which was pretty much all he could do.

Just as Elian returned to the docking bay, the lights went out, and were replaced by dim, backup ones. Everyone stopped laughing at once.

'What's happening?' asked Skye.

Elian touched the com-link on her chest. 'Bridge, report.' There was no answer, so she ordered the officers to go and check it out. 'Skye, go with them, and send me the Chief. We need to get your friends out of that sky-jet, double-quick.'

Skye nodded, threw one last glance at his mates, and joined the officers.

'Bridge, come in,' continued Elian, growing frustrated. Again, there was no reply, so she plucked up an Omni-gizmo and set to work at the front panel of the jet. 'I'm going to bypass the safety mech—'

Just then, there was an almighty rumble, which shook the whole ship. Elian fell to the floor, still holding onto the tool.

'Elian!' cried Julius.

A siren began to blare, signalling that the ship had entered into a state of red alert.

Elian sat up, and massaged her left arm. She turned her head towards the entrance, and a look of panic washed over her face. Julius followed her gaze and instantly understood: a red light was flashing above the closed door, which meant that the room had automatically sealed itself off from the rest of the ship, and was losing pressure. He would have no time to use his mind-skills. 'Get on the sky-jet!' he shouted desperately to her.

Elian leapt up, sprinted to the nearest scooter, hopped on and activated the cupola, not a moment too late, as the trapdoor below them began to open. The ensuing vacuum sucked the jets up and spun them out into space.

It took a couple of frantic minutes before Faith was able to regain control and, when he did, he quickly realised that they were now far away from the Ahura Mazda, and that the ship was under attack.

'Fly close to Elian, Faith!' urged Julius. Then he sent a mind-message to her. '*What is your tag-name?*'

'*Aurora!*' came the reply.

Julius repeated the name to Faith, who typed it onto the control screen, before opening up a channel.

Faith zoomed over to her; when she spotted him, she came about, beside his jet.

'Elian, are you OK?' asked Julius through their newly opened channel.

'Yes, I am,' she said. 'But we can't stay here, or we'll get caught in the crossfire. We've ended up in the Arneshians airspace, and they could be on us at any moment.'

'Where do we go?' asked Julius.

'Faith? Do you still have the com-link for the mission?'

'Yeah, it's in here.'

'Then let's not waste this opportunity and start the scouting mission, pronto.'

The determination in her voice was enough for Julius. 'Let's do it.'

'Faith, turn off your lights and follow my tracks precisely,' she said. 'Julius, keep your eyes open.'

'Roger, Aurora,' responded Faith, pressing several buttons on his screen.

'Roger that; will do ... if I can turn my head, that is,' said Julius. He could just about see the dark bulk of Moonrising, getting smaller as they moved further away from it. The Ahura Mazda, and the attacking Arneshian ships, were now directly behind them so he had lost sight of them completely. 'Faith, can we contact the captain?'

'Elian's sent him a distress call already. Let's hope he picks it up soon, even though he has more pressing matters at hand.'

Julius tried to pull his head up as much as possible, so he could turn it both ways. A wave of Cougars was flying in their direction, engaging any enemy ships that were trying to come at them. Below him, the planet was getting closer. Even without the aid of scanners, he could tell there was a large deployment of Arneshian ships, and they were waiting for the assault to start.

'I can see the camp on the map,' said Faith. 'It's massive.'

'It's a big mission,' answered Elian. 'I've sent you the co-ordinates of our landing point. Can you see it?'

'Yes, it's flashing.'

'Good, stay with me.' Elian took them by the most hidden way she could find, skirting past debris, and in and out of tunnels of meteorites. She used every natural shelter she could find, to protect them from any stray hits, and from being spotted.

Julius could see now that she was a natural pilot, just like Morgana and, given their predicament, he was grateful that Faith was able to keep up with her so well. After a while of this, the tower came into view; they drew closer and continued past it for about 2000 yards, before slowly lowering their altitude. Julius could see that there was some sort of energy field covering the holding area like a dome and assumed that it worked in much the same way as the Zed shield did. After all, if humans were being kept there, they would need oxygen to breathe.

The scooters landed in among thick bushes, which consisted of exotic plants, the likes of which Julius had never seen before.

The leaves were blue-grey, rather than the green that they were all accustomed to, creating an eerie atmosphere. Tall trunks grew at odd angles, forming an impressive barrier, almost impossible to penetrate. Using the cascading foliage as cover, Elian inched her sky-jet slowly forward, closely followed by the boys, until they were in sight of the rectangular tower beneath the protective shield. 'This is it,' she said. 'According to our initial readings, the structure itself is empty, save for the backup terminals.'

'How do we know that we won't set off any alarms, by going in?' asked Julius, over the com-channel.

'We don't. I'll go first and, if all's well, you follow. If not, drive the other way, as fast as you can.'

'No way!' said Faith. 'Kelly would kill us if he found out we'd abandoned you like that!'

'Well, he won't. And, it's an order,' she replied.

Julius focused ahead, into the distance, and saw that there were several guards patrolling the compound. He sighed. He hated it when adults pulled rank like Elian had just done. Why was it that only grown-ups got to do all the dangerous stuff?

Elian began to move forward again, towards a spot far away from the guards. As the nose of her jet touched against the shield, there was no resistance, so she pressed on. To their relief, no alarm sounded. 'You can enter now,' she said.

Faith pushed toward the same portion of shield and they were soon through it without being detected.

They came to a stop, and the boys watched as Elian climbed off her jet. She had the Omni-gizmo tool in her hand and, as she reached them, she knelt in front of their scooter and started to tamper with the safety mechanism. A few minutes later, there was a click, and the cupola vanished. Faith almost fell out onto the ground, but Julius caught him at the last minute. He let go of his friend, once he had steadied him, and they eased out of the vehicle. Julius stood and stretched out his arms and legs, to get the blood circulating again.

'You guys up for some telekinesis?' asked Elian. 'We need to hide these two jets in the bushes somewhere.'

Both Julius and Faith nodded eagerly and, starting with their own jet, they locked their minds on it and shifted it back outside the shield, where they manoeuvred it out of sight, behind a large purple bush.

Once the second jet had been hidden, Elian moved stealthily towards an access grating set into the side of the tower, being careful not to be seen, and once more pulled out the Omni-gizmo.

'Does that thing have a laser cutter too, or something?' asked Julius, surprised. He had seen it in action the year before, aboard the Arneshian ship, a present from

Valentina to Skye.

'It has pretty much everything you want,' said Elian, using the screwdriver function, to remove the grating. 'It's custom made, see?'

'I'll get you one for your birthday, McCoy,' said Faith. 'If you get to celebrate another birthday that is …'

'Thanks, mate.'

'Hold the grill and pull,' said Elian.

Julius grabbed hold of one end, with Faith at the other and, together, they began to pull at it. The grating popped off in a puff of dust.

Elian looked around anxiously to make sure that no one had detected them, then motioned for the boys to crawl inside the opening. Once they were in, she joined them, replacing the grid from within.

'I've found the terminal,' said Faith excitedly.

Julius stood up and moved on to join Faith. They were in a small rectangular area, where several crates were piled along its sides. There was just about enough space for the main frame and 5 or 6 people to stand. The grey, concrete walls rose to 60 feet above them, where they ended in a flat skylight.

'Can you find the blueprints for this camp on there?' asked Elian.

Faith began to shift items around on the terminal screen, his fingers moving fast. 'Here they are. It's much bigger than I thought.'

Julius examined the sprawling levels in dismay. Every one of them was as big as a city, large enough to contain roughly 4 million people.

'So, let's say we want to choose *this* spot here on the ground floor,' said Faith, lifting the com-link. 'We enter the co-ordinates in this self-teleporting thing, right? Like this …'

'That's it, Faith,' said Elian. 'You've done it.' Her PIP vibrated just then, so she opened it up. 'It's JD,' she said, excitedly. 'Aurora here.'

'Elian!' said Kelly, obviously ecstatic to hear her voice. 'Are you all OK?'

'Yes. We've made it! We're inside the tower. What's going on up there?'

Kelly didn't answer straight away. 'The Arneshians have come out to play, but we're giving them a run for their money. Are you safe?'

'We are at the moment,' she answered.

'Captain, we have access to the backup terminal,' said Faith.

'There are more than a hundred subterranean levels here,' explained Elian. 'It's massive and the grounds are packed with guards. Plus, the airspace is choked.'

'Send me all you can, from that terminal,' said Kelly.

'Doing it right now, Captain,' said Faith.

'It looks like we're not going to be able to do what we did for Oceania. We don't have enough portals for that. I'll call a meeting with the GMs and the Curia right now, and we'll get back to you shortly. Stay put.'

'Roger that,' answered Elian, sounding miffed. She added a, 'Humph' for good measure at the end.

'He's just worried about you,' said Faith, trying to cheer her up.

'There was a time when he would have considered this situation his idea of a date, you know?' she said. 'Since he became Captain of the Mazda, his life has changed so much. *He* has changed so much.' She sat down on the dusty floor, and tried to get as comfy as she could. 'Then, of course, there's this issue with his dad.'

'Don't they get along at all?' asked Julius, eager for this opportunity to learn more about Kelly.

'They're really tight, but they just don't want to admit it. JD wants his approval but, for one reason or another, they always end up fighting. It's been like that since he graduated from the academy. That year, things really got messy. He argued with his dad and fought with his best friend — that's how he got that scar, by the way — until they both got locked in the brig for several days.'

'Wow,' said Julius. 'That bad, huh? What were they fighting about?'

Elian looked down, and started to play with her Omni-gizmo. 'JD fell for his best friend's girl, and told him so. It ended in a brawl, with the girl in question breaking all ties with them both, until one of them gained some maturity. Eventually, they went their separate ways, both working hard for their posts. I guess in the end they *did* grow up.'

'Why did you choose Kelly?' asked Julius. 'I mean, *you're* that girl, aren't you?' Julius had seen how she had become enveloped in various multi-coloured wisps, something that wouldn't have happened if she were just telling a story about someone else. It had to be her.

Elian looked up at him, with a smile. 'He's my destiny,' she said, simply.

'If I were Morgana, I would have cried at this point,' said Faith.

'Mind you,' she added, 'it did take him the best part of fifteen years to ask me out. Faith, don't play with that com-link, please. It's very sensit-'

There was a puff of air, and Faith was gone in an instant.

'Faith!' cried Julius, groping at the space where he had been standing a moment earlier. 'Where did he go?'

'I think he just got teleported inside the compound,' Elian said, getting to her feet.

Julius' PIP vibrated and he answered it. 'Faith? Are you OK?'

'Yeah, but I think I gave a couple of folks here a heart attack. They're staring at me really weird-like.'

'Are there any guards in there?'

'They say no; just surveillance cameras.'

'Ask them where they're from?' said Elian.

There was silence for a couple of minutes, before Faith came back on the line. 'There's a mixture of people here. They say Canada, Peru, Illinois … and various other places around there.'

'It's the Americas, then,' she said. 'OK, you need to find Ackley Smith. He's the Voice of the Earth for the Americas, but don't go below ground, to any of the lower levels, you hear? Send someone else to fetch him if you must.'

'All right, I'm on it, but don't you dare leave me behind again!'

'We'll come up with a plan, I promise,' said Julius. 'And I'll need your help.'

'Yeah, I've heard that one before,' he replied. Then Faith's voice became softer and slightly muffled as if he was covering his mouth. 'Make it quick, McCoy. Most of these folks look like you after that inorganic draw you did, three years ago. I'm not sure what's happening, but their energy levels are way low.'

Julius wasn't sure what to make of that comment, nor did Elian for that matter apparently, as she just shrugged her shoulders when he looked at her. He dismissed it from his thoughts, and started to examine the blueprints again, an idea forming in his mind. 'Now that Faith is inside there, do you think they can lock onto his com-link from the teleportation pads on Moonrising?'

'Why?' asked Elian.

'It's just an idea, but … can we try to contact Moonrising?'

Elian nodded and opened up a channel on her PIP. 'Moonrising, this is Aurora. Do you read me?'

'Go ahead, Aurora. Cress speaking.'

'We've infiltrated the ground level,' she said, winking at Julius.

'You were told to hold your position in the tower,' said Cress, sounding slightly agitated. 'Who's with you?'

'McCoy and Shanigan.'

'What?' spluttered Cress. 'Who … How … What is he … What are they doing there?'

'There's no time for this, Nathan! I need you to listen to McCoy, please!'

'Put him on,' said Cress, still sounding rather shaken.

'Master Cress,' said Julius. 'Did you receive the data from Captain Kelly?'

'I did. What are you thinking?'

'The Arneshian fleet is busy with our Cougars, which leaves only the ground guards around the compound to take care of. There are only surveillance cameras inside, but no guards. If you can use the modified com-link as a receiver, and teleport several smaller versions of the portals into the room, then we can activate them from inside and people can just walk through them and hit the portal sequence, just like the Storks and Herons did with Oceania. There's too many of them for uplift — it would take forever. Am I making any sense?'

'One moment,' replied Cress. There were muffled voices on his end of the line, as Cress checked if what Julius had proposed was actually possible.

'He may be angry, but he's not stupid,' said Elian to Julius, quietly. 'If the plan is good, he'll go with it.'

Julius nodded, then decided it would be a good idea to contact Faith and update him on the plan. 'Mate, we need a clear way in. Can you get rid of the guards outside the main entrance?'

'There are plenty of people around me here nodding, and cracking their knuckles,' answered Faith. 'I think I'll have plenty of support.'

'Great. Tell someone to cover the cameras on that floor only. After that, get ready to receive a shipment of portals. You'll need to get folks to go through them. Do you understand?'

'Right. I'll try,' he said, sounding a little unsure. 'But, given how they reacted when I appeared out of thin air, I hope they're not thinking of burning me at the stake as a witch.'

'Cress says they'll do it,' said Elian suddenly, closing her PIP. 'Now all we have to do is actually get in there. Are you ready for some action, McCoy?'

'You bet. By the way, why did you tell him we were in there already?' asked Julius, as he removed the grating from the wall once more.

'What's done is done. We've given him one less thing to worry about, trust me.'

Julius couldn't argue with that. He paused in front of the opening and pulled his Gauntlet from his leg pocket, wearing it on his right hand. He turned to Elian. 'Listen, if these guards are anything like the others, they'll have some sort of device embedded in the palms of their hands, which they can use to attack with. They emit electricity …

or something like that, so watch out for them.'

Elian looked at him, intrigued.

'I found out last year,' he explained. 'T'Rogon's helpers – K'Ssander and A'Trid.'

'Thanks for the tip,' she said. 'I'll cover us, you do the shooting, OK?'

'Sounds good to me.'

As soon as they were outside, and out of the shadow of the tower, Elian activated her shields in a way that Julius had never seen before. She held her palms facing up, and streams of energy sprung into the air from them, like jets from a water fountain, which then fell around them, enveloping them in a protective cocoon.

'I feel like a hamster in a ball,' said Julius, admiring the sphere.

'It's a very special shield,' she said. 'You'll get one too, after graduation.'

They began to jog along the perimeter of the compound defence, Julius sticking close, just in front of Elian. Every now and then, she pointed her hands forward, whenever she needed the cocoon to stretch ahead of them, to give Julius some space. It had an appearance like a curtain of shimmering, thin cobwebs, constantly shifting about them in fluid movements.

'To the right!' called Elian suddenly, halting and reinforcing that portion of the shield.

Julius turned on the spot and saw a guard, holding his right arm towards them, looking quite startled. The man's palm was starting to glow, as if an internal neon light had been switched on inside it. He made a flicking gesture in their direction and a thin bolt of electricity shot out at them.

There was no hesitation from Julius, as he threw both of his hands forward, channeling a mind-push. Two single-bursts of golden energy shot out of the cocoon from Julius' Gauntlet. The Arneshian's electric bolt crashed harmlessly against the shield, and he flew backwards as he was lifted off the ground by the force of Julius' push, before crumpling in a heap a few feet away.

'Keep going!' called Julius.

Elian started to run. As they drew closer to the entrance, the number of guards increased considerably. It seemed that they had finally been alerted to the fact that there were intruders on the loose.

Julius noticed two of the Arneshians heading their way, open handed, ready to strike. He wasn't about to let them get any closer, and immediately fired off a volley from his Gauntlet which propelled them up and away. Instinctively, he whirled around, and threw another blast in the direction of a guard that was trying to sneak up on them from behind.

'There's too many of them!' shouted Elian. 'What is that useless husband of mine doing?'

As if in answer to her question, two ferocious blasts shook the protective shield around the camp. Most of the guards stopped in their tracks, distracted by the new attack.

'Um, I hope our guys are remembering we're all still out here,' said Julius, nervously looking up to the sky.

'Actually they wouldn't,' said Elian, tensely. 'I told them we were inside, remember? Let's keep moving.'

From nowhere, two Herons came into view; they hovered in midair for a minute, before attempting to push through the shield. As they did this, the Arneshian guards, atop the towers surrounding the camp, targeted them. From below, it looked like an electric storm was raging high above, as waves of defensive strikes pummelled the Zed ships.

Julius saw that the cocoon of energy around him began to shift again, telling him that Elian was on the move. Being careful to remain inside its protection, Julius started to blast a path forward, occasionally throwing a burst of energy or a fireball to either side, whenever one of the Arneshians tried to flank them. He could see that the gate wasn't far off now, and there was something going on just outside, because there were Arneshians being lifted and dropped several feet away. As they got closer, he could see this was courtesy of Faith who was zipping left to right, up and down, deftly avoiding the guards' fire, and scattering them with mind-pushes.

Just then, Elian stumbled on a rock, and the shield clicked off as she fell.

Julius grabbed her by the arm, trying desperately to steady her. She slipped from his grasp and landed on the ground, but he at least succeeded in breaking the force of her fall. 'Get up. Get up!' he cried, aware of a group of Arneshians heading straight for them.

Elian scampered back up, but she wasn't quick enough to activate the shields again before the enemy got off several shots at them. Julius felt a sharp pain in his right shoulder, and he jerked sideways. It was followed by a burning sensation, which spread down his arm and up to his neck. There was no time to stop and check it out though so, grabbing Elian by her jumper, they ran the last few feet towards Faith and the entrance, while a barrage of electric energy bolts flew past their heads. Julius returned fire over his left shoulder, knowing that, even if he didn't actually manage to hit any of their assailants, at least he was making their life more difficult.

'Get back inside!' Elian shouted to Faith and the group of people helping him.

They stared at Elian for a second, not comprehending, then realised what was going on and dashed back through the door. As they reached the entrance, Julius pushed Elian inside first, then spun around, and projected a last burst of energy, which acted like a shockwave for five pursuing Arneshians, propelling them backwards into the air. He felt someone grab his jumper and pull him away, into the safety of the building.

'Quick, shut the doors!' shouted Faith.

Several people to either side of the entrance swung two vast wrought-iron doors closed. It momentarily struck Julius how odd that seemed, that they didn't have the automated doors he was so used to.

'That was close,' said Faith, shoving his back against the door.

'I never thought I would say this,' grunted a tall, dark haired man who, along with a host of burly men, was leaning against it too, 'but we *really* need to keep this shut and stay in here.'

'Julius,' called Elian, moving to the corner of the room. 'Help me with this furniture.'

Elian was standing in what looked like an impromptu office space. He saw a clump of metal desks and a group of large, heavy-looking filing cabinets scattered around the room, and understood immediately what she was looking to do. Quickly, the two of them began to lift the items with their minds, and shifted them towards the exit.

Faith, meanwhile, had turned to face the doors, and was using his own mind-skills to keep them closed, while his helpers edged out of the way as the furniture was stacked against the entrance. All this happened under the stares of a dozen or so other people, who looked scared, but also quite relieved that Zed had actually come.

'That should hold it for the moment,' said Elian. 'Besides, I think they have more pressing matters out there.'

'Hey Julius, you're bleeding, man,' said Faith, moving over to him.

Now that the adrenaline rush had passed, Julius remembered that he had been hit and, as he thought about it, his arm began to throb.

'Let me see that,' said Elian. 'Take off your jumper.'

Julius winced as he lifted his right arm to free it from the uniform.

'Hmm … nasty gash, but it looks worse than it is,' said Elian, examining it; a small stream of blood was trickling down his arm, but the wound was mostly cauterised, as it was singed around its edges. 'Come over here.' She led him to a nearby sink and carefully washed the excess blood away with cold water. Julius watched as it seeped down into the drain.

When she was happy that it was clean enough, Elian tore off a strip from the bottom of her t-shirt and ripped it in two. She wet one half, and used it to clean the wound as best as she could, then took the remaining strip and wrapped it around his arm, in a tight field-bandage. 'This will have to do for now.'

'Thanks,' said Julius, gently moving his arm.

'Let me through, y'all,' said a male voice, from the back of the small room. 'Please, let me through.'

Julius turned and saw a plump man, with sandy hair, probably in his mid-fifties, advancing towards them. He took Elian's right hand in both of his and shook it furiously.

'It's so good to see y'all! I'm Ackley Smith, Voice of the Earth for the Americas.' He kept Elian's hand tight, then he threw his arms around her and embraced her, swept up by emotion. 'I never thought I'd see this blue uniform ever again.'

It seemed everything about Ackley Smith was expansive, including the healthy twang in his accent.

Julius just stood there, next to Faith, surprised, and slightly amused, by the reaction of this high status man, but fully appreciative of his feelings nonetheless. The room had gone quite, but he could hear a few sobs from somewhere in the midst of the small crowd gathered behind them. He also noticed how there were various threads of green and gold floating above their heads. The faces of these men and women, who had been so unceremoniously removed from their homes against their will, made Julius' heart ache. Some of them where wearing tattered dressing gowns, others dirty pyjamas — a sign that they had been abducted at dead of night. It was their sense of gratitude that he felt the most in that moment. Right then, Zed's existence, and importance made perfect sense to him. Being there, bringing hope back to these people, was what he had been trained to do, and it filled him with a welcome sense of satisfaction.

'Mr Smith,' said Elian, once he had let go of her, 'we have a plan for rescuing all of you, but I'm going to need your help.'

'Ah'll see to it,' he replied, promptly.

'How many people can we use to manage the crowds on each floor?'

'Everyone in this room has been in charge of maintaining control, since the start,' explained Smith. 'Each of them has also been in charge of others, on each floor. But, I have to warn you, the majority of folks in there don't look quite as … perky as we do.'

'What do you mean?' asked Elian.

'It's been that way ever since we got here,' said Smith, looking for confirmation from among his people, and receiving several nods in return. 'It's like people are tired or somethin', which is mighty strange because we've had food an' plenty sleep.'

'The people we rescued from Oceania were exactly the same,' said Faith.

'You found Oceania?' asked a man, barging to the front, excited.

'We did,' confirmed Julius. 'Just a few weeks back. They're all safe and back on Earth.'

'That's incredible!' said Smith. 'How did you do that? An entire continent?'

'It's a bit of a long story,' explained Elian, 'but we used the same technology the Armeshians used to bring you here. And we're about to do the same with all of you.'

'How long will it take?' asked Smith.

'Once the preparations are done,' said Julius, 'I'd say, just short of a month.'

'A *month*?' said an incredulous female voice from the crowd.

'I know it seems a long time,' said Elian, 'but these portals we're using to teleport you back home cannot cope with more than a million people per hour, and you have a lot of people here.'

Ackley Smith nodded in agreement. 'Ah'm not sure I fully understand how it all works, but it explains how this young man here,' he said, pointing at Faith, 'appeared out of nowhere, a while ago.'

'That's right; I used this device here,' said Faith, showing them the com-link.

'We want to use it to get some serious portals onto this floor,' explained Julius. 'All you'll have to do is walk through them and they'll take you back to Earth. It's perfectly safe, by the way.'

As Smith looked at the people behind him, checking for signs of approval, Julius could understand their doubts, but they really had no choice.

Smith turned to face Julius again. 'Tell us what you need.'

*

Cress had run Julius' idea by the technicians of Moonrising, which believed that it was a doable solution. The first thing they did, was to teleport into the compound a receiver larger than the link-com in Faith's possession, then a third one, larger than the previous one and so on, until the receiving platform was large enough to allow for the teleportation of the portals, which were roughly 40 inches high and 400 wide.

Once the first portal had been put into place, a small platoon of Zed officers appeared in the middle of the room, to everyone surprise. They were led by none other than Master Cress himself.

Elian and Ackley went to meet him, while half of the officers went to secure the exit door properly and the other half went towards the doors leading to the lower levels.

Julius noticed how visibly relieved Cress was to see that Elian was unharmed, before turning his attention to him and Faith.

'Master Cress,' began Julius, 'we're sorry, but it wasn't our fault! You have to believe us. The sky-jet malfunctioned and-'

'I'm aware of that, McCoy,' said Cress, nodding. 'It seems you have both redeemed yourselves from your previous foolishness. However, I still don't understand why you were on the Ahura Mazda to begin with.'

'They asked us to make a delivery, sir,' answered Faith, quickly.

'And you conveniently forgot that you were grounded on Tijara, did you?'

Julius was at least grateful that Cress wasn't shouting at them in front of everyone, but he was still getting rather tired of all this scolding business. However, he decided it would be wisest to keep his mouth shut for now, and avoid any further trouble.

'Get your things,' said Cress, looking at Julius' bandage. 'Grand Master Freja wants to see you, McCoy. And you, Mr Shanigan, will need to visit engineering.'

'Why?' asked Faith. Cress said nothing, and lowered his eyes. He followed the master's gaze, and saw that one of the bottom panels of his skirt was dangling loosely. 'Uh, right. I hadn't noticed that,' he said. 'So that's why I felt so ... tilted.'

'Come on, said Elian, and escorted them to the portal. 'Thanks, boys. You really stood up for Zed today. I'll make sure I write that in my report.' As she said that, she glanced at Cress, and Julius got the distinct feeling that a mind-message had just passed between them. As if to confirm that, Cress looked down, a little smile formed briefly on his lips, before disappearing just as quickly.

Julius looked at the portal, and hesitated. All of the people in the room were observing with curiosity, waiting to see what happened when they walked through it. Cress strode over to Julius and Faith, placed his hands on their shoulders, and gently pushed them through, before following them. They were all gone in an instant.

*

Julius opened his eyes on Moonrising, checking that he was all in one piece. To his relief, he felt just fine, as if he had just done a simple hyperjump.

Cress led them towards Freja's office. When they arrived there, he said, 'McCoy, you wait here. Mr Shanigan, let's see to your skirt.'

Julius did as he was told. After grabbing a glass of water from the cooler in the corridor, he checked the time on his PIP, and was astonished to see that, in less than 30 minutes, it would be New Year. He wondered where Morgana was, and whether she knew what had happened. There hadn't been any ball organised this year, so it wasn't as if she would be at that. 'She's probably with Maks, anyway,' he thought. On impulse, he selected Farrah from his address book and typed her a message, ignoring the throbbing pain from his wound. "At Freja's office, about to get thrown out the air-lock, most likely. If not, I'll be spending New Year in the infirmary. Whoop-de-doo. Hope yours goes better. X"'

'Julius? What are you doing here?' It was Kelly.

Julius stood up. 'Freja wants to see me,' he answered, 'and I think that Cress is going to kill me this time.'

'Nah,' said Kelly. 'Once maybe, but he's calmed down a lot in recent years. He can be a hot head, but he's not stupid.'

'You seem to know him well, sir.'

'I do ... I did. He was my best friend at the academy, you see,' replied Kelly.

Julius almost choked on his water when he heard that. 'Wait till I tell the others,' he thought. So that surely meant that Elian had been Cress' girlfriend before, and therefore the cause of his friendship ending with Kelly. He had never really given much thought to Cress' private life. As his teacher, he was ... well, just Cress. He began to wonder then how many of the Tijaran staff had families, somewhere out there, waiting for them. Even Freja's had to have a family, it occurred to him.

Suddenly, the Grand Master's door opened and Freja stepped into the corridor. Upon seeing Kelly, his eyes widened in surprise. 'Captain Kelly?'

'Grand Master,' said Kelly, 'I need to speak to you.'

'Not now, I'm afraid,' replied Freja.

'Yes, *now*!'

Julius couldn't believe his ears. Had he really just heard Kelly ordering the GM to talk to him?

'McCoy needs to go to the infirmary, in case you hadn't noticed, before he passes out on your carpet.'

Freja instantly switched his attention to Julius. 'Are you wounded?'

'I don't think it's serious, sir,' he said, showing him the bandage under his t-shirt, which was now soaked in dark blood.

'Go, McCoy,' said Freja. 'We will speak at another time.' Then he turned to the Captain, coldness in his voice. 'Step into my office.'

Julius remained where he was as Kelly and Freja disappeared inside the room. As soon as the door had shut, Julius moved closer to it, eager to hear if Kelly would be decapitated for his insubordination.

'How could you have been so insensitive?' shouted Kelly.

'And how could *you* have been so selfish and reckless?' Freja cried back.

'Don't you dare accuse *me* of being selfish! If there's anyone here who tramples all over students' dreams, it's you! You've always cared more for this school than its pupils!'

'Don't give me that old story again. You should know better than that.'

'You always liked *him* better than me, and I know you wish she had stayed with him!'

'For the love of Tijara, John Dean ... don't be such a dramatic fool!'

'My name is JD.'

'I know that!' snapped Freja. '*I gave it to you!*'

Julius was so shocked, he barely even noticed as the glass of water in his hand slipped from his grasp and landed with a thunk on the floor at his feet. *Freja's son ...*

'McCoy!' cried Kelly, from inside the room. 'To the infirmary! Now!'

Julius plucked the glass from the floor, plonked it down on a nearby coffee table, and ran down the corridor.

When he arrived at the infirmary, Nurse Primula was sitting behind the reception desk, beneath a row of colourful fairy lights, chatting with a colleague. When she saw him, she quickly stood and approached him, a look of concern on her face. 'What's happened to you?'

Julius, who was still mulling over the avalanche of news he had discovered about Kelly over the last 12 hours, snapped out of his reverie. 'Oh, I got hit by Arneshian fire.'

'Again?' she sighed, half-amused. 'Go to the usual room. I'll be right there.'

Julius made his way to the end of the foyer, beginning to feel quite tired and achy, and just a little lonely. It was about to toll midnight, and even Freja would have someone from his family to be with, even if that person was a "dramatic fool", as he had put it. Julius wondered where his parents were right now, and how they were spending the night. He imagined them huddled in each other's arms, in one of the Arneshian compounds, surrounded by countless strangers. He wished with all his heart that they were well, and nothing bad had happened to them. As for Michael, he had no idea where he could be, or with whom, even though he had a horrible feeling that he may be with Billy Somers.

It appeared that most of the infirmary beds were free at the moment; a situation Julius was sure would change as the rescue missions wore on. He entered the last room on the left, which was the one he used when he came for his Gene Therapy, and immediately dimmed the lights, inexplicably annoyed by their brightness. Gently, he removed his bloodied t-shirt and sat down on the bed, absently thinking that he would need to order a new jumper for his uniform.

Nurse Primula came in with a trolley and set to work at once. After removing the dirty bandage, she washed the cut properly. Next, she applied a disinfectant salve and held the Derma-Fix tool over the wound for a few seconds. Once it looked less inflamed, she prepared a new, waterproof bandage, containing a slow releasing healing paste, and wrapped it around his arm. 'There,' she said, standing up. 'Sorry you'll have to spend the night here, but tomorrow you'll be good as new.'

'Thanks.'

'Here,' she said, placing a pair of clean ward slacks on his bed. 'Shower's over there. You'll find towels and soap too.'

'A shower sounds great.'

'Well, happy New Year then,' she said, smiling.

'Let's hope so,' he replied.

Nurse Primula exited the room, leaving the door ajar.

Julius switched off the light completely and walked over to the window. He placed his left arm against the cold glass, and rested his forehead on it. From where he was, only stars and empty space were visible, no Cougars or Herons, and certainly no Arneshians. All was silent. Too many thoughts were passing through his mind, so he pushed them away. He would try to meditate a little to see if it helped him slee-

The light touch of small fingers stroking his shoulder blade, stopped his breath and sent shivers of goosebumps across his bare skin. Julius turned slowly, aware of how the hand hadn't moved away. He found Farrah's eyes looking back at him, close enough that he could see the stars reflected in them. She placed her other hand on his chest, gently, and Julius felt the muscles in his abdomen tensing, while a hot wave ran through his body. For a moment he was totally at a loss for words, the surprise of seeing her in the infirmary too big to handle. But it didn't last long. It's now or never, he thought. He brought his hand up to her face, and lifted her chin towards him, all the while convinced that she must surely be able to feel his heart pounding wildly against her palm. Her lips glistened in the cold stellar light and, as they parted, her teeth shone like pearls. Julius ran his hand through her hair, to behind her head and gently pulled her closer, until his lips found hers. They kissed for a very long time.

PRIORITIES

Wake up, McCoy.'

The voice seemed to be coming closer, but Julius couldn't quite tell to whom it belonged. Not that he cared really, since he was presently lying on a beach, with the sun warming his skin. There was a tall coconut tree casting shade over his spot. When he looked at it, he saw that the initials, "J & F" had been scratched into the bark; an empty green towel was laid out next to him, and he gazed towards the water, for any sign of her.

'Look at him. He's chasing rabbits.'

'Mmm … gway …' he mumbled, shooing the air, with a limp arm, desperately trying to cling onto the dream.

'Shake him,' said Skye.

'Oh, sweetie!' called Faith, shaking Julius, earthquake style.

'Nnnnn. Whasamatterwidya!' groaned Julius, waking up with a start, and looking, wide-eyed around the room. 'Where is she?'

Faith looked at Skye, puzzled. 'Where's *who*?'

'Hold it, hold it,' said Skye. 'Did you just say *she*? Was there a girl in this room last night?'

Julius stared at him, lost for words, as his brain tried to recall the events of the previous night.

'I don't believe it!' said Skye, grinning. 'Was it Farrah?'

'Farrah was here?' piped in Faith, looking around the room, as if he was expecting to find her hiding in the corner or something.

'Shhh!' said Julius, quickly. 'You want to get her into trouble?'

'You little sly thing. Oh, come here you!' and with that, Skye leapt on Julius, and rubbed his knuckles against his head. 'You finally managed!'

'Did you kiss her?' asked Faith, eagerly. 'Did you?'

'Geroffme!' said Julius, half laughing and half attempting to shove Skye off his chest. 'What are you like?!'

'Congrats!' said Faith, making himself comfortable at the bottom of the bed. 'So?'

Skye let go of him. 'Come on, tell us all about it!'

Julius sat up straight, trying not to grin too much. 'There's not much to tell, you know.'

'Will you tell us, already?' said Faith, impatiently.

Julius duly obliged them, in the most gentlemanly terms that he could. When he finished, he slumped back against his pillow and drew a long sigh.

'That beats me New Year's Eve in engineering,' said Faith, disconsolately.

'I can't believe the nurses didn't see her,' said Skye. 'You lucky sod.'

'I know, right?' said Julius. 'What about you, Skye, where were you?'

'With this Irishman,' he answered, patting Faith on the shoulder. 'When I heard you were back, I came looking for you. They told me you would be spending the night in sickbay, and that Faith was getting his skirt fixed, so I went to pester him.'

'He gave up Valentina for me,' said Faith. 'And I'm much hairier.'

'And Morgana?' asked Julius.

'She popped in to see us, with Maks,' said Skye. 'When we told her you were fine and stuck in here, she went back to New Satras.'

Julius nodded, pleased to know that she had at least tried to see him. 'I have some serious news for you both, by the way.'

'About what?' asked Faith.

'I have the perfect ending to the Kelly saga,' said Julius, smugly. 'But it'll have to wait till I get my breakfast.'

'OK, OK,' said Skye, standing up. 'Get dressed and meet us in the mess hall then. And don't take too long. The rescue mission is still ongoing, and they can call on us at any moment.'

'Roger,' said Julius, climbing out of bed. He lifted one corner of his bandage, and peered under it; seeing that the wound was dry, he took it off. A clean uniform had been placed on the chair next to the bed, and a pair of shiny boots had been left on the floor, probably by the nurse. He went off to shower, still very much unable to wipe the dreamy look off his face, wondering exactly how and when Farrah had managed to leave without being seen.

*

When Julius entered the mess hall, Morgana was sitting with Faith and Skye, eating her breakfast. He was glad to see her, and he also wanted to let her know that he too was now seeing someone, although he wasn't quite sure why. He grabbed some food from the counter and made his way over to their table. When he got there, the first thing he did was to wish her a belated happy birthday.

In reply, Morgana stood up and gave him a big hug. 'I'm so sorry, Julius,' she said, still holding him. 'I was mad at you when I left, and what if something had happened out there? I would never be able to forgive myself.'

Julius felt strangely unprepared to hear her apologies. He had been sure that she would still be cross about his behaviour, but obviously he had been wrong. 'I'm sorry too. I shouldn't have said those things.'

'That's sweet,' said Skye, vigorously chewing a rasher of bacon. 'And now, let's hear it.'

'They already told me about Kelly and Elian's marriage,' said Morgana, letting go of Julius and sitting down again. 'I'm so happy for them.'

'Guess who's not?' said Julius.

'We know that Kelly's dad doesn't know and wouldn't be too happy about it either,' said Faith. 'But who is he?'

Julius moved his head closer to the centre of the table; the others did likewise, and waited with bated breath. Julius gave it an extra couple of seconds for effect, then whispered, '*Freja* is Kelly's dad.'

'You're kidding, right?' said Skye, incredulous.

Faith and Morgana were staring at Julius in wide-eyed amazement.

'Everyone needs a dad, I guess,' said Julius.

'Wow,' said Faith. 'But Freja …'

'Uh huh. I know, but don't even think about telling anyone else,' added Julius. 'Kelly and Freja know that I know, and if the story gets around, they'll be after me for sure.'

'Don't worry,' said Morgana. 'We'll not tell a soul.'

'Good. And did you tell them about Cress and Elian, Faith?'

'He did,' confirmed Skye. 'I never thought our master had the punch-up-for-love type of fight in him.'

'So *that's* how Kelly got the scar,' said Morgana, dreamily. 'That's so romantic. Has Kelly told Freja about the marriage?'

'I'm not sure. Maybe last night,' said Julius, shrugging his shoulders. 'He'll have to, eventually.'

'That'll sure make Cress cross,' said Faith. He winked, and added, 'See what I did there?'

'Yeah, shenanigans of Shanigan,' replied Julius, quick as a flash. 'See what I did there?'

Faith rolled his eyes and went back to his breakfast.

As far as the first of January's went, thought Julius as he tucked into his porridge, this one hadn't been too bad at all. While the others laughed and commented on Kelly's family tree, his mind was filled with images of Farrah. Even the mere thought of her made his stomach constrict, and the yearning to see her again soon even more painful. He found himself craving her kisses and longing to have her in his arms, so he could hold her tight and breathe in her scent. Honestly, was this normal or was he losing it? He wondered absently if it was maybe a little of both. He tried to focus on his food again, hoping that his feelings weren't too noticeable to the rest of the world. The real question though was, when would he next get to see her?

*

Even though Julius and Faith had contributed greatly to the Americas rescue mission, their ban from Satras hadn't been lifted, which they both found utterly unfair. As a result, Julius was limited to seeing Farrah by way of vid-call on his PIP, which wasn't nearly good enough, but it was all he had. Every free moment brought with it the perfect excuse to call, or text each other. Julius was getting well practiced at disguising these from the others although, to Skye's trained eye, it was all too clear what was going on.

Freja had still not summoned Julius to his office yet, which left him with a slight sense of dread hanging over his head. In fact, he hadn't seen him around the ship at all, and hadn't heard from Cress either. They were now a week into January and he was beginning to think that perhaps the Grand Master had forgotten about it.

Meanwhile, the mission was proceeding well, according to Professor Clavel. The Cougars and Herons were still stationed in the planet's orbit, to ensure that no Arneshians got back in. The guards patrolling the ground had all either been captured, or killed, during the fighting, but so too had some of the Zed officers. A ceremony was held in New Satras to commemorate the victims, with each of the coffins draped in a Zed flag. Not all of the bodies had been recovered, like those of the pilots who had died out in space; for each of them, a small urn was used, embellished with the Zed emblem, their names and ranks engraved on them. Julius and his classmates watched this on the TV in the mess hall, all of them deeply moved by the words that the GMs spoke. It was the first time they had witnessed a mass funeral in space and, when all of the coffins and urns had been ejected from the airlock, a few sobs were heard in the room.

Despite this, much to everyone's surprise, Zed met with very little resistance after that initial confrontation. Clavel told the Mizkis that, after losing their first foothold at the end of October, the Arneshians had been expected to focus their defences on the rest of the kidnapped Earthlings. Instead, all they had left to defend this new compound was a relatively small group of guards, which made everyone wonder what was *really* going on.

Mizki apprentices throughout Moonrising had been given a different task this time: that of compiling a massive database of all the people that had been rescued from Oceania. The Curia, who were particularly short on staff, had given them access to lists of names according to the latest Earth census, with the students being required to check each of the rescued earthling's names against this database. It was, without a doubt, the most boring job that Julius had ever done, but he realised how important it was to know that no one had been left behind, or was missing. Because he understood this, Julius continued to scan the database, day in and day out, hour after hour, without any complaint.

Even their classes had been cut down to a minimum, until their current assignment was completed, leaving just Clavel's and Chan's lessons to run as normal.

It was only in mid-January that Julius finally got the opportunity to leave the confinement of Tijara on an errand. To him though, what that really meant was a chance to see Farrah in person. Professor Turner was supervising the Mizkis as they went about their database chores, when she received a call. By chance, Julius was standing next to her desk, seeking help with a surname that he couldn't find.

'I can't right now,' she was saying to her earpiece. 'I won't be free for a few more hours, actually.'

Professor Turner listened for a moment, and her facial expression told Julius that no, whatever the caller wanted, it couldn't wait. She looked at Julius and raised an eyebrow, as if an idea had just popped into her head. 'I'm sending you one of my students: 4MA McCoy. Give it to him, please. Goodbye.'

'So,' said Julius, 'where am I going?'

I need you to head over to the Curia, by the main entrance. There's a package at reception which you need to bring back to me. Can you do that?'

'Of course,' said Julius. He was so eager to get out of Tijara for a while that he would have said yes to pretty much anything.

'Get there and get back quick as you can,' continued Turner. 'You're still grounded, so no excursions, understood?'

'Yes, Ma'am,' he said. He winked at the Skirts, got the thumbs-up from Skye and Faith, while Morgana limited herself to a small smile.

Julius took the corridor at a stride texting Farrah as he went, asking her to meet him by the Curia's entrance if she could, in five minutes.

'Please be there,' he murmured to himself, as he hopped on the lift to the fourth layer of the ship, which housed both the Curia and Moonrising's main hospital. A few minutes later, as soon as the lift doors opened, he lunged out into the foyer, and scanned the ground for Farrah. He could see the main entrance and the reception desk beyond it; fortunately not many people were milling about. To the right of the Curia was a recess, partially hidden by a large, holographic hydrangea bush. Julius strolled towards it, trying to blend in as much as possible and, when he was sure that no one was looking, he dived into it. Once hidden from view, he poked his head back out, and scanned the area for Farrah. He saw her pop into view a few moments later and a massive grin broke out on his face.

Farrah entered the large, well lit foyer, and nervously started scouting around for Julius. She walked past the entrance of the Curia and peered inside the glass doors, before moving on and stopping in front of the bush, twisting a corner of her jumper. Just as it looked like she was about to move again, a hand shot out from the hydrangea, grabbed her arm and pulled her through the bush. 'What—', she started.

'Shhh!' said Julius.

Farrah looked at him, and her eyes lit up. 'Julius! I've missed you so much!'

'So have I,' he said, the blood rushing to his face. He kissed her eagerly, wrapping his arms around her. Her body was pushed flush against his, as she passionately returned the kisses. Her scent called images of tropical, white beaches to his mind, while the taste of her strawberry balm melted in his mouth. He found himself wishing for that moment to last forever, as he revelled in feelings and emotions he had never experienced before. Right then, he didn't care that Professor Turner was waiting for him, or that she may be sending someone to look for her missing Mizki. He was ready to face a whole string of T'Rogons and Frejas, all mixed together, with Cress on top and Foster for dessert, rather than let Farrah go.

'Ahem,' said a voice from the other side of the bush, suddenly.

Julius and Farrah froze, lips still glued together.

'I'm sure I haven't just seen two students kissing in the bushes,' said the voice. 'How could I? Students couldn't possibly be in there. I must be tired.'

'Mr Hastings?' called Julius, afraid to let him see Farrah.

'Mr McCoy? How's the hydrangea today?'

'I'll call you later,' Julius whispered to Farrah.

'You better,' she said seductively in his ear, before planting a light kiss on the tip of his nose.

Julius got lost in her eyes for a moment, then let her sneak away through the back before he moved. Straightening his uniform, he stepped out of the bush.

Ben Hastings was standing there, arms crossed and head cocked to one side. 'I must have missed the briefing,' he said, sounding amused. 'Do active duties now extend to gardening?'

Julius flattened his hair, and looked down, sheepishly.

Hastings laughed, obviously enjoying the situation. 'I take it that's your girl, then?'

Julius nodded, still feeling quite embarrassed, but pleased to be able to answer yes to that particular question. 'I hadn't seen her for a while,' he began to explain.

'Don't worry about it,' said Hastings, waving his hand. 'But you need to be more careful in the future. And why here, of all places?'

'Actually, I'm supposed to pick up a package for one of my teachers,' he said pointing at the main entrance to the Curia.

'Well, you best go do that then,' said Hastings. 'I'll wait for you.'

Julius nodded and hurried away.

As he entered the building, the stout, bald man at reception looked up from his desk. 'Are you McCoy?'

'Yes, sir,' replied Julius, bowing.

'Retinal scan, please,' he said, lifting a hand in front of him. 'Look at my palm.'

The centre of the man's hand glowed brightly as Julius looked at it, and there was a beep, followed by a green light. 'We have to be careful,' the man said, then grabbed a small parcel from under the desk and handed it to Julius.

Once outside, Julius walked over to Hastings.

'Let me escort you to the lift,' the Curiate said. 'In case you should get lost again.'

Julius grinned, thankful that Hastings was being so relaxed about it; not so much for himself, but for Farrah.

'I heard about your latest adventure, in the Americas compound,' said Ben. 'That was well done. Risky, but well done.'

'It was Lieutenant Elian Flywheel who took the initiative, actually.'

'So I've heard. Still, you and Mr Shanigan played your part well, so don't be modest and take a bow.'

'Thank you, sir,' replied Julius, pleased that at least someone was able to see that he wasn't just being reckless.

'I take it you're still banned from New Satras, yes?'

'Hence the hydrangea,' sighed Julius.

'Well, you're not the first student to think of that,' said Hastings, chuckling. 'Don't worry though, the ban will be lifted soon.'

'Really?' said Julius, stopping. 'How do you know?'

'A benefit of my job. The Curia does have *some* powers over the schools, you know?' replied Hastings, knowingly.

'That's a serious piece of good news, sir.'

'Don't go tiring yourself out though, McCoy. You look tired enough as it is.'

'Everyone is, I think,' replied Julius, starting to walk again. 'We're all doing our part.'

'Sure, I know, but ...' Hastings looked at him, with concern. 'Listen, I can't really say too much, but you really should rest whenever you can. When you get back to New Satras, try not to overdo the games, or the dating.'

Julius wondered what he meant by that and why he was being so insistent about the R&R. Then he remembered the classified file he had found in Cress' office, and it dawned on him that Ben Hastings may have more information than he did. He needed to find out if this was the case. 'Sir, since you seem to have a good opinion of me and my abilities as a Mizki, would it be too much to ask for a little more information? I won't tell anybody, I promise.'

Hastings looked at him seriously. 'We — the Curia, that is — know that Freja has his eyes on you for a *very* important mission.'

This, Julius knew already. He wondered if he should tell Ben about the file. Hastings had been cool about covering up for him and Farrah, but what would he do if he knew of Julius' breaking-and-entering activities? He was still a Curiate, after all, with his own responsibilities. Perhaps it would be best to fake ignorance and let him talk. 'A mission?' he said, trying to sound surprised.

'Think about all you've been through as a White Child already,' continued Ben.

'Freja has allowed you to do more than a lot, for a Mizki. Not forgetting your special DNA augmentations over the past two years. His plans for you are big.'

Julius had read all of this in the file. He decided to change tactic. 'Sir, should I be worried?'

Hastings shifted his weight from one foot to the other, looking suddenly uneasy. 'Freja's a clever man. He always has been. I'd be careful if I were you. Sometimes I think that he loves his school more than his students.'

Julius had heard that before, coming from none other than the GM's own son, Captain Kelly. But what did it all mean for Julius? Would Freja really send him on a one-way mission? Suddenly, the joy he had felt with Farrah just a few minutes earlier was gone, replaced by a growing sense of anxiety. As they approached the lift, he stopped and bowed to the Curiate. 'Thanks for the heads-up, Mr Hastings,' he said. 'I'll keep my strength.'

'You do that, McCoy,' replied Ben. Then he opened his PIP and typed something quickly. 'I've just sent you my direct number. Call me if you need.'

'Thank you, sir' said Julius, and stepped into the lift.

*

The mission continued throughout that month, until it was brought to a successful end on Wednesday the 22nd of January. After the last million Earthlings had been rescued, the Americas' compound was blasted off the face of the planet by the Zed fleet, and its destruction was broadcasted on all of Moonrising's screens. Iryana Mielowa was, of course, there to give a detailed account of all the proceedings, with live interviews from the three hangars of the schools. It was the second cause for celebration they had had since leaving the Lunar Perimeter, and everyone gathered to toast the occasion, some in New Satras and others in the schools' mess halls.

Julius chatted to Farrah pretty much all of that night, and couldn't refrain from telling her that his ban would soon be over. He didn't mention his talk with Ben about Freja's plans for him: their time together was already so short that he didn't want to worry her needlessly.

Julius however, had underestimated the true level of his anxiety about this whole secret mission business because, as the last weekend of January passed him by, he began to feel increasingly nervous and heavy-hearted.

Unknown to him, his downcast mood did not escape some of his friends and, on Sunday, after lunch, he received a message from Morgana: "Meet me in room H2B, Training Area, 3PM. M."

Julius wondered what she could want. He hadn't seen her all weekend, but had a pretty good idea who she had been with. When the time came he made his way towards the south end of Tijara. He could tell from the name of the room that it was a holographic class on the second level. He went down the stairs and along the corridor, until he reached the door. 'Computer, activate 4MA Ruthier,' he said. Then pressed the entry button, and walked in.

Morgana had activated a countryside programme, which didn't surprise Julius in the least. Whenever she had been feeling troubled about something, or needed peace, she always went back to nature. The afternoon sun was shining warm and bright over lush, green pastures. Julius took his jumper off and left it on the ground by the entrance, which was hidden behind a large boulder. He could hear the bleating of sheep in the distance, rolling towards him from beyond one of the small hills. The landscape reminded him a lot of the Scottish Borders back home, but he couldn't tell for sure if that was what the holographic setting had been modelled after. He took a few steps, looking around; then he spotted Morgana sitting beside a stream, her silhouette dark against the sunlight, and made his way over there.

'Hi,' he said, as he reached her.

Morgana looked up at him, and smiled. She had taken her boots off and had her feet in the water. 'Thanks for coming. Join me.'

Julius sat down, took his own boots off, and rolled his trousers up to his knees, before dipping his feet into the water. It was cool, and he immediately felt refreshed by it. He threw a glance sideways and saw that Morgana had her head tilted back, as she basked in the sun's glow. Her dark hair was alight with sparkling reflections that flitted about as the breeze rippled through it. For a moment, he thought about the dance they had had, the previous year when, for the first time, he had looked at her like a boyfriend might, rather than just a friend. He shook the thought from his mind, as a feeling of guilt crept into his consciousness, given that he was with Farrah now.

'I know we haven't spoken much, lately,' said Morgana, not noticing his passing moment of discomfort. 'I've missed you.'

Julius wasn't sure what to reply to that.

'You weren't there for my birthday, for the first time since we've met. Times change, I guess.'

There was no blame in her words, Julius felt, just a hint of sadness.

'So, how's things?' she asked, more lightly. 'You seem happy with Farrah.'

'I am,' he said. 'You'd like her.'

Morgana nodded. 'We should all go out, for sure.'

'Skye wants to organise a dinner or something, so we just need to get Siena and Faith to team up.'

'He'll need some *serious* help,' said Morgana.

Julius could sense the tension easing a little. Despite that, and as much as he was happy to just chat with her like this, he was also quite curious as to why she had invited him here. 'So, what did you want to talk to me about?'

'You,' she answered, simply. 'Lately you've seemed a little on edge, and tired, like there's something on your mind that you don't want to share with any of us.'

'Did the guys ask you to come speak to me?'

'No. It was just me, actually. I can always tell when you're stressed. So I decided to meet you. Was that wrong of me?'

'No, of course not,' he said, wondering how much he should tell her.

'Look,' continued Morgana, 'I don't care what you do in your spare time, Julius, because you're old enough to decide that for yourself. But I'm your friend, even if we haven't seen each other much lately. And, even if you tell me not to be your friend anymore, I'll always be here for you.'

'You'll *always* be my friend; don't be silly,' he said, surprised that she would even think something like that. 'It's just that … you're right, I *am* stressed.' Morgana was listening intently now, and that encouraged him to go ahead. 'I feel under pressure. My head is cluttered and, no matter how much I try, I can't seem to sort it out.'

'What's burdening you?'

'*Everything*,' he said. 'I worry about Mum and Dad. I think about Michael spending time with Billy Somers. I wonder how long the rescue missions will continue for, or this stupid ban, for that matter. And, on top of all this, there's that classified file business and that mission they have in stock for me.'

'I wouldn't stress over that one,' she said. 'You don't even know if Freja would actually ask you to do it.'

'But I *do*,' he replied. 'One of the Curiates, Ben Hastings, told me that Freja has plans for me.'

'A Curiate? When?'

Julius told her about Hastings and all of their past meetings, ending with the latest one, in which he had recommended that he take it easy.

Morgana was silent, and thoughtfully smoothed the creases in her skirt.

'What is it?' Julius asked her.

'Nothing … except, why would a Curiate give you the heads-up on a classified mission before the GM? It's a bit unprofessional, don't you think?'

'It's probably because I pushed him to find out. That, and the fact that he likes me, I guess. Anyway, it's not an issue.'

Morgana didn't seem too convinced, but let it go.

'So, how do I declutter my head, then?' he asked. 'You're the expert on this stuff.'

'I think you need to get your priorities right,' she said, lightly splashing the surface of the water with her feet. 'Most of the worries you mentioned are outside of your control, Julius, and there's nothing you can do to change them at this point in time. You need to let them go.'

'What am I left with, then?'

'Yourself, and what you can become if you focus on that.'

'What do you mean?'

'I mean that your concern should be for the development of your true nature to its full potential. You were born a White Child for a reason, and you have a duty to yourself not to waste that gift. And not because others want you to, but because *you* want to.'

'Ben told me the same thing,' said Julius, quietly. 'He said that I should use this gift to bring hope back to people.'

Morgana rummaged through her bag and pulled out a card. 'Here,' she said, handing it to him. 'Early birthday present.'

Julius took it, puzzled. On the cover was the picture of a dragonfly, its vivid blue and black colours in stark contrast to the paleness of the water.

'It symbolises victory in Japan,' she explained. 'Open it.'

He did so and read the inscription.

"If you can't choose the song,
You'll have to dance to the music that's playing."

Julius felt a fleeting heartache as he read the words and realised how well she knew him. The words may not have been the same as his own personal maxim, but the meaning was — adapt and survive.

Morgana lifted her feet out of the water and stood up. She picked up her boots and socks, but didn't move. 'What are you *really* afraid of, Julius?'

'What?' he replied, startled. 'I'm not afraid of anything. I'm just worried, that's all.'

'You've been in dire straits before, and you came through it without breaking a sweat. What's different this time?'

Julius shook his head. 'I don't know what you want me to say.'

'What is your fear?'

'I don't know.'

'Then you'll need to find out.'

*

Julius spent the next few days thinking about his talk with Morgana. He had placed the dragonfly card on his bedside table, and would stare at it, as he recalled their meeting. Her words had deeply troubled him, and he couldn't quite understand the reason why that was. He kept asking himself about what his biggest fear was, but somehow the answer seemed to elude him, as if, subconsciously, he didn't want to find it. She had been right about the fact that he was worrying too much, about many things that he couldn't change, but he wasn't doing it on purpose.

Faith and Skye had asked him if he was all right on a couple of occasions, when he got lost in himself, to which he simply replied that he was tired. He avoided telling Farrah anything too, and had to use the same excuse with her, only she wasn't really buying it, and told him as much. Still, she didn't press him into telling her either, for which Julius was immensely grateful.

On Thursday 31st January, the 4MAs were working with Professor Turner, updating the Americas database, starting with Mexico. Since that was Manuel Valdez's home country, he had prepared a personal list of family and friends, which he had sent to his classmates, asking them to prioritise it, if it wasn't too much trouble. Occasionally the silence was broken by a spontaneous expression of joy, whenever one of the Mizkis spotted one of the names from the list; each time this happened, Manuel would run up to them to see who it was. Julius could have sworn that he saw his eyes welling up a few times and definitely once, when he saw his mom and dad's names.

Around 16:30, Professor Turner approached Julius' station. 'The Grand Master would like to see you, McCoy.'

'Thank you, Professor,' replied Julius. He turned to the Skirts, and grinned. 'Fingers crossed, guys, but it looks like my detention may be over.'

'In that case, don't forget about me,' added Faith. 'I'm sick and tired of being confined to this ship.'

'I won't,' he said, standing and darting out of the room.

When he arrived at Freja's office, he paused to allow his breathing to calm a little, then straightened his uniform and knocked on the door. It slid open and Julius stepped into the GM's office.

Freja was sitting at his desk and bowed his head to Julius as he entered. 'Please, sit,' said Freja, indicating the chair opposite him.

'Good evening, sir,' said Julius, sitting.

'I was meant to meet with you earlier in the month,' began Freja, 'but it has been rather hectic. How are you? I take it your wound wasn't serious?'

'Oh no. Ms Primula took care of that, sir.'

'Very well,' he said. After looking at Julius for a few moments, he said, 'Aren't you going to ask me about Captain Kelly?'

Julius was taken aback, but then again, Freja did know that he knew. 'It *was* a surprise, sir. I guess a student never imagines that everyone has family, even teachers.'

Freja nodded, and smiled. 'JD took his mother's surname. He said he'd rather keep his family tree hidden. He was never one for favouritism.'

'You have a great son, sir. I owe him a lot, already. I haven't spoken about his family with anybody … well, except the Skirts that is. They were with me when Captain Kelly and Lieutenant Flywheel were discussing their …'

'Thank you, McCoy. I know now. We appreciate your discretion.'

Julius nodded, all the time wondering when Freja would get around to his ban. Instead, the GM asked him an unexpected question.

'I can imagine you've been under a lot of stress, lately. I hope your friends have helped take your mind off things. Perhaps a girlfriend, even?'

Julius did his best not to betray his surprise. Was Freja really asking about his love life? Suddenly, the image of his classified file sprung to mind, with that note at the end of the page about FH; just in case it really was referring to Farrah, Julius decided to lie about it. He couldn't risk being banned from seeing her. 'No time for girls, sir,' he said. 'You keep us far too busy for that.'

'Mr Miller seems to manage,' answered Freja.

'He's a particular case, as you probably know.'

Freja laughed. 'I believe I've heard,' he said. He studied Julius for a moment, then changed topic. 'I read Lieutenant Flywheel's report. You did well, McCoy. You and Mr Shanigan.'

'Thank you, sir,' he said, relieved and surprised that Freja wasn't still mad at him, for leaving Tijara.

'It was a good piece of improvisation, that kick started our mission without any further delays. I won't hide the fact that we were very worried when we heard but … well, it's done now. And their opposition was minimal enough to pose no real threat to us.'

'About that, sir,' blurted out Julius, before he could stop himself.

'Yes?'

Seeing as Freja seemed inclined to listen, he went on. 'There's something *off* about their lack of defence. And about the lack of Nuarns, for that matter. I thought perhaps you knew why.'

'As a future captain of the fleet, I would hope you'd have your own answer for that.'

'Ideas, mainly,' he replied, tentatively.

'Try me.'

Julius thought about it, then said, 'Well, why go to all the bother of kidnapping the humans, just to give them back so easily, continent by continent and unharmed? Not that I'm unhappy about that, of course, but it feels … staged.'

'In what way?'

'Like we're being led from A to B, just to keep us busy. And never mind how we *found* A in the first place.'

Freja nodded. 'It did occur to us as well, I must say. So, what about the Nuarns?'

'T'Rogon said before that they had enough of them to last a lifetime of experiments.'

'That tape was a fake, remember? There's no proof that they're being harmed in any way.'

'Then where are they, sir?'

'There's only one place left that we know of,' said Freja.

'Arnesh?' wondered Julius aloud.

'Why not? It's their stronghold after all. Their entire defence system is sure to be there.'

Julius mulled it over, weighing up the likelihood of Freja's guess. As he thought about it, his eyes wandered to the Arneshian artifact, which was lying on a stand on the Grand Master's desk, and grew wider as he noticed something.

Freja followed his gaze. 'What is it?'

'Two of the sections are switched off now,' said Julius. He stood up and moved closer to the object. 'It was only one when I first found it.' He turned to the GM. 'When did this happen?'

'Last week, after we completed the Americas mission,' answered Freja, watching Julius. 'Any theories as to how and why?'

Julius carefully studied the silver object. The four arms all branched out into two symmetrical portions at the end of each one: a small sphere with three short arms, each ending in a little square. Both portions of one of the arms were now turned off. 'I think that they represent two of the five continents. Oceania and the Americas are the smallest in population, since the Chemical Wars, so they're are both at the end of the same arm,' explained Julius. 'The rest of the arms are for the remaining, largest continents.'

Freja nodded. 'Go on.'

Julius picked up the artifact, and ran his fingers along the length of the four arms, feeling all of the holes as he did so. Suddenly, he caught sight of something glinting on the floor and, without thinking, he moved the artifact until one of the holes was right above it, which allowed him to see that it was clearly a loose screw. An idea formed in his mind and he looked up at Freja.

The GM sat up straight, intrigued by Julius' reaction.

'I don't know what each of these squares, spheres and triangles mean, exactly, or what they stand for,' began Julius, 'but the only other idea I can think of, is that this artifact is actually a guide. Grand Master, do we have a star-map that shows the exact locations of the first two missions?'

Freja nodded and activated his desk. He quickly found what he was looking for and, plucking the virtual map by its corners with the tips of his fingers, he stretched it out so that it covered the entire length of his desk.

Julius passed the silver object to him. 'Can you align the planets where we found Oceania and the Americas with the two holes on the lit off arm, in such a way that-'

'...all the other holes are filled with a planet ...' finished Freja, excitedly.

Julius watched as he moved the artifact over the desk, not even aware that he was holding his breath.

Freja adjusted its position a few times, and the size of the map, to ensure that the two planets they had already visited would remain visible through the holes. Once he was happy, he placed the object flat on the map and dimmed the main light. 'Look,' he said.

Julius stepped over to the desk and examined it from above. The room was bathed in eerie blue light, emanating from the map and the artifact. Each of the holes was now filled with a bright dot, which represented a planet. 'Thank you, Julius,' said Freja. 'If you're right, our people won't be waiting long.'

Julius nodded, unable to answer, on account of the knot in his throat; he knew that one of those dots was sure to be a planet which held the citizens of Europe, where his mum and dad would be waiting to be rescued.

Freja didn't switch the lights back on, but instead sat down on his chair, his face looking thoughtful. 'You can tell Mr Shanigan that your ban is lifted. And now, if you'll excuse me, I have three missions to plan.'

'Yes, sir!' said Julius, thrilled by this news. He bowed to the GM and hurried out of the room. He checked his PIP and saw a message from Faith, saying that they were all in one of the booths in the mess hall. Julius started to jog: he was eager to tell his friends all about his discovery and, after that, he would dash to New Satras to give Farrah the good news, in person.

BEFORE THE STORM

After the lifting of the ban, Julius and Faith were finally able to spend more time in New Satras with the rest of the Skirts. The group had naturally expanded to include the respective love interests, much to everyone's satisfaction. As well as Maks and Valentina, Farrah was now also a fixed feature. Although they weren't actually going out, Siena and Faith were simply considered the fourth couple; everyone, except perhaps for Faith, knew that it was only a matter of time before they hooked up. As well as "couple time", many of their free afternoons and weekends were spent in group activities, whether that was in a sim-room, or in one of New Satras' many cafes.

It was a new experience for the Skirts, a new phase of life, which Julius liked very much. Having Farrah by his side, her head resting on his shoulder, was not an issue and did not make him feel embarrassed, especially because everyone else was doing much the same. Julius found fascinating watching Siena trying to get closer to Faith, doing things like casually leaving her hands where he could find them but, inevitably, Faith never picked up on it. Whether this was down to him simply not noticing, or because he was pulling one of his nervous, inept-at-dating stunts, was unclear, however, it was agreed that they really needed to help him out before Siena decided that it was no longer worth it.

One Saturday afternoon, near the end of February, Julius, Morgana, Skye and Siena were having lunch at Eat Your Mama Blind. They had worked hard all week finishing the database for the Americas, and were now reaping the satisfaction of a job well done. The Mizkis had been told that while Moonrising was preparing for the next mission, all students would return to a more-or-less regular timetable, with most of their classes opening up once more.

'I think we should organise a proper meal soon,' said Skye, stretching in his chair. 'We've worked hard and I bet we could find a few reasons to gussy up.'

'I'd like that,' said Morgana. 'One fancy dinner to make up for the lost New Year's ball, missed birthdays and, of course, to celebrate the successful missions.'

'I wish I had something to celebrate too,' said Siena, sulking.

'Awww,' said Morgana, hugging her. 'He's such a silly, isn't he? I bet he thinks about you all day, and he doesn't know how to tell you.'

'Speaking of ...' said Julius, pointing out the window.

Zooming in and out of the crowd, Faith was on his way to the restaurant, looking slightly crazy. Julius was immediately worried and leapt up from his chair, hurrying to the entrance. A second later, Faith crashed through the doors, straight into Julius' arms, and dragged him back to the table.

'What's the matter?' asked Morgana. 'Is everything OK?'

Faith, it seemed, was unable to talk properly, but he was grinning, which at least put the others at ease.

'What is it?' pleaded Julius, growing ever more curious.

A soft whisper of a reply escaped Faith's mouth, which they all had to lean in close to hear. 'I did it. I won Pete's spaceship design competition!'

'Awesome!' exclaimed Julius. 'I'm so proud of you, mate!'

'Congrats!' cried Skye, patting him on the back.

'Well done!' said Morgana, hugging him tight. 'I knew you could win it!'

'Cheers. It was tough, though,' said Faith. 'The other competitors were all older than me. I knew I had to come up with something really special to beat them.'

'So what did you do then?' asked Skye.

'I created a couple of things. One is a new engine, to help make longer jumps,' he explained. 'Pete said he wants to call it the Shanigan's Relay.'

'That is amazing,' said Morgana, awestruck. 'And what was the other thing?'

'A space coffin,' said Faith, a little more tentatively.

'A what?' asked Skye, 'Why?'

'Well, it's just that when we release one of our people into space, I always wonder what happens to them — you know, how long their bodies will look nice for, or their coffins will last and the like. Everyone deserves a proper rest ... afterwards.'

'You're so thoughtful, Faith,' said Morgana. 'I think it's a splendid idea.'

'Are they really going to build your inventions?' asked Siena, excitedly.

'Absolutely,' answered Faith. 'Although, they might have to do it a little bit here and a little bit there, with the missions taking top priority and what-not.'

'Oh, Faith,' said Siena, smiling proudly, but still seemingly too shy to move any closer.

'There!' said Julius. 'Now, we have the perfect excuse for that fancy dinner!'

'You've got that right!' agreed Morgana, standing and picking her things up from the chair. 'I'm gonna go see Maks and find out when he's free.' She hugged Faith again. 'You and your magnificent brain!'

As she left, Faith slumped down into a chair, exhausted, but clearly over-the-moon. 'So, what's this dinner thing?'

'It will be a great night,' said Skye. 'A celebration of all the good things that have happened this year. It's for the Skirts only, and their partners.'

'Or whoever you'd like to invite,' added Julius, hinting at Siena with his head.

Faith stared at Julius for a moment, studying his head movements, mystified. Thankfully, it dawned on him to look in the right direction and, when he saw Siena, he grinned. Casually, he turned to her and said loudly, 'Well, paint me brown and call me a turd!' followed by a cheeky wink.

A moment of stunned silence descended on the table, while Siena stared at him, in disbelief. After a brief, uncomfortable few seconds, she snapped her head in the other direction and stormed out of the restaurant.

Julius and Skye watched as she left, and then turned back to Faith, incredulous.

'Really, Faith? Really?' groaned Julius. 'A turd?'

'For the love of Zed!' cried Skye. 'What possessed you to say something like that?'

'Why?' asked Faith, sounding genuinely puzzled. 'What did I say?'

'Come with me,' growled Skye. He grabbed Faith by the arm and dragged him outside.

Julius, eager not to miss any of this, hurried after them.

'Where are we going?' said Faith.

'Shut up and hover,' replied Skye, fuming.

When they reached the holographic sector, Skye selected the sim-dating programme and turned to Faith. 'It's time you use that voucher we gave you for your birthday. I don't care how you do it, or how long it takes, but this will be your home until that meal. I'll get you two together if it's the last thing I do, or my name isn't Black-Hole Miller. Am I clear?'

'Yeah, sure thing, buddy,' said Faith, nodding and looking slightly frightened.

'Good. Get in there!' He nodded to Julius. 'I'll see you later, McCoy.'

Julius watched as they disappeared inside the room, and burst out laughing. He was still chuckling when he got back to Farrah and was unable to stop, even after he had told her the story a couple of times.

Once he had himself under control again, they decided to forget Faith's lady troubles for a while and found a nice, quiet, very isolated corner where they could spend the next few hours in peace.

*

As March got underway, Julius' mood had lifted slightly, thanks mainly to the thought that if the artifact really was a map, they would soon be able to locate another continent. With the regular classes underway, a sense of normality had returned to the students, bringing a feeling of spring to their hearts.

Julius continued to enjoy his Twist lessons, and it didn't take long for him to improve his rebinding of molecules to a satisfactory level. While most of his classmates were still tackling small objects, Morales had moved Julius to one side of the room and given him bigger and more complicated things to twist; everything from engine cores to Sky-jets. Whenever he grew bored of those, he turned his attention to other, more interesting objects, such as the classroom door, whenever Morales wasn't looking. The resulting laughs from the Mizkis would prompt her to turn around, but Julius had become a fast hand and was able to rebind it before she could catch him out. Eventually though, he had to stop this when, one day, an unaware student on his way out to the toilet, almost got trapped inside the very fabric of the door, scaring them both almost to death.

In Telekinesis class, Professor King continued his obstacle course training, where students practiced moving each other along it, using their mind-skills. Faith had been very careful never to pair up with Siena, just in case he accidentally dropped her in front of everyone and really killed his chances with her. Skye and Julius agreed that it was probably the sensible thing to do.

It took a lot of back-and-forth before the Skirts were able to find a date for the meal that suited everyone; eventually, it was decided that it would take place on Saturday the 23rd of March, in one of the holographic rooms in New Satras. Then began the problem of deciding the virtual setting and, as everyone had completely different ideas on the matter, they resorted to a lucky draw, where the chosen person would be the one calling the shots.

To her delight, Farrah won. She hopped up and down several times, clapping her hands happily. 'I'll send the invitations out soon!'

A few days later, all the guests received a little parcel in the mail. Julius opened his with Morgana and Siena, in the lounge.

'Oh my,' said Morgana. 'It's a shell!' She held it up for the others to see, delicately touching the shiny inner surface.

'Mine is a piece of red coral,' said Siena, admiring it. 'What do you have, Julius?'

Julius opened the small envelope, and a stream of white, fine sand ran out into his cupped hand. 'I get the feeling that we're going somewhere tropical,' he said, rubbing the sand between his fingertips. It reminded him of the dream he had had on the night when they had first kissed, and was amazed at the coincidence.

'Where did she get these things?' wondered Morgana.

'Her folks have a shop of old Earth stuff on level 2,' explained Julius.

'That's right. I've seen it!' said Siena. 'Auld Oddities, yeah?'

'That's the one,' answered Julius.

'Dress code is smart-casual,' read Morgana, from her invite. She looked at Siena. 'We need to check out some pictures of people at beach parties and see what kind of things the guests wear.'

'Absolutely,' said Siena.

'I seem to remember white being a prominent colour,' added Morgana helpfully.

'You're right!' agreed Siena. 'Also, linen is a good material for the clothes.'

'It does crease a lot though,' said Morgana, sounding almost crestfallen.

Julius stared blankly at the pair of them, feeling quite lost and confused. 'I'm gonna leave that particular search to your good selves. Just tell me what to wear and I'll do it.'

'Let's go see Farrah,' said Siena. 'We should help her out with the preparations!'

As it turned out, the Skirts had chosen the best possible time to celebrate since, a few days later, it was announced that a new continent had been located and that the third mission would began on Monday the 25th of March. Judging by the number of bio-signatures present, they believed it was Africa. The excitement spread through Moonrising like wildfire, tempered slightly by the frustration of those who still had missing relatives and friends from the remaining, unfound two continents.

To his great surprise, Julius received a short message from Freja that read, "It is a map! Well done." Feeling quite pleased with himself, he showed it to the others and, of course, to Farrah, although he couldn't help telling her a slightly more colourful version of the story; how he had discovered the true nature of the artifact, preventing Freja from making a fatal mistake that could have led Moonrising off course by several light years. Farrah listened intently to him, enraptured, before hugging him tight and showering him with kisses.

Julius had come to associate his time with Farrah as the only time in which he could truly relax, leaving his anxiety behind. She had that effect on him, and he couldn't imagine ever letting her go. These feelings both astonished and excited him, and left him craving for more.

*

At 18:30, on the night of the meal, Julius, Skye and Faith set off to meet Maks in New Satras. Morgana had told them that the matrix for their clothing had been embedded into the simulation programme, so they didn't need to worry about anything except turning up. This news had made them all very happy, as it took some of the pressure off.

'How're you feeling?' asked Julius, to Faith.

'As ready as I'll ever be,' he said, nervously.

'Be confident,' said Julius. 'You've worked hard for tonight.'

'That's right,' added Skye. 'Just be calm, relaxed and delicate. No sudden movements. And think before you speak. In fact, remember that you have two ears and one mouth; use them in that order.'

'Right,' nodded Faith, making mental notes. 'Listen first, talk later.'

'Correct,' continued Skye. 'Girls like an attentive listener. And don't forget the details; little things are important to them. Let her sit first, fill her glass if necessary, ask her questions that require more than just a yes or no answer, like I taught you.'

'What, who, why, which,' recited Faith, diligently.

'And after dinner, when we all go for a walk along the beach-'

'How do you know *that* will happen?' asked Faith, flustered.

'Why else do you think we're going to a romantic tropical island?' answered Skye. 'They want us to walk them along the shore in the moonlight. It's romantic. It gets them all fuzzy and dreamy.'

'You should write a book, man,' said Julius, enjoying the lesson.

'I kinda did, actually,' replied Skye. 'When List asked for my help with the sim-dating programme, I had to write a lot of this stuff down for the software.'

Julius chuckled. 'Please continue, master.'

'The moonlight walk is the right time to compliment her on a thing or two, like her dress, or her hair. Your mum's Italian, and Siena comes from Italy, so talk about that. Her reaction should tell you if she's ready.'

'For what?' asked Faith.

'You'll need to take her hand, no? Assuming she lets you, you can then move to arm-over-shoulder.'

'Like when?'

'I can't time you, now can I?'

'Oh, right, sure.'

'When you see a nice spot, lead her there and sit down. Talk some more and then … then …'

'Then *what*?'

'Well, then you're on your own.'

'Don't worry, Faith,' said Julius. 'You'll know what to do.'

'I hope so,' said Faith taking a deep breath.

When they got to the holographic sector, Maks was waiting by one of the entrances. They greeted him and walked to their holosuite, growing more curious by the minute. Skye entered the password Farrah had sent them and, when the door slid open, the four of them stepped inside.

Julius was once again reminded of how fantastic the holoworld was; as his sandal-clad feet sunk into the cool evening sand, there was nothing to remind him where he really was. His heavy-cottoned uniform had transformed into a loose, white linen outfit, comprising a shirt with rolled up sleeves, and trousers, which felt comfortable against his skin.

'Grand!' said Faith. 'Me legs are back!'

Julius grinned. It was a nice touch, and one that would certainly boost Faith's confidence. Looking around at the others, he noticed that they were all wearing similar, light coloured clothing and leather sandals. 'I'm sure they loved creating our clothes,' he said.

'And I bet you even our underwear is matching,' added Maks, peaking inside his trousers. 'Yep ... White.'

The others confirmed the same, after a quick check.

'I wish I could have dressed *them*,' said Skye, dreamily.

'Knowing you, I'm not sure *they* would have liked that,' said Julius.

'Yeah, probably,' admitted Skye, as an afterthought.

Julius began to stroll away from the entrance, and was soon followed by the others. As he looked around, a sense of familiarity grew in him, as if somehow, he had been here before, though he had no clear memory of when, or even where exactly this was. The sun had already sunk beyond the horizon, leaving streaks of oranges and pinks in the evening sky. The sea was calm, and waves gently lapped against the shore, creating a serene melody all of their own.

'Over there,' said Faith, pointing towards a hut in the distance.

Julius looked, and saw that it was a circular structure, with a roof seemingly made of knitted palm leaves. An open-air kitchen stood to one side of it, and a bar on the other; at the front of the hut was a long patio, which held a wonderfully decorated table, set for eight people. Everything was beautifully illuminated by the flickering light of the many tall torches, planted in the sand, creating a soft atmosphere.

As they approached the small structure, a virtual waiter approached them, carrying a tray of colourful looking drinks. He was wearing a bright, flowery shirt, which matched the rest of the tropical appearance of the place. 'Good evening!' he greeted. 'Make yourselves at home.'

'Don't mind if I do,' said Skye, grabbing one the glasses.

Julius picked a cream coloured one, with a wedge of pineapple stuck to the rim. 'Cheers, guys,' he said, lifting his glass.

'Likewise,' replied Maks.

'Cheers,' said Faith and Skye.

Just then, the noise of girlish giggles carried to them from the other side of the bar.

'They're coming,' said Maks.

Julius detected a hint of excitement in his voice, and suddenly realised how excited he personally was, as well. Even after 82 days of going out with Farrah — not that he was counting or anything — the thought of seeing her, still made him feel as if it was for the first time. On cue, his palms began to sweat. He decided it might be wise to put his glass down before he could drop it, and wiped his hands on his trousers.

The girls emerged from behind the bar and Skye stepped forward promptly, heading for Valentina, arms opened. Julius opted to follow him, rather than wait for the girls to approach them. Using Skye as a sort of shield, he went straight over to Farrah. He was aware of Morgana as she walked past him, but he didn't look at her: first of all, he just wanted to see *his* girl.

Farrah was wearing a long, fuchsia, fitted dress, with thin shoulder straps. Her hair was softly gathered up, leaving only a few honey coloured curls loose to bounce against her slender neck. A pink lily was fixed one side of her head, matching a smaller one, which was pinned to a wrist strap.

As she stepped towards him, one long, tanned thigh slipped briefly into view, leaving Julius simply mystified. 'She comes with legs ...' he whispered, as a pleasant warm feeling rose in the pit of his stomach.

'And cleavage …' breathed Faith, to his left, admiring Siena as if for the first time.

Farrah stopped in front of Julius, and they stared at each other for a few seconds.

'How do I look?' she asked, nervously.

'Drop dead gorgeous,' he said, proudly.

Farrah blushed, as one of her huge, gorgeous smiles lit up her face. She stepped forward and kissed him gently. 'Come.'

Julius let her led him over to the table, where he greeted the other girls. Morgana was wearing a short, black summer dress; her long, dark hair was gathered in a ponytail. He couldn't help but notice how good she looked, as always. He sat down on the same side of the table as her, but with Faith and Siena between them. Farrah took the chair opposite him, with Skye, Valentina and Maks seated to her right.

'This looks wonderful,' said Faith.

'Aye,' added Julius. 'A great idea.'

'Farrah did most of the thinking,' said Siena.

'I couldn't have done it without you, girls,' she replied quickly.

'Let's toast then,' said Skye, encouraging the others to take up their glasses. 'To our amazing ladies, who were able to concoct the perfect setting for our celebrations.'

'Hear, hear,' said Morgana cheerfully.

'A toast to the success of our missions,' continued Skye. 'To those that have been, and those that are still to come. And, last but not least, to Faith, for fulfilling one of his dreams. Well done, mate.'

'Thank you, guys,' said Faith, blushing.

'All right,' said Valentina, 'that's enough toasts for one night. Let's eat.'

'She's definitely with *you*,' said Julius to Skye.

'And for good reason,' he replied, flexing his biceps.

Farrah gestured to the waiter, who quickly summoned the help of several others. They brought a host of large, wooden trays, filled with grilled langoustines, king prawns, crabs and scallops, garnished with fresh herbs and wedges of large, juicy lemons.

Julius' mouth began to water at the sight. 'Bring it on,' he said, unfolding a napkin over his legs.

'Wow,' said Skye. 'Food that fights back. I like it.'

The first course was indeed a challenge, with the boys determined to get every last bit of meat from the shellfishes, using all of the cutlery at their disposal. At one point, Skye even tried to pull out his Omni-gizmo to help him with the lobster, but Valentina held him back. 'Leave room for dessert, dear,' she told him.

The shellfish was followed by more, equally tasty dishes, like spicy plaice with mango, black olive and tomato salsa; pesto and olive-crusted monkfish, and plenty of salad to accompany everything.

As a tribute to her boyfriend, Farrah had even ordered a whale-sized, beer-battered, fish and chips, which left Julius gaping. 'Fish supper …' he said, his Scottish accent resurfacing strongly.

'I never thought I would see one again,' said Morgana, similarly impressed. 'Well done, Farrah!'

'I thought you'd like it,' she said sweetly to him.

'What's this? What's this?' asked Skye, excited at the prospect of trying a new food.

'You're gonna love it, mate,' said Julius, dividing it into small portions and dishing them out to everyone.

'Here,' said Morgana, passing around a bowl that came with it. 'Put some Tartare sauce on it.'

Julius excitedly explained how important it was to have a good "Chippy" on your street — something his dad had always raved about — with Morgana nodding approvingly. Faith was possibly the only other one who could properly appreciate Julius' little speech, while the rest of the group listened curiously.

'And you may some people put *vinegar* on it?' asked Maks.

'Or brown sauce,' added Morgana. 'At least in Edinburgh, we do.'

'Brown, you say?' said Skye, as if he was making mental notes.

'It's sort of vinegary too, but thick ... and brown,' she explained, before tucking into her fish with gusto.

After the last chip had disappeared from their plates, everyone agreed that it was time for dessert. The waiters promptly returned with small pastries, Italian style, in honour of Siena, along with coffee and tea.

'So, Africa's next,' said Maks, stirring his coffee. 'Anyone in your year from there?'

'Chiddy Dumisai is from Zimbabwe,' said Faith, passing the sugar to Siena.

'And there's Femi,' added Morgana, 'from Egypt. Mariam Richards is from Lebanon, but we don't know if her family will be there, or with the Asian folks.'

'It'll be a big one,' said Maks. 'I'd say roughly 40 days, if they manage to port an average of 20 million people per day.'

'That sounds about right,' agreed Julius. 'I still can't believe that the artefact was really a map.'

'Aye,' said Morgana. 'Well worth the detention we got for it.'

'Who's the Voice for Africa?' asked Farrah.

'Hasani Yeboah,' answered Skye. 'From Ghana.'

'I still think that finding the first location was kind of a miracle,' said Maks.

'Don't get me started on that one,' said Faith. 'I can't believe that we did that just by following the Taurus One's signature.'

'Yes, but since they won't tell us the truth, we'll just have to be content with that explanation,' said Valentina.

Julius was sure that Faith was right, but he had no way of proving it either.

As people finished their coffees, Julius heard Faith whispering to Siena, and asking if she would like to go for a walk. It must have taken all of his courage, and made Julius all the more proud of him; he was delighted to see Siena nodding enthusiastically in reply.

'Ladies,' said Faith, standing. 'I must thank you all once more for a splendid dinner.'

Skye winked at Julius, satisfied by this show of gallantry.

'Siena and I are going to admire the scenery,' he continued, helping her up.

'It was a pleasure, Faith,' replied Farrah. 'See you later!'

'I want to go too,' said Valentina dragging Skye from his chair.

'As you wish,' he said, grinning. 'Later, guys!'

At that point, Farrah and Morgana also stood, hinting that the others should follow suit.

Julius left his sandals behind and, when he was sure that the others had all gone ahead, he pulled Farrah to him, so that her body was pressed against his, and kissed her. 'It was a great dinner,' he said, afterwards. 'Thank you.'

'Glad you liked it.' She slipped her left hand into his right, and led him toward the shore.

The moon was full, bathing the sand and palm trees around them in milky light. Far ahead, Julius could see Faith and Siena walking side by side, while the others had gone off in the opposite direction. They walked in silence for a while, just enjoying the moment. Eager as he was to have her close to him whenever possible, he passed his arm around her shoulders, kissing her head as she drew near. It was then that he spotted the tall coconut tree from his dream, or at least one that looked just like it.

'What is it?' asked Farrah.

'That tree ... I've seen it before.'

'Let's go sit there, then,' she said.

Julius followed her, and the first thing he did was examine the base of its trunk. A look of disappointment crossed over his face. 'Hmm ... I was sure I was going to find a little carving there.'

'Something like "J+F"?' she said, grinning.

Julius looked at her, puzzled. 'As a matter of fact, yes. That's *exactly* what I was thinking. Are you reading my mind now?'

'I can read you like an open book, mister,' she said, teasingly.

Julius sat down on the sand, his back against the trunk. He let Farrah sit between his legs, resting with her back against him. 'Are you cold, Miss I-know-everything?'

In reply, she wrapped his arms around her, like a shawl. 'There, now it's better. I love to feel your arms around me. It makes me feel safe.'

Julius kissed her left cheek, breathing in her scent. 'You know,' he said, looking at her, 'it may sound odd but, every time I see you, there's something different about you.'

'What do you mean?'

'I'm not sure how to explain it, but you're not like the other 4th year girls.'

'Are you saying I look old?' she said, pretending to be offended.

'Never mind. I didn't mean it like that,' he said, poking her in the side.

'Well, what did you mean? Why am I not like the other girls?'

Julius thought that through, before answering. 'You're more mature, I think, like a *grown up.*'

'Maybe,' she said, giggling. 'And that is a nice thing to hear. Does that mean you're not bored of me yet?'

'How could I be?' he said, nuzzling her neck. 'You're ... addictive.' Each word was punctuated with a kiss.

'Hey, did I ever tell you about my secret hideout?'

'No,' answered Julius.

'It doesn't actually exist,' she explained. 'At least I don't think so. It's a place I've seen in my dreams, ever since I was really young.'

'Tell me about it,' said Julius, curious to find out more.

'It happens only when I'm in hospital. See, they need to put me into a sort of induced coma every time I go in,' she told him, candidly.

Julius nodded, although the news made him even more worried about her mysterious condition.

'I can't remember when the first time I dreamt about it was, but it felt good ... safe. After that, every time I was called back for check-ups, I knew that I could hide in Eneamar.'

'Eneamar? So you've even named it?'

Farrah shook her head. 'I think that's its *actual* name. I heard it spoken when I walked through the city streets, by the locals. Am I making sense?'

Julius laughed. 'No actually, but I'm having fun. Go on.'

'The city is beautiful, built on a sea of emerald green water. Clean air, clean streets, and blue skies. The sky-scrapers are bent in the shapes of arches, all made of glass. There are flower beds along the pavements, full of colourful plants and there is music in the air, a soft, soothing melody. It talks to you. "Everything will be alright," it says.'

Julius could tell by her voice, that she really liked this place and that it certainly had a strong effect on her. 'What about the people?'

'They aren't human,' she answered. 'They look a lot like us, but they are different. The most advanced beings in their galaxy. Their features are more delicate, their necks longer. Their skin is almost translucent and their eyes are always shining like crystals, no matter what colour they are. The women wear their hair in plaits, gathered to the back in the most beautiful hairstyles. I really wish it was real.' Farrah was silent for a while, as if her mind was still lost in this city. Then she turned around to look at Julius, a serious expression on her face. 'If I should … go away, would you still remember me?'

'What?' said Julius, startled.

'Good things don't always last,' she said. There was a calm certainty in her voice, which scared him.

'What's going on? Is this because of your illness?'

Farrah smiled at him, but her eyes began to well up. To Julius, it looked as if she was struggling mentally with something. 'You know we can talk about anything, right?' he told her, gently.

'You're the best thing that has ever happened to me,' she said, 'and I'm really, really scared of losing you.'

'You won't,' he answered, holding her by the shoulders. 'I'll be by your side till the end.'

She lunged forward and kissed him. Julius held her tight, kissing her back, a mixture of feelings taking hold of him. Why had she said that? Had the doctor recalled her to the hospital? He needed to find out, but maybe now wasn't the right time. As he lay on the sand with her, wiping the tears from her face with his lips, he knew it wasn't. Tonight was for them.

INTO THE NIGHT

The African mission hit the ground running. The Mizkis' lessons had once again been suspended, and the students prepped in advance so that, when the small red planet finally came into view, they were all ready to go. A fleet of Zed officers had been sent ahead to scout the airspace above the underground compound where they had registered the presence of the bio-signatures, and its landing area. They returned, confirming what everyone had already been expecting: the resistance found was nothing more than a show. A brief and vicious struggle had taken place between a dozen Arneshian planes and the Cougars, which had ended with the enemy being completely wiped out. With the coast clear, the huge portals were fitted around Moonrising, as they had done during the Oceania rescue and, just like then, Julius and his classmates boarded the Cougars, to provide aerial support.

The mood was light and cheery that morning, and the sense of satisfaction was tangible among the students: it was the first day of the rescue mission, but victory was already in the air.

'Goshawk, ready to go,' confirmed Julius to the tower, before lifting off. He could see Faith up ahead of him, leaving the hangar with a brio he hadn't shown in months, and that was all thanks to Siena. Julius chuckled as he recalled how his friend had come knocking at his door the morning after the meal, to share some good news, and thank Skye for the extra lessons. Apparently, he must have made quite an impression, since Siena hadn't just kissed him back, but had also immediately agreed to go steady with him. So now, Faith was all loved-up, grinning like a loon and using phrases like 'me wild nymph', whenever he mentioned her.

Speaking of being loved-up, Julius knew he really needed to be careful himself because, the more time he spent with Farrah, the more he felt utterly under her spell. Just thinking about that Saturday night left him feeling all flustered, as images of his hand running along her toned, soft thigh kept repeating on a loop in his head. One of his favourite highlights was when he had slid his hand up the back of her leg and up toward her-

'Watch it, McCoy!' cried Morgana, through their toon channel com-link.

Julius veered just in time to avoid bumping into the side of her Cougar. 'Sorry!' he said, panicking. 'Are you all right?'

'Yeah,' she said, sounding a little miffed. 'Just watch where you're going.'

'I know what he's watching,' said Skye with a chuckle. 'And I'm sure it wasn't the portal!'

'Very funny,' said Julius, drily.

'In fact, I've been meaning to ask you, it was you who triggered the safe-relationship protocol on Saturday night, right?'

'Look who's talking!' joined in Faith.

'Yeah!' added Julius, 'As far as I know, it could have been *you*, Miller.'

'Hey, I wrote that programme, remember? That's why we left early!'

'Why, you sneaky son-of-a-gun. You could have told us!'

Skye was laughing his head off at that point. 'Anyway,' he said, once he had composed himself, 'I bet it was Morgana. It's always the quiet ones.'

'Just you wait till we get out of these planes, Skye Miller,' said Morgana, only half-seriously, 'and I'll show you *quiet*.'

'Oh yeah, baby. I'll be waiting,' he added in a husky voice that made her giggle.

'OK, that's enough! Let's focus, people,' cut in Julius quickly. 'We have a mission at hand.' To Julius it didn't matter that he was happy with Farrah, and that he had worked past his old, strange feelings for Morgana; there was still simply no way he could be part of a conversation which required him to imagine her doing anything that would trigger the safe-relationship protocol. Actually, now that he thought about it, it might even have been him who had set it off, possibly when Farrah had removed his- No that was *not* good. He shook his head clear of such thoughts, and put aside all memories of the party. Much safer that way.

*

Over the next three weeks, all the Mizkis had their days divided up into three, eight-hour shifts, filled with aerial support, rest and data entry. The absence of any Arneshian counterattack made Julius quite nervous. He kept asking himself why. Where were the Nuarns, and why had T'Rogon moved them to Arnesh — if that's where they really were. Julius tried hard to guess what Freja would do next. On the one hand, there were two more continents to rescue, which were quite a fair distance away from each other; on the other hand, the Taurus constellation, home of Salgoria, was relatively close to their current position — a matter of a few small hyperjumps, in fact.

'I wish adults were more open with us,' he said to himself one night as he was returning, inside his Cougar, to Tijara's hangar. It wasn't only the mission he was thinking about; he was, of course, thinking about his classified file and whatever plans Freja had in store for him. 'And when is all that supposed to happen, anyway?' he wondered. Julius knew that he had had little enough time to see Farrah properly, but they were now halfway through the rescue, and his birthday was only a few days away. Surely they would give him a break for that.

*

On Thursday the 18th of April, Julius received a most welcome present. The Skirts had decided to pull a few double shifts, in order to get him the whole day off. Once Clavel had given his permission for this, they met with him at breakfast and told him the news.

'You guys are the best!' he said, hugging them each in turn. 'Thank you!'

'Oh, it's all right,' said Faith. 'But don't forget to meet us tonight for dinner.'

'I won't,' said Julius. 'Where are we going, by the way?'

'Not sure yet,' said Morgana. 'New place, perhaps. We'll text you later.'

Julius left them with a spring in his step, destination New Satras. He thought he would surprise Farrah by telling her that they had time for more than just dinner together. She had already arranged to get the evening off from duties, by working the afternoon shift. Because of that, he hoped she would be free this morning too. As he headed to her parents' shop, he was as excited as a kid in a candy store.

When Julius entered Auld Oddities, the door swung inwards, and a little bell tinkled. This unfamiliar feature took him aback, as all of the doors in his life were of the automatic, sliding variety. 'It must be part of the shop's presentation,' he thought, amused.

The front room was empty, but he could hear a female voice talking in the back of the shop, possibly Farrah's mother. It sounded like she was on a call, so Julius decided to wait and peruse the shelves, which were laden with all manner of curious and bizarre items. He felt a little awkward being there; after all, he had never been properly introduced to Farrah's parents. A thought hit him then: what if she hadn't mentioned him to them? What if they didn't even know that she had a boyfriend? Maybe he should pretend that he was just a schoolmate, to avoid causing any trouble for Farrah. Agreeing with himself that this was the sensible thing to do, he resumed his rounds. He was just examining a curious item, labelled "record player", when his eyes caught sight of something unexpected. A picture had been placed above the counter, in a beautiful gold, wooden frame. The scene portrayed a young couple holding a little blonde girl, of no more than six or seven years old, who was wearing a red-and-white dress, with shiny black shoes and short, white socks. Surrounding the happy family were none other than the three GMs of Zed: Freja, Milson and Kloister. What really caused Julius to do a double-take on it, however, was that he knew exactly when and where that picture had been taken; it had been on the 1st of December of the previous year, in Satras, the day of the deadline for Faith's spaceship competition. Julius clearly remembered how, after visiting Pete's shop, they had all gone to eat at Hallouminati and that, while they had been sitting there, he had noticed the little girl lifting huge objects with a mere flick of her wrist. The mother had called her by name that day — what was it again? Indeed, the woman holding the girl in the picture was Mrs Hendricks, and Julius assumed the man to be her husband. He wondered if the girl was Farrah's cousin, or something, because he could definitely see a resemblance there, and she had certainly never mentioned having a sister.

'Can I help you?'

Julius whirled around, startled. 'Uh, good morning, ma'am. I'm a friend of Farrah. Is she here?'

The woman looked at him with what seemed like just a hint of diffidence. 'What is your name?'

'Julius, ma'am; Julius McCoy,' he said, bowing slightly.

'Oh,' she said, instantly becoming more relaxed. 'In that case, Farrah is at the hospital.'

'The hospital? Is she all right?'

'Oh, yes. It's just a regular checkup. She'll be back later on in the afternoon. Can you return then?'

'Of course,' he said quickly. 'Is there something I can do for her?'

Mrs Hendricks paused at that question, as if some internal dilemma was taking place in her mind. Eventually, she shook her head and smiled. 'Thank you, Julius, but there's nothing you can do right now. Be here before dinner though. Farrah will be looking forward to seeing you.'

Those words reassured him a little, and made him feel even happier; she was fine and it appeared she had told her parents about him. In the meantime, though, he wasn't sure how to spend the rest of the morning, so he headed toward the lifts, where he knew there was a large interactive map of New Satras. The games were down while the mission was ongoing, so he hoped to get some inspiration on what to do, from exploring the directory.

As the escalator took him up to his destination, Julius noticed a door, set within a recess, and his mind took a quick leap back in time. He recalled now that it was in fact the same door he had waited in front of, while a wave of Mizkis passed him by, on the day when he had first met Farrah. He remembered the strange heat that had emanated from it, so hot that it had almost burned his neck, and the strange symbol etched into its surface, of 4 interlinked stars, forming a diamond shape. Suddenly, Julius' eyes grew wide, as he remembered exactly where else he had seen that symbol, not once, but twice before. He took the remaining escalator steps two at the time, and boarded the lift for Tijara, everything else instantly forgotten.

Ten minutes later, Julius was in the training sector, staring at a closed door. He had returned to the little storage room where Foster had sent him and Faith for their detention. The corridor was empty, so no-one was about to question what he was doing there; quickly, he opened the door and stepped into the room. Using his PIP to light the way, he found the light switch and flicked it on. The shelves were filled with the items that he and Faith had unpacked that night, seemingly untouched and unused since then.

'Where are you?' he muttered, as he searched the shelves. He quickly worked his way from the top shelf towards the bottom one. 'Bingo,' he said out loud, a few minutes later. It was still there after all. "Tijara's Ultimate Sacrifice", he read, as he pulled it out, looking at the cover of the microchip: it had the same emblem of four stars joined by straight lines, in the shape of a diamond. Julius searched the room for a chip reader, and found one lying on top of a stack of boxes. It was a circular device, not larger than his own hand; he placed it on the floor, and sat in front of it. Delicately, he inserted the chip into the empty slot and waited.

A hologram of Marcus Tijara sprang suddenly to life above the pad. It wasn't actual size, so Julius was able to look him straight in the eyes. Marcus looked just like he did in his many portraits: short dark hair, tall and sturdy, with a curious glint in his light brown eyes. It was a likeable face, welcoming and friendly. To each side of Tijara, there were various text headings, which Julius began to scan quickly. One entry simply read "Tijara's Heart", a title Julius instantly recognised from his file. He touched his right index finger to the heading and leaned back against the wall, holding his breath.

'The device is now completed,' said Marcus, a strange mix of sadness and satisfaction etched across his features.

Julius liked his voice immediately: it was deep and caring; somehow perfectly fitting with the image of Marcus he had built up in his head.

'I didn't think it was possible, but there it is: Tijara's Heart. This is my last gift to Zed; its last defence. They asked me why I've called it so. I have used my own name for it, because only I can use it, a White Child. As for the Heart, well, let's just say that a lot will be given up for the sake of humanity. That, and the fact that the device is for the undying love of my life, to whom my heart had already been given a long time ago. Maybe afterwards, we shall once again be able to live as a family, in peace. For her, this is a sacrifice I am willing to make. I only wish I had more time to test the crys—'

The recording crackled and stopped abruptly. Frustrated, Julius switched the reader off. He knew that Marcus was referring to Clodagh Arnesh, when he spoke of his undying love. The rest of the message however, was a little too cryptic to understand. Tijara's Heart was to be used for the defence of Zed that much was clear; it involved some sort of sacrifice on the part of the giver and, by all accounts, it looked like he was next in line. He needed to know more, so he opened his PIP, and called the only person he thought would be able to help him. 'Mr Hastings?'

'Julius?' replied the Curiate. 'Are you OK?'

'I am, sir. Sorry to disturb you at work, but … I need to ask you … what do you know about Tijara's Heart?'

Ben seemed to consider his answer for a minute. 'Let's meet.'

*

Julius went back to the holo-floor of New Satras, where Ben was waiting for him by the large screens. As he joined the Curiate and they found a seat in the courtyard, a feeling of dread spread over him.

'What do you know of Tijara's death?' asked Ben.

'Only that he died in the final battle with Clodagh,' answered Julius.

'Technically yes, he did, but it was by his own hand.'

'How so?'

'The Heart was a machine he had built for that last stand and, as he used it against the Arneshians, he also gave himself up. He was the sacrifice. There was no other way to power the weapon, except with his own life energy. But, why are you asking about this?'

Julius had turned white. It took him a while before he could speak again. 'I found a chip in a storage room, called "Tijara's Ultimate Sacrifice". It had a symbol on it, the same one that was on my classified file. You were right: Freja has marked me down for one final mission. He wants me to activate Tijara's Heart again.'

'How do you know that?' asked Ben, looking perplexed.

'I broke into his office, and saw the file,' replied Julius.

Hastings seemed at a loss for words.

'Don't feel bad,' said Julius. 'I knew you weren't supposed to tell me, but now I need to know everything.'

'I'm sorry all the same, Julius,' said Ben. He stood up and took a few steps into the arena, before turning back to him. 'What do you want to know?'

'If Tijara's Heart was the *ultimate* weapon, why are we having this conversation? Why weren't the Arneshians killed off once and for all?'

'Because that was not the purpose of the device,' answered Ben. 'Marcus wasn't a mass murderer; he just wanted the Arneshians out of the game. The Heart does not remove life, but power. You need to understand how the Arneshians work, Julius. All of them have what we call a "Pearl" of White skills inside them, which activates their Grey skills.'

'Is that why my brother could levitate socks?'

'Yes. It's also why some people can be misread during the induction test.'

Julius thought of Billy Somers, a proper case of *misreading*, if ever there was one.

'The Heart was invented to block these Pearls,' continued Ben, 'which in turn would deactivate their Grey skills, transforming the Arneshian carrier into a simple, albeit slightly more logical, human, but nothing more.'

'What happens to Nuarns and people like us?'

'There were *no* Nuarns back then, so I don't know. As for us, our Pearls are far too big to be damaged by the weapon. Anyway, when Clodagh arrived with the largest fleet humanity had ever seen, Marcus was ready. The machine delivered in full and the *new* Arneshians had to kneel before its superiority. The war ended in that instant. They retreated with their tails between their legs, all except for Clodagh.'

'How did she die?'

'Before the device went off, she went looking for Marcus where the Heart was kept. People saw her shuttle docking beside his and, after a while, there was an explosion. And that, as they say, was that.'

'I have to ask again,' said Julius. 'Why are we having this conversation if Marcus was successful?'

'Many reasons,' replied Ben, sitting back next to him. 'Not all the Arneshians were in the fleet. The ones left behind bided their time, repopulated their planet, regrouped, all those things. Also, Marcus wasn't as strong as you are now, nor did he have your augmented powers. The Curia really believes that this time would be the last, if we attack their home-world directly.'

'Am I supposed to ... die too?' asked Julius, eventually.

'*What*? Of course not,' said Ben, putting his hand on Julius' shoulder. 'I told you that Freja is reckless when it comes to the school, but he's no murderer.'

'So ... what am I supposed to sacrifice, then?'

Ben looked at him. 'Your powers, Julius. All of them.'

The words landed like a stone hitting the bottom of a well, leaving Julius breathless and stupefied. He tried to say something, but his mouth had gone dry and his lips wouldn't part. He watched as Ben sat quietly by his side, waiting. 'You might as well kill me,' he managed, eventually.

Ben chuckled humourlessly. 'Yeah, I'm with you on that, as you well know.'

'So that's it,' said Julius. 'Freja has set me apart for this one-way trip, without even asking me.'

'I suppose he should have,' said Ben. 'Or at least one of us was supposed to break it to you. When you called me before, I let him know that I would be the one to do it. I hope you don't mind — believe me, he was relieved that someone else took the job. Technically you're the only one that can man that machine, Julius; and your life belongs to Zed, after all. You didn't sign up for your own glory, you know?'

'This feels like "humanity's last hope" type of crap,' said Julius, who was too furious to worry about watching his words anymore. 'Why now? Why can't I try some other way? Why do I have to sacrifice all I have, all I *am*? Why?' In his mind, those words were really translating as, 'Why, now that I have Farrah?'

'Look, you're a good kid; if you really wanted to, I could give you a way out. I could guarantee safe passage to somewhere on the regular colonies where no one knows who you are. You'd be in hiding yes, but with your mind-skills intact. But, do you really want that?'

Julius didn't answer. He took a breath and asked, 'When is this supposed to happen?'

'1st of May,' replied Ben. 'On that day, we'll be at the closest co-ordinates to the Taurus constellation, where Arnesh is. You have 12 days to inform Freja of your decision.'

'Huh,' grunted Julius, running his fingers through his hair. 'I really don't think I want to talk to him, actually.'

'Call me, then. If it's of any consolation, your girlfriend wasn't going to be sticking around either.'

Julius looked up quickly. 'What do you mean?'

'Since you've already read your file, you know that you weren't supposed to meet FH,' he said knowingly.

'She is the one from my file, then. Why not?'

'She's not who you think she is, Julius. I feel bad telling you this, but given the kind of decision you're about to make, I think it's fair someone levels with you. It may even help you.'

'Go on,' he said. His voice had gone cold.

'She's 15, going on 21. Every one of your years, is roughly seven of hers. She's the Oracle's treasure, the one you rescued from Angra Mainyu; the daughter of Marcus and Clodagh.'

'That's impossible!' he cried, leaping up. 'It was destroyed. The GMs said so. You're just making this up.'

Ben shook his head. 'She wasn't supposed to try the Solo game, but she did anyway. Of course, she beat you and everyone else on that scoreboard, being who she is, but that's why her game and score haven't been broadcasted. They are classified. If you think your powers are strong, you haven't seen anything yet. Compare to her you're a newbie.'

'But … her parents?'

'They're undercover Zed officers. They took her in as an infant, a couple of years ago. Even without this chat we're having, she would have had to disappear, in the near future. That's why she joined Sield this year; she wasn't old enough before then. Think of it like this, Julius: by the time you're 20, she'll be close to her fifties.'

Julius slumped back down, feeling utterly bewildered. The picture in Auld Oddities had been of Farrah. He had seen her with his own two eyes, only a year ago. No wonder she seemed different to him every time they met — she was ageing. It would also explain why her mother didn't look anything like her. And what about the tropical setting of their dinner? All those details, from the palm tree to the white sand. "I can read you like an open book" she had told him on the beach. It looked like she wasn't kidding. 'How do I know you're not lying to me?' said Julius, grasping at one last glimmer of hope.

'Ask her yourself,' he said, standing up. 'You have a big decision ahead of you.'

'You said I have no choice.'

'We *always* have a choice. This is yours and yours alone. I wish I could help you more, but … Happy birthday, for what it's worth, Julius.'

Julius didn't stand to say goodbye, nor did he watch Ben as he walked away. He just sat there, for what felt like an eternity.

*

'Julius!' cried Farrah, before running across Rowan Square to meet him.

Julius didn't move, nor did he uncross his arms. He just stood there, by the tree where he had first met her.

Farrah must have felt that something was wrong because, as she drew nearer, her run had turned to a walk. 'What's happened?'

Against every bit of his will, which made him want to hold her tight, he steeled himself away from her. 'Why did you lie to me?'

The words, spoken quietly, had the effect of cold water on Farrah, who stopped dead in her tracks, the smile disappearing from her face. 'I didn't know what else to do,' she said simply, and slumped down on the bench facing the tree.

'You didn't, huh?' said Julius, bitterly. 'How about NOT letting me into my life in the first place, knowing that you were going to leave me sooner or later? How did you put it, the other night, on the beach? "Good things don't always last." Smooth, Farrah. Very smooth.'

'Do you think I chose this?' she retorted, starting to lose her cool. She stood and walked up to him. 'Did I *choose* to be abandoned by my own mother even before I was born? Did I *choose* to be found by you, or to be handed over to a couple of soldiers for parents? No, I did not! And, most definitely, I did *not* choose to fall in love with you!'

'This isn't love,' replied Julius, his voice raising. 'Love means sacrifice, but you've been selfish.'

'How?' she asked, her eyes widening in surprise.

'You *knew* this couldn't last and you let it happen anyway. You should have let me go,' he said, not caring that he probably sounded unfair or illogical just then.

Farrah it seems, couldn't find a reply to that. Tears began to well in her eyes, but she didn't wipe them away. 'You said you'd be by my side till the end ...'

'This *is* the end,' replied Julius. He turned and walked away, without looking back.

*

Julius didn't show up for his birthday meal. He simply texted Skye to say that he had broken up with Farrah. It worked perfectly, because no one asked him any questions about his skulking mood. The Skirts must have warned a few of the other Mizkis too, who did their best to stay away from him with any probing questions.

To the eyes of all, Julius was dealing with a harsh case of a broken heart, but inside, in spirit, he was in agony. Every time he had to use his powers, which was quite a lot since he was piloting the Cougars for the rescue mission, he couldn't help but think about how it would soon be his last time using them. Whenever he crossed one of his teachers in the corridors of Moonrising, he remembered all that he had accomplished over the past four years of training. It was the exceptional things he could do that made it particularly hard to decide; like the inorganic draws he could perform, or the cascade of colourful wisps he was able to see, that made his view of the world so special.

To say that he was miserable was an understatement. Freja had asked him to let go of all the things in his life that made him who he was; but how could he let go of all his friends, or his future career as fleet captain? Even Michael would be more powerful than he was, if he went through with this.

The absence of Farrah from his life was crushing. It felt as if a part of his being had been removed and left empty. Sometimes, it was even physically painful. With the passing hours, he had distributed the blame equally between all of the GMs, on account of how they had lied the previous year when they had said the embryo would be destroyed; Farrah should have been better guarded and not allowed to interact with anybody. How they could possibly think it was good idea for her to join Sield, was beyond Julius to comprehend. After all, Freja practically knew how many times Julius went to the toilet, so he must have known that they were seeing each other. If they weren't meant to meet, then why had Freja allowed it to happen? On a logical level, Julius could see that they had let her live, for a while anyway, like a normal girl. It would be her only chance at that, but it was a broken-hearted young man who had to deal with the pain and there was no logic to set that particular wrong right. Frustrated by all of these thoughts, Julius would spend his evenings pacing up and down the corridors, avoiding making eye contact with anybody. He could see that Morgana was itching to talk to him, but he kept her at a distance and she didn't push him.

Ben had told him that he had a choice, even offering him an escape route. But the more he thought about it, the more he knew there was no easy way out. There was no honour in avoiding his responsibilities, and that is what it came down to in the end. He clearly remembered the talks he had had with Faith and Morgana. Their words had been haunting Julius in all the waking hours of these past few days. Faith had spoken about inner strength and how choosing his cousin's life over his own freedom to walk could never be questioned. "We all have responsibilities. She was mine," he had told Julius. His friend hadn't faltered then and, given the choice, Julius knew he would do it all over again. As for Morgana, she had clearly told him that he had been born a White Child for a reason — who was he to waste that gift? Even Ben had said that such a gift should be used to bring hope back to the people. And as far as his own fear was concerned, Julius now knew now what it was: to be normal and powerless.

The final push towards making a decision came on Tuesday night. Part of Julius really could not believe that Freja would send him on such a mission, without as much as a single word. Determined to hear it from the GM's own mouth, he walked towards his office to confront him. As he approached the corridor, he heard Cress and Freja talking behind the corner, so he stopped.

'We need to get McCoy ready,' said Freja.

'What if he says no?' asked Cress.

'It isn't his choice, Nathan.'

Julius was startled by the curtness of Freja's tone. Was there even a point in talking to him if he had no alternatives? Hurt, he turned on his heels and walked back to the dorms, a sense of betrayal growing in his heart.

When dawn broke on Wednesday the 1st of May, Julius was sitting cross-legged on the floor of his room, staring into space. A single tear had dried on his cheek, marking the end of his inner struggle. His mind was made up: he was no hero, but he was a very necessary link in an important chain. He had been dealt a special hand, and he was going to play it well. When Skye left the room, he called Hastings. 'I'm ready.'

'Do you want me to accompany you, or shall I call the GM?' asked Ben.

'I'd rather not see him,' said Julius. A brief thought went to Captain Kelly, but he felt it was too late to ask for that. Who knew where he was, anyway? 'Do you mind coming with me?'

'I'd be honoured,' he replied. 'Meet me in thirty minutes by the door in New Satras. You know the one I mean, right?'

Julius nodded. 'Till then,' he finished, before closing his PIP.

He went for a shower, and toyed with the idea of leaving a note for the others. He had decided not to tell them directly, in case they tried to stop him and, in truth, he was afraid that his resolve would falter if they pressed him hard enough. He dressed, took a good look around the room, not knowing if he would be allowed back once his powers had gone, and made his way to New Satras.

His heart was heavy, and he could hardly breathe properly. As he waited for the lift, he suddenly decided to send a short message. He selected the Skirts' group mail address and typed, "I've accepted Freja's mission. I'm going to use Tijara's Heart on Arnesh. Ben Hastings is taking me. I'll see you guys later." It was done; he would send it on his way to the Heart. There was nothing left to do now, except fulfill his duty.

JULIUS' HEART

Morning, folks,' said Skye, sitting down with his breakfast tray.

'Hi there,' replied Morgana, stifling a yawn.

'Where's WC?' asked Faith, stretching to look behind Skye, to see if he was following.

'I left him in the room. I think he was meditating.'

'Who? Julius?' said Morgana. 'Yeah, right.'

'Well, either that or he'd fallen asleep cross-legged, staring out the window.'

'Did we actually figure out what happened between him and Farrah?' asked Faith, poking at his cereal.

'Not me,' answered Skye. 'He's been very private about this whole business. He looks thoroughly miserable, though. What about you, Morgana?'

'No. In fact, no one has even seen Farrah at Sield since Julius' birthday, or so Maks told me. I wonder …'

'Hmm?' said Skye, his mouth full.

'Just wondering if a split-up is all this is, actually. Julius has been so strange lately, like he's had something on his mind.' She shook her head. 'You know what he's like; he'd rather keep things to himself than ask for help.'

'Yeah, I know,' said Skye. 'Maybe it's time we corner him. What do you think?'

Faith looked at his PIP. 'We have some time before reporting for duty. We should go fetch him.' At that moment, Faith's screen beeped. 'Wait, Skirts mail,' he said.

The others opened theirs too and read the message, as a mixture of shock and surprise took hold of them.

'I knew there was something else,' said Morgana, who was now extremely upset. 'Why didn't he talk to us?'

'Is he referring to the mission from the classified file?' asked Faith.

'It has to be,' answered Skye. 'Look at the name, *Tijara's Heart*, it's the same one that was on his file. And who's this Ben?'

'He's one of the Curiate,' said Morgana. 'You probably know them all.'

'Yes, I *do* know the Curiates, but none of them are called Ben,' said Skye, suddenly worried.

'What?' she said, stunned.

'Let's go find Freja,' said Faith, standing up and hurrying them out of the mess hall.

They ran across Moonrising at full pelt, past the dorms and the engine room, raising a few eyebrows as they went, until they reached the teacher's floor. As they turned one of the corners, they collided head-on with Freja and Master Cress.

'Watch where you're going, Mizkis,' said Cress, steadying Skye from falling.

'Sorry, sir,' said Faith, bowing quickly.

Something in their faces put Freja on alert. 'What's going on?'

'It's Julius, Grand Master,' said Morgana, panting. 'He's gone.'

Freja's astonishment instantly spread over his face. 'Explain yourself.'

In reply, Morgana opened her PIP and showed him the message.

Freja's eyes grew wide. 'When did you receive this message?'

'About 5 minutes ago,' answered Skye. 'What's happening?'

'Cress, get Kelly to track the Heart's signature and follow it. Prepare a fleet for Arnesh. Go!'

'Right away,' said Cress, sprinting towards the hangar.

'You three, come with me!' The urgency in his voice made the others realise just how serious the situation was.

'Grand Master,' asked Morgana, as she ran beside him. 'Is it true that Hastings isn't a Curiate? That he's not one of us?'

'There's no one by that name among the Curiates, Miss Ruthier,' replied Freja, coldly. 'But he's one of us all right. Or so we thought.'

Morgana looked at the others, her panic rising.

Freja entered one of the control rooms and walked straight to a monitor. The technician working there moved out of the way without uttering a word. The surveillance camera was pointed dead centre at the door by the lifts, in New Satras. Freja first checked the time, then placed his finger on the corner of the screen, moving it anti-clockwise, to rewind the recording.

The Skirts had gathered behind him, focusing intently on the screen, for a sign of anything unusual. A few seconds later, they found what they were looking for. Freja stopped, and turned the sound up. A heavy silence had fallen on the room. Julius came into view a few seconds later, and stopped by the door. He seemed extremely serious, with a deep line creasing his brow. Then he looked up, and stretched his hand forward. A man came into view and shook his hand, before patting him on the shoulder in a reassuring manner.

'You're very brave, Julius,' said Ben, his voice loud in the stillness of the surveillance room. 'Braver than I could ever be. Zed will not forget what you're about to do.'

Julius nodded. 'Let's go, before I change my mind.'

Hastings pulled out some sort of key from his pocket — the sight of it seemed to stun Freja greatly — and placed it against the door. Immediately, the diamond emblem glowed into life, and the door unlocked.

'Welcome to Tijara's Heart,' said Ben.

Julius looked beyond the door, hesitating. Then he took a deep breath and stepped inside.

Ben followed him and the door swished shut behind him, leaving the camera staring at the symbol in its center.

Freja passed his hands over his face, looking momentarily lost. He seemed to have aged considerably in these last few minutes. He moved to the next monitor, which showed a view of space. Steadily, he rewound the recording, until the clock marked the time just after Julius had entered through the door. On the monitor, a ship flew out of Moonrising. It was a smaller craft, of a kind that hadn't been seen since the time of Marcus Tijara, flat as a disk and bronze in colour. A ring of lights, which revolved slowly around its circular hull, surrounded it. Steadily, it made its way away from Moonrising's orbit, then slipped into warp and disappeared from view.

'Sir,' said Skye, taking advantage of the silence. 'Even if Ben lied about his job, you were going to send Julius on that mission anyway. So why the bad feeling?'

Freja ignore the question, and asked one of his own in return. 'How did McCoy find out about Tijara's Heart?'

'Accidentally,' answered Morgana, quickly, avoiding any mention of Julius and Faith breaking into Cress' office. 'Ben Hastings confirmed it afterwards. Julius told me so himself.'

'Do you know what will happen to him if he uses the weapon?' asked Freja, seemingly dismissing Morgana's feeble explanation. He appeared to be calm, but his eyes told another story.

They shook their heads, their worries now surfacing fast.

'Assuming that Hastings really intends for McCoy to activate the Heart and use it against Arnesh, he will sacrifice every last strand of mind-skills he has. Forever. Without mentioning that he could very well die.'

'What?' cried Skye.

Faith looked horrified. 'But you … you were going to send him there too!'

'Yes, I was,' said Freja, now visibly angry, 'but not without this!' he lifted a long, white crystal from his pocket and held it in front of them. 'Marcus Tijara himself designed it to preserve his own powers when he used the Heart, so that he could get them back afterwards.'

'Then we need to stop them!' implored Morgana.

'We will try, but it may be too late.'

'Don't say that, please,' she begged, tears beginning to flow down her cheeks. 'There must be something we can do. I don't care about his powers; I want *him* back!'

'Damn you, McCoy,' shouted Freja, slamming his fist on the console. 'Of all the stubborn Mizkis that ever passed through this school, why did it have to be *you*?' He turned to face the Skirts. 'How many times did I tell you not to go off on one, before talking to me? How many? Do you think I would have let him go on a trip like this without talking to him myself, or taking precautions? Huh? But no, you always know best. With this stunt he's jeopardising an entire mission, all that we've been working for in the last few years, not to mention his own powers. If that happens he will have brought it upon himself, and if you knew that he was going to go on this mission alone, then you are just as guilty as he is!'

The Skirts stood there in complete silence. Seeing Freja so upset was a unique and shocking experience. But the Grand Master was right, and there was nothing they could say back to him.

'Sir,' said Cress, entering the room. 'Kelly was able to track their signatures and he's now in pursuit.'

'Send the coordinates to our fleet. He'll need back-up when he enters into Arnesh's airspace.'

'There's something else too,' continued Cress, looking at the Skirts, as if he was unsure if he should say it in front of them.

Freja decided for him. 'Well?'

'Miss Hendricks is also missing.'

The Grand Master looked stunned. He turned to the Mizkis, gravely. 'Go back to your duties. That's an order.'

Morgana was about to say something, but Skye pushed her gently out of the room before she could. 'If anyone can find them,' he whispered to her, 'Kelly will.'

The last thing they heard, before they left the room, was Freja demanding to know how they could have allowed this to happen.

*

Captain Kelly was in the ready room of the Ahura Mazda, sitting at the head of the table. Elian was to his left, with Master Cress on his right. Even now, Kelly felt the need to be physically separating them. His crew was still in pursuit of the Heart, along with a large Zed fleet, which had also joined them. The Tijara portion of Moonrising had also split from the rest of the battlestar, and Professor Deloi was trying to contact Julius telepathically as they moved in closer, in the vague hope of stopping him before it was too late.

'Nathan,' said Elian, 'how did this happen? Why did Julius go with the Arneshian without speaking to you or Carlos, first?'

'For starters, we didn't know McCoy had found out about the mission, let alone that we had a traitor in the Curia itself.'

'What do you mean?' asked Elian, looking shocked.

'Ben Hastings isn't an Arneshian; he's one of ours, a Zed officer working in the Curia.'

'What?'

'We don't know exactly when he switched sides, but last year must have been his big chance to impress Ambassador T'Rogon, and he obviously succeeded.'

'But how did Julius find out about this dratted mission?' said Kelly, feeling thoroughly frustrated.

'He broke into my office, if you really want to know,' answered Cress, with a raised eyebrow. 'He saw a classified file with his name on it by chance, when he came to see me, and snuck back in to read it. I cornered Shanigan earlier and, eventually, he admitted it. McCoy went with Hastings to use the weapon willingly; he may be a fool, but he has honour. He must have truly believed that he was doing the right thing. This Ben has been very clever: using the truth about the Heart and what it does, he led McCoy to do what Tijara himself had done before, appealing to his sense of duty. The only lie he told was in convincing Julius that we were working together.'

'If only you had been more open with him from the start,' said Kelly, coldly, 'all this would never have happened.'

'We made a mistake,' replied Cress.

'A mistake that could cost Julius his life. You're just like my father, Nathan: the school comes first. No wonder you get along so well.'

'What's *that* supposed to mean?' asked Nathan, angrily sitting up in his chair.

'Enough!' shouted Elian. 'The pair of you! What's done is done, so let's focus on the next bit, shall we?'

'Humph,' said Cress, but he did as Elian had asked.

Kelly also curbed his temper, he certainly didn't need an upset wife on top of all this. 'We'll be entering Arnesh's orbit very soon. Any idea what we're likely to find there?'

'Plenty of hostility, no doubt,' answered Cress. 'Only a handful of their fleet was deployed to guard the three compounds holding our people, which leads us to believe that the rest of them are still there, back on their home world. We're heading for serious fire.'

Kelly nodded. For a brief moment, he even considered asking Nathan to order Elian back to Moonrising, just in case things went bad, but he knew there was more chance of Salgoria surrendering than of Elian stepping away from the action. 'We'll be ready,' he said, silently hoping that they actually would be.

*

On and off, for the last ten minutes, Julius had begun to feel pretty uncomfortable. He had the definite feeling that something wasn't right. For starters, he could hear a strange sort of distant echo in the deep recesses of his mind but, no matter how hard he tried, he couldn't figure out what it was, or where it was coming from. It reminded him of a telepathic link under construction, yet, out here in the deep emptiness of space, who could possibly be trying to contact him? Then, there was the matter of *the smell*. It was too faint to clearly tell what it was, but it had distinctive traces of sweetness to it. Again, Julius struggled to identify it, knowing that it was somehow familiar to him. The truth was, that the closer they drew to Arnesh, the more it dawned on him that his destiny was coming to meet him with open arms: very soon, he would be just another human being; he would have to return to Earth, and wait eagerly for his mates to storm the European compound and rescue his parents. Then, with his family reunited — most of them, anyway — he would try to learn a trade or something like that, and find a job that didn't bore him too much. Perhaps he could become a history professor at Edinburgh University; Freja could surely pull some strings for him, especially in light of what he was giving up for humanity.

'... us ... lius ...'

Startled by the clipped sound, Julius sat up in his chair. He glanced at Ben, but he sat casually piloting the Heart, seemingly unaware of any strange occurrence.

'... Julius ...'

His eyes grew wide; there was no mistaking that it had been the voice of Professor Beloi. But what would he be doing out here? Had something happened? Maybe they had changed their plans, but then, why didn't they just hail them over the ship's com-link? He tried to clear his mind as best as he could, given the circumstances, and began searching for the voice, reaching out to it with his mind.

It wasn't long before Beloi found him again. '*Julius ... if you can hear me, don't say anything out loud ...*'

'*Professor? What are you doing here?*'

'*... trap ... don't use the Heart ... we're coming to get you ...*'

Julius was stunned. Please, say that is a joke, he thought, anything except that he had been lured into a trap. '*What ...*'

'*... don't use the Heart ... don't trust Hastings ...*' came the reply. Then the link was gone.

As Beloi's words hit home, Julius had a sudden moment of clarity, which made him blush in embarrassment. 'You are a complete and utter pillock, Julius and, quite frankly, you deserve everything that's coming to you,' he thought bitterly to himself. With that out of his system, his mind clicked into gear again. He tried to link back to Beloi, but failed. Still, his teacher had told him that they were coming for him, so he needed to stall Ben for as long as possible. 'Ben?' he said, trying to sound as if all was normal. 'How far are we from Arnesh?'

'Very close, actually. Are you curious to see the planet of your enemies?'

'Actually, yes I am. Too bad it'll be the last time.'

'It's sad having to lose all those brains,' continued Ben. 'Life could have been much more interesting if they had collaborated with us from the start. It would have benefited us all.'

'Sure,' said Julius. He began looking around the ship — which didn't take long, given its size — for anything that he could use to stop them from advancing. Faith would have come up with something, he was sure of that, but of course, he wasn't here. What could he do?

'Here we are, Julius,' said Ben.

Julius turned his head to look and saw it: the planet Arnesh, home of Queen Salgoria and all her subjects. It looked very much like a smaller version of Earth, but with much less green to it. Land and sea were visible in equal measure, painting the surface brown and blue. He couldn't see any docking stations or fleet in its surrounding airspace, and wondered why that was.

Ben piloted the Heart steadily onwards, until they reached the planet's orbit, where he brought the vessel to a stop. Quickly, he reached for a panel to his right and began to type on it, before repeating the action on the Heart's main computer.

'What are you doing?' asked Julius.

'You'll see,' he answered, focusing on his preparations.

Suddenly, a field not dissimilar to the Zed Shield sprung into life, completely enclosing Arnesh. Promptly, a second one appeared, larger and thicker, which closed over the first one. Julius watched as the Heart slowly pierced the first layer, creating bright sparks of silver and gold, fizzling against the front of the ship. Once through, the craft came to a stop in the buffer zone between the two fields.

Ben relaxed in his chair. 'Great. Now we can talk in private. Beloi won't be able to link to you from the other side of this field.'

'What?' said Julius, alarmed.

'Let's stop pretending, shall we?' Ben replied, turning to face him. A cold glint was in his eyes. 'And, before you do anything stupid, think again, or someone else very dear to you will pay for it.'

As he said this, Julius heard a sound like a large panel swishing open, from the back of the Heart. He looked behind him, and saw a partition sliding down, revealing a small enclosure beyond it. Inside, was a glass container; from where he sat, he could just about discern the outline of a body within it. He stood and strode to it, a gasp escaping his lips as he got closer. There were in fact not one, but two bodies in the large container: those of Farrah and Michael, lying still side-by-side. Seeing her, he immediately remembered the scent from before — it was her perfume. She was so beautiful, and Julius felt a sudden pang of regret that almost knocked the breath out of him. He was overwhelmed by the urge to hold her and tell her how sorry he was for leaving her like he had.

As for Michael, he looked taller than the last time Julius had seen him, and he realised just how much he had missed his brother. 'What did you do to them?' he growled at Ben.

'Nothing, actually; they're just asleep, otherwise what kind of leverage would they be?'

Julius stormed back toward him, fury mounting within.

'As I was saying,' continued Ben, 'all I need to do is simply think about that red button inside their chamber, and it will open into space. Instant death!'

'You're lying,' said Julius, flatly. 'Arneshians don't have the skills for that.'

'Oh, but I'm not an Arneshian, Julius. I'm just like you — hence why I heard Beloi. I guess you were too shocked to realise that.' As he said this, he pointed his open palm at a medical kit, causing it to fly across the room with his mind skills. 'You believe me now?' The kit landed back on the shelf.

'Are you going to level with me, Ben?' asked Julius, sitting back down in his chair. With the hostages in danger, and for lack of a better plan, he decided to get Ben talking, hoping it would give enough time for his rescuers to reach them.

'Sure, I can spare a few moments while I set up here,' said Ben, approaching one of the terminals and setting to work on it. 'Salgoria needs to get rid of *all* of the Arneshians, and *you* are going to do it for her.'

'What?'

'Her people have become redundant, you see. Over the centuries, the impact of Tijara's attack with this machine, has had great repercussions on the entire population. The unaffected Arneshians mated with those who had lost their white pearls, diluting their abilities. Salgoria has always strived to create the most evolved species in the universe, and her new plan involves the Nuarns and a small group of pure Arneshians.'

'Where are they?'

'That is not your concern. All you need to focus on, is cleaning up that planet which, in case you've forgotten, is what the heads of Zed have always dreamt about. You'll be doing everyone a favour. And, if you're wondering, spreading the humans across the galaxy was just a way of keeping Zed busy, while I worked on the *real* hero of this mission: you.'

A thought occurred to Julius. 'How did you know I would go with you? What if I had gone to Freja instead? I almost did, you know? Your story would have been blown.'

Ben chuckled. It made Julius want to jump up and punch him in the face. 'To be honest, I'm surprised you didn't. I had another plan in place, again using your brother as leverage. Farrah was an added bonus, as were you, making my life easier by coming to me directly.'

Julius restrained himself, knowing his anger wouldn't help him right now. 'I won't do it. You can't make me.'

'True; but I'll tell you what I *can* do,' he said, continuing his preparations. 'I can kill Farrah, and I can kill Michael; I can even make sure Mielowa receives the proof that you killed K'Ssander last year.'

'Wha … K'Ssander? No, I didn't!' cried Julius, stunned.

'I knew they wouldn't tell you, but I'm afraid he didn't survive the draw you did on him, who could, quite frankly? Anyway, Q&A time is over. Let's get to work. All I ask is that you use the Heart. Do that and you'll *all* live through this — you'll all live through this,' he said, pointing at the back container. 'You have my word.'

Julius was at a loss for what to do. As his brain tried to cope with the news that he had willingly killed another person — because, in truth, he had *wanted* to kill K'Ssander — he realised that no rescue would reach him. He had run out of time and didn't doubt for one moment that Ben would kill his brother and Farrah. Could he risk challenging him to do it? No, he thought, he couldn't afford that. And even if he attacked him, Ben would only need a second to focus on the button in the container and all would be lost. He tried one last time to find Beloi with his mind, but he caught only static. Did it really have to end like this?

'Looks like the cavalry is here,' said Ben, sounding amused. 'You want to say hi?'

Behind the container, a back screen was revealed. Julius ran to it, his heart thumping hard in his chest. As he passed Farrah and Michael, his hope rekindled momentarily. At the back, he saw a fleet of ships, their outlines slightly blurred by the outer shield; at the head of them was the unmistakable nose of the Ahura Mazda. He fancied that he could just about make out the shapes of people behind the bridge, but that could merely have been wishful thinking. He wondered if they could see him, and he tried hard to link to Beloi and Kelly. The field dividing them must have been really strong however because, after several failed attempts, Julius had to give up. Kelly had found him in the end, but it was too late and, although it was a meager consolation, he knew that at least he would not be left to die alone. Suddenly, the noise of air escaping made him look down. With horror, he realised that Ben had lowered the partition of the glass container of a fraction, letting oxygen out into space. 'Wait!' he cried to Ben. 'I'll do it. Stop it!' The fissure closed up instantly.

'Place your hands here, Julius,' said Ben, inviting him to take a seat at the front. A glass pad had been uncovered on the main console. 'You really have no choice.'

At that moment, Julius knew that Hasting was right. He had accused Farrah of being selfish; now it was his time to show her what it truly meant to love someone. He turned away from the screen and trudged over to Ben. There, he sat down, opened his hands and gently lowered them over the glass control pad as directed, ignoring the ice-cold of its surface.

'It'll be over soon,' said Ben. He sat back down beside Julius and flicked a switch.

Julius felt the panel getting warmer, and a small blue light appeared below his hands. 'It looks like a crystal,' he thought. 'Like the one sketched on the door.' He couldn't feel any pain, as Ben had said, but his body was tingling all over, as if a low current, instead of blood, was now coursing through his veins.

'On the count of three, I want you to push hard against the glass,' said Ben. 'One … Two … Three.'

Julius took a deep breath and pushed. The heat beneath his hands intensified, making him wonder if he would have blisters afterwards. He was expecting something dramatic to occur, like flashes of light engulfing them, but nothing like that happened. He felt the hair on his body rise up, electrified, while his powers simply poured out of him, through his hands and into the Heart. More spectacular was what was happening outside the ship. A thick, yellow beam shot out towards Arnesh and, when it reached the inner field, closer to the planet's surface, it spread over it like a cocoon, in a dazzling flash of light.

It lasted just over a minute, before the voice of the computer came online: 'Transfer completed.'

Julius felt the flow diminishing, until it trickled down to nothing. The glass below his palm went cool and suddenly he felt incredibly tired. He collapsed in the chair, his hands flopping down into his lap. His head lolled to the side, and his eyes began to close, even as he fought against sleep. He forced them open a fraction. He could see Ben sliding the glass panel up, and gently lifting something blue from beneath it, before pocketing it. Whatever it was, it reflected the light like a prism. Julius tried hard to follow Ben's movement around the ship, but his head was heavy and kept lolling onto his chest. All sound had gone soft too, as if his ears had been stuffed with cotton. His eyes closed again.

Julius woke a little later, although he couldn't tell for sure how long he had been out, with fresh air blowing on his face. He was still in the Heart, sitting limply and with no strength to speak of. A light twitch had started in his legs, slowly working its way up. He couldn't understand why they were doing it, and that scared him. He realised that the air was coming from an open hatch. Julius tried to look in its direction by tilting his head a little. As he did so, he saw the shadow of someone standing on the threshold. It took him a few seconds but, as he lifted his head a little more and saw who it was, he gasped. Ambassador T'Rogon was there, holding the blue crystal object from the panel, high above his head, admiring it. Julius could hear footsteps drawing nearer, from behind him, and he saw first a pair of dangling, female boots then legs: Ben was carrying Farrah into the Arneshian vessel, which had docked with the Heart at some point while Julius had been asleep. T'Rogon looked greedily at the girl. Julius was desperate to leap up out of the chair and stop them, but he couldn't move. 'I'll find you, Farrah. I promise,' he whispered. He watched as Ben carried her away from him, leaving only her scent behind.

'Come,' said T'Rogon, looking to the back of the craft. 'He is spared, as promised.'

Julius didn't understand what T'Rogon meant; then a shadow fell over him and, when he looked up, he saw his brother.

'Now we're equal,' muttered Michael, leaning over him. He turned and moved over beside T'Rogon.

The Ambassador placed a hand on his shoulder and didn't move until the hatch between the two vessels had completely closed.

With that image etched in his mind, Julius passed out.

A LONG SLEEP

'He's coming to.'

Julius opened his eyes and squinted against the light. As they adjusted, he noticed that there was a sheet of glass. He ran his eyes across its surface, and saw that it curved over him, disappearing into either side of the bed he was lying on. He tried to look down and examine himself, but found that he couldn't lift his head. What he saw however, was enough to get his heart beating fast. There were tubes filtering in and out of his arms and legs, with electrodes stuck to his chest; he couldn't feel his legs and a faint throbbing pulsated rhythmically in the back of his head. Beyond the glass he could see that he was in an unfamiliar place, possibly a sickbay, but not Tijara's. However, he did recognise Dr Walliser, when he leaned over the chamber and smiled at him.

'You'll need to be brief, Mizkis,' said the doctor, moving away.

The Skirts walked into Julius' view, and he thought that they looked quite drawn and pale, as well as scared.

Morgana placed her palms against the glass, fresh tears still smearing her cheeks. 'You stupid, stupid boy!' she cried suddenly. 'You could have died. What on Earth were you thinking?'

'I couldn't agree more,' said Freja's from behind them, out of view. His friends moved aside, and the Grand Master came to stand over him. He looked tired and gaunt. 'Did you really think me so ruthless as to send you off to sacrifice yourself like that, without a word, or any precautions?' said Freja, blankly.

He sounded disappointed, and to Julius that was worse than him just being upset.

'We know what happened,' continued Freja. 'The Heart's internal security cameras showed us everything.'

It was a relief to hear that, since he had no strength to explain himself, nor the skills to mind-talk to him anymore.

'I thought you'd be smarter than that. How could you believe him? Do you really think Ben would have been allowed to hurt Farrah? The daughter of Tijara and Arnesh is far too precious a gift to be airlocked at the whim of a traitor. Your brother is a Nuarn, a much needed breed in Salgoria's new world order; Ben told you so himself. And as for K'Ssander, he's alive and well. After he recovered from your draw, he was made to reveal the first location for our mission, which, in hindsight, was also part of T'Rogon's plan. That's why he was left behind in the first place.'

As Julius made sense of these words, he cursed his own stupidity.

'The only positive is that the Arneshians have no powers anymore — thanks to you — and their threat to us is now restricted to Salgoria and her elite group. But at what cost …'

Julius closed his eyes, trying to digest all of this.

'Salgoria wanted your powers all along,' said Freja, 'and Farrah's. Now she has both.' He was about to turn away, but stopped, 'I thought we were family.'

Those words hit Julius harder than he could have believed possible, and silent tears began to fall from his face onto his pillow.

After Freja had left, no one moved for a while, until Dr Walliser came back to his patient, working fast at a terminal by the side of the chamber. 'Julius,' he called, 'the loss of your powers has greatly damaged your organs. The recovery will be long and painful. You have been placed into a stasis chamber, where you will sleep for some time. We are hopeful that this will accelerate the healing process.'

Julius mouthed the words, 'How long?'

Dr Walliser hesitated before answering. 'A few months should be sufficient.'

In response, Julius' tears increased, as he realised his impotence to say or do any differently.

'You must say your goodbyes now,' he said, turning to the Skirts.

They came forward, huddling around the chamber once more, and all put their palms on the glass. Julius could tell by their red eyes that Freja's news had affected them all.

'We'll find a way out of this, you'll see,' said Skye, trying to look tough.

'You just hibernate in there, WC,' said Faith. 'We'll take care of you this time.'

He felt so glad to have his friends there, that he temporarily forgot that he would never be a White Child again.

Lastly, he looked at Morgana. She sniffed first, then managed a smile, before her lips formed a few silent words. He wanted to ask her to repeat what she had said, to speak up, because he hadn't got it properly, and he felt somehow that it had been something very important. But a feeling of heaviness was overwhelming him, and he knew that the stasis was about to begin. So he just looked at her. It was the last image he saw before he fell into a deep sleep and for a long time, he knew no more.

TIJARAN TALES
BOOK V

THE GUARDIAN'S
TRAIL

CONTENTS

PROLOGUE

The sun shone brightly on the vast, icy expanses of planet Mah, sending shards of reflected light in all directions. A high ridge of harsh peaks created a natural perimeter around the city of Mahin — a grey mass of low buildings and deep dark shafts that sunk down into the core of the planet. The cold blasts of wind that swept the plains for most of the year made it very difficult for anything to grow; rough bushes and slender fir trees stood lonely along the lower slopes of the mountains, while every other kind of vegetation was confined to the protective heat of the numerous greenhouses.

Ruxshin fastened the clasp of her hood, tightening it around her neck. As the moving platform reached the surface, she stepped out onto the frozen ground and began to walk eastwards, to where one of the winter gardens was waiting for her. A flurry of snow buffeted her suddenly, making the soft reddish fur on the sides of her face stand on end. An icy shiver ran down the back of her body, which was covered by hair, all the way down to her ankles. The cold had been unbearable this year, like no other time in her life, all nineteen years of it. She couldn't imagine how the Mahini would ever survive in this environment without their natural fur coats, and she was glad that hers was still thick and luscious — quite the envy of her friends, and an allure for her suitors. In three months, the ice would melt, leaving behind gurgling streams and pregnant lakes, the snow replaced by rain; it wasn't *that* much better, but at least it was warmer.

'Chief! Over here!' called a voice from the threshold of a nearby hut.

Ruxshin looked up and saw Hutan beckoning for her to join him, while holding a steaming mug in his other hand. She waved back and hurried toward him. 'Put that hood on,' she told him, watching the way his chestnut mane was being ruffled by the wind. 'You'll catch your death.'

'I'm too warm for that!' he grinned.

'How is it?' she asked, eyeing the dark liquid in the mug with curiosity.

'Try it,' he answered, offering it to her.

She accepted it eagerly, and blew gently over its surface. As she took the first sip, her green eyes closed and she savoured the taste. It was slightly bitter, but very strong, and it quickly heated her up. She looked at Hutan with delight. 'You did it.'

Hutan was visibly relieved to hear the approval in her voice. '*We* did it,' he said. 'You're the best Chief we've ever had. If you hadn't fixed that greenhouse the way you did — getting temperature settings right and all — there wouldn't have been any berry bushes to pick.'

'Well, if you insist, I'll take my share of bows.'

'You'd better. So, where are you off to now?'

'Heading to GH5. The heating system is acting up again. You?'

'Going back to my lab. I want to have this brewing system down perfect before I approach the Council.'

'You'll be fine. Mah Gira will love it.'

'So, will you come tonight?'

Ruxshin noticed that Hutan was looking at his feet, slightly embarrassed. She had been growing increasingly aware that his feelings for her had developed in an unexpected way; unfortunately for him, she only saw him as friend — closer than others, but still nothing more than a friend. She knew she couldn't encourage him in any way; even though it mighthurt, she had to create some sort of barrier between them. 'Will Khavar be there?' she asked, smiling coyly.

Hutan's eyes grew wide for a moment, his disappointment clear as day; it lasted only for a moment though. 'Sure,' he said, trying to sound as casual as possible. 'He never misses a party, that one.'

'See you tonight then,' she said, and before Hutan could say anything else, she headed back to the road. She hated herself for hurting him, but the very fact that he had backed down so easily confirmed that he wasn't right for her. She wanted a strong companion, someone she could follow with undying loyalty. Out here on the surface, she was one of the Chief Engineers. People depended on her for their food; her workers followed her every order. But in the underground, in the cosiness of her little home, she wanted to be led and cared for. Hutan wasn't right for that job. *Someone will be*, she thought. She knew it was only a matter of time before she found him.

Ruxshin saw her greenhouse coming into view and smiled, thinking about the heat that would soon be enveloping her. For the next few hours she would be working in there, surrounded by fragrant fruit trees and berry-laden bushes. She swiped her keycard in the slot to unlock the door and stepped inside, pulling the door shut behind her. The warmth was delightful and she began to remove her suit, unzipping the front. With the top part dangling around her waist, she took off her snow boots. Then she stepped out of the thick, heavy trousers and socks, remaining in shorts and a halter neck top, designed to cover only her chest and stomach, leaving the fur on the back exposed. Finally, she took a tub of plant extract lotion from her backpack, and began to apply it to the front side of her legs and arms, where no hair grew. All these jumps in temperature were really harsh on the skin, and Ruxshin took great care of her body.

It was at that moment that she noticed the light. A quick flash entered her field of vision, and made her look up; she saw a little, bright point in the sky — it didn't seem to be moving. Perhaps it was a comet. *Or maybe*, she thought excitedly, *visitors from another planet*. She decided to check with the astronomers after work. They would surely know.

*

The Taurus One was morphing. It had travelled through the wormhole in a semi-shapeless state, emerging inside an uncharted solar system. Gradually, a structure appeared from the stretched black mass, which solidified into a steel, sphere shape. On the war deck, the commander gave the all clear, restoring a condition one throughout the ship.

Manuel T'Rogon took a deep breath, before rising from his chair. He had just sat through a wormhole passage *as well as* a morphing — two of his least favourite things — and he felt queasy. He knew very well that shapeless travel cut down the journey length by half and prevented a person from ageing, but he also knew that he would pay the price for that shortcut; the human body seemed to lose the ability to sleep for about a day following a morphing, due to the after-effects from the rebinding of its molecular structure. *One day*, he thought, *something will go wrong with the ship's mainframe and we'll be lost forever, condemned to roam the universe in a shapeless state, never ageing, never dying.* Still, he had a good feeling about the day ahead: a treasure mine had been found and a new life form discovered. His mood brightened.

T'Rogon lifted his head, and spoke to the room computer. 'K'Ssander, Michael; join me please.' A few seconds later, there was a long beep, confirming that they had heard him and were on their way. T'Rogon stepped in front of one of the vertical glass panels of the ship deck and adjusted his long, silver robe. His pearl-white hair framed a pair of pale blue eyes and a thin, pointy nose. He straightened the circlet around his forehead, knowing that soon this metal band would be redundant. 'Very soon, yes,' he said.

The noise of the door sliding open alerted T'Rogon that his officer and the boy had arrived.

'Ambassador,' said K'Ssander, stepping into the room.

'Sir,' said Michael.

T'Rogon turned. 'At ease,' he replied. His eyes wandered to K'Ssander first. Like all Arneshians, the young man's hair was pure white, making his blue eyes stand out more against the natural greyness of his skin. He had grown so much in the last year, thought T'Rogon, reflecting on the fact that he had come to think of him as a sort of adopted stray, loyal for the most part, but still to be kept at a safe distance. K'Ssander had left his biological parents back on Arnesh to join the military path, never once expressing the wish to see them again. At nineteen, he was the brightest among his peers, vicious too, and T'Rogon had taken advantage of these traits from the start. Leaving him behind, two years ago, aboard the Zed shuttle, had been one such instance. Banking on the sense of honour of his enemies, T'Rogon had planned for K'Ssander to be imprisoned, rather than killed, so that he could slowly feed information that would help Zed discover the locations of their own captured people. And, as Freja led his fleet on a merry chase across the galaxy, the traitor Ben Hastings was working from the inside on the White Child, Julius McCoy. Luckily for them all, and thanks to the help of McCoy's own brother, Michael, his plan had succeeded. Julius had been convinced to sacrifice all his powers to wipe away any trace of Grey Skills from the people of Arnesh. By eliminating those lesser Arneshians from the equation, Julius had left Salgoria's selected people free to grow into the purest specimens of their kind: the most technologically gifted humans in the galaxy.

His gaze then moved over to the young boy standing next to K'Ssander. At fifteen, Michael McCoy was rather tall for his age. Hoodwinking him had been far too easy — the discovery that he wasn't fit to follow his brother at Zed had made him more pliable when it came to steering his course towards joining the Arneshians. And of course, there had been that chance encounter on Satras the year before. Realising that Julius

McCoy's own brother was a Nuarn had opened up a whole lot of opportunities to T'Rogon. The ambassador had subsequently taken great care to send Michael the most appealing recruitment material in his possession — highlighting what he could achieve if he fulfilled his Arneshian potential. After that, it had been as easy as drinking cool water. Michael had shown great courage in challenging his family's wishes and leaving all of them behind; a good sign, in truth, given the plans T'Rogon had in store for him. Another good sign, although somewhat surprising, had been Michael's happiness at his brother's loss of powers. With the threat that Julius represented eliminated, he could build Michael in any way he wanted; he could choose to give him Julius' lost powers, augment his body and, of course, their new queen could distil her special serum to make him invincible. There was even the possibility of a trip to the Halls of Ahriman. After all, if the old stories were true, Tijara's treasure lay there, waiting to be found. Indeed, the possibilities were endless. 'Come, look,' he said to the boys. 'We have arrived.'

K'Ssander and Michael stepped up to the glass and looked down, towards the small planet, which was surrounded by a thin blue layer. There were no clouds to obscure the view and, as far as the eye could see, the land was smothered in a white coat of snow. The image zoomed in, showing great mountain chains crisscrossing the vast planes and dividing the surface into different sectors. Standing out among all that white was a dark grey area, stretching like a cobweb in all directions; it appeared to be a large city.

'Where are we?' asked Michael.

'Actually, we do not know its name,' answered T'Rogon. 'New system, new planet.'

'It seems pretty cold to me.'

'It is. Our scouts have been observing it for the last year or so and have detected a most unfriendly weather pattern,' explained T'Rogon. 'Six months of snow and six months of rain.'

'Why are we here, sir?'

'A couple of reasons. The inhabitants of this little planet are sitting on the biggest deposit of Strullium outside our system, and all but a wormhole away from ours.'

'*Strullium* — what is that?'

'It's a metal, without which we could not make core engine parts.'

'Are we running out of it — back home, I mean?'

'Not in the immediate future, but its location has always been … a source of unease for us, shall we say.'

'And the second reason?' asked K'Ssander.

'We're looking for a new home — although, given the weather here, I doubt we'll choose this one.'

K'Ssander looked at him, surprised.

'Arnesh's days are numbered,' explained T'Rogon. 'Besides, it is no longer the house of the Grey Arts — Julius McCoy has seen to that.'

'Why abandon it?' K'Ssander pressed.

It was T'Rogon's turn to be taken aback, as he detected real concern in his voice. He didn't think the boy would care about his home world. 'You *know* why. The current inhabitants of that planet are no longer our kindred, just humans.'

'But the queen …'

'All in good time, K'Ssander,' he replied enigmatically. 'Our queen is fine where she is, and that's what matters. We have other concerns at hand. That city you see below us is the entrance to enormous riches, and I intend to claim them. Our fleet depends on it.'

K'Ssander nodded and didn't question him further.

'Commander,' said T'Rogon, contacting the war deck. 'Let's send a proper greeting card to the locals.'

'Yes, Ambassador,' came the reply.

'Make yourselves at home, gentlemen,' he told his charges, an amused smile on his face. 'We'll be here for a while.'

Michael moved forward keenly, until his forehead was pressed against the glass. A few seconds later, the Taurus One opened fire on the dark city below.

The Arneshians had arrived.

THE LIGHT

Nurse Primula began her morning shift as she always did, by walking straight over to the stasis chamber and tapping lightly against its glass. 'Good morning, Julius.' The fact that the patient sleeping inside it wasn't able to hear the greeting or respond to it didn't bother her: healing took time and this particular one had suffered a great deal.

She headed over to her desk, where her colleague had left a handover from the previous shift. Quickly, she read the page, scanning through the data recorded by the machine during the night. All the values seemed stable, with the exception of twenty or so electric peaks. She had been noticing these fluctuations for the past three weeks, and kept a chart on the number of occurrences per day. Even though Dr Walliser believed they were normal in a stasis, she couldn't ignore the fact that they had increased steadily, with every passing day. 'A girl can hope, right?' she said, looking over her shoulder at the chamber.

She activated her palm-screen and the holodisplay appeared in the space between her and her open left palm. When she logged into the sickbay network, there was a message flashing in the corner. She touched it and it popped open. "Please create a full new record for JM. Old files corrupted by teleportation. Thanks, Dr Walliser." Nurse Primula sent a quick reply, saying that she would do so right away. With her shift being so quiet, it would give her something to do.

She had known Julius since the first day of his life at the Zed Academy, one of the brightest and nicest kids she had ever met in her long service on the Lunar Perimeter. To be completely honest, he was part of a rare group, as far as students went. Julius was a White Child, a mind-skill user who possessed the most powerful White and Grey Arts, unlike the Arneshians whose total lack of White skills was the reason why they had separated themselves from the rest of humanity in the first place.

Grand Master Freja and the whole of Zed had hoped that Julius would be the one to bring an end to the war between Earth and Arnesh and, for four years, it had appeared that he would accomplish this. Then, everything changed. Julius lost all his powers, turning into a regular human who, once fully recovered, would be sent home to an ordinary life, and thank you very much for your time. The Mizki students of Zed were always hard at work, but no one had been pushed as much as Julius had. 'And for what?' Primula said to herself. She shook her head; there was no point in getting upset now. She would take care of him and let life run its course.

'Computer, begin recording,' she said to the room. 'Julius McCoy, 6MS,' and then halted. The stark reality hit her, and not for the first time. Dr Walliser had induced Julius' stasis in May 2859. Its purpose was to hibernate the body while it was healed at a subatomic level. No one could interfere with this process: the subject could only wake up naturally, once the cycle was completed. What made her stop was the fact that it was Monday the 13th of October 2860. Julius was now a seventeen-year old Mizki, on the last leg of his student life on Zed. 'How am I going to break that to you?' she whispered to him.

The young man in the chamber continued to sleep blissfully, his dark hair pushed back by a hairnet of sensors. Numerous tubes linked his body to the large machines below his bed, where all the data was gathered and stored.

The nurse touched a few keys on a pad and, once the glass case dematerialised, she gently took his hand, realising that it was time to trim his nails again; perhaps she would shorten his hair as well, as it kept getting entangled in the wires. She took a deep breath and began recording again. 'The subject has been in full stasis for 15 months and 13 days. He received severe injuries to the majority of his internal organs, due to the total removal of his mind-skills through the unauthorised use of the weapon called Tijara's Heart, by the Arneshians — see file 125B.'

As she spoke, she began her routine check of the machinery that kept Julius alive: blood filters, food and liquid dispensers; everything had to be calibrated just right. She then selected a download of all the records stored since the beginning of the stasis to date and sent it to the main network. 'Sending files now.'

There were many daily actions to perform on a patient in stasis, from maintaining the muscular tone and joints to pressure area care — the list went on and on. Mouth, eyes and skin also needed attention and, while no medical trial had backed it up, talking to the patient was also something recommended by Dr Walliser. Nurse Primula had some great help with that particular aspect, as Julius' classmates were always popping in or out of sickbay; especially Morgana, who did this every single day. After the first week of stasis, Nurse Primula had an armchair brought in for her, since she would keep vigil by his bed until she fell asleep, often having cried herself dry. The weeks passed, and so did the months, but Morgana kept visiting him, sometimes for hours and sometimes for a few minutes. Primula thought of alerting Grand Master Freja about this, but how could she really? Morgana was Julius' best friend and being there brought her closure. What she did do, however, was to call the rest of Julius' group, Skye and Faith, who would always come pick her up or make sure that she ate and functioned. After all, they were still in deep space, aboard Battlestar Moonrising, trying to teleport all the abducted humans back to Earth, and it was paramount that she remained fit for duties.

As if summoned by these thoughts, Morgana appeared at the door. 'Morning!'

Primula looked at the tall young woman leaning against the doorframe. 'Come in,' she said warmly. 'I've just finished my dailies.'

Morgana stepped over to Julius' side and immediately took his hand. 'Any news?' she asked hopefully.'

'I did record a few more of those electric peaks,' said Primula, smiling.

'That's good, right?'

'Yes, it is,' she answered. Nothing wrong with giving her a little hope. 'You look tired. What have you been doing?'

'I've been studying all the data on Tijara's Heart, from around the time of the explosion that killed Marcus and Clodagh.'

Primula looked at her and sat down at her desk. 'What are you expecting to find?'

Morgana shook her head and flicked her long, black hair behind her shoulders. 'I know it's ancient history, but I'm on to something — I just know it.'

The sparkle in her eyes intrigued Primula, who nodded. 'Very well, but try not to overdo it: those black bags don't match your pretty green eyes. And eat, girl! You're getting far too slim.'

'I am,' she said, not sounding too convincing.

'All right then,' said Primula. 'Before you go to your class, be a darling and pass me that tray by his pillow, will you?'

'Sure,' she replied. The tray had several scanners on it, and she lifted it gently, trying to balance them all. 'Where do you want me to-' Morgana's grip on the tray loosened, and the devices crashed to the floor.

'What's the matter?' cried Primula, leaping up and rushing to her. Then she followed her gaze and took a step back in disbelief.

Julius' eyes were open.

THE TIME THAT WAS

'I know it hurts, mate,' said Faith, hovering to the left of the treadmill. 'But you've got to push through it. Trust me.'

Julius kept running, sweat streaming down his forehead, but he felt as if his quadriceps were about to burst. 'I can't ... take this ... any longer,' he panted.

Faith checked his watch and looked at the nurse, who nodded. 'All right then, I guess you can take a break.'

Julius eased the machine to a halt before dismounting with shaky legs. He grabbed the towel from Faith, and collapsed on a nearby chair.

'You did well, McCoy,' he said, patting his shoulder. 'Look, I've got to go back to Tijara and meet Professor De Boer, but we'll pick you up at lunch, all right?'

'For sure,' said Julius. 'At one, by the lifts. Thanks Faith.'

'You'll get there, mate. Don't you worry.'

Julius watched him leave the room. He had to hover low and duck as he passed through the door. Faith, like Skye and his other classmates for that matter, had grown considerably since Julius had been put into stasis. His own body looked different too, for that matter: he was taller and had lost most of his muscle mass. Ironically, that didn't matter, as he would have all the time in the world to lift weights in a gym, now that his career in space was over. At least Nurse Primula had done a good job keeping the black, jagged strands of his hair under control — one less thing to worry about. When he had seen himself in the mirror for the first time, he had been taken by surprise. Staring back at him was a young man, no longer the boy Julius remembered. 'I've lost fifteen months of my life,' he had said to himself, 'and I'll never get them back. How could they have let me sleep for so long?'

Then there was Morgana, more like a woman and more beautiful than ever. Seeing her had brought back waves of memories, from their childhood together to the jealousy he had felt when she had started going out with Maks. The fact that he himself had hooked up with Farrah not long after that had always raised suspicions in his heart. He knew that his feelings for Farrah had been true but then, why had Morgana never been too far from his mind? He had felt plenty guilty all right, even just thinking about it, as if he had somehow been betraying his girlfriend with his thoughts.

Knowing that he was about to see Morgana at lunchtime though, felt good on so many levels, that he had to wonder if there was more going on than just plain old friendship. However, he shook his head and decided not to work himself up just yet. Maks would probably be there too. But then again, what had she been doing there that morning in sickbay, when he had woken up? Surely she had come to see *him*? 'Stop it, McCoy' he mumbled, forcing his thoughts elsewhere, as he stretched his legs.

Since his return to life, Julius had spent the past three weeks under constant monitoring from the sickbay staff, the Grand Masters, the Curia and of course his family and friends. Everyone wanted to know how he was, and everyone wanted to see him, even if only by way of a vidcall monitor. Given how fragile his mental state had been when he had heard how long he had been in stasis — he couldn't talk for two whole days when he found out that he was seventeen — Dr Walliser had decided to cut down all visits. For Julius, who had not taken part in the rescue of his parents and Nana, to know that they were well and in the safety of their own home, even if a little older, had been the only consolation. There were no others really. He had lost his brother Michael to the Arneshians, possibly forever; he had jeopardised the life of his ex girlfriend Farrah, of whom no one now knew her whereabouts. And to cap it all off, he had lost the only thing that made him whole: without his powers, he was no longer an asset to Zed and, once his rehab was over, he would be shipped back to Earth on the first shuttle.

Thinking about these things made him feel lost and frustrated. He breathed deeply and banished all thoughts from his mind, until the anger dissipated. He wasn't allowed to return to Tijara or to his dorm, but had to stay in the main hospital of the Citadel. He didn't have the new uniform; in fact, he didn't even have the new timetable. He felt like a visitor in his own home, and that was heartbreaking. It was only in the last week of October that Freja had given permission to his classmates to stop for short visits and, although Julius was grateful for their attention, he also felt envious, because he would never be like them again. Even Barth Smit, Faith's roommate and the clumsiest student in Zed, was now better than him, and if that wasn't an injustice, what was? The Skirts had been allowed to see him a little more often, and when Faith had offered his help during the physio sessions, Julius had accepted it gladly. Faith couldn't walk, but his disability had also been his strength and that was what Julius needed to learn now.

Finally, Dr Walliser had given him permission to spend some quality time outside of sickbay, and today he would meet his friends in New Satras for the first time.

'Are you going to take that shower,' said Primula cheekily, 'or are you going to stink the place up for me?'

Julius smiled, and stretched his legs in front of him. 'As a matter of fact, I was thinking that the world has moved on without me and left me alone. I wish I were someone else. How's that for self-esteem?'

'I'd say the worst kind of loneliness is to not be comfortable with yourself,' she said kindly. 'As for wanting to be someone else ... well, that's a waste of a perfectly good Julius McCoy.'

'Mmph,' he grunted. 'Sorry if I don't share your enthusiasm, but I'm a broken man ... literally.'

'Nonsense,' she said waving her hand at him. 'If only you knew how many people have been worried about you these past months. Some a lot more than could be expected, even from a friend.'

'Like who?' he blurted out, hoping that maybe she would say Morgana.

'Never you mind. Shower now. Off you go.'

'You're just saying all this to make me feel better,' he answered, but he *did* feel better nonetheless. Struggling, he heaved himself up, while his body complained at that unexpected request for energy. He made his way to the shower, looking forward to a long, hot soak before lunch.

*

Eager as he was to get out of the hospital, Julius arrived by the lifts a full ten minutes early and was surprised to see that the Skirts were already there, waiting for him.

'We know you so well, McCoy,' said Skye, calling the lift.

Julius couldn't help but notice that they were all wearing the 6 Mizki Senior badges on their jumpers, while he was wearing a simple blue Tijara uniform, without name tags or ranks. He forced himself to hide his disappointment, and smiled.

'How are you feeling today?' asked Morgana cheerfully.

'Better, thanks. The mad Irishman here is training me for a space marathon,' he said, motioning at Faith, who hovered beside him, grinning.

Julius felt immediately better for being with them, and for the first time since waking up, he felt positively hungry. 'So, where are you taking me?'

'There's a new joint in town,' said Skye, as always the expert in food matters. 'It's called — wait for it — "Eat It While It's Down". Cool name, huh?'

'Seriously?' said Julius wearily. 'I mean, we don't have to kill our own food, do we? 'Cause let me tell you, I don't think I have the strength for it.'

'It depends what you order,' answered Skye seriously.

They all looked at him, before bursting out laughing.

'We missed you, McCoy,' said Skye, stretching his hand forward.

Julius placed his own over it, followed by Faith and Morgana.

'We missed you very much,' he said again.

'Thanks guys.' He didn't think he could trust himself to say more, but he was sure they knew how he felt.

They arrived at the ground floor and made their way to the front exit. Julius stretched blissfully under the artificial sunlight flooding the main concourse. There were potted plants and hydrangea bushes, paired up with wooden benches — a cheery place where patients could spend time with their visitors. As he looked at the colourful surroundings, Julius remembered that nothing around him was real. When Battlestar Moonrising was in Citadel mode, with all the different school ships stacked together, the holocore transformed the environment, giving colour to each object. When they had first boarded BM, two years ago, he had seen it in battle mode, in all its grey glory, a sight that had managed to depress the students right away. Sadly, he realised that he would miss these little things, once they sent him back to Earth.

'Hey,' said Faith, stopping suddenly. 'Isn't that Elian?'

'Yes, but-' said Morgana. 'Oh dear!' she said, sprinting ahead.

Julius stood staring at Elian, who was bent over a nullifying bin. 'What is she … Oh,' he said, realisation dawning on him.

Faith and Skye stayed where they were, unsure what to do.

Elian had obviously been sick, but thankfully she had reached the bin just in time.

Morgana was standing by her side, offering a napkin. When it was clear that Elian was feeling better, she accompanied her to the nearest bench. Only then the boys joined them.

'All right, Lieutenant?' asked Skye, sounding concerned.

Elian took a deep breath and, as the colour slowly returned to her cheeks, it was clear that she was. 'Much better,' she replied, with her usual brightness. 'Thank you guys.' Then she saw Julius, and her smile widened considerably. She had visited him with Kelly, after he had awakened from the stasis, but to see him out and about was obviously a sign of great progress. 'It's so good to see you back, Julius,' she said, squeezing his arm.

'It's good to be back,' replied Julius. 'But what about you? Have you eaten something funny?'

Elian took a few seconds before answering. It looked like she was trying to decide how much to say. 'Actually, it has been quite a regular thing the last couple of weeks. Mind you, I *am* eating all sorts of weird stuff.'

'Nothing can be weirder than what Skye here eats. Believe me,' said Faith, matter-of-factly.

Morgana nodded, then stopped and drew her hands up to her mouth. 'Omygodyouarepregnant!'

'I just caught the pregnant bit,' said Julius, perplexed. Then it hit him, and he added, 'Wait a minute; pregnant? *How?*'

Elian looked at him and grinned, her head tilted to one side. 'Really, Julius? How?'

'No, no, I didn't mean it like that!' he replied, blushing. 'I mean, pregnant? But … but that's great!'

'Yes, Elian!' Morgana said, jumping onto her seat. 'I'm *so* excited for you guys!'

'And how did Kelly take it?' asked Faith.

'He didn't …' she said, her cheeriness dampened.

'He doesn't know?' asked Morgana, perplexed.

'No, and I would ask you not to tell him.'

'Sure, but why?' asked Julius.

'He's been under a lot of stress lately, and his father has put him on standby for a big mission — you know how demanding Freja can be. He simply doesn't need the extra worry,' she answered.

The word "mission" evoked a painful feeling in Julius' heart. That kind of thing existed in his previous life, as he had come to think of the time before the stasis, and there would be no more trips on the Ahura Mazda for him, or battling against the Arneshians. He had played his part, but someone else would put an end to Salgoria's reign; someone that wasn't him.

'We'll keep your secret, Elian,' said Morgana.

'Thank you, guys,' she said. 'I need to go now. I have an ultrasound appointment.' She stood up. 'Take care, Skirts!'

'Bye!' replied Morgana, waving. When Elian disappeared inside the hospital, she was still looking in her direction, dreamily.

'What's up with you?' asked Skye.

'She's so cool,' said Morgana, in awe. 'I *absolutely* adore her.'

'Wow,' said Skye, 'I didn't know Kelly had competition.'

Morgana slapped him on the arm. 'Silly,' she said, beginning to walk.

The boys followed her, waiting to hear more.

'She's the kind of woman I want to be,' explained Morgana. 'She's a brilliant pilot, who lives on a spaceship; she's gutsy, clever and married to an adventurer! That's exactly what I want!'

That practically rules me out, thought Julius, his stomach closing a little. Powerless as he was, there was nothing he could offer her anymore. Better to start forgetting about it, and make things easier for himself later on.

They walked through the different sectors, passing shops that had slipped from Julius' memory. Students from the three schools were milling about in pairs or small groups. He caught snippets of conversations as they passed him by. The holo-games were on the minds of many, as always, followed by chats about new subjects or teachers. Occasionally they bumped into some of his classmates, who would stop him to shake his hand or pat him on the shoulder.

'Where are the Mizki Juniors?' asked Julius, suddenly noticing the lack of young students.

'They've sent them back,' answered Faith. 'All Juniors and Apprentices have returned to Zed to continue their training. Only seniors and Zed officers are here.'

'And the teachers?'

'Most of them have gone with them,' said Morgana. 'The Curia decided that we could stay and help the fighters out. We still do classes, mainly practical stuff with Clavel or Chan. The rest is through the network.'

Julius nodded. 'And what about Kaori?'

'My sister graduated in June,' continued Morgana. 'She's now here on active duties, and I must confess, I'm really pleased about that.'

When they finally reached the restaurant, it turned out to be a Brazilian churrascaria, where all sorts of barbecued meat was served. Skye waltzed in with the ease of a habitual client.

The owner, a tall man with dark curls, walked towards him with open arms. '*Boa tarde amigo*! *Tudo bem?*'

Skye embraced the man. '*Bem, obrigado! E você?*'

'*Bom!*'

'Rogerio,' said Skye, pointing at Julius, 'this is Julius.'

Rogerio embraced Julius, like a long lost brother. 'You don't need introduction, Hulius. I am honoured to meet you. Lunch is on me!'

'*Hermano!*' cried Skye, embracing the chef again, even happier.

Julius was rather stunned by the greeting he had just received. He had no idea there were people — besides Zed personnel — who had this kind of consideration for him. He was grateful, but at a loss for what to say.

Morgana, possibly aware of this, gently pushed him towards a wooden table in the corner.

'I see you haven't changed a bit,' said Julius to Skye, impressed by the never-ending relationship between his friend and the chefs of the universe.

'The more I live, the more I believe that chefs are truly inspired beings.'

'That means yes,' added Faith, pouring some yellow juice into four glasses. 'It's mango, by the way.'

'Cheers then,' said Julius. The liquid was fresh and naturally sweet. It tasted delicious. 'Well guys, I'm ready. Bring me up to speed. What happened to Arnesh?'

'Are you sure you want to talk about that?' asked Skye.

'Yeah, it's not a problem. I need to get on with things, you know,' said Julius, trying to sound casual.

Skye looked at the others, before carrying on. 'Well, like Freja told you, using the weapon on the planet *did* work. The Arneshians lost their Grey Arts and they were turned into regular humans. The Curio Maximus offered them the chance to start again on Earth-'

'Really?' Julius cut in.

'Roversi believes that it's the quickest way to heal the wounds,' explained Faith, sounding unconvinced.

'And did they accept?'

'Only a minority,' continued Skye. 'The rest decided to stay there, in their own homes, although Arnesh belongs to Earth now. The Curia agreed to that and we left them behind — without a single spacecraft, may I add.'

'Well, it's not like they lack the technology to survive in space, anyway,' observed Julius.

'Guess who else stayed behind: K'Ssander.'

'And they let him?' Julius was astonished. The boy was a treacherous person, who had shown no remorse for his actions. Julius recalled their last encounter, when he had tried to strangle Skye. If Kelly hadn't intervened when he had, Julius would have killed him.

'Apparently no one wanted the responsibility of keeping him on Earth or on Zed. His family was there, anyway.'

Julius nodded. 'So, what's the plan now?'

'We're looking for Salgoria,' answered Faith. 'Meantime, we've been doing a bit of exploration — charting routes, new planets, and the lot.'

'Tell him about your ship, Faith,' said Morgana.

'Of course!' said Julius, pleased. 'You won Pit-Stop Pete's competition.'

'You remember?' said Faith. 'She's under construction on Zed,' he said, sounding like a proud father. 'Pete sends me updates all the time, and pictures! He says it'll be one of the best ships he's ever built.'

'That's great. Really proud of you, Faith.'

Faith flashed his best grin.

'And are you still seeing Siena?'

'Yeah,' he replied, blushing.

'He's all loved up!' said Skye, nudging him.

'Oh shush!' Faith replied, but he was still grinning.

'And what about you, loverboy?' asked Julius, looking at Skye. 'Who are you gracing right now?'

'No one, actually. I'm in a in-between period.'

'Not even Valentina?' asked Julius, surprised.

'She left last year, you know, and went to work back on Zed — Colonial Affairs,' he explained. 'I do miss her though. She was a good laugh.'

'I'll tell you who was really lonesome when you went all sleeping beauty on us,' said Faith.

'For me? Who?'

'Isolde! She was inconsolable for a while.'

'And then what happened?'

'Skye consoled her.'

Julius burst out laughing, immediately joined by the other boys. Morgana couldn't refrain a giggle either and, as she headed to the toilet, she was properly laughing.

As the laughter subsided, Julius nodded in the direction of the toilets. 'And how is *she*?'

'She came to visit you every single day, mate' said Skye, lowering his voice.

'Worried sick, she was,' added Faith.

'Oh,' said Julius, surprised.

'And when she wasn't with you or in class,' continued Skye, 'she was pouring over the database, looking for a way to cure you.'

'Was she? And Maks had nothing to say about that?'

'Maks?' said Faith. 'She left him a few days after your stasis began.'

Julius didn't know what to say. It was good news all round, although he hadn't meant for her to worry so much. But, a cure? Surely that was just wishful thinking. At that moment, Morgana reappeared, so Julius refrained from asking any more questions about her. 'And how's Barth?'

'A menace, as always, but there's a twist,' answered Skye.

'What did he do?'

'He locked himself inside the Sim dating programme for a month,' explained Faith. 'Then one day, he walked up to Leanne North and asked her out.'

'No way!' cried Julius. Leanne was tall as a tree, and with all the finesse of a tank. 'What happened?'

'She punched him right on the nose — what you think?' said Faith, laughing madly. 'Then she picked him up and kissed him, right in front of everybody!'

'Good man,' said Julius, grinning. 'I didn't know he had it in him.'

'I know, right.' Faith went serious again. 'Look, we're sorry about Michael and Farrah. We saw what happened on the Heart.'

'You saw my brother betray me then?' asked Julius, his voice cold, but steady. He hadn't wanted to have this particular conversation today. He knew however, that he couldn't avoid it, not with the Skirts and, once done, they could all move on. 'Everyone on that ship lied to me. Ben had me wrapped around his finger all along. My brother was working with T'Rogon and the Arneshians behind my back. And Farrah … well, she didn't even have the guts to tell me the truth.'

'Do you miss her?' asked Faith.

Morgana shifted in her seat, which Julius noticed. It was an uncomfortable topic, but perhaps it was good for her to hear this. 'I've thought about her a lot since waking up, but it's different now — knowing who she really is, the fact that she ages five times faster than I do …' He stopped and shrugged his shoulders. 'The Farrah I knew doesn't exist anymore. All I want now is for Freja to find her … make sure she's all right.'

'He will — we will, Julius,' said Skye. 'Now that you're back, we will.'

'I don't think so, guys. In case you haven't noticed, I'm no longer wearing a uniform, I don't share your dorm and, last but not least, the only way I can move an object is if I actually push it with my hands. Why they're still keeping me here is beyond me.'

Skye and Faith didn't have an answer to that.

Morgana, on the other hand, had watched and listened carefully, as if there was something more going on in her mind than she was willing to share. 'Look, Julius,' she said, eventually, 'Freja doesn't do anything for no reason. He *wants* you here.'

Julius nodded, but didn't really believe her. As Rogerio began to bring their food over to the table Julius realised that, this time, not even Freja could fix him.

WHEN HOPE IS LOST

As November got underway, Julius was allowed to resume his gym sessions, accompanied by his own personal physio. The hospital was well equipped with exercise machines and, as each of them had a screen with a network link, he was able to catch up with the latest on the exploration missions of Moonrising and its crew. For all the distance travelled by Zed over the centuries, he was still astonished that they hadn't yet encountered any other species in the universe. It went against all odds, quite frankly. On the other hand, having to contend with the rotten half of his *own* race was challenging enough.

'Julius, you need to take a break now,' said Nurse Primula, entering the room.

'But I feel fine, honestly.'

'I can see that,' she observed, looking amused. 'Looks like you're trying to enter a bodybuilding competition.'

'What? No ... I just want to get back in shape,' he said, lowering the set of weights he was holding to the ground. 'Besides, what else *can* I do?'

'Read this: it'll exercise the muscle inside your skull,' she said, lifting up her palm-screen.

Julius opened his own PIP screen, and waited for the message to arrive. As he did so, he realised that at least *that* particular body augmentation would go back to Earth with him, as it didn't need any mind-skills to work. The only parting gift he would get from Zed. 'What is it?'

'I don't generally read someone else's mail, you know,' she replied, before leaving the gym.

Julius saw the new message blinking in his inbox, and pressed on it. When it opened, the name of Tijara's Master immediately caught his attention.

"McCoy, please report to the Grand Master's office today at midday. Take all your belongings with you. Master Cress."

'This is it,' said Julius, his heart sinking. 'Time to go home.' He felt tears mounting, but blinked hard and forced them back. He would not cry. He had nothing to be ashamed of. In fact, if Freja had any sense of honour, he would write his name in the history books of Zed. After all, when Julius had sacrificed his powers, he had done what only the great Marcus Tijara had done before him. The only difference was that Julius was still alive. Taking a deep breath, he grabbed his towel. He would shower first, and then call home while he packed. And, maybe afterwards, he would take a walk through New Satras, to look at it for the last time.

*

'Are you serious?' cried Rory from the other end of the vidscreen. He sounded surprised, but pleased.

Julius looked at his parents, Rory and Jenny McCoy, father and mother to both a White Child and a Nuarn, the most unlikely combination to come from any couple: one child with the same powerful mind-skills as those of Marcus Tijara and the other with all the technological skills of Clodagh Arnesh. And now they were enemies.

His folks had aged a fair amount in the last year, he noticed. Rory's hair had gone full grey, while Jenny's long, dark locks were now speckled with silver strands. 'Yes, I'm serious, although I'm not as thrilled as you are, if you can believe it.'

'Look, Julius,' said Rory, 'we know how hard this must be for you. But put yourself in our shoes. We spent last year thinking that we had lost both our sons for good. Now you're coming home, and that makes us the happiest people on Earth.'

Julius understood that perfectly well, but it didn't make it any easier.

'You'll be amazed when you get here,' said Jenny. 'The absence of humans has done wonders for the environment. The air is fresher and clearer, like never before. It is truly beautiful.'

'Sounds like fun,' said Julius.

'You'll see,' she continued, ignoring his sarcasm. Then, quietly, 'Any news of Michael?'

Julius was sorely tempted to tell them both about how their precious little son had betrayed them all, by helping to steal his own brother's power. But, when he looked at his mum and dad, he saw sadness, and a vague hope that maybe one day they would be reunited again with both their children, and he bit his lip. 'No news, sorry. We are looking, Mum. You'll be the first to know when we find him.'

Jenny replied confidently, 'Of course baby, I know. I guess he must be happy enough with his new friends then.'

Julius nodded, but it sounded distinctly like she was trying to convince herself.

'So, have you given any thought to a possible career?' asked Rory, changing the subject. 'Surely with your experience you could work at the Zed Test Centre.'

'As what — a receptionist?'

'Nonsense,' said Jenny. 'Everyone will know who you are and what you sacrificed for us. They'll look after you, you'll see.'

'I doubt it. Either way, I'd rather cut all ties with Zed, when I'm back. I was thinking more along the lines of joining a Shaolin monastery — you know, forget space ever existed and all that.'

'All right, Julius,' said Jenny crossing her arms in front of her. 'I see there's very little point in having this conversation with you at the moment. Let us think about that when you get here, shall we?'

'Yes, let's,' he replied, with a deep sigh. 'Gotta go now.'

'Goodbye son,' waved Rory. 'And let us know when you'll be arriving in Prague. Your Mum and I will take you for a little holiday.'

'Will do. Speak soon.'

Julius turned off the screen and grabbed a bag. At some point they had brought his belongings over to the hospital; Skye had packed them for him, at Cress' request, a year into his stasis. Since waking up, he had only worn his gym clothing, washing them at need, and hadn't bothered checking the bottom of the bag. He just assumed that Skye had found everything he owned. Between his clothes and the various microchips, he had enough to fill a large rucksack.

He left his room and headed towards the reception area. A blonde nurse was there, busy writing notes on her terminal. He looked around for Nurse Primula, but couldn't see her anywhere. *Shame*, he thought. He really wanted to thank her. *I'll try to find her in Tijara.* He took the lift to the ground floor and left the hospital. There was still one hour to kill before his meeting with Freja, so he headed straight for the Holographic sector. He refused to leave without saying goodbye to Mrs Mayflower.

As he walked, he made a point of observing everything around him: the bright colours of the shops' neon signs, the various enticing food smells from the restaurants and cafes, and even the little odd noises of the sliding doors and ventilation systems. He would miss all of it. Although his walk had purposely skirted around Rowan Park, where he had met Farrah for the first time, he now found himself staring at her parents' closed-down shop — *fake* parents, actually, as it had turned out. The empty windows of *Auld Oddities* stared blankly at him, like ghostly eyes. The place had been no more than a cover for Farrah's background and, now that she was gone, the Zed officers who had been posing as her mother and father had been reassigned to active duties elsewhere. He moved on, feeling as empty as the shop.

Eventually he reached the game arena, which was rather quiet. A small group of soldiers, who had been gathered on the steps, hurried away after checking the time. Julius wondered where they were going before looking greedily at their officer uniforms. They weren't too dissimilar from his old Tijaran one: jumper, combat trousers and boots. The main difference was the colour, from the students' navy to a deeper shade of blue, almost black. On the forearms they had a patch with their name and rank, while on their hearts, they displayed the symbol of their class. This lot had the design of a stylised Glove embroidered on the jumper, which told Julius they were fighters. After graduation, Morgana would receive the Cougar badge of the pilots, Faith the Tools of the Tinkerer for technicians and Skye would get the Globe, symbol of the politicians of the Curia. Julius would have been in line for the Star, the symbol of the captains, but now it would go to someone else, probably Isolde.

He forced these thoughts from his mind and headed for the booking kiosk. Soon however, he realised that the woman behind the glass was not Mrs Mayflower. *Great*, he thought. *Where is everyone today?*

As he approached, the woman saw him and opened the little window, smiling. 'I knew I would eventually see you,' she said.

'Did you?' he said, surprised.

'Mrs Mayflower knew you would wake up sooner or later, and that when you did, you would come straight here for a game with the Skirts. This is for you,' she said, rummaging through the objects in a small drawer. She picked up a microchip and handed it to Julius. 'She wanted me to give you this.'

Julius took it, a little surprised. 'Thanks. What is it?'

'It's a record of your entire gaming history, from your very first flight with the Skirts, to your Solo run. Even the Zed Toon game is in there.'

'This is brilliant,' he said, chuffed. 'Where is she? Can I see her?'

The woman became suddenly somber, her smile fading. 'Oh my ... Don't you know?'

Right then, even without his mind-reading abilities or the colourful auras he used to see around people, Julius knew that Mrs Mayflower was no longer among them and felt incredibly sad. 'When did she die?'

'Last April. She became ill around January, and they decided to move her back to Zed, hoping that her home would make her more comfortable. Unfortunately, she didn't last the spring.'

Julius nodded to her. 'Thank you,' he said, the cheerfulness her gift had brought him quickly forgotten. As he walked away, he wondered why the Skirts hadn't told him about her. Perhaps they didn't want to upset him, given what he was going through already. Either way, her loss was another marking of the end for Julius; the end of an era.

*

When he entered Freja's office, he wasn't surprised to see that Captain Kelly and Master Cress were also there; they had obviously come to say their goodbyes. He bowed to them and stood to attention, waiting to be told what to do.

Freja bowed briefly to him, then left his armchair and walked into an adjacent room, where three platforms stood empty. He stepped onto the middle one, with his back to the rest of the room. Julius had definitely seen a change in the Grand Master. His eyes were now harder and sterner, his stance more rigid and calculated. He wondered when this change had come about, and if he was partly responsible for it.

'Leave your bag by the door, McCoy,' said Cress.

Julius relaxed. Kelly gave him a friendly pat on the shoulder, for which he was grateful.

Cress checked his palm-screen, before looking at Freja. 'They are ready, Grand Master.'

Julius was starting to get curious now. *Ready for what?* he thought.

Cress pressed a few buttons on the wall, and a widescreen appeared in front of Freja. Julius gasped when he saw all the Mizki Seniors seated in rows, looking at them. He recognised a few familiar faces — Lopaka, Barth, Siena — although he couldn't see the Skirts, he knew that they were there as well. To the left and right of the screen, Zed officers came into view, puzzling Julius even more. Then all three platforms began to glow faintly, and soon the outer two were filled with the holographic forms of the GM of Sield Roland Kloister, and the GM of Tuala, Edwina Milson. The three leaders exchanged a quick bow, before facing forward, towards their audience. Suddenly, Julius realised that the Mizkis and the officers would soon be addressed by the holograms. Whatever this was, it looked official and important.

It was Freja who spoke first. 'Officers. Mizkis. You stand here today as testament that our war with the Arneshians still rages on. In the past months, we have been able to celebrate success, in the rescue of our people and the defeat of the Arneshian forces on their own home world.'

The audience murmured its approval enthusiastically. Julius found himself nodding involuntarily, mirroring the atmosphere in the Assembly Hall of Moonrising.

'Arneshians are like brothers to us,' continued Freja. 'Brothers who have turned their backs on their own family. They have been given countless opportunities to see the error of their ways and we were punished for our acts of compassion with treachery and betrayal,' said Freja, slamming his fist on the control panel in front of him, allowing his anger to surface. 'I don't know if we are alone in the universe or not, but should we *ever* meet someone, I don't want the Arneshians to represent the human race. I don't want them to speak for *me*!'

Julius began to feel the powerful effect of this speech, while open approval was spreading among the listeners. As Freja's voice grew louder, so did the assent of his people.

'There's only one human race — and *we* are it!'

Cheers erupted freely from the audience, from both Mizkis and officers alike.

'We stand here today,' he continued, motioning to the GMs to his left and right, 'to tell you that we are *done* waiting for the next time the Arneshians come at us. We have set a course for what was once our post, the Halls of Ahriman, and we shall reclaim it, like we did with planet Arnesh. The time has come to free the universe once and for all from the worst part of humanity. We are set on a path of destruction, and if history blames us for it, so be it!'

The cheers became wild applause, with cries of 'Zed, Zed, Zed'. Julius' hair stood on end, charged by the electric atmosphere, while his heart sank deeper, knowing that he would have no part in this.

'Zed: you have become the hunters!'

'So let it be!' all in the crowd cried back, now on their feet, clapping wildly.

Cress shut down the widescreen and, as Freja took leave of his colleagues, Julius knew he had to pick himself up. For everybody else, this had been the kind of speech that moves mountains, but to him it meant regret and anguish. Why had Freja brought him in to see this? It would have been kinder to just let him go.

'Sit down, McCoy,' said Freja, pointing at a chair in front of his desk.

Julius did so, while Cress and Kelly sat to either side of him.

'It took me more than a year to let go of my anger,' began the GM, looking straight at him. 'When you joined Zed, you became our hope for a better future, and you did not disappoint us. With your foolish stunt, you gave up everything you had, for Zed. And *if* your story concludes here, you have earned your place in history.'

At least he's being direct, thought Julius. He asked the GM, 'What do you mean "if", sir?' The question had escaped his mouth, before he even realised.

'I mean that we may still have one last card to play, McCoy.'

Julius felt the tiniest spark of hope kindling in his heart.

'We spent months trying to figure out a way to restore your mind-skills, but with no luck. We were at a deadlock when someone came to us with the only idea left unexplored: recovering Tijara's own crystal, the Heart he used way back. If that crystal could be found, then its powers *could* be transferred back to you.'

'Is it even possible?' asked Julius, his desperation forgotten. 'Who thought of this?'

Freja paused briefly, before answering. 'Miss Ruthier did.'

'Morgana?' Julius suddenly remembered that his friends had told him about her looking for a cure, only at the time it had sounded like wishful thinking. Now however, even Freja believed it was possible.

'Yes. Her determination to heal you led her to the solution before we did.'

'Where is this crystal now?' asked Julius eagerly.

'You've heard of the plan to retake the Halls. According to some, that's where the crystal was stored.'

'But I thought that the craft carrying the Heart, with Marcus and Clodagh Arnesh was destroyed. How did the crystal make it out of there?'

'We never really looked into it, as we had no need to do so, until recently. While watching the footage from that day, Miss Ruthier focused on the activities that went on outside the craft. She saw Clodagh's ship docking with the Heart, preceded by another ship. As you know she died with Marcus in the explosion, but not before the first vessel took off again, carrying someone — and *maybe* the crystal — to safety.'

'We don't know who that person was,' said Julius, 'but you believe they took the crystal to the Halls.'

'Correct,' said Freja. 'At the time, Ahriman was still under our control, and it was the safest place outside of Zed. Underneath the facilities, there was a maze of tunnels and caves, excavated to be used as a refuge in an emergency. By the time Arnesh took over the place, this underground area had been sealed off and, as far as we know, they never reopened it. If they did, however, we can be sure they didn't find the crystal, or they wouldn't have gone after you.'

Julius couldn't believe his ears. He had practically given up all hope, and now here was this news, turning his world the right way up again.

'You must understand that this is no guarantee of a happy ending,' said Freja somberly. 'There may be no crystal and, if there is, the transfer may not even be possible.

'I am aware of that, Grand Master,' he replied, trying to keep his voice steady. 'But really, it's not like I have a better alternative.'

Freja nodded. 'One last thing; are you finally ready to trust us? Or will we still to pass as some sort of enemy to you?'

He sounded hurt, and it made Julius blush. 'Yes, sir.'

Freja studied him for a while, before speaking again. 'We all need to prepare for this. In the meantime, you shall resume certain Grey Classes. Whatever happens, you will graduate with your classmates.'

Julius' eyes lit up. This went beyond his wildest expectations.

'Professor Chan and Professor Clavel will be expecting you, and Mr Miller told me that he could do with a roommate again.'

Julius couldn't believe his ears, but there was still something he needed to ask. 'Grand Master, what about Farrah and Michael?'

'I don't believe that Miss Hendricks has been hurt. When we find Salgoria, she will be there. As for your brother, don't forget that T'Rogon took the crystal with your powers. It is possible that they may have been given to Michael already.'

'Would they work on a Nuarn?' asked Julius. The thought that his mind-skills could be now residing inside his brother unsettled him.

'We don't know, McCoy, but the Arneshians are resourceful enough to make it happen. Don't dwell on this right now. You have far more pressing matters to attend to.'

Julius nodded.

'McCoy,' said Cress, 'head to your room. On the bed you'll find your new uniform. A copy of your timetable has also been sent to your PIP.'

Julius got up and bowed to them all. 'Thank you,' he said, feeling the emotion of the last hour twisting inside his stomach. He threw a quick glance at Kelly, who was looking at him, and smiling.

He ran along the corridor, amazed that he remembered exactly where to go. When he reached the dorm, he skidded to a halt in surprise; Skye, Faith and Morgana were waiting for him at the start of the corridor, wearing the biggest grins he had ever seen.

SPACEWALK

On Monday the 17th of November, Julius woke up with the 7 o'clock alarm. The first thing that came to his mind was, *Why have I set the alarm?* followed by the recollection that he would shortly be returning to Professor Clavel's classes. It was a thought so good that he gave himself a few more minutes beneath the warmth of his blanket, smiling contentedly at the day ahead. Skye was snoring lightly to his right — an old, familiar sound to Julius — only this time he didn't mind at all. Eventually he got up and, by the time he emerged from the shower, Skye was slowly waking from his slumber.

'I can't believe you're up before me, McCoy,' he said, groggily.

'I think I've had enough sleep to last me a lifetime,' Julius replied, beginning to dress. 'Hey, I wanted to ask you ...' said Skye, before trailing off.

'What is it?'

'How ... What does it feel like to be without ...'

Julius looked at him, puzzled; then his eyes grew wider as he realised what his friend was trying to ask. 'You mean without mind-skills?'

Skye nodded, looking slightly embarrassed.

'Physically, there's no difference really,' answered Julius, shrugging his shoulders. 'I don't feel any different. It's only when I try to use my powers to move something, or to send a message and nothing happens, that I remember they aren't there anymore.'

'I'm sorry, mate.'

'Yeah, same here.'

'But we have a plan, right?'

'That we do,' replied Julius, trying to sound convinced.

'Let's get you back into the swing of things then, starting with a good ol' breakfast.'

It was an invite that Julius accepted gladly and, as soon as Skye was washed and dressed, they headed for the mess hall.

The news that Julius would be rejoining some of the classes had already made its way around the Mizkis over the course of the past weekend, which meant that he could attend breakfast without too many questions — the curious stares came mainly from the 5MS students, who Julius didn't really know all that well. A few more of his classmates joined them at the long table that morning: Siena next to Faith, Isolde between Morgana and Skye, then Lopaka, Yuri and Gustavo. Barth and Leanne sat with them too, surprising Julius with how sweet they acted to each other — he really hadn't seen that one coming.

Freja's speech had quite obviously had a massive impact on everyone's morale. Between the prospect of bringing the reign of the Arneshians to an end, and the fact that, in less than one year they would all be graduating, the Mizkis were in high spirits. Seeing his friends so excited about their futures made Julius fully realised how much he wanted to be part of it, more than anything else. If there was even a remote chance that his powers could be restored, he would do all he could to make it happen.

At 08.50 the 6MS students left the canteen and headed for the hangar, following the usual illuminated lines on the walls that guided them to their selected destinations. The Mizkis had been told that today they would be learning to use spacesuits for the very first time, and not just in theory. In the hangar, they were directed toward a small door, which led into a vast room with a row of lockers on one side. Clavel was standing at the opposite end of the entrance and, as the Mizkis walked in, he raised seats from gaps in the floor with a sweeping gesture of his hands.

'Come on in and take a seat, please,' he said. When he saw Julius he grinned. 'A pleasure to have you back in class, Mr McCoy.'

'Great to be back, sir!'

The students hurried to their chairs, hushing each other excitedly until the room was silent.

'I can tell you're more eager than usual,' began Clavel, observing his students. 'I feel exactly the same, believe me.' Happy to have the attention of the class, the teacher pressed a few buttons on his palm screen, and a 3D image of a white, bulky spacesuit appeared, revolving in mid air above his position.

Julius recognised it as a model that he had seen during his History studies.

'A spacesuit,' began Clavel, 'is like your personal spacecraft, and it will protect you from the harsh space environment. Whenever you leave your ship, you'll do what we call an EVA — Extravehicular Activity. During such activity, you'll protect yourself by wearing an EMU — no Mr Liway, I don't mean the Australian bird.'

'Sorry ...' whispered Lopaka, who had been mimicking a chicken-like action.

'EMU stands for Extravehicular Mobility Unit,' resumed Clavel. 'Although our technology allows us to interact with space from the safety of our ships, human presence will always be needed out there, whether it be for fixing something or for building it.'

The 3D suit moved to the left and several different models appeared to its right. They varied in shape and colour, but it was obvious that they ranged from ancient to the more recent ones.

'As you can see, EMUs have changed much over the centuries. From those connected to the craft by a hose,' said Clavel, pointing at the first one, 'to others which gave much more freedom of movement, but with only a few hours of autonomy. These images of past suits show you much bulkier ones from today's slimmer models. Our technology has allowed us to compress all protective and insulating layers into a more compact material. Moreover, we have made use of force fields to give an ulterior protection to our astronauts, and to allow their mind-skills to be channeled through it. EMUs have not been used inside a Cougar for decades, due to the advances in craft technology, but also because of this.' Clavel removed a small button-like device from his pocket, and pinned it over his heart.

'Isn't that an Exoskin?' asked Skye.

'Close enough, Mr Miller,' answered Clavel. 'As you know, the Exoskin wraps your body within an energy field, which then turns into solid armour. The new EMUs have been created following the same principle, except they don't offer protection from weapons-fire. Watch.' He touched the device and a layer of energy crackled into life around his body, from head to toe, before solidifying into a layered, dark silver suit.

Julius saw immediately that it was thicker than a regular Exoskin, but much lighter than an old fashioned suit. The helmet was nothing like the big, early ones, but thinner, like a cap. The gap for the face was covered by a face-shield. All in all, it reminded Julius of a thick, shiny wetsuit, with no part of the body left exposed.

Clavel moved around the students, showing them the suit up close. He was able to walk smoothly enough, his movements not too clumsy. When he reached the back of the room, he pressed the button again and the suit vanished, with the usual static, crackling sound.

'How do we breathe, sir?' asked Isolde.

'In essence, photosynthesis without solar light. The air trapped within the suit is all you'll ever need in terms of quantity, even for a week-long mission. You breathe in the oxygen, and breathe out CO_2. At the same time the field of the suit does the reverse, providing you with oxygen.'

'Awesome!' commented Faith.

'To communicate,' continued Clavel, 'you have telepathy. To move through space, you use your telekinetic skills, and whenever you see an object floating around you, use it like a trampoline by pushing yourself away from it. Or, if it's heavy enough, you could even try pulling it, as that will slowly move you towards it. In case of emergency, you can even use each other like stepping stones, to progress further.'

Julius felt suddenly worried. How was he supposed to do that without mind-skills?

'If these two should fail, for whatever reason,' added the teacher right on cue, 'then you'll find a microphone at the bottom of the face-shield, and thrusters in your belt.' As he said this, he moved over to one of the lockers, and picked up what looked like a utility belt. 'This is one of the two separate parts of your suit. As well as the thrusters, it will carry whatever tools you need on your walk, and it has a hook too, in case you need to secure yourself onto another object. The second one,' he said, leaning into the locker again, 'is the drink-bag. It's rather flat, so you can strap it around your lower back, pass the tube up and over your shoulder and fix it next to your mouth.'

It seemed pretty straightforward to Julius, who at this point was just itching to try it.

Professor Clavel asked the Mizkis to go to the lockers and retrieve a drink-bag and a belt each, before showing them how to fix them over their clothing. He spent a little more time with Julius, explaining to him the most effective ways to use his thrusters. 'Skirts, I want you to guide Mr McCoy out with your minds.' Then, to Julius, 'Use your thrusters only once you're out there.'

'Will do, sir,' answered Faith.

When Clavel was satisfied that his students were all ready to go, he made them line up in two rows, in front of the large airlock. 'Today is all about getting comfortable in your EMUs and learning to move in null-gravity, but don't go too far, understood?'

'Yes, Sir!'

'Very well, Mizkis. Suit up.'

A series of deep buzzing noises filled the room as they each did as instructed.

Julius felt a tingle as his body was wrapped in the insulating layers, and the shield closed gently over his face. He breathed deeply and slowly, relaxing as the fresh air hit his lungs, then adjusted the belt, so that it was sitting comfortably on his hips. He was thrilled at being given the chance to add EVA to the list of his experiences in space; a chance that may have never happened hadn't been for Morgana.

'Computer, open airlock one,' requested Clavel.

'Airlock one opening,' the computer confirmed.

The wide metal wall began to slide slowly upwards, replaced by the thin shield that kept the room pressurised.

Julius stared at that emptiness with the greed of a man who had been deprived of his dream for too long.

'Ready, Julius?' called Faith.

He nodded.

Faith began to rise upwards in a straight line. Once he had gathered some momentum, he locked his eyes on Julius and pulled with his mind.

Julius' feet left the ground and, as he was led through the membrane and out of the airlock, he felt the weight leaving his body, as they abandoned the gravity of Moonrising. Faith moved away from the metal body of the battlestar, and Julius felt an unexpected twinge of fear creeping over him — without telepathy he wasn't sure he could feel too safe by himself. What if he got lost and out of range from the scanners? He turned around to look at the ship and gasped: it was positively gigantic. He started to think that, of all the times he had been out in space, this was the one that really put things into perspective. Humans were so small, so incidental in the grand scheme of things, and yet the spaceship floating up ahead told a different story. For hundreds of years, humans had transformed their planet so as to suit mankind, and when they couldn't alter an environment — like space — they had found ways of living in it by building their spaceships. The universe had existed for billions of years; how would the human race compare? By experience, Julius thought it was a miracle they were still around, given their history of wars and genocides. Lost in these thoughts, he began to notice that he was moving in a very strange, back and forth manner. It took him a few seconds to realise that Faith, to his side, was causing this. 'I'm not a yo-yo, you know?' he said into his mike.

'I couldn't resist!' he laughed. 'A little payback for old time's sake.'

'I don't think this suit deals well with vomit, Faith, and I'd rather not test it out here.'

'Oh, all right! You're no fun,' he said, lying on his back and moving his arms as if he was swimming. 'I don't even need me legs! Isn't that grand?'

Skye and Morgana came to join them just then.

'Look guys!' cried Faith, propelling himself forward, and twirling as he went.

Julius and Morgana couldn't remain serious for long, as Faith's laughter was rather contagious.

'I'm gonna retrieve the dolphin there, before we lose him to a black hole,' said Skye heading in Faith's direction. 'Morgana, stay with Julius, will you?'

'Roger,' she said, smiling. 'Julius, give me your hand,' she said, moving forward. Julius let her grab his right hand, wondering what she had in mind.

'Try to lie down, like this,' she said. She slowly stretched her body, until it was like she was floating on water.

Julius did the same, using her hand to steady himself. 'Are we stargazing?'

'Yes,' she giggled. 'I can't think of a better place for it.'

Julius turned to look at her. He could see the awe in her eyes, as she held her free hand up, her fingers tentatively reaching out to the empty space before her. She was so beautiful. 'Morgana,' he began, on impulse.

'What is it?' she asked.

'I wouldn't be here right now if it wasn't for you. Freja told me how you came up with a plan. Even if it doesn't work … I just wanted to thank you.'

She squeezed his hand in reply. 'Whatever Freja may have told you the day you came back from Arnesh, everything you've done since joining Zed, you did for us, for me, for Earth. You're no fool, Julius, but incredibly selfless.'

Julius could have sworn she was blushing under the pale light of the stars. Right then, he wanted to turn over and hold her in his arms, but she slyly drifted away, leaving him alone with her words.

Shortly afterwards, Skye and Faith returned, and together they kept an eye on Julius while he tried out his thrusters. Eventually, Clavel gathered them all to him, to observe their progress in the basic manoeuvres. Only once he was satisfied that everyone knew how to move in all directions and spin effectively, did he allow them to return to base.

Inside the airlock the Mizkis made two surprising discoveries: using an EMU made them sweat quite profusely, and their legs felt like rubber when going from null to full gravity. Clavel allowed them to sit on the floor for a while, until they were ready to go for a wash.

'Julius, we'll meet you at lunch, mate,' said Faith, heading out of the shower room. 'We need to go to a Twist class.'

'All right,' he replied from his cubicle, trying his best not to sound disappointed. 'I'll see you there.'

When the last classmate had left, Julius dried off, thinking that maybe he could go back to the gym in the afternoon, since there were no more Grey Classes for that day. He grabbed his bag and made to leave. As he arrived at the door, he heard two familiar voices coming from the adjacent corridor — Siena and Morgana — and he stopped where he was.

'Did you tell him?' asked Siena.

'There's nothing to tell,' answered Morgana.

'Are you sure? Because, from where I stand, I see a whole different story.'

Julius moved closer to the door, as quietly as possible.

'I remember picking you up from sickbay every night,' continued Siena, 'and handing you hankies when you couldn't stop crying because you thought he would never wake up.'

Julius froze, realising he was the subject of their chat.

'He's my best friend; of course I was worried,' replied Morgana. 'Besides … someone else is still in his heart.'

'Farrah, you mean?' she asked, sounding surprised.

'Who else?'

'Two years ago, maybe; now, I'm not so sure.'

'How do you know that?'

'Apart from the fact that she's currently twice his age and will be fifty in two years' time, she's just not a possibility.'

'What do you mean?' asked Morgana.

Yes, what do you mean, Siena? thought Julius, leaning in.

'Think about it; you started to go out with Maks, *then* she came along and now she's not there anymore.'

'So what you're saying is that I should be second best.'

'Wake up, girl; I'm saying *she* was.'

That statement was met with silence, followed by a shuffling of feet and the opening and closing of a door. Julius remained where he was. The way Siena spoke, it sounded like Morgana might be interested in him too. Wasn't Siena right, though? Hadn't Julius started to have feelings for Morgana, even before Maks and Farrah had come along? Julius felt his stomach closing. Even if — and it was a *big* if — Morgana was interested in him, there was nothing he could offer her now, not without his powers. Without a career of his own, and no access to Zed or its colonies, Morgana would not be able to pursue her dream of becoming a pilot. If she stayed with him, she risked being sent home, back to Earth. He knew she would never want that. Her admiration for Elian's life, married to her dream man and to her dream job all in one neat package, was what she wanted, and Julius couldn't give her that. He would not be the one to take that away from her either. If he couldn't get his powers back, he would just have to let her go forever.

*

Julius had two full weeks of lessons with Clavel and Chan. Although Professor Farshid had asked permission to have him back in Spaceship Management, Freja hadn't allowed it, deciding that it was slightly premature. He also wanted Julius to prioritise getting his body space, and combat, ready. In line with this, his new timetable saw him spending his mornings with Clavel, wearing his EMU or practicing driving a sky-jet, and the afternoons with Chan, who had devised a proper fitness regime for Julius to follow, even when he was busy teaching a class. To make up for the lack of mind-skills and the inability to practice mind-katas, Chan had introduced him to more traditional forms of martial arts, something that Julius was enjoying very much. Freja hadn't left anything to chance: assuming they would find the crystal, they didn't know how Julius' body would react. To minimise the risks, the Grand Masters had Dr Walliser create a special diet for him, so that his immune system would also be healthy and strong.

With some sort of routine back in his life, Julius began to feel useful again and, when his classmates left him to go to a different lesson, he was no longer disappointed, but kept busy working towards a clear goal. Thanks to all these preparations, he felt the best he had ever been. He still couldn't shake off a slight sense of uneasiness, due to the uncertainty surrounding their mission, but he pushed that back into the recesses of his mind whenever it threatened to surface and distract him.

At the start of December, they finally reached the constellation where the Halls of Ahriman were located, and Moonrising began the preparations for landing, amidst the excitement of its passengers.

THE HALLS OF AHRIMAN

Freja and Cress had spent the entire morning of Thursday the 4th of December in the ready room of Tijara looking over the reports that had come back from the probes. The Halls were built on the surface of a small planet called Funesto, which was not human friendly — its atmosphere was quite poisonous in fact, and EMUs were required at all times when going outside the main complex. From the start, it had served several functions for Zed, but primarily that of star-shipyard and research base. The little planet was quite unremarkable, except for being rich in Strullium, the most important metal in the making of core engine parts. Freja hadn't forgotten that, and it was his intention to replenish Moonrising's stock and to also fill extra loads to send back to Zed.

'Where should we look for the crystal, Carlos?' asked Cress, looking at a blueprint of Ahriman's main building.

'Kloister has sent us a map of the foundations of the Halls,' replied Freja, opening a new file. 'He found it in the Tijaran archives.'

'Why down there?'

'At the time of Marcus' death, this place had just opened for business,' explained Freja. Conscious of the presence of Strullium, our people began to excavate long tunnels and caves, perhaps with a view to expanding underground. Then Marcus used the Heart on the Arneshians, putting them out of the game for a long time, as you know. When they regrouped, the first thing they did was to take over the Halls. Tijara's followers fought to defend the facility, but they lost. However, before giving up and retreating, the access to the underground tunnels was sealed off, like the records state.'

'And you think that the crystal could be down there.'

'Yes, I do. It would have been the most secure place on Funesto. Besides, the Arneshians have occupied Ahriman for centuries now, and found nothing, or we wouldn't be having this conversation.'

Cress nodded. 'All right then, where should we-'

The door slid open suddenly and Kelly entered the ready room. 'Sorry to interrupt, but we have company.'

Freja watched his son activate his screen palm and select the projector mode. As a series of pictures scrolled over it, Cress' expression grew darker.

'When were these taken?' asked Freja somberly.

'In the last twenty minutes,' answered Kelly, 'using the spy-drones of the Ahura Mazda.'

Freja stood up and walked closer to the screen. In one picture, the western courtyard of Ahriman was bustling with people; in another, a group of men were clearly excavating the ground of one of the gardens. 'They're trying to reach the caves,' he said, almost to himself.

'Could they be after Strullium?' asked Cress.

'I don't think so,' answered Kelly, magnifying a new picture. 'Look at this.'

Freja's brow knotted. The picture showed Ambassador T'Rogon and Ben Hastings deep in conversation, surrounded by diggers.

'They're here for the crystal,' said Kelly. 'I have no doubt about it.'

Freja nodded. 'I agree. I don't know how they found out, but we must find it before they do.'

'We still can,' said Kelly. 'They don't know we're here.'

Freja turned to Cress, 'The Mizkis must be informed of the situation. We will set up camp at the foot of the eastern plateau and enter the tunnels through the Seffira Cave. If we work fast and quietly, we should reach the centre before they do.'

'What about McCoy?' asked Kelly.

'The presence of Hastings could upset him. Besides, if we are treating him like any of the other students, he only needs to know that the Arneshians are here. Nathan, I want a protocol ready to be sent out when excavation begins. Mizkis and officers will be involved in the mining of Strullium, but we need to make sure that if any of them find the crystal, we know about it.'

'That's easy enough. We have the composition of the actual crystal container, left by Marcus himself, and we can calibrate their PIP and screen palm chips to trigger an alarm as soon as they get close to it.'

'I want the best software designer on this, Nathan. You know as much as I do how important this crystal is.'

'It'll be ready for download by tomorrow,' he said.

'Assemble the Mizkis then, and let's get going.'

*

'How many Arneshians are we talking about, sir?' asked Julius, the surprise clear on his face. Professor Clavel had gathered the 6MS students in his classroom on Friday morning for the briefing and was now showing them the pictures that Captain Kelly had taken, bar the one with T'Rogon and Hastings.

'Scanners have revealed a small fleet, about 500 strong. Most of them are Arneshians who didn't get caught in the blast of the Heart, but there are also some from the new powerless group — incidentally, we're calling them Numans: new humans.'

'Why are they here?' asked Morgana, voicing everyone's question.

Julius reached Freja's conclusion pretty quickly, and his heart sunk: the Arneshians must also be after the crystal; there was no doubt in his mind. What he wondered though, was if Clavel would tell his classmates about Zed's main purpose for coming to the Halls.

'For the same reasons we are, Miss Ruthier,' answered Clavel. He selected another image, which showed a rock with small lilac crystals and blue veins running across its surface.

'That's pretty,' said Leanne. 'What is it?'

'It's Strullium,' answered Faith. 'I've worked with the stuff before, in Professor de Boer's class.'

'That is correct, Mr Shanigan. We mine it for the construction of core engines and we are counting on stocking up before leaving the Halls. Mizkis and officers will be in charge of extraction, so I'd advise you to refresh your memory on how to use the appropriate tools.'

Skye leaned over to Julius. 'Don't worry,' he whispered, 'I'll teach you once we get there.'

Julius nodded.

'We are also looking for something else,' said Clavel. 'There are many crystals present under Funesto. Some of them have healing properties, and we strongly believe that one of these may be able to restore Julius' powers.'

'That would be brilliant!' cried Barth.

Ferenc and Lopaka patted Julius on the shoulder, while others let out hollers of approval.

Julius blushed against his will at this reaction of solidarity amongst his classmates. He also noticed how Clavel hadn't revealed the true nature of the crystal, which he thought was a wise idea.

'Indeed, Mr Smit. Therefore, before we begin operations, your PIP will receive an update — an alarm software, triggered by the vicinity of these special crystals.'

'Only an update?' asked Faith eagerly. 'So me body isn't going to be augmented this year?'

Body augmentations were a regular occurrence in this line of work, and Faith had never been too keen on them, especially because of his own disability, which already required him to wear the hovering metal frame around his waist.

'It's still early, Shanigan,' cried Manuel Valdez from the back, accompanied by a few laughs.

'Don't I know,' he replied, knocking loudly on the side of his metallic skirt.

A new picture replaced the previous one, and everyone hushed.

'This is a map of the land adjacent to Ahriman. We land here,' said Clavel, pointing to an area beside a protruding ridge. 'It's called the Seffira Cave; we can set up camp just outside it. The cave itself has a disused conduit leading into the tunnels. Once it's reopened, the ore will come up from there, into our storks and back to Moonrising. We'll try to be out of their scanner's range for as long as possible, but there's no guarantee this will work.'

'Surely they won't attack us,' said Siena. 'We outnumber and outpower them.'

'Let them try,' replied Leanne, slamming her fist into her open palm.

'No, I don't think they will,' volunteered Clavel. 'Still, better safe than sorry. The fleet will be on standby as a precaution, while we carry out our work. Which leads us to the next point … you have one hour to pack your bags. Report to Tijara's hangar at noon. Dismissed.'

Julius left the briefing with mixed emotions: he was excited at the prospect of finding Tijara's crystal, but also worried that the Arneshians may find it first. He followed Skye back to their room, and began to stuff clothes into his rucksack, plus his usual handful of chips containing books and music. He picked up a tiny chip with "Hits 2858" and grimaced. 'Skye, have you got anything recent to give me?' he asked.

'Got plenty, mate. The last two years have been pretty decent actually. There's this new band back home, called Memories of Pluto, and they hit those chords something fierce.'

'Sounds good to me,' he said, thinking about how a good soundtrack always made his workouts go faster.

With their bags packed, they collected Faith on the way and headed for the hanger. They were early, but the place was filling up fast with the students and officers assigned to the mission. Captain Foster was directing the Mizki Seniors towards a desk, so the boys made their way there.

'Press your thumb on the sign-in sheet and collect your EMU for the mission,' cried Foster over their heads.

'I have never seen that man smile in five years,' whispered Faith, as he moved forward in the line. 'How does he do it?'

'It's 'cause he has to look at your ugly face every day,' answered Skye smartly.

Faith turned, zoomed up into the air and then swiftly down, landing his elbow on Skye's right shoulder, flooring him, bag and all. 'Revenge!' he cried.

They were laughing so much that they didn't see Foster leaning over them; they were only aware when he grabbed them by the scruffs of their necks and pulled them up onto their tiptoes. Skye remained perched where he was but Faith's skirt lifted him upwards, above the crowd, until he became lodged between two beams.

'McCoy!' barked Foster.

'Yes, sir!' answered Julius, standing to attention.

'Retrieve the Irish pest — that's an order!' He turned to Skye. 'Miller, give me twenty, right here.'

Skye obeyed and began a quick series of push-ups, accompanied by the curious looks and giggles of officers and Mizkis alike.

Morgana and Siena arrived just as Julius was jumping up and down, trying to grab the bottom of Faith's skirt.

'What are you two doing?' asked Morgana, trying not to laugh.

'I'm trying … to … retrieve him …' huffed Julius. 'But, without powers, it's kinda hard.'

'Let me,' said Siena, stepping in. She locked her eyes on Faith and, in a few seconds he was free and landed by her side. 'How did you even get up there?' she asked him, brushing some dust off his uniform.

'Just Foster acting like a girl having her period,' blurted out Faith.

Siena's tenderness gave way to an icy stare, while Julius face-palmed himself.

'I … I didn't mean it like that, I swear! You're nothing like him!' implored Faith.

Five seconds later he was stuck between the beams again, and Julius had to wait for Skye to get him back down.

Eventually, the 6MSs were all kitted up and ready to board the Storks. Foster sent them out in groups of four, as the crafts were half filled with the equipment they would need to set up camp.

Julius, Lopaka, Skye and Faith were transporting food crates to the landing spot Clavel had assigned them.

'Touchdown,' said Faith, landing the Stork with ease. 'Suit up, guys.'

Julius touched his EMU button and the heavy layers wrapped around his body instantly. He touched it once more to activate his helmet, before giving them the thumbs-up.

Faith made sure that everyone was ready before opening the hatch.

Julius stepped outside, shielding his eyes from the intense sunlight. After months in the darkness of stasis and several more under artificial lighting, getting used to the real thing again would definitely take some time. 'A desert … who would have thought?'

he said, observing the sandy plains, which were framed by angular hills of red rocks. The entrance to Seffira Cave was clearly visible from their position, a black, yawning mouth that opened out over the sands. Slowly, the other Storks started to land and their occupants poured out of the hatches.

'Come on, let's start unloading,' said Lopaka.

Julius and Skye grabbed the first crate by the door and carried it to a spot outside, as directed by one of the older officers. Although Skye could have done this with his mind, he instead physically helped to carry it, a gesture that Julius appreciated. They were done in ten minutes and, with their Stork now empty, they were sent back to Moonrising. At 14.00 Faith landed on Funesto for the last of their trips. Julius and Skye grabbed the final load and headed for the gathering point.

'I hope you're not tired already, Mizkis,' said Professor Clavel. 'This mission is all about the sweat of your brow, believe me.'

'Professor Chan will be happy,' said Julius, the heat rising uncomfortably inside his suit.

'I am indeed,' said Professor Chan, appearing suddenly from the mouth of the cave. 'Think of it as extra training.'

Julius, as always, welcomed the physical exercise, since it was the only thing he could actually do, apart from reading and watching the Space Channel or the games on Satras.

'Ah, good,' said Clavel, pointing west. 'The camp has arrived.'

Julius turned to look and saw several students carrying cubic boxes the size of footballs. Professor Morales was coordinating them, and moved from one to another, getting them to position their loads at exact locations. From where he was standing, Julius couldn't see any specific pattern, but assumed that there must be one. Besides, he wasn't particularly focusing on that just then. His eyes had just caught Morgana, advancing slowly through the desert haze, the EMU suit fitting her body like a glove. The shiny material of the suit made her seem like some beautiful mirage, with the reflection of the red sands and blue sky shimmering over her body.

'Ahriman to Julius,' said Skye, grinning. 'Do you copy?'

'Huh? What?' he murmured, snapping out of it.

'I see some things haven't changed,' Skye commented merrily.

Julius shrugged his shoulders and said nothing.

'Place your boxes on the floor, please,' called Morales. 'Then step well back.'

Morgana retreated to Julius' side, followed by Siena and Leanne. They all watched as Morales activated her palm-screen and typed something on it.

'There!' she said, pushing one last button.

There was a loud popping sound as each box suddenly inflated into a series of large, igloo-shaped tents. Each one of them was the colour of the desert and, as they touched, they linked up to each other, as if their sides had merged, like human cells would do. Some of the igloos were much wider than the rest, so creating larger spaces.

'It's like a giant anthill-stroke-beehive,' said Faith, astonished.

'Pretty much,' said Morales. 'They come in all sizes — handy for camping too. And now for the last touch …'

With a sharp buzz, a protective shield sprung up from each of the boxes, and merged together to form a dome above the camp. Immediately, groups of officers began to file in, carrying crates of various shapes and sizes.

'6MS, grab your bags and go through the main entrance,' called Chan, waving the students inside.

Julius was just about to do this when he noticed Chan whispering something in Morales' ear. She giggled, blushed and briefly placed one hand in his, before moving away again. There was no mistaking the intimacy of the gesture. *Good on you*, thought Julius, grinning. It was a memory from before his stasis but, now that he thought about it, he clearly recalled Chan and Morales dancing around each other. He wondered which one of them had taken the plunge first and if they would have to keep their relationship a secret, like Kelly and Elian did. Either way, in the midst of all the fighting, it was a good thing to see. He stepped through the invisible shield covering the main entrance, aware of the strange sensation of its energy field seeping into his muscles for just a second, before he was inside and free to deactivate his EMU.

'This is pretty cool,' said Skye as he entered, tapping the gummy floor with one foot. He moved over to a directory screen, and typed in "6MS DORMS". 'There they are,' he said, pointing at a point on the map that was lit up in red. 'So we walk straight up to the pop-up bar-'

'We have a bar?' asked Lopaka, suddenly interested.

'Then left, until we reach the blue lounge,' continued Skye. 'From there it's left again for the boys and right for the girls.'

They headed there together, looking around them in amazement as they went. For Julius the enjoyment of this all was even greater — in his new outlook, he saw everything related to life in space as an unexpected gift. They walked through what would soon be the bar, where a couple of officers were assembling a long counter, accompanied by the eager cheers of several passing students. Someone had brought some furniture in — small tables, chairs and some speakers. The Mizkis voiced their appreciation all the way through to the lounge, where they split and headed to their respective corridors.

Julius stopped outside an odd-looking opening. There was no door as such, but he clearly couldn't see through it. He pressed his finger forward and instantly realised that there was a force field across the opening. As soon as he touched it, the field shone green and dissolved. 'I guess this is my room then,' he said, walking in. 'Skye, you're in here too.'

Skye followed him inside, staring in puzzlement at the empty floor. 'Where are we supposed to sleep?'

'In here,' said a voice from the entrance.

Julius turned and found himself staring at a familiar face. 'Docherty! What are you doing here?'

'It's good to see you too!' he said, throwing a couple of sleeping bags into the centre of the room.

Docherty had graduated three years earlier and was now sporting an officer uniform with the Star badge on his chest. He looked just as Julius remembered him, tall and jovial.

'Sorry,' said Julius, stretching his hand forward. 'It's good to see you again, Bernard.'

'Likewise,' replied Docherty, shaking his hand. 'Miller,' he added, nodding to Skye.

Skye nodded back, then grabbed the sleeping bags and made himself busy, giving them some privacy.

'I thought you were heading for the Curia,' said Julius, pointing at his badge.

'So did I, but something happened: I met someone, so …'

Him too, thought Julius, with a silent groan. It didn't surprise him though, since girls had always flocked to him on account of his charisma and good nature.

'She's a heck of a pilot,' continued Docherty, 'and I wanted to work with her.'

'That's great, man, seriously.'

'Hey look,' he added in a lower voice, 'I wanted to tell you that I'll do everything in my power to find those healing crystals. What you did for us, it's worth more than all the Solo scores in the world.'

Julius was speechless for a moment. He had always thought that Docherty was a decent man — a gracious winner, as he had described him once — but this was different: Bernard was showing personal gratitude for what Julius had done. Coming from the former Solo champion, it meant a lot to him. 'Thanks, man,' he replied.

At that moment, Morgana appeared around the corridor. When she saw Bernard she grinned and walked over. He passed his arm around her shoulder and gave her a quick squeeze.

Julius' confusion at this scene became panic as the idea that she could be the reason for Bernard's change of career popped into his mind.

'Julius,' said Morgana, excitedly, 'I forgot to tell you about this!'

Nononono, please no! he thought.

'Kaori and Bernard got together last summer!'

THANKYOU THANKYOU THANKYOU! he shouted in his mind.

Bernard smiled and sunk his hands into his pockets. 'Well, I'm gonna finish handing out these sleeping bags. Meantime, don't use the nullifying toilets at the end of the corridor: they're not working yet and the techs are trying to fix them.'

'Gross,' said Morgana, scrunching up her nose. 'Anyway, Morales wants us to finish setting up some of the rooms. Let's go guys. Bye Bernard!' With that, she spun on her heels, her EMU sending reflections of light every which way, and headed back toward the blue lounge.

Julius stared at her for a little longer than necessary, until a polite, 'Ahem' from Docherty made him turn.

'I'll be off then,' he said, with a cheeky grin. 'See you around, McCoy.'

'Later,' he replied, as Bernard moved on to the next room. He really needed to control himself more. What if Docherty went back to Kaori and mentioned about how Julius was ogling her sister? He didn't even want to think about that.

When he stepped back into the room, Skye had already opened their sleeping bags, only they looked nothing like the ones he had used many times before, whilst camping in Scotland, all those years ago. These had a three feet-thick mattresses attached to them, and were wider than usual.

'Bernard is going out with Kaori,' he told Skye, as he tested the softness of his bed. 'Did everyone catch a love bug while I was asleep?'

'You've just got some catching up to do, mate,' he replied.

'Not in a hurry here.'

'Then let's get back to work. Your time will come.'

Julius shrugged his shoulders and followed Skye out of the room.

For the rest of the day, the Mizkis helped with the setup of the camp, by partitioning spaces, carrying crates and boxes into the right areas and checking that all entrances and exits were sealed properly, in case of a shield failure. By the time they finished it was well past nine in the evening, and they were all released for dinner. Julius slept well that night, the thought of the crystal keeping him focused on the mission they would soon be starting.

*

On Saturday morning, Professor Clavel gathered all the Mizki Seniors into the main lounge and split them into small groups of eight. 'Before you head out,' he said, 'stop by Operations to get the updated software for your PIPs. As I mentioned, it contains an alarm system, which is triggered by the vicinity of the special healing crystals. A map of the tunnels and coordinates for where you need to go has been sent to you this morning. You'll find it in your inbox. Let's go, Mizkis.'

Julius followed his group to Ops, where he filed in a queue for the downloader. He remembered using one of them on the Gea One, but these models were smaller and more modern, even though they still looked like hand dryers. When it was his turn, he stepped up to the machine and placed the PIP chip embedded in his left hand under the sensor, walking on once he heard the beeping noise to signal it was finished. He moved over to a corner of the room, and waited for his group to gather. Skye, Faith, Morgana, Siena, Isolde, Lopaka and George Lowet joined him shortly afterwards, one after the other, and together they headed back through the lounge, where they took the corridor that led to the Seffira Cave. Two storage rooms sat off to the left and right, soon to be filled with Strullium.

The tunnel ended in a transparent membrane, positioned well inside the cave mouth. From the threshold, Julius could see several spotlights fixed onto the rocks beyond, which made the area very bright.

Captain Foster was waiting by the exit. 'You'll need to suit up from here to the entrance of the Halls, which looks exactly like this one. Let's move out.'

Julius activated his EMU and stepped through the jelly-like membrane. He followed the row of lights all along the path, until he reached the gate. Once there, he stepped delicately through it and found Professor Chan waiting on the other side.

'You can remove your suit now,' said the teacher.

Julius did so and, as soon as the rest of the group joined him, Chan sent them down the left tunnel. Ahriman's atmosphere was quite stifling, but that didn't prevent Julius from walking briskly along, eagerly examining the rocky walls to either side, looking for any trace of crystals. A few minutes later he arrived in a large cave, with three more tunnels branching off at odd angles. His PIP map confirmed that this was the sector they were supposed to work in, so he stopped and began to remove his jumper.

'This is far too hot,' said Lopaka, following his example. 'As soon as we get a break I'm going to change into shorts, or I'll pass out.'

'Well,' began Julius, 'we have three caves — four with this one.'

'Two in each cave then,' proposed Faith.

'All right,' said Lopaka. 'George, let's head for the next one.

Skye grabbed Julius and walked toward the middle tunnel. Morgana and Isolde took the last remaining cave, while Faith and Siena stayed and set to work in the main chamber.

'Look,' said Skye pointing at the floor of their cave. 'Santa's been here.'

A bunch of tools had been left there for them. There were brushes, scalpels, hammers and spades, all neatly arranged by size, plus several L shaped, silver coloured devices and at least twenty containers, each the size of footballs, with extraction nozzles sticking out of their tops. Four spotlights had been fitted, already switched on, illuminating the entire room and giving off dazzling blue reflections wherever they lit the veins of Strullium.

Julius passed his fingers over the metal; it felt cold and smooth to the touch. 'How are we supposed to remove this stuff from the walls again?'

In reply, Skye grabbed one of the devices from the floor and held it close to the vein. 'It's a type of blowtorch,' he explained. 'They taught us how to use it last year.' He pressed the ON button and a small flame ignited at the tip of the horizontal bar. Skye brought it close to the rock face and, a few seconds later, the blue metal began to melt and slowly slide down. 'Quick, bring one of those containers here.'

Julius picked up the one closest to him, hurried back to Skye, and placed its nozzle close to the rock. He switched it on and the melting metal was instantly sucked into the glass chamber.

'That's it. Keep it there,' said Skye, passing the torch up and down the ore. When there was nothing left to extract, he turned the torch off.

Julius did the same with his nozzle. There was about four inches of blue goo at the bottom of the jar, sloshing gently as he moved. 'Simple as that, huh?'

'Now we need to grab this little pickaxe and see if we can find some more embedded in the rock,' said Skye, beginning to chip away at the surface. He kept on going until a new blue vein appeared. 'There it is. So we melt it, then we store it and so on. Got it?'

'OK,' replied Julius. 'I'll go grab my tools.'

'Start with that rock over there then,' he said, pointing behind him. 'It's big enough to keep you busy until break time.'

Julius dried his face with a corner of his t-shirt, sweat forming on his forehead already, picked up his tools and got to work. His rock proved to be rich with Strullium and, when Foster appeared to call them back for a break, he had already filled three containers. He grabbed them all and took them back to the storage rooms inside the camp, before heading to the canteen for a well-deserved fruit juice and toast.

'I think I've just lost half my weight in water,' said Morgana, fanning herself with a napkin. She gathered her hair up and fixed it into a bun, before gulping her glass of juice down in one.

'How much metal did you get?' asked Julius.

'Isolde and I got about five jars.'

'I got seven!' said Faith, clearly pleased with himself. 'And me lovely lady got another three.'

'Yeah, but this is like home advantage for you,' said Isolde. 'You're used to working with this stuff.'

'Mizkis!' thundered Foster from the door. 'Time to go! Let's move it!'

Skye groaned and heaved himself up. 'He could have given us a few more minutes. I've only managed to eat five muffins.'

'Poor starving you,' said Julius, grabbing his remaining slice of toast. He held it between his teeth as he picked up his tray and returned it to the food counter. He was hot and tired too, but he had every reason in the world to keep going back in until he found that crystal. He didn't say this though, because he didn't want to put more pressure on his friends.

*

The December days passed, following a practical routine of food, work and sleep. With the officers starting to work night shifts, the bar quickly became a lively hub where friends could be found at all hours of the day. The 5MS students tended to keep mainly to themselves, but Julius and his classmates were quick to befriend the older Zed members. The Mizki girls in particular had started to revolve around them at any opportunity and it was a common sight to catch them in their vicinity, pretending to be busy with the most absurd tasks. At one point, Julius even saw Evita Suarez and Jiao Yu pretending to fall, so that two tall officers could come to their rescue.

'They better watch it,' said Faith one afternoon, observing one of Docherty's friends flirting with Isolde. 'It's against regulation and, if Foster catches them, it's goodbye Ahriman for them.'

Julius was slightly encouraged by those words, especially considering the amount of attention Morgana was getting whenever she entered a room. She seemed pretty oblivious of it most of the time, but Julius couldn't be certain of that and felt little stabs of jealousy every time another man talked to her. On the other hand, when had Foster's presence, or school rules, ever stopped Skye from hooking up with the girl he wanted?

On Wednesday the 24th of December, Julius, Skye and Faith were called out of their regular tunnel to help elsewhere for the afternoon.

'Everyone else stay here for the moment,' said Foster to the rest of the group. 'I'll send some of you over later on, to gather their containers.'

Faith seemed to know where he was going, so Julius and Skye followed him as best they could, as he zig-zagged in and out of tunnels, looking for their new team. Eventually they arrived at a large cave, which had plumes of steam seeping from the walls. It was so hot that the four officers there had already removed their t-shirts, large beads of sweat forming on their foreheads and torsos.

'Who left the heating on?' gasped Skye.

'You'll get used to it,' answered a blonde officer, not unkindly. 'The tools are over there,' he said pointing to the corner of the room.

Julius nodded and fetched a blowtorch and an empty container. He spotted a fat rock at ground level and went straight for it, as it meant that he would be able to sit down while he worked, where it was cooler. He set to it, and it wasn't long before he noticed a small Strullium crystal protruding from the rock. He knew it wasn't what he was looking for, but it shone with a delicate lilac shade — Morgana's favourite colour. It would make a prefect present for her birthday — after all it was only a week away — and what chance would he have to find something better than that? He gripped it lightly and carefully tried to prise it from the rock face. It budged a little, so he grabbed a scalpel and began to scratch away at the earth all around it, until it had fully loosened and he was able to dislodge it. As he held it in the palm of his hand and examined it, he knew he'd need to polish it and maybe get a little chain to go with it. He could ask Docherty to find him one in New Satras, since he was going back and forth regularly between Moonrising and the camp. He pocketed the crystal and resumed his work, his mood raised by the unexpected find.

Around six o'clock in the afternoon, Foster sent the rest of group to pick up their supplies. As they walked closer, the volume of their voices and laughter increased, bouncing off the rocky tunnels.

As Julius heard them approaching, he turned, and saw that only Lopaka and George had actually entered the cave. Behind them, rooted by the entrance, were the girls, their cheeks bright red. Every one of them was gaping in awe at the muscular prowess of the four officers. The blonde one, who had spoken to them the first time, was now lifting the containers with the greatest of ease — four in each hand — and passing them to Lopaka and George, who almost fell forward from the weight of them. He plucked up another nearby container and walked right up to Isolde, who found herself face-to-face with a six-pack of lean muscle.

'Thank you,' she quivered, still unable to do much more than ogle.

'Anytime,' the officer replied in a sultry voice, before moving on to Morgana with a second container.

Julius noticed how her jaw dropped a little. Not good.

Just then, possibly anticipating that the next in line would be his girlfriend, Faith hovered between them and unceremoniously loaded Morgana and Siena with a container each. 'Thank you ladies,' he said, ushering them out of the cave. 'Off you go now. I can hear Foster calling you. Thanks for your help. We'll be right behind you. Bye!'

The officer stood there — hands on hips, showing off his alluring biceps — watching the girls disappear down the tunnel, enveloped in their own giggles. When they were out of sight, he walked back to his mates, where he was welcomed with laughter and cheers.

Julius breathed a little easier, inwardly thanking Faith for his intervention and, at the same time, cursing himself for not having removed his own t-shirt. After all the workouts he had put himself through, he was pretty sure his abs were every bit as glorious as those other guys. *But I didn't want to show off*, he thought, feeling peeved.

Skye, on the other hand, had paid attention only to one thing. 'You are amazing!' he gushed, furiously shaking the blonde officer's hand. 'I have never seen that level of blushingness coming on so quickly! I mean, even their toes must have been red!'

Lopaka and George were in agreement with Skye and were nodding their appreciation.

'How did you do it?' Skye demanded to know, sitting down on the floor and opening his PIP so he could take notes.

Julius and Faith looked at each other in resignation, before resuming their work.

For the last hour of their shift, Julius kept his eyes on the rock, while he listened to a lecture on the virtues of sweat, scars and muscle definition, and their effect on women.

Eventually, even Faith was dragged into the discussion. 'I don't mean to disappoint you, but I think a brain goes further than just muscle. Look at me — yet, me girl fancies me.'

'Of course you need a brain,' answered a brown-haired guy, 'but you can't deny that fitness is a major turn-on, for both sexes. It's just human nature: we are attracted to healthy specimens because it leads to reproduction, survival of the species and all the rest. And on top of that, a Zed officer can run circles around any old human from Earth.'

'That's right,' piped in a third guy, who had remained quiet so far. 'If you make it into Zed, it goes without saying that you have a brain, mind-skills and a body to go with it, since we are not really allowed to be unfit. Simple as that.'

Julius had to admit that the guy was right, even though at the moment he himself was only half a Zed regular, without his mind-skills. He wondered what would happen if he never found Tijara's crystal; would Morgana even consider him? Because he didn't really believe that his muscles alone would cut it. Not with her.

Foster arrived to break up the debate club at 7 o'clock, allowing them to return to their lodgings for a well-deserved shower.

*

'McCoy, over here,' cried Docherty over the loud music. He was waiting at the entrance of the bar lounge, waving one hand in the air.

Julius waded through the New Year's revellers, towards him. 'You made it!' he said, pleased.

'Sorry it took me so long, but the air traffic was fearsome tonight. Here it is,' he said, handing Julius a little green box.

'You're fine, mate. Thanks for doing this,' he replied. He peeked inside it and smiled when he saw the fine, silver chain, with the polished crystal pendant. 'It looks great.'

'My pleasure. Gonna head back to Kaori now,' he said, shaking his hand. 'Enjoy the party!'

Julius pocketed the present and moved back to his table, where Faith had just deposited a tray filled with bottles of Martian Bile. Siena and Morgana were right behind him. Judging by the rosy complexions of their cheeks and their not-so-sure-walks, he could tell that they were enjoying the party.

'Cheers, everyone!' said Skye, grabbing one bottle. 'To good things and all that.'

'Cheers,' echoed the others.

'And happy eighteenth birthday, Morgana,' toasted Siena, once again followed by all.

'Thank you guys!' she replied, negotiating gravity in order to stand up. 'To my last birthday as a Mizki!' she said, swaying forward.

Siena grabbed her quickly by the side pockets of her trousers and pulled, managing only to make her land on her own lap.

The boys were on their feet in a second, trying to help, but the pair of them were just giggling merrily, as they tried to re-emerge from the depths of the sofa.

'Oh dear,' said Faith, amused. 'And it's not even midnight.'

Julius couldn't help but laugh, although the chances that Morgana could really appreciate his gift now were growing slimmer with every sip of Bile she took. If things went downhill, he could always give it to her in the morning. He decided to sit back and enjoy the evening — still no chance of him dancing — determined to make up for the one he had missed the previous year.

The party had started in the bar, but as more officers were coming in from Moonrising, ready to start an early shift in the mines, it had naturally spilled out throughout the rest of the compound to accommodate the rising numbers. There were neither long dresses nor the traditional champagne, but it felt like a genuine party nonetheless. Julius could see that Foster was quite against the whole situation, his face twitching with every drink sold. He paced the room like a lion in a cage, paying particular attention at the corridor leading off to the dorms, interrogating anyone that went that way as to their intentions — he even stopped Chan and Morales by mistake at one point, with the result of being glared at by the only man on Zed with a bigger monobrow than his. The music blared from the speakers, travelling from tent to tent. It was so loud that Julius had to wonder if the Arneshians would be able to hear them, with the bass thumping so hard.

Around eleven, Faith decided to turn the party up a notch, and proceeded to hand out small pieces of glass, which he had salvaged from broken Strullium containers, to those around him, who in turn began to glue them all over his skirt.

Julius watched, mystified, until Faith shooed everyone away and hovered up high, to the centre of the lounge. 'Hit me!' he cried to Lopaka.

A spotlight was promptly aimed in his direction and Faith began to spin. As he did this the shards of glass sent sparkling reflections across the room, turning him into the weirdest disco ball Julius had ever seen. By then all logic had abandoned ship and the crowd was laughing and hollering.

'Oh, it hurts!' cried Skye, doubled over in his chair, howling his head off.

Julius stared in wonder at Faith and was pleased to see him sporting his trademark grin, fully satisfied with his performance. He cried with laughter when Foster tried to ninja him down, jumping stealthily at him from the top of the counter, and missing.

'That's enough, Shanigan!" said Foster, trying to make him land.

But Faith was quicker even than the captain's mind-skills and zoomed around the room, forcing Foster to try and claw him down. When Faith took the corridor at high speed, lit up like a runway, Foster was still after him, oblivious of the fact that a couple of people back in the lounge had actually collapsed on the floor in hysterics.

'I'm sooo gonna miss Foster when I leave this place,' said Skye, trying to catch his breath.

Meantime, Faith's strobe lights had attracted more people to the dance floor so, when midnight arrived, most of the camp's occupants were gathered together, ready to welcome the New Year in en masse.

Julius couldn't see Morgana anywhere and felt bitterly disappointed about that. Just then, Isolde decided to show up, pretty much begging for some form of New Year's greeting from him. Julius couldn't exactly avoid her without being rude, so he smiled and moved forward. 'Happy New Y … OOF!' he gasped, as Isolde propelled herself into his arms, knocking the wind out of him at the same time.

'Oh Julius,' she cooed in his ear. 'I'm so happy you're back. I suffered so much when you weren't here. I was inconsolable!'

'Yeah, I heard,' he replied, thinking about her and Skye with a raised eyebrow. *Damn it*, he thought, trying to wriggle out of her embrace as politely as possible.

'But now here we are,' she continued, holding him even tighter. 'And perhaps we could go … there …' she said, hinting at the dorms with her head.

'Where … What … No! Bad idea,' he said, shaking his head, a cold sweat forming on his brow. 'Foster and all that, you know. Why don't we have a drink here, instead?'

'It will do … for a start,' she said, winking. 'Don't go anywhere.'

As soon as she turned and disappeared into the crowd, Julius was grabbed by a pair of hands and dragged backwards.

'You're so smooth, McCoy!' said Skye, laughing.

'Come on, let's split before she gets back,' he replied, hurrying out of the lounge.

'This way,' said Faith, popping into view suddenly and leading them to the storage room. 'Foster is still after me.'

It seemed that another party was in full swing there, amidst the crates of Strullium.

Empty bottles of Martian Bile covered the floor, filling all the shelves and ledges; yet, there seemed to be a never-ending stock somewhere, because everyone was holding one. In the middle of a small group, perched on top of a crate — her crossed legs swinging in time with the music — Morgana was holding court for several officers, who seemed to be thoroughly enjoying her company.

Julius recognised one of them from their shift the week before, and remembered all too well how he had made Morgana blush that day. However, he needn't have worried because, when she saw him entering the tent, she stopped talking, the officers suddenly forgotten.

'Julius!' she cried, clearly more excited and tipsier than earlier. 'It's my birthday!' she said, jumping off the crate and running more or less in a straight line over to him.

This time he didn't hesitate, and held his arms wide open to catch her. 'I know, silly. And I see you're celebrating in style.'

'Indeed I am! Where were you?' she said, almost pleadingly. 'I wanted you at midnight.'

Julius' heart skipped a beat: had he heard her right? 'What about now?' he asked tentatively. Och … he might as well.

She laughed cheekily. 'What do you think?'

The light made her eyes sparkle, and he remembered holding her, three years ago to the day, aware for the first time of his feelings for her; he remembered how soft her skin had been as his fingertips touched it during the last dance of that evening. He looked at her now, a beautiful woman, who may never have a part in his life. The thought made his heart ache.

Morgana must have felt something change because suddenly she stared intently back at him, as if she had read something in his eyes.

Julius could have kept her there for the rest of the night. Instead though, he lowered his arms, convincing himself that now wasn't the right time to find out if she really wanted him or not. It had to come from her, not the Martian Bile. But what a sensation to hold her close to him like that — she made his soul resonate.

'I think it's time we go for a little shut-eye,' said Siena, appearing from nowhere and wrapping her arms around Morgana's shoulders.

'But I don't want to go to bed,' she said, still staring at Julius, while swaying slightly.

'Yes you do,' he encouraged her. 'I'll see you tomorrow.'

Siena managed to drag her away, and struggled to steer her back into the corridor, as she tried to change course several times, complaining that the night was young and she wasn't really tired.

'I think I need a drink,' he said, turning to Skye and Faith.

'I bet you do,' said Skye, passing him his bottle. 'That was pretty intense, McCoy, even by my standards.'

'Ah, but this guy is a gentleman, don't you know?' Faith piped up, patting him on the shoulder.

'A gentleman who's sleeping alone tonight,' remarked Skye. 'Unless of course, you don't manage to get rid of her.'

'Rid of who?' asked Julius, watching Skye and Faith sidestepping quickly.

Before he could say another word, Isolde had literally jumped on his back, and was holding on for dear life.

'Found you!' she giggled.

'Is…ol…de,' he said, trying to shake her off. 'For the love of the wee man, geroffme.' At this point, a few of the officers nearby stopped their chatting and took to watching them instead.

'Skye! A little help here,' called Julius, feeling like a branch with a heavy koala wrapped around it.

'All right,' sighed Skye, finally stepping in. 'Come Isolde, he doesn't deserve you.'

'Yes he does,' she insisted.

'No, he really doesn't!' cried Morgana, suddenly re-entering the room.

Julius managed to turn his head just enough to see her take a running jump and crash into Skye who, in turn, knocked over Isolde and Julius, sending them flying across the floor.

At that point the crowd began to applaud and cheer.

'What the …' said Julius, staggering up and massaging his elbow. He saw Morgana and Isolde regaining their feet and, before either of them could do anything, he went straight to Morgana, bent forward and hoisted her over his shoulder, struggling to hold her legs still as she vigorously punched his back.

'Let me at her,' she cried.

Skye did the same with Isolde and followed Julius down the corridor, accompanied by the amused bellowing of the crowd.

Neither of them was too bothered that the girls were still clawing at each other as they dangled behind their backs.

'Well done mate,' said Skye. 'Your very own cat-fight.'

'They're both drunk,' said Julius even though deep down he was pretty chuffed about the jealous scene Morgana had just made over him.

'I feel unneeded,' continued Skye, 'like a fourth corner in a triangle.'

'I'm sure you can rectify that,' answered Julius, adjusting Morgana so she wouldn't slide off his shoulder. 'I think this one's asleep already. Unbelievable.'

Hoping to avoid any curious remarks, they hurried through the bar area and headed straight for the dorms where, of course, Captain Foster was standing guard.

Julius pretended that everything was business as usual, and walked past him as vaguely as possible. 'Sir,' he saluted. 'She's out for the count. Just taking her to bed …' he trailed off.

'Just you watch where you put those hands, McCoy,' growled Foster.

'Yessir, will do sir,' he replied, breaking into a cold sweat.

'Don't worry about Skye, sir,' mumbled Isolde, raising herself up as they walked past the captain. 'He knows what to do with his ha-'

'Shhhh!' hissed Skye. Then to Foster, 'I don't know what she's talking about, sir.'

Julius grunted, trying to suppress his laughter, especially since Foster had already caught Skye out a few times before. When he reached the girls' dorm, he looked for Morgana's room. 'Hey,' he said, tapping the back of her knee. 'Can you open the door please?' But she wasn't exactly in a helping mood. Julius twisted, grabbed one of her hands and pressed it against the door, which immediately opened. Thankfully, her roommate wasn't in yet, so he walked over to the bed, hoping it was the right one, and gently lowered her onto it.

Morgana immediately snuggled up and wrapped herself in the duvet. 'Are we at the party?' she said, her eyes closed.

'Party's over,' he answered amused, kneeling beside the bed and switching on one of the smaller lights.

'Maybe I'll close my eyes a little then,' she said.

'Great idea.'

'Jules?'

'Mm?'

'You're my most precious friend.'

'I know.'

'Will you always be with me?'

'I will,' he answered.

With that, Morgana fell asleep, a blissful smile on her face.

He remained where he was for a few minutes, just looking at her, taking in every single line of her face. He decided he would give her the present another time. Before leaving, he delicately removed a strand of dark hair from her forehead, kissed it and turned off the light.

THE ROAD TO BURUWANG

The sleepy faces that filled the canteen on the morning of the first of January wore the signs of a late night, and a mighty good one at that. Julius was having breakfast — a triple dose of strong, black coffee, bacon galore and scrambled eggs — with Faith and Skye, when Siena and Morgana joined their table.

'Happy New Year, me nymph,' said Faith, kissing Siena as she sat near him, creating a chorus of awwwww followed by mock puking sounds from Skye and Julius.

'Don't listen to them, my flying saucy,' she told him. 'They're just jealous.'

'And how are you, gorgeous?' asked Skye to Morgana.

'Why am I feeling so crappy again?' she replied.

'Maybe because you drank your weight in Martian Bile?' volunteered Faith.

'Please don't tell me I embarrassed myself. I remembered discussing something with Isolde … Did we fight?'

Julius grinned. 'Nah. You were fine and so was she.'

'Incidentally,' added Faith, 'I wouldn't mention anything if I were you.'

'Oh. Ok,' she replied, sounding surprised. 'How did I get to bed again?'

'On his shoulder, darling,' answered Siena, pointing at Julius.

'I'm so sorry,' said Morgana, blushing. 'I hope I didn't spoil your party or anything.'

Julius thought that "spoil" was definitely the wrong word to describe how he had felt the night before, but he wasn't going to tell her that, not in front of the others at least. 'All good. It was time to go to bed anyway.'

After breakfast, and still half asleep, he resumed his first working shift of the year, heartened by the fact that the Arneshians hadn't given them any trouble yet. However, if Julius had started the year with renewed optimism, it didn't last the week. He worked hard in the caves, from dawn till dusk, often sneaking in a quick night shift, if Foster wasn't on guard by the Seffira Cave. But no matter how much he tried, the search was always fruitless.

Morgana must have read the frustration on his face, because eventually she stopped beside him, before carrying her containers through to the storage rooms and said quietly, 'Don't lose hope. I know it's here. We'll find it.'

He had just nodded, thankful for her words, although his hope was faltering with each passing day. But that would not do: he couldn't be the one who gave up first. So he buckled his belt and worked on.

It wasn't until the 6th of January that his luck began to change.

*

The Skirts had spent the morning working inside a new cave, while Isolde, Lopaka, Siena and George were tidying up the storage room. To Julius' relief, since New Year,

Isolde had tried to stay clear of him as much as possible, which hadn't gone unnoticed by the others — although no one had made any funny comments about her behaviour. At lunchtime, they left their post only to find themselves in the middle of a long tunnel, stretching to the left and right.

'Hold on,' said Skye, looking puzzled. 'I don't think we came through here.'

Julius opened his PIP and tried to locate their position on the map. 'Mine is dead,' he said poking at the screen, his finger passing straight through it. 'Dead, or we're totally lost.'

Faith hovered first to one side of the tunnel, then the other, trying to remember the way. 'I'm pretty sure we came from there,' he said eventually, pointing to one end. 'And anyway, we have enough microchips inside us to be traceable from Earth. If we get lost, they'll find us.'

That seemed to convince the others, so they all followed him toward the south-bearing direction.

It was Morgana who first voiced her concern after they had been walking for about ten minutes. 'Are you sure this is the right way?' she asked, sounding a little panicky.

'Not anymore,' answered Faith. 'Maybe I should have taken a left back at that weird rock formation that looked like a mutant banana, or maybe a sharp right when we saw the Strul-'

A sharp beeping sound interrupted Faith, followed immediately by another four.

'It's the alarm!' cried Morgana, a smile breaking out on her face.

Julius fumbled open his PIP and saw the words "Crystal Alert" flashing bright red on his screen — the link to the network might have been down, but it hadn't prevented the PIP from scanning the area. He felt his stomach contract. He glanced around and saw that the others were looking as amazed as he felt.

'Where's it coming from?' asked Morgana, spinning on her heels, as she tried to use her PIP like a compass.

Julius did likewise, and stepped forward with his hand held open in front of him, listening intently as the alarm's beeping grew more insistent. 'This way,' he said. He walked for what felt like an eternity, hypnotised by the sound. He could barely hear his friends breathing. 'In here,' he said suddenly, taking a sharp right. He stopped abruptly, making Skye walk straight into him.

'What is it?' asked Skye, peeking over Julius' shoulder.

Julius selected the torch from his PIP display, shone the light to the far end of the room and gasped.

Crouched on the floor were two men gathering something from a hole in the rock. When the beam of light hit them, they whirled around, their faces looking startled beneath the hoods of their long, brown tunics. One of them stretched out a hand and plucked up a small parcel from the floor, showing a tanned arm covered in blue, spiraling tattoos.

The men sprung into action and sprinted down a side tunnel.

As they ran off, the beeping of Julius' PIP began to fade. 'They have the crystal!' he cried.

'Go!' urged Morgana. 'I'll call Freja!'

Julius launched himself forward, closely followed by the others. 'No, no, no!' he kept repeating in his mind as he ran. 'Please don't take it away.'

'Julius,' cried Skye, 'try to stop them!'

'What am I supposed to use? Harsh language?' he replied, redoubling his effort.

Faith zoomed over his head, his hand stretched forward. 'Stop, or I'll shoot!' he cried. The men didn't turn, and kept running.

A jet of energy flashed past Julius' shoulder — possibly from Skye — and he moved aside, aware that, without his powers, he could only hope to outrun the thieves. Skye fired several shots, none of which found their targets. Julius could have sworn that one or two of the jets of energy had deflected off the men's bodies, absurd as that seemed.

'There's a dead end up ahead,' cried Faith. 'I can see it!'

Julius redoubled his efforts, ignoring the painful stitch mounting in his left side: the men were trapped now, and he would be able to get his crystal back. Suddenly, the fugitives veered off to the right, and disappeared from view. Julius hurtled after them and crashed into a wall of solid rock. Skye and Faith piled into him, unable to stop in time.

Julius' right cheekbone scraped against the rock, but he ignored the sharp pain, confused by what had just happened. 'Where are they?' he growled, slamming his fists against the wall.

'Move aside,' said Skye, lighting up his torch to examine the rocks.

Julius pulled back, running his eyes over every nook and cranny that was illuminated by the torch. Skye pushed, pulled and even tried to use his powers against the rock face, trying to shift it, but it was no good.

'There's something on the floor,' said Faith.

Skye looked down. 'It's a hood,' he said, picking up the crumpled piece of material. 'Who are these people?'

Julius backed up against the wall, and let himself slide down to the floor. 'I don't know, but they got what they came for.'

*

Twenty minutes later, the Skirts were gathered in the encampment's ready room, where they had been summoned by Freja. He didn't look pleased.

'They took the crystal, sir,' said Julius, unable to hide his distress, as he entered.

'Take a seat, McCoy,' the GM replied, pouring a glass of water. 'Drink.'

Julius was so at a loss for what to do that he took it and gulped it down, vaguely realising how thirsty he was.

'Who were they, sir?' asked Morgana. 'I thought they might be aliens, but they looked so ... human.'

'It appears that they are, Miss Ruthier,' he answered. 'We've analysed the hood you found, and it contains *traces* of human DNA. There's no doubt about it, but that is all we know for now, I'm afraid.'

'Well, where are they now?' asked Skye.

'An unknown ship left orbit, right after this incident. It went to warp before we could intercept them and, once again, the signature was unusual but still very similar to that of an Earth vessel's.'

'So what you're saying ...' blurted out Julius, growing frustrated '... is that they stole the crystal, walked right through the wall and vanished?'

Freja didn't reply, choosing to ignore the impatience in Julius' voice.

Master Cress entered the room at that moment. He was panting, as if he had just been running a marathon. 'Freja, you must come to the centre of Ahriman. You too Julius,' he said. 'They can come too,' he said as an afterthought, looking at the Skirts.

Julius looked at the others in surprise, and followed the GM as he left the ready room. 'What's happened?' asked Freja, as they headed for the main exit.

'After the ship went to warp, an encrypted message was sent to Moonrising,' Cress replied, hurrying on. He turned to the Mizkis as he walked and said, 'Suit up. We're going out.'

Julius activated his EMU and followed, eager to know more.

A stork was standing by just outside the camp. Cress opened the hatch, and ushered the GM and the Skirts inside. Once the cabin was pressurised, he signaled to them that it was safe to remove their suits. 'Miss Ruthier,' he said, turning to Morgana, 'follow the coordinates and take us to the rendezvous point.'

'Yes, sir,' she said, taking the pilot seat.

'Well?' asked Freja, impatiently. 'What was this message? Who are they?'

Everyone was eagerly waiting for the answer, and Julius had to refrain from shaking Cress by the shoulders to hurry him up.

'It has been confirmed. They are humans, Grand Master, just like us,' answered Cress, excitedly. 'Well, maybe not exactly like us — their bio-signatures have revealed different wavelengths concerning their mind-skills. It's an incredible discovery for Zed … a colony of humans outside of Earth, Zed and Arnesh.'

Julius was astonished at the news, and could see that everyone else was too, Freja included. However, it still didn't explain why they had taken his crystal. 'What did the message say, Master Cress?' he pressed.

'They want to meet our leader at the centre of Ahriman … us and the Arneshians'.

'What?' cried Julius. 'Why?'

'I don't know,' answered Cress. 'It also said that the "Powerless Seekers" involved in the search for the crystal must be present. A powerless seeker,' he repeated, looking at Julius.

'Wait a minute — seekers?' remarked Faith. 'In the plural?'

'What is the meaning of this, Cress?' demanded Freja.

'I'm sorry Grand Master, this is all I know. Kelly and Moonrising are on standby, in case things get out of hand.'

Freja nodded his approval at the security measure, and settled into his seat, looking apprehensively ahead of him.

Julius exchanged a quick glance with Skye and Faith, aware that he couldn't hide his worry. That crystal was his only chance of setting things right, for Farrah, Michael, Morgana and Zed. He was not going to let it get away.

*

Morgana began her descent towards Ahriman's front gate. She had to change course a couple of times, as more Arneshian vessels were also approaching the landing area.

Julius watched as the whitewashed walls of a tall building came into view. He was surprised by the overall brightness of the place. In his mind, Ahriman had always been a dark, smoky place rife with dangers, and certainly not this clean-lined building. The vast area below them was devoid of decorations, but he could see where trees had once grown — the Arneshians were obviously not too bothered with that sort of stuff. A few windows opened up onto the front facade, surrounding a large gate-like structure that functioned as an entrance. The gate was wrought from some kind of metal, which was darkened now, but Julius could see that it must have been much lighter at some point; stylised stars decorated the two large doors, and he wondered what it must have looked like in the time of Clodagh and Marcus. Everything they had built together had been useful and pleasant to the eyes, and he was sure that Ahriman had been no exception.

'Get ready,' said Morgana, once they had touched down safely. As soon as her passengers had suited up, she opened the hatch.

Freja stepped out first, motioning for the Mizkis to follow. 'Stay close please.'

As soon as they were in the open, several of the Arneshians turned to stare at them, hostility clear on their faces. No one tried to hinder them though, as if they had been warned against this already. Still, Julius made sure that Morgana was kept safe between him and Skye: he didn't trust the Arneshians one bit. And what if K'Ssander had left Arnesh to rejoin T'Rogon? After all, his powers were still intact — why Roversi had let him go back was beyond his comprehension, quite frankly. The guy was a viper, ready to bite at the first opportunity.

The group walked through the main gate with their heads held high, Freja in front, sending a clear message that the Arneshians around him didn't matter and that the place belonged to Zed first and foremost. Julius noticed the same angry resolution on his face now as he had seen on the day in which he had addressed Moonrising with plans of war, and that filled him with confidence.

The gate opened into a vast atrium, with arches all along the sides and a wide, central staircase branching out into two thinner sections, to the left and to the right, which curled their way up to the second floor. Julius saw a group of people standing around a circular podium. One man in particular stood out. Even from a distance he could recognise T'Rogon, with his shimmering white hair, greyish skin, a metal circlet crowning his head and wearing a long, silver tunic — the mere sight of him made Julius reel with anger. Then another figure moved into the light and Julius stopped.

Ben Hastings took a step forward, facing the newcomers with an air of smugness. He leaned closer to T'Rogon, and whispered something. The Ambassador turned to them, and smirked.

If the sight of T'Rogon had shaken Julius, the presence of Hastings made him positively furious. Without thinking twice, he launched forward, only to be stopped by Freja's hand grabbing his shoulder. Julius looked at him, but Freja only shook his head firmly.

'Grand Master,' said T'Rogon, 'welcome to our Halls.'

'I do not need to be welcomed to my own home, Ambassador,' replied Freja coldly.

T'Rogon's smile disappeared and he turned to Julius. 'I did not expect to see you again.'

Julius' barely contained anger exploded. 'Where's Farrah?' he cried. 'Where's my brother?'

Skye had to grab him by the shoulders to stop him moving forward.

T'Rogon looked at him with contempt. 'Farrah belongs to us now. Stop your whining.'

'We'll see about that,' growled Julius. He looked at Ben. 'Traitor.'

Ben was about to reply when a static field crackled into life over the podium, making every head turn.

Standing tall, clad in a brown tunic, was a man that Julius didn't recognise and, judging by the surprise on everyone's faces, neither did they. The same blue tattoos that he had seen on the men from the cave decorated his face, spiralling from his neck, over his cheeks and up to his forehead in a tribal fashion.

'I bid you welcome,' he said. His voice was calm, but it had an edge that made Julius wary. 'I am Daku Derain, Leader of the Ocluths and Guardian of Tijara's Crystal. Those who wish to claim it must gather in Buruwang at month's end. Will the powerless Seekers show themselves?'

Julius looked at Freja, who nodded, and he stepped forward.

'Who will challenge him?' asked the projection.

Yes, thought Julius, *who's your powerless hero, T'Rogon?*

In response, a small group of Arneshians, who had been standing to the side, now parted, letting a young man through.

Julius heard Morgana gasp, then saw what she had. His stomach closed as his brother advanced towards the podium, and stopped by his side. Michel had grown to be as tall as him, his hair and eyes the same light brown colour of their father. There was a cunning resemblance between them that would mark them as brothers to all. 'How could you?' he whispered in shock, but Michael just stared ahead and didn't reply.

'Seekers, state your names and origin,' said Derain.

Julius had to force his eyes away from Michael. 'Julius McCoy, planet Earth.'

'Michael McCoy, planet Earth.'

Not even his voice sounded familiar to Julius anymore.

A light flashed across their faces, as if someone had taken a scan of them.

'The Guardian's Trail has now been activated,' said Derain. 'Follow the co-ordinates and meet us on our planet. Farewell, Seekers.'

The hologram hadn't even dissolved completely when Cress, Faith and Skye gathered around Julius, dragging him away. In truth, Julius was too stunned to even think of doing something.

'Go,' ordered Freja. 'I'll take care of the directions.'

Cress didn't need to be told twice, and ushered the Mizkis outside, back to the shuttle.

*

Julius spent the first few days after the meeting alone, struggling to process the pain of this latest betrayal. He didn't leave his room, or even eat; he slept badly, and very little. Skye would leave food on the table for him at night, only to find it still sitting there the next morning. Worried and astonished as they all were, they let him deal with it in his own way, for which Julius was grateful. It was only on the following Friday that he received a message from Freja, practically ordering him to meet Professor Chan in the dojo, to resume his training. By then, the balance in his feelings had shifted greatly, whereby anger had replaced the sorrow in his heart.

The base camp on Funesto had been disbanded and, while the Mizkis had returned to Moonrising, a large presence of Zed officers had remain behind, with the intent of regaining control of the Halls of Ahriman. By the time Julius' spirits had begun to rise again, the last group of Arneshians had been defeated after a brief but gruesome battle and forced out of the facility.

*

One afternoon, at the end of a long day of training, Julius went to the mess hall, feeling famished. He grabbed a couple of sandwiches from the food counter and looked for an empty seat. It was then that he noticed Faith, working away at one of the tables.

'Hey, Julius,' said Faith, moving several pads to the side with a sweeping gesture of his hand. 'How are you?'

'You can choose between knackered and pissed off,' he replied, sitting down in front of him. 'But I would go for an equal mix of the two. No one knows what this challenge is about, but since there's not a lot I can do, except physical stuff, Freja just left me in the capable hands of Chan and his torture-dojo.'

'Ouch,' grinned Faith. 'Erm … listen, did you tell your folks about, you know …'

'About what? That we found their traitor son?' he said bitterly. 'No, I didn't.'

'I wonder if it's better this way, actually,' volunteered Faith. 'I mean, they are now half resigned to the fact that Michael lives happily with the Arneshians — it has been more than a year, after all. Maybe they don't need to know about this.'

Julius thought about it for a few seconds, as he readjusted the contents of his sandwich, and nodded. 'Perhaps you're right. It's kinder this way. It lets them keep the good memories.' He began to eat his food, agreeing silently that it was the best solution. And if something should happen, well, maybe then he would tell them, but there was no point at the moment.

'I want to show you these,' said Faith, opening his PIP. 'Pete just sent them to me.'

Julius realised immediately that they were parts of the spaceship Faith had created for Pit-Stop Pete's competition, which was now under construction. 'It's coming on so fast. You must be really proud, mate.'

'I am. You can't quite see the whole picture yet, but wait until he starts to assemble all the parts. It's gonna be grand. Here, see this panel?'

Julius leaned over to take a better look. 'What is it?'

'That's where the name of this baby will go, and I want you to name it for me.'

'What? No, Faith, I couldn't possibly do that!'

'Of course you can. Don't you remember, Julius? It's your birthday present from three years ago, on Gassendi.'

It took him a moment to remember what he was going on about. Then his eyes widened. 'But it's your creation.'

'Look, you're me best mate, Jules. Besides, a gift is a gift.'

'All right,' he said, finally. 'But I need to think about it properly.'

'Sure you do. I wouldn't accept any old pet name, you know?'

Julius grinned. 'Thank you … for sticking by me, all these years.'

'You gave all you had for us,' replied Faith candidly. 'That changes people. It changed me.'

Julius was touched and at a loss for what to say.

Faith began to play with his teaspoon and, still staring at his cup, he continued. 'When you were in stasis, I had a lot of time to think. You were just lying there, unable to live. It made me realise how precious time is and that I should do something about the things that are important to me, before it's too late. Siena, me career as a shipbuilder, me friends. I feel like I have lived more in the past year than in me whole life.'

'So what you're saying is that you've had the best time of your life when I was out for the count. Great,' said Julius, cheekily.

'You know what I mean,' said Faith, throwing a napkin at him.

'Just kidding mate. I'm glad things are working out for you. I really am.'

*

That night, as he rested in his bed, Julius was still reflecting on Faith's words. Time was indeed precious, and you never knew when the show would end. What if he had a more permanent accident, before he had a chance to tell Morgana how he felt about her? Did he really need to have his powers in order to show her his feelings? Then it dawned on him, that his flatmate was none other than Skye "Loverboy" Miller, and who could give better advice than the man who had invented the Zed sim-dating programme? He turned to look at him, and saw that he was intently watching a movie; he was laughing and had his headset on.

Julius decided to wait until he was done and, to pass the time, listen to some music instead. He stretched out his arm to retrieve his rucksack, sure that he had put the new music chips somewhere in there. As he rummaged around for them, his hand closed around a sheet of thick paper. He stopped, puzzled. Slowly, he pulled it out and leaned back. It was Michael's letter.

He remembered finding the envelope lying under his pillow, in his bedroom back in Edinburgh, just a few months after the Arneshians had taken everyone. "TO JULIUS. M." was written in blue ink on it, in Michael's steady handwriting. Julius placed his finger under the top fold and ripped it open. There was a single sheet of white, lined paper in it. He opened it, feeling his heart start to beat faster.

"Dear Julius,

If you are reading this letter, it means that I have made up my mind and am no longer with you.

You'll probably think me selfish and ungrateful and you're not the only one: Mum and Dad have practically stopped talking to me already.

I wish there was another way to fulfill my dreams, here with you all, or on Zed. But there isn't. On Arnesh I will be given all the chances for a career in space that I cannot get on Earth. I'm heading for the Nuarn Academy, and I'll have my own place on campus. I've already met many others like me, cool kids from all over the world. I guess you know what I mean — Zed isn't very different from this.

They also told us that excellent students will get a chance to actually meet Queen Salgoria, but apparently you need loads of prep before you can do that — going through a meteorite field followed by a wormhole, and a flision field (whatever that is) is not kind on the untrained, or so they say.

You'll probably think I'm mad, being so excited to go, but once again, this is my life Julius, and I'll make my own decisions. After all, it was you who taught me that we must pursue our dreams no matter what.

Thank you for looking after me all these years. You've been the best brother anyone

could have. I hope you make all your wishes come true.
    Michael"

Julius crushed the letter in his fist, and his hands began to shake. Glad now that Skye was too busy to notice him, he just lay there, staring at the ceiling with his heart thumping in his ears, as if someone had just slapped him across the face.

*

He never showed the letter to the others. He had uncrumpled the letter, put it back inside its envelope, and placed it at the bottom of his rucksack again. As Moonrising drew closer to Buruwang, Julius tried hard to understand what could have pushed Michael to do what he had. As he trained, his brother was never too far from his mind. The boy who wrote the letter was a different person from the one who had stepped up to the podium in Ahriman: a boy with dreams, one who didn't know about T'Rogon's real intentions and, for that, Julius could forgive him for leaving his family behind. It had been the impetus of youth to make that decision. But what of the choices he had made after that? The more he thought about it, the less he could justify them. Working with the Arneshians to trap his own brother and then challenging him to acquire the only thing that could give Julius his hope back. Those things were not easy to excuse. Somewhere in his heart, Julius knew that those actions had sealed the rift between him and Michael, and that their relationship was now forever lost.

On the last day of January, Julius was on the running track situated on Tijara's top deck. The large windows on its outer side granted a clear view of space, while the neon blue overhead lights gave a cold, wintery feeling to the whole environment. He liked to run here in the evening; it felt peaceful and was rarely busy. He ended his last lap by the water fountain, where he closed his PIP monitor. Thirteen miles that night — not bad, he thought. His t-shirt was drenched and he felt his tracksuit sticking to his legs. A shower and some food were in order.

He bent over the fountain and began to drink. After a few seconds he heard approaching footsteps. He continued drinking but saw a pair of trainers come into view to his right. Long, bare legs followed, ending in a pair of tight, blue shorts. He would have known those legs anywhere. He stopped drinking, as his eyes drifted up Morgana's body, enticed by a single drop of sweat running down her flat stomach, ready to disappear into the elastic band of her shorts. Finally, he let go of the water valve and slowly raised himself, drying his mouth with the back of his hand — his eyes now gliding over the curves below her top. When eventually he looked at her face, he felt as if an eternity had passed.

'Hi,' she said, placing one foot behind her, and resting against the wall.

Julius had to swallow before he could speak, as his mouth had gone dry again. He really hoped he'd sound normal, rather than the hormonal wreck he felt inside. 'I didn't see you coming up.'

'I was downstairs, in the gym.'

He nodded. Sweat or no sweat, she still looked good to him, with her hair gathered in a cute ponytail and her cheeks flushed from the exercise.

'How are you feeling?' she asked, seemingly oblivious of the way he had just looked at her. Or maybe she had simply decided to ignore it.

'Getting there … but kinda empty, if that makes any sense.'

Morgana nodded.

'Hey, have you eaten yet?' he asked her suddenly, the words just blurting out of their own accord. 'We could go to New Satras for some food.'

'You mean with the guys?'

'I mean,' he waved his hand vaguely, 'us, you know?'

Morgana had just started to smile, when Julius' PIP beeped loudly. Startled, he opened the screen to find Master Cress staring at him. 'Evening, sir,' he said.

'McCoy, we are approaching Buruwang's orbit. Shower, get changed and report to the GM's office as quick as you can.'

'Yes, sir,' he replied, closing the link. He looked up at Morgana apologetically.

'First things first,' she said. 'Go now!'

He nodded and, as he ran up the stairs — a cheeky grin building on his face — it dawned on him that she would have said yes.

THE GUARDIAN'S TRAIL

Julius was sitting in the front seat of the Stork, peering at the screen in the hope of gaining a better view of Buruwang, but night was falling and large, thick clouds blanketed the sky. Piloting the shuttle was Freja, his eyes focused on the radar as he negotiated the way down. Daku Derain had only given permission for the two of them to land on the planet. 'Sir,' he said, after a while, 'do you think T'Rogon will respect Derain's request as well?'

'Under the circumstances, I don't think he has a choice,' replied Freja. 'Moonrising has detected an advanced defence system protecting their planet. T'Rogon has no interest in starting a battle; he wants that crystal too much.'

'For Michael, you mean.'

Freja looked at him briefly. 'Yes, for your brother.'

'I have no brother,' said Julius curtly.

'You can choose your friends, McCoy, but you cannot choose your relatives.'

'He shamed my parents,' said Julius. 'How could he? That's not how they raised us.'

'The world judges you by your actions, not your connections. Michael's choices have paved his road, just as yours have. When this is over, everyone will find their rightful place in history, where mistakes are not forgotten.'

Pretty words, thought Julius, but they didn't remove the bitter taste of betrayal.

'Soon you'll have to face Michael,' continued Freja, 'and it may be that you're not as angry at him as you may think.'

'Oh, but I am,' Julius cut in.

'Be that as it may, remember that blood is thicker than water. Before this is over, you'll have to deal with it.'

Julius silently mulled over his words.

'It is obvious that Michael did not receive your powers, or he wouldn't be able to compete in this challenge,' said Freja. 'The question is, where are they?'

It didn't seem like Freja was expecting an answer, and Julius couldn't have given him one in any case.

The shuttle emerged from the clouds, over the sea, distracting him from these thoughts. A strip of red lights guided Freja to the landing area and, in a few minutes, they touched down.

When the hatch opened and Julius stepped out, a wave of warm air met him. It smelled of sea and trees. The very fact that the air was breathable though, reminded him that he was among humans.

'Welcome to Burawang,' said a man, walking up to them. 'I am Walamai.'

Julius bowed to him. Blue markings decorated the man's skin, similar to those worn by Derain. The only difference was his clothes: instead of a long, brown tunic, he wore soft leather trousers and strips of suede across his chest, from the left side to the right shoulder. Julius could see a staff of some sort attached to his back, tied to the clothes. He wore sandals on his feet, with leather straps around his ankles. Julius was reminded of some of the ancient tribes he had studied when he was in school, back on Earth; warrior people who had roamed the vast lands many centuries ago.

'Please, come with me,' said the man.

As he followed, Julius observed the lush vegetation all around and, although he couldn't see the ocean from there, he could hear it clearly, as the waves lapped gently againstthe shore. Several round, whitewashed buildings came into view among the trees, none of them taller than two stories high. They looked a bit like upside down bowls, with tiny windows dotted randomly across their walls. People were starting to emerge from these homes, men, women, and children too, all bearing the blue marks and similar leather clothing. He felt quite out of place with his woollen jumper and combat boots, not to mention quite hot.

Walamai stopped at the beginning of a path, which wound its way down through thick bushes. 'Daku Derain is waiting for you,' he told them, pointing at the slope.

Freja went first and Julius stayed close to him. The smell of the crisp night air and the fresh grass was strong and soothing. Eventually, the trees gave way to a circular, sandy area, where a bonfire burned brightly. Daku Derain was standing before it, clad in the familiar brown tunic, and beckoned the visitors to step forward. There were benches all around the fire; two figures were already seated to the right hand side of the fire. As soon as Julius saw who they were, a surge of anger sparked in him: T'Rogon and Michael.

'Come,' called Derain. 'Welcome to our home.'

Freja bowed, as did Julius, trying not to look at the Ambassador or his brother. He let his GM sit closest to T'Rogon, using him as a shield from their sight.

'I am the Guardian of Tijara's crystal, Daku Derain, Sand of the Mountain. Who stands before me?' With that, he turned to T'Rogon.

'I am Ambassador T'Rogon,' began the Arneshian, 'a human, and humble messenger of Queen Salgoria, direct descendant of Clodagh Arnesh. On that, I lay my claim to the crystal, for the sake of the people of Arnesh.'

'Why do your people need the crystal, Ambassador?' asked Derain.

'To repair the harm done by the boy sitting over there,' answered T'Rogon, pointing at Julius.

Before Julius could even move a muscle, Freja lifted his hand. 'All in good time,' he whispered.

'We lived in peace for centuries,' continued T'Rogon, 'until this meddling lot came to our home world and unleashed a terrible weapon that wiped out all of our powers. It is this harm that we want to repair, by putting forward our Seeker.'

Derain looked at both Freja and Julius deeply, for a long time. 'Has this man spoken the truth?'

'He has,' answered the Grand Master.

Julius saw Derain's eyes widen momentarily and it worried him. *I hope Freja knows what he's doing*, he thought.

The Guardian motioned for Freja to continue.

'I am Carlos Freja, Grand Master of Tijara Academy in the Zed Lunar Perimeter, founded by Tijara and Arnesh at the end of the Chemical War. After defending that legacy from repeated attacks from the Arneshians, we unleashed our most powerful weapon against them, to rid them of their powers and stop their attacks forever.'

'And why do you seek the crystal?' asked Derain.

'Because this boy,' he said, indicating Julius with a movement of his head, 'has sacrificed all he had, his greatest powers, so that we could live free from attack. We owe it to him.'

T'Rogon dismissed Freja's words with disdain. 'If he gets the crystal, Master Derain, then my people will be forever at their mercy. It cannot be allowed.'

'Says who?' grunted Julius, bending forward. Michael looked at him for the first time and Julius was startled by the hatred he saw in his eyes.

'The Ambassador,' said Freja to Derain, 'is responsible for countless deaths and for breaking up families in the most subtle and evil of ways.'

'Hah!' smirked T'Rogon. 'I can only divide what is already broken.'

'My family was not broken,' growled Julius.

'Purposely,' continued Freja, 'he removed that child, Michael, from his family, and turned him against them. I trust you have guessed the Seekers are brothers, yes?'

Derain nodded. 'I have, Grand Master. As the Guardian, I cannot make a decision as to the value of each champion — it is not for me to decide. Tijara wanted the crystal to go to a powerless heir, someone worthy of such a gift. He entrusted it to Gelar Ganan, founder of Buruwang, who hid it in a secure location. To obtain it, each contestant will need to prove himself to our ancestor, in the spirit world.'

A few seconds of uneasy silence followed that statement.

'I beg your pardon?' said T'Rogon, finally.

'It is far too precious a decision to be left in the hands of mere mortals like us. Gelar Ganan will show us who the chosen one is. But be warned, there may not be a winner. Both your Seekers could be proven unworthy.'

Before anyone could reply, Walamai stepped out of the shadows and ushered Daku Derain away, before returning to the bonfire. 'The Seekers will be housed in the village tonight, under our care, in preparation for their journey. Grand Master, Ambassador — you will return to your vessels, and wait to be summoned again.'

Julius could see that neither Freja nor T'Rogon were happy to leave them there, but it seemed they were in no position to negotiate.

Freja placed a hand on Julius' shoulder and walked him away from the group.

'Sir,' whispered Julius, 'what does he mean by *the spirit world*?'

'Derain spoke of ancestors. I can only assume he refers to some sort of shamanic practice, where a person enters the spirit world by going into a trance.'

Julius looked at him in surprise. 'I thought this would be a physical challenge.'

'Don't underestimate it,' replied Freja. 'I'm certain it will test your mind more than your body, and that is often harder. If I were you I would take a leaf out of Miss Ruthier's book and spend the next few hours meditating. And, whatever you do, stay away from Michael.'

Julius nodded.

'Stay true to your heart and remember, you are the true heir of Tijara. Don't be afraid to claim what is rightfully yours.' With that, he turned and climbed up the path.

Julius waited for T'Rogon to do the same, before walking back to the fire.

'Come with us,' Walamai told them, as he headed for a thin opening in the trees.

Julius let his brother go first but, just as Michael was turning sideways to slip through the gap, he grabbed his arm. 'Why are you doing this?'

Michael stared at him. 'I'm a McCoy, remember? I'll do anything to fulfill my destiny.'

'If you really want to be like me, then why don't you use my crystal?'

'Who says that I want to be like you? They have better plans for me.' He stared at Julius' hand, and looked up again. 'Do you mind?'

Julius let go, taken aback by his coldness and his words. What could they possibly want with Michael?

Once beyond the trees, they arrived at a long, white beach. A small wooden hut came in to view, and he followed the others there.

'You will sleep here tonight,' Walamai told him. 'Check the top drawer — you'll need to get changed for the challenge. I will pick you up at eight.'

He bowed and remained where he was, watching Michael walk away from him. Even though he was taller, older and more distant than the little brother he remembered, still, in that moment, Julius' heart ached.

*

Julius woke up to the cawing of seagulls. It had been a long time since he had heard such a sound — not since his days back in Edinburgh. A pale light was filtering in through the leather mat covering the windows of the hut. He stretched, shivering a little in the crisp morning air. The mattress had been comfy enough for a good night's sleep — in the end, the tiredness had taken over. He looked around the hut, which comprised the one room, plus a small shower and toilet. There was a desk with a chair and a small chest of drawers, all made of wicker. His uniform was lying on the floor, by the door, where he had left it the night before.

He was starting to feel quite nervous about the trial ahead, and hoped to be able to relax properly before the start. He got up and quickly showered, before putting on the items that had been left for him — a pair of loose, buckskin leggings, an animal hide shirt with three quarter sleeves and a pair of soft moccasins. There were no decorations on them, and they were comfortable to wear.

He stepped outside and took in the view: white sand led to a vast expanse of water, stretching as far as the eye could see. He wondered what the rest of the planet was like. He took a few steps toward the sea and saw a couple of surfers riding the early waves. He immediately thought of Faith and Lopaka, and how much they would have loved to surf here, in this strange new world. Perhaps after all this was over, they could return here together.

'Good morning,' called Walamai, as he walked briskly to him.

Julius bowed. 'And to you, sir.'

'Come for some food. It will be a long day.'

Julius followed him back to the same bonfire they had been gathered around the night before which, to his surprise, was still burning strong.

'We never allow it to go out,' explained Walamai, anticipating his question. He picked up a bowl from a low bench and passed it to Julius.

'It reminds me of porridge,' said Julius, poking at the food in it with a wooden spoon.

'I've never heard of that.'

'Och, it's just something we eat in Scotland, where I come from. Michael likes it too, especially with hon-' He stopped as he remembered that those days were gone.

Walamai smiled. 'I also have a sibling,' he told him, sitting down. 'He's thirty now, but he's always going to be my little brother.'

'Yeah well, I don't think Michael cares about that anymore,' answered Julius, tasting his porridge. 'So, what do I need to do?'

'Before you can begin, you need to choose your guides in the spirit world.'

'How do I pick them?'

'Tijara believed that worthy people are recognisable by the friends they keep. Choose from those that matter most in your life. You must be able to rely on them.'

'That's easy then,' he replied. 'Morgana, Faith and Skye.'

Walamai nodded. 'If you had to describe each of them in one word, what would that be?'

Thinking about his relationship with them, he said, 'Faith is resilience. He never gives up. Skye is excitement. He's in love with life and, well, anything that moves really. Morgana … she's hope …' He trailed off, knowing that she was much more than that to him. 'When I'm lost, she gets me back on track.'

'It sounds like you have the perfect spirit guides. Are they on Moonrising?'

Julius nodded.

'Very well then. I will arrange for them to be brought over.'

'That's great. Thank you, sir. Can I ask you something? How come you're here, on this planet?'

'Our founder, Gelar Ganan, decided to leave Earth at the time when the relationship between Marcus and Clodagh broke down. He was a friend to both of them, but couldn't stand the thought of another fight, so soon after the Chemical War. So he left, taking with him all that would follow.'

'I see. And do your people have any of the White or Grey Skills?'

'We have all sorts among us, yes, including those with no skills to speak of. Gelar didn't care for divisions. We are a simple people, Julius. We cherish nature and, most of all, the gift of life. This is our legacy from the Chemical War. Finish your breakfast now. I shall return shortly.'

Julius did so, reflecting on what he had just heard. Certainly he now understood why this place felt more like a nature reserve rather than the kind of dwelling that he was used to, back on Earth. If only he had known about them before, maybe Michael could have moved here, where being a Nuarn wasn't an issue, and where he wouldn't have had to wear a choker around his neck. Once his bowl was empty, he took a drink from a nearby water fountain, and began to pace around the bonfire, practicing some breathing exercises.

Walamai returned an hour later, followed by Michael, who was wearing the same outfit as Julius. They exchanged no more than a brief glance.

'Come,' Walamai told both of them, heading up the path. Eventually, they arrived outside an oval shaped tent, made of large pieces of leather, decorated with the blue tribal designs that the Ocluths wore on their bodies. Walamai lifted one of the hide entrance-flaps, revealing an opening. 'Go through it,' he said, ushering them.

When Julius stepped in, he was surprised at how wide the floor space was. Hides covered the ground, except for a small space in the middle, where a couple of thin logs were burning fast. He followed the smoke with his eyes and watched it disappear through an opening above his head. The air smelled sweet and he felt a slight head rush as he inhaled.

'Julius, over here,' he heard Faith whisper.

He turned and saw the Skirts sitting along one side of the tent. Skye and Faith were wearing his same leather clothing, while Morgana looked lovely in her short suede skirt and soft boots. Julius lingered a second longer on her, before turning to examine the other side of the tent.

Michael had also chosen his guides, whose sight disappointed Julius greatly. Ben Hastings, K'Ssander — whom Julius had known would run back to T'Rogon — and Billy Somers, still evidently convinced that the world revolved around him, judging by the arrogant look on his face. What saddened him most was the fact that they were the only people his brother could count among his closest friends.

'Seekers,' said Walamai, 'lie beside your guides. When you are ready, put on your mind-visors.' He handed them a metal band each. 'It will take you into the dream world and interacts with your thoughts.'

Julius took his, a platinum coloured band, bent to fit around the forehead. He knelt down on the floor and waited for Skye and Faith to part, before lying down between them. Morgana put her hand on his shoulder.

'Don't you fall asleep, McCoy,' whispered Skye.

'I'm far from sleepy, mate,' he replied.

'Guides, your circlets please,' Walamai instructed them. Julius watched as ach of them put a circlet on.

'It's supposed to help us enter your vision,' explained Morgana.

'Or so he says,' added Faith, adjusting his so that it wouldn't shift about.

'Your visors now, Seekers,' continued Walamai.

Julius placed the metal band over the bridge of his nose, and felt it closing gently, but tightly, around his head and ears. All light and sound disappeared in an instant and, shortly afterwards, he saw a rendition of himself standing at one end of a long, dark room. This was the first example of technology he had experienced from the Ocluths, and he was curious to see how powerful it was. Two buttons appeared in his field of vision, allowing him to select the point of view. He switched from third to first person, which made the virtual version of him disappear, bringing him right into the action. It was much better.

The only light in the room dimly illuminated a square platform ahead of him, in the centre, and the four steps leading up to it. Unsure of what to do, he moved tentatively forward; as soon as he did so, the light grew in intensity. By the time he reached the bottom step, it was bright enough to see the outline of his brother approaching from the opposite end and climbing his own set of steps.

A blue suede carpet covered the platform, with two cushions placed at the top of both stairs. Michael took the lead and reached the flat surface first. He sat on the side closest to him, and crossed his legs. Julius watched his face for a moment longer, wondering if he truly realised what he was doing. His eyes were scouting the room with an appearance of mild curiosity, but Julius knew he was only pretending. Without noticing, Michael was nibbling at his lower lip, just as he used to do back home, whenever he had been nervous or anxious. The familiarity of that gesture felt completely out of place in the empty room, bringing Julius abruptly back to reality.

He climbed the last two steps and settled down on his cushion. The softness of the carpet under his hands took him by surprise – it seemed that the Ocluths had also mastered the holographic world.

A dot of light appeared in the space between the boys, like a tiny star. 'Welcome, Seekers,' it said. The greeting had been spoken by a young female voice, which sounded almost like a child's. 'Tijara's crystal can only be given to the most deserving one. The first part of the trail will test the strength of your will. Prove yourself.' With that, the light began to tremble and grew to the size of an apple. Two streams of bright blue phosphorescence emerged from either side of the orb and extended out towards the boys. As the stream reached Julius, it touched the centre of his forehead and melted upwards, covering his head. He saw the same thing happening to Michael.

The sight of this frightened Julius, making him wonder if Michael would have access to his thoughts. He tried to search his brother's mind, but found nothing. Perhaps the link wasn't meant for that, but instead served another purpose. Julius relaxed.

'Seekers,' said the young voice once more, 'it's time to see the future.'

The room around them disappeared, leaving Julius and Michael suspended in midair. A few seconds later, they both landed heavily in the middle of a white sand desert, which stretched out to the horizon.

Julius climbed to his feet and shook the sand off his clothes. The air was dry and all too realistically hot. The sun reflected off the ground, blinding him with its intensity, but he had nothing to shield his face with. He looked around, feeling lost, just like he had felt at the start of his first Solo game. There was nothing to see except sandy flatlands. He tried to activate his PIP to use the compass, but with no success. Judging by the position of the sun, he figured it must be some time past midday; keeping it to his left, he began to walk towards what he believed to be north. He had no particular reason to pick that course but, given the circumstances, did it matter? He saw that Michael had also started to walk, heading in the same direction. Without even noticing, he started to walk faster, until he was actually jogging. His brother followed suit.

Ten minutes later, Julius was completely drenched in sweat. The desert began to rise slightly and formed a small dune. He slowed down as he reached its edge and, looking beyond it, he gasped. A wide canyon opened at his feet, black and unwelcoming. The sunrays were unable to penetrate its darkness and were lost a few feet into the abyss. He looked to both sides, but could not see any crossing or an end to the ravine.

As if in answer to his hesitation, a message flashed in the middle of his vision: "JUMP!"

Julius didn't need to be told twice, and took a few steps back, preparing for a running jump. As his feet left the ground, a vortex of streaming images opened beneath him, trapping him inside its core, suspending him in midair. He saw his brother jump as well and soon they were facing each other at the centre of the swirling twister. Eventually, the images slowed, enough for him to see that they represented cityscapes from Earth. When the familiar outline of Edinburgh Castle caught his eyes, it spread like a virus through the other frames, until all the pictures were showing an identical scene. Then everything stopped abruptly, and they found themselves standing outside their home, in Scotland. A part of Julius' brain knew that his body had not actually moved from the raised platform, yet here he was, on his feet and about to knock on his own door.

As suddenly as he had arrived, the sky turned dark red and was filled with thousands of spacecraft opening fire over the roofs of the city, creating fireballs wherever they shot. A missile of some sort swooshed over his head, too low for comfort, and he ducked instinctively. He watched it make a straight line for the Castle and recoiled as it hurtled into St. Margaret's Chapel, blowing it to smithereens. 'What the heck is going on?' he said to himself.

'Looks like Earth has met its match,' commented Michael. 'It's the future, remember?'

Julius turned away from the smoke-filled street and the raging sky battle. However fake it was, he wanted to shut out these images of war and death. The front door was unlocked so he pushed it open and stepped inside, followed by his brother.

Of all the things he was expecting to see, the image of his parents and his grandmother — winter coat on and suitcases at her side — was the last he could have thought of.

'Mum? Dad?' he said, flabbergasted. 'Nana?'

'Thank Zed you're here!' cried Jenny, throwing her arms around him. 'We didn't know when you would come!'

'What ...'

'The net is down,' explained his dad. 'We lost communication with the Curia a few days ago.'

'What did they tell you?' asked Michael.

Julius heard coldness in his voice, but also a practical edge, of someone used to speeding things forward.

'Just that you would come pick us up and take us to Moonrising.'

'For the evacuation, you know?' added Jenny, hopefully. 'We almost ran out of food, but it doesn't matter. You're here now — why are you wearing those clothes?'

Julius was unsure how to continue. He knew there was no war on Earth, but the thought of his family in danger made his heart ache.

"TWO PEOPLE ONLY. CHOOSE." The message popped up suddenly in his optical screen.

'No!' he cried.

'Julius?' asked his father. 'What's wrong, son?'

'Nothing, Dad,' said Michael, stepping in. 'There's been a change of plans.'

'Change?' asked Jenny, fear surfacing in her eyes.

'We can only take two people. I'm sorry.'

Julius looked as startled as his family. How was he supposed to choose who to leave behind? Game or not, it was a nasty thing to ask of them.

'I don't understand,' said Nana, gripping her handkerchief tightly. 'Why?'

No one spoke for a few seconds, while the explosions outside continued.

'How ...' said Rory, clearly shaken. He slumped down on the sofa, and looked at his sons.

'I'll choose for you, Dad,' said Michael.

Julius watched sadly as his father stared at the floor, with the expression of one who is trapped on his face.

'Nana should stay,' Michael said, his voice loud and clear in the silence. 'I'm sorry Nana,' he told her, going to kneel by her feet and holding her wrinkled hand. 'It pains me to do this, but time is short and we need our race to survive. Mum and Dad are still young. They can still contribute much. You understand that, right Nana?'

Julius gasped at his speech. 'No way,' he said, stepping forward. 'You all go. I'll give you my place. I'm a fighter and have the most chance of survival.'

These words seemed to shake Rory McCoy into action once again. He stood up and gathered Jenny by Nana's side.

Michael left them and returned to Julius, while his family began to talk in hushed voices. 'You're weak,' he said. 'How can you be a real leader?'

'You're spending far too much time with T'Rogon, Michael,' he replied. 'What makes you think you can decide for others when it's something so important?'

'That is exactly what a leader does,' continued his brother. 'He makes decisions for everyone, even the tough ones.'

Julius knew that leaders were responsible for all; Professor Farshid had taught him that. But he also believed that the life of a man was his own to live. People didn't follow a leader because they had to, but because they wanted to. It was the only way to gain respect and trust, in his book. He looked at his family, and saw how distressed they all were, trying to decide what to do as the city was being destroyed.

Just as the explosions began to intensify, the bright light returned, engulfing the Seekers and removing them from that scene without revealing their choice.

When Julius opened his eyes, he was sitting on the sand once more, while Michael had landed several feet away to his right. The sun was much lower than it had been and the temperature had dropped considerably, he noticed with relief. There was something else too. A mountain range now loomed in the distance, its rocks bathed in orange from the afternoon sun. He guessed a distance of twenty miles between where he was and its base. If he jogged and walked he reckoned that he could do it in three hours or so. As he took his first steps, another thought came to his mind. Walking wasn't going to be an issue, but water would soon become one. Let's hope Ganan thought this through, he thought.

Julius walked for two hours, jogging as much of it as he could without overdoing it. Any curiosity he might have had about the brilliance of the Ocluths' technology was out of his mind as, quite frankly, he was actually starting to believe that he was in an actual desert. His pale skin was red from the sun, his lips dry, his stomach rumbling and he could feel a couple of blisters forming under his feet. Michael had always been either 50 feet ahead, or behind him, in a sort of strange relay. The only thing keeping him pushing forward was the mountain getting closer, bringing the hope of refreshment. Ahead of him, he could see a couple of large boulders, positioned like a gateway of some sort, marking the road he needed to take. Just then, he noticed that Michael had stopped short of the rocks, and was examining something on the ground. He then brought a pouch of sorts to his mouth. 'Water,' whispered Julius, and hurried his way.

Before he could reach him though, Michael threw the pouch on the ground and started walking again. Julius had no inclination to stop him, as he had just realised what the bundle on the ground was: Nana McCoy had been left behind.

He rushed to kneel at her side, and grabbed her small, cold hands. Her body was lying there, composed as if laid out inside a coffin. He felt his eyes welling up, remembering his life with her and what she had done for him. 'I bet you ordered them to leave you behind, right Nana?' he said. 'Ever the practical one.' He looked at her purple woolen jumper, and saw something bulging in one of her front pockets. When he checked, he found half a packet of sugar-encrusted ginger sweets. He opened them hungrily, and pushed all the remaining candy into his watering mouth. He let the juice coat his tongue, before crunching the sugar under his teeth. 'Thank you, Nana,' he said.

He sat there by her side, savouring his granny's favourite treat and resting his tired body. He noticed the empty water pouch lying on the sand and felt a stab of hatred for Michael — he was rapidly running out of excuses for his brother's choices of late, almost as if he had been replaced by an empty shell that merely looked like him.

The cry of an eagle pulled him from his thoughts and Julius got back to his feet. He grabbed the pouch from the ground and fixed it to his trousers, tying the leather strings around his belt – perhaps he would find water by the mountain. He couldn't leave his granny like this however. 'It's not real, Nana, I know, but I'm still going to bury you by the boulder.' He lifted her with ease, as she was now lighter than in life, and walked towards the taller of the two rocks. He chose the side that looked the most sheltered and, just as he knelt down, Nana's body turned into fresh, moist dark soil. Julius fell backwards, surprised by the sudden transformation. Her purple jumper was filled with it, while the rest of her clothes just lay there empty.

Julius stood up, wondering what to do. The sun was low and would soon disappear over the horizon. He needed to get to the mountain before it got too dark and, thanks to the sugar boost, he felt ready to continue. Before leaving though, he reached down to the jumper and tied each arm to one corner of the waistband, creating a sort of satchel to carry the soil inside. He placed it over his shoulder and began walking again. He didn't believe that this trail offered up anything without a good reason: if they gave him soil, then he was sure he should be keeping it.

Julius reached the base of the mountain a little while after twilight. The air was cold now and he felt incredibly tired. He caught the scent of roasted meat in the air and his stomach rumbled loudly, so he followed it eagerly. Once again, Michael was ahead, this time sitting by a small campfire with an animal roasting on a spit. Ten feet from him was another campfire, with a white goat tethered to a stand. Julius stepped toward this free camp and eyed the goat suspiciously. The head of the animal was secured through the stanchion, so that it couldn't slip back through. Feed had been placed in a container by its head, allowing it to eat while at the stand. On the ground was a sharp stone, a sack of feed and a bowl. He examined the goat closely and saw that it was female, and clearly ready to be milked. She had a little brown leather collar with the word "Oddball" written on it. Julius looked at her in amusement. 'And what am I supposed to do with you?' he asked. The goat bleated at him curtly and resumed feeding.

Julius picked up the sharp stone, which was shaped like a primitive knife, and threw a glance at his brother. Michael was currently eating his own newfound friend, but Julius wasn't too keen on a slaughtering end to his already long day. Besides, what if they kept them in the desert for days without food? If he had the goat and fed her, he could milk her and get proteins and liquid at the same time. The meat would be his last resort. He put the stone-knife down and grabbed the bowl instead, then placed it beneath the goat's udder and knelt by her side. 'Goat … Oddball,' he said, remembering the inscription on her collar. 'I've never done this before, so I apologise in advance. Please don't move.'

Oddball bleated in reply.

'If you say so,' said Julius. He rubbed his palms together and focused. 'Here we go.' It took Julius several attempts before he was able to draw the milk out. Oddball was not at all pleased with his unprofessional milking technique and proceeded to kick and struggle. He gave her more food, tickled her ears and even tried to talk some sense into her head, until the goat became more accommodating. Needless to say, Michael was thoroughly enjoying the scene, nibbling at a rib with his legs stretched out in front of him. Every so often he would hurl some bit of unhelpful advice at Julius, punctuated by laughter that was meant only to annoy him. By the time he turned in for the night, Julius' stomach had at least been placated. He freed the goat from the stand, but kept her tied to it, then lay close to the fire with the soil and the water pouch cradled in his arms. The purple jumper gave off the familiar scent of his grandmother, and he let his thoughts turn to her, as he was swept off into a deep sleep.

Julius woke at first light, feeling stiff and cold. The goat was currently nibbling at his hair and happily licking his forehead. 'Ouch! You're the worse alarm clock I've ever had,' he said, pushing her away. Oddball's bleat echoed off the face of the mountain, in a weird sort of morning greeting. He sat up and saw that his brother had already gone, leaving a smoking campfire behind. Julius stretched his limbs, feeling the blood start to flow again. There was still some milk in the bowl, so he drank it before putting the bowl and the knife in the soil pouch. He picked up the feed and nibbled at a few grain seeds, beneath Oddball's stare. 'Not bad,' he told her, offering her the remaining ones from the palm of his hand. The goat looked at them, bleated and turned away. 'Suit yourself,' he said, finishing the rest.

When Julius examined the mountain in front of him, he realised that carrying the milking stand along with everything just wasn't going to be an option. The rock face wasn't too sharp, but it looked like he would need both hands at several points. With that decision made, he loaded himself with the items he had gathered so far, and grabbed Oddball's line. He was grateful for the fact that the sun was still low and not too hot, although it wouldn't stay so for too long. He needed to hurry. 'Let's go.'

A clear path began to take shape as Julius climbed, winding its way upward. Oddball made it look easy, finding the best places to step, while Julius had to struggle to balance himself and his load. Looking ahead made him even more worried. The top of the ridge looked pretty steep to climb without a rope, so much so that he wondered if Michael had actually gone through there. And now that he thought of it, where was his brother? Julius didn't know when he had set off from the base camp — had he made the right choices or was he too late to catch up with him? Lost in this reverie, he arrived at a split in the path. He followed both ways with his eyes, trying to determine which would lead to the top, but there were so many protruding parts, which could hide all sorts of obstacles. 'Oddball,' he called. 'As a goat, which path would you pick?'

Oddball bleated and pulled towards the left path, dragging Julius behind.

'Can you slow down, please?' said Julius, tugging her back.

The goat had no intention of cooperating though, and pulled even harder.

'Fine,' he conceded. The animal led him for almost an hour, navigating the harsh surroundings with ease. Julius followed as best he could. He was once again too hot as the sun nipped at his exposed skin. He wondered how much further they had to go; fatigue was creeping back into his joints. Just then, Oddball stopped. Julius took a few steps further and saw a small opening in the rock to their left, large enough for them to pass through. 'Good goat,' he said.

It was an opening for a tunnel, carved into the mountain. Jagged shards of rocks crept out at odd angles, forcing Julius to bend and twist to avoid getting cut. When the tunnel finally started to expand in diameter, he was able to stand upright and drew a sigh of relief. Several side tunnels opened up to the left and right, but Julius decided to stick with the centre route, no matter how hard the goat pulled. They had been walking like this for a few minutes, when Oddball suddenly began to retreat.

'What's the matter?' asked Julius. The goat looked scared and pretty keen to go back the way they had come. Julius focused on the tunnel ahead and heard a low droning noise. 'Let's check it out. Come on.'

Oddball followed reluctantly.

As he moved further ahead, the noise grew louder. 'It sounds like … bees,' said Julius.

'Beh-eh,' added the goat.

Soon, the source of the noise came into view and it was Julius' turn to take a step back, completely baffled by what he saw. A wall of bees swarmed in front of them, blocking the tunnel and their path. On the ground was a bunch of cut flowers, which had seemingly already been visited by the buzzing colony. It occurred to Julius that Michel could have passed through there already, and that the flowers had been his way of distracting the bees so he could get through the tunnel. If that was the case, and he wouldn't put it past his brother, he needed to get hold of more flowers if he wanted to proceed as well. He looked around the walls of the tunnel, and didn't see any, so he walked back towards the exit until he reached one of the side tunnels. 'You wanted to go in here before, Oddball,' he said. 'Let's see if you can find some fresh food.'

The goat had been waiting for just such an opportunity and raced full steam ahead. 'Are you sure you're not a sniffer dog?'

'Beh-eh.'

'Just checking,' said Julius, unable to hold back a grin. Oddball led him a few yards further, and came to a stop in front of a thick bush of wild flowers growing out from between the grooves. Julius bent over them and a beautiful mossy scent washed over him. The flowers had long dark green stems; each flower was a vivid blue and six-petalled, ripe with nectar. 'They'll do,' he said.

Carefully, he began to pick a big bunch of them. The goat was clearly interested in the flowers too, but for different reasons. Julius noticed and gathered a few extra to bring along. 'Since I've eaten your grain, you should have something else in return.' He placed the spare ones in the bowl.

'Beh-eh.'

Satisfied that he had enough, Julius led Oddball back toward the bees. Cautiously, he placed the flowers to the left of the tunnel and took a step back. After a few seconds the bees shifted to the side around the flowers, slowly revealing an opening. Julius waited a moment longer, adjusted his load and led Oddball through the new exit, making sure he stuck to the right and hoping that the bees wouldn't be attracted to the few flowers he was carrying in the bowl behind his back. Once past the cloud of bees, he eased away from the wall, checking that they weren't being followed.

At the end of the tunnel was a large cavern, cut in two halves by a wide, placid stream. 'Now what?' he mumbled to himself.

'The game is broken,' said a voice to his right, catching him off guard.

Julius turned and saw Michael sitting on a rock, looking sulkily at a small rowing boat on the shore. 'Are you stuck?'

'I've been up and down the shore a few times already, but I can't cross anywhere — there's some sort of field. It's probably due to the Ocluths' rubbish technology, actually.'

'When did you become so cynical?' said Julius, walking to the edge of the stream.

Michael didn't reply. 'Why have you brought the zoo with you? You were supposed to eat the thing.'

'I felt like it,' he answered curtly. He set the satchel of soil down on the ground, along with the flowers in their bowl and kept the goat on a tight leash, so that she couldn't eat them. Seeing that the flowers were off bounds, Oddball approached the water and began to drink.

Julius immediately remembered his water pouch and, removing it from his belt, he refilled it.

'Hey!' said Michael, sounding annoyed. 'That's my water pouch.'

'Correction,' replied Julius, angrily, 'it's Nana's. You used it and left it behind, just like you did with all of us. Finders keepers. The pouch is mine now.'

Michael, it seemed, didn't have an apt answer to that.

Julius drank from the pouch, relishing the fresh water in his parched mouth. At that point he didn't even care what the water tasted like or even if it was poisoned. After he had had enough, he filled the pouch again and placed it on the ground, beside the rest of the stuff. He tried wading into the water, but knocked against an invisible wall. Michael had been right there: he couldn't swim across it. He washed his face and stood up. There were two boats on the shore and Julius moved to examine the one closest to him. It was large enough to carry one person. He noticed a tiny carving on one side and looked closer. "Carries Only 2", it read.

Taking advantage of the distraction, Oddball had another go at reaching the flowers.

Julius spotted her out of the corner of his eye and scooped the flowers up, away from the animal. 'That's it. I'm taking them with me. Stay!'

'Beh-eh,' argued the goat, but didn't move.

Julius stepped inside the boat, and sat down, balancing the flowers on his lap. As soon as he had done that, the boat shifted unexpectedly off the bank and began to cross the stream.

'How did you …' stammered Michael.

Julius thought about the sign on the boat, "Carries Only 2" — right now there was him and the flowers, and that made two. Still, he wasn't going to share that tip with Michael. When he reached the other side, he climbed out and walked the path to the exit. As soon as Julius moved one hand toward the opening, he found another invisible barrier. Unsure of what to do next, he put the flowers down. As they touched the ground, a beep echoed in the cave, the surface underneath them turned bright green and a small hole appeared at the centre of the barrier blocking the exit.

'What was that?' called Michael.

Julius stuck his finger inside the hole and smiled as it passed right through without finding any resistance.

Michael, meanwhile, was trying to get his boat moving, but it still wouldn't budge. 'Do it again, Julius!'

Intrigued, Julius picked up the flowers again; as soon as he did, the green light disappeared and the hole closed. 'It's the flowers,' whispered Julius. He placed them down once more and, sure enough, there was a loud beep, followed by the green light, and the small opening reappeared. He took a step back to observe the scene. Obviously he needed the hole to widen enough for him to get through it and the gap itself had only occurred when he had placed an object on the ground. What else did he have? He examined himself and immediately spotted the water pouch. He plucked it off his belt and placed it next to the flowers. As predicted, he heard the beep, the ground below the object turned bright blue and the hole widened enough to allow his head and one arm through.

'I need more,' he said. He peered at his things on the other side of the stream, then leapt into the boat and was instantly carried back — it looked like the boat could handle the return journey with only one item in it. Under the puzzled stare of Michael, Julius scooped up the purple jumper holding the soil and crossed back to the other shore. He placed it on the ground and the usual echo greeted him. This time a brown light bathed the ground and the hole grew considerably. Technically, he could have made it through as it was, but he wasn't about to leave the goat behind. For the last time, he returned to the boat.

It was at this point that Michael wised up about how to escape from the cavern and decided to take Julius' last item.

'Hey! Leave that goat alone!' shouted Julius from the boat.

Michael however, was having more serious problems, as he hadn't taken into account the power of Oddball. First he tried to pull it towards his boat, but to no avail. Then, avoiding the horns as best as he could, he tried to grab it around its body.

Julius had to wait for the boat to clear the invisible field before he could leap out of it and onto Michael. He grabbed him, trying to force him to let go of the animal.

Michael retaliated by elbowing him in the stomach. Julius felt the air leaving him and gasped, but didn't let go of his brother. Michael however, in doing this, lost his hold on the goat. 'Beh-eh-eh,' added Oddball amid the chaos.

With his remaining strength, Julius shook Michael off with a last twist of his torso. Michael rolled to the ground in a cloud of dust, unaware that the goat was now charging him. Before he could get out of the way, Oddball had pushed its little horns into his backside, and then turned to kick him with her rear legs.

When Julius and Oddball were safely back in the boat, Michael was still howling on the floor. 'Good job, girl,' he said, caressing her soft head.

'Beh-eh-eh.'

'Yeah, to you too.'

The boat landed on the far shore and, as soon as Oddball touched the ground there was another loud beep, followed by a red light that flashed into life beneath the animal. The exit was now completely open.

Just as Julius was taking his first step into the tunnel beyond, he heard four popping sounds and, turning, he saw that the objects he had brought across were now floating a couple of feet above the ground, encased in individual bubbles, corresponding to the colours of the lights he had seen before: green, blue, brown and red. He watched, mesmerised, as they floated past him, as if being pushed by a light wind. Oddball was resting, seated inside the cocoon, and looking quite smug.

'You can't leave me here!' cried Michael.

'Watch me,' Julius answered coldly.

The wall of the cavern closed behind him, trapping Michael beyond it.

Turning away, Julius followed the procession of floating cocoons, until they arrived in another chamber. At the centre of the chamber was a large hole in the ground; the four balloons came to a standstill above it. Julius watched keenly as the they blended together, separated and then blended again. As he watched in awe, the bubbles formed into one larger sphere, and the colours took up specific positions within it. It wasn't long before Julius realised what he was looking at. A small-scale representation of a brand new world teeming with land, sea, vegetation and life revolved above the ground before his marvelling eyes.

'Welcome to the future, Seeker,' said the childlike voice.

At that moment, he was plunged into darkness. He was starting to panic when the lights slowly returned and he saw a rendition of himself standing inside a white room with no doors. Then Michael appeared, standing by his side. He looked angry with his brother, but said nothing.

The voice continued. 'You're about to begin the last part of your trail, Seekers, where you can change the past, if you wish to do so. One can tell a lot about a man by the company he keeps. Is your sense of judgment worthy of the power that lies ahead?'

Julius felt invigorated. Thinking of Morgana, Faith and Skye made him sure that he had what it took. On the other hand, he couldn't say the same for his brother. 'K'Ssander, Hastings and Somers — are those your best pals out there?' he asked, unable to restrain himself.

'So what if they are?'

'Then you'll need more luck than you think,' he replied coldly.

Michael faltered slightly, and he didn't look quite so cocky anymore.

Suddenly, two openings appeared on one of the walls. Julius didn't wait, and stepped assuredly through the one on the right. When the wall slid shut behind him, he was sure his brother hadn't moved yet.

He was standing at the beginning of a long corridor, where several doors opened on either side. He couldn't shake the feeling that he had been here before, a sense of familiarity almost but, try as he might, no clear recollection came to mind. Unsure of what else to do or what to expect, he walked forward. Michael was nowhere to be seen and Julius wondered if he was also standing in a similar place. A shaft of light splashed the floor outside one of the doors. He approached it, hoping to find some answers. As he reached the door, he saw a plaque on the wall. "Grand Master Marcus Tijara" was engraved on it. Julius gasped in surprise. No wonder the place seemed so familiar; he was back on Zed, in his school, centuries ago. Heart beating furiously, he stepped into the room.

Marcus Tijara was sitting at his desk, poring over a clump of paper files. Julius remembered the day he had first seen his portrait hanging up in the Zed Test Centre. In it, Tijara was in full Zed uniform, proud and tall. Julius drew closer to him, pretty confident that he couldn't be seen. To confirm that, Tijara didn't even lift his head, but just kept on shuffling the papers in front of him. From that distance, Julius could see that he was probably in his late forties, and sporting a full head of thick, dark hair. There was an air of sadness about him, coupled with a knotted brow, as of someone facing a serious decision.

Julius looked at the closed folder on the desk, and his eyes widened as he examined the drawing on the cover: four stars — one at the top, two below it at either side and one at the bottom — joined together by lines, to form a diamond; Tijara's Heart. Frantically, he wondered when this was, before or after the construction of the weapon. His hand stretched towards the document, but his fingers merely passed through the paper. He sighed, feeling like a helpless spectator. It was at that moment that the door opened.

'Come in, Eronan,' called Tijara, looking up.

The person who had just walked into the room, with all the confidence of a regular visitor, looked like a human, but upon closer scrutiny it became evident that he wasn't. His grey eyes were the first thing that struck Julius. They weren't smooth, but had tiny surfaces, like a cut diamond; as they caught the light, it made the irises appear like tiny crystals. His neck was long and his facial features extremely delicate — as if someone had sketched them lightly on a canvas — befitting the frail hue of his skin. He wore a red tunic and had a kindly smile. There were no markings on his clothes to identify his rank or origin but, whoever he was, his relationship with the Grand Master must have been a close one. Although Julius felt a positive, safe vibe emanating from him, he began to wonder about the nature of this strange visitor. Was this even real? If Marcus Tijara had befriended an alien, surely someone would have noticed.

'How are you feeling, Marcus?' Eronan asked, taking the chair opposite the Grand Master. His voice was calm and gentle.

Julius stepped back and quietly observed the scene.

'Scared, to tell you the truth.'

Eronan nodded pensively. 'You don't need to do this, you know?'

Tijara looked at him with a raised eyebrow. 'And what other choice do I have, pray tell?'

'You could come with me to Eneamar and leave the others to their squabbles.'

Eneamar, thought Julius. He was sure he had heard that name before.

'Leave the Solar System?' said Freja.

'We're only a wormhole away — the closest one from here. It's so well hidden that no one would ever find you. You can join me later, if you prefer. Once you're through it, it's only a matter of looking for the Archer, on the highest peak of the tallest mountain of Mah. He will show you the way,' finished Eronan, with a flourish of his hand.

Marcus stared at him, unmoved.

'Alternatively, we can counteract the effect of the Chemical War, if you really want us to, but it would not be quick.'

'Time is a luxury I don't have.'

'Then,' continued Eronan, 'we do have time to prepare an all out attack. Or ...' he added quickly, seeing as Tijara was shaking his head firmly, '... we organise yet another diplomatic mission with Clodagh.'

'Which you know very well will fail, just like the previous two,' said Marcus.

'Have you tried talking to her? Privately, I mean.'

Tijara nodded. 'I told her that if she didn't back down and remove her forces from our solar system, I would build it.'

He must be referring to the weapon, thought Julius.

'And?'

'She laughed,' said Tijara, sadly. 'She doesn't believe I have the technology to do it. She says if they can't build it, we surely have no chance.'

'I take it you haven't told her about the partnership between *us* then?'

Tijara shook his head. 'Not in light of recent events. I decided to pay for the sins of our parents alone, without dragging your lot into all this.'

'They meant well,' said Eronan, delicately. 'We all did.'

'The road to hell is paved with good intentions, we say here. I guess your people have never heard that one before.'

Julius was confused, no matter how much he tried to make sense of this conversation. His eyes kept passing back to Eronan, captivated by his strange features.

'Your parents were visionaries, Marcus. They knew the Chemical War was the only way to start the change,' he said softly. 'The least painful.'

'For the billions who died, or for those who survived?' asked Tijara. There was bitterness in his voice. 'Those deaths are only the beginning Eronan, mark my words, even with my sacrifice. Half of your creation has turned against you.'

Eronan took some time before answering. 'Then maybe,' he ventured tentatively, 'it will be your sacrifice that shows Clodagh what love can do.'

Julius flinched, as the thought of his last words to Farrah came swirling suddenly to the surface of his memories.

Eronan stood up. 'We don't have a lot of time left, Grand Master. You need to make a decision soon. Are you going to give me that file, or are you going to bin it?'

To Julius' surprise, everything froze and all went still. As he looked around perplexed, another figure emerged from the shadows. It was Faith. Only, he didn't look as real to Julius as Tijara or Eronan; he was more ethereal, like a ghost.

'How did you get here?' asked Julius in astonishment.

'Beats me,' he replied, looking at his transparent hands with curiosity. He hovered forward, and examined Eronan. 'He looks weird — I heard everything, by the way,' he added, pointing at the two men. 'So, what's it gonna be? I think they want you to make a decision, McCoy.'

'Faith, haven't you noticed the alien in the chair or the weird conversation about the war they've just had?'

'Forget the funny man and his games,' he answered, oddly dismissive. 'If you were Tijara, what would you have done?'

Julius struggled to think, but tried to focus despite this. He was daunted by the task and stood still, staring at the file. 'Well, Tijara could save himself a lot of grief by binning that document — he would live, for one thing. And, with his powers, he could deliver a final blow to Arnesh. He could also …'

'Yes?' prompted Faith, as Julius paused mid-sentence.

'He could raise Farrah properly,' he blurted out, 'rather than allowing her mom to turn her into a frozen embryo, a prize for a treasure hunt — besides, Tijara's sacrifice didn't actually stop the Arneshians, as we well know. Why would he go and choose such a stupid, self-harming way to solve a situation that could have been dealt with by the best-trained officers in the universe? Tell me that!'

'Anything else?' asked Faith. He seemed to be enjoying Julius' little rant.

'As a matter of fact, yes. It hurts so damn much having your powers ripped from you. I wouldn't recommend it to anyone! But I guess you couldn't understand that.'

Faith, patting the side of his skirts with his hand, replied, 'I'd say I do know what it means to give up something dear for a good cause, even if it hurts. Or have you forgotten that?'

Julius shook his head. 'I had no choice.'

'Actually you did. Hastings gave you a way out. He said he would have shipped you off Zed, to spend the rest of your life in some remote outpost. Now, whether or not he was lying, you could have done that, but you didn't. Why is that?'

Julius mulled over the reasons for his actions. 'I was angry at Farrah, for lying … and I believed I could make a difference; that I could stop it for good.'

'And you did, Julius. We wouldn't be here if you hadn't. There's only a handful of Arneshians left in the whole universe, thanks to you.'

Julius dismissed the words with a wave of his hand.

'And FYI, I had a choice too,' continued Faith. 'I didn't have to jump in front of that car to save me cousin Patty, you know. But, like I told you once before, the important things sometimes come at a price. So what's it gonna be?'

Those last words hung in the air and, when Julius turned to look at his friend, he realised that Faith was gone. Sighing deeply, he came to the conclusion that he couldn't make a decision based on what he knew now. If Tijara hadn't used the weapon, was there any guarantee that the war would have ended? And as for Clodagh's actions regarding her daughter ... how could he prevent that, and what if it had already happened? Tijara had struck the first blow against the Arneshians, and Julius had merely picked up where he had left off, to bring the story to an end. Everything else was circumstantial, a backdrop for the main plot. Marcus had been the protagonist then and this was Julius' moment, but he needed the crystal if he wanted to end this once and for all. 'I'm ready,' he said.

The air crackled, and an action grid appeared before him. To the left was a square with the writing, "Build Heart" and to his right another that said, "Bin file". Julius took a deep breath, then stretched his fingers towards the left button and pushed it. As soon as he did this, the grid disappeared and he found himself staring into Tijara's eyes.

The Grand Master hesitated for a moment, then picked up the papers and shoved them into Eronan's waiting hand. 'Set it up.'

A bright light engulfed Julius and the room, and everything vanished. He was startled to find himself back inside the white room from the beginning of his mission. There was no trace of Michael, and Julius wondered what his brother had chosen.

It was a while before a new door opened in the wall. Julius wasn't sure how many minutes had passed; his perception of space and time had gone completely off kilter. He walked to the door and poked his head through the gap, realising immediately that he was standing inside a small ship. The deck was empty, except for Tijara, who was steering them away from Zed. Although there was no trace of Pit-Stop Pete's in the vicinity, Julius knew that airspace all too well — they were leaving Zed orbit, so that Tijara's Heart could be used safely.

They flew for a few minutes, before Tijara brought the ship to a standstill, and checked the radar. Julius looked past the Grand Master and saw a massive enemy presence surrounding the Zed fleet, essentially cutting off any escape routes. Seeing this, Julius now knew that, if Tijara hadn't used the Heart, Arnesh would have wiped them all out for good, and then taken over Earth. Relief washed over Julius as he realised that he had made the right decision, back in the room with Eronan.

A flickering dot blipped into life on the radar, moving closer to their position. To Julius' surprise, Tijara allowed it to dock and board the vessel. He watched as the Grand Master hurried towards the main hatch. When the green light beside it blinked on, the porthole opened, allowing a tall, olive-skinned man to enter. Julius didn't recognise him, but he was wearing clothing made of animal hides, similar to the ones worn by the Ocluths. Tijara and the man embraced, as old friends do.

'Marcus Tijara,' said the man warmly.

'Gelar Ganan, my brother from the West,' replied the Grand Master.

Julius' eyes widened when he heard the name. He was standing in front of the founder of Buruwang, ancestor of the Ocluths and keeper of Tijara's crystal.

'I wasn't sure you would come,' continued Tijara, 'since your people have already left Earth.'

'You needed me, so here I am.'

Tijara ushered him towards the deck, where they stopped in front of a console. 'Julius!'

Julius turned with a jolt, as he of course wasn't expecting to be addressed by anybody just then. It seemed that another passenger had come aboard; another ghostly one. 'Skye, over here, quick,' said Julius, beckoning when he saw his friend, before turning back to the two men.

Tijara was caressing the cold, flat surface of the pedestal before him. 'Will you keep it safe, Gelar?'

'I will. Until you come back to claim it.'

The Grand Master didn't reply, and continued rubbing the panel beneath his fingers.

'Marcus?' said Gelar, sounding worried. 'You are coming back for it, right?' The look on Tijara's face was answer enough. 'But why?'

'It's the only way to end this war,' he replied tiredly. 'One day perhaps, someone worthy of it will come seeking. I trust you'll know such a person when the time comes.'

Gelar stared into Marcus' eyes for a moment, and nodded. 'Of course, my friend.'

'Let us begin then,' he said. He moved over to the navigation panel, and pointed at the radar. 'The Arneshians are grouped along this section of our quadrant, and have been for some time. We managed to position the field beams all around them — practically under their noses.' Tijara pressed a few buttons. 'There, the field is now on.'

Julius remembered how Ben Hastings had also had to activate a similar field around planet Arnesh, before unleashing Julius' powers on it. It was clear that its function was to distribute the energy beam evenly, and ensure everything within its radius was affected.

'My powers will enter the Heart, which acts as a catalyst but also as an activator of certain subatomic particles, which will seek out the white pearls of every Arneshian, killing those pearls instantly.'

'Are you sure it will work?' asked Gelar nervously.

'There's only one way to find out, my friend, but I'm willing to take the risk.'

A loud beeping sound suddenly echoed around the deck, startling all present. Tijara and Ganan looked at each other in disbelief.

'What's happening?' whispered Julius to Skye, but he found no answer.

'On screen,' ordered Tijara.

Clodagh Arnesh's face filled the frame. She looked from Tijara to Gelar and back, seemingly flustered. 'Will you not let me in?'

That was when time froze again.

Julius stood staring at the beautiful woman with delicate features, her long blonde hair curled over her shoulders. Julius had seen her once before, during his second year at Tijara, as the Oracle of Life; what struck him now though, was her striking resemblance to Farrah.

'We didn't even recognise her when we first saw her,' said Skye. 'Remember, Julius?'

He was right, of course. Not until it was too late, at least.

'She wants to come aboard,' said Julius, growing worried. 'What if she tries to stop them?'

In reply, Skye walked up to the screen and began observing Clodagh, like a critic in front of a painting. Occasionally he would step back and tilt his head a little, before moving forward again to examine something that had caught his attention.

Julius watched, puzzled. 'What on Zed are you doing, Skye?'

'I think it's safe to let her in,' he said after a while, sounding satisfied. 'She won't harm them.'

'How do you know?' he asked. 'I mean, I also get that impression, but how do you actually know?'

'Women are my territory, McCoy. She's here to make amends.'

'But how can you tell?' asked Julius, examining her face closely.

Skye pointed at various parts of the screen, like a teacher in an art class. 'Look at her body language: the way her shoulders are slightly hunched forward, her head tilted downwards, the downcast eyes. She's not wearing elaborate hairdos or fancy make-up; her robe is somber, without frills — penitent, I would say.'

'And you can tell all that from a picture?'

'Yep, the Miller can. And if that isn't enough, look at her eyes. I haven't seen that kind of sadness since the look in your eyes, when Michael left Earth.'

Julius had to admit that Skye's description seemed quite accurate. He was right about her sadness too, although he hadn't expected Skye's observation of his feelings. 'All right then. Thanks Skye. I'm ready.'

As soon as the words left his mouth, Skye's form faded away, and the grid appeared in front of him again. This time the options were to either let her aboard or not. Julius selected the first one.

Time returned to normal, and Marcus Tijara was preparing his vessel to be boarded. With Gelar by his side, he turned to face the hatch, waiting for her to enter.

When Clodagh appeared, Julius noticed how Tijara tried to look stern and serious, the shadow of tiredness suddenly gone.

'Gelar, what are you still doing here?' asked Clodagh. There was concern in her voice, and genuine surprise.

'I'll be on my way soon enough,' he answered.

Julius thought that they must have known each other in better times and, although neither of them spoke with resentment, the awkwardness of the situation was evident.

Clodagh turned to Tijara. 'Have you really built it?'

'I did,' he said, motioning toward the pedestal with his head.

Clodagh's eyes widened and Julius saw a look of fear passing over her face.

'Come with me, Marcus. It's not too late,' she cried in distress. When he didn't reply, she tried a different tactic. 'Gelar, you cannot let him do this. It could kill him!'

'Since when have you been concerned with our welfare?' asked Tijara.

'Don't be ridiculous,' she replied. 'I've always cared about you, you know that.'

'And I have always cared about our people.'

Clodagh flushed and turned away, clearly trying to hide her face from them.

Without warning, Tijara hurried away, catching them all by surprise. He flipped open the panel over the pedestal and spread both palms against the glass, activating the weapon.

'No!' cried Clodagh, dashing towards him.

Gelar stepped in and grabbed her before she could reach him. 'You can't stop the procedure! It's too dangerous.'

Julius watched, aghast, as the memories and feelings of his own transfer of energy came flooding back to his mind, from the cold glass panel under his hands to the sense of emptiness that had followed. He watched sadly as Tijara slumped over the console, eyes closed, face contorted in pain. Some of the hairs on his body were standing on end, and Julius knew that his powers were running out of his body like a current.

'Look,' said Gelar to Clodagh.

Julius turned towards the front of the ship, and saw a thick yellow beam shoot out of the vessel, into the Arneshian fleet. When the beam struck the field, which was encasing the enemy ships, it spread over it, like a bucket of paint being poured over a transparent sphere. The blinding flash that followed made him shield his eyes, but it didn't last long. After that, there was darkness and silence.

Julius watched in astonishment as Tijara let go of the pedestal, still holding the crystal in one hand, and collapsed to the floor.

Clodagh was quickly by his side, and cradled his head in her lap. 'Marcus ... Marcus! Can you hear me?'

Suddenly, the security system of the ship came to life, and a deep vibration caused the ship to shudder.

Gelar ran to the navigation panel. 'The Heart has drawn too much energy from the core of the ship. It won't last long. We must leave now!'

Tijara stirred a little, and opened his eyes.

'You fool!' Clodagh said to him, ignoring Gelar's warning. 'Why did you have to do this?'

'You ... you know why, Clodagh,' he replied feebly. 'It has to end ... I have done my part. Withdraw your troops, and let Earth become a better place.'

Clodagh stared at him in silence. Then she saw the crystal in his hand and delicately took it. 'Everything I need to fulfill my plan is in this little blue crystal.'

'Clodagh,' said Gelar hurriedly, 'there's no time for this nonsense now. Help me get him up!'

'I won't be going anywhere,' said Marcus. 'There's nothing left inside me worth saving. Gelar, my friend, take Clodagh and protect her from herself.' He looked at her, and smiled. 'Go, my dear ... beloved Clodagh.'

As time froze around him, Julius realised that his mouth was wide open, he was so captivated by the intensity of the moment. He didn't even notice Morgana as she stepped out of the shadows.

'Julius,' she called.

He turned, startled. 'Did you see that?'

She nodded, then walked over to the couple and knelt by their side. Her eyes were shining. 'They must have loved each other very much,' she said quietly. 'Even after all they went through.'

'Am I to decide if she stays or goes then?' he asked.

'I think so,' said Morgana.

'The ship is about to explode and she doesn't seem in a hurry to leave,' he said, feeling confused. 'Why isn't she going?' Tijara is powerless ... finished. He has nothing else to offer her — nothing she could ever want ...' He looked around him, expecting the grid to appear and give him the choice, but there was nothing. 'Just go already!'

he shouted at her.

'She won't,' added Morgana.

'Why not?'

'Don't you remember?' she asked, looking up to him. 'All we ever knew was that Tijara and Arnesh died together, ending the conflict for a very long time and giving Zed a chance to grow stronger. This is how they did it. Clodagh loved him so much that, in the end, she sacrificed all she had for him, as broken as he was, so that Zed's victory would be complete. I would have done the same for the man I loved ... powerless or not.'

Julius mulled over her words and wondered if they could have really been meant for him — was she trying to tell him something more than just solving this case? He forced his thoughts away from that spark of hope, and moved them back onto Clodagh and Marcus. He knew their story, but was still torn. It showed on his face.

'What is it?' asked Morgana, noticing this. 'Talk to me.'

'Well, it's just that, if Clodagh survived, so would ... Farrah,' said Julius. 'She would have a chance at a proper life and maybe that would be enough to keep her mother from going mental, or something.'

'If Clodagh is here it means that Farrah has already been frozen. Besides, I don't believe Farrah would have been strong enough to stop her. Not even Marcus was able to do that with his love, never mind an infant. With that crystal, Clodagh could take over everything, even with her people defeated. She knows that and that's why she's not going. Let her stay.'

Julius remained dubious, even though he could hear a ring of truth in Morgana's words. And besides, did it really matter? Whatever he chose, he couldn't actually change the past, could he? 'I'm ready.'

As Morgana's shape faded away, the grid appeared. As predicted, the options were to do with Clodagh's next decision. Julius followed Morgana's advice and let her stay.

When time began to flow normally once more, Clodagh slowly handed the crystal to Gelar. 'Go, and keep it safe.'

Gelar grabbed it, as the rattling of the ship became more violent. 'Come with me,' he said, extending his hand out to her, but she only shook her head.

'Clodagh,' said Tijara weakly, 'you must go.'

'No, my love,' she said, tenderly caressing his hair. 'My place is here with you, for all eternity.'

Julius saw Gelar wavering for a moment, before pocketing the crystal and leaving the lovers behind. The floor shook beneath his feet and, even though he knew this was only a dream, his heart began to race. The ship alarm was beeping insistently now, and he had to grab one of the wall handles to steady himself. Just before the ship exploded, Julius saw Clodagh bending over Marcus and kissing his lips in one last embrace.

Light erupted all around Julius, making him wonder if he had actually been caught in the explosion. But everything had gone quiet, and he felt no pain, or flames licking at his skin. He forced his eyes open, and saw that he was back in the foyer. Michael was nowhere to be seen but, lying in the centre of the floor, unadorned and simple, was Tijara's crystal. The sight of it there drove everything else from his mind.

He lunged at it and grasped the crystal with both hands. The blue liquid inside it swayed from left to right, causing sparkles of light all around it. Julius removed its cap with shaky hands, being careful not to spill even one drop. He brought it under his nose, but the liquid had no smell. Everything he had hoped for was now in his hands — his chance to set things right and fulfill all of his dreams. Without a second thought, he gulped back the content.

A warm feeling spread through his body, from his chest, to his arms, then down his legs. As it reached the tips of his fingers and toes, it became so hot it felt like it was burning him. Julius waggled his hands, trying to shake off the pain, but it was no good. He could feel Tijara's powers filling every fibre of his body in waves; there was so much of it that it began to seep out his pores, like sweat. A golden aura formed around his body, and he tingled all over, as if someone had connected him to a power socket. Eventually, all the power converged back into his chest for a few seconds, before shooting up into his head where it exploded in an invisible blast of energy. Julius tilted his head back and cried out — a long shout of victory and pain. Then he fell backwards and the room went dark as night.

THE GALACTIC FEDERATION OF EARTH

When Julius opened his eyes, he realised that he was lying on the ground, back inside the tent. He was aware of the shuffling of feet around him and people moving, but couldn't recognise the voices. His head felt heavy and, when he let it roll to the right, he saw through bleary eyes his brother Michael asleep by his side. He wanted to reach out to him, but no part of his body was willing to answer his summons. Several figures appeared in his field of vision and he watched as they bent over Michael, lifted him up and carried him out of the tent. Knowing that he was alone once again, he forced the muscles of his neck to turn his head upwards. The smoke from the fire was still rising, squeezing out into the open air through a gap at the top of the tent. No matter how much he tried, he was struggling to keep his eyes open, he was so tired. At some point, he felt arms and hands grabbing him around the back of his chest and he was lifted like a sack of rocks, unable to move or help. Then he passed out.

He came to in the open, by the familiar bonfire glade, some time later. He couldn't tell how long he had been asleep, but it was nighttime. The logs were burning brightly at the centre of the clearing, and he realised he was sitting on some sort of stone armchair. The flames warmed his naked chest, while his animal-hide trousers were becoming hotter. The rhythmic, slow beat of a drum filled the air, causing his heart to vibrate with each stroke. There were hands on his shoulders, propping him up — he knew that he was still unable to do so by himself. His eyes kept opening and closing and, in a daze, he saw that Daku Derain was sitting opposite him, holding a brush. Each time the man leaned in and painted his skin, Julius felt cold, wet lines forming wherever the brush made contact. The air smelled sweet, and the perfume was making him drowsy, so he dozed off once more.

A chill breeze woke him. This time his eyes were willing to open and remain so, and he had regained control over his body once again. He looked around, wondering where everyone had gone, and why they had left him there by himself. The steady beating of the drum still filled the air though; it had grown a little faster than before. He examined himself and noticed that his arms were covered in jet-black markings. His torso and face had been decorated too – he could feel dried lines on his cheeks and forehead. He touched one of the lines on his chest, transferring some of the paint to his fingertips. Carefully, he stood up, using the armrests as support. His head wasn't completely clear and his entire body felt on edge, as if a current was running through it. The once familiar drops of energy were back, seeping out from the pores of his fingers and falling onto the ground at his feet, in fluorescent yellow pools. Whenever Julius had seen them before, they had been as a side effect of intense anger, even rage. Now however, they were simply surplus energy. He was so charged up with Tijara's power — his powers now — that his body couldn't contain it all. It should have been scary, but Julius had never felt more exhilarated in his entire life.

The drum continued to beat in the distance; it seemed to be coming from the direction of the beach. Julius breathed deeply, which steadied him enough that he felt he would be able to walk. Blood was rushing like a torrent through his veins, energising his muscles wherever it flowed. He walked towards a gap in the trees, peering ahead, looking for the source of the sound. The moon made the sand shine white, but the beach was empty as far as he could see. In the dark night air, Julius' body was glowing with Tijara's essence. Another light — the only other one on the beach — appeared to his left. It was coming from the open door of his hut. Julius turned towards it, the drummer suddenly forgotten, and headed for the open door. He couldn't hear any voices but, as he approached, a red glare appeared and washed over the floorboards. Cautiously, he walked up to the opening and looked inside.

Morgana was leaning against the chest of drawers, the heels of her hands propped on the counter at either side of her hips, her legs stretched out in front of her. She was still wearing the top and skirt made of soft hides. A chunky candle burned brightly behind her, creating shadows on the walls, like dancing spirits. When he appeared, she looked up. Her eyes examined the designs on his body with eagerness, as if she was reading a story in them.

Julius didn't realise how much he had missed his ability to see the auras around people whenever they felt strong emotions, until now, as he noticed the red glare emanating from her. He knew exactly what it meant and what she wanted, because it was also his wish. He stepped inside, closing the door behind him, aware of his rising heartbeat. He walked towards her, feeling scared and excited at the same time. Morgana stood up confidently, bringing her face an inch from his and Julius lost himself in her eyes. He bent and kissed her mouth gently, enjoying the light-headed rush it gave him. His hands slid down from her shoulders, along her arms, searching for her hips, where he began to slowly gather the thin material of her skirt in his palms, until he found bare, soft skin beneath it. He pulled her to him and felt her quiver against his body. Then her fingers were on his arms, his chest, following the outline of his muscles. Julius kissed her harder, pushing her back against the counter. Morgana let him lift her up, wrapping her legs around his waist, while he stubbed out the candle flame between his fingertips.

With the darkness, the drumbeat stopped.

*

Julius dreamt of Eneamar for the first time that night. He saw waves crashing on sandy beaches; arched skyscrapers dotting the city line; the monorail and fly-cars; blue sky and warm sun. He walked through the clean streets of the city, surrounded by a soothing music that reassured him that better times were just ahead. The people looked like Eronan, with eyes like crystals. They all smiled at him as they passed him, as if they knew him already. Julius inhaled the fresh air and walked on, captivated by all the sounds and scrolling images projected from the rectangular screens that wrapped themselves around the buildings. He didn't know where he was, or when he was, but it didn't matter — here, no one would harm him. He arrived at a fountain in the centre of a square; the water gurgled out from the top of a giant metal sphere, to then gather in a basin below it, before flowing away along a thin canal. The sphere looked oddly familiar to Julius, with its surface decorated by bas-reliefs. He looked at it for a while, before following the little duct, wondering where the water would end.

The passage continued through a park, where tall trees let only shards of sunbeams through to lighten up the fresh carpet of new grass. When the ground began to rise, Julius followed. A hill was growing under his feet, and the fact that the water was also running upwards didn't bother him in the least. As the trees receded he saw the summit, where the sunlight caught the silver base of a statue. He shielded his eyes until he reached it, and then examined it properly. It was humanoid in shape, but there was something peculiar about it – a mane of thick hair grew on the back of the body, from head to toes. The male figure was standing with his legs apart, firmly fixed to the ground, he held a bow in his stretched, left arm, while the right one pulled the rope back towards his face. He wore a linen cloth around his waist and padded leather boots. Curious, Julius touched the point of the arrowhead; as soon as he did this, a beam of light shot off into the distance, startling him, and was lost in the blue sky above.

'Mah,' said a voice.

Julius turned, and found himself face to face with Eronan, who was pointing in the direction of the beam. He looked just like he had during the dream quest, wearing the same red tunic. 'What did you say?' he asked.

Eronan repeated, 'Mah.'

Julius began to toss and turn in his bed, an uneasy feeling seeping into his mind. When morning came, however, the feeling had gone and only fleeting images from the dream remained, tucked away in a corner of his mind.

*

When Morgana opened her eyes she saw Julius laying by her side, watching her, with his head held up on his right hand. She smiled coyly, gathering the pillow under her head. 'Hi.'

'Hi,' he replied, barely able to refrain from grinning.

'I seem to have smudged your beautiful designs,' she said, passing a finger over his chest.

'They look better on you anyway.'

Morgana looked down, examining the dried black traces on her arms. 'I'm going to need a serious shower.' She smiled at him. 'You got them back, huh? How do you feel?'

He knew she was talking about his powers. 'Great,' he said, rolling over onto his back, and stared at the ceiling, feeling elated. 'Fully charged. But for some reason I can't really remember what happened in the dream quest.'

'Neither can I, nor the guys,' said Morgana, baffled. 'At first, we just sat there, watching you. We didn't know what was going on and no one came to give us directions. I clearly remember sitting in the tent and then suddenly, I heard your summon. I became drowsy and the next thing I knew, I was back in the tent again, as if awakening from a deep sleep. The memory of it disappeared in that moment, the way dreams do in the morning. They are right on the edge of consciousness, but you just can't reach them.'

'That's weird. And what about Freja and Derain? Did they see any of it?'

'Apparently not. Like us, they saw you asleep throughout the journey, until the end when you got the powers. You were thrashing on the floor most of the time; then your body began to glow — which was really freaky! And speaking of powers, Derain says not to use them yet. You have a medical at noon.'

'I suppose,' he said.

'You've waited for this long,' she said, reading his disappointment. 'Waiting a few more hours won't hurt.'

Julius nodded. In truth, he didn't mind staying right where he was for a while longer, a blissful zone where he felt full of power and life. For the first time in months, he was truly at peace with himself. Lying there, next to her, he felt no embarrassment; it was a moment as natural as their friendship, but richer in complicity and intimacy. Not even with Farrah had he felt this way, and for some reason, he didn't care to know why that was. 'I've been wondering,' he said, looking at her. 'The day they put me in stasis, you came by the chamber and said something to me through the glass, just before I closed my eyes. What did you say?'

Morgana's cheeks flushed slightly. 'I said that I'd be waiting.'

Julius leaned towards her, and kissed her.

She shifted under the sheet, getting closer to him, caressing his face tenderly.

Suddenly, an urgent knock rattled the wooden door. 'McTijara, are you awake yet?' called Faith from the other side.

'Shoot!' whispered Julius, panicking. 'Just a sec!' he cried towards the door, while Morgana tried to hide under the covers.

Faith, taking Julius' answer as an invitation to enter, swung the door wide open and hovered inside. 'It's so good to have you back, WC! We must celebraAAAAHHH!' he finished, backtracking fast.

'What's the matter?' cried Skye, hurrying into the room. 'Faith? Julius? Are you all right?' He immediately stopped too, once he saw Morgana's head popping out from under the sheet.

A moment of awkward silence followed, until Skye took the situation back into his hands. 'Good morning!' he said, merrily. 'And congrats! About time too, may I add!'

Seeing as the guys were just staring at them, Julius cleared his throat. 'Was there something you came to tell me?'

'Wha-?' began Skye, startled. 'Oh! Yes of course … Your meeting with Freja is soon. You better be there in twenty.'

'Thanks,' said Julius, vaguely.

Faith was still standing there, mouth wide open, so Skye grabbed him by the waist of the skirt and dragged him out.

Once the door had closed, Julius turned to Morgana. 'He did say twenty, right?'

Morgana nodded, a cheeky look on her face. She grabbed the sheet and pulled it over their heads.

*

Half an hour later, Julius arrived jogging at the bonfire glade. Walamai was waiting for him. 'I'm so sorry for being late,' he said.

'No need to worry,' Walamai replied jovially. 'You must have needed the rest after yesterday.'

'Yes,' he answered. 'And I could have remained in bed for a few more days too,' he added, under his breath.

Walamai walked him towards the upper part of the village. They passed many huts along the way, bustling with daily activities. Julius looked around him as if it was the first time; he observed all the details, the faces, noises and soaked them all in. In truth, he felt like a new person, and he knew that it was also due to Morgana. The villagers seemed to be studying him too, and Julius wondered if they knew what had happened the day before. When they reached a low, whitewashed building, Walamai invited him to enter.

The interior decor surprised Julius for its highly technological content. It could have been any of the rooms on Moonrising. There were numerous machines, panels, screens and displays, and Julius was reminded of the day he took his first medical in the Zed Test Centre. Freja and Derain were thick in conversation, and only stopped when Julius was a step away from them. 'Grand Master, sir,' he said, bowing to both.

Surprisingly, Freja placed his hands on Julius' shoulders, looking satisfied. 'We are all very proud of you, Julius.'

'The true Seeker,' said Derain, bowing to Julius. 'Whatever you did in the dream, it must have been very well played. As a guardian, I couldn't have wished for a better contestant.'

'Thank you,' he replied. 'I still can't believe it myself.'

'We can only guess what tough choices you must have faced in there,' continued Freja. 'And I think you owe a lot to your friends.'

'I know, sir. I won't forget,' he added. Then, as an afterthought, 'Why can't we remember what happened during the quest?'

'Spiritual journeys are not meant to be shared or viewed by spectators,' explained Derain. 'Outsiders understand them by seeing the changes affecting the seeker, and we can all see that your search was successful. I bet you're eager to try out your new powers, are you not, Mr McCoy?'

'I am, sir,' answered Julius.

'Then we shall prepare the machines. It won't be long,' he said.

Julius nodded, and drew closer to Freja. 'Sir … is my brother … is he all right?'

'He is,' said Freja. 'T'Rogon and Hastings took him away. They left orbit last night.'

'Have they gone?' he asked, worried.

'We are guests here Julius,' replied Freja, lowering his voice. 'I had no inclination to attack them under these circumstances. There's something else that requires our attention now, and hopefully it will be an asset in our final assault on Salgoria.'

Julius was eager to find out more, but didn't press the matter further.

'I had them followed,' added the Grand Master, as an afterthought.

Typical of Freja to hold back on such a tiny detail, he thought. Still, the news made him feel much better, so he approached the few hours of testing ahead in the best of spirits. And to keep his mind better occupied, he focused on Morgana and their future together.

The testing took longer than Julius had imagined. Doctor Walliser had come in from Moonrising to help out. Together with Freja and Derain, they checked every inch of his brain and body with scanners and probes. In a way, it was a test very similar to the one that Dr Flip, his family Mind Doctor, had performed on him at birth, and he made a mental note to ask his parents how long that one had lasted. Speaking of, he really needed to let them know about his achievement — he would contact them once the tests were finished.

Dr Walliser called it a day around 18:00, looking exhausted but pleased. 'Well, Mr

McCoy,' he said, removing sensors from Julius' chest. 'It looks like you've made it into the science books once again.'

'That's good, right?'

'It is. Not just you were able to receive someone else's powers, but your own genes as a natural White Child seem to have heightened them.'

'What does that mean?'

'It means that Freja might consider giving you a cutoff valve implant, to help control your mind-skills.'

Julius smiled, removing the last of the sensors from his neck.

'Seriously though,' continued Walliser. 'You ought to be extremely careful from now on. You could really hurt someone without even trying.'

'I will, sir,' replied Julius. Of course he would be careful; he had never used his powers unless he meant to. And this time wouldn't be any different.

'And now,' said the doctor, standing up and moving towards Freja and Derain, 'show us something.'

Julius looked up, surprised. 'Here?'

Walliser nodded. 'Start with the basics: telekinesis.'

Julius moved to the centre of the room, looking around for something to move using his mind. He thought that he should probably start with something small, so he focused on the nullifying bin in front of him. He tried to reach that place in his mind, where the skills clicked and came alive; he struggled at first, hindered by the long months of inactivity. But it didn't last too long. He found the path and the feeling flooded back into him, as if it had never been gone. He closed his eyes and opened his hands, palms up, raising them slowly, focusing on lifting the bin up into the air.

'Ahem … McCoy,' said Freja, 'whatever you do next, don't let go.'

Julius opened his eyes, perplexed by the request. Then he gasped, but kept his mind focused. Freja, Derain and Walliser were currently floating below the ceiling, trying to keep themselves upright by holding on to the walls. They were surrounded by every single piece of machinery in the area, now unceremoniously jumbled up on the top half of the room. The nullifying bin, however, was still on the floor, with no intention of going anywhere. 'I am so sorry,' he fumbled.

'Nonsense!' cried Walliser, laughing. 'This is marvellous! You just need a little recalibration, that's all.'

'Hold on to something,' said Julius. He changed his focus from the bin to the whole room, and willed his mind into lowering every object, people included, gently to the floor. He managed successfully, and when he finally let go, he felt as is a great weight had lifted from his shoulders.

'I think you should take a break now,' said Freja, straightening his uniform. 'But I'd hold off for the night with the party tricks,' he said, raising an eyebrow. 'No matter how much Mr Shanigan implores you.'

'Yes, sir,' he answered promptly.

'You'll resume your training tomorrow, back on Moonrising. We'll be at the landing pad at 07.00.'

'Understood.' An unexpected question rose from the depths of his mind. 'Grand Master?' he asked, quietly.

'Yes?'

'Do the names Mah or Eronan mean anything to you?'

Freja thought about it for a moment, and then shook his head. 'I'm sorry, but I've never heard of them. Why do you ask?'

'I think they are from the quest. Never mind, sir. If they were, I wouldn't be able to remember that anyway.'

Freja pondered this for a moment. 'Very well. Go enjoy the rest of your evening.'

'Thank you, sir.' He bowed to Walliser and Derain. 'Thank you for your help.'

*

Once out of the room, Julius jogged back to the bonfire glade, but the Skirts weren't there. He was about to open his PIP, to locate them, when he stopped and slapped his forehead. 'Surely a little telepathy won't hurt me,' he thought. He concentrated on Morgana, and began looking for her with his mind, calling her name.

'Is it really you?' she said, almost immediately.

'Aye! Where are you?'

'We are all by the sea. Come here!'

Julius jogged down the path, through the gap in the trees until he arrived at the beach. Skye, Faith and Morgana were sitting in a circle, surrounded by three surfboards, laughing and talking animatedly, their swimming costumes still wet. When they saw him, rivers of greens and golds erupted around them — they were as excited to see him as he was to see them. He ran to the shore and was swept up in Morgana's embrace first, then Faith's and Skye's. After that, they settled around the campfire to enjoy what remained of the day. They talked about the elusive dream quest and how amazing it was to be there, discovering another inhabited planet. Their minds were also drawn to the fact that, in a few months, they would graduate and become ZED officers, free at last to explore more of the galaxy and the world outside Tijara. They cooked food on the fire and managed to forget about the dangers still ahead, for a few hours. That night, after Faith and Skye had retired, he lay on the sand with his head on Morgana's lap. She was stroking his hair soothingly. The embers shone pale red, flickering brighter whenever the wind kindled them to life.

'You're very quiet,' said Morgana. 'What's wrong?'

It had been a good night, yet Julius felt uneasy. 'This thing with Michael ... it's like a shadow has been cast over us.'

'On your relationship, you mean?'

Julius nodded. 'Freja says that I'll have to face him, before this is over, and it may get ugly.'

Morgana was silent for a while, before speaking again. 'Could you hurt him, if it came to that?'

Julius shifted uncomfortably. 'If it came down to a choice between you or him, then yes, I would.'

*

On Tuesday morning, Julius and the Skirts met at the landing pad. Morgana had sneaked back to her lodging one hour before, to avoid any trouble from Freja. The Grand Master wasn't there, however, and had sent Lopaka to pick them up, while Barth, Leanne and Siena had also slipped in, eager to see Julius. They waited until the

Skirts were onboard before jumping out of their hiding places, giving Julius a fright along with their congratulations. Morgana took Siena to the side straight away, and proceeded to talk to her very fast and excitedly, drawing all sorts of giggly reactions from her, leaving Julius in no doubt what the topic of their conversation was.

'Everyone is just dying to see you, mate,' said Lopaka. 'We've been trying to get as much news as we could, but Freja wouldn't talk.'

'Will you tell us, Julius?' asked Barth hopefully.

Julius grinned. 'Sure, and thanks for your help guys, especially in Ahriman. It means a lot to me.'

'Nonsense,' cut in Leanne, abrupt as always. 'What's due is due.'

Unfortunately, the relaxing atmosphere didn't last long. Once they took off, Lopaka broke some seriously bad news to them.

'What do you mean, Moonrising has lost T'Rogon's vessel?' asked Faith.

'Unfortunately it's true,' added Leanne. 'We lost communication last night.'

It was a major setback for their mission, one that could have been avoided, according to Julius, and he didn't waste time venting his frustration. 'Seriously?' he shouted, at no one in particular. 'We are travelling on one of the most powerful battlestars in the galaxy and we lose a tiny vessel?'

'Not saying I don't agree,' said Faith, 'but you're talking about an Arneshian vessel, tiny as it may be.'

'Why did Freja let them go in the first place?' asked Skye.

Julius shook his head. 'Something to do with being guests and some other plan of his in the making.'

'So what are we supposed to do now?' continued Skye.

'We stay put until we track them down,' said Siena. 'And in the meantime, lessons, training, you name it.'

'And speaking of Freja's plan,' said Lopaka, 'there are rumours that he's working out some sort of alliance with Derain.'

'Really?' said Skye, suddenly interested. 'I can see myself working on this planet … you know, as a diplomat for Zed.'

'That means that the Ocluth ladies are hot then, huh?' said Lopaka, grinning.

'And the waves are great too,' added Skye, giving him a high five.

Julius couldn't quite bring himself to join the chitchat at that moment; he was too worried about Michael and where T'Rogon had taken him. His brother hadn't gotten hold of the crystal, so would he still have his uses in the new Arneshian order, or would he be discarded? He had also hinted at the fact that Salgoria had different plans for him — would things change now that he had failed?

When they returned to Moonrising, the 6MS students were all assembled in the hangar, waiting for Julius to emerge from the ship. The cheers that erupted as he stepped out took him by surprise, but filled him with pride. He spent the next half an hour answering their questions. When it was time to return to duty, the Mizkis left the hangar and Julius grabbed his bag from the Stork, before joining Morgana who was waiting for him. She passed her arm around his waist as they walked back to the dorms.

'Don't forget to call your folks,' she told him.

'I meant to do that yesterday actually, but I got … distracted,' he said, kissing her head. Morgana giggled, which prompted Julius to stop, drop his bag on the floor and kiss her properly.

'Wow,' she said, a few minutes later, her aura glowing bright pink. 'Where did that come from?'

'Your kiss reservoir.'

'And what's my daily allowance?' she asked, moving a little closer.

'No limit for you,' he whispered in her ear, before finding her lips again. Julius couldn't believe how much he craved her. It was like every fibre of him needed to hold her close, feel the softness of her skin under his hands, and smell her perfume. He was too busy wondering how much time they had before the next lesson to notice that Master Cress had approached them and was now standing there, arms and face equally crossed.

'Mister McCoy,' he said.

Julius and Morgana turned to face him, flushed cheeks and all.

'Sir,' they said in unison, standing to attention.

'Miss Ruthier, your next lesson starts in fifteen minutes. I'd suggest you go get ready.'

'Yes, sir,' she replied promptly. She grabbed her bag and ran off down the corridor. Master Cress then turned his attention to Julius. 'I believe congratulations are in order, McCoy.'

'Why thank you, sir,' said Julius, surprised, but pleased nonetheless. 'I mean, we've known each other since we were kids, and I always liked her, but I never thought that I, or she … that we-'

'McCoy,' Cress cut in, raising an eyebrow, *'on your powers* – congratulations on getting your powers back.'

'Oh,' fumbled Julius, blushing even more. 'Sorry sir, of course. Thank you.'

'Walk with me,' said Cress.

Julius did so, hoping to lose his beetroot red shade before meeting anyone else.

'Before you can resume your training, Dr Walliser needs to see you in Professor Clavel's room. Wear your training clothes and be there in thirty minutes from now.'

'Yes sir, I will,' answered Julius. 'Master Cress, sir?'

'What is it?'

'I know I'd focus better on my training if you could tell me what's going to happen next.'

Cress didn't slow down, but merely glanced at Julius briefly. 'It's no secret, McCoy. We are going to remain in Buruwang's orbit until we know exactly where to go. Captain Kelly is tracing T'Rogon's vessel, and he's not alone either. I don't know how long it will take, but we will find them. I suggest you use this time wisely and get your skills back in synch. Zed knows we'll need all the help we can get soon enough.'

'Thank you, sir. That's all I needed to hear.'

When they reached the main lift, Julius saluted the Master and stopped by the dorm to get changed. Afterwards, he headed to Clavel's room, wondering where the others were. 'Faith!' he called with his mind. 'Can you hear me?'

'Drat!' Came a voice in reply. 'Are you trying to kill me? You gave me a heart attack!'

Julius grinned. 'Just checking where you are.'

'In engineering, fixing a holocore system. You?'

'I'm going to Clavel to meet Doc Wally.'

'Why?'

'Who knows? Anyway, I'll see you later?'

'For sure. Got some new pics of me ship to show you. And don't forget to come up with a name!'

'Will do, dearie.'

'Later, honey,' replied Faith, with a chuckle.

Julius arrived at his appointment right on time and, when he entered, he halted in surprise. As well as the doctor and Professor Clavel, he found himself staring at Chan, King, Beloi, Gould, Clavel and Morales.

'Come in, Julius,' called Walliser.

Julius moved forward, feeling slightly intimidated. Clavel and Morales were wearing their usual warm smiles, which made him feel more at ease.

'We are so proud of you, Julius,' said Morales.

'Thank you,' was all he could say to this unexpected welcome. Even Chan was betraying something close to a human expression of approval, which confused Julius greatly.

Gould bowed his head briefly, evidently satisfied.

'*Well done, Julius,*' said the voice of Professor Beloi, inside his head.

'*Professor!*' answered Julius, telepathically. '*Still not speaking?*'

'*55 years and counting!*'

'Well done, Mr McCoy,' said King, looking as rosy and shiny as always.

Julius felt genuinely moved and gratefully bowed to his teachers. 'Thank you.'

'Doctor Walliser told us about you lifting the Grand Master,' continued King. 'I cannot believe I never thought of that!'

'It was quite a spectacle, I can assure you,' remarked Walliser. 'But that's why we are here. Before we unleash the new improved McCoy, we need to make sure his powers are under control.'

Julius groaned inwardly, already foreseeing a series of boring medical tests ahead of him.

'How would you like to get that Solo Champion title back, McCoy?' Gould asked him.

Julius felt his jaw drop, and his mouth then widened into a perfectly contented grin. 'I'd like that very much, sir.'

'And make sure to beat your old record too,' added Chan, ever the practical one.

Julius nodded. 'I'll give it my all.'

Professor Clavel pressed a few buttons on his PIP screen and a section of the floor slid sideways, to reveal an opening; Professor King stretched his hands over it and, a few seconds later, a Solo tank emerged from it, rising until it was just above floor level. After Clavel had closed the gap, King gently lowered the tank to the ground.

'Julius, go get geared up,' said Clavel, pointing to the changing room.

Julius nodded and, as he headed there, he kept an eye on the preparations. Morales and Beloi had selected some holographic furniture from their own PIPs, and a large screen had appeared next to the tank, while several rows of seats had sprung out of the floor, like a stairwell, facing it. Inside the changing room, Julius found a holosuit waiting for him and, as he put it on, he realised that, never in a million years could he have imagined playing again. When he came out, the teachers had taken their seats, as if they were about to watch a movie. Julius walked to the contraption by the tank.

Although it had been four years since his last Solo game, he remembered how the game technician had operated it. Holding on to the railing, he activated the pedestal, which rose upwards until it was level with the top of the tank. He grabbed the face shield that he would need to breathe inside the jelly-like substance that filled the container, and checked its thick rubber rim for faults, but he found none.

'Julius,' called Walliser from the seats, 'this will be a slightly different game from your average Solo. The computer has been calibrated to use exclusively Arneshian technology as your enemy. We have learned about their machinery over the centuries, and today it will be used against you, by your own teachers.'

That sounds interesting, thought Julius.

'The normal rules of Solo still apply,' continued Walliser. 'You will use your real powers to progress and, as you do, your skills will be monitored and recorded. This will help us to assess the situation and help you in controlling them properly. Understood?'

'Yes, sir.'

'When you're ready then.'

Julius sat on the edge of the tank, with his legs in the warm liquid. He took a deep breath, put the face shield on, and slowly lowered himself into the tank. Only when he was completely submerged did he allow himself to breathe again. The familiar sensation of weightlessness took over his body, and he turned until he was facing his teachers. He gave the thumbs-up to Walliser, who nodded in return, before activating the game. When he did this, Julius felt the water vibrating all around him, before a flash of blinding light flooded the tank.

*

Julius' second Solo run became the main topic of conversation on Moonrising for the next couple of weeks. The footage from his game had made its way around the general network, and was watched on repeat by pupils and officers alike. From the teachers' perspective, it was simply astonishing the way in which Julius had whisked through every obstacle, without breaking so much as a sweat.

Doctor Walliser was able to gather enough data to create a wrist implant that acted as a valve, so that Julius could regulate the flow as he saw fit and, of course, he had to write a few more chapters to add to the medical history of mind-skills. Seeing as the Solo ring, which was worn by the reigning champion, had remained with Farrah, Master Cress had a new one made for the occasion; like the original ring, it was a black metal band that self-adjusted itself around the wearer's finger, only this time the word "Solo" was engraved on its outer side. For his part, Julius was thrilled to have regained his title, even though it had been much easier than expected. Upon learning of his victory, he had spared a thought for Mrs Mayflower, who had talked him into trying his first Solo game, back when he was in first year. He wished she was still alive so she could know that he had done it, that he had reached the top again.

The weeks that followed proved to be a rollercoaster of emotions for Julius. On the one hand, Michael and Salgoria were never too far from his mind, like grey clouds on the horizon; on the other, there was the thrill that Morgana had brought to his life, and the excitement of training with his new powers. But he carried on, focusing on the only goal that mattered: ending the war with the Arneshians.

On Wednesday the 5th of March, Julius and Faith were told to meet Freja at lunchtime.

'I wonder what's going on,' said Faith, as they made their way along to the staff area. 'You may be used to this, but I don't get called to see the boss that often.'

Julius didn't know what it was about either, and he became even more curious when they stepped into the Grand Master's office and found him in the company of Daku Derain. Julius threw an inquisitive glance at Faith, before bowing to them.

'Please,' said Freja, motioning for Derain and the Mizkis to sit at a small round table.

'It is a pleasure to see you again, Julius,' said Derain, affably. 'Are your skills under control?'

'Thank you sir, they are. Doctor Walliser saw to that.'

'This is Faith Shanigan,' said Freja, 'the young man I mentioned to you earlier.'

Julius saw Faith straightening up with pride when he heard that, and was very happy for him.

'Ah!' said Derain. 'The youngest winner of Pete's competition. My sincere congratulations!'

'Thank you, sir,' said Faith, grinning with delight.

'It is a marvellous design,' continued Derain. 'One of the finest ships I've ever seen. And that new space coffin — truly ingenious!'

Faith's grin couldn't grow any wider, so he bowed his head a few times, bashfully offering his thanks.

'We have some news to share with you, Mizkis,' began Freja. 'In the past couple of weeks, there has been much talk between the Ocluths and Zed, about our present situations.'

Julius nodded, unsure as to why Freja would want to tell them about these meetings.

'My people,' explained Derain, 'have lived on Buruwang for the last 232 years. Although we began primarily as a colonial refuge for those fleeing the war, you now know that our purpose became that of guarding Tijara's crystal. With your success, Julius, our mission has ended, leaving us free to pursue other ventures.'

'Which is … good, right sir?' asked Julius hesitantly.

'Indeed,' answered Derain. 'Very good indeed.'

'Like the Ocluths, we are also about to experience change,' continued Freja. 'Our showdown with Salgoria is drawing closer each day and soon Zed will no longer be embroiled in this mindless war, but free to explore, grow and perhaps meet other species.'

'What if we don't win?' The words were out before Julius could stop himself.

Freja didn't seem to mind. Instead, he threw a brief glance in the direction of Derain, as if they had just shared an inside joke that wasn't altogether funny.

'Even more reason to proceed with our plan,' answered Derain.

Freja nodded. 'The Earth Leader, the Curio Maximus, the GMs, Derain and the Hands — leaders — of the Zed and Earth colonies, have signed a treaty to create a new power structure that will bring us all together. From now on we shall be known as the Galactic Federation of Earth.'

'That is good news, sir,' said Faith. 'Unity makes us stronger.'

'It does, Mr Shanigan,' said Derain. 'We want a stable, peaceful galaxy, and the new federation will do just that. Our new council will reside in the Halls of Ahriman, and the Curia will represent the people who live on planet Earth.'

'We're moving the Curia?' asked Julius, surprised. It had been the political heart of Zed since Tijara's time, and he couldn't imagine the Lunar Perimeter without it.

'Ahriman is in a more central location,' explained Freja, 'accessible to all of us — the old building on the Moon will be used as a liaison centre between the schools and Earth. Our technicians are already building additional teleportation gates along the main routes, in the orbits of all of our locations, plus a few more at important crossways. And, thanks to the Shanigan Relay, it will make space travel faster and safer.'

Julius was astonished at this news, while Faith turned redder than ever. He believed inside that it was the right move, especially now that they had come across the Ocluths. It would also strengthen relationships with the inhabitants of Colonial 1 and the three Terra colonies, where most of his Mizki friends were from. Still, it didn't explain why they had been called to receive this news in private.

As if reading his thoughts, Freja continued. 'As to the reason why I called you here, Mizkis: there will be a second council beside the Curia, called the Forum. It will be a social gathering place, where everyone not involved in politics, and not residing on Earth, can meet to discuss problems or any other matters that may arise.'

'A place to be heard,' commented Julius.

'Precisely,' said Freja. 'Together with the GMs, we have appointed key figures to be present at Forum meetings, experts if you like. These people will keep up to date with all developments in their fields and will provide support and knowledge to those who have something to discuss. Mr Shanigan, we would like you to be the Forum's expert in the technology field.'

Faith's jaw dropped open. 'Seriously, sir? But aren't there more qualified people than me?'

'There are, yes, but they have been working in Zed for too long. You, on the other hand, will be able to bring a fresh perspective, besides being one of the most skilled technicians we have. Your Grey Arts are so advanced that you could pass for an Arneshian.'

Julius watched Faith's aura going from pink to fuchsia to bright red in one second. His friend deserved the praise and, in fact, it was about time that someone recognised that publicly. It would do his confidence a great deal of good.

'As for you, McCoy,' continued the Grand Master, 'we would like you to become the leader of the Forum.'

'Sir?'

'You are known by all humans, on Earth, Buruwang and the colonies.'

'You're more than qualified for the job, Julius,' said Derain. 'Especially now, I should think.'

'Job?' said Julius, alarmed. 'I was thinking more of a career as a captain, sir.'

'And you can have that,' explained Freja. 'These Forum meetings should only be scheduled a few times a year, and will not interfere with your regular duties. The rest of the time, people will be able to contact you through the network and, if you cannot attend a meeting, you can always select a deputy to go in your place or be there holographically.'

Julius nodded, but still felt uncertain.

'You have some time to think about it,' said Freja, standing up.

Julius and Faith did likewise. They thanked them, bowed and left the room.

'Can you believe it?' said Faith ecstatically. He was hovering quite erratically along the corridor, gesticulating wildly.

'Try not to poke me in the eye, please,' said Julius ducking a couple of times. 'And yes, I can believe it, Faith. You're a bit of a genius, in case you haven't noticed.'

'Siena will be so proud of me,' he said cheerily. 'I'm definitely going to say yes to Freja. A brand new federation! This is really exciting. You'll be the best leader ever, Julius!'

'Thanks for the vote of confidence,' he said, 'but I don't know if I really want to do it. It sounds a lot like politics, and that's not my game at all. He should have asked Skye.'

'But he didn't,' replied Faith. 'Skye can smooch his way forward as much as he wants, but people need someone to trust, to look up to. And that's you.'

Julius threw a glance at Faith, his cheeks flushed. 'Is that what you think of me?'

Faith stopped, and turned to him. 'Do you need to ask me after all these years? Your funny powers should be able to tell you that I'm true. I would follow you, no matter what.'

Julius held his gaze for a few more seconds, before lifting his hand forward for Faith to grab. Being leader of the Forum would be worth it, even just for the chance to see Faith again after graduation. 'Thanks mate.'

'However,' he added cheekily, 'your girlfriend may get to name me ship if you don't get a move on.'

'Is that right?'

'She came up with a few crackers, you know. Me favourites so far are *Serenitatis* or *Tranquillitatis*. See, they are both seas on the Moon. Serenity is where the Zed docks are built — and you know how Morgana loves the docks — and Tranquility is Satras' location, which means Hologram Palace.'

'Why doesn't that surprise me? And when did this betrayal happen?'

'Last night. Her and Siena were helping me out with the space coffin project — don't ask. Anyway, they couldn't stop laughing. Those two are mental when they're together.'

'I bet. Come on, let's go find them and settle this once and for all.'

OCCUPATION

The underground dwellings of Mahin were linked together in a hive-like structure, with larger open spaces between them, where people met to trade or socialise. An intricate system of streets had been laid out to allow the passage of electric vehicles, used to carry stock and people. The natural darkness of the rocks was brightened by beautiful sculptures of Strullium, wired internally with neon lamps. The Mahini didn't encourage ownership. Resources were shared equally and individual skills were utilised for the advancement and sustenance of the citizens; for all that, they did believe in leadership and key roles were assigned through elections, to ensure the smooth running of everyday life.

This peaceful and orderly world no longer existed though, and not one day began without Ruxshin being painfully aware of this. Her new daily routine, enforced by the Arneshians pretty much from the beginning of the occupation, did not start in the coziness of her bedroom anymore, because it was now used to house soldiers. Instead, she had made herself a nest in a corner of her own living room, using whatever pelts and blankets she could find. At first light, she would quickly use the bathroom to wash, comb her mane and get dressed, before preparing breakfast; then she would wake her guests up, lay the food on the table, and leave for work. To her surprise, the majority of the soldiers using her home had been rather tidy, often even pulling the bed covers up; there was a sense of order about them, reflected in their neat haircuts and blunt manners. She wondered who had pressed their uniforms to make them always look so pristine; then again, she wouldn't have been surprised if she had discovered that the material itself never creased — after all, these people had already turned her world upside-down with their technology. She had never really believed that there could be people living on other planets, let alone intelligent ones and, for all the hatred she felt towards them for crashing into their lives uninvited, she couldn't stop marvelling at the things they had introduced them to. For one, these people didn't need to grow food, as they had machines — they called them *replicators* — to create a dish out of nothing. She had tried her first one a few weeks after the occupation started, and she had liked it very much; they called it "Mac and Cheese", and it had materialised in a little vapour of sparkles, piping hot inside the empty plate. It had felt wrong, unnatural even, but they had had no choice, as the greenhouses had been destroyed during the first attack. The rations weren't plentiful, but at least no one was going hungry. As long as the Mahini collaborated with the Arneshians, excavating Strullium, there were no problems.

Once she left her home, Ruxshin turned left instead of right, where the path that led towards the winter gardens had once been. As her people were relatively safe, she would allow herself to mourn the loss of her plants and all the years spent creating a thriving environment to keep her people fed every day of their lives.

Since then, she had been reassigned to another job, more interesting than mining Strullium — on that score, she still couldn't see what they would do with it or why they needed so much of it. Her new duty was to help the Arneshians create a vocabulary of their language for a translation device. Working on this machine was a priority for everyone, as the lack of communication between them was making things worse, by straining relationships and delaying potential peace talks. Mah Gira himself had begged Ruxshin to take up the job when they requested — demanded — suitable helpers, and she could not have refused the Supreme of the Mahini.

Creating a database of their words and their equivalent in the Arneshian language was at least a stimulating challenge, one that kept her busy and interested for the whole duration of her long shift. There would be five other people working with her, but she was the head of her group. At night, another team would take over, because this project had high priority and there were no days off to be had. Every member of the translation group had been paired up with an Arneshian; Ruxshin's co-worker was a tall man by the name of A'Krad who, after a rough start, in which he was keen to assert his superiority, had become slightly more affable, making her work experience bearable. At first, the job had been rather easy, as they set about creating a noun section: A'Krad would pick up an object or point at it, and say its name out loud, clearly and slowly; Ruxshin would then do the same in her language, and they would both then type it into the database, matching the two. Of course, things like the plural version of a word, or the article to go with it, had to be recorded too. The hardest part came with the creation of sentences, which required a basic understanding of their grammar; it was a process that involved a lot of fine-tuning, and it felt like it would never end.

It was at the close of their first month of work that Ruxshin and A'Krad had exchanged their first proper conversation. She could still remember the excitement of that moment, when A'Krad had sat her at the table, placed the translator between them and turned it on, changing gibberish into sense.

'Hi, Ruxshin,' he had said.

'Hello, A'Krad.'

'How are you today?'

The satisfaction of a job well done turned sour at those words, as she remembered exactly why she was sitting there, working on the project. 'Why are you here? Why don't you go away?'

A'Krad had smiled. 'It seems like we are doing a great job with this project. I'll tell my boss to go easy on you.'

With that, he had left her at the table, staring at the device with tears in her eyes. It seemed so long ago now and, as the hope of freedom slowly waned, she felt that she had no choice but to co-operate — even if not at the speed they wished.

Ruxshin followed the road through the centre of her quadrant, and headed for the platforms. Most of the soldiers were also emerging from the surrounding houses, pouring out into the streets, swapping places with the nightshift. She avoided making eye contact because she didn't want to see them staring at her mane; some were repulsed by it and looked away disgusted, but others couldn't help themselves, some even reaching out to touch it. For a Mahin, that was the ultimate taboo: no one was allowed to touch someone else's mane, unless they were the parents or the companion. A few fights had already erupted on that account, resulting in such violent reactions from the prisoners that the Arneshian soldiers had been instructed to refrain from this.

Once she reached the platform, she saw that her friend Hutan was already there, together with the other three translators. Seeing him made her smile.

'Hi Rux,' he said.

'Hey there. Slept well?'

'A little. My *guest* couldn't, so I had to *entertain* him for a while — three hours, to be precise.'

'The joys of babysitting,' she sighed.

'At least I don't have to put up with the guy that's always with their leader — Xander or something.'

'K'Ssander, they call him,' she said. 'He's a nasty piece of work.'

'I'll tell you who really gives me the creeps though,' added Hutan in a whisper. 'The little one. His hair isn't like the others — I don't even think he's of the same breed. But there's something about him that unsettles me. It's like he's in awe of the other two, and would do anything to impress them.'

Ruxshin had seen this boy many times before, and knew exactly what Hutan meant. He was dangerous, a boy who didn't know his place yet, or had an agenda, but was set to follow his leader until the end. She could only hope he found his own voice before it was too late, before he became a puppet forever.

Just then, a group of soldiers stepped off one of the platform lifts, walking towards them and holding eight pairs of handcuffs. This was the part that Ruxshin really didn't like — being tied by the ankles and wrists to the others was unnecessary, especially when the soldiers had long-range weapons that could kill in seconds. The rain season would soon be replaced by the long, snowy winter; they had no food and no spare clothing — where could they go? In the end she complied, as she did every morning. The guard handed the cuffs to Hutan, who kneeled on the ground to fasten them around his own left ankle, then around Ruxshin's right one — an operation he repeated for their wrists; each of them would do the same until all five prisoners were linked.

Slowly, they stepped forward and onto the lift, bringing their hoods up, to shelter themselves from the inclement weather.

The rain was indeed waiting for them. As they reached the surface, it seemed to grow in intensity, from a light drizzle to a downpour in the space of a few seconds. They trudged along as best they could. Then a gust of wind blew the hood off Ruxshin's head, and her mane was soaked through instantly.

'Cover yourself, woman!' growled one of the guards. 'I don't want to spend the day having to smell your wet dog fur.'

Hutan looked at him with hatred in his eyes, and perhaps he would have let it slide if the man hadn't stretched his hand towards Ruxshin's head.

Ruxshin saw what was going to happen; she even had a quick thought that the guard had stretched his hand to pull her hood back up, given that she was chained, rather than to touch her, but there was nothing she could do to prevent the events that followed. 'Hutan, no!' she cried.

That was when the fight started.

*

Ambassador T'Rogon wasn't pleased. His index finger was slowly moving a file around the screen built into the surface of his desk, following an imaginary figure of eight.

His chin rested on the heel of his left hand, while one of his moccasin-clad feet tapped the floor rhythmically. He felt restless and out of sorts. Michael had failed to retrieve Tijara's crystal, leaving him no choice but to turn to plan B: Julius' powers would be transferred to him, while K'Ssander would need to visit Salgoria's space station to begin the distillation of the queen's essence. Only these two operations combined would give them a renewed leader, capable of taking over what he considered to be the wrong side of humanity once and for all. And of course, a large stock of Strullium was the necessary fuel to make this possible.

He stood and walked briskly to the large window overlooking the main square of Mah. The rain season was at its close, due to be replaced by six months of snow. It was absurdly precise, as he had been told by his men, but on the 1st day of Primani – or what the Arneshians thought of as April — the rain would suddenly stop, as if someone had just closed a tap. Then a few snowflakes would start to fall here and there; within an hour those few flakes would turn into a full-blown storm, laying a white blanket wherever they landed. T'Rogon had no problem believing this, since he had witnessed the reverse on the first day of the previous October, when the snow had simply vanished between one moment and the next, leaving centre stage to the pouring rain.

His attention was caught by a group of five natives, emerging from one of the shafts and heading towards their daily job, whatever that was. They were chained to each other by their ankles, their hands bound together. He noticed one of the males closing his hood over his dark mane. T'Rogon smirked. Evolution was all over the Universe, it seemed.

Their fur protected them from the harsh conditions of their weather system in quite a successful way. Back in June, when they had taken over the city, T'Rogon had donated a couple of locals, a female and a male, to his physician. He wanted them studied, inside and out. It was important to know about a new species — were they gifted in some way, were they dangerous and could they pose any threats? As it turned out, the Mahini were in fact humans, much to his surprise, with the exception of their extensive posterior fur. Their diet was slightly different, as different food was available on this planet, but they ate, slept, breathed and reproduced in the same way as people on Earth did.

Their society was moderately advanced, with a sort of peaceful, democratic structure already in place. The harsh weather conditions had pushed the natives below the surface, where they had created an impressive underground city, with running water and electricity. To make the most of the thin sunbeams, they had built several greenhouses to grow what they needed to survive, both animals and plants. Ingenious, really.

Still, technologically they were far behind. All their engineering relied on hydroelectric power, and they had no use for Strullium, except for decorative purposes. They studied the skies, but had never flown. After the first attack, they had been unable to retaliate, stunned as they were to meet another species — and a special one at that.

Overall it had been an easy takeover, even though he had not been able to figure out how the human species had found its way to a new system. What was annoying the ambassador, however, was their inability to communicate, which was hindering and slowing down the whole operation. His men were working on a simultaneous translator, he knew that, but they didn't appear to be working fast enough. He had sent

K'Ssander to light a fire under their chairs, since he could be extremely persuasive when he wanted to be.

The group of captives continued to trudge along the road under the curious stare of T'Rogon. They walked hunched forward, as the rain drenched their coats. Unexpectedly, a gust of wind blew the hood off of one of the female prisoners, revealing her red mane underneath. One of the guards stopped to talk to her, before stretching his hand forward. Quick as lightning, the other prisoners stopped, turned and encircled the guards. Immediately, T'Rogon stepped forward, his hands banging on the glass, trying to get the attention of a patrol stationed not too far from where the brawl had erupted. Then, from the right of the path, came the shouting of more soldiers. As they parted, T'Rogon saw K'Ssander striding through them; he stretched his hand forward and sent a bolt of electricity straight into the men on the ground, uncaring if he hit his own or just the prisoners. The electric shock enveloped them all in a white cocoon, which had the effect of visibly scaring the few Mahini that had gathered to watch the attempted rebellion. The red-haired woman was screaming, while K'Ssander directed the Arneshians to take care of all the bodies, with an ease that made the ambassador smile. 'Trust you to sort things out,' he said to himself, relieved. At that moment, K'Ssander looked up, towards the control tower. T'Rogon pressed the com-link on his chest. 'I want to see you.'

'On my way,' came the reply.

When K'Ssander stepped into the office, he was dragging Ruxshin by the hood. He pushed her towards the corner of the room, where she landed badly, a trickle of blood wetting her lower lip. The right sleeve of her coat was dark, singed by the electric shock created by K'Ssander during the brawl. It was clear that she had been crying. Michael followed them quietly and moved over to the sofa, watching the young woman with curiosity.

'I'm sick and tired of this wet hole,' said K'Ssander abruptly. 'I feel the dampness soaking right through my bones.'

T'Rogon listened with mild interest. 'What is she doing here?' he asked, ignoring his officer's remark.

'I thought you wanted to know why the translator was coming on so slowly,' he replied, moving towards the sofa. 'She's in charge of her team. Ask her.'

T'Rogon saw the red mane and recognised her as the one whose hood had been blown off by the wind a few minutes before. She was quite good-looking for her kind; a touch of freckles gave life to chiseled cheekbones, a life which extended to her green eyes — yes, he thought, without the fur she would have been a very popular woman. He opened one of his drawers and took a translation device from it, before placing it on the table. 'Come closer,' he told her, using his hand to beckon her.

Ruxshin looked scared, but she shuffled to the desk, the cuffs clashing with every small step she took.

'Sit,' T'Rogon invited, again using his hand to communicate. He switched on the little black box between them, and waited until the light changed from red to green. 'What's your name?'

The box repeated the question in Mahin, highlighting an edgy, guttural sound.

'Ruxshin,' she answered.

Again, her name was repeated by the device.

T'Rogon nodded, satisfied. That had been a quick answer, a sign that the translator could at least be tested further. He turned to his first officer. 'K'Ssander, remind me to ask our crew to make this process more immediate, somehow. I don't want to waste time listening to the talking box. When she speaks in Mahin, I want to hear her in my language.'

'I'm sure that can be arranged,' he replied.

'Good. Let's try something more complicated now,' continued T'Rogon. 'Tell me about your leader, Mah Gira.' Ruxshin's fear hadn't left her face, but now she seemed focused, which pleased T'Rogon, as he would get more out of her that way.

'Mah Gira is the Supreme of the Mahini. He's the leader of the … and we … his …'

T'Rogon's eyebrows lifted up. The translator had gone silent three times, unable to convey some of the woman's words. He glared at K'ssander, his patience waning. 'Is this the best the device can do?' His question was repeated in Mahin. T'Rogon thought about it for a moment, and decided to leave it on.

'Apparently,' he replied sarcastically. 'As one of the translation team-leaders, maybe she needs a little push in the right direction.'

'Any suggestions?' said T'Rogon.

'I know how to do that,' said Michael suddenly.

As those words were translated, the ambassador was immediately aware of a change of atmosphere in the room: the boy was sitting on the edge of the sofa, eager to please, while the woman's fear had suddenly resurfaced in her eyes. Even K'Ssander was listening, his curiosity piqued. This could be fun, thought the ambassador.

Seeing as they were all looking at him, Michael continued. 'She's not human enough to understand our language. She doesn't look the part.'

'Oh?' said T'Rogon. 'And how would you rectify that, young Michael?'

'Shave her.'

'No!' cried Ruxshin, retreating towards the back of the room. 'Don't do this!'

The device translated her plea, as if mocking her.

K'Ssander began to laugh, while patting Michael on the back.

'Who would have thought?' said T'Rogon, pleased. The boy was coming on all right — the perfect machine to bring his plans to fruition.

'It's such a good idea that I'll do it myself,' said K'Ssander, standing up.

'No, please!' Ruxshin implored them, unable to restrain her tears anymore.

K'ssander pointed his palm at her and sent out a low intensity electroshock, strong enough to render her unconscious. She hit the floor like a heavy sack. 'Michael,' he said, turning towards him. 'Do you want to watch?'

In reply, the boy climbed off the sofa and moved over to his side.

T'Rogon leaned back in his chair, silently approving. Let K'Ssander teach him the nitty-gritty of war.

THE HIDEOUT

March was coming to an end, but there was still no trace of Michael or anybody else. Captain Kelly and his search party were running out of luck and, with every new report, the spirits in Moonrising were dampened. To keep his people focusing on different matters, Freja had begun releasing information on the GFE, the new re-housing of the Curia and the creation of the Forum; all he kept private were the appointments of Julius and Faith. The rest of the Skirts, however, had already been informed; Morgana was ecstatic and, to everyone's relief, Skye hadn't taken his exclusion to heart, but was really happy for them both.

'Besides,' he told them, with a cheeky smile, 'you'll need me for advice more than you know. I'll be the puppet master behind the curtains.'

On Sunday the 6th of April, Julius and Morgana were relaxing in New Satras, waiting for the others to join them for lunch. Like all other Mizkis and officers, they went to visit the new Ocluth shop. To everyone's liking, they had been given permission to open trade, selling a vast array of their crafted products. Freja believed that, to strengthen the ties with this lost branch of the human race, he needed to integrate them right away into their world, by insuring their presence on Moonrising, and then on all the other human outposts. With time, people would become used to their presence, helping the Galactic Federation of Earth to develop in a true, friendly spirit. Daku Derain had even managed to find a few young men and women willing to relocate aboard the battlestar, obviously eager to experience a new life in space.

'Skye has to see that surfboard!' said Morgana, pointing at one of the walls. 'He's so going to buy it.'

'That is if Lopaka doesn't see it first,' added Julius, before resuming his browsing. 'Hey, I wonder if they sell any of those little suede numbers you were wearing on Buruwang,' said Julius, rummaging through the ladies' clothing rack.

'Is that right?' said Morgana, laughing. 'I guess you liked it, huh?'

'Everything looks good on you, actually,' he replied, matter-of-factly. 'But that could be our ... you know ... anniversary outfit.'

She giggled before planting a kiss on his lips.

'Wait, wait!' said Julius suddenly, pulling away.

'What's the matter?'

'I almost forgot ... again.' He dipped his hand into the side pocket of his trousers and retrieved her birthday present. 'Happy belated birthday. I've been meaning to give you this since New Year, but you were possessed by the Martian Bile.'

Excited, Morgana took the little green box. 'Thank you!' she said. She opened the lid delicately and, when she saw the cylindrical, lilac crystal her eyes widened in surprise and joy. 'Julius,' she gasped, 'it's gorgeous! Where does it come from?'

'Funesto. I found it when we were working underground. I'm glad you like it.'

'Like it? I love it!' she said. 'Help me put it on.'

Julius opened the chain and, when Morgana had lifted her hair up, he slipped it around her neck, fastening the clasp securely. 'Done,' he said. She turned around and showed him the pendant with delight. He passed his fingers over it, satisfied with the elegant look of it. 'It goes with your eyes.' In reply, Morgana lunged forward for a full body hug, something that always made Julius look for nearby secluded places — in this case, the changing rooms. He was slowly and vaguely moving her in that general direction, when Faith hovered inside the shop.

'Lovebirds!' he called out, focusing the attention of every customer on them.

'Right on time,' said Julius ironically.

'We're all outside, come on!'

As they headed to the exit, Julius couldn't help but notice the chuckles and whispers of the groups of Mizkis browsing the shelves, as they walked past them. It was now common knowledge, even among the 6MSs, that he was seeing Morgana; to a certain extent, people were already used to seeing them together, but not necessarily *that* together. Isolde took it really badly and stopped talking to both of them all of a sudden; whenever they walked into a room, she theatrically turned the other way or stormed off. For his part, Julius wasn't too subtle when it came to showing his affection for Morgana; in fact, it was fair to say that he was barely able to restrain himself most of the time. It was like a dam had been broken, and all his emotion were pouring out of him. He suspected that she knew how much he needed her support to stay focused during this trying time, because she was never too far away, and loved her even more for that.

'Over here,' called Faith, standing with Siena and Skye by a park bench.

When they joined them, Faith motioned for them to sit down, while Siena went to stand in front of them, activating her PIP.

'What's going on?' asked Julius.

'Me mum wants a picture of the Skirts, for her lounge,' explained Faith, going slightly red. 'She's really proud of us,' he added quietly, before taking his place between Julius and Skye.

'Say cheese!' prompted Siena.

'Halloumi!' replied Skye, with his mouth wide open, before bursting into laughter. Faith slapped him upside the head, while Morgana fell into a fit of giggles.

'I don't think his mum needs to see your intestines through your mouth, Skye,' commented Julius, giving him another slap. As he waited for Skye and Morgana to pull themselves together, he noticed two Zed officers walking in the direction of their bench, sipping coffees and very much absorbed in some sort of discussion. His ears tuned in on their words, without meaning to.

'You don't know that,' said the blonde man.

'I'm telling you,' answered the taller of the two, 'it's true. The meteorite field was strange enough, but to add a traversable wormhole and a flision field is just mental — I mean, they are so rare and all.'

Julius caught the word *flision*, and his brain froze. Around him, he was vaguely aware that the Skirts had stopped laughing.

'All right, all right,' answered Skye. 'Forget the cheese.'

'One … Two … Three.' The flash lit their faces, but Siena lowered the PIP, half exasperated. 'Darn! Julius, stay still!'

To everyone's surprise, Julius stood up and walked off camera.

'What's wrong?' asked Morgana.

'McCoy?' called Skye, following him with his eyes.

Julius didn't hear them, but kept on walking until he reached the officers. 'Excuse me, did you say, "flision field"?'

The men stopped and turned to him.

'Aren't you the Solo champion?' asked the tall one. 'I want your autograph, man!'

'Yes, yes. But can you please tell me about that field?' continued Julius, unswayed.

'The flision field?'

'Yes. Where is it? How did you find it?'

By then the Skirts and Siena had walked up to them and were listening with curiosity.

'One of the Herons sent a report this morning with its coordinates,' he explained. 'The crew was examining a wormhole in the Uruplatus system, when they came across it.'

'You mentioned a meteorite field as well, right? Is this before the wormhole?'

'So they said,' answered the officer.

Julius took a step back, as if in a trance. He turned to the others. 'I know where Salgoria is hiding.'

*

Julius ran to his dorm to rummage through his bag before heading for Freja's office, with his friends in tow. The others stopped by the door, eagerly watching on, while Julius stood in front of the GM's desk waiting for him to finish reading his brother's letter.

'"… going through a meteorite field followed by a wormhole, and a flision field (whatever that is) is not kind on the untrained, or so they say …"' read Freja, aloud. He looked up. 'Where does this come from?' he asked, holding the sheet of paper.

'Michael left it on my bed, on Earth, after the Arneshians took our people. I didn't read it until Buruwang. That particular part didn't mean much to me until those officers mentioned the flision field. It *has* to be the same place,' he said animatedly.

'It is possible, yes,' answered Freja, growing thoughtful. 'We would need to test if the wormhole is stabilised already, or it may collapse on us.'

Julius watched as Freja's eyes skimmed over the rest of the letter. He knew that he was reading some of the more personal stuff as well, but he didn't mind; the possibility that he could have found Salgoria's hiding place was far more important than any privacy issues.

Eventually, Freja looked up. 'It's the best trace we have. Let's go for it.'

'Yes, sir,' replied Julius eagerly. He spun around and, gathering the others on his way, left the GM to prepare for the new mission.

To everyone's satisfaction, it took only a couple of days to organise the fleet. Given the nature of the obstacles to surpass, it was decided that Moonrising would separate, allowing Tijara, Sield, Tuala and the fourth section — which carried the hospital and the Curia — to follow the fleet, while New Satras remained in Buruwang's orbit. All senior Mizkis would make the journey in the safety of their schools' ships until they reached the wormhole.

*

On the 7th of April, Tijara's hangar was bustling with activity. The technicians were readying the Cougars, lined up along the several stackable floors of the ship, while the teachers directed their students towards the west and east parts of the area.

Julius was standing with his classmates in the centre of the room, his EMU activator safely pinned to his t-shirt. There was an eerie calm among the Mizkis, and it was clear for all to see that they were nervous. Lopaka, Barth and Leanne stood fidgeting in one corner, looking around expectantly. Skye was shifting his weight from one foot to the other, while Faith couldn't stop hovering up and down, as if he was waiting for someone; Morgana and Siena were scanning their PIPs apprehensively, trying to take their minds off the long wait. Julius glanced around. All he could see were grey threads coiling down and pooling around the legs of his classmates. He had been focusing all morning on Salgoria, bending his mind to the mission; there was a high chance that he would meet Farrah and Michael again and he didn't want to become distracted by his emotions. He had allowed himself only a brief private moment with Morgana, after breakfast, but she needed focus time just as much as he did so, after a few recommendations on safety and a long comforting embrace, they left each other free to prepare in their own ways.

'Citadel mode offline,' bellowed a voice over the intercom. 'FTL engaged in ten, nine …'

Startled, Julius took a deep breath, grabbed hold of a banister with one hand and Morgana with the other.

'… three, two, one. Skip.'

Julius felt the familiar sensation of stepping out of his own body, and closed his eyes to minimise his nausea. It didn't last long though and the room came back into sharp focus all around him. A few of the teachers began to move towards the students, grouping them up as they went.

'Gather up, 6MS,' called Clavel. 'The hyperjump has taken us past the meteorite field and it seems that we've remained undetected by the Arneshians. You'll continue through the wormhole in the Cougars, which have been shielded to protect you from the high radiation of the flision field. I want you to keep your PIPs switched on throughout the mission. Film your surroundings as much as possible, without jeopardising your safety, of course. We need to learn all we can about their hideout and, between all your audio-visual images, we will do just that. You'll be under the guidance of Commander Fletcher and his Lynx Army. They are all veteran fighters and will look after you. Follow orders and don't play hero.'

'Is he looking at us?' whispered Faith, leaning towards Julius.

'I wonder why,' he answered sarcastically.

'Board your rides. Hunt hard, Mizkis,' concluded Clavel.

The students bowed to him and walked briskly towards their planes.

Julius grabbed Morgana by the shoulders and held her quickly to him, as he kissed her head. 'Be careful.'

'Likewise,' she said, as she headed off. Then she stopped, and turned back to him.

Julius stood, waiting for her to say something. She didn't though, and he noticed a serious look in her eyes, while a thin, grey thread began to rise from the top of her head. It wasn't like her to be scared before a mission. Julius couldn't let her go in that state; he walked to her and hugged her tightly, until the grey eased out of her aura. 'What's wrong?'

'I guess someone just walked over my grave.'

He was about to say something when she smiled at him, and let go. Julius winked at her and watched her head to her plane, his sense of unease not totally appeased.

His Cougar was the first to come into view. He climbed onboard and placed his thumb against the recognition plate, allowing his tag-name to appear in bright yellow letters on the side-displays of the plane's body.

'Ready check, Goshawk,' said the computer.

'Goshawk ready and in standby,' answered Julius, turning on the last system.

'Permission to initiate departure procedure granted. Hunt hard.'

Julius' engine came to life and, as the last red light turned green, he grabbed the catalyst and slowly rolled along the runway, heading for the hangar door. He would have to fly through the protective membrane that maintained the right pressure inside the hangar so, when he reached the correct position, he willed his plane forward, causing it to accelerate. Flying the Cougar had been one of the most enjoyable things he had done during his training, since acquiring Tijara's powers. Although he still preferred the path of the captain, piloting this plane brought him the thrill of the more raw elements of fighting. He could be truly at one with his vessel, linked only by the strength of his mind-skills. Once outside Moonrising, he waited for all the Mizkis to join him. It didn't take too long and, shortly after, Commander Fletcher hailed them.

'I want you to make a three-by-three formation, Mizkis, right behind my army,' he said, flying forward. 'The wormhole is essentially a tunnel, and we are about to pass through it. Match the speed of the vessels in front of you and you'll be fine. Enjoy the ride.'

Julius felt his excitement kicking up a notch — going through a wormhole was a first, and probably one of the scariest things he would ever do, together with the FTL jump and teleportation. He saw three officers' planes lining up in front of him, so he flew behind the first one at the recommended distance, and saw Skye and Faith flying by his right side. Morgana was just behind them, together with Siena and Isolde. He adjusted his speed to keep a steady distance from his guide and relaxed a little. 'Here we go,' he thought, as the mouth of the tunnel loomed over his head. Looking into the opening was extremely peculiar: it was like space had become a two dimensional sheet, with an invisible hand pulling it downwards at its middle, creating a funnel of bright concentric circles. As he crossed the threshold, all manner of shadows and lights appeared around him, delineating the tubular structure of the tunnel. To his surprise and relief, he didn't feel claustrophobic about being inside it, just quite apprehensive.

'We are all in,' said Fletcher. 'Increase velocity to level 10 until I say so.'

Given that his powers could push his Cougar much faster than the others, Julius was glad to use the standard speed system onboard. He prepared himself and, carefully watching the officer ahead, he matched his speed, level by level, until he reached the mark. They were still flying very fast, following the regular structure of the tunnel. The passageway bent off to either side at times, but these curves were gentle enough and did not cause any trouble. Eventually, Fletcher ordered them to slow down.

'As you come out of the tunnel, keep following your guides at speed level 5. The flision field creates thick vapours which are highly radioactive. I want you all to suit up right now.'

Julius touched his EMU gadget and the suit enveloped his body. He shifted in his seat, trying to get comfy. There was a pink cloud at the end of the tunnel and, as he got closer to it, it became luminous, shimmering with red iridescence. It was beautiful to look at and Julius was thrilled to see it up close, as opposed to in a picture — after all, a flision field was a rarity.

It lasted about five minutes and, as the vapours began to thin, Fletcher instructed them further. 'This is it, Mizkis. Our fleet is on standby ahead of us, at the edge of a small solar system called Uroplatus. They have opened a breech for us to fly through. You are now receiving a reading of the positions of the planets and their moons. The hideout is on a space station, which has been reported as moving constantly in an erratic pattern. The goal is to board it. Expect enemy fire, so make your six years of training count.'

'Or five in my case,' muttered Julius. He adjusted his grip on the catalyst and followed the pilots ahead of him. He looked at the sensors of his Cougar, and saw that the airspace ahead was dotted with asteroids, which could provide some level of cover in combat. Unfortunately, the radar was also picking up a host of Arneshian crafts, which were moving in tight formations, patrolling the system. 'Faith, can we already see her hideout on the radar?'

'For the sake of their reputation, I would hope not,' he replied. 'We can track its signature though — it's unique within the system.'

'Do it.'

'Tracking now,' answered Faith.

Julius watched his screen intently. A stripe of red dots appeared just off his map, Northeast of their current position. 'I can see a contrail. She could be hiding behind that asteroid belt on the radar.'

'I'll send the coordinates to Fletcher,' said Faith.

'Sneaky lady,' commented Skye. 'She's playing hide and seek with us.'

'Good job, Baza,' came Fletcher's voice in reply. 'Take three pilots and follow me. We're going to find the back door.'

Julius thought he heard Siena complaining about being separated from Faith, but she followed orders and continued on with the rest of the Mizkis.

'You heard the man,' said Faith, obviously chuffed at the sudden bestowal of responsibility. 'Skirts, if you please.'

Fletcher and two other Lynx pilots veered away from the rest of the group, followed by the new toon. Julius gradually increased his speed and, soon enough, he was back at level 10. The Commander must have trusted their piloting skills, as he led them through several tight turns and twists that matched the viciousness of the Holo Palace games. The Skirts lived up to their reputation and followed with ease.

'Baza, get your toon to the right side. You'll have to blast your way through, but we need to open a path for the others.'

'Yes, sir,' said Faith. 'Skirts, spread out in a line and shoot at will.'

'You loved saying that, didn't you?' said Morgana, amused.

'Not as much as I love me engines, but it'll do for now,' he replied happily.

'Err … not to spoil the party, but we have company,' said Skye. 'Six bogies ahead, hiding behind that large asteroid. And with real pilots onboard this time.'

'I see them,' said Julius, checking his radar. 'Faith, can you distract them?'

'Boy, can I?'

'Take them for a loop, heading right back here.'

'And what will you do?'

'We'll be the ones doing the ambush,' added Morgana.

'I like it,' said Skye.

Julius was glad to hear that Morgana's fighting spirit had resurfaced. Whatever had happened in the hangar was now gone. He watched as Faith accelerated, and then flew straight past them, catching them by surprise. 'Darn. Three of them aren't following!'

'It's because they're waiting for me,' cried Morgana. 'Come to mama!' she taunted, diving into the middle of their group.

'This way, McCoy,' called Skye, flying slowly towards the rocks.

Julius waited for Morgana to disappear from view before getting into position. He had to admit, watching her jump into the midst of the enemies like that had made his heart ache with worry. The sooner he got her piloting a big old spaceship, the better he would feel — a selfish thought perhaps, but a safer option for sure. He moved forward, behind Skye, and landed his Cougar on one of the asteroids to Skye's left. The Cougar's engine rolled gently into a hum as it waited, poised.

'Guys!' shouted Faith over the com. 'I'm coming back. Be ready with the welcome committee.'

'Roger, Faith,' said Julius. 'Party hats are on.' He looked at the radar, and saw Faith's Cougar advancing fast, followed by the three Arneshians. Another dot blinked onto screen. 'Morgana, are you ready?'

'Coming on like a tornado!' she said, sounding exhilarated.

Suddenly, Faith's aircraft sprung into view from the right, while Morgana's came to meet him from the opposite direction. The two Cougars were seemingly on course for a collision. Julius gripped his Catalyst, instantly anxious. A fraction of a second later, the two planes rotated on their axes, passing each other belly-to-belly, like two huge black sharks. The high manoeuvrability of the Cougars, and the fine piloting skills of Faith and Morgana, were too great for the Arneshians; the six pilots converged towards the same central point at breakneck speed, and only two of them were able to steer away at the last second. That was when Julius saw the Arneshian fast-crafts for the first time: they were small and their surfaces were coated in dark red dye; their shape reminded him of a boomerang, with the two parted wings pointing backwards, like the tail of a swallow; the cockpit was enclosed in a copper- coloured capsule, triangular in shape, in fitting with the pointy design of the front of the craft. The explosion sent debris from the ships hurtling outwards, but Julius had no time to worry about that. As soon as the two surviving planes changed course, he began to shoot. Skye followed suit and, a few moments later, the Arneshian patrol was completely destroyed.

'Ace job, guys,' said Julius.

'Just don't ask me to do that too often,' said Faith. 'I'm exhausted! Be a darling and call Fletcher for me, McCoy. I relinquish all responsibilities.'

'Commander Fletcher, sir?' said Julius. 'This side has been secured.'

'Roger that, Goshawk,' he replied. 'You're getting closer to the target. Continue on that trajectory and approach with caution. We'll join you shortly — a few loose ends to tie up here.'

'Roger and out, sir,' concluded Julius.

'Siena, can you hear me?' said Faith, once the channel was clear.

Julius detected worry in his voice.

'Siena, come in,' he repeated.

'There's loads of movement here,' came Siena's reply. 'The Lynx Army is doing a grand job, and so are our classmates.'

'Please be careful,' said Faith.

'I'll be fine, I promise. I'm pretty much to the side of this whole thing. I was told to follow another group. But Lopaka, Barth and some of the others are right in the middle of it.'

Julius tensed, hoping that they would all come out of the fight unscathed. His group couldn't go back though, as they had their orders to carry out. 'Faith, scan ahead,' he said, 'beyond that last meteorite field. There's too much cover to be had for the bogies. I'll scout us a path.'

'Roger that.'

Flying ahead, Julius saw a larger rock floating amongst the belt, and decided to use it as a shield. He willed his plane forward and, when he reached it, began to turn his plane on its axis, following the rotation of the rock. He could see from the radar that the others were still behind him, but no other dots were blinking on his screen. 'Talk to me, Faith.'

'Coast is clear,' he said. 'We're coming in.'

Julius relaxed in his chair and veered away from his cover, edging forward tentatively. The nose of the Cougar emerged into the empty space beyond the rocks; that was when the space station appeared from the shadows to greet him. Julius froze.

The hideout was shaped like an hourglass, with a large metal belt around its middle, turning counterclockwise. It was a sizeable vessel — probably as big as the Tijara section of Moonrising. Although the system was packed with patrols, the station itself seemed rather forlorn. *Who's protecting it?* thought Julius.

Suddenly, as if it had somehow sensed him thinking about it, the space station awoke. Several portholes opened like ominous black eyes around the perimeter of the outer belt, from which poured out hundreds of small aircrafts, like a thick flight of blood-red swallows.

Julius hoped that his Cougar would blend in with the shadows of the asteroids, but it was too late; although the majority of the planes were heading towards the centre of the system, a few of them had branched off and were now heading straight for him. 'Get back!' he cried to the others. Then, to Fletcher, 'We are under attack. I repeat, we are under attack.'

'We're almost done here. Can you handle them, McCoy?'

'We'll sure try, sir.'

'Stay alive until we get there.'

'Roger that, Commander,' he answered.

'They're almost on us!' cried Skye.

'I'm going to meet them!' said Morgana, accelerating towards the Arneshian patrol. Julius watched her arrow past his right side. 'I'm right behind you,' he said, following. They both began to shoot as they propelled their Cougars forward, twisting and dodging the return fire. Julius was unleashing his new powers through the catalyst, keen to get rid of the danger before it could find Morgana or the others. They struck two planes with the yellow energy pulses from their catalysts. They exploded and crashed into the midst of their squadron, taking three more enemy ships with them.

Morgana whooped triumphantly as she flew through them, unscathed, making

Julius smile. She's something else, all right, he thought, suddenly feeling the urge to be back in the hut on Buruwang with her.

'Watch your tail, McCoy,' warned Faith.

Julius turned just in time to see an Arneshian opening fire on him. He halted, tilting the Cougar down, so that the enemy ship flew by over him, and found itself in the middle of his target. Julius locked his mind onto it and opened fire. 'Bull's-eye!' he cried, as the craft exploded in front of him. He quickly scanned the radar and realised that the remaining Arneshians had been divided between the others. The three red dots following Morgana blinked suddenly and disappeared from the radar, courtesy of Skye, who had snuck up on them from behind. There was only Faith left now, giving chase to a couple of fighters. It looked like he was heading his way. Julius turned his plane, waiting for him to emerge from the asteroid belt. He also saw Morgana and Skye shooting out of the shadows toward him. He didn't notice the lone craft emerging from the hideout, and sneaking up on him.

Julius' Cougar rocked forward as one of its wings was halved by enemy fire. 'I'm hit!' he cried.

'There's a small runway ahead,' said Skye, flanking him. 'Can you make it?'

Julius twisted his head left and right to try spot it. His plane was swaying wildly. 'I can see it, Skye!' The strip stuck out for about half a mile before disappearing inside a dock of the space station. There was no way of telling if it would be empty inside, but he had no other choice. 'Come on,' he whispered through gritted teeth. The Cougar was becoming increasingly difficult to steer and he had to bend all his will to keep it straight.

'You're almost there, Julius,' said Morgana, flying to his left side. 'Skye, go to his right. We'll use our powers to keep him on course.'

'On my way,' replied Skye, taking up position.

To Julius, it felt as if two giant hands had suddenly grabbed his plane and steadied it. He was coming in fast to the landing strip now. With a last effort he prepared to touch down and avoid crashing in the process. The Cougar's nose landed first; Julius realised that, without the help of Morgana and Skye, it would have tumbled forward. There was a flash of light on his controls, which told him that he had crossed the threshold into the pressurised area. The plane lost momentum and the tail end crashed back down to the floor. It was only thanks to the others that his Cougar skidded to a halt before the back wall. Julius exhaled. 'That was close. Thanks guys.'

'Hey,' said Skye, 'where's Faith?'

'Incoming!' was the loud reply. Faith's plane zoomed into the hangar faster than any safe protocol would have allowed, skidding sideways as soon as it touched the strip. 'A little help here!' he shouted, as he hurtled toward them.

Julius turned in his seat, locked his mind on the Cougar, and pushed it backwards to slow it, while at the same time steadying it. The plane came to a halt a few inches from Morgana's.

'That was one heck of an entrance,' said Skye, impressed.

'I think I'm gonna be sick,' said Faith feebly.

'McCoy, come in,' said Fletcher over the com-link.

'Commander, we're inside the hideout. It's a side hangar. Ruthier, Miller and Shanigan are here too.'

'You'll need to fly out again.'

'Sir, this place is empty. It doesn't look like they've detected us.'

Fletcher seemed to be thinking about this, because the channel went quite.

'Commander?' said Julius, after a while.

'What's happening?' asked Morgana.

'Fletcher isn't answering, and I can't get through to him,' he said. He tried all the other channels but there was no reply.

Then the intercom beeped. 'McCoy, can you hear me?' It was Freja.

'Grand Master?' said Julius, surprised. There had been a hint of urgency in his voice, which hadn't escaped Julius.

'Are you all safe?'

'Yes, sir, but my plane isn't. What happened to Commander Fletcher?'

'The enemy has engaged him. He'll get to you as soon as he can, but your classmates need him most right now.'

'Is Siena all right?' said Faith anxiously.

'She's fighting, Mr Shanigan, so let her do her job while you do yours. You need to suit up, get out of your Cougars and find shelter right now.'

'But …'

'No buts. Film your surroundings and everything you can. Keep yourself safe until Lynx army joins you; and don't engage Salgoria. I repeat, do not engage Salgoria!'

'Roger that, Grand Master,' said Julius. He switched his attention to the others. 'You heard Freja.' He pressed the EMU button on his chest, making sure that his suit was indeed active before releasing the roof of his plane – although he had detected a pressure barrier on entry, he needed to be sure. He stood up and looked for the easiest way to get to the floor, which turned out to be by stepping onto the Cougar's left wing, and jumping down from there, landing heavily.

The readings on his PIP came back safe, so Julius removed his helmet and hurried over to Morgana; she was sitting on the right wing of her plane. Julius stretched his arms out towards her and helped her down.

'Thanks,' she said, gratefully, removing her helmet.

'You hurt?' he asked, checking her face for bruises.

'I don't think so. Just a bit stiff.'

He nodded. 'Great bit of flying out there, as always.'

'You know me,' she said cheekily.

He kissed her and held her tight — her perfume filled the air around him, making it feel almost homely. 'Yeah, I know you.' He took her by the hand and walked over to the others.

'Get your Gauntlets online,' said Skye, activating his EMU's inbuilt hand-catalyst.

Julius activated his too, keeping the safety locks on.

'Faith, have you been able to reach Siena?' asked Morgana.

He just shook his head. 'I'm sure she's fine,' he said, trying to sound confident.

'Of course she is,' replied Morgana, smiling reassuringly.

Faith nodded, before hovering around the hangar, scouting all the corners from bottom to ceiling. 'Freja wants us to keep safe,' he said, checking out a door on a small mezzanine. 'I say that we need to get inside to do that. There's a shooting gallery out there and someone could fly in at any moment.'

'Agreed,' said Skye. 'We're sitting ducks in here'

'I think we can use this passage,' continued Faith. 'Come on, I'll help you.'

Julius moved to just below Faith's position; using telekinesis, Skye and Morgana lifted him upwards, while Faith pulled him up towards him, in the same way. Julius landed gently by Faith's side, and looked down. 'Morgana's next.'

They repeated the manoeuvre with her, then with Skye, until they were all safely on the platform. There was a panel to the right of the door. Faith removed its cover and opened his PIP, using its software to bypass the security lock. It took him a minute or so, while the others were aiming their Gauntlets at the entrance, ready for any potential danger. Once the door opened, Faith stepped inside, and motioned for the others to follow.

Julius threw another glance at their Cougars before facing the dark opening ahead. Beyond the threshold, Salgoria was waiting.

SACRIFICES

As soon as Julius passed over the threshold, a sense of dread began to slowly creep over him. He was standing in a long corridor, positioned at the rear of the group; strong overhead lamps cast a cold white light over the walls and floor, against which their dark EMUs made them stand out like sore thumbs. Julius felt all too exposed and kept looking around for cameras or sensors of any sort, but saw none — if they were being watched, he couldn't tell.

'It's so quiet here,' whispered Morgana.

'*Let's keep it that way*,' said Skye, beginning to use telepathy. '*Which way should we go?*'

'*Nowhere?*' said Morgana. '*Freja said to stay safe, and not go looking for Salgoria.*'

'*He said safe, not put,*' Skye chipped in.

'*Fine,*' said Morgana, giving in.

'*Any ideas, McCoy?*'

Julius looked up and down the passageway, trying to decide. He took a few steps southwards, and felt the sense of unease diminishing. He stepped the other way and, as he did, he began to feel anxious. '*This way.*'

'*You seem pretty sure,*' said Faith.

'*It's giving me bad vibes.*'

'*Shouldn't that be a cue to go the other way?*' said Skye.

'*Come on,*' said Julius, leading them forward.

'*I guess not,*' added Faith, bringing up the rear.

They could hear the sounds of heavy things being moved and unexplainable swishing noises, echoing around the station. Julius couldn't pinpoint exactly where these sounds were coming from, which made him nervous. He walked to the end of the corridor, slowing down as he reached the first turn, then flattened himself against the left wall, before peering around the corner. Two men in grey uniforms were standing there, talking by a niche in the wall; he couldn't tell if there were more guards within the niche but, somehow, he didn't think so. '*Two guards ahead,*' he told the others.

In reply, Faith moved in front of him, and his shields hummed into life. Skye and Morgana knelt by Julius, their Gauntlets readied.

'*One,*' began Julius, '*Two ... Three!*'

Faith stepped into the corridor, positioning his shields to form a barricade. At the same time, three Gauntlets found the nearest gaps and opened fire in unison. The Arneshians had no time to turn, run or call for help, and collapsed as they were shot down.

The Skirts waited a few seconds, but heard no further noise. Skye and Morgana ran to the bodies as quietly as they could, at the same time pushing them into the recess in the wall telekinetically. Julius and Faith quickly joined them. Bunched up, they kept advancing, each with an arm-shield turned on and their Gauntlets leaning against it, ready to channel their energies. They went up two long flights of stairs, before encountering more enemies; this time there were three of them.

Julius saw the tip of a boot appearing from around a corner, as its owner descended the steps. It was enough for him to stop where he was and shoot both foot and leg. The Arneshian guard stumbled and fell forward, crashing onto the landing between them. Faith hit him again, while Skye and Julius shot at the empty space in front, to discourage any more guards from coming down to help. Shielded and laying down cover fire, they turned the corner.

A guard was standing right there, ready to retaliate. Morgana quickly crouched down between Julius and Skye's legs, and grabbed the man by the bottom of his trousers. With her left hand she held onto him, and with the right she pushed him using her mind-skills. He flipped backwards, as if someone had removed a carpet from underneath his feet. Once down, he was soon finished off by Faith.

Julius' shield buzzed as it was bombarded by a series of electric shocks from the top of the stairs, where a guard was attacking them from behind the next corner. '*Let's move,*' he said to the others. Slowly but steadily, they continued up the steps. Julius didn't want the man to run off anywhere so, as soon as he saw his hand appear again, he grabbed it with his mind, and pulled. There was a loud crack and a scream, and the guard stumbled into view. He was instantly silenced by more mind-skill hits. As the man lay on the steps, Julius realised that he had broken his arm. *Tough,* he thought, treading over him.

Once they reached the top of the stairs, they stopped.

'*Where to?*' asked Skye, as the corridor split in opposite directions.

Julius decided to trust his instincts once more and walked to the front of the group, feeling for any hint of that strange, initial sense of unease. Annoyingly, it seemed to be emanating from both sides, making his choice harder. '*That feeling … it's everywhere.*'

'*Then focus on the small differences,*' said Morgana.

He wasn't convinced, but did as she had suggested. After moving in both directions he began to realise that Morgana was right — there were differences. The left side was colder and, as odd as this seemed, it smelt of damp. The other side was definitely warmer, but it carried the scent of something really wrong, something not quite human. Yet, for all that, there was a familiar smell to it, a weak undercurrent that reminded him of the sea. Automatically, he began to move to the right, feeling the sense of dread returning. He had chosen the right path.

'*Hold it,*' said Skye, stopping in his tracks.

They had just turned a corner, when a door ahead and to the left of them slid open. It was too late to scamper back, so Julius turned on all four of his shields, and stepped to the front. An Arneshian walked into the corridor, turned towards them and froze — a look of surprise on his face. Quick as lightning, Faith lifted the guard with his mind, and slammed him against the ceiling, while Morgana stunned him with a shot from her Gauntlet. As a second guard stuck his head out to check on his colleague, Faith released his hostage, and the man fell on top of the other, bringing them both to the floor. For good measure, Skye stunned them, before stepping inside the room to make sure it was empty.

Only then did Julius feel safe enough to close down his shields. '*That was close,*' he said.

'*Faith,*' asked Morgana. '*How big is this place? Any chance that you can access its blueprints?'*

'Probably, but I'd need a terminal.'

'In here,' said Skye, from inside the room. *'Plenty of toys.'*

'I don't know what I would do without him,' said Faith, sounding amused.

Julius let them go inside, while he stayed on the door, covering the corridor. He reckoned he could find the source of his dread just by feel but, if Faith could find them a path there, without too long a detour, that would be even better.

'All the energy seems to be routed into this large area,' said Faith, after a few minutes. *'It's not too far from here and I think it's worth searching.'*

'But what if Salgoria is there?' argued Morgana. *'You heard the Grand Master.'*

'Yes, but this room isn't the safest place either,' he replied.

They were both right, thought Julius, but he couldn't wait cooped up in here, without knowing what was causing him to feel these strange vibes. Yet, in the light of what had happened to him in the past for acting of his own accord, he decided to play it safe. *'Skye, check the door,'* he said, stepping into the room, and moving to the back. He opened his PIP and tried to make contact with Freja. He was answered by a few seconds of crackling of static, making him fear that he wouldn't be able to connect, but it worked: Freja's face popped into view on the screen.

'McCoy, is everything all right?'

'Yes, sir,' he whispered. 'We had to leave the hangar — too exposed there. We're inside a control room now.'

'Enemies?'

'We took a few down already.'

Freja looked worried. 'Lynx Army is still engaged with the Arneshians. The whole fleet is.'

'Sir, there's a large central area a few doors from here.'

'Absolutely not, McCoy! Not without support.'

'What do you want us to do then, sir?' he said, aware that his frustration was seeping through in his voice.

'You must stay put. Barricade the door. We'll not be lon- Miller, watch out!'

Freja's eyes had grown wider as they shifted to a point beyond Julius. Startled, Julius turned on his heels, Gauntlet at the ready. Skye was holding an Arneshian by his arms trying to immobilise him, while at the same time using him as protection from someone else's electric blasts. Faith and Morgana took refuge behind their shields as they traded fire with more guards. Julius sprinted forward, delivering a strong mind-push ahead of him, which sent Skye's assailant flying against the wall. Quickly, he activated his own shield, sheltering both Skye and himself, while twisting his body to the left and shooting at the three remaining guards. With all of their combined powers, the guards were swiftly dispatched.

Julius checked his PIP again and tried to re-establish a connection with Freja, but he was answered only by static. Faith hovered back the way they had come, to check that the coast was still clear.

'He zapped me,' said Skye, telepathy forgotten, holding a hand up to his neck.

Julius took a look at it, and nodded. 'It's a light wound. The main thing is that your EMU is intact.'

'Incoming guards! They know we're here!' cried Faith suddenly, also not bothered about being heard anymore.

'We have to move out,' urged Julius. 'Let's head for the centre!'

They slipped back into a tight formation, using their shields as best as they could, all the while getting further away from the safety of their Cougars and into the belly of the station.

*

From the comfort of his control room, K'Ssander watched them go. His face betrayed mild surprise at seeing them there. 'Taurus 1,' he said, using his com-link. 'Tell the Ambassador that the Queen has visitors.' Following their escape on the larger monitor, he caught sight of Morgana and his lips curled into a smile. He slowly stood up and opened his hands. The disks embedded in his palms began to glow, sending little electric sparks up into the air.

*

Faith steered their course, using the blueprint he had downloaded from the terminal. 'We take the next right, then the first left. The door is at the end of that corridor.'

Julius could hear the sound of hurried footsteps behind them, drawing closer. He tried not to panic, and instead focused on Faith's directions, aware that there could be more guards ahead.

On cue, as they turned the last corner, they were welcomed by a thick discharge of electricity, which crashed against their shields.

'Don't stop, guys,' said Julius, moving steadily forward. They pushed on. Julius lifted his hand towards the guards ahead of him, lifted them up and pinned them against the wall, while the others hit them repeatedly with their mind-skills. Only when he saw their heads lulling to the side did Julius set them down, unconscious, on the floor.

'Faith,' said Skye, 'open this door fast. We'll cover you.'

Faith moved to the door's release pad, opened his PIP and quickly bypassed the security code. 'There,' he said. 'Get in.'

Julius didn't need to be asked twice. Grabbing Morgana, he entered the room and moved to the left, holding still against the wall. Faith managed to close the door again not a moment too soon, as the Arneshians had just turned into the corridor and opened fire again.

Inside the room, it took Julius a few moments to adjust to the poor illumination. The area was larger than he had imagined, and it bent in an L shape, hiding from view where the source of the light was. All around them were hundreds of ledges, holding long, rectangular metal containers. From their position, all he could see was a layer of eerie green brightness covering the top of each box. Holding Morgana's hand, he cautiously moved away from the door.

Faith hovered behind them, followed by Skye, and headed towards one of the shelves.

'It's so hot in here,' said Morgana, deactivating her EMU.

Then Faith let out a cry.

'What's wrong?' asked Julius, running forward.

Faith had recoiled away from the shelf and Julius followed his gaze back to the metal container in front of him. Carefully, he peeked inside, vaguely aware that he had stopped breathing. As his eyes moved over the rim and saw the contents within it, his stomach lurched. The box was filled with an oily substance all the way to the brim, the green light turning it into a malevolent-looking slime; at the bottom of the tank, wearing only a pair of boxer shorts, was the still body of Billy Somers. The small monitor against the wall recorded a slow heartbeat, confirming that the boy was in a sort of coma, but alive nonetheless. Numerous thin tubes emerged from his body, from his feet to the head, linking him to a central pump. All the anger Julius had ever felt on account of Somers' obnoxiousness, from their first day of school to Buruwang, dissipated quickly from his consciousness, and was replaced by a deep sense of pity. He took a step back, now fully aware of the thousands of tanks filling the shelves around them — it seemed they had found the missing Nuarns.

'This isn't right,' said Morgana feebly.

Julius could see she was close to tears and hugged her tightly to him. There was nothing he could tell her to make things better, so he just held her. The feeling of dread that had guided him to this room hadn't subsided however, as if there was something worse still to come. He began to look around, anxious as to why the noises outside the door had completely ceased.

'Let's get him out of here,' said Faith. 'He's a douchebag, but me conscience can't stand this.'

Skye moved closer and began fiddling with the life monitor above Somers' tank. Faith touched the liquid with one fingertip; when nothing happened, he dipped his whole hand into it and placed it under the boy's head.

'His skin is all slippery,' he said, creasing his nose in disgust.

'Faith, try to pull that big tube off the main pump,' volunteered Skye.

'I wouldn't do that if I were you,' boomed T'Rogon's voice, from the other side of the wall. 'It might kill him.'

Skye and Faith froze in mid action. Julius stepped away from Morgana, opened his shield and readied his Gauntlet. The Ambassador was around the corner, he was sure of that. Behind him, the others grouped up and followed cautiously. He edged forward, noticing how the light was growing brighter and stronger. There was a faint noise of water bubbling, along with a familiar sweet fragrance. Slowly, he advanced around the corner and his eyes grew wide, his sense of bewilderment at what he saw punctuated by the sharp intakes of breath from behind him.

A large tank sat before them; it must have been fifteen by twenty feet at least, lit by a warm internal light and filled with what appeared to be water. The tunic-clad body of a woman floated peacefully inside it, like a white cloud, surrounded by tiny bubbles working their way up to the surface. The beautiful, sad woman before him was at least thirty, with long hair framing her body like golden deep-sea algae, dancing slowly in a perennial undercurrent. He knew it was Farrah he was looking at. As he stared at her, he now fully realised what Ben Hastings had meant when he had told him she was aging faster than was humanly possible. Julius stepped to the glass, and touched his fingers to its cold surface, unsure if she could actually see him or not. There were tubes converging from the top of the tank, into the back of her body, to a point below her shoulder blades that Julius couldn't see. She looked like some sort of surreal sea creature, crowned by the bright light behind her. Suddenly, her eyes shifted slightly and Julius could have sworn they had just focused on him, and grown a little wider. That small action was enough to shake him from his daze and send ripples of anger through his body.

He turned to the left, and saw T'Rogon. The Ambassador looked back at him from an unknown location, from the safety of a large monitor. 'I have to admit, very few people surprise me these days, but you … How on Earth did you find us?' asked the Ambassador, a mixture of amusement and genuine incredulity in his voice.

'What have you done to Farrah?' he replied calmly, completely disregarding the question. 'Where is Salgoria?'

T'Rogon's expression grew sterner. 'Salgoria is dead, and has been for some time. In fact, she died the night you lost your powers.'

Julius stepped back from the tank, allowing himself a better view of the Ambassador. 'What do you mean?'

'Your people have been acting under many misguided assumptions, McCoy,' he replied in a patronising tone. 'You seem to believe that the queen is like us — a human — when, in fact, our ruler is more than just a symbol of power. It is the repository of knowledge of every single Arneshian that has ever lived, since Clodagh's death.'

Julius watched as T'Rogon brought his hands up to his temple, and began to slowly pull at his circlet; as the metal band was slipped off, it revealed a dark circular hole in the middle of his forehead.

'You've seen this before,' said T'Rogon. 'Clodagh couldn't give her people Telepathy, so we've come up with a different way of communicating. The circlet taps directly into our brains, recording all the technological knowledge we can ever think of. When we die, the device is brought here to become part of our greatest treasure: the Grey Skills Database. The human brain is good, McCoy, but limited by our own humanity. Only a computer can analyse 236 years of hard data, connect the dots and make the kind of leaps that give birth to great discoveries. The ruler, whether a king or a queen, represents the apex of Grey Skill creativity; the most technologically evolved being in the universe — the Arneshian afterlife. And each ruler is better than their predecessor; an upgraded model if you like, since they carry all the knowledge of a few generations. So you see, we have already achieved immortality — through her,' he concluded, pointing at the tank.

Julius was struggling to make sense of it all. These people, with their holographic army and their powerful spaceships, were all linked to each other in a way that other humans could only dream of. Through the queen, their technological contribution to life would never be forgotten, no matter how small it had been. 'You mean to tell me you've been through all these centuries of war for the sake of … knowledge?'

'Ah, McCoy, you're but a child still. Knowledge is power. It's a trampoline to everything you could ever hope to achieve. Nothing can be accomplished without it.'

'I might be a child, but I understand you all too well. The difference between us is that my parents taught me to respect other people – but what's the point in talking about morality with you? You need to have a soul to do that.' Without waiting for T'Rogon's reply, he turned to Farrah, dismayed. 'Is she … Salgoria's successor now?'

'Temporarily,' answered T'Rogon coldly – Julius' accusation had hit its target. 'You know full well that she will age and die in a few years. No, we needed a longer-term solution. Farrah is more of a high-maintenance, mid storage facility for us. Because of her rapid decay, we must keep her full of fresh nutrients, using Nuarns — the closest, expendable thing to an Arneshian there is; hence our visit to your planet. She's worth the nuisance though because, as she processes all this information, she is also filtering it from all impurities gathered over the centuries, by removing obsolete or faulty data.'

Julius thought about it logically, keeping his feelings out of it and his temper at bay. He couldn't hear a single noise from the others, but he knew they were there, listening, mystified. 'So, you knew that she survived Angra Mainyu and you knew about her condition all along,' he said, as understanding dawned on him.

'Yes. Clodagh had implanted a cellular tracker in the foetus, so we knew that Freja hadn't destroyed it. As for the rest, it was only a theory at first, based on past experiments with genetic engineering, but a little observation of your lunar facilities showed that she had grown from zero to five years in the space of one.'

Julius shook his head. 'I bet you're dying to take over the role, aren't you, *King* T'Rogon?'

'You flatter me,' he answered affably. 'But no; too much limelight, in my opinion. I'd rather be at the right hand. Besides, we have already chosen her successor. Your powers have set him up properly and Farrah here is transmitting her knowledge to him as we speak. Imagine that: an Arneshian king with White Skills from two White Childs – our next ruler will be invincible! Can you guess who this is?'

'Michael!' cried Skye.

With that, the last piece of the puzzle clicked into place and Julius knew his friend was right. The realisation brought a chill to his heart, as he could only begin to imagine how powerful Michael would be with two centuries of knowledge and the highest form of mind-skills in existence. He walked to the monitor, as close to T'Rogon's image as he could. 'I'm coming to get you,' he told him, looking him square in his eyes. 'Before this is over, you will pay for what you've done to my family.' The Ambassador's smirk seemed to falter a little, and Julius slammed his open hand against the glass, unleashing a discharge of fire that smashed the monitor to pieces. The fury that had been mounting inside him in the last few minutes had been unleashed, leaving a familiar trace of yellow liquid-energy seeping from his fingers and dripping gently to the ground. He felt better for it and, with a clearer head, he could now focus on their next step. He turned to the tank again and pressed his hands against it. Before doing anything else, he looked at Morgana quickly; there was a part of him that was worried that she may still be jealous of Farrah. It seemed ridiculous, considering the circumstances but, with that glance, he wanted her to know that she was the one he loved.

Whether Morgana felt it or not, she smiled reassuringly.

Julius then tapped the glass lightly. 'Farrah, can you hear me?'

She lifted her head in his direction, a gentle smile appearing on her tired features. 'You came for me,' she said. Her voice was delicate and seemed to come from afar, apparently unhindered by the liquid in the container.

Julius recognised that smile immediately and felt a stab in his heart, as he recalled the way in which he had left her. 'I'm sorry I couldn't protect you. What can I do to make things right?'

Those words seemed to give her some strength. 'The line of Arneshian rulers must end. Their stored knowledge cannot be allowed to grow any further.'

'What did T'Rogon mean about Michael? What are they doing to him?'

'Two centuries of knowledge are being processed through my body. I am distilling the data into its purest form, before passing it on to him. Michael will have the entire Arneshian treasure within him as well as your powers. All we can do now is to prevent the last transfer because, once it's done, he will be the most powerful being in existence and not even Tijara's powers will be enough to stop him.'

Julius nodded. 'How do I interrupt the transfer?'

Farrah turned to Faith, who was standing by a terminal. 'You must begin the process by pressing the pad in the centre of the monitor.'

Faith identified it and followed her instructions. A distant noise of engines winding down filled the room.

'I think we did it,' said Julius eagerly. 'What else can we do?'

'There's nothing more for you to do.'

'What?'

Farrah's smiled fondly at him. 'You told me I wasn't capable of loving, because true love means sacrifice. You were wrong.'

Suddenly, a cavernous rumble surged up from the depths of the space station, spreading through the walkways and into the walls. The vibrations caused the containers on the shelves to slowly shift towards their edges, until they toppled and fell, spreading their contents in a jumbled mess onto the ground. The liquid in the individual tanks flooded the floor, and disappeared into various fissures and ridges.

'What's happening?' cried Skye, looking around him, as the bodies of the Nuarns began to stack up on top of each other, in a last undignified pose.

The black tubes attached to Farrah's back began to snap out, coiling and twisting around her head, releasing a golden fluid into the water.

'Her sensors are shutting down,' said Faith, wildly searching the interface of her monitor for a way to stop it. 'She's overriding the system!'

'Farrah,' cried Julius, banging his hands against the glass. 'Stop! What are you doing? There has to be another way. Wait Farrah, please!' A sudden panic had replaced his logic. He had come to save her, not to watch her die.

'Every advantage the Arneshians ever had, they have now played,' she told them. 'There is only Michael left. You must find him and stop him Julius, and it will all be over.'

'Where is he, Farrah?' asked Morgana urgently.

'Mah,' she answered.

Julius flinched at the name. Was it the place from his dream? He pushed it to the back of his mind for the moment. 'I won't let you die, Farrah!'

'My death is the beginning of the end. Leave before it's too late. I have the power to stop my army. I will clear the way for you.'

The last, larger tube detached from her, flowing backwards and releasing a golden stream onto her hair. As her eyes closed, her gaze was still fixed on Julius. Then, an odd calm spread over her face and her body sunk slowly, enveloped in the golden cloud saturating the water. She was finally at peace.

Julius looked at her, until she disappeared from his view forever, his hands still pressed against the glass. A crack appeared beside his right hand, slowly creeping outwards like a streak of lightning.

'Get back,' said Skye. 'It's gonna break open.' Seeing that Julius wasn't moving, he grabbed his arm and pulled him back. 'Come on, mate. She's gone.'

'Julius, please.' Morgana's voice had an edge of fear in it, which made Julius snap back to reality.

He turned to her and, passing his arm around her waist, hurried her back towards the entrance at the other side of the room. They had to step over the Nuarns, their bad choice to follow the Arneshians now cruelly displayed in the form of their dying bodies. The rumbling was getting stronger, and it seemed to be spreading to the whole station.

'We need to get back to the Cougars,' said Skye. 'This place doesn't sound steady anymore. McCoy, you fly with me.'

Julius opened his PIP again, trying to get in touch with Freja. He thought he caught a glimpse of a face, but the image was still too distorted.

Meantime, Faith was hovering above the carnage and making a straight line for the door. He opened his shield, positioning himself to the side. 'Be ready, guys.'

They watched the door sliding open and held their breaths, expecting enemy fire, but there was none.

'Where is everybody?' said Morgana.

Skye moved forward, stepping into the corridor with his Gauntlet resting on his left wrist. 'Clear,' he confirmed, from over his shoulder.

They all followed him, keeping close to each other to maximise the shield-wall area. The very structure of the hideout was groaning now, as if the metal sheets that held it together were being pulled from all sides. Overhead, live cables had fallen down in some of the corridors, and they had to duck under them to avoid being electrocuted. Around one of the corners, they stumbled upon the body of an Arneshian guard, who had died under the weight of a fallen steel beam. A small streak of blood was etched from the corner of his mouth to the skin of his cheek. Except for Faith, they had to climb over him to get across, which involved adding their body weight to that of the beam.

When Julius pushed his hands down on the cold steel, he saw the chest of the man lowering, as a sickening crunch of broken ribs filled the air. He climbed over it as fast as he could, trying to ignore it, even though his stomach was threatening to rebel.

'Come on, let's hurry out of here,' said Morgana edgily.

Faith guided them back the way they had come as, all around them, the station was falling to pieces. Some of the passageways had collapsed or were now blocked by debris, so they had to use the blueprint to find different routes back. By the time they reached the control room they were practically running, dodging burst pipes and jumping over large gaps which had opened in the floor.

Soon, they came to the main stairwell. 'It's not far now,' said Skye, taking the steps in long jumps.

Guided by Morgana, Julius tried to contact Freja as he walked. 'Come on …' he said to the screen above his palm. After several failed attempts, he turned it off, frustrated.

They finally arrived at the last corridor, which now looked very different. The far side of it was completely gone, collapsed by what could only have been an explosion. There were more live cables snaking their way above the chasm, sending sparks in every direction. They edged slowly to the side, thankful that they could at least reach the hangar hatch in relative safety.

'Farrah wasn't joking when she said she would clear the way for us,' said Skye, panting. 'We haven't met a soul.'

'Yeah, but her way of clearing a path is tearing down the house,' added Faith. 'Let's hope it doesn't stop us too.'

As they reached the exit, however, they saw a red light flashing on the access panel, indicating a full loss of pressure.

'Look!' said Morgana, flustered. She peered through the glass opening.

Julius joined her, and realised the magnitude of their predicament in an instant. Half of the hangar was missing, possibly blown apart by one of the later explosion, and their planes were gone.

'I can still see one of the Cougars floating away,' said Skye. 'McCoy, do you think we can get it back with telekinesis?'

Julius tried to lock his mind onto it, but it was well outside his range, hindered by the station's walls. 'I can barely grab it.'

'Damn,' cried Skye.

In reply, Julius opened his PIP again. The others huddled over it, watching the static on the screen. A glimpse of Freja came into view. 'Grand Master!' he called with relief. It took him a few attempts before the link could be established with some form of success.

'What's happening? Are you safe?' said Freja.

'Sir, the hideout is coming apart. Our planes have all gone. A pickup would be great,' answered Julius quickly.

Freja turned to someone to his right, and they saw him exchanging a quick word. 'Kelly is heading your way, but there's far too much debris for speed. Twenty minutes, I'd say.'

'As quickly as possible, please sir. I don't know how much time we've got left.'

'Suit up and activate your trackers … should you need to get out.'

Julius nodded and closed his PIP. He turned to the others, feeling reassured. 'Kelly will find us. He always does.'

'Let's create a little safety here,' said Faith, drawing closer to the door and positioning all his shields in such a way that he was almost cocooned against the wall. In case of another explosion, or sudden attack, they would be fine.

Julius realised that it was a good idea and, as he busied himself with the preparations, he didn't notice that Morgana had backtracked along the corridor, her shield and Gauntlet at the ready, as if investigating something.

'K'Ssander!' she cried. She opened fire but, just then, the station rumbled and shook, throwing her off balance, her shield deactivated. A deep, scraping sound in two short blasts cut through the air.

Alarmed, Julius turned and saw Morgana standing in front of K'Ssander, staring blankly at him. The Arneshian ran to the left, disappearing from view. Morgana didn't chase him, but looked down, where her hands were now gathered, then slowly sunk to her knees and then onto her side.

'No!' cried Julius, terrified. He bolted into action and ran to her. He was already bending from a few feet away, and reached her as he slid down on his knees. 'Morgana!' he cried, as Faith and Skye joined him to either side of her. He turned her face up, and held her head so that she could breathe properly. Morgana's eyes were half closed and the colour was draining slowly from her cheeks.

'Oh,' said Faith, aghast, looking at the wound under her cupped hands.

Julius pushed her hands out of the way and drew breath. The blue of her uniform was singed, and there was a hole the size of a coin passing through it. Using his right hand, which was underneath her, he began to prod her back for an exit wound. What he found made his stomach lurch: her t-shirt had a gash in it and it was wet and sticky.

His fingertips found the edges of a deep circular wound and he moved them aside, sickened. Slowly, he pulled his hand out and brought it up for all to see. It was covered in blood.

'Suit her up!' said Faith. 'We need to put pressure on the wounds.'

Julius pressed the device on her chest and immediately her EMU enveloped her body tightly. 'Morgana, talk to me, please!' he said, holding her face and tapping her cheek gently with his clean hand.

She opened her eyes slowly, a look a fear veiling them. 'K'Ssander ...' she trailed off.

Julius snapped at that, and started to climb to his feet, murder on his mind.

'Don't ...' said Morgana feebly. Her hand weakly gripped his arm.

Julius looked down at her, his face still flushed with hatred.

'Don't leave me,' she repeated, mustering her strength.

The look in her eyes made him falter. He knew she would be all right soon and he really wanted to get his hands on that treacherous scumbag, but when he tried to stand up again, her hold on his arm tightened. K'Ssander would have to wait.

'Mate,' said Skye, looking pale. 'I don't think we can wait for Kelly.'

Julius could feel panic creeping over him, afraid to make the wrong decision. He held her hands, pretending that the blood staining his skin wasn't there. Faith and Skye were looking at him expectantly; if anyone had to make a decision concerning Morgana, it had to be him. The station's gravitational system was going askew, and the entire structure was tilting dangerously. He had no time to lose. 'Skye, grab that piece of metal,' he said, pointing to their right. 'We're going to make a stretcher. We'll suit up and get out, using our thrusters to clear the debris. Kelly will meet us half-way.'

'Ok,' said Skye. He stood up and went to retrieve the fallen panel. When he returned, he placed it on the floor, by her left side.

'Morgana,' said Julius gently, leaning over her, 'we're going to move you now. We'll be quick, I promise. We're going to meet Elian.' She looked at him, but Julius got the feeling that she wasn't really aware. The shock caused by the loss of blood was slowly creeping over her. He moved with renewed energy. 'Help me out,' he said to the guys, aware of the almost pleading tone in his voice.

Using their mind-skills, Skye and Julius lifted her by the shoulders, while Faith took care of her legs.

As soon as they moved her, Morgana cried in pain, her awareness resurfacing.

'I'm sorry, baby,' he said, trying to soothe her. Her cry had made his skin crawl, while a new wave of fear was clutching at his stomach. He focused on lowering her down onto the metal panel, which was large enough to fit most of her body comfortably. 'It's ok,' he told her. 'We don't have to do that again.' He turned to Faith. 'Push her my way — gently — if we do it manually it may be less painful.' As Julius slid his hand under her, around her waist, he felt something that shouldn't have been there. The back of the suit was slightly swollen and, when he touched it, it caused the liquid inside it to move around.

Faith must have felt it too, because he looked up at Julius, with a look of horror on his face. They both knew what that liquid was. 'We need to go. Now!' he urged, leaving her as she was. He headed towards the hatch and began to override the door mechanism that kept it shut against the depressurization beyond it.

Julius and Skye positioned themselves at either side of the stretcher, lifting it with their minds. They each held her by one shoulder, to make sure she wouldn't fall off.

When they reached the door, Julius bent over her and saw how pale her face had become. The familiar light of her beautiful green eyes was almost spent. 'Don't you go anywhere,' he told her. 'Don't you leave me.'

Morgana shifted her gaze to him, finding his eyes. 'Never,' she whispered.

Her lips offered a hint of a smile, and he kissed them tenderly for what felt like too short a time. He then pressed her EMU device again to activate her helmet.

The space station rumbled more violently this time, causing several sections of the area around them to collapse into the widening gap. They had very little floor space left.

'Trackers on,' said Faith. 'Hold on to Morgana and the stretcher with all you've got. Here we go.' He pushed the release pad and the door slid open.

The vacuum sucked them into the hangar suddenly, pulling them into a tumble, as they held on to the metal panel protecting Morgana's limbs and head with their bodies. Julius had to shoot brief mind-pushes to various points around him, so they wouldn't go off course or smash against the walls of the hideout. Once they'd cleared the space station and begun to slow down, they took up positions all around her, lying flat by her side.

Faith was checking his PIP screen through the glove of his EMU, for what direction to take. 'I can see the Ahura,' he said, 'but it's well beyond the asteroid field.'

'Let's clear it then,' said Julius, activating his thrusters. Immediately, they began to move faster, getting closer to the obstacles. Between the rocks and the debris from the battle, Kelly's rescue would be greatly hindered and time was not a luxury they had. As they moved forward, Julius kept looking at Morgana, the reflection of the stars streaming over her visor. His thoughts went back to November, when Clavel had let them outside, for their first EVA. Morgana had taken his hands then, guiding him into the darkness, savouring the freedom it offered her. He had floated in space by her side, stargazing. He remembered the awe he had seen in her eyes and how, in that moment, in his heart, he had known that he loved her. He squeezed her hand and felt her doing the same, a sign that she was still fighting.

They blasted rocks and debris from their path as they advanced, so they wouldn't need to slow down. Faith was still tracking Kelly's ship on the radar on his PIP but, for some reason, the captain's progress was really slow.

After several minutes, which were more like an eternity given the circumstances, Julius felt a sudden urge to speed things up. 'Faith, where's Kelly?'

'Dead ahead,' he replied. 'We're on the right coordinates.'

Julius made a sharp turn towards a huge rock on the outer side of the belt, dragging the stretcher with him.

'What are you doing?' asked Skye, slowing down to a stop.

Julius planted his boots firmly against two gaps in the rock, as if he was readying himself to launch forward. 'Both of you, lie down by her side, hold her and don't let go. There's only one way to get her to Kelly on time and only I have the power to do it.'

'What-' started Faith.

'I'm going to push you towards him and I'll use this rock to prevent me from going backwards. When you get there, send someone to fetch me.'

'That's insane!' replied Skye.

'It's the only way,' he insisted, in a tone that didn't need approval. 'When I tell you, turn your thrusters back on.' He looked at Morgana one more time, before letting go of her hand. She was either asleep or unconscious but, right now, as hard as it was to accept, there was nothing else he could do for her. Only a doctor could patch her up. He positioned himself against the rock to gain maximum hold, then closed his eyes and began to breathe deeply. Everything was cleared from his mind — T'Rogon, K'Ssander, Michael. He focused on a source of heat from within his chest and allowed it to grow. As it swelled, he visualised a thick, yellow ball of energy bubbling inside him. Slowly, he stretched his right hand forward and said calmly, 'Ready, steady, go.'

Faith and Skye turned on their thrusters, while a full blast of power erupted from Julius' open palms, engulfing them. The three of them were propelled forward at incredible speed, resembling a shooting star flying across space, until they were too far away to clearly distinguish.

The rock behind Julius had moved backward under the pressure, but not too much, as he had also activated his thruster to hold him steady. 'Please, get there in time,' he said. He took a sip of his sugary drink before he could go any further, as the effort of the mind-push had left him weak. At the same time though, he didn't want to wait to be found. So he pushed away from the asteroid, following their course. Alone, as he drifted in the emptiness of space, he began to feel panic gnawing at him again, suffocating him. His mind was filled with all kinds of horrible thoughts, causing him to shudder. He wasn't moving fast enough, and he had nothing to grab with his mind to propel himself forward.

After several minutes, which felt more like hours, he was starting to think that they would never find him. Oppressed by the vastness of space and worried sick about the state of Morgana, he fumbled his PIP open, trying to figure out where he was. The radar on his screen scanned his surroundings meticulously, but there was nothing there. He followed the circular motion of the gauge in an effort to hold onto his sanity, as he began to think that maybe he had gone off course.

You need to stay cool, he told himself, taking slow, long breaths. When he had managed to push his desperation below the surface of his mind and restored some sense of calm, he looked all around, as far as his eyes could see. It was at that moment that he caught a glimpse of something familiar.

Emerging from the shadows was the streamlined shape of a Cougar, advancing slowly towards him. A wave of relief swept over him.

The pilot was none other than Commander Fletcher, who looked as pleased as Julius was. He halted his craft beside him, and sent a mind-message to Julius. 'Hold on to the fin, McCoy, and secure yourself. We're not far.'

Julius straddled the plane and grabbed the fin with both hands. Then he stretched out the hook on his belt and fixed it onto one of the loops attached to the back edge of the fin. 'Ready,' he said.

Fletcher turned the plane around and accelerating slowly, headed back towards the Ahura.

Julius knew that the commander wouldn't risk high speed with him perched on top of the Cougar, but a sense of urgency was once again growing in his heart. Finally, the spaceship came into view, and Julius forced himself to relax. He could see that they were heading straight towards one of the side ports, so he propped himself up on one knee and released the hook on his belt. As soon as Fletcher had cleared the pressurisation layer at the entrance of the hangar, and before the craft had even stopped, Julius jumped down to the floor, rolled smoothly forward and sprinted along the passageway. Thanks to his previous visits, he now knew the layout of the ship by heart, and exactly where the sickbay was. He headed for the stairwell, taking the steps three at a time and removed his helmet just before he turned into the final corridor. What he saw, however, slowed his run to an unsteady walk.

Kelly, and a heavily pregnant Elian, were standing outside the medical room, next to Faith and Skye. A thick, black smoke went from their heads to the ground, surrounding their ankles like a pestilential lake. They were all facing the doctor, who had just emerged through the door. His light blue medical gown was stained with large darker patches, and he had his hands in his front pockets. Looking at Kelly, he shook his head sadly, which made Elian bury her face in her husband's shoulder and Faith drop his arms to his side. Skye stepped forward, enraged, and grabbed the doctor by the front of his uniform; then, as he heard the sound of steps approaching, he turned his head to the side, his cheeks flushed. Immediately, he let go of the doctor and walked towards Julius, keeping his hands forward, as if he was getting ready to catch him. Tears were streaming down his cheeks.

Julius' mind and body drew to a standstill at once. His brain, however, continued to process the scene unfolding before his eyes, confirming what his heart already knew: Morgana was dead.

DAWNLESS SLEEP

The Battle of Uruplatus, as it came to be known in the history logs, counted the most severe Zed losses to date. Although casualties in the dozens were felt among the officers on active duty, the schools had also suffered heavily. Tuala had lost ten senior Mizkis, who had all been caught in a deadly ambush together with one of the Zed armies, while Sield had sacrificed four and Tijara one. That the battle had ultimately been won, the new system claimed for Earth and Salgoria's hideout destroyed, did only a little to mend the heartache brought about by the loss of human life.

Zed began its rescue mission immediately after the fight, re-deploying those who were not hurt to aid the operations. A myriad of sky-jets, Herons and Storks spread throughout the Uruplatus system, searching for fallen pilots and any salvageable parts. Inexplicably, the Arneshian fleet had come to a sudden halt in the middle of the battle, leaving their pilots stuck inside their planes, like insects trapped in a web. Zed wasn't taking prisoners and obliterated every last one of them.

The fragmentary video recordings taken by the Skirts during their infiltration of the hideout were reviewed thoroughly by Freja, Kloister and Milson. The GMs hoped to learn something of the whereabouts of T'Rogon, but the word Mah, uttered by Farrah, didn't aid them in the least. Freja remembered Julius mentioning this particular word to him, after Buruwang. At the time, it hadn't registered much; it was an issue he would need to investigate further, but not while Julius was in his present state.

Given the delicate situation brought about by the presence of the bodies of the Nuarns and Farrah, the three Grand Masters were the first people to set foot in the dilapidated space station, leaving their security detail outside the central room. When Edwina Milson saw the body of the young woman at the bottom of the tank, she had started to cry, remembering how, only a few years earlier, she had held her in her arms, feeding her from a bottle. Freja had passed an arm around her shoulder, trying to console her but, in truth, he had also been deeply affected.

It was Kloister who had shown them the silver lining among the misery and destruction. 'We kept Farrah alive for a reason,' he told them. 'We should never regret that act. It was a good deed, and she repaid us tenfold by stopping the Arneshian line at the cost of her own life. We'll find Michael and end this war forever.'

After that visit, Moonrising split into two sections. It was decided that all the Mizkis should return to the Lunar Perimeter ahead of the others, using only Tijara's ship, while Tuala and Sield remained behind with New Satras and the hospital. On Friday the 11th of April, all the students joined together and began their re-entry to the Moon. The Mizkis' funerals would be held on the Saturday, away from the battleground, inside their own solar system, making it a much more intimate affair for the victims' classmates, teachers and those family members that could be reached among the officers.

Moonrising personnel were working hard to prepare the hangar for the ceremony. It would be a brief one, but it was unthinkable not to have it. It was a longstanding tradition among spacefarers, and an honour bestowed to the departed. The Grand Masters had the necessary powers to perform a burial in space and it was agreed that Milson would lead it, since her school had suffered the most losses. Doctor Walliser and Nurse Primula had the heart wrenching task of washing Morgana, closing her wounds, cleaning and dressing her, in an ultimate gesture of love. With the exception of hers, the other bodies couldn't be recovered, given the fact that they had died during a space battle; as a result, their names would be etched onto empty urns.

The Mizkis were all extremely tired and subdued, torn between mixed feelings of elation at their victory, and grief for the passing of their friends. No one enrolled in Zed thinking that it would be an easy space walk, but somehow, and partially due to age and lack of experience, most of the students still believed that bad things wouldn't happen to them, because they were the good guys. A lot of those beliefs were shattered in that battle, more painfully for some than others.

The death of Morgana affected the Tijaran Mizkis at a very personal level. She was the kind of person who had known how to ease her way into a person's heart from the get-go, always ready to forgive and encourage, always there to comfort and bring sunshine with her liveliness. Each of the 6MS students had at least a handful of experiences to confirm that. Once the news of her death had reached Tijara, Siena had locked herself in her bedroom for two days, only allowing Isolde to come in. Faith was dealing with his grief in a similar way and welcomed the solitude from his girlfriend and his friends. On the other hand, Skye hadn't been able to stay away from Julius, as if being near him made the loss more bearable somehow. He didn't talk, but merely followed him around.

Julius hid his own feelings in the most remote place he could find, in the deepest recess of his mind — a room with no windows and walls painted black. On the outside he seemed to be functioning normally — he walked, ate, slept, saluted his teachers and superiors — but inside he was bleeding. It was as a part of his brain had completely shut down, preventing him from shedding even a tear. Whenever one of his classmates patted his arm, telling him how sorry they were, he would nod, pat their arm in return, and thank them sincerely. Then he would walk on, knowing that Skye wouldn't be too far behind. His presence created a buffer between him and the world, for which he was glad.

*

That fateful day, on the Ahura Mazda, Skye had tried to stop him and Julius had to struggled to get past him. In the end, he had used a mind-push to clear his friend out of his path, which had pressed Skye flat against the wall. By the time Julius had reached the medical room, he was ready for a fight. However, Faith hadn't moved a muscle, shell-shocked as he was. Kelly had merely stood there holding his sobbing wife and the doctor had taken a single step to the right, allowing him to enter. Julius' eyes had immediately been drawn to the pool of blood covering the floor and realised that it must have splashed down when they had deactivated her EMU. Red drops tinged the walls and the cabinets surrounding the examination bed, and they were already beginning to dry. Her t-shirt had been cut to allow access to the wound, leaving her in her black bra and trousers. Julius' first thought had been to cover her, because he didn't want the others to see her so exposed but, when he had stepped up to her body and seen the large hole that had perforated her abdomen, he had felt sick to his stomach. Turning to the side, he had put his hands on his knees and thrown up on the floor — over her blood — unable to stop himself. It had taken him a while before he was steady enough to stand straight again. Afterwards, he had buried his face beside hers, throwing his arms around her shoulders and lifting her up as he held her tight. The nightmare had unfolded around him, enveloping both their bodies in its cold embrace.

Julius had no memory of being taken back aboard Moonrising. He had woken up inside his cabin the day after, drenched in sweat and aching all over from the battle. The memory of Morgana had flooded back to him in an instant, oppressing his spirit in a way he never knew could be possible. That was when he had taken refuge inside himself, while his body had resumed a sort of basic daily routine.

*

The morning of the funeral, Julius left his room with Skye and headed for the hangar. He felt numb and not quite present, but he welcomed that feeling, as it kept him apart from what was going on around him. As he walked, he caught snippets of conversations among the students. The only one that caught his attention involved Faith's new coffin. Everyone knew that he had won Pete's competition with it and that it would be put to use on this occasion.

'She will look peaceful, like she's asleep,' he heard Leanne saying to a forlorn Barth. 'Forever young.'

'I hope so,' he sniffled.

'I know so,' she replied. 'Faith has built that thing as strong as a Cougar.'

'She was always nice to me, even after I chopped her hair off. I'll miss her so much.' Leanne hugged Barth while Julius walked on, carrying those words in his heart.

As he approached the entrance, he saw Faith waiting to the side. He caught his attention by placing a hand on his shoulder and, when he turned, Julius saw that his eyes were red. They didn't need to say anything, just a quick nod was sufficient. Skye led the way, then Faith. As Julius began to walk, someone grabbed his arm.

'Julius,' whispered Siena.

She looked tired, he thought. It dawned on him that he hadn't spoken to her since that day.

Siena lifted a storage box up between them, which was full of small items and microchips. 'It's for Kaori,' she said quietly. 'I thought you might want something from it.'

Julius looked down and realised that the items belonged to Morgana — a red bow, a make-up dispenser, her Zed Toon t-shirt. An invisible hand closed around Julius' heart. His eyes caught her handwriting on the case of one microchip: "My holo-dream place". Slowly, he reached for it and pulled it out of the box. 'Thanks.'

She looked at him for a few seconds, before a fresh wave of tears poured down her cheeks.

Julius passed his arm around her shoulders, waiting for the sobbing to subside. Then, he ushered her into the hangar, where she rejoined Faith. At the opposite end of the room, he spotted Kaori, nestled in Bernard Docherty's arms. He really couldn't face speaking to her just then, so he looked elsewhere.

The silver coffin lay on the floor, surrounded by 14 egg-shaped urns, in front of a large port; they rested over a platform, which would eventually move them inside the airlock compartment, before being jettisoned into space. The Grand Masters stood between these and the port, while the schools had been asked to gather along the remaining side.

Julius took his place among the 59 Tijaran Mizkis, who stood to the left of the GMs; Tuala followed them, facing the airlock, and then Sield, closing off the area along the right side. When the students were ready, the lights were dimmed.

It was in that darkness that the coffin and the urns began to shimmer, attracting everyone's attention. Each of them glowed the colour of its occupant's school, and many sobs were heard when ten of them turned green. Morgana's blue coffin stood alone, surrounded by four red urns. The colours faded and were slowly replaced by moving images. Flowers of various shapes and shades floated peacefully along the edges of Morgana's coffin, against a blue, summer sky. They twirled, as if controlled by a gentle breeze, then ducked and dived around the corners of the coffin before disappearing from sight. At first, Julius thought that it was simply a beautiful, holographic decoration, but then it dawned on him that it was more than that. Hana-chan was Morgana's pet name which, in Japanese, meant flower. Faith had selected that particular design because of that. Julius looked at the urns before him and noticed how each of them had their own distinct scenes or objects moving over their surfaces — the sea, the face of a woman, wild horses on a plain — and he realised that there was a purpose, a reason for all of them. Every design represented a person and what had been important to them in life, making death personal and intimate. Julius breathed deeply.

Grand Master Edwina Milson waited a few moments before speaking, so that they could all observe the images in front of them a little longer. Her voice was soft and calm, like a mother's embrace. 'A dream,' she began, 'is what has led us here. The dream of a life without fear, without hate, and without greed. This is what we celebrate today. Not death, not weakness or failure, but the strength of fifteen brave souls, who offered themselves in the pursuit of that dream.'

The sound of a lone sob marked a brief silence.

'Ask yourselves, Mizkis,' she said, looking around the room, catching their eyes. 'What do you want to be remembered for? Let me tell you!' Milson's voice rose steadily. 'For how well you loved. For how fully you lived. And for how deeply you committed to that dream! The people resting before us made a choice between hopelessness and hopefulness, between kneeling to the oppressors and standing up to them. That is why we honour them. Today, we salute them as heroes, and we swear by them that we will see that dream fulfilled. And so it shall be!'

'So let it be!' they all cried in reply.

Julius clenched his jaw, looking straight ahead, fighting back the tingling at the corners of his eyes. The pressure on his chest increased, making it hard to breathe.

The Grand Masters walked slowly towards their respective schools and moved to stand among their students. The large port began to slide upwards, revealing the airlock looming behind. A humming sound rose from the floor, as the platform moved slowly outward, until it was locked into place. Then the port closed again. Involuntarily, some of the students shuffled forward, keeping their gaze fixed on their fallen friends.

Julius stood were he was, suddenly alone, unable to move. He felt his mind reaching for her, searching for her aura, but there was only emptiness. When the airlock opened, the Mizkis gasped, and only then did Julius turn his head to the porthole, behind which the stars streamed past. One by one, the urns and the coffin were lifted and carried into space by the vacuum that had just been created. They floated around each other without colliding, on their own individual path to eternity.

Morgana's final resting place drifted away, destined to be part of the universe, in a never-ending night. Julius followed her with his eyes for as long as he could, then closed them and let her go.

TIJARAN TALES
BOOK VI

THE GIRL FROM
THE SKY

CONTENTS

THE GIRL FROM THE SKY

Mah Gira stepped out of his home, and stretched his aging joints in familiar, reassuring movements. The white mane covering the entire rear side of his body from head to heel, shimmered in the lights of the street lamps and the purple glare of their Strullium encasings. The Arneshian occupation had prevented him from doing regular exercise, but because of his status as Supreme of the Mahini, Ambassador T'Rogon had showed him some leniency, allowing him to remain in his house and most importantly, ordered him to knock some sense into any hot-blooded "furcoat" that dared step out of line.

'Furcoats,' muttered Mah Gira, starting to get a bit worked up. 'How dare they? Awful people, with grey skin and bad manners. Constantly complaining about the snow or the rain or our underground city. Who invited them here, anyway? I did not invite you here.' He shook his head indignantly and slowly walked over to the edge of his tiny, slate yard. Looking at the bench, he negotiated a way to sit that wouldn't hurt too much. Eventually, he placed a hand on the stony seat and used it as a lever to turn and lower himself. Out of habit, he bent forward to check that the smooth black rock was still under there, completely tucked away in the right corner. It was, and he smiled to himself.

When he looked up, a couple of soldiers were just leaving one of the local's home, before walking past his gate. They didn't even glance at him, but strutted on as if they *actually* owned the place, rather than being intruders.

As well as scaring the daylights out of the Mahini, showing up as they had in the first place and proving that there *was* life beyond Mah, the Arneshians had invaded their city, enslaved their people, killed those who rebelled and stole the only precious thing that the planet had to offer — Strullium. As a matter of fact, thought Mah Gira, he hadn't even realised that Strullium was so precious outside of their world — here they only ever used it for decoration, from lampshades to toilet bowls.

The ground beneath his feet trembled, not for the first time that day. Mah Gira, and everyone else on Mah, was getting used to these short episodes. Not knowing what caused them was the alarming part, but the Arneshians had never volunteered an explanation, so they had stopped asking. He smoothed the fur on his left arm distractedly, as he continued his reflections on the past months of occupation. The rate at which the Arneshians were mining, the veins would be dried out soon. And then what? They'd probably leave, abandoning them to certain death. They had destroyed all their greenhouses; the sole means of sustenance they had. The Mahini could rebuild them, of course they could — their Chief Engineer, Ruxshin, was very skilled and could definitely set up new winter gardens in a short enough time — but it would take months before the crops could grow in enough quantities to feed the whole city. However he looked at it, the situation was grim and getting grimmer by the day.

Just then, as if summoned, the voices of Ruxshin and Khavar drew closer to Mah

Gira's home. It was one of the Supreme's jobs to spend time with the teenage Mahini, until they reached their fifteenth birthdays. It created important bonds between the older generation and the younger ones, making for a more stable and caring society. Both Ruxshin and Khavar had showed leadership skills right from the start, becoming focal points among their peers for very different reasons — there was nothing that Ruxshin couldn't grow, and there was nothing that Khavar couldn't hunt with his bow. Hutan had been another youth of such quality, with his knack for growing unusual berries to brew into weird and marvellous concoctions. Alas, he was dead now, killed by an Arneshian while defending Ruxshin. His heart ached at the memory and he pushed it away, into the place where all his dearly departed were remembered.

The Supreme waited for the pair to come into view before hailing them softly. It looked like they had just come from their day shift, as they were still wearing the protective leather suits they used above ground, which was handy, as they would shortly need to return outside. As soon as they saw him, the slender frame of Ruxshin and the bulky one of Khavar rushed over to the Supreme's feet, and knelt deeply before him, their right hands gently touching his knees as a display of respect.

'Mah Gira!' said Ruxshin, plainly happy to see him out of the house.

'Dear girl,' he answered, patting her hand, which was covered in short red fur. 'See, I still have the strength to walk about.'

'Of course you do!' stated Khavar. 'You are our leader. You'll always be strong enough.'

'Bless you, Khavar. Full of life as always. Come, both of you. Sit by my side.'

It was evident from the surprise on their faces that they hadn't expected this request, but they quickly obliged.

'I hear some of the soldiers have been misplacing their boots lately,' he started, to no one in particular.

Ruxshin suppressed a grin and looked down between her feet.

Khavar scratched his dark brown mane, blushing ever so slightly. 'They're very distracted, Mah Gira,' he replied.

'So it seems. Let's make sure they *remember* where they left them soon, yes?'

There was no anger in his voice, and perhaps even a hint of amusement, but Khavar got the message right away. 'Of course.'

'And make sure the other jokers know that too, please.'

'I'll see to that,' he answered.

'Good,' said Mah Gira, satisfied. 'Not that I object to a little fun, but these people don't seem to share our sense of humour.'

'Among other things,' added Ruxshin, ironically.

Mah Gira nodded. 'It won't last forever, you'll see.'

'Let's hope there's someone left alive to see that day, then,' blurted out Khavar. 'I wish there was something we could do to get rid of them ... before it's too late.'

'We have no food of our own left,' said Ruxshin dejectedly. 'Nothing has survived — no seed, no soil, no compost. The land around Mahin is either frozen or flooded. From the moment they go, it'll be a countdown for us.'

Mah Gira leaned over to Ruxshin in a conspiratorial way. 'What if you had the chance to build a small nursery ... in secret? Would that help?'

Ruxshin's eyes widened. 'If I could start the seeds now, then yes, it could. We may still need time, but it would give us a fighting chance.'

'But where can we build it?' asked Khavar. 'The Arneshians have the whole place under surveillance.'

'I disagree,' said Mah Gira, smiling. 'Follow me.'

Khavar offered him his arm, to help him stand easily and threw a curious glance at Ruxshin, who didn't seem to know any more than he did.

The Supreme opened his front door and ushered them into a small lounge; a sofa, a table and a wooden chest comprised the only furnishing in the room. A passageway opened out to the right, leading to other areas of the house. 'Close the door,' said Mah Gira to Khavar.

'What's going on?' asked Ruxshin, once they were safely alone.

In reply, the Supreme moved towards the chest and placed himself on its left side. He leaned over it and began to push.

Quickly, Khavar stepped up. 'Let me,' he said. He then leaned his body weight against it and pushed it easily along the wall, revealing a rectangular hole beyond.

'Goodness!' exclaimed Ruxshin, hurrying forward.

The cavity was large enough to allow an adult through and it opened onto a tunnel, carved into the rock. A cold breeze filtered into the room, bringing with it the smell of pine trees.

'It leads to the back of the house, outside. I've never told anybody about this … gateway,' said Mah Gira, with a cheeky little smile. 'It's a secret handed down from one Supreme to the next. Understand, had circumstances been different, I would not have disclosed this to you.'

'Of course, Mah Gira,' said Ruxshin. 'We will not tell anybody.'

'You're doing us a great honour sharing this with us,' added Khavar, bowing his head.

Mah Gira knew they wouldn't betray his trust. 'Let's cover this up while we talk.'

*

The snow crunched under their boots, while new flakes quickly filled the depressions left by their feet. To their right, far beyond the line of trees, were the ruins of their once great winter gardens, reduced now to skeletal frames.

'Are you sure this is the place?' asked Ruxshin, shivering. Dusk was setting in, soon to be replaced by the moonlit night.

Khavar stopped. They had emerged from the mouth of the tunnel and then walked quietly for about five minutes between thick trees. 'Mah Gira said that he buried the box by the White Glade, under a thin fir. We should be coming up on it soon.'

'I'm just conscious of the time, that's all,' she muttered.

'Don't worry Rux. We'll head back before they even know we've gone. Besides, it's our downtime. They'll think we're resting or something.'

Ruxshin looked around. The snow-laden firs and bushes grew along the base of the mountain — the only vegetation on the icy planes of Mah and, right now, their only shelter from the vigilant eyes of the soldiers. 'All right, but let's hurry.'

Khavar nodded.

Having him making decisions for her had been easy in the last few months. Since Hutan's death, she had become quieter — *withdrawn* was perhaps the right word — and unwilling to look past the end of the day. Working on the translator device for the

Arneshians was all that took up her time. Not that she believed communicating with these people would do them any good, but what was the alternative? Her supervisor, A'Krad, was impressed enough by the work she had done on the *dictionary* to treat her with less contempt, especially since the day of shame — the *Memory*, as she had come to think of it — and the time spent in the holding cell. The excited face of the boy Michael as he had watched K'Ssander lowering the laser razor down on her back again and again in long steady strokes, removing clumps of her red mane; the hands of the guards pinning her, face down, on the floor - the images swirled around her mind. *No!* she screamed inside her head. *Stop it.* Those memories were poisonous and only made her weaker. She took a deep breath and unclenched her fists.

'Look!' said Khavar, pointing ahead. 'The White Glade.'

Glad for the diversion, she looked to where he was pointing and saw a wide empty circle in the forest, delineated by trees. It was the only place where the light was able to touch the ground, reflecting off the snow and bouncing onto the surrounding trunks, making them appear white. She looked at Khavar, and nudged him to go on ahead.

Khavar stepped cautiously into the area, checking that the coast was clear. He walked along the perimeter, looking behind every tree and peering into the snow laden bushes. Then he stopped, examining the base of a thin trunk. An X was engraved there, with the design of a bow and arrow, pointing to the right. He motioned for Ruxshin to join him and hunched down.

'What are you doing?' asked Ruxshin.

In reply, Khavar peered behind the tree, where a thick evergreen bush grew. Delicately, he began to move the branches out of the way, creating an opening large enough to fit his gloved hands. 'There's something in here,' he told her.

Ruxshin helped him pull back some more foliage, so he could dig deeper.

'It's a container of some sort,' he said, stretching his arms forward. He drew his hands back out and began to snap the twigs directly behind the tree, freeing up access to the under-bush.

Ruxshin bent forward, and poked her head into the hole they had created. 'It's … a tiny greenhouse!' she squealed excitedly. Removing her gloves, she pushed her head further in, ignoring the branches catching the fur on the back of her head and the snow melting against her neck, trickling beneath her coat.

Khavar tried to free a passage for her as fast as he could but, in her excitement, Ruxshin wasn't paying him any attention.

'Bless you, Mah Gira!' she exclaimed. 'There are at least twenty plants in here — all healthy and growing!'

'I cannot believe that the old man went back into the ruins to gather the seeds,' said Khavar.

'That's why he's our Supreme,' she answered proudly.

'So, what do we do now? Bring it in?'

Ruxshin thought for a moment. 'This box has been here for months now, surviving the soldiers and the weather. I need to talk to Mah Gira before we move it.'

'All right. Let me cover it up again,' he said, gathering the broken branches from the ground.

Ruxshin stood up, a smile on her face for the first time in who knew how long. The memory of the tender leaves between her fingertips brought back a spark of hope, a precious treasure these days. Her mind had already switched to working mode — her *real* work, that is — and she had started mentally listing all the nutrients she would need to take the plants to the end of the snow season and through the wet six months that would follow. Putting her gloves back on, she walked to the side of the bush; she was so taken by this new project, that she didn't notice the object sticking out of the ground. Her foot caught it full on, sending her flying into the snow, face first. 'Oomph!' she exhaled, as the air was knocked from her lungs.

'Did you say something, Rux?' asked Khavar, from over his shoulder.

'Mmph,' came the reply.

'What was that?' Khavar stood up and turned around, then looked down in surprise.

Ruxshin sat herself up, snow capping her face and mane, and massaged her ankle. 'Not a word,' she admonished him.

Khavar refrained a smile and offered her his hand.

'Where is that dratted thing?' said Ruxshin, ignoring his help and checking the ground.

The snow had been pushed further back by her shoe, revealing what appeared to be the tip of a metallic blue object. Ruxshin moved towards it and poked it with a finger. When nothing happened, she looked up at Khavar, who quickly knelt in front of her. Together, they began to clear the snow away, their curiosity growing by the minute. 'It's a box,' she said, eventually.

'A long one at that,' added Khavar, perplexed.

Once the metal frame had been freed, Ruxshin used both hands to wipe the snow off a portion of the surface. 'Glass ...' she mused. She placed her face close to it, trying to look through it. A few seconds later, she screamed and fell back, scrambling away.

'What is it?' cried Khavar, retreating in panic.

Ruxshin pointed at the box, her hand shaking. 'There's ... there's *someone* in there!'

'What?' Khavar's eyes widened and he returned quickly to the box.

Ruxshin watched as he lowered his nose to the glass and placed his palms around his eyes to shield out the light.

'It's a girl,' he said, surprised. 'Come, look.' He started to briskly wipe more snow off the box.

Ruxshin joined him cautiously and leaned forward, eyeing it with suspicion. The girl inside looked perhaps a couple of years younger than her - maybe eighteen - and she seemed to be sleeping peacefully. Her long black hair framed delicate features, and her skin was as light as the snow. She was clothed in a white, full-length robe, which was wrapped around her body, right side over left, and held fast with a sash; a pair of sandals lay at her sock-clad feet.

'Is she one of them?' asked Khavar.

'An Arneshian? I don't think so,' replied Ruxshin. 'Her hair isn't white and her skin isn't grey. She looks more like the boy, Michael, than the rest of the soldiers.'

'Hmm ...'

'What is it?'

Khavar shook his head. 'Don't you think it's strange that out of two species we meet from outer space, they both look remarkably like us?'

Ruxshin observed the girl. Like their invaders, she had no fur that could be seen, but her body was the same shape as hers. Of course she had noticed the similarities — it had made the Arneshians look less threatening when they had first arrived. 'Maybe that's all there is out there.'

'Maybe.'

'I'm more concerned with how she ended up here.'

Khavar looked around, then upwards. 'Some of those branches have been snapped,' he said.

'What are you saying: that she fell from the sky?'

'Nastier things have fallen from our sky recently,' he replied.

'Hey, look at her necklace!'

'That's a Strullium crystal,' said Khavar. 'How did she get that?'

Ruxshin shook her head. She examined the blue frame of the box, sliding her fingers under the lid. She stopped the moment she felt a little depression with something like a button in it, which she pressed. There was a loud click, and the lid popped up. When she pushed it aside, it moved without any resistance.

'Now, that is something else,' said Khavar, clearly impressed.

Ruxshin agreed – it was pretty astonishing what they were seeing. The girl was protected by a sort of transparent cocoon that swayed in the breeze, reflecting the shapes and the colours of the objects around them. Ruxshin removed her gloves once more, and gently touched it. Suddenly a screen popped into life above the girl's midriff, giving both of them a massive fright.

'It's like those Arneshians' weird machines,' said Khavar, recomposing himself.

Ruxshin nodded, and examined the screen. On it, the girl in the box was sitting on a bed, laughing. She wore blue clothing, very different from her current ones, and her expression was one of happiness. Two other voices could be heard around her: a female and a male.

'I can't understand what they're saying,' said Khavar eventually.

'Yes, well, if she is one of them there *is* a way around that,' replied Ruxshin.

'The translator?'

She nodded. Her hand returned to the cocoon and she pushed through, until she touched the lilac stone. The air inside the layer was warm on her skin and she didn't like it — the girl might look like she was merely sleeping, but Ruxshin knew full well that it was the permanent kind of sleep, never mind the fact that she was clearly in a coffin. 'Close it, Khavar. We have to hide her until Mah Gira decides what to do.'

Khavar slid the lid back into place, until it clicked shut. Then, with Ruxshin's help, he began to shovel snow onto it, trying to cover every bit of the blue metal. 'Do you think it's safe to leave her here?'

'They haven't found her so far. Besides, she's not going anywhere.'

CLASS OF 2861

Julius woke with a jolt, drenched in sweat, the bed sheet tangled around his legs. He stared at the blue sky of the scenery screen before him, waiting for his breathing to settle. Since returning to his old room on Zed, the dream had become more regular. No matter how much meditation he did before going to bed, he still ended up in the sickbay of the Mazda, holding Morgana's body. On those nights, he ran along the corridor that led to the infirmary, believing that she was waiting for him, hurt but alive. Instead, it was the blood on the floor that told another story. As he buried his face against her neck, the darkness rising up to meet him, he would try to believe that he was about to wake up, only to find that the terror was real and his nightmare had become reality.

When he looked to his right, Skye was watching him from the bathroom archway — he was almost as tall as the door. Julius registered that his hair was combed back and distractedly wondered why.

'Mazda again?' asked Skye, tucking his shirt inside his white trousers.

'I preferred it when all I dreamt of was Eneamar.'

'Farrah's imaginary place?' he asked, buckling his belt.

Julius nodded. 'It was her hideout when she was in the hospital. I was hoping it could be mine too, instead of ...' he trailed off. That was when he finally realised that there was something odd going on. He focused on Skye again. 'Where are you going?'

Skye glanced at him sideways, while buttoning up his white jacket. 'Graduation ceremony, remember? That thing at the end of school, where they send you off into the big bad world with a handshake?'

Julius fell back in his bed and pulled the sheet over his head. It had completely slipped his mind.

'You have thirty minutes to get ready. I want you to join me and Faith in the garden.'

The garden — Julius knew why. 'I'll be there,' he replied quietly. After a few seconds of silence, he heard Skye walking past his bed to leave the room.

His friend's request had sounded pretty matter-of-fact to Julius, like someone who has grown tired of talking to a whining kid. He had noticed this progressively over the summer, and could tell that his downcast mood had had an effect on their relationship. But what was he supposed to do about it? He couldn't just pretend that Morgana was still with them. He opened his PIP under the sheet and saw that it was nine in the morning. His parents would already be on Zed by now, probably at the reception breakfast that was organised by the school for the families. Grudgingly, he pulled himself out of bed and headed for the toilet. After a quick shower, he laid the ceremonial suit on his bed and, with a heavy heart, began to dress.

The fitted jacket had the Gold Star embroidered inside an ivory shield badge on the chest, to the left. It was the class symbol for captains and, since Julius had only just started down this career path, the star only had one line underneath it. He combed his dark hair back and straightened his suit. The ceiling light made his white, varnished shoes gleam, lending him an air of legitimacy. Julius looked at the smiling picture of Morgana, stuck to one side of the mirror. 'How do I look?' he asked. He buttoned up his jacket and sighed. 'You would have looked great.'

*

As Julius crossed the mess hall, he was vaguely aware of the small clusters of 6MS students dotted around the room. Their anticipation at the impending ceremony was visible to his eyes in the form of green threads floating up from their heads. He had the painful suspicion that for most of them the memories of the Battle of Uruplatus were beginning to fade, replaced by the thrill of life and an exciting future ahead. To Julius however, it seemed like yesterday, and at the same time felt like he was stuck in the longest and bleakest summer of his life.

Leanne, Barth and Lopaka were huddled to one side, just before the garden door. They were so happy and loud that Julius was able to hear every word they were saying.

'My parents have booked us a great holiday,' said Lopaka, buzzing.

'Where to?' asked Leanne. She was holding Barth's hand tenderly.

'Out to Terra 2, actually.'

'That's amazing, Lopaka! I so want to go see it and-'

'Shhh,' said Barth, blushing, as Julius drew near.

'Hi Julius,' said Lopaka, a lot less energetically.

'Hi there,' he replied, but didn't stop. He had seen a lot of those guilty expressions since returning to Zed. It was as if his friends had moved on, except for when he was around — his presence was the painful reminder of what they were trying hard to forget.

Julius stepped into the garden, feeling the warmth of the artificial sun on his face. The oak tree stood green and imposing by the stream, a point of continuity for the Tijaran pupils. Skye was chatting to Faith, and leaning against the tree trunk. Faith had had his mechanical skirt painted cream for the occasion and Julius could see that the usual extra panel had been added to the bottom rim to cater for his growth. He walked over the soft grass, heading their way and, when they saw him, they both turned, showing the class symbols on the fronts of their ceremonial jackets. Skye had the Globe, the sign of those who were embarking on a career in politics, and Faith had the Tool of the Tinkerer, the emblem of engineers; a class which contained many sub classifications, such as navigators, like Barth. Their symbols had also been underscored with a single line.

They looked pleased to see him, even a little surprised he had come at all, but said nothing. He knew full well why they had wanted to meet here and, although it hurt, it had to be done. Three years before, Zed had left the Moon to rescue the kidnapped people of Earth. Before boarding Moonrising, Skye had placed a metal plaque at the base of their favourite tree, engraving the caption, "The Skirts were here", followed by "Skye, Faith, Julius and Morgana". Looking at it now, fixed to the oak trunk, it felt more like an epitaph to Julius.

'Fifteen,' said Faith. 'It seems like ages ago. Even me handwriting was different.'

'The last three years have flown by,' added Skye. 'Our life in school is over.'

Her life is over, period, thought Julius.

Faith dipped his hand inside his jacket and retrieved an origami lilac rose, which he laid on the grass at the base of the oak.

Julius wondered where he had got it from and was about to ask him when Faith put his left arm across his shoulders. He just stood there, watching the flower for a few moments.

'Guys,' called Siena from the garden door, breaking the spell. 'It's almost ten.'

Julius waited for Faith to move his arm away and, after glancing at the rose one last time, he headed back.

When Faith reached Siena, he kissed her on the forehead. Then, with his arm around her waist, they headed towards the Assembly Hall. Julius couldn't avoid noticing the intimacy of their relationship; although he was happy for them, his heart ached all the more. He forced himself to look elsewhere and kept his eyes on the small crowd of students on the concourse as they made their way to the ceremony. When they reached the entrance, Master Cress asked them all to wait outside while he adjusted the students' uniforms at random, making sure that they looked as pristine as he was.

Peering into the Hall, Julius was taken aback by the brightness of the room. Although the sliding roof was completely retracted, it was impossible to see the stars beyond it with all the spotlights turned on. Even the black walls were somehow glowing, as if the light was emanating from within them. In front of him, the floor was packed with parents and young children, all looking at their best, being ushered towards the rows of seats by the Mizki Seniors in Tijaran uniforms. There was a definite feel of euphoria in the crowd, which Julius could understand even in his current mindset. These people had been freed from captivity and their sons and daughters had returned home after two very long and tough years. Most of them, anyway. Flags were hanging all around the room, each of them representing one of the graduates' countries. Branches of green luxurious ivy snaked their way all across the walls of the Hall, some of them bearing large flowers of different colours. Julius couldn't smell their scent in the air, and began to wonder if the vegetation was in fact holographic. They extended to the far wall, behind the main stage. There was a new flag above the podium, which Julius had never seen before: a planet, easily identifiable as Earth, was enclosed in the centre of a white oval space, surrounded by eight golden stars.

'Here, McCoy,' said Master Cress, from his right.

Julius turned to him, startled.

'Your last button is undone,' he said, fastening it.

Julius could tell that Cress was just as excited as any of the parents that had come to the event. His students were his life and Julius would not have been able to find fault with him in all his years at Tijara — especially considering the amount of times he himself had caused the Master's temper to rise.

'What are you thinking about?' Cress asked, straightening Julius' jacket for good measure.

'Nothing, sir,' he answered. Then a thought occurred to him, and he added, 'The Solo ring. I need to give it back.'

'You can keep it a while longer, you know?'

'I'd rather give it back, if it's all the same to you, sir.'

'Very well.'

Julius pulled the black metal band off his finger, wiped it with the corner of his jacket, and handed it back to Cress.

'When will we find the likes of you again, McCoy?' he said, with a hint of a smile.

'It'll happen,' he replied, feeling a little sad.

Cress looked at him intently. 'The Grand Master and I agree that your parents should be told about Michael. *Today.*'

'Why?' he answered sceptically. 'Do you think they'd be able to change his mind?'

'For starters, they are his parents and they deserve to know. Besides, this burden you decided was yours to bear is only dragging you down, even if *you* can't see it.'

'I don't know …' he said, unconvinced.

'If you won't, *I* will.'

Julius realised that there was no point in arguing, so he just bowed his head and moved over to the left, where he allowed the various conversations to distract him.

'Have you packed your bags?' Isolde was asking Manuel Valdez.

'All ready to be moved into our temp dorms,' he replied.

'I didn't even know there was a floor -7!' Dhara Sundaram piped in.

Neither did I, thought Julius distractedly. But there it was: the floor of the graduates, where they would stay for a few more days before leaving the academy for good.

'It's almost time,' whispered Isolde to Yuri Slovich, who nodded vigorously. 'They're all seated, look!'

Julius turned along with them and saw a sea of combed hair and colourful hats.

'*Mizkis,*' said Cress, telepathically.

Julius turned to face him and saw that Grand Master Freja had just joined their group. Behind him were the Tijaran teachers in their ceremonial uniforms – even Lao-Tzu and Chan had ditched their tunics for the occasion. He noticed that their class symbol wasn't like any other he had seen so far. Regardless of what they taught at the academy, they all wore a rectangular gold label with their name and the school name on it, which Julius assumed was a teacher's privilege to wear. Freja had GM Tijara embroidered on his golden shield, and Cress had M Tijara on his.

'*As we rehearsed, Mizkis,*' continued Cress. '*Once the last two teachers have entered, you'll follow in alphabetical order, two by two. The line behind Professor Clavel will be seated in the first two rows on the right side of the hall and the line behind Professor Morales will do the same, on the left. Get ready.*'

Julius knew he was the sixth student after Lopaka Liway, so he waited for him to take his place before standing behind him, with George Lowet to his left. What he really didn't have any desire to do was to turn around and see Morgana's empty place. Morgana's roommate, Mariam Richards, would have to face the audience's gazes alone, since everyone knew why she was walking into the Hall by herself.

As Freja entered the room solemnly, rolling drums began to beat the cadence of the steps, while the low murmur of the crowd turned to loud applause, which did not die down until the last two students had finally been seated. As he walked up the aisle, Julius turned to his right and saw Jenny and Rory applauding as hard as they could, expressions of pride on their faces that followed him all the way to his seat. He loved them for that, despite the hurt and the absurdity of the situation and, most of all, given that the war hadn't actually been won.

Once all the teachers had taken their seats on the stage, Freja stepped up to the podium, using his hands to gently hush the audience.

'Welcome to Zed,' he began, smiling warmly. 'Thank you all for being here with us today, to celebrate the graduation of our Mizkis.'

A brief applause greeted his words.

'The Class of 2861 has already made history,' he continued. 'Since their very first year on Zed, the growth and development of these students has gone hand in hand with the resurgence of the Arneshian threat, as you all well know. The events of the past few years have seen drastic changes to the way we live. Since many of you were kidnapped from Earth and eventually safely returned, many things have changed. We have new environmental laws, better relationships between countries and even a new part of the population, made up of those Arneshians who decided to turn their lives around. We have also achieved much in fostering alliances, by strengthening ties with new friends, far from here.'

Julius watched as Freja turned around and pointed at the starry banner on the wall.

'*That* is our future,' he said. 'The Galactic Federation of Earth is now a reality, made up of Zed, the colonies, Buruwang and the Halls of Ahriman; each one represented by a golden star, surrounding our planet.'

Murmurs of assent spread throughout the room, from parents and students alike.

So that's what it is, thought Julius.

'Hey,' said George, leaning over towards him. 'Freja mentioned four places, but there are eight stars on that flag. I don't get it.'

'It's because the colonies have five stars: Terra 1, 2 and 3, plus Colonial 1 and 2. With Zed, Ahriman and Buruwang, it makes eight.'

'Ah!' said George, satisfied. 'I like it.'

Julius couldn't match his classmate's enthusiasm; he felt largely indifferent about the entire thing in fact, just going through the motions, with no great expectations for the future.

'We have plenty reason to celebrate,' resumed Freja, bringing the audience's focus back to him, 'but we also have many reasons to grieve.' The GM's eyes darted to Morgana's empty seat for a moment. 'Your sons and daughters have endured a great deal, especially in this past year. But, as you know, there is one family in particular among you who has given more than anyone could ask for our cause.'

Freja took a moment before continuing while Julius, knowing what was coming, simply wanted this moment over as soon as possible.

'Morgana Ruthier is not here today. She will not collect her diploma and she will not toast to the future with us at the end of this ceremony. By no means the only loss that Zed has suffered, but she is *our* loss and nothing will ever heal that wound.'

Julius, not willing to linger on Freja's words, stopped listening and turned his thoughts instead to the conversation he would have to have with his parents.

'Mr and Mrs Ruthier have not come today but, as do you, they too know that we haven't yet reached the end of the road. Their other daughter, Kaori, has already started life as a Zed Officer, just like your children will do from today. It is one last sacrifice that we ask of you. Be strong for them in this final leg of the journey. We won a great battle at Uruplatus, but to win the war we must deliver the finishing blow. Rise now, Mizkis, and proclaim who you are.'

The students stood and prepared for the school salute.

'You will soon leave these walls as men and women of Zed,' said Freja solemnly. 'You will bear the mark of Tijara in your hearts for the rest of your days. You will live, fight and die with that name etched in your souls. Show us your commitment. To your earth!'

'TI-JA-RA!' cried the Mizkis, as one voice.

The audience, carried by the emotional strength of Freja's words and the impact of their children's proud cries, erupted in thunderous applause, which even brought several parents to tears.

As he sat down again, Julius knew that something was really wrong with him. For the first time in his life he felt nothing at that rallying cry — no stirring or shivers — just a flat state of being.

Freja was shortly flanked by Master Cress, who was now getting ready to hand the certificates to each of the students.

'Zolin Acalan,' called Professor Farshid, from the podium.

Julius watched his classmate from Colonial 1 walking proudly towards the stage. There, he shook hands with Freja and Cress, before receiving a ten-by-six inch frame, containing a certificate and a still unfolding, recorded feed of the ceremony. Faith had explained to them that, once put on display in the individual's home, the video would be replayed on a loop, with the graduate in question as the focus. Julius knew he wasn't giving his best smile at all and wondered what his folks would make of it.

Farshid continued calling the students up one by one and eventually reached George Lowet. Julius was asked to stand beside one of the ushers, since he would be up next.

'Julius McCoy,' she called, smiling proudly.

Julius let the applause shield him from the audience as he walked to the centre of the stage. There, he stood before Freja, waiting for his diploma. However, when Freja looked into his eyes, he hesitated, as if he had seen something behind them that worried him deeply. Julius held the GM's inquisitive gaze without faltering.

It was Master Cress who got things moving again, nudging Freja's arm with his elbow and handing him the frame.

'Congratulations, Julius.'

'Thank you, Grand Master,' he replied taking the certificate and bowing.

'Siena Migliori,' called Farshid, moving on.

*

After the ceremony had ended, Julius knew he didn't want to meet anybody or waste time with niceties. He grabbed his parents and whisked them away from the Hall and the buffet, making a straight line for Tijara's garden. The benches were all empty, so he sat them down on the closest one he found, before proceeding to tell them Michael's full story, from his betrayal, to Buruwang. Incredibly enough, as the words left his mouth, crashing like waves against his flabbergasted parents, a sense of relief swept over him. Master Cress had been right.

'What I don't understand is why you didn't tell us sooner,' said Rory McCoy, visibly upset.

Jenny looked as if she was in shock, like her brain was trying to digest the enormity of the situation, but failing miserably.

'I didn't see the point, Dad.'

'You *what*?' fumed Rory.

'Don't go giving yourself a heart attack, all right?'

Rory stared at him for a few seconds, his anger barely contained. He paced briefly, back and forth, in front of the bench, before sitting down, breathing deeply. 'Bear with me, lad' he said in the broadest Scottish accent Julius had ever heard him use. 'You just told me that my youngest son is a two-timing, back-stabbing traitor; a killer of his own people and, potentially, the future leader of Arnesh. Forgive me, but I think a heart attack is the least of my concerns right now.'

Julius nodded, worried about his dad's purple face and the way his right eyelid was twitching.

Jenny broke from her stupor. 'Don't be mad at Julius now, Rory.'

'I'm not mad at him, woman! I'm furious at that wee screwball of a scumbag we call our son!' he said, standing up again, hands flailing.

At that moment, Julius spotted Faith and Skye by the garden entrance, rooted to the spot and staring at them. They were followed by their own families who, no doubt, they'd wanted to introduce to the McCoys.

'*Please guys, not now!*' he told them with his mind quickly.

'*Do you need a hand?*' asked Skye, visibly worried.

'*Just tell Nurse Primula to be on standby, will you? I think Dad is having a fit.*'

'*Call if you need a hand,*' said Faith, before turning and ushering everyone out of the garden.

'Dad, you need to calm down now,' said Julius, walking up to him. He put his hands on his shoulders, realising how much taller than his dad he now was. 'I've got this.'

Rory looked his son in the eyes for a few seconds. Then, a little calmer, he sat back down, and allowed Jenny to take his hand.

'Julius will take care of this,' she told her husband. She looked up, with an uncertain smile on her face. 'Zed wouldn't hurt him, would they? I'm sure it's not his fault and deep down you know that too. What if the Arneshians made him act like that? You must find him and bring him back to us!'

Julius chose to ignore part of what his mom had just said. That was the mother in her talking, trying to reassure herself more than anything else. 'If I bring him back, he'll be in prison for the rest of his life.'

Jenny's eyes widened. 'They can't think it's his fault! He's only a child!'

'To you he'll always be one, Mum. But that's not who he is anymore and I'm done covering for him.'

Jenny buried her face in her hands and began to sob. Rory let her head rest on his left shoulder, while he patted the bench to his right, inviting his son to sit.

Julius did that, and grabbed his father's hand, now older and marked by age.

'You'll do what needs to be done, son.' His voice was steady and under control once more. 'I trust you with all my heart.'

Julius felt the mixed emotions of that morning bumping around uneasily in his mind. As long as Michael was left unchecked, they could have no peace. He knew that, as he knew that he needed to solve this, for everyone's sake. The problem was that he didn't know exactly *how* to do it or even where to find the strength to get back on the saddle. The loss of Morgana had left him feeling ineffective and unsure, filled with guilt for her death and searching for a way out that he just couldn't see.

THE DEATH MAIL

Freja had just brewed a fresh pot of coffee. The smell was strong and had spread throughout his office. Savouring the intensity that he would soon taste, he filled three cups, which were resting on a red tray. He added one teaspoon of sugar for himself, half for Cress, and then stopped. 'Still two sugars, JD?'

'Shouldn't you know by now?' replied Kelly, with a little frown.

'I don't like to assume,' said Freja amiably. 'Not even with my own blood.'

'Two will do.'

Freja took the tray over to the coffee table, leaving his son and Cress to help themselves. September was underway and a fresh batch of 1 Mizki Juniors had just finished their first week at Tijara. The Grand Master liked that time of the year and being back in his Zed office was having a positive effect on his spirits. He felt recharged and optimistic — more than he had in the last year, anyway — and he was determined to take advantage of this period of calm before the storm. 'Gentlemen,' he said, 'before the last stretch, we have two problems to resolve: Mah and McCoy.'

'I went through the Curia archives several times,' said Cress dejectedly. 'There's no record of a planet or a constellation called Mah. Even Professor Brown, who's a Spaceology expert, has never heard of it.'

'I sent out a message to all fleet captains,' added Kelly, scratching the scar on his left cheek distractedly, 'but no one has come across such a place. I even checked with the Colonies, but no joy.'

'In the footage from the hideout,' said Freja, 'Farrah clearly says, "Mah". One reason I have for believing that this place exists is that McCoy asked me about it after he won his powers back.'

'When was this?' asked Kelly.

'During his medical, on Buruwang. He asked me if the name Mah meant anything to me. In fact, he mentioned another name as well, but I can't remember what it was.'

'We'll just ask McCoy then,' offered Kelly.

'That leads us to the second problem, JD,' said Freja. 'He's not in a good place right now.'

'Morgana's death has hit him harder than we thought,' explained Cress. 'We believed that the thirst for revenge would be enough to recharge him, but it's not happening.'

'We need to *steel* him for this last task,' said Freja.

'You need to be careful, that's what,' said Kelly. 'Bend him too much and you risk breaking him.'

Freja nodded. 'He's no longer the boy who joined the academy. We have changed him beyond repair — the Arneshians and us. And you're right: it's not about how hard he can hit, but how much he can take and still go on. Resilience is all he's got left.'

'Then let him come with me,' cut in Kelly. 'He needs a change. He can wait for the battle plans on the Mazda.'

Freja agreed that it was a good idea — too many memories in Tijara — besides, he knew Julius liked being with Kelly. Maybe it would shake him out of his daze. 'I have no objections to that. McCoy has signed up for a captain's career path and you're more than qualified to start his training. His year group will be able to leave Tijara by the middle of the month. You can have him then.'

*

It was Monday the 8th of September and the graduates were about to start their last week in Tijara school. To distinguish them from the regular students, they had already been allowed to wear officer uniforms, which comprised of the usual items of jumper over tee, combat trousers and boots, but of a deeper shade of blue, almost black, instead of the usual navy ones. That morning they had been sent a document titled "Leaving Procedures", which contained a particularly busy schedule for the next seven days.

Julius sat having breakfast with Skye, Faith and Siena, going through his appointments. As well as plenty of paperwork to be filled out, he would have to spend a long time in the Infirmary for his PIP and shield upgrades. Under normal circumstances, the mere words "Leaving Procedures" would have filled him with excitement. Instead, all that was to come — from finding T'Rogon, to beginning his career — had been locked away in a padded room in his heart; a buffer space that tinged everything in grey tones, sucking the joy and anticipation out of it. Whenever he tried to break it open, he was overwhelmed by a feeling of impotence and despair.

Just then, a small young boy stopped by the table, looking awfully shy. He was a 1MJ.

'You all right, kid?' asked Faith.

'Are you guys the Skirts?' he said, in a little voice.

'Guilty as charged,' said Skye pleasantly.

'I just wanted to say that you're awesome,' he said, breaking into a smile. 'Can I have your autographs please?'

'Sure, little man,' he said, grabbing the pad and stylus that the boy was holding. He signed and passed it on to Faith. When he was done, Siena took the pad from him and handed it over to Julius.

'Won't you sign too?' asked the boy, looking at her.

'Oh,' she said, startled. 'I'm not a Skirt. Morgana Ruthier is, not-'

'Morgana is dead!' cut in Julius. 'And so are the Skirts.' With that, he stood up, taking his tray with him.

The boy looked a mixture of frightened and disappointed. 'I'm sorry,' he said. 'I didn't know.'

From the food counter, Julius heard Siena telling the Junior that it wasn't his fault, but he also heard a sort of annoyed grunt from Skye. *Who cares*, he thought. *Games are over anyway, whether he likes it or not.* He headed for the 6MS common room, looking for a quiet place to work. A few students were already there and, as he walked in, he was aware of a few hushed comments directed his way. He chose to ignore them and went straight to one of the tables at the back, where he opened his PIP screen and activated his holographic keyboard. There was a new folder in his inbox called "Captaincy — a leading career". He touched it with his fingertips and it opened up, revealing a dozen files within. He sighed, wondering who in their right mind would ever consider taking orders from him right now.

Around midday, Faith and Skye came to find him.

'Cress wants our whole class to talk to the 1MJs this afternoon,' said Faith. 'Thirty minute slots each.'

Julius closed his PIP and leaned back in his chair, stretching. 'About what?'

Faith showed him a list of topics on his own screen, the majority of which had been scored off, with only two left.

'I'll take "Hologram Palace",' said Skye coolly, 'since it's quite obvious you don't want it anymore.'

Julius could tell that he was still annoyed with him, but had no intention of apologising. 'It's all yours,' he answered, equally coldly.

Faith raised his eyes skyward. 'That leaves the two of us to talk about "Safety on Zed" … even though I could think of *more qualified people* to teach about this particular topic …'

Julius couldn't agree more. In fact, it would be easier to just tell the Juniors about their adventures on Zed and then tell them to do the opposite. 'I take it we have to.'

The words had barely left his mouth when Skye turned on his heels and stormed out, looking very much like he was restraining himself from saying something harsh.

'Yes, McCoy,' said Faith. 'Part of our last duties for this week. I'll meet you at the end of lunch by the Grey Arts lift. *On* time.'

'I know, I know,' said Julius, noticing the impatience in Faith's voice as well. A little ashamed at his indifference, he realised that his sense of duty was unravelling fast, like a thread slipping between his fingers.

*

After lunch, Julius made his way downstairs; he knew he was late for the event, but still didn't hurry. When he reached floor -1 he saw that the Mizkis were gathered in the third classroom to the left and that the door had been left ajar. He couldn't remember receiving these kinds of talks when he was a first year student, and wondered when they had introduced them. As he reached the door, he stood to the side, listening to what Faith was saying, taking care not to be seen.

'And that brings us to curfew times.'

'Is there a curfew?' came the heartbroken voice of a boy. 'Why? What can possibly happen to us in here?'

'You'd be surprised,' replied Faith, clearly enjoying himself.

Julius closed his eyes and thought back to how Morgana had been kidnapped by Red Cap, right inside the Zed perimeter, during their Gassendi trip. He had cried her name out so hard that his voice had gone. He remembered thinking then how he would never forgive himself if anything happened to her … and then, that day had come after all. No, there was nothing for him to do here. Quietly, he returned upstairs.

*

At the end of the event, the 1MJs left the room in high spirits, talking mostly about Faith's hovering skirt in absolute, deferential awe.

Faith was gathering up his things when, unexpectedly, Freja stepped into the class and sat on one of the desks in the front row.

'Grand Master,' said Faith, surprised. 'Err … you just missed McCoy.'

'I appreciate your loyalty, but you don't need to cover for him.'

Faith blushed and turned off the last piece of equipment. 'He didn't come.'

'How is he?'

'I think he hit rock bottom around the end of June.'

'How so?' asked Freja, concerned.

'He was disappearing every night, so in the end we decided to follow him. He was in Satras, using the Sim-dating programme to talk to Morgana. We told him it wasn't healthy and eventually he stopped.'

'You did well,' nodded Freja. 'And now?'

'Aside from the nightmares, he eats and sleeps,' answered Faith with a shrug of his shoulders. 'He seems normal enough, but inside it's like he's waiting for something — waiting to see what the end will be.' Faith hovered towards the GM. 'It feels as if he's already left.'

Freja, who was looking past Faith to a point on the far wall, remained immersed in his own thoughts for a few more seconds. 'Mr Shanigan,' he said eventually, 'since the passing of Morgana, have you ever seen Julius cry?'

Faith thought long and hard. 'Now that you mention it, sir, no I haven't, and Skye would have told me if it had happened at night. He's probably the only one who hasn't shed a tear — not even *that* day, when he entered sickbay. I was a mess meself, but I noticed it. At the time I thought he was in shock.'

Freja brought his eyes back to Faith. 'Julius is lost right now.'

'No offence, sir, but this isn't the right time to be lost; not now that we need him more than ever.'

'He's struggling with guilt. Even with his new powers, he wasn't able to save her. A burden like that could squash the hardest of men.'

'Whatever you want me to do, sir, I'll help you. I can't stand seeing him like this anymore. And Skye is ready to punch him in the face … which theoretically could make him cry for a bit.'

Freja smiled. 'I believe that, but it's not the kind of tears he needs to shed. Do you still have a copy of Miss Ruthier's Death Mail?'

Faith's eyes widened. 'Do you think it would help?'

'We've both seen it, Mr Shanigan, and I'm sure you are also aware of its potential impact. Morgana left us the only absolution he needs. If she can't make him see sense …'

He didn't complete the sentence, but Faith knew exactly what he meant. He bowed to Freja, and left the room.

*

That evening, Julius headed back to his new dorm for a shower before dinner. When he stepped out of the lift, he halted at the sight of Faith, Siena and Skye, deep in conversation outside his room. From the looks of things, Faith was trying to reason with Skye, without success. Julius could see an angry red thread lifting up from Skye's head. 'What's going on?' he asked, walking forward.

Skye turned his way and squared up to him.

'Stop it,' said Faith, trying to grab his arm, but Skye shook him off easily.

'Why did you chicken out this afternoon?'

'What? I didn't *chicken* out,' he replied bitterly. He could feel his own temper rising — if Skye wanted a fight, he might just get it.

'Is this how you're honouring her death?'

Julius' face betrayed his surprise at those words. Then his anger got the better of him and he moved forward, an inch away from Skye's nose. 'Don't you dare,' he hissed.

'You think you're the only one grieving?' Skye pressed.

'Maybe I am, you know,' he replied, the stress of the summer finally bubbling up to the surface. 'It seems that folks around here forget easily enough.'

Skye pushed him to the side, his right forearm pressed against Julius' collarbone, pinning him against the wall. 'I've had enough of your moping. We risked our lives to get your powers back for you, and you've been dragging your heels all summer, instead of helping us find your brother. Stop feeling guilty and stop feeling sorry for yourself!' With that, he let go and stormed back upstairs.

'Skye,' Faith called after him. 'You promised you'd be there!'

Skye dismissed him with a brusque wave of his hand before he disappeared from view.

Julius tried to move away from the wall, but found that he couldn't. Suddenly, the anger that had built so quickly inside him faded from his heart, and was replaced by a sense of hopelessness. Siena must have noticed this change in mood, because she went quickly to his side.

'I miss her,' he whispered. 'I miss her so much, it hurts. Laughing feels wrong; doing things — eating, feeling, living — everything feels wrong. Like I have no right to keep doing any of it.' It wasn't easy saying these things but, now that he had started, he couldn't stop. He didn't *want* to stop. 'I ... I had no time to say goodbye. One minute she was there and the next ... She can never forgive me.'

Siena grabbed his trembling hands and held them tight.

'You're to blame as much as *we* are, for that matter,' said Faith. 'We were there too, remember? Besides, if Morgana heard us talking about blame, she would give us a piece of her mind and you know that. But it doesn't matter me telling you this. You need to hear it from her.'

Slowly, Siena opened one of Julius' hands and placed a microchip in it. 'We think you should see this.'

Julius looked at them, feeling completely shaken. 'What is it?'

'Morgana's Death Mail,' she answered.

Julius stared at the chip resting in the palm of his hand, stunned. His heart was beating furiously as he thought about its content.

Then Faith showed him something else: a small, square case, containing a holographic programme. Written on it, in Morgana's handwriting, was "My holo-dream place". 'Skye got it from your rucksack.'

Julius looked at them both and nodded, finally willing to be led and helped. Together, they went back upstairs and, once on the concourse, they headed for the White Arts block. Faith was sure Professor Lao-Tzu wouldn't mind letting them use one of the Meditation classrooms. They found an empty one right away and went in. The control screen was by the door and Siena activated all the right switches, as she had done many times before. After this, she opened the case, slotted Morgana's chip into the simulator slot, and pressed the activation button.

At first, Julius didn't move, but stayed where he was with his eyes closed. He felt the air grow fresh and the void of an empty space behind his shoulders, instead of the door. An eagle screeched high above him; there were no other sounds. He recognised familiar smells —pine trees, heather bushes and even water. Morgana had taken him home.

Julius opened his eyes slowly, to find himself at the top of a hill overlooking a loch. 'Where are we?' asked Siena, marvelling at the panorama.

'It's Loch Achray,' answered Julius, 'in the Trossachs area. Her family took all us kids here for Morgana's tenth birthday.' He pointed at a chalet on the shore of the lake below them. 'We ate there, before climbing the peak behind it: Ben Venue.' Julius had clear memories of that day, like stills from a movie.

'We'll take a walk,' said Faith, patting him on the shoulder. He took Siena's hand and moved down the hill, towards the water.

Julius breathed deeply. From his position, he could see a myriad of multi-coloured leaves, showing that autumn was underway. It was gorgeous. The grass was still thick and soft, so he decided to remain where he was. He lay on his stomach facing the lake, prepared his PIP screen and pressed PLAY.

Morgana is sitting on a sofa, her legs gathered under her. Her long black hair is dancing, because she cannot stop laughing.

'Will you be serious already?' says Faith, out of shot. 'Siena, don't even start.'

'Sorry babe,' she says, somewhere off screen, to the right.

Morgana sits, adjusts her uniform, and her hair. She throws a last wink at Siena before looking straight at the camera.

'Right,' says Faith, 'let's start. Death Mail test, Take One.'

Morgana bursts into laughter, echoed by Siena. The camera tilts.

'Death Mail?' says Siena. 'You ought to find another name, you know?'

'Can we record please?' says Faith, sounding exasperated. 'I'll think of something. Just roll with it, OK?'

'Sorry,' says Morgana, stifling a last giggle.

'Death Mail test, Take Two. Action.'

Morgana smiles. 'Hi, my name is Morgana Ruthier and if you're watching this, it means I'm dead.'

'Go on,' says Faith quietly.

Morgana tries to remain serious, but her lips are betraying her. 'I'm a 6MS at Tijara School, Zed, Moon, Earth, Solar System, Milky Way, and I'm a heck of a pilot.'

'That she is,' confirms Siena from the sideline.

'It's my last year at the Academy and soon I'll graduate. I hope the war with the Arneshians will be over by then.'

'Don't go too video-diary now,' Faith directs.

'Oh-oh! Excuse me for living!' she replies, giggling again.

The camera tilts to one side.

'OK, OK,' she says. 'Ahem. If you're watching this, it means that I have left behind someone

very precious to me. He's the man of my life, my destiny, my perfect half. Her eyes grow serious, like when a cloud obscures the sun. Then she smiles again. 'Julius McCoy, leaving you behind is the biggest tragedy of all. You're probably in total depression right now, going all "woe to me" on the others, mourning the loss of your beloved Hana-Chan.' She giggles. 'Don't be sad, my love. Your life must go on, brilliant and exciting! You'll be leading the fleet through the stars, exploring new galaxies and meeting new people. It's in your nature. Be a captain and a leader!' She opens her arms wide. 'Live big and hunt hard!' Now she's quiet again. 'Never forget me, Julius. If you do . . . I'll be really gone. Forever.' Morgana looks hesitantly at Faith.

'Wow,' he says. 'That was good.'

'I love you, Julius McCoy!' shouts Morgana, blowing kisses to the camera.

Siena jumps onto the bed next to her. 'We love you Julius!' she cries.

The camera is placed down on something and Faith enters the shot. In a broken, deep voice, he joins in, 'We-lo-ve-you-Ju-lius-Mc-Coy,' his arms bent rigidly, moving up and down, like a robot.

In the chaos, Morgana moves towards the camera, her hands stretched forward as if to touch the lens. Behind her, Faith and Siena continue their joyous chanting, improvising a waltz. She looks into the camera one last time, her eyes sparkling. 'I love you,' she whispers.

Fade to black.

Julius hadn't realised it but, as he watched the video, he had finally begun to well up. It felt as if the dam inside his heart was on the brink of bursting. He had taken in every word she had said, every movement she had made, craving to hear and see more, wanting to walk into the video and hold her in his arms. One of his hands closed around a clump of long grass and he pulled hard at it, as if looking for support. With her last words to him ringing in his ears, he dropped his forehead onto his arm, unable to resist the rising waves of tears. He let them flow, and take with them some of the layers of sorrow and despair that had been haunting him since her death. As he lay there, a strong hand gripped his right shoulder and he was amazed at how much relief it brought to him.

'You're not alone,' said Skye gently. 'You'll never be.'

THE MESSAGE IN THE DREAM

Freja's suggestion had worked. Morgana's Death Mail hadn't solved Julius' problems, but it had given him some much needed perspective back. As he went to bed that night, Julius reflected on how his tears had helped wash away so much of the lingering pain that had been eating at him. It still hurt but, strangely, he felt a renewed sense of purpose now. In the video she had told him to be a leader — was he at least prepared to follow her advice? He forced himself to examine the war situation, focusing only on the positives. Morgana had helped him regain his powers, enabling him to reclaim his place in the fight. Farrah had brought them a step closer to T'Rogon and his circle, giving them a location. Her sacrifice had also destroyed part of the Arneshian repository of knowledge, striking an important victory for Zed. Julius was now left with one clear goal: find his brother Michael and stop him once and for all. That was his objective. If he focused on that, the pain could be kept at bay, at least until his mission was over. After that, he could worry about his sanity, or what was left of it. And as for K'Ssander … his days were numbered.

*

On Tuesday morning, Julius awoke refreshed and hungry. Skye had left him to sleep a little longer, for which he was grateful. For a change, he hadn't had the usual recurring nightmare, but a welcome deep, restful sleep instead.

After a quick shower, he headed for the mess hall, where the others were waiting for him. He sat at their table with a full Scottish breakfast.

'Are you following Skye's diet?' asked Faith, stealing a strip of crunchy bacon.

Julius grinned and tucked into the haggis. The atmosphere was much lighter between them, even compared to the day before, and the appreciation of this had him in a good mood. He knew his problems hadn't just disappeared, but it was a start. 'So, what's the plan today?'

'Infirmary,' said Skye. 'All day. I bet you're in rapture about it, Faith.'

'I'll be *ruptured* all right, by the end of it,' he said, making them all chuckle. 'I don't know though: maybe it's because it's the last time, but I'm not too bothered about it.'

'Last time on Zed, you mean,' said Siena.

'Yeah. I'm sure they'll find the time to download new stuff into me body at a later stage.'

'True that,' she said.

At 09:00 hours, the school-leavers began to head off for their appointments.

'That's us,' said Skye, stealing the last strip of bacon from the plate.

Julius threw him a dirty glance, before returning his tray and following the others.

Dr Walliser gathered them all in the waiting area of the Infirmary, surrounded by his assistants.

Julius saw Nurse Primula and gave her a wave. She winked back, delighted to see him.

'Gather round, officers!' called the doctor.

'No one else has called me an officer since graduation,' commented Siena proudly.

'Welcome to Mr Shanigan's favourite hangout,' continued Walliser, drawing laughter from the crowd and bowing to Faith, who grinned back. 'It seems like yesterday that you came in here, as Juniors, to get your first PIP implant. And look at you now, ready to leave Tijara for good, though you will never leave our thoughts.'

Julius could tell that he was speaking genuinely, thanks to the fuzzy, warm aura surrounding his body.

'Today, your PIP implants will be connected to the Officer Network. Its most important feature is your personal account, which will reflect your career path — assignments, promotions and the like — and will be accessible to all employers in the GFE. Keep it up to date and make it count. The majority of the other features are similar to what you had in school, but I'll leave you to discover them. And, FYI, Zed Officers get some really good discounts in the federation — a perk of the job that you'll want to keep in mind when shopping.'

'Sir,' said Isolde, 'will Buruwang's network be available as well?'

'Indeed. Anyone belonging to the GFE is part of the network. It's only the permissions that change, according to your rank and role.'

Julius thought about Daku Derain and Walamai. He would have liked to see them again; however, he had no intention on setting foot in their town for a long time, where his memories of Morgana were at their strongest and most intimate.

'This upgrade will be quick and you'll get it either before or after the ones for your shields. Let's begin.'

The first ten students on the register were called up by the nursing staff and led into the private rooms.

Dr Walliser moved over to a wall station and activated it. He dragged two chairs over and sat down on one of them. 'Can I have the next in line please?' he called.

Julius stood and moved over to him.

'Sit here, McCoy.' Walliser patted the chair.

Julius did so and, knowing the drill, placed his arm inside the transparent glass cylinder, palm up.

'It'll only take a moment,' said the doctor, inputting the information in his terminal.

Julius nodded, and watched the little green dot that had appeared on his skin. He knew it was seeking out the chip embedded in his wrist. As he glanced up at Walliser, it occurred to him that, once he left school, he may never see him again. In fact, most of his teachers would remain behind, leaving the last leg of the journey to the fleet. He wasn't even sure if the GMs could come, given that the schools were full once again.

'There,' said the doctor. 'All done.'

Julius pulled his arm out and carefully tapped his wrist to check for any discomfort. 'Thanks, Doctor; for everything.' He felt embarrassed saying it, but he had to say how grateful he was. Without Walliser's medical expertise, his stasis could have lasted a lot longer. *Try, forever long*, he thought.

'It is I who should thank you,' he answered cheerfully. 'You made me famous among my peers, with all the articles I wrote about you.'

'Then it was quid pro quo,' replied Julius, standing up.

'Such is life. Nurse Primula will see you soon. She'll kill me if you go to another nurse.'

'I'll wait,' said Julius, grinning. He returned to the sofa area, while George Lowet took his place.

'Let's check out the new interface,' said Faith, leaning over his shoulder.

Julius opened his left hand and willed the virtual screen to pop up. A personalised greeting message appeared in the centre of the screen. In the bottom left corner was the Captain class emblem.

'I bet that's your personal account menu,' said Faith, touching it.

The icon opened a list of options, showing different forms for Julius to complete. 'I'll check that later,' he said, moving the menu off his screen with the flick of a finger. Several circular icons now replaced the welcome message. 'Look, there's one for the Forum. You should have one too, Faith.'

'I think everyone has it, but yours will also have unrestricted permissions, since you're the leader. I'm the techy expert. I bet they gave me some leeway too.'

Julius touched the screen and it opened up a new sub menu. 'There's even a calendar,' said Julius. 'Do I need to set meeting dates already? We don't even know where we'll be in the next few months.'

'Eventually you'll have to. As for the agenda, I can help you get started. Zed knows some of our fleet protocols need a change. Besides, people will bring their own issues to discuss. Believe me, I don't think you'll ever have a problem filling meetings.'

Julius nodded and touched the second icon, which was titled "GFE Forum Database". A list of names appeared, seemingly going on forever.

'You have every single contact in the federation on that thing,' said Faith, in awe. 'Power-trip, anyone?'

'Wow,' said Julius, a little less in awe and more worried about the size of the file.

'It looks like fun,' said Faith, nudging him.

'It looks like a lot of work actually; and not at the right time either.'

'Hmm. Let's get this week out of the way first, I say.'

Julius closed the Forum menu and quickly checked the other icons on his screen. Maps, directories, job listings and housings were only a few of the many pages he could explore. It seemed like his future was being facilitated in more than one way. Still, he couldn't even consider buying his folks a house on Colonial 1 at the moment. As long as Michael was out there, there was no space for other projects.

'McCoy!' called Nurse Primula, from one of the rooms.

Julius closed his PIP and stood up. 'Later, Faith.'

'So good to see you,' she told him when he arrived. She ushered him inside and pointed at a small changing room to the side. 'There's an overall for you behind there. I'll be back in five minutes.'

Julius did so, and swapped his clothes for a blue overall, which he tied behind his neck and back. Barefoot, he hopped onto the bed and waited for the nurse to return.

Primula came back into the room, and tied her long brown hair in a ponytail. 'How are you?'

'Better, I guess.'

'How's your sleep?'

Julius hesitated, thinking that she had been through enough with him to not have to lie about his sleep. 'Not great, although last night was fine.'

Primula looked at him with concern. She started up the machine to the left of the bed. 'Bad dreams?'

He nodded. 'And not even there can I save her.'

'Stop,' she said, putting her hand on his arm. 'Don't do this to yourself. If you really must blame someone, blame the bastard that killed her and use your anger to find him.'

Julius was taken aback hearing her speak like this. It must have shown on his face, because Primula removed her hand, and blushed.

'When you were in stasis,' she said, continuing the preparations, 'Morgana came to see you every day. No matter how bad a week she was having, she never lost focus on her priority — to find a cure for you. I have never met anyone so resilient, or more dedicated to a friend than she was. She did this because she believed that you had a job to finish.'

Julius saw her eyes welling up as she spoke. It had never occurred to him to ask her about those days in the Infirmary, after her death. The nurse had probably spent more time with Morgana than the boys had that year. He didn't trust himself enough to speak, as her words had created a knot in his throat, so he just nodded firmly. '*Thank you,*' he told her with his mind.

Primula wiped her eyes and smiled. 'You're welcome.'

*

Julius woke up in the Infirmary bed late that afternoon. They had had to put him to sleep before they could implant the new shields. He stretched, feeling groggy and thirsty. 'Ouch,' he said, flinching. His hand went to his head, to a spot behind his right ear. There was a plaster there.

'Don't touch it yet,' said Primula, entering the room.

'What is it?'

'Your last ever implant: the core of the other four chips. It's linked directly into your brain, to activate your shields quicker, among other things.'

Julius was still feeling too out of sorts to really understand the mechanics of it.

'The dizziness will pass,' she told him kindly. 'By the way, they won't be activated until you leave school. Get dressed now and go get some dinner.'

'Dinner? How long was I out for?'

'Most of the day, I'm afraid. It's almost nine in the evening.'

Julius didn't like losing time like that without knowing. It reminded him too much of his stasis. However, he thanked her and slowly climbed out of bed.

When he returned to the waiting room, Siena and Skye were chatting away on the sofa.

'There you are,' said Siena. 'Faith won't be out for another hour or so. We should go eat.'

Julius had no objections to that and headed for the mess hall with them.

With the exception of a few Seniors, there were mainly leavers in the room, all looking tired. On her way to the counter, Siena stopped to wake Astra Evangelou, who was just about to slump into her soup, face first.

'That's how I feel,' muttered Skye, watching her stand and sway out of the canteen like a zombie.

Julius nodded. 'I just hope that the tiredness means no dreams tonight.'

They had a quick nibble and decided to go straight to their dorms. After leaving Siena, the boys made their way down to their room.

'So, what's the schedule for tomorrow?' asked Julius.

'In theory, leavers should apply for their first assignment. But with the mission still on, who knows what Freja will want us to do?'

Julius nodded. 'Given the choice, I wondered how many in our class would pick active duties. And we still don't know where to go.'

'Faith and I will be there, McCoy. Don't you worry about that.'

What remains of the Skirts, thought Julius.

*

Julius was walking through Eneamar, navigating the streets with the confidence of a local. Everything around him was clean and tidy as it always was and he felt refreshed. He made his way toward the metal sphere at the centre of the square and sat on a bench, watching the people walking by. The soothing music in the air and warmth of the sun made him feel relaxed and, after several minutes, he decided to close his eyes for a while.

He couldn't tell how long he rested for, but when he woke, Eneamar had changed. He stood up, realizing that the sun had gone, leaving behind a light mist and drizzle. There was a chill in the air and the music had stopped, while all the people had disappeared, taking all other sounds with them. Julius shivered. Gradually, one noise resurfaced — the water in the canal had begun to flow towards the globe. He took a step forward and saw that it was rushing into the square, as if it were a mountain torrent. Anxiety gripped his heart and he knew that he had to reach the hill, where the statue of the Archer stood.

He turned right, following the stream back to its source. The leaves in the trees above him had turned dark, as if autumn had suddenly arrived. Julius saw the water change colour, from clear to dark red. Scared, he ran towards the hill, trying to ignore the river of blood now gurgling by his side. As the slope approached, he didn't stop, but spurred himself forward, scrambling upwards. Just as he reached the summit, his foot caught on something; he fell forward, and landed hard on the ground. Winded, he looked up, only to recoil in horror. The grassy hilltop was strewn with bodies; their backs were covered in fur. They had burn-wounds and dried blood all over them. The statue of the Archer was gone, replaced by one of K'Ssander holding Morgana's lifeless body in his arms. The arrow that used to be perched, cocked in the bow, was now protruding from her chest, pointing at the sky. Blood gushed from her wound, cascading into the canal and forming the stream at their feet. That was when Morgana's eyes flew open and she slowly raised her hand, a frightening crackle from her stiff joints accompanying the movement. She pointed into the far distance and said, 'Mah.' As the air flew back into his lungs, Julius opened his mouth and screamed.

*

'Julius! Wake up!'

The voice arrived from afar, growing closer. Julius forced himself to focus on it and suddenly there he was, back in his bed, on Zed.

'Shh. It's me. Calm down.'

Julius looked up, panting, and saw Skye sitting on the bed, holding his arms. 'What …'

'Just relax. It's over now.'

Julius lay back down, his skin covered in sweat. A hurried knock at the door made him flinch.

'It's fine,' Skye said, before opening the door.

Freja entered the room, followed by Doctor Walliser. 'Mr Shanigan,' he said, turning towards the corridor, 'send the others back to their rooms, please.'

'Yes, sir,' came Faith's reply from outside.

The doctor took Skye's place on the bed and passed his handheld medical scanner over Julius' head and chest.

'What happened, Mr Miller?' asked Freja, worried.

'He had another dream, sir. Only … this time it was really bad. I was woken up by his screams and couldn't get him to stop. The whole floor heard us and that's when I told Faith to call you.'

'You did well. Have a glass of water.'

'Don't mind if I do. He scared the heck out of me.'

Walliser closed his device and gave Julius an injection in the side of his neck. 'It's a R.E.M. inhibitor. It'll get rid of all dreams for the next few hours, as well as helping you sleep.'

Julius nodded, already feeling the effects of the drug on his body. He watched as the doctor joined Freja and Skye, but his vision was beginning to blur as his eyelids drooped, so he saw them only as silhouettes.

'How long has he been having these dreams for?' asked Freja quietly.

'Since Morgana,' he replied, throwing a side glance at Julius. 'This was different though. He kept saying, "Mah".'

'The Arneshian location?'

Skye nodded.

'Does he know where it is?'

'Ene … amar,' whispered Julius, before falling asleep.

*

When he woke up, Julius felt refreshed, although the images of the dream still lingered in the back of his mind. He remembered crying out, and the GM having to be called for, and he felt ashamed. So far, Eneamar had been a safe place to be, but last night things had changed, as if someone had hijacked his mind to show him what *they* wanted him to see. Did it mean something, or had his subconscious simply been playing tricks on him? Perhaps, after breakfast, he could talk to the doctor about it, and ask him for a repeat prescription of that dream-stopper of his. He got up, showered and headed upstairs.

As he walked along the central concourse, he saw Freja and Walliser exiting the mess hall, followed by Skye and Faith.

'The very man,' said Doctor Walliser. 'How are you feeling this morning?'

Julius saw Freja's inquisitive gaze and wondered if he thought that Julius had finally lost it. 'Better, I guess,' he said vaguely.

'I need you to come to sickbay with us, Julius,' Freja told him. 'We're at an impasse, and I believe your mind may hold the key to Mah's location.'

'I really don't know where it is, sir.'

'Let me worry about that. Nurse Primula will give you something to eat. We start in fifteen minutes.'

As the doctor and the GM walked away, Julius and the guys walked over to the Infirmary.

'That was some show you put on last night,' said Skye. 'Never seen you freak out like that before.'

'I heard you through me own walls,' added Faith. 'I thought Skye had gone nuts and stabbed you to death for eating his food, or something.'

'Sorry,' he replied. 'It was the worst one for sure. K'Ssander ...' he trailed off.

'You don't have to talk about it,' said Faith quickly. 'Go in and grab your coffee.'

Julius nodded gratefully and headed for the reception desk, where Nurse Primula was busy on a work call. She smiled at him and handed him a tray with two slices of toast and a glass of juice. He took the food to one of the sofas and began to eat.

'I thought Eneamar was good for you,' said Skye, sitting down with him.

'It was, until last night. Morgana ... she-'

'McCoy,' called Walliser from one of the rooms, 'we're ready for you. Miller, Shanigan, you too.'

Julius finished the last of the juice in one gulp and followed the others. The doctor ushered them into a large room that Julius had never seen before. It looked more like an office than a medical bay. It had a brown leather couch, with a chair by its side and a desk, piled with files and old books. Like Freja, it looked like the doctor enjoyed owning old-fashioned paper books. Julius glanced at their titles and realised that they were mainly medical tomes.

'Am I late?'

Julius turned around and was surprised to see Professor Len Lao-tzu entering the room. He was followed by Cress.

'Not at all,' replied Walliser. Then, to Julius, 'Lie on the couch, please.'

'What's happening?' asked Julius, perplexed.

'After you obtained the crystal,' explained the doctor, 'you mentioned Mah for the first time on Buruwang, way before Farrah spoke of it. As this is not a place we've discovered yet, you're the only one that may be able to help. We are going to use different methods of data retrieval on you, including hypnosis, which is why Professor Lao-tzu is here.'

'Hypnosis, sir? Will it work?'

'The way we do it now, yes.'

'Miller and Shanigan,' said Freja, 'could you please sit over here.'

Julius took his place and got comfortable, while his old teacher sat by his side.

'This will help you slip into a trance in a few minutes, without falling asleep,' said Walliser, injecting him in the neck.

Julius flinched, but the pain was short-lived. He watched as the doctor dimmed all the lights in the office, before taking a seat next to Freja. From his position, all he could see was the empty wall in front of him.

'Close your eyes now,' began Lao-tzu. 'I want you to focus only on my words.' His voice was calm, soothing and it felt to Julius like it was coming to him from afar. 'Turn your thoughts to Buruwang. I want you to remember the place and its sounds.'

Julius remembered them all, although, in his present state, the images were out of focus. His head felt heavy and couldn't even lift his fingers.

'Can you see it?'

'Yes,' he answered.

'You are there,' said Lao-tzu.

At those words, Julius felt a cold spot in the middle of his forehead and all the images appeared in sharp definition. He saw the ocean and heard the waves and the seagulls, but felt nothing, as if it was someone else there, walking on the sand.

In the office, the empty wall had become a screen, showing the images from Julius' brain. They all saw him standing on the beach.

'It is the morning of your medical test. You have just woken up. Where are you?'

'I'm in my bed,' answered Julius quickly.

The screen showed him inside the hut. There was someone else under the sheet, next to him.

'Who is that there with you?'

'Morgana.'

There was an embarrassed shuffling of feet at the back of the room, followed by a little cough from Faith.

'Did you dream?'

'Yes.'

'What did you see?'

'Eneamar, where Farrah used to go when she was in hospital.'

Lao-tzu turned to look at Freja, puzzled, before resuming his questioning.

'Describe Eneamar.'

'It's a clean city, built beside the ocean.' As he spoke, the images on the wall reflected his descriptions. 'The people are friendly and elegantly dressed. You are safe walking its streets. It is very green, with hanging gardens everywhere. Even the glass buildings have gardens on their balconies.'

'What do you do in Eneamar?'

'I start to walk and I reach the main square. There's a fountain that looks like a planet. I know it's Earth.'

Skye and Faith exchanged a quick glance. Even Freja sat up. The globe did look like Earth, with the bas-relief showing the familiar continental shapes.

'I see water flowing into the square and I want to know where it comes from. I walk along the canal and it takes me through a field, beneath tall trees. There's a hill at the edge of the forest, covered in grass. I begin to climb up it, wanting to see the view from its top.'

'What do you see?' asked Lao-tzu, peering at the screen.

'I see a statue. It is an archer, ready to shoot an arrow into the air. It has fur.'

Freja stood and quietly walked over to the screen.

'Is he wearing the fur?'

'No, only short strips of suede. The fur grows on his skin, all over the back of his body.'

'Wha-' began Skye, but Freja hushed him with a raised hand. He also looked mystified and pointed at the fur on the back of the statue.

'Is the Archer from Eneamar?' asked Lao-tzu.

'No. He comes from beyond. The arrow points to it.'

'Where does it point to, Julius?'

'Mah. Eronan says so.'

The name made Freja turn to Julius suddenly, as if he had just remembered something. 'Who is he, Julius?'

'Eronan can reverse the effects of the Chemical War. He's Marcus' friend.'

The statement about the War took everyone by surprise, leaving them to ponder its meaning.

'Marcus Tijara?' asked Lao-tzu, after a few moments. The surprise in his voice was plain even to himself, so he steadied it. 'Is he a friend of Marcus Tijara?' he continued.

'Yes. He wears a red tunic and he looks just like he did in Marcus' office.' An image of the office promptly appeared on the screen.

Lao-tzu turned to Freja, who motioned for him to continue. 'Julius, when did you see Tijara?'

'When I was on the Guardian's Trail. I saw Eronan come to see Marcus on Zed and tell him to go to Eneamar. Mah points to Eneamar and Eneamar points to Mah.'

Lao-tzu took a few seconds, as if he was thinking about how to put the next question to Julius. 'I want you to remember what they said about those two locations, in Marcus' office. Word for word.'

The screen now showed Eronan and Marcus sitting opposite each other, on either side of a desk.

'He doesn't look right,' whispered Skye, pointing at Eronan.

Everyone examined the stranger's facial details for as long as Julius' view stayed on him. His eyes were far from those of a human.

When Julius began to recall their dialogue, the view drew back to include both Eronan and Marcus. His voice had no emotion.

"And what other choice do I have, pray?" says Tijara.

"You could come with me to Eneamar and leave the others to their squabbles," Eronan tells him.

"Leave our solar system?"

"We're only a wormhole away — the closest one from here. It's so well hidden that no one would ever find you. You can join me later, if you prefer. Once you're through it, it's only a matter of looking for the Archer, on the highest peak of the tallest mountain of Mah. He will show you the way."

'Is there more?' asked Lao-tzu, after Julius had gone quiet.

On the screen, Julius walked towards Eronan and tried to touch his face, but his fingers went right through his skin. On the sofa, he became agitated, as if he was having a bad dream.

'We need to bring him back,' said Walliser.

Lao-tzu nodded. 'Julius, I want you to follow my voice and focus on your body. Now.'

On the screen, everyone saw Julius lying on the couch, as if there was a camera looking down on him from the ceiling.

'I am going to count to three, and when I say the word "Awake", you will leave the trance and come back to reality. One … Two … Three … Awake.'

Julius opened his eyes and the room sprung back into focus. He saw Freja standing at the foot of the couch. 'What happened? Did it work?'

'Take a look for yourself,' answered Freja. The GM pressed a button on the wall-screen and rewound the film back to Eronan's entrance.

Seeing his face plainly on the screen startled Julius, and more so when he saw Tijara sitting in the office. The scene was familiar, but he couldn't quite place it. 'Is this from the Guardian's Trail?'

'It appears so.'

Doctor Walliser turned to Skye and Faith. 'We are aware that the Trail left no clear memories with either of you or Mr McCoy. However, since you were his guides, do you recognise the encounter with Tijara from any part of your experiences?'

'Yes,' replied Faith. 'I was in that room as Julius' guide. When I saw it on the screen, it felt way too familiar, and so did Eronan. I just don't know how I could have forgotten about it.'

'Doctor,' said Freja, 'how sure can we be that Julius' recollection was genuine?'

'One hundred per cent, actually. We have just unpacked a memory that had been stored away.'

'Very well. Master Cress, you have an undiscovered wormhole to find.'

Cress bowed and hurried out of the room.

'Professor, what do you make of the message?'

Lao-tzu thought about it for a few seconds. 'Aside from the directions for reaching Eneamar from Mah, it seems to me that he was offering Tijara a way out. Judging by Marcus' facial characteristics, I would also place this event around the time of his death. It is likely that the "squabbles" Eronan mentioned referred to the situation with Clodagh.'

'Yes, I agree with that timeline. Julius, you said that Eronan can reverse the effects of the Chemical War — what does that mean?'

'I'm sorry, sir,' he said, shaking his head, 'I don't know.'

Freja nodded, and grew thoughtful. 'There must be a reason Eronan appeared when you were on the Guardian's Trail. And if he can really help us, then we must find Eneamar before we deal with T'Rogon. McCoy, your first assignment as a Zed Officer will be to discover all you can about Eronan. Miller and Shanigan can accompany you, if they don't have other plans.'

'Wha-' said Faith, shocked that the Grand Master would even think of separating him from Julius. 'I'm seeing this through to the end, sir.'

'I couldn't do anything else, sir,' added Skye firmly.

'I thought as much, but I had to ask. All of you will need to go to the Curia Archive.'

'To Ahriman?' said Julius, surprised.

He nodded. 'A transporter is leaving at lunch for Colonial 1. They'll drop you off on the way. The new teleportation system will make it a very quick trip — especially thanks to the Shanigan Relay.'

Faith grinned and immediately blushed.

'Once you get there, I want you to dig out everything you can on Eronan. Start from March 2628 — the time of Tijara's death — and work your way back to the present. Doctor Walliser will send you a still of Eronan's face from the video we just watched. In the meantime, we'll get the fleet organised. Please understand that time is of the essence. As soon as Cress and his team discover the wormhole, you'll be recalled, even if your assignment is unsuccessful.'

'Understood, sir,' replied Skye.

'Good. That will be all. McCoy, a word if you please.'

Julius thanked Professor Lao-tzu for his help.

'Here, McCoy,' said Walliser handing him a small tub of pills. 'If you wake up from another cracker like last night, take one of these. But only if it's *that* bad.'

'Thanks,' he said, putting the container in his side pocket.

'We'll start packing,' Faith told him, as he left the room.

Freja walked towards the window as the door slid shut. He touched a button which let light back into the room and the glass of the window became clear. He crossed his arms in front of him and looked quietly outside for a few moments. 'When JD was nine, my wife Kathryn died suddenly, in her sleep.'

Julius was taken aback by this unexpected disclosure.

'Every night I gave her a goodnight kiss, but not *that* night. The Zed shield was malfunctioning and, even though it wasn't an emergency, nor was I an engineer that could fix the problem, I felt I had to go and check nonetheless. Duty, above all. I spent a whole year in utter dejection before being able to look at the world again with any interest, and before some of the guilt, for not being there, finally left me. The people around me bore the brunt of my sadness; especially, I regret to say, my son.' Freja took a deep breath and turned around.

Julius thought about his last moments with Morgana. Before they left the hideout, she said she would never leave him. He had kissed her lips then, for the very last time. The memory made his stomach tighten. It had been too brief. He had to swallow before he could speak. 'How did you manage to recover, sir?'

'Mostly through time and friendship — though it never really leaves you. You just … *adapt*. We all grieve in different ways, McCoy, but I'm afraid you don't have the luxury of time. Friendship, *that* you have, but not time.'

Julius nodded, painfully aware of the pressure he was under.

'I need you back. I want you to use your grief to get you back in the race, because you are our champion and we believe in you. I don't know why, but you've been chosen to lead our mighty fleet through this chaos. I don't intend to leave this war as an inheritance to my granddaughter, and I need your help to make it so.'

Julius was deeply moved by Freja's words. Over the years, he knew that the Grand Master had supported him above and beyond expectations, believing in his abilities. To be told all this openly, along with such personal details of his own past, made it all the more powerful and true.

'I won't let you down, sir.'

*

'Where are you guys going?' asked Lopaka. It was midday and he had just arrived in the dorm corridor, in time to see Julius and Skye leaving their rooms with their rucksacks shouldered.

'First assignment, my friend,' replied Skye. 'Off to Ahriman.'

'Oh. You'll miss the graduation party in Satras.'

'I know, but there's stuff to do before *the mission* starts.'

Lopaka nodded and Julius realised that the "mission" now meant only one thing for everyone — the end of Arnesh.

'I'll find you in space then,' said Lopaka. 'I'll be in an engine room somewhere.'

'For sure,' said Julius. 'Stay safe.'

'Yeah. You too. Hey, speaking of engines, where's Faith?'

'He's been saying goodbye to Siena for the last four hours,' said Skye, grinning.

'Who could blame him, right?'

I couldn't, thought Julius. He smiled too, though — Faith's happiness was as important to him as his welfare was. He couldn't really sulk about the fact that *his* girlfriend was still alive.

After leaving Lopaka, they made their way to the main entrance, where Faith and Siena were waiting, cuddling on one of the couches. They stood up quickly when they heard them approaching, but not quick enough to go unnoticed.

'Tut tut, naughty Irish boy' said Skye, pretending to be shocked.

'Don't you even start,' Faith admonished him, finger raised.

Siena giggled, then went over to Skye to say goodbye.

'We won't be gone long, you'll see,' he told her, giving her a peck on the cheek.

'Look after each other,' she said, moving to Julius and hugging him.

She remained at the top of the stairs that led to the Zed underground until they had disappeared from view. The boys lingered a bit as they walked through the hustle and bustle of the hangar, reminiscing about the times spent in there. To recall them from their reveries was the vision of Captain Foster, standing on the main platform. When he saw them, he waved them his way.

'This here is your lift to Pit-Stop Pete,' he said, pointing at a Stork behind him. 'Good luck out there, boys.'

'We'll make our own luck, sir,' Julius told him, shaking his hand.

'That's the spirit, McCoy.'

'And don't let your guard down with the Juniors, sir,' added Skye. 'They're pretty pesky this year.'

'After you, Miller, everyone's a doddle.'

As they climbed aboard, it didn't escape them that Foster was actually smiling.

'Now I've really seen it all,' remarked Faith.

The shuttle took them to the Zed docking station, where they registered at the arrival desk. They had only a few minutes to spare before the transporter would leave, but Faith insisted on touching base with Pete, his inspiration and mentor. By one o'clock, they were seated in a small passenger lounge, heading for the first of the portals which would take them to Ahriman in a series of skips.

Later that afternoon, the transporter entered planet Funesto's orbit over a strip of desert, which they immediately recognised as the eastern plateau. The search for Tijara's crystal had started there, by the Seffira Cave, over a year ago.

Julius looked out of the shuttle window, wanting to see what had changed since the Arneshians had been expelled, and he wasn't disappointed. The Halls had been completely revamped. A new atmosphere shield, like the one on Zed, had been built to encapsulate the main complex, removing the need for using an EMU while on Curia ground. The central building, where Julius had met his brother Michael for the first time after his stasis, was now completely restructured and brought back to its original splendour. The whitewashed walls had been cleaned and repaired, the iron doors polished, the fountains refilled and new plants potted. Earth had definitely left its stamp.

As the shuttle landed gently outside the main entrance, Julius saw the square filled with Zed Officers and Curia workers walking around looking busy. When he stepped outside, he had to force himself not to think about the fact that it had been Morgana who made that landing on their last visit. Fortunately, a distraction arrived in the form of a short man, who was waving and walking quickly in their direction. When he reached them, he snapped to attention and bowed low, catching Julius and the others off guard.

'Welcome to Ahriman, sirs,' he said obsequiously. 'I am Milan Todorov, Secretary to the Curiates.'

'*Sirs?*' whispered Faith sideways. 'Is he talking to us?'

'Thank you, my good man,' said Skye, stepping forward. 'Take us to your leader. Our business cannot wait.' With that, he let the man go ahead, raised his chin and followed him theatrically.

'*Take us to your leader?*' repeated Faith. 'Has he gone insane?'

'A long time ago,' replied Julius wryly.

They followed Skye through the large main gate. Its light-coloured metal had been restored like the rest of the building and shone brightly in the sun, revealing the stylised stars that decorated the two doors. The gate led them to a large atrium, its marble floors polished to reflect the sunlight shining through the glass roof. Wide arches opened onto the main area, showing the many doors that opened onto the different sections of the building. Directly opposite the gate, a central staircase began, branching out into two thinner sections, curling their way up to the mezzanine on the first floor.

The guide halted at the foot of the staircase and looked up, towards the stout woman who was descending towards them. 'Curiate Alohalani Kaula will organise your stay in the Halls.'

'Great news,' whispered Skye. 'She's a really nice lady – from Tonga. And she likes me.'

Julius had never personally met any of the other Curiates; only Aldobrando, their leader. Knowing that this particular member of Roversi's council was an easy-going person heartened him, as it would make their job much easier. The woman had long, wavy hair, gathered in a ponytail that reached down to her waist. Its colour was matched by the deep brown shade of her eyes. On her uniform, she sported the class emblem – the globe on a grey shield, completely boxed in by four lines. Only Roversi, as the Curio Maximus, was allowed to have a gold shield, to distinguish him above all others. Curiates also wore three pale blue stripes on the sleeves of their jackets.

'Good day, officers,' she said kindly.

They bowed to her promptly.

'Curiate Kaula,' said Skye, 'it's a pleasure to see you again.'

'I was very pleased to hear that you would be working with us again, Mr Miller.' She turned to Julius and Faith, smiling. 'He has worked so hard in his placements that Colonial Affairs has already offered him a position.'

'You don't say,' commented Faith, with a cheeky wink to Julius.

'Once the mission is over, I will be only too glad to accept it,' replied Skye.

It was a fleeting moment but, right then, Julius realised that life would not necessarily keep them together forever, and that their friendship would have to go through the test of distance as well as time. It made him sad thinking about it, but it was inevitable.

'Follow me, please,' said Kaula, heading across the square. 'Lodgings have been arranged for you within the main complex. Todorov will send you the blueprints for the building shortly.' When she reached the last door in the south-west corner, she stopped and turned around. 'Grand Master Freja has explained your mission. Mr Todorov will be on standby to attend to your needs. He will give you access to the records you seek.'

'Thank you, Curiate Kaula,' replied Julius.

'Your mission concerns us all, Mr McCoy. You have our full support.'

They bowed to her and let Todorov usher them inside the archive.

Back on Earth, Julius had visited the National Museum of Scotland many times, passionate as he was about history. There was a special section in the basement, with a perfect replica of a vast library from ancient times. Once paper books had gone out of fashion and the world had fully switched to digital, Britain had decided to save some of them for posterity. Walking along the aisles, between high shelves loaded with colourful tomes of all sizes, had been something quite wondrous. Julius' eyes would travel along the hundreds of titles printed on the spines, wondering about the secret worlds they contained. By contrast, the archive of Ahriman was very different from the basement of the museum – bright and light, furnished with desks and terminals – and rather disappointing, thought Julius.

'All the records from 2628 have been made accessible to you. We have a mixture of sources, from official documents to news bulletins. The classified material has already been searched by our own people, but there was nothing there.'

'Can we access files from Earth and the colonies as well?' asked Faith.

'It's all there – the entire written history of humankind.'

'A walk in the park then,' said Skye, sighing.

'I will return at dinner time and escort you to your quarters,' said Todorov.

'Thanks,' answered Julius, heading towards the closest table to dump his rucksack. 'We don't have much time. We must make this search as efficient as possible,' he said, activating his terminal, before opening his PIP to retrieve Eronan's picture. Faith and Skye took their places at terminals either side of him, ready to start. 'In the video, Eronan looks like he's in his forties maybe? We should limit ourselves to going back as far as 2580, I'd say.'

'Sounds good to me,' said Faith. 'I'll do '28, Julius can take '27, and Skye '26. Then, after that, '25 for me, '24 for Julius, '23 for Skye and so on.'

'Deeply convoluted, but OK,' said Skye. 'How do we start?'

'Use the search box – top right corner,' said Julius. 'Enter your year, and in the key word field, type "Eronan".'

'Good idea,' said Faith. 'I would also add, "alien".'

'If people knew about an alien on Zed, surely we wouldn't be here,' commented Skye.

'Yes, but perhaps a journalist noticed his weird features. And on that note, add "crystal eyes" too, for good measure.'

His eyes were certainly peculiar, agreed Julius, but he doubted those key words could really help. *I'll start with his name*, he thought. As he hit Enter, the screen began to scan a thick list of names. The whole process took a few seconds, but the result brought back a blank screen. 'Not found,' said Julius.

'Same here.'

'Yup.'

They repeated the process a few more times, ending on the same blank screen. Eagerly, they kept going, until a search of every year back to 2580 was completed.

'No sign of Eronan,' said Faith, leaning heavily back in his chair.

'No sign of his name, you mean,' Skye added. 'We need to check pictures next.'

'Yes,' agreed Julius, opening the search field again. 'Faith, go for pictures containing unnamed people. Skye, you search for a combination of unnamed and people of the Curia, and I'll look for unnamed pictured with Marcus Tijara.'

They all agreed, put their heads down and trawled through the records once again. It was close to 20:00 hours before they had a breakthrough.

'Come check this out,' said Skye eagerly.

Julius and Faith moved to his station and, from over his shoulders, peered at the monitor.

'This is from the opening of the Lunar Perimeter, in 2620,' explained Skye. 'There's Tijara, with Clodagh to his left.'

'There he is, behind her …' said Faith, astonished.

Julius immediately recognised him. Eronan was standing a few steps behind the front row, in his red tunic. He was wearing a pair of dark shades, and smiling at someone beside him. Although dated, the digital picture had retained the vibrancy of its original colours. 'Look at his neckline.'

Skye clicked on Eronan and magnified his head and neck as much as possible, without losing any definition. 'Is it … *glowing?*'

'Well, I'll be air-locked,' said Faith, looking closer. 'Could it be an effect of the light?'

'Probably,' replied Julius. 'Weird though.'

'They all look so young,' said Skye, bringing the zoom over the faces of Marcus and Clodagh. 'They must have been very happy back then. Way before she went cuckoo.'

Marcus had loved her very much; Julius was sure of that. No matter what she had done to him, he had still loved her. They had been destined for each other. Morgana's face floated up to the surface of his consciousness – it was never too far away. Had she been his destiny? The silence that followed in his mind made his heart ache.

'Hey, Jules,' said Skye, tapping him on the shoulder.

'Huh?'

'Todorov is here. Let's go get some food.'

                                        *

The following morning, after a quick breakfast, they returned to the archives with renewed energy. Finding proof of Eronan's presence on Zed had given them hope of discovering more evidence, so they decided to stick to their plan until they had searched every year. In the middle of the morning, Julius took a coffee break, during which he sent the link over to Freja, to share the findings. He was hoping to receive good news from him as well, but there were none – the wormhole was still eluding the scouts.

When the second day of searches was brought unsuccessfully to an end, Julius began to grow restless. What if they never found out who he was, or Mah's location? Farrah had told him that Michael was there and he believed her. *Perhaps tomorrow …* he thought. As it turned out, it took them another three days before a new clue was discovered.

'Golly,' said Faith one evening. His eyes were red from staring at the screen for so long. 'Reading about the aftermath of the Chemical War isn't pretty.'

'Chemical War?' said Skye. 'Why are you looking so far back?'

'At this point anything goes, quite frankly.'

'Did Eronan look 80 to you?'

Julius could tell they were getting tired from their stroppy chit-chat – maybe it was time to call it a night.

'I'll tell you what then: I'll do a last search for Eronan of … forever, shall I?'

'And waste time we don't have?'

'Dinner?' Julius cut in.

Unperturbed, Faith said, 'All history – Eronan. Search. Dinner it is.' With that, he got ready to leave.

Julius stretched in his chair before standing up. 'Faith, wait up.' He turned his terminal off and headed for the door.

Skye was about to follow them when a tiny beep sounded in the room, rooting everyone to the spot. 'It found something,' he said, staring at the terminal.

Julius and Faith quickly joined him, their eyes fixed on the monitor. There were two entries on the screen, dated 2431 and 2020.

'Open the first link,' Faith commanded the terminal.

The computer obeyed and an article appeared, titled "Inauguration of the orbital aereodock". Below it was a picture of a plump man in a fluorescent green suit, holding a bottle of bubbly, amidst a small, cheering crowd. Standing to his left, applauding, was a man in a red tunic and shaded glasses. The caption read, "Mr Jankowksy seals the deal with his new associate, Mr Eronan."

'It's him,' said Faith, astonished.

'It can't be,' replied Julius. 'He would have been 197 when Tijara died.'

'I'm telling you, it's him,' insisted Faith. 'Look at his neck.' He moved the cursor over the man's head, magnifying it several times. The line created by his tunic against his skin was glowing almost imperceptibly, but unmistakably.

'He kinda does look like Eronan too,' added Skye.

'Open the second link,' commanded Faith once more.

The picture was from a small American newspaper. This time it showed a crowd standing in front of a shuttle plane. There were ordinary women, men and children with suitcases at their feet. On the side of the plane, in red letters, were the words "Mahin Space Enterprise". Two men stood in the foreground, shaking hands. The caption read, "Captain Gorghinian and his sponsor, Mr Eronan, before leaving Earth." The *sponsor* was wearing the usual red tunic and dark glasses. He even had the same unusual glow at the base of his neck. To all effects, he looked identical to the man in the previous two pictures.

'So now he's 278,' blurted out Skye. 'And what does it mean, *leaving Earth*? In 2020 there was no colonisation of other planets, or space stations open to civilians.'

Julius was at a loss for what to say. Common sense told him that it was impossible for that man to be Eronan, but gut instinct told him otherwise. 'Freja will find it hard to believe.'

'Well, this is all we have,' said Faith. 'Send him the links and let him decide. We'll keep looking in the meantime.'

FINDING THE WAY

Push, Ruxshin. Come on!' grunted Khavar.

'I ... am ... pushing!'

The coffin was heavier than it looked, and carrying it from the snowy glade to the secret tunnel had taken over an hour. Thankfully, Mah Gira had been able to provide them with a long strip of sturdy leather to slip underneath it. Whenever they got stuck, they used it to lift the front of the box upwards and overcome the obstacle. The tunnel, however, was posing a different set of problems.

'Why can't this tunnel be straight?' moaned Ruxshin. 'I can't get past the last corner. I think we're stuck.'

Khavar looked around and assessed the situation. 'All right, go ahead and prepare a space in the house with Mah Gira. I'll take care of this.'

Ruxshin knew his friend enough to know that he would. She stepped over the coffin and headed towards the concealed entrance. A chest of drawers was blocking the access, so she knocked lightly against it. Soon after, hurried steps were heard coming her way, followed by the sound of someone loudly clearing their throat. 'It's us – open up,' she said.

Mah Gira started to push the chest to one side, helped by Ruxshin from within the tunnel.

'Where is it?' he asked her, worried.

'Khavar is handling it – the box is awkward to steer. Where will we put it?'

'Under my bed, I'd say.'

'Are you sure?'

'Young lady, at my age, death is always nearby anyway.'

She grinned at him. Then she heard a noise coming from the tunnel. 'Here he is. Watch out.'

They moved aside, leaving as much space as possible for Khavar to enter. Somehow, he had heaved the coffin onto his shoulders and walked with it for the last stretch. His face was red from the strain and big pearls of sweat wet his brow. He was carrying the leather strip between his teeth.

'This way,' said Mah Gira, grabbing the leather and showing him to his bedroom.

Ruxshin followed them inside and, once Khavar had placed the coffin down on the bed, she helped him lower it onto the floor, where Mah Gira had placed the leather like a rug.

'Dizzy,' muttered Khavar, sitting down heavily on the bed.

'Well done,' said the Supreme. Eagerly, he bent over the coffin to look at the girl inside, compassion on his face. 'What a pity to die so young.'

'We need to know what her message is about,' said Ruxshin. 'Do you think she's one of them?'

'Like Michael, yes. And *he* speaks the language of the Arneshians.'

'I must get hold of a translator then. I can do it this afternoon.'

'I'll do it,' said Khavar seriously. 'If they catch you … they already-'

'I'm the only one that can do it,' she interrupted. 'I work there.' She could see in his eyes that he was thinking about what K'Ssander had done to her – it was sweet of him to worry, but pointless.

Mah Gira patted Khavar on the shoulder. Although he was also concerned, she really was the only one that could enter the building in broad daylight without raising suspicion. 'Be careful,' he told her.

Ruxshin nodded. She kissed Mah Gira's hand and headed out.

*

Ruxshin pushed the door of her workplace open and walked inside. As foreseen, the guard by the entrance knew who she was and let her in without thinking twice. Her face betrayed no emotion but inside her heart was thumping hard. *Stay calm*, she thought.

The building was comprised of a corridor with four rooms, two on either side. Her team worked in the first one to the right, which was now empty, as her shift had ended at lunchtime, while the second team was always in the room opposite hers. She could see them right now sitting around a large table, compiling the dictionary, unaware of her presence. 'Good,' she whispered, moving along swiftly.

Her goal was to reach the second room on the left, where the translators were stored. Unfortunately, that meant having to pass in front of her supervisor A'Krad's room. The odds of him being away from his desk were zero, so she thought of a quick excuse, in case he saw her. Stepping as lightly as she could without looking conspicuous, she took the plunge and walked right to the end of the corridor, without looking back. Her trembling hand was stretching towards the touchpad that released the door lock, when a small cough made her jump and made all the hair on her body stand on end in panic.

'I didn't mean to scare you, Ruxshin,' said A'Krad, looking surprised. 'What are you doing back here?'

He was wearing the translator around his wrist, allowing this conversation to happen. Digging out her best smile, she shook her head affably. 'I'm sorry, I should have come to see you first. It's just that I forgot to close today's log at the end of the shift and I didn't want to disturb you.'

A'Krad held her gaze for a moment, before his face relaxed. 'But of course. Please continue.'

Ruxshin watched as he turned back towards his office, feeling a little faint after that sudden adrenaline rush. Taking a deep breath, she stepped inside the storage room and waited for the door to slide shut behind her. A few boxes were stacked against the walls, ready to be shipped out to the Arneshian troops. She knew this because she had prepared them herself, over the course of the last week. She accessed the terminal log and quickly removed one device from the stock, as if it had never been packaged. The transaction required her thumbprint identification in order to be authorised, so she went ahead and pressed her finger against the screen. 'There,' she whispered, satisfied. Opening the box nearest to her, she collected one translator wristband, or

Unilogus, as A'Krad had renamed them. It had taken the Arneshians over a year, but they had managed to transform the original box-shaped device into this slimmer, portable model. It worked much better than its prototype; the translation was indeed faster, but not quite simultaneous, much to T'Rogon's annoyance and Ruxshin's secret delight. Carefully, she closed the box and turned off the terminal, quickly exiting the storage. When she reached her supervisor's room, she stopped at the door. 'Thank you, A'Krad. See you tomorrow.'

'Goodbye, Ruxshin,' he replied from his desk.

Had Ruxshin not been in such a hurry to return to Mah Gira, she might have noticed the live feed monitors in A'Krad's room. Each of them showed one of the four rooms of that building, including the storage area. Unknown to her, A'Krad had watched her every move as soon as he had returned to his office. He couldn't understand why she would steal a Unilogus, but he was determined to find out, so he followed her cautiously.

*

> ... she moves towards the camera, her hands stretched forward as if to touch the lens. Behind her, the boy and the other girl begin to dance together. Morgana looks into the camera one last time, her eyes sparkling. 'I love you,' she whispers.
>
> Fade to black ...

Ruxshin's eyes were moist with tears and she wiped them lightly. The words of the girl called Morgana had made her heart ache. And what of her lover, Julius? Did he know she was dead? If he was the one who had put her in that coffin, why would he let her go, away from him?

'I don't think I understood half the things she said,' said Khavar, shaking his head. 'What's a *6MS*?'

Mah Gira leaned back in his chair, struggling to take in all the words he had just heard. 'I couldn't say, but her world is at war with the Arneshians too, that much is clear.'

'She said she was a pilot at Tijara school,' added Ruxshin. 'If they know how to fight against them, maybe her people can help us.'

'Even so, where do we find them, and how?' said Khavar. 'We can't exactly leave Mahin.'

Ruxshin, however, wasn't bothered by that. The message she had just watched had acted like a catalyst, strengthening her resolve to act against her captors 'This school, Tijara, is somewhere ... in one of these places she talked of – these systems and ways. We just need to find them!'

'I'll tell you what: why don't we make A'Krad take us there in one of their flying machines?'

Ruxshin gave him a look, as if to say, *I just might*. Carefully, she pushed her hand through the cocoon layer, reaching for Morgana's Strullium pendant.

'What are you doing?' asked Khavar, grabbing her wrist.

She looked at him, a serious expression on her face. 'If I don't, her story will be forgotten.'

Khavar threw a quick glance at Mah Gira, who just nodded, so he let her continue.

Ruxshin shivered when her fingers touched the girl's neck – her skin was cold as marble and there was no give when her knuckles pressed against it. Deftly, she unclasped the pendant and pulled it loose, trying not to mess her hair up. She gathered the delicate silver chain inside her cupped palm and put it away safely inside her coat. 'We need to go back to A'Krad,' she told the others. 'He'll know where these places are.'

Khavar looked thoughtful. 'How do we get him to talk?'

Suddenly, a shadow blocked the light from the open window, making them turn. An arm shot inside the room and pulled the curtain aside, revealing A'Krad's stern features.

Ruxshin yelped, while Khavar instinctively threw himself in front of her and Mah Gira. They were far too surprised to speak. The fact that the Arneshian had his palms opened towards them, charged and ready to fire, had also rooted them to the spot. Even without the Unilogus, they knew they were in big trouble.

'I'm curious,' said A'Krad, swinging a leg over the low window ledge to get inside, 'how did you plan to make me talk exactly?' He was now inside the small bedroom, readjusting his aim, while crackling energy sparked from the disks under his skin. He advanced slowly toward the coffin, motioning for the Mahin to move away. 'Back! Back!' he barked at them.

They scampered against the wall, which gave Ruxshin an opportunity to glance into the lounge. Thankfully, the chest of drawers was back in place. *The tunnel is safe*, she thought. That single moment of relief helped her to refocus on her current situation. There was no way they could allow A'Krad to report back or take the coffin. 'A'Krad …' she started, almost pleading. Her supervisor, however, hushed her unceremoniously, while his eyes never left the object on the floor. Ruxshin couldn't tell what he was thinking, but he looked as stunned as they had been when they had found the coffin.

'Zed … This is impossible,' he muttered. 'How did you …'

'So you *do* know of Tijara!' said Ruxshin.

A'Krad didn't reply, but kept staring at the girl in disbelief. His hesitation was not long-lived, but those few seconds turned out to be more than enough for him to lose the upper hand.

Khavar jumped forward, planting his right shoulder in the man's midriff, winding him. The momentum of his lunge carried them both over the bed and beyond it, where they tumbled onto the stone floor.

As this happened, Ruxshin shook herself from her daze and, grabbing Mah Gira's blanket, she threw it, with her on top, over the struggling men, hoping to hinder A'Krad somehow. Instead, the Arneshian fought back harder. An electric shock scorched through the blanket and struck the ceiling. The hot flux missed Ruxshin's head by an inch, but it still burned a patch of skin and hair away from her right temple. She screamed, but kept her weight over the wriggling mass below her, not caring about the kicks and elbows that her body was receiving. Out the corner of her eye, she saw Mah Gira running to close the window and the curtain, before he too joined the fight.

He grabbed the lamp from his bedside, which was made from an intricate – and heavy – block of Strullium. 'Uncover him!' he cried at her.

A'Krad shot out a hand from underneath the blanket, grabbed the Supreme's ankle and pulled, causing Mah Gira to fall hard on his back, while the lamp tumbled noisily to the floor. Then the Arneshian curled his hand into a fist and punched the twitching shape of Khavar under the cover. The Mahini man cried out in pain as the wrestling resumed.

The wound on Ruxshin's head was burning, making her wish for the cold snow outside. But there was no time to think about that, as Mah Gira was struggling back to his feet and reaching for the lamp. He held it high above his head and nodded to her. Ruxshin pulled the cover back, revealing A'Krad's head. 'Now!' she cried.

Mah Gira brought the lamp down, striking him on the side of the head, bringing the fight to an abrupt end.

Khavar was sweating heavily, and let his head rest between the Arneshian's neck and shoulder, overcome by fatigue.

'Are you okay, Mah Gira?' asked Ruxshin, temporarily forgetting her wound.

The old man placed the lamp back on the stand and sat down on his armchair, exhausted. He nodded though, reassuring her that he wasn't hurt.

Ruxshin climbed off the heap on the floor before helping Khavar to his feet.

'We need to tie him up,' he said. 'What can I use?'

'In the kitchen,' said Mah Gira. 'There are bindings under the sink. And bring a wet cloth for Ruxshin.'

Khavar disappeared into the room to the right, while Ruxshin moved over to the window to check outside. Thankfully, all was quiet in the street and no one seemed to have notice what had happened in the Supreme's home. She turned and looked at her unconscious supervisor. 'This is bad. When T'Rogon finds out, he'll be after you.'

'You needn't worry about me,' he replied. 'We wanted A'Krad's help and now we have it.'

She could tell that Mah Gira was worried just as much as she was. This unplanned fight had pushed them into a corner, with not many choices left. 'If he doesn't tell us where to go, he'll have to come with us.'

Khavar returned to the room just then, carrying a bundle of thick leather strips. He passed a wet sponge to Ruxshin, which she used to gently dab at her wound. He then turned A'Krad onto his back, grabbed his wrists, and positioned his palms together. 'Tie him while I hold him.'

Ruxshin nodded and proceeded to wrap the leather around his wrists, and all the way down to his fingers. It was a clever idea, she thought, realising that the man's weapons were now neutralised.

'If he tries to use them,' said Khavar, 'he'll fry his own hands first.'

Ruxshin used one last binding to gag him, before taking a step back. 'So, it turns out that this was the easy part.'

'You can't leave him behind,' said Mah Gira. 'He could lie about the location of Tijara, and you need a pilot.'

'But how do we get him out of here?' asked Khavar. 'The city is crawling with soldiers, and we would never make it past the lifts.'

'Use the tunnel then. You'll have to go behind and around the hill of the White Glade, but the trees and the snow will cover you until you reach the Arneshian aerodock.'

'We wait for darkness then,' said Khavar. 'In the meantime, we drag this scumbag back into the tunnel, where he can't call for help.'

They agreed that it was a good idea so, while Ruxshin helped Mah Gira free the tunnel entrance from the chest of drawers, Khavar scooped up A'Krad. The Arneshian was a big man and it wasn't easy to manoeuvre him out of the room – Ruxshin noticed his head banging against the wall one too many times to be just accidental, but found that she didn't really care.

Once in the tunnel, Khavar put him down, checked that his restraints were still holding, bound his feet and pulled one of Mah Gira's pillowcases over his head.

'There,' he said. 'Let's hide Morgana now.'

They discussed if it was sensible to leave the coffin under the bed, after what had just happened. In the end, they agreed to carry it back into the tunnel, where no one could find it, even if they searched the house.

An hour later, with the tunnel concealed once again, Mah Gira heated up a thick broth for them to eat and served it along with a generous handful of nuts.

'We can't take your rations,' said Khavar. 'Hand-out day is two sunrises away.'

'You're about to spend the night in the snow; you'll need this more than I do. Besides, if I'm really starving, I'll go to your house and take yours,' he replied.

Khavar chuckled. 'If you say so.'

A knock at the door made them all jump in their seats.

'Mah Gira, open the door.' There was no mistaking K'Ssander's voice.

Ruxshin's hand began to tremble, making her spoon rattle against the bowl. She had to put it down on the table, for fear it would give her away.

Mah Gira stood up. 'Be calm,' he told them quietly. 'We'll be all right.' He went to open the door, his head held high.

K'Ssander had brought three guards along, who were standing behind him and trying to peer suspiciously into the house.

'What is it?' asked the Supreme briskly.

K'Ssander looked at the old man with disdain, as if he were an insect. 'Where's the red-fur girl?'

'There's no one here by that name, young man. However, if you're looking for the Mahini's Chief Engineer, Ruxshin, then she is sitting in my house.'

The Arneshian didn't seem to enjoy being patronised by a slave, so he pushed the man aside and stepped inside. Ruxshin and Khavar were on their feet in an instant, and moved over to their leader protectively.

'Where is A'Krad?' asked the Arneshian.

'How should I know?' she replied.

K'Ssander stretched his hand forward and grabbed her by the front of her coat, moving her over to the opposite wall.

Khavar tried to stop this, but the guards immediately surrounded him.

'Where is he?' repeated K'Ssander.

'I don't know,' she answered, managing somehow to keep her voice steady.

'Why did you go back to his office this afternoon?'

Ruxshin could feel his eyes burning into her, trying to catch her out. 'I had forgotten something. He helped me with it, and then I left and returned here.'

'He followed you here; the guards saw him.'

'He never came here, I swear.'

'She's telling the truth,' said Khavar, trying to sound convincing. 'We came to visit our leader, and that was all. No one else was here.'

'You can search my *vast* dwelling, if it pleases you,' said Mah Gira. 'Although I doubt you'll find what you seek.'

K'Ssander motioned for his men to search the place, something they did pretty quickly, on account of the lack of hiding places.

Ruxshin was secretly thankful that they'd decided to move the coffin into the tunnel, and hoped that A'Krad was still out cold, and unable to hear their voices.

'Nothing, sir,' said one of the soldiers, returning to the front room.

K'Ssander paused for a moment, not looking pleased. 'Guards, take the *Supreme* away.'

'No!' cried Khavar and Ruxshin together, stepping forward.

'Stay where you are,' Mah Gira ordered. 'This is all a misunderstanding and I am sure the Ambassador will see that.'

Ruxshin was torn, but realised that he was right. If they reacted and were also taken, their chances of leaving Mah would disappear in an instant. She backed down.

'The quicker A'Krad returns,' said K'Ssander, looking at her, 'the quicker *he* gets out.'

They waited for the Arneshian to leave with Mah Gira, then locked the door.

'I hate him so much,' said Ruxshin, throwing herself onto the small couch. Just hearing his voice made her shake with anger, never mind having to talk to him. 'I have never met anyone so ... *broken* in my whole life.'

'We can't waste any more time,' said Khavar. 'We must leave now, before they come back.' He went to the chest and pushed it out of the way. 'Quickly now.'

Ruxshin fastened her coat and entered the tunnel, pleased to see that their prisoner was still unconscious. She turned back to the opening and helped Khavar drag the cabinet back into place, making absolutely sure there were no gaps. 'This is the best we can do from this side.'

'Yeah. Come on, let's see if this one is ready to walk.' He adjusted the rope around A'Krad's ankles, giving him enough slack so he could walk in small steps, then shook him by the shoulder, and heaved him up. The Arneshian began to regain consciousness and low muffled noises could be heard coming from under the hood. Khavar pulled it off.

Surprise mixed with fear was spread all over the supervisor's face. His eyes darted from Ruxshin to Khavar, to his surroundings, clearly unable to tell where he was. 'Mmph ...'

'I wouldn't bother,' Khavar told him coldly. He moved closer to A'Krad, pulling the meanest face he could muster. 'Let me tell you how it is: you're going to come on a night walk with us and you're going to behave. If you don't, I'll knock you out again, and drag you by your feet. We're going to board one of your ships so you can take us to Tijara. Understood?'

A'Krad tried to move back, and made a grunting noise in reply.

Khavar grabbed him by the collar and pressed his knuckles into his neck, deep enough to stop him breathing. '*Understood?*'

The man was visibly struggling for air and had no choice but to give in. He nodded his head vigorously.

Satisfied, Khavar let go and pulled the hood back down. 'Grab his other arm,' he said to Ruxshin.

Slowly, they walked out into the open, careful that their prisoner wouldn't trip and fall. With the cold night air enveloping them and thick snow crunching under their boots, A'Krad hesitated, but the Mahini pulled him forward.

'Lift your feet!' Ruxshin ordered.

Khavar took charge of steering. Being an experienced hunter, he knew the land better than most. He followed the path in the direction of the White Glade and, after ten minutes or so, he veered to the left, up a smaller trail that was sheltered by snow-laden shrubs.

An hour passed and the night grew darker. A series of small tremors accompanied the group on their trail. It was unusual to have more than one in any given hour, let alone several. At one point, the ground shook hard enough to halt them in their tracks.

'You wouldn't know anything about this now, would you, Arneshian?' asked Khavar.

'Our leader is restless,' he said.

'Who are you talking about?'

'*She* knows him – the same one who had the great idea to give you that hair trim.'

Khavar hit him on the side of the head. 'Watch your mouth, *ferech*.'

Ruxshin stepped forward, stunned. 'Michael? *Leader*?'

'Surprising, isn't it? He may be young, but oh so powerful. You'll all see. They're testing his latest creation tonight.'

Ruxshin looked at Khavar, perplexed. Whatever could he mean? A boy like him, with untold powers, could only spell trouble for Mah. Uneasy, she motioned for Khavar to keep moving, eager more than ever to reach their destination.

When they reached the hill summit, Ruxshin stopped to catch her breath. She glanced towards the lights stretching out on the plane below her, and looked at her city. The round elevator shafts appeared like bright eyes opening onto the surface of Mah, revealing the powerful reflectors that had been installed underground by the Arneshians. There were people working in the mines day and night, and they would continue to do so until all the Strullium had been removed from their land. Spiralling columns of smoke wafted upwards from the Mahini dwellings, glowing now in the surrounding lights. *I wonder if my fireplace has been lit yet*, she thought, feeling a little melancholy. The soldiers staying in her home were used to that small comfort and soon they would be wondering why there were no logs burning brightly, and where on Mah their "maid" had gone. That worried her. 'We need to hurry before they realise we've left.'

Khavar must have noticed the edge to her voice, or at any rate shared her fear, because he nodded right away. 'This way,' he said, grabbing A'Krad by the elbow and leading the group down a new path. 'The trail will lead us past the ruins of Greenhouse 4.'

'What about guards?' asked Ruxshin, walking carefully but briskly on the other side of A'Krad.

'Not so many at this time.'

Ruxshin didn't look too convinced.

'Look,' said Khavar, 'there will be guards every way we go. Other paths would take us too far away from the aerodock. It makes sense.'

'I know,' she said. 'It's just that …'

Khavar stretched his arm behind A'Krad and over her shoulders. 'We'll make it,' he said reassuringly.

They walked for most of the night, struggling to find sure footing in the soft snow. The gentle fall of flakes turned into a storm on a couple of occasions, forcing them to seek shelter; once by a group of trees and the second time at the base of a long, low rock formation. They huddled against each other, all three facing inwards and downwards, to keep the swirling flurry at bay. Ruxshin and Khavar had to press against the pillowcase over A'Krad's head to keep it in place – given the situation, the Arneshian didn't complain about their proximity, probably welcoming the short-lived cosiness it created. Despite the brighter white clouds in the sky, the night had grown increasingly dark, hiding both path and obstacle. They couldn't risk carrying torches for fear of being spotted by patrols, so they endured the struggle as best they could, pushing and pulling their prisoner along.

Ruxshin's stomach was beginning to grumble but, in the hurry to leave Mah Gira's home, they had packed no extra food. 'How long?' she asked, shouting over the wind.

Khavar stopped to get his bearings. 'Once we get to the bottom of the hill, it will be about half an hour to GH4. From there, maybe ten or twenty minutes more to the aerodock.'

'Will we make it before sunrise?'

'We have to.'

Ruxshin sighed and started walking again, ignoring the fact that she could barely feel her legs. Fur or not, the icy cold night had no mercy to dish out.

*

The prison block was tucked away in a corner of the underground. It had been hastily built by the Arneshians using the local resources. To K'Ssander, anything involving wood and mechanical locks should have been kept inside a museum, but they hadn't had any choice. Glumly, he headed to the holding cell where Mah Gira was being kept. He hooked the fingers of his left hand over the lower ledge of the little window that was cut into the door's surface and began to tap his fingers lightly on the wood. For some reason, he couldn't sleep and he didn't know why. Uneasy, he peered inside the room.

Mah Gira had spent the night locked in the small cell in the company of a high-backed chair, a cup of water and a bowl of reconstituted food. He had complained at first, and even asked to speak to T'Rogon. Then he had drifted off with his chin resting on his chest, and was now snoozing peacefully, emitting a low snoring.

In K'Ssander's mind, the man looked far too frail to act as a leader for these people, though he did have charisma – he had to grant him that. The way the Mahini worshipped him, bowed, and even kissed his hand, was an unmistakable sign of respect. The temptation to get rid of him was strong, but the Ambassador had forbidden anyone to harm him. And he was right. The murder of the Supreme would surely cause an insurrection; even if the Arneshians out-powered them and could squash them all in an instant, it would gain them nothing. No Mahini meant no miners and no knowledge of the subterranean tunnels – it would slow their operation down and they had no time to lose. Zed was still a problem that needed resolving and the Arneshians required Strullium to deliver the final blow. If this wasn't enough, there was the matter of A'Krad's disappearance to deal with. K'Ssander had better things to do than play detective or babysit geriatric citizens, but T'Rogon had insisted, so he adjusted the Unilogus on his wrist and switched it on – it was time to wake the old man up.

He unlocked the door with a long iron key and stepped inside. There was a spare chair in the room and he dragged it noisily to in front of the prisoner, meaning to wake him up; it worked. Mah Gira looked startled and it seemed to K'Ssander that, for a second there, he hadn't been too sure where he was. 'You're not telling me the truth, Supreme,' he began, hoping to catch him off guard.

Mah Gira regarded him with a puzzled expression, then brought his finger to his right ear, tapped it and shook his head.

'Have you gone deaf now?'

The old man pointed at his empty wrist and said, 'Unilogus.'

K'Ssander understood the word, but wondered what he meant by it. 'He lifted his own wrist, showing the bracelet. 'You don't need one - I have mine.'

Mah Gira shook his head again.

'Great,' muttered K'Ssander. His Unilogus must have stopped working. Frustrated, he stormed out, slamming the cell door behind him. He barged into the technician's office, making the brown-haired Arneshian jump out of his skin. 'It's broken,' K'Ssander growled at him, taking the band off his wrist and throwing it into the man's lap. 'Fix it.'

'Yes, sir. Right away,' he replied quickly. He took a hand-held tool and began to scan the device. He tinkered with it for a few more minutes, opening panels and tightening dials, before returning it. 'I can't fix it. I'm sorry,' said the man, positively worried about having to disappoint his superior. 'It's missing a part.'

'Well, where did the part go?'

'It was never there. A mistake in the assembly line probably.'

'Excuses! It worked just fine today.'

'It ... it couldn't have; this Unilogus was never activated.'

It was K'Ssander's turn to look confused. He stood there, speechless, feeling a sense of unease resurfacing slowly, but surely. That very afternoon, he had talked to three Mahini using this very wristband. His men hadn't been wearing one – of that he was sure. Then it dawned on him, and the surprise in his eyes was replaced by a cold realisation: the only way to explain the conversation was if one of them had been wearing a Unilogus too, a thing which was strictly forbidden for any furcoats. As he turned on his heels and stormed out of the room and into the corridor, he knew beyond doubt that Ruxshin had been the one wearing the band – that had to be why she had returned to work and why A'Krad had followed her back to the underground. When he passed Mah Gira's holding cell, he stopped briefly and leaned inside. The Supreme must have felt the change in him, because he shrank in his seat. 'I'll get you for this,' he said coldly. 'Ruxshin better be home and have some answers, or I'll do far worse than just give her a *shave*.'

*

'This is worse than I thought,' said Khavar, peeking over the edge of a large metal crate. He pointed at two groups of guards, stationed at either side of a small transporter.

Ruxshin nibbled her lower lip anxiously and nudged A'Krad. 'Why is there only one ship?'

Her former supervisor shook his head and remained silent.

She scowled at him. 'There's no way we can get aboard that ship unseen.'

'We need a diversion,' said Khavar. 'Something to-'

A blaring siren broke the still of the night, making all three of them jump.

'What's happening?' cried Ruxshin over the noise.

In reply, Khavar grabbed A'Krad's forearm in a tighter grip, readying him to sprint. 'I don't know, but it's the diversion we were looking for. Come on.'

Ruxshin held the Arneshian's free arm and followed, keeping herself low enough to hide behind the odd crate. The soldiers had moved forward as one, and they were now huddled around a newcomer. She squinted her eyes, trying to work out who it was through the falling snowflakes, and when she did, she gasped out loud. 'It's K'Ssander! Khavar, he knows!'

'We can't go back now. This way!'

Ruxshin's heart skipped a beat but she kept moving along the shadowed perimeter. Under their leader's orders, the soldiers were spreading out in different directions, but still two of them remained on the landing pad. K'Ssander wasn't far from them, and was carefully searching the aerodock. She heard him bark something, a single word, and four powerful spotlights flooded the pad as if it was broad daylight.

'Get down!' ordered Khavar, crouching suddenly and dragging the others down with him. When A'Krad made a noise, trying to communicate, he quickly removed the gag. 'What?'

'You won't make it,' said A'Krad, gloating.

'Shut up, or I'll *make* you.'

Ruxshin could see the shuttle clearly, only a hundred feet or so away. Its hatch was yawning open invitingly, but just out of reach.

'Listen carefully,' whispered Khavar. 'I'll backtrack, as far away as possible from the shuttle. From there I can distract the guards while you two get on board.'

'No way,' replied Ruxshin. 'Too risky. You'll never make it in time.'

Khavar grabbed one of her hands. 'If I don't, no one will get on that transporter and you know that. You and A'Krad must leave now and look for help, or we're all lost.'

Ruxshin felt her throat closing and tears welling in her eyes. What if they caught him? K'Ssander would kill him without hesitation. Still, how much more pain could her people endure before the Arneshians crushed their spirits?

'If he's here,' continued Khavar, trying to reason with her, 'it means that he knows something and that Mah Gira is in danger. Very soon everyone else will be too. Go and bring back help. Zed is the only hope we have.' He squeezed her hand. 'Look at me - you can do this.'

Ruxshin saw the urgency in his eyes and felt the last of her objections crumble. 'Promise you'll be here when I return.'

Khavar smiled. 'I will.'

She let go of his hand and watched him sneak back the way they had come. Soon the snow hid him from view, as if he had never existed. Ruxshin readied herself and A'Krad to sprint towards the shuttle.

'You'll fail,' he told her coldly.

'Shut up!'

'K'Ssander will kill your friend and your leader. As for you-'

'Shut up!' she growled in his face, her hatred resurfacing, fuelled by the memory of her humiliation at their hands.

'You don't even know how to pilot that ship, let alone make it to the wormhole.'

Ruxshin bit her lip, storing the word "*wormhole*" in the back of her head. It would surely help her later. A'Krad had kept quiet throughout the night, obviously waiting to be alone with her to rattle her cage. She wouldn't let him, however. It was true that she had never piloted a spaceship before, but she still knew a thing or two about engines. Besides, she had learned a very useful word when working on the dictionary. She looked at the man assuredly. 'Autopilot.'

A'Krad flinched at that.

'You thought I'd forgotten, didn't you?' she mocked. 'Your ship will take me to Zed, whether you help or not.'

Just then, Khavar's cry echoed in the darkness: 'Over here, you naked *ferechs*!'

Immediately, a flood of electric discharges shot out from the guards.

'Get them!' shouted K'Ssander, charging in the direction of the voice.

Ruxshin knew this was her moment. As soon as the guards left their post, she leapt up and ran onto the pad, dragging her prisoner behind her. She could tell he was purposely slowing her down. 'Move!' she yelled, yanking him forward by his arm. There were still sixty feet to go to the shuttle but, at their speed, the distance seemed greater. Then A'Krad stumbled and fell flat on his face. Ruxshin was pulled to the ground, and her shin banged against his bent knee. Pain shot up her leg and she had to stifle a cry for fear of being heard. 'Get up!' she ordered, struggling to get back to her feet.

'Make me,' shouted A'Krad cruelly.

'Be quiet! Up!' she hissed, fearing that someone would hear them. 'I said UP!' He wasn't budging though. In fact, he had relaxed his body completely, and become almost impossible to shift. She was now a sitting duck beneath the spotlights.

Two guards materialised right behind them, at the edge of the pool of light. 'STOP!' they cried.

Frantic with terror, Ruxshin saw one of the men start running towards her, while the other bellowed their position to the whole landing area. Time was up. She looked at the useless Arneshian on the ground, then at the open hatch of the shuttle. She had no choice. 'I can do this,' she said, letting go of A'Krad's arm. Just then, K'Ssander appeared in her field of vision.

'Grab A'Krad,' he told his men. '*She's* mine!'

Ruxshin hesitated for only a couple of seconds, then turned and ran, adrenaline pumping through her veins. A couple of lightning strikes zipped past her, and fizzed into the snow ahead of her. A third one grazed the outside of her left thigh; searing pain spread across her skin. There was no time to check how bad it was but, since she was still able to run, she ignored it. Thirty feet now … Twenty. A flurry of electric fire charged the air all around her, charring the outer layer of her winter suit. Snow sprayed up to either side of her. Ten feet … a bolt whizzed right between her legs, striking the ground in a blinding flash. The hatch was close now and Ruxshin readied herself to jump. A few steps from it, she leapt forward and landed nimbly inside. She whirled and saw K'Ssander advancing, his palm open, pointed at the shuttle. Catching her breath, she ordered, 'Autopilot, engaged.'

The shuttle came to life, its panels lighting up all at once.

'Lock the door!' she cried, still amazed that it had worked.

The hatch began to close, all too slowly.

She flattened herself against the back wall, hypnotised by the sight of the Arneshian running at her and the outer light decreasing as the gap diminished. K'Ssander fired a shot through the opening. Ruxshin jolted to the side, a second too late. The bolt sunk into her left calf. She cried out in pain and fell to the floor, clutching her wound.

'Door locked,' said the on-board computer calmly. 'State your destination.'

A mighty thump on the side of the shuttle made her scream again. She was so scared that she even managed to climb back to her feet and move painfully over to the pilot chair, ignoring her injuries.

'Open the hatch!' growled K'Ssander, banging against the metal. 'I'll kill you. I swear I'll kill you for this!'

Terrified, Ruxshin stared out the windscreen and saw a handful of soldiers converging on the ship. Time was running out. 'Computer,' she said, steadying her voice as best she could, 'take me to Zed!'

'Location not found,' replied the machine.

Ruxshin panicked. What else had Morgana said? Her focus was all over the place, especially now that drilling noises had replaced the pounding on the outer hull – they were breaking in. 'Think,' she told herself, trying to recall the recording. After mentioning Zed, the girl had talked about a system. She couldn't begin to guess where it was, but given that the coffin had made it to her planet, it would surely have to be close enough. 'What is the nearest system to Mah?' she asked, changing tactics.

'The Solar System, in the Milky Way Galaxy.'

'That's the one!' she cried, recognising the name. 'Go! Now!'

'Calculating route. Please fasten your seatbelt.'

Ruxshin did just that, before clutching the armrests of her seat and taking a deep breath. Even if the destination was wrong, she needed to get out of here before they breached the hull. Just as the shuttle began to lift-off, K'Ssander appeared on the ground in front of her and looked up. There was so much hatred in his eyes that she recoiled in her seat. Then a soldier came into view and held up a light fur coat for her to see. It was Khavar's snow jacket. Ruxshin's heart sank. As tears gathered in her eyes, the front of the shuttle began to lift, pushed upwards from beneath. She felt the engine burst into life and a pressure growing in her chest, as gravity pinned her back against the seat. She closed her eyes and hoped with all her might that Khavar hadn't been killed.

The ascent seemed to last an unbearably long time. She was scared to bits about being inside a flying machine, piloted by a computer and heading for an unknown destination. She didn't know the first thing about space, or how she would survive if she ended up on another planet. But what choice did she have? She was lost in these thoughts when the shuttle was struck by something and tilted to the right. 'What's happening?'

The computer replied as if all was normal. 'The craft is under attack. Do you wish to halt and negotiate?'

'Wha- No! Don't you dare!'

'Understood. Maintaining course. Wormhole locked on ideal trajectory.'

That word: *wormhole* … A'Krad had told her about it – whatever it was. 'I'm on the right course,' she said, allowing herself to hope. Another wave rocked the craft. 'Can't we go faster?'

'Affirmative.'

'Well?' she pressed, seeing as there was no change in speed.

'Do you wish to go faster?'

'Yes! I damn well wish to go FASTER!'

'Velocity increasing.'

'And while we're at it, see if you can lose them!'

'Affirmative.'

Honestly, thought Ruxshin. *Who created these machines?* Still, she counted her blessings for, without this autopilot, her race wouldn't have even started. She saw a handlebar attached to the panel in front of her and guessed that it was the steering mechanism for the real pilot. It was jerking in all directions, and she was thankful that someone else was doing the driving. Unable to do anything else except panic, she clutched the armrests, stiffening her body during the sharp bends they were making, to avoid whiplash.

'Wormhole proximity increasing. Entry on ten … nine … eight …'

'Here goes nothing,' she said, not knowing what to expect. Her eyes were fixed on something that looked like a giant orb, slowly filling the screen of the shuttle. Its surface shifted, as if it wasn't really part of the space surrounding it. *Will it hurt?* she thought suddenly. For the second time, she closed her eyes and hoped for the best.

THE WORMHOLE

'Coochy coochy coo! Who's me favourite snuggle bunny?' cooed Faith, holding Elian's baby girl carefully. His index finger wiggled over her perfect little button nose, making her giggle.

'Faith, you're a splendid babysitter,' said Elian, watching them in delight.

'With such an angel, who wouldn't be?' he replied, not taking his eyes off her. 'Isn't that right, little Savannah? Coochy-coochy-coo!'

Julius grinned, surprised at Faith's paternal instincts. He had been lulling Kelly's baby for almost an hour without showing any sign of tiredness, and it seemed that her mum was also appreciating this unplanned moment of rest – she looked tired out from a recent spate of sleepless nights. The rhythmic bouncing of a ball brought his attention back to the basketball match underway in the Ahura Mazda's rec-bay, where Kelly and Skye were taking on a couple of officers from engineering. Julius watched as Kelly leapt into the air before slam-dunking the ball in the basket.

'Show them who's the daddy, babe!' hollered Elian, clapping for her husband.

Kelly bowed to her before giving a high five to Skye. 'And that, my friends,' he said to the other team, 'is the end of the game.'

'Well played, Captain,' said the officers, before saluting quickly and leaving.

Kelly moved towards the large steps around the field, drying his face with the bottom of his t-shirt. He caressed his daughter's cheek with the back of his finger, before going to sit by his wife.

Skye, who was a bit red from all the exercise, plonked himself down next to Julius. 'I haven't run like that in a while,' he said, panting.

'Glad to see you still can,' said Julius.

'Very funny,' he replied, nudging him.

Julius stretched out on the step, resting forward on his elbows and forearms. He could feel the vibration of the ship through the palms of his hands and body. He loved the soothing sensation of it. As a matter of fact, being on the Mazda was always a sure way to rid him of the blues, at least in part, and he was glad that Freja had sent his son to fetch them from the Halls. They had explored the archives as much as possible and there was really nothing left to do.

'Now, Savannah,' said Faith, propping the baby in front of a window, 'see that marvellous place over there that looks like a daisy?'

Savannah cooed with delight.

'That, me lovely, is Pit-Stop Pete, your uncle Faith's true home.'

Elian looked at Julius sideways and chuckled, while Kelly and Skye shook their heads.

'And see that absolute marvel – not you this time – parked right underneath it? That is me own baby. Isn't she gorgeous?'

Savannah giggled, patting the reinforced glass with her tiny hand.

'And what's your baby's name, Faith?' asked Elian.

Faith looked immediately at Julius. Although it was supposed to have been his birthday present to name Faith's first ship, they had decided to go with Morgana's choice in the end. '*Tranquillity*,' he said, proudly.

Kelly went to stand by him and looked at it. 'She truly is a beauty, Faith. If ever the Mazda decides to pack up on me, I know what model I'd want next.'

'Really?' he said, visibly touched.

'Yeah,' he said. '*Tranquillity* … it's a good name. Though, I'd feel more tranquil if we found that bloody wormhole. We scouted everywhere around Earth and all available charts, but nothing. And what you guys found, those pictures with Eronan, don't make things any clearer.'

Julius nodded. If anything, tracing the alien back to 2020 had only made things worse. How was it even possible? Then he thought about another impossible find. 'Hey, what's the story with the Mahin Space Enterprise? I mean, those people didn't really leave Earth, did they?'

'That picture you recovered,' said Elian, 'it really surprised me. The MSE has been a regular ghost story of the fleet for almost 900 years.'

'Ghost story?' asked Skye.

'Space colonisation didn't really begin until Marcus Tijara's time, around 2600,' explained Kelly. 'In the 21st Century, Earth had the International Space Station up and running, plus several probe missions with the use of robots, but no space travel as we know it. A lot of private companies began to experiment with space tourism and, for a while, people did think that it would work, but it didn't. Earth was overridden by economic crisis, global warming, conflicts and epidemics and, in the end, the governments decided to reroute the funds into the betterment of the planet – which didn't really work for a long time, but that's another story. Then, one day, this newspaper article appears, saying that a group of willing humans, led by Captain Gorghinian, is all packed up and ready to leave Earth.'

'People thought it was a hoax,' continued Elian, 'or the latest bunch of space crazies, ready to follow the whims of some unknown rich corporation – and it had to be filthy rich to have anything that could take people up when the governmental agencies couldn't.'

'Who were these folks who left?' asked Skye.

'Mostly they were fans of a TV series about space exploration: "Mahini 2.5". Apparently it was very famous back then.'

'Oh yes, I forgot about that,' added Kelly. 'They loved the show so much that they'd learned to speak one of its made-up languages as well. Anyhow, their shuttle was filmed taking off from Earth without a hitch, but thirty minutes into the flight they lost all contact.'

'What do you mean?' asked Julius who, like Skye, was now sitting up, captivated by the story.

Elian shrugged her shoulders, looking pensive. 'They just vanished. Off all radars. Either their shuttle crashed back into the ocean – which is why it was never found – or they actually left.'

'I'd like to think they made it,' said Faith in a hushed tone.

Elian stood up and walked over to him. Savannah was sleeping peacefully in her soft white blanket. 'Good job,' she whispered. 'I'll take her to our room now and see if I can squeeze a nap in there too.'

Faith handed the girl to her mother, looking pleased with his effort.

'What do you think, Captain?' asked Julius.

'I used to believe they just crashed, but since you found that picture with Eronan in it, I'm a bit iffy. And if he's the same guy from Tijara's time, then we have a bigger problem than-'

'Bridge to Kelly,' a voice said over the ship's computer.

Savannah woke with a start and began to cry.

'Damn it,' said Elian, hurrying out of the bay.

The captain touched the com-link on his chest. 'Go ahead, Lieutenant Steele.'

'We've detected a strange anomaly a few light years from here, sir. It's expanding.'

'On my way,' said Kelly, standing quickly. 'Come along.'

Julius and the others followed him, exchanging puzzled glances among themselves.

Kelly entered the bridge and went straight to his pilot, a fragile looking individual, who was analysing the steady flow of data. 'What is it, Lieutenant?'

'I think we've just found the wormhole.'

A wave of excitement washed over Julius.

'Can you give us a visual?'

Lieutenant Steele did so and, as the orb appeared in its fullness, the entire bridge was stunned.

Julius had travelled through a wormhole before so he recognised its shape immediately. 'How could we have missed it?'

'Send a message to Freja immediately,' ordered Kelly. 'We'll go take a closer look.'

'Captain, there's something else in there.'

Kelly turned back to Steele's screen, trying to interpret the readings. 'It can't be.'

'What is it?' asked Skye, still staring at the wormhole.

'There's a ship coming out of it.'

'Make that four, Captain,' added his lieutenant.

Kelly ran towards his chair, ordering a tactical alert. Immediately, the main lighting system dimmed while the power was rerouted to more important parts of the ship. 'Action stations on the double. Faith, go to engineering. Julius and Skye, lower war-deck.'

'Yes, sir,' replied Julius, sprinting out of the room. He knew the path to the war-deck as if it were his own home, as did Skye. A few minutes later they reached their post and took position at two free catalysts, surrounded by the ship's veteran fighters. Like all war-decks, its walls and ceiling could turn transparent, showing the outer space beyond, overlaid by a grid with important information. Julius had never fought from the lower deck, but he knew that it was the floor that disappeared there, something not all fighters could stomach. He grabbed the handles of the catalyst and prepared his mind to call upon the energy needed to fire it.

An eerie silence fell among the soldiers as they waited to hear from the bridge. Shortly after, Steele's voice began to report. 'Four crafts confirmed. The first will enter visual contact in 30 seconds.'

'Fighters on standby,' said Kelly.

'Ready, Captain.'

The reply was from a rough looking man, a couple of catalysts to the left of Julius.

He knew him as Lieutenant Velasquez, a veteran fighter with many years of experience. On his chest was the Cougar emblem, which was the symbol of pilots and fighters.

'Here they come,' said Steele.

Everyone stared at the screen, holding their breath.

'It's an Arneshian craft!'

'Lock on target,' ordered Kelly. 'Steele, scan for bio-signs.'

'There's one, sir; a bio-signature.'

'At least they haven't sent holograms this time,' said Skye.

Julius nodded, and then spotted three more crafts emerging from the wormhole, all Arneshian. To their surprise, the latecomers opened fire on the first ship. 'They're not here for us, Captain,' cried Julius. 'They're chasing that shuttle!'

'Affirmative,' confirmed Steele. 'And all bio-signatures are human, sir.'

'All right,' said Kelly, 'let's save number one. Any enemy of the Arneshians is a friend of mine. Disable the other's engines. If they shoot back, blow them out of the sky. Steele, get us closer. I want the lower war-deck crew on that first ship to beam her in.'

Julius locked onto the craft that was furthest away, knowing that only his range was broad enough to reach it. Using the overlay grid, he identified its engine, drew on his powers, and waited to get a clear shot before unleashing on the target. 'Just a little closer,' he muttered, following the ship with the catalyst. 'Now.' A yellow beam hurtled out of the cannon and crashed into its target. The ship slowed and turned its weapons on the Mazda.

'Now you've done it,' said Velasquez. 'Fire at will,' he ordered.

Julius let loose. It was a brief battle. The three crafts were no match for the Mazda and, within a few minutes, they had been destroyed.

The first ship was the only one left standing now, and was soon enveloped inside the protective yellow cocoon of the Mazda's tractor beam. It was drawn towards them, before disappearing from view below the hull.

'Velasquez,' said Kelly, 'take your team to Bay 2.'

'Aye, sir. Let's move, people.'

Julius and Skye followed them, curious to find out who was piloting the shuttle and why the Arneshians had been in pursuit. When they reached the bay, Kelly was already there, pointing his Gauntlet at the shuttle hatch. He signalled for the fighters to do likewise, so Julius readied his weapon.

Faith was stationed behind a console, his fingers lightly tapping at a control panel; a secondary energy field sprung to life around the craft. 'Ready, Captain,' he told Kelly.

'Release the hatch.'

Slowly, the door began to open, revealing a crouched figure, with both arms over its head in a protective gesture, clutching something in one hand that looked like a metal band.

Julius shifted to the side, trying to get a better view. Whoever they were, they were shaking uncontrollably. The thick coat they were wearing had burnt patches in several places, which he recognised immediately as ones that must have been made by an Arneshian's palm-weapon. The pilot was sporting a larger wounded area along their left leg, which would need to be tended to by a doctor.

Kelly moved forward cautiously. 'Who are you?' he asked, not unkindly.

The figure made a little noise, and lowered its arms, bringing the metal strip to face-height. 'Help me …' It was a woman's voice. She slowly raised her head, revealing herself to her rescuers. Loose strands of red hair escaped from under the hood of her coat, framing bright green eyes. She tried to stand, propping herself against the shuttle for balance. 'Julius McCoy …' she said, speaking through the strange metal band; they all saw her lips moving, but the words were quite clearly coming from it – her own words were unintelligible.

Julius stepped forward hesitantly. When she spotted him, it seemed as if a shadow had slipped from her features. Mustering her strength, she spoke again: 'She says you have a fleet. She says you can save us …'

'Who told you that?' he asked.

'The girl in the box…' That was all she could manage, before fainting.

Kelly jolted forward, and caught her just in time. 'Velasquez, alert sickbay and get engineering to analyse this shuttle. Faith, get that language gizmo and check it out. Julius, follow us.'

Julius was completely baffled and couldn't understand how she knew his name. As he hurried alongside Kelly, with Skye in tow, he looked at the girl lying in the captain's arms, trying to remember if he had seen her before, but to no avail. At the same time, a painful thought occurred to him: he hadn't been to the sickbay since the day Morgana had died, and that was exactly where he was heading now. He was struck by a horrible sense of déjà vu just then, but forced his mind away from it.

'Was she talking about Farrah?' asked Skye.

While it was true that Farrah had been kept contained inside a glass tank, it just didn't add up that this was who the strange newcomer had been referring to. On the other hand, how many "girls-in-a-box" did Julius know? 'I don't think so. I mean, why wouldn't Farrah have told us there was someone looking for us … for *me*?'

'We'll just have to ask *her* then,' he answered.

When they reached sickbay, the boys stood to the side, allowing Kelly to enter first.

Doctor Bato was the Mazda physician, a jovial middle-aged woman, of Filipino descent. 'What do we have here, Captain?' she enquired, motioning for the girl to be placed on the medical bed.

'She just fainted,' he replied, shaking his head. 'I'm not sure about the rest.'

Bato examined the wounded leg immediately, but didn't seem too worried. 'Leave her with me.' She gently pulled back the injured newcomer's hood and, as she did so, it revealed her unusual hairline.

Kelly shifted the coat away from her neck, marvelling at how it grew all the way down the back of her head and down between her shoulders.

Julius, who had stepped forward to take a closer look, gasped at the familiar sight. 'The statue of the Archer …' he said, trailing off.

'The one on Eneamar?' asked Skye.

'Yes.'

Kelly nodded as well. He had been told about the hypnotherapy session. 'Can you check her DNA, Doc?'

Bato took a device against the skin of her neck and pressed a button. For a few seconds it analysed the result, while the room went completely quiet. She raised an eyebrow. 'It's human.'

'Are you sure?' asked Kelly.

'Positive. There are some minor modifications to her genetic structure – possibly accounting for the fur – but other than that, she's as human as us.'

'Check for mind-skills too.'

'I will, Captain. Give me an hour.'

Satisfied, Kelly led Julius and Skye out of sickbay and back to the bridge.

When they got there, Elian was leaning against the Captain's chair, deep in conversation with Faith.

'Any news?' asked Julius, upon entering the room.

'The shuttle is definitely Arneshian,' replied Faith, 'and this device is a translator.'

'From what language?'

'None we've heard before. Sounds harsh though, guttural.'

'Did the Arneshians make it?' asked Kelly.

'Oh yes. It's got their tech-magic written all over it. I want to take it apart to study it, but I figured you might want to use it with our guest first.'

Elian looked at her husband worriedly. 'How's the girl, JD?'

'Bato is taking care of her now. She's human, apparently.'

Faith's eyebrows shot up in surprise. 'Did I miss something during Spaceology classes? Whenever did we colonise space, pre-Tijara?'

'You were never awake in Brown's class,' replied Julius. 'But it still doesn't make any sense. She has fur like the Archer – how can she be human?'

'Fur?' said Faith. 'Then, couldn't she be from Mah?'

'What makes you say that?' asked Kelly.

'The Archer is in Eneamar, but the people of that city, as Julius told us already, look nothing like fur-covered folks – they're more like Eronan, you know?'

Skye nodded in agreement. 'I think you're right. The statue points to Mah and maybe that's where she's from too.'

Julius seemed troubled. 'How do you explain the DNA then?'

'Don't forget the people of Buruwang,' said Elian. 'We didn't know about them, but they exist – humans on another planet.'

She was right, of course, but to Julius the thought created more questions than answers. 'Aye, but this is getting ridiculous. I mean, have we been leaking humans left, right, and centre for the last few centuries without knowing?'

'It certainly looks like it,' said Kelly. 'What bothers me though is that those Arneshian crafts have come out of the wormhole we were looking for. Since she was inside one of *their* shuttles, it is likely that they've landed on her planet. And if it is Mah, then T'Rogon has beaten us to it.'

'Is this why she wants our help?'

'You can bet your fancy Draw it is.'

Julius was uneasy and, like everyone else, he could do nothing more but wait for Bato to end her examination. Kelly and Skye took the opportunity to go for a quick shower, while Elian returned to her quarters to check on Savannah. Julius followed Faith to the sickbay's waiting room and watched him play with the translator, listening in fascination to the new sounds it made when a word was spoken into it. Mercifully, the wait came to an end and, upon the others re-joining them, Doctor Bato came out to meet them.

'How is she?' asked Kelly.

'Recovering. Her leg wound wasn't serious – it will mend in a few days. The hypothermia will require my attention overnight – she almost froze to death. Captain, I know you need to talk to her, but I cannot give you more than five minutes – and I mean it.'

'It will do for now. Thanks, Doc.'

Bato ushered them back in, halting by a glass divider. 'Only the captain can go in. You will be able to see and hear quite well from here.'

Disappointed, Julius followed the others while Kelly stepped inside the room, holding the translator in his hand. He watched as the doctor moved a curtain aside, revealing the girl as she lay on the bed. Her thick coat had been removed, while a thermal blanket covered her entire body, up to her collarbones. He could see that she was wearing a green sickbay camisole. Her red hair jutted out to either side of the pillow in uneven lengths, as if someone had attempted a haircut with an axe. He wondered how old she was and how scared she must have been when the Arneshians were chasing her through the wormhole. It was a miracle that she had made it out of there alive.

The doctor walked to the top of the bed, while the captain stood by the right side of the girl, facing the glass. Bato injected something into her neck and, within a matter of seconds, she opened her eyes and stared directly at Kelly. The sight must have startled her, because she began to thrash in the bed, kicking at her blanket, clearly frightened. Immediately, Kelly placed his hands over her legs, to avoid being hit. Bato was quickly by her side, hands pressed down on her shoulders. 'Everything is fine; hush. You are safe and among friends.'

The captain made sure the device was close enough to translate their words, so as to reassure her. It seemed to work, because the girl stopped kicking.

'Hi, sweetheart,' continued Bato, full of motherly concern. 'We need to talk to you briefly, and then we'll let you sleep again. Is that okay?'

The girl looked at her suspiciously at first, then looked at the man holding the device. Perhaps she recognised him from before, because she seemed to relax a bit and nodded.

Bato looked up and whispered, 'Five minutes.'

Kelly nodded. 'Hi ... my name is Captain Kelly, of the Galactic Federation of Earth. You are now aboard my ship, the Ahura Mazda.'

'Zed?' she asked timidly.

Kelly smiled, 'Yes, we are Zed. What is your name?'

'Ruxshin, of the Mahini.'

Kelly looked at the people behind the glass in astonishment.

'Could it really be ...' whispered Julius.

Kelly turned to her once more. 'What is the name of your planet, Ruxshin?'

'Mah,' she answered. She shivered and closed her eyes for a moment.

'Quickly, Captain,' said Bato.

'Is your planet under attack?'

The girl nodded. 'The ... Arneshians did ... this.'

'Was there a man named Ambassador T'Rogon?'

'Yes, he's in charge.'

Kelly let out a sigh. 'Thank you. One last question, please: who told you to look for help? For us?'

Ruxshin was evidently struggling to talk, but mustered her last strength. 'Morgana did ... she spoke of Julius.'

The silence that followed those words lingered heavily in the room. As if in a trance, Julius stepped forward from behind the glass. 'What did you just say?'

Ruxshin turned her head towards the voice. '... In my coat ...' she whispered, before closing her eyes.

'That's enough now,' said the doctor.

'Where is her coat?' asked Kelly.

Bato pointed at a chair in a corner, and Julius hurried to it. With trembling fingers, he began to search every pocket he could find, unaware that the others had gathered around him and were looking on, quite shaken by what they'd heard. His fingertips closed around something and, even before pulling it out, Julius knew immediately what it was. As his hand re-emerged, the light caught the silver chain and the Strullium lilac crystal, making them sparkle brightly.

*

Julius had troubled sleep. He spent the best part of the night reflecting on the impossibility of what Ruxshin had told them; yet, she had given him a proof that he couldn't refute. He had had the necklace specially made for Morgana, and he knew it was hers beyond all shadow of a doubt. Images of the pendant, and of the moment he had given it to her, passed in and out of his mind, condemning him to a restless night that left him tired and cranky. When the dark dawn of space arrived, he was glad to get out of bed, hoping that a cold shower would remove the last dregs of sleep from his thoughts. He had a long day ahead of him. Freja would join them at 09:00 hours for a briefing on the situation as well as for a chance to meet Ruxshin. He looked at the sleeping shape of Skye, then at Faith's empty bed, and quietly left the room, heading for the mess hall. Coffee could always make *some* wrongs right.

The ready room of the Mazda was at the front of the ship, below the war-deck. When Julius arrived, Faith was already there fitting the translator over a large metal cube. 'I didn't see you at breakfast. What are you up to?'

'I know; I haven't had the time. I'm fitting a multidirectional receiver and amplifier, so we can all be translated and heard properly. It doesn't look great, but I made it last night – no time to embellish it.'

Julius examined it closely, once again amazed by Faith's ingenuity. He took a seat, his right hand clasped around the pendant, which was in the safety of his trouser leg pocket. 'Faith ...'

'Uh-huh?'

'Is it possible that Morgana ... that the coffin travelled through the wormhole? I mean, the pendant is real enough, but ...'

Faith stopped what he was doing to look at him. 'I'd say so, yes,' he answered. 'It's built well enough to withstand that kind of pressure - it was a special one off, that coffin was. Ruxshin must have seen the death mail, Julius. You know that Morgana didn't actually talk to her, right?'

The death mail – of course. 'I was so spaced out last night, I forgot you'd put that in there with her.'

Faith smiled and continued setting up the device. 'It's true what they say – we can't really see all ends.'

Julius mulled over those words for a moment. The death of Morgana had proven to be an important link in a chain of events. Without it, or the special coffin, they would not have found the way to Mah and Michael. 'It didn't need to be her though,' he said bitterly.

Faith looked up once more. 'And what life would you have traded hers for?'

Julius felt an immediate sense of guilt at his own selfish thought and had no answer to give.

Shortly afterwards, Freja arrived at the meeting, accompanied by Master Cress. Once they were all settled around the table, Kelly called for his wife to bring the girl in. There was an excited anticipation preceding her arrival for, as well as meeting a representative of another planet, they were about to learn potentially important information about their enemies.

When she entered the ready room, Julius saw that Ruxshin was wearing clothes made of stitched leather cloths and furs, together with a pair of sturdy leather boots. A rosy complexion had returned to her cheeks and she confidently held all in the room with her gaze. As her hosts stood up, bowing their heads slightly in greeting, she returned the gesture gratefully. The fact that there was a grey wisp over her head also told Julius that she was still very anxious.

'You can sit here,' said Elian, offering the chair between her and Kelly.

When she sat, Julius noticed red fur growing along the back of her hand. His first impulse was to reach over and touch it, but of course he knew better than that. The girl turned briefly towards him, and when their eyes met, he noticed how she backed away in surprise, as if she had recognised him from sickbay. She smiled and turned her attention to the rest of the group.

'Welcome among us, Ruxshin. I am Freja, Head of Tijara, one of the Zed schools. This is my second, Cress,' he continued, pointing. 'Captain Kelly and Lieutenant Flywheel you know already. These here are Julius, Skye and Faith. I am very glad you have found us.'

'Thank you,' she replied, looking briefly around the table. 'And thank you for saving me from the Arneshians.'

'We want to do more than that, but we need to know all the facts first. Will you help us?'

'The Mahini will do anything to see *them* out of our homeland.'

There, she had used that word again: *Mahini*. Julius immediately thought of the picture they had seen of Eronan standing in front of a shuttle with the words "Mahin Space Enterprise" on it. Coincidence or not, they would need to discuss that possibility. The wisp over Ruxshin's head turned briefly scarlet. Julius saw the determination in her eyes and was pleased – time was ticking and they would work faster with a smart and resolute guide.

'We understand that your planet, Mah, is currently occupied by Arneshian troops. Is this correct?' asked Freja.

'It is. The occupation started ...' Ruxshin began to count on her fingers before answering, '... a year and a half ago. You use *years* too, right? A'Krad, my supervisor, said so.'

'We do,' answered Kelly. 'What does this A'Krad *supervise*, exactly?'

'We've been doing all sorts of work for them. Mining Strullium and-'

'Strullium?' cut in Freja.

'Yes, it's a blue metal when it's liquid. Our planet is filled with it.'

Freja exchanged a quick glance with Cress, who had been taking notes on his PIP screen since the meeting had begun. 'We use Strullium too, to run our fleet. The Arneshians will help themselves to it, believe me.'

'That has become apparent,' she replied. 'We don't even mind, to be honest, as we have no real use for it – we make furniture out of it. But unfortunately they have destroyed our greenhouses and every other means we had of creating food. Mah is not a very hospitable place as it is, and now it's even worse.'

'In what way?' asked Cress.

'Six months of snow and six months of rain.'

'Hmm,' said Kelly. 'I take it it's the snowy season now, judging by the state you got here, right?'

'It is. The rain will start on the day the Arneshians call the 1st of October, uninterrupted, for six months.'

'Sounds just like home,' muttered Julius vaguely.

'We'll make sure we plan for it then,' added Cress, matter-of-factly.

'Ruxshin,' continued Freja, 'have you ever seen or heard of a young man named K'Ssander among the Arneshians?'

The girl's facial reaction at the name was enough to confirm she did. Still, she nodded. 'He almost caught me on the landing pad. I think they got Khavar, my friend. He may be dead by now.'

'I'm sorry,' replied Freja.

'Look, it may be too late for Khavar, but Mah Gira is still alive. He's our chief and they have captured him. If we don't work or don't do what they ask, they kill us ... or do *things* to us.'

Julius saw a strange wisp emanating from her aura: a mix of red and grey, indicating shame. *What did they do to her, to make her feel this way?* he wondered.

'It is very likely that your leader is still alive,' Freja reassured her. 'T'Rogon is a diplomat at heart and knows the value of negotiation. He will not kill him, especially if his life means a lot to your people. He's leverage.'

'Death is not the worst thing they can impose on us. There are some among them who take joy in humiliating us. Like this boy, Michael, who they're now calling their *leader*.'

The room grew suddenly quiet.

'Do you know him?' asked Ruxshin, seeing the reaction she had caused.

Julius remained quiet, leaving the others to answer for him.

'We do, Ruxshin,' answered Freja. However, he did not volunteer any more information. 'When was the last time you saw him?'

'About seven months ago. I know he's still on Mah, because the soldiers talk about going to "*Michael's Chamber*" often enough, whatever that is, and of strange tests that cause the very ground we walk on to shake; but none of us have seen him since. And, quite frankly, good riddance. If there's anyone worse than K'Ssander, it's him. I would kill him with my own hands if I could.'

Freja risked a quick glance at Julius, before continuing. 'Ruxshin, we need to find a statue on Mah.'

'What kind of statue?'

'It depicts an archer; a Mahini archer. Do you know where it is?'

'I've never seen any such statue in Mahin – our city. It could be somewhere on the planet, though. Mah Gira will definitely know.'

'Another reason to find him then.'

'Will you really help me?' said Ruxshin, leaning forward. She sounded almost incredulous.

Freja nodded. 'We believe that statue holds the key to defeating the Arneshians. We must find it before we can deal with them.'

The wisp around her body turned to emerald green, as if she hadn't heard such good news in a long time. She looked at Elian and squeezed her hand, overjoyed, making the lieutenant smile.

Freja looked at Julius once more. '*Do you want to hear this?*' he asked, telepathically. Julius knew he was going to ask about Morgana. '*I do.*'

Freja looked back at the girl. 'How did you come across Morgana?'

*

The meeting went on longer than planned, as questions on the Mahini, and their oppression at the hands of the Arneshians, began to emerge naturally, painting a very sad state of affairs, but a very useful one all the same. They were about to infiltrate the city and they would need all the information they could get.

Around 11:00 hours, they all began mapping a 4D rendering of the city of Mahin and the surrounding area. The girl proved to have a prodigious memory because she was able to relay the geography of her plateau in great detail, from trees to glades, to the position of all the former greenhouses and access lifts to the underground. Her knowledge of the Arneshian compounds, due to her work with A'Krad and her previous visit to the holding cells, proved to be very useful.

At midday, the GM sent Faith to engineering to work on replicating the Unilogus – Ruxshin had told them its name – while his son had been asked to co-ordinate the invasion with Julius and Skye.

'If it wasn't for her people, I would be inclined to nuke the whole planet,' said Kelly, pouring over their quadrant route-chart, which was now sporting a brand new wormhole.

'Amen to that,' replied Skye.

Julius could see their point, but although the temptation to get rid of Michael in such a way was strong, it was nothing compared to how much he wanted to deal with him and K'Ssander *personally*. Besides, Morgana's body was there too now. Ruxshin's story of how they'd found the coffin had caught him unprepared. He had to restrain himself from asking her all sorts of questions in front of everybody, about how she looked, or if Khavar had thought her beautiful the way he did. He was tremendously glad that she had been found by them, and that the casket had remained undiscovered by the Arneshians.

Later that afternoon, Freja came to see them in the ready room. 'Did you get our schematics, JD?'

'Yes. They look very accurate.'

'She's got a good memory. Run me through your plan then,' he said, going to stand next to Julius and Skye.

Kelly touched his com-link. 'Computer, activate Mahin 1.'

The long, glass table-top lit up green as it came to life. The familiar 4D rendering of the plateau emerged until it took centre stage. 'This, here, is Mahin,' he said, using a laser pen to circle the structure in the middle. The landing pad is to the north, next to the main Arneshian compounds. All the shafts you see dotted around are lifts to the underground – there is no other access to it.'

'All except Mah Gira's secret tunnel,' said Julius.

'That's right,' said Kelly, pointing the laser at a small forest to the south. 'Ruxshin and Khavar made it to the landing pad undetected, by skirting the city along the eastern border. If the tunnel is still hidden, it's our best bet to enter the lower level. Anywhere else would involve an attack, and I don't think it's what we're planning for, right?'

'Yes,' replied Freja. 'T'Rogon is expecting an invasion, but not an infiltration party, at this stage. However, this means that the wormhole will be guarded too. They'll detect us as soon as we enter their quadrant.'

'That's what we're counting on,' he said. 'We'll be using our Cougars as shields – not to engage, but as a diversion. They chase our fighters, we split away and land on Mah.'

'Won't they be able to detect your signatures?'

'Scan this room for bio-signs, please,' Kelly requested.

Freja looked perplexed, but did as indicated, using his PIP. 'Four people.'

In reply, Kelly looked to his right. 'Faith?'

At that moment, Faith materialised in a corner of the room, smiling brightly. 'Et voila!'

Julius enjoyed the expression on the GM's face – he looked impressed. 'We managed to cloak his signature using the Arneshian technology left behind during their visit to Earth,' he explained. 'They'll have no indication of intruders.'

'Once on the ground,' continued Kelly, 'we hit the east road and get in through the tunnel.'

'I take it a full port is out of the question?' enquired Freja.

All eyes turned to Faith, who shrugged his shoulders. 'We've never ported through a wormhole, sir,' he explained. 'Testing may take too long and I wouldn't send a soul without one.'

'Damn right you wouldn't,' mumbled Skye.

'It's kinda far, truth be told, but I can run some trials if you want me to. I've been working on a portable version of the Shanigan Relay, and it may just do the trick.'

'Yes, please,' said Freja. 'I want you to give one portal to Captain Kelly. He will release it near Mah's orbit, for us to use.'

It was Faith's turn to be impressed. 'Great idea, sir. We can start testing as soon as they drop it.'

Freja nodded. 'What happens once you get to the tunnel?'

'Computer, activate Mahin 2,' said Kelly.

A new 4D map appeared, this time of the underground level.

'This here is Mah Gira's house,' explained Skye. 'And this one, across town, is the holding cellblock. All we need to do is go to him and ask for the location of the Archer.'

Freja remained silent for a while, pondering the feasibility of the plan. 'I guess it's easy enough to replicate Ruxshin's clothing, but the rest … if you could just turn into Mahini, then yes, it would be a perfect plan.'

'Actually, sir,' said Faith, 'we sort of can.'

Julius, Skye and Kelly didn't seem too surprised at that; in fact, they looked quite chuffed. Freja, on the other hand, looked at him with interest - when it came to Faith and his inventions, expectations were generally high. 'Astonish me then, since the rest of the room seems to already be in the know.'

'Wait for it, sir,' piped up Skye, looking excited. 'This is something else.'

'Well, so,' began Faith, holding everyone's attention, 'the two things that could give us away are the language and the fur. After downloading the vocabulary into the Officer Network, I went to talk to Doctor Bato and we came up with a throat implant – a different version of the Unilogus - linked to the PIP. So basically, when the translation feature is activated, it triggers the chip in your voice box; you open your mouth and what comes out is the language of choice. Like so.' Faith pressed a button on his PIP and began to speak,

Freja looked completely stunned at the sounds reaching his ears – so guttural and completely unlike Faith's Irish ones.

'Would you believe it?' was all he could say.

'And that's not all,' said Faith, reverting to the common speech. 'Check my back out!' And with that, he turned around and pulled his t-shirt over his head.

'Zed's beard!' Freja exclaimed, rushing over to examine Faith's hairy back. 'How …'

Julius stepped closer as well. He had already seen it and touched it plenty, but it was still amazing. 'It's just a DNA alteration, sir,' he explained. 'Dr Bato will be able to reverse it when we get back. She's a genius, by the way.'

'Unbelievable,' the GM murmured. He turned to his son. 'And how will the party get back afterwards?'

The enthusiasm quickly left their faces.

'I see,' said Freja, understanding that was no plan for that.

'Once we make it to the Archer,' said Kelly, 'and retrieve the coordinates, you'll need to pick us up.'

'Hopefully the portal you drop will work. Otherwise, we'll think of something else,' replied Freja. 'Leave that to us. Once you make it safely to the Archer, you stay put until we contact you – and bring plenty of provisions.'

*

Preparations completely took up the following couple of weeks. Julius was itching to ask Ruxshin various questions about Morgana, but he had no opportunity. The girl was either in sickbay or in long, drawn out meetings with Cress and the GM, dishing out every bit of information she possessed on Mah. And, when she was free, Julius was busy elsewhere. Part of the groundwork involved installing a trace on the Arneshian shuttle, altering the DNA of the infiltration party, implanting them with the translation chip and gearing them up for cold weather and snow. Julius, Skye and Kelly made up the entire team, while Faith would help to co-ordinate things from the Mazda. 'I can't imagine any of the Mahini wearing a skirt like mine, to be honest,' he had told them candidly. They knew he was right – no amount of camouflage could conceal his metallic hovering device.

Ruxshin, on the other hand, didn't seem too happy about being left behind. Towards the end of the second week, she took to roaming the guest areas of the Mazda like a lion in a cage, asking for updates whenever she saw an officer. It was understandable given the circumstances, but it wasn't helping either.

On Monday the 22nd, Julius walked into Bay 2 to find Ruxshin arguing with one of the technicians. By the looks of things, he seemed more uncomfortable than she was, practically hiding inside the shuttle as he worked, while she stood by the hatch, determined to convince him why she had to be in the landing party.

Upon hearing steps, the engineer shot out of the craft, looking exasperated. 'Why don't you ask *him?*' he told her over his shoulder, while hurrying for the exit.

Ruxshin fell quiet and looked at Julius, as if studying him.

'Hi,' he said. Then he remembered his new throat implant and turned his PIP on. 'Hi,' he said again. Only, this time, he could barely recognise his own voice.

'That's a pretty neat trick your friends came up with,' she said, pointing at her own throat.

'Aye, it's really strange though,' he said. 'My thoughts don't match my words. Hard to get used to.'

Ruxshin smiled. 'You all look like Arneshians, you know that, right? And you invent things, just like they do.'

Julius couldn't detect any sarcasm in her voice. She was just stating a fact. He wondered what she would say if she saw his mind-skills in action. 'We are both humans … and so are you, apparently.'

'Yes, the doctor told me. But she doesn't know why we look different from you.'

'Neither do I,' he answered truthfully. He was toying with the idea of asking her about Morgana, when she stepped up to him, quickly and eagerly. He was taken aback, not least because he hadn't been physically close to a woman for some time, and right now he could count her freckles.

'You must take me with you,' she begged.

Julius was caught off guard, distracted by her scent – a distant reminder of pine trees and sweet resins. 'I can't,' he replied eventually.

'It is *my* home,' she continued, standing up to him. 'I know the land, the access to the tunnel and every nook and cranny of the underground. You'll look lost and out of place, and they will catch you!'

Julius could understand her feelings perfectly – he would have done the same in her place – but he couldn't afford to babysit her. Determined not to be dragged into a fight, he took a step back. 'I'm sorry, but the Grand Master has been clear about that. His word goes.'

Ruxshin tilted her head to the side, as if trying to suss him out. The fight reappeared in her eyes. '*She* said you'd be a leader. It seems to me that it's quite the opposite.'

It was like being slapped. Julius knew exactly who Ruxhin was referring to, and why she had said it. It was his turn to step up to her, barely containing his anger. He planted his index finger in the middle of her chest and stared her down. 'Don't you ever use her like that again. *Ever.*'

Ruxshin lost her edge and cowered back.

Again, the sudden change stopped Julius in his tracks. She looked scared, as if she was expecting him to hit her. Confused by her reaction and shaken by guilt at his outburst, he stepped back and walked out of the bay.

'McCoy, is everything all right?'

Kelly had just crossed his path in the corridor. 'I'm fine,' he growled.

'What was that? I can't understand you.'

Julius stopped and realised that his Unilogus was still turned on. 'Great,' he said, deactivating it. 'I just had my first argument in Mahin.'

Kelly raised an eyebrow.

'Ruxshin wants to tag along,' he explained, leaving out the rest of their exchange.

'She can't,' he replied, 'and that is that. Now, go get ready. The shuttle will leave in one hour.'

He nodded and headed for his quarters, trying to push away the discomfort of his first proper encounter with Ruxshin.

*

Elian had taken the Mazda right up to the wormhole, surrounded by the Zed fleet. Two teams had been positioned on the upper and lower decks of her ship, ready to defend the fleet if any enemy decided to pay them a visit.

'Is everyone ready?' asked Freja. He was standing in Bay 2 with the landing party, who were wearing Mahini style clothing.

'As ready as we'll ever be,' replied Faith. 'The shuttle has been cloaked.'

'Very well. Good luck, Team 1. You know what's at stake,' said Freja. 'Mr Shanigan, you can join me on the bridge.'

'Aye, sir,' he replied, hovering around the craft for one last check.

While Kelly exchanged a last minute word with his father, Julius shouldered his small backpack and did a mental check of his gear. The fur coat was really heavy and he had to leave it open for as long as he was on the shuttle, or it would be too hot. He had packed several highly caloric bars rich in proteins, fat and grains. He also carried a bottle of concentrated hydration fluid; a mouthful of it made up for a whole glass of water. The EMU device was pinned to his chest, underneath all the layers – if it was good enough for deep space, it was good enough to keep him from the cold of Mah. Satisfied, he stepped into the craft and secured his luggage in a side compartment. Then he went to the front, occupying one of the two pilot seats. A few minutes later, Kelly joined him, taking the other place, while Skye strapped himself into the seat behind Julius.

'Hey,' said Skye, grinning, 'do you know what Ruxshin told me about the female Mahini the other night?'

'Here we go,' sighed Julius, rolling his eyes.

'They tend to be quite *affectionate* people – not sure what she meant, but I intend to find out.'

'Whatever you do,' said Kelly, turning to him, 'don't you dare bring back any kittens.'

'Skye, are we going to have a problem with you?' said Julius.

'The local gals might ... but it doesn't follow that they won't like it!'

'Like what?' asked Faith, his head peaking inside the hatch.

'Take a wild guess,' said Julius, nodding at Skye.

'The Miller is going *hunting*?'

'I told you,' Kelly piped in, index finger waving, 'I don't want any tiny fur balls on my ship.'

'No offense, Captain,' said Skye, 'but right now you're as hairy as she is.'

'And anyway ... why did Ruxshin mention that, exactly? Were you asking her funny questions?'

'*Moi?*' he said, looking all innocent. 'Never!'

'You fancy her?'

'She's kinda hot, actually. Red hair, green eyes, those cute little freckles of hers. And she gave the slip to K'Ssander – feisty!'

'You're hopeless,' Julius told him, shaking his head.

'Not that you're wrong, mind you,' added Faith as an afterthought, 'but that's beside the point.'

'I'm only representing my people. You know: inter-space relationsh-'

The ship intercom came to life, cutting him short. 'Team 1,' called Freja, 'stand by.'

'Roger that, bridge,' replied Kelly over his com-link. 'Take your positions.'

'Good luck guys,' said Faith. 'And remember that your powers won't work through the cloak. And don't forget to eject the portal.'

'Will do. See you on the other side,' replied Julius, sadly aware that Faith wasn't going with them on this mission.

The captain closed the hatch and checked the controls. He had spent a lot of time familiarising himself with the Arneshian craft and felt pretty confident. He turned the engine on without a hiccup.

'The Cougars are in position,' said Freja. 'Team 1, ready check.'

'Bay 2, depressurising now,' replied Kelly. 'Team 1, we're good to go.'

Julius watched the port slide open underneath them, revealing the darkness below. He checked his straps again and cracked his knuckles nervously, while Michael's face appeared at the edge of his consciousness.

A NEW SOLAR SYSTEM

The Arneshian shuttle carrying Team 1 approached the group of Cougars that had been deployed to escort them through the wormhole. Five of them would be sent ahead and five more would follow the shuttle.

'We're going to have two former Solo champions in that wormhole,' said Kelly, taking his position in the convoy. 'What are the odds?'

'Is Docherty here?' asked Julius, suddenly interested. He hadn't seen him since the funeral and wondered where Kaori was.

Kelly pointed at his Cougar in reply. 'He's leading the toon.'

The tag name "Arrow" shone on the name plate on the side of that craft in the front group and Julius knew it was Bernard's.

'Arrow, Team 1 in position and ready to go,' said Kelly.

'Captain!' Docherty replied, sounding surprised. 'You really snuck up on us.'

'That's what I wanted to hear. It means the cloak is working just fine.'

Julius allowed himself a sigh of relief – they would need all the stealth they could get. He looked ahead and saw the Cougars beginning to enter into the wormhole. Kelly matched their speed and guided them smoothly inside the sphere that marked the entrance to the conduit. Since he wasn't in charge of piloting the craft, Julius gave himself the chance to observe his surroundings properly, marvelling at its beauty as he went. There were no defined edges around him, but a layer of undulating, shimmering surfaces instead. It made him think his eyes were playing tricks on him, bringing the images in and out of focus. As Kelly accelerated, the blurring increased, creating strands of light that streamed past them.

'I wish we could use our mind-skills,' said Skye, breaking the silence. 'It would make me feel much safer.'

'The only way to do that,' said Kelly, 'is by leaving the craft and surfing it to the surface.'

'Now *that's* an idea!'

'Yeah, well, let's hope it doesn't come to that.'

Julius hand wandered to the EMU button on his chest without realising it. It wouldn't be the first time he had hitched a ride on top of a ship.

The Cougars cruised smoothly ahead, flying steady and sure. Bernard's scouting group would be exposed to the enemy right from the start, and would need to fly by them quickly, as well as taking the brunt of any opposition. He had to give them enough time to-

'Atchoo!'

'What was that?' started Kelly, before being interrupted by a second sneeze.

Julius and Skye were on their feet in an instant, Gauntlets pointed towards the rear of the shuttle. They exchanged a quick, wary glance.

'Who's there?' called Skye.

There was a shuffling noise from inside one of the cabinets built into the back wall. Julius advanced cautiously and released the latch, without lowering his weapon. As the door swung open, a huddled Ruxshin tumbled out into the open.

'Don't shoot! Don't shoot please!' she cried, shielding herself with her arms, while speaking into her Unilogus.

'Shoot? What- No!' replied Skye, astonished.

'What are you doing here?' said Julius, barely able to contain his temper.

'I'm sorry! I just *had* to come, but you wouldn't listen!'

'Ruxshin,' said Kelly, over his shoulder. He sounded disappointed. 'This is not how we do things. There were serious reasons for leaving you behind, including the fact you're a wanted fugitive. You're less of a help than you think.'

Ruxshin blushed, her gaze falling to her feet. 'It's my home,' she answered quietly.

Julius lowered his weapon and returned to his seat, feeling annoyed. The way she had used Morgana that very morning had marked her in his bad books right away, and this latest stunt wasn't going to change that sentiment.

'You better sit down and buckle up,' Skye told her, helping her to her feet. 'It's going to get rough.'

'Arrow, come in,' said Kelly.

'Yes, Captain?'

'When you re-enter, please advise the GM that we have a stowaway on board.'

'Sir?'

'The Mahini girl.'

'Oh,' he replied, sounding uncertain. 'Is ... there something I should do?'

'Just clear us safe passage, Arrow; that's all I ask for.'

'Roger that, Captain. Two minutes to go.'

Kelly turned to Julius. 'There's a spare EMU in my rucksack – try the inside pocket. Give it to her. Then turn on your translator, since she's here.'

Julius nodded and got up – time was short and he had to focus on the mission rather than on personal matters. He rifled through Kelly's belongings and found the EMU badge. He turned to her and showed her his own activator, fixed to his t-shirt. 'Put this on, as close to your body as possible.'

Ruxshin nodded, grabbed the badge and opened the top half of her coat. 'This good?' she said, pointing above her left breast.

'It'll do,' he replied.

She fixed it onto her chest and looked up apprehensively. 'I'm sorry,' she whispered.

Julius saw her blush when he looked at her, noticing little pink dots in her otherwise grey aura – he couldn't read them, but they made him feel uncomfortable. He nodded curtly, before going back to his seat.

'It's fine,' said Skye, trying to reassure her. 'I'll tell you if you need to use it.'

'Thirty seconds, Captain,' said Docherty.

Kelly took a deep breath and readjusted his grip on the piloting levers. 'Enter the coordinates, McCoy. The computer will alert us when it's time to drop the portal.'

Julius did so quickly. They were going to land in a hilly area east of the tunnel entrance, where Ruxshin had said there were no soldiers.

Finally, the end of the wormhole came into view and a thick silence fell over the crew.

'Arrow is out,' Docherty informed them.

Julius tensed as he watched the scouts disappearing into the new system, one after the other. Sitting there, unable to do anything but watch, made him feel restless and uneasy. He stared at the new controls which the Mazda's engineers had added, to check the vitals of all the Cougars in the party, hoping that no lights would turn red.

Kelly brought them into the open smoothly, and kept moving forward until the back group had joined them too. 'Here comes trouble,' he said, 'as expected.'

Julius saw at least ten Arneshian crafts converging toward them. The Cougars began their evasive manoeuvres by splitting outwards from their balled-up position, like sparks from fireworks. The confusion left the enemy disorganised for a few seconds, before they also split to follow the individual fighters.

With the front guard gone, Kelly decelerated slightly, allowing the rear group to move forward and surround his shuttle. They were covered once again.

Julius didn't know the pilots, but they were flying competently, shielding them from all angles. 'Enemies approaching at ten o'clock,' he warned.

'I see them,' replied Kelly. 'Shields up.'

Julius obeyed promptly, not a second too soon, as a stray shot from one of the enemy crafts found its way into the group. Their shuttle shook, but held intact. 'Docherty is coming back,' he said, watching the plane on the radar. 'He's being followed.'

'Let's hope he doesn't bring them too close to us,' replied Kelly.

'Can you see the others?' asked Skye.

'The scan range of this craft is pretty shabby – they keep passing in and out of radar,' said Julius.

'Wings,' called Kelly, 'make some white noise for us.'

'Aye, sir,' came the reply from a female voice.

Julius didn't know who the pilot was, but knew that "white noise" was a manoeuvre designed to confuse the readings of scanner sensors by way of mind-skill impulses – in this case, the aim was to protect the Arneshian shuttle even more. The Cougars where moving clockwise around his craft, each of the pilots unleashing a series of mind-pushes to confuse the Arneshians. At the same time, they all had to fly in formation, to avoid being hit.

The six planes twisted and turned their way ahead like a flock of birds, forging a path towards Mah, amidst the shimmering enemy-fire. Kelly's face was like a mask, focused on piloting and removed from all the rest.

Julius couldn't do anything, except hold his breath during the countless corkscrew manoeuvres, ignoring the odd little whimpering sounds from Ruxshin. His eyes kept creeping back to the radar, waiting for the proximity alarm to go off. 'Watch out!' he cried suddenly. Instinctively, he pushed back in his seat, as he saw an Arneshian ship chasing a Cougar, before veering away from its prey. 'He's coming right at us!'

Kelly banked sharp left, bringing them outside the safety of the group, but he had no other choice. Following the coordinates, he stayed his course, hoping that the enemy wouldn't notice.

Two Zed crafts appeared to either side of the shuttle, giving them all a chance to catch breath.

'Captain Kelly?'

'Wings, talk to me.'

'The group is scattered, but they'll keep the Arneshians distracted for as long as they can. Mah is right ahead. You can make it.'

The pilot had just finished speaking when a violent shock pushed the shuttle to the left. Ruxshin screamed in fear.

'Wings!' cried Kelly. 'Come in, Wings!'

'She's gone, sir,' came the nervous reply from the second Cougar.

As if to confirm his words, several shards of metal bounced off their shuttle, before ricocheting out into space.

'Captain,' said Julius, checking their own craft's vitals, 'our shield has been damaged. We cannot take another hit!'

'Blackie,' ordered Kelly to the remaining pilot, 'take that craft away from us *now* – our cloaking device may not last for long.'

'Roger that, Captain.'

Julius watched as the Cougar to his right flipped backwards and began firing at the enemy craft behind. It was a daring manoeuvre given their speed, but it paid off. The enemy had to take evasive action, leaving Kelly free to accelerate forward. As they sped away, Mah came into view, looking starkly bright against the darkness around it.

'Get ready to eject the portal, McCoy. We want it to remain outside the planet's orbit.'

Julius keyed in the code given to him by Faith to open the outer locker where the portal was being stored. The button went from red to green, indicating that it was ready to be fired. 'Let's hope it works,' he said, as he ejected it.

Just as they zoomed out of the fighting zone, an alarm echoed inside their craft.

'What's happening?' cried Ruxshin.

'We're losing speed,' said Kelly, testing his controls. 'Miller, check the back!'

Skye unbuckled his seatbelt and moved to the rear. He opened one of the covers to see if they had taken any damage and a plume of smoke escaped. He quickly took an extinguisher and put the fire out. 'Not good.'

'We're drifting,' admitted Kelly. I can steer, but that's about it.'

'And the cloak?' asked Skye.

'Its core engine was in the back. We probably lost that too,' he said, leaning back in his seat.

Julius ran his fingers through his hair, trying to think of a solution. He used their radar to scan for objects but, between them and Mah, there were no structures or debris of any kind - without any solid objects, there was no way he could pull them closer using his skills.

'Oh no,' said Kelly, staring at the radar.

Julius and Skye leaned forward and saw two incoming crafts heading their way. One of the Cougars had taken a long detour, bringing the enemy with it. Unable to move out of the way, there was nothing they could do but wait.

The beeping sound of the proximity alert became more insistent as the chase drew closer to their location. Then, just as it was beginning to slow again, a stray hit slammed against the tail of their shuttle, making it spin out of control and sending Skye crashing forward.

Julius tried to grab him to break his fall, while Kelly used the handles to counteract the spin. As successfully as he did this, the momentum was still accelerating them onwards.

'They've pushed us towards the planet's orbit!' cried Kelly. 'We'll land all right -

gravity will see to that pretty soon.'

'Yes, but not where we want to go,' added Skye, massaging his head. We're heading way beyond the eastern forest.'

'Better than the middle of the city,' replied Kelly. 'McCoy, if you have any bright ideas, now's the time.'

Julius felt a sting of panic. He could see the dark patch that was Mah disappearing fast to their right, together with their designated landing spot. Ahead there was only snow, just as Ruxshin had described. No matter how he looked at it, there was only one way they could survive the one-way trip without crashing. He unbuckled his seatbelt and looked at them. 'Suit up, people.'

'Thinking of sharing?' asked Kelly, as he activated his own EMU underneath the fur coat.

'You're not going to like this.' He turned to Skye. '*You'll* certainly like this.'

'We're going out, aren't we?' Skye said gleefully.

'It ain't normal that you're this excited about it,' replied Kelly, helping Ruxshin with her suit.

'We fly down, then?' continued Skye, unperturbed.

'Er ... no. If we leave the shuttle to crash, they'll know we're there.' Julius said.

'Then how are we ...'

Julius cracked on. 'Ruxshin, you'll be fine,' he said to her, tightening her straps. 'Just stay there and keep the face shield on at all times – it will allow you to breathe and hear us.'

She was too shocked to say anything, so just nodded anxiously.

'We are going to act as the thrusters for this craft,' Julius explained. 'You hold on to whatever you can find in here. I open the port door and the three of us push against the ground until we slow ourselves down.'

Skye's smile fell from his face, and he looked at Kelly. 'I love this man.'

Kelly, on the other hand, didn't seem to share his enthusiasm. 'Are you insane?'

'We've done it before, Captain,' Julius answered. 'Thirty of us halted a Heron ship in its track.'

'There are three of us here,' pointed out Kelly, unconvinced.

'Yeah, but the ship is smaller. Come on, we need to secure ourselves to something – but make sure we can reach the hatch.'

Kelly raised his hands in resignation.

'There's some sort of rope in the cupboard where I was hiding,' volunteered Ruxshin. 'Although I'm not sure I understood your plan properly.'

Ignoring her last remark, Julius got straight to it. He rummaged for a few seconds, then turned around, holding a length of rope and two grapples.

At that moment, the craft jolted and gained speed. The orbital pull had sucked them in.

'Let's do this quickly then,' said Kelly.

They secured the hooks to two handles on either side of the hatch, then fastened the rope around their waists and knotted it at the base points of the grapples. They had purposely kept it short and tight, to prevent them being sucked outside once the door was opened.

'Focus on the ground,' Julius told them. 'Skye, you get the door.'

'Wait!' said Ruxshin. 'What are you doing?'

'Counting down,' continued Skye. 'Three, two, one … Unlock.'

The door didn't even finish opening before it was sucked clear off its hinges by the vacuum. Ruxshin screamed as she was dragged forward against her safety harness. The rope around their waists tightened, making them groan in pain, but they tensed their abdominal muscles and held fast.

'Take a deep breath,' hollered Julius. He could see the ground speeding up toward them. Still, they had to wait until they were in range, or there would be nothing to push against but air.

'The craft is tilting!' cried Skye. 'We'll lose sight of the ground.'

'Hit the starboard wall … as gently as you can,' replied Kelly.

Skye forced himself sideways, pointing his right hand behind him, and let out a quick burst.

It did the trick and the hatch faced the onrushing surface below once more.

'Here we go!' shouted Julius. 'Push with everything you've got.' He felt a familiar inner click in the recesses of his mind, stretched his hands forward and unleashed a powerful push towards the planet.

Three beams of yellow light shot out of the craft and struck the ground in a flurry of snowflakes. The candid white blanket turned black, as the heat scorched the grass beneath.

'Skye!' cried Kelly, as the shuttle began to tilt again, this time as a result of their mind-skills.

'I'm on it.'

Julius kept going, ignoring the sharp pain at the back of his head. 'Keep pushing!' he urged them. They were visibly losing speed and with a couple of hundred feet to go, Julius knew they'd made it. He mustered the last of his strength and unleashed a further wave, which slowed the shuttle down even more.

Skye turned to starboard and gave a last push to ensure they landed the right way up.

Now under control, the Arneshian spacecraft touched down. As soon as they eased off with the mind-push, a violent gust of snow blasted into them, forcing them all to the floor.

They had made it.

THE ARCHER

Kelly was the first to his feet and started to undo one of the knots.

Shaken, but unhurt, Ruxshin staggered out of her seat and went to work on the other one, ignoring the raging storm. She was regarding these men in a new light now, a mixture of fear and awe.

Julius' head and ribcage throbbed. He tried to loosen the rope around his waist, enough to push it down, past his hips. When he managed to wriggle free, he rushed to the front, to check the radars. The scanner sensors seemed to be working fine and there was no trace of incoming visitors. He sighed, relieved.

Skye had retrieved their bags from the locker, and handed Julius his. 'My clock says it's night time,' he added, 'but the sky is pretty light here.'

'I've noticed,' agreed Kelly. 'Can you tell what time it is, Ruxshin?'

'The middle of the day, give or take.'

'It'll do. Listen up then. The map in our PIPs will take us back toward the forest. The storm should cover our tracks well enough. Ruxshin, as soon as you recognise the area, I want you to take us straight to the secret tunnel. No point in backtracking now.'

Ruxshin seemed on the verge of asking something, but changed her mind and simply nodded.

When Julius stepped outside, the stormy wind wrapped around his body, buffeting him from all sides. He turned to the craft and was pleased to see that the snow had practically covered it already. He motioned for Kelly to move on, making sure that Ruxshin was right in front of him – the last thing they needed was to lose her. As she walked, she turned her head briefly and gave him a strange look, as if she was seeing him for the first time – Julius knew that their display of mind-skills would require some further explanation, but he would worry about that later.

The EMU turned out to be the perfect protection from the storm, keeping them cosy in a way that a regular fur coat couldn't have. The visors allowed them to talk to each other without using their mind-skills and without the need to shout over the elements. Still, the walk was far from enjoyable, as they had to negotiate their path amidst the dips hidden under the soft white layers. Kelly, as the first in the line, was taking the brunt of all the falls and missteps, but bore it quite stoically. Skye had his PIP open as well, to double check they didn't stray from the path.

After an hour Ruxshin stopped and turned to the others. 'Do you feel it?'

A deep tremor sprung up beneath their feet at that moment.

'What was that?' asked Skye.

'One of those *Michael-tests* I was telling you about.'

'What's beyond that low hill?' asked Julius, pointing east. 'The rumbling is coming from there.'

'A valley. There's a forest, a lake, and some rocky outcrops.'

'Give me a minute,' he said to the others. 'I want to check it out.'

Kelly seemed unsure about this detour, but nodded. 'Let's go together. Come on, Ruxshin.'

The tremors intensified as they drew closer to the hill and, by the time they climbed to the top, the rumbling had become so strong that they had to scramble on all fours.

'Over here. Keep low,' Julius told them, lying down, and trying to ignore the weird sensation of the tremors in his bones.

The snow continued to fall, coating everything in white. Still, the landscape was visible enough for them to recognise the landmarks mentioned by Ruxshin a few moments before.

'I can see the lake and th-' began Kelly, before the words died in his throat. 'Look there, to the right.'

Julius did so. On top of a mound stood a group of people, surrounding a machine of sorts. An eerie purple light spread like a fog all around them.

'What the heck are they doing?' asked Skye to no one in particular.

The light around the machine grew stronger, until the lake itself was tinged with it. The small forest to the left of the water began to tremble, gently at first, as if a light breeze had just blown through the treetops, but the breeze quickly became a heavier wind, causing their peaks to bend in all directions. At the same time, a new rumbling emerged, which appeared to be strongest in the ground below the forest. The trees were shaking so much that they became a blur of green and brown. After a few seconds of this, the entire mass of land broke free from the soil below and lifted into the air. Their roots were in full view, dragging clumps of earth and stone up with them. Then, suddenly, it stopped and the forest hovered above the ground, no longer shaking.

This didn't last long before a further tremor began, this time below the lake. The water bubbled, as if it were in a pan that someone had lit a massive fire beneath. A sinister screech broke the air from the edges of the lake, as the rocks around it cracked and split, and slid over each other. As if a giant hand had scooped it up, the body of water levitated into the sky. Some of the icy liquid cascaded over the rim of this invisible field and down into the newly created hole in the ground below it. The lake, once in the air, stopped and hovered peacefully.

When the body of water and the trees moved towards each other, Ruxshin yelped in fear, shaking Julius from his trance. 'How is this possible?' he asked.

No one replied though, as the show wasn't over yet. Accelerating through the snow, the circular surface of the lake floated to the side of the forest, tilted forward and wrapped itself around the trees, like a hand gripping a bunch of flowers. The water poured over the pine needles their roots, and finally down to the ground below. With the trees grasped firmly, the watery tentacles slammed them down to the surface, sending shockwaves along the ground for miles. It took a couple of minutes before the tremors completely subsided.

'I can't believe this,' began Kelly. 'That machine tampered with every law of physics we know. If this is an indication of Michael's latest achievements, we have some serious planning to do.'

'He's practicing telekinesis and mixing it with technology,' said Julius, matter-of-factly. 'He was given mind-skills from Farrah, remember?'

'He's a fast learner then,' said Skye.

Julius nodded, a new set of worries weighing on his heart. He looked at Ruxshin, fear spread across her face, and felt sorry for her.

*

When the forest came into view, everyone drew a sigh of relief. They had been happy to leave the scene of Michael's demonstration behind them for the minute, and push on. That was a worry for another day.

Fortunately, Ruxshin had a good recollection of her journey with Khavar and A'Krad, and Kelly was happy to let her steer their course. By the time they reached the shelter of the trees, the sky had darkened considerably.

Julius had to admit that Ruxshin's knowledge of the landscape was helping them advance much faster, but he had no intention of admitting it – he was still ticked off at her.

They climbed the eastern slopes of the hills, trudging over snapped branches and ducking under snow-laden boughs. Their helmets muffled the howling of the wind, but they knew it was still blowing strong from the flurry of white all around them.

'This is the last hill,' announced Ruxshin, sounding relieved and stopping to catch her breath.

The others gathered around her, and stared down the face of a slope that was riddled with firs.

'It's about an hour to the White Glade from here.'

'We'll be quicker than that,' said Kelly. 'You had A'Krad to drag when you were coming up this way.'

Ruxshin nodded and headed down the slope.

Kelly had been right, thought Julius, as he negotiated his way down: thirty minutes in and already the landscape had changed. The tall firs had thinned, to be replaced by larger bushes and feet-entangling roots. A path began to appear in the snow, marked by flat boulders on either side.

Ruxshin must have recognised it, because there was an extra spring in her step as she completed the last portion of the path. 'We made it,' she said, turning to the others. 'The Glade is to the left, but we're going right. Not long now.'

Julius glanced to one side, trying to imagine the place where Morgana's casket had landed. He paused a few extra seconds there, trying to keep his emotions at bay, before re-joining the party.

Eventually, they reached the entrance to the secret tunnel, where Ruxshin turned and looked directly at Julius.

'What … what is it?' he asked.

'She's in there, in the tunnel.'

Kelly and Skye appeared to have been caught off guard as much as Julius and, for a moment, were unsure how to proceed.

Julius felt his stomach tighten as a flurry of memories rushed to mind. Suddenly he didn't know which way to go. Part of him wanted to see her beautiful face again; on the other hand, he knew that even a glimpse of her would probably jeopardise the tenuous healing process that had just started to mend his heart. Ruxshin didn't need to know this, so he used his mind-skills to speak to the others instead. *'Can you go ahead, please? I don't think I can.'*

'*You can both stay behind,*' said Kelly. '*I'll take care of it and call you when the coast is clear.*'

Julius nodded and saw a tinge of green in Skye's aura as well - it seemed he wasn't ready for this either.

Maintaining the pretence for Ruxshin's benefit, Kelly motioned for her to join him. 'I want you boys to stay behind and watch our back. I'll go ahead with Ruxshin to check the place out.'

Once the two of them had disappeared inside the tunnel, Skye and Julius moved over to the entrance without speaking, both secretly knowing what the other was thinking. The snow kept falling, wrapping each of them in their own reflections.

It was at least ten minutes before Kelly returned and called them inside.

Julius stooped as he walked along the tunnel, using his hands for balance. His eyes scouted ahead, exploring the rocky path and wondering when he would catch a glimpse of the coffin. As he approached the light at the end of the tunnel, he realised that Kelly was standing to the right hand side, as if to block his view.

'Don't linger! Keep going straight now,' he told them.

Julius swallowed and had to force himself to focus ahead. His eyes were attracted to the shadow on his right, like magnets to iron. When he emerged in Mah Gira's lounge and was able to stand up straight again, he drew a deep, relieved breath.

Kelly stepped inside behind Skye and helped Ruxshin reposition the chest of drawers in front of the opening.

'We made it,' he said, removing his EMU.

Julius did the same and felt the new hair on the back of his body spring up. It was a strange sensation, but oddly pleasant too. He readjusted his outer clothing and fur coat, while his eyes took in the spartan room around him. As the Mahini's leader, he would have expected Mah Gira's home to be more richly furnished than this - in truth though, he preferred it this way; it made him instinctively develop a liking for the man.

'Ruxshin,' said Kelly, 'you will remain here with Skye.'

'But I-'

'You nothing!' he cut her off. 'I'm in charge. Skye has an instrument that will allow you to see Mah Gira and talk to him when we get there. You need to be content with that.'

She didn't seem to like the idea, but was smart enough to know when to let go. 'Fine,' she said despondently. 'Don't get lost, at least.'

'We'll do our best, trust me.'

'Don't worry, Ruxshin,' said Skye, 'I know how to keep you entertained.'

Kelly threw him a serious warning glare, making Skye grin guiltily.

'Err ... I'll tell you all about our awesome abilities; that's what I meant! I bet you're dying to know how we stopped that shuttle in mid-air, aren't you?'

Julius shook his head, before pulling his hood up and opening the door onto Mah Gira's small courtyard.

The underground was quite different from what Julius had expected. It was cleaner and brighter, with beautiful Strullium decorations embellishing the streets. Groups of Mahini passed from home to home, their mood sombre and their voices hushed. There were also Arneshian patrols, not en masse, but enough to remind the locals that they were being watched. Julius felt anger rising in him. The Arneshian corruption had finally seeped out of their solar system to infest another. He wondered where Michael was, and what the soldiers had meant when they talked about his "Chamber". The word made him think of Farrah's glass cage - was Michael floating, suspended like she had been? A human computer; a vessel for all Arneshian knowledge? For some reason though, he doubted that.

'*We turn right here,*' said Kelly telepathically, as they crossed one of the squares.

Julius saw two guards hanging around at the corner of one the houses, overseeing the path they were about to take, and tensed.

'*Relax,*' said Kelly. '*Keep your head down and carry on.*'

Julius followed the captain's lead and kept walking, trying to act as inconspicuous as possible. Fortunately, the guards were too busy discussing their R&R plans to pay them much attention, and soon were out of earshot.

The holding block had been an Arneshian addition to the underground, and it stuck out like a sore thumb - a dark rectangular wooden structure, positioned against the natural rocks. The only hint of colour was the reflection of the many Strullium crystals protruding above it.

Julius' eyes moved immediately to the entrance, where one Arneshian was standing guard. '*Any ideas?*'

Kelly slowed and took a good look around. Then he saw something that made him grin. '*Watch this.*'

Julius saw the captain locking his eyes somewhere on the ceiling above the block, and past the soldier. He wasn't sure what Kelly was doing until he noticed a protruding crystal starting to shake in its cradle, slowly at first, but getting steadily faster. Suddenly, it popped out of place, shot off to the right, and crashed against the rocky wall behind the building.

The soldier jumped in fright, before sheepishly checking that no one had seen him. Then he opened his palms, activating the electric disks in them, and edged around the corner in search of the cause of the noise.

Kelly tapped Julius on the shoulder and nodded towards the now unguarded entrance. As soon as the guard disappeared behind the corner, they sprinted forward and sneaked inside, unchallenged.

Julius stared along the long empty corridor ahead. There were four doors on the right hand side, each with a small square window cut into the top halves of the panels. The third one, unlike the others, was ajar. Following Kelly's lead, he moved forward slowly and quietly, observing the opening mechanism for each door. They were old lock-and-key devices, which he had only ever seen in books or museum displays. He wondered how easy it would be to try and force them. The first two cells were empty, but they could hear noises from the open doorway of the next one along. They stopped.

Kelly opened his PIP and selected the camera option, and used it to take a sneaky peek inside, by moving the sensor just beyond the edge of the entrance.

Julius tilted forward to look at the image on the screen. He saw a man sitting at a computer terminal, absorbed in his work. He scanned the surface of the desk and its surroundings; something caught the light, causing a tiny glint. When Julius looked closer, he realised it was a long metal key, resting to the left-hand side of the screen, but still too close to the guard. He pointed it out to Kelly.

'*It's your turn now, McCoy,*' Kelly told him.

Julius went back to the projection on the Captain's PIP, exploring the room further.

He spotted a waste bucket on the floor beyond the Arneshian, and grinned. Quietly, he swapped places with Kelly and knelt down, peering around the corner, until his eyes were locked onto the bin. He opened his left hand towards the room and took a deep breath. A small yellow orb began to form above his palm, before turning bright orange as tiny flames erupted all around it, like a miniature sun. Slowly he willed it forward, keeping it so low that it was practically skimming along the floor. The fireball moved silently ahead, dodging the chair's leg until it reached the bucket. There, it began to ascend slowly towards the rim, where it stopped. Julius released more energy and, as the ball grew, he dropped it into the bucket. Whatever was in there instantly caught alight, and the small flame became a lively fire.

Shocked, the man leapt up and hurried around the room erratically, looking for something to put the fire out with. Julius didn't have the luxury of time, so he quickly found the keys with his mind, lifted them from the desk and dragged them towards him, where Kelly was waiting to catch them. They couldn't afford to wait and see the end of the impromptu comedy sketch Julius had created so, with grins on their faces, they tiptoed to the door at the end of the corridor.

Kelly inserted the key in the lock and turned it to the right a few times, until he heard a click. Julius heard footsteps approaching the corridor. Worried that the guard would leave his room, he readied himself to unleash a barrage of mind-skills.

'You need to turn it to the left,' someone whispered from inside the room.

Startled, Kelly did as advised and the door unlocked. He waited for Julius to sidestep inside, then followed and closed the door.

An old man was standing in the middle of the room, a serene expression on his face, his fingers interlaced against his chest. 'Welcome,' he said quietly.

'Mah Gira?' replied Kelly, keeping his voice low.

The man nodded. 'I must be getting older than I thought. There was a time when I knew the faces of all my people.'

'We are not what you think,' replied Kelly, gently pushing Julius away from the door and into a corner, where they both knelt.

Mah Gira moved closer to them, as if waiting to be told a secret.

'I'm Captain Kelly and he's Julius McCoy. We come from Earth.'

'Ruxshin ...' said the man, a trace of hope creeping onto his face.

Julius nodded and opened his PIP, ignoring the stupefied expression of Mah Gira at the sight of this new technology. When the video came to life, Ruxshin's face appeared next to Skye's.

'Mah Gira!' she cried.

Quickly, Skye clamped his hand over her mouth to shush her, while Julius turned the volume down and Mah Gira broke into a fit of pretend coughing.

'Sorry,' she whispered. 'I was so worried about you!'

'My dear girl,' said the Supreme, 'you did it! K'Ssander never said a word – I was afraid you ... Well, I was wrong.'

'Where is Khavar?'

Mah Gira's eyes grew troubled and he looked at his visitors.

'We believe he was taken,' explained Kelly. 'Only Ruxshin made it to us.'

'If he was captured, they haven't brought him here. Knowing Khavar though, I doubt he let them take him without a fight.'

'We'll find him,' said Skye to Ruxshin. He even put an arm around her shoulders for good measure.

'We need your help,' said Kelly. 'We can defeat the Arneshians, but in order to do that-'

'Mah Gira,' interrupted Ruxshin, 'they need to find a statue. Is there an archer statue in Mah?'

The Supreme looked amazed once more. '*The* Archer?'

'Is it real?' asked Julius, wanting to know that his dreams had meant something.

'Yes, but ... how do you know about it?'

'It's a long story,' replied Kelly. 'Suffice it to say that this *Archer* holds the key to another planet – a place where we hope to find powerful allies.'

The old man observed them quietly, while an inner debate was obviously taking place inside his head. He looked at Ruxshin, as if looking for reassurance. 'Hope doesn't amount to much, but it's what has brought you here,' he said eventually. 'What you seek is on top of Mount Mahtab, a ten day trek from here. By the time you reach it, the rainy season will have started – it will be treacherous.'

'We can handle that,' said Kelly.

'Who put it there?' asked Julius.

'The first colony of Mahini brought it with them, when they settled on this planet. We have passed on their story from chief to chief - although, now that you've explained your reasons for wanting to reach it, it seems that there is more to it than meets the eye.'

'I'll want to hear that story when we get back, if you don't mind,' said Kelly, standing. He went to the door to check that the corridor was still clear. 'We will return – that's a promise.'

'I pray you do, Captain. My people didn't stand a chance against the invasion and still aren't able to fight back alone. We are food gatherers - some hunters, by necessity - not soldiers.'

'Hunters, huh? That's a start. They can protect your people when we help you make a stand.'

'Is there someone you can trust?' asked Julius.

Mah Gira thought about that. Then he looked at Skye. 'Young man, go into my courtyard please, and see if there is a black stone tucked under the bench.'

Skye hurried to the window. He peered through the curtain, checking first that the coast was clear, before poking his head out and looking for the object. 'I can see it,' he said, being careful to keep his PIP inside the room.

'I need you to move it to the opposite side,' explained Mah Gira. 'All the way to the left.'

Skye nodded, and turned his PIP off.

In the cell, everyone waited with bated breath for a few, long minutes.

When the link came back up, Skye was once again in the safety of the house. 'Done.'

'The stone is a signal,' explained Mah Gira. 'The man I trust will know what to do.'

'Nice trick,' said Julius.

'We need to go now,' said Kelly. 'How do we get to this mountain?'

Mah Gira bent forward. 'There is an underground tunnel that passes under the plateau ...'

*

They reached the foot of Mount Mahtab as the last dregs of sunlight were seeping from the sky. In the darkness they made a small camp, using a pop-up tent.

Seeing the tent, Julius thought of the Seffira Cave, when they had set up their base camp on Ahriman the year before. He remembered Morgana advancing through the desert haze like a mirage, carrying one of the larger tents, red sand and blue sky reflecting off her EMU. For a moment, he could almost feel the heat of that day warming his body, but the sensation didn't last long. The sound of the tent popping open brought him back to reality. Its surface was designed to reflect the surroundings, so camouflaging it. As he helped Kelly lay the tent on the ground, it became obvious that it was only large enough for three people. They would need to squeeze in if they all wanted shelter from the icy wind, but perhaps the extra body heat wouldn't be completely unwelcome. He ducked inside and began to remove his boots. Ruxshin entered next, followed by Skye, and they followed suit, placing all the shoes in a recess near the tent's entrance.

Kelly joined them after a few minutes. 'I've set up a protective perimeter,' he said. 'If anything comes close to us, it will trigger our defences.'

'Here,' said Skye, handing a food bar to Ruxshin. 'It will fill you up.'

Julius noticed how she hesitated. When she took it, her aura was tinged with red-and-grey specks of shame, because she knew that neither the food, nor the tent, had been meant for her. Seeing this genuine reaction from her softened his disposition towards her a little.

Kelly grabbed a cup from his rucksack and opened the tent-flap. He scooped some snow into it, before quickly withdrawing his arm. He poured some of the concentrated hydration fluid over the melting snow and stirred it with a metal spoon. 'I hope your snow's edible,' he said to Ruxshin.

They watched him drink the content in one gulp, waiting to see how he would react.

'It ain't Martian Bile, but it'll do,' he said, before scooping up some more snow for the others.

Under the glow of a small orange tube-light, they ate and drank in silence, the howling sound of the storm muffled by the tent. From the moment Kelly sealed the entire structure by activating the electromagnetic field, the wind simply washed over it, without even causing a ripple. One by one they lay down, trying not to take up too much space.

Julius was on the edge of the mat, with Ruxshin between him and Kelly. He was tired from the long walk, but sleep didn't seem to be forthcoming. He rolled onto his back as gently as he could, but his movements were hindered by the many layers he was wearing. He decided to deactivate his EMU suit and that gave him more breathing space, although he definitely felt cooler than he would have liked. He began to stroke the fur growing on the backs of his hands; it was soft, long and comforting. He found it strange how easy it had been to get used to it.

The light breathing of Ruxshin caught his ear and he turned towards her. She was lying on her left side with both her hands gathered to her face. She seemed peaceful, save for a little crease between her eyebrows. Julius could see her eyes moving beneath the lids and wondered what she was dreaming about. He knew nothing of her, her family or friends. It was obvious that Mah Gira trusted her deeply, or he would not have sent her on such a rescue mission. She definitely seemed a resourceful sort of girl, not easily put down. But then, why did she hate Michael so much? It was clear that something serious had happened between them, something that had scared her. Should he tell her that Michael was his brother?

Ruxshin made a little noise. The dream was obviously agitating her and the furrow on her brow grew deeper. Delicately, he placed his right hand on her shoulder. 'Shhh,' he whispered. 'Shhh.' She stopped fidgeting almost immediately and her breathing became calm again.

A wave of deep sadness washed over him as he observed her delicate features. Not far from him, Morgana slept her endless sleep, with no one to comfort her.

*

With each passing day, the path became steeper and trickier. The snow continued to fall relentlessly, but softer than it had been on their arrival.

'It's close to the change of season,' explained Ruxshin.

Knowing how long the march would take, they had rationed the food and drinks to make them last until they reached the Archer, although feeding a fourth mouth meant that there was definitely less to go around. In exchange for using up part of their provisions, Ruxshin proved herself to be a really useful guide, using her experience of the land to pick the path efficiently, avoiding the most treacherous ways. It was her home world, after all, and she was an experienced hill walker.

Day followed night and they carried on for over a week, seeing nothing but snow. Then, on the morning of Wednesday the 1st of October, Ruxshin stopped onto a large flat ridge, and inspected the sky. 'Captain Kelly,' she said eventually, 'this would be a good time to open that tent of yours and that field thingy you use at night.'

'We can't stop now,' replied Skye. 'We just got up.'

'It's the rain,' she explained. 'It's coming.'

Kelly didn't seem overly convinced, but he had no reason not to trust her, so he opened the tent. 'All aboard.'

Once inside they sat, waiting curiously for this famous Mah downpour, and secretly enjoying the unplanned break. After about ten minutes, they heard a heavy *tock-tock* sound on the top of the tent.

'It's starting,' she told them.

Julius looked up, puzzled. *TOCK. TOCK-TOCK.* He flinched, startled by the loudness of it.

Then, as if a waterfall had materialised right above them, the rain came crashing down. It had happened in a matter of seconds.

'What the-' cried Skye, placing his hands protectively against the roof of the tent, as if he expected it to collapse on their heads.

'You should have seen the Arneshians when they got caught in it, last year,' said Ruxshin, with a cheeky smile. 'One of their guards got himself electrocuted when he tried to use his palm weapon on one of us. Black smoke everywhere.'

The thought made them all grin, then laugh out loud; it seemed a strange sound, because it hadn't been heard for a while, but it was definitely welcome.

'Ahh ... priceless,' said Kelly, wiping a tear from his eye.

'Are these fur coats waterproof?' asked Skye.

'If you have replicated them well enough, they will keep you dry. Besides, it's only one more night before we reach the statue.'

'That's good news and no mistake,' said Kelly. 'Suit up, people. We're going swimming.'

One by one, they filed out of the tent, while the rain lashed at their visors. It didn't relent until after sunset, when they reached the top of the last hill.

Julius stopped to catch breath, trying to keep his footing in the muddy river that was washing over his boots. 'This place is *dreich* and dreary,' he vented.

'You should feel right at home then, McCoy,' replied Skye.

'Maybe we could camp here tonight,' volunteered Ruxshin. 'The top isn't far, as you can see, but I wouldn't climb up there in the darkness.'

Julius followed her gaze. He could see the summit easily enough, but the rocky slope leading to it was already covered in a shady curtain. The night would catch them in mid climb and, with the rain turning the ground into slush, heading up was too big a risk. Kelly must have thought the same thing, because he began to set up camp.

They were awake at first light. No one spoke as they got ready, but Julius could tell they were all as excited as he was, judging by the scarlet blotches in their auras. It was, of course, still raining relentlessly and Kelly insisted that they walked within grabbing distance of each other, since there was no rope at hand.

At two thirds of their climb, Julius began to feel uneasy, but didn't know why. At first he thought it was the effect of the altitude making his ears buzz, but then his head began to ache; a dull, remote pain, somewhere in the back of his skull.

'Everything all right, McCoy?' asked Kelly, noticing his distress.

Julius stopped and began to scout the grey sky.

'Did you feel something?'

'I'm not sure. There's some sort of interference though. Don't you feel it too?'

Skye shook his head, but Kelly paused for a moment, his eyes closed.

'What's going on?' asked Ruxshin warily. 'Is it the Arneshians?'

In answer to their questions, there was a rumbling from the lip of the mountain behind them. The ground shook under their feet in one single, long growl.

'Oh crap,' said Skye. 'I say we leg it.'

'Come on then,' said Kelly, hurrying them. 'And watch your feet.'

Julius didn't know what the rumbling was, but he also agreed that they needed to reach the top on the double.

They scampered up the slope, boots slipping on the wet gravel. As they climbed to the peak, the path became narrower as the slopes to either side dropped off. They couldn't see the ground below and, powers or not, they wouldn't survive a fall like that. As the noise behind them grew louder, they began to climb faster, a sense of urgency in their steps. Kelly grabbed Ruxshin by the arm and pulled her along with him.

Skye, who was climbing on all fours, had just turned his head back to check on Julius, when his face lit up in surprise. 'It's the Mazda! The portal worked!'

They all stopped and turned, pointing in excitement at the shadow growing over them. The thunderous noise hadn't subsided though, but seemed to be increasing and coming from different directions.

'Why aren't they stopping?' asked Skye.

In answer, five small Arneshians aircrafts shot up from the bottom of the valley, appearing all around them like water jets in a fountain, and converged on the Mazda, firing as they flew.

'Run!' cried Kelly, starting to sprint, with Ruxshin following.

Julius and Skye were right behind them, keeping their heads low and hoping none of the crafts would notice them.

'Mazda, this is Kelly. Do you read me?' he cried over the noise. 'Do you read me?'

The fight intensified above them. Julius could see the enemy crafts crisscrossing each other as they tried to push the Mazda against the rocky face of the surrounding peaks. Just as he was considering opening his shield, a stray hit burst a hole in the ground a foot away from him. He halted just in time.

Thankfully, Elian's voice carried to them through their EMU systems. 'JD, do you read me?'

'Elian?' he answered, relieved. 'Loud and clear!'

Another voice came through on their coms, that of the Grand Master. 'Kelly, make your way to the statue. We'll cover you.'

'Roger that. How many are in pursuit?'

'Seven at the moment, but there'll be more. You must hurry!'

Julius activated his new shield implants, creating a dome-shaped capsule around him and Skye, who in turn opened his own device to shelter Kelly and Ruxshin. In this tight formation they covered the last six-hundred feet, keeping a wary eye on the battle raging above them.

Having scampered, rather than walked up, they didn't see the statue until they were practically at its feet. The size of the pedestal stopped them in their tracks and they took shelter against its grey, wet stone.

'This thing is so big I actually thought it was part of the mountain,' said Skye, catching his breath.

'I had no idea …' said Ruxshin, her voice trailing off, equally mystified by its size.

The base was extremely wide. Julius had to take a few steps back before he could actually see the whole statue. 'It's at least sixty feet tall,' he said, awestruck. The statue of the Mahini man looked exactly like it had in his dream, from the fur growing on the back of his body, to his cocked arrow pointing towards an unknown location beyond the grey sky.

'What do we do now?' asked Ruxshin, looking at each one of them in turn, an edge of fear returning to her voice.

A stray shot bounced off their shields, making them all jump.

'I'll not be used for target practice,' said Kelly. 'Skye, double up your shield on top of mine. We'll walk around the base to see if we can activate the arrow somehow. Julius, you'll do the exploring, seeing as you know this *guy* better than we do.'

With the protection in place, Julius began to circle the statue, his palms opened flat against the surface, in case of hidden pressure pads. He looked up and down the smooth rock, keen not to miss anything, but also aware that their shields couldn't withstand a direct attack from several crafts. After a couple of frustrating minutes, he looked at Kelly and shook his head. 'Nothing here.'

'You'll need to go up, then,' he replied. 'How much do you weigh?'

Julius looked confused for a second, but quickly realised what Kelly was thinking. 'I haven't had a doughnut in ages.'

'Skye, cover us while I send McCoy on a mini mission,' he said, closing his shield. 'Huh? Where to?'

'I wish Faith was here,' muttered Julius. 'All right, I'm ready.'

As Kelly focused on Julius, Skye caught on to what the captain was about to do and gave a fresh burst of energy to his shield, which was the only active one they had now.

Julius relaxed and focused on the statue's right arm, which was bent, drawing the string of the bow; as Kelly pushed him up with his mind, he began to use his own skills to pull himself towards it. He let his eyes explore the massive limbs in front of him: feet, legs, knees then thighs. The stone looked as smooth as marble, any signs of age washed away by the constant snow and rain. The ascent was steady, thanks to Kelly's experienced mind-skills, so Julius ceased his own mind-pull and used his hands to explore the material, unsure what he should be looking for.

'Kelly!' cried Skye. 'Craft incoming!'

Julius turned his head, left to right, and spotted it. Kelly must have flinched too, because Julius dropped down a few inches. Adrenaline surged through him and he scrambled to try grab the Archer's arm. His fingertips scraped the huge forearm, which was too big to grab for human-sized hands, but a sudden push forced him upwards again. It was just enough for him to reach the top of the forearm, which was pressed flush against the statue's torso, where he quickly hunkered under the folds of its sculpted clothes. He couldn't see Kelly anymore, as he was now stuck a good 30 feet above the captain, with a perfect view of the enemy shuttle making a beeline for the group at the base.

The Arneshian pilot opened fire as the craft made a fly-by of the ground, sending up a spray of debris and water. Stones and water drops ricocheted off their shields. Ruxshin balled up next to the pedestal, while Skye and Kelly stood over her, focusing on keeping up the protective layers.

'Julius,' called Kelly over their com-system, 'we need both shields to keep us safe from that craft. We'll be distraction enough, but you need to activate that arrow on your own and double-quick.'

'I'm on it …' he replied, '… somehow.' He waited for the craft to move out of sight, then straddled the forearm and slowly began to drag himself towards its wrist. He knew the enemy was no doubt veering back to renew its attack. However, it was tricky going, as the pouring rain had rendered the stone too slippery for hurrying. He edged forward, focusing on the statue's cupped hand. He could see the stony feathers at the back of the arrow, clasped within the Archer's thick fingers and palm. A sort of alcove had been created within it, and Julius knew he would have to pass through it in order to go further.

When he reached the base of the thumb, he twisted and stretched his left hand forward towards the fletching, but couldn't quite reach it. He tensed and pushed his body towards it to cover the last few inches. His hand grasped the top line of the feathers, and he dragged himself forward, sliding off the hand. Julius did his best to avoid looking down as he dangled in the air. With his right hand, he grabbed another section of fletching. His nose was almost touching the nock, the little notch in the rearmost end of the arrow - he could see the string, delicately sculpted, passing through it, as the bow was being drawn. The shaft ran between the index and forefinger of the Archer's right hand, creating a gap wide enough for him to squeeze through. Edging slowly, he moved as close to it as he could, before heaving himself up and planting the tip of his right boot on one of the protruding fingertips. There, perched like a bird, he gave himself a moment to look around for anything unusual.

'Captain,' he said to Kelly, 'I'm on the arrow.'

'Anything?'

'Nope. I think I need to move forwa-'

'Damn!' Kelly interrupted. 'He's back.'

Julius looked down, fighting a sense a vertigo, and saw the craft flying toward the pedestal. He tried to lock onto it, hoping to push it away with his mind, but it was flying erratically, and dipped from view just when he thought he had a clear shot. Skye and Kelly were firing blasts of energy at the shuttle, but they weren't strong enough to do any real damage. Only the Ahura could save them at this point.

On cue, Freja's voice came over the com: 'McCoy, what's your position?'

Julius scouted the sky and saw the Mazda surrounded by an increasing swarm of small crafts, in the middle of a frantic battle. 'Precarious, sir,' he replied. 'I'm on the arrow shaft, but there's nothing here that looks useful.'

'We're kiting the enemies for the moment, so they keep focusing on us, but it's a game that can't last too long. We'll have to fire back soon – their number is growing fast.'

It was true, but what was he supposed to do about that? It was a miracle he had reached this spot at all.

'Julius,' said Freja, 'think of your dream. Any detail may help at this point.'

'Roger, sir,' he replied. Closing his eyes, he turned his mind to Eneamar and his visions of it. Whenever he had reached the statue in his dream, there had been someone there waiting for him. Generally, it was Eronan, though Morgana had also been there once. He revisited the sequence of events, but nothing stood out immediately. Neither Eronan, nor Morgana, had touched anything on the statue, yet the beam of light had emitted from the arrowhead every time. 'Yes, but every time after *what*, exactly?' he said aloud.

'Are you talking to us, Julius?' said Skye.

He ignored the question and stayed focused. 'What's the damn constant of all the dreams?' he said aloud again.

'McCoy?' said Kelly, this time sounding worried.

Julius could feel the right memory dancing at the edge of his consciousness. He forced all other thoughts from his mind and took a deep breath, creating an inner space of calm and concentration. As the chaos and anxiety drifted away, the answer appeared to him clear as day. 'The name! They both said *its name* ...'

'McCoy, what's going on?' pushed Kelly.

'I think I know how to do it!' he cried, excited. 'Grand Master, you need to pick the team up now. Then get the Arneshians away from here and be ready to do a flyby to get me as soon as I say so.'

'Sure, but ...' started Freja.

'Trust me, sir, there's not much time left.'

He looked towards the Mazda and saw it veering their way, with a thick train of Arneshian planes on its tail. He stuck his head between the Archer's fingers and began to pull himself onto the shaft, until he was fully resting on it. The raindrops bounced off the surface, splashing against his visor, making it harder to see clearly. His EMU was supposed to help him blend against the rock surface, making him a less obvious target for the enemies, but unfortunately it was buried under the thick leather coat. As he dragged himself forward, he saw the Mazda coming to a halt between the crafts and the group, before opening one of its lower ports.

'We have a teleportation gate, Julius!' cried Skye. 'We'll come get you.'

'Just go, Skye. Now!' he shouted, shimmying along. The left hand of the statue was right in front of him, with the thick bow secured in its palm and the arrowhead just beyond the fingers. He climbed over the left index and stood tall, with his arms fastened around the bow. He looked down, briefly, and saw that the others had been safely retrieved by Freja. The sky was getting ever darker, not because of rainclouds, but on account of the growing number of Arneshian shuttles.

The Mazda's shields were taking strain from all directions, until one section became fully exposed, allowing the enemy to land a couple of direct blows. Julius saw smoke drifting from the hull, before the ship regained altitude and zoomed away, with the Arneshians in pursuit.

'You're clear, McCoy,' said Freja. 'Whatever you want to try, do it fast.'

'Roger, sir,' he replied. He waited for the group to move completely away, before attempting to activate the beam – the last thing he needed was an Arneshian spectator. When he felt safe enough, he crouched down, holding on to the Archer's finger, and removed his visor. The wind and rain lashed at his face, but he ignored them. Taking a deep breath, he shouted the only word he had ever heard uttered in his dreams with the Archer: 'Mah.'

There was a slow rumbling and the statue began to shake. It felt as if whatever was causing it was rising from the very depths of the mountain. Julius tightened his hold on the bow, to prevent himself from slipping off. Then he looked at the arrowhead, and was gobsmacked by what he saw. The point had become piping hot, boiling the droplets of water on its surface and evaporating any raindrops before they struck it. The grey stone had turned yellow as a result of the intense heat, and Julius tried to shield his face behind the bow, fearing that the rock would explode. The heat converged at the tip of the arrow, where it lingered for a moment, before shooting outward so violently that Julius had to hold on for dear life. The beam pierced the grey clouds, vaporising every drop in its path, and disappeared out beyond view.

'You did it!' Skye said over his com-link. 'Now what?'

Unfortunately, Julius didn't really know how to answer that. 'Can't we just follow it?' he said.

'What, with the Arneshians in tow?'

'Any other ideas, then?'

No one answered him for a while, which wasn't reassuring in the least. Then, unexpectedly, Faith came online.

'McCoy, do me a favour, will you?'

'As long as it doesn't involve me climbing down.'

'Find something to throw – something heavy.'

Julius paused, baffled. But, this was Faith, and he had no reason to argue with that kind of brain. He opened his coat and searched the utility belt of his EMU. There was a spare retractable snap-hook attached to it. 'Got it.'

'I want you to cast it into the beam.'

'What for?'

'Testing a theory. Indulge me.'

'All right then. Here goes nothing.' Cradling the hook in the palm of his hand, he focused his mind on it and slowly lifted it using his mind-skills. The steel carabiner floated up and forward until it was right above the beam. Carefully, he lowered it towards the yellow ray.

At least, that was what he had planned to do. As soon as the object was within a few inches of the beam, it was sucked into it and whisked away by the stream. A millisecond later, he was pulled after it.

THE COUNCIL OF ENEAMAR

He found himself in a conduit that appeared to have no solidity, zooming forward so fast that all he could make out was bright, cold light streaming past him. The speed at which he was moving kept his arms pinned alongside his body; no matter how much he tried, he couldn't shift them an inch. After the first immediate reaction of shock, fear started to force its way into his consciousness, as it dawned on him that he was going to be lost in space until death took him; this seemed to be the only outcome he could see.

Abruptly, he was brought to a halt, as if someone had grabbed the back of his suit at the waist, and held fast. His arms and legs shot forward and the air was forced from his lungs. Sharp pain jolted through his body, wiping all thoughts away, leaving him in a state of clarity.

He was floating in space, a foot away from a blanket of interweaving beams – "energy beams" was the closest description that sprung to his mind. They contained lights and colours, of the same kinds he knew, but in the coldest tones he'd ever seen. Interspersed throughout them was a nebula, a sort of dust that filled the voids of this unnatural tapestry, bestowing it with a kind of sandy appearance. Julius stuck his fingers through one of the beams, but nothing happened, except that the flow of particles – or whatever they were – flowed around the obstacle. There was no apparent pattern he could see, and yet, there was an indefinable order. The problem though was that there was nothing for him to aim for – no planet, or station; nothing that equated to *safety*. Was he even in space, or was this a pocket within it?

Julius turned around, to see if there was something behind him that he had missed, refusing to let panic take over completely. That was when the Ahura Mazda materialised a short distance from him. He screamed inside his helmet, watching helplessly as the massive bulk of the ship ploughed towards him. 'STOP!' he cried with his mind, hoping someone would hear him; but the ship just kept on coming. Julius lifted his arms in front of him, bracing for the impact.

A few seconds passed, and nothing happened, so he dared to open one eye. That was when he saw Faith and a furless Skye behind the glass of the Upper War Deck, banging against it, to try attract his attention. It seemed like they couldn't hear him over his com-link, or even telepathically. Relief washed over Julius. Just like him, it seemed that the Mazda had been halted before it could hit the weave of beams. Faith was motioning for him to wait there, but then stopped, eyes fixed to a point beyond Julius.

'What?' he mouthed. 'What is it?' Faith didn't answer. Julius looked at Skye, who motioned for him to turn around, so he did.

There was a bright spot inside the weave. It illuminated the space around it for a moment, before settling into a more subdued tone. It moved towards them. Julius flinched backward instinctively; he bumped against the hull of the Mazda and began to scamper upwards, until he was perched against the window. To his left and right, his friends, together with Kelly, who was now also furless, and Freja, were mesmerised, witnessing this phenomenon.

When the nebula reached Julius, it stopped, illuminating his face and suit as if it was dawn. Julius stared at it, transfixed. Cautiously, he reached his hand toward it and touched its surface. This made it glow a little brighter. He retracted his hand again.

A face began to emerge from the vapour, one that they all knew well. Soon, Eronan was gazing at them, smiling. He wasn't wearing any sunglasses, as he had been many of the other times they had seen him; in such close proximity, this allowed Julius to really appreciate the peculiarity of his eyes – they reflected the light off the many tiny sections that made up their surface, just like a diamond would. In this way, they didn't seem to have any one discernible colour, except for the dark pupils. Eronan's body began to slowly materialise in front of them, from his red robe to the eerie luminescence around the collar that had puzzled them for so long, but that now made sense. *No wonder he's been around for ages*, thought Julius. *He's incorporeal.*

'I have not seen humans for some time,' said Eronan suddenly. He looked at the Mazda, then at the faces behind the ship's glass, before settling his eyes on Julius. 'And from Zed, no less. Why have you come?'

Julius had to swallow before he could manage to speak – his mouth had gone dry. 'You … you said you can help us defeat the Arneshians … when I was on the Guardian's Trail.'

'A seeker of the crystal, I see.' Eronan seemed pleased.

Julius nodded. 'I'm the one who won it.'

'Then you better come in.' With that, he lifted his arms to his sides, his hands touching the energy beams around him.

As if activated by an unspoken command, the beams started to shift, still surrounded by the sandy dust. They bent and twisted, slowly at first, then faster, until the dust became a whirlwind, eventually obscuring the view like a desert storm.

A sudden gust of wind blew the nebula towards the Ahura. Julius instinctively brought his arms up to shield his face, but he felt no push against his body, as a real wind would have done. He looked up and, to his perfect astonishment, the sand washed away, leaving him and the ship docked on what appeared to be the seaport of a marine city. He looked behind at the rest of the crew, but they were just as hypnotised by the scenery as he was.

A spaceship the size of the Mazda could never have landed on a planet like a shuttle could, let alone dock like a sea vessel. Yet here it was, resting in a huge enclosure filled with ocean water, like a majestic cruise liner. Noisy flocks of seagulls dotted the blue skies over the city, their shapes crisp and defined in the clean air. Tall glass buildings littered the skyline, some of them bent into arches over lower edifices. Parks and green spaces were planted around the city, including numerous hanging gardens that clung to the structures.

Julius was the only one who had seen this city before – albeit only in his dreams – and instantly knew he was in Eneamar. He slid down the front of the Mazda, and landed safely on the pier, then watched as the crew emerged from one of the escape hatches above water level.

'Julius, are you all right?' called Faith, hovering over to him. He wasn't wearing his EMU. 'You have no idea the fright you gave us when you disappeared on Mah!'

'You're telling me. I thought I was done for.'

'Here,' he said, pulling out an injector. 'For your *de-furring* ... and remove your suit – we seem to be fine without them.'

Julius did this, and allowed Faith to administer the antidote to the left side of his neck. 'That stings,' he said, as an unpleasant tingling nipped at the areas of his body that were covered in fur. He looked at the backs of his hands and saw that the fur was slowly retracting, as if growing smaller, before disappearing completely. It was as odd a sensation as he'd ever felt.

Freja, Kelly, Ruxshin and Skye joined them shortly afterwards, while the rest of the crew remained aboard the ship.

Eronan, who had just silently stood watching, finally moved towards them. Unsure what to do, they bowed to him and Ruxshin followed suit.

'True Tijarans,' he said, bowing back. 'Welcome to Eneamar. And also to you,' he added, to Ruxshin, 'child of the Mahini.'

'Thank you ...' Freja paused, unsure how to address him.

'Eronan will do.'

'I am Carlos Freja.'

'Tijara's Grand Master,' he said, admiring his uniform. 'I am given to understand that you need my help?'

'We do. I'm sure you remember the Arneshians. They must be stopped, and it seems we are losing that fight.'

Eronan regarded him intently before answering. 'Let us go inside.'

It seemed to Julius that Freja sighed with relief at the invitation and could understand why – now they would have a chance to plead their case. These people - or whatever they were - constituted their only hope, so they followed Eronan along the dock towards the city entrance.

'Sir,' said Faith eagerly, 'let me tell you, this place is grand, if I may say so.'

Eronan smiled, but didn't stop walking.

Faith took this as an invitation to ask a few questions. 'Where are we? I mean, I can tell this isn't like our cities, but ... how do you do it?'

'Eneamar is a vision, you could say; a construct. Normally I exist as energy, but I can interact with matter. The shapes you see all around you are the forms I choose to assume in order to interact with you. This,' he said, gesturing at the city around him, 'makes sense to you humans, and so I project it for your benefit.'

'So the beams we saw ... it was you?'

'Precisely. That is how I exist.'

'You are a network ... of one?'

'Yes, you could say that.'

'Wow. And do you have a name? I mean, how do we call your kind?'

'Names of this sort are an enjoyment of Earthlings; I have no need for it. Perhaps *you* can think of something suitable.'

'That would be awesome!'

'This part of the city seems to be empty,' ventured Ruxshin, 'but you're saying it isn't?'

'I *am* the city, young Mahini. There is no need for more than my appearance right now; but rest assured, the whole place is listening.'

'Wow,' said Faith, awestruck at his surroundings. 'So I'm actually hovering *through* you. Just wow.'

'You populated it for Farrah,' said Julius, before he could stop himself.

'She told you, did she?' he replied, amused, but volunteered no further explanation.

Julius didn't think it was the right moment to probe further, so didn't push it, but his curiosity hadn't been appeased. Certainly, Eronan was real and standing in front of them, but he, or *it*, was something unlike anyone or anything they had ever met: the first alien life form they'd encountered. He felt a sense of awe at this long awaited moment.

Eronan ushered them inside a small, cubic glass building. It contained a silver rectangular table surrounded by chairs, with potted plants along the walls. It was illuminated by the sunlight, but it didn't feel hot or stuffy – a cool breeze drifted across the room, even though there was no sign of wind, judging by the stillness of the plants.

They sat around the table, leaving the top chair for their host. Julius could sense hesitation in the Grand Master, as if he didn't know where to start.

It was Faith who broke the ice. 'Are you God, by any chance?'

The fact that no one scoffed at him was sign enough that it was a mighty good question, thought Julius.

'Ah! An interesting word that, is it not?' Eronan smiled inscrutably. 'I'm more of a *custodian* though – you could call me that.'

'Of what? Who are *you*?' Faith was determined to get to the bottom of this.

'I simply am and always was, young Earthling. I choose to make, to watch, to nurture. My dealings with your planet span thousands of years – you have always fascinated me. I have observed you, unseen, encouraging life to flourish in the midst of natural upheaval; gave you ways of surviving when the planet said *stop*. Sometimes it worked, sometimes it didn't.'

'For some people,' said Kelly, 'that would be reason enough to quit meddling.'

Though Freja raised an eyebrow at his son's tone, Eronan didn't seem offended by the implication; on the contrary, it brought back his enigmatic smile. 'You could say that I enjoy directing humanity towards improvement – and I say *directing*, not forcing. With every attempt, I change the circumstances, but leave you free rein as to what to do with it. I offer my help, without assuming it will be accepted. You're a very adaptable race.' Behind his head, a picture formed, similar to a holographic representation. It showed the North Pacific Ocean, with an unfamiliar feature: what looked like an island, surrounded by four smaller ones.

'Um … where is that?' Skye wasn't the only one looking confused at the image.

'Or you could ask, *when*? Earth was young then. This was my first project and, although it didn't work out quite as planned, it served its purpose. It brought you Marcus Tijara as a matter of fact. But that is another story.'

'So the fact that you keep coming back means we aren't improving very much, right?' Kelly still felt the need to dig deeper.

'Yes and no. I found it fascinating that a species such as yours survived despite the limitations of your physical bodies and your propensity for self-annihilation. However, in the twenty-first century, it became clear that, in order to avoid extinction, you would need to expand outside the boundaries of your planet. I decided to help the humans once more, starting with *her* people,' he said, pointing at Ruxshin. As he talked, a new image appeared.

Immediately Julius, Skye and Faith sat up, recognising the scene as the one they had found in the archives of Ahriman. It was 2020, and Eronan was shaking hands with Captain Gorghinian, surrounded by families and their suitcases.

'Mahin Space Enterprise,' he continued. 'They were eager to leave, so I helped them. I believed that one day they could provide a safe haven for their mother planet.'

'I don't look like those people,' said Ruxshin, observing the hairless features of the families in the scene.

'I gave them modifications once they were on Mah,' answered Eronan. 'Your planet was the closest habitable one available. Its atmosphere was chemically similar to that of Earth, only colder and damper. I had no choice but to introduce some genetic mutations into the colonists, like the fur. After that, the colony settled down and a new life began. Hopeful, I moved on, but not before leaving them with a means of getting in touch.'

'The Archer,' said Ruxshin.

'Precisely. It was to be the duty of your leaders to pass on its secret to their successors.'

'Hmm … I think that part didn't come out so well,' observed Kelly. 'A *Chinese Whisper* problem.'

'You are here, no?' replied Eronan, satisfied. '400 years after the Mahin mission left, it was evident that Earth was heading towards a slow, painful death with no space expansion to speak of.'

Julius knew what he meant, as he had studied this in his History classes: the complete breakdown of society had exacerbated deeper unresolved issues; drought, famine, depletion of resources; wars and diseases had worsened, leaving Earth on the brink of collapse.

'The people of Mah,' continued Eronan, 'had surprisingly reverted to a lower level of technology than the one they had left behind and were in no shape to become the rescuers I had envisioned. That is why I came back, to save your people from themselves.'

'And how exactly did you do that?' asked Kelly.

Eronan looked at Freja, who stared back in anticipation. 'It was agreed that the only way out was to help you become more … efficient, and better equipped to overcome your technological setbacks. I gave you the White and Grey skills, creating people like Marcus and Clodagh. And they did it; they brought the change.'

'But *how* did you give them those skills?' urged Kelly.

'It happened as a result of the Chemical War; that is how I gifted you.'

'*Gifted us?*' said Kelly, sitting up. 'You killed 12 billion people. How is that a gift?'

'JD,' began Freja, putting his hand on his son's forearm.

Kelly motioned for his father to wait. He wasn't finished by a long stretch. 'And who allowed this to happen?'

'Some of your own people did, on behalf of the human race. It was their intelligence that put them in charge.'

'Sorry to burst your bubble, Eronan, but humans aren't always renowned for their intelligence, otherwise we would not have needed your help.'

'So what are you renowned for then, Captain?'

'Our heart. Our *goodness*. That's how we function, and that's what has kept Earth from extinction for billions of years.'

'Alas, your time will come.'

'Then why help us? Why help Marcus?'

'Because sometimes, just sometimes, the odds are tipped by the smallest improbability, with the power to affect the whole universe.'

Freja gripped Kelly's arm again, and this time he did settle back in his chair.

Julius' felt his very soul stirred by Kelly's questioning of Eronan, along with the answers he'd received; he could see the others had been similarly affected. The War obviously had a whole hidden story behind it that he would never know about. But another question needed to be asked: 'I saw you when I was on the Trail. You told Tijara that you could reverse the effects of the Chemical War.'

'And why would you wish me to do that?' he asked calmly.

'The Arneshians strive to become the most evolved group there is, no matter how, or what it costs. Besides, you said it yourself: they could be *the smallest improbability with the power to affect the whole universe*; they could tip the odds.'

'And what is wrong with that? Isn't their victory survival also?'

Julius was about to tell him what they had witnessed of Michael's new abilities, back on Mah, but the Grand Master was ready to have his say.

'The skills you gave us worked for the majority of people, but not all. You know that the Arneshians went rogue from the time of Marcus and Clodagh. Centuries later, they are still bringing death; only, this time, in another system – yours. You said you *nurture* life, but it *has* to matter what kind of life you allow to flourish. My son is a hothead,' he said, placing his hand on Kelly's shoulder, 'but he said it right: it is humanity's goodness that has kept us alive for so long. No more, no less. And I think you know that, Eronan.'

'You're partly correct,' said Eronan. 'You think it is goodness that defines your race because you are good people – or at least as close to this as the concept of goodness allows – however, it is adaptability that has allowed humans to survive; your greater ability to evolve and tame the world around you. Good and bad are relative concepts and so don't define my choices.'

Freja pressed on: 'We could argue semantics all day, but your trail of *interventions* on Earth speaks for itself – you've always helped the *right* sort of people, the ones willing to bring *improvement*. The land of Mah that you created is no more. Arnesh has seen to that. Her people,' he said, pointing at Ruxshin, 'are enslaved as we speak, dying under the Arneshians' fists. And Zed isn't strong enough. They've reached a point that puts them beyond our grasp, creating an invincible leader for themselves. That's why we're here. That's why we risked everything to find you. It was based on Julius' dream and his memories of the Trail, but it was all we had left. Now, you said you can help us, like you wanted to help Marcus. You built the Trail for Gelar Ganan, to protect Marcus' legacy and you planted the information in the crystal for the right seeker to find – otherwise, why show Julius those conversations? Tell me I'm not right.'

Eronan stood and went to stand by the window overlooking the dock and the Mazda anchored in it. 'Yes, the Ocluths were my doing. They got out before it was too late, unlike Tijara, and accepted becoming the guardians of his powers. And yes, there is *always* a solution,' he said, finally facing his guests, 'but it could be worse than the problem itself. Are you sure you want to hear this?'

Julius nodded and so did the others.

'Purification,' he said. 'I deactivate all the pearls, permanently. A complete reset.'

'You don't mean another "Heart" machine, do you?' said Julius, alarmed.

'No. I can remove the skills once and for all – the pearls are all linked to my …

network, for want of a better word – I can shut them all down at once, although the Arneshian leader will require something extra, I wager.'

'Hey … we have pearls too,' said Skye, getting worried. 'You don't mean *us* too, do you?'

'As I said, all the pearls, *permanently*. It would cause a levelled restart to all.'

Julius' jaw dropped, and a heavy silence descended on the room.

'Once their leader is defeated,' continued Eronan, 'I can begin with the humans on Mah – the Arneshians are a priority, you would agree. Then I would move on to your system. In my pure form I can purge all human habitats, even simultaneously if you wish me to.'

Along with trying to cope with the absurd finality of the plan, Julius' mind kept returning to the *defeat of the leader* part - did he mean killing Michael right before handing over all his powers for a second time? There was no way he could go through with that.

'If this is all you can offer us, it is an important decision to make, Eronan,' said Freja eventually. 'Unlike my ancestors, I cannot speak for humanity. I will need to bring it to our people. We will need a referendum.'

'You can't be seriously consid-' began Julius, stupefied, but Freja raised his hand, motioning for him to be quiet.

'I understand,' answered Eronan. 'I can help you return to your system, unhindered and unseen.'

'How much time will you give us?'

'How much time can *her* people hold out?'

Freja nodded and stood. 'Give us a month, then,' he said.

'It's too long!' complained Ruxshin, visibly unhappy.

Freja ignored her though. 'We shall return with an answer.' He beckoned for his crew to follow him outside, leaving Eronan within.

Julius looked at Skye and Faith. He really didn't much care about Ruxshin's feelings just then – she'd never had mind-skills and so wouldn't know the difference they made. How could they give it all up? The others stared back at him miserably, like animals in a cage, trying to look for a way out that wasn't there.

THE FORUM SPEAKS

Julius observed the people in the Mazda's ready room as they quietly talked to each other in small groups. Freja was deep in conversation with the GMs of Tuala and Sield, Roland Kloister and Edwina Milson, while Kelly sat to one end of the table with the Earth Leader, Paulo Trent, and the Curio Maximus, Aldobrando Roversi. He looked deeply upset, and with more grey hair than ever.

First, Freja had to explain the importance and impact of Eronan's actions on human space history, and the improbable, yet real, form of existence of the alien: a being of pure energy. His hand reached far, and he had proven to be a trustworthy ally to Earthlings. Then Freja broke the news in the clearest possible way, explaining how Eronan's solution came with the heaviest price tag any of them would ever have to pay. Just like Julius, their reaction was one of incredulity. Eventually, considering Eronan's knowledge of Earth's history, and confirmation from the Ocluths that he had indeed been responsible for their settlement, they were convinced that he truly intended to help them.

'I need to return to Earth,' announced Trent to the room, at the end of the consultation.

'Very well, Paulo,' replied Freja. 'We have agreed to hold the referendum on Friday the 31st of October – it should give us enough time to inform the people and organise the voting.'

'I will send an envoy to the five members of the Federation,' added Roversi, 'and when this is over, we shall add another star to our new flag, for the Mahini.'

'So let it be,' said Milson.

'So let it be,' echoed everyone in the room.

The meeting ended then and, as he was walking past, Freja stopped by Julius. 'You will need to assemble the Forum. Once the information is out, you must be there for them, and so must Shanigan. You will leave tomorrow at noon. Miller and Ruxshin too, if they wish to join you.'

Julius didn't feel particularly excited at the prospect, which didn't escape the Grand Master.

'What is it?'

Julius had been quiet throughout the conference, but he could not leave the room without speaking his mind. 'Permission to speak freely, sir.'

'Granted.'

'Quite frankly, I find it baffling that everyone went right ahead with the referendum without considering other options first.'

'Such as?'

'How about fighting the Arneshians without giving up who we are, for example?' He was aware that his voice was rising slightly, and he tried hard to keep it at bay. 'All of you in this room have had less than four days to digest the news. Yet today you all voted for the referendum. You told Eronan that you couldn't decide for the race, but don't you see that today's call to vote has already set the wheels in motion? You have decided for us all.'

Freja pondered his words. 'I cannot live with the alternative, Julius,' he said eventually. 'Removing the choice from our people altogether is essentially deciding for them. I'm sorry.' And with that, he left the room.

Faith and Skye walked in as soon as the coast was clear, but one look at Julius' face told them all they needed to know.

'When?' asked Skye, downcast.

'The end of the month. And Faith, we are off to the Forum tomorrow. Freja says you and Ruxshin can come too, Skye.'

'Back to Ahriman then, huh? I can't imagine what else I would do here, anyway,' he said.

Faith's expression, on the other hand, improved visibly and Julius knew why. 'Siena will be happy to see you.'

'When did she move there?' asked Skye.

'Her post started on the 1st of October,' replied Faith. 'She's Junior Assistant to one of the Curiates: the Vietnamese De Bui. So yes, at least I'll get to see her this month. What about you, Skye? Any news from Valentina?'

'Nah,' he said, sounding quite chilled. 'Distances don't agree with us very much. We'll probably have clandestine affairs until old age takes us and we can't boogie anymore.'

'Amen to that,' said Faith.

Ruxshin was quite excited at the prospect of landing on a new planet. Deep down, Julius could understand this: a plan to rescue her people would shortly materialise, while she was travelling to Funesto, where she would meet new people and even have access to some of her own Mahin history. But, for some reason, tiredness being one of them, her happiness ticked him off, until he could no longer restrain it. 'Hey, Ruxshin,' he said, just before they landed.

She looked up, smiling.

'You know that you will have to vote too, right? As a representative of the Mahini, no less.'

Her smile faltered. 'I … I guess so?'

'And I'm guess you'll vote a big fat Yes too.'

Skye and Faith turned to him.

'What are you doing, Jules?' asked Faith. 'It's not her fault, you know?'

Julius knew this, but he still felt like he needed to vent a bit more. 'All you ever wanted was for your people to be free – that's why you came to us, right? And if it takes all we have to help *you*, then so be it.'

Ruxshin looked away, growing visibly uncomfortable.

'She has no skills; why should she vote?' he continued.

'That's a fair point,' said Skye, stepping in, 'but still not her fault. Bring it to Freja - the first feedback

for the Forum.'

Julius sighed, and finally let it rest. He knew it was petty, but he felt better for having said it; a little payback for her using Morgana against him like she had, back on the Mazda. He was slowly discovering that a little bit of coldness went a long way when releasing stress. No one else seemed to care about what really mattered, so why should he?

Just like the first time they'd arrived there, Milan Todorov welcomed them on the landing pad. He stood there in his usual obsequious manner, but he faltered a little when he saw Ruxshin's fur.

'He's the Secretary of the Curiates,' Faith explained to her quietly. 'A bit bonkers, but nice.'

Todorov was too well trained to betray more than the smallest hint of surprise. He took them to their quarters, before showing them the Forum room, which was accessible from the main courtyard of the Hulk. Just as they were about to enter, Siena called out to them.

'Hey! You made it!'

Faith welcomed her with open arms, followed by Julius and Skye. Julius was always happy to see her, perhaps because of the close connection she'd had with Morgana.

'You must be Ruxshin,' she said, giving the Mahini a hug.

Ruxshin was taken aback by the gesture, but the kind expression on Siena's face relaxed her immediately. 'Hello,' she ventured.

'Come inside, guys,' she said, opening the door. 'The preparations are already underway.'

The Forum was shaped like an amphitheatre, with marble steps descending towards a circular inner floor. Large screens were dotted around the room, positioned at different heights.

'It reminds me of the Hologram Palace's waiting area,' said Skye. 'I like it.'

'I've been assigned to liaise between you and the Curiates,' Siena explained. 'I shall pass on all orders to Julius, as the Forum Leader, and to you Faith, as one of the people's experts.'

'When do we start?' asked Julius, stepping down to the lower floor.

'A full broadcast has been sent out to all humans one hour ago and you can expect the delegates to arrive from as early as tomorrow.'

Julius turned and looked up at her, surprised. 'So soon?'

'With a decision like this to make, you'll have a full house. And the press, of course. I suggest you spend today getting familiar with the issue, because people will come to you for advice.'

'Well, that's easy enough,' said Skye. 'He'll just tell them to vote *No*.'

'Even more reason to be prepared. There will be some who would prefer a reset for everyone – especially those who have been jealously wishing they had mind-skills.'

Julius knew she was right. 'Sure. Send me what you have and I'll get ready.'

That afternoon, while Todorov escorted Ruxshin on a tour of the complex, Julius, Skye and Faith lay sprawled across the steps, poring over the videos and the communications that had gone out to the GFE that morning. Whoever had written the reports had managed to stay neutral, stating the facts as plainly as possible – even Julius had to admit that. Every so often, one of them would ask a question, pretending to be a *Yes* voter, and they took it in turns coming up with convincing counterpoints.

Around 20:00 hours, Siena took them for dinner in the Curia's social complex, a more relaxing place than the daily canteen used by the workers. It was the kind of place where visitors and diplomats could be seen, as well as the off-duty officers. It had several areas, from bars to cafes to different food outlets – it wasn't as big as Satras, but it had enough choice. They opted for a pizzeria and it wasn't until they sat down that they realised Ruxshin didn't know what they were talking about.

'Pizza?' she asked, curiously eyeing the large wood-fire oven.

'I think the best way is to just try one,' said Siena, showing her a menu. 'What do you like?'

Ruxshin looked at the list of ingredients, completely baffled, and had to admit defeat after a minute or so. 'You couldn't order for me, could you?'

'I'll take care of it,' said Skye. When the waiter arrived, he asked for a margherita with extra mozzarella and a glass of beer. 'Let's start simple,' he said. 'You'll like it.'

And of course, he was right. The pizza had a thin and crispy base, with slightly charred edges, courtesy of the wood fire. The smell of oregano and cheese wafted to Ruxshin's nostrils, making her stomach gurgle. She took up the beer tanker, aware of the little cold droplets covering the outside of the glass. Hesitantly, she brought it to her lips and took a sip.

Julius, like everybody else, was watching her, waiting to see her reaction. When she looked up and smiled, he couldn't help but grin, at least for a few seconds. He had decided to be mad at her, and he wasn't done yet.

They stayed at their table for a couple of hours, discussing the situation. Siena wanted to know everything about Eronan and, only after hearing it all, she allowed Faith to take her away for a walk. Julius had half a mind to ask Ruxshin what had happened between her, K'Ssander and Michael, to make her so frightened, but changed his mind. He had enough reasons to hate them as it was; besides, he didn't need to take on her problems too, on top of those of her whole planet. With that in mind, he also took his leave, but not before sending Skye a mind-message reminding him about what might happen to any illegitimate *kittens*.

Siena had been right: the first delegates began to arrive from the early hours of Tuesday morning. Todorov was busy ushering them all inside, first to their rooms and then to the Forum, logging their presence in the central system, so that Julius would know exactly who was there and where they were from. By lunchtime, Todorov had to enlist the help of several colleagues, because the number of people landing had shot to the stars in a way they could not have anticipated.

'Schedule the first meeting tonight at 16:00,' Siena advised Julius. 'You'll need two a day until the referendum.'

And so Julius did. He scheduled one for that evening, then a morning slot, from 10 to noon, and a later one from 16:00 to 18:00. He knew that, as they got closer to the vote, he would need more time, but this would do to start with.

That afternoon, the Forum was officially declared open and a stream of people entered the room, sitting down on the steps until there was no space left. Siena was seated at a table on the lower floor, ready to take notes and moderate as needed. Julius stood next to her, looking around calmly. He had reminded himself that, in order to win the referendum, he would need to use his weight as a White Child, so he needed to look assured and credible – no space for stage-fright. He waited for the last of the delegates to arrive before motioning to Skye to close the doors.

Julius had decided to begin the meeting by replaying the broadcast they had all received. He knew people had seen it already, but it was essential that Eronan's solution, proposed by the Curio Maximus, was understood thoroughly. When the video ended, the assembly turned in his direction.

'Welcome to the Forum of the Galactic Federation of Earth,' he began, his voice steady and clear. 'I am Julius McCoy and I have been appointed as leader of this assembly. Thank you all for coming.'

The crowd murmured its assent and a few shouts of "Hear, hear!" echoed around the room.

Heartened, Julius continued. 'It seems that the first decision this council will discuss may very well also be the last; because, rest assured, a *No* vote will bring consequences that none of us can foresee.'

'And what would you recommend?' called a voice from the crowd.

Julius looked around until he found its owner: a male in his twenties, wearing civilian clothes.

'Can you state your name, please?' called Siena, professionally, but firmly.

'Alano Tirosky, from Colonial 2.'

'As a civilian from one of the Earth colonies, I assume you have no mind-skills, correct?' he asked him, trying to sound non-confrontational.

'I am. Is this a problem?'

'Not at all, but your situation gives me the opportunity to raise the first question of this meeting, and I would ask each and every one of you to take it back to your people tonight.' He cleared his throat, gathering some courage. 'Should non-skilled people be allowed to vote?'

Immediately, thick chatter broke out in the previously quiet room, which pleased Julius.

'Order, please,' called Siena. It took a minute but, eventually, she was able to give the floor back to Julius.

'The Referendum has two choices,' he continued. 'A *Yes* vote will see a permanent removal of all mind-skills from this solar system. Now, for half of our people, there will be no tangible difference to their lives, except that their DNA will be altered in such a way that passing on the mutation will become impossible. For the other half of humanity, life as they know it will disappear in an instant. All they fought for, all they worked hard to study and master, will be gone. And never mind all the technology that will become useless, because it requires mind-skills to be operated.' He looked around, wanting to strike up a connection with those in front of him. 'Since the establishment of Zed and the development of White skills, we gave ourselves a fighting chance against all threats, a chance that can still be guaranteed by a *No* vote. The countless lives that have been lost protecting and defending Earth, and humans across our galaxy, will be honoured if you choose *No*. Anything else would be an insult to their memory; to what they lived and died for.'

Applause broke out around the room; not from everyone, but it was something, thought Julius. 'You may think that my position is an obvious one, given that I have skills but, trust me, I do believe that a purge would drag us all backwards, and nowhere near an end to the war with the Arneshians, nor prevent future threats.'

As a new wave of applause died down, a female voice piped up: 'I'm not so sure, Julius.'

Julius looked up to the top tier, scouting the crowd – he knew that voice all too well. Sitting beside a dejected Bernard Docherty was Kaori, Morgana's sister.

'Kaori Ruthier, Earth,' she stated for Siena, standing up.

She looked tired, but she was resolute in her gaze. It was the look of someone who had finally made a hard decision. Julius didn't like that.

'I used to believe,' she began, 'that life without skills was nothing. I used to think that if I trained hard enough I would put a stop to the fighting and the war. In all these years, nothing of the sort has happened, except death upon death of friends and family members. I believed in that so much that I convinced my entire family of it. When my little sister was old enough to join Zed, I convinced her too. And now, the most important person in my life … has gone. She died because of it!'

Julius felt his heart shrink in his chest, completely unprepared for her words and the emotion of them.

'It is crucial to remember,' continued Kaori, 'that the Purge will remove every single mind-skill, from the Arneshians *and* us. Once it's done, we will *all* be equal and, although we will still need to fight, it will be a fair fight; an equal fight. And we can win it, because we have our hearts in the right place; because we are the righteous!' She looked around the crowd, parts of which appeared to be incensed by her words. 'I am willing to give up *my* way of life and *my* way of being for the greater benefit of humanity.' She turned back to Julius. 'Can you say the same?'

Applause rippled around the room, this time louder than ever.

Julius wasn't sure he could talk, let alone reply to her.

'*End the meeting,*' said Faith telepathically.

But Julius didn't trust himself to speak and was glad that the applause was protracted.

Faith hovered over to the middle of the room and did it for him. 'The Forum will remain open until 18:00. Feel free to stay and continue the discussion among yourselves. Don't forget to bring the first point back to your groups: should non-skilled people be allowed to vote? Thank you.'

The delegates stood up almost immediately and milled about, forming clusters with people of similar views.

Julius' eyes were still on Kaori, who was looking straight back at him. He moved forward and climbed the steps to her tier but, as he did so, she turned and left the room. Docherty's hand shot out as he passed by and stopped him.

'Not now, Julius,' he said.

'What's going on?' he asked, feeling frustrated. 'Of all the people … Why?'

Bernard slumped down on the step, crestfallen. 'She's been like this since Morgana died. She's changed: blaming Zed … our mind-skills …'

Julius sighed and sat down next to him.

'I thought it would just be a matter of giving her some time - you know, to move on. But when the news came out yesterday, she totally flipped. She told me that this was the best thing that had ever happened to us and that I was a fool not to see that.'

'So you don't agree?'

'How could I? I'm a Solo champion, Julius,' he said, with a tired grin.

Julius nodded. 'I'm sorry, man.'

'I love her, Julius, but this referendum is going to break us up … I can feel it.'

As he sat there beside Bernard, he wondered what Morgana would have said to her sister. Somehow, he knew in his heart that she would never have voted *Yes*.

*

One day followed another, faster than Julius could ever have anticipated. The Forum meetings had become the most intense parts of the day, around which everything else revolved. The gatherings began to stretch well over the designated starting and closing times as the number of delegates increased, and the issues to discuss multiplied. The Curia ran out of accommodation and the visitors had been confined to sleeping in their ships, which were docked in orbit. To allow for all visitors having a chance to physically enter the Forum room, they had to assign particular days to the delegates. He had tried to find Kaori so he could speak properly with her but, every time he went looking, she was never available. Julius knew she was avoiding him, but there was nothing he could do. He actually felt particularly sorry for Bernard, who was facing the possible end of more than just one important thing.

Together with Siena, Julius was always on his feet, replying to requests, relaying decisions back to the leaders and generally making himself present and available. Faith and Skye gave all the help they could, and even broke up a few fights when tempers rose. Ruxshin, meanwhile, eagerly listened to all the arguments that were being made, trying hard to make up her mind about something that really had nothing to do with her or her own life experience. She understood why Julius didn't want people like her to vote but, since she was about to become a part of this new Galactic Federation of Earth, she figured she might as well be prepared for what was to come – that is, if they managed to defeat the Arneshians.

On Monday the 27th of October, Julius entered the Forum to find an unexpected addition. Overnight, a large interactive screen had been fitted to the central wall, showing different maps and locations.

'Would you look at that?' remarked Skye, his head raised.

Faith, on the other hand, hovered up to it, and observed it as if he was standing in front of an art piece, tilted head and all. Julius stopped halfway up the steps, to get a good vantage point. Earth was fully displayed according to its political map, with all five continents shown. To its right were the colonies, their names beside them, one above the other: Earth Colonies and Zed Colonies, including the Lunar Perimeter; next was Buruwang.

'Where's Mah?' asked Ruxshin, perplexed. 'I thought you said I might get to vote too.'

'Technically the vote is secret,' explained Siena, 'and since you are the only voter from Mah, you'll probably be counted with Earth.'

'If at all,' added Julius. 'We still don't know if they'll let people without skills vote.' Julius hadn't meant it to sound churlish, but it was the truth – they still hadn't confirmed who would be eligible to vote.

'Ahriman is in the Federation, but it's missing too,' added Skye. 'Probably because no one has been born here since the War.'

'Except for Arneshians,' added Faith.

Julius' stomach closed a little. It was going to be a tense week and he wasn't looking forward to the outcome. In all honesty, he had purposely avoided talking about the reality of a Yes victory with the others as if, by doing so, it would make the threat less real. Even though he had lived without powers once before, this was different. Back then, he had chosen to give up his powers, for what he believed to be the greater good of all – now he would be forced to do that. And there was no turning back.

The newly erected screen became one of the main topics of conversation within the Forum, given that voting instructions hadn't yet been released. They had to wait until Thursday night, when a galaxy-wide communication was broadcast. Julius took his seat on the steps, between Faith and Skye, and waited for the news with bated breath.

At 8PM that night, Iryana Mielowa came online for what was the most important broadcast of her career.

'Gosh, I've never seen her quite so fidgety,' said Siena. 'Still, her hair is immaculate as ever.'

'I'd be fidgeting too with that lot behind me,' added Skye.

Julius knew what he meant and couldn't have agreed more. While Mielowa did some introductory chit-chat, he could see that, behind her, was a long table occupied by a serious line-up: Kloister, Milson and Freja, followed by Roversi, Trent and Daku Derain. 'They look as tense as I feel, funnily enough.'

Mielowa ended her introduction and turned to the panel behind her. 'The Curio Maximus will address this meeting tonight,' she said, moving out of frame.

The Curio Maximus cleared his voice before speaking. 'Thank you, Iryana. Citizens of the Federation, it is with a heavy heart that I am here tonight. We have chosen a live transmission in order to be with you all, on the eve of the most important day we have faced since the Chemical War. By now, you have had many days of discussions and, I am sure, quite a few sleepless nights. I know I have. After listening to your feedback and, after much deliberation, we are now going to lay down the two eligibility criteria for the vote.'

Julius tried to read Freja's expression, but the Grand Master just stared ahead impassively.

'The vote is open to all human beings from the age of 11 upwards,' he said.

A murmur spread around the Forum, as people expressed their feelings on this to one other.

'I like that,' said Skye, nodding. 'If we're old enough to train on Zed at 11, then we're old enough to vote.'

Julius agreed – it was a good start.

'The second criterion has been the hardest, and it concerns the eligibility of voting for those without skills.' Roversi shifted in his seat. 'When the Chemical War happened, no one could foresee the repercussions. As the years passed, some of us began to display the mutations that would eventually be developed by Marcus Tijara and Clodagh Arnesh, with results that are familiar to us all. No citizen was asked if they wanted these mutations or not – chance made that decision, affecting their lives and that of their descendants. We all had to get on with it, on Earth and in space. The people who live outside of planet Earth have all been affected by these mutations, - that is, except for the humans on Mah.'

Julius saw the eyes of the Forum shifting in Ruxshin's direction, making her aura turn red from the embarrassment of suddenly being the centre of attention.

'The Mahin Space Enterprise left Earth many years before the War broke out, avoiding contamination. It is because of this that Ruxshin, as representative of her colony, will not be allowed to vote in this referendum.'

Assent spread through the room at that. Julius was satisfied; for some reason, he also believed that Ruxshin would be relieved too at not having to make the call on behalf of her people. Sure enough, her aura took on a tinge of green, confirming Julius' suspicions.

'As for those humans without mind-skills,' continued Roversi, 'it is the will of this council that you be allowed to vote.'

A cacophony of noise erupted from the crowd, some cheering and some yelling in protest. Julius looked at the others in frustration - he knew that full participation could very well change the result; and not necessarily in their favour.

'It's not over yet,' said Faith. 'You'll see.'

Roversi's voice hushed the room once again. 'Voting will take place tomorrow at noon, standard time throughout the Galaxy. It will remain open for a one-hour window and will be accessible from all personal terminals and PIP screens. The Federation map will show the results live, and each territory will take the colour of the majority vote: yellow for *Yes* and blue for *No*. The colour will continue to shift until 13:00 hours, when the voting will close. We have one last night to think about our choice; our own *personal* choice. I can only advise that you look into your hearts, examine your lives and think of the repercussions that each vote will bring. Ask yourself, if my choice wins out, can I live with that? Humans, I bid you goodnight.'

The transmission ended just as Freja was beginning to stand. Julius did the same and stretched. There was nothing else for him to do that night. He only hoped that his vote would count.

*

After a sleepless night, Julius met the others for breakfast around 09:00. Siena didn't stay long, and returned to her office with the promise of joining them at noon. They were all nervous but, with nothing else to do, they went to the Forum to try gauge the overall feeling.

It was obvious that most of the delegates wanted to watch the results together, although the room was far too small to accommodate them all. When they saw Julius arriving, they immediately asked him to create a similar space elsewhere and he set to work eagerly, glad to have something to occupy him for a few hours. Together with Todorov and his colleagues, they managed to transmit the feed from the Federation map to a new temporary screen in the main atrium of the Halls, where large numbers of people could assemble; then, to make sure that no one would miss a beat, they tuned all screens in the social areas in to show the map in the Forum. Only when everyone seemed to have settled down somewhere, did Julius allow himself to take a seat on the steps with Faith and Skye. At 11:50, Siena and Ruxshin arrived, and sat behind them.

Julius noticed that Bernard and Kaori were at the end of the row to his right. He nodded towards Docherty, who greeted him back. Knowing that it was too late now to change Kaori's mind, he opened his PIP and selected his mail inbox. He saw that he had a new message from home. Anxiously, he opened it first. A video recording of Rory and Jenny showed the pair of them on their sofa smiling. "We are voting NO, Julius! And so is Nana! You'll have our support!" Julius couldn't refrain a grin at that. Immediately, he typed a big thank you, followed by a string of *NOs*, before hitting reply. His eyes then went to a message from the Curia; the same one that had been received by all humans. It contained the link to the online ballot and he re-read the instructions one more time, just to be sure. His stomach was now completely closed and his mouth dry. He kept cracking his knuckles distractedly, watching as the seconds ticked down.

When noon arrived, a wave of silence fell over the Halls of Ahriman and no one spoke.

Julius saw the link on his mail turn from red to green and he pressed it quickly. The new screen showed the ballot paper with only one question. Julius forced himself to read it again, afraid to make a mistake. It said: "Do you agree to the complete, final and permanent removal of mind-skills from all human beings belonging to the GFE?" Below it there were two boxes, one yellow saying YES and one blue with a NO on it. 'Do I agree to the end of my life as I know it?' Julius asked himself. 'No, I certainly don't.' As he pressed his thumb on the NO box, a message appeared, confirming his identity via print authentication and delivered a receipt to show he had indeed voted. The ballot paper disappeared from the screen and, with that, he closed his PIP.

'Look at the screen,' said Skye. The areas on the map were shifting colour from blue to yellow as the votes came in.

'It's interactive,' said Faith, linking his PIP to it by scanning the map on his hand device. 'Shall we check what our own people are voting?'

'Start with me then,' said Siena excitedly.

Faith's PIP showed a projection of Italy, with two columns representing both outcomes. At the moment they were moving up and down erratically, making it impossible to predict results. Faith then checked Ireland, Scotland and finally Terra 3, but it was still too early to predict where the majority was going. Ruxshin, in the meantime, was looking around mystified, fascinated by people's reactions.

Julius' eyes were darting from one end of the main screen to the other, following the changes in colour of all the different places. At 12:20, the area representing Buruwang seemed to have stopped on the yellow colour. 'Damn,' he growled.

'I thought they'd stick with Marcus' people,' said Skye.

'Actually, they left Earth because of all the fights caused on account of mind-skills,' remarked Siena. 'I'm not surprised in the least.'

As the minutes ticked by, tensions continued to rise.

'Terra colonies are blue!' cried Skye, pointing frantically at the screen. 'I knew they wouldn't let us down!'

'Come on, Zed Colonies,' said Julius. 'Show me some more blue love.'

'Come on, Zed … come on …' urged Skye.

When the remaining colony shone an unchanging blue, they all jumped to their feet. Faith and Siena hugged each other excitedly.

Julius threw a glance towards where Docherty was sitting and saw him grinning back at him with his thumbs up. Only Earth was left now. He sat down again and waited.

A new graph appeared to the left of the screen, showing the overall percentage of votes in two columns. At the moment, the *No* vote was winning, strengthened by results from the colonies, but the *Yes* was also slowly rising.

'Faith,' called Julius, 'can we see what the individual continents are voting?'

'Sure,' he replied, before selecting a new link. 'Oceania is gone, I'm afraid.'

Julius looked and, sure enough, he saw the continent tinted yellow. Europe, however, had turned blue. He looked up at the overall screen and saw that the No vote was still holding. Five minutes later, America had also turned dark, to their delight.

'This is killing me,' said Skye, rubbing his face in his hands. 'Come on!'

Suddenly Africa stopped shifting hues and solidified on a bright yellow shade. The Yes column in the overall graph shot up, overtaking the No, and Julius' heart sunk. They had one last chance now – the fate of their skills rested with the people of Asia.

Julius sat down, not realising that he had brought his hands up and cupped them in front of his mouth, as if he was warming them up from the cold. His eyes were focused on the shape of the Asian continent, his mind blank. Then all the noise around him disappeared and the crowd blurred away. It was as if he was staring along a tunnel at the shape that lay beyond it. There was light there: a bright, yellow light. Julius closed his eyes in despair.

ERONAN'S CHOICE

Julius was standing in front of a screen, waiting for the video-call to start. Behind him, and to the left, were Skye, Faith, Siena and Ruxshin. It was eight o'clock at night and the Forum was empty, now that the delegates had returned to their homes. He shifted from one foot to the other, vaguely remembering that he still needed to pack his belongings, as few as they were. He would have time to do that afterwards – Kelly wouldn't arrive until midnight.

Finally, the display came to life, with the screen split into two halves. On the left side of the screen stood Freja, from the Ahura's ready room; to the right was Roversi, who was travelling back to the Halls from Earth.

Julius bowed to them, barely able to keep his face free from the disappointment of that day.

'McCoy,' said Roversi cordially, 'a job well done with the Forum. You have our thanks.'

'Only doing my duty, sir,' he replied.

'Be that as it may, it was an important job. And now that the people have spoken, we know what to do once the war is over.'

Julius couldn't refrain a "*hmph*", which didn't go unnoticed.

'Is something the matter?' asked Roversi.

Julius looked at Freja briefly, before answering. 'Actually there is, sir, if I may speak my piece.'

'You may,' replied Roversi, leaning back in his chair.

'It is obvious that you wouldn't want us to fight without mind-skills. Useful things, aren't they? I wonder what's going to happen next time we're threatened. Are we planning to call on Eronan when that happens?'

'Julius!' cut in Freja.

'Leave it, Carlos,' said Roversi. 'I understand exactly how you feel, McCoy, but Eronan's help comes at this price. We had a choice to make - all or nothing - and our people feel that *all* is better. We will just be ourselves after the purge, as we were intended to be; no more, no less.'

'*Intended?* And what about adaptation and evolution? We are who we are because of our capacity for hanging on, no matter what. What if we don't take Eronan's help? What if we fight *our* way?'

'Unfortunately, I don't think we have that option anymore,' answered Freja. 'I do believe we can beat the Arneshians without powers, but not Michael. You told us about the machine he created and the testing that went with it. And that was weeks ago. Your brother will be several stages ahead of us once the Arneshians have finished shaping him into their perfect vessel and, to stop him, we would need your powers, along with any other help Eronan could give us.'

'I agree with Freja,' said the Curio. 'Once this is over, we will initiate the purge throughout our race and start again. Granted, *some* of the technology will become obsolete, but we have resourceful people among us - we will succeed in the end.'

'Sir, it isn't just some technology. All the ships rely on our skills to function. It would cost us less to do away with the entire fleet than to replace the individual war decks. The Cougars, on the other hand, will be ready for Pete's graveyard.'

'Yes, McCoy, I am aware of that. As too am I aware that our current FTL and hyperjump functions will receive the hardest knock.'

Julius shook his head. 'After all we've been through - the effort; the deaths - it would be a choice worse than the one that caused all this in the first place. It's who we are! You can't be serious.'

'The people have spoken, and that vote has won.'

'Of course it did,' continued Julius. 'The skill-less are many more than we are, and they're all jealous. I bet they were delighted at the chance to get even. How is this fair? We are the good guys!'

'Even if I agreed with you, Zed belongs to Earth and its colonies - it serves them - and their decision is binding. Zed will continue to exist, training people for space exploration and expansion, but in a natural way; a real, human way.'

Julius groaned. 'But what is *real*? I am a real human being, just the way I am! Please don't do this to us!' He was pleading now, but he didn't care. It was all he had left.

'Enough,' said Roversi firmly. 'McCoy, you have this mission to see to; the most important thing you'll ever do. Don't worry about matters outside of your control.'

'*Back down,*' said Faith in his mind.

'We'll dock in a couple of hours, McCoy,' said Freja. 'Make sure you're ready to leave.'

Julius stared back at the two men, then bowed. 'We will be ready, sir.'

*

Arriving in Eneamar the second time wasn't as traumatic for Julius from inside the safety of the Mazda. He was able to appreciate the tapestry of colour in all its grandiosity and vastness as they slowly approached it. This time, as soon as the hull touched the energy beams, the transformation was immediate, and they found themselves anchored at port, in Eneamar's impossible ocean.

Eronan was waiting for them on the pier, his countenance serene. Freja took Julius and Kelly to meet him, leaving everyone else on-board.

'Eronan,' said the Grand Master, bowing.

'Do you have an answer for me, Freja?'

'We do. Our people have spoken: the purge has been authorised.'

Eronan nodded. 'Follow me then.' He led them inside the familiar small building they had used before; only, this time, the table had been replaced by a large 3D map of Mahin, split into two layers: above ground and beneath.

If Julius thought that their reconstruction on the Mazda had been good, this was ten times better. Every building was perfectly detailed and, when he touched one, it grew larger and opened up to show the internal layout. Faith would have had a fit at the sight of it.

'Are these ... Arneshians?' asked Kelly, pointing at tiny figures moving around the streets.

'Indeed they are. And look, there goes the Ambassador,' he said, pointing at a little shape of a man, moving from building to building.

'How is this possible? Are they real?' said Julius.

'Oh, they are very real,' answered Eronan, with a hint of a smile. 'Mah has been under strict observation for the last month. They obviously don't know about it.'

'I must say,' added Freja, 'knowing that it is still doable to pull one over on these people fills me with confidence.'

'Is Mah Gira still in prison?' asked Kelly.

'He is. They haven't harmed him.'

'Ruxshin will be pleased to know that.'

'I think she would be happier to find out where her friend Khavar is,' commented Julius.

'I'm not sure who that person is,' said Eronan, 'but I have seen a group of Mahini sneaking suspiciously in and out of this building.' As he said that, the top layer of Mahin lifted, fully revealing the underground. Eronan tapped on one of the dwellings, causing it to expand in size.

'That's Mah Gira's house!' said Julius. 'I bet anything Khavar's got back inside it and is using the secret tunnel.'

'I saw the tunnel being used, yes,' confirmed Eronan. 'It is possible they are using the house as a meeting place.'

'When we saw Mah Gira,' said Julius pensively, 'he asked us to move a black stone he kept in his courtyard.'

'That's right,' said Kelly. 'He told Skye to move it to the left, under the bench. Can you tell if it's still there?'

Eronan manipulated the hologram of the building until he pinpointed the bench. There was a small black spot in the left-hand corner. 'Maybe it was a signal.'

'It was, yes,' said Kelly.

'This building here, at the end,' continued Eronan, pointing at a house by the cliff, 'is the focal point of the map. The Ambassador and one of his men visit it daily, but, worryingly, I cannot see inside. I can only assume the Arneshian leader to be there.'

'Sounds plausible,' said Kelly. 'What do we do now?'

'Julius' job is to deal with the Arneshian leader and I will help him prepare for that. Yours is with the soldiers.'

Freja walked around the map, observing it intently. 'We will need to keep the troops occupied.'

'And stun them,' added Kelly. 'When we're done, I want to leave behind a stream of sleeping Arneshians, ready to get their medicine.'

'That is right, Captain,' continued Eronan. 'Once their leader is down, and you are safely in orbit, I will begin the purification of the planet. It won't have any effect on the Mahini, but anyone else carrying a pearl will be immediately purged. Do you understand?'

'Trust me,' said Kelly, 'we'll be well out of range. If I have to be purged, I'd rather be among my own folk.'

'What will happen to the Arneshians afterwards?' asked Julius.

'What you do with them is your business,' replied Eronan.

'We can't leave them there, can we?'

'You could consider relocating them to Arnesh, and get rid of their fleet altogether. They'd be stranded for a long time. Or you could relocate them and then destroy their world, once and for all.'

'Wow,' said Kelly. 'You don't mince your words, do you? I like it.'

Freja threw a sideways-glance at his son, obviously not quite as keen on that plan.

'Be that as it may, it is your choice to make. Shall we start?'

'Very well. I will leave the Curia to decide on the aftermath. May I use this graphic to plan our attack? We have nothing quite as sophisticated.'

'It has already been transferred to your ship, Grand Master.'

'Thank you. Julius, I will see you later then. Good luck.'

Julius bowed, and waited for Freja and Kelly to leave before turning to Eronan unenthusiastically. 'I'm all yours.'

Eronan waved his hands once, making the room instantly disappear. Julius tried to hold on to something, but even the ground had vanished under his feet. He thought he would fall into darkness; instead, he found himself seated in a reclining chair, not dissimilar to a dentist's. Lights and machines appeared all around him, almost masking the fact that there was still no floor and no walls around him. Julius looked down, but he had to turn away, as a hint of nausea crept over him.

Eronan approached the chair and sat on a stool by his side. 'Freja has explained to me the true nature of their leader-'

'Michael,' cut in Julius. 'His name is Michael.'

Eronan nodded. 'Michael. Truly a remarkable technological miracle. I did not expect Clodagh to set up such a machine: a treasure of knowledge, instantly accessible to all its followers. Still, for all its greatness, this device contains the same pearl all humans have and, once you remove the distilled powers that Farrah gave him, Michael will become vulnerable to the purge, just like everyone else, rendering his knowledge useless.'

'Go on.'

Eronan waved his hand again and a 3D human shape appeared in front of them. 'Farrah's knowledge has been distilled into a tiny package which has attached itself to Michael's pearl, using it as a medium to express itself. The package may have been absorbed,' explained Eronan, 'but it's still a foreign body to Michael, so we can build a vaccine to debilitate it.'

'And how do you make it so that it attacks the right bit?'

'That's where you come in handy. See, the package comes from Farrah – it has her genetic code in it - and you and her share a portion of the same DNA: Marcus Tijara's.'

Julius' eyes widened. 'She's his daughter and I have his powers – I drunk that liquid when I won on the Guardian's Trail.'

'Exactly. Using the DNA introduced into your body by the Buruwang crystal, I am creating a vaccine so that it finds Tijara's DNA within Michael. Once it has locked onto it, it will be destroyed.'

Another thought occurred to him then. 'How come Farrah could see you?' he asked. 'In fact, why was I able to dream of you too? Neither of us had ever been here.'

Eronan seemed to be lost in thought for a moment. 'I had hoped Tijara would follow me,' he said eventually. 'I left an imprint in him about Eneamar; a vision to recall at will. He must have passed that imprint on to his daughter.'

'And since I essentially *drank* part of Tijara, I also got it. Is that it?'

'It certainly looks like it,' he replied.

Julius was trying to determine if there was more – he had a feeling Eronan wasn't telling the whole truth. He was about to ask one more question, when Eronan changed the subject.

'Do you know how to locate the pearl, young man?'

'I don't.'

Eronan opened up an image of a brain and rotated it until the lower side was facing them. 'See the four lobes of the brain? It is right at their centre. The mutation brought about by the Chemical War creates a bridge between them which grows into the pearl.'

Julius' moment of hope faltered slightly. 'Hold on; am I supposed to walk up to him and *inject* him in the head?'

'If he refuses, you'll need to find another way. That is *your* task.'

Julius closed his eyes and lay back in the chair, leaving Eronan free to work. *Another way*, he thought. He couldn't really perform open surgery now, could he? 'It won't end well,' he muttered disconsolately.

*

Eronan took the whole morning and the best part of the afternoon to create the vaccine. He made several doses, in case Julius needed extra. Each one was encased in a metallic container, ready to be loaded into a syringe. How he would get close enough to inject them into Michael was anybody's guess though.

At sunset they returned to the Mazda. Julius halted before boarding, and watched the sun disappear into the sea. 'Eneamar System,' he said. 'Faith has named this solar system the Eneamar System. And your species is now known as the *Dathannach*. It means multi-coloured in Irish.'

Eronan looked genuinely touched. 'Thank him for me. The name will be mine from now on.'

Julius nodded. 'So ... you said that you *choose* to nurture. Why help humans? At all, I mean.'

Eronan stared at the horizon for a while. 'Eternity alone is a mighty long time, if you must know.'

For the first time, Julius noticed a hint of sadness in his features, and he could partly share this sentiment. The prospect of the years to come without Morgana by his side made him feel extremely lonely. And, in truth, even losing Michael had deepened that feeling. 'Did you know that the Arneshian leader is my brother?'

Eronan looked at him inquisitively. 'I did not. For some reason though, I sense that this is not why you are full of anger right now.'

'That obvious, huh?'

'Tell me.'

Julius thought about it for a moment, then decided to talk straight. 'I hate this. You know what I went through to get Tijara's crystal and win my skills back. It's all been for nothing and it isn't right. I am who I am, and I have no intention of changing. They can't make me. No one can.'

'I offered Marcus a way out once,' he replied. 'You were there with us in his office when it happened. To you, and anyone who would follow you, I could offer another path – this system is small and exhausted - there is nothing for you here. However, it does hold the door to a new one. You could leave all you know behind after this, with your powers intact, and head out into the unknown.'

Julius remembered when Ben Hastings had offered him the same thing. At least this time he knew that Eronan's offer was genuine though. 'Is ... is there more to see? More life?' he asked hesitantly.

'Are there stars in the universe?' replied Eronan, with an enigmatic smile. With that, he turned back towards the city.

*

Over the next four days, the crew of the Mazda worked hard to organise the mission. Most of the fleet was moved into Mahi's system, thanks to Eronan's advanced relay junctions, which sent Faith into a tizzy. At one point, he tried sneaking up to one of them to see if he could draw its schematics. It was only after Kelly promised he would ask Eronan to send these to him that he was able to be dissuaded from boarding one.

Julius sat in the ready room, observing the comings and goings of the officers, without saying much. Although he would land on Mahin with the others, his only job was to get to Michael and deal with him. He had hoped that his friends would join him - Kelly too - but at the moment they were being assigned to other missions.

As he sat in his chair, tucked away in a corner, he kept thinking about Eronan's words. Could he really defect? Because that is what he was contemplating. His mind turned to the samurai of feudal Japan. He had loved and read so much about them that he knew what they would have done in his place. A samurai was loyal to his master; the order of committing *seppuku* — taking one's own life - would have been embraced on the spot, without any second thoughts. Disobedience was not an option. No self-respecting samurai would have challenged the Curia's order. 'Hmph. I guess I'm not a samurai after all,' he muttered to himself.

On Thursday evening, the eve of battle, the mess hall was filled with hushed voices and a sombre atmosphere. Freja had retired to his quarters early, to go over the attack one more time, while Ruxshin stared at Eronan's map of Mahin with renewed interest. Since finding out that it showed her city in real time, she was taking it all in, checking on her friends and family and, most of all, trying to discover if Khavar was still alive. Julius sat at a table with Skye, Faith, Elian and Kelly, staring at his food.

'Eat something,' Elian told him. 'You'll need your strength tomorrow.'

'What is it, Julius?' asked Kelly eventually. 'You've been acting very weird lately, and I mean more than usual.'

'Like he doesn't have a reason,' said Elian, but Kelly kept looking at him, ignoring her remark.

Julius glanced around, to make sure they were out of earshot. 'It's something Eronan said,' he told them quietly.

The others leaned in a little.

'After this is over, he could help us escape, powers and all. Would you do it?'

Silence descended on the table, as everyone looked at each other hesitantly.

'Tempting,' said Kelly, after a minute. 'But not for us. We have a kid now. Living as fugitives isn't exactly a great legacy for Savannah.'

Skye and Faith looked at each other, but couldn't think of any reply.

Julius was disappointed at their lack of enthusiasm. 'What's the matter? I thought you two at least would understand.'

'It's … deserting, Julius,' said Faith. 'It never really occurred to me as an option.'

'I mean, it's Zed we're talking about,' added Skye. 'Our family and friends. We would never be able to come home again.'

Julius bit his lip and backed down. 'Sure. Let's forget about it.'

Kelly stood up, and grabbed his tray. 'It won't be easy, Julius, for any of us, but we'll need to make do together.'

'Focus on your mission now,' said Elian, following her husband. 'If we fail, we'll have far worse scenarios to deal with.'

*

Around 2AM, Julius got out of bed, unable to sleep. He took a wander around the Mazda, relaxing among the engine noises and the general quiet. There were people still milling around, but no one paid him much attention. When he passed through the canteen, he stopped to grab a cup of hot chocolate and, with it, he resumed his stroll.

Without realising it, he found himself in engineering, on one of the upper gangways. He put his cup on the floor and sat down, letting his legs hang out. One of the engineers looked up and gave him a wave, before returning to his work. There were many reasons why he couldn't sleep that night, the latest being a sense of disappointment at being let down by his friends. It was obvious that they all had something worth staying for, and he wondered what Morgana would have done. She had been his partner in crime, so to speak, many times, and he felt sure she would have gone with him; even to the edge of the universe if need be.

At that moment, a figure appeared to his right, interrupting his thoughts. He looked up and saw Freja. 'Grand Master,' he said, surprised.

Freja smiled and slowly, using the bannister, lowered himself down next to him. 'I don't think I've ever sat on a walkway before,' he said, sounding as surprised as Julius was. 'Can't sleep?'

Julius shook his head and finished the last sip of his chocolate.

'I never sleep well the night before a big battle,' Freja told him. 'Granted, I didn't see that many battles until *you* joined Zed.'

That made Julius smile. 'That bad, huh?'

'It's okay to be scared, you know? A little fear keeps things real. This battle, humans against humans, is our responsibility. I can't promise you it will be the last time, but it is *our* battle. I can understand that the thought of facing Michael is daunting, but-'

'I'm not really worried about tomorrow, sir,' cut in Julius. 'At least not now. It's the rest that bothers me; being robbed of my identity, and you know that.' *You started this*, thought Julius defiantly.

'A true White Child,' said Freja kindly. 'You want to talk about *after*, so let me tell you about it. The world will need a leader; someone to take the GFE forward; a man of his time. Tijara was the man that brought us into the space era, and you will be the man to take us into a new one. A symbol to unite the systems of the Milky Way; an explorer and ambassador for the human race.'

For a moment, Julius felt warmth in his heart, as if the sun had come out from behind a cloud. There was hope in Freja's words of what things could be like, and that brought a sense of peace. Then he saw Morgana's body, lying in sick bay covered in blood, and the sun was obscured once more. 'I don't think I care.'

'But you *have* to care,' replied Freja, more urgently. 'When our powers go, people will still look to us for guidance and safety. We must make that transition smooth and seamless. A White Child is the hero of our times and you need to rise up to that challenge. That's what maturity is – facing up to facts. If Morgana was here …'

Julius glared at him.

'… If she was here,' continued Freja, unperturbed, 'you know what she would say to you. Deep down, in that stubborn heart of yours, you know what *she* would want you to do.' With that, he pulled himself up and walked away.

Julius felt like screaming. Maybe that was the problem, he thought. No matter how much he tried, he couldn't tell what Morgana would have done anymore. He felt more alone than ever.

THE SIEGE OF MAHIN

Julius was standing inside a Stork, holding on to the handrail, waiting to jump out. There was a reinforced inner pocket concealed inside his suit, where the vaccine had been stored, and his hand kept going back to it, to check it was still there. Skye, Faith and seven other soldiers were standing next to him, ready for launch. The fleet had arrived in Mah's orbit ten minutes before, counting on the element of surprise. Julius knew that, without Eronan's technology, this would not have been possible. The alien had boosted all their basic shields and cloaking devices, as well as improving their Exoskin suits. Most importantly, he had introduced a special device into the Gauntlets to heighten the effect of the stun setting, so it would induce a deep sleep in the target.

'Are you sure these boosters will work?' asked Skye, touching the two cylinders attached to either side of his Exoskin belt.

'If you three halted a falling shuttle just by using your hands as outlets,' said Faith, 'those two thrusters will be way more stable.'

'We'll soon find out, won't we?'

'Just be glad that they didn't see us coming.'

Julius couldn't have agreed more. The element of surprise was all they had. As soon as the Storks released the infantry, the Cougars and Herons would enter the fray to deal with the enemy crafts and lend aerial support to the ground troops.

'One minute to launch,' said the pilot.

'This is it, guys,' said Skye to his friends. 'Let's make it count.'

'For Morgana,' said Julius, putting his hand forward.

Skye and Faith placed theirs over his, briefly giving rise to green wisps in their otherwise red auras.

Julius' heart was heavy, but he couldn't allow himself to worry about the Curia's decision now. His mission was to find Michael and bring this war to an end.

The emergency light over the hatch flashed and Julius activated the helmet on his Exoskin. They were high above the ground, but not enough to need their EMUs. When the door slid open, he felt someone pat his shoulder a couple of times. He took a deep breath and jumped.

He stretched his body fully, cutting through the air like a bullet. In a few seconds Skye, Faith and the soldiers from their shuttle were at his side. In that moment, everything below him was still peaceful and, as he flew to meet the ground, he saw hundreds of Zed soldiers all around him, falling to Mah like silent spears amidst the raindrops. A storm was falling on Mahin.

The first anti-aircraft gun opened fire a few seconds later. Julius had no desire to slow up just yet, so he opened his shield to full, creating a protective bubble around him. The rain pelted against it to either side.

Skye pointed at a turret, where Arneshian soldiers were firing at them, and fired up his boosters. He changed course immediately, swerving to the left and soaring parallel to the ground. As he drew closer, he shot at them from his Gauntlets. Faith followed, while Julius aimed for the portion of ground directly below the enemy. He activated his boosters at the latest possible second to break his freefall, creating a thick wave of jet-stream around him and causing a puddle of raindrops at his feet to fly off in every direction, as if he was landing on the sea. Once on the ground, he tore down the turret's entrance door with a burst of energy and marched in, taking the steps two at a time. When he reached the top, one of the soldiers was lying on the floor, while the other shot at Skye and Faith, who were hovering above his head. Julius stunned the first man unconscious, just as Skye and Faith laid out the soldier who'd been firing at them. Julius strode forward and obliterated the artillery gun with a mind push.

Skye and Faith landed by his side and crouched down. As per orders, they quickly sent their personal co-ordinates to mission control, confirming they had landed safely.

'That was a welcome-party and no mistake,' commented Skye, drawing breath.

Julius looked at the city below the turret. The infantry had all landed now and bursts of lightning and energy flashed all around. At the same time, Cougars were performing dangerous flybys over the offensive positions, demolishing the Arneshian guns with their shots. With the enemy crafts tight on their tails, though, this wasn't the easiest thing to do. Troops of soldiers poured from the various lift shafts like ants from a hill, spreading over the ground, hunting their attackers. Among them were Mahini prisoners, some still in shackles, fleeing the crossfire and seeking shelter. Soon there would be no safe place left.

Faith used his PIP to activate a holographic display of the layers of the buildings in front of him. This was linked to Eronan's live map and so capable of showing exactly what each building was and how many people were in them. He moved around, trying to identify their mission hotspots. 'Right, so, Mah Gira's prison is straight ahead, below that shaft,' he said, pointing at his screen. 'Kelly and his team are in charge of that. We're heading east, past T'Rogon's office – over there.'

'Let's go then,' said Julius, not wanting to stay out in the open much longer. Using his boosters, he leapt from the tower and landed safely on the ground. 'Quickly!'

Shields up, they advanced, skirting whatever shelter they could find, staying out of sight as much as possible. The collapsed greenhouses were the best hiding places along their path, so they cut through them as they ran to their goal. Faith made use of his hovering skirt whenever he could, warning the others of possible dangers. Aided by the power of his boosters, he was able to zoom back and forth quicker than usual, helping Julius and Skye overwhelm the small groups of Arneshians along their path.

'To the right!' cried Faith, as they approached one of the largest gardens.

Julius whirled in, Gauntlets blazing, even before he had laid eyes on the enemy. As he turned a corner, three guards sprang out in front of him, but were repelled by his shields. As the guards retreated, Faith and Skye moved behind them and shot them in their backs with powerful mind-pushes, propelling them against what remained of a nearby support wall. They were knocked out cold.

'In here,' shouted Faith, leading them inside the ruins.

Shards of broken pots were strewn across the floor, at the feet of dead stubs that had once been living trees. Fallen leaves lay scattered over the ruined tables, whose wooden tops were rotting away in the pouring rain.

Julius edged around the room, wary of any guards waiting in ambush. As he moved, he heard a rustling noise over the sound of the rain, coming from a large wooden container, that was possibly an old compost bucket. He stopped and gestured for the others to halt, and pointed to the source of the noise. Skye immediately moved to its side, blocking any escape route.

Slowly, Julius locked his eyes on the lid and began to raise it open with his mind. The cover moved a few inches before slamming back down again. Julius hadn't expected that. He aimed his Gauntlet at the box, and pulled; this time the wooden top flew off to the left.

A frazzled Ambassador T'Rogon jumped up like an overgrown jack-in-the-box. 'You can't shoot me!' he cried, red-faced.

In all truth, Julius was too stupefied to even speak. Of all the things he had been expecting to see, the Arneshian ambassador was the least of them.

T'Rogon must have sensed Julius' surprise, because he recomposed himself and assumed his more familiar, controlling persona. 'You should not have come here,' he said. 'Putting yourself in the path of Arnesh is neither sensible, nor wise. Your brother will destroy yo … ooooh!' He managed to say that much, before slumping to the ground unconscious, courtesy of a right hook from Skye.

Again, Julius' mouth fell open. 'I did not see that coming either,' he said.

'I'm sorry to spoil the moment,' said Skye, massaging his hand, 'but I've heard quite enough from that pompous prick.'

'Way to go, Miller,' said Faith, hovering over to the Ambassador and checking that he was still breathing. He grabbed the hem of T'Rogon's tunic and ripped a piece off, before using it on its owner as a gag. 'Let's put this Jack back in his box.'

Julius looked around the greenhouse and spotted several small lengths of rope hanging to one side. He pulled them towards him with his mind and tied T'Rogon's feet and hands. Once this was done, Skye lifted the Arneshian and placed him back inside the container.

'Move over,' said Faith. With a quick gesture, he used his mind to scoop up dirt and leaves from the ground and poured it into the box, all around and over the man, leaving only his face sticking out.

'That's the ugliest cabbage I've ever seen,' said Faith, patting the soil down around the Ambassador.

T'Rogon opened his eyes groggily and, when he realised his predicament, he tried to scream, but managed only a few incoherent, muffled wailings, thanks to the gag in his mouth.

'Say *cheese*!' said Faith, taking a picture with his PIP. 'Freja will love this one. In fact, the whole fleet will; let me just send it since we're here. It's sure to go viral.'

'MMMMMM!' protested T'Rogon.

Julius strode up to him and stared into his eyes. 'You have no idea how lucky you are to be breathing right now.' With that, he slammed the lid shut over the prisoner. 'He cannot get out, understood?' he said to Faith.

'I'll take care of him,' he replied, plonking himself down on top of the crate with his full shield on. 'Freja is on his way. I'll join you soon.'

Julius nodded and motioned for Skye to move forward. They hopped over a wall and onto the street beyond, advancing swiftly through the rain.

When they reached the outskirts of the city, they stopped in the shadow of a crumbling shelter. Skye opened his PIP and used the map overlay to get their bearings.

There was only one building remaining, before the face of a high cliff. There were guards outside, watching the unfolding battle not too far from them. Eronan's map identified the building as Michael's Chamber.

'Get down,' said Julius, pulling Skye with him. 'There's a vehicle coming.'

To their right, a small, open-topped hover-car skidded through the rain, aiming for the building's entrance. Next to its pilot, K'Ssander stood tall, holding on to the top of the windscreen, oblivious of the rain lashing at his face. The car had barely stopped before the Arneshian jumped out effortlessly, but didn't head inside. Instead, he jogged back towards the city, and entered a smaller, newly built home to the left.

Julius experienced a surge of hatred so strong that he could feel his powers seeping out through his fingertips, inside his Exoskin suit. The noise around him had faded. All he could hear was his heart, pounding furiously inside his brain.

'... lius ... Julius ...'

It took him a minute before he was able to focus on Skye's voice. He turned.

'K'Ssander is mine. You have your mission,' Skye told him resolutely.

Julius knew this, but all he could see was that horrible moment: Morgana crumpling to the floor; K'Ssander fleeing. The person who had taken everything from him, and he was right there within his grasp.

Seeing that Julius was obviously considering disobeying orders, Skye placed his hand on his friend's shoulder and looked him straight in the eyes. 'He tried to kill me,' he said. 'He killed Morgana. Do you think for one moment that he will see the end of this day?'

Julius mulled over those words, weighing his options. The aura surrounding Skye was the darkest shade of red he had ever seen - he meant business. Julius backed down. 'Make sure that he doesn't.'

'If it's the last thing I do,' replied Skye, full of determination, before leaving the shelter and disappearing through the maze of ruined buildings.

Alone, Julius focused on the guards patrolling the Chamber. He needed to distract them if he wanted access to his brother. He left the safety of his hideout and moved to the right, giving it a wide berth before heading toward it again. He used the rocks, the trees and his Exoskin in camouflage mode, so that they wouldn't be able to see him. He even closed his shield, in case the raindrops bouncing off it gave him away. It took him almost five minutes before he reached the side of the building, and stopped by a large boulder to catch his breath.

On the other side, where Skye had followed K'Ssander, all was quiet – maybe his friend was also waiting for the right moment. Julius looked around and, when his eyes settled on the hover-car, he realised that it could act as the diversion that would help them both. He focused on it, simultaneously creating a fireball. When he felt he had accumulated enough, he lifted the vehicle, making sure the guards would see it; then, with a jerk, he threw it in the direction of the building and the house, followed by his fireball, which set it on fire in mid-air, causing it to explode. The guards recoiled, then recovered and ran to investigate the burning wreckage. Using the distraction, Julius fired up his boosters and flew to the roof of the Chamber, where he landed on it, like a cat. He scampered to the edge, looking for an entry point below the eaves of the roof. There was a window cut into the top floor, so he activated his boosters again and hovered down to it, before kicking the glass in and swinging into the room. His entrance surprised a guard, who had very little time to react, but still managed to shoot a bolt of energy at Julius. He ducked just in time, and flung himself head-first into the man's midriff. They grappled on the ground, each fighting to get the upper hand. Finally, Julius managed to strain and get his Gauntlets up to the man's head, where he unleashed enough power to stun him. Julius lay motionless for a minute, listening for any footsteps coming his way, but all seemed calm. Then a second explosion shook the entire building. He staggered to his feet and steadied himself against a nearby wall, hoping the explosion was one of his own people's doing.

When he was sure that the coast was clear, he stepped into a corridor beyond the room he was in. There were no other areas on this level, so he moved quietly downstairs. The main entrance was wide open and unguarded, with another exit opposite it. Julius selected the camouflage setting again, activated his full shield and moved towards this secondary door. It was closed firmly and, when he tried to push, it didn't budge. Finally, he noticed a thin pressure pad running alongside the right hand side of the frame. *Here goes nothing*, he thought, and pushed it. He heard a click beneath him and looked down, but too late; the trapdoor had already swung open, leaving Julius to tumble into a dark hole.

BROTHERS

He fell into a conduit, and was unable to stop himself bouncing from side to side as he slid downwards; the only thing he had managed, as an instinctive reaction, was shielding his head with his folded arms. After a few seconds that felt more like an eternity, he found himself freefalling. Instinct kicked in and he flipped on his boosters, just in time to halt his fall.

He looked around and saw that he was hovering in the middle of a huge, circular, iced cave, its roof lined with stalactites. When he looked down to the ground, a range of razor-sharp rock-shards jutted up from the surface of a frozen lake – without his boosters he could have fallen to his death. By all accounts, this natural opening had been turned into a trap of sorts, to keep out intruders. There were no openings in the ceiling that he could see but, somehow, light was creeping in, allowing him to see a little of his surroundings. There was a frozen lake below him and a suspended ice bridge in the middle of the cave. Carefully, he lowered himself onto it, turning the boosters off as he landed, for fear of melting the ice. He found his footing and waited to see if the structure would hold his weight. It creaked a little, but didn't break. Using the light on his Gauntlet, he explored the cavern, looking for a path. There was nothing leading off from the lake below, except for a narrow slit in the rock for the water to trickle through. He checked the two sides of the bridge, but the exits at both ends had caved in long ago. Lastly, he looked at his PIP, hoping to identify his coordinates but, not only were there none, he couldn't even send a signal out.

'Damn,' he muttered, creating a sudden, eerie echo in the room, while his breath spread out in a white cloud. There was clearly no one here and nowhere else to go – Julius' only choice seemed to be to use the boosters to try to make his way up the conduit he had fallen from. He looked up, trying to gauge its position and, just as he was about to lift off, he noticed an alcove.

Excavated within one of the walls was a large recess of smooth brown rock. It was pretty dark but, with his torch, Julius could just make out the beginning of a path. He flew over to it and landed, feeling the temperature rising immediately. Cautiously, he followed the path and was soon descending along a spiral tunnel. A few times, his feet stumbled, but he always managed to steady himself against the rocky walls. He was getting worried though, wondering whether he was going in the right direction, or if he had just fallen into a new trap.

Eventually he reached the bottom of the passageway, where an arch, protected by a film of energy, led into a sophisticated control room. He stepped inside, unhindered by the field. The new room was clean and well lit, its walls functioning as computer terminals. It reminded him immediately of the hideout where they had found Farrah, only this time there was no floating tank in sight, or Nuarn bodies. As he moved around the place, he became aware that even the air around him was coated with green cyphers and bits of code scrolling in every direction. The only way he could explain this to himself was thinking of a glass of salty water: the glass was the room, containing a mixture of some sort, with him in the middle of it. He had the feeling that, if he poked his tongue out, he might even be able to taste it, but thought better of it. He reached toward a random spot in front of him and, as he touched it, hundreds and hundreds of tiny letters and numbers flocked to his fingertips, swirling around his hand and arm, as if attracted by curiosity. If it wasn't for the seriousness of his mission, Julius might have found it enchanting – Faith surely would have fainted from excitement.

'I thought I recognised you,' said a male voice suddenly.

Julius instantly knew it was Michael's. He raised his Gauntlet, and spun round. No one there. He jerked back in the other direction again, but there was no trace of his brother.

'Can't you see me?' Michael taunted.

Julius didn't like this – how was it possible? He could have sworn Michael had been behind him! And his voice … it sounded so innocent; childlike.

'Can't you feel me?' he continued.

Julius turned again, and saw nothing but the exit. *This won't do*, he thought. He made an effort to calm himself, and took a proper look around. 'Where are you?'

'All around you.'

There was a hint of playfulness in his voice, but what really hit Julius hard was that he hadn't heard that particular tone in his brother's voice since before Zed – no malice, or hate; just his little brother. 'What do you mean? I can't see you, Michael.'

Suddenly, a cluster of letters and numbers began to assemble in front of Julius, and formed into the outline of a man. The shape lifted its hand. 'Here I am.'

Julius stumbled, stopping only when his back met the wall. His heart was racing. Was this the real meaning of the Arneshians' knowledge? 'What did they do to you?' he asked shakily. It didn't matter that his brother was now the leader of the Arneshians because, right then, Julius had even forgotten his brother's betrayal, seeing only a child who had fallen prey to ruthless enemies.

The Michael-shape shrugged its shoulders. 'I've evolved, Julius. I am the people. I'm their legacy, you see. It's *all* in here,' he said, tapping his head with his finger. 'And I feel great!'

'This … this can't be. It isn't natural, Michael. You've given up your identity to become these people's vessel!'

'I don't understand why you're so upset about it, Julius. Had I stayed in my corporeal form, like you, what could I have accomplished? My life would have ended in a few decades time, leaving virtually no trace of my existence behind. In this way, not only have I carved my name in the history of my people – I have become their future.'

Julius' initial shock began to wane, leaving in its place a slowly rising sense of anger and frustration. This didn't bode well at all. How was he supposed to inject the vaccine now? Was the distillation from Farrah even there anymore? Without a physical body to interact with, Julius didn't think he could win this battle. He had to find another way; he had to know more. 'Will you listen to yourself?' Julius said, changing tactic. 'Actually, Michael, scrap that. I bet you *can't* listen to yourself, because there's nothing *left* of you to begin with!'

That seemed to irk Michael, who stopped and suddenly dissolved into the air again. 'That is not nice,' he said, his voice coming from all around.

Julius kept his gaze fixed ahead – there was no point in looking for a source that didn't exist. He was pleased, however, that his words had shaken him a little. Maybe there was more Michael left within than he had initially thought. He needed to use this to his advantage and pry him out again. He moved forward, and strolled around the room, as if window shopping. 'So,' he said, 'is this your new home then? I mean, do you actually live under this frozen mountain?'

'For now,' he answered. 'The heat in here allows me to change state; it keeps me fluid and efficient, and my chamber can be moved.'

'What's the fun in that? No more swimming, no running about; no dating! What kind of a life is this?'

'I'm past those needs, brother. Although, if I really wanted to, I could do all those things – I'm not a prisoner; I'm the King of Arnesh.'

Julius made a mental note of that; what did he mean by *fluid*? The thought that the Arneshians had mastered chemical transformations to this degree was alarming as well as mind-blowing. His mind conjured up the earlier vision of a salty water mixture within a glass. Pretending to ponder what he had just heard, he turned towards the exit and observed the door. The energy field in its frame needed to go; without it, he could draw Michael out. He could short the mechanism, or at least try.

'What do you want from me, Julius?'

'I guess I'm here to convince you to stop this nonsense. Even Clodagh saw the error of her ways, or have you forgotten what we saw on the Trail?'

The particles in the air slowed.

Julius took advantage of the silence and continued. 'Clodagh was the ultimate Arneshian, and she said, *enough*. It was someone else's greed that brought centuries of hostilities upon us. But we can stop it! We have the power to do it, you and I.'

'It's too late, Julius.'

'No, it isn't. Help me set things right and be my brother again.'

'It's too late! I know too much,' he said, in anger and frustration. 'You don't understand. I don't need you anymore. You are no match for the King - stop bothering me!'

Those words were like ice water to Julius, and he flinched. Whatever pity he had felt before had now been pushed aside, and replaced by a welcome coldness of thought. 'You lost on the Trail because you were thinking like an Arneshian. You're right: you're not one of us and you're certainly not fit to have anyone's powers; not Tijaras, or mine.' With that, he made straight for the door.

'Wait … where are you going?' Michael sounded outraged. 'How *dare* you walk out on me?'

'Come and get me then!' he shouted over his shoulder. As he crossed the threshold, he discharged a full blast of energy into the sensor grid, sending sparks everywhere and shorting it. The field disappeared with a crackle and Julius turned. The room had gone quiet and nothing moved. The little letters and numbers were nowhere to be seen. *Come out, Michael*, he thought.

A whooshing sound filled the air as the cyphers appeared again, circling the room in a whirlwind. The maelstrom expanded until it was bigger than the doorframe, before changing into the shape of a man again. Michael faced the exit and lunged forward, rushing at his brother.

Julius couldn't see much more than a green, code-filled shape coming his way, but his instincts told him to run. He scampered up the path, unsure what to do next. He could feel the wind behind him drawing closer, so he fired up his boosters enough to stay ahead of it. The whirlwind continued to give chase, until it was almost on him. Julius veered left and out into the rocky alcove. Just as he emerged into the cave, the wind propelled him forward and slammed him down onto the icy bridge. Sharp pain jagged up his leg, from just above the ankle, and he cried out. He was panting, his breath drifting from his mouth in a mist. With difficulty, he sat up, sure that he had broken something. Meanwhile, the whirlwind had left him and was now hovering above the lake.

'Come on, coward! Are you afraid to show yourself?' he said, trying to goad his brother. Michael's shape appeared again at that, this time almost to perfection. Julius couldn't see a face as such, but he could tell it was his brother's from a lot of little details. However, there was something odd about the way he moved. As Michael flew at him, Julius realised two things: the cold was making him less fluid in his mobility and, secondly, if he could draw him into the snow, he was sure this would accelerate the process.

Before Michael could reach him, Julius rolled off the bridge, fired up his boosters and flew directly at his brother. The two clashed in mid-air and tumbled towards the ground. Not wanting to use the boosters too much, in case they heated the air around Michael, Julius instead had to use his mind-skills to cushion their fall. He doubted that Michael would feel any pain in that form if they crashed, but Julius might not make it out in one piece. He managed to break their descent just enough, but his wounded ankle jarred against the floor, and a fresh burst of pain shot up his leg. They rolled along the ground, Michael becoming increasingly tangible as the cold took effect. Julius used all his strength to roll him along the snowy floor – it had turned into a wrestling match, as if they were two young brothers again, just messing about.

But there was nothing playful about this contest. The change from code to a flesh-and-blood version of Michael happened so quickly that Julius was caught off guard. As his brother fully materialised, he planted his feet against Julius' chest and levered himself away. Julius saw Michael rushing back for him, so he opened up his boosters and flew from his grasp at the last second.

'Come down where I can get you,' snarled Michael, glaring as his brother hovering above him. 'Don't make me change shape.'

'I don't think you can, actually,' replied Julius. 'You're too cold for that, and now that you're just a little boy again, you can't even fly back to the alcove.' Michael's expression changed from one of rage to uncertainty, no doubt realising the truth in Julius' words. 'Are you ready to listen now?'

Michael looked around frantically, like a caged animal trying to find a way out that didn't exist. He paced up and down near to the icy walls, searching for any kind of opening.

'I brought you a vaccine,' said Julius. 'If you let me use it, I can cure you and you will be Michael again.'

'This is not a virus,' he growled. 'I am not ill. Don't you dare speak to me like I'm any different from you!'

'Soon, we'll really be exactly the same, Michael, more than you can imagine.'

His brother stopped and looked up. 'How?'

'The being that gave us our Grey and White Skills is ready to purge us all, and turn us back to norm- to the way we were before. The Curia held a referendum and every human in the system has voted on it. We'll all be stripped of our powers.'

'It's a lie,' he said, incredulous.

'I wish it was.'

'Even more so then, I have no intention of standing down. You'll have to find another way.' He turned suddenly, shooting two lightning beams from the disks in his hands.

Taken by surprise, Julius managed to veer to the side, but one of the shots brushed his back and he felt a surge of heat searing his skin. He gritted his teeth and focused again, knowing he couldn't afford to let Michael use the disks on the surroundings, or he would be able to heat the air and change shape once more. He veered down at him, but Michael was too quick and fired off a barrage of shots as he ran along the snowy banks around the lake. Some of the stray rounds crashed into the stalactites high above, and they rained down and smashed onto the frozen water, causing several cracks in its surface. It took every ounce of dexterity and reflexes that Julius possessed to avoid being struck by his brother's weapons or the falling shards of ice.

He spotted a protruding rock and quickly hovered behind it, catching his breath. 'I'm going to ask you one more time, Mickey,' he shouted. 'Stand down and come back to us.' It occurred to him that Freja had been right after all: blood was thicker than water, and he couldn't bring himself to deny Michael one last chance.

There was silence, then a shot skimmed his right thigh. He fell the couple of feet to the ground and landed painfully on the ice. He could hear Michael running towards him, and realised that he couldn't allow him to get hold of his boosters and escape. There were no excuses left for his brother anymore. He rolled on to his side, stretched his hand forward, and pushed Michael back with his mind, giving enough of an opening to heave himself up. Keeping the weight off his broken ankle, he focused all of his mind on the young man in front of him. All White Skills worked through balance – he had learned that in school. Right now though, Julius needed *imbalance*. He was going to try something new, something drastic, and he needed the right fuel. He needed to fill himself with righteous anger. He thought of all the faces of the fallen, their pain and anguish, suffered at the hands of the Arneshians. To top it off, he filled his mind with the image of Morgana lying dead on the hospital bed, her dark hair matted in blood; the hole in her stomach; the cold lips that would never kiss him again. It worked as a powerful catalyst, toppling the towering rage building inside his mind. When Michael squared up to him, Julius brought his hands forward and *unbound* his brother.

The world had suddenly stopped, leaving them enveloped in the cold stillness of the cave. Where before was nothing, now countless small red clusters floated in the air, revolving gently like tiny frozen pebbles. Julius stood there, the realisation of what he had done too great to handle. His eyes darted around the room, staring at the molecules that made up his little brother. No hair, or entrails – he didn't see eyeballs or floating ears either - this particular *Twist* had gone well beyond that. He was too petrified to move; if he tried to grab the vaccine, he could lose his grip, and Michael would be killed. There was no way out that he could see. He was stuck. For want of a better plan, he waited, trying not to move a muscle.

He wasn't sure how much time passed as he had stood there, ignoring the searing pain in his ankle, but he did know that he was really cold. He tried to open his mouth, but his jaw was stiff and he wondered if his lips were turning blue. What if he passed out? Would Morales be able to put Michael together again? Just as desperation was beginning to seep into his mind, Julius heard a noise, nothing more than a faint echo, but a noise nonetheless. He jammed his broken ankle on the ground, using the sharp pain to wake himself up. He screamed hard, but he felt better; vigilant.

He heard a second noise, like a padded explosion, and the cave shook; debris fell to the ground. The noise grew in intensity: a whooshing sound that echoed around the cavern. It was coming from the opening in the ceiling; the very conduit that Julius had fallen down. He listened carefully, making sure not to let any part of Michael drop from his field of focus. The echo became ever louder as whatever the source of it was drew closer; he began to think there were voices in the midst of it. Could it be …

'Julius!' Skye's voice exploded into the cave.

Julius allowed himself to breathe out, relief washing over him. The sound of boots landing on the ice belonged to more than one person though. In a flash, he was surrounded by his friends, along with Kelly and Freja.

'What are you doing, McCoy?' asked Faith, hovering towards the cluster that was Michael.

Julius forced his jaw open and cried, 'Don't touch them!'

There was enough desperation in his voice that Freja stepped forward. 'Stay where you are,' he told the others. He moved closer to Julius, observing his stance and the way his eyes were focusing so intently on the particles floating in the air. Then he turned and slowly approached them. He allowed himself to take it all in, before turning back to Julius. 'Is this who I think it is?'

Julius nodded slowly.

'What are you talking about?' asked Kelly.

'The vaccine is in my p-pocket, sir,' said Julius, teeth chattering from the cold.

Freja looked shaken, but he went ahead and closed Julius' Exoskin, in order to retrieve the little box, before activating it again. Inside was the injector with a few samples of the vaccine.

'You need to find the pearl and inject it,' explained Julius.

'Why would the pearl be among those fragments?' asked Faith. 'I mean, only people have pearls, right?' The silence coming from Freja told its own story, and his eyes widened. 'Crikey, McCoy! Did you Twist your brother?'

'Mr Shanigan, please!' said Freja nervously. 'I need your help, all of you.'

The others stepped forward to join Freja.

'You're something else all right,' mused Skye as he walked past, with a mixture of admiration and incredulity.

'I don't know what a pearl looks like,' said Freja truthfully, 'because I've never seen one, but we're going to learn today.'

Julius watched anxiously as they moved cautiously among his brother's parts, trying to identify the right cluster. He was beginning to feel weak and wondered how long he could last in this cold.

Beyond everyone's expectations, Freja called them to him after only a few minutes. 'Over here,' he said. 'This particular clump has an odd growth to its side – not organic, I don't think.'

They gathered around him as he pointed at it; even Julius was able to get a glimpse of it. From afar, he could only make out that the pearl was off-white in colour and that it shimmered in the light; he watched as Freja injected the vaccine into it, trying not to touch it with his fingers. As soon as it had been administered, the odd growth fell to the floor and, to everyone's astonishment, shattered as if it was made of glass - the freezing temperature had done its job. Immediately, the cluster turned black and shrivelled, like a rotten fruit.

Freja moved away from the dead pearl and ushered everyone back with him. 'It's time to fix this, Julius,' he said gently. 'He cannot harm anyone now.'

Julius didn't respond for a moment, toying with the possibility that he wouldn't be able to put his brother back together.

'I know you can do it,' said Faith, reassuring him.

'Not like this,' replied Julius. 'It's too cold.'

'Leave it to us,' said Kelly, stepping forward and directing the others into a circle.

They positioned themselves around the area where Michael was and created fireballs in each of their hands, until the clusters were surrounded by a circle of fire.

Even Julius benefited from the warmth, as some of the heat touched the skin on his face.

The ice began to thaw quickly and the clusters to lose the shine they'd been given by the crystallised liquid. There were no drops of water falling to the floor though, as the clusters were still very much encased in the hold of the Twist.

'Whenever you are ready now,' Freja told him calmly.

Julius dearly hoped that all the training he had gone through wouldn't let him down now. He bent his will on the particles in front of him and, with one single click of his mind, he willed them back together, just like he had done countless times before on inanimate objects. He feared it wouldn't work, but it was the only way he knew how.

There was a snapping sound, instantly followed by a *whoosh*, and Michael appeared in front of them, looking dazed and with much shorter hair. He swayed for a moment, not looking at anyone in particular, then fainted.

Julius lowered his arms and fell to his knees, exhausted and unable to stand any longer.

'Excellent job, Julius, but you cannot rest yet,' said Freja, lifting him up with the help of Skye and Faith. 'We need to leave, or we'll be caught in Eronan's purge.'

Julius was tempted to ask why that mattered anyway, but let it go. He bent over and massaged his ankle with a grimace.

Noticing this, Skye moved back to his side to support him, taking most of his weight on himself. 'Get those boosters on; I'll take you up.'

Julius didn't move at first, but merely looked him in the eyes, wanting to know what had happened to K'Ssander. Skye's upper lip was split and his right eye was on the way to turning black; he also had several spots of dried blood on the front of his Exoskin.

He opened his mouth but, before he could talk, Skye cut him off. 'It's done,' he said quietly, so only Julius could hear him.

Julius tightened his grip on his friend's shoulder and nodded gratefully. It was all he needed to know.

Freja went ahead, followed by Kelly, who was carrying Michael. Next came Skye and Julius, with Faith last. They zoomed back up through the chute and emerged in the foyer of the home; Julius took note of how they had made the trapdoor chute much larger – in fact, it was fair to say that they had blasted half the floor away. They must have taken some serious power tools to the conduit. Julius grinned.

The group exited from the house, into the twilight, and waited by a boulder for a Stork to pick them up. Julius stood on one foot, his arms on Faith and Skye's shoulders for balance. He didn't think he needed all that support in reality, but he guessed that they too were keen for some closure - the remaining Skirts, standing together. Warm rain began to fall and he turned his face up to it, letting it wash away the memories of his last fight, not quite fully appreciating that it was all over. He could feel blood pumping through his veins, reminding him he was still alive. He had fought and won and, although the future was hidden, he knew that something important in him had changed. The detachment he had experienced towards an increasing number of things - situations, people, even emotions themselves – hadn't quite left him, even now, at the end of it all. It was as if the icy cold of the cave had escaped with him – *inside* him – and, without the warmth of Morgana to melt it away, Julius knew it was there to stay.

He looked at his brother, resting against the rock, fast asleep. It would take a while to explain his new predicament to him, and he was glad to not have that task. Prison was the most likely ending to his story; it would break their parents' hearts, but he couldn't see any other solution. One thing that war taught was how to handle yourself in order to survive. Michael had obviously lost that fight the moment he forgot who he really was.

Julius' gaze turned to the city of Mahin; it was quiet again, and there were bodies on the ground as far as the eye could see - he didn't believe all of them were merely stunned. Zed officers were uplifting the surviving Mahini; at least until Eronan had performed his duties on the planet. Once this was done, they would be allowed to return home and start afresh, while the purged Arneshians awaited their fate in the holding cells of the fleet. Perhaps taking them back to Arnesh wouldn't be such a bad idea after all.

The Stork landed ten minutes later, and shuttled them all to the safety of the Mazda. Mahin had witnessed the end of an era: the long-standing conflict between Arnesh and Earth was over.

A NEW BEGINNING

'It seems that the Mahini's Winter Gardens are one of the most successful exhibitions at this year's Mid-Winter Festival in Oulu,' said Iryana Mielowa, wearing a fur-lined hood and full-length snow-coat. 'Mah Gira has invited us all to see them in their natural environment, on Mah. I, for one, intend to accept that invitation.'

Julius, who was getting dressed, stopped and looked at the screen. Mah Gira was standing next to the reporter, surrounded by Ruxshin, Khavar and a couple of Norwegian delegates. They seemed to be having a great time, eating new food and learning new words. As it turned out, Kelly had had an easy job during the Supreme's rescue. The black stone Skye had moved on his behalf, back on Mah, had alerted a few selected Mahini, including Khavar, to organise a full scale insurrection. When Kelly had arrived at the prison cell, he practically had no choice but to join a large number of hunters, bent on making the Arneshians' lives a misery. Mah would certainly benefit from being in the federation, thought Julius. And maybe Ruxshin and Khavar would take on roles in the Forum, as spokespersons.

'As a symbol of unity between Earth and the Mahini, a memorial has been erected at the feet of the Archer, to preserve Morgana Ruthier's coffin. Without her arrival on Mah, things would have been very different.'

Julius had already been told of that decision. Perhaps housing her on Mah was the best way to protect her from further dangers. He didn't like to think about it though, so he focused back on the screen, ignoring the feeling it stirred within him.

'In other news,' continued the anchorman in the studio, 'After the successful purge of the GFE, Zed readies itself for the purification session this afternoon. Zed is the last remaining place in the Federation where skills are still active.'

Julius watched as images of the previous purges flashed across the screen. The nebula that was Eronan appeared and surrounded the planets. The phenomenon lasted for almost thirty minutes before the beams slowly dissipated into the atmosphere, leaving all pearls deactivated.

'There are still tickets available to watch the Zed Purge. Purchase is possible through MoonBee box office. And now, the weather ...'

'Like a bloody circus,' he muttered, turning the screen off. He moved to the mirror and finished adjusting his suit. They had been asked to wear their white ceremonial uniforms to mark the occasion; something he found completely unacceptable and in poor taste. He had tried to change the Curio's mind one last time, after leaving Michael in his custody, but to no avail – the world had already moved on, leaving him behind.

His PIP beeped and he opened the vid-screen. His parents smiled at him, but he could see their eyes were red and puffy. The news about Michael had not been easy to digest.

'Hello son,' said Rory. 'Are you all set?'

'Almost, Dad,' he replied, continuing to adjust his jacket.

'You look so handsome,' said Jenny.

'Indeed, our little guy is now a man. We are so proud of you, son.'

Julius felt a lump in his throat and couldn't speak.

'You'll always be our White Child. Walk with your head held high, son. It isn't an honour bestowed on many.'

Jenny couldn't hold back her tears and Rory hugged her to him. 'Write soon!' he said, wiping the corners of his eyes.

'I will.' He looked up at them, a sense of finality on his heart. 'I love you.' He didn't know if he would ever see them again in his lifetime. Eventually, he closed his PIP, taking a last look around the room. Nothing would ever be the same again.

He took the lift back to the Tijaran promenade and headed right. There were several students milling about, since all lessons had been suspended. Some, like him, had already changed into their uniforms, waiting nervously for the afternoon. He saw a few of his former classmates, huddled together chatting in the garden, but had no real inclination to talk to anyone, so he kept on walking. He passed the technician's den where Mister List had fitted him with the infamous Holopal, the infirmary where Nurse Primula had patched him up countless of times, and the mess hall, where Felice Buongustaio was shouting orders to his chefs around the stoves, as per tradition.

When he reached the main entrance, he headed swiftly for the stairs that led to the school's hangar; he didn't want to attract the attention of Mister Leven, or the security guards. Still, he paused on the first step and looked up. The sign, "TIJARA – HANGAR ACCESS" looked exactly the same as it had six years ago, when a much shorter Julius, along with Morgana, had seen it for the first time. "*That'll be my bedroom, then!*" she had cried out enthusiastically. He sighed and moved on.

A couple of officers walked past him, and nodded in his direction in greeting. It looked like they were about to say something so Julius nodded in return, but didn't slow and they didn't call after him.

When he arrived in the hangar, he couldn't help but notice an eerie quiet - all Zed personnel and students had already arrived and no one was scheduled to leave the perimeter until the evening, after the purge. Julius took the stairs down unchallenged, floor after floor, and eventually reached the lowest deck.

As he stepped onto the runway, he looked for his shuttle, dreading the possibility that something had gone wrong, and that there might be no one waiting for him.

'Come on!' called Skye suddenly, standing in front of a Stork's hatch with Faith. Behind them, he could see Siena plus a couple of other people he couldn't quite make out. They were all wearing their white uniforms. 'We thought you'd changed your mind!'

Julius beamed. 'No chance.' He began to move towards them, when two figures emerged from the shadows to either side of him. He saw Skye and Faith's expressions freeze and he was instantly glued to the spot.

'Mr McCoy,' said Master Cress. 'Going somewhere, are we?'

A look of panic spread over his face. They had been caught. With a last glance at Faith and Skye, he turned, preparing himself for a fight. Surprisingly, Freja was wearing a familiar enigmatic smile and his aura was bright green. Whatever the Grand Master had come to do, it wasn't to stop him.

'It seems that, the next time we meet, I will have to arrest you for deserting,' he said jovially.

'I'd like to see you try that, sir, without your powers,' he replied with a grin.

Freja and Cress smiled. Julius could tell though, despite their efforts to appear relaxed, that they were both visibly emotional about this last farewell.

'Are you sure you don't want to join us?'

'And leave Tijara?' said Cress. 'Thank you, McCoy. I'm sure we'll have plenty chance to regret this, but we've decided to stay. We taught you well,' he said, gesturing to him and the group by the Stork, 'and you've learned well. You'll make us proud, no matter where you go. In your heart ...'

'... Tijara,' Julius said, his right fist touching his own heart. 'Always. I will not forget you, Master Cress. I will not forget you,' he said, bowing low. Then he turned to the Grand Master, who was smiling, though his eyes were teary. For the first time Julius saw an older man, rather than the Tijaran GM, burdened by everyone else's troubles, not least Julius'.

'Take care of my granddaughter, White Child,' he said.

'Wha- Kelly?' he asked, delighted.

'And Elian. The Mazda is waiting for you at Eronan's, with a few other ... escapees.'

Julius' pleasure at this news was written all over his face. He straightened up for a final salute, his heart swelling with pride, just like the first time he had met him. "It has been an honour serving with you, sir.'

The Grand Master stepped forward unexpectedly and hugged him tightly. 'Good luck, son.'

Julius felt tears welling in his eyes. At this moment, in Freja's arms, he felt as if Rory and Jenny were also there holding him, and he didn't want to let go.

It was his mentor who eventually stepped back, bowing to him along with Cress.

Julius bowed gratefully, then turned and ran to the Stork, joining Faith and Skye on its steps. For one last moment, the three remaining Skirts stood there staring at each other, almost as if to check that they were really going ahead with their plan. After a final glance at their former teachers, they disappeared inside the shuttle.

They took off without delay, aiming for the black hole that would lead them to the Eronan System and, from there, to a new life beyond.

Lightning Source UK Ltd.
Milton Keynes UK
UKHW011313160820
368300UK00001B/209

9 781913 387297